SHADOW
OF THE
GIANT

BY ORSON SCOTT CARD
FROM TOM DOHERTY ASSOCIATES

ENDER UNIVERSE

ENDER SAGA
Ender's Game
Ender in Exile
Speaker for the Dead
Xenocide
Children of the Mind

SHADOW SERIES
Ender's Shadow
Shadow of the Hegemon
Shadow Puppets
Shadow of the Giant
Shadows in Flight

THE FIRST FORMIC WAR
(WITH AARON JOHNSTON)
Earth Unaware
Earth Afire
Earth Awakens

THE SECOND FORMIC WAR
(WITH AARON JOHNSTON)
The Swarm
The Hive

Children of the Fleet

ENDER NOVELLAS
A War of Gifts
First Meetings

THE MITHERMAGES
The Lost Gate
The Gate Thief
Gatefather

THE TALES OF ALVIN
MAKER
Seventh Son
Red Prophet

Prentice Alvin
Alvin Journeyman
Heartfire
The Crystal City

HOMECOMING
The Memory of Earth
The Call of Earth
The Ships of Earth
Earthfall
Earthborn

WOMEN OF GENESIS
Sarah
Rebekah
Rachel & Leah

THE COLLECTED
SHORT FICTION OF
ORSON SCOTT CARD
*Maps in a Mirror: The Short
    Fiction of Orson Scott Card*
Keeper of Dreams

STAND-ALONE FICTION
Invasive Procedures (with
    Aaron Johnston)
Empire
Hidden Empire
The Folk of the Fringe
Hart's Hope
Lovelock (with Kathryn H. Kidd)
*Pastwatch: The Redemption of
    Christopher Columbus*
Saints
Songmaster
Treason
The Worthing Saga
Wyrms
Zanna's Gift

SHADOW OF THE GIANT

Orson
Scott
Card

TOR®

A TOM DOHERTY ASSOCIATES BOOK
NEW YORK

This is a work of fiction. All of the characters, organizations, and events portrayed in this novel are either products of the author's imagination or are used fictitiously.

SHADOW OF THE GIANT

Copyright © 2005 by Orson Scott Card

A Tor Book
Published by Tom Doherty Associates
120 Broadway
New York, NY 10271

www.tor-forge.com

Tor® is a registered trademark of Macmillan Publishing Group, LLC.

ISBN 978-0-8125-7139-4

Our books may be purchased in bulk for promotional, educational, or business use. Please contact your local bookseller or the Macmillan Corporate and Premium Sales Department at 1-800-221-7945, extension 5442, or by email at MacmillanSpecialMarkets@macmillan.com.

First Edition: March 2005
First Mass Market Edition: March 2006

Printed in the United States of America

19 18 17 16 15 14 13 12

To ED and KAY MCVEY,
who are saving the world
one kindness at a time

CONTENTS

X CONTENTS

SHADOW OF THE GIANT

1

MANDATE OF HEAVEN

From: Graff%pilgrimage@colmin.gov
To: Soup%battleboys@strategyandplanning.han.gov
Re: Free Vacation Offer

Destination of your choice in the known universe. And . . .
we pick you up!

Han Tzu waited until the armored car was completely out of
sight before he ventured out into the bicycle-and-pedestrian-
packed street. Crowds could make you invisible, but only if
you were moving in the same direction, and that's the thing
Han Tzu had never really been able to do, not since he came
home to China from Battle School.

He always seemed to be moving, not upstream, but cross-
ways. As if he had a completely different map of the world
from the one everyone around him was using.

And here he was again, dodging bikes and forward-
pressing people on their ten thousand errands in order to get
from the doorway of his apartment building to the door of
the tiny restaurant across the street.

But it was not as hard as it would have been for most
people. Han Tzu had mastered the art of using only his

peripheral vision, so his eyes stared straight ahead. Without eye contact, the others on the street could not face him down, could not insist that he yield the right of way. They could only dodge him, as if he were a boulder in the stream.

He put his hand to the door and hesitated. He did not know why he had not been arrested and killed or sent for re-training already, but if he was photographed taking this meeting, then it would be easy to prove that he was a traitor.

Then again, his enemies didn't need evidence to convict—all they needed was the inclination. So he opened the door, listened to the tinkle of the little bell, and walked toward the back of the narrow corridor between booths.

He knew he shouldn't expect Graff himself. For the Min-ister of Colonization to come to Earth would be news, and Graff avoided news unless it was useful to him, which this would certainly not be. So whom would Graff send? Some-one from Battle School, undoubtedly. A teacher? Another student? Someone from Ender's Jeesh? Would this be a re-union?

To his surprise, the man in the last booth sat with his back toward the door, so all Han Tzu could see was his curly steel-grey hair. Not Chinese. And from the color of his ears, not European. The pertinent fact, though, was that he was not facing the door and could not see Han Tzu's approach. How-ever, once Han Tzu sat down, *he* would be facing the door, able to observe the whole room.

That was the smart way to do it—after all, Han Tzu was the one who would recognize trouble if it came in the door, not this foreigner, this stranger. But few operatives on a mis-sion this dangerous would have the brass to turn their backs on the door just because the person they were meeting would be a better observer.

The man did not turn as Han Tzu approached. Was he un-observant, or supremely confident?

"Hello," the man said softly just as Han Tzu came up be-side him. "Please sit down."

Han Tzu slid into the booth opposite him and knew that he knew this old man but could not name him.

"Please don't say my name," said the man softly.

"Easy," said Han Tzu. "I don't remember it."

"Oh, yes you do," said the man. "You just don't remember my face. You haven't seen me very often. But the leader of the Jeesh spent a lot of time with me."

Now Han Tzu remembered. Those last weeks in Command School—on Eros, when they thought they were in training but were really leading far-off fleets in the endgame of the war against the Hive Queens. Ender, their commander, had been kept separate from them, but they learned afterward that an old half-Maori cargo-ship captain had been working closely with him. Training him. Goading him. Pretending to be his opponent in simulated games.

Mazer Rackham. The hero who saved the human race from certain destruction in the Second Invasion. Everyone thought he died in the war, but he had been sent out on a meaningless voyage at near-lightspeed, so that relativistic effects would keep him alive so he'd be there for the last battles of the war.

He was ancient history twice over. That time on Eros as a part of Ender's Jeesh seemed like another lifetime. And Mazer Rackham had been the most famous man in the world for decades before that.

Most famous man in the world, but almost nobody knew his face.

"Everyone knows you piloted the first colony ship," said Han Tzu.

"We lied," said Mazer Rackham.

Han Tzu accepted that and waited in silence.

"There is a place for you as head of a colony," said Rackham. "A former Hive world, with mostly Han Chinese colonists and many interesting challenges for a leader. The ship leaves as soon as you board it."

That was the offer. The dream. To be out of the turmoil of

Earth, the devastation of China. Instead of waiting to be executed by the angry and feeble Chinese government, instead of watching the Chinese people writhe under the heel of the Muslim conquerors, he could board a beautiful clean starship and let them fling him out into space, to a world where human feet had never stepped, to be the founding leader of a colony that would hold his name in reverence forever. He would marry, have children, and, in all likelihood, be happy.

"How long do I have to decide?" asked Han Tzu.

Rackham glanced at his watch, then looked back at him without answering.

"Not a very long window of opportunity," said Han Tzu.

Rackham shook his head.

"It's a very attractive offer," said Han Tzu.

Rackham nodded.

"But I wasn't born for such happiness," said Han Tzu. "The present government of China has lost the mandate of heaven. If I live through the transition, I might be useful to the new government."

"And that's what you were born for?" asked Rackham.

"They tested me," said Han Tzu, "and I'm a child of war."

Rackham nodded. Then he reached inside his jacket and took out a pen and laid it on the table.

"What's that?" asked Han Tzu.

"The mandate of heaven," said Rackham.

Han Tzu knew then that the pen was a weapon. Because the mandate of heaven was always bestowed in blood and war.

"The items in the cap are extremely delicate," said Rackham. "Practice with round toothpicks."

Then he got up and walked out the back door of the restaurant.

No doubt there was some kind of transport waiting there.

Han Tzu wanted to leap to his feet and run after him so he could be taken out into space and set free of all that lay ahead.

Instead he put his hand over the pen and slid it across the table, then put it into the pocket of his trousers. It was a weapon. Which meant Graff and Rackham expected him to need a personal weapon soon. How soon?

Han Tzu took six toothpicks out of the little dispenser that stood on the table against the wall, beside the soy sauce. Then he got up and went to the toilet.

He pulled the cap off the pen very carefully, so he didn't spill out the four feather-ended poison darts bunched in it. Then he unscrewed the top of the pen. There were four holes there, besides the central shaft that held the tube of ink. The mechanism was cleverly designed to rotate automatically with each discharge. A blow-gun revolver.

He loaded four toothpicks into the four slots. They fit loosely. Then he screwed the pen back together.

The fountain pen writing tip covered the hole where the darts would emerge. When he held the top of the pen in his mouth, the point of the writing tip served as the sighting device. Point and shoot.

Point and *blow*.

He blew.

The toothpick hit the back wall of the bathroom more or less where he was aiming, only a foot lower. Definitely a close-range weapon.

He used up the rest of the toothpicks learning how high to aim in order to hit a target six feet away. The room wasn't large enough for him to practice aiming at anything farther. Then he gathered up the toothpicks, threw them away, and carefully loaded the pen with the real darts, handling them only by the feathered part of the shaft.

Then he flushed the toilet and reentered the restaurant. No one was waiting for him. So he sat down and ordered and ate methodically. No reason to face the crisis of his life with an empty stomach and the food here wasn't bad.

He paid and walked out into the street. He would not go home. If he waited there to be arrested, he would have to deal with any number of low-level thugs who would not be worth wasting a dart on.

Instead, he flagged down a bicycle taxi and headed for the ministry of defense.

The place was as crowded as ever. Pathetically so, thought Han Tzu. There was a reason for so many military bureaucrats a few years ago, when China was conquering Indochina and India, its millions of soldiers spread out to rule over a billion conquered people.

But now, the government had direct control only over Manchuria and the northern part of Han China. Persians and Arabs and Indonesians administered martial law in the great port cities of the south, and large armies of Turks were poised in Inner Mongolia, ready to slice through Chinese defenses at a moment's notice. Another large Chinese army was isolated in Sichuan, forbidden by the government to surrender any portion of their troops, forcing them to sustain a multimillion-man force from the production of that single province. In effect, they were under siege, getting weaker—and more hated by the civilian population— all the time.

There had even been a coup, right after the ceasefire—but it was a sham, a reshuffling of the politicians. Nothing but an excuse for repudiating the terms of the ceasefire.

No one in the military bureaucracy had lost his job. It was the military that had been driving China's new expansionism. It was the military that had failed.

Only Han Tzu had been relieved of his duties and sent home.

They could not forgive him for having named their stupidity for what it was. He had warned them every step of the way. They had ignored every warning. Each time he had shown them a way out of their self-induced dilemmas, they had ignored his offered plans and proceeded to make decisions based on bravado, face-saving, and delusions of Chinese invincibility.

At his last meeting he had left them with no face at all. He had stood there, a very young man in the presence of old men of enormous authority, and called them the fools they were. He laid out exactly why they had failed so miserably. He even told them that they had lost the mandate of heaven—the traditional excuse for a change of dynasty. This was the unforgivable sin, since the present dynasty claimed not to be a dynasty at all, not to be an empire, but rather to be a perfect expression of the will of the people.

What they forgot was that the Chinese people still believed in the mandate of heaven—and knew when a government no longer had it.

Now, as he showed his expired i.d. at the gate of the complex and was admitted without hesitation, he realized that there was only one fathomable reason why they hadn't already arrested him or had him killed:

They didn't dare.

It confirmed that Rackham was right to hand him a four-shot weapon and call it the mandate of heaven. There were forces at work here within the defense department that Han Tzu could not see, waiting in his apartment for someone to decide what to do with him. They had not even cut off his salary. There was panic and confusion in the military and now Han Tzu knew that he was at the center of it. That his silence, his waiting, had actually been a pestle constantly grinding at the mortar of military failure.

He should have known that his *j'accuse* speech would have more effects than merely to humiliate and enrage his "superiors." There were aides standing against the walls listening. And *they* would know that every word that Han Tzu said was true.

For all Han Tzu knew, his death or arrest had already been ordered a dozen times. And the aides who had been given those orders no doubt could prove that they had passed them along. But they would also have passed along the story of Han Tzu, the former Battle Schooler who had been part of Ender's Jeesh. The soldiers ordered to arrest him would have also been told that if Han Tzu had been heeded, China would not have been defeated by the Muslims and their strutting boy-Caliph.

The Muslims won because they had the brains to put *their* member of Ender's Jeesh, Caliph Alai, in charge of their armies—in charge of their whole government, their religion itself.

But the Chinese government had rejected their own Enderman, and now were giving orders for his arrest.

In these conversations, the phrase "mandate of heaven" would certainly have been spoken.

And the soldiers, if they left their quarters at all, seemed unable to locate Han Tzu's apartment.

For all these weeks since the war ended, the leadership must already have come face to face with their own powerlessness. If the soldiers would not follow them on such a simple matter as arresting the political enemy who had shamed them, then they were in grave danger.

That's why Han Tzu's i.d. was accepted at the gate. That's why he was allowed to walk unescorted among the buildings of the defense department complex.

Not *completely* unescorted. For he saw through his peripheral vision that a growing number of soldiers and functionaries were shadowing him, moving among the buildings in paths parallel to his own. For of course the gate guards would have spread the word at once: He's here.

So when he walked up to the entrance of the highest headquarters, he paused at the top step and turned around. Several thousand men and women were already in the space between buildings, and more were coming all the time. Many of them were soldiers under arms.

Han Tzu looked them over, watching as their numbers grew. No one spoke.

He bowed to them.

They bowed back.

Han Tzu turned and entered the building. The guards inside the doors also bowed to him. He bowed to each of them and then proceeded to the stairs leading to the second floor office suites where the highest officers of the military were certainly waiting for him.

Sure enough, he was met on the second floor by a young woman in uniform who bowed and said, "Most respectfully, sir, will you come to the office of the one called Snow Tiger?"

Her voice was devoid of sarcasm, but the name "Snow Tiger" carried its own irony these days. Han Tzu looked at her gravely. "What is your name, soldier?"

"Lieutenant White Lotus," she said.

"Lieutenant," said Han Tzu, "If heaven should bestow its mandate upon the true emperor today, would you serve him?"

"My life will be his," she said.

"And your pistol?"

She bowed deeply.

He bowed to her, then followed her to Snow Tiger's office.

They were all gathered there in the large anteroom—the men who had been present weeks ago when Han Tzu had scorned them for having lost the mandate of heaven. Their eyes were cold now, but he had no friends among these high officers.

Snow Tiger stood in the doorway of his inner office. It was unheard of for him to come out to meet anyone except members of the Politburo, none of whom were present.

"Han Tzu," he said.

Han Tzu bowed slightly. Snow Tiger bowed almost invisibly in return.

"I am happy to see you return to duty after your well-earned vacation," said Snow Tiger.

Han Tzu only stood in the middle of the room, regarding him steadily.

"Please come into my office."

Han Tzu walked slowly toward the open door. He knew that Lieutenant White Lotus stood at the door, watching to make sure that no one raised a hand to harm him.

Through the open door, Han Tzu could see two armed

soldiers flanking Snow Tiger's desk. Han Tzu stopped, regarding each of the soldiers in turn. Their faces showed nothing; they did not even look back at him. But he knew that they understood who he was. They had been chosen by Snow Tiger because he trusted them. But he should not have.

Snow Tiger took Han Tzu's pause as an invitation for him to enter the office first. Han Tzu did not follow him inside until Snow Tiger was seated at his desk.

Then Han Tzu entered.

"Please close the door," said Snow Tiger.

Han Tzu turned around and pulled the door all the way open.

Snow Tiger took his disobedience without blinking. What could he do or say without making himself seem pathetic?

Snow Tiger pushed a paper toward Han Tzu. It was an order, giving him command over the army that was slowly starving in Sichuan province. "You have proved your great wisdom many times," said Snow Tiger. "We ask you now to be the salvation of China and lead this great army against our enemy."

Han Tzu did not even bother to answer. A hungry, ill-equipped, demoralized, surrounded army was not going to accomplish miracles. And Han Tzu had no intention of accepting this or any other assignment from Snow Tiger.

"Sir, these are excellent orders," said Han Tzu loudly. He glanced at each of the soldiers standing beside the desk. "Do you see how excellent these orders are?"

Unused to being spoken to directly in such a high-level meeting, one of the soldiers nodded; the other merely shifted uncomfortably.

"I see only one error," said Han Tzu. His voice was loud enough to be heard in the anteroom as well.

Snow Tiger grimaced. "There is no error."

"Let me take my pen and show you," said Han Tzu. He took the pen from his shirt pocket and uncapped it. Then he drew a line through his own name at the top of the paper.

Turning around to face the open door, Han Tzu said, "There is no one in this building with the authority to command me."

It was his announcement that he was taking control of the government, and everyone knew it.

"Shoot him," said Snow Tiger behind him.

Han Tzu turned around, putting the pen to his mouth as he did.

But before he could fire a dart, the soldier who had refused to nod had blown out Snow Tiger's head, covering the other soldier with a smear of blood and brains and bone fragments.

The two soldiers bowed deeply to Han Tzu.

Han Tzu turned back around and strode out into the anteroom. Several of the old generals were heading for the door. But Lieutenant White Lotus had her pistol out and they all froze in place. "Emperor Han Tzu has not given the honorable gentlemen his permission to leave," she said.

Han Tzu spoke to the soldiers behind him. "Please assist the lieutenant in securing this room," he said. "It is my judgment that the officers in this room need time to contemplate upon the question of how China came into her current difficult situation. I would like them to remain in here until each of them has written a complete explanation of how so many mistakes came to be made, and how they think matters should have been conducted."

As Han Tzu expected, the suck-ups immediately went to work, dragging their compatriots back to their places against the walls. "Didn't you hear the emperor's request?" "We will do as you ask, Steward of Heaven." Little good it would do them. Han Tzu already knew perfectly well which officers he would trust to lead the Chinese military.

The irony was that the "great men" who were now humiliated and writing reports on their own mistakes were never the source of those errors. They only believed they were. And the underlings who had really originated the problems saw themselves as merely instruments of their commanders' will. But it was in the nature of underlings to use power recklessly, since blame could always be passed either upward or downward.

Unlike credit, which, like hot air, always rose.

As it will rise to me from now on.

Han Tzu left the offices of the late Snow Tiger. In the corridor, soldiers stood at every door. They had heard the single gunshot, and Han Tzu was pleased to see that they all looked relieved to learn that it was not Han Tzu himself who had been shot.

He turned to one soldier and said, "Please enter the nearest office and telephone for medical attention for the honorable Snow Tiger." To three others, he said, "Please help Lieutenant White Lotus secure the cooperation of the former generals inside this room who have been asked to write reports for me."

As they rushed to obey, Han Tzu gave assignments to the other soldiers and bureaucrats. Some of them would later be purged; others would be elevated. But at this moment, no one even thought of disobeying him. Within only a few minutes he had given orders to have the perimeter of the defense complex sealed. Until he was ready, he wanted no warning going to the Politburo.

But his precaution was in vain. For when he went down the stairs and walked out of the building, he was greeted by a roar from the thousands and thousands of military people who completely surrounded the headquarters building.

"Han Tzu!" they chanted. "Chosen of Heaven!"

There was no chance the noise would not be heard outside the complex. So instead of rounding up the Politburo all at once, he would have to waste time tracking them down as they fled to the countryside or tried to get to the airport or onto the river. But of one thing there could be no doubt: With the new emperor enthusiastically supported by the armed forces, there would be no resistance to his rule by any Chinese, anywhere.

That's what Mazer Rackham and Hyrum Graff had understood when they gave him his choice. Their only miscalculation was how completely the story of Han Tzu's wisdom had swept through the military. He hadn't needed the blowgun after all.

Though if he hadn't had it, would he have had the courage to act as boldly as he did?

One thing Han Tzu did not doubt. If the soldier had not killed Snow Tiger first, Han Tzu would have done it after—and would have killed both soldiers if they had not immediately submitted to his rule.

My hands are clean, but not because I wasn't prepared to bloody them.

As he made his way to the department of Planning and Strategy, where he would make his temporary headquarters, he could not help but ask himself: What if I had taken their initial offer, and fled into space? What would have happened to China then?

And then a more sobering question: What will happen to China *now?*

2

MOTHER

From: HMebane%GeneticTherapy@MayoFlorida.org.us
To: JulianDelphiki%Carlotta@DelphikiConsultations.com
Re: Prognosis

Dear Julian,

I wish I had better news. But yesterday's tests are conclusive. Estrogen therapy has had no effect on the epiphyses. They remain open, even though you definitely do not have any defect in the estrogen receptors on the growth plates of your bones.

As to your second request, of course we will continue to study your DNA, my friend, whether any of your missing embryos are found or not. What was done once can be done again, and Volescu's mistakes may be repeated with some other genetic alteration in the future. But the history of genetic research is fairly consistent. It takes time to map and isolate an unusual sequence and then perform animal experiments in order to determine what each portion of it does and how to counteract its effects.

There is no way to expedite such research. If we had ten thousand working on the problem, they would perform the same experiments in the same order and it would take the same amount of time. Someday we will understand why your astonishing intellect is so incurably linked with uncontrolled growth. Right now, to be candid, it seems to be almost malicious on the part of nature, as if there were some law that the price for the unleashing of human intellect is either autism or giantism.

If only, instead of military training, you had been taught biochemistry so that at your present age you could be up to speed in this field. I have no doubt that you would be more likely to have the kind of insights we need than we of fettered intellect. That is the bitter irony of your condition and your personal history. Even Volescu could not have anticipated the consequence of his alteration of your genes.

I feel like a coward, delivering this information in an email instead of face to face, but you insisted on no delay and a written report. The technical data will, of course, be forwarded to you as the final reports become available.

If only cryogenics had not proven to be such a barren field.

Sincerely,
Howard

As soon as Bob left for his shift as night manager of the grocery store, Randi sat down in front of the screen and started the special on Achilles Flandres over again from the beginning.

It galled her to hear how they slandered him, but by now she was adept at tuning it out. Megalomaniac. Madman. Murderer.

Why couldn't they see him as he really was? A genius like

Alexander the Great, who came *this* close to uniting the world and ending war forever.

Now the dogs would fight over the scraps of Achilles's achievements, while his body rested in an obscure grave in some miserable tropical village in Brazil.

And the assassin who had ended Achilles's life, who had thwarted his greatness, *he* was being honored as if there were something heroic about putting a bullet into the eye of an unarmed man. Julian Delphiki. Bean. The tool of the evil Hegemon Peter Wiggin.

Delphiki and Wiggin. Unworthy to be on the same planet with Achilles. And yet they claimed to be his heirs, the rightful rulers of the world.

Well, poor fools, you're the heirs of nothing. Because I know where Achilles's true heir is.

She patted her stomach, though that was a dangerous thing to do, what with her puking at a moment's notice ever since the pregnancy really took hold. She didn't show yet, and when she did, it was a fifty-fifty chance whether Bob would throw her out or keep her and accept the child as his own. Bob knew he couldn't father children—they'd had enough tests—and there was no point in pretending since he'd ask for a DNA test and then he'd know anyway.

And she had sworn never to tell that she had received an implant after all. She would have to pretend that she had had an affair with somebody and wanted to keep the baby. Bob would *not* like that at all. But she knew that her baby's life depended on keeping the secret.

The man who interviewed her at the fertility clinic had been adamant about that. "It doesn't matter whom you tell, Randi. The enemies of the great man know that this embryo exists. They'll be searching for it. They'll be watching all the women in the world who give birth within a certain time-frame. And any rumor that a baby was implanted rather than naturally conceived will bring them like hounds. Their resources are unlimited. They will spare no effort in their search. And when they find a woman that they even think *might* be the mother of his child, they will kill her, just in case."

"But there must be hundreds. Thousands of women who have babies implanted," Randi protested.

"Are you a Christian?" asked the man. "You've heard of the slaughter of the innocents? However many you have to kill, it's worth it to these monsters, as long as it means they can prevent the birth of this child."

Randi watched the stills of Achilles during his Battle School days and soon after, during his time at the asylum where his enemies had him confined after it became clear that he was a better commander than their precious Ender Wiggin. She had read it on the nets in many places, the fact that Ender Wiggin actually used plans devised by Achilles in order to beat the Buggers. They could glorify their phony little hero all they wanted—but everyone knew it was only because he was Peter Wiggin's little brother that Ender was given all the credit.

It was Achilles who had saved the world. And Achilles who had fathered the baby she had been chosen to bear.

Randi's only regret was that she could not be the biological mother as well, and that the child could not have been naturally conceived. But she knew that the bride of Achilles must have been very carefully chosen—a woman who could contribute the right genes so as not to dilute his brilliance and goodness and creativity and drive.

But *they* knew about the woman Achilles loved, and if she had been pregnant when he died, they would have torn the womb out of her so she could lie there in agony and watch them burn the fetus before her eyes.

So to protect the mother and the baby, Achilles had arranged for their embryo to be taken secretly and implanted in the womb of a woman who could be trusted to take the child to term and give him a good home and raise him with full awareness of his vast potential. To teach him secretly who he really was and whose cause he served, so he could grow up to fulfil his father's cruelly-blocked destiny. It was a sacred trust, and Randi was worthy of it.

Bob was not. It was that simple. Randi had always known that she married beneath herself. Bob was a good provider, but he hadn't the imagination to understand anything more important than making a living and planning his next fishing trip. She could just imagine how he would respond if she told him that not only was she pregnant, but the baby was not even hers.

Already she had found several places on the web where people were searching for "lost" or "kidnapped" embryos. She knew—the man who spoke to her had warned her—that these were likely to originate from Achilles's enemies, trolling for information that would lead them to . . . to her.

She wondered if maybe the very act of searching for people searching for embryos would alert them. The search companies claimed that no government had access to their databases, but it was possible that the International Fleet was intercepting all the messages and monitoring all the searches. People said that the I.F. was really under the control of the United States government, that America's isolationism was a façade and it ran everything through the I.F. Then there were the people who said that it was the other way around—the U.S. was isolationist because that was the way the I.F. wanted it, since most of the space technology they depended on was developed and built in the U.S.

It couldn't be an accident that Peter the Hegemon was American himself.

She would stop searching for information about kidnapped embryos. It was all lies and traps and tricks. She knew she would seem paranoid to anyone else, but that's only because they didn't know what she knew. There really were monsters in the world, and those who kept secrets from them had to live with constant vigilance.

There on the screen was that terrible picture. They showed it over and over again: Achilles's poor broken body lying on the floor in the Hegemon's palace, looking so peaceful, not a wound on his body. Some on the nets said that Delphiki didn't shoot him through the eye at all; that if he had, Achilles's face would have been powder-burned and there would have been an exit wound and blood all over.

No, Delphiki and Wiggin imprisoned Achilles and faked some kind of phony standoff with the police, pretending that Achilles was taking hostages or something, so they'd have an excuse for killing him. But in fact they gave him a lethal injection. Or poisoned his food. Or infected him with a hideous disease so he died writhing on the floor in agony while Delphiki and Wiggin looked on.

Like Richard III murdering those poor princes in the tower.

But when my son is born, Randi told herself, then all these false histories will be destroyed. The liars will be eliminated, and so will their lies.

Then this footage will be used in a *true* story. My son will see to that. No one will ever even hear the lies they're telling now. And Achilles will be known as the great one, even greater than the son who will have completed his life's work.

And I will be remembered and honored as the woman who sheltered him and gave him birth and raised him up to rule the world.

All I have to do to accomplish that is: nothing.

Nothing that calls attention to me. Nothing that makes me unusual or strange.

Yet the one thing she couldn't bear to do was *nothing*. Just to sit here, watching the television, worrying, fretting—it had to be harmful for the baby, to have so much adrenalin coursing through her system.

It was the waiting that was making her crazy. Not waiting for the baby—that was natural and she would love every day of her pregnancy.

It was waiting for her life to change. Waiting . . . for Bob. Why should she wait for Bob?

She got up from the couch, switched off the television, went into the bedroom, and started packing her clothing and other things into cardboard boxes. She emptied out Bob's obsessive financial records in order to empty the boxes—let him amuse himself by sorting them out later.

Only after she had packed and taped up the fourth box did it occur to her that the *normal* pattern would have been to tell him about the baby and then make *him* move out.

But she didn't want a connection with him. Didn't want any dispute about paternity. She just wanted to be gone. Out of his ordinary, meaningless life, out of this pointless town.

Of course she couldn't just disappear. Then she'd be a missing person. She'd be added to databases. Someone would be alerted.

So she took her boxes of clothing and a few favorite pots, pans, and recipe books and loaded them into the car that she had owned before she married Bob and that was still in her name alone. Then she spent half an hour writing different versions of a letter to Bob explaining that she didn't love him anymore and was leaving and didn't want him to look for her.

No. Nothing in writing. Nothing that can be reported to anyone.

She got in the car and drove to the grocery store. On the way in from the parking lot she took a cart that someone had left blocking a parking space and pushed it into the store. Helping keep the parking lot clear of abandoned carts proved that she wasn't vindictive. She was a civilized person who wanted to help Bob do well in his business and his ordinary, ordinary, ordinary life. It would *help* him not to have such an extraordinary woman and child in that life.

He was out on the floor and instead of waiting in his office, she went in search of him. She found him supervising the unloading of a truck that was late because of a breakdown on the highway, making sure that the frozen foods were at a low enough temperature to be safely offloaded and shelved.

"Can you wait just a minute?" he said. "I know it's important or you wouldn't have come down here, but . . ."

"Oh, Bob, it won't take more than a second." She leaned close to him. "I'm pregnant and it's not yours."

Being a two-part message, it didn't entirely register right away. For a moment he looked happy. Then his face started to turn red.

She leaned in close again. "Don't worry, though. I'm leaving you. I'll let you know where to mail the divorce papers. Now, you get back to work."

She started to walk away. "Randi," he called after her.

"Not your fault, Bob!" she called over her shoulder. "Nothing was your fault. You're a great guy."

She felt liberated as she walked back through the store. Her mood was so generous and expansive that she bought a little container of lip balm and a bottle of water. The tiny amount of profit from the sale would be her last contribution to Bob's life.

Then she got into the car and drove south, because that way was a right turn coming out of the parking lot, and traffic was too heavy to wait for a chance to go left. She'd drive wherever the currents of the traffic led her. She wouldn't try to hide from anybody. She'd let Bob know where she was as soon as she decided she was there, and she'd divorce him in a perfectly ordinary way. But she wouldn't bump into anyone she knew or anyone who knew her. She would become effectively invisible, not like someone *trying* to hide, but like someone who had nothing to hide at all but who never became important to anyone.

Except to her beloved son.

3

COUP

From: JulianDelphiki%milcom@hegemon.gov
To: Volescu%levers@plasticgenome.edu
Re: Why keep hiding when you don't have to?

Look, if we wanted you dead or punished, don't you think it would have happened already? Your protector is gone and there's not a country on Earth that will protect you if we lay out the facts of your "achievements."

What you did, you did. Now help us find our children, wherever you've hidden them.

Peter Wiggin had brought Petra Arkanian with him because she knew Caliph Alai. They had both been in Ender's Jeesh together. And it was Alai who had sheltered her and Bean in the weeks before the Muslim invasion of China—or liberation of Asia, depending on which propaganda mill you shopped at.

But now it seemed that having Petra with him meant nothing at all. Nobody in Damascus acted as if it even mattered that the Hegemon had come like a supplicant to see the Caliph. Not that Peter had arrived with any publicity—this was a private visit, with him and Petra passing themselves off as a tourist couple.

Complete with bickering. Because Petra had no patience with him. Everything he did and said and even *thought* was wrong. And last night, when he finally demanded, "Tell me what you really hate about me, Petra, instead of pretending it's all this trivial stuff."

Her answer had been devastating: "Because the only difference I ever saw between you and Achilles was that you let others do your killing for you."

It was so patently unfair. Peter had devoted himself to trying to avoid war.

At least now he knew why she was so furious at him. When Bean went into the besieged Hegemony compound to face Achilles alone, Peter understood that Bean was putting his own life on the line and that it was extremely unlikely that Achilles would give him what he had promised—the embryos of Bean's and Petra's children that had been stolen from a hospital soon after in vitro fertilization.

So when Bean put a .22 slug through Achilles's eye and let it bounce around a few dozen times inside his skull, the only person who absolutely got everything he needed was Peter himself. He got the Hegemony compound back; he got all the hostages safely returned; he even regained his tiny army trained by Bean and led by Suriyawong, who had turned out to be loyal after all.

While Bean and Petra did not get their babies, and Bean was dying, Peter couldn't do a thing to help either of them except provide office space and computers for them to conduct their search. He also used all his connections to get them whatever cooperation he could from the nations where they needed access to records.

Right after Achilles's death, Petra had simply been relieved. Her irritation with Peter had developed—or merely resurfaced—in the weeks after, as she saw him trying to reestablish the prestige of the office of Hegemon and try to put together a coalition. She began making snotty little comments about Peter playing in his "geopolitical sandbox" and "outstrutting the heads of state."

He should have expected that actually having her travel along with him would only make it worse. Especially because he wasn't following her advice about anything.

"You can't just show up," she told him.

"I have no choice."

"It's disrespectful. As if you think you can drop in on the Caliph. It's treating him like a servant."

"That's why I brought *you*," Peter patiently explained. "So you can see him and explain that the only way this can happen is if it's a secret meeting."

"But he already told me and Bean that we couldn't have access to him like we used to. We're infidels. He's Caliph."

"The Pope sees non-Catholics all the time. He sees *me*."

"The Pope isn't Muslim," said Petra.

"Just be patient," said Peter. "Alai knows we're here. Eventually he'll decide to see me."

"Eventually? I'm pregnant, Mr. Hegemon, and my husband is dying in a big way, ha ha ha, and you're wasting some of the time we have together and that pisses me off."

"I invited you to come. I didn't compel you."

"It's a good thing you didn't try."

But now it was out. In the open. Clear at last. Of course she was really irritated at all the things she complained about. But underneath it all was resentment about how Peter had let Bean do his killing for him.

"Petra," said Peter. "I'm not a soldier."

"Neither is Bean!"

"Bean is the finest military mind alive," said Peter.

"So why isn't he Hegemon?"

"Because he doesn't want to be."

"And you do. And *that's* why I hate you, since you asked."

"You know why I wanted this office and what I'm trying to do with it. You've read my Locke essays."

"I also read your Demosthenes essays."

"Those also needed to be written. But I intend to govern as Locke."

"You govern nothing. The only reason you even have your little army is because Bean and Suriyawong created it and decided to let you have the use of it. You only have your precious compound and all your staff because Bean killed Achilles and gave it back to you. And now you're back to putting on your little show of importance, but you know what? Nobody's fooled. You're not even as powerful as the Pope. He's got the Vatican and a billion Catholics. You've got nothing but what my husband gave you."

Peter didn't think this was quite accurate—he had labored for years to build up his network of contacts, and he had kept the office of Hegemon from being abolished. Over the years he had made it mean something. He had saved Haiti from chaos. Several small nations owed their independence or freedom to his diplomatic and, yes, military intervention.

But certainly he was on the verge of losing it all to Achilles—because of his own stupid mistake. A mistake that Bean and Petra had warned him about before he made it. A mistake that Bean had rectified only at a grave risk.

"Petra," said Peter, "you're right. I owe everything to you and Bean. But that doesn't change the fact that whatever you think of me and whatever you think of the office of Hegemon, I hold that office, and I'm trying to use it to avoid another bloody war."

"You're trying to use your office to make your office into 'dictator of the world.' Unless you can figure out a way to extend your reach out to the colonies and become 'dictator of the known universe.'"

"We don't actually have any colonies yet," said Peter.

"The ships are all still in transit and will be until we're all dead. But by the time they arrive, I'd like them to send their ansible messages back home to an Earth that is united under a single democratic government."

"It's the democratic part I missed," said Petra. "Who elected you?"

"Since I don't have any actual authority over anybody, Petra, how can it possibly matter if I'm not legitimately authorized?"

"You argue like a debater," she said. "You don't actually have to have an idea, you just have to have a seemingly clever refutation."

"And you argue like a nine-year-old," said Peter. "Sticking your fingers in your ears and going 'La la la' and 'same to you.'"

Petra looked like she wanted to slap him. Instead she put her fingers in her ears and said, "Same to you" and "La la la."

He did not laugh. Instead he reached out a hand, intending to pull her arm away from her ear. But she whirled around and kicked his hand so hard that he thought she might have broken his wrist. As it was, he staggered and stumbled over the corner of the bed in his hotel room and ended up on his butt on the floor.

"There's the Hegemon of Earth," said Petra.

"Where's your camera? Don't you want this to be public?"

"If I wanted to destroy you, you'd be destroyed."

"Petra, I didn't send Bean into that compound. Bean sent himself."

"You let him go."

"Yes I did, and in any event I was proven right."

"But you didn't know he'd live. I was carrying his baby and you sent him in to *die*."

"Nobody sends Bean anywhere," said Peter, "and you know it."

She whirled away from him and stalked out of the room.

She would have slammed the door, but the pneumatics prevented it.

He had seen, though. The tears in her eyes.

She didn't hate Peter. She wanted to hate him. But what she really was furious about was that her husband was dying and she had agreed to this mission because she knew it would be important. If it worked, it would be important. But it wasn't working. It probably wouldn't work.

Peter knew that. But he also knew that he had to talk to Caliph Alai, and he had to do it now if the conversation was to have any good effect. If possible, he'd like to have the conversation without risking the prestige of the office of Hegemon. But the longer they delayed, the greater the likelihood of word of his trip to Damascus getting out. And then if Alai rebuffed him, the humiliation would be public, and the office of Hegemon would be greatly diminished.

So Petra's judgment of him was obviously unfair. If all he cared about was his own authority, he wouldn't be here.

And she was clever enough to know that. *She* got into Battle School, didn't she? *She* was the only girl among Ender's Jeesh. That certified her as his superior—at least in the area of strategy and leadership. Surely she must see that he was putting the goal of preventing a bloody war above his own career.

As soon as he thought of this, he heard her voice inside his head, saying, "Oh, isn't that fine and noble of you, to put the lives of hundreds of thousands of soldiers ahead of your own indelible place in history. Do you think you get a prize for that?" Or else she'd say, "The only reason I'm along is specifically so you can avoid risking anything." Or else, "You've always been bold as a risk-taker—when the stakes are high enough and your own life isn't on the line."

This is great, Peter, he thought. You don't even need her in the room with you and you can still carry on an argument with her.

How did Bean stand her? No doubt she didn't treat him like this.

No. It was impossible to imagine that being nasty was something she could switch on and off. Bean *had* to have seen this side of her. And yet he stayed with her.

And loved her. Peter wondered what it would be like, to have Petra look at him the way she looked at Bean.

Then he corrected himself at once. Wonderful to have *a woman* look at him the way Petra looked at Bean. The last thing he wanted was a lovelorn Petra making googly eyes at him.

The telephone rang.

The voice made sure it was "Peter Jones" and then said, "Five in the morning, be downstairs outside the north lobby doors." Click.

Well, what brought *that* on? Something in Petra's and his argument? Peter had swept the room for bugs, but that didn't mean they couldn't have some low-tech device like somebody in the next room with his ear pressed against the wall.

What did we say to make them let me see the Caliph?

Maybe it was what he said about avoiding another bloody war.

Or perhaps it was because they heard him admit to Petra that maybe he didn't have any legitimate authority.

What if they recorded that? What if it suddenly surfaced on the web?

Then it would happen, and he'd do his best to recover from the blow, and either he'd succeed or he'd fail. No point fretting about it now. Somebody was meeting him at the north door of the lobby tomorrow morning before daylight. Maybe they'd lead him to Alai, and maybe he'd achieve what he needed to achieve, save all that he needed to save.

He toyed with the idea of not telling Petra about the meeting. After all, she had no pertinent office at all. She had no particular right to be at the meeting, especially after their quarrel tonight.

Don't be spiteful and petty, Peter told himself. One spiteful act brings too much pleasure—it just makes you want to do another, and another. And sooner each time.

So he picked up the phone and on the seventh ring she picked it up.

"I'm not going to apologize," she said curtly.

"Good," he said. "Because I don't want some smarmy I'm-sorry-you-got-so-upset fake apology. What I want is for you to join me at five A.M. at the north door of the lobby."

"What for?"

"I don't know," said Peter. "I'm just passing along what I was just told on the telephone."

"He's going to let us see him?"

"Or he's sending thugs to escort us back to the airport. How can I possibly know? You're the one who's his friend. You tell *me* what he's planning."

"I haven't the slightest idea," said Petra. "It's not like Alai and I were ever *close*. And are you sure they want me to come to the actual meeting? There are plenty of Muslims who would be horrified at the thought of an unveiled married woman speaking face to face with a man—even the Caliph."

"I don't know what they want," said Peter. "*I* want you at the meeting."

———

They were ushered into a closed van and driven along a route that Peter assumed was convoluted and deceptively long. For all he knew, the Caliph's headquarters was next door to their hotel. But Alai's people knew that without the Caliph there was no unity, and without unity Islam had no strength, so they were taking no chances on letting outsiders know where the Caliph lived.

They were driven far enough that they might be outside Damascus. When they emerged from the van, it was not in daylight, it was indoors . . . or underground. Even the porticoed garden into which they were ushered was artificially lighted, and the sound of running and trickling and falling water masked any faint noises that might have seeped in from outside and hinted where they were.

Alai did not so much greet them as notice their presence as he walked in the garden. He did not even face them, but sat a few meters away, facing a fountain, and began to speak.

"I have no desire to humiliate you, Peter Wiggin," he said. "You should not have come."

"I appreciate your letting me speak with you at all," Peter answered.

"Wisdom said that I should announce to the world that the Hegemon had come to see the Caliph, and the Caliph refused to see him. But I told Wisdom to be patient, and let Folly be my guide today in this garden."

"Petra and I are here to—"

"Petra is here," said Alai, "because you thought her presence might get you in to see me, and you needed a witness that I would be reluctant to kill, and because you want her to be your ally after her husband is dead."

Peter did not let himself glance at Petra to see how she took this sally from Alai. She knew the man; Peter did not. She would interpret his words as she saw fit, and nothing he could see in her face right now would help him understand anything. It would only weaken him to show he cared.

"I'm here to offer my help," said Peter.

"I command armies that rule over more than half the population of the world," said Alai. "I have united Muslim nations from Morocco to Indonesia, and liberated the oppressed peoples in between."

"It's the difference between 'conquered' and 'liberated' that I wanted to talk about."

"So you came to rebuke me, not to help after all," said Alai.

"I see I'm wasting my time," said Peter. "If we can't speak together without petty debate, then you are past receiving help."

"Help?" said Alai. "One of my advisers said to me, when

I told them I wanted to see you, 'How many soldiers does this Hegemon have?' "

"How many divisions has the Pope?" quoted Peter.

"More than the Hegemon has," said Alai, "if the Pope should ask for them. As the old dead United Nations found out long ago, religion always has more warriors than some vague international abstraction."

Peter realized then that Alai was not speaking to him. He was speaking past him. This was not a private conversation after all.

"I do not intend to be disrespectful to the Caliph," said Peter. "I have seen the majesty of your achievement and the generosity of spirit with which you have dealt with your enemies."

Alai visibly relaxed. They were now playing the same game. Peter had finally understood the rules. "What is to be gained from humiliating those who believe they stand outside the power of God?" asked Alai. "God will show them his power in his own good time, and until then we are wise to be kind."

Alai was speaking as the true believers around him required him to speak—always asserting the primacy of the Caliphate over all non-Muslim powers.

"The dangers I came to speak of," said Peter, "will not ever come from me or because of the small influence I have in the world. Though I was not chosen by God, and there are few who listen to me, I also seek, as you seek, the peace and happiness of the children of God on Earth."

Now was the time, if Alai was completely the captive of his supporters, for him to rant about how it was blasphemous for an infidel like Peter to invoke the name of God or pretend that there could be peace before all the world was under the rule of the Caliphate.

Instead Alai said, "I listen to all men, but obey only God."

"There was a day when Islam was hated and feared throughout the world," said Peter. "That era ended long ago, before either of us were born, but your enemies are reviving those old stories."

"Those old lies, you mean," said Alai.

"The fact that no man can make the Hajj in his own skin and live," said Peter, "suggests that not all the stories are lies. In the name of Islam terrible weapons were acquired and in the name of Islam they were used to destroy the most sacred place on Earth."

"It is not destroyed," said Alai. "It is protected."

"It's so radioactive that nothing can live within a hundred kilometers," said Peter. "And you know what the explosion did to Al-hajar Al-aswad."

"The stone was not sacred in itself," said Alai, "and Muslims never worshipped it. We only used it as a marker to remember the holy covenant between God and his true followers. Now its molecules are powdered and spread over the whole Earth, as a blessing to the righteous and a curse to the wicked, while we who follow Islam still remember where it was, and what it marked, and bow toward that place when we pray."

It was a sermon he had surely said many times before.

"Muslims suffered more than anyone in those dark days," said Peter. "But that is not what most people remember. They remember bombs that killed innocent women and children, and fanatical self-murderers who hated any freedom except the freedom to obey the very narrowest interpretation of Shari'ah."

He could see Alai stiffen. "I make no judgment myself," Peter immediately said. "I was not alive then. But in India and China and Thailand and Vietnam, there are people who fear that the soldiers of Islam did not come as liberators, but as conquerors. That they'll be arrogant in victory. That the Caliphate will never allow freedom to the people who welcomed him and aided him in overcoming the Chinese conquerors."

"We do not force Islam on any nation," said Alai, "and

those who claim otherwise are liars. We ask them only to open their doors to the teachers of Islam, so the people can choose."

"Forgive my confusion, then," said Peter. "The people of the world see that open door, and notice that no one passes through it except in one direction. Once a nation has chosen Islam, then the people are never allowed to choose anything else."

"I hope I do not hear the echo of the Crusades in your voice."

The Crusades, thought Peter, that old bugbear. So Alai really has joined himself to the rhetoric of fanaticism. "I only report to you what is being said among those who are seeking to ally against you in war," said Peter. "That war is what I hope to avoid. What those old terrorists tried, and failed, to achieve—a worldwide war between Islam and everyone else—may now be almost upon us."

"The people of God are not afraid of the outcome of such a war," said Alai.

"It's the process of the war that I hope to avoid," said Peter. "Surely the Caliph also seeks to avoid needless bloodshed."

"All who die are at the mercy of God," said Alai. "Death is not the thing to fear most in life, since it comes to all."

"If that's how you feel about the carnage of war," said Peter, "then I've wasted your time." Peter leaned forward, preparing to rise to his feet.

Petra put her hand on his thigh, pressing down, urging him to remain seated. But Peter had had no intention of leaving.

"But," said Alai.

Peter waited.

"But God desires the willing obedience of his children, not their terror."

It was the statement Peter had been hoping for.

"Then the murders in India, the massacres—"

"There have been no massacres."

"The *rumors* of massacre," said Peter, "which seem to be

supported by smuggled vids and eyewitness accounts and aerial photographs of the alleged killing fields—I am relieved that such things would not be the policy of the Caliphate."

"If someone has slain innocents for no other crime than believing in the idols of Hinduism and Buddhism, then such a murderer would be no Muslim."

"What the people of India wonder—"

"You do not speak for the people of any place except a small compound in Ribeirão Preto," said Alai.

"What my informants in India tell me that the people of India wonder is whether the Caliph intends to repudiate and punish such murderers or merely pretend they didn't happen? Because if they cannot trust the Caliph to control what is done in the name of Allah, then they will defend themselves."

"By piling stones in the road?" asked Alai. "We are not the Chinese, to be frightened by stories of a 'Great Wall of India.' "

"The Caliph now controls a population that has far more non-Muslims than Muslims," said Peter.

"So far," said Alai.

"The question is whether the proportion of Muslims will increase because of teaching, or because of the slaughter and oppression of unbelievers?"

For the first time, Alai turned his head, and then his body, to face them. But it was not Peter he looked at. He only had eyes for Petra.

"Don't you know me?" he said to her.

Peter wisely did not answer. His words were doing their work, and now it was time for Petra to do what he had brought her to do.

"Yes," she said.

"Then tell him," said Alai.

"No," she said.

Alai sat in wounded silence.

"Because I don't know whether the voice I hear in this garden is the voice of Alai or the voice of the men who put him into office and control who may or may not speak to him."

"It is the voice of the Caliph," said Alai.

"I've read history," said Petra, "and so have you. The Sultans and Caliphs were rarely anything but holy figureheads, when they allowed their servants to keep them within walls. Come out into the world, Alai, and see for yourself the bloody work that's being done in your name."

They heard footsteps, loud ones, many footsteps, and soldiers trotted out of concealment. Within moments, rough hands held Petra and were dragging her away. Peter did not raise a hand to interfere. He only faced Alai, staring at him, demanding silently that he show who ruled in his house.

"Stop," said Alai. Not loudly, but clearly.

"No woman speaks to the Caliph like that!" shouted a man who was behind Peter. Peter did not turn. It was enough to know that the man had spoken in Common, not in Arabic, and that his accent bore the marks of a superb education.

"Let go of her," Alai said to the soldiers, ignoring the man who had shouted.

There was no hesitation. The soldiers let go of Petra. At once she came back to Peter's side and sat down. Peter also sat down. They were spectators now.

The man who had shouted, dressed in the flowing robes of an imitation sheik, strode up to Alai. "She uttered a *command* to the Caliph! A challenge! Her tongue must be cut out of her mouth."

Alai remained seated. He said nothing.

The man turned to the soldiers. "Take her!" he said.

The soldiers began to move.

"Stop," said Alai. Quietly but clearly.

The soldiers stopped. They looked miserable and confused.

"He doesn't know what he's saying," the man said to the soldiers. "Take the girl and then we'll discuss it later."

"Do not move except at my command," said Alai.

The soldiers did not move.

The man faced Alai again. "You're making a mistake," he said.

"The soldiers of the Caliph are witnesses," said Alai. "The Caliph has been threatened. The Caliph's orders have been countermanded. There is a man in this garden who thinks he has more power in Islam than the Caliph. So the words of this infidel girl are correct. The Caliph is a holy figurehead, who allows his servants to keep him within walls. The Caliph is a prisoner and others rule Islam in his name."

Peter could see in the man's face that he now realized that the Caliph was not just a boy who could be manipulated.

"Don't go down this road," he said.

"The soldiers of the Caliph are witnesses," said Alai, "that this man has given a command to the Caliph. A challenge. But unlike the girl, this man has ordered armed soldiers, in the presence of the Caliph, to disobey the Caliph. The Caliph can *hear* any words without harm, but when soldiers are ordered to disobey him, it does not require an imam to explain that treason and blasphemy are present here."

"If you move against me," the man said, "then the others—"

"The soldiers of the Caliph are witnesses," said Alai, "that this man is part of a conspiracy against the Caliph. There are 'others.'"

One soldier came forward and laid a hand on the man's arm. He shook it off.

Alai smiled at the soldier.

The soldier took the man's arm again, but not gently. Other soldiers stepped forward. One took the man's other arm. The rest faced Alai, waiting for orders.

"We have seen today that one man of my council thinks he is the master of the Caliph. Therefore, any soldier of Islam who truly wishes to serve the Caliph will take every member of the council into custody and hold them in silence until the Caliph has decided which of them can be trusted and which must be discarded from the service of God. Move quickly, my friends, before the ones who are spying on this conversation have time to escape."

The man wrenched one hand free and in a moment held a wicked-looking knife.

But Alai's hand was already firmly gripping his wrist.

"My old friend," said Alai, "I know that you were not raising that weapon against your Caliph. But suicide is a grave and terrible sin. I refuse to allow you to meet God with your own blood on your hands." With a twist of his hand, Alai made the man groan with pain. The knife clattered on the flagstones.

"Soldiers," said Alai. "Make me safe. Meanwhile, I will continue my conversation with these visitors, who are under the protection of my hospitality."

Two soldiers dragged the prisoner away, while the others took off at a run.

"You have work to do," said Peter.

"I've just done it," said Alai. He turned to Petra. "Thank you for seeing what I needed."

"Being a provocateur comes naturally to me," she said.

"I hope we've been helpful."

"Everything you said has been heard," said Alai. "And I assure you that when it's actually in my power to control the armies of Islam, they will behave as true Muslims, and not as barbarian conquerors. Meanwhile, however, I'm afraid that bloodshed is likely, and I believe you will be safest here with me in this garden for the next half hour or so."

"Hot Soup has just taken over in China," said Petra.

"So I've heard."

"And he's taking the title of emperor," she added.

"Back to the good old days."

"A new dynasty in Beijing now faces the restored Caliphate in Damascus," said Petra. "It would be a terrible thing, for members of the Jeesh to have to choose up sides and wage war against each other. Surely that's not what Battle School was ever meant to accomplish."

"Battle School?" said Alai. "They may have identified us, but we already were who we were before they laid a hand on us. Do you think that without Battle School, I could not be where I am, or Han Tzu where he is? Look at Peter Wiggin—*he* didn't go to Battle School, but he got himself appointed Hegemon."

"An empty title," said Peter.

"It was when you got it," said Alai. "Just as my title was until two minutes ago. But when you sit in the chair and wear the hat, some people don't understand that it's just a play and start obeying you as if you had real power. And then you *have* real power. Neh?"

"Eh," said Petra.

Peter smiled. "I'm not your enemy, Alai," he said.

"You're not my friend, either," said Alai. But then he smiled. "The question is whether you'll turn out to be a friend to humanity. Or whether I will." He turned back to Petra. "And so much depends on what your husband chooses to do before he dies."

Petra nodded gravely. "He'd prefer to do nothing except enjoy the months or perhaps years he'll have with me and our child."

"God willing," said Alai, "that's all he'll be required to do."

A soldier came pounding across the flagstones. "Sir, the compound is secure and none of the council have escaped."

"I'm happy to hear that," said Alai.

"Three councilmen are dead, sir," said the soldier. "It could not be helped."

"I'm sure that's the truth," said Alai. "They are now in God's hands. The rest are in mine, and now I must try to do what God would have me do. Now, my son, will you take these two friends of the Caliph safely back to their hotel? Our conversation is finished, and I wish them to be free to leave Damascus, unhindered and unrecognized. No one will speak of their presence in this garden on this day."

"Yes, my Caliph," said the soldier. He bowed, and then

turned to Peter and Petra. "Will you come with me, friends of the Caliph?"

"Thank you," Petra said. "The Caliph is blessed with true servants in this house."

The man did not acknowledge her praise. "This way," he said to Peter.

As they followed him back to the enclosed van, Peter wondered whether he might have unconsciously planned for the events that happened here today, or whether it was just dumb luck.

Or whether Petra and Alai planned it, and Peter was nothing more than their pawn, thinking foolishly that he was making his own decisions and conducting his own strategy.

Or are we, as the Muslims believe, only acting out the script of God?

Not likely. Any God worth believing in could make up a better plan than the mess the world was in now.

In my childhood I set my hand to improving the world, and for a while I succeeded. I stopped a war through words I wrote on the nets, when people didn't know who I was. But now I have the empty title of Hegemon. Wars are swirling back and forth across swathes of the Earth like a reaper's scythe, vast populations are seething under the whips of new oppressors, and I am powerless to change a thing.

4

BARGAIN

From: PeterWiggin%private@hegemon.gov
To: SacredCause%OneMan@FreeThai.org
Re: Suriyawong's actions concerning Achilles Flandres

Dear Ambul,

At all times during Achilles Flandres's infiltration of the Hegemony, Suriyawong acted as my agent inside Flandres's growing organization. It was at my instructions that he pretended to be Flandres's staunch ally, and that was why, at the crucial moment when Julian Delphiki faced the monster, Suriyawong and his elite soldiers acted for the good of all humankind—including Thailand—and made possible the destruction of the man who, more than any other, was responsible for the defeat and occupation of Thailand.

This is the "public story," as you pointed out. Now I point out that in this case the public story also happens to be the complete truth.

Like you, Suriyawong is a Battle School graduate. China's new Emperor and the Muslim Caliph are both Battle School graduates. But they are two of those chosen to take part in my brother Ender's famous Jeesh. Even if you discount their actual brilliance as military commanders, the public perception of their powers is at the level of magic. This will affect the morale of your soldiers as surely as of theirs.

How do you suppose you will keep Thailand free if you reject Suriyawong? He is no threat to your leadership; he will be your most valuable tool against your enemies.

Sincerely,
Peter, Hegemon

Bean stooped to pass through the doorway. He wasn't actually tall enough to bang his head. But it had happened often enough, in other doorways that once would have given him plenty of room, that now he was overcautious. He didn't know what to do with his hands, either. They seemed too big for any job he might need them for. Pens were like toothpicks; his finger filled the trigger guard of many a pistol. Soon he'd have to butter his finger to get it out, as if the pistol were a too-tight ring.

And his joints ached. And his head hurt sometimes like it was going to split in two. Because, in fact, it was trying to do exactly that. The soft spot on the top of his head could not seem to expand fast enough to make room for his growing brain.

The doctors loved that part. To find out what it did to the mental function of an adult to have the brain grow. Did it disrupt memory? Or merely add to capacity? Bean submitted to their questions and measurements and scans and bloodlettings because he might not find all his children before he died, and anything they learned from studying him might help them.

But at times like this he felt nothing but despair. There was no help for him, and none for them, either. He would not find them. And if he did, he could not help them.

What difference has my life made? I killed one man. He was a monster, but I had it in my power to kill him at least once before, and failed to do it. So don't I share in the responsibility for what he did in the intervening years? The deaths, the misery.

Including Petra's suffering when she was his captive. Including our own suffering over the children he stole from us.

And yet he went on searching, using every contact he could think of, every search engine on the nets, every program he could devise for manipulating the public records in order to be ready to identify which births were of his children, implanted in surrogates.

For of that much he was certain. Achilles and Volescu had never intended to give the embryos back to him and Petra. That promise had only been a lure. A man of less malice than Achilles might have killed the embryos—as he pretended to do when he broke test tubes during their last confrontation in Ribeirão Preto. But for Achilles, killing itself was never a pleasure. He killed when he thought it was necessary. When he actually wanted to make someone suffer, he made sure the suffering lingered as long as possible.

Bean's and Petra's children would be born to mothers unknown to them, probably scattered throughout the world by Volescu.

But Achilles had done his work well. Volescu's travels were completely erased from the public record. And there was nothing about the man to make him particularly memorable. They could show his picture to a million airline workers and another million cab drivers throughout the world and half of them might remember seeing a man who looked "like that" but none of them would be sure of anything and Volescu's path could not be retraced.

And when Bean had tried to appeal to Volescu's lingering shreds of decency—which he hoped existed, against all evidence—the man had gone underground and now all Bean could hope for was that somebody, some agency somewhere, would find him, arrest him, and hold him long enough for Bean to . . .

To what? Torture him? Threaten him? Bribe him? What could possibly induce Volescu to tell him what he needed to know?

Now the International Fleet had sent him some officer to give him "important information." What could they possibly know? The I.F. was forbidden to operate on the surface of Earth. Even if they had agents who had discovered Volescu's whereabouts, why would they risk exposing their own illegal activities just to help Bean find his babies? They had made a big deal about how loyal they were to the Battle School graduates, especially to Ender's Jeesh, but he doubted it went *that* far. Money, that's what they offered. All the Battle School grads had a nice pension. They could go home like Cincinnatus and farm for the rest of their lives, without even having to worry about the weather or the seasons or the harvest. They could grow weeds and still prosper.

Instead, I stupidly allowed children of my deformed and self-destructive genes to be created *in vitro* and now Volescu has planted them in foreign wombs and I must find them before he and people like him can exploit them and use them up and then watch them die of giantism, like me, before they turn twenty.

Volescu knows. He would never leave it to chance. Because he still imagined himself to be a scientist. He would want to gather data about the children. To him, it was all one big experiment, with the added inconvenience of being illegal and based on stolen embryos. To Volescu, those embryos belonged to him by right. To him, Bean was nothing but the experiment that got away. Anything he produced was part of Volescu's long-term study.

An old man sat at the table in the conference room. It took

Bean a moment to decide whether his skin was naturally dark or merely weathered into a barnwood color and texture. Both, probably.

I know him, thought Bean. Mazer Rackham. The man who saved humanity in the Second Bugger Invasion. Who should have been dead many decades ago, but who surfaced long enough to train Ender himself for the last campaign.

"They send *you* to Earth?"

"I'm retired," said Rackham.

"So am I," said Bean. "So is Ender. When does *he* come to Earth?"

Rackham shook his head. "Too late to be bitter about that," he said. "If Ender had been here, do you think there's any chance he would be both alive and free?"

Rackham had a point. Back when Achilles was arranging for all of Ender's Jeesh to be kidnapped, the greatest prize of all would have been Ender himself. And even if Ender had evaded capture—as Bean had done—how long before someone else tried to control him or exploit him in order to achieve some imperial ambition? With Ender, being an American as he was, maybe the United States would have stirred from its torpor and now, instead of China and the Muslim world being the main players in the great game, America would be flexing its muscles again and then the world really would be in turmoil.

Ender would have hated that. Hated himself for being part of it. It really was better that Graff had arranged to send him off on the first colony ship to a former Bugger world. Right now, each second of Ender's life aboard the starship was a week to Bean. While Ender read a paragraph of a book, a million babies would be born on Earth, a million old people and soldiers and sick people and pedestrians and drivers would die and humanity would move forward another small step in its evolution into a starfaring species.

Starfaring species. That was Graff's program.

"You're not here for the fleet, then," said Bean. "You're here for Colonel Graff."

"For the Minister of Colonization?" Rackham nodded gravely. "Informally and unofficially, yes. To inform you of an offer."

"Graff has nothing that I want. Before any starship could arrive on a colony world, I'd be dead."

"You'd undoubtedly be an . . . interesting choice to head a colony," said Rackham. "But as you said, your term in office would be too brief to be effective. No, it's a different kind of offer."

"The only things I want, you don't have."

"Once upon a time, I believe, you wanted nothing more than survival."

"It's not within your power to offer me."

"Yes it is," said Rackham.

"Oh, from the vast medical research facilities of the International Fleet there comes a cure for a condition that is suffered by only one person on Earth?"

"Not at all," said Rackham. "The cure will have to come from others. What we offer you is the ability to wait until it's ready. We offer you a starship, and lightspeed, and an ansible so you can be told when to come home."

Precisely the "gift" they gave Rackham himself, when they thought they might need him to command all the fleets when they arrived at the various Bugger worlds. The chance of survival rang inside him like the tolling of a great bell. He couldn't help it. If there was anything that had ever driven him, it was that hunger to survive. But how could he trust them?

"And in return, what do you want from me?"

"Can't this be part of your retirement package from the fleet?"

Rackham was good at keeping a straight face, but Bean knew he couldn't be serious. "When I come back, there's going to be some poor young soldier I can train?"

"You're not a teacher," said Rackham.

"Neither were you."

Rackham shrugged. "So we become whatever we need to

be. We're offering you life. We'll continue to fund research on your condition."

"What, using my children as your guinea pigs?"

"We'll try to find them, of course. We'll try to cure them."

"But they won't get their own starships?"

"Bean," said Rackham. "How many trillions of dollars do you think your genes are worth?"

"To me," said Bean, "They're worth more than all the money in the world."

"I don't think you could pay even the interest on that loan."

"So I don't have as high a credit rating as I hoped."

"Bean, take this offer seriously. While there's still time. Acceleration is hard on the heart. You have to go while you're still healthy enough to survive the voyage. As it is, we'll be cutting it rather fine, don't you think? A couple of years to accelerate, and at the end, a couple more to decelerate. Who gives you four years?"

"Nobody," said Bean. "And you're forgetting. I have to come home. That's four more years. It's already far too late."

Rackham smiled. "Don't you think we've taken that into account?"

"What, you've figured out a way to turn while traveling at lightspeed?"

"Even light bends."

"Light is a wave."

"So are you, when you're traveling that fast."

"Neither of us is a physicist."

"But the people who planned our new generation of messenger ship are," said Rackham.

"How can the I.F. afford to build new ships?" asked Bean. "Your funding comes from Earth and the emergency is over. The only reason the nations of Earth even pay your salaries and continue to supply you is because they're buying your neutrality."

Rackham smiled.

"Somebody's paying you to keep developing new ships," said Bean.

"Speculation is pointless."

"There's only one nation that could afford to do that, and it's the one nation that could never keep it secret."

"So it's not possible," said Rackham.

"Yet you're promising me a kind of ship that couldn't exist."

"You go through acceleration in a compensatory gravity field, so there's no additional strain on your heart. That lets us accelerate in a week instead of two years."

"And if the gravity fails?"

"Then you're torn to dust in an instant. But it doesn't fail. We've tested it."

"So messengers can go from world to world without losing more than a couple of weeks of their lives."

"Of their *own* lives," said Rackham. "But when we send someone out on such a voyage, thirty or fifty lightyears, everyone they ever knew is dead long before they come back. Volunteers are few."

Everyone they ever knew. If he got on this starship, he'd leave Petra behind and never see her again.

Was he heartless enough for that?

Not heartless at all. He could still feel the pain of losing Sister Carlotta, the woman who saved him from the streets of Rotterdam and watched over for him for years, until Achilles finally murdered her.

"Can I take Petra with me?"

"Would she go?"

"Not without our children," said Bean.

"Then I suggest you keep searching," said Rackham. "Because even though the new technology buys you a bit more time, it's not forever. Your body imposes a deadline that we can't put off."

"And you'll let me bring Petra, if we find our children."

"If she'll go," said Rackham.

"She will," said Bean. "We have no roots in this world, except our children."

"Already they're children in your imagination," said Rackham.

Bean only smiled. He knew how Catholic it made him sound, but that's how it felt to him and Petra both.

"We ask only one thing," said Rackham.

Bean laughed. "I knew it."

"As long as you're waiting around anyway, searching for your children," said Rackham. "We'd like you to help Peter unite the world under the office of the Hegemon."

Bean was so astonished he stopped laughing. "So the fleet intends to meddle in earthside affairs."

"We aren't meddling at all," said Rackham. "You are."

"Peter doesn't listen to me. If he did, he would have let me kill Achilles back in China when we first had the chance. Peter decided to 'rescue' him instead."

"Maybe he's learned from his mistake."

"He thinks he learned from it," said Bean, "but Peter is Peter. It wasn't a mistake, it's who he is. He can't listen to anyone else if he thinks he has a better plan. And he always thinks he has a better plan."

"Nevertheless."

"I can't help Peter because Peter won't be helped."

"He took Petra along on his visit to Alai."

"His top secret visit that the I.F. couldn't possibly know about."

"We keep track of our alumni."

"Is that how you pay for your new-model starships? Alumni donations?"

"Our best graduates are still too young to be at the really high salary levels."

"I don't know. You have two heads of state."

"Doesn't it intrigue you, Bean, to imagine what the history of the world would have been like if there had been two Alexanders at the same time?"

"Alai and Hot Soup?" asked Bean. "It'll all boil down to which of them has the most resources. Alai has most at the moment, but China has staying power."

"But then you add to the two Alexanders, a Joan of Arc here and there, and a couple of Julius Caesars, maybe an Attila, and . . ."

"You see Petra as Joan of Arc?" asked Bean.

"She could be."

"And what am I?"

"Why, Genghis Khan of course, if you choose to be," said Rackham.

"He has such a bad reputation."

"He doesn't deserve it. His contemporaries knew he was a man of might who exercised his power lightly upon those who obeyed him."

"I don't want power. I'm not your Genghis."

"No," said Rackham. "That's the problem. It all depends on who has the disease of ambition. When Graff took you into Battle School, it was because your will to survive seemed to do the same job as ambition. But now it doesn't."

"Peter's your Genghis," said Bean. "That's why you want me to help him."

"He might be," said Rackham. "And you're the only one who *can* help him. Anybody else would make him feel threatened. But you . . ."

"Because I'm going to die."

"Or leave. Either way, he can have the use of you, as he thinks, and then be rid of you."

"It's not as he thinks. It's what you want. I'm a book in a lending library. You lend me to Peter for a while. He turns me in, then you send me out on another chase after some dream or other. You and Graff, you still think you're in charge of the human race, don't you?"

Rackham looked off into the distance. "It's a job that, once you take it on, it's hard to let go. One day out in space I saw something no one else could see, and I fired a missile and killed a Hive Queen and we won that war. From then on, the human race was my responsibility."

"Even if you're no longer the best qualified to lead it."

"I didn't say I was the leader. Only that I have the responsibility. To do whatever it takes. Whatever I can. And what I can do is this: I can try to persuade the most brilliant military mind on Earth to help unify the nations under the leadership of the only man who has the will and the wit to hold them all together."

"At what price? Peter's not a great fan of democracy."

"We're not asking for democracy," said Rackham. "Not at first. Not until the power of nations is broken. You have to tame the horse before you can let it have its head."

"And you say you're just the servant of humanity," said Bean. "Yet you want to put a bridle and saddle on the human race, and let Peter ride."

"Yes," said Rackham. "Because humanity isn't a horse. Humanity is a breeding ground for ambition, for territorial competitors, for nations that do battle, and if the nations break down, then tribes, clans, households. We were bred for war, it's in our genes, and the only way to stop the bloodshed is to give one man the power to subdue all the others. All we can hope for is that it be a decent enough man that the peace will be better than the wars, and last longer."

"And you think Peter's the man."

"He has the ambition you lack."

"And the humanity?"

Rackham shook his head. "Don't you know by now how human you are?"

Bean wasn't going to go down that road. "Why don't you and Graff just leave the human race alone? Let them go on building empires and tearing them down."

"Because the Hive Queens aren't the only aliens out there."

Bean sat up.

"No, no, we haven't seen any, we have no evidence. But think about it. As long as humans seemed to be unique, we could live out our species history as we always had. But now we know that it's possible for intelligent life to evolve twice, and in very different ways. If twice, then why not three times? Or four? There's nothing special about our corner of the galaxy. The Hive Queens were remarkably close to us. There could be thousands of intelligent species in our galaxy alone. And not all of them as nice as we are."

"So you're dispersing us."

"As far and wide as we can. Planting our seed in every soil."

"And for that you want Earth united."

"We want Earth to stop wasting its resources on war, and spend them on colonizing world after world, and then trading among them so that the whole species can profit from what each one learns and achieves and becomes. It's basic economics. And history. And evolution. And science. Disperse. Vary. Discover. Publish. Explore."

"Yeah, yeah, I get it," said Bean. "How noble of you. Who's paying for all this now?"

"Bean," said Rackham. "You don't expect me to tell you, and I don't expect you to have to ask."

Bean knew. It was America. Big sleepy do-nothing America. Burned out from trying to police the world back in the twenty-first century, disgusted at the way their efforts earned them nothing but hatred and resentment, they declared victory and went home. They kept the strongest military in the world and closed their doors to immigration.

And when the Buggers came, it was American military might that finally blew up those first exploratory ships that scoured the surface of some of the best agricultural land in China, killing millions. It was America that mostly funded and directed the construction of the interplanetary warships that resisted the Second Invasion long enough for New Zealander Mazer Rackham to find the Hive Queen's vulnerability and destroy the enemy.

It was America that was secretly funding the I.F. now, developing new ships. Getting its hand into the business of interstellar trade at a time when no other nation on Earth could even attempt to compete.

"And how will it be in *their* interest for the world to be united, except under their leadership?"

Rackham smiled. "So now you know how deep our game has to be."

Bean smiled back. So Graff had sold his colony program to the Americans—probably on the basis of future trade and a probable American monopoly. And in the meantime, he was backing Peter in the hope that he could unite the world under one government. Which would mean, eventually, a showdown between America and the Hegemon.

"And when the day comes," said Bean, "when America expects the I.F., which it's been paying for and researching for, to come to its aid against a powerful Hegemon, what will the I.F. do?"

"What did Suriyawong do when Achilles ordered him to kill you?"

"Gave him a knife and told him to defend himself." Bean nodded. "But will the I.F. obey you? If you're counting on the reputation of Mazer Rackham, remember that hardly anybody knows you're alive."

"I'm counting on the I.F. living up to the code of honor that every soldier has drummed into him from the start. No interference on Earth."

"Even as you break that code yourself."

"We're not interfering," said Rackham. "Not with troops or ships. Just a little information here and there. A dollop of money. And a little, tiny bit of recruitment. Help us, Bean. While you're still on Earth. The minute you're ready to go, we'll send you, no delays. But while you're here . . ."

"What if I don't believe Peter's as decent a man as you think he is?"

"He's better than Achilles."

"So was Augustus," said Bean. "But he laid the foundation for Nero and Caligula."

"He laid a foundation that survived Caligula and Nero and lasted for a millennium and a half, in one form or another."

"And you think that's Peter?"

"We do," said Rackham. "I do."

"As long as you understand that Peter won't do a thing I say, won't listen to me or anyone, and will go on making idiotic mistakes that I can't prevent, then . . . yes. I'll help him, as much as he'll let me."

"That's all we ask."

"But I'll still give my first priority to finding my children."

"How about this," said Rackham. "How about if we tell you where Volescu is?"

"You know?"

"He's in one of our safe houses," said Rackham.

"He accepted the protection of the I.F.?"

"He thinks it's part of Achilles's old network."

"*Is* it?"

"Somebody had to take over his assets."

"Somebody could only do that if they knew where his assets were."

"Who do you think maintains all the communications satellites?" asked Rackham.

"So the I.F. is spying on Earth."

"Just as a mother spies on her children at play in the yard."

"Good to know you're looking out for us, Mummy."

Rackham leaned foward. "Bean, we make our plans, but we know we might fail. Ultimately, it all comes down to this. We've seen human beings at their best, and we think our species is worth saving."

"Even if you have to have the help of non-humans like me."

"Bean, when I spoke of human beings at their best, whom do you think I was talking about?"

"Ender Wiggin," said Bean.

"And Julian Delphiki," said Rackham. "The other little boy we trusted to save the world."

Bean shook his head and stood up. "Not so little now," said Bean. "And dying. But I'll take your offer because it gives me a hope for my little family. And apart from that, I have no hope at all. Tell me where Volescu is, and I'll go see him."

"You'll have to secure him yourself," said Rackham. "We can't have I.F. agents involved."

"Give me the address and I'll do the rest."

Bean ducked again to leave the room. And he was trembling as he walked through the park, back toward his office in the Hegemony compound. Huge armies prepared to clash, in a struggle for supremacy. And off to one side, not even on the surface of Earth, there were a handful of men who intended to turn those armies to their own purposes.

They were Archimedes, preparing to move the Earth because they finally had a lever big enough.

I'm the lever.

And I'm not as big as they think I am. Not as big as I seem. It can't be done.

Yet it might just be worth doing.

So I'll let them use me to try to pry the world of men loose from its age-old path of competition and war.

And I'll use them to try to save my life and the lives of my children who share my disease.

And the chance of both projects succeeding is so slim that the odds are much better of the Earth being hit by a disastrously huge meteor first.

Then again, they probably already have a plan to deal with a meteor strike. They probably have a plan for everything. Even a plan they can turn to if . . . when . . . I fail.

5

SHIVA

From: Figurehead%Parent@hegemon.gov
To: PeterWiggin%Private@hegemon.gov
Password: * * * * * * * *
Re: Speaking as a mother

After all these years of posing as the Madonna in your little Pietà, it occurs to me that I might whisper something in your oh-so busy ear:

Ever since Achilles's little kidnapping venture, the not-so-secret weapon in everyone's arsenal is whatever array of Battle School graduates they're able to acquire, keep, and deploy. Now it's even worse. Alai is Caliph in fact as well as name. Han Tzu is emperor of China. Virlomi is . . . what, a goddess? That's what I hear, coming out of India.

Now they will go to war against each other.

What are YOU doing? Betting on the winner and choosing up sides?

Quite apart from the fact that many of these children were Ender's friends and fellow soldiers, the whole human race owes them our very survival. We took away their child-hood. When do they get a life they can call their own?

Peter, I've read history. Men like Genghis and Alexander were deprived of a normal childhood and absolutely focused on war and you know what? It deformed them. They were unhappy all the days of their lives. Alexander didn't know who he was when he stopped conquering people. If he stopped moving forward, slaughtering all the way, he died.

So how about setting these children free? Have you given any thought to that? Talk to Graff. He'll listen to you. Give these children an out. A chance. A life.

If for no other reason than because they're Andrew's friends. They're *like* Andrew. They didn't choose themselves for Battle School.

You, on the other hand, didn't go to Battle School. You volunteered to save the world. So you have to stay and see it through.

Your loving and ever-supportive mother

A woman's face appeared on the screen. She was dressed in the simple work-stained clothing of a Hindu peasant woman. But she bore herself like a lady of the highest caste—a concept that still had meaning, despite the long-ago banning of all outward markers of caste.

Peter did not know her. But Petra did. "It's Virlomi."

"All this time," said Bean, "she hasn't shown her face. Till now."

"I wonder," said Petra, "how many thousands of people in India already know her face."

"Let's listen," said Peter. He moused the PLAY button.

"No one is faithful to God who has no choice. That is why Hindus are truly faithful, for they may choose not to be Hindus and no harm comes to them.

"And that is why there are no true Muslims in the world, because they may not choose to cease to be Muslims. If a Muslim tries to become a Hindu or a Christian or even a simple unbeliever, some fanatical Muslim will kill him."

Pictures were flashed on the screen of beheaded bodies. Well-known images, but still potent as propaganda.

"Islam is a religion that has no believers," she said. "Only people who are compelled to call themselves Muslims and live as Muslims under fear of death."

Standard pictures of Muslims en masse, bowing down to pray—the very footage that was often used to show the piety of Muslim populations. But now, framed as Virlomi had framed it, the images seemed to be those of puppets, acting in unison out of fear.

Her face reappeared on the screen. "Caliph Alai: We welcomed your armies as liberators. We sabotaged and spied and blocked Chinese supply routes to help you defeat our enemy. But your followers seem to think they conquered India rather than liberating us. You did not conquer India. You will never conquer India."

Now there was new footage: Ragged Indian peasants bearing modern Chinese arms, marching like old-fashioned soldiers.

"We have no need of false Muslim soldiers. We have no need of false Muslim teachers. We will never accept any Muslim presence on Indian soil until Islam becomes a true religion and allows people the freedom to choose *not* to be Muslim, without any penalty."

Virlomi's face again. "Do you think your mighty armies can conquer India? Then you do not know the power of God, for God will always help those who defend their homeland. Any Muslim that we kill on Indian soil will go straight to hell, for he does not serve God, he serves Shaitan. Any imam who tells you otherwise is a liar and a shaitan himself. If you obey him, you will be condemned. Be true Muslims and go home to your families and live at peace, and let us live in peace with our own families, in our own land."

Her face looked calm and sweet as she uttered these condemnations and threats. Now she smiled. Peter thought she must have practiced the smile for hours, for days in front of a mirror, because she absolutely looked like a god, even though he had never seen a god and did not know how one should look. She was radiant. Was it a trick of the light?

"My blessing upon India. I bless the Great Wall of India. I bless the soldiers who fight for India. I bless the farmers who feed India. I bless the women who give birth to India and raise India to manhood and womanhood. I bless the great powers of the Earth who unite to help us regain our stolen freedom. I bless the Indians of Pakistan who have embraced the false religion of Islam: Make your religion true by going home and letting us choose not to be Muslim. Then we will live at peace with you, and God will bless you.

"My blessing above all blessings on Caliph Alai. O noble of heart, prove that I am wrong. Make Islam a true religion by giving freedom to all Muslims. Only when Muslims can choose *not* to be Muslims are there any Muslims on Earth. Set your people free to serve God instead of being captives of fear and hate. If you are not the conqueror of India, then you will be the friend of India. But if you intend to be the conqueror of India, then you will make yourself nothing in the eyes of God."

Great tears rolled out of her eyes and down her cheeks. This was all done in a single take, so the tears were real enough. What an actress, thought Peter.

"Oh, Caliph Alai, how I long to embrace you as a brother and friend. Why do your servants make war on me?"

She made a strange series of movements with her hands, then drew three fingers backhanded across her forehead.

"I am Mother India," she said. "Fight for me, my children." Her image remained on the screen as all motion stopped.

Peter looked from Bean to Petra and back again. "So my question is simple enough. Is she insane? Does she really believe she's a god? And will this work?"

"What was that business at the end, with the fingers on her forehead?" asked Bean.

"She was drawing the mark of Shiva the Destroyer on her forehead," said Peter. "It was a call to war." He sighed. "They'll be destroyed."

"Who?" said Petra.

"Her followers," said Peter.

"Alai won't let them," said Bean.

"If he tries to stop them, he'll fail," said Peter. "Which may be what she wants."

"No," said Petra. "Don't you see? The Muslim occupation of India absolutely counts on supplying their armies from Indian produce and Indian revenues. But Shiva will be there first. They'll destroy their own crops rather than let the Muslims have it."

"Then they'll die in famine," said Peter.

"And they'll absorb many bullets," said Petra, "and beheaded Hindu bodies will litter the ground. But then the Muslims will run out of bullets and they'll discover that they can't get more because the roads are blocked. And for every Hindu they killed, there will be ten more to overwhelm them with their bare hands. Virlomi understands her nation. Her people."

"And all of this you understand," said Peter, "because you were a prisoner in India for a few months?"

"India has never been led into war by a god," said Petra. "India has never gone to war with perfect unity."

"A guerrilla war," insisted Peter.

"You'll see," said Petra. "Virlomi knows what she's doing."

"She wasn't even part of Ender's Jeesh," said Peter. "Alai was. So he's smarter, right?"

Petra and Bean looked at each other.

"Peter, it's not about brains," said Bean. "It's about playing the hand you're dealt."

"Virlomi has the stronger hand," said Petra.

"I don't see it," said Peter. "What am I missing?"

"Han Tzu won't just sit there while the Muslim armies try to subdue India. The Muslim supply lines either run across the vast Asian desert or through India or by sea from Indonesia. If the Indian supply lines are cut, how long can Alai hold his armies there in numbers sufficient to keep Han Tzu contained?"

Peter nodded. "So you think Alai will run out of food and bullets before Virlomi runs out of Indians."

"I think," said Bean, "that what we just saw was a marriage proposal."

Peter laughed. But since Bean and Petra weren't laughing . . . "What are you talking about?"

"Virlomi *is* India," said Bean. "She just said so. And Han Tzu *is* China. And Alai *is* Islam. So will it be India and China against the world, or Islam and India against the world? Who can sell that marriage to their own people? Which throne will sit beside the throne of India? Whichever one it is, that's more than half the population of the world, united."

Peter closed his eyes. "So we don't want either to happen."

"Don't worry," said Bean. "Whichever happens, it won't last."

"You're not always right," said Peter. "You can't see that far ahead."

Bean shrugged. "Doesn't matter to me. I'll be dead before it all shakes out."

Petra growled and stood up and paced.

"I don't know what to do," said Peter. "I tried to talk to Alai, and all I did was provoke a coup. Or rather, Petra did that." He couldn't hide his annoyance. "I wanted him to control his people, but they're out of control. They're roasting cows in the streets of Madras and Bombay and then killing the Hindus who riot. They're beheading any Indian that someone accuses of being a lapsed Muslim—or even the *grandchild* of lapsed Muslims. Do I just sit here and watch the world collapse into war?"

Petra snapped at him. "I thought that was part of your plan. To make yourself seem indispensable."

"I don't have a great plan," said Peter. "I just . . . respond. And I'm asking you about it instead of figuring things out on my own because the last time I ignored your advice it was a disaster. But now I find out you don't actually have any advice. Just predictions and assumptions."

"I'm sorry," said Bean. "It didn't cross my mind you were asking for advice."

"Well, I am," said Peter.

"Here's my advice," said Bean. "Your goal isn't to avoid war."

"Yes it is," said Peter.

Bean rolled his eyes. "So much for listening."

"I'm listening," said Peter.

"Your goal is to establish a new order in which war between nations becomes *impossible*. But to get to that utopian place, there's going to have to *be* enough war that people will *know* the thing they're desperate to avoid."

"I'm not going to encourage war," said Peter. "It would discredit me completely as a peacemaker. I got this job because I'm Locke!"

"If you stop objecting and listen," said Petra, "you'll eventually get Bean's advice."

"I'm the great strategist, after all," said Bean with a wry smile. "And the tallest man in the Hegemony compound."

"I'm listening," said Peter again.

"You're right, you can't encourage war. But you also can't afford to try to stop wars that can't be stopped. If you're seen to try and *fail*, you're weak. The reason Locke was able to broker a peace between the Warsaw Pact and the West was that neither side wanted war. America wanted to stay home and make money, and Russia didn't want to run the risk of provoking I.F. intervention. You can only negotiate peace when both sides want it—badly enough to give up something in order to get it. Right now, nobody wants to negotiate. The Indians can't—they're occupied, and their occupiers don't believe they pose a threat. The Chinese can't—it's politically impossible for a Chinese ruler to settle for any boundary short of the borders of Han China. And Alai can't because his own people are so flushed with victory that they can't see any reason to give anything up."

"So I do nothing."

"You organize relief efforts for the famine in India," said Petra.

"The famine that Virlomi is going to cause."

Petra shrugged.

"So I wait until everybody's sick of war," said Peter.

"No," said Bean. "You wait until the exact moment when peace is possible. Wait too long, and the bitterness will run too deep for peace."

"How do I know when the time is right?"

"Beats me," said Bean.

"You're the smart ones," said Peter. "Everyone says so."

"Stop the humble act," said Petra. "You understand perfectly what we're saying. Why are you so angry? Any plan we make now will crumble the first time somebody makes a move that isn't on our script."

Peter realized that it wasn't them he was angry at. It was his mother and her ridiculous letter. As if he had the power to "rescue" the Caliph and the Chinese emperor and this brand new Indian goddess and "set them free" when they had all clearly maneuvered themselves into the positions they were in.

"I just don't see," said Peter, "how I can turn any of this to my advantage."

"You just have to watch and keep meddling," said Bean, "until you see a place where you can insert yourself."

"That's what I've *been* doing for years."

"And very well, too," said Petra. "Can we go now?"

"Go!" said Peter. "Get your evil scientist. I'll save the world while you're out."

"We expect no less," said Bean. "Just remember that you asked for the job. We didn't."

They got up. They started for the door.

"Wait a minute," said Peter.

They waited.

"I just realized something," Peter said.

They waited some more.

"You don't care."

Bean looked at Petra. Petra looked at Bean. "What do you mean we don't care?" said Bean.

"How can you say that?" said Petra. "It's war, it's death, it's the fate of the world."

"You're treating it like . . . like I was asking advice about a cruise. Which cruise line to go on. Or . . . or a poem, whether the rhymes are good."

Again they looked at each other.

"And when you look at each other like that," said Peter. "It's like you're laughing, only you're too polite to show it."

"We're not polite people," said Petra. "Especially not Julian."

"No, that's right, it's not that you're polite. It's that you're so much wrapped up in each other that you don't *have* to laugh, it's like you already laughed and only you two know about it."

"This is all so interesting, Peter," said Bean. "Can we go now?"

"He's right," said Petra. "We aren't involved. Like he is, I mean. But it's not that we don't care, Peter. We care even more than you do. We just don't want to get involved in *doing* anything about it because. . . ."

They looked at each other again and then, without saying another word, they started to leave.

"Because you're married," said Peter. "Because you're pregnant. Because you're going to have a baby."

"Babies," said Bean. "And we'd like to get on with trying to find out what happened to them."

"You've resigned from the human race is what you've done," said Peter. "Because you invented marriage and children, suddenly you don't have to be part of anything."

"Opposite," said Petra. "We've *joined* the human race. We're like most people. Our life together is everything. Our children are everything. The rest is—we do what we have to. Anything to protect our children. And then beyond that, what we have to. But it doesn't matter to us as much. I'm sorry that bothers you."

"It doesn't bother me," said Peter. "It did before I understood what I was seeing. Now I think . . . sure, it's normal. I think my parents are like that. I think that's why I thought they were stupid. Because they didn't seem to care about the outside world. All they cared about was each other and us kids."

"I think the therapy is proceeding nicely," said Bean. "Now say three Hail Marys while we get on with our limited domestic concerns, which involve attack helicopters and getting to Volescu before he makes another change of address and identity."

And they were gone.

Peter seethed. They thought they knew something that nobody else knew. They thought they knew what life was about. But they could only *have* a life like that because people like Peter—and Han Tzu and Alai and that wacko self-deifying Virlomi—actually concentrated on important matters and tried to make the world a better place.

Then Peter remembered that Bean had said almost exactly what his mother said. That Peter chose to be Hegemon, and now he had to work it out on his own.

Like a kid who tries out for the school play but he doesn't like the part he's been given. Only if he backs out now the show can't go on because he has no understudy. So he's got to stick it out.

Got to figure out how to save the world, now that he's got himself made Hegemon.

Here's what I want to have happen, thought Peter. I want every damn Battle School graduate off Earth. *They* are the complicating factor in every country. Mother wants them to have a life? Me too—a nice long life on another planet.

But to get them offplanet would require getting the cooperation of Graff. And Peter had the sneaking suspicion that Graff didn't actually want Peter to be an effective, powerful Hegemon. Why should Graff accept the Battle School kids into colony ships? They'd be a disruptive force in any colony they were in.

What about this? A colony of nothing *but* Battle School grads. If they bred true, they'd be the smartest military minds in the galaxy.

Then they'd come home and take over Earth.

OK, not that.

Still, it was the seed of a good idea. In the eyes of the people, it was the Battle School that won the war against the Buggers. They all wanted their armies to be led by Battle Schoolers. Which was why the Battle Schoolers were virtually the slaves of their nations' military.

So I'll do as Mother suggested. I'll set them free.

Then they can all marry like Bean and Petra and live happily ever after while other people—responsible people—did the hard work of running the world.

———

In India, the response to Virlomi's message was immediate and fierce. That very night, in a dozen incidents scattered across India, Muslim soldiers committed acts of provocation—or, as they saw it, retaliation or defiance to Virlomi's blasphemous, outrageous accusation. Thereby, of course, proving those accusations in the eyes of many.

But it wasn't riots they faced this time. It was an implacable mob determined to destroy them no matter what the cost. It was Shiva. So yes, the streets were littered with the dead bodies of Hindu civilians. But the Muslim soldiers' bodies could not be found. Or at least, could not be reassembled.

Reports of the bloodshed flowed into Virlomi's mobile headquarters. Including plenty of video. She had a selected version out on the web within hours. Lots of pictures of Muslims committing acts of provocation, and then firing on the rioters. No footage of human waves swarming over the machine-gun-firing Muslim soldiers and tearing them to pieces. What the world would *see* was Muslims offending Hindu religion and then massacring civilians. They would only hear about the fact that among the Muslim soldiers, there were no survivors.

———

Bean and Petra boarded attack helicopters and headed out across the ocean to Africa. Bean had heard from Rackham and knew where Volescu was.

6

EVOLUTION

From: CrazyTom%WackoMack@sandhurst.england.gov
To: Magic%Legume@IComeAnon.com
Forwarded and Posted by IcomeAnon
Encrypted using code ********
Decrypted using code ***********
Re: England and Europe

I hope you're still using this address, now that you're official and not hiding from Mr. Tendon anymore. I don't think this should go through channels.

I keep getting these feelers from Wiggin. I think HE thinks he's got some special affinity for members of the Jeesh, just because he's Ender's brother. Does he? I know he's got his fingers in everything—the items the Hegemony seems to know before we do are sometimes quite amazing—but does he have his fingers in us?

He's asked me for an assessment of the European willingness to surrender sovereignty to a world government. Given that the whole history of the past two hundred years consists of Europe flirting with a real European government, and always backing away, I wonder if the question comes from an idiot child or a deep thinker who knows more than I do.

But if you think his question is a legitimate one, then let me say that surrendering sovereignty to any existing world or regional body is laughable. Only little countries like Benelux or Denmark or Slovenia are eager to join. It's like communes—people with nothing are always willing to share. Even though Europe now speaks a version of English as its native tongue (except a few diehard enclaves) we are as far from unity as ever.

Which is not to say that under the right pressure, at the right time, each proud nation of Europe might not trade sovereignty for safety.

Tom

It would have to be Fortress Rwanda, of course. The Switzerland of Africa, they called it sometimes—but it only maintained its independence and neutrality because meter for meter, it was probably the most fortified nation on Earth.

They could never have fought their way into Rwandan airspace. But a chatty phone call from Peter to Felix Starman, the prime minister, won them a safe passage for two Hegemony jet choppers and twenty soldiers—along with uploads of detailed maps of the medical center where Volescu was operating.

Under another name, of course. For Rwanda had been one of the places where Achilles maintained safe houses and spy cells. What Volescu could not have known was that Peter's computer experts had been able to enter Achilles's clandestine computer network through Suriyawong's computer, and cell by cell, Achilles's organization had either been coopted, subverted, or destroyed.

Volescu was depending on a Rwandan cell that had been

reported to the Rwandan government. Felix Starman had chosen to continue to operate the cell through intermediaries, so the members of the cell did not realize that they were actually working for the Rwandan government.

So it was no small thing for Starman—who insisted that his self-chosen name should be translated, so that everyone was aware of the rather odd image he wished to convey—to give up this asset. While Bean and Petra took Volescu, the Rwandan police would be arresting all the other members of Achilles's organization. They even promised that Hegemony experts could monitor the Rwandan deconstruction of the Achillean computers.

The beat-beat-beat of chopper blades was as good as a police siren when it came to announcing their approach, so they set down a kilometer away from the medical center. Four soldiers on each chopper were equipped with slimline motorcycles, and they took off to secure all the vehicle exit points. The rest advanced through the yards and parking lots of houses, apartment buildings, and small businesses.

Since the entire population of Rwanda was trained as soldiers, they knew enough to stay indoors as they watched the dark-green-clad soldiers of the Hegemony jog cross-lots, from cover to cover. They might try to telephone the government to find out what was happening, but cellphones were getting a "we're making your service better, please have patience" message and landlines were hearing that "all circuits are busy."

Petra was pregnant enough now that she didn't jog along with the troops. And Bean was so distinctively large that he, too, remained in the choppers with the pilots. But Bean had trained these men and had no doubt of their ability. Besides, Suriyawong, still trying to rehabilitate himself even though Bean had assured him that he had his full trust, was eager to show that he could fulfil the mission perfectly without Bean's direct supervision.

So it was only fifteen minutes before Suriyawong texted them "fa," which either meant *fait accompli* or the fourth note of the musical scale, depending on what mood Bean was in. This time when he saw the message he sang it out, and the choppers rose into the air.

They came down in the parking lot of the medical complex. As befitted a rich country like Rwanda, it was state of the art; but the architecture was designed to make the place feel homelike to its patients. So it looked for all the world like a village, with every room that did not need a controlled environment open to whatever breezes blew.

Volescu was being held in the climate-controlled lab where he was arrested. He nodded gravely to Bean and Petra when they came inside. "How nice to see you again," he said.

"Was anything you told us true?" asked Petra. Her voice was calm, but she wasn't going to pretend that pleasantries were in order.

Volescu gave a little smile and shrug. "Doing what the boy wanted seemed to be a good idea at the time. He promised me . . . this."

"A place to conduct illegal research?" asked Bean.

"Oddly enough," said Volescu, "in our new days of freedom now that the Hegemony is powerless, my research is not illegal here. So I don't have to be prepared to dispose of my subjects at a moment's notice."

Bean looked at Petra. "He still says 'dispose of' instead of 'murder.'"

Volescu's smile grew sad. "How I wish I had all your brothers," he said. "But that's not why you're here. I already served my time and was legally released."

"We want our babies back," said Petra. "All eight of them. Unless there are more."

"There were never more than eight," said Volescu. "I was observed the whole time, as you arranged, and there is no way I could have faked the number. Nor could I have faked the destruction of the three discards."

"I've already thought of several," said Bean. "The most obvious being that the three you pretended to find that had

Anton's Key turned had already been taken away. What you destroyed were someone else's embryos. Or nothing at all."

"If you know so much, why do you need me?" asked Volescu.

"Eight names and addresses," said Bean. "The women who are bearing our babies."

"Even if I knew," said Volescu, "what purpose would be served by telling? None of them have Anton's Key. They aren't worth studying."

"There *is* no nondestructive test," said Petra. "So you don't know which of them had Anton's Key turned. You would have kept them all. You would have implanted them all."

"Again, since you know more than I do, by all means tell me when you find them. I'd love to know what Achilles did with the five survivors."

Bean walked up to his biological half-uncle. He towered over him.

"My," said Volescu. "What big teeth you have."

Bean took him by the shoulders. Volescu's arms seemed so small and fragile within the grasp of Bean's huge hands. Bean probed and pressed with his fingers. Volescu winced.

Bean's hands wandered idly along Volescu's shoulders until his right hand nested the back of the man's neck, and his thumb played with the point of Volescu's larynx. "Lie to me again," whispered Bean.

"You'd think," said Volescu, "that someone who used to be small would know better than to be a bully."

"We all used to be small," said Petra. "Let go of his neck, Bean."

"Let me crush his larynx just a little."

"He's too confident," said Petra. "He's very sure we'll never find them."

"So many babies," said Volescu genially. "So little time."

"He's counting on us not torturing him," said Bean.

"Or maybe he wants us to," said Petra. "Who knows how his brain works? The only difference between Volescu and

Achilles is the size of their ambitions. Volescu's dreams are so very, very small."

Volescu's eyes were welling up with tears. "I still think of you as my only son," he said to Bean. "It grieves me that we don't communicate any better than this."

Bean's thumb massaged the skin of Volescu's throat in circles around the point of his larynx.

"It surprises me that you can always find a place to do your sick little brand of science," said Petra. "But this lab is closed now. The Rwandan government will have its scientists go over it to find out what you were doing."

"Always I do the work while others get the credit," said Volescu.

"Do you see how I nearly encircle his throat with just one hand?" said Bean.

"Let's take him back to Ribeirão Preto, Julian."

"That would be nice," said Volescu. "How are my brother and his wife doing? Or do you see them anymore, now that you've got to be so important?"

"He's talking about my family," said Bean, "as if he were not the monster who cloned my brother illegally and then murdered all but one of the clones."

"They've gone back to Greece," said Petra. "Please don't kill him, Bean. Please."

"Remind me why."

"Because we're good people," said Petra.

Volescu laughed. "You live by murder. How many people have you both killed? And if we add in all the Buggers you slaughtered out in space. . . ."

"All right," said Petra. "Go ahead and kill him."

Bean tightened his fingers. Not that much, really. But Volescu made a strangled sound in his throat and in moments his eyes were bugging out.

At that moment Suriyawong entered the lab. "General Delphiki, sir," he said.

"Just a minute, Suri," said Petra. "He's killing somebody."

"Sir," said Suriyawong. "This is a war materials lab."

Bean relaxed his grip. "Still genetic research?"

"Several of the other scientists working here had misgivings about Volescu's work and the sources of his grants. They were collecting evidence. Not much to collect. But everything points to Volescu breeding a common-cold virus that would carry genetic alterations."

"That wouldn't affect adults," said Bean.

"I shouldn't have said war materials," said Suriyawong, "but I thought that would stop your little game of strangulation faster."

"What is it, then?" asked Bean.

"It's a project to alter the human genome," said Suriyawong.

"We know that's what he worked with," said Petra.

"But not with viruses as carriers," said Bean. "What were you doing here, Volescu?"

Volescu choked out some words. "Fulfilling the terms of my grants."

"Grants from whom?"

"The grant granters," said Volescu.

"Lock this place down," said Bean to Suriyawong. "I'll call the Hegemon to request a Rwandan perimeter guard."

"I think," said Petra, "that our brilliant scientist friend had some bizarre notion of remaking the human race."

"We need Anton to look at what this sick little disciple of his was doing," said Bean.

"Suri," said Petra. "Bean wasn't really going to murder him."

"Yes I was," said Bean.

"I would have stopped him," said Petra.

Suri barked out a little laugh. "Sometimes people need killing. So far, Bean's record is one for one."

———

Petra stopped going along on the interviews with Volescu. They could hardly be called interrogations—direct questions led nowhere, threats seemed to mean nothing. It was maddening and stressful and she hated the way he looked at her. Looked at her belly, which was showing her pregnancy more and more every day.

But she still kept on top of what they were calling, for lack of a better name, the Volescu project. The head of electronic security, Ferreira, was working most intensely on trying to track down everything Volescu had been doing with his computer and tracking his various identities through the nets. But Petra made sure that the database searches and indexes that they already had under way continued. These babies were out there somewhere, implanted in surrogate mothers, and at some point they were going to give birth. Volescu wouldn't risk their lives by forbidding the mothers access to good medical care—in fact, that was bound to be a minimum. So they would be born in hospitals, their births registered.

How they would find these babies in the millions that would be born in that timeframe, Petra couldn't begin to guess. But they'd collect the data and index it on every conceivably useful variable so it was there to work with when they finally figured out some identifying marker.

Meanwhile, Bean conducted the interviews with Volescu. They were yielding some information that proved accurate, but it was hard for Bean to decide whether Volescu was unconsciously letting useful information slip, or deliberately toying with them by bleeding out little bits of information that he knew would not be terribly useful in the end.

When he wasn't with Volescu, Bean was with Anton, who had come away from retirement and accepted a heavy level of drugs to control his aversive reaction to working in his field of science. "I tell myself every day," he said to Bean, "that I'm not doing science, I'm merely grading a student's assignments. It helps. But I still throw up. This is not good for me."

"Don't push any harder than you can."

"My wife helps me," said Anton. "She's very patient with

this old man. And you know what? She's pregnant. In the natural way!"

"Congratulations," Bean said, knowing how hard this was for Anton, whose sexual desires did not tend in the same direction as his reproductive plans.

"My body knows how, even at this old age." He laughed. "Doing what comes unnaturally."

But his personal happiness aside, the picture Anton began to paint looked worse and worse. "His plan was simple enough," said Anton. "He planned to destroy the human race."

"Why? That makes no sense. Vengeance?"

"No, no. Destroy and *replace*. The virus he chose would go straight to the reproductive cells in the body. Every sperm, every ovum. They infest, but they don't kill. They just snip and replace. All kinds of changes. Strength and speed of an East African. A few changes I don't understand because nobody's really mapped that part of the genome— not for function. And some I don't even know where they fit on the human genome. I'd have to try them out and I can't do that. That would be real science. Someone else. Later."

"You're sidestepping the big change," said Bean.

"My little key," said Anton. "His virus turns the key."

"So he has no cure. No way to switch the key for intellectual ability without also triggering this perpetual growth pattern."

"If he had it, he'd use it. There's no advantage not to."

"So it *is* a biological weapon."

"Weapon? Something that affects only your children? Makes them die of giantism before they're twenty? Oh, that would make armies run in panic."

"What then?"

"Volescu thinks he's God. Or at least he's playing dress-up with God's clothing. He's trying to jump the whole human race to the next stage of evolution. Spread this disease so that *no* normal children can be born, ever again."

"But that's insane. Everybody dying so young—"

"No, no, Julian. No, not insane. Why do humans live so long? Mathematicians and poets, they burn out in their mid-twenties anyway. We live so long because of grandchildren. In a difficult world, grandparents can help ensure the survival of their grandchildren. The societies that kept their old people around and listened to them and respected them—that *fed* them—always do better. But that's a community on the edge of starvation. Always at risk. Are we at risk so much today?"

"If these wars keep getting worse—"

"Yes, war," said Anton. "Kill off a whole generation of men, yet the grandfathers keep their sexual potency. They can propagate the next generation even if the young ones are dead. But Volescu thinks we're ready to move beyond planning for the deaths of young men."

"So he doesn't mind having generations that are less than twenty years."

"Change society's patterns. When were you ready to assume an adult role, Bean? When was your brain ready to go to work and change the world?"

"Age ten. Earlier, if I'd had good education."

"So you get good education. All our schools change because children are ready to learn at age three. Age two. By age ten, if Volescu's gene change takes place, the new generation is completely ready to take over for the old. Marry as early as possible. Breed like bunnies. Become giants. Irresistible in war. Until they keel over from heart attacks. Don't you see? Instead of spending the young men in violent death, we send the old men—the eighteen-year-olds. While all the work in science, technology, building, planting, everything—all done by the young men. The ten-year-olds. All of them like you."

"Not human anymore."

"A different species, yes. The children of Homo sapiens. Homo lumens, maybe. Still capable of interbreeding, but the old style of human—they grow to be old, but they are never big. And they are never very smart. How can they compete? They are gone, Bean. Your people rule the world."

"They wouldn't be my people."

"It's good that you're loyal to old humans like me. But you are something new, Bean. And if you have any children with my little key turned, no, they won't be fast like what Volescu has designed, but they'll be brilliant. Something new in the world. When they can talk to each other, instead of being alone like you, will you be able to keep up with them? Well, maybe yes, for *you*. But will *I* be able to keep up with them?"

Bean laughed bitterly. "Will Petra? That's what you're saying."

"You had no parents to be humiliated when they found out that you were learning faster than they can teach."

"Petra will love them just as much."

"Yes, she will. But all her love won't turn them human."

"And here you told me that I'm definitely human. Not true after all."

"Human in your loves, your hungers. In what makes you good and not evil. But in the speed of your life, the intellectual heights, are you not alone in this world?"

"Unless that virus is released."

"How do you know it won't still be released?" asked Anton. "How do you know he hasn't already completed a batch and disseminated it? How do you know he didn't infect himself and now he spreads it wherever he goes? In these past weeks since he got here, how many people in the Hegemony compound have had a cold? Sniffly nose, itchy penis, tender nipples—yes, he used *that* virus as his base, he has a sense of humor, an ugly kind."

"I haven't checked on the subtler symptoms, but we've had the normal number of colds."

"Probably not," said Anton. "He probably didn't make himself a carrier. What would be the point? He wants other people to spread it."

"You're saying that it's already out there."

"Or he has a website that he has to check every week or every month. And then one month he doesn't do it. So a signal is sent out to some of Achilles's old network. The virus gets broken out and used. And all Volescu had to do to trigger it was . . . be a captive with no access to computers."

"Was his research that complete? *Could* he have a working virus?"

"I don't know. All his records were changed when he moved. When you sent him a message, you told me about that, yes? You sent him a message and he moved to Rwanda. Before that maybe he had an earlier version of the virus. Maybe not. Maybe this is the first time he put the changed human genes into the virus. If that's the case, then no, it has not been released. But it could be. It's ready. Ready *enough*. Maybe you caught him just in time."

"And if it *is* out there, what?"

"Then I hope the baby my wife is pregnant with, I hope it's one like you, and not one like me."

"Why?"

"Your tragedy, Bean, is that you are the only one. If all the world will soon be like you, then you know what that makes you."

"A damn fool."

"It makes you Adam."

Anton was unbearably complaisant about this. What Bean was, what was happening to him, he wouldn't wish that on anyone. Not his child, and not Anton's. But Anton could be forgiven for his idiotic wish. He had not been so small; he had not been this large. He could not know how . . . how larval the early stage was.

Like silkworms, the larva of my species does all the work of its life while it's young. Then the big butterfly, that's what people see, but all it has left to do in its life is get laid, then lay eggs, then die.

Bean talked it through with Petra, and then they went to

Ferreira and Peter. Now the computer search was geared—with some urgency—toward detecting any kind of dead-man switch that Volescu was signing on to every day or every week. No doubt the dead-man switch was set to destroy itself as soon as its message was sent. Which meant that if it *was* already sent, it wouldn't be there anymore. But somewhere there were tracks. Backups. Records of one kind or another. Nobody traveled the networks clean.

Not even Bean. He had made himself untraceable by constantly changing everything. But Volescu had stayed rooted in a lab here or a lab there, as long as he could. He might not have been as careful in his maneuvers through the nets. After all, Volescu might think he was brilliant, but he was no Bean.

7

AN OFFER

From: PeterWiggin%private@hegemon.gov
To: Vlad%Impaled@gcu.ru.gov
Re: my brother's friends

I'd like to have a chance to talk with you. Face to face. For
my brother's sake. On neutral territory.

Peter arrived in St. Petersburg ostensibly to be an observer
and consultant at the Warsaw Pact trade talks that were part
of Russia's ongoing effort to set up an economic union to rival the western European one. And he did attend several
meetings and kept his suite humming with conversations.
Of course, his agenda was quite different from the official
one, and he made good headway with—as expected—
representatives from some of the smaller or less prosperous
countries. Latvia. Estonia. Slovakia. Bulgaria. Bosnia. Alba-
nia. Croatia. Georgia. Every piece in the puzzle counted.

Not every piece was a country. Sometimes it was an individual.

That's why Peter found himself walking in a park—not
one of the magnificent parks in the heart of St. Petersburg,
but a smallish park in Kohtla-Järve, a town in northeastern

Estonia with delusions of cityhood. Peter wasn't sure why Vlad had chosen a town that involved crossing borders—nothing could have made their encounter more obvious. And being in Estonia meant there'd be two intelligence services watching them, Estonia's *and* Russia's. Russia hadn't forgotten history: They still watched over Estonia using their domestic spy service rather than the foreign one.

This park was, perhaps, the reason. There was a lake—no, a pond, a skating pond in winter, Peter was sure, since it was almost perfectly round and over-equipped with benches. Now, in the summer, it was undoubtedly advertised with a "suck blood and lay eggs all in one place" campaign among the mosquitos, which had shown up in profusion.

"Close your eyes," said Vlad.

Peter expected some kind of spy ritual and, sighing, complied. His sigh left his mouth open, however, just enough to get a good taste of the insect repellant that Vlad sprayed in his face.

"Hands," said Vlad. "Tastes bad but doesn't kill. Hands."

Peter held out his hands. They were sprayed, too.

"Don't want you to lose more than a pint during our conversation. Horrible place. Nobody comes here in summer. So it isn't prewired. Lots of clear meadows. We can see if anybody's watching us."

"Are you that closely watched?"

"Russian government not as understanding as Hegemon. Suriyawong stays in your confidence because you believe he always opposed Achilles. But me? Not trusted. So if you think I have influence, very wrong thinking, my friend."

"Not why I'm here."

"Yes, I know, you're here for the trade talks." Vlad grinned.

"Not much point to trade talks when smuggling and bribery make any kind of customs collection a joke anyway," said Peter.

"I'm glad you understand our way of doing things," said

Vlad. "Trust no one that you haven't bribed within the last half hour."

"Don't tell me you really have that thick a Russian accent, by the way," said Peter. "You grew up on Battle School. You should speak Common like a native."

"I do," said Vlad—still in a thick Russian accent. "Except when my future depends on giving people no reason to remember how different I am. Accents are hard to learn and hard to hold on to. So I will maintain it now. I am not by nature a good actor."

"May I call you Vlad?"

"May I call you Peter?"

"Yes."

"Then yes also. Lowly strategic planner cannot be more formal than Hegemon of whole world."

"You know just how much of the world I'm Hegemon over," said Peter. "And as I said, that's not why I'm here. Or not directly."

"What then? You want to hire me? Not possible. They may not trust me here, but they certainly don't want me going anywhere else. I'm a hero of the Russian people."

"Vlad, if they trusted you, what do you think you'd be doing right now?"

Vlad laughed. "Leading the armies of Mother Russia, as Alai and Hot Soup and Virlomi and so many others are already doing. So many Alexanders."

"Yes, I've heard that comparison," said Peter. "But I see it another way. I see it as being the arms race that led up to World War I."

Vlad thought for a moment. "And we Battle School brats are the arms race. If one nation has it, then another must have more. Yes, that's what Achilles's little venture in kidnapping was about."

"My point is: Having a Battle School graduate—particularly one of Ender's Jeesh—makes war more, not less, probable."

"I don't think so," said Vlad. "Yes, Hot Soup and Alai are in the thick of things, but Virlomi wasn't in the Jeesh. And the rest of the Jeesh—Bean and Petra are with you, struggling for world peace, yes? Like beauty pageant contestants? Dink is in a joint Anglo-American project which means he has had his balls cut off, militarily speaking. Shen is marking time in some ceremonial position in Tokyo. Dumper is a monk, I think, or whatever they call them. A shaman. In the Andes somewhere. Crazy Tom is at Sandhurst confined to a classroom. Carn Carby is in Australia where they may or may not have a military but nobody cares. And Fly Molo . . . well, he's a busy boy in the Philippines. But not their president or even an important general."

"That squares with my tally, though I think Carn would argue with you about the value of the Australian military."

Vlad waved the objection aside. "My point is, most nations that have this 'treasured national resource' are far more concerned to keep us under observation and away from power than to actually use us to make war."

Peter smiled. "Yes. Either they have you up to your elbows in blood, or they have you locked in a box. Anybody happily married?"

"We're none of us even twenty-five yet. Well, maybe Dink. He always lied about his age. Most of us are in our teens or barely out of them."

"They're afraid of you. All the more so now, because the nations that actually *used* their Jeesh members in war are now governed by them."

"If you can call 'worldwide Islam' a nation. I, personally, call it a riot with scripture."

"Just don't say that in Baghdad or Tehran," said Peter.

"As if I could ever go to those places."

"Vlad," said Peter. "How would you like to be free of all this beauty?"

Vlad hooted with laughter. "So you're here representing *Graff*?"

Peter was taken aback. "Graff came to you?"

"Be head of a colony. Get away from it all. All-expenses-paid vacation . . . that takes the rest of your life!"

"Not a vacation," said Peter. "Very hard work. But at least you *have* a life."

"So Peter the Hegemon wants Ender's Jeesh offplanet. Forever."

"Do you want my job?" said Peter. "I'll resign it today if I thought it would go to you. You or any member of Ender's Jeesh. You want it? Think you can *hold* it? Then it's yours. I only have it because I wrote the Locke essays and stopped a war. But what have I done lately? Vlad, I don't see you as a rival. How could I? What freedom do you have to oppose me?"

Vlad shrugged. "All right, so your motives are pure."

"My motives are realistic," said Peter. "Russia is not using you right now, but they haven't killed you or locked you up. If they ever decide that war is desirable or necessary or unavoidable, how long before you get promoted and put into the thick of things? Especially if the war goes badly for a while. You are their nuclear arsenal."

"Not really," said Vlad. "Since my brain is supposed to be the payload of this particular missile, and my brain was defective enough to *seem* to trust Achilles, then I must not be as good as the other Jeesh members."

"In a war against Han Tzu, how long before you commanded an army? Or at least were put in charge of strategy?"

"Fifteen minutes, give or take."

"So. Is Russia more or less likely to go to war, knowing they have you?"

Vlad smiled a little and ducked his head. "Well, well. So the Hegemon wants me out of Russia so Russia won't be so adventurous."

"Not quite so simple," said Peter. "There'll come a day when much of the world will have merged their sovereignty—"

"By which you mean they will have surrendered it."

"Into one government. It won't be the big nations. Just a bunch of little ones. But unlike the United Nations and the League of Nations and even the Hegemony in its previous form, it will *not* be designed to keep the central government as powerless as possible. The nations in this league will maintain no separate army or navy or air force. They will not have separate control over their own borders—and they will collect no customs. Nor will they maintain a separate merchant marine. The Hegemony will have power over foreign policy, period, without rival. Why would Russia ever join such a confederacy?"

"It never would."

Peter nodded. And waited.

"It never would unless it thought that it was the only safe thing to do."

"Add the word 'profitable' into that sentence and you'll be closer to right."

"Russians are not Americans like you, Peter Wiggin. We don't do things for profit motive."

"So all those bribes go into charitable causes."

"They keep the bookmakers and prostitutes of Russia from starving," said Vlad. "Altruism at its finest."

"Vlad," said Peter. "All I'm saying is, think about this. Ender Wiggin did two great deeds for humanity. He wiped out the Buggers. And he never returned to Earth."

Vlad turned on Peter with real fire in his eyes. "Do you think I don't know who arranged for that?"

"I advocated it," said Peter. "I wasn't Hegemon then. But do you dare to tell me I was wrong? What would have happened if Ender himself were here on Earth? Everybody's hostage. And if his homeland managed to keep him safe, what then? Ender Wiggin, the Bugger-slayer, now at the head of the armed forces of the dreaded United States. Think of the jockeying, the alliances, the preemptive attacks, all because this great and terrible weapon was in the hands of the nation that still thinks it has the right to judge and govern all the world."

Vlad nodded. "So it's just a happy coincidence that it left you without a rival for the Hegemony."

"I have rivals, Vlad. The Caliph has millions of followers who believe that he's the one God chose to be ruler over the earth."

"Aren't you making the same offer to Alai?"

"Vlad," said Peter. "I don't expect to persuade you. Only to inform you. If there comes a day when you think your best hope of safety is to leave Earth, post a note to me at the website I'll link to you in an email. Or if you realize that the only chance your nation has of peace is for all its Battle School grads to disappear from Earth, tell me, and I'll do all I can to get them safely out and off."

"Unless I go to my superiors and tell them all that you just told me."

"Tell them," said Peter. "Tell them and lose the last shreds of freedom that you have."

"So I won't tell them," said Vlad.

"And you'll think about it. It will be there in the back of your mind."

"And when all the Battle School grads are gone," said Vlad, "there will be Peter. Brother of Ender Wiggin. The natural ruler of all humankind."

"Yes, Vlad. The only chance we have of unity is to have a strong consensus leader. Our George Washington."

"And that's you."

"It could be a Caliph, and we'd have a future as a Muslim world. Or we might all be made into vassals of the Middle Kingdom. Or—tell me, Vlad—should we prefer to be ruled over by the government that now treats you so kindly?"

"I'll think about this," said Vlad. "And *you* think about something else. Ambition was part of the basis by which we were chosen for Battle School. Just how self-sacrificing do you think we'll be? Look at Virlomi. As shy a person as Battle School could possibly admit. But to achieve her purpose, she made herself into a god. And she does seem to play the part with enthusiasm, doesn't she?"

"Ambition balanced against survival instinct," said Peter. "Ambition leads you to great risk. But ambition never leads you to certain destruction."

"Unless you're a fool."

"There are no fools in this park today," said Peter. "Unless you count the spies lying underwater breathing through straws in order to overhear our conversation."

"It's the best the Estonians can do," said Vlad.

"I'm glad to know that Russians haven't forgotten their sense of humor."

"Everybody knows a few dozen Estonian jokes."

"Who do Estonians tell jokes about?" asked Peter.

"Estonians, of course. Only they don't realize that they're jokes."

Laughing, they left the park and headed back, Peter to his chauffered car, Vlad to the train back to St. Petersburg.

———

Some Battle School graduates came to Ribeirão Preto to hear Peter's invitation. Others, Peter contacted through mutual friends. Members of Ender's Jeesh, Peter met with directly. Carn Carby in Australia. Dink Meeker and Crazy Tom in England. Shen in Tokyo. Fly Molo in Manila. And Dumper amid a council of Quechuas in the ruins of Macchu Picchu, his unofficial headquarters as he worked steadily to organize the Native Americans of South America.

None of them accepted his offer. All of them listened and remembered.

Meanwhile, the guerrilla fighting in India grew more savage. More and more Persian and Pakistani troops were withdrawn from China. Until the day came when there was no one penning in the starving Chinese army in Sichuan province. Han Tzu set it in motion.

The Turks withdrew to Xinjiang province. The Indonesians got back in their boats and withdrew to Taiwan. The Arabs joined in the occupation of India. Han China was free of foreign occupiers, without the Emperor firing a shot.

At once, the Americans and Europeans and Latin Americans were back, buying and selling, helping China recover from empty wars of conquest. While the Muslim nations continued to bleed weapons and wealth and men in the ever-more-brutal war to control India.

Meanwhile, a new pair of essayists emerged on the nets.

One styled himself "Lincoln" and spoke of the need to put an end to bloody wars and oppression, and to secure the rights and freedoms of all societies by giving an honest, law-abiding world government exclusive control of all weapons of war.

The other called himself "Martel," harking back to Charles the Hammer, who stopped the Muslim advance into Europe at Poitiers. Martel kept pounding at the grave danger the world faced from the existence of a Caliph. The Muslims, who now made up more than a third of the population of some European countries, would be emboldened, seize power, and force all of Europe to live under brutal Muslim law.

There were some commentators who saw in these two new essayists a similarity to the days when Locke and Demosthenes dueled, with a similar division between statesmanlike peace-seeking and warnings of war. Those had turned out to be written by Peter and Valentine Wiggin. Only once did Peter answer a question about "Lincoln": "There are several ways the world could be united. I'm glad that I'm not the only one who hopes it will be through a liberal democracy rather than a conquering despotism."

And only once did Peter comment when questioned about "Martel": "I don't believe it helps the cause of peace in the world to stir up the kind of fear and hatred that leads to expulsions and genocide."

Both answers only added to the credibility of the two essayists.

8

ENDER

From: Rockette%Armenian@hegemon.gov
To: Noggin%Lima@hegemon.gov
Re: I'm having fun so don't carp

Beloved husband,

What ELSE can I do while I'm sitting around with a belly the size of a barn except type? It's actually hard work, considering the keyboard is at arm's length. And it's not as if anti-Muslim propaganda is harder than breathing. I'm Armenian, O Father of the Balloon I'm Carrying Around Inside My Abdomen. We learn about how Muslims—Turks in particular, of course—have been slaughtering Armenian Christians from time immemorial. How they can never be trusted. And guess what? When I look for evidence, ancient and contemporary, I don't have to get out of my chair.

So I will continue to write the Martel essays and continue to laugh while they accuse Peter of writing them. Of course I AM doing it at his request, which is what I understand Valentine did for him when she wrote Demosthenes's essays back when we were all in school. But you know that nobody will listen to his Lincoln stuff unless they're also terrified. Either terrified of Muslims taking over the world (id est, more particularly, their neighborhood) or terrified of the hideous bloodshed that would ensue if nations with Muslim minorities actually started restricting them or expelling them.

Besides, Bean, I think that what I'm saying is true. Alai means well but he clearly is not in control of his fanatical supporters. They really are murdering people and calling it "executions." They really are trying to rule over India. They really are agitating and rioting and committing the odd atrocity in Europe right now, pushing to have European nations declare for the Caliph and cease trading with China, which really is supplying Virlomi.

And now this essay will end because the stomach aches I've been having are clearly not stomach aches. This baby thinks it's coming, two months prematurely. Please get back here right away.

Peter waited outside the delivery room with Anton and Ferreira.

"Does this premature birth mean anything?" he asked Anton.

"They wouldn't let the doctors amnio the baby," said Anton, "so I didn't have any reliable genetic material to work with. But we know that in the early stages, maturity is highly accelerated. It seems possible to me that premature birth is consistent with the key being turned."

"My thought," said Peter, "is that this might be the break we need to find the other babies and unravel Volescu's network."

"Because the others might be premature too?" asked Ferreira.

"I think Volescu had a deadman switch and sometime after he was arrested, a warning went out and all the surrogate mothers bolted. That wouldn't help us before, because we didn't know when the signal went out, and pregnant women may be one of the more stable demographic groups, but they do move around by the hundreds of thousands."

Ferreira nodded. "But now we can try to correlate premature births with abrupt moves at the same time as other women with similarly premature births."

"And then check funding. They'll have the best possible hospital care, and somebody's paying for it."

"Unless," said Anton, "this baby is premature because Petra herself has some kind of problem."

"There's no history of premature births in her family," said Peter. "And the baby has been developing quickly. Not in size, mind you—but the parts were all in place before schedule. I think this baby is like Bean. I think the key is turned. So let's use it as a key to finding where Volescu went and where those viruses might be waiting to be released."

"Not to mention finding Bean's and Petra's babies," said Anton.

"Of course," said Peter. "That's the main purpose." He turned to the managing nurse. "Have someone call me when we know anything about the condition of the mother and baby."

———

Bean sat down beside Petra's bed. "How do you feel?"

"Not as bad as I expected," she said.

"That's one good thing about premature delivery," he said. "Smaller baby, easier birth. He's doing fine. They're only keeping him in neonate intensive care because of his size. All his other organs are working."

"He's got . . . he's like you."

"Anton is supervising the analysis right now. But that's my guess." He held her hand. "The thing we wanted to avoid."

"If he's like you," she said, "then I'm not sorry."

"If he's like me," said Bean, "then it means Volescu really

didn't have any kind of test. Or he had one, and discarded the babies that were normal. Or maybe they're all like me."

"The thing you wanted to avoid," she whispered.

"Our little miracles," said Bean.

"I hope you're not too disappointed. I hope you. . . . Think of it as a chance to see what your life might have been like if you had grown up with parents, in a home. Not barely escaping with your life and then scrabbling to survive on the streets of Rotterdam."

"At the age of one."

"Think what it will be like to raise this baby surrounded by love, teaching him as fast as he wants to learn. All those lost years, recovered for our baby."

Bean shook his head. "I hoped the baby would be normal," he said. "I hoped they'd all be normal. So I wouldn't have to consider this."

"Consider what?"

"Taking the baby with me."

"With you where?" asked Petra.

"The I.F. has a new starship. Very secret. A messenger ship. It uses a gravity field to offset acceleration. Up to light-speed in a week. The plan is that once we find the babies, I take the ones like me and we take off and keep traveling until they find the cure for this."

"Once you're gone," said Petra, "why do you think the fleet will bother even looking for a cure?"

"Because they want to know how to turn Anton's Key without the side effects," said Bean. "They'll keep working on it."

Petra nodded. She was taking this better than Bean expected.

"All right," she said. "As soon as we find the babies. Then we go."

"We?" said Bean.

"I'm sure, in your normal legumocentric view of the universe, it didn't cross your mind that there's no reason I shouldn't go along with you."

"Petra, it means being cut off from the human race. It's different for me because I'm *not* human."

"That again."

"What kind of life is that for the normal babies? Growing up confined to a starship?"

"It would only seem like weeks, Bean. How grown up will they be?"

"You'd be cut off from everything. Your family. Everybody."

"You stupid man," she said. "*You* are everybody now. You and our babies."

"You could raise the normal babies . . . normally. With grandparents. A normal life."

"A fatherless life. And their siblings off on a starship, so they'll never even meet. I don't think so, Bean. Do you think I'm going to give birth to this little boy and then let somebody take him away from me?"

Bean stroked her cheek, her hair. "Petra, there's a whole bunch of rational arguments against what you're saying, but you just gave birth to my son, and I'm not going to argue with you now."

"You're right," said Petra. "By all means, let's avoid this discussion until I've nursed the baby for the first time and it becomes even more impossible for me to consider letting you take him away from me. But I'll tell you this right now. I will never change my mind. And if you maneuver things so you sneak off and steal my son from me and leave me a widow without even my child to raise, then you're worse than Volescu. When he stole our children, we knew he was an amoral monster. But you—you're my husband. If you do that to me, I'll pray that God puts you in the deepest part of hell."

"Petra, you know I don't believe in hell."

"But knowing that I'm praying such a thing, *that* will be hell for you."

"Petra, I won't do anything you don't agree to."

"Then I'm coming with you," she said, "because I'll never agree to anything else. So it's decided. There's no discussion to have later when I'm rational. I'm already as rational as I'll ever be. In fact, there's no rational reason why I shouldn't come along if I want to. It's an excellent idea. And being raised on a starship has to be better than being orphaned on the streets of Rotterdam."

"No wonder they named you after rock," said Bean.

"I don't give up and I don't wear down. I'm not just rock, I'm *diamond*."

Her eyelids were heavy.

"Go to sleep now, Petra."

"Only if I can hold on to you," she said.

He took her hand; she gripped it fiercely. "I got you to give me a baby," she said. "Don't think for a minute I'm not going to get my way in this, too."

"I promised you already, Petra," said Bean. "Whatever we do, it'll be because you agree that it's the right thing."

"Think you *want* to leave me. Voyage to . . . nowhere. Think nowhere's *better* than living with me. . . ."

"That's right, baby," said Bean, stroking her arm with his other hand. "Nowhere is better than living with you."

———

They had the baby christened by a priest. He came into neonate intensive care; not the first time he'd done it, of course, baptizing distressed newborns before they died. He seemed relieved to learn that this baby was strong and healthy and likely to survive, despite how tiny he was.

"Andrew Arkanian Delphiki, I baptize you in the name of the Father, the Son, and the Holy Ghost."

It was quite a crowd gathered around the neonate incubator to watch. Bean's family, Petra's family, and of course Anton and Ferreira and Peter and the Wiggin parents and Suriyawong and those members of Bean's little army who weren't actually on assignment. They had to wheel the incubator cart out into a waiting room to have space enough to hold everybody.

"You're going to call him Ender, aren't you," said Peter.

"Until he makes us stop," said Petra.

"What a relief," said Theresa Wiggin. "Now you won't have to name a child of your own after your brother, Peter."

Peter ignored her, which meant that her words had really stung.

"The baby is named for Saint Andrew," said Petra's mother. "Babies are named for saints, not soldiers."

"Of course, Mother," said Petra. "Ender and our baby were *both* named for Saint Andrew."

———

Anton and his team learned that yes, the baby definitely had Bean's syndrome. The Key was turned. And having two sets of genes to compare confirmed that Bean's genetic modification bred true. "But there's no reason to suppose that all the babies will have the modification," he reported to Bean, Petra, and Peter. "The likelihood is that the trait is dominant, however. So any child who has it should be on the fast track."

"Premature birth," said Bean.

"And we can guess that statistically, half the eight babies should have the trait. Mendel's law. Not ironclad, because randomness is involved. So there might be only three. Or five. Or more. Or this might be the only one. But the likeliest thing—"

"We know how probability works, Professor," said Ferreira.

"I wanted to emphasize the uncertainty."

"Believe me," said Ferreira, "uncertainty is my life. Right now we've found either two dozen or nearly a hundred groups of women who gave birth within two weeks of Petra, and who moved at the same time as others in their group, since the day Volescu was arrested."

"How can you not even know how many groups you have?" asked Bean.

"Selection criteria," said Petra.

"If we divide them into groups that left within six hours of each other, then we get the higher total. If we divide them into groups that left within two days of each other, the lower total. Plus we can shift the timeframes and the groups also shift."

"What about prematurity in the babies?"

"That supposes that the doctors are aware that the babies are premature," said Ferreira. "Low birth weight is what we went for. We eliminated any babies that were higher than the low end of normal. Most of them will be premature. But not all."

"And all of this," said Petra, "depends on all the babies being on the same clock."

"It's all we can go on," said Peter. "If it turns out that Anton's Key doesn't make them all trigger delivery after about the same gestation time . . . well, it's no more of a problem than the fact that we don't know when the other embryos were implanted."

"Some of the embryos might have been implanted much more recently," said Ferreira. "So we're going to keep adding women to the database as they give birth to low-birthweight children and turn out to have moved at about the time Volescu was arrested. You realize how many variables there are that we don't know? How many of the embryos have Anton's Key. When they were implanted. *If* they were all implanted. *If* Volescu even had a deadman switch."

"I thought you said he did."

"He did," said Ferreira. "We just don't know what the switch was about. Maybe it was for release of the virus. Maybe for the mothers to move. Maybe both. Maybe neither."

"A lot of things we don't know," said Bean. "Remarkable how little we got from Volescu's computer."

"He's a careful man," said Ferreira. "He knew perfectly well that he'd be caught someday, and his computer seized.

We learned more than he could have imagined—but less than we had hoped."

"Just keep looking," said Petra. "Meanwhile, I have a baby-shaped suction cup to go attach to one of the tenderest parts of my body. Promise me that he won't develop teeth early."

"I don't know," said Bean. "I can't remember not having them."

"Thanks for the encouragement," said Petra.

———

Bean got up in the night, as usual, to get little Ender so Petra could nurse him. Tiny as he was, he had a pair of lungs on him. Nothing small about his voice.

And, as usual, once the baby started suckling, Bean watched until Petra rolled over to feed the baby on the other side. Then he slept.

Until he awoke again. Usually he didn't, so for all he knew it was like this every time. Because Petra was still nursing the baby, but she was also crying.

"Baby, what's wrong?" said Bean, touching her shoulder.

"Nothing," she said. She wasn't crying anymore.

"Don't try to lie to me," said Bean. "You were crying."

"I'm so happy," she said.

"You were thinking about how old little Ender will be when he dies."

"That's silly," she said. "We're going off in a starship until they find a cure. He's going to live to be a hundred."

"Petra," said Bean.

"What. I'm not lying."

"You're crying because in your mind's eye you can already see the death of your baby."

She sat up and lifted the now-sleeping baby to her shoulder. "Bean, you really are bad at guessing things like this. I was crying because I thought of you as a little baby, and how you didn't have a father to go and get you when you cried in the night, and you didn't have a mother to hold you and feed you from her own body, and you had no experience of love."

"But when I finally found out what it was, I got more of it than any man could hope for."

"Damn right," said Petra. "And don't you forget it."

She got up and took the baby back to the bassinet.

And tears came to Bean's eyes. Not pity for himself as a baby. But remembering Sister Carlotta, who had become his mother and stayed with him long before he learned what love was and was able to give any back to her. And some of his tears were also for Poke, the friend who took him in when he was in the last stages of death by malnutrition in Rotterdam.

Petra, don't you know how short life is, even when you don't have some disease like Anton's Key? So many people prematurely in their graves, and some of them I put there. Don't cry for me. Cry for my brothers who were disposed of by Volescu as he destroyed evidence of his crimes. Cry for all the children that no one ever loved.

Bean thought he was being subtle, turning his head so Petra couldn't see his tears when she came back to bed. Whether she saw or not, she snuggled close to him and held him.

How could he tell this woman who had always been so good to him and loved him more than he knew how to return—how could he tell her that he had lied to her? He didn't believe that there would ever be a cure for Anton's Key.

When he got on that starship with the babies that had his same disease, he expected to take off and head outward into the stars. He would live long enough to teach the children how to run the starship. They would explore. They would send reports back by ansible. They would map habitable planets farther away than any other humans would want to travel. In fifteen or twenty years of subjective time they would live a thousand years or more in real time, and the data they collected would be a treasure trove. They would be the pioneers of a hundred colonies or more.

And then they would die, having no memory of setting foot on a planet, and having no children to carry on their disease for another generation.

And it would all be bearable, for them and for Bean, because they would know that back on Earth, their mother and their healthy siblings were living normal lives, and marrying and having children of their own, so that by the time their thousand-year voyage was over, every living human being would be related to them one way or another.

That's how we'll be part of everything.

So no matter what I promised, Petra, you're not coming with me, and neither are our healthy children. And someday you'll understand and forgive me for breaking my word to you.

9

PENSION

From: PeterWiggin%personal@hegemon.gov
To: Champi%T'it'u@QuechuaNation.Freenet.ne.com
Re: The best hope of the Quechua and Aymara
peoples

Dear Champi T'it'u,

Thank you for consenting to visit with me. Considering that
I tried to call you "Dumper" as if you were still a child in Battle School and a friend of my brother, I'm surprised you
didn't toss me out on the spot.

As I promised, I am sending you the current draft of the
Constitution of the Free People of Earth. You are the first
person outside the innermost circle of Hegemony officials to
look at it, and please remember that it is only a draft. I
would be grateful for your suggestions.

My goal is to have a Constitution that would be as attractive to nations that are recognized as states as to peoples
that are still stateless. The Constitution will fail if the language is not identical for both. Therefore there are aspira-
tions you would have to give up and claims you would

have to relinquish. But I think you will see that the same will be true for the states that now occupy territory you claim for the Quechua and Aymara peoples.

The principles of majority, viability, contiguity, and compactness would guarantee you a self-governing territory, albeit one much smaller than your present claim.

But your present claim, while historically justifiable, is also unattainable without a bloody war. Your military abilities are sufficient to guarantee that the contest would be far more evenly matched than the governments of Ecuador, Peru, Bolivia, and Colombia would anticipate. But even if you won a complete victory, who would be your successor?

I speak candidly, because I believe that you are not following a delusion but embarking on a specific, attainable enterprise. The route of war might succeed for a time—and the operative word is "might," since nothing is certain in war—but the cost in blood, economic losses, and ill will for generations to come will be steep.

Ratifying the Hegemony Constitution, on the other hand, will guarantee you a homeland, to which those who insist on being governed only by Quechua and Aymara leaders and raising their children to be Quechua and Aymara speakers may migrate freely, without needing anyone's permission.

But take note of the irrevocability clause. I can promise you that this will be taken very seriously. Do not ratify this Constitution if you and your people do not intend to abide by it.

As for the personal question you asked me:

I don't believe it matters whether I'm the one who unites the world under one government. No individual is irreplaceable. However, I am quite certain that it will need to be a person exactly like me. And at present, the only person who meets that requirement is me:

Committed to a liberal government with the highest degree of personal freedom. Equally committed to tolerating no breach of the peace or oppression of one people by another. And strong enough to make it happen and make it stick.

Join with me, Champi T'it'u, and you will not be an insurrectionary hiding out in the Andes. You'll be a head of a state within the Hegemony Constitution. And if you are patient, and wait until I have won the ratification of at least two of the nations at issue, then you and all the world can see how peacefully and equitably the rights of native peoples can be handled.

It only works if every party is determined to make the sacrifices necessary to ensure the peace and freedom of all other parties. If even one party is determined on a course of war or oppression, then someday that party will find itself bearing the full weight of the pressure the Free Nations can bring to bear. Right now that isn't much. But how long do you think it will take me to make it a considerable force indeed?

If you are with me, Champi T'it'u, you will need no other ally.

Sincerely,
Peter

Something was bothering Bean, nagging at the back of his mind. He thought at first that it was a feeling caused by his fatigue, getting so little uninterrupted sleep at night. Then he chalked it up to anxiety because his friends—well, Ender's and Petra's friends—were involved in a life-or-death struggle in India, which they couldn't possibly all win.

And then, in the middle of changing Ender's diaper, it came to him. Perhaps because of his baby's name. Perhaps, he thought bitterly, because of what he had his hands in.

He finished diapering the baby and left him in the bassinet, where Petra, dozing, would hear him if he cried.

Then he went in search of Peter.

Naturally, it wasn't easy to get in to see him. Not that there was so huge a bureaucracy in Ribeirão Preto. But it was large enough now that Peter could afford to pay for a few layers of protection. Nobody who just stood there being a guard. But a secretary here, a clerk there, and Bean found he had explained himself three times—at five-thirty in the morning—before he even got to see Theresa Wiggin.

And, now that he thought about it, he wanted to see her.

"He's on the phone with some European bigwig," she told him. "Either sucking up or getting sucked up to, depending on how big and powerful the country is."

"So that's why everybody's up early."

"He tries to get up early enough to catch a significant part of the working day in Europe. Which is hard, because it's usually only a few hours in the morning. *Their* morning."

"So I'll talk to you."

"Well, that's a puzzler," said Theresa. "Business so important that you'd get up at five-thirty to see Peter, and yet so unimportant that when you find out he's on a phone call, you can actually talk to me about it."

She said it with such verve that Bean might have missed the bitter complaint behind her words. "So he still treats you like a ceremonial mother?" asked Bean.

"Does the butterfly consult with the cocoon?"

"So . . . how do your other children treat you?" asked Bean.

Her face darkened. "This is your business?"

He wasn't sure if the question was pointed irony—as in,

that's none of your business—or a simple question—this is what you came for? He took it the first way.

"Ender's my friend," said Bean. "More than anybody else except Petra. I miss him. I know there's an ansible on his ship. I just wondered."

"I'm forty-six years old," said Theresa. "When Val and Andrew get to their destination, I'll be . . . old. Why should they write to me?"

"So they haven't."

"If they have, the I.F. hasn't seen fit to inform me."

"They're bad at mail delivery, as I recall. They seem to think that the best family therapy method is 'out of sight, out of mind.' "

"Or Andrew and Valentine can't be bothered." Theresa typed something. "There. Another letter I'll never send."

"Who are you writing to?"

"Whom. You foreigners are wrecking the English language."

"I'm not speaking English. I'm speaking Common. There's no 'whom' in Common."

"I'm writing to Virlomi and telling her to wise up to the fact that Suriyawong is still in love with her and she has no business trying to play god in India when she could do it for real by marrying and having babies."

"She doesn't love Suri," said Bean.

"Someone else, then?"

"India. It's way past patriotism with her."

"Matriotism. Nobody thinks of India as the fatherland."

"And you're the matriarch. Dispensing maternal advice to Battle School grads."

"Just the ones from Ender's Jeesh who happen now to be heads of state or insurrectionary leaders or, in this case, fledgling deities."

"Just one question for you," said Bean.

"Ah. Back to the subject."

"Is Ender getting a pension?"

"Pension? Yes, I think so. Yes. Of course."

"And what is his pension doing while he's puttering along at lightspeed?"

"Gathering interest, I imagine."

"So you're not administering it?"

"Me? I don't think so."

"Your husband?"

"I'm the one who handles the money," said Theresa. "Such as it is. *We* don't get a pension. Come to think of it, we don't get a salary, either. We're just hangers-on. Camp followers. We're both on leave of absence at the University because it was too dangerous for potential hostages to be out where enemies could kidnap us. Of course, the main kidnapper is dead, but . . . here we stay."

"So the I.F. is holding on to Ender's money."

"What are you getting at?" asked Theresa.

"I don't know," said Bean. "I was wiping my little Ender's butt, and I thought, there's an awful lot of shit here."

"They drink and drink. The breast doesn't seem to get smaller. And they poop more than they could possibly get from the breast without shriveling it into a raisin."

"And then I thought, I know how much I'm getting in my pension, and it's kind of a lot. I don't actually have to work at anything as long as I live. Petra, too. Most of it we simply invest. Roll it back into investments. It's adding up fast. Pretty soon our income from invested pension is going to be greater than the original pension we invested. Of course, that's partly because we have so much inside information. You know, about which wars are about to start and which will fizzle, that sort of thing."

"You're saying that somebody ought to be watching over Andrew's money."

"I'll tell you what," said Bean. "I'll find out from Graff who's taking care of it."

"You want to invest it?" asked Theresa. "Going into brokering or financial management when Peter has finally achieved world peace?"

"I won't be here when Peter—"

"Oh, Bean, for heaven's sake, don't take me *seriously* and make me feel bad for acting as if you weren't going to die. I prefer not to think of you dying."

"I was only saying that I'm not a good person to manage Ender's . . . portfolio."

"So . . . who?"

"Wouldn't that be *whom?*"

She grimaced. "No it would not. Not even if you spoke English."

"I don't know. I've got no candidate."

"And so you wanted to confer with Peter."

Bean shrugged.

"But that would make no sense at all. Peter doesn't know anything about investing and . . . no, no, no. I see what you're getting at."

"How, when I'm not sure myself?"

"Oh, you're sure. You think Peter is financing some of this from Andrew's pension. You think he's embezzling from his brother."

"I doubt Peter would call it embezzling."

"What would he call it, then?"

"In Peter's mind, Ender's probably buying government bonds issued by the Hegemony. So when the Hegemon rules the world, Ender will get four percent per year, tax free."

"Even I know that would be a lousy investment."

"From a financial point of view. Mrs. Wiggin, Peter has the use of more money than the scant dues the few dues-paying nations still pay to the Hegemony."

"The dues go up and down," said Theresa.

"He tells you?"

"John Paul is closer to these things. When the world is

worried about war, money flows into the Hegemony. Not a lot, just a little extra."

"When I first got here there were Peter, you two, and the soldiers I brought with me. A couple of secretaries. And a lot of debt. Yet Peter always had enough money to send us out in the choppers we brought with us. Money for fuel, money for ammunition."

"Bean, what will be gained if you accuse Peter of embezzling Ender's pension? You know Peter isn't making himself rich with it."

"No, but he *is* making himself Hegemon. Ender might need that money someday."

"Ender will never come back to Earth, Bean. How valuable will money be on the new world he's going to colonize? What harm is it causing?"

"So you're all right with Peter cheating his brother."

"*If* he's doing that. Which I doubt." Theresa's smile was tight and her eyes flashed just a little. Mother bear, guarding cub.

"Protect the son who's here, even if he's cheating the son who's gone."

"Why don't you go back to your place and take care of your own child instead of meddling with mine?"

"And the pioneers circle the wagons to protect from the arrows of the Native Americans."

"I like you, Bean. I'm also worried about you. I'll miss you when you die. I'll do my best to help Petra get through the hard times ahead. But keep your hippo-sized hands off my son. He has the weight of the world on his shoulders, in case you didn't notice."

"I think maybe I won't have that interview with Peter this morning after all."

"Delighted to be of service," said Theresa.

"Do avoid telling him I stopped by, will you?"

"With pleasure. In fact, I've already forgotten that you're

here." She turned back to the computer and typed again. Bean rather hoped she was typing meaningless words and strings of letters because she was too angry to be writing anything intelligible. He even thought of peeking, just to see. But Theresa was a good friend who happened to be protective of her son. No reason to turn her into an enemy.

He sauntered away, his long legs carrying him much farther, much faster than a man walking so slowly should have gone. And even though he wasn't moving quickly, he still felt his heart pump faster. Just to walk down a corridor, it's as if he were jogging a little.

How much time? Not as much as I had yesterday.

———

Theresa watched him go and thought: I love that boy for being so loyal to Ender. And he's absolutely right to suspect Peter. It's just the sort of thing he'd do. For all I know, Peter got us back onto full salary at the University, too, only he didn't tell us and he's cashing our checks.

Then again, maybe he's secretly getting paid by China or America or some other country that values his services as Hegemon.

Unless they value his services as Lincoln. Or . . . as Martel. If he was really writing the Martel essays. Such a thing smacked of Peter's propaganda methods, but the writing sounded nothing like him, and it could hardly be Valentine this time. Had he found another surrogate writer?

Maybe somebody was contributing in a big way to "Martel's" cause and Peter was pocketing the money to advance his own.

But no. Word of such contributions would get out. Peter would never be so foolish as to accept money that might compromise him if it were found out.

I'll check with Graff, see whether the I.F. is paying out the pension to Peter. And if it is, I'll have to kill the boy. Or at least make my disappointed-in-you face and then curse about him to John Paul when we're alone.

———

Bean told Petra he was going to train with Suri and the boys. And he did—go where they were training, that is. But he spent his time in one of the choppers, making a scrambled and encrypted call to the old Battle School space station, where Graff was assembling his fleet of colony ships.

"Going to come visit me?" said Graff. "Want to take a trip into space?"

"Not yet," said Bean. "Not till I've found my lost kids."

"So you have other business to discuss?"

"Yes. But you'll immediately realize that the business I want to talk about is none of my business."

"Can't wait. No, got to wait. Call I can't turn down. Wait just a minute please."

The hiss of atmosphere and magnetic fields and radiation between the surface of the Earth and the space station. Bean thought of breaking off the connection and waiting for another time. Or maybe dropping the whole stupid line of inquiry.

Just as Bean was going to terminate the call, Graff came back on. "Sorry, I'm in the middle of tricky negotiations with China to let breeding couples emigrate. They want to send us some of their surplus males. I told him we were forming a colony, not fighting a war. But . . . negotiating with the Chinese. You think you hear yes, but the next day you find out they said no *very* delicately and then tittered behind their hands."

"All those years controlling the size of their population, and now they won't let go of a measly few thousand," said Bean.

"So you called me. What is it that's none of your business?"

"I get my pension. Petra gets hers. Who get's Ender's?"

"My, but you're to the point."

"Is it going to Peter?"

"What an excellent question."

"May I make a suggestion?"

"Please. As I recall, you have a history of making interesting suggestions."

"Stop sending the pension to anybody."

"I'm the Minister of Colonization now," said Graff. "I take my orders from the Hegemon."

"You're in bed so deep with the I.F. that Chamrajnagar thinks you're a hemorrhoid and wakes up scratching at you."

"You have a vast untapped potential as a poet," said Graff.

"My suggestion," said Bean, "is to get the I.F. to turn Ender's money over to a neutral party."

"When it comes to money, there *are* no neutral parties. The I.F. and the colony program both spend money as fast as it comes in. We have no idea where to begin an investment program. And if you think I'm trusting some earthside mutual fund with the entire savings of a war hero who won't even be able to inquire about the money for another thirty years, you're insane."

"I was thinking that you could turn it over to a computer program."

"You think we didn't think of that? The best investment programs are only two percent better at predicting markets and bringing a positive return on investment than closing your eyes and stabbing the stock listings with a pin."

"You mean with all the computer expertise and all the computer facilities of the Fleet, you can't devise a neutral program to handle Ender's money?"

"Why are you so set on software doing it?"

"Because software doesn't get greedy and try to steal. Even for a noble purpose."

"So what if Peter *is* using Ender's money—that's what you're worried about, right?—if we suddenly cut it off, won't he notice? Won't that set back his efforts?"

"Ender saved the world. He's entitled to have his full pension, when and if he ever wants it. There are laws to protect child actors. Why not war heroes traveling at lightspeed?"

"Ah," said Graff. "So you *are* thinking about what will happen when you take off in the scoutship we offered you."

"I don't need you to manage my money. Petra will do it just fine. I want her to have the use of the money."

"Meaning you think you'll never come back."

"You're changing the subject. Software. Managing Ender's investments."

"A semi-autonomous program that—"

"Not semi. Autonomous."

"There *are* no autonomous programs. Besides which, the stock market is impossible to model. Nothing that depends on crowd behavior can be accurate over time. What computer could possibly deal with it?"

"I don't know," said Bean. "Didn't that mind game you had us play predict human behavior?"

"It's very specialized educational software."

"Come on," said Bean. "It was your shrink. You analyzed the behavior of the kids and—"

"That's right. Listen to yourself. *We* analyzed."

"But the game also analyzed. It anticipated our moves. When Ender was playing, it took him places the rest of us never saw. But the game was always ahead of him. That was one cool piece of software. Can't you teach it to play Investment Manager?"

Graff looked impatient. "I don't know. What does an ancient piece of software have to do with . . . Bean, do you realize how much effort you're asking me to go to in order to protect Ender's pension? I don't even know that it needs protecting."

"But you *should* know that it doesn't."

"Guilt. You, the conscienceless wonder, are actually using guilt on me."

"I spent a lot of time with Sister Carlotta. And Petra's no slouch, either."

"I'll look at the program. I'll look at Ender's money."

"Just out of curiosity, what is the program being used for now that you don't have any kids up there?"

Graff snorted. "We have *nothing* but kids here. The adults are playing it now. The Mind Game. Only I promised them never to let the program do analyses on their gameplay."

"So the program *does* analyze."

"It does pre-analysis. Looking for anomalies. Surprises."

"Wait a minute," said Bean.

"You *don't* want me to have it run Ender's finances?"

"I haven't changed my mind about that. I'm just wondering—maybe it could look at a really massive database we've got here and analyze . . . well, find some patterns that we're not seeing."

"The game was created for a very specific purpose. Pattern finding in databases wasn't—"

"Oh, come on," said Bean. "That's *all* it did. Patterns in our behavior. Just because it assembled the database of our actions on the fly doesn't change the nature of what it was doing. Checking our behavior against the behavior of earlier children. Against our own normal behavior. Seeing just how crazy your educational program was making us."

Graff sighed. "Have your computer people contact my computer people."

"With your blessing. Not some foot-dragging fob-them-off-with-smoke-and-mirrors 'effort' that deliberately leads nowhere."

"You really care about what we do with Ender's money?"

"I care about Ender. Someday he may need that money. I once made a promise that I'd keep Peter from hurting Ender. Instead, I did nothing while Peter sent Ender away."

"For Ender's own good."

"Ender should have had a vote."

"He did," said Graff. "If he had insisted on going home to Earth, I would have let him. But once Valentine came up to join him, he was content."

"Fine," said Bean. "Has he given consent to have his pension pillaged?"

"I'll see about turning the mind game into a financial manager. The program is a complex one. It does a lot of self-programming and self-alteration. So maybe if we ask it to, it can rewrite its own code in order to become whatever you want it to be. It *is* magic, after all. This computer stuff."

"That's what I always thought," said Bean. "Like Santa Claus. You adults pretend he doesn't exist, but *we* know that he really does."

When he ended the conversation with Graff, Bean immediately called Ferreira. It was full daylight now, so Ferreira was actually awake. Bean told him about the plan to have the Mind Game program analyze the impossibly large database of vague and mostly useless information about the movements of pregnant women with low-birth-weight babies and Ferreira said he'd get right on it. He said it without enthusiasm, but Bean knew that Ferreira wasn't the kind of man to say he'd do something and not do it, just because he didn't believe in it. He'd keep his word.

How do I know that? Bean wondered. How do I know that I can trust Ferreira to go off on wild goose chases, once he gives his word to do it? While I know without even knowing that I know it, that Peter is partly financing his operations by stealing from Ender. That was bothering me for days before I understood it.

Damn, but I'm smart. Smarter than any computer program, even the Mind Game.

If only I could control it.

I may not have the capacity to consciously deal with a vast database and find patterns in it. But I could deal with the database of stuff I observe in the Hegemony and what I know about Peter and without my even *asking the question,* out pops an answer.

Could I always do that? Or is my growing brain giving me ever-stronger mental powers?

I really should look at some of the mathematical conundrums and see if I can find proofs of . . . whatever it is they can't prove but want to.

Maybe Volescu isn't so wrong after all. Maybe a whole world full of minds like mine . . .

Miserable, lonely, untrusting minds like mine. Minds that see death looming over them all the time. Minds that know they'll never see their children grow up. Minds that let themselves get sidetracked on issues like taking care of a friend's pension that he'll probably never need.

Peter is going to be so furious when he finds out that those pension checks aren't going to him anymore. Should I tell him it was my meddling? Or let him think the I.F. did it on their own?

And what does it say about my character that I am absolutely going to tell him I did it?

———

Theresa didn't actually see Peter until noon, when she and John Paul and their illustrious son sat down to a lunch of papaya and cheese and sliced sausage.

"Why do you always drink that stuff?" asked John Paul.

Peter looked surprised. "Guaraná? It's my duty as an American to never drink Coke or Pepsi in a country that has an indigenous soft drink. Besides which, I like it."

"It's a stimulant," said Theresa. "It fuzzes your brain."

"It also makes you fart," said John Paul. "Constantly."

"*Frequently* would be the more accurate term," said Peter. "And it's sweet of you to care."

"We're just looking out for your image," said Theresa.

"I only fart when I'm alone."

"Since he does it in front of us," said John Paul to Theresa, "what exactly does that make us?"

"I meant 'in private,'" said Peter. "And flatulence from carbonated beverages is odorless."

"He thinks it doesn't stink," said John Paul.

Peter picked up the glass and drained it. "And you wonder why I don't look forward to these little family get-togethers."

"Yes," said Theresa. "Family is so inconvenient for you. Except when you can spend their pension checks."

Peter looked back and forth between her and John Paul. "You aren't even *on* a pension. Either of you. You're not even fifty yet."

Theresa just looked at him like he was stupid. She knew that look drove him crazy.

But Peter refused to bite. He simply went back to eating his lunch.

His very incuriosity was proof enough to Theresa that he knew exactly what she was talking about.

"You mind telling me what this is about?" asked John Paul.

"Why, Andrew's pension," said Theresa. "Bean thinks that Peter's been stealing it."

"So naturally," said Peter with his mouth full, "Mother believes him."

"Oh, haven't you, then?" asked Theresa.

"There's a difference between investing and stealing."

"Not when you invest it in Hegemony bonds. Especially when a circle of huts in Amazonas has a higher bond rating than you."

"Investing in the future of world peace is a sound investment."

"Investing in *your* future," said Theresa. "Which is more than you did for Andrew. But now that Bean knows, you can be sure that source of funding will dry up very quickly."

"How sad for Bean," said Peter. "Since that was what was paying for his and Petra's search."

"It wasn't until you decided it was," said John Paul. "Are you really that petty?"

"If Bean decides unilaterally to cut off a funding source, then I have to reduce spending somewhere. Since spending on his personal quest has nothing to do with Hegemony goals, it seems only fair that the meddler's pet project be the first to go. It's all moot anyway. Bean has no claim on Ender's pension. He can't touch it."

"He's not going to touch it himself," said Theresa. "He doesn't want the money."

"So he'll turn it over to you? What will *you* do, keep it in an interest-bearing debit account, the way you do with your own money?" Peter laughed.

"He seems unrepentant," said John Paul.

"That's the problem with Peter," said Theresa.

"Only the one?" said Peter.

"Either it doesn't matter or it's the end of the world. No in between for him. Absolute confidence or utter despair."

"I haven't despaired in years. Well, weeks."

"Just tell me, Peter," said Theresa. "Is there no one you won't exploit to accomplish your purposes?"

"Since my purpose is saving the human race from itself," said Peter, "the answer is no." He wiped his mouth and dropped his napkin on his plate. "Thanks for the lovely lunch. I do enjoy our little times together."

He left.

John Paul leaned back in his chair. "Well. I think I'll tell Bean that if he needs any next-of-kin signatures for whatever he's doing with Andrew's pension, I'll be happy to help."

"If I know Julian Delphiki, no help will be needed."

"Bean saved Peter's whole enterprise by killing Achilles at great personal risk, and our son's memory is so short that he'll stop paying for the effort to rescue Bean's and Petra's children. What gene is it that Peter's missing?"

"Gratitude has a very short half-life in most people's hearts," said Theresa. "By now Peter doesn't even remember that he ever felt it toward Bean."

"Anything we can do about it?"

"Again, my dear, I think we can count on Bean himself. He'll expect retaliation from Peter, and he'll already have a plan."

"I hope his plan doesn't require appealing to Peter's conscience."

Theresa laughed. So did John Paul. It was the saddest kind of laughter, in that empty room.

10

GRIEF

From: FelixStarman%backdoor@Rwanda.gov.rw
To: PeterWiggin%personal@hegemon.gov
Re: Only one question remains

Dear Peter,

Your arguments have persuaded me. In principle, I am prepared to ratify the Constitution of the Free People of Earth. But in practice, one key issue remains. I have created in Rwanda the most formidable army and air force north of Pretoria and south of Cairo. That is precisely why you regard Rwanda as the key to uniting Africa. But the primary motivation of my troops is patriotism, which cannot help but be tinged with Tutsi tribalism. The principle of civilian control of the military is, shall we say, not as preeminent in their ethos.

For me to turn over my troops to a Hegemon who happens to be not only white, but American by birth, would run a grave risk of a coup that would provoke bloodshed in the streets and destabilize the whole region.

That is why it is essential that you decide in advance who the commander of my forces will be. There is only one plausible candidate. Many of my men got a good look at Julian Delphiki. Word has spread. He is viewed as something of a god. His record of military genius is respected by my officer corps; his enormous size gives him heroic stature; and his partial African ancestry, which is, fortunately, visible in his features and coloring, makes him a man that patriotic Rwandans could follow.

If you send Bean to me, to stand beside me as the man who will assume command of Rwandan forces as they become part of the Free People's army, then I will ratify and immediately submit the issue to my people in a plebiscite. People who would not vote for a Constitution with you at its head will vote for a Constitution whose face is that of the Giant Julian.

Sincerely, Felix

Virlomi spoke on the cellphone with her contact. "All clear?" she asked.

"It's not a trap. They're gone."

"How bad is it?"

"I'm so sorry."

That bad.

Virlomi put away the phone and walked from the shelter of the trees into the village.

There were bodies lying in the doorway of every house they passed. But Virlomi did not turn to the right hand or the left. They had to make sure they got the key footage first.

In the center of the village, the Muslim soldiers had spitted a cow and roasted it over a fire. The bodies of twenty or so Hindu adults surrounded the roasting pit.

"Ten seconds," said Virlomi.

Obediently, the vidman framed the shot and ran the camera for ten seconds. During the shot, a crow landed but did not eat anything. It merely walked a couple of steps and then flew again. Virlomi wrote her script in her head: The gods send their messengers to see, and in grief they fly away again.

Virlomi walked near the dead and saw that each corpse had a slab of half-cooked, bloody meat in its mouth. No bullets had been spent on the dead. Their throats were split and gaping open.

"Close up. These three, each in turn. Five seconds each."

The vidman did his work. Virlomi did not touch any of the bodies. "How many minutes left?"

"Plenty," said the vidman.

"Then take every one of them. Every one."

The vidman moved from body to body, taking the digital shots that would soon go out over the nets. Meanwhile, Virlomi now went from house to house. She hoped that there would be at least one person living. Someone they could save. But there was no one.

In the doorway of the village's largest house, one of Virlomi's men waited for her. "Please do not go in, Lady," he said.

"I must."

"You do not want this in your memory."

"Then it is exactly the thing that I must never forget."

He bowed his head and moved aside.

Four nails in a crossbeam had served the family as hooks for clothing. The clothing lay in a sodden mass on the floor. Except for the shirts that had been tied around the necks of four children, the youngest only a toddler, the eldest perhaps nine. They had been hung up on the hooks to strangle slowly.

Across the room lay the bodies of a young couple, a middle-aged couple, and an old woman. They had made the adults in the household watch the children die.

"When he is finished by the fire," said Virlomi, "bring him here."

"Is there enough light inside, Lady?"

"Take down a wall."

They took it down in minutes, and then light flooded into the dark place. "Start here," she told the vidman, pointing to the adults' bodies. Pan very slowly. And then pan, just a little faster, to what they were forced to watch. Hold on all four children. Then when I enter the frame, stay with me. But not so close that you can't see everything I do with the child."

"You cannot touch a dead body," said one of her men.

"The dead of India are my children," she said. "They cannot make me unclean. Only the ones who murdered them are made filthy. I will explain this to the people who see the vid."

The vidman started, but then Virlomi noticed the shadows of the watching soldiers in the frame and made him start over. "It must be a continuous take," she said. "No one will believe it if it is not smooth and continuous."

The vidman started again. Slowly he panned. When he had focused on the children for a solid twenty seconds, Virlomi stepped into the frame and knelt before the body of the oldest child. She reached up and touched the lips with her fingers.

The men could not help it. They gasped.

Well, let them, thought Virlomi. So would the people of India. So would the people of the whole world.

She stood and took the child in her arms, raising him up. With no tension on the shirt, it came away easily from the nail. She carried him across the room and laid him in the arms of the young father.

"O Father of India," she said, loudly enough for the camera, "I lay your child, the hope of your heart, in your arms."

She got up and walked slowly back to the children. She knew better than to look to see if the camera was with her. She had to act as if she didn't know the camera was there. Not that anyone would be fooled. But looking toward the camera reminded people that there were other observers. As long as she seemed oblivious of the camera, the viewers would forget that there must be a vidman and would feel as if only they and she and the dead were in this place.

She knelt before each child in turn, then rose and freed them from the cruel nails on which they once hung shawls or school bags. When she laid the second child, a girl, beside the young mother, she said, "O Mother of the Indian house, here is the daughter who cooked and cleaned beside you. Now your home is permanently washed in the pure blood of the innocent."

When she laid the third child, a little girl, across the bodies of the middle-aged couple, she said, "O history of India, have you room for one more small body in your memory? Or are you full of our grief at last? Is this one body at last too many to bear?"

When she took the two-year-old boy from his hook, she could not walk with him. She stumbled and fell to her knees and wept and kissed his distorted, blackened face. When she could speak again, she said, "Oh, my child, my child, why did my womb labor to bring you forth, only to hear your silence instead of your laughter?"

She did not stand again. It would have been too clumsy and mechanical. Instead, she moved forward on her knees across the rough floor, a slow, stately procession, so that each dip and lurch became part of a dance. She propped the little body on the corpse of the old woman.

"Great grandmother!" cried Virlomi. "Great grandmother, can't you save me? Can't you help me? Great grandmother, you are looking at me but you do nothing! I can't breathe, Great grandmother! You are the old one! It is your place to die before me, Great grandmother! It is my place to walk around your body and anoint you with ghi and water of the holy Ganges. In my little hands there should have been a fistful of straw to do pranam for you, for my grandparents, for my mother, for my father!"

Thus she gave voice to the child.

Then she put her arm around the shoulder of the old woman and partly raised her body, so the camera could see her face.

"O little one, now you are in the arms of God, as I am. Now the sun will stream upon your face to warm it. Now the Ganges will wash your body. Now fire will purify, and the ashes will flow out into the sea. Just as your soul goes home to await another turn of the wheel."

Virlomi turned to face the camera, then gestured at all the dead. "Here is how I purify myself. In the blood of the martyrs I wash myself. In the stink of death do I find my perfume. I love them beyond the grave, and they love me, and make me whole."

Then she reached out toward the camera.

"Caliph Alai, we knew you out among the stars and planets. You were one of the noble ones then. You were one of the great heroes, who acted for the good of all humankind. They must have killed you, Alai! You must be dead, before you would let such things happen in your name!"

She beckoned, and the vidman zoomed in. She knew from experience with this vidman that only her face would be visible. She held herself almost expressionless, for at this distance any kind of expression would look histrionic.

"Once you spoke to me in the corridors of that sterile place. You said only one word. Salaam, you said. Peace, you said. It filled my heart with joy."

She shook her head once, slowly.

"Come forth from your hiding place, O Caliph Alai, and own your work. Or if it is not your work, then repudiate it. Join me in grieving for the innocent."

Because her hand could not be seen, she flicked with her fingers to tell the vidman to zoom away and include the whole scene again.

Now she let her emotions run free. She wept on her knees, then wailed, then threw herself across the bodies and howled and sobbed. She let it go on for a full minute. The version for western eyes would have captions over this part, but for Hindus, the whole shocking scene would be allowed to linger, uninterrupted. Virlomi defiling herself upon the bodies of the unwashed dead; but no, no, Virlomi purified by their martyrdom. The people would not be able to look away.

Nor would the Muslims who saw it. Some would gloat. But others would be horrified. Mothers would see themselves in her grief. Fathers would see themselves in the corpses of the men who had been unable to save their children.

What none of them would hear was the thing she had not said: Not a single threat, not a single curse. Only grief, and a plea to Caliph Alai.

To the world at large, the video would excite pity and horror.

The Muslim world would be divided, but the portion that rejoiced at this video would be smaller each time it was shown.

And to Alai, it would be a personal challenge. She was laying responsibility for this at his door. He would have to come out of Damascus and take command himself. No more hiding indoors. She had forced his hand. Now to see what he would do.

———

The video swept around the world, first on the nets, then picked up by broadcast media—high-resolution files were conveniently provided for download. Of course there were charges that the whole thing was faked, or that Hindus had committed the atrocities. But no one really believed that. It fit too well with the record that Muslims had created for themselves during the Islamic wars that raged in the century and a half before the Buggers came. And it was unbelievable to imagine Hindus defiling the dead as these had been defiled.

Such atrocities were meant to strike terror in the hearts of the enemy. But Virlomi had taken this one and turned it into something else. Grief. Love. Resolve. And, finally, a plea for peace.

Never mind that she could have peace whenever she wanted, merely by submitting to Muslim rule. The world would understand that complete submission to Islam would not be peace, but the death of India and its replacement by a land of puppets. She had made this so clear in earlier vids that it did not need to be repeated.

They tried to keep the vid from Alai, but he refused to let them block what he saw on his own computer. He watched it over and over again.

"Wait until we can investigate and see if it's true," said Ivan Lankowski, the half-Kazakh aide he trusted to be closest to him, to see him when he was not acting the part of Caliph.

"I know that it's true," said Alai.

"Because you know this Virlomi?"

"Because I know the soldiers who claim to be of Islam." He looked at Ivan with tears streaming down his cheeks. "My time in Damascus is done. I am Caliph. I will lead the armies in the field. And men who act this way, I will punish with my own hand."

"That is a worthy goal," said Ivan. "But the kind of men who massacred that village in India and nuked Mecca in the last war, they're still out there. That's why your orders are not being obeyed. What makes you think you can reach your armies alive?"

"Because I truly am Caliph, and if God wants me to lead his people in righteousness, he will protect me," said Alai.

11

AFRICAN GOD

From: H95TqwOqdy9@FreeNet.net
Posted at site: ShivaDaughter.org
Re: Suffering daughter of Shiva, the Dragon grieves at
the wounds he caused you.

May not the Dragon and the Tiger be lovers, and bring
forth peace? Or if there is no peace, may not the Tiger and
the Dragon fight together?

Bean and Petra were surprised when Peter came to see them
in their little house on the grounds of the Hegemony compound. "You honor our humble abode," said Bean.

"I do, don't I," said Peter with a smile. "The baby's
asleep?"

"Sorry, you don't get to watch me nurse him," said Petra.

"I have good news and bad news," said Peter.

They waited for him to tell them.

"I need you to go back to Rwanda, Julian."

"I thought the Rwandan government was with us," said
Petra.

"It's not a raid," said Peter. "I need you to take command

of the Rwandan military and incorporate it into the Hegemony forces."

Petra laughed. "You're kidding. Felix Starman is going to ratify your Constitution?"

"Hard to believe, but yes, Felix is ambitious the way I'm ambitious—he wants to create something that will outlive him. He knows that the best way for Rwanda to be safe and free is for there to be no armies in the world. And the only way for that to happen is to have a world government that will maintain the liberal values he has created in his Rwanda—elections, individual rights, the rule of law, universal education, and no corruption."

"We've read your Constitution, Peter," said Bean.

"He asked for you in particular," said Peter. "His men saw you when you took Volescu. They call you the African Giant now."

"Darling," said Petra to Bean. "You're a god now, like Virlomi."

"The question is whether you're woman enough to be married to a god," said Bean.

"I shade my eyes and it keeps me from going blind."

Bean smiled and turned to Peter. "Does Felix Starman know how long I'm not expected to live?"

"No," said Peter. "I regard that as a state secret."

"Oh no," said Petra. "Now we can't tell each other."

"How long will you expect me to stay?"

"Long enough for the Rwandan army to transfer its loyalty to the Free People."

"To you?"

"To the Free People," said Peter. "I'm not creating a cult of personality here. They have to be committed to the Constitution. And to defending the Free People who have accepted it."

"In practical terms, a date, please," said Bean.

"Until after the plebiscite, at least," said Peter.

"And I can go with him?" asked Petra.

"Your choice," said Peter. "It's probably safer there than here, but it's a long flight. You can write the Martel essays from anywhere."

"Julian, he's leaving it up to us. We're Free People now too!"

"All right, I'll do it," said Bean. "Now what's the good news?"

"That *was* the good news," said Peter. "The bad news is that we've had a sudden and unexpected shortfall in revenue. It will take months, at least, to make up what we abruptly stopped receiving. Therefore we're cutting back on projects that don't contribute directly to the goals of the Hegemony."

Petra laughed. "You have the cheek to ask us to help you, when you're cutting off funding for our search?"

"You see? You immediately recognized that your search was not contributing."

"You're searching, too," said Bean. "To find the virus."

"If it exists," said Peter. "In all likelihood, Volescu is teasing us, and the virus doesn't actually work and hasn't been dispersed."

"So you're going to bet the future of the human race on that?"

"No I'm not," said Peter. "But without a budget for it, it's beyond our reach. However, it is *not* beyond the reach of the International Fleet."

"You're turning it over to them?"

"I'm turning Volescu over to them. And they're going to continue the research into the virus he developed and where he might have dispersed it, if he did."

"The I.F. can't operate on Earth."

"They can if they're acting against an alien threat. If Volescu's virus works, and it's released on Earth, it would create a new species designed to completely replace humanity in a single generation. The Hegemon has issued a secret finding that Volescu's virus constitutes an alien invasion, which the I.F. has kindly agreed to track down and . . . repel for us."

Bean laughed. "Well, it seems we think alike."

"Really?" said Peter. "Oh, you're just flattering me."

"I already turned over our search to the Ministry of Colonization. And we both know that Graff is really functioning as a branch of the I.F."

Peter regarded him calmly. "So you knew I'd have to cut the budget for your search."

"I knew that you didn't have the resources no matter how much budget you have. Ferreira was doing his best, but ColMin has better software."

"Well, everything's working out happily for everyone, then," said Peter, standing up to go.

"Even for Ender," said Bean.

"Your baby's a lucky little boy," said Peter, "to have such attentive parents." And he was out the door.

———

Volescu looked tired when Bean went to see him. Old. Confinement wasn't good for him. He was not suffering physically, but he seemed to be growing wan as a plant kept in a closet without sun.

"Promise me something," said Volescu.

"What?" asked Bean.

"Something. Anything. Bargain with me."

"The one thing you want," said Bean, "you will never have again."

"Only because you're vindictive," said Volescu. "Ungrateful—you exist because I made you, and you keep me in this box."

"It's a good-sized room. It's air-conditioned. Compared to the way you treated my brothers. . . ."

"They were not legally—"

"And now you have my babies hidden away. And a virus with the potential to destroy the human race—"

"Improve it—"

"Erase it. How can you be given your freedom again? You combine grandiosity with amorality."

"Rather like Peter Wiggin, whom you serve so faithfully. His little toad."

"The word is 'toady,'" said Bean.

"Yet here you are, visiting me. Could it be that Julian Delphiki, my dear half-nephew, has a problem I could help him with?"

"Same questions as before," said Bean.

"Same answer," said Volescu. "I have no idea what happened to your missing embryos."

Bean sighed. "I thought you might want a chance to square things with me and Petra before you leave this Earth."

"Oh, come on," said Volescu. "You're threatening me with the death penalty?"

"No," said Bean. "You're simply . . . leaving Earth. Peter is turning you over to the I.F. On the theory that your virus is an alien invasion."

"Only if *you're* an alien invasion," said Volescu.

"But I am," said Bean. "I'm the first of a race of short-lived giant geniuses. Think how much larger a population the Earth can sustain when the average age at death is eighteen."

"You know, Bean, there's no reason for you to die young."

"Really? You have the antidote?"

"Nobody needs an antidote to destiny. Death from giantism comes from the strain on your heart, trying to pump so much blood through so many kilometers of arteries and veins. If you get away from gravity, your heart won't be overtaxed and you won't die."

"You think I haven't thought of that?" said Bean. "I'll still continue to *grow*."

"So you get large. The I.F. can build you a really big ship. A colony ship. You can gradually fill it up with your protoplasm and bones. You'd live for *years*, tied to the walls of the ship like a balloon. An enormous Gulliver. Your wife could come visit you. And if you get too big, well, there's always amputation. You could become a being of pure mind. Fed intravenously, what need would you have of belly and bowels? Eventually, all you really need is your brain and spine, and they need never die. A mind eternally growing."

Bean stood up. "Is that what you created me for, Volescu? To be a limbless crippled monster out in space?"

"Silly boy," said Volescu, "to ordinary humans you already *are* a monster. Their worst nightmare. The species that will replace them. But to me, you're beautiful. Even tethered to an artificial habitat, even limbless, trunkless, voiceless, you'd be the most beautiful creature alive."

"And yet you came within one toilet-tank lid of killing me and burning my body."

"I didn't want to go to jail."

"Yet here you are," said Bean. "And your next prison is out in space."

"I can live like Prospero, refining my arts in solitude."

"Prospero had Ariel and Caliban," said Bean.

"Don't you understand?" said Volescu. "*You're* my Caliban. And all your little children—they're my Ariels. I've spread them over the earth. You'll never find them. Their mothers have been taught well. They'll mate, they'll reproduce before their giantism becomes obvious. Whether my virus works or not, your children are my virus."

"So that's what Achilles plotted?"

"Achilles?" Volescu laughed. "That bloody-handed little moron? I told him your babies were dead. That's all he wanted. Fool."

"So they're not dead."

"All alive. All implanted. By now, perhaps, some of them born, since those with your abilities will be born two months premature."

"You knew that and didn't tell us?"

"Why should I? The delivery was safe, wasn't it? The baby was mature enough to breathe and function on its own?"

"What else do you know?"

"I know that everything will work out. Julian, look at yourself, man! You escaped at the age of *one*. Which means that seventeen months after conception, you were able to survive without parents. I don't have even the tiniest worry about the health of your babies, and neither should you. They don't need you, because you didn't need anybody. Let them go. Let them replace the old species, bit by bit, over the generations to come."

"No," said Bean, "I love the old species. And I hate what you did to me."

"Without 'what I did to you,' all you'd be is Nikolai."

"My brother is a wonderful person. Kind. And very smart."

"Very smart, but not as smart as you. Would you *really* trade with him? Would you really like to be as dull-witted as he is, compared to you?"

Whereupon Bean left, having no answer to Volescu's last question.

12

ALLAHU AKBAR

From: Graff%pilgrimage@colmin.gov
To: Borommakot%pinto@IComeAnon.com
Forwarded and Posted by IcomeAnon
Encrypted using code * * * * * * * *
Decrypted using code * * * * * * * * * * *
Re: Investment Counselor

Your idea of converting the Fantasy Game software into an investment counselor is going surprisingly well. We haven't had time to do more than short-term testing, but so far it has outpicked all the experts. We are paying Ender's pension funds to it. As you suggested, we are making sure that all investments are under false identities; we are also making sure the software is hooked widely over the nets in endlessly self-varying forms. It will be effectively untraceable and un-killable unless someone is making a systematic international effort to wipe it out, which is unlikely to happen as long as no one suspects it's there.

Ender will have no need of this money on his colony, and he'll do a better job if he's not aware that it's there. The first time he enters the nets after his subjective twenty-first birthday, the software will reveal itself to him along with the extent of his investments. Given the amount of time in travel alone, Ender will come of age with a noticeable fortune. Considerably more, I might add, than even the most optimistic projections of the value of Hegemony bonds,

But Ender's finances are not an emergency, and your children are.

A different team is tweaking the database your Ferreira sent us so it yields us more useful information. It involves a lot of additional research, not by raw data-seeks, but by individual operators trawling various medical, voting, tax, real estate, moving company, transportation and other databases, some of them not legally available. Instead of getting thousands of positives, of which none is likely to be useful, we are now getting hundreds of positives of which some might actually go somewhere.

Sorry it takes time, but once we get a decent positive, we have to check it out, often with landside personnel. And for obvious reasons, we don't have many of those to work with.

Meanwhile, I suggest you keep in mind that our deal depends on your making Peter Hegemon in fact as well as name before you go. You asked me what my standard of success would be. You can go when: Peter has firm control over more than 50% of the world's population, or Peter has sufficient military force that he is assured of victory whether or not any potential opponent is led by Battle School graduates.

Therefore: Yes, Bean, we expect you to go to Rwanda. We are your best hope for your and your children's survival, and you are our best hope for assuring Peter will prevail and achieve unity and general peace. Your task begins with getting Peter that irresistible military force, and our task begins with finding your babies.

Like you, I hope both our tasks turn out to be achievable.

Alai had thought that once he took control of the complex in Damascus, he'd be free to rule as Caliph.

It didn't take long to learn otherwise.

All the men in his palace complex, including his body-guards, obeyed him implicitly. But as soon as he tried to leave, even to ride around in Damascus, those he trusted most would begin to plead with him. "It's not safe," Ivan Lankowski would say. "When you got rid of the people controlling you here, it panicked their friends. And their friends include those who are commanding our armies everywhere."

"They followed my plan in the war," said Alai. "I thought they were loyal to the Caliph."

"They were loyal to victory," said Ivan. "Your plan was brilliant. And you . . . were in Ender's Jeesh. His closest friend. Of course they followed your plan."

"So they believed in me from Battle School, but not as Caliph."

"They believe in you as Caliph," said Ivan. "But more as the figurehead kind of Caliph who makes vague religious pronouncements and encouraging speeches, while you have wazirs and warlords to do all the nasty tedious work like making decisions and giving commands."

"How far does their control reach?" asked Alai.

"It's impossible to know," said Ivan. "Here in Damascus, your loyal servants have caught and eliminated several dozen agents. But I would not let you board an aircraft in Damascus—military or commercial."

"So if I can't trust Muslims, drive me over the Golan Heights into Israel, and let me fly on an Israeli jet."

"The same group that refuses to obey you in India is also

saying that our accommodation with the Zionists was an offense against God."

"They want to start *that* nightmare all over again?"

"They long for the good old days."

"Yes, when Muslim armies were humiliated left and right, and the world feared Muslims because so many innocents were murdered in the name of God."

"You don't have to argue with *me*," said Ivan pleasantly.

"Well, Ivan," said Alai, "if I stay here, then someday my enemies will finish in India—either they'll win or they'll lose. Either way, they'll come here, made mad by victory or by defeat, it doesn't matter which. Either way, I'll be dead, don't you think?"

"Oh, definitely, sir. We do have to find a way to get you out of here."

"No plan?"

"All kinds of plans," said Ivan. "But they all involve saving your life. Not saving the Caliphate."

"If I run away, then the Caliphate is lost."

"And if you stay, then the Caliphate is yours until the day you die."

Alai laughed. "Well, Ivan, you've analyzed it well. So I have no choice. I have to go to my enemies and destroy them."

"I suggest you use a magic carpet," said Ivan, "as the most reliable form of transportation."

"You think only a genie could get me to India to face General Rajam?"

"Alive, yes."

"Then I must contact my genie," said Alai.

"Is this a good time?" asked Ivan. "With the madwoman's latest vid all over the nets and the media, Rajam is going to be a crazy man."

"That's the best time," said Alai. "By the way, Ivan, can you tell me why Rajam's nickname is 'Andariyy'?"

"Would it help if I told you that he chose the nickname 'thick rope' himself?"

"Ah. So it doesn't refer to his tenacity or strength."

"He would say it does. Or at least the tenacity of a particular part of his body."

"And yet . . . rope is limp."

"Thick rope isn't."

"Thick rope is as limp as any other," said Alai, "unless it's very short."

Ivan laughed. "I'll make sure to repeat this joke at Rajam's funeral."

"Just don't repeat it at mine."

"I will not be at your funeral," said Ivan, "unless it's a mass grave."

Alai went to his computer and began to compose a few emails. Within a half hour of sending them, he received a telephone call from Felix Starman of Rwanda.

"I'm sorry to tell you," said Felix, "that I cannot allow Muslim teachers into Rwanda."

"Fortunately," said Alai, "that isn't why I called."

"Excellent," said Felix.

"I am calling in the interest of world peace. And I understand you have already made your decision about who is the best hope of humankind for achieving that goal—no, say no names."

"Since I have no idea what you're talking about—"

"Excellent," said Alai. "A good Muslim always assumes that unbelievers have no idea." They both laughed. "All I ask is that you let it be known that there is a man crossing the Rub' al Khali on foot because his camel won't let him mount and ride."

"And you wish someone to help this poor wanderer?"

"God watches over all his creatures, but the Caliph cannot always reach out a hand to do God's will."

"I hope this poor unfortunate will be helped as soon as possible," said Felix.

"Let it be soon. I am ready at any time to hear good news of him."

They said their good-byes, and Alai got up and went in search of Ivan.

"Pack," he said.

Ivan raised his eyebrows. "What will you need?"

"Clean underwear. My most flamboyantly Caliph-like costume. Three men who will kill at my command and will not turn their weapons on me. And a loyal man with a video camera with a fully charged battery and plenty of film."

"Should the vidman be one of the loyal soldiers? Or a separate person?"

"Let all the loyal soldiers be part of the video crew."

"And shall I be one of these three?"

"That is for you to decide," said Alai. "If I fail, the men who are with me will surely die."

"Better to die quickly before the face of God's servant than slowly at the hands of God's enemies," said Ivan.

"My favorite Russian," said Alai.

"I'm a Kazakh Turk," Ivan reminded him.

"God was good to send you to me."

"And good when he gave you to all of the faithful."

"Will you say so when I have done all that I mean to do?"

"Always," said Ivan. "Always I am your faithful servant."

"You are a servant only to God," said Alai. "To me, you are a friend."

An hour later, Alai received an email that he knew was from Petra, despite the innocent signature. It was a request that he pray for a child that was undergoing an operation at the largest hospital in Beirut at seven o'clock the next morning. "We will begin our own prayers at five in the morning," said the letter, "so that dawn will find us praying."

Alai merely answered, "I will pray for your nephew, and for all those who love him, that he may live. Let it be as God wills, and we will rejoice in his wisdom."

So he would have to go to Beirut. Well, the drive was easy enough. The problem was doing it without alarming anyone that his enemies had set to spy on him.

When he left the palace complex, it was in a garbage truck. Ivan had protested, but Alai told him, "A Caliph who is afraid to be filthied on God's errand is unworthy to rule." He was sure this would be written down and, if he lived, would be included in a book of the wisdom of Caliph Alai. A book he hoped would be long and worth reading, instead of brief and embarrassing.

Dressed as a pious old woman, Alai rode in the back seat of a little old sedan driven by a soldier in civilian clothes and a false beard much longer than his real one. If he lost, if he was killed, then the fact that he dressed this way would be taken as proof that he was never worthy to be Caliph. But if he won, it would be part of the legend of his cleverness.

The old woman accepted a wheelchair to take her into the hospital, pushed by the bearded man who had driven her to Beirut.

On the roof, three men with ordinary, scuffed suitcases were waiting. It was ten minutes to five.

If someone in the hospital had noticed the disappearance of the old woman, or looked for the wheelchair, or wondered about the three men who had arrived separately, each carrying clothing for a family member to wear home, then word might already have gone out to Alai's enemies. If someone came to investigate, and they had to kill him, it would be as good as setting off an alarm by Rajam's own bed.

Three minutes before five, two young doctors, a man and a woman, came onto the roof, ostensibly to smoke. But soon they withdrew out of the sight of the men waiting with their suitcases.

Ivan looked at Alai questioningly. Alai shook his head. "They are here to kiss," he said. "They are afraid of us reporting them, that's all."

Ivan, being careful, got up and walked to where he could see them. He came back and sat down. "More than kissing," he whispered.

"They should not do that if they aren't married," said

Alai. "Why do people always think that the only two choices are either to follow the harshest shari'ah or else discard all the laws of God?"

"You have never been in love," said Ivan.

"You think not?" said Alai. "Just because I can't meet any women does not mean I haven't loved."

"With your mind," said Ivan, "but I happen to know that with your body you have been pure."

"Of course I'm pure," said Alai. "I'm not married."

A medical chopper approached. It was exactly five o'clock. When it came close enough, Alai could see that it was from an Israeli hospital.

"Do Israeli doctors send patients to Beirut?" asked Alai.

"Lebanese doctors send patients to Israel," said Ivan.

"So must we expect that our friends will wait until this chopper leaves? Or are these our friends?"

"You have hidden in garbage and dressed as a woman," said Ivan. "What is riding in a Zionist helicopter compared to that?"

The chopper landed. The door opened. Nobody got out.

Alai picked up the suitcase that he knew was his because it was light—filled only with clothes instead of weaponry—and walked boldly to the door.

"Am I the passenger you came for?"

The pilot nodded.

Alai turned to look back toward where the couple had gone to kiss. He saw a flurry of motion. They had seen. They would speak of it.

He turned back to the pilot. "Can this chopper carry all five of us?"

"Easily," said the pilot.

"What about seven?"

The pilot shrugged. "We fly lower, slower. But we often do."

Alai turned to Ivan. "Please invite our young lovers to come with us." Then Alai climbed into the helicopter. In moments, he had the women's clothing off. Underneath, he was wearing a simple western business suit.

In moments, a pair of terrified doctors climbed into the helicopter at gunpoint, in various stages of deshabille. Apparently they had been warned to maintain absolute silence, because when they saw Alai and recognized him, the man went white and the woman began to weep while trying to re-fasten her clothing.

Alai came and knelt in front of her. "Daughter of God," he said, "I am not concerned about your immodesty. I am con-cerned that the man you offered your nakedness to is not your husband."

"We *will* be married," she said.

"Then when that happy day comes," said Alai, "your nakedness will bless your husband, and his nakedness will belong to you. Until then, I have this clothing for you." He handed her the costume he had worn. "I do not ask that you dress like this all the time. But today, when God has seen how your heart intended to sin, perhaps you might cover yourself in humility."

"Can she wait to dress until we're in the air?" asked the pilot.

"Of course," said Alai.

"Everybody strap down," said the pilot.

There weren't enough seats along the sides; the center was meant to hold a gurney. But Alai's driver grinned and in-sisted on standing. "I've ridden choppers into battle. If I can't keep my feet in a medical chopper, I deserve some bruises."

The chopper tilted as it rose into the air, but soon it found a workable equilibrium, and the woman unstrapped and awkwardly dressed herself. All the men looked away, except her companion, who helped her.

Meanwhile, Alai and the pilot conversed, making no at-tempt to lower their voices.

"I don't want these two with us for the main enterprise," said Alai. "But I don't want to kill them either. They need time to find their way back to God."

"They can be held in Haifa," said the pilot. "Or I can have them taken on to Malta, if that would suit you better."

"Haifa will do."

It wasn't a long journey, even flying low and slow. By the time they arrived, the doctors were quiet and looked penitent, holding hands and trying not to look at Alai too much. They landed on the roof of a hospital in Haifa, and the pilot turned off the engine and got out to converse for a moment with a man dressed like a doctor. Then he opened the door. "I have to lift off again," he said, "to make room for your transportation. So you need to come out now. Except those two."

The doctors looked at each other, frightened.

"They'll be safe?" asked Alai.

"Better if they don't see your transportation come and go," said the pilot. "It will soon be dawn and there's a little light. But they'll be safe."

Alai touched them both as he left the chopper.

He and his men watched as the medical chopper lifted off. Instantly, another chopper arrived, but this time a long-range battlejet, large enough to carry many soldiers into battle, and armed heavily enough to get them past a lot of obstacles.

The door opened, and Peter Wiggin stepped out.

Alai walked up to him. "Salaam," he said.

"And in you, too, let there be peace," said Peter.

"You still look more like Ender than the public photographs show."

"I have them retouched by computer to make me look older and smarter," said Peter.

Alai grinned. "It was nice of you to give us a ride."

"When Felix told me the sad story of that lonely pedestrian in the Empty Quarter, I couldn't pass up the chance to help."

"I thought it would be Bean," said Alai.

"It's a whole bunch of men trained by Bean," said Peter. "But Bean himself is on another errand. In Rwanda, as it happens."

"So that's happening now?" asked Alai.

"Oh, no," said Peter. "We won't make a *move* until we see how your little adventure turns out."

"Then let's go," said Alai.

Peter invited Alai to take precedence, but then he himself entered before any of Alai's soldiers. Ivan made as if to protest, but Alai gestured for him to relax. Alai had already bet everything on Peter's being cooperative and trustworthy. Now was not the time to worry about assassination or kidnapping. Even though there were twenty Hegemony soldiers already inside, as well as a sizable amount of equipment. Alai recognized the Thai-looking commander as someone he knew from Battle School. Had to be Suriyawong. Alai nodded to him. Suriyawong nodded back.

Once they were under way and on jet power—this time without any embarrassed woman having to be officially rebuked and forgiven and dressed—Peter indicated the men who were with him.

"I assumed," said Peter, "that the lone hitchhiker our mutual friend told me about didn't need a large escort."

"Only enough to get me to where a certain thick rope is coiled like a snake."

Peter nodded. "I have friends currently trying to find his exact location."

Alai smiled. "I assume it's far from the front."

"If he's in Hyderabad," said Peter, "then he will be under extremely heavy guard. But if he's across the border in Pakistan, security will not be unusually heavy."

"Either way," said Alai, "I will not have your men exposed to danger."

"Or observed," said Peter. "It wouldn't do for too many people to know you were brought to real power with the help of the Hegemon."

"You do seem to be at hand whenever I make a play for power."

"This is the last time, if you win," said Peter.

"This is the last time either way," said Alai, then grinned. "Either the soldiers will follow me or they won't."

"They will," said Peter. "If they get the chance."

Alai indicated his small escort. "That's what my camera crew is here to ensure."

Ivan smiled and lifted his shirt enough to show that he was wearing a bulletproof vest and carrying grenades and clips and a machine pistol.

"Oh," said Peter. "I thought you had gained weight."

"We Battle School boys," said Alai, "we always have a plan."

"You're not going to fight your way in, then."

"We're going to walk in as if we expected to be obeyed," said Alai. "With cameras rolling. It's a simple plan. But it doesn't have to work for very long. That thick rope, it always did love a camera."

"A vain and brutal man, my sources say," said Peter. "And not stupid."

"We'll see," said Alai.

"I think you're going to succeed," said Peter.

"So do I."

"And when you do," said Peter, "I think you're going to do something about the things Virlomi has been complaining about."

"It's because of those things that I could not wait for a more opportune time. I must wash Islam clean of this bloody stain."

"I believe that with you as Caliph, the Free People of Earth can coexist with a united Islam," said Peter.

"I believe so as well," said Alai. "Though I can never say so."

"But what I want," said Peter, "is insurance that I can use in case you don't survive. Either today or at some future point, I want to make sure I don't have to face a Caliph I can't coexist with."

Peter handed Alai a couple of sheets of paper. It was a script. Alai began to read.

"If you die a natural death and pass on your throne to someone you have chosen, then I'll have no need of this," said Peter. "But if you were murdered or kidnapped or exiled or otherwise dethroned by force, then I want this."

"And what if *you* are killed or otherwise forcibly removed from office?" asked Alai. "What happens to this vid then, assuming I say these things for the camera?"

"Try to encourage your followers not to think that killing me would be good for Islam," said Peter, "and my soldiers and doctors will guard against any other possible causes of my untimely death."

"In other words, I just have to risk it," said Alai.

"Come now," said Peter, "the only way this vid will be useful is if you aren't around to repudiate it. And if I'm dead, it will have no value to my unworthy successor."

Alai nodded. "True enough."

He stood up, opened his suitcase, and dressed in the flamboyant costume of a Caliph as the Muslim people expected to see him. Meanwhile, Peter's vidman set up his equipment—and the backdrop, so it wouldn't be obvious it was taped on a battlecraft, surrounded by soldiers.

At the gate of the heavily guarded military complex at Hyderabad—once the headquarters of the Indian military, then of the Chinese occupiers, and now of the Pakistani "liberators"—three motorcycles pulled up, two of them carrying two men each, and the third a single rider with a satchel on the seat behind him.

They stopped well back from the gate, so no one would suppose it was an attempt at a suicide bombing. They all held up their hands so some trigger happy guard wouldn't take a shot at them while one of the men pulled a video camera out of the satchel and fitted a satellite feed to the top of it.

That got the attention of the guards, who immediately phoned for advice from someone in authority.

Only when the camera was ready did the man who had been alone on his cycle peel back the traveling coat that had covered him. The guards were almost blinded by the whiteness of his robes, and long before he had his kaffia-cloth and 'agal-rope in place on his head.

Even the guards who weren't close enough to recognize him by face guessed from the clothing and from the fact that he was a young black man that their Caliph had come to see them. None of the common soldiers and few of the officers suspected that General Rajam would not be happy to have a visit from the Caliph. So they raised their voices in cheers— some of them in an ululation meant to suggest the cries of Arab warriors riding into battle, though all the soldiers here were Pakistani.

The camera rolled as Alai raised his arms to receive the adulation of his people.

He strode through the checkpoint unmolested.

Someone brought him a jeep, but he refused and kept walking. But the vidman and his crew got into the jeep and rode along beside and then ahead of the Caliph. While the Caliph's aide, Ivan Lankowski, dressed in civilian clothes like the vid crew, explained to the officers who trotted alongside him that the Caliph was here to bestow upon General Rajam the honors he had earned. He expected General Rajam and those men he wished to have share this honor greet the Caliph in the open square before all of the Caliph's soldiers.

This word quickly spread, and before long, Alai's progress was accompanied by thousands of uniformed soldiers, cheering and calling his name. They kept a path clear for the vid crew, and those who thought they might be within line of sight of the camera made an especially exuberant show of their love for the Caliph, in case someone from home was watching and might recognize them.

Alai was reasonably confident that whatever Rajam might be planning, he wouldn't do it in front of a live satellite feed, with thousands of soldiers looking on. Rajam would have had Alai die in a plane crash on the way, or be assassinated somewhere far from Rajam himself. Now that he was here, Rajam would play a waiting game, to see what Alai was up to, meanwhile looking for some innocent-seeming way for Alai to be gotten rid of—killed, or trundled back to Damascus and kept under closer guard.

As Alai expected, Rajam waited for him at the top of the imposing stairs leading up to the finest-looking building in the compound. But Alai walked up only a few steps and stopped, turning his back on Rajam and facing the soldiers . . . and the camera. The light was good here.

The vid crew took their places at the bottom of the steps.

Alai held up his arms for silence and waited. The shouting died down.

"Soldiers of God!" he shouted.

A huge roar, but it subsided at once.

"Where is the general who has led you?"

Another cheer . . . but one that was noticeably less enthusiastic. Alai hoped that Rajam wouldn't be too resentful of the difference in their popularity.

Alai did not look—he counted on Ivan to signal him when Rajam was near. He saw Ivan beckoning to Rajam to take his place at Alai's left hand, directly in front of the camera.

Ivan signaled. Alai turned and embraced and kissed Rajam.

Stab me to death right now, Alai wanted to say. Because this is your last chance, you treasonous, murdering dog.

Instead, he spoke softly into Rajam's ear. "As my old friend Ender Wiggin used to say, Rajam, the enemy's gate is down."

Then he let go of the embrace, ignoring the puzzled look on Rajam's face, and took his hand, offering him to the cheering of the soldiers.

Alai raised his hands for silence and got it.

"God has seen all the deeds that have been done in his name here in India!"

Cheering. But also, on some faces, uncertainty. They had seen Virlomi's vid, including the most recent one. Some of them, the brightest of them, knew that they could not be sure what Alai meant by this.

"And God knows, as you all know, that nothing has been done in India except by the will of General Rajam!"

The cheering was definitely half-hearted.

"Now is the day God has appointed to pay the debt of honor that is owed!"

The cheer had barely started when the camera crew pulled out their machine pistols and filled Rajam's body with bullets.

At first many of the soldiers thought it was an assassination attempt on the Caliph, and there was a roar. Alai was glad to see that these were not the Muslim soldiers of history—few fled from the bullets, and many rushed forward. But Alai raised his arms and strode to a higher position, above the body of Rajam. At the same time, as he had instructed them, Ivan and the two men who were not holding the camera bounded up the steps and stood in line with Alai and raised their weapons above their heads.

"Allahu akbar!" they cried in unison. "Muhammed is his prophet! And Alai is Caliph!"

Again Alai raised his hands, and waited until he had relative silence and the rush toward the steps had ceased. Now there were soldiers all around him.

"The crimes of Andariyy Rajam have made a stink throughout the world! The soldiers of Islam came to India as liberators! In the name of God they came, as friends to our brothers and sisters in India! But Andariyy Rajam betrayed God and his Caliph by encouraging some of our people to commit terrible crimes!

"God has already declared the penalty for such crimes! Now I have come to cleanse Islam of such evil. Never again will any man or woman or child have reason to fear the army of God! I command all the soldiers of God to arrest any man who committed atrocities against the people we came to liberate! I command the nations of the world to give no shelter to these criminals. I command my soldiers to arrest any man who ordered such atrocities, and any man who knew of the atrocities but did nothing to punish the offenders. Arrest them and bear witness against them, and in the name of God I will judge them.

"If they refuse to submit themselves to my authority, then they are in rebellion against God. Bring them to me for judgment; if they do not resist you, and they are innocent, they have nothing to fear. In every city and fortress, in every camp and airfield, let my soldiers arrest the offenders and bring them to the officers who are loyal to God and the Caliph!"

Alai held his pose for a long ten seconds while the soldiers cheered. Then he saw the camera lowered, as some soldiers already dragged various men toward him and others ran for nearby buildings, in search of others.

It was a very rough kind of justice that was going to go on now, as the Muslim army tore itself apart. And it would be interesting to see where such men as Ghaffar Wahabi, the prime minister of Pakistan, aligned themselves. It would be a shame to have to use this army to subdue a Muslim government.

But Alai had to act quickly, even if it was messy. He could not afford to let any of the offenders get away to plot against him.

And as he watched the accused men being lined up in front of him, under the direction of Ivan and his men, who seemed unlikely to be killed today after all, Alai spoke inside his mind: There, Hot Soup! See how Alai adapted your trick to his purposes.

We still learn from each other, we soldiers of Ender's Jeesh.

As for you, Peter, keep your little vid. It will never be needed. For all men are only tools in the hand of God, and I, not you, am the tool God has chosen to unite the world.

13

FOUND

From: Graff%pilgrimage@colmin.gov
To:PADelphiki@TutsiNet.rw.net
Re: Can you travel?

Since your husband is busy in Rwanda right now, I wonder if you are able to travel? We expect no physical danger apart from the normal rigors of air travel. But with little Ender still so young, you will probably want to leave him behind. Or not—if you wish to bring him, we will do our best to accommodate you.

We have confirmed the identity of one of your children. A daughter. Naturally, we are finding the children who share Bean's genetic condition first. We have already accessed blood samples from the child, taken at the hospital because the birth was premature. The genetic match is absolute: She is yours. In all likelihood this will be difficult for the erstwhile parents, especially for the mother, who, like the victim of the proverbial cuckoo, has just borne another female's child. I will understand completely if you prefer not to be present. Your presence, however, might also help them believe in the reality of the true mother of "their" child. Your call.

Petra was furious with Peter—and with Graff. These plotters, so sure they know what's best for everyone. If they were holding off on the announcement of ratification while the turmoil—no, the bloodbath—in the Muslim world continued, then why couldn't Bean come with her to pick up the first of their missing children to be found?

No, that was impossible, he needed to cement the allegiance of the Rwandan military, and so on and so on, as if it really mattered. And most maddening of all, why did Bean go along with it? Since when had Bean become *obedient?* "I have to stay," he said, over and over, without any further explanation, despite her demand for some kind of justification.

Was Bean a plotter too? But not against *her*, surely. Why would he conceal his thinking from her? What secrets would he keep?

But when it became clear that Bean would not come with her, Petra packed baby clothes, diapers, and a change of clothes for herself into a single bag, then scooped up little Ender and headed for Kayibanda Airport.

She was met there by Mazer Rackham. "You came to Kigali instead of meeting me there?" she said.

"Hello to you too," said Rackham. "We're not trusting commercial flights on this matter. We believe Achilles's network has been broken, but we can't risk having your baby kidnapped or you harmed en route."

So Achilles still bends us and costs us time and money, even after death. Or else he's just your excuse for making sure you supervise everything directly. Why are Bean's and my children so important to you? How do I know that you, too, don't have some plan to harness our children to the yoke of some noble world-saving project?

What she said aloud was, "Thank you."

They took off on a private jet that pretended to belong to one of the big solar desalinization companies that were developing the Sahara.

Nice to know which companies the I.F. is using as a cover for planetside operations.

They overflew the Sahara, and Petra couldn't help but be pleased at the sight of a restored Lake Chad and the vast irrigation project surrounding it. She had read that the desalination on the Libyan coast was now proceeding faster than evaporation, and that Lake Chad was already affecting weather in the surrounding area. But she had not been prepared to see so many kilometers of grassland, or the herds of animals grazing on it. The grass and vines were turning sand and sahel into fertile soil again. And the dazzling surface of Lake Chad was dotted with the sails of fishing boats.

They landed in Lisbon and Rackham took her first to a hotel, where she nursed Ender, cleaned herself up, then put the baby into a sling in front of her. Carrying him she went back down to the lobby, where Rackham met her and led her to the limo waiting outside.

To her surprise, she felt a sudden stab of fear. It had nothing to do with this car, or their destination today. She remembered the day in Rotterdam when Ender was implanted in her womb. Bean emerged from the hospital with her and the drivers of the first couple of taxis were smoking. So Bean made her get in the third one. He got into the first one himself.

The first two cabs had been part of a kidnapping and murder plot, and Bean only narrowly escaped death. The cab she entered was part of an entirely different plot—one to save her life.

"You know this driver?" asked Petra.

Mazer nodded gravely. "We leave nothing to chance," he said. "The driver is a soldier. One of ours."

So the I.F. had trained military personnel on Earth, wearing civilian clothes and driving limousines. Such a scandal.

They drove up into the hills, to a large and lovely home with an astonishing view of the city and the bay and, on a clear day, the Atlantic beyond. The Romans saw this place, ruled in this city. The Vandals took it, and then the Visigoths. The Moors got it next, and then the Christians took it back. From this city, sailing ships went out and rounded Africa and colonized in India and China and Africa and, eventually, Brazil.

And yet it was nothing more than a human city in a lovely setting. Earthquakes and fires had come and gone, but people still built in the hills and on the flat. Storms and calms and pirates and war had taken ship after ship, and yet people still put out to sea with nets or trade goods or guns. People made love and grew babies, in the mansions just as in the tiny houses of the poor.

She had come here from Rwanda, as humans had come out of Africa for fifty thousand years. Not as part of a tribe that climbed down into caves to paint their stories and worship their gods. Not as part of a wave of invaders. But . . . wasn't she here to take a baby out of a woman's arms? To claim that what came from this stranger's womb would belong to *her* from now on? Just as so many people had stood on the hills overlooking the bay and said, This is mine now, and it always was mine, regardless of the people who happen to think it belongs to them and have held this place all their lives.

Mine mine mine. That was the curse and power of human beings—that what they saw and loved, they had to have. They could share it with other people but only if they conceived of those people as being somehow their own. What we own is ours. What you own should also be ours. In fact, you own nothing, if we want it. Because you are nothing. We are the real people, you are only posing as people in order to try to deprive us of what God means us to have.

And now she understood for the first time the magnitude of what Graff and Mazer Rackham and, yes, even Peter were all trying to do.

They were trying to get human beings to define themselves as all belonging to one tribe.

It had happened briefly when they were threatened by creatures who truly were strangers; then the human race had felt itself to be one people, and united in order to repel an enemy.

And the moment victory was achieved, it all fell apart, and long-pent-up resentments erupted into war. First the old rivalry between Russia and the West. And when that was quelled by the I.F., and the old polemarch fell and was replaced by Chamrajnagar, the wars moved to different killing fields.

They even looked at the Battle School grads and said, Ours. Not free people, but the property of this nation or that.

And now those same children, once property, were at the heads of some of the most powerful nations. Alai, mortaring the bricks of his fragmented empire with the blood of his enemies. Han Tzu, restoring the prosperity of China as quickly as possible in order to emerge from defeat as a power in the world. And Virlomi, out in the open now, refusing to join any party, standing above politics, but Petra knew that she would not release her hold on power.

Hadn't Petra sat with Han Tzu and Alai and controlled fleets and squadrons in distant wars? They thought they were only playing a game—all of them thought that, except Bean, the secret-keeper—but they were saving the world together. They loved being together. They loved being one, under the leadership of Ender Wiggin.

Virlomi hadn't been with them then, but Petra remembered her as well, as the girl she turned to when she was a captive in Hyderabad. She had given her a message and Virlomi had taken the burden as if Petra were a real person; she had delivered it to Bean and had helped Bean to come and save her. Now Virlomi had created a new India out of the wreckage of the old; she had given them something more powerful than any mere elected government. She had given them a divine queen, a dream and a vision, and India was poised to become, for the first time, a great power commensurate with her great population and her ancient culture.

All three of them are making their nations great, in a time when the greatness of nations is the nightmare of humanity.

How will Peter ever gain mastery over them? How will he tell them, No, this city, that mountain, these fields, that lake, they do not belong to you or to any group or individual, they are part of Earth, and Earth belongs to all of us, a single tribe. One overgrown troop of baboons that have taken shelter in the shade of this planet's night, that draw their life from the heat of this planet's day.

Graff and his ilk did their work too well. They found all of the children best suited to rule; but part of the mix they selected for was ambition. And not just the desire to achieve or even surpass others—it was aggression, the desire to rule and control.

The need to have our own way.

I certainly have it. If I had not fallen in love with Bean and focused on our children, wouldn't I be one of them? Only I would be hampered by the weakness of my country. Armenia has neither the resources nor the national will to rule over great empires. But Alai and Han Tzu inherit centuries of empire and a sense of entitlement to rule. While Virlomi is making her own myth and teaching her people that their day of destiny has come.

Only two of these great children have stepped outside the pattern, the great game of slaughter and domination.

Bean was never selected for aggression. He was selected for brilliance alone. His mind far outshone any other. But he was not one of us. He could solve the strategic and tactical problems more easily than anyone—more easily than Ender. But he didn't care whether he ruled; he didn't care whether he won. When he had an army of his own, he never won a battle—all his effort was spent on training his soldiers and trying out his ideas.

That's why he was able to be the perfect shadow to Ender Wiggin. He did not need to surpass Ender. All he wanted was to survive. And, without knowing it, to belong. To love and be loved. Ender gave him that. And Sister Carlotta. And me. But he never needed to rule.

Peter is the other one. And he *does* need to rule, to surpass all others. Especially because he wasn't selected for Battle School. So what tames him?

Ender Wiggin? Is that it? Peter must be greater than his brother Ender. He can't do it by conquest because he isn't a match for these Battle Schoolers. He can't take the field against Han Tzu or Alai—or Bean, or me, for that matter! Yet he must somehow be greater than Ender Wiggin, and Ender Wiggin saved the human race.

Petra stood at the edge of the hill, across the street from the house where her second child waited for her—a daughter she intended to take away from the woman who bore her. She looked out over the city and saw herself.

I am as ambitious as Hot Soup or Alai or any of them. Yet I fell in love with and determined to marry—against his will—the only Battle Schooler who had no ambition of his own. Why? Because I wanted to have the next generation. I wanted the most brilliant children. Even as I told him that I wanted none of them to have his affliction, in fact I wanted them to have it. To be like him. I wanted to be Eve to a new species. I wanted my genes to be part of the future of humanity. And they will be.

But Bean will also die. I knew that all along. I knew that I would be a young widow. In the back of my mind, I thought of that all along. What a terrible thing to realize about myself.

That's why I don't want him to take our babies away from me. I must have them all, the way conquerors have had to have this city. *I* must have them. That is my empire.

What kind of life will they have, with me for their mother?

"We can't put this off forever," said Mazer Rackham.

"I was just thinking."

"You're still young enough to believe that will get you somewhere," said Rackham.

"No," she said. "No, I'm older than you think. I know that I can't think my way out of being who I am."

"Why would you want to?" said Mazer Rackham. "Don't you know that you were always the best of them?"

She turned to him, suppressing the rush of pride, refusing to believe it. "That's nonsense. I'm the least. The worst. The one that broke."

"The one that Ender pressed hardest, relied on most. *He* knew. Besides, I didn't mean the best at war. I meant the best, period. The best at being human."

The irony of hearing him say that right after she realized just how selfish and ambitious and *dangerous* she was—she almost laughed. Instead she reached out and touched his shoulder. "You poor man," she said. "You think of us as your children."

"No," said Rackham, "that would be Hyrum Graff."

"Did you have children? Before your voyage?"

Rackham shook his head. But she couldn't tell if he was saying, No, I had no children, or No, I won't talk to you about this. "Let's go inside."

Petra turned around, crossed the narrow street, and followed him through the gate of the garden and up to the door of the house. It stood open in the early autumn sunlight. Bees hummed among the flowers of the garden but none came into the house; what business did they have in there, when all they needed was outside?

The man and woman waited in the dining room of their house. A woman in civilian clothes—who nevertheless seemed to Petra like a soldier—stood behind them. Perhaps watching to make sure they didn't try to run.

The wife sat in an armchair and held their newborn daughter. Her husband leaned on the table. His face was a mask of despair. The woman had been crying. So they already knew.

Rackham spoke at once. "I didn't want you to turn your baby over to strangers," he said to the man and woman. "I wanted you to see that the baby is going home to her mother."

"But she already has a baby," said the woman. "You didn't tell me that she already—"

"Yes he did," said the man.

Petra sat down in a chair across from the man, cornerwise from the woman. Ender wriggled a little but stayed asleep. "We meant to save the others, not to have them born all at once," said Petra. "I meant to bear them all myself. My husband is dying. I meant to keep having his children after he was gone."

"But don't you have more? Can't you spare this one?" The woman's voice was so piteous that Petra hated herself for saying no.

Rackham spoke before she could. "This child is already dying of the same condition that is killing her father. And her brother. That's why they were born prematurely."

This only made the woman cling more tightly to the baby.

"You'll have children of your own," said Rackham. "You still have the four fertilized embryos you already created."

The would-be father looked up at him blandly. "We'll adopt next time," he said.

"We're all very sorry," Rackham went on, "that these criminals stole the use of your womb to deliver another woman's child. But the child is truly hers, and if you adopt, you should have children that were willingly given up by their parents."

The man nodded. He understood.

But the woman had the baby in her arms.

Petra spoke up. "Would you like to hold her brother?" She reached down and lifted Ender out of the sling. "His name is Andrew. He's a month old."

The woman nodded.

Rackham reached down and took her daughter out of her arms. Petra handed Ender to her.

"My . . . the girl is . . . I call her Bella. My little Lourinha." She wept.

Lourinha? The baby's hair, such as it was, was brown. But apparently it didn't take much lightness of hair to earn the appellation "blonde."

Petra took the girl from Rackham's hands. She was even smaller than Ender, but her eyes were just as intelligent and searching. Ender's hair was as black as Bean's. Bella's hair was more like Petra's. It startled her, how happy it made her that the baby took after her.

"Thank you for bearing my daughter," said Petra. "I grieve for your grief, but I hope you can also rejoice at my joy."

Weeping, the woman nodded and clung now to Ender. She turned her face to the baby and spoke in a small babytalk voice. "Es tu feliz em ter irminha? Es tu felizinho?" Then she burst into tears and handed Ender to Rackham.

Standing, Petra laid Bella into the sling where Ender had been. Then she took Ender from Rackham and held him against her shoulder.

"I'm so sorry," said Petra. "Please forgive me for not letting you keep my baby."

The man shook his head. "Não ha de que desculpar," he said.

"Nothing to forgive," murmured the stern-looking woman who was apparently not just a guard, but also an interpreter.

The woman wailed in grief and leapt to her feet, upsetting the chair. She sobbed and babbled and clutched at Bella and covered her with kisses. But she didn't try to take the baby.

Rackham pulled Petra away as the guard and the husband pulled the mother back and held her, still wailing and sobbing, while Petra and Rackham left the house.

Back in the car, Rackham sat in back with Petra and took Ender out of her arms for the ride back to the hotel. "They really are small," he said.

"Bean calls Ender a toy person," said Petra.

"I can see why," said Rackham.

"I feel like a really polite kidnapper," said Petra.

"Don't," said Rackham. "Even though they were embryos

when they were stolen from you, it was a kidnapping, and now you're getting your daughter back."

"But these people did nothing wrong."

"Think again," said Rackham. "Remember how we found them."

They moved, she remembered. When Volescu's deadman switch triggered a message, they moved. "Why would they knowingly—"

"The wife doesn't know. Our deal with the husband was that we wouldn't tell. He's completely sterile, you see. *Their* attempt at in vitro fertilization didn't take. That's why he took Volescu's offer and pretended to his wife that the baby was really theirs. He's the one that got the message and made up a reason for them to move to this house."

"He didn't ask where the baby came from?"

"He's a rich man," said Rackham. "Rich people tend to take it for granted that things they want simply come to them."

"The wife meant no harm, though."

"Neither did Bean, and yet he's dying," said Rackham. "Neither did I, and yet I was sent on a voyage that jumped me decades into the future, costing me everyone and everything. And you'll lose Bean, even though you've done nothing wrong. Life is full of grief, to exactly the degree we allow ourselves to love other people."

"I see," said Petra. "You're the Ministry of Colonization's resident philosopher."

Rackham grinned. "The consolations of philosophy are many, but never enough."

"I think you and Graff planned the whole history of the world. I think you chose Bean and Peter for the roles they're playing now."

"You're wrong," said Rackham. "Flat wrong. All that Graff and I ever did was choose the children we thought might win the war and try to train them for victory. We failed again and again until we found Ender. And Bean to back him up. And the rest of the Jeesh to help him. And when the last battle ended and we had won, Graff and I had to face the fact that the solution to the one problem was now the cause of another."

"The military geniuses you had identified would now tear the world apart with their ambition."

"Or be used as pawns to satisfy the ambitions of others, yes."

"So you decided to use them as pawns in your own game once again."

"No," said Rackham softly. "We decided to find a way to set most of them free to live human lives. We're still working on that."

"*Most* of us?"

"There was nothing we could do for Bean," said Rackham.

"I guess not," said Petra.

"But then something happened that we hadn't planned on," said Rackham. "Hadn't hoped for. He found love. He became a father. The one we could do nothing for, you made him happy. So, I have to admit, we feel a lot of gratitude to you, Petra. You could have been out there playing the game with the others." He chuckled. "We would never have guessed it. You're off the charts when it comes to ambition. Not quite like Peter, but close. Yet somehow you set it all aside."

She smiled as beatifically as she could.

If only you knew the truth, she thought.

Or maybe he does know, but telling her that he admires her is a way of manipulating her . . .

Nobody ever completely means what they say. Even when they think they're telling the truth, there's always something hidden behind their words.

It was dark when she got back to her own house in the military headquarters compound just outside Kigali. Mazer Rackham did not come inside with her. So she carried both babies, Ender in the sling again, and Bella at her shoulder.

Bean was there, waiting for her. He ran to her and took the new baby from her and pressed his cheek to the baby's cheek.

"Don't smother her, oaf," said Petra.

He laughed and kissed her. They sat together on the edge of the bed, holding the two children, and then trading, back and forth.

"Seven to go," said Petra.

"Was it hard?" asked Bean.

"I'm glad you weren't there," said Petra. "I'm not sure you would have been tough enough to go through with it."

14

VIRLOMI'S VISITORS

From: ImperialSelf%HotSoup@ForbiddenCity.ch.gov
To: Suriyawong@hegemon.gov
Re: We have found Paribatra

Suriyawong, I am relieved to tell you that Paribatra, the former prime minister of Thailand, has been located. His health is not good but with proper attention it is believed that he will recover as well as can be expected for a man his age.

The former government had nearly perfected the art of making people disappear without actually killing them, but we are still tracking down other Thai exiles. I have great hopes of finding and releasing your family members.

You know that I opposed all these illegal actions against Thailand, its citizens, and its government. I have now moved at the first opportunity to undo as much of the damage as I can.

For internal political reasons I cannot release Paribatra directly to Ambul's Free Thai organization at this time, even though I fully expect that his group will be the core of the new government of Thailand and look forward to an early reconciliation.

As we free Paribatra into the care of the Hegemon, it seems appropriate that you who tried so hard to save Thailand should be the one to receive him.

Virlomi came to Hyderabad, and in front of the gate of the military complex where she once worked in virtual captivity, drawing up plans for wars and invasions she did not believe in, she now built a hut with her own hands.

Each day she went to a well and drew water, even though there were few villages in India that did not already have clean running water. Each dawn she buried her night soil even though most villages had working sewer systems.

Indians came to her by the hundreds, to ask her questions. When she was tired, she came out and wept for them and begged them to go home. They went, but the next morning others came.

No soldiers came near her, so there was no overt provocation to the Muslims inside the military compound. Of course, she was controlling the Indian military, which grew in strength every day, through her encrypted cellphones, which were swapped out daily for freshly charged ones by aides posing as ordinary supplicants.

Now and then someone from another land would come to see her. Her aides would whisper to them that she would not speak to anyone who was not barefoot, and if they wore western business suits she would offer them appropriate clothing, which they would not like, so it was better to be clad already in Indian clothing of their own choosing.

Three visitors came to her in one week of her vigil.

The first was Tikal Chapekar. Emperor Han had freed him, along with many other Indian captives. If he had expected some kind of ceremony when he returned to India, he was disappointed.

He assumed at first that the silence from the media was because the Muslim conquerors would not allow any mention of the return of the imprisoned Prime Minister to India.

So he went to Hyderabad to complain to the Caliph himself, who now ruled over his vast Muslim empire from within the walls of the military compound there. He was allowed to enter the compound, though while he waited in line at the checkpoint, he was curious about the hut a few dozen meters away, where a great many more Indians waited in line than waited to see the rulers of the nation.

"What is that hut?" he asked. "Do ordinary citizens have to go there first before coming to this gate?"

The gate guards laughed at his question. "You're an Indian, and you don't know that's where Virlomi lives?"

"Who is Virlomi?"

Now the guards grew suspicious. "No Hindu would say that. Who are you?"

He explained that he had been in captivity until just a few days ago, and was not aware of the news.

"News?" said one guard. "Virlomi isn't on the *news*. She makes her own news."

"Wish they'd just let us shoot her," muttered another.

"And then who would protect you as they tore us all limb from limb?" said another, quite cheerfully.

"So . . . who is she?" asked Chapekar.

"The soul of India is a *woman*," said the one who had wanted to shoot her. He said "woman" with all the contempt he could put into a single word. Then he spat.

"What office does she hold?" asked Chapekar.

"Hindus don't hold offices anymore," said another guard. "Not even you, former Prime Minister."

Chapekar felt a wave of relief. Someone had recognized his name.

"Because you forbid the Indian people to elect their own government?"

"We allow it," said the guard. "The Caliph declared an election but nobody came."

"No one voted?"

"No one ran for office."

Chapekar laughed. "India has been a democracy for hundreds of years. People run for office. People vote."

"Not when Virlomi asks them not to serve in any office until the Muslim overlords leave India."

Now Chapekar understood everything. She was a charismatic, like Gandhi, centuries ago. Rather a sad one, since she was imitating a primitive Indian lifestyle that hadn't been the rule through most of India in many lifetimes. Still, there was magic in the old icons, and with so many disasters befalling India, the people would look for someone to capture their imagination.

Gandhi never became ruler of India, however. That job was for more practical people. If he could just get the word out that he was back. Surely the Caliph would want a legitimate Indian government restored to help keep order.

After a suitable wait, he was ushered into a building. After another wait, he was brought to the anteroom of the Caliph's office. And finally he was brought into the Presence.

Except that the person he met with was not the Caliph at all, but his old adversary, Ghaffar Wahabi, who had been prime minister of Pakistan.

"I thought to see the Caliph," said Chapekar, "but I'm glad to see you first, my old friend."

Wahabi smiled and nodded, but he did not rise and when Chapekar made as if to approach him, hands restrained him. Still, they did not stop him from sitting in an armless chair, which was good, because Chapekar tired easily these days.

"I am glad to see that the Chinese have come to their senses and set their prisoners free. This new emperor they have is weak, a mere boy, but a weak China is better for all of us, don't you think?"

Chapekar shook his head. "The Chinese people love him."

"Islam has ground the face of China into the dust," said Wahabi.

"Has Islam ground the face of India into the dust as well?" asked Chapekar.

"There were excesses, under the previous military leadership. But Caliph Alai, may God preserve him, put a stop to that some time ago. Now the leader of the Indian rebels sits outside our gate, and we are untroubled, and she and her followers are unmolested."

"So now Muslim rule is benign," said Chapekar. "And yet when the Indian Prime Minister returns, there is not a word on television, not an interview. No car waiting for him. No office."

Wahabi shook his head. "My old friend," he said. "Don't you remember? As the Chinese surrounded and swallowed up your armies, as they swept across India, you made a great public pronouncement. You said, if I remember rightly, that there would be no government in exile. That the ruler of India from then on would be . . . and I say this with all modesty . . . me."

"I meant, of course, only until I returned."

"No you were very clear," said Wahabi. "I'm sure we can get someone to play you the vid. I can send for someone if you—"

"You are going to hold India without a government because—"

"India has a government. From the mouth of the Indus to the mouth of the Ganges, from the Himalayas to the waves that lap the shores of Sri Lanka, the flag of Pakistan flies over a united India. Under the divinely inspired leadership of Caliph Alai, may Allah be thanked for him."

"Now I understand why you suppress news of my coming," said Chapekar, rising to his feet. "You are afraid of losing what you have."

"What I have?" Wahabi laughed. "We are the government, but Virlomi rules India. You think *we* blacked out the news about you? *Virlomi* asked the Indian people not to look at television as long as the Muslim invaders retained their unwelcome presence in Mother India."

"And they obey her?"

"The drop in national power consumption is noticeable. No one interviewed you, old friend, because there *are* no reporters. And even if there were, why would they care about you? You don't rule India, and I don't rule India, and if you want to have anything to do with India, you'll take off your shoes and get in that line in front of the hut outside the gate."

"Yes," said Chapekar. "I'll do that."

"Come back and tell me what she says," said Wahabi. "I've been contemplating doing the same thing myself."

So Chapekar walked back out of the military compound and joined the line. When the sun set and the sky began to darken, Virlomi came out of the hut and wept with grief that she could not hear and speak to everyone personally. "Go home," she said. "I pray for you, all of you. Whatever is the desire of your heart, let the Gods grant it, if it would bring no harm to another. If you need food or work or shelter, go back to your city or your village and tell them that Virlomi is praying for that city, that village. Tell them that my prayer is this: Let the gods bless the people to exactly the degree that they help the hungry and jobless and homeless. Then help them make this prayer a blessing upon them instead of curse. *You* try to find someone less fortunate than you, and help him. In helping him, you will also rise."

Then she went back inside the hut.

The crowd dispersed. Chapekar sat down to wait until the morning.

One of the others who had been in the line said, "Don't bother. She never sees anyone who spends the night. She says that if she lets people gain an advantage by doing that, soon the plain will be covered with snoring Indians and she will never get any sleep!"

He and several others laughed, but Chapekar did not laugh. Now that he had seen his adversary, he was worried. She was beautiful and gentle-seeming, and moved with unspeakable grace. She had mastered it all—the perfect demagogue for India. Politicians had always shouted to whip an audience into a frenzy. But this woman spoke quietly, and made them hunger for her words, so she hardly had to say anything, and they felt blessed to hear her.

Still, she was only a lone woman. Chapekar knew how to command armies. More important, he knew how to get legislation through Congress and keep party members in line. All he needed to do was attach himself to this girl and soon he would be the real ruler of her party.

Now all he needed was to find a place to spend the night and come back in the morning to see her.

He was leaving when one of Virlomi's aides touched his shoulder. "Sir," said the young man, "the Lady has asked to see you."

"Me?"

"Aren't you Tikal Chapekar?"

"I am."

"Then you're the one she asked for." The young man eyed him up and down, then knelt, scooped up some dirt, and flung it at Chapekar's suit and began to rub it in.

"What are you doing! How dare you!"

"If I don't make you look like your suit is old and you have seen much suffering, then—"

"You idiot! My suit *is* old, and I have suffered in exile!"

"The Lady will not care, sir. But do as you wish. It's this or the loincloth. She keeps several in her hut, so she can humble proud men."

Chapekar glared at the young man, then squatted, scooped up dirt, and began rubbing it into his own clothing.

A few minutes later, he was inside the hut. It was lighted by three small flickering oil lamps. Shadows danced on the dried-mud walls.

She greeted him with a smile that seemed warm and friendly. Maybe this would go better than he had feared.

"Tikal Chapekar," she said. "I'm glad that our people are returning from captivity."

"The new emperor is weak," said Chapekar. "He thinks that he'll appease world opinion by letting his prisoners go."

She said nothing.

"You've done an excellent job of annoying the Muslims," he said.

She said nothing.

"I want to help you."

"Excellent," she said. "What weapons are you trained to use?"

He laughed. "No weapons."

"So . . . not as a soldier, then. Do you type? I know you can read, so I assume you can handle record keeping on our military computers."

"Military?" he asked.

"We're a nation at war," she said simply.

"But I'm not a soldier of any kind," said Chapekar.

"Too bad."

"I'm a governor."

"The Indian people are doing an excellent job of governing themselves right now. What they need are soldiers to drive out their oppressors."

"But you have government right here. Your aides, who tell people what to do. The one who covered me with dirt."

"They help people. They don't govern them. They give advice."

"And this is how you rule all of India?"

"I sometimes make suggestions, and my aides put the vid

out over the nets," said Virlomi. "Then the people decide whether to obey me or not."

"You can reject government now," said Chapekar. "But someday you'll need it."

Virlomi shook her head. "I will never need government. Perhaps someday India will choose to have a government, but *I* will never need it."

"So you wouldn't stop me from urging exactly that course. On the nets."

She smiled. "Whoever comes to your site, let them agree or disagree with you as they see fit."

"I think you're making a mistake," said Chapekar.

"Ah," said Virlomi. "And you find this frustrating?"

"India needs better than a lone woman in a hut."

"And yet this lone woman in a hut held up the Chinese Army in the passes of the east, long enough for the Muslims to have their victory. And this lone woman led the guerrilla war and the riots against the Muslim occupiers. And this lone woman brought the Caliph from Damascus to Hyderabad in order to seize control of his own army, which was committing atrocities against India."

"And you're very proud of your achievements."

"I'm pleased that the gods saw fit to give me something useful to do. I've offered you something useful, too, but you refuse."

"You've offered me humiliation and futility." He stood to go.

"Exactly the gifts I once had from your hand."

He turned back to her. "Have we met?"

"Have you forgotten? You once came to see the Battle School graduates who were planning your strategy. But you discarded all our plans. You despised them, and followed instead the plans of the traitor Achilles."

"I saw all your plans."

"No, you saw only the plans Achilles wanted you to see."

"Was that my fault? I *thought* they were from you."

"I foresaw the fall of India as Achilles's plans overextended our armies and exposed our supply lines to attack from China. I foresaw that you would do nothing except futile rhetoric—like the monstrous act of appointing Wahabi as ruler of India—as if the rule of India were yours to bequeath to another in your will. I saw—we all saw—how useless and vain and stupid you were in your ambition, and how easily Achilles manipulated you by flattery."

"I don't have to listen to this."

"Then go," said Virlomi. "I say nothing that doesn't play over and over again in the secret places in your heart."

He did not go.

"After I left, to notify the Hegemon of what was happening, so that perhaps my friends from Battle School could be saved from Achilles's plan to murder them all—when that errand was done, I set up resistance to Chinese rule in the mountains of the East. But back in Battle School, led by a brilliant and brave and beautiful young man named Sayagi, the Battle Schoolers drew up plans that would have saved India, if you had followed them. At risk of their own lives, they published it on the nets, knowing that Achilles would let none of it get to you if they submitted it through him. Did you see the plans?"

"I was not in the habit of getting my war plans from the nets."

"No. You got your plans from our enemy."

"I didn't know that."

"You should have known. It was plain enough what Achilles was. You saw what we saw. The difference is, we hated him, and you admired him—for exactly the same traits."

"I never saw the plans."

"You never asked the most brilliant minds in India for a shred of advice. Instead, you trusted a Belgian psychopath.

And followed his advice to make unprovoked war on Burma and Thailand, pouring out war on nations that had done no harm to us. A man who embraces the voice of evil when it whispers in his ear is no less evil than the whisperer."

"I'm not impressed by your ability to coin aphorisms."

"Sayagi defied Achilles to his face, and Achilles shot him dead."

"Then he was foolish to do it."

"Dead as he is, Sayagi has more value to India than you have ever had or will ever have in all the days of your life."

"I'm sorry he's dead. But I'm not dead."

"You're mistaken. Sayagi lives on in the spirit of India. But you are dead, Tikal Chapekar. You are as dead as a man can be, and still breathe."

"So now it comes to threats."

"I asked my aides to bring you to me so I could help you understand what will now happen to you. There is nothing for you in India. Sooner or later you will leave and make a life for yourself somewhere else."

"I will never leave."

"Only on the day you leave will you begin to understand Satyagraha."

"Peaceful noncompliance?"

"Willingness to suffer, yourself and in person, for a cause you believe is right. Only when you are willing to embrace Satyagraha will you begin to atone for what you have done to India. Now you should go."

Chapekar did not realize anyone had been listening. He might have stayed to argue, but the moment she said those words, a man came into the hut and drew him out.

He had thought they would let him go, but they didn't, not until they led him into the town and sat him down in the back room of a small office and brought up a notice on the nets.

It was his own picture. A short vid taken as the young man tossed dirt onto him.

"Tikal Chapekar is back," said a voice.

The picture changed to show Chapekar in his glory days. Brief clips and stills.

"Tikal Chapekar brought war to India by attacking Burma and Thailand without any provocation, all to try to make himself a great man."

Now there were pictures of Indian victims of atrocities. "Instead, he was taken captive by the Chinese. He wasn't here to help us in our hour of need."

The picture of him with dirt being flung on him returned to the screen.

"Now he's back from captivity, and he wants to rule over India."

A picture of Chapekar talking cheerfully with the Muslim guards outside the gates of the compound. "He wants to help our Muslim overlords rule over us forever."

Again with the dirt-flinging.

"How can we rid ourselves of this man? Let us all pretend he doesn't exist. If no one speaks to him, waits on him, shelters him, feeds him, or helps him in any way, he will have to turn to the foreigners he invited into our land."

That was when they ran the footage of Chapekar turning the government of India over to Wahabi.

"Even in defeat, he invited evil upon us. But India will not punish him. India will simply ignore him until he goes away."

The program ended—with, of course, the dirt-flinging picture.

"Clever set-up," said Chapekar.

They ignored him.

"What do you want from me, so you won't publish that piece of trash?"

They ignored him.

After a while, he began to rage, and tried to fling the computer to the ground. That was when they restrained him and put him out of doors.

Chapekar walked down the street, looking for lodging. There were houses with rooms to rent. They opened the door when he called out, but when they saw his face, they closed the doors again.

Finally he stood in the street and shouted. "All I want is a place to sleep! And a bite to eat! What you would give a dog!"

But no one even told him to shut up.

Chapekar went to the train station and tried to buy a ticket out, using some of the money the Chinese had given him to help him make his way home. But no one would sell him a ticket. Whatever window he went to was closed in his face, and the line moved over to the next one, making no room for him.

At noon the next day, exhausted, hungry, thirsty, he made his way back to the Muslim military compound and, after being fed and clothed and given a place to bathe and sleep by his enemies, he was flown out of India, then out of Muslim territory. He ended up in the Netherlands, where public charity would support him until he found employment.

———

The second visitor followed no known road to come to the hut. Virlomi merely opened her eyes in the middle of the night, and despite the complete darkness, she could see Sayagi sitting on the mat near the door.

"You're dead," she said to him.

"I'm still awaiting rebirth," he said.

"You should have lived," Virlomi told him. "I admired you greatly. You would have been such a husband for me and such a father for India."

"India is already alive. She does not need you to give birth to her," said Sayagi.

"India does not know she's alive, Sayagi. To wake someone from a coma is to bring them to life as surely as a mother brings forth life when she bears a baby."

"Always have an answer, don't you? And the way you talk now—like a god. How did it happen, Virlomi? Was it when Petra chose you to confide in?"

"It was when I decided to take action."

"Your action succeeded," said Sayagi. "Mine failed."

"You should not have spoken to Achilles. You should simply have killed him."

"He said he had the building wired with explosives."

"And you believed him?"

"There were other lives besides mine. You escaped in order to save the lives of the Battle Schoolers. Should I then have thrown their lives away?"

"You misunderstand me, Sayagi. All I say now is, either you act or you don't act. Either you do the thing that makes a difference, or you do nothing at all. You chose a middle way, and when it comes to war, the middle way is death."

"Now you tell me."

"Sayagi, why have you come to me?"

"I haven't. I'm only a dream. You're awake enough to realize that. You're making up both sides of this conversation."

"Then why am I making you up? What do I need to learn from you?"

"My fate," said Sayagi. "So far all your gambits have worked, but that's because you have always played against fools. Now Alai is in control of one enemy, Han Tzu another, and Peter Wiggin is the most dangerous and subtle of all. Against these adversaries, you will not win so easily. Death lies down this road, Virlomi."

"I'm not afraid to die. I've faced death many times, and when the gods decide it's time for me to—"

"See, Virlomi? You've already forgotten that you don't believe in the gods."

"But I do, Sayagi. How else can I explain my string of impossible victories?"

"Superb training in Battle School. Your innate brilliance. Brave and wise Indians who awaited only a decisive leader to show them how to act like people worthy of their own civilization. And very, very stupid enemies."

"And couldn't it be the gods who arranged for me to have these things?"

"It was an unbroken network of causality leading back to the first human who wasn't a chimp. And farther back, to the coalescing of the planets around the sun. If you wish to call that God, go ahead."

"The cause of everything," said Virlomi. "The *purpose* of everything. And if there are no gods, then my own purposes will have to do."

"Making you the only god that actually exists."

"If I can call you back from the dead by the power of my mind alone, I'd say I'm pretty powerful."

Sayagi laughed. "Oh, Virlomi, if only we had lived! Such lovers we could have been! Such children we could have had!"

"You may have died, but I didn't."

"Didn't you? The real Virlomi died the day you escaped from Hyderabad, and this impostor has been playing the part ever since."

"No," said Virlomi. "The real Virlomi died the day she heard you had been killed."

"*Now* you say it. When I was alive, not one little kiss, nothing. I think you didn't even fall in love with me until I was safely dead."

"Go away," she said. "It's time for me to sleep."

"No," he said. "Wake up, light your lamp, and write down this vision. Even if it is only a manifestation of your unconscious, it's a fascinating one, and it's worth pondering over. Especially the part about love and marriage. You have some cockeyed plan to marry dynastically. But I tell you the only way you'll be happy is to marry a man who loves you, not one who covets India."

"I knew that," said Virlomi. "I just didn't think it mattered whether I was happy."

That's when Sayagi left her tent. She wrote and wrote and wrote. But when she woke in the morning, she found that she had written nothing. The writing was also part of the dream.

It didn't matter. She remembered. Even if he denied that he was really the spirit of her dead friend and mocked her for believing in the gods, she did believe, and knew that he was a spirit in transit, and that the gods had sent him to her to teach her.

———

The third visitor did not have to have help from the aides. He came walking in from empty fields, and he already wore the garb of a peasant. However, he was not dressed as an Indian peasant. He wore the clothing of a Chinese rice-paddy worker.

He placed himself at the very end of the line and bowed himself to the dust. He did not move forward when the line moved forward. Every Indian he allowed to pass in front of him. And when dusk came and Virlomi wept and said good-bye to all, he did not go.

The aides did not come to him. Instead, Virlomi emerged from the hut and walked to him in the darkness, carrying a lamp.

"Get up," she said to him. "You're a fool to come here unescorted."

He stood up. "So I was recognized?"

"Could you have possibly looked more Chinese?"

"Rumors are flying?"

"But we're keeping them off the nets. For now. By morning, there's no controlling it."

"I came to ask you to marry me," said Han.

"I'm older than you," said Virlomi. "And you're the emperor of China."

"I thought that was one of my best features," said Han.

"Your country conquered mine."

"But *I* didn't. I gave the captives back and as soon as you said the word, I'll come here in state and get down on my knees in front of you—again—and apologize to you on behalf of the Chinese people. Marry me."

"What in the world do relations between our nations have to do with sharing a bed with a boy that I didn't have all that high an opinion of in Battle School?"

"Virlomi," said Han, "we can destroy each other as rivals. Or we can unite and together we'll have more than half the population of the world."

"How could it work? The Indian people will never follow you. The Chinese people will never follow me."

"It worked for Ferdinand and Isabella."

"Only because they were fighting the Moors. And Isabella and her people had to fight to keep Ferdinand from trampling on her rights as Queen of Castile."

"So we'll do even better," said Han. "Everything you've done has been flawless."

"As a good friend recently reminded me, it's easy to win when you're opposed by idiots."

"Virlomi," said Han.

"Now are you going to tell me that you love me?"

"But I do," said Han. "And you know why. Because all of us who were chosen for Battle School, there's only one thing we love and one thing we respect: We love brilliance and we respect power. You've created power out of nothing."

"I've created power out of the love and trust of my people."

"I love you, Virlomi."

"Love me . . . and yet you think that you're my superior."

"Superior? I've never led armies in battle. You have."

"You were in Ender's Jeesh," said Virlomi. "I wasn't. You'll always think I'm less than you because of that."

"Are you really telling me no? Or merely to try harder or come up with better reasons or prove my worth in some other way."

"I'm not going to set you to a series of lovers' tests," said

Virlomi. "This isn't a fairy tale. My answer is no. Now and always. The dragon and the tiger don't have to be enemies, but how can a mammal and an egg-laying reptile ever possibly mate?"

"So you got my letter."

"Pathetically easy cipher. Anybody with half a brain could get it. Your code was just to type an obvious version of your nickname with your fingers moved one row higher on the keyboard."

"And yet only you, of all the thousands who access the nets, figured out it was from me."

Virlomi sighed.

"Just promise me this," said Han.

"No."

"Hear the promise first," said Han.

"Why should I promise you anything?"

"So I don't preemptively invade India again?"

"With what army?"

"I didn't mean *now*."

"What's the promise you want me to make?"

"That you won't marry Alai, either."

"A Hindu, marrying the Caliph of all Islam? I never knew you had such a sense of humor."

"He'll offer," said Han.

"Go home, Han. And, by the way, we saw the choppers arrive and let them pass. We also asked the Muslim oppressors not to shoot you down, either."

"I appreciated that. I thought it meant you liked me, at least a little."

"I do like you," said Virlomi. "I just don't intend to let you diddle me."

"I didn't know a mere diddle was on the table."

"Nothing's on the table. Back to your chopper, Boy Emperor."

"Virlomi, I beg you now. Let's be friends, at least."

"That would be nice. Someday, maybe."

"Write to me. Get to know me."

She shook her head, laughing, and walked back to her hut. Han Tzu walked back out into the fields as the night wind rose.

15

RATIFICATION

From: RadaghasteBellini%privado@presidência.br.gov
To: PeterWiggin%private@hegemon.gov
Re: Please consider carefully

If your goal is to establish world peace, my friend, why would you begin our Constitution with a deliberate act of provocation against two widely separated nations, one of which might call upon the whole weight of Islam against you?

Is peace to be founded on war after all? And if you did not have Julian Delphiki commanding 100,000 friendly African troops, would you attempt it?

From: PeterWiggin%private@hegemon.gov
To: RadaghasteBellini%privado@presidência.br.gov
Re: We must make it real

History is strewn with the corpses of attempted world governments. We must demonstrate immediately that we are serious, that we are capable, and that we are transformative.

And without Delphiki, I would follow your more prudent counsel, because I would not count on our African troops.

The ceremony was simple enough. Peter Wiggin, Felix Starman, Klaus Boom, and Radaghaste Bellini stood on a platform in Kiyagi, Rwanda. There was no attempt to bring in crowds of citizens to cheer; neither was there any kind of military presence. The audience consisted entirely of reporters.

Copies of the Constitution were provided on the spot. Felix Starman explained the new government very briefly; Radaghaste Bellini informed them of the unified military command; Klaus Boom explained the principles under which new nations could be admitted to the Free People of the Earth.

"No nation will be admitted that does not already provide human rights, including a free and universal adult franchise." Then he dropped the bombshell. "Nor do we require that a nation already be recognized by any existing nation or body of nations, provided it meets our other requirements."

The reporters murmured to each other as Peter Wiggin walked to the dais and the map appeared on the screen behind him. As he named each country that had already secretly ratified the Constitution, it was lighted in pale blue on the map.

South America provided the largest swathes of blue, with Brazil lighting up half the continent, along with Bolivia, Chile, Ecuador, Suriname, and Guyana. In Africa, the blue was not so dominant, but it represented most of the African nations that had maintained stability and democracy for at least a hundred years: Rwanda, Botswana, Cameroon, Mozambique, Angola, Ghana, Liberia. No two ratifying nations bordered on each other. No one missed the fact that South Africa and Nigeria were not participating, despite their long record of stability and freedom; nor did anyone fail to notice that no Muslim nation was included.

In Europe, the map was even sparser: The Netherlands, Slovenia, Czechland, Estonia, and Finland.

Elsewhere, blue was rare. Peter had hoped the Philippines would be ready for the announcement, but at the last minute the government chose to wait and see. Tonga had ratified; so had Haiti, the first nation where Peter's abilities had been tested. Several other small Caribbean nations were also blue.

"At the earliest opportunity," said Peter, "plebiscites will be held in all the ratifying nations. In the future, however, plebiscites will precede a nation's entry into the Free People of Earth. We will maintain capitals in three places: Ribeirão Preto, Brazil; Kiyagi, Rwanda; and Rotterdam in the Netherlands. However, because the official language of the FPE is Common, and few people find the pronunciation of Ribeirão Preto . . . comfortable . . ."

The reporters laughed, since they were the ones who had to bear the brunt of learning to pronounce the Portuguese nasals.

". . . therefore," Peter continued, "the Brazilian government has kindly allowed us to translate the name of the city for world government purposes. From now on, you may refer to the South American capital of the FPE as 'Blackstream,' one word."

"Will you do the same with Kiyagi!" shouted a reporter.

"Since you are able to pronounce it," said Peter, "we will not."

More laughter.

Peter's acceptance of the question, however, opened the floodgates, and they began calling out to him. He raised his hands. "In a minute, be patient."

They quieted down.

"There is a reason why we have chosen the name 'Free People of Earth' for our Constitution, instead of, say, 'United Nations.' "

Another laugh. They all knew why *that* name wouldn't be used.

"This Constitution is a contract among free citizens, not between nations. The old borders will be respected insofar as they make sense, but where they don't, adjustments will be made. And people who have long been deprived of legally recognized national boundaries and self-government will receive those things within the FPE."

Two new lights appeared, blinking a deeper blue. One cut a large swathe across the Andes. The other took a chunk out of southwestern Sudan.

"The FPE immediately recognizes the existence of the nations of Nubia, in Africa, and Runa, in South America. Plebiscites will be held immediately, and if the people of these regions vote to ratify the Constitution, then the FPE will act vigorously to protect their borders. You will notice that part of the territory of Runa has been voluntarily contributed by the nations of Bolivia and Ecuador as one of the terms of their entry into the FPE. The Free People of Earth salute the far-sighted and generous leaders of these nations."

Peter leaned forward. "The FPE will act vigorously to protect the electoral process. Any attempt to interfere with these plebiscites will be regarded as an act of war against the Free People of Earth."

There was the gauntlet.

The questioning afterward, as Peter had hoped, focused on the two new nations whose boundaries included territory belonging to nations that had not ratified—Peru and Sudan. Instead of being peppered with skeptical questions about the FPE itself, Peter had already settled the question of how serious they were. Taking on Peru was bad enough—no one doubted the ability of the FPE to crush the Peruvian military. It was Sudan. A Muslim country, which had given its allegiance to Caliph Alai.

"Are you declaring war against Caliph Alai?" demanded a reporter for an Arab news service.

"We declare war against no one. But the people of Nubia have a long history of oppression, atrocities, famine, and religious intolerance committed against them by the government of Sudan. How many times in the past two hundred years has international action caused Sudan to promise to do better? Yet in the aftermath of Caliph Alai's astonishing unification of the Muslim world, the outlaws and criminals in Sudan immediately took this as permission to renew their genocidal treatment of the Nubians. If Caliph Alai wishes to defend the criminals of Sudan even as he repudiates those of India, that is his choice. One thing is certain: Any right the Sudanese might once have claimed to rule over Nubia has long since expired. The Nubian people have been united by war and suffering into a nation that deserves statehood—and protection."

Peter ended the press conference soon afterward, announcing that Starman, Bellini, and Boom would each hold press conferences two days later in their home countries. "But the armed forces, border guards, and customs services of these nations are now all under the control of the FPE. There is no such thing as a Rwandan or Brazilian military. Only the military of the FPE."

"Wait!" cried one reporter. "There's no 'Hegemon' in this whole Constitution!"

Peter returned to the microphone. "Fast reading," he said.

Laughter, then expectant silence.

"The office of Hegemon was created to meet an emergency that threatened the entire Earth. I will continue as Hegemon under both the original authority under which I was selected for the office, and under temporary authorization from the FPE, until such time as no serious military threat against the Free People of Earth exists. At that time, I will resign my office and there will be no successor. I am the last Hegemon, and I hope to give up the office as quickly as possible."

Peter left again, and this time ignored the shouted questions.

———

As expected, Peru and Sudan didn't even declare war. Since they refused to recognize the legitimacy of the FPE *or* the new nations carved from their territory, whom would they declare war against?

Peruvian troops moved first, heading for known hideouts of Champi T'it'u's revolutionary movement. Some of them were empty. But some of them were defended by highly trained Rwandan soldiers. Peter was using Bean's Rwandans so that it wouldn't be perceived as another war between Brazil and Peru; it had to be the FPE defending a member state's borders.

The Peruvian armies found themselves caught in well-laid traps, with sizable forces moving in across their lines of supply and communication.

It quickly became known throughout Peru that the Rwandan troops were better trained and better equipped than the Peruvian Army—and they were led by Julian Delphiki. Bean. The Giant.

Morale collapsed. Rwandan troops accepted the surrender of the entire Peruvian Army. The Peruvian Congress immediately voted almost unanimously to petition the FPE for membership. Radaghaste Bellini, as interim president of the South American region of the FPE, declined their offer, stating the principle that no territory would be added to the FPE by conquest or intimidation. "We invite the nation of Peru to hold a plebiscite, and if the people of Peru choose to join the Free People of Earth, we will welcome them to join with their brothers and sisters of Runa, Bolivia, Ecuador, and Chile."

It was over in two weeks, plebiscite and all: Peru was part of the FPE, and Bean and the bulk of the FPE's Rwandan troops were transported back across the Atlantic to Africa.

As a direct result of this decisive action, Belize, Cayenne, Costa Rica, and the Dominican Republic announced that they would hold plebiscites on the Constitution.

The rest of the world waited to see what would happen in Sudan.

Sudanese troops were already spread throughout Nubia; they were already engaged in military actions against the Nubian "rebels" who were resisting the renewed attempt to impose Shari'ah on the Christian and pagan region. So while there were plenty of acts of defiance against Peter's proclamation of Nubia's new status, there was no actual change.

Suriyawong, leading the elite core of the FPE military that he and Bean had created years before and used so effectively since, conducted a series of raids designed to demoralize the Sudanese military and cut them off from their supplies. Ammunition dumps and arsenals were destroyed. Convoys were burned. But since Suri's choppers returned to Rwanda after every raid, there was no one for the Sudanese military to strike back against.

Then Bean returned with the bulk of the Rwandan soldiers. Burundi and Uganda both granted permission for him to transport his army across their territory.

As expected, the Sudanese army tried to strike at Bean's army inside the borders of Uganda, before they reached Nubia. Only then did they discover that this army was an illusion—there was nothing to strike but a bunch of old and empty trucks whose drivers fled at the first sign of trouble.

But it was a strike on Ugandan territory. Uganda not only declared war on Sudan, it also announced a plebiscite on the Constitution.

Meanwhile, Bean's army had already traversed the eastern reaches of Congo and were inside Nubia. And Suriyawong's strike force took over the two airbases to which the planes that had taken part in the attack on the decoy convoy had to return. The pilots landed without suspecting any problem, and were taken prisoner.

The trained jet pilots among Suriyawong's soldiers immediately took off again in Sudanese planes and carried out a demonstration bombing against the air defenses of Khartoum. And Bean's army made simultaneous attacks on all the Sudanese military bases inside Nubia. Unprepared to fight against a real army, the Sudanese forces surrendered or were overwhelmed within the day.

Sudan called on Caliph Alai to intervene and bring the wrath of Islam down on the heads of the infidel invaders.

Peter held an immediate press conference.

"The Free People of Earth do not conquer. The Muslim portions of Sudan will be respected, and all prisoners will be returned, as soon as we have the pledge of Caliph Alai and of the Sudanese government that they recognize Nubia as a nation and as part of the Free People of Earth. The Sudanese Air Force will be returned to Sudan, along with their air bases. We respect the sovereignty of Sudan and of all nations. But we will never recognize the right of any nation to persecute a stateless minority within their borders. When it is within our power, we will grant such minorities a state within the Constitution of the Free People of Earth and defend their national existence.

"Julian Delphiki is commander of all FPE forces within Nubia and temporarily occupying portions of Sudan. It would be a tragedy if two old friends from the war against the Buggers, Julian Delphiki and Caliph Alai, should face each other in combat over an issue as ridiculous as whether Sudan should have the right to continue persecuting non-Muslims."

Negotiators soon redrew the boundaries so that a significant portion of what Peter had originally declared to be Nubia would remain in Sudan. Of course, he had never expected to keep that territory and the Nubian leaders already knew that. But it was sufficient for Caliph Alai to save face. In the end, Bean and Suriyawong spent their efforts returning prisoners and protecting the convoys of non-Muslims who chose to leave their homes inside Sudanese territory and find new homes in their new nation.

In the aftermath of this clear victory, the FPE was so wildly popular in black Africa that nation after nation petitioned to hold a plebiscite. Felix Starman informed most of them that they had to reform their internal government first, providing human rights and elections. But the plebiscites in the democracies of South Africa, Nigeria, Namibia, Uganda, and Burundi proceeded immediately, and it was clear that the Free People of Earth had real existence as an intercontinental state with convincing military power and resolute leadership. As Colombia now accepted the borders of Runa and petitioned to become part of the FPE, it seemed inevitable now that all of Latin America and sub-Saharan Africa would be part of the FPE, and sooner rather than later.

There was movement elsewhere, too. Belgium, Bulgaria, Latvia, Lithuania, and Slovakia began to plan for their own plebiscites, as did the Philippines, Fiji, and most of the tiny island nations of the Pacific.

And of course the FPE capitals were flooded with pleas from minorities that wanted the FPE to grant them nationhood. Most of these had to be ignored. For now.

———

On the day that Sudan—under enormous pressure from Caliph Alai—recognized both Nubia and the FPE, Peter was surprised to see his office door open and his parents come in.

"What's wrong?" Peter asked.

"Nothing's wrong," said Mother.

"We came to tell you," said Father, "that we're very proud of you."

Peter shook his head. "It's only the first step on a long road. We don't have twenty percent of the world's population yet. And it will take time to integrate these new nations into the FPE."

"First step on the *right* road," said Father.

"A year ago, if somebody had put up a list of these nations," said Mother, "and said that they would ever unite into one coherent nation under a single Constitution, and surrender command of their armed forces to the Hegemon . . . is there anyone who would not have laughed?"

"It's all thanks to Alai and Virlomi," said Peter. "The atrocities committed by the Muslims in India, and the publicity Virlomi gave those actions, combined with all the recent wars . . ."

"Terrified everybody," said Father. "But the nations joining the FPE are *not* the ones that were most afraid. No, Peter, it was your Constitution. It was *you*—your achievements in the past, the promises you were making for the future . . ."

"It was the Battle Schoolers," said Peter. "Without Bean's reputation—"

"So you used the tools you had," said Mother. "Lincoln had Grant. Churchill had Montgomery. It's part of their greatness that they weren't so jealous of their generals that they had to depose them."

"So you won't let me talk you out of this," said Peter.

"Your place in history was already assured by your work as Locke, before you ever became Hegemon," said Father. "But today, Peter, you became a great man."

They stood in the doorway for long moment.

"Well, that's what we came to say," said Mother.

"Thanks," said Peter.

They left, pulling the door closed behind them.

Peter went back to the papers on his desk.

And then discovered that he couldn't see them because of the tears blurring his eyes.

He sat up and found himself gasping. No, sobbing. Quietly—but his body was wracked with sobs as if he had just been relieved of a terrible burden. As if he had just learned that his terminal disease had spontaneously healed itself. As if he had just had a long-lost child returned to him.

Not once in that whole conversation had anybody said the name "Ender" or referred to him in any way.

It was a full five minutes before Peter got control of himself. He had to get up and wash his face in the tiny bathroom in his office before he could get back to work.

16

JEESH

From: Weaver%Virlomi@MotherIndia.in.net
To: PeterWiggin%private@hegemon.gov
Re: Conversation

I have never met you, but I admire your achievements. Come visit me.

v

From: PeterWiggin%private@hegemon.gov
To: Weaver%Virlomi@MotherIndia.in.net
Re: Meeting

I also admire your achievements.

I will happily provide safe transportation for you to the FPE or any other site outside of India. While it is still under Muslim occupation I do not travel to India.

pw

From: Weaver%Virlomi@MotherIndia.in.net
To: PeterWiggin%private@hegemon.gov
Re: Place

I will not set foot on any country but India; you will not enter India.

Therefore: Colombo, Sri Lanka. I will come in a boat. Mine will not be comfortable. If you bring a better one, we'll enjoy our visit much more.

v

Fly Molo met Bean at the Manila airport and did his best not to look shocked at how tall Bean was.

"You said your business was personal," said Fly. "Forgive my suspicious nature. You are the head of FPE armed forces, and I am head of Filipino armed forces, and yet we have nothing to discuss?"

"I'm assuming that your military is superbly trained and well equipped."

"Yes," said Fly.

"Then until it's time for us to deploy somewhere, our planning and logistics departments have far more to say to each other than you or I do. Officially speaking."

"So you're here as a friend."

"I'm here," said Bean, "because I have a child in Manila. A boy. They tell me his name is Ramón."

Fly grinned. "And yet this is your first time here? Who was the mother, a flight attendant?"

"The baby was stolen from me, Fly. As an embryo. In vitro fertilization. The child is mine and Petra's. It's especially important to us, because it's the first we know of that definitely does not have my condition."

"You mean it isn't ugly?"

Bean laughed. "You've done well here in the Philippines, my friend."

"It's easy. Somebody argues with me, I just say, 'I was in

Ender's Jeesh,' and they shut up and do what I say."

"It's just like that for me, too."

"Except for Peter."

"Especially Peter," said Bean. "I'm the power behind the throne, didn't you know? Don't you read the papers?"

"I notice the papers love to mention your zero-wins record as a commander in Battle School."

"Some achievements are so extraordinary," said Bean, "that you never live them down."

"How's Petra?" asked Fly. And they talked about people they both knew and reminisced about Battle School and Command School and the war with the Buggers until they got to a private home in the hills east of Manila.

There were several cars in front. Two soldiers wearing their new FPE uniforms stood at either side of the door.

"Guards?" asked Bean.

Fly shrugged. "Not my idea."

They did not have to prove who they were. And when they got inside, they realized that this was not the meeting either of them expected.

It was a reunion, apparently, of Ender's Jeesh—those that were available. Dink, Shen, Vlad on one side of a long table. Crazy Tom, Carn Carby, and Dumper—Champi T'it'u—on the other. And at the head of the table, Graff and Rackham.

"Now all are here that were invited," said Graff. "Please, Fly, Bean, take your seats. Bean, I trust that you will tell Petra all that goes on here. As for Han Tzu and Caliph Alai, they're now heads of state and don't travel easily or surreptitiously. However, everything we say to you will be said to them."

"I know some people who'd like to bomb this room," said Vlad.

"There's still someone unaccounted for," said Shen.

"Ender is voyaging safely. His ship is functioning perfectly. His ansible works well. Remember, though, that for him it has been scarcely a year since this group destroyed the Hive Queens. Even if you could talk to him, he would seem . . . young. The world has changed, and so have you." Graff glanced back at Rackham. "Mazer and I are deeply concerned, about you and about the world as a whole."

"We're doing all right," said Carn Carby.

"And thanks to Bean and Ender's big brother, maybe the world is, too," said Dumper. He said it a little defiantly, as if he expected to be argued with.

"I don't give a rat's ass about the world," said Bean. "I'm being blackmailed into helping Peter. And *not* by Peter."

"Bean is referring to a bargain he entered into with me of his own free will," said Graff.

"What's this meeting about?" asked Dink. "You're not our teacher any more." He glanced up at Rackham. "You're not our commander, either. We haven't forgotten how you both lied to us continually."

"We never *could* convince you of our sincere devotion to your welfare back in school, Dink," said Graff. "So as Dink requests, I won't waste time on preliminaries. Look around this table. How old are you?"

"Old enough to know better," muttered Carn.

"What are you, Bean, sixteen?" asked Fly.

"I was never actually born," said Bean, "and the records of my decanting were destroyed when I was about a year old. But sixteen is probably close."

"And all the rest of us must be around twenty, give or take," said Fly. "What's your point, Colonel Graff?"

"Call me Hyrum," said Graff. "I'd like to think we're colleagues now."

"Colleagues in *what*," muttered Dink.

"Back when you last met," said Graff, "when Achilles arranged for your kidnapping in Russia—you were already held in high esteem throughout the world. You were regarded as having . . . potential. Since then, however, one of your number has become Caliph, unified the ununifiable Muslim world, and masterminded the conquest of China and the . . . liberation of India."

"Alai's lost his mind, that's what he's done," said Carn.

"And Han Tzu is Emperor of China. Bean is commander of the undefeated armies of the FPE, plus being known as the man who finally brought Achilles down. All in all, what once was viewed as potential is now regarded as a certainty."

"So what have you assembled here?" said Crazy Tom. "The losers?"

"I've assembled the people that national governments will turn to to stop Peter Wiggin from uniting the world."

They looked around at each other.

"Nobody's talked to *me* yet," said Fly Molo.

"But they turned to you to put down the Muslim rebellion in the Philippines, didn't they?" said Rackham.

"We're citizens of our countries," said Crazy Tom.

"Mine rents me out," said Dink. "Like a taxi."

"Because you always get along so well with authority," said Crazy Tom.

"Here's what will happen," said Graff. "Some combination of China, India, and the Muslim world destroy each other. Whichever one emerges on top, Bean destroys on the battlefield on behalf of the FPE. Does anyone doubt he can do it?"

Bean raised his hand.

No one else did.

And then Dink did.

"He's not hungry," he said.

No one argued with him.

"Now, what could Dink possibly mean by that?" said Graff. "Any ideas?"

No one seemed to have any.

"You don't want to say it, but I will," said Graff. "It's well known that Bean scored higher on the Battle School tests than anyone else in history. No one else was *close*. Well, Ender, but 'close' is such a relative term. Let's say Ender scored *closest*. But we don't know how close because Bean was off the charts."

"How?" said Dink. "He answered questions you didn't ask?"

"Exactly," said Graff. "That's what Sister Carlotta showed me. He had time to spare in taking the tests. He commented on them and mentioned how the test could have been improved. He was unstoppable. Irresistible. That's what the world knows about Julian Delphiki. And yet when we put him in charge of all of you on Eros, in Command School, while we were waiting for Ender to make up his mind about whether to continue his . . . education—how did that go?"

Again silence.

"Oh, why must we pretend that things weren't as they were?" said Graff.

"We didn't like it," said Dink. "He was younger than all of us."

"So was Ender," said Graff.

"But we knew Ender," said Crazy Tom.

"We loved Ender," said Shen.

"Everybody loved Ender," said Fly.

"I can give you a list of people who hated him. But *you* loved him. And you didn't love Bean. Why is that?"

Bean barked out a laugh. The others looked at him. Except the ones who were embarrassed and looked away. "I never learned how to be cuddly," said Bean. "In an orphanage that would have got me adopted, but on the street, it would have got me killed."

"Nonsense," said Graff. "Cuddly wouldn't have cut it with this group anyway."

"And you actually *were* cuddly," said Carn. "No offense, but you were spunky."

"If that's your word for 'bratty little asshole,' " said Dink mildly.

"Now now," said Graff. "You didn't dislike Bean personally. Most of you. But you didn't like serving under him. And you can't say that it's because you were too independent to serve under anybody, because you gladly served under Ender. You gave Ender everything you had."

"More than we had," said Fly.

"But not Bean." Graff said it like it was proof of something.

"Is this a therapy group?" asked Dink.

Vlad spoke up. "Of course it is. He wants us to reach the same conclusion he's already reached."

"Do you know what it is?" asked Graff.

Vlad took a breath. "*Hyrum* thinks that the reason we didn't follow Bean the way we followed Ender was because we knew something about Bean that the rest of the world doesn't know. And because of that, we're likely to be willing to challenge him in battle, while the rest of the world would just give up and surrender to him because of his reputation. Isn't that about it?"

Graff smiled benignly.

"But that's stupid," said Dumper. "Bean really *is* a good commander. I've seen him. Commanding his Rwandans in our campaign in Peru. It's true that the Peruvian Army wasn't well led or well trained, but those Rwandans—they worshipped Bean. They would have marched off a cliff if he asked them to. When he twitched, they sprang into action."

"And your point is?" asked Dink.

"My point is," said Dumper, "*we* didn't follow him well, but other people do. Bean's the real thing. He's still the best of us."

"I haven't seen his Rwandans," said Fly, "but I've seen him with the men he and Suriyawong trained. Back when the forces of the Hegemon were a hundred guys and two choppers. Dumper's right. Alexander the Great couldn't have had soldiers more devoted and more effective."

"Thanks for the testimonials, boys," said Bean, "but you're missing Hyrum's point."

"'Hyrum,'" muttered Dink. "Aren't we cozy."

"Just tell them," said Bean. "They know it, but they don't know that they know it."

"You tell them," said Graff.

"Is this a Chinese reeducation camp? Do we have to indulge in self-criticism?" Bean laughed bitterly. "It's what Dink said right at the start. I'm not hungry. Which might seem stupid, considering I spent my whole infancy starving to death. But I'm not hungry for *supremacy*. And all of you are."

"That's the great secret of the tests," said Graff. "Sister Carlotta gave the standard battery of tests we used. But there was an additional test. One that I gave, or one of my most trusted aides. A test of ambition. Competitive ambition. You all scored very, very high. Bean didn't."

"Bean's not ambitious?"

"Bean wants victory," said Graff. "He likes to win. He *needs* to win. But he doesn't need to beat anybody."

"We all cooperated with Ender," said Carn. "We didn't have to beat *him*."

"But you knew he would lead you to victory. And in the meanwhile, you were all competing with each other. Except Bean."

"Only because he was better than any of us. Why compete if you've won?" said Fly.

"If any one of you came up against Bean in battle, who would win?"

They rolled their eyes or chuckled or otherwise showed their derision for the question.

"That would depend," said Carn Carby, "on the terrain, and the weather, and the sign of the zodiac. Nothing's sure in war, is it?"

"There wasn't any weather in the Battle Room," said Fly, grinning.

"You can conceive of beating Bean, can't you?" said Graff. "And it's possible. Because Bean is only better than the rest of you if all else is equal. Only it never is. And one of the most important variables in war is the hunger that makes you take ridiculous chances because you intuit that there's a path to victory and you have to take that path because anything other than winning is inconceivable. Unbearable."

"Very poetic," said Dink. "The romance of war."

"Look at Lee," said Graff.

"Which one?" said Shen. "The Chinese or the American?"

"Lee L-E-E the Virginian," said Graff. "When the enemy was on Virginia soil, he won. He took the chances he needed to take. He sent Stonewall Jackson out on a forest path at Chancellorsville, dividing his forces and exposing himself dangerously against Hooker, exactly the sort of reckless commander who could have exploited the opportunity if he'd realized it."

"Hooker was an idiot."

"We say that because he lost," said Graff. "But would he have lost if Lee had not taken the dangerous move he took? My point isn't to refight Chancellorsville. My point is—"

"Antietam and Gettysburg," said Bean.

"Exactly. As soon as Lee left Virginia and entered Northern territory, he wasn't hungry anymore. He believed in the cause of defending Virginia, but he did *not* believe in the cause of slavery, and he knew that's what the war was about. He didn't want to see his state defeated, but he didn't want to see the southern cause win. All unconsciously. He didn't know this about himself. But it was true."

"It had nothing to do with the North's overwhelming force?"

"Lee lost at Antietam against the second stupidest and *most* timid commander the North had, McClellan. And Meade at Gettysburg wasn't terribly imaginative. Meade saw the high ground and he took it. And what did Lee do? Based on how Lee acted in all his Virginia campaigns, what would you have expected Lee to do?"

"Refuse to fight on that ground," said Fly. "Maneuver.

Slide right. Steal a march. Get between Meade and Washington. Find a battlefield where the Unions would have to try to force *his* position."

"He *was* low on supplies," said Dink. "And he didn't have the information from his cavalry."

"Excuses," said Vlad. "No excuses in war. Graff is right. Lee didn't act like Lee, once he left Virginia. But that's Lee. What does that have to do with Bean?"

"He thinks," said Bean, "that when I don't believe in a cause, I can be beaten. That I would beat myself. The trouble is that I *do* believe in the cause. I think Peter Wiggin is a decent man. Ruthless, but I've seen how he uses power, and he doesn't use it to hurt anybody. He really is trying to create a world order that leads to peace. I want him to win. I want him to win *quickly*. And if any of you think you can stop me."

"We don't have to stop you," said Crazy Tom. "We just have to hold out till you're dead."

Utter silence.

"There it is," said Graff. "There's the whole point of this meeting. Bean only has a little while. So while he lives, the Hegemon is perceived as unbeatable. But the moment he's gone, what then? Dumper or Fly would probably be appointed commander after him, since they're already inside the FPE. But every one of you at this table would feel perfectly free to take on either of them, am I right?"

"Hell, *Hyrum*," said Dink, "we'd take on Bean."

"And so the world would be torn apart, and the FPE, even if it was victorious, would stand on the bodies of millions of soldiers who died because of *your competitive ambition*." He looked fiercely around the table.

"Hey," said Fly, "we haven't killed anybody yet. Talk to Hot Soup and Alai about that."

"Look at Alai," said Graff. "It took him two purges to get real control over the Islamic forces, but now he has it, and what has he done? Has he left India? Has he withdrawn from

Xinjiang or Tibet? Have the Indonesian Muslims left Taiwan? He remains face to face with Han Tzu. Why is that? It makes no sense. He can't hold India. He couldn't rule over China. But he has Genghis dreams."

"It always comes back to Genghis," said Vlad.

"You all want the world united," said Graff. "But you want to do it yourselves, because you can't stand the thought of anyone else standing on top of the hill."

"Come on," said Dink. "In our hearts we're all Cincinnatus. We can hardly wait to get back to the farm."

They laughed.

"At this table sits fifty years of bloody war," said Graff.

"What about it?" said Dink. "We didn't invent war. We're just good at it."

"War gets invented every time there's somebody so hungry for domination that he can't leave peaceful nations alone. It is precisely people like you that invent war. Even if you have a cause, like Lee did, would the South have struggled on for all those bloody years of Civil War if they hadn't had the firm belief that no matter what happened, 'Marse Robert' would save them? Even if you don't make the decision for war, nations will enter into wars only because they have *you*."

"So what's your solution, Hyrum?" said Dink. "You have little cyanide pills for us all to swallow so we can save the world from ourselves?"

"It wouldn't help," said Vlad. "Even if what you're saying is true, there are other Battle School graduates. Look at Virlomi—she's outmaneuvered everybody."

"She hasn't outmaneuvered Alai yet," said Crazy Tom. "Or Hot Soup."

Vlad insisted on his point. "Look at Suriyawong. *That's* who Peter will turn to after Bean . . . retires. We weren't the only kids at Battle School."

"Ender's Jeesh," said Graff. "You're the ones who saved the world. You're the ones with the magic. And there are hundreds and hundreds of Battle School grads on Earth. Nobody is going to think that just because they happen to have one or two or five, they can conquer the world. Which *one* of them would it be?"

"So you want to be rid of us all," said Dink. "And that's why you brought us here. We're not leaving here alive, are we?"

"Lighten up, Dink," said Graff. "You can all go home as soon as this meeting is over. ColMin doesn't assassinate people."

"Now, that's an interesting point," said Crazy Tom. "What *does* ColMin do? It packs people into starships like sardines, and then it sends them off to colony worlds. And they'll never come back, not to the world they left. Fifty years out, fifty years back. The world would have forgotten all of us by then, even if we went to a colony and came right home. Which of course he wouldn't let us do."

"So this isn't an assassination," said Dink, "it's another damn kidnapping."

"It's an offer," said Rackham, "which you can accept or decline."

"I decline," said Dink.

"Hear the offer," said Rackham.

"Hear this," said Dink, with a gesture.

"I offer you command of a colony. Each one of you. No rivals. We don't know of any enemy armies for you to face, but there will be worlds full of danger and uncertainty, and your abilities will be highly adaptable. People will follow you—people older than you—partly because you *are* Ender's Jeesh, and partly because—*mostly* because—of your own abilities. They'll see how quickly you grasp important information, rank it by priority, foresee consequences, and make correct decisions. You'll be the founders of new human worlds."

Crazy Tom put on a babytalk voice. "Wiw dey name da pwanets aftew us?"

"Don't be such a dullbob," said Carn.

"Sowwy."

"Look, gents," said Graff. "We saw what happened to the Hive Queens. They bunched up on one planet and they got wiped out in a single blow. Any weapon we can invent, an enemy can also invent and use against us."

"Come on," said Dink. "The Hive Queens spread out and colonized as many planets as you're colonizing—in fact, all you're doing is sending ships to colonize the worlds they already settled because they're the only ones you know about that have an atmosphere we can breathe and flora and fauna we can eat."

"Actually, we're taking our own flora and fauna with us," said Graff.

"Dink's right," said Shen. "Dispersal didn't work for the Hive Queens."

"Because they didn't disperse," said Graff. "They had Buggers on all the planets, but when you boys blew up their home world, *all* the Hive Queens were there. They put all their eggs in one basket. We're not going to do that. Partly because the human race isn't just a handful of queens and a whole bunch of workers and drones, every damn one of us is a Hive Queen and has the seeds of recapitulating the whole of human history. So dispersing humanity *will* work."

"Like coughing in a crowd spreads the flu," said Crazy Tom cheerfully.

"Exactly," said Graff. "Call us a disease, I don't care—I *am* a human, and I want us to spread everywhere like an epidemic, so we can *never* be stamped out."

Rackham nodded. "And to accomplish that, he needs his colonies to have the best possible chance of survival."

"Which means you," said Graff. "If I can get you."

"So we make your colonies work," said Carn, "*and* you get us off Earth, too, so Peter can end all war and bring the millennial reign of Christ."

"Whether Christ comes or not isn't my business," said Graff. "All I care about is saving human beings. Collectively and individually."

"Aren't you the noble one."

"No," said Graff. "I created you. Not you individually—"

"Good thing you said that," said Carn, "because my dad would have had to kill you for that aspersion on my mother."

"I found you. I tested you. I assembled you. I made the whole world aware of you. The danger you represent, I created it."

"So you're really trying to atone for your mistakes."

"It wasn't a mistake. It was essential to winning the last war. But it's not unusual in history for the solution to one problem to become the root of the next one."

"So this meeting is clean-up," said Fly.

"This meeting is to offer you a chance to do something that will satisfy your own irresistible craving for supremacy, while ensuring the survival of the human race, both here on Earth and out there in the galaxy."

They thought about that for a moment.

Dumper was the first to speak. "I've already chosen my life's work, Colonel Graff."

"It's *Hyrum*," Dink whispered loudly. "Because he's our buddy."

"You chose it," said Graff, "and you accomplished it. Your people have a nation, and you're part of the FPE. That struggle is over for you. All that's left is for you to chafe under Peter Wiggin's rule until you either rebel against him or become his military commander—and then his replacement as Hegemon. Ruling the world. Am I close?"

"I have no such plans," said Dumper.

"But it resonates with you," said Graff. "Don't pretend otherwise. I know you boys. You're not crazy. You're not evil. But *you can't stop*."

"That's why you didn't invite Petra," said Bean. "Because then you couldn't have said 'you boys' all the time."

"You forget," said Dink, "we're his colleagues now. So we can call him and Rackham 'you boys' too."

Graff stood up from his seat at the head of the table. "I've made the offer. You'll think about it whether you mean to or not. You'll watch events unfold. You all know how to contact me. The offer is open. We're done here for today."

"No we're not," said Shen. "Because you aren't doing anything about the real problem."

"Which is?"

"We're just potential warmongers and baby killers," said Shen. "You're not doing a thing about Hot Soup and Alai."

"And Virlomi," added Fly Molo. "If you want somebody who's dangerous, it's *her.*"

"They will get the same offer as you," said Rackham. "In fact, one of them already has."

"Which one?" asked Dink.

"The one who was in a position to hear it," said Graff.

"Hot Soup, then," said Shen. "Because you couldn't even get in to meet Mr. Caliph."

"What smart fellows you all turned out to be," said Graff.

" 'Waterloo was won,' " quoted Rackham, " 'on the playing fields of Eton.' "

"What the hell does *that* mean?" asked Carn Carby. "You never even went to Eton."

"It was an analogy," said Rackham. "If you hadn't spent your entire childhood playing war games, you'd actually know something. You're all so uneducated."

17

BOATS

From: Champi%T'it'u@Runa.gov.qu
To: WallabyWannabe%BoyGenius@stratplan/mil.gov.au
Re: "Good Idea"

Of course Graff's "offer" sounded like a good idea to YOU. You live in Australia.

—Dumper

From: WallabyWannabe%BoyGenius@stratplan/mil.
gov.au
To: Champi%T'it'u@Runa.gov.qu
Re: Ha ha

People who live on the moon—pardon me, the Andes—shouldn't joke about Australia.

—Carn

From: Champi%T'it'u@Runa.gov.qu
To: WallabyWannabe%BoyGenius@stratplan/mil.gov.au
Re: "Who was joking?"

I've seen Australia and I've lived on an asteroid and I'd take the asteroid.

—Dumper

> From: WallabyWannabe%BoyGenius@stratplan/mil.gov.au
> To: Champi%T'it'u@Runa.gov.qu
> Re: Asteroid

Australia doesn't need life support like an asteroid or coca like the Andes to be livable. Besides, you only liked the asteroid because it was named Eros and that's as close to sex as you've ever gotten.

—Carn

> From: Champi%T'it'u@Runa.gov.qu
> To: WallabyWannabe%BoyGenius@stratplan/mil.gov.au
> Re: At least

At least I have a sex. Male, by the way. Open your fly and check to see what you are. (You grip the handle of the zipper and pull downward.) (Oh, wait, you're in Australia. Upward, then.)

—Dumper

> From: WallabyWannabe%BoyGenius@stratplan/mil.gov.au
> To: Champi%T'it'u@Runa.gov.qu
> Re: Let's see . . . zipper . . . fly . . . pull . . .

Ouch! Ow! Oweeee!

—Carn

The sailors were so nervous to have The Lady aboard their dhow that it was a wonder they didn't swamp the boat just getting out to sea. And sailing was slow, with lots of tacking; even turning the ship seemed to require as much work as the reinvention of navigation. Virlomi showed none of her impatience, though.

It was time for the next step—for India to reach for the world stage. She needed an ally to free her nation from the foreign occupiers. Even though the atrocities had ended—nothing filmable now—Alai persisted in keeping his Muslim troops all over India. Waiting for Hindu provocations. Knowing that Virlomi couldn't control her people as tightly as Alai now controlled his troops.

But she wasn't going to bring Han Tzu into the picture. She had fought too hard to get the Chinese out of India to invite them back again. Besides, even though they had no religion to force on people like Alai's Muslims, the Chinese were just as arrogant, just as sure they were entitled to rule the world.

And these Jeeshboys, they were *so* sure they could be her masters. Didn't they understand that her whole life was a repudiation of their sense of superiority? They had been chosen to wage war against aliens. The gods fought on their side in that war. But now the gods fought on Virlomi's side.

She hadn't been a believer when she began. She exploited her knowledge of the folk religion of her people. But over the weeks and months and years of her campaign against China and then against the Muslims, she had seen how everything bent and turned to fit her plans. Everything she thought of worked; and since there were tests proving that Alai and Han Tzu were smarter than she was, it must be that entities wiser than they were providing her with her ideas.

There was only one person now who could give her the help she needed, and only one man in the world whom it would not demean her to marry. After all, when she married it would be all India marrying; and whatever children she bore would be the children of a god, at least in the eyes of the people. Since parthenogenesis was out of the question, she needed a husband. And that's why she had summoned Peter Wiggin.

Wiggin, the brother of the great Ender. The *older* brother. Who then could doubt that her children would carry the best genes available on Earth? They would found a dynasty that could unite the world and rule forever. By marrying her, Peter would be able to add India to his FPE, transforming it from a sideshow into more than half the population of the world. And she—and India—would be raised above any other nation. Instead of being the leader of a single nation, like China, or the head of a brutal and backward religion, like Alai, she would be the wife of the enlightened Locke, the Hegemon of Earth, the man whose vision would bring peace to all the world at last.

Peter's boat wasn't huge—clearly he wasn't a wasteful man. But it wasn't a primitive fisherman's dhow; Peter's boat had modern lines and it looked as if it was designed to rise up and fairly fly over the waves. *Speed.* No time to waste in Peter Wiggin's world.

She had once belonged to that world. For years now she had slowed herself down to the pace of life in India. She had walked slowly when people were watching her. She had to maintain the simple grace they expected of someone in her position. And she had to hold silence while men argued, speaking only as much as was appropriate for her to say. She could not afford to do anything to diminish herself in their eyes.

But she missed the speed of things. The shuttles that took her to and from Battle School and Tactical School. The clean polished surfaces. The quickness of games in the Battle Room. Even the intensity of life in Hyderabad among other Battle Schoolers before she fled to let Bean know where Petra was. It was closer to her true inclinations than this pose of primitiveness.

You do what victory requires. Those with armies, train the armies. But when Virlomi started, she had only herself. So she trained and disciplined herself to seem as she needed to seem.

In the process, she had become what she needed to *be*.

But that didn't mean she had lost her ability to admire the sleek, fast vessel that Peter had brought to her.

The fishermen helped her out of the dhow and into the rowboat that would take her between the two vessels. Out in the Gulf of Mannar, there were undoubtedly much heavier waves, but the little islands of Adam's Bridge protected the water here, so it was only slightly choppy.

Which was just as well. There was a faint nausea that had been with her ever since she got aboard. Vomiting was not something she needed to show these sailors. She hadn't expected seasickness. How could she have known she was susceptible? Helicopters didn't bother her, or cars on winding roads, or even freefall. Why should a bit of chop on the water nearly do her in?

The rowboat was actually better than the dhow. More frightening, but less nauseating. Fear she could deal with. Fear didn't make her want to throw up. It only made her more determined to win.

Peter himself was at the side of his boat, and it was his hand that she took to help her climb aboard. That was a good sign. He wasn't trying to play games and force her to come to him.

Peter had her men tie the dinghy to his craft, and then brought them aboard to rest in relative comfort on the deck while she went inside the main cabin with Peter.

It was beautifully and comfortably decorated, but not overly large or pretentious. It struck just the right note of restrained opulence. A man of taste.

"It's not my boat, of course," said Peter. "Why would I waste FPE money on owning a boat? This is a loan."

She said nothing—after all, saying nothing was part of

who she was now. But she was just a little disappointed. Modesty was one thing; but why did he feel compelled to tell her that he didn't own it, that he was frugal? Because he believed her image of seeking traditional Indian simplicity— no poverty—as something she really meant, and not just something she staged in order to hold on to the hearts of the Indian people.

Well, I could hardly expect him to be as perceptive as me. He wasn't admitted to Battle School, after all.

"Have a seat," he said. "Are you hungry?"

"No thank you," she said softly. If only he knew what would happen to any food she tried to eat at sea!

"Tea?"

"Nothing," she said.

He shrugged—with embarrassment? That she had turned him down? Really, was he such a *boy* as that? Was he taking this personally?

Well, he was supposed to take it personally. He just didn't understand how or why.

Of course he didn't. How could he imagine what she came to offer him?

Time to be Virlomi. Time to let him know what this meeting was about.

He was standing near a bar with a fridge, and seemed to be trying to choose between inviting her to sit with him at the table or on the soft chairs bolted to the deck.

She took two steps and she was with him, pressing her body against his, entwining the arms of India under his and around his back. She stood on her toes and kissed his lips. Not with vigor, but softly and warmly. It was not a girl's chaste kiss; it was a promise of love, as best she knew how to show it. She had not had that much experience before Achilles came and made Hyderabad a chaste and terrifying place to work. A few kisses with boys she knew. But she had learned something of what made them excited; and Peter was, after all, scarcely more than a boy, wasn't he?

And it seemed to work. He certainly returned the kiss.

It was going as she expected. The gods were with her.

"Let's sit down," said Peter.

But to her surprise, what he indicated was the table, not the soft chairs. Not the wide one, where they could have sat together.

The table, where they would have a slab of wood— *something* cold and smooth, anyway—between them.

When they were seated, Peter looked at her quizzically. "Is that really what you came all this way for?"

"What did you think?" she said.

"I hoped it had something to do with India ratifying the FPE Constitution."

"I haven't read it," she said. "But you must know India doesn't surrender its sovereignty easily."

"It'll be easy enough, if *you* ask the Indian people to vote for it."

"But, you see, I need to know what India gets in return."

"What every nation in the FPE receives. Peace. Protection. Free trade. Human rights and elections."

"That's what you give to Nigeria," said Virlomi.

"That's what we give to Vanuatu and Kiribati, too. And the United States and Russia and China and, yes, India, when they choose to join us."

"India is the most populous nation on Earth. And she's spent the past three years fighting for her survival. She needs more than mere protection. She needs a special place near the center of power."

"But I'm not the center of power," said Peter. "I'm not a king."

"I know who you are," said Virlomi.

"Who am I?" He seemed amused.

"You're Genghis. Washington. Bismarck. A builder of empires. A uniter of peoples. A maker of nations."

"I'm the breaker of nations, Virlomi," said Peter. "We'll

keep the *word* nation, but it will come to mean what *state* means in America. An administrative unit, but little more. India will have a great history, but from now on, we'll have *human* history."

"How very noble," said Virlomi. This was not going as she intended. "I think you don't understand what I'm offering you."

"You're offering me something I want very much—India in the FPE. But the price you want me to pay is too high."

"Price!" Was he really that stupid. "To have me is not a *price* you pay. It's a sacrifice *I* make."

"And who says romance is dead," said Peter. "Virlomi, you're a Battle Schooler. Surely you can see why it's impossible for me to marry my way into having India in the FPE."

Only then, in the moment of his challenge, did the whole thing become clear. Not the world as *she* saw it, centered on India, but the world as he saw it, with himself at the center of everything.

"So it's all about you," said Virlomi. "You can't share power with another."

"I can share power with *everybody*," said Peter, "and I already am. Only a fool thinks he can rule alone. You can only rule by the willing obedience and cooperation of those you supposedly rule over. They have to *want* you to lead them. And if I married you—attractive as the offer is on every count—I would no longer be seen as an honest broker. Instead of trusting me to lead the FPE's foreign and military policy to the benefit of the whole world, I would be seen as tilting everything toward India."

"Not everything," she said.

"More than everything," said Peter. "I would be seen as the *tool* of India. You can be sure that Caliph Alai would immediately declare war, not just on India, which has his troops all over it, but on the FPE. I'd be faced with bloody war in Sudan and Nubia, which I don't want."

"Why would you fear it?"

"Why wouldn't I?" he said.

"You have *Bean*," she said. "How can Alai stand against you?"

"Well," said Peter, "if Bean is so all powerful and irresistible, why do I need *you?*"

"Because Bean can never be as fully trusted as a wife. And Bean doesn't bring you a billion people."

"Virlomi," said Peter, "I'd be a fool to trust you, wife or not. You wouldn't be bringing India into the FPE, you'd be bringing the FPE into India."

"Why not a partnership?"

"Because gods don't need mortal partners," said Peter. "You've been a god too long. There's no man you can marry, as long as you think you're elevating him just by letting him touch you."

"Don't say what you can't unsay," said Virlomi.

"Don't make me say what's so hard to hear," said Peter. "I'm not going to compromise my leadership of the whole FPE just to get one country to join."

He meant it. He actually thought his position was above hers. He thought he was greater than India! Greater than a god! That he would *diminish* himself by taking what she offered.

But now there was nothing more to say to him. She wouldn't waste time with idle threats. She'd show him what she could do to those who wanted India for an enemy.

He rose to his feet. "I'm sorry that I didn't anticipate your offer," said Peter. "I wouldn't have wasted your time. I had no desire to embarrass you. I thought you would have understood my situation better."

"I'm just one woman. India is just one country."

He winced just a little. He didn't like having his foolish, arrogant words thrown in his face. Well, you'll have more than that thrown at you, Ender's Brother.

"I brought two others to see you," said Peter. "If you're willing."

He opened a door and Colonel Graff and a man she didn't know entered the room. "Virlomi, I think you know Minister Graff. And this is Mazer Rackham."

She inclined her head, showing no surprise.

They sat down and explained their offer.

"I already have the love and allegiance of the greatest nation on Earth," said Virlomi. "And I have not been defeated by the most terrible enemies that China and the Muslim world could hurl against me. Why should I wish to run and hide in a colony somewhere?"

"It's a noble work," said Graff. "It's not hiding, it's building."

"Termites build," said Virlomi.

"And hyenas tear," said Graff.

"I have no need for or interest in the service you offer," said Virlomi.

"No," said Graff, "you just don't *see* your need yet. You always were hard to get to change your way of looking at things. It's what held you back in Battle School, Virlomi."

"You're not my teacher now," said Virlomi.

"Well, you're certainly wrong about one thing, whether I'm your teacher or not," said Graff.

She waited.

"You have not yet *faced* the most terrible enemies that China and the Muslim world can hurl against you."

"Do you think Han Tzu can get into India again? I'm not Tikal Chapekar."

"And he's not the Politburo or Snow Tiger."

"He's *Ender's Jeeshmate*," she said in mock awe.

"He's not caught up in his own mystique," said Rackham, who had not spoken till now. "For your own sake, Virlomi, take a good hard look in the mirror. You're what megalomania looks like in the early stages."

"I have no ambition for myself," said Virlomi.

"If you define India as whatever you conceive it to be," said Rackham, "you'll wake up some terrible morning and discover that it is not what you *need* it to be."

"And you say this from your vast experience of governing . . . what country was it, now, Mr. Rackham?"

Rackham only smiled. "Pride, when poked, gets petty."

"Was that already a proverb?" asked Virlomi. "Or should I write it down?"

"The offer stands," said Graff. "It's irrevocable as long as you live."

"Why don't you make the same offer to Peter?" asked Virlomi. "He's the one who needs to take the long voyage."

She decided she wasn't going to get a better exit line than that, so she walked slowly, gracefully, to the door. No one spoke as she departed.

Her sailors helped her back into the rowboat and cast off. Peter did not come to the rail to wave her off; just another discourtesy, not that she would have acknowledged him even if he had. As for Graff and Rackham, they'd soon enough be coming to her for funding—no, for *permission* to operate their little colony ministry.

The dhow took her back to a different fishing village from the one she had sailed from—no point in making things easy for Alai, if he had discovered her departure from Hyderabad and followed her.

She rode a train back to Hyderabad, passing for an ordinary citizen—if any Muslim soldiers should be so bold as to search the train. But the people knew who she was. Whose face was better known in all of India? And not being Muslim, she didn't have to cover her face.

The first thing I will do, when I rule India, is change the name of Hyderabad. Not back to Bhagnagar—even though it was named for an Indian woman, the name was bestowed by the Muslim prince who destroyed the original Indian village in order to build the Charminar, a monument to his own power, supposedly in honor of his beloved Hindu wife.

India will never again be obliterated in order to appease the power lust of Muslims. The new name of Hyderabad will be the original name of the village: Chichlam.

She made her way from the train station to a safe house in the city, and from there her aides helped get her back inside the hut where she had supposedly been meditating and praying for India for the three days she had been gone. There she slept for a few hours.

Then she arose and sent an aide to bring her an elegant but simple sari, one that she knew she could wear with grace and beauty, and which would show off her slim body to best advantage. When she had it arranged to her satisfaction, and her hair was arranged properly, she walked from her hut to the gate of Hyderabad.

The soldiers at the checkpoint gawped at her. No one had ever expected her to try to enter, and they had no idea what to do.

While they went through their flurry of asking their superiors inside the city what they should do, Virlomi simply walked inside. They dared not stop her or challenge her— they didn't want to be responsible for starting a war.

She knew this place as well as anyone, and knew which building housed Caliph Alai's headquarters. Though she walked gracefully, without hurry, it took little time for her to get there.

Again, she paid no attention to guards or clerks or secretaries or important Muslim officers. They were nothing to her. By now they must have heard Alai's decision; and his decision was obviously to let her pass, for no one obstructed her.

Wise choice.

One young officer even trotted along ahead of her, opening doors and indicating which way she should go.

He led her into a large room where Alai stood waiting for her, with a dozen high officers standing along the walls.

She walked to the middle of the room. "Why are you afraid of one lone woman, Caliph Alai?"

Before he had time to answer the obvious truth—that far from being afraid, he had let her pass unmolested and uninspected through his headquarters complex and into his own presence—Virlomi began to unwrap her sari. It took only a moment or two before she stood naked before him. Then she reached up and loosened her long hair, and then swung it and combed her fingers through it. "You see that I have no weapon hidden here. India stands before you, naked and defenseless. Why do you fear her?"

Alai had averted his eyes as soon as it became clear that she was undressing. So had the more pious of the other officers. But some apparently thought it was their responsibility to make sure that she was, in fact, weaponless. She enjoyed their consternation, their embarrassment—and, she suspected, their desire. *You came here to ravish India, didn't you? And yet I am out of your reach. Because I'm not here for you, underlings. I'm here for your master.*

"Leave us," Alai said to the other men.

Even the most modest of them could not help but glance at her as they shuffled out of the room, leaving the two of them alone.

The door closed behind them. She and Alai were alone.

"Very symbolic, Virlomi," said Alai, still refusing to look at her. "*That* will get talked about."

"The offer I make is both symbolic and tangible," she said. "This upstart Peter Wiggin has gone as far as he should go. Why should Muslim and Hindu be enemies, when together we have the power to crush his naked ambition?"

"His ambition isn't as naked as you are," said Alai. "Please put on clothing so I can look at you."

"May not a man look at his bride?"

Alai chuckled. "A dynastic marriage? I thought you already told Han Tzu what he could do with that idea."

"Han Tzu had nothing to offer me. You are the leader of the Muslims of India. A large portion of my people torn away from mother India in fruitless hostility. And why? Look at me, Alai."

Either the force of her voice had power over him, or he could not resist his desire, or perhaps he simply decided that since they were alone, he need not keep up the show of perfect rectitude.

He looked her up and down, casually, without reaction. As he did, she raised her arms above her head and turned around. "Here is India," she said, "no longer resisting you, no longer evading you, but welcoming you, married to you, fertile soil in which to plant a new civilization of Muslim and Hindu united."

She faced him again.

He continued to look at her, not bothering to keep his eyes only on her face. "You do intrigue me," he said.

I should think so, she answered silently. Muslims never have the virtue they pretend to have.

"I must consider this," he said.

"No," she said.

"You think I'll make up my mind in an instant?"

"I don't care. But I will leave this room in moments. Either I'll do it dressed in that sari, as your bride, or I'll do it naked, leaving my clothing behind. Naked I'll pass through your compound, and naked I'll return to my people. Let them decide what they think was done to me within these walls."

"You'd provoke such a war as that?" said Alai.

"Your presence in India is the provocation, Caliph. I offer you peace and unity between our peoples. I offer you the permanent alliance that will enable us, together, India and Islam, to unite the world in a single government and along the way cast Peter Wiggin aside. He was never worthy of his brother's name; he's wasted enough of the time and attention of the world."

She walked closer to him, until her knees touched his.

"You have to deal with him eventually, Caliph Alai. Will you do it with India in your bed and by your side, or will you do it while most of your forces have to remain here to keep us from destroying you from behind? Because I'll do it. Either we're lovers or enemies, and the time to choose is now."

He made no idle threat to detain her or kill her—he knew that he could no more do that than let her walk out of the compound naked. The real question was whether he would be a grudging husband or an enthusiastic one.

He reached out and took her hand.

"You've chosen wisely, Caliph Alai," she said. She leaned down and kissed him. The same kiss she had given Peter Wiggin, and which he had treated as if it were nothing.

Alai returned it warmly. His hands moved on her body.

"Marriage first," she said.

"Let me guess," he said. "You want the wedding now."

"In this room."

"Will you dress so we can show video of the ceremony?"

She laughed and kissed his cheek. "For publicity, I'll dress."

She started to walk away, but he caught her hand, drew her back, kissed her again, passionately this time. "This is a good idea," he said to her. "It's a bold idea. It's a dangerous idea. But it's a good one."

"I'll stand beside you in everything," she said.

"Not ahead," he said. "Not behind, not above, not below."

She embraced him and kissed his headdress. Then she pulled it off his head and kissed his hair.

"Now I'll have to go to all the trouble of putting that back on," he said.

You'll take whatever trouble I want you to take, she thought. *I have just had a victory here today, in this room, Caliph Alai. You and your Allah may not realize it, but the* gods of India rule in this place, and they have given me victory without another soldier dying in useless war.

Such fools they were in Battle School, to let so few girls in. It left the boys helpless against a woman when they returned to Earth.

18

YEREVAN

From: PetraDelphiki@FreePeopleOfEarth.fp.gov
To: DinkMeeker@colmin.gov
Re: Can't believe you're at this address

When Bean told me what happened at that meeting, I thought: I know one guy who's never going to go along with any plan of Graff's.

Then I got your letter informing me of your change of address. And then I thought some more and realized: There's no place on Earth where Dink Meeker is going to fit in. You have too much ability to be content anywhere that they're likely to let you serve.

But I think you were wrong to refuse to be the head of the colony you're joining. Partly it's because: Who's going to do it better than you? Don't make me laugh.

But the main reason is: What kind of living hell will it be for the colony leader to have Mr. Insubordinate in his colony? Especially because everybody will know you were in Ender's Jeesh and they'll wonder why you AREN'T leader . . .

I don't care how loyal you think you're going to be, Dink. It's not in you. You're a brat and you always will be. So admit what a lousy follower you are, and go ahead and LEAD.

And just in case you don't know it, you stupidest of all possible geniuses: I still love you. I've always loved you. But no woman in her right mind would ever marry you and have your babies because NOBODY COULD STAND TO RAISE THEM. You will have the most hellish children. So have them in a colony where there'll be someplace for them to go when they run away from home about fifteen times before they're ten.

Dink, I'm going to be happy, in the long run. And yes, I did set myself up for hard times when I married a man who's going to die and whose children will probably have the same disease. But Dink—nobody ever marries anybody who ISN'T going to die.

God be with you, my friend. Heaven knows the devil already is.

Love, Petra

Bean held two babies and Petra one on the flight from Kiev to Yerevan—whichever one was hungriest got mama. Petra's parents lived there now; by the time Achilles died and they could return to Armenia, the tenants in their old home in Maralik had changed it too much for them to want to return.

Besides, Stefan, Petra's younger brother, was quite the world traveler now, and Maralik was too small for him. Yerevan, while not what anyone would call one of the great world cities, was still a national capital, and it had a university worth studying at, when he graduated from high school.

But to Petra, Yerevan was as unfamiliar a city as Volgograd would have been, or any of the cities named San Salvador. Even the Armenian that was still spoken by many on the street sounded strange to her. It made her sad. I have no native land, she thought.

Bean, however, was drinking it all in. Petra got into the cab first, and he handed her Bella and the newest—but largest—of the babies, Ramón, whom he had picked up in the Philippines. Once Bean was inside the taxi, he held Ender up to the window. And since their firstborn son was beginning to show signs that he understood speech, it wasn't just a matter of playfulness.

"This is your mama's homeland," said Bean. "All these people look just like her." Bean turned back to the two that Petra was holding. "You children all look different, because half your genetic material comes from me. And I'm a mongrel. So in your whole life, there'll be no place you can go where you'll look like the locals."

"That's right, depress and isolate the children from the start," said Petra.

"It's worked so well for me."

"You weren't depressed as a child," said Petra. "You were desperate and terrified."

"So we try to make things better for our children."

"Look, Bella, look, Ramón," said Petra. "This is Yerevan, a city with lots of people that we don't know at all. The whole world is full of strangers."

The taxi driver spoke up, in Armenian: "Nobody in Yerevan is a stranger to Petra Arkanian."

"Petra Delphiki," she corrected him mildly.

"Yes, yes, of course," he said in Common. "I just meaning that if you want a drink in a tavern, nobody let you pay!"

"Does that go for her husband?" asked Bean.

"Man big like you?" said the driver. "They don't tell you the price, they ask you what you wanting to give!" He roared with laughter at his own joke. Not realizing, of course, that

Bean's size was killing him. "Big man like you, little tiny babies like these." He laughed again.

Think how amused he'd be if he knew that the largest baby, Ramón, was the youngest.

"I knew we should have walked from the airport," said Bean in Portuguese.

Petra grimaced. "That's rude, to speak in a language he doesn't know."

"Ah. I'm glad to know that the concept of rudeness *does* exist in Armenia."

The taxi driver picked up on the mention of Armenia, even though the rest of the sentence, being in Portuguese, was a mystery to him. "You wanting a tour of Armenia? Not a big country, I can take you, special price, meter not running."

"No time for that," said Petra in Armenian. "But thanks for offering."

The Arkanian family now lived in a nice apartment building—all balconies and glass, yet upscale enough that there was no hanging laundry visible from the street. Petra had told her family she was coming, but asked them not to meet her at the airport. They had gotten so used to the extraordinary security during the days when Petra and Bean were in hiding from Achilles Flandres that they accepted this unquestioningly.

The doorman recognized Petra from her pictures, which appeared in the Armenian papers whenever there was a story about Bean. He not only let them go up unannounced, but also insisted on carrying their bags.

"You two, and three babies, this all the luggage you have?"

"We hardly ever wear clothes," said Petra, as if this were the most sensible thing in the world.

They were halfway up in the elevator before the doorman laughed and said, "You joking!"

Bean smiled and tipped him a hundred-dollar coin. The

doorman flipped it in the air and pocketed it with a smile. "Good thing *he* give me! If Petra Arkanian give, my wife never let me spend!"

After the elevator doors closed, Bean said, "From now on, in Armenia *you* tip."

"They'd *keep* the tip either way, Bean. It's not like they give it back to us."

"Oh, eh."

Petra's mother could have been standing at the door, she opened it so quickly. Maybe she was.

There were hugs and kisses and a torrent of words in Armenian and Common. Unlike the cabdriver and doorman, Petra's parents were fluent in Common. So was Stefan, who had cut his high school classes today. And young David was obviously being raised with Common as his first language, since that's what he was chattering in almost continuously from the moment Petra entered the flat.

There was a meal, of course, and neighbors invited in, because it might be the big city, but it was still Armenia. But in only a couple of hours, it was just the nine of them.

"Nine of us," said Petra. "Our five and the four of you. I've missed you."

"Already you have as many children as we did," said Father.

"The laws have changed," said Bean. "Also, we didn't exactly plan to have ours all at once."

"Sometimes I think," said Mother to Petra, "that you're still in Battle School. I have to remind myself, no, she came home, she got married, she has babies. Now we finally get to see the babies. But so small!"

"They have a genetic condition," said Bean.

"Of course, we know that," said Father. "But it's still a surprise, how small they are. And yet so . . . mature."

"The really little ones take after their father," said Petra, with a wry smile.

"And the normal one takes after his mother," said Bean.

"Thank you for letting us use your flat for the unofficial meeting tonight," said Bean.

"It's not a secure site," said Father.

"The meeting is unofficial, not secret. We expect Turkish and Azerbaijani observers to make their reports."

"Are you sure they won't try to assassinate you?" asked Stefan.

"Actually, Stefan, they brainwashed *you* at an early age," said Bean. "When the trigger word is said, you spring into action and kill everybody at the meeting."

"No, I'm going to a movie," said Stefan.

"That's a terrible thing to say," said Petra. "Even as a joke."

"Alai isn't Achilles," said Bean to Stefan. "We're friends, and he won't let Muslim agents assassinate us."

"You're friends with your enemy," said Stefan, as if it were too incredible.

"It happens in some wars," said Father.

"There *is* no war yet," Mother reminded them.

They took the hint, stopped talking about current problems, and reminisced instead. Though since Petra had been sent to Battle School so young, it's not as if she had that much to reminisce about. It was more like they were briefing her about her new identity before an undercover mission. *This* is what you should remember from your childhood, if you'd had one.

And then the Prime Minister, the President, and the Foreign Minister showed up. Mother took the babies into her bedroom, while Stefan took David out to see a movie. Father, being Deputy Foreign Minister, was allowed to stay, though he would not speak.

The conversation was complex but friendly. The Foreign Minister explained how eager Armenia was to join the FPE, and then the President echoed everything he had said, and then the Prime Minister began another repetition.

Bean held up a hand. "Let's stop hiding from the truth. Armenia is a landlocked country, with Turks and Azerbaijanis almost completely surrounding you. With Georgia refusing to join the FPE at present, you worry that we couldn't even supply you, let alone defend you against the inevitable attack."

They were obviously relieved that Bean understood.

"You just want to be left alone," he said.

They nodded.

"But here's the truth: If we don't defeat Caliph Alai and break up this strange and sudden union of Muslim nations, then Caliph Alai will eventually conquer all the surrounding nations. Not because Alai himself wants to, but because he can't remain Caliph for long if he isn't aggressively pursuing an expansionist policy. He says that's not his intent, but he'll certainly end up doing it because he'll have no choice."

They didn't like hearing this, but they kept listening.

"Armenia will fight Caliph Alai sooner or later. The question is whether you'll do it now, while I still lead the forces of the FPE in your defense, or later, when you stand utterly alone against overwhelming force."

"Either way, Armenia will pay," said the President grimly.

"War is unpredictable," said Bean. "And the costs are high. But *we* didn't put Armenia where it is, surrounded by Muslims."

"God did," said the President. "So we try not to complain."

"Why can't Israel be your provocation?" asked the Prime Minister. "They are militarily much stronger than we are."

"The opposite is true," said Bean. "Geographically their position is and always has been hopeless. And they have integrated so closely with the Muslim nations surrounding them that if they now joined the FPE, the Muslims would feel deeply betrayed. Their fury would be terrible, and we could not defend them. While you—let's just say that over the centuries, Muslims have slaughtered more Armenians than they ever did Jews. They hate you, they regard you as a terrible intrusion into their lands, even though you were here long before any Turks came out of central Asia. There's a burden of guilt along with the hatred. And for you to join the FPE would infuriate them, yes, but they wouldn't feel *betrayed*."

"These nuances are beyond me," said the President skeptically.

"They make an enormous difference in the way an army fights. Armenia is vital to forcing Alai to act before he's ready. Right now the union with India is still merely formal, not a fact on the ground. It's a marriage, not a family."

"You don't need to quote Lincoln to me."

Petra inwardly winced. The quote about "a marriage, not a family" did not come from Lincoln at all. It came from one of her own Martel essays. It was a bad sign if people were getting Lincoln and Martel confused. But of course it was better not to correct the misattribution, lest it appear that she was way too familiar with the works of Martel and Lincoln.

"We stand where we've stood for weeks," said the President. "Armenia is being asked too much."

"I agree," said Bean. "But keep in mind that we're asking. When the Muslims finally decide that Armenia shouldn't exist, they won't ask."

The president pressed his fingers to his forehead. It was a gesture that Petra called "drilling for brains." "How can we hold a plebiscite?" he asked.

"It's precisely the plebiscite that we need."

"Why? What does this do for you militarily except overextend your forces and draw off a relatively small part of the Caliph's armies?

"I know Alai," said Bean. "He won't want to attack Armenia. The terrain here is a nightmare for a serious campaigning. You constitute no serious threat. Attacking Armenia makes no sense at all."

"So we won't be attacked?"

"You will absolutely be attacked."

"You're too subtle for us," said the Prime Minister.

Petra smiled. "My husband is *not* subtle. The point is so obvious that you think it couldn't be *this* that he means. Alai will not attack. But Muslims will attack. It will force his hand. If he refuses to attack, but other Muslims do attack, then the leadership of the jihad moves away from him to someone else. Whether he strikes down these freelance attackers or not, the Muslim world is divided and two leaders compete."

The President was no fool. "You have higher hopes than this," he said.

"All warriors are filled with hope," said Bean. "But I understand your lack of trust in me. For me it's the great game. But for you, it's your homes, your families. That's why we wanted to meet here. To assure you that it is our home and our family as well."

"To sit and wait for the enemy to act is the decision to die," said Petra. "We ask Armenia to make this sacrifice and take this risk because if you don't, then Armenia is doomed. But if you join the Free People of Earth, then Armenia will have the most powerful defense."

"And what will that defense consist of?"

"Me," said Petra.

"A nursing mother?" asked the Prime Minister.

"The Armenian member of Ender's Jeesh," she answered. "I will command the Armenian forces."

"Our mountain goddess versus the goddess of India," said the Foreign Minister.

"This is a Christian nation," said Father. "And my daughter is no goddess."

"I was joking," said Father's boss.

"But the truth that underlies the joke," said Bean, "is that Petra herself is a match for Alai. So am I. And Virlomi is no match for any of us."

Petra hoped that this was true. Virlomi now had years of experience in the field—if not in the logistics of moving huge armies, then in exactly the kind of small operations that would be most effective in Armenia.

"We have to think about it," said the President.

"Then we're where we were before," said the Foreign Minister. "Thinking."

Bean rose to his feet—a formidable sight, these days—and bowed to them. "Thank you for meeting with us."

"Wouldn't it be better," said the Prime Minister, "if you could get this new Hindu-Muslim . . . thing . . . to go to war against China?"

"Oh, that would eventually happen," said Bean. "But when? The FPE wants to break the back of Caliph Alai's Muslim League now. Before it grows any stronger."

And Petra knew they were all thinking: Before Bean dies. Because Bean is the most important weapon.

The President rose from his seat, but then laid a restraining hand on the other two. "We have Petra Arkanian here. And Julian Delphiki. Couldn't we ask them to consult with our military on our preparations for war?"

"I notice there are no military men here," said Petra. "I don't want them to feel that we've been thrust on them."

"They won't feel that way," said the Foreign Minister blandly. But Petra knew that the military was not represented here because they were eager to join the FPE, precisely because they did not feel adequate, by themselves, to defend Armenia. There would be no problems with a tour of inspection.

After the top leadership of Armenia left the Arkanian flat, Father and Petra flung themselves down on the furniture and Bean stretched out on the floor, and at once began discussing what had just happened and what they thought *would* happen.

Mother came in as the conversation was winding down. "All asleep, the little darlings," she said. "Stefan will drop David off after the movie, but we have a little while, just us grown-ups."

"Well, good," said Father.

"We were just discussing," said Petra, "whether it was a waste of time for us to come here."

Mother rolled her eyes. "How can it be a waste of time?" And then, to everyone's surprise, she burst into tears.

"What is it?" At once she was enveloped in the concern of her husband and daughter.

"Nothing," she said. "I just . . . you didn't come here and bring these babies because you had negotiations. Nothing happened here that couldn't have happened by teleconference."

"Then why do you think we're here?" asked Petra.

"You came to say good-bye."

Petra looked at Bean and, for the first time, realized that this might be true. "If we are," she said, "it wasn't our plan."

"But it's what you're doing," said Mother. "You came in person because you might not see us again. Because of the war!"

"No," said Bean. "Not because of the war."

"Mother, you know Bean's condition."

"I'm not blind! I can see that he's giraffed up so he can hardly get into houses!"

"And so are Ender and Bella. They have Bean's same condition. So once we get all our other children, we're going out into space. At lightspeed. So we can take advantage of relativistic effects. So that Bean will be alive when they finally find a cure."

Father shook his head.

"Then we'll be dead before you come home," said Mother.

"Pretend I'm away at Battle School again," said Petra.

"I get these grandchildren, but . . . then I don't get them." Mother cried again.

"I won't leave," said Bean, "until we've got Peter Wiggin safely in control of things."

"Which is why you're in such a hurry to get this war started," said Father. "Why not just tell them?"

"We need them to have confidence in me," said Bean.

"Telling them that I might die in mid-campaign won't reassure them about joining the FPE."

"So these babies will grow up on a starship?" asked Mother, skeptically.

"Our joy," said Petra, "will be to see them grow old—without any of them growing as big as their father."

Bean raised one enormous foot. "These are tough shoes to fill."

"It really is true," said Petra, "that this war—in Armenia—is the one we want to fight. All these hills. It will go slowly."

"Slowly?" asked Father. "Isn't that the opposite of what you want?"

"What we want," said Bean, "is for the war to end as soon as possible. But this is one case where going slow will speed us up."

"You're the brilliant strategists," said Father, heading for the kitchen. "Anybody else want something to eat?"

———

That night, Petra couldn't sleep. She went out onto the balcony and looked out over the city.

Is there anything in this world that I can't leave?

I've lived apart from my family for so much of my life. Does that mean I'll miss them more or less?

But then she realized that this had nothing to do with her melancholy. She couldn't sleep because she knew that war was coming. Their plan was to keep the conflict in the mountains, to make the Turks pay for every meter. But there was no reason to think that Alai's forces—or whatever Muslim forces they were—would shrink from bombing the big population centers. Precision bombing had been the rule for so long—ever since Mecca was nuked—that a sudden reversion to anti-population, saturation bombing would come as a demoralizing shock.

Everything depends on our being able to get and keep

control of the air. And the FPE doesn't have as many planes as the Muslim League.

Damn those short-sighted Israelis for training the Arab air forces to be among the most formidable in the world.

Why was Bean so confident?

Was it only because he knew that he'd soon leave Earth and wouldn't have to be here to face the consequences?

That was unfair. Bean had said he'd stay until Peter was Hegemon in fact as well as name. Bean did not break his word.

What if they never find a cure? What if we sail on through space forever? What if Bean dies out there with me and the babies?

She heard footsteps behind her. She assumed it would be Bean, but it was her mother.

"Awake without the babies waking you?"

Petra smiled. "I have plenty to keep me from sleeping."

"But you *need* your sleep."

"Eventually, my body takes it whether I like it or not."

Mother looked out over the city. "Did you miss us?"

She knew her mother wanted her to say, Every day. But the truth would have to do. "When I have time to think about anything at all, yes. But it's not that I miss you. It's that . . . I'm glad you're in my life. Glad you're in this world." She turned to face her mother. "I'm not a little girl anymore. I know I'm still very young and I'm sure I don't know anything yet, but I'm part of the cycle of life now. I'm no longer the youngest generation. So I don't cling to my parents as I once would have liked to. I missed a lot up there in Battle School. Children need families."

"And," said Mother sadly, "they make families out of whatever they have at hand."

"That will never happen to my children," said Petra. "The world isn't being invaded by aliens. I can stay with them."

Then she remembered that some people would claim that some of her children *were* the alien invasion.

She couldn't think that way.

"You carry so much weight in your heart," said Mother, stroking her hair.

"Not as much as Bean. Far less than Peter."

"Is this Peter Wiggin a good man?"

Petra shrugged. "Are great men ever really good? I know they *can* be, but we judge them by a different standard. Greatness changes them, whatever they were to start with. It's like war—does any war ever settle anything? But we can't judge that way. The test of a war isn't whether it *solved* things. You have to ask, Was fighting the war better than not fighting it? And I guess the same kind of test ought to be used on great men."

"*If* Peter Wiggin is great."

"Mother, he was Locke, remember? He stopped a war. Already he was great before I came home from Battle School. And he was still in his teens. Younger than I am now."

"Then I asked the wrong question," said Mother. "Is a world that he rules over going to be a good place to live?"

Petra shrugged again. "I believe he means it to be. I haven't seen him being vindictive. Or corrupt. He's making sure that any nation that joins the FPE does it through the vote of the people, so nothing is being forced on them. That's promising, isn't it?"

"Armenia spent so many centuries yearning to have our own nation. Now we have it, but it seems the price of keeping it is to give it up."

"Armenia will still be Armenia, Mother."

"No, it won't," she said. "If Peter Wiggin wins everything he's trying to win, then Armenia will be . . . Kansas."

"Hardly!"

"We'll all speak Common and if you go from Yerevan to Rostov or Ankara or Sofia, you won't even know you've gone anywhere."

"We all speak Common *now*. And there'll never be a time you can't tell Ankara from Yerevan."

"You're so sure."

"I'm sure of a lot of things. And about half the time, I'm right." She grinned at her mother, but her mother's return smile wasn't real.

"How did you do it?" asked Petra. "How did you give up your child?"

"You weren't 'given up,'" said Mother. "You were taken. Most of the time I managed to believe it was all for a good cause. The other times I cried. It wasn't death because you were still alive. I was proud of you. I missed you. You were good company almost from your first word. But so ambitious!"

Petra smiled a little at that.

"You're married now," said Mother. "Ambition for yourself is over. It's now ambition for your children."

"I just want them to be happy."

"*That* is something you can't do for them. So don't set that as your goal."

"I don't have a goal, Mother."

"That's nice. Then your heart will never break."

Mother looked at her with a deadpan expression.

Petra laughed a little. "You know, when I've been away for a while, I forget that you know everything."

Mother smiled. "Petra, I can't save you from anything. But I want to. I would if I could. Does that help? To know that somebody wants you to be happy?"

"More than you know, Mother."

She nodded. Tears slipped down her cheeks. "Going off into space. It feels like closing yourself in your own coffin. I know! But that's how it feels to *me*. I just know that I'm going to lose you, as sure as death. You know it too. That's why you're out here saying good-bye to Yerevan?"

"To Earth, Mother. Yerevan's the least of it."

"Well, Yerevan won't miss you. Cities never do. They go on and we don't make any difference to them at all. That's what I hate about cities."

And that's true of the human race, too, thought Petra. "I

think it's a good thing, that life goes on. Like water in a pail. Take some out, the rest fills in."

"When it's my child that's gone, nothing fills in," said Mother.

Petra knew that Mother was referring to the years that she spent without Petra, but what flashed into Petra's mind was the six babies they still hadn't found. The two ideas put together made the loss of those babies—if they even existed—too painful to contain. Petra began to cry. She hated crying.

Her mother put her arms around her. "I'm sorry, Pet," she said. "I wasn't even thinking. I was missing one child, and you have so many and you don't even know whether they're alive or dead."

"But they aren't even real to me," said Petra. "I don't know why I'm crying. I've never even met them."

"We're hungry for our children," said Mother. "We *need* to take care of them, once we bring them into existence."

"*I* didn't even get to do *that,*" said Petra. "Other women got to bear all but the one. And I'm going to lose *him.*" And suddenly her life felt so terrible it could not be borne. She sobbed as her mother held her.

"Oh, my poor girl," her mother kept murmuring. "Your life breaks my heart."

"How can I complain like this?" said Petra, her voice high with crying. "I've been part of some of the greatest events in history."

"When your babies need you, history doesn't bring much comfort."

And as if on cue, there was a faint sound of a baby crying inside the flat. Mother made as if to go, but Petra stopped her. "Bean will get her." She used the hem of her shirt to dab at her eyes.

"You can tell from the crying which baby it is?"

"Couldn't you?"

"I never had two infants at the same time, let alone three. There aren't many multiple births in our family."

"Well, I've found the perfect way to have nontuplets. Get eight other women to help." She managed a feeble laugh at her own black humor.

The baby cried again.

"It's definitely Bella, she's always more insistent. Bean will change her, and then he'll bring her to me."

"I could do that and he could go back to sleep," Mother offered.

"It's some of our best time together," said Petra. "Caring for the babies."

Mother pecked her on the cheek. "I can take a hint."

"Thanks for talking to me, Mother."

"Thanks for coming home."

Mother went inside. Petra stood at the edge of the balcony. After a while, Bean came padding out in bare feet. Petra pulled her T-shirt up and Bella started slurping noisily. "Good thing your brother Ender got my milk factory started," said Petra. "Or it would have been the bottle for you."

As she stood there, nursing Bella and looking out over the nighttime city, Bean's huge hands held her shoulders and stroked her arms. So gentle. So kind.

Once as tiny as this little girl.

But always a giant, long before his body showed it.

19

ENEMIES

From "Note to Hegemon: You Can't Fight an Epidemic
With a Fence"
By "Martel"
Posted on "Early Warning Network"

The presence of Julian Delphiki, the Hegemon's "enforcer,"
in Armenia might look like a family vacation to some, but
some of us remember that Delphiki was in Rwanda before it
ratified the FPE Constitution.

When you consider that Delphiki's wife, Petra Arkanian,
also one of Ender's Jeesh, is Armenian, what conclusion
can be reached except that Armenia, a Christian enclave
nearly surrounded by Muslim nations, is preparing to
ratify?

Add to that the close ties between the Hegemon and Thailand, where Wiggin's left-hand man, General Suriyawong,
is now "consulting" with General Phet Noi and Prime Minister Paribatra, newly returned from Chinese captivity, and
the FPE's position in Nubia—and it looks like the Hegemon
is surrounding Caliph Alai's little empire.

Many pundits are saying that the Hegemon's strategy is to "contain" Caliph Alai. But now that the Hindus have gone over to the Muslim bed—er, I meant to say, "camp"—containment is not enough.

When Caliph Alai, our modern Tamerlane, decides he wants a nice big pile of human skulls (it's so hard to get good decorators these days), he can field huge armies and concentrate them wherever he wants on his borders.

If the Hegemon sits passively waiting, trying to "contain" Alai behind a fence of alliances, then he'll find himself facing overwhelming force wherever Alai decides to strike.

Islam, the bloodthirsty "one-way religion," has a track record only slightly less devastating to the human race than the Buggers.

It's time for the Hegemon to live up to his job title and take decisive, preemptive action—preferably in Armenia, where his forces will be able to strike like a knife into the neck of Islam. And when he does, it's time for Europe, China, and America to wake up and join him. We need unity against this threat as surely as we ever needed it against an alien invasion.

> From: PeterWiggin%personal@FreePeopleOfEarth.fp.gov
> To: PetraDelphiki%getlost@FreePeopleOfEarth.gov
> Re: Latest Martel essay

Encrypted using code:******
Decrypted using code:*********

"Strike like a knife into the neck of Islam" indeed. Using what enormous army? What vast air force to neutralize the Muslims AND airlift that enormous army over the mountainous terrain between Armenia and the "neck" of Islam?

Fortunately, while Alai and Virlomi will know that Martel is full of kuso, the Muslim press is famous for its paranoia. THEY should believe there's a threat. So now the pressure is on and the game's afoot. You're a natural rabble-rouser, Petra. Promise me you'll never run against me for anything.

Oh, wait. I'm hegemon-for-life, aren't I . . .

Good work, mommy.

Caliph Alai and Virlomi sat beside each other at the head of a conference table in Chichlam—which the Muslim press still called Hyderabad.

Alai couldn't understand why it bothered Virlomi that he refused to insist that the Muslims call the city by its pre-Muslim name. He had problems enough to worry about without a needlessly humiliating name change. After all, the Indians hadn't *won* their independence. They had married their way to self-government. Which was a far better method than war—but without having won a victory on the field of battle, it was unseemly for Virlomi to insist on tokens of triumph like making your undefeated conquerors change the name *they* used to refer to their own seat of government.

In the past few days, Alai and Virlomi had met with several groups.

At a conference of heads of Muslim states they had listened to the woes and suggestions of such widely separated peoples as Indonesians, Algerians, Kazakhs, and Yemenis.

At a much quieter conference of Muslim minorities, they had indulged the revolutionary fantasies of Filipino, French, Spanish, and Thai would-be jihadists.

And in between, they had put on banquets for—and listened to stern counsel from—the French, American, and Russian foreign ministers.

These lords of the ancient, weary empires—hadn't they noticed that their nations had long since retired from the world? Yes, the Russians and Americans still had a formidable military, but where was their will to empire? They thought they could still boss around people like Alai, who had power and knew how to use it.

But it did Caliph Alai no harm to pretend that these nations still mattered in the world. Placate them with wise nods and palliative words, and they would go home and feel good about having helped promote "peace on Earth."

Alai had complained to Virlomi afterward. Wasn't it enough for the Americans that the whole world used their dollar and let them dominate the I.F.? Wasn't it enough for the Russians that Caliph Alai was keeping his armies away from their frontier and was doing nothing to support Muslim rebel groups inside their borders?

And the French—what did they expect Alai to *do* when he heard what their government's opinion was? Didn't they understand that they were spectators now in the great game, by their own choice? The players were not going to let the fans call the plays, no matter how well they played back in their day.

Virlomi listened benignly and said nothing in all these meetings. Most of the visitors came away with the impression that she was a figurehead, and Caliph Alai was in complete control. This impression did no harm. But as Alai and his closest advisers knew, it was also completely false.

Today's meeting was far more important. Gathered at this table were the men who actually ran the Muslim empire—the men Alai trusted, who made sure that the heads of the various Muslim states did what Alai needed them to do, without chafing at how thoroughly they were under the Caliph's thumb. Since Alai had the ecstatic support of most of the Muslim people, he had enormous leverage in gaining the cooperation of their governments. But

Alai did not yet have the clout to set up an independent system of finance. So he was dependent on contributions from the various republics and kingdoms and Islamic states that served him.

The men at this table made sure that the money flowed inward toward Hyderabad, and obedience flowed outward, with the least possible friction.

The most remarkable thing about these men was that they were no richer now than they had been when he appointed them. Despite all their opportunities to take a bribe here or exact a bit of a kickback there, they had remained pure. They were motivated by devotion to the Caliph's cause and pride in their positions of trust and honor.

Instead of one wazir, Alai had a dozen. They were gathered at this table, to counsel him and hear his decisions.

And every single one of them resented Virlomi's presence at the table.

And Virlomi did nothing to help alleviate this. Because even though she spoke softly and briefly, she persisted in using the quiet voice and enigmatic attitude that had played so well among Hindus. But Muslims had no goddess tradition, except perhaps in Indonesia and Malaysia, where they were especially alert to stamp out such tendencies where they found them. Virlomi was like an alien being among them.

There were no cameras here. The role wasn't working for this audience. So why did she persist in acting the goddess here?

Was it possible she believed it? That after years of playing the part in order to keep Indian resistance alive she now believed that she was divinely inspired? Ridiculous to think she actually believed she was divine herself. If the Muslim people ever believed she thought *that,* they would expect Alai to divorce her and have done with this nonsense. They accepted the idea that the Caliph, like Solomon of old, might marry women from many kingdoms in order to symbolize the submission of those kingdoms to Islam as a wife submits to a husband.

She couldn't believe she was a goddess. Alai was sure of that. Such superstitions would have been stamped out in Battle School.

Then again, Battle School was over years ago, and Virlomi had lived in isolation and adulation during most of that time. Things had happened that would change anybody. She had told him about the campaign of stones in the road, the "Great Wall of India," how she had seen her own actions turn into a vast movement. About how she first became a holy woman and then a goddess in hiding in eastern India.

When she taught him about Satyagraha, he thought he understood. You sacrifice anything and everything in order to stand for what's right without causing harm to another.

And yet she had also killed men with a gun she held in her own hand. There were times when she did not shrink from war. When she told him of her band of warriors who had stood off the whole Chinese army, preventing them from flooding back into India, from even resupplying the armies that Alai's Persians and Pakistanis were systematically destroying, he realized how much he owed to her brilliance as a commander, as a leader who could inspire incredible acts of bravery from her soldiers, as a teacher who could train peasants to be brutally efficient soldiers.

Somewhere between Satyagraha and slaughter, there had to be a place where Virlomi—the girl from Battle School—actually lived.

Or perhaps not. Perhaps the cruel contradictions of her own actions had led her to put the responsibility elsewhere. She served the gods. She was a god herself. Therefore it was not wrong for her to live by Satyagraha one day, and wipe out an entire convoy in a landslide the next.

The irony was that the longer he lived with her, the more Alai loved her. She was a sweet and generous lover, and she talked with him openly, girlishly, as if they were friends in school. As if they were still children.

Which we are, aren't we?

No. Alai was a man now, despite being in his teens. And Virlomi was older than he was, not a child at all.

But they had had no childhood. Alone together, their marriage was more like *playing* at being husband and wife than anything else. It was still fun.

And when they came to a meeting like this, Virlomi could switch off that playfulness, set aside the natural girl and become the irritating Hindu goddess that continued to drive a wedge between Caliph Alai and his most trusted servants.

Naturally, the counsel was worried about Peter Wiggin and Bean and Petra and Suriyawong. That Martel essay was taken very seriously.

So naturally, in order to be irritating, Virlomi dismissed it. "Martel can write what he wants, it means nothing."

Careful not to contradict her, Hadrubet Sasar— "Thorn"—pointed out the obvious. "The Delphikis really are in Armenia and have been for a week."

"They have family there," said Virlomi.

"And they're on vacation taking the babies to visit grandfather and grandmother," said Alamandar. As usual, his irony was so dry you could easily miss the fact that he was utterly scornful of the idea.

"Of course not," said Virlomi—and her scorn was not subtle. "Wiggin *wants* us to think they're planning something. We withdraw Turkish troops from Xinjiang to invade Armenia. Then Han Tzu strikes in Xinjiang."

"Perhaps al-Caliph has some intelligence indicating that the Emperor of China is in alliance with the Hegemon," said Thorn.

"Peter Wiggin," said Virlomi, "knows how to use people who don't know they're being used."

Alai listened to her and thought: That principle might as easily apply to the Armenians as to Han Tzu. Perhaps *they're* being used by Peter Wiggin without their consent. A simple matter to send Bean and Petra to visit the Arkanians, and then plant a false story that this means the Armenians are about to join the FPE.

Alai raised a hand. "Najjas. Would you compare the language in the Martel essays with the writings of Peter Wiggin, including the Locke essays, and tell me if they might be written by the same hand?"

A murmur of approval around the table.

"We will not take action against Armenia," said Caliph Alai, "based on unsubstantiated rumors from the nets. Nor based on our longstanding suspicion of the Armenians."

Alai watched their reaction. Some nodded approvingly, but most hid their reactions. And Musafi, the youngest of his wazirs, showed his skepticism.

"Musafi, speak to us," said Alai.

"It makes little difference to the people," said Musafi, "whether we can prove that the Armenians are plotting against us or not. This isn't a court of law. They are being told by many that instead of gaining India peacefully by marriage, we lost it the same way."

Alai did not look at Virlomi; nor did he sense any stiffening or change in her attitude.

"We did nothing when the Hegemon humiliated the Sudanese and stole Muslim land in Nubia." Musafi raised his hand to the inevitable objection. "The people *believe* the land was stolen."

"So you fear that they will think the Caliph is ineffective."

"They expected you to spread Islam throughout the world. Instead, you seem to be losing ground. The very fact that Armenia cannot be the source of a serious invasion also means that it's a safe place to take some limited action that will assure the people that the Caliphate is still watching over Islam."

"And how many men should die for this?" said Alai.

"For the continued unity of the Muslim people?" asked Musafi. "As many as love God."

"There's wisdom in this," said Alai. "But the Muslim people are not the only people in the world. Outside of Islam, Armenia is perceived as a heroic victim nation. Isn't there a chance that any kind of action in Armenia will be seen as proof that Islam is expanding, just as Martel charges? Then what happens to the Muslim minorities in Europe?"

Virlomi leaned forward, looking each of the counselors boldly in the face, as if she had authority at this table. Her stance was more aggressive than Alai ever showed to his friends. But then, these were not her friends. "You care about unity?"

"It's always been a problem in the Muslim world," said Alamandar. Some of the men chuckled.

"The 'Free People' can't invade us because we're more powerful than they are at any point where they might attack," said Virlomi. "Is our goal to unite the world under the leadership of Caliph Alai? Then our great rival is not Peter Wiggin. It's Han Tzu. He came to me with plots against Caliph Alai. He proposed marriage with me, so India and China could unite against Islam."

"When was this?" asked Musafi.

Alai understood why he was asking. "It was before Virlomi and I even considered marriage, Musafi. My wife has behaved with perfect propriety."

Musafi was satisfied; Virlomi showed no sign that she even cared what the interruption had been about. "You don't fight wars to enhance domestic unity—to do that, you pursue economic policies that make your people fat and rich. Wars are fought to create safety, to expand borders, and to eliminate future dangers. Han Tzu is such a danger."

"Since he has taken office," said Thorn, "Han Tzu has

taken no aggressive action. He has been conciliatory with all his neighbors. He even sent home the Indian prime minister, didn't he?"

"That was no conciliatory gesture," said Virlomi.

"The expansionist Snow Tiger is gone, his policies failed. We have nothing to fear from China," said Thorn.

He had gone too far, and everyone at the table knew it. It was one thing to make suggestions, and quite another to flatly contradict Virlomi.

Pointedly, Virlomi sat back and looked at Alai, waiting for him to take action against the offender.

But Thorn had earned his nickname because he would say uncomfortable truths. Nor did Alai intend to start banishing advisers from his council just because Virlomi was annoyed with them. "Once again, our friend Thorn proves that his name is well chosen. And once again, we forgive him for his bluntness—or should I say, sharpness?"

Laughter . . . but they were still wary of Virlomi's wrath.

"I see that this counsel prefers to send Muslims to die in cosmetic wars, while the real enemy is allowed to gather strength unmolested, solely because he has not attacked us yet." She turned directly to Thorn. "My husband's good friend Thorn is like the man in a leaky boat, surrounded by sharks. He has a rifle, and his fellow passenger says, 'Why don't you shoot those sharks! Once the boat sinks and we're in the water, you won't be able to use the rifle!'

"'You fool,' says the man. 'Why should I provoke the sharks? None of them has bit me yet.'"

Thorn seemed determined to press his luck. "The way I heard the story, the boat was surrounded by dolphins, and the man shot at them until he ran out of ammunition. 'Why did you do that?' his friend asked, and the man said, 'because one of them was a shark in disguise.'

"'Which one?' said his companion.

"'You fool,' says the man. 'I told you he's in disguise.'"

Then the blood in the water drew many sharks. But the man's gun was empty."

"Thank you all for your wise counsel," said Alai. "I must now think about all that you have said."

Virlomi smiled at Thorn. "I must remember your alternate version of the story. It's hard to decide which one is funnier. Maybe one is funny to Hindus, and the other to Muslims."

Alai stood up and began shaking hands with the men around the table, in effect dismissing each one in turn. It had already been rude for Virlomi to continue the conversation. But still she would not let up.

"Or perhaps," she said to the group as a whole, "Thorn's story is funny only to the sharks. Because if *his* story is believed, the sharks are safe."

Virlomi had never gone this far before. If she were a Muslim wife, he could take her by the arm and gently lead her from the room, then explain to her why she could not say such things to men who were not free to answer.

But then, if she were a Muslim wife, she wouldn't have been at the table in the first place.

Alai shook hands with the rest of them, and they showed their deference to him. But he also saw a growing wariness. His failure to stop Virlomi from giving such outrageous offense—to a man who had admittedly gone too far himself—looked like weakness to them. He knew they were wondering just how much influence Virlomi had over him. And whether he was truly functioning as Caliph any more, or was just a henpecked husband, married to a woman who thought she was a god.

In short, was Caliph Alai succumbing to idolatry by being married to this madwoman?

Not that anyone could say such a thing—even to each other, even in private.

In fact, they probably weren't thinking it, either.

I'm thinking it.

When he and Virlomi were alone, Alai walked out of the room to the conference room toilet, where he washed his face and hands.

Virlomi followed him inside.

"Are you strong or weak?" she asked. "I married you for your strength."

He said nothing.

"You know I'm right. Peter Wiggin can't touch us. Only Han Tzu stands between us and uniting the world under our rule."

"That's not true, Virlomi," said Alai.

"So you contradict me, too?"

"We're equals, Virlomi," said Alai. "We can contradict each other—when we're alone together."

"So if I'm wrong, who *is* a greater threat than Han Tzu?"

"If we attack Han Tzu, unprovoked, and it looks as if he might lose—or he does lose—then we can expect the Muslim population of Europe to be expelled, and the nations of Europe will unite, probably with the United States, probably with Russia. Instead of a mountain border that Han Tzu is not threatening, we'll have an indefensible border thousands of kilometers long in Siberia, and enemies whose combined military might will dwarf ours."

"America! Europe! Those fat old men."

"I see you're giving my ideas careful consideration," said Alai.

"Nothing's certain in war," said Virlomi. "This *might* happen, that *might* happen. I'll tell you what *will* happen. India will take action, whether the Muslims join us or not."

"India, which has little equipment and no trained army, will take on China's battle-hardened veterans—and without the help of the Turkish divisions in Xinjiang and the Indonesian divisions in Taiwan?"

"The Indian people do what I ask them," said Virlomi.

"The Indian people do what you ask them, as long as it's *possible*."

"Who are you to say what's possible?"

"Virlomi," said Alai. "I'm not Alexander of Macedonia."

"*That* much is abundantly clear. In fact, Alai, what battle have you *ever* fought and won?"

"You mean before or after the final war against the Buggers?"

"Of course—you were one of the sacred Jeesh! So you're right about everything forever!"

"And it was my plan that destroyed the Chinese will to fight."

"Your plan—which depended on *my* little band of patriots holding the Chinese army at bay in the mountains of eastern India."

"No, Virlomi. Your holding action saved thousands of lives, but if every single Chinese they sent over the mountain had faced us in India, we would have won."

"Easy to *say.*"

"Because my plan was for the Turkish troops to take Beijing while most of the Chinese forces were tied up in India, at which point the Chinese troops would have been called back from India. Your heroic action saved many lives and made our victory quicker. By about two weeks and an estimated hundred thousand casualties. So I'm grateful. But you've never led large armies into combat."

Virlomi waved it away, as if such a gesture could make the fact of it disappear.

"Virlomi," said Alai. "I love you, and I'm not trying to hurt you, but you've been fighting all this time against very bad commanders. You've never come up against someone like me. Or Han Tzu. Or Petra. And definitely no one like Bean."

"The stars of Battle School!" said Virlomi. "Ancient test scores and membership in a club whose president got outmaneuvered and sent into exile. What have you done lately, Caliph Alai?"

"I married a woman with a bold plan," said Alai.

"But what did I marry?" asked Virlomi.

"A man who wants the world to be united in peace. I thought the woman who built the Great Wall of India would want the same thing. I thought our marriage was part of that. I never knew you were so bloodthirsty."

"Not bloodthirsty, realistic. I see our true enemy and I'm going to fight him."

"Our *rival* is Peter Wiggin," said Alai. "He has a plan for uniting the world, but his depends on the Caliphate collapsing into chaos and Islam ceasing to be a force in the world. That's what the Martel essay was designed to do—provoke us into doing something stupid in Armenia. Or Nubia."

"Well, at least you see through *that*."

"I see through all of it," said Alai. "And you don't see the most obvious thing of all. The longer we wait, the closer we come to the day when Bean will die. It's a cruel and terrible fact, but when he's gone, then Peter Wiggin loses his greatest tool."

Virlomi looked at him with withering scorn. "Back to the Battle School test scores."

"All the kids in Battle School were tested," said Alai. "Including you."

"Yes, and what did that get any of them? They sat here in Hyderabad like passive slaves while Achilles bullied them. *I* escaped. *Me*. Somehow I was different. But did that show up on any of their tests in Battle School? There are things they didn't test for."

Alai did not tell her the obvious: She was different only because Petra asked her for help, and not someone else. She would not have escaped without Petra's request.

"Ender's Jeesh didn't come from the tests," said Alai. "We were chosen because of what we *did*."

"Because of what you did that *Graff* thought was important. There were qualities that he didn't know were important, so he didn't watch for them."

Alai laughed. "What, you're jealous because you weren't in Ender's Jeesh?"

"I'm disgusted that you still believe that Bean is irresistible because he's so 'smart.' "

"You haven't seen him in action," said Alai. "He's scary."

"No, you're just scared."

"Virlomi," said Alai, "don't do this."

"Don't do what?"

"Don't force my hand."

"I'm not forcing anything. We're equals, right? You'll tell your armies what to do, and I'll tell mine."

"If you send your troops on a suicide attack against China, then China will be at war with me, too. That's what our marriage *means*. So you're committing me to war whether I like it or not."

"I can win without you."

"Don't believe your own propaganda, my beloved," said Alai. "You aren't a god. You aren't infallible. And right now, you're so irrational that it scares me."

"Not irrational," said Virlomi. "*Confident*. And determined."

"You studied where I did. You already know all the reasons why an attack against China is insane."

"That's why we'll achieve surprise. That's why we'll win. Besides," said Virlomi, "our battle plans will be drawn up by the great Caliph Alai. And *he* was a member of Ender's Jeesh!"

"What happened to the idea of our being equals?" said Alai.

"We *are* equals."

"I never forced you to do anything."

"And I'm not forcing you, either."

"Saying that over and over won't make it true."

"I'm doing what I choose, and you're doing what you choose. The only thing I want from you is—I want your baby inside me before I lead my troops to war."

"What do you think this is, the middle ages? You don't lead your troops to war."

"I do," said Virlomi.

"You do if you're a squad commander. There's no point

when you have an army of a million men. They can't *see* you so it doesn't help."

"You reminded me a minute ago that you aren't Alexander of Macedon. Well, Alai, I *am* Jeanne d'Arc."

"When I said I'm not Alexander," said Alai, "I wasn't referring to his military prowess. I was referring to his marriage to a Persian princess."

She looked irritated. "I studied his *campaigns*."

"He returned to Babylon and married a daughter of the old Persian Emperor. He made his officers marry Persians, too. He was trying to unite the Greeks with the Persians and form them into one nation, by making the Persians a little more Greek, and the Greeks a little more Persian."

"Your point?"

"The Greeks said, We conquered the world by being Greek. The Persians lost their empire by being Persian."

"So you aren't trying to make your Muslims more Hindu or my Hindus more Muslim. Very good."

"He tried to combine soldiers of Persia and soldiers of Greece into one army. It didn't work. It fell apart."

"We're not making those mistakes."

"Exactly," said Alai. "I'm not going to make mistakes that destroy my Caliphate."

Virlomi laughed. "All right, then. If you think invading China is such a mistake, what are you going to do? Divorce me? Void our treaty? What then? You'll have to retreat from India and you'll look like even more of a zhopa. Or you'll try to stay and then I'll go to war against *you*. It all comes crashing down, Alai. So you're not going to get rid of me. You're going to stay my husband and you're going to love me and we'll have babies together and we'll conquer the world and govern it together and do you know why?"

"Why?" he said sadly.

"Because that's how I want it. That's what I've learned over the past few years. Whatever I think of, if I decide I want it, if I do what I know I need to do, then it happens. I'm the lucky girl whose dreams come true."

She came to him, wrapped her arms around him, kissed him. He kissed her back, because it would be unwise of him to show her how sad and frightened he was, and how little he desired her now.

"I love you," she said. "You're my best dream."

20

PLANS

From: ImperialSelf%HotSoup@ForbiddenCity.ch.gov
To: Weaver%Virlomi@MotherIndia.in.net;
Caliph%Salaam @caliph.gov
Re: Don't do this

Alai, Virlomi, what are you thinking? Troop movements can't be hidden. Do you really want this bloodbath? Are you bent on proving that Graff is right and none of us belong on Earth?

Hot Soup

From: Weaver%Virlomi@MotherIndia.in.net
To: ImperialSelf%HotSoup@ForbiddenCity.ch.gov
Re: Silly boy

Did you think that Chinese offenses in India would be forgotten? If you don't want bloodshed, then swear allegiance to Mother India and Caliph Alai. Disband your armies and offer no resistance. We will be far more merciful to the Chinese than the Chinese were to India.

From: Caliph%Jeeshman@caliph.gov
To: ImperialSelf%HotSoup@ForbiddenCity.ch.gov
Re: Look again

Take no precipitate action, my friend. Things will not go as
they appear to be going.

Mazer Rackham sat across from Peter Wiggin in his office in
Rotterdam.

"We're very concerned," said Rackham.

"So am I."

"What have you set in motion here, Peter?"

"Mazer," said Peter, "all I've done is keep pressing, using
what small tools I have. *They* decide how to respond to that
pressure. I was prepared for an invasion of Armenia or Nubia. I was prepared to take advantage of a mass expulsion of
Muslims from some or all European nations."

"And war between India and China? Are you prepared for
that?"

"These are *your* geniuses, Mazer. Yours and Graff's. You
trained them. You explain to me why Alai and Virlomi are
doing something so stupid and suicidal as to throw badly
armed Indian troops against Han Tzu's battle-hardened,
fully equipped, revenge-hungry army."

"So that's not something you did."

"I'm not like you and Graff," said Peter, irritated. "I
don't think I'm some master puppeteer. I've got *this*
amount of power and influence in the world, and it doesn't
amount to much. I have a billion or so citizens who have
not yet become a genuine nation, so I have to keep dancing
just to keep the FPE viable. I have a military force which is
well trained and well equipped, has excellent morale, and
is so small it wouldn't even be noticed on a battlefield in
China or India. I have my personal reputation as Locke and

my not-so-empty-anymore office as Hegemon. And I have Bean, both his actual abilities and his extravagant reputation. That's my arsenal. Do you see anything in that list that would allow me to even *think* of starting a war between two major world powers over whom I have no influence?"

"It just played into your hands so nicely, we couldn't help but think you had something to do with it."

"No, *you* did," said Peter. "You made these kids crazy in Battle School. Now they're all mad kings, using the lives of their subjects as playing pieces in a tawdry game of one-upmanship."

Rackham sat back, looking a little sick. "We didn't want this either. And I don't think they're crazy. Somebody must see some advantage in starting this war, and yet I can't think who. You're the only one who stands to gain, so we thought . . ."

"Believe it or not," said Peter, "I would not start a war like *this*, even if I thought I could profit from picking up the pieces. The only people who start wars that are bound to depend on human waves getting cut down by machine guns are fanatics or idiots. I think we can safely rule out idiocy. So . . . that leaves Virlomi."

"That's what we're afraid of. That she's actually come to believe her image. God-blessed and irresistible." Rackham raised an eyebrow. "But you knew that. You met with her."

"She proposed marriage to me," said Peter. "I turned her down."

"Before she went to Alai."

"I have a feeling that she married Alai on the rebound."

Rackham laughed. "She offered you India."

"She offered me an entanglement. I turned it into an opportunity."

"You knew when you turned her down that she'd be angry and do something stupid."

Peter shrugged. "I knew she'd do something spiteful. Something to show her power. I had no idea she'd try Alai, and I certainly had no idea he'd actually fall for it. Didn't he know she was crazy? I mean, not clinically, but drunk on power."

"You tell *me* why he did it," said Rackham.

"He was one of Ender's Jeesh," said Peter. "You and Graff must have so much paper on Alai that you know when he scratches his butt."

Rackham only waited.

"Look, I don't know why he did it, except maybe he thought he could control her," said Peter. "When he came home from Eros, he was a naive and righteous Muslim boy who's been sheltered ever since. Maybe he just wasn't ready to deal with a real live woman. The question now is, how will this play out?"

"How do *you* think it will play out?"

"Why should I tell you what I think?" said Peter. "What possible advantage will I get from you and Graff knowing what I'm expecting and what I'm preparing to do about it?"

"How will it hurt?"

"It'll hurt because if you decide your goals are different from mine, you'll meddle. Some of your meddling I've appreciated, but right now I don't want either the I.F. or ColMin doing one damn thing. I'm juggling too many balls to want some volunteer juggler to come in and try to help."

Rackham laughed. "Peter, Graff was so right about you."

"What?"

"When he rejected you for Battle School."

"Because I was too aggressive," said Peter wryly. "And look what he actually *accepted*."

"Peter," said Rackham. "Think about what you just said."

Peter thought about it. "You mean about juggling."

"I mean about why you were rejected for Battle School."

Peter immediately felt stupid. His parents had been told

that he was rejected because he was too aggressive—dangerously so. And he had wormed that information out of them at a very young age. Ever since then, it had been a burden he carried around inside—the judgment that he was dangerous. Sometimes it had made him bold; more often, it had made him not trust his own judgment, his own moral framework. Am I doing this because it's right? Am I doing this because it will really be to my benefit? Or only because I'm aggressive and can't stand to sit back and wait? He had forced himself to be more patient, more subtle than his first impulse. Time after time he had held back. It was because of this that he had used Valentine and now Petra to write the more dangerous, demagogic essays—he didn't want any kind of textual analysis to point to him as the author. It was why he had held back from any kind of serious arm-twisting with nations that kept playing with him about joining the FPE—he couldn't afford to have anyone perceive him as coercive.

And all this time, that assessment of him was a lie.

"I'm not too aggressive."

"It's impossible to be too aggressive for Battle School," said Rackham. "Reckless—now, that would be dangerous. But nobody has ever called you reckless, have they? And your parents would have known that was a lie, because they could have seen what a calculating little bastard you were, even at the age of seven."

"Why thanks."

"No, Graff looked at your tests and watched what the monitor showed us, and then he talked to me and showed me, and we realized: You weren't what we wanted as commander of the army, because people don't love you. Sorry, but it's true. You're not warm. You don't inspire devotion. You would have been a good commander *under* someone like Ender. But you could never have held the whole thing together the way he did."

"I'm doing fine now, thanks."

"You're not commanding soldiers. Peter, do Bean or Suri

love you? Would they die for you? Or do they serve you because they believe in your cause?"

"They think the world united under me as Hegemon would be better than the world united under anyone else, or not united at all."

"A simple calculation."

"A calculation based on trust that I've damn well earned."

"But not personal devotion," said Rackham. "Even Valentine—she was never devoted to you, and she knew you better than anyone."

"She pretty much hated me."

"Too strong, Peter. Too strong a word. She didn't trust you. She feared you. She saw your mind like clockwork. Very smart. She always figured you were six steps ahead of her."

Peter shrugged.

"But you weren't, were you?"

"Ruling the world isn't a chess game," said Peter. "Or if it is, it's a game with a thousand powerful pieces and eight billion pawns, and the pieces keep changing their capabilities, and the gameboard never stays the same. So just how far ahead can you possibly see? All I could do was put myself into a position with the most possible influence, and then exploit whatever opportunities came."

Rackham nodded. "But one thing was certain. Your off-the-charts aggressiveness, your passion to control events, we knew that you would place yourself in the center of everything."

It was Peter's turn to laugh. "So you left me home from Battle School so I would be what I am now."

"As I said, you weren't suited for military life. You don't take orders very well. People aren't devoted to you, and you aren't devoted to anyone else."

"I might be, if I found somebody I respected enough."

"The only person you ever respected that much is on a colony ship right now and you'll never see him again."

"I could never have followed Ender."

"No, you never could. But he's the only person you respected enough. The trouble was, he was your younger brother. You couldn't have lived with the shame."

"Well, all this analysis is nice, but how does it help us now?"

"We don't have a plan either, Peter," said Rackham. "We're also just moving useful pieces into place. Taking others out of play. We have some assets, just as you do. We have our arsenal."

"You have the whole I.F. You could put a stop to all of this."

"No," said Rackham. "Polemarch Chamrajnagar is adamant about it, and he's right. We could force the world's armies to come to a halt. They would all obey us or pay a terrible price. But who would be ruling the world then?"

"The fleet."

"And who is the fleet? It's volunteers *from Earth*. And from that moment on, who would be our volunteers? People who love the idea of going out into space? Or people who want to control the government of Earth? It would turn us into an Earth-centered institution. It would destroy the colonization project. And the Fleet would be hated, because it would soon be dominated by people who loved power."

"Makes you sound like a bunch of nervous virgins."

"We are," said Rackham. "And that's a strange line, coming from a nervous virgin like you."

Peter didn't bother responding to that. "So you and Graff won't do anything that would compromise the purity of the I.F."

"Unless somebody brings out the nukes again. We won't let that happen. Two nuclear wars were enough."

"We never had a nuclear war."

"World War II was a nuclear war," said Rackham. "Even if only two bombs were dropped. And the bomb that destroyed Mecca was the end of a civil war within Islam being fought out through surrogates and terrorism. Ever since then, nobody has even considered using nukes. But wars that are ended by nukes are nuclear wars."

"Fine. Definitions."

"Hyrum and I are doing everything we can," said Rackham. "So is the Polemarch. And believe it or not, we're trying to help you. We want you to succeed."

"And now you're pretending that you've been rooting for me all along?"

"Not at all," said Rackham. "We had no idea whether you'd be a tyrant or a wise ruler. No idea of what method you'd use or what your world government would be like. We knew you couldn't do it by charisma because you don't have much. And I'll admit you emerged with greater clarity after we got a good look at Achilles."

"So you didn't really get behind me until you realized I was better than Achilles."

"Your achievements were so extraordinary that we were still wary of you. Then Achilles showed us that you were actually cautious and self-restrained, compared to what *could* have been done by somebody who was truly ruthless. We saw a tyrant on the make, and we realized you weren't one."

"Depending on how you define 'tyrant.'"

"Peter, we're trying to help you. We want you to unite the world under *civilian* government. Without any advice from us, you've determined to do it by persuasion and plebiscite instead of using armies and terror."

"I use armies."

"You know what I mean," said Rackham.

"I just didn't want you to have any illusions."

"So tell me what you're thinking. What you're planning. So we *won't* interfere with our meddling."

"Because you're on my side," Peter said scornfully.

"No, we're not 'on your side.' We're not really in this game, except insofar as it affects us. We're in the business of dispersing the human race to as many worlds as possible.

But so far, only two colony ships have taken off. And it will be another generation before any of them lands. Far longer before we know whether the colonies will take hold and succeed. Even longer than that before we know if they'll become isolated worlds or trade will be profitable enough to make interstellar travel economically feasible. That's all we care about. But to accomplish it, we have to get recruits from Earth, and we have to pay for the ships—again, from Earth. And we have to do it without any hope of financial return for a hundred years at the best. Capitalism is not good at thinking a hundred years ahead. So we need government funding."

"Which you've managed to get even when I couldn't raise a dime."

"No, Peter," said Rackham. "Don't you understand? Everybody except the United States and Britain and a handful of smaller countries has stopped paying their assessments. We're living off our huge cash reserves. It's been enough to outfit two ships, to build a new class of gravity-controlled messenger ships, a few projects like that. But we're running out of money. We have no way to finance even the ships we already have under construction."

"You want me to win so I'll pay for your fleet."

"We want you to win so that the human race can stop spending its vast surpluses on ways to kill each other, and can instead send all the people that would have been killed in war out into space. And all the money that would have been spent on weapons can be spent on colony ships, and on trading ships, eventually. The human race has always produced a vast surplus of human beings and of wealth, and it has used up almost all of it either on stupid monuments like the pyramids or on brutal, bloody, pointless wars. We want you to unite the world so that this waste can finally stop."

Peter laughed. "You are such *dreamers*. Such idealists!"

"We were warriors and we studied our enemy. The Hive Queens. They failed because they were too unified. Human beings are a better design for a sentient species. Once we get over this war thing. What the Hive Queens tried, we can *do*. Spread out the species so it can develop truly new cultures."

"New cultures? When you insist that each colony be made up entirely of people from one nation, one language group?"

"We're not absolutely rigid on that, but yes. There are two ways of looking at species diversity. One is that every colony should contain a complete copy of the whole human race—every culture, every language, every race. But what's the point of that? Earth already has that! And look how well it's worked.

"No, the great colonies of the past have succeeded precisely because they were internally unified. People who knew each other, trusted each other, shared the same purposes, embraced the same laws. Each one monochromatic to begin with. But when we send out fifty monochromatic colony ships, but all different colors, so to speak—fifty different colonies, each with a separate cultural and linguistic root—*then* the human race can perform fifty different experiments. Real species diversity."

"I don't care what you say," said Peter, "I'm not going."

Rackham smiled. "We don't want you to."

"The two colony ships you've launched. One of them was Ender's."

"That's right."

"Who's the commander of the second ship?"

"Well, the *ship* is commanded by—"

"Who's going to rule the *colony*," said Peter.

"Dink Meeker."

So that was the plan. They meant to take Ender's Jeesh and anybody else who was dangerously talented in a military way and send them off into space. "So to you," said Peter, "this war between Han Tzu and Alai is your worst nightmare."

Rackham nodded.

"Don't worry," said Peter.

"Don't worry?"

"All right," said Peter. "Worry if you want. But your offer

to Ender's Jeesh, to take them all off planet, to give them colonies—now I understand what it's about. You care about these kids whose lives you coopted. You want to get them off to worlds where there's no rival. They can use their talents to help a community triumph over a new world."

"Yes."

"But the most important thing is, they won't be on Earth." Rackham shrugged.

"You knew that nobody could ever unite the world as you need it to be united while those highly trained, highly aggressive, publicly certified geniuses are still in it."

"We didn't see a way it could happen."

"Well, that's a lie," said Peter. "You saw the way it would happen, because it's obvious. One of *them* would be the ruler of Earth, and all the others would be dead."

"Yes, we saw that, but it wasn't an option."

"Why not? It's the human way of settling things."

"We love these kids, Peter."

"But love them or not, they'll all die eventually. No, I think you would have been content to let them work it out, if you thought it would work. If you thought one of them would emerge triumphant. What you couldn't stand was the knowledge that they were so evenly matched that none of them would win. They'd use up the resources of Earth, all that surplus population, and *still* there'd be no clear winner."

"That wouldn't help anything," said Rackham.

"So if you could have found a cure for Bean's condition, you wouldn't need me. Because Bean could do it. He could defeat the others. He could unite the world. Because he's so much better than they are."

"But he's going to die," said Rackham.

"And you love him," said Peter. "So you're going to try to save his life."

"We want him to help you win first."

"That's not possible," said Peter. "Not in the time he has left."

"By 'win,' " said Rackham, "I mean, we want him to help you get into a position where your victory is inevitable, given your abilities. Right now, you could be stopped by all kinds of chance events. Having Bean increases your power and influence. Another thing that would help is if we could get the rest of the Jeesh off this planet. If we've removed from the board all the pieces that could challenge you—if, in effect, you're the queen in a game of knights and bishops—then you won't need Bean anymore."

"I'll need somebody," said Peter. "I'm not trained for war the way these Battle School kids were. And as you said, I'm not the kind of guy that soldiers want to die for."

Rackham leaned forward. "Peter, tell us what you're planning."

"I'm not planning anything," said Peter. "I'm simply waiting. When I met Virlomi, I realized that she was the key to everything. She's volatile, she's powerful, and she's drunk. I knew that she'd do something destabilizing. Something that would break things apart."

"So you think the war between India and China will happen? And that Alai's Muslim League will be drawn into it?"

"That's possible," said Peter. "I hope it won't happen."

"But if it does, you'll be poised to attack Alai when his forces are tied up fighting China."

"No," said Peter.

"No?"

"We're not going to attack anybody," he said.

"Then . . . what?" said Rackham. "Whoever emerges from that war—"

"I don't think that war's going to amount to much," said Peter, "if it happens at all. But if it does happen, then both sides will be weakened by it. There's no shortage of ambitious nations ready to step in and pick up the pieces."

"So what do *you* think is going to happen?"

"I don't know," said Peter. "I wish you'd believe me. There's only one thing I'm sure of. Alai's and Virlomi's marriage is doomed. And if you want either or both of them to command any of your precious colonies, you'd better make sure you're ready to get them off planet fast."

"Are you planning something?" asked Rackham.

"No! Aren't you listening? I'm watching the whole damn thing just like you are! I've already played my cards—making the Muslim leadership suspicious of my intentions. Provoking them. Plus a little quiet diplomacy."

"With whom?"

"With Russia," said Peter.

"You're trying to get them to join with you in attacking Alai? Or China?"

"No, no, no," said Peter. "If I tried anything like that, word would get out, and then what Muslim nation would ever, *ever* join the FPE?"

"So what are you doing with your diplomacy?"

"Begging the Russians to stay out of it."

"In other words, pointing out the opportunity and telling them that you're not going to interfere in any way."

"Yes," said Peter.

"Politics is so . . . indirect."

"That's why conquerors rarely make great rulers."

"And great rulers are rarely conquerors."

"You closed the door on my becoming a conqueror," said Peter. "So if I'm to be the ruler of the world—a good one—then I have to win that position in such a way as not to have to keep killing people in order to stay in power. It does the world no good if everything depends on me, if it all collapses when I die. I need to build this thing piece by piece, bit by bit, with powerful institutions that have their own momentum, so that it will make very little difference who's at the head. It's what I learned from growing up in America. It was a nation created out of nothing—nothing but a set of ideals that they never measured up to. Now and then they had great leaders, but usually nothing but political hacks, and I mean right from the start. Washington was great, but

Adams was paranoid and lazy, and Jefferson was as vile a scheming politician as a nation has ever been cursed with. I learned a lot from *him* about destroying your enemies with demagoguery conducted under pseudonyms."

"So you were praising him."

"I'm saying that America shaped itself with institutions so strong that it could survive corruption, stupidity, vanity, ambition, recklessness, and even insanity in its chief executive. I'm trying to do the same thing with the Free People of Earth. Base it on some simple but workable ideals. Bring nations into it because they freely choose to join. Unite them with a language and a system of laws, and give them a stake in institutions that take on a life of their own. And I can't do any of that if I conquer a single country and force it to join. That's a rule I can never violate. My forces will defeat enemies who attack the FPE, and we'll carry war into their territory to do it. But when it comes to joining the FPE, they can only do it if a majority of the people want to. If they choose to be subject to our laws and take part in our institutions."

"But you're not above getting other nations to do your conquering for you."

"Islam," said Peter, "has never learned how to be a religion. It's a tyranny by its very nature. Until it learns to let the door swing both ways, and permit Muslims to decide not to be Muslim without penalty, then the world has no choice but to fight against it in order to remain free. As long as Muslim nations remained divided, working against each other, they weren't going to be a problem for me, because I could pick them up one by one, especially after the FPE becomes large enough for them to see how the people within my borders prosper."

"But united under Alai—"

"Alai is a decent guy," said Peter. "I think he has some idea of liberalizing Islam from the top. But it can't be done. He's simply wrong. He's a general, not a politician. As long as ordinary Muslims believe it's their duty to kill any Muslim who tries to quit being a Muslim, as long as they think they have a holy duty to resort to arms to compel unbelievers to obey Islamic law—you can't liberalize that, you can't make it a decent system for anybody. Not even for Muslims. Because the cruelest, narrowest, most evil people will always rise to power because they'll always be the ones most willing to wrap themselves in the crescent flag and murder people in God's name."

"So Alai is doomed to fail."

"Alai is doomed to die. The moment the fanatics realize that he's not as fanatically pure a Muslim as they are, they'll kill him."

"And install a new Caliph?"

"They can install whoever they want," said Peter. "It won't matter to me. Without Alai, there's no Islamic unity, because only Alai can lead them to victory. And in defeat, Muslims don't stay united. They move like a great wave— until they meet a wall of rock that doesn't move. Then they crash and recede."

"As they did after Charles Martel defeated them."

"It's Alai who made them powerful," said Peter. "The only trouble is, Alai doesn't like the things he has to do in order to rule a totalitarian system like Islam. He's already killed a lot more people than he wanted to. Alai's not a killer, but he's become one, and he likes it less and less."

"You think he's not going to follow Virlomi into war."

"It's a race," said Peter. "Between followers of Alai who plan to kill Virlomi in order to free Alai from her influence, and fanatical Muslims who plan to kill Alai because he betrayed Islam by marrying Virlomi in the first place."

"Do you know who the conspirators are?"

"I don't have to," said Peter. "If there weren't any conspirators planning murder, it wouldn't be a Muslim empire. And there's another race. Can they kill Alai or Virlomi before China or Russia attacks? And even if they do kill one or both of them, will that stop China or Russia from attacking, or simply encourage them to think that victory will be more likely?"

"And is there any scenario where you'll go to war?"

"Yes," said Peter. "If they get rid of Virlomi, and Russia and China don't attack, then Alai—or his successor, if they kill him, too—will be pushed into attacking Armenia and Nubia. And *that's* a war I'm ready to fight. We'll destroy them. We'll be the rock against which Islam crashes and breaks into pieces."

"And if Russia or China does attack them before they can turn to you, then you still profit from the war as frightened nations unite with you against either Russia or China— whichever country is seen as the aggressive, dangerous one."

"It's like I said," Peter answered. "I have no idea how things will turn out. I just know that I'm ready to take advantage of every situation I can think of. And I'm watching very closely so that if something happens that I haven't foreseen, I can take advantage of it."

"So here's the key question," said Rackham. "It's the information I came here to get."

"I'm dying to hear."

"How long are you going to need Bean?"

Peter thought about that one for a while. "I've had to make my plans knowing that he was going to die. Or, once you made your offer, leave. So the answer is, as long as I have him, of course I'll use him, either to intimidate would-be enemies, or to command my forces when we go to war. But if he dies or leaves, I can make do. My plans don't depend on having Bean."

"So if he left in three months."

"Rackham, have you already found his other children? Is that what you're saying? Have you found them and you aren't telling him and Petra because you think I need Bean?"

"Not all of them."

"You're cold. You're such bastards," said Peter. "You're still using children as your tools."

"Yes," said Rackham. "We're bastards. But we mean well. Just like you."

"Give Bean and Petra their babies. And save his life, if you can. He's a good man who deserves better than to have you toy with him any longer."

21

PAPERS

From: The Impaled One
To: HonestAbe%Lincoln@RailSplitter.org/
WriteToTheAuthor
Re: God help me

Sometimes you give advice assuming that no one will take it. I just hope the man upstairs will forgive me and still find a place for me. Meanwhile, tell the big guy he's got to do something about the cup I broke.

From: PeterWiggin%private@hegemon.com
To: Graff%pilgrimage@colmin.gov
Fwd: Re: God help me

Dear Hyrum,

As you'll see from below, our Slavic friend has apparently offered suggestions to his government that they actually took, and he regrets it. Assuming that you're the guy upstairs, I would guess this open encryption suggests he wants out. My sources last put him in Florida but if they're watching him closely, they would have moved him to Idaho.

As for the cup he broke, I think he means that instead of Russia looking for a chance to attack Alai, they've made a deal with the Muslim League and while China looks south to fight India, Russia is going to move on Han Tzu from the north while the Turks move from the west, the Indonesians from Taiwan, and Virlomi's insane invasion will go on over the mountains. Not so insane now.

However, on the chance that by "the big guy" Russian Boy meant somebody other than "the man upstairs," he could only mean a certain giant we both know. I'll confer with him and Mrs. Giant about what, if anything, we can do to deal with the situation.

Peter

Alai had given his orders, and now he was going to make sure he was out of Hyderabad when they were carried out. The Caliph could not be tainted with the arrest of his own wife.

But the Caliph could not be ruled by her, either. Alai knew that the wazirs of his council hated her; if he did not have her arrested by men loyal to him, then she would certainly be killed.

Later, after things had settled down, after she had regained her senses and stopped thinking she was unstoppable, he would take her out of prison. He could not release her in India—that was out of the question. Maybe Graff would take her. She wasn't one of Ender's Jeesh, but by the same reasoning Graff had used in his invitation, the world would certainly be a safer place with her gone from it, while a colony might be lucky to have someone of such ability and ambition at its head.

Meanwhile, without Virlomi there was no reason for him to govern from Hyderabad. He would continue to respect his treaty with India and withdraw his forces. Let them try to rebuild without Virlomi's madness trying to throw them prematurely into war. India would not be in shape to mount a meaningful military campaign against anything more substantial than a flock of starlings for many years to come.

Alai would spend the next few years putting Islam's house in order and trying to forge a real nation out of this mishmash that history had left for him to deal with. If Syrians and Iraqis and Egyptians couldn't get along with each other and despised each other the moment they heard the other's accent, how could anyone expect Moroccans and Persians and Uzbeks and Malays to see the world in the same way just because a muezzin called them to prayer?

Besides, he had to deal with the stateless peoples—the Kurds, the Berbers, half the nomad tribes of ancient Bactria. Alai knew perfectly well that these Muslims would not follow a Caliph who kept the status quo—not when Peter Wiggin was tempting revolutionaries everywhere with his promise of statehood and the examples of Runa and Nubia.

We brought Nubia on ourselves, thought Alai. The ancient Muslim contempt for blackest Africa still seethed under the surface; if Alai had not been a member of Ender's Jeesh, it would have been inconceivable for him, as a black African, to be named Caliph. It was in Sudan, where the races met face to face, that the ugliness had emerged with so much virulence. The rest of Islam should have disciplined Sudan long ago. And now they all paid the price, with the humiliation of Sudan at the hands of the FPE.

So we have to give the Kurds and Berbers their own governments. Real ones, not sham "autonomous regions." That would not be popular in Morocco and Iraq and Turkey, Alai knew. That's why it was stupid in the extreme to imagine embarking on wars of conquest when there was no peace or unity inside the world of Islam.

Alai would govern from Damascus. It was far more central. He would be surrounded by Muslim culture instead of Hindu. It would be a civilian-centered government, not an obvious military dictatorship. And the world would see that

Islam was not interested in conquering the world. That Caliph Alai had already liberated more people from oppressive conquerors than Peter Wiggin ever could.

As Alai left his office, two of the guards fell in step beside him. Ever since Virlomi simply walked into his office the day they got married, Alamandar had insisted that it not be so easy to walk into highly sensitive areas of the compound. "We *are* in occupied enemy country, my Caliph," he had said, and he was right.

Still, there was something that made Alai uneasy about having to be accompanied by guards as he moved about the compound. It felt wrong. The Caliph should be able to move among his own people with perfect trust and openness.

As Alai stepped through the door into the parking garage, two more guards joined the two who had walked with him from upstairs. His limousine sat idling at the curb. The back door opened.

He saw someone jogging toward him from among the parked cars.

It was Ivan Lankowski. Alai had rewarded him for his loyal service by putting him in charge of the administration of the Turkish nations of central Asia. What was he doing here? Alai had not called him back from service, and Ivan had not written or called about coming.

Ivan reached into his jacket. Where a gun would be, if he was armed with a shoulder holster.

And he *would* be armed; he had carried a gun for too many years to be comfortable without one now.

Alamandar got out of the open back door of the limo. As he rose to his feet, he shouted at the guards. "Shoot him, you fools! He's going to kill the Caliph!"

Ivan's gun was out. He fired, and the guard to Alai's left dropped like a rock. The sound was strange—the barrel had a silencer, but Alai was close to being directly in front of it, so it wasn't so much silenced as shaped.

I should drop to the ground, thought Alai. To save my life, I should get out of the line of fire. But he couldn't take the danger seriously. He didn't feel as though he were in danger at all.

The other guards had their guns out now. Ivan shot another one, but then the bullets—not silenced—flew in the other direction, and Ivan fell to the ground. His gun did not slip from his hand; he maintained his grip on it to the end of his life.

Or maybe he wasn't dead. Maybe he could spend his last moments explaining to Alai how he could betray him like this.

Alai walked to Ivan's body and felt for a pulse. Ivan's eyes were open. He was already dead.

"Come away, my Caliph!" shouted Alamandar. "There may be other conspirators!"

Conspirators. There was no possibility of other conspirators. Ivan didn't trust anybody enough to conspire with them. The only person Ivan absolutely trusted was . . .

Was me.

Ivan was a perfect shot. Even at a run, he could not have aimed at me and then clumsily hit two guards.

"My guards," said Alai, looking up at Alamandar. "The ones he shot—will they be all right?"

One of the other guards jogged back to look. "Both dead," he said.

But Alai already knew that. Ivan had not been aiming at Alai. He had come here with one purpose in mind, the purpose that had guided him for years. Ivan was here to protect his Caliph.

It flashed into Alai's mind with immediate clarity. Ivan had learned of a conspiracy against the Caliph, and it involved people so close to Alai that there was no way for Ivan to warn him from a distance without running the risk of alerting one of the conspirators.

Alai reached with one hand to close Ivan's eyes, while with the other he pulled Ivan's pistol from his slackened fingers. Still not taking his eyes off of Ivan's face, Alai fired the pistol upward into the guard who was standing over him. Then he calmly aimed at the guard who had gone back to the bodies and fired. Alai had never been as good a shot as Ivan. He could not have done this while running. But kneeling, he was all right.

The guard he had shot without looking was lying on the pavement, twitching. Alai shot him again, then turned to Alamandar, who was getting back into the limo.

Alai shot him. He fell into the car and it screeched away from the curb. But the door was not closed yet, and Alamandar was in no shape to close it. So as it passed Alai, there would be a brief moment when the driver would be unprotected by the heavy armoring and bulletproof glass. Alai laid down three quick shots in order to have a better chance of catching that moment.

It worked. The car did not turn. It ran into a wall.

Alai jogged over to the still-open back door of the car, where Alamandar was panting and holding his chest. His eyes were on fire with rage and fear as Alai leveled Ivan's pistol to fire.

"You are no Caliph!" gasped Alamandar. "The Hindu woman is more of a Caliph than you are, you black dog."

Alai shot him in the head and he fell silent.

The driver was unconscious, but Alai shot him, too.

Then he went back to the bodies of the guards, who were dressed in western business suits. Ivan had shot one of them in the head. He was larger than Alai but his clothing would do. Alai had his white robe off in a moment. Underneath he wore jeans as he always did. After wrestling with the corpse for a few moments, he got the shirt and jacket off the man, and without popping any of the buttons off.

Alai took the pistols from the two guards who had never gotten off a shot and dropped them into the pockets of the jacket he now wore. Ivan's silenced pistol had to be nearly out of bullets, so Alai slid it across the pavement back toward Ivan's body.

Where do I imagine an African man can hide in Hyderabad? No one's face was more recognizable than the

Caliph's, and those who didn't know his face knew his race. They would also know that he spoke no Hindi. He would not make it a hundred meters outside in Hyderabad.

Then again, there was no chance he could get out of the compound alive.

Wait. Think.

Don't wait. Get away from this murder scene.

Ivan jogged through the parked cars. The garage would have been cleared of any observers by Alamandar's men; that meant Ivan must have been hidden inside a car. Where was that car?

Keys in the ignition. Thank you, Ivan. You planned for everything. No time would be wasted fumbling with keys, as you dragged me to your car to get me out of here.

Where were you going to take me, Ivan? Whom do you trust?

Alamandar's last words rang in his ears. The Hindu woman is more of a Caliph than you are.

He thought they all hated her. But now he realized that she was the one advocating war. Expansion. The restoration of a great empire.

That's what they wanted. And all his talk of peace, of consolidation, of reforming Islam from the inside before reaching out to the rest of the world, of competing with Peter Wiggin using the same methods, inviting other nations to join the Caliphate without requiring them to become Muslim or live under Shari'a—they had listened, they had agreed, but they hated it.

They hated *him*.

So when they saw the break between him and Virlomi, they exploited it.

Or . . . was Virlomi behind this?

Was Virlomi pregnant with his child?

The Caliph is dead. But here is his baby, born after he died but infused with the gifts of God from his birth. In the name of the baby Caliph, the council of wazirs will rule. And since the mother of the new Caliph is ruler of India, he will join the two great nations in one. With Virlomi as regent, of course.

No. Virlomi could not have wanted him *murdered*.

Ivan would have an airplane waiting. The airplane that brought him. With his own trusted crew.

Alai drove at a normal pace. But he did not drive to the checkpoint where he normally entered the airport grounds. In all likelihood, that place would be manned by the conspirators. Instead, he went to a service gate.

The guard sauntered over and started to tell him only authorized service vehicles could use this gate.

"I'm the Caliph, and I want to go through this gate."

"Oh," said the guard, looking confused. "I see. I—"

He pulled out a cellphone and started to punch at it.

Alai didn't want to kill this man. He was an idiot, not a conspirator. So he swung the door open, bumping into the man. Not hard. Just enough to get his attention. Then he closed the door and reached through the window. "Give me that cellphone."

The soldier gave it to him. Alai switched it off.

"I'm the Caliph. When I say to let me through, you don't have to ask *anyone* else's permission."

The soldier nodded and ran to the controls and the gate slid open.

As soon as Alai was through the gate, he saw a small corporate jet with Cyrillic lettering under the Common letters naming the corporation. The kind of plane Ivan would have used.

The engines started up as Alai approached. No, as Ivan's car approached.

Alai stopped the car and got out. The door of the jet was open, forming steps to the ground. Holding one hand on the pistol in his pocket—for he was taking this plane whether it was Ivan's or not—Alai walked up the steps.

A businessman—or so he seemed—waited for him inside. "Where's Ivan?" he asked.

"We're not waiting for him," said Alai. "He died saving me."

The man nodded once, then went to the door and pushed the button to raise it. Meanwhile he shouted, "Let's go!" and then said to Alai, "Please sit down and fasten your seat belt, my Caliph."

The plane began taxiing before the door was closed.

"Do nothing out of the ordinary," said Alai. "Nothing to alert them. There are weapons here that could easily shoot down this plane."

"Our plan exactly, sir," said the man.

What would the conspirators do, when they found out that Alai had escaped?

They would do nothing. They would say nothing. As long as Alai might turn up alive somewhere, they dared not be on record as saying anything.

In fact, they would continue to act in his name. If they followed Virlomi's plans, if her insane invasion went forward, then Alai would know they were with her.

When they were in the air—having waited for ordinary permission from the controllers—Ivan's man came back and stood diffidently two meters away.

"My Caliph, if I may ask?"

Alai nodded.

"How did he die?"

"He was busy shooting the guards surrounding me. He got two of them before they cut him down. I used his weapon to kill the others. Including Alamandar. Do you know how far the conspiracy went?"

"No sir," said the man. "We only knew that you would be killed on the airplane to Damascus."

"And this airplane? Where is it taking me?"

"It has a very long range, sir," said the man. "Where will you feel safe?"

———

Petra's mother was tending the babies while Petra and Bean oversaw the last preparations for the opening of hostilities.

Peter's message had been terse: How busy can you keep the Turks, while watching out for Russians in the rear?

Turks and Russians allies, or potentially so. What game was Alai playing? Was Vlad in it? Trust Peter not to share any more information than he thought he had to—which was invariably less than other people actually needed.

Still, she and Bean had been spending every spare moment working out ways, using limited, undertrained, and under-equipped Armenian forces to cause maximum disruption.

A raid on the most highly visible Turkish target, Istanbul, would enrage them without accomplishing anything.

Blocking the Dardanelles would be a harsh blow against all the Turks, but there was no way to project that much force from Armenia to the western shore of the Black Sea, and maintain it.

Oh, for the days when oil was strategically important! Back then, the Russian, Azerbaijani, and Persian wells in the Caspian would have been a prime target for disruption.

But now the wells had all been dismantled, and the Caspian was mostly used as a source of water, which was desalinated and pumped over to irrigate fields around the Aral Sea, with the runoff being used to replenish that once-dying lake. And to strike at the water pipeline would impoverish poor farmers without affecting the enemy's ability to wage war.

The plan they finally came up with was simple enough, once you bought the concept. "There's no way to strike the Turks directly," said Bean. "Nothing is centralized. So we'll strike Iran. It's highly urbanized, the big cities are all in the northwest, and there'll be an immediate demand for Iranian troops to come home from India to fight us. The Turks will be under pressure to help, and when they launch a very badly planned attack against Armenia, we'll be waiting."

"What makes you think it will be badly planned?" Petra asked.

"Because Alai isn't running the show on the Muslim side."

"When did *this* happen?"

"If Alai were in control," said Bean, "he wouldn't let Virlomi do what she's doing in India. It's too stupid and it will kill too many men. So . . . somehow he's lost control. And if that's the case, the Muslim enemy we're facing is incompetent and fanatic. They're acting out of anger and panic, with poor planning."

"What if this *is* Alai's doing, and you don't know him as well as you think?"

"Petra," said Bean. "We *know* Alai."

"Yes, and he knows us."

"Alai is a builder, like Ender. He always has been. An empire won through audacious and bloody conquest isn't worth having. He wants to build his Muslim empire the way Peter is building the FPE, by transforming Islam into a system that other nations will want, voluntarily, to join. Only somebody's decided not to follow his path. Either Virlomi or the hotheads within his own government."

"Or both?" asked Petra.

"Anything's possible."

"Except Alai controlling the Muslim armies."

"Well, it's simple enough," said Bean. "If we're wrong, and the Turkish counterattack is brilliantly planned, then we'll lose. As slowly as possible. And hope Peter has something else up his sleeve. But our assignment is to draw Turkish forces and attention away from China."

"And meanwhile, we'll be putting pressure on the Muslim alliance," said Petra. "No matter what the Turks do, the Persians won't believe they're doing enough."

"Sunni against Shi'ite," said Bean. "It's the best I could think up."

So for the past two days they had been drawing up plans for the quick, audacious airborne attack on Tabriz, and then, when the Iranians started to react to that, an immediate evacuation and airborne attack on Tehran. Meanwhile, Petra, in command of the defense of Armenia, would be prepared to make the Turkish counterattack pay for every meter of progress through the mountains.

Now everything was ready, awaiting only the word from Peter. Petra and Bean weren't really necessary while the troops began their deployment and the supplies were moved to depots in the areas where they'd be needed. Everything was in the hands of the Armenian military.

"What scares me," Petra told Bean, "is how they have absolute confidence that we know what we're doing."

"Why does that scare you?"

"Doesn't it scare *you?*"

"Petra, we *do* know what we're doing. We just don't know why."

It was in that lull, between planning and getting the order to go ahead, that Petra got a call on her cellphone. From her mother.

"Petra, they say they're friends of yours, but they're taking the babies."

Panic stabbed through her. "Who's with them? Put the one in charge on the phone."

"He won't. He just says, the 'teacher' says to meet them at the airport. Who's the teacher? Oh, God help us, Petra! This is like the time they kidnapped you."

"Tell them we'll be at the airport and if they've hurt the babies I'll kill them. But no, Mother, it's not the same thing at all."

Unless it was.

She told Bean what was happening, and they calmly made their way to the airport. They saw Rackham waiting at the curb and made the driver let them off there.

"I'm sorry to frighten you," said Rackham. "But we don't have time for arguments until we get on the plane. Then you can scream at me all you like."

"Nothing is so urgent you have to steal our babies," said Petra, putting as much venom into her voice as she could.

"See?" said Rackham. "Arguing instead of coming with me."

They followed him then, through back passages and out to a private jet. Petra protested as they went. "Nobody knows where we are. They'll think we ran out on them. They'll think we were kidnapped."

Rackham just ignored her. He moved very quickly for a man so old.

The babies were on the plane, each one being cared for by a separate nurse. They were fine. Only Ramón was still nursing, because the two with Bean's syndrome were eating more-or-less solid food now. So Petra sat down and fed him, while Rackham sat down opposite them in the luxury jet and, as the plane took off, began his explanation.

"We had to get you out of there now," he said, "because the airport at Yerevan is going to be blown to bits in an hour or two, and we need to be out over the Black Sea before it happens."

"How do you know?" demanded Petra.

"We have it from the man who planned the attack."

"Alai?"

"It's a Russian attack," said Rackham.

Bean blew up. "Then what was all that *kuso* about distracting the Turks!"

"It all still applies. As soon as we see the attack planes take off from southern Russia, I'll let you know and you can give the word to launch *your* attack on Iran."

"This is Vlad's plan," said Petra. "A sudden preemptive strike to keep the FPE from doing anything. To neutralize me and Bean."

"Vlad wants you to know he's very sorry. He's used to none of his plans actually being used."

"You've been talking to him?"

"We got him out of Moscow about three hours ago and debriefed him as quickly as possible. We think they don't know he's gone. Even if they do know, it's no reason for them not to go ahead with their plan."

The telephone beside Rackham's seat beeped once. He picked it up. Listened. Pressed a button and handed it over to Petra. "All right, the rockets have launched."

"I assume I need the country code?"

"No. Put in the number as if you were still in Yerevan. As far as they'll know, you are. Tell them that you're conferring with Peter and you'll rejoin them with the attack in progress."

"Will we?"

"And then call your mother and tell her you're all right and not to talk about what happened."

"Oh, *that's* about an hour too late."

"My men told her that if she called anyone but you until she heard from you again, she'd be very sorry."

"Thank you for terrifying her even more. Do you have any idea what this woman has been through in her life?"

"It always turns out all right, though. So she's better off than some."

"Thanks for your cheery optimism."

A few minutes later, the strike force was launched and a warning was given to evacuate the airport, reroute all incoming flights, evacuate the parts of Yerevan nearest the airport, and alert the men at all possible military targets inside Armenia.

As for Petra's mother, she was crying so hard—with relief, with anger at what had happened—that Petra could hardly make herself understood. But finally the conversation ended and Petra was more pissed off than ever. "What gives you the right? Why do you think you—"

"War gives me the right," said Rackham. "If I'd waited till you could come home and *get* your babies and then meet us at the airport, this plane would never have taken off. I have my men's lives to think of here, not just your mother's feelings."

Bean put a hand on Petra's knee. She accepted the need for calm, and fell silent.

"Mazer," said Bean, "what's this about? You could have warned us with a phone call."

"We have your other babies."

Petra was already emotional. She burst into tears. Quickly she controlled herself. And hated the fact that she had acted so . . . maternal.

"All of them? At once?"

"We've been watching some of them for several weeks," said Rackham. "Waiting for an opportune moment."

Bean waited only a moment before saying, "Waiting for Peter to tell you that it was all right. That you didn't need us any more for his war."

"He still needs you," said Rackham. "As long as he can have you."

"Why did you wait, Mazer?"

"How many?" said Petra. "How many are there?"

"One more with Bean's syndrome," said Rackham. "Four more without it."

"That's eight," said Bean. "Where's the ninth?"

Rackham shook his head.

"So you're still looking?"

"No, we're not," said Rackham.

"So you have definite information that the ninth wasn't implanted. Or it's dead."

"No. We have definite information that whether it's alive or dead, we have no search criteria left. If the ninth baby was ever born, Volescu hid the birth and the mother too well. Or the mother is hiding herself. The software—the mind game, if you will—has been very effective. We wouldn't have found any of the normal children without its creative searches. But it also knows when it has nothing more to try.

You have eight of the nine. Three of them have the syndrome, five are normal."

"What about Volescu?" asked Petra. "Can we drug him?"

"Why not torture?" said Rackham. "No, Petra. We can't. Because we need him."

"For what? His virus?"

"We already have his virus. And it doesn't work. It's a bust. Failure. Dead end. Volescu knew it, too. He just enjoyed tormenting us with the thought that he had endangered the entire world."

"So what do you need him for?" demanded Petra.

"We need him to work on the cure for Bean and the babies."

"Oh, right," said Bean. "You're going to turn him loose in a lab."

"No," said Rackham. "We're going to put him in space, on an asteroid-based research station, closely supervised. He's been tried and is under sentence of death for terrorism, kidnapping, and murder—the murders of your brothers, Bean."

"There's no death sentence," said Bean.

"There is in military court in space," said Rackham. "He knows he's alive as long as he's making progress on finding a legitimate cure for you and the babies. Eventually, our team of co-researchers will know everything he knows. When we don't need him anymore . . ."

"I don't want him killed," said Bean.

"No," said Petra. "I want him killed *slowly.*"

"He might be evil," said Bean, "but I wouldn't exist if not for him."

"There was a day," said Rackham, "when that would be the biggest crime you charged him with."

"I've had a good life," said Bean. "Strange and hard sometimes. But I've had a lot of happiness." He squeezed Petra's knee. "I don't want you to kill him."

"You saved your own life—*from* him," said Petra. "You owe him nothing."

"It doesn't matter," said Rackham. "We have no intention

of killing him. When he's no longer useful, he goes into a colony ship. He's not a violent man. He's very smart. He could be useful in understanding alien biota. It would be a waste of a resource to kill him. And there's no colony that will have equipment he could adapt to create anything . . . biologically destructive."

"You've thought of everything," said Petra.

"Again," said Bean, "you could have told us this over the telephone."

"I didn't want to," said Rackham.

"The I.F. doesn't send a team like this or a man like you on an errand like this just because you didn't want to use the phone."

"We want to send you now," said Rackham.

"In case you haven't been listening to yourself," said Petra, "there's a war on."

Bean and Rackham ignored her. They just looked at each other for a long time.

And then Petra saw that Bean's eyes were welling up with tears. That didn't happen very often.

"What's happening, Bean?"

Bean shook his head. To Rackham he said, "Do you have them?"

Rackham took an envelope out of his inside jacket pocket and handed it to Bean. He opened the envelope, removed a thin sheaf of papers, and handed them to Petra.

"It's our divorce decree," said Bean.

Petra understood at once. He wasn't taking her with him. He was leaving her behind with the normal children. He was going to take the three children with the syndrome out into space with him. He wanted her to be free to remarry.

"You are my husband," she said. She tore the papers in half.

"Those are copies," said Bean. "The divorce has legal force whether you like it or not, whether you sign them or not. You're no longer a married woman."

"Why? Because you think I'm going to *remarry?*"

Bean ignored her. "But all the children have been certified as legitimately ours. They aren't bastards, they aren't orphans, they aren't adopted. They're the children of divorced parents, and you have custody of five of them, and I have custody of three. If the ninth one is ever found, then you'll have custody."

"That ninth one is the only reason I'm listening to this," said Petra. "Because if you stay you'll die, and if we both go, then there might be a child who . . ."

But she was too angry to finish. Because when Bean planned this, he couldn't have known there'd be one child missing. He'd already *done* this and kept it secret from her for . . . for . . .

"How long have you been planning this?" asked Petra. Tears were streaming down her face, but she kept her voice steady enough to speak.

"Since we found Ramón and we knew there *were* normal children," said Bean.

"It's more complicated than that," said Rackham. "Petra, I know how hard this is for you—"

"No you don't."

"Yes I damn well do," said Rackham. "I left a family behind when I went out into space on the same kind of relativistic turnaround voyage that Bean's embarking on. I divorced my wife before I went. I have her letters to me. All the anger and bitterness. And then the reconciliation. And then a long letter near the end of her life. Telling me about how she and her second husband were happy. And the children turned out well. And she still loved me. I wanted to kill myself. But I did what I had to do. So don't tell me I don't know how hard this is."

"You had no choice," said Petra. "But I could go with him. We could take all the children and—"

"Petra," said Bean. "If we had conjoined twins, we'd separate them. Even if one of them was sure to die, we'd separate them, so that at least one of them could lead a normal life."

Petra's tears were out of control now. Yes, she understood his reasoning. The children without the syndrome could have a normal life on Earth. Why should they spend their childhood confined to a starship, when they could have the normal chance of happiness?

"Why couldn't you at least let me be part of the decision?" said Petra, when she finally got control of her voice. "Why did you cut me out? Did you think I wouldn't understand?"

"I was selfish," said Bean. "I didn't want to spend our last months together arguing about it. I didn't want you to be grieving for me and Ender and Bella the whole time you were with us. I wanted to take these past few months with me when I go. It was my last wish, and I knew you'd grant it to me, but the only way I could *have* that wish is if you didn't know. So now, Petra, I ask you. Let me have these months without you knowing what was going to happen."

"You already have them. You stole them!"

"Yes, so now I ask you. Please. Let me have them. Let me know that you forgive me for it. That you give them to me freely, now, after the fact."

Petra couldn't forgive him. Not now. Not yet.

But there was no later.

She buried her face in his chest and held him and wept.

While she cried, Rackham spoke on, calmly. "Only a handful of us know what's really happening. And on Earth, outside of the I.F., only Peter will know. Is that clear? So this divorce document is absolutely secret. As far as anyone else will know, Bean is not in space, he died in the raid on Tehran. And he took no babies with him. There were never more than five. And two of the normal babies that we've recovered are also named Andrew and Bella. As far as anyone knows, you will still have all the children you ever did."

Petra pulled back from her embrace of Bean and glared savagely at Rackham. "You mean you're not even going to let me grieve for my babies? No one will know what I've lost except you and *Peter Wiggin*?"

"Your parents," said Rackham, "have seen Ender and Bella. It's your choice whether to tell them the truth, or to stay away from them until enough time has passed that they can't tell that there's been a change."

"Then I'll tell them."

"Think about it first," said Rackham. "It's a heavy burden."

"Don't presume to teach me how to love my parents," said Petra. "You know and I know that at every point in this you've decided solely on the basis of what's good for the Ministry of Colonization and the International Fleet."

"We'd like to think we've found the solution that's best for everyone."

"I'm supposed to have a funeral for my husband, when I know he's not dead, and that's best for me?"

"I will be dead," said Bean, "for all intents and purposes. Gone and never coming back. And you'll have children to raise."

"And yes, Petra," said Rackham, "there *is* a wider consideration. Your husband is already a legendary figure. If it's known that he's still alive, then everything Peter does will be ascribed to him. There'll be legends about how he's going to return. About how the most brilliant graduate of Battle School really planned out everything Peter did."

"This is about *Peter?*"

"This is about trying to get the world put together peacefully, permanently. This is about abolishing nations and the wars that just won't stop as long as people can pin their hopes on great heroes."

"Then you should send *me* away, too, or tell people *I'm* dead. I was in Ender's Jeesh."

"Petra, you chose your path. You married. You had children. Bean's children. You decided that's what you wanted more than anything else. We've respected that. You have Bean's children. And you've had Bean almost as long as you would have had him if we had never intervened. Because he's dying. Our best guess is that he wouldn't make it another six months without going out into space and living weightlessly. We've done everything according to *your* choice."

"It's true that they didn't actually requisition our babies," Bean said.

"So live with your choices, Petra," said Rackham. "Raise these babies. And help us do what we can to help Peter save the world from itself. The story of Bean's heroic death in the service of the FPE will help with that."

"There'll be legends anyway," said Petra. "Plenty of dead heroes have legends."

"Yes, but if they *know* we put him in a starship and trundled him off into space, it won't be just a legend, will it? Serious people would believe in it, not just the normal lunatics."

"So how will you even keep up the research project?" demanded Petra. "If everybody thinks the only people who need the cure are dead or never existed, why will it continue?"

"Because a few people in the I.F. and ColMin *will* know. And they'll be in contact with Bean by ansible. He'll be called home when the cure is found."

They flew on then, as Petra tried to deal with what they'd told her. Bean held her most of the time, even when her anger surged now and then and she was furious with him.

Terrible scenarios kept playing themselves out in her mind, and at the risk of giving Bean ideas, she said to him, "Don't give up, Julian Delphiki. Don't decide that there's never going to be a cure and end the voyage. Even if you think your life is worthless, you have my babies out there too. Even if the voyage goes on so long that you really are dying, remember that these children are like you. Survivors. As long as somebody doesn't actually kill them."

"Don't worry," said Bean. "If I had the slightest tendency toward suicide, we would never have met. And I would never do anything to endanger my own children. I'm only taking this voyage for them. Otherwise, I'd be content to die in your arms here on Earth."

She wept again for a while after that, and then she had to feed Ramón again, and then she insisted on feeding Ender and Bella herself, spooning the food into their mouths because when would she ever get a chance to do it again? She tried to memorize every moment of it, even though she knew she couldn't. Knew that memory would fade. That these babies would become only a distant dream to her. That her arms would remember best the babies she held the longest—the children she would keep with her.

The only one she had borne from her own body would be gone.

But she didn't cry while she was feeding them. That would have been a waste. Instead she played with them and talked to them and teased them to talk back to her. "I know your first word isn't going to be too long from now. How about a little 'mama' right now, you lazy baby?"

It was only after the plane had landed in Rotterdam, and Bean was supervising the nurses as they carried the babies down onto the tarmac, that Petra stayed back in the plane with Rackham, long enough to put her worst nightmare into words.

"Don't think that I'm not aware of how easy it would be, Mazer Rackham, for this fake death of Bean's not to be a fake at all. For all we know there is no ship, there is no project to find a cure, and Volescu is going to be executed. The threat of this new species replacing your precious human race would be gone then. And even the widow would be silent about what you've done to her husband and children, because she'll think he's off in space somewhere, traveling at lightspeed, instead of dead on a battlefield in Iran."

Rackham looked as if she had slapped him. "Petra," he said. "What do you think we *are?*"

"What you are," said Petra, "is *not denying it.*"

"I deny it," said Rackham. "There *is* a ship. We *are* seeking a cure. We *will* call him home."

Then she saw the tears streaming down his cheeks.

"Petra," said Rackham, "don't you understand that we

love you children? All of you? We already had to send Ender away. We're sending them all away, except for you. *Because* we love you. *Because* we don't want any harm to you."

"So why are you leaving *me* here?"

"Because of your babies, Petra. Because even though they don't have the syndrome, they're also Bean's babies. He's the only one who had no hope of a normal life. But thanks to you, he had one. However briefly, he got to be a husband and a father and have a family. Don't you know how much we love you for giving him that? As God is my witness, Petra, we would never harm Bean, not for any *cause* and certainly not for our *convenience*. Whatever you think we are, you're wrong. Because you children are the only children we have."

She wasn't going to feel sorry for *him*. It was her turn right now. So she pushed past him and went down the stairs and took the hand of her husband and followed the nurses that were carrying her children toward a closed van.

There were five new children that she hadn't met yet, waiting for her and Bean. Her life hadn't ended yet, even though it felt like she was dying with every breath she took.

22

RUMORS OF WAR

From: Graff%pilgrimage@colmin.gov
To: PeterWiggin%private@FreePeopleOfEarth.fp.gov
Re: debriefing

Attached are the data to the division level, including names of commanders. But the gist is simple enough: Russia is gambling everything on the quiescence of eastern Europe. They're all supposed to be terrified of a newly aggressive Russia. This is the move they thought they were going to be able to make when they had Achilles with them and kidnapped all of Ender's Jeesh.

What you can tell them, with authority, is this: Russia IS newly aggressive, they ARE bent on proving they're a world power again. They're dangerous. But:

1. They don't have Vlad. They have his plan, but can't adapt to any changes.

2. We have Vlad's plan, so we can anticipate every move they make while they follow it, and the generals in command are going to follow it with religious devotion. Expect

no flexibility, even after they know we have it. Vlad knows the men in command. In the Russian military these days, any leaders with the imagination to improvise don't rise to the level where it will matter.

3. Han Tzu is being provided with their plan, so their main army will meet with disaster in the East.

4. They stripped their western defenses. A fast-moving army, competently led, should take St. Petersburg in a walk and Moscow in a week. That's Vlad's opinion. Bean has been over this information and concurs. He suggests you take Petra out of Armenia and put her in charge of the campaign in Russia.

When Suriyawong got the word from Peter, he was ready. Prime Minister Paribatra and Minister of Defense Ambul had kept their affiliation with the FPE secret for just this occasion. Now, armed with Burmese and Chinese permission to pass through their territory, the Thai army was going to have the chance to face the Indians who had begun all this nonsense with their vicious, unprovoked invasion of Burma and Thailand.

The troops went by train all the way into Chinese territory; Chinese trucks with Chinese drivers ferried them the rest of the way to the spots that Suriyawong had mapped out as soon as Peter suggested it as a contingency. At the time, Peter had said, "It's a remote possibility, because it requires incredible stupidity on the part of some nonstupid people, but be ready."

Ready to defend China. That was the irony.

But Han Tzu's China was not the China that had embraced Achilles's treacherous plan and crushed everyone, carrying away the entire Thai leadership and Suriyawong's parents. Han Tzu promised friendship, and Bean vouched for him. So

Suriyawong had been able to persuade his top leadership, and they had persuaded his men, that defending China was nothing more or less than a forward defense of Thailand.

"China has changed," Suriyawong told the officers, "but India has not. Once again, they're pouring over the border of a nation that believes itself to be at peace with them. This goddess they follow, Virlomi—she's just another Battle School graduate, like me. But *we* have what she doesn't have. We have Julian Delphiki's plan. And we *will* win."

Bean's plan, however, was simple enough. "The only way to end this once and for all is to make it a disaster. Like Varus's legions in the Teutoburger Wald. No guerrilla action. No chance of retreat. Virlomi alive if possible, but if she insists on dying, oblige her."

That was the plan. But Suriyawong needed no more than that. The mountainous country of southwestern China and northern Burma was ambush country. Virlomi's ill-trained troops were advancing on foot—ridiculously slowly—in three main columns, following three river valleys with three inadequate roads. Suriyawong's own plans called for a simple, classical ambush on all three routes. He hid relatively small but heavily armed contingents at the heads of the valleys, where they would be passed by the Indian troops. Then far, far down the valley, he had far larger contingents with plenty of transport to move up the valley upon command.

Then it was a matter of waiting for two things.

The first thing came on the second day of waiting. The southernmost outpost notified him that their column had entered the valley and was moving briskly. This was no surprise—they had had a much easier trip than the two northern armies.

"They're not careful about probing ahead," said the general in charge of that contingent. "Raw troops, marching blind. As I watched them, I kept thinking, this must be an attempt to deceive us. But no—they keep passing, with large gaps in the line, stragglers, and only a few regiments that put out scouts. None of them came close to finding us. They haven't put a single observer on either ridge. They're *lazy*."

When, later in the day, the other two hidden contingents reported a similar story, Suriyawong relayed the information back to Ambul. While he waited for the next triggering event, he had his lookouts make a particular point of searching for any sign that Virlomi herself was traveling with any of the three armies.

There was no mystery about it. She was traveling with the northernmost Indian army, riding in an open jeep, and the troops cheered when she passed, moving up and down the line—slowing down her own army's advance in the process, since they had to move off the road for her.

Suriyawong heard this with sadness. She had been so brilliant. Her assessment of how to undo the Chinese occupation had been dead on. Her holding action to keep the Chinese from returning to India or resupplying when the Persians and Pakistanis invaded had been of Thermopylaean proportions. The difference was that Virlomi was more careful than the Spartans—she had already covered all the back roads. Nothing got past her Indian guerrillas.

She was beautiful and wise and mysterious. Suriyawong had rescued her once, and cooperated in the little drama that made the rescue possible—and played upon her reputation as a goddess.

But in those days, she had known she was just acting.

Or had she? Perhaps it was her intimations of godhood that had caused her to reject Suriyawong's overtures of friendship and more-than-friendship. The blow had been painful, but he wasn't angry with her. She had an aura of greatness about her that he had seen in no other commander, not even Bean.

The troop deployments she was showing here were not what he would have expected from the woman who had been so careful of her men's lives in all her previous actions. Nor from the woman who had wept over the bodies of the victims of Muslim atrocities. Didn't she see that she was leading the soldiers to disaster? Even if there were no ambush in these mountains—though it was absolutely predictable that there would be—an army this ragged could be destroyed at will by a trained and determined enemy.

As Euripides wrote, Whom the gods would destroy, they first make mad.

Ambul, knowing how Suriyawong felt about Virlomi, had offered to let him command only that part of the army that wouldn't face her directly. But Suri refused. "Remember what Bean said Ender taught. 'To know the enemy well enough to defeat him requires that you know him so well you can't help but love him.'"

Well, Suriyawong already loved this enemy. And knew her. Well enough that he even thought he understood this madness.

She wasn't vain. She never thought she'd survive. But all her plans kept succeeding. She couldn't believe that it was because of her own ability. So she thinks that she has some kind of divine favor.

But it *was* her abilities and training, and she isn't using them now, and her army is going to pay for it.

Suriyawong had left plenty of room for the Indians to move down the valleys before they reached the ambush. They weren't traveling at the same pace, so he had to make sure all three ambushes were sprung at the same time. He had to make sure all three armies passed through the top of the trap in their entirety. His instructions to his men were clear: Accept the surrender of any soldier who throws down his weapon and puts up his hands. Kill anyone who doesn't. But let no one out of the valley. *All* killed or captured.

And Virlomi alive, if she lets us.

Please let us, Virlomi. Please let us bring you back to reality. Back to *life*.

Han Tzu went among his troops. There was no nonsense about an invisible emperor. The soldiers of the Chinese army had chosen him and sustained his authority. He was theirs, and they would see him often, sharing their privations, listening to them, explaining to them.

It was what he had learned from Ender. If you give orders and explain nothing, you might get obedience, but you'll get no creativity. If you tell them your purpose, then when your original plan is shown to be faulty, they'll find another way to achieve your goal. Explaining to your men doesn't weaken their respect for you, it proves your respect for *them*.

So Han Tzu explained, chatted, pitched in and helped, shared the meals of common soldiers, laughed at their jokes, listened to their complaints. One soldier had complained about how no one could sleep on ground like this. Han Tzu promptly took over the man's tent and slept in it himself, exactly as it was, while the man took Han Tzu's tent. In the morning, the man swore that Han Tzu's bed was the worst one in the army, and Han Tzu thanked him for his first good night's sleep in weeks. The story made its way through the army before nightfall.

Han Tzu's army did not love him any more than Virlomi's loved her. And there was no hint of worship in it. The key difference was that Han Tzu had worked to train this army, had made sure that it was as well equipped as possible, and they knew the stories about the last war, when Han Tzu had constantly warned his superiors about all their mistakes before they made them. The belief was that if Han Tzu had been emperor all along, they would not have lost the lands they conquered.

What they didn't understand was that if Han Tzu had been their emperor, there would have been no conquests to lose. Because Achilles would have been arrested the moment he entered China and turned over to the I.F., under whose authority he had been confined to a mental hospital. There would have been no invasion of India and southeast Asia, only a holding action to block the Indian invasion of Burma and Thailand.

A real warrior hates war, Han Tzu well understood. He had seen how devastated Ender was when he learned that the last game, the final exam, had been the real war, and that his enemy had been utterly destroyed by Ender's victory.

So his men trusted him as Han Tzu kept retreating, farther and farther into China, moving from one strong position to another, but never allowing his army to engage with the Russian invaders.

He heard what the men said, the questions they asked. His answers were honest enough. "The farther they come, the longer their supply lines." "We want them so deep inside China that they can't get home again." "Our army grows the deeper we move back into China, and theirs shrinks, as they have to leave men behind to guard their route."

And when they asked him about the rumors of a huge Indian army invading in the south, Han Tzu only smiled and said, "The madwoman? The only Indian who ever conquered China was Gautama Buddha, and he did it with teachings, not artillery."

What he couldn't tell them was that they were waiting.

For Peter Wiggin.

———

Peter Wiggin stood in front of the microphones in Helsinki. Beside him stood the heads of government of Finland, Estonia, and Latvia.

Aides were on secure cellphones connected to diplomats in Bangkok, Yerevan, Beijing, and many capitals in eastern Europe.

Peter smiled at the gathered reporters.

"At the request of the governments of Armenia and China, both of which were the victims of simultaneous unprovoked aggression by Russia, India, and the Muslim League of Caliph Alai, the Free People of Earth have decided to intervene.

"We are joined in this effort by many new allies, many of which have agreed to hold plebiscites to determine whether or not to ratify the Constitution of the FPE.

"Emperor Han Tzu of China assures us that his armies are capable of dealing with the combined Russian and Turkish forces that are now operating well within the Chinese border in the north.

"In the south, Burma and China have opened their borders to safe passage for an army led by our old friend General Suriyawong. Right now, in Bangkok, Prime Minister Paribatra is holding a press conference to announce that Thailand will hold a plebiscite on ratification, and that as of this moment, the Thai Army is regarded as being under the provisional command of the FPE.

"In Armenia, where it is not possible to hold a press conference right now because of the exigencies of war, a nation under attack has turned to the FPE for help and leadership. I have placed the Armenian military under the direct command of Julian Delphiki, where they are resisting unprovoked Turkish and Russian aggression and have carried the war deep inside Muslim territory, in Tabriz and Tehran.

"And here in eastern Europe, where Finland, Estonia, Latvia, Lithuania, Slovakia, Czechland, and Bulgaria had already joined the FPE, we are joined by our new allies Poland, Rumania, Hungary, Serbia, Austria, Greece, and Belarus. They have all repudiated the Warsaw Pact, which never obligated them to join in an offensive war in any event.

"Under the command of Petra Delphiki, the combined allied armies are already making rapid progress toward capturing key targets inside Russia. They have met little resistance so far, but they are prepared to deal with any forces the Russians care to throw against them.

"We call upon the aggressors—Russia, India, and the Muslim League—to lay down their arms and accept an immediate ceasefire. If this offer is not accepted within the next twelve hours, then a ceasefire will only be accepted by us upon our terms and at a time of our choosing. The enemies of peace can expect to lose all the forces they have committed to this immoral war.

"I would now like to play for you a video that was recently recorded at a safe haven. In case you don't recognize him, since the Russians have kept him under wraps for many years now, the speaker is Vladimir Denisovitch Porotchkot, a citizen of Belarus who until several days ago was kept against his will in the service of a foreign power, Russia. You may also remember him as one of the team of young warriors who defeated the enemy that threatened the existence of the human race."

Peter stepped away from the microphone. The room was darkened; the screenwall came alive.

There stood Vlad, in front of what looked like an ordinary office in an ordinary room on Earth. Only Peter knew that this was recorded in space—in the old Battle School space station, as a matter of fact, which was now the Ministry of Colonization.

"I offer my apologies to the people of Armenia and China, whose borders were violated and citizens were killed by Russians who were using plans I created. I assumed that the plans were for contingency only, in response to aggression. I did not know that they would actually be used, and without the slightest provocation. As soon as I understood that this was how my work was to be used, I escaped from Russian custody and am now in a safe place, where I can finally speak the truth.

"It came to my knowledge just before I left my captivity in Moscow that the leaders of Russia, India, and the Muslim League have divided up the world among them. To India will go all of southeast Asia and most of China. To Russia will go part of China and all of eastern and northern Europe. To the Muslim League will go all of Africa and the western European countries with large Muslim populations.

"I repudiate this plan. I repudiate this war. I refuse to let my work be used to enslave innocent people who did no harm and do not deserve to live under tyranny.

"Therefore I have provided to the Free People of Earth a complete knowledge of all the plans I drew up for Russian use. There is no movement they are now making which is not completely anticipated by the forces acting in concert with the FPE.

"And I urge the people of Belarus, my true homeland, to vote to join the Free People of Earth. Who else has stood relentlessly against aggression and in favor of freedom and respect for every nation and every citizen?

"As for me—my talents and training are entirely geared toward warfare. I will no longer put my abilities at the service of any nation. I gave my childhood to fighting an alien enemy that was trying to destroy the human race. I did not fight off the Buggers so that millions of humans could be slaughtered and hundreds of millions conquered and enslaved.

"I am on strike. I urge every other graduate of Battle School except those who serve the FPE to join me in that strike. Do not plan war, do not wage war, except to help the Hegemon Peter Wiggin to destroy the armies of the aggressors.

"And to the common soldiers I say, Do not obey your officers. Surrender at the first opportunity. Your obedience makes war possible. Take responsibility for your own actions and join me in my strike! If you surrender to the forces of the FPE, they will make every effort to spare your life and, at the earliest opportunity, to return you to your families.

"Again, I beg the forgiveness of those whose lives were lost because of plans I drew. Never again."

The video ended.

Peter strode back to the microphone. "The Free People of Earth and our allies are now at war with the aggressors. We have already told you everything we can say without compromising ongoing military operations. There will be no questions."

He walked away from the microphone.

Bean stood in the midst of the small wheeled beds that held his five normal children. The ones he would never see again, once he left them today.

Mazer Rackham put a hand on his shoulder. "It's time to go, Julian."

"Five of them," said Bean. "How will Petra manage?"

"She'll have help," said Rackham. "The real question is, how will *you* manage on that messenger ship? They'll outnumber you three to one."

"As I can attest, children with my particular genetic defect become self-sufficient at a very early age," said Bean.

He touched the bed of the baby named Andrew. The same name as the eldest of the siblings. But this Andrew was a normal infant. Not undersized for his age.

And this second Bella. She would lead a normal life. As would Ramón and Julian and Petra.

"If these five are normal," Bean said to Rackham, "then the ninth child—it's most likely . . . defective?"

"*If* the odds are fifty-fifty of the traits getting passed on, and we know that five of the nine didn't get them, then it stands to reason that the missing one has a higher likelihood of having the traits. Though as any expert on probability would tell you, the probability for each child was fifty-fifty, and the distribution of the syndrome among the other infants will have no effect on the outcome for the ninth."

"Maybe it's better if Petra never finds . . . the last one."

"My guess, Bean, is that there is no ninth baby. Not every implantation works. There could easily have been an early miscarriage. That would be a complete explanation of the lack of any record that was traceable by the software."

"I don't know whether to be comforted or appalled that you would think I'd find that the death of one my children might be comforting."

Rackham grimaced. "You know what I meant."

Bean took an envelope from his pocket and laid it under Ramón. "Tell the nurses to leave that envelope there, even if he leaks and wets all over the thing."

"Of course," said Rackham. "For what it's worth, Bean, your pension will also be invested, like Ender's, and run by the same software."

"Don't," said Bean. "Give it all to Petra. She'll need it, with five babies to raise. Maybe six someday."

"What about when you come home, when they find the cure?"

Bean looked at him as if he were crazy. "Do you really think that will happen?"

"If you *don't,* why are you going?"

"Because it might," said Bean. "And if we stay here, early death is certain for all four of us. *If* the cure is found, and *if* we come home, then we can talk about a pension. I'll tell you what. After Petra dies, after these five all grow old and die, then start paying my pension into a fund controlled by that investor software."

"You'll be back before then."

"No," said Bean. "No, that's . . . no. Once we're ten years out—and there's no hope of a cure before that—then even if you find the cure, don't call us back until . . . well, until Petra would be dead before we got here. Do you understand? Because if she remarries—and I want her to—I don't want her to have to face me. To face me looking as I do right now, the boy she married—the *giant* boy. This is cruel enough, what we're doing now. I'm not going to cause her one last torment before she dies."

"Why don't you let her decide?"

"It's not her choice," said Bean. "Once we leave, we're dead. Gone forever. She can never have back the life that will have been lost. But I'm not worried, Mazer. There *is* no cure."

"You know that?"

"I know Volescu. He doesn't want to find a cure. He doesn't think it's a disease. He thinks it's the hope of humanity. And except for Anton, nobody else knows enough to proceed. It was an illegal field of study for too long. It's still tainted. The methods Volescu used, the whole process surrounding Anton's Key—nobody's going to turn that key again, and therefore you're not going to have any scientists who know what they're doing in that area. The project will have less and less importance for your successors. Someday—not too long from now—somebody will look at the budget item and say, We're paying for *what?* And the project will die."

"It won't happen," said Mazer. "The Fleet doesn't forget its own."

Bean laughed. "You don't get it, do you? Peter is going to succeed. The world is going to be united. International war will end. And along with it, the sense of loyalty among the military will also die. There'll just be . . . colony ships and trading ships and scientific research institutes that will be scandalized at the thought of wasting money doing a personal favor for a soldier who lived a hundred years ago. Or two hundred. Or three hundred."

"The funding won't be contingent," said Rackham. "We're funding it using the same investment software. It's really good, Bean. This is going to be one of the best-funded projects ever, in a few years."

Bean laughed. "Mazer, you just don't understand how far people will go to get their hands on money that they think is being wasted on pure research. You'll see. But no, I take that back. You won't see. It'll happen after you're dead. *I'll* see. And I'll raise a glass to you, among my little children, and I'll say, Here's to you, Mazer Rackham, you foolish old optimist. You thought humans were better than they are, which is why you went to all the trouble of saving the human race a couple of times."

Mazer put an arm around Bean's waist and clinched tight for a moment. "Kiss the babies good-bye."

"I will not," said Bean. "Do you think I want them to have nightmares of a giant bending over them and trying to eat them?"

"*Eat* them!"

"Babies fear being eaten," said Bean. "There's a sound evolutionary reason for it, considering that in our ancestral homeland in Africa hyenas would always have been happy to carry off a human baby and eat it. I guess you've never read the child-rearing literature."

"Sounds more like Grimm's Fairy Tales."

Bean walked from bed to bed, touching each child in return. Perhaps spending a bit longer with Ramón, since he had spent so much time with him, compared to mere minutes with the others.

Then he left the room and followed Rackham out to the enclosed van that was waiting for him.

———

Suriyawong heard the report and the order: The press conference has been held; Thai participation in the FPE has been announced; now begin active operations against the enemy.

Suri timed the departure of all six contingents so that they would arrive simultaneously, more or less. He also ordered the Chinese battle choppers into position, ready to join in the battle as soon as surprise was achieved.

One of them would take him to where Virlomi would be.

If there are any gods looking out for her, thought Suriyawong, then let her live. Even if a hundred thousand soldiers die for her pride, please let her live. The good she did, the greatness in her, should count for something. The mistakes of generals can kill many thousands, but they're still mistakes. She set out for victory, not destruction. She should be punished only for her intent, not the result.

Not that her intent was all that good.

But you—you gods of war! Shiva, you destroyer!—what

was Virlomi, ever, except your servant? Will you let your servant be destroyed, solely because she was so good at her job?

———

St. Petersburg had fallen more quickly than anyone expected. The resistance hadn't even been enough to count as "token." Even the police had fled, and the Finns and Estonians ended up working to maintain public order rather than fight a determined enemy.

But that was all just a matter of reports to Petra, who was improvising her way across Russia. Without a huge air force, there was no way to airlift her army of Brazilians and Rwandans to Moscow. So she was bringing them in on passenger trains, carefully watching from what looked like recreational aircraft so she'd know as soon as there was any kind of problem. The heavier ordnance was being carried on the highway by big Polish and German moving vans, of the kind that plied the highways across Europe all the time, stopping only to eat and pee and visit roadside whores. Now they carried the war that the Russians had begun straight to Moscow.

If the enemy was determined, they would be able to track Petra's army's progress. After all, there was no concealing what the trains were carrying as they raced through stations without stopping and demanded that the tracks be cleared in front of them "or we'll blast you and your station and your stupid little village of baby-killing Russians to smithereens!" All rhetoric—a single telephone pole dropped across the tracks here and there would have slowed them down considerably. And they weren't about to start killing civilians.

But the Russians didn't know that. Peter had told her that Vlad was sure the commanders who were left in Moscow would panic. "They're runners, not fighters. That doesn't mean nobody will fight—but it will be local people. Scattered. Wherever you meet resistance, just go around. If the Russian army in China is stopped and international vids show Moscow and St. Petersburg in your hands, either the government will sue for peace or the people will revolt. Or both."

Well, it had worked for the Germans in France in 1940. Why not here?

The loss of Vlad had a devastating effect on Russian morale. Especially because the Russians all knew that Julian Delphiki himself had planned the counterattack, and Petra Arkanian was leading the army that was "sweeping across Russia."

More like "chugging across Russia."

At least it wasn't winter.

———

Han Tzu gave the orders, and his retreating troops moved to their positions. He had timed his retreat exactly right, to lure the Russians to the exact spot he needed them to reach at the exact time he wanted them there. Well ahead of Vlad's original schedule—the only deviation from his plan.

The satellite information forwarded to him by Peter Wiggin assured him that the Turks had withdrawn westward, heading toward Armenia. As if they could get there in time to make any difference at all! Caliph Alai had apparently not solved the perpetual problem of Muslim armies. Unless they were under iron control, they were easily distracted. Alai was supposed to *be* that control. It made Han Tzu wonder if Alai was even in command anymore.

No matter. Han Tzu's objective was the huge, overextended, weary Russian Army that was still rigidly following Vlad's plan despite the fact that their pincer movements had encountered an empty Beijing, with no Chinese forces to crush or Chinese government to seize. And despite the fact that panicky reports must be coming from Moscow as they kept hearing rumors of Petra's advance without knowing where she was.

The Russian commander he was facing was not wrong to persist in his campaign. Petra's advance on Moscow was ultimately cosmetic, as Petra no doubt knew: designed to cause panic, but without sufficient force to hold any objective for long.

In the south, too, Suri's Thai army would do important work, but India's army wasn't a serious threat in the first place; Bean, in Armenia, had drawn off the Turkish armies, but they could easily come back.

Everything came down to this battle.

As far as Han Tzu was concerned, it had better not be a battle at all.

They were in the wheatfield country near Jinan. Vlad's plan assumed that the Chinese would seize the high ground to the southeast of the Hwang Ho and dispute the river crossing. Therefore the Russians were prepared with portable bridges and rafts to move across the river at unexpected places and then surround the supposed Chinese redoubt.

And, just as Vlad's plan predicted, Han Tzu's forces were indeed gathered on that high ground, and were shelling the approaching Russian troops with reassuring ineffectiveness. The Russian commander had to feel confident. Especially when he found the bridges over the Hwang Ho ineptly "destroyed," so repairs were quick.

Han Tzu couldn't afford to have a grinding battle, matching gun for gun, tank for tank. Too much materiel had been lost in the previous wars, and while Han's soldiers were battle-hardened veterans, and the Russian army hadn't fought in years, Han's inability to get his army back to full material strength in the short time he had been emperor would inevitably be decisive. Han was not going to use human waves to overwhelm the Russians with numbers. He couldn't afford to waste this army. He had to keep it intact to deal with the much more dangerous Muslim armies, should they get their act together and join in the war.

The Russian drones were easily a match for the Chinese; both commanders would have an accurate picture of the battlefield. This was wheatfield country, perfect for the Russian tanks. Nothing Han Tzu did could possibly surprise his en-

emy. Vlad's plan was going to work. The Russian commander had to be sure of it.

His forces that had been concealed behind the Russian advance now reported that the last of the Russians had passed
the checkpoints without realizing what the small red tags on
fences, bushes, trees, and signposts signified.

For the next forty minutes, Han Tzu's army had only one
task: To confine the Russian army between those little red
flags and the highlands across the Hwang, while none of the
Chinese army strayed into that zone.

Didn't the Russians notice that every single civilian had
been evacuated? That not a civilian vehicle was to be found?
That the houses had been emptied of belongings?

Hyrum Graff had once taught a class in which he told
them that God would teach them how to destroy their enemy, using the forces of nature. His prime example was the
way God used a flood of the Red Sea to destroy Pharaoh's
chariots.

The little red flags were the highwater mark.

Han Tzu gave the order for the dam to be blown up. It
would take the wall of water forty minutes to reach the Russian army and destroy it.

———

The Armenian soldiers had achieved all their objectives.
They had forced a panicky Iranian government to demand
the recall of their troops from India. Soon an overwhelming
force would arrive and they would all be lost.

They thought, when the black choppers came flying low
over the city, that their time had come.

Instead, the soldiers that emerged from the choppers
were Thais in the uniform of the FPE. The original strike
force trained by Bean and led in so many raids by him or
Suriyawong.

Then Bean himself stepped out of the chopper. "Sorry I'm
late," he said.

Within minutes, the FPE troops had secured the perimeter and the Armenian troops were embarking on the choppers. "You're going to be taking the long way home," one of the Thais said, laughing.

Bean made a big deal about how he was going to go down the hill to see how things were going with the forward defense. The Armenians watched as Bean ducked to go through the door of a half-bombed-out building. A few moments later, the building blew up. Nothing left standing. No walls, no chimney. And no Bean.

The chopper took off then. The Armenians were so happy to have been rescued that it was hard to remember the terrible news they were going to have to take to Petra Arkanian. Her husband was dead. They'd seen it. There was no way anyone in that building could have survived.

23

COLONIST

From: BlackDog%Salaam@IComeAnon.com
To: Graff%pilgrimage@colmin.gov
Encrypted using code: *******
Decrypted using code: *********
Re: Vlad's farewell message

Why I'm writing to you from hiding should be obvious; I'll give you the detailed story at a later date.

I want to take you up on your invitation, if it's still open. I learned recently that while I'm a real whiz at military strategy, I'm a dimwit about what motivates my own people—even those I thought were closest to me. For instance, who would have guessed that they would hate a modernizing, consensus-building black African Caliph a lot more than they hated a dictatorial, idolatrous, immodest Hindu woman?

I was going to simply disappear from history, and was feeling quite sorry for myself in my exile, while grieving for a dear friend who gave his life to save mine in Hyderabad, when I realized that the news reports that endlessly replayed Vlad's message were showing me what I needed to do.

So I've made arrangements to make a vid inside a nearby mosque. In a country where I'll be safe showing my face, so don't worry. I'm not going to let this one be released through you or Peter—that would discredit it immediately. It's going to move out through Muslim channels only.

The thing I realized is this: I may have lost the support of the military, but I'm still Caliph. It's not just a political office, it's also a religious one. And not one of those clowns has the authority to depose me.

Meanwhile, I know now what they called me behind my back. "Black dog." They're going to hear those words back from me, you can be sure.

When the vid is released, then I'll let you know where I am. If you're still willing to take me.

Randi watched the news reports avidly. It seemed so hopeful at first, when they heard that Julian Delphiki had been killed in Iran. Maybe the enemies hunting her baby would be crushed, and she'd be able to come out in the open and proclaim that she was carrying Achilles's son and heir.

But then she realized: the evil in this world would not die just because a few of Achilles's enemies were killed or defeated. They had done too good a job of demonizing him. If they knew who her son was, he would at least be scrutinized and tested constantly; at worst, they'd take him away from her. Or kill him. They'd stop at nothing to erase Achilles's legacy from the earth.

Randi stood by her son's little traveling bed in the former motel room that now was as cheap a one-room hot-plate apartment as northern Virginia offered. A traveling bed was all he needed. He was so small.

His birth had taken her by surprise. Months too early. And

he came so fast. She couldn't get to a hospital. Not that they would have taken her. She was in the midst of changing her identity. She had no health insurance.

But because he was so small, the birth was easy. He just . . . came out. And small as he was, he didn't have any problems. He didn't even look like one of those premature babies, the ones who looked so . . . fetal. Fishlike. Not her boy. He was beautiful, completely normal looking. Just . . . small.

Small and brilliant. It almost frightened her sometimes. He had said his first word just a couple of days ago. "Mama," of course—who else did he know? And when she spoke to him, explained things to him, told him about his father, he seemed to be listening intently. He seemed to understand. Was that possible?

Of course it was. Achilles's child would be wiser than normal. And if he was small, well, Achilles himself had been born with a twisted foot. An abnormal body to contain extraordinary gifts.

Secretly, she had named the baby Achilles Flandres II. But she was careful. She didn't write that name anywhere but in her heart. Instead the birth certificate called him Randall Firth. She was going by the name Nichelle Firth now. The real Nichelle Firth was a retarded woman in a special school where she had worked as an aide. Randi looked old enough, she knew, to pass for the right age—being on the run and working so hard and worrying all the time gave her a kind of tired look that aged her. But what did she care about vanity? She wasn't trying to attract a man. She knew men well enough to know that none of them would want to marry a woman only to have her spend all her care on another man's baby.

So she made herself up only enough to be hirable in decent jobs that didn't require a long resume. They'd say, Where have you worked before, and she'd say, Nothing since college, they wouldn't even remember me, I was a stay-at-home mom, but my husband wasn't a sleep-at-home guy, so here I am, no resume except my baby's healthy and my house is clean and I know how to work like my life depended on it cause now it does. That line got her hired anywhere she bothered to apply. She'd never be an executive but she didn't want to be. Just put in her hours, get "Randall" out of daycare, and then talk to him, sing to him, and study about how to be a good mother and raise a healthy, confident baby who would have the strength of character to overcome the bigotry against his father and take on the whole world.

But these wars, and Peter Wiggin's hideous face on the camera, announcing *this* nation was now in the FPE and *that* nation was allied with the FPE, it worried her. She couldn't hide forever. Her fingerprints couldn't be changed, and there was that shoplifting arrest when she was in college. It was so stupid. She really had sort of forgotten that she took the thing. If she'd remembered she would have changed her mind and paid for it, like the other times. But she forgot and they stopped her outside the store so she had actually done the theft, they said, and she wasn't a minor so she got the whole arrest treatment. They let her off, but her prints were in the system. So someday somebody would know who she really was. And the man who approached her, who gave her Achilles's baby—how could she be sure he wouldn't tell them? Between what he told them and her fingerprints, they could find her no matter how often she changed her name.

That was when she decided that for the first time in human history, when a person was not safe anywhere on Earth, he had somewhere else to go.

Why should her little Achilles Flandres II be raised here, in hiding, with bloodthirsty monsters out to kill him in order to punish his father for being better than them? When instead he could grow up on a clean new colony world, where no one would care that the baby wasn't really hers or that he was small, if he was smart and worked hard and she raised him right? They promised that there would be trade back and forth between colony worlds, and visits from starships.

When the time was right for Achilles II to claim his heritage, his legacy, his *throne*, she would bring him aboard one of those starships and they'd come back to Earth.

She had studied the relativistic effects of star travel. It might be as much as a hundred years or more—fifty years out and fifty years back, say—but it would only be three or four years of voyaging. So all of Achilles's enemies would be long since dead. Nobody would bother spreading vicious lies about him anymore. The world would be ready to hear of him with fresh ears, with open minds.

She couldn't leave him alone in the apartment. It was a drizzly afternoon, though. Was it worth risking him catching cold?

She bundled him well and carried him in a sling in front of her. He was so *small*, it felt like he was lighter than her purse. Her umbrella shielded them both from the rain. They'd be fine.

It was a long walk to the Metro station, but that was the best—and the driest—way to get to the liaison office of the Ministry of Colonization, where she could sign up. That would be a risk, of course. They might fingerprint her. They might run a check. But . . . surely they knew that many people would choose to go on a colony ship because they needed to get away from their old lives. And if they found that she had changed her name, the shoplifting arrest might explain it. She had been drifting into crime and . . . what would they assume? Drugs, probably . . . but now she wanted a fresh start, under a new name.

Or maybe she should use her real name.

No, because under *that* name she had no baby. And if they questioned whether "Randall" was really hers and ran a genetic test, they'd find that he had none of her genes. They'd wonder where she had kidnapped him. He was so small they'd think he was a newborn. And the birth had been so easy, there'd been no tearing—did they have tests to determine if she had ever given birth? Nightmares, nightmares. No, she'd give them her new name and then be prepared to run if they came looking for her. What else could she do?

It was worth the risk, to get him off planet.

On the way to the Metro she walked past a mosque, but there were cops outside, directing traffic. Had there been a bombing? Those were happening in other places—Europe, she kept hearing—but not in America, surely. Not *lately*, anyway.

No, not a bombing. Just a speaker. Just . . .

"Caliph Alai." She heard someone say it, almost as if they had been speaking to her.

Caliph Alai! The one man on Earth who seemed to have the courage to stand against Peter Wiggin.

Luckily she had a scarf over her head—she looked Muslim enough for this secular town, where plenty of Muslims wore no special clothing at all. Nobody challenged her, a woman with a baby, though they did make everybody leave things like umbrellas and purses and jackets at the security counter.

She walked into the women's section of the mosque. She was surprised at how the carved and decorated latticework interfered with her ability to see what was going on in the men's part of the mosque. Apparently even liberal American mosques still thought women did not need to see the speaker for themselves. Randi had heard about such things, but the only church she had ever attended was Presbyterian and families sat together there.

There were cameras all over the men's section, so maybe the view from here was as good as most men were getting. She wasn't converting to Islam, anyway, she just wanted to catch a glimpse of Caliph Alai.

He was speaking in Common, not Arabic. She was glad of that.

"I remain Caliph, no matter where I live. I will take with me in my colony only Muslims who believe in Islam as a religion of peace. I leave behind me the bloodthirsty false Muslims who called their Caliph a black dog and tried to murder me so they could make war on their harmless neighbors.

"Here is the law of Islam, from the time of Muhammed and forever: God gives permission to go to war only when we are attacked by an enemy. As soon as a Muslim raises his hand against an enemy who has not attacked him, then he is not engaged in jihad, he has become shaitan himself. I declare that all those who plotted the invasion of China and Armenia are not Muslims and any good Muslim who finds these men must arrest them.

"From now on Muslim nations may only be governed by leaders who were freely elected. Non-Muslims may vote in these elections. It is forbidden to molest any non-Muslim, even if he used to be a Muslim, or deprive him of any of his rights, or put him at any disadvantage. And if a Muslim nation votes to join the Free People of Earth and abide by its constitution, that is permitted by God. There is no offense in it."

Randi was heartsick. This was just like Vlad's speech. A complete capitulation to Peter Wiggin's phony "ideals." They had apparently blackmailed or drugged or frightened even Caliph Alai.

She picked her way carefully over and around the woman seated and standing and leaning in the packed women's chamber. Many of them looked at her as if she were sinning by leaving; many others were looking toward Caliph Alai with love and longing.

Your love is misplaced, thought Randi. Only one man was pure in his embrace of power, and that was my Achilles.

And to one woman who glared at her with special ferocity, Randi pointed to baby Achilles's diaper and made a face. The woman at once relaxed her grimace. Of course, the baby had messed himself, a woman had to take care of her baby even before she heard the words of the Caliph.

If the Caliph cannot stand against Peter Wiggin, then there is nowhere on Earth for me to raise my son.

She walked the rest of the way to the Metro as the rain came down harder and harder. Her umbrella did its job, though, and the baby stayed dry. Then she was in the Metro station and the rain had stopped.

That's how it will be in space. All the sheltering of this baby will be needless then. I can put away the umbrella and he will have nothing to fear. And on the new world, he can walk in the open, in the light of a new sun, like the free spirit he was born to be.

When he returns to Earth, he will be a great man, towering over these moral dwarfs.

By then, Peter Wiggin will be dead, like Julian Delphiki. That's the only disappointment—that my son will never be able to face his father's murderers directly.

24

SACRIFICE

From: Mosca%Molo@FilMil.gov.ph
To: Graff%pilgrimage@colmin.gov
Re: My ticket

Just when things were getting interesting here on Earth, I keep getting this nagging feeling that you were right. I hate it when that happens.

They came to me today, excited as babies. Petra took Moscow with a ragtag army traveling by passenger train! Han Tzu wiped out the entire Russian Army without taking more than a few dozen casualties! Bean was able to decoy the Turkish forces toward Armenia and keep them from getting involved in China! And of course Bean also gets the credit for Suriyawong's victory in China—everybody wants to assign all glory to the boys and girl of Ender's Jeesh.

You know what they wanted from me?

I'm supposed to conquer Taiwan. No joke. I'm supposed to draw up the plans. Because, you see, my poor little ragtag island nation has me, Jeeshboy, and that makes them a great power! How dare those Muslim troops remain on Taiwan!

I pointed out that now that Han Tzu had won against the Russians and the Muslims probably wouldn't dare attack, he'd probably be looking to put Taiwan back in his fold. And even if he didn't, did they really think Peter Wiggin would sit idly by while the Philippines committed an act of unprovoked aggression against Taiwan?

They wouldn't listen. It was: Do as you're told, genius boy.

So what's left for me, Hyrum? (I feel so wicked calling you by your first name.) Do as Vlad did, and draw up their plans, and let them fall into their own pit? Do as Alai did and repudiate them openly and call for revolution? (That is what he did, isn't it?) Or do as Han did and stage an internal coup and become Emperor of the Philippines and Master of the Tagalog-Speaking World?

I don't want to leave my home. But there's no peace for me on Earth. I'm not sure I want the burden of running a colony. But at least I won't be drawing up blueprints for death and oppression. Just don't put me in the same colony with Alai. He thinks he's so the man because he's the successor of the Prophet.

Even the tanks had been washed downstream, some of them for kilometers. Where the Russians had been spreading out for their offensive against Han Tzu's forces on the high ground, there was nothing, not a sign that they had been there.

Not a sign that the villages and fields had been there either.

It was a muddy version of the moon. Except for a couple of deep-rooted trees, there was nothing. It would take a long time and a lot of work to restore this land.

But now there was work to do. First, they had to glean the survivors, if there were any, from the countryside downstream. Second, they had to clean up the corpses and gather up the tanks and other vehicles—and, most important, the live armaments.

And Han Tzu had to swing a large part of his army north, to retake Beijing and sweep away whatever remnants of the Russian invasion might be left behind. Meanwhile, the Turks might decide to come back.

The work of war wasn't over yet.

But the grinding, bloody campaign he had feared, the one that would tear China apart and bleed a generation to death, that had been averted. Both here in the north and in the south as well.

And then what? Emperor of China indeed. What would the people expect? Now that he had won this great victory, was he supposed to go back and subjugate the Tibetans again? Force the Turkic-speakers of Xinjiang back under the Chinese heel? Spill Chinese blood on the beaches of Taiwan to satisfy old claims that the Chinese had some inherent right to rule over the racially-Malay majority on that island? And then invade any nation that mistreated its Chinese minorities? Where would it stop? In the jungles of Papua? Back in India? Or at the old western border of Genghis's empire, the lands of the Golden Horde on the steppes of Ukraine?

What frightened him most about these scenarios was that he knew he could do it. He knew that with China he had a people with the intelligence, the vigor, the resources, and unified will—everything a ruler needed to go out into the world and make everything he saw his own. And because it was possible, there was a part of him that wanted to play it out, see where this path led.

I know where it leads, thought Han Tzu. It leads to Virlomi leading her pathetic army of half-armed volunteers to certain death. It leads to Julius Caesar bleeding to death on the floor of the Senate, muttering about how he was betrayed. It leads to Adolf and Eva dead in an underground bunker while their empire crumbles in explosions above their corpses. Or it leads to Augustus, casting about him for a successor, only to realize that it all has to be handed over to his revolting pervert of a . . . stepson? What *was* Tiberius, really? A sad statement about how empires are inevitably led. Because what rises to the top in an empire are the bureaucratic infighters, the assassins, or the warlords.

Is that what I want for my people? I became Emperor because that's how I could bring down Snow Tiger and keep him from killing me first. But China doesn't need an empire. China needs a good government. The Chinese people need to stay home and make money, or travel through the world and make even more money. They need to do science and create literature and be part of the human race.

They need to have no more of their sons die in battle. They need to have no more of them cleaning up the bodies of the enemy. They need peace.

———

The news of Bean's death spread slowly out of Armenia. It came to Petra, incredibly enough, on her cellphone in Moscow, where she was still directing her troops in the complete takeover of the city. The news of Han's devastating victory had reached her, but not the general public. She needed to be in complete control of the city before the people learned of the disaster. She needed to make sure they could contain the reaction.

It was her father on the telephone. His voice was very husky, and she knew at once what he was calling to tell her.

"The soldiers who were rescued from Tehran. They came back by way of Israel. They saw . . . Julian didn't come back with them."

Petra knew perfectly well what had happened. And, more

to the point, what Bean would have made sure people thought they had *seen* happen. But she let the scene play out, saying the lines expected of her. "They left him behind?"

"There was . . . nothing to bring back." A sob. It was good to know that her father had come to love Bean. Or maybe he only wept in pity for his daughter, already widowed, and only barely a woman. "He was caught in the explosion of a building. The whole thing was vaporized. He could not have lived."

"Thank you for telling me, Father."

"I know it's—what about the babies? Come home, Pet, we—"

"When I'm through with the war, Father, then I'll come home and grieve for my husband and care for my babies. They're in good hands right now. I love you. And Mother. I'll be all right. Good-bye."

She cut off the connection.

Several officers around her looked at her questioningly. What she had said about grieving for her husband. "This is top-secret information," she said to the officers. "It would only encourage the enemies of the Free People. But my husband was . . . he entered a building in Tehran and it blew up. No one in that building could possibly have survived."

They did not know her, these Finns, Estonians, Lithuanians, Latvians. Not well enough to say more than a heartfelt but inadequate, "I'm sorry."

"We have work to do," she said, relieving them of the responsibility to care for her. They could not know that what she was showing was not iron self-control, but cold rage. To lose your husband in war, that was one thing. But to lose him because he refused to take you with him. . . .

That was unfair. In the long run, she would have decided the same way. There was one baby unfound. And even if that baby was dead or had never existed—how did they know how many there were, except what Volescu told them?—the five normal babies shouldn't have their lives so drastically deformed. It would be like making a healthy twin spend his life in a hospital bed just because his brother was in a coma.

I would have chosen the same *if I'd had time.*

There was no time. Bean's life was too fragile already. She was losing him.

And she had known right from the start that one way or another, she would lose him. When he begged her not to marry him, when he insisted he wanted no babies, it was to avoid having her feel as she felt now.

Knowing it was her own fault, her own free choice, all for the best—it didn't ease the pain one bit. If anything, it made it worse.

So she was angry. At herself. At human nature. At the fact that she was a human and therefore had to *have* that nature whether she wanted it or not. The desire to have the babies of the best man she knew, the desire to hold on to him forever.

And the desire to go into battle and win, outwitting her enemies, cutting them off, taking all their power away from them and standing astride them in victory.

It was a terrible thing to realize about herself—that she loved the contest of war every bit as much as she missed her husband and children, so that doing the one would take her mind off the loss of the others.

———

When the gunfire began, Virlomi felt a thrill of excitement. But also a sick sense of dread. As if she knew some terrible secret about this campaign that she had not allowed herself to hear until the gunfire brought the message to her consciousness.

Almost at once, her driver tried to take her out of harm's way. But she insisted on heading toward the thick of the fighting. She could see where the enemy was gathered, in the hills on either side. She immediately recognized the tactics that were being used.

She started to issue orders. She ordered them to notify the

other two columns to withdraw up their valleys and reconnoiter. She sent her elite troops, the ones that had fought
with her for years, up the slopes to hold the enemy off while
she withdrew the rest of her troops.

But the mass of untrained soldiers were too frightened to
understand their orders or execute them under fire. Many of
them broke and ran—straight up the valley, where they
were exposed to fire. And Virlomi knew that not far behind
them would be the trailing force which they had carelessly
passed by.

All because she didn't expect Han Tzu, preoccupied with
the Russians, to be able to send a force of any size here to
the south.

She kept reassuring her officers—this is only a small
force, we can't let them stop us. But the bodies were falling
steadily. The firing only seemed to increase. And she realized that what she was facing was not some aging Home
Guard unit thrown together to pester them as they marched.
It was a disciplined force that was systematically herding her
troops—her hundreds of thousands of soldiers—into a
killing ground along the road and the riverbank.

And yet the gods still protected her. She walked among
the cowering troops, standing upright, and not a bullet struck
her. Soldiers fell all around her, but she was untouched.

She knew how the soldiers interpreted it: The gods protect her.

But she understood something completely different: The
enemy has given orders not to harm me. And these soldiers
are so well trained and disciplined that they are obeying the
order.

The force opposing them was not huge—the firepower
wasn't overwhelming. But most of her soldiers weren't
shooting at all. How could they? They couldn't see a target
to shoot at. And the enemy would concentrate its fire on any
force that tried to leave the road and get up the hills to sweep
over the enemy lines.

As far as she could see, if any of the enemy had died, it was by accident.

I am Varus, she thought. I have led my troops, as Varus led the Roman Legions, into a trap, where we will all die. Die without even damaging the enemy.

What was I thinking? This terrain was made for ambush. Why didn't I see that? Why was I so sure the enemy couldn't attack us here? Whatever you're sure the enemy *can't* do, but which would destroy you if they did it anyway, you must plan to counter. This was elementary.

No one from Ender's Jeesh would have made such a mistake.

Alai knew. He had warned her from the start. Her troops weren't ready for such a campaign. It would be a slaughter. And here they were now, dying all around her, the whole highway thick with corpses. Her men had been reduced to piling up the dead as makeshift bulwarks against enemy fire. There was no point in her issuing commands, because they would not be understood or obeyed.

And yet her men fought on.

Her cellphone rang.

She knew at once that it was the enemy, calling her to ask her to surrender. But how could they know her cellphone number?

Was it possible that Alai was with *them?*

"Virlomi."

Not Alai. But she knew the voice.

"This is Suri."

Suriyawong. Were these FPE troops? Or Thai? How could Thai troops get across Burma and all the way up here?

Not Chinese troops at all. Why was it suddenly so clear now? Why hadn't it been clear before, when Alai was warning her? In their private talks, Alamandar said it would all work because the Russians would have the Chinese army fully involved in the north. Whichever attack Han Tzu defended against, the other side would be able to rampage through China. Or if he tried to fight both, then each would destroy that part of his army in turn.

What neither of them had realized was that Han Tzu was just as capable of finding allies as they were.

Suriyawong, whose love she had spurned. It felt like so many years ago. When they were children. Was this his vengeance, because she had married Alai instead of him?

"Can you hear me, Vir?"

"Yes," she said.

"I would rather capture these men," he said. "I don't want to spend the rest of the day killing them all."

"Then stop."

"They won't surrender while you're still fighting. They worship you. They're dying for you. Tell them to surrender, and let the survivors go home to their families when the war is over."

"Tell Indians to surrender to *Siamese?*"

As soon as she said it, she regretted it. Once she had cared first for the lives of her men. Now, suddenly, she found herself speaking out of injured pride.

"Vir," said Suri. "They're dying for nothing. Save their lives."

She broke the connection. She looked at the men around her, the ones that were alive, crouching behind piles of their comrades' bodies, searching for some kind of target out in the trees, up the slopes . . . and seeing nothing.

"They've stopped shooting," said one of her surviving officers.

"Enough men have died for my pride," said Virlomi. "May the dead forgive me. I will live a thousand lives to make up for this one vain, stupid day." She raised her voice. "Lay down your weapons. Virlomi says: Lay down your weapons and stand up with your hands in the air. Take no more lives! Lay down your weapons!"

"We will die for you, Mother India!" cried one of the men.

"Satyagraha!" shouted Virlomi. "Bear what must be

borne! Today what you must bear is surrender! Mother India commands you to live so you can go home and comfort your wives and make babies to heal the great wounds that have been torn in the heart of India today!"

Some of her words and all of the meaning of her message were passed up and down the highway of corpses.

She set the example by raising her hands and walking out beyond the wall of bodies, into the open. Of course no one shot at her, because no one had during the whole battle. But soon others joined her. They lined up on the same side of the corpse wall that she had chosen, leaving their weapons behind them.

From out of the trees on both sides of the highway, wary Thai soldiers emerged, guns still at the ready. They were covered with sweat and the frenzy of killing was only just leaving them.

Virlomi turned and looked behind her. Emerging from the trees on the other side of the road was Suriyawong. She walked back over the walls of corpses to meet him in the grass on the other side. They stopped when they were three paces apart.

She gestured up and down the road. "So. This is your work."

"No, Virlomi," he said sadly. "It's yours."

"Yes," she said. "I know."

"Will you come with me to tell the other two armies to stop fighting? They'll only give up when you tell them to."

"Yes," she said. "Now?"

"Phone them and see if they obey. If I try to lead you away right now, these soldiers will take up arms again to stop me. For some reason they still worship you."

"In India we worship the Destroyer along with Vishnu and Brahma."

"But I never knew that you served Shiva," said Suriyawong.

She had no answer for him. She used her cellphone and made the calls. "They're trying to stop the men from fighting."

Then there was silence between them for a while. She could hear the barked commands of the Thai soldiers, forming her men into small groups and beginning their march down the valley.

"Aren't you going to ask about your husband?" said Suri.

"What about him?"

"Are you so sure your Muslim co-conspirators killed him, then?"

"Nobody was going to kill him," she said. "They were only going to confine him until after the victory."

Suri laughed bitterly. "You spent this long fighting the Muslims, Vir, and you still don't understand them any better than that? This isn't a chess game. The person of the king is not sacred."

"I never sought his death."

"You took away his power," said Suri. "He tried to stop you from doing *this* and you plotted against your own husband. He was a better friend to India than you ever were." His voice cracked with passion.

"You cannot say anything to me that's crueller than what I am now saying to myself."

"The girl Virlomi, so brave, so wise," said Suri. "Does she still exist? Or has the goddess destroyed her too?"

"The goddess is gone," said Virlomi. "Only the fool, only the murderer remains."

A field radio crackled at his waist. Something was said in Thai.

"Please come with me now, Virlomi. One army is surrendering, but the other shot the officer you telephoned when he tried to give the order."

A chopper approached them. Landed. They got on.

In the air, Suriyawong asked her, "What will you do now?"

"I'm your prisoner. What will *you* do?"

"You're Peter Wiggin's prisoner. Thailand has joined the Free People."

She knew what that would mean to Suriyawong. Thailand—even the name meant "land of the free." Peter's new "nation" had coopted the name of Suriyawong's homeland. And now, his homeland would no longer be sovereign. They had given up their independence. Peter Wiggin would be master of all.

"I'm sorry," she said.

"Sorry? Because my people will be free within their borders, and there'll be no more wars?"

"What about my people?" she asked.

"You're not going back to them," said Suri.

"How could I, even if you let me? How could I possibly face them?"

"I was hoping that you *would* face them. By vid. To help undo some of the damage you've done today."

"What could I possibly say or do?"

"They still worship you. If you disappear now, if they never hear of you again, India will be ungovernable for a hundred years."

Virlomi answered truthfully: "India has always been ungovernable."

"*Less* governable than ever," said Suri. "But if you speak to them. If you tell them—"

"I will not tell them to surrender to yet another foreign power, not after they've been conquered and occupied by Chinese and then Muslims!"

"If you ask them to vote. To freely decide whether to live in peace, within the Free People—"

"And give Peter Wiggin the victory?"

"Why are you angry with Peter? What did he ever do but help you win your nation's freedom in every way that was possible to him?"

It was true. Why was she so angry?

Because he had beaten her.

"Peter Wiggin," said Suriyawong, "has the right of conquest. His troops destroyed your army in combat. He showed mercy he didn't have to show."

"*You* showed mercy."

"I followed Peter's instructions," said Suriyawong. "He

does not want any foreign occupiers in India. He wants the Muslims out. He wants only Indians to govern Indians. Joining the FPE means exactly that. A free India. But an India that doesn't need, and therefore doesn't *have,* a military."

"A nation without an army is nothing," said Virlomi. "Any enemy can destroy them."

"That's the Hegemon's work in the world. He destroys the aggressors, so peaceful nations can remain free. India was the aggressor. Under your leadership, India was the invader. Now, instead of punishing your people, he offers them freedom and protection, if they only give up their weapons. Isn't that Satyagraha, Vir? To give up what you once valued, because now you serve a greater good?"

"Now you teach *me* about Satyagraha?"

"Hear the arrogance in your voice, Vir."

Abashed, she looked away from him.

"I teach you about Satyagraha because I lived it for years. Hiding myself utterly so that I would be the one Achilles trusted in the moment when I could betray him and save the world from him. I had no pride at the end of that. I had lived in filth and shame for . . . forever. But Bean took me back and trusted me. And Peter Wiggin acted as if he had known all along who I really was. They accepted my sacrifice.

"Now I ask you, Vir, for your sacrifice. Your Satyagraha. Once you put everything on the altar of India. Then your pride nearly undid what you had accomplished. I ask you now, will you help your people live in peace, the only way that peace can be had in this world? By joining with the Free People of Earth?"

She felt the tears streaming down her face.

Like that day when she was making the video of the atrocities.

Only today she was the one who had caused the deaths

of all these Indian boys. They came here to die because they loved and served her. She owed their families something.

"Whatever will help my people live in peace," she said, "I'll do."

25

LETTERS

From: Bean@Whereverthehelliam
To: Graff%pilgrimage@colmin.gov
Re: Did we actually do it?

I can't believe you still have me hooked up to the nets. This continues by ansible after we're moving at relativistic speeds?

The babies are fine here. There's room enough for them to crawl. A library big enough I think they won't lack for interesting reading or viewing material for . . . weeks. It will only be weeks, right?

What I'm wondering is: did we do it? Did I fulfil your goal? I look at the map, and there's still nothing inevitable about it. Han Tzu gave his farewell speech, just like Vlad and Alai and Virlomi. Makes me feel cheated. They got to bid the world farewell before they disappeared into this good night. Then again, they had nations to try to sway. I never really had anybody who followed me. Never wanted them. That's the thing, I guess, that set me apart from the rest of the Jeesh—I was the only one who didn't wish I were Ender.

So look at the map, Hyrum. Will they buy Han Tzu's plan of dividing China into six nations and all of them joining the Free Peoples? Or will they stay unified and still join? Or look for another Emperor? Will India recover from the humiliation of Virlomi's defeat? Will they follow her advice and embrace the FPE? Nothing's assured, and I have to go.

I know, you'll tell me by ansible when anything interesting happens. And in a way, I don't care. I'm not going to be there, I'm not going to have any effect on it.

In another way, I care even less than that. Because I never did care.

Yet I also care with my whole heart. Because Petra is there with the only babies I actually wanted—the ones that don't have my defects. With me I have only the cripples. And my only fear is that I'll die before I've taught them anything.

Don't be ashamed when you see your life coming to an end and you haven't found a cure for me yet. I never believed in the cure. I thought there was enough of a chance to take this leap into the night, and cure or not, I knew that I didn't want my defective children to live long enough to make my mistake and reproduce, and keep this valuable, terrible curse going on, generation after generation. Whatever happens, it's all right.

And then it occurs to me. What if Sister Carlotta was right? What if God is waiting for me with open arms? Then all I'm doing is postponing my reunion. I think of meeting God. Will it be like when I met my father and mother? (I almost wrote: Nikolai's parents.) I liked them. I wanted to love them. But I knew that Nikolai was the child she bore, the child they raised. And I was . . . from nowhere. And for me, my father was a little girl named Poke, and my mother was Sister Carlotta, and they were dead. Who were these other people really?

Will meeting God be like that? Will I be disappointed with the real thing, because I prefer the substitute I made do with?

Like it or not, Hyrum, you were God in my life. I didn't invite you, I didn't even like you, but you kept MEDDLING. And now you've sent me into outer darkness with a promise to save me. A promise I don't believe you can keep. But at least YOU aren't a stranger. I know you. And I think that you honestly meant well. If I have to choose between an omnipotent God who leaves the world in this condition, and a God who has only a little bit of power but really cares and tries to make things better, I'll take you every time. Go on playing God, Hyrum. You're not bad at it. Sometimes you kind of get it right.

Why am I writing like this? We can email whenever we want. The thing is, nothing's going to happen here, so I'll have nothing to tell you. And nothing you have to tell me is going to matter to me all that much, the farther I get from Earth. So this is the right time for these valedictories.

I hope Peter succeeds in uniting the world in peace. I believe he's still got a couple of big wars ahead of him.

I hope Petra remarries. When she asks you what you think, tell her I said this: I want my children to have a father in their lives. Not some absent legend of a father—a real one. So as long as she chooses somebody who'll love them and tell them they've done ok, then do it. Be happy.

I hope you live to see colonies established and the human race thriving on other worlds. It's a good dream.

I hope these crippled children I have with me find something interesting to do with their lives after I'm dead.

I hope Sister Carlotta and Poke are there to meet me when I die. Sister Carlotta can tell me I told you so. And I can tell them both how sorry I am that I couldn't save their lives, after all the trouble they went to to save mine.

Enough. Time to switch on the gravity regulator and get this boat out to sea.

From: Graff%pilgrimage@colmin.gov
To: Bean@Whereverthehelliam
Re: You did enough

You did enough, Bean. You only had a little time, and you sacrificed so much of it to helping Peter and me and Mazer. All that time that could have belonged to Petra and you and your babies. You did enough. Peter can take it from here.

As for all that God business—I don't think the real God has as bad a track record as you think. Sure, a lot of people have terrible lives, by some measure. But I can't think of anybody who's had it tougher than you. And look what you've become. You don't want to give God the credit because you don't think he exists. But if you're going to blame him for all the crap, kid, you got to give him credit for what grows from that fertilized soil.

What you said about Petra getting a real father for your kids. I know you weren't talking about yourself. But I have to say it, because it's true, and you deserve to hear it.

Bean, I'm proud of you. I'm proud of myself because I actually got to know you. I remember sitting there after you figured out what was really going on in the war against the

Buggers. What do I do with this kid? We can't keep a secret from him.

What I decided was: I'll trust him.

You lived up to my trust. You exceeded it. You're a great soul. I looked up to you long before you got so tall.

You did ok.

The plebiscite was over in Russia and it joined the FPE. The Muslim League was broken up and the most belligerent nations had been subdued, for now. Armenia was safe.

Petra sent her army home on the same civilian trains that had brought them to Moscow.

It had taken a year.

During that time she missed her babies. But she couldn't bear to see them. She refused to let them be brought to her. She refused to take even a brief leave to see them.

Because she knew that when she came home, there would only be five of them. And the two she knew the best and therefore loved the best would not be there.

Because she knew that she would have to face the rest of her life without Bean.

So she kept herself busy—and there was no shortage of important work to do. She told herself—next week I'll take a leave and go home.

Then her father came to her and bulled his way past the aides and clerks that fenced her off from the outside world. Truth to tell, they were probably glad to see him and let him through. Because Petra was hell on wheels and terrified everybody around her.

Father came to her with an attitude of steel. "Get out of here," he said.

"What are you talking about?"

"Your mother and I lost half your childhood because they *took you away*. You're cheating yourself out of some of the sweetest time in the lives of your children. Why? What are you afraid of? The great soldier, and babies terrify you?"

"I don't want this conversation," she said. "I'm an adult. I make my own decisions."

"You don't grow out of being my daughter." Father said. Then he loomed over her, and for a moment she had a childish fear that he was going to . . . to . . . *spank* her.

All he did was put his arms around her and hug her. Tight.

"You're suffocating me, Papa."

"Then it's working."

"I mean it."

"If you have breath to argue with me, then I'm not done." She laughed.

He let her out of the hug but still held her shoulders. "You wanted these children more than anything, and you were right. Now you want to avoid them because you think you can't bear the grief of the ones that aren't there. And I tell you, you're wrong. And I *know*. Because I was there for Stefan, during all the years you were gone. I didn't hide from *him* because I didn't have *you*."

"I know you're right," said Petra. "You think I'm stupid? I didn't decide *not* to see them. I just kept putting it off."

"Your mother and I have written to Peter, begging him to *order* you home. And all he said was, She'll come when she can't help it."

"You couldn't listen to him? He *is* the Hegemon of the whole world."

"Not even half the world yet," said Father. "And he might be Hegemon of nations, but he's got no authority inside my family."

"Thank you for coming, Papa. I'm demobilizing my troops tomorrow and sending them home across borders where they won't need passports because it's all part of the Free People of Earth. I did something while I was here. But now I'm done. I was going home anyway. But now I'll do it because you told me to. See? I'm willing to be obedient, as long as you order me to do what I was going to do anyway."

———

The Free People of Earth had four capitals now—Bangkok had been added to Rwanda, Rotterdam, and Blackstream. But it was Blackstream—Ribeirão Preto—where the Hegemon lived. And that was where Peter had had her children moved. He hadn't even asked her permission and it made her furious when he informed her what he had done. But she was busy in Russia and Peter said that Rotterdam wasn't home to her and it wasn't home to him and he was going home, and keeping her kids where he could make sure they were getting cared for.

So it was Brazil she came home to. And it did feel good. Moscow's winter had been a nightmare, even worse than Armenia's winters. And she liked the feel of Brazil, the pace of life, the way they moved, the football in the streets, the way they were never quite dressed, the music of the Portuguese language coming out of the neighborhood bars along with batuque and samba and laughter and the pungent smell of pinga.

She took a car part of the way but then paid him and told him to deliver her bags to the compound and she walked the rest of the way. Without actually planning it, she found herself walking past the little house where she and Bean had lived when they weren't inside the compound.

The house had been changed. She realized: It was connected to the house next door by a couple of rooms added in, and the garden wall between them had been torn down. It was one big house now.

What a shame. They can't leave well enough alone.

Then she saw the name on the little sign on the wall beside the gate.

Delphiki.

She opened the gate without clapping hands for permission. She knew now what had happened, but she also couldn't believe that Peter had gone to such trouble.

She opened the door and walked in and . . .

There was Bean's mother in the kitchen, making something that had a lot of olives and garlic in it.

"Oh," said Petra. "I'm sorry. I didn't know you—I thought you were in Greece."

The smile on Mrs. Delphiki's face was all the answer Petra needed. "Of course you come in, it's your house. I'm the visitor. Welcome home!"

"You came to—you're here to take care of the babies."

"We work for the FPE now. And our jobs brought us here. But I couldn't stand to be away from my grandchildren. I took a leave of absence. Now I cook, and change nasty diapers, and scream at the empregadas."

"Where are the . . ."

"Naptime!" said Mrs. Delphiki. "But I promise you, little Andrew, he's only faking. He *never* sleeps, whenever I go in his eyes are just a little tiny bit open."

"They won't know me," said Petra.

She dismissed that with a wave. "Of course not. But you think they're going to remember that? Nothing that happens before age three."

"I'm so glad to see you. Did . . . did he say good-bye to you?"

"He wasn't sentimental that way," said Mrs. Delphiki. "But yes, he called us. And sent us nice letters. I think it hit Nikolai harder than us, because he knew Julian better. From Battle School, you know. But Nikolai is married now, did you know? So pretty soon, maybe another grandchild. Not that we have a shortage. You and Julian did *very* well by us."

"If I'm very quiet and don't wake them, can I go see them?"

"We divided them into two rooms. Andrew shares one room with Bella, because he never sleeps, but she can sleep through anything. Julian and Petra and Ramón are in the other room. They need it dimmer. But if you wake them, it's not a problem. All their cribs have the sides down because they climb out anyway."

"They're walking?"

"Running. Climbing. Falling off things. They're more than a year old, Petra! They're normal children!"

It almost set her off, because it reminded her of the children who weren't normal. But that wasn't what Mrs. Delphiki meant, and there was no reason to punish her for a chance remark by bursting into tears.

So the two who bore the names of the children she grieved for most were sharing a room. She had courage enough to face this. She went there first.

Nothing about these babies reminded her of the ones who were gone. They were so big. Toddlers, not babies now. And, true to reputation, Andrew's eyes were already open. He turned to look at her.

She smiled at him.

He closed his eyes and pretended to be asleep.

Well, let him retreat and decide what he thinks of me. I'm not going to demand that they love me when they don't even know me.

She walked to Bella's crib. She was sleeping hard, her black curls tight and wet against her head. The Delphiki genetic heritage was *so* complicated. Bella really showed Bean's African roots. Whereas Andrew looked Armenian, period.

She touched one of Bella's curls and the girl didn't stir. Her cheek was hot and damp.

She's mine, thought Petra.

She turned and saw that Andrew was sitting up in bed, regarding her soberly. "Hello, Mama," he said.

It took her breath away.

"How did you know me?"

"Picture," he said.

"Do you want to get up?"

He looked at the clock on the top of the dresser. "Not time."

These were *normal* children?

How would Mrs. Delphiki know what normal was, anyway? Nikolai wasn't exactly stupid.

Though they weren't *so* brilliant. They were both wearing diapers.

Petra walked over to Andrew and held out her hand. What do I think he is, a dog that I give my hand to sniff?

Andrew took hold of a couple of her fingers, just for a moment, as if to make sure she was real. "Hello, Mama."

"May I kiss you?"

He lifted his face and puckered up. She leaned down and kissed him.

The touch of his hands. The feel of his little kiss. The curl on Bella's cheek. What had she been waiting for? Why had she been afraid? Fool. I'm a fool.

Andrew lay back down and closed his eyes. As Mrs. Delphiki had warned, it was completely unbelievable. She could see the whites of his eyes through the partly-open slits.

"I love you," she whispered.

"Loveyoutoo," murmured Andrew.

Petra was glad that someone had said those words to him so often that the answer came by rote.

She crossed the hall into the other room. It was much darker. She couldn't see well enough to dare to cross the room. It took a few moments for her eyes to grow used to the dark and make out the three beds.

Would she know Ramón when she saw him?

Someone moved to her left. She was startled, and she was a soldier. In a moment she was in a defensive crouch, ready to spring.

"Only me," whispered Peter Wiggin.

"You didn't have to come and—"

He held a finger to his lips. He walked over to the farthest crib. "Ramón," he whispered.

She came and stood over the crib.

Peter reached down and flipped something. A paper.

"What is it?" she asked. In a whisper.

He shrugged.

If he didn't know what it was, why had he pointed it out to her?

She pulled it out from under Ramón. It was an envelope, but it didn't contain much.

Peter took her gently by the elbow and guided her out the door. Once they were in the hall, he said softly, "You can't read in that light. And when Ramón wakes up, he's going to look for it and be very upset if it isn't there."

"What is it?"

"Ramón's paper," said Peter. "Petra, Bean put it there before he left. I mean, not *there*. It was in Rotterdam. But he tucked it under Ramón's diaper as he was lying asleep in bed. He meant you to find it there. So it's been there every night of his life. It's only been peed on twice."

"From Bean."

The emotion she could deal with best was anger. "You knew he had written this and—"

Peter kept the both of them moving out of the hall and into the parlor. "He didn't give it to me or anyone else to deliver. Unless you count Ramón. He gave it to Ramón's butt."

"But to make me wait a year before—"

"Nobody thought it would be a year, Petra." He said it very gently, but the truth of it stung. He always had the power to sting her, and yet he never shrank from doing it.

"I'll leave you alone to read it," he said.

"You mean you didn't come here for my homecoming so you could find out what was in it?"

"Petra." Mrs. Delphiki stood in the doorway to the parlor. She looked mildly shocked. "Peter didn't come here for *you*. He's here all the time."

Petra looked at Peter and then back and Mrs. Delphiki. "Why?"

"They climb all over him. And he puts them down for their nap. They obey him a *lot* better than me."

The thought of the Hegemon of Earth coming over to play with her children seemed freakish to her. And then it seemed worse than freakish. It seemed completely unfair. She pushed him. "You came to *my* house and played with *my* children?"

He didn't show any reaction; he also stood his ground. "They're great kids."

"Let me find that out, will you? Let me find it out for myself!"

"Nobody's stopping you."

"*You* were stopping me! I was doing your work in Moscow, and you were *here* playing with my kids!"

"I offered to bring them to you."

"I didn't want them in Moscow, I was busy."

"I offered you leave to come home. Time after time."

"And let the work fall apart?"

"Petra," said Mrs. Delphiki. "Peter has been very good to your children. And to me. And you're behaving very badly."

"No, Mrs. Delphiki," said Peter. "This is only *slightly* badly. Petra's a trained soldier and the fact that I'm still standing—"

"Don't tease me out of this." Petra burst into tears. "I've lost a year of my babies' lives and it was my own fault, do you think I don't know that?"

There was a crying sound from one of the bedrooms.

Mrs. Delphiki rolled her eyes and went down the hall to rescue whoever it was that needed rescuing.

"You did what you had to do," said Peter. "Nobody's criticizing you."

"But *you* could take time for my children."

"I don't have any of my own," said Peter.

"Is that my fault?"

"I'm just saying I had time. And . . . I owed it to Bean."

"You owe more than that."

"But this is what I can do."

She didn't want Peter Wiggin to be the father figure in her children's lives.

"Petra, I'll stop if you want. They'll wonder why I don't come, and then they'll forget. If you don't want me here, I'll understand. This is yours and Bean's, and I don't want to intrude. And yes, I did want to be here when you opened that."

"What's in it?"

"I don't know."

"Didn't have one of your guys steam it open for you?"

Peter just looked a little irritated.

Mrs. Delphiki came into the room carrying Ramón, who was whimpering and saying, "My paper."

"I should have known," said Peter.

Petra held up the envelope. "Here it is," she said.

Ramón reached for it insistently. Petra handed it to him.

"You're spoiling him," said Peter.

"This is your mama, Ramón," said Mrs. Delphiki. "She nursed you when you were little."

"He was the only one that wasn't biting me by the time . . ." She couldn't think of a way to finish the sentence that wouldn't involve speaking of Bean or the other two children, the ones that had to go on solid food because they got teeth so incredibly young.

Mrs. Delphiki wasn't giving up. "Let your mama see the paper, Ramón."

Ramón clutched it tighter. Sharing was not yet on his agenda.

Peter reached out, snagged the envelope, and held it out to Petra. Ramón immediately began to wail.

"Give it back to him," said Petra. "I've waited this long."

Peter got his finger under the corner, tore it open, and extracted a single sheet of paper. "If you let them get their way just because they cry, you'll raise a bunch of whiny brats that nobody can stand." He handed her the paper, and gave the envelope back to Ramón, who immediately quieted down and started examining the transformed object.

Petra held the paper and was surprised to see that it was shaking. Which meant her hand was shaking. She didn't *feel* like she was trembling.

And then suddenly Peter was holding her by her upper arms and helping her to the sofa and her legs weren't working very well. "Come on, sit here, it's a shock, that's all."

"I've got your snack all ready," said Mrs. Delphiki to Ramón, who was trying to get his whole forearm inside the envelope.

"Are you all right?" Peter asked.

Petra nodded.

"Want me to go now so you can read this?"

She nodded again.

Peter was in the kitchen saying good-bye to Ramón and Mrs. Delphiki as Andrew padded down the hall. He stopped in the archway of the parlor and said, "Time."

"Yes, it's time, Andrew," said Petra.

She watched him toddle on toward the kitchen. And then a moment later she heard his voice. "Mama," he announced.

"That's right," said Mrs. Delphiki. "Mama's home."

"Bye, Mrs. Delphiki," Peter said. A moment later, Petra heard the door open.

"Wait a minute, Peter!" she called.

He came back inside. He closed the door. As he came back into the parlor she held the paper out to him. "I can't read it."

Peter didn't ask why. Any fool could see the tears in her eyes. "You want me to read it to you?"

"Maybe I can get through it if it isn't his voice I hear," she said.

Peter opened it. "It isn't long."

"I know."

He started reading aloud, softly so only she could hear.

"I love you," he said. "There's one thing we forgot to decide. We can't have two pairs of children with the same name. So I've decided that I'm going to call the Andrew that's with me 'Ender,' because that's the name we called him when he was born. And I'll think of the Andrew that's with you as 'Andrew.' "

The tears were streaming down Petra's face now and she could hardly keep herself from sobbing. For some reason it tore her apart to realize that Bean was thinking about such things before he left.

"Want me to go on?" asked Peter.

She nodded.

"And the Bella that's with you, we'll call Bella. Because the one that's with me, I've decided to call her 'Carlotta.' "

She lost it. Feelings she'd had pent up inside her for a year, feelings that her underlings had begun to think she didn't have, burst out of her now.

But only for a minute. She got control of herself, and then waved to him to continue.

"And even though she isn't with me, the little girl we named after you, when I tell the kids about her, I'm going to call her 'Poke' so they don't get her confused with you. You don't have to call her that, but it's because you're the only Petra I actually know, and Poke ought to have somebody named after her."

Petra broke down. She clung to Peter and he held her like a friend, like a father.

Peter didn't say anything. No "It's all right" or "I understand," maybe because it wasn't all right and he was smart enough to know he couldn't understand.

When he did speak, it was after she was much calmer and quieter and another of the children had walked past the archway and loudly proclaimed, "Lady crying."

Petra sat up and patted Peter's arm and said, "Thank you. I'm sorry."

"I wish his letter had been longer," said Peter. "It was obviously just a last-minute thought."

"It was perfect," said Petra.

"He didn't even sign it."

"Doesn't matter."

"But he was thinking of you and the children. Making sure you and he would think of all the children by the same names."

She nodded, afraid of starting again.

"I'm going to go now," said Peter. "I won't come back till you invite me."

"Come back when you usually do," she said. "I don't want my homecoming to cost the children somebody they love."

"Thanks," he said.

She nodded. She wanted to thank him for reading it to her and being so decent about her crying all over his shirt, but she didn't trust herself to speak so she just sort of waved.

It was a good thing she had cried herself out. When she went into the kitchen and washed her face and listened to little Petra—to Poke—say, "Lady crying" again, she was able to be very calm and say, "I was crying because I'm so happy to see you. I've missed you. You don't remember me, but I'm your mama."

"We show them your picture every morning and night," said Mrs. Delphiki, "and they kiss the picture."

"Thank you."

"The nurses started it before I came," she said.

"Now I get to kiss my boys and girls myself," she said. "Will that be all right? No more kissing the picture?"

It was too much for them to understand. And if they wanted to keep kissing the picture for a while, that would be fine with her, too. Just like Ramón's envelope. No reason to take away from them something that they valued.

By your father's age, Petra said silently, he was on his own, trying not to starve to death in Rotterdam.

But you're all going to catch up with him and pass him by. When you're in your twenties and out of college and getting married, he'll still be sixteen years old, crawling through time as his starship races through space. When you bury me, he'll not have turned seventeen yet. And your brothers and sister will still be babies. Not as old as you are. It will be as if they never change.

Which means it's exactly as if they had died. Loved ones who die never change, either. They're always the same age in memory.

So what I'm going through isn't something so different. How many women became widows in the war? How many mothers have buried babies that they hardly had time to hold? I'm just part of the same sentimental comedy as everyone else, the sad parts always followed by laughter, the laughter always by tears.

It wasn't until later, when she was alone in her bed, the children asleep for the night, Mrs. Delphiki gone next door—or, rather, to the other wing of the same house—that she was able to bring herself to read Bean's note again. It was in his handwriting. He had done it in a hurry and in spots it was barely legible. And the paper was stained— Peter hadn't been joking about Ramón peeing on the envelope a couple of times.

She turned the light out and meant to go to sleep.

And then something occurred to her and she switched on the light again and fumbled for the paper and her eyes were so bleary she could hardly read, so maybe she had actually fallen asleep, and this thought had woken her out of a sound slumber.

The letter began, "There's one thing we forgot to decide."

But when Peter read it, he had started with "I love you."

He must have scanned over the letter and realized that Bean never said it. That it was just a note that Bean had jotted at the last moment, and Peter worried that she might be hurt by the omission.

He couldn't have known that Bean just didn't put that kind of thing in writing. Except obliquely. Because the whole note said "I love you," didn't it?

She turned the light off again, but still held the letter. Bean's last message to her.

As she drifted off again, the thought passed briefly through her mind: When Peter said it, he wasn't reading at all.

26

SPEAK FOR ME

From: PeterWiggin%hegemon@FreePeopleOfEarth.fp.
gov
To: ValentineWiggin%historian@BookWeb.com/
AuthorsService
Re: Congratulations

Dear Valentine,

I read your seventh volume and you're not just a brilliant writer (which we always knew) but also a thorough researcher and a perceptive and honest analyst. I knew Hyrum Graff and Mazer Rackham very well before they died, and you treated them with absolute fairness. I doubt they would dispute a word of your book, even where they did not come off as perfect; they were always honest men, even when they lied their zhopas off.

The work of the Hegemon's office is pretty slight these days. The last actual military ventures that were needed took place more than a decade ago—the last gasp of tribalism, which we managed to mostly put down with a show of force. Since then I've tried to retire half a dozen times—no, wait, I'm talking to a historian—twice, but they don't believe I mean it and they keep me in office. They even ask my advice sometimes, and to return the favor I try not to reminisce about how we did things in the early days of the FPE. Only the good old USA refuses to join the FPE and I have hopes they'll get off their "don't tread on me" kick and do the right thing. Polls keep saying that Americans are sick of being the only people in the world who don't get a chance to vote in the world elections. I may see the whole world formally united before I die. And even if I don't, we've got peace on earth.

Petra says hi. Wish you could have known her, but that's star travel. Tell Ender that Petra is more beautiful than ever, he should eat his heart out, and our grandchildren are so adorable that people applaud when we take them out for walks.

Speaking of Ender. I read The Hive Queen. I heard about it before, but never read it till you included it at the end of your last volume—but before the index, or I would never have seen it.

I know who wrote it. If he can speak for the buggers, surely he can speak for me.

Peter

Not for the first time, Peter wished they made a portable ansible. Of course it would make no economic sense. Yes, they miniaturized it as much as possible to put it on starships. But the ansible only made an important difference in communication across the void of space. It saved hours for within-system communication; decades, for communication with the colonies and the ships in flight.

It just wasn't a technology designed for chatting.

There were a few privileges that came with the vestiges of power. Peter might be over seventy—and, as he often pointed out to Petra, an *old* seventy, an *ancient* seventy—but he was still Hegemon, and the title had once meant enormous power, it once meant attack choppers in flight and armies and fleets in motion; it once meant punishment for aggression, collection of taxes, enforcement of human rights laws, cleaning up political corruption.

Peter remembered when the title was such an empty joke they gave it to a teenage boy who had written cleverly on the nets.

Peter had brought power to the office. And then, because he gradually stripped away its functions and assigned them to other officials in the FPE—or "EarthGov" as people now called it as often as not—he had returned the position to a figurehead position.

But not a joke. It was no longer a joke and never would be again.

Not a joke, but not necessarily a good thing, either. There were plenty of people left alive who remembered the Hegemon as the coercive power that shattered their dream of how Earth ought to be (though usually their dream was everyone else's nightmare). And historians and biographers had often had at him and would do it again, forever.

The thing about the historians was, they could arrange the data all neatly in rows, but they kept missing what it was for. They kept inventing the strangest motives for people. There was the biography of Virlomi, for instance, that made her an idealistic saint and blamed Suriyawong, of all people, for the slaughter that ended Virlomi's military career. Never mind that Virlomi herself repudiated that interpretation, writing by ansible from the colony on Andhra. Biographers were always irritated when their subject turned out to be alive.

But Peter hadn't bothered to answer any of them. Even the ones that attacked him quite savagely, blaming him for everything that went badly and giving others the credit for everything that went well . . . Petra would fume over some of them for days until he begged her not to read them anymore. But he couldn't resist reading them himself. He didn't take it personally. Most people never had biographies written about them.

Petra herself had only had a couple about her, and they were both of the "great women" or "role models for girls" variety, not serious scholarship. Which bothered Peter, because he knew what they seemed to neglect—that after all the other members of Ender's Jeesh left Earth and went out to the colonies, she stayed and ran the FPE defense ministry for almost thirty years, until the position became more of a police department than anything else and she insisted on retiring to play with the grandchildren.

She was there for *everything*, Peter said to her when he was griping about this. "You were Ender's and Bean's friend in Battle School—you taught Ender how to *shoot*, for heaven's sake. You were in his Jeesh—"

But at those points Petra would shush him. "I don't want those stories told," she said. "I wouldn't come off very well if the truth came out."

Peter didn't believe it. And you could skip all of that and start when she returned to Earth and . . . wasn't it Petra who, when the Jeesh was almost all kidnapped, found a way to get a message out to Bean? Wasn't she the one who knew Achilles better than anybody that he didn't succeed in killing? She was one of the great military leaders of all time, and she also married Julian Delphiki, the Giant of legend, and then Peter the Hegemon, another legend, and on top of all that raised five of the children she had with Bean and five more that she had with Peter.

And no biography. So why should he complain that there were dozens about him and every one of them got simple, obvious things wrong, things that you could actually *check*, let alone the more arcane things like motive and secret agreements and . . .

And then Valentine's book on the Bugger wars started to come out, volume by volume. One on the first invasion, two on the second—the one Mazer Rackham won. Then four volumes on the Third Invasion, the one that Ender and his Jeesh fought and won from what they thought was a training game on the asteroid Eros. One whole volume was about the development of Battle School—short biographies of dozens of children who were pivotal to the improvements in the school that eventually led to truly effective training and the legendary Battle Room games.

Peter saw what she wrote about Graff and Rackham and about the kids in Ender's Jeesh—including Petra—and even though he knew part of her insight came from having Ender right there with her in Shakespeare colony, the real source of the book's excellence was her own keen self-questioning. She did not find "themes" and impose them on the history. Things happened, and they were connected to each other, but when a motive was unknowable, she didn't pretend to know it. Yet she understood human beings.

Even the awful ones, she seemed to love.

So he thought: Too bad she isn't here to write a biography of Petra.

Though of course that was silly—she didn't have to be there, she had access to any documents she wanted through the ansible, since one of the key provisions of Graff's ColMin was the absolute assurance that every colony had complete access to every library and repository of records in all the human worlds.

It wasn't until the seventh volume came out and Peter read The Hive Queen that he found the biographer that made him think: I want him to write about me.

The Hive Queen wasn't long. And while it was well written, it wasn't particularly poetic. It was very simple. But it painted a picture of the Hive Queens that was as they might have written it themselves. The monsters that had frightened children for more than a century—and continued to do so even though all were now dead—suddenly became beautiful and tragic.

But it wasn't a propaganda job. The terrible things they did were recognized, not dismissed.

And then it dawned on him who wrote it. Not Valentine, who rooted things in fact. It was written by someone who could understand an enemy so well that he loved him. How often had he heard Petra quote what Ender said about that? She—or Bean, or somebody—had written it down. "I think it's impossible to really understand somebody, what they want, what they believe, and not love them the way they love themselves."

That's what the writer of The Hive Queen, who called himself Speaker for the Dead, had done for the aliens who once haunted our nightmares.

And the more people read that book, the more they wished they had understood their enemy, that the language barrier had not been insuperable, that the Hive Queens had not all been destroyed.

The Speaker for the Dead had made humans love their ancient enemy.

Fine, it's easy to love your enemies after they're safely dead. But still. Humans give up their villains only reluctantly.

It had to be Ender. And so Peter had written to Valentine, congratulating her, but also asking her to invite Ender to write about him. There was some back and forth, with Peter insisting that he didn't want approval of anything. He wanted to talk to his brother. If a book emerged from it, fine. If the book painted him to be a monster, if that's what Speaker for the Dead saw in him, so be it. "Because I know that whatever he writes, it'll be a lot closer than most of the kuso that gets published here."

Valentine scoffed at his use of words like *kuso*. "What are you doing using Battle School slang?"

"It's just part of the language now," Peter told her in an answering email.

And then she wrote, "He won't email you. He doesn't know you anymore, he says. The last he saw of you, he was five years old and you were the worst older brother in the world. He has to talk to you."

"That's expensive," Peter wrote back, but in fact he knew the FPE could afford it and would not refuse him. What really held him back was fear. He had forgotten that Ender had only known him as a bully. Had never seen him struggle to build a world government, not by conquest, but by free choice of the people voting nation by nation. He doesn't know me.

But then Peter told himself, Yes he does. The Peter that he knew is part of the Peter who became Hegemon. The Peter that Petra agreed to marry and permitted to raise children with her, that Peter was the same one that had terrorized Ender and Valentine and was filled with venom and resentment at having been deemed unworthy by the judges who chose which children would grow up to save the world.

How much of my achievement was the acting out of that resentment?

"He should interview Mother," Peter wrote back. "She's still lucid and she likes me better than she used to."

"He writes to her," said Valentine. "When he has time to write to anyone. He takes his duties here very seriously. It's a small world, but he governs it as carefully as if it were Earth."

Finally Peter swallowed his fears and set a date and time and now he sat down at vocal interface of the ansible in the Blackstream Interstellar Communication Center. Of course, BICC didn't communicate directly with any ansible except ColMin's Stationary Ansible Array, which relayed everything to the appropriate colony or starship.

Audio and video were so wasteful of bandwidth that they

were routinely compressed and then reinflated at the other end, so despite the instantaneity of ansible communications, there was a noticeable timelag between sides of the conversation.

No picture. Peter had to draw the line somewhere. And Ender hadn't insisted. It would be too painful for both of them—for Ender to see how much time had passed during his relativistic voyage out to Shakespeare, and for Peter to be forced to see how young Ender still was, how much life he still had ahead of him while Peter was looking coolly at his own old age and approaching death.

"I'm here, Ender."

"It's good to hear your voice, Peter."

And then silence.

"No small talk, is there?" said Peter. "It's been too long a time for me, too brief a time for you. Ender, I know I was a slumbitch to you as a kid. No excuses. I was full of rage and shame and I took it out on you and Valentine but mostly on you. I don't think I ever said a kind thing to you, not when you were awake anyway. I can talk about that if you want."

"Later maybe," said Ender. "This isn't a family therapy session. I just want to know what you did and why."

"Which things I did?"

"The ones that matter to you," said Ender. "What you choose to tell me is as important as what you say about those events."

"There's a lot. My mind is still clear. I remember a lot."

"Good. I'm listening."

He listened for hours that day. And more hours, more days. Peter poured out everything. The political struggles. The wars. The negotiations. The essays on the nets. Building up intelligence networks. Seizing opportunities. Finding worthwhile allies.

It wasn't until near the end of their last session that Peter dredged up memories of when Ender was a baby. "I really loved you. Kept begging Mom to let me feed you. Change you. Play with you. I thought you were the best thing that ever existed. But then I noticed. I'd be playing with you and have you laughing and then Valentine would walk into the room and you'd just rivet on her. I didn't exist anymore.

"She was luminous, of course you reacted that way. Everybody did. *I* did. But at the same time, I was just a kid. I saw it as, Ender loves Valentine more than me. And when I realized you were born because they regarded me as a failure—the Battle School people, I mean—it was just one more resentment. That doesn't excuse anything. I didn't have to be a bastard about it. I'm just telling you, I realize now that's where it started."

"OK," said Ender.

"I'm sorry," said Peter. "That I wasn't better to you as a kid. Because, see, my whole life, all the things I've told you about in all these incredibly expensive conversations, I would find myself thinking, that was OK. I did OK that time. Ender would like that I did that."

"Please don't tell me you did it all for me."

"Are you kidding? I did it because I'm as competitive a marubo as ever was born on this planet. But my standard of judgment was: Ender would like that I did that."

Ender didn't answer.

"Aw, hell, kid. It's way simpler than that. What you did by the time you were twelve made my whole life's work possible."

"Well, Peter, what you did while I was voyaging, that's what made my . . . victory worth winning."

"What a family Mr. and Mrs. Wiggin had."

"I'm glad we talked, Peter."

"Me too."

"I think I can write about you."

"I hope so."

"Even if I can't, though, it doesn't mean I wasn't glad. To find out who you grew up to be."

"Wish I could be there," said Peter, "to see who *you* grow up to be."

"I'm never going to grow up, Peter," said Ender. "I'm frozen in history. Forever twelve. You had a good life, Peter. Give Petra my love. Tell her I miss her. And the others. But especially her. You got the best of us, Peter."

At that moment, Peter almost told him about Bean and his three children, flying through space somewhere, waiting for a cure that didn't look very promising now.

But then he realized that he couldn't. The story wasn't his to tell. If Ender wrote about it, then people would start looking for Bean. Somebody might try to contact him. Someone might call him home. And then his voyage would have been for nothing. His sacrifice. His Satyagraha.

They never spoke again.

Peter lived for some time after that, despite his weak heart. Hoping the whole time that Ender might write the book he wanted. But when he died, the book was still unwritten.

———

So it was Petra who read the short biography called, simply, The Hegemon, and signed Speaker for the Dead.

She wept all day after reading it.

She read it aloud at Peter's grave, stopping whenever any passersby came near. Until she realized that they were coming in order to hear her reading. So she invited them over and read it aloud again, from the beginning.

The book wasn't long, but there was power in it. To Petra, it was everything Peter had wanted it to be. It put a period on his life. The harm and the good. The wars and the peace. The lies and the truth. The manipulation and the liberty.

The Hegemon was a companion piece, really, to The Hive Queen. The one book was the story of an entire species; and so was the other.

But to Petra, it was the story of the man who had shaped her life more than any other.

Except one. The one who lived now only as a shadow in other people's stories. The Giant.

There was no grave, and there was no book to read there. And his story wasn't a human one because in a way he hadn't lived a human life.

It was a hero's life. It ended with him being taken away into heaven, dying but not dead.

I love you, Peter, she said to him at his grave. But you must have known that I never stopped loving Bean, and longing for him, and missing him whenever I looked in our children's faces.

Then she went home, leaving both her husbands behind, the one whose life had a monument and a book, and the one whose only monument was in her heart.

ACKNOWLEDGMENTS

Thanks to Joan Han, M.D., who works in pediatric endocrinology at the National Institutes of Health in Bethesda, for advice on what kinds of legitimate therapy might be tried to stop Bean's unstoppable growth. Along the same lines, M. Jack Long, M.D., brought up the ideas that became Volescu's suggestions for how Bean might live a long life. My thanks to Dr. Long—along with my relief that he realized they were truly appalling ideas. (His letter ended "Yikes—I hope not!")

Thanks to Danny Sale for suggesting that Bean might have a hand in the decision to convert the Fantasy Game from Battle School into the program that eventually became Jane. Farah Khimji of Lewisville, Texas, reminded me of the need for a world currency—and the fact that the dollar already is one. Andaiye Spencer let me know that I could not let the old Battle School relationship between Petra Arkanian and Dink Meeker die without at least some mention.

Mark Trevors of New Brunswick reminded me that Peter and Ender conversed once before Peter died, and expressed the wish that he could see that scene more fully, and from Peter's point of view. Since this idea was *much* better than the one I had for ending the book, I seized upon it immediately, with gratitude. I also had reminders and help from

Rechavia Berman, my Hebrew translator, and from David Tayman.

I'm not good with calendaring my books or aging my characters. I don't pay attention to those things in real life, and so I have a hard time keeping track of the passage of time in my fiction. In response to a plea at our Hatrack River Web site (www.hatrack.com), Megan Schindele, Nathan Taylor, Maureen Fanta, Jennifer Rader, Samuel Sevlie, Carrie Pennow, Shannon Blood, Elizabeth Cohen, and Cecily Kiester all pitched in and sorted through all the age and time references in *Ender's Game* and the other *Shadow* books to help sort it out for me. In addition, Jason Bradshaw and C. Porter Bassett caught a continuity error between the original *Ender's Game* and this novel. I'm grateful for readers who know my books better than I do.

I'm grateful for the willingness of my good friends Erin Absher, Aaron Johnston, and Kathy Kidd, who set aside many other more important concerns in order to join my wife, Kristine, in giving me quick feedback on each chapter as it was written. It never ceases to amaze me how many errors—not just typos, but also continuity lapses and outright contradictions—can slip past me and three or four very careful readers, only to be caught by the next. If there are such mistakes still in this book, it's not their fault!

Beth Meacham, my editor at Tor, went the extra mile on this book. Still in pain from major surgery and drugged to the gills, she read this manuscript while the bits and bytes were still sizzling, and gave me excellent advice. Some of the best scenes in this book are here because she suggested them and I was smart enough to recognize a great idea when I heard it.

The whole production team at Tor went to extraordinary lengths to help us bring out this book in time for a good publishing window, and I appreciate their patience with an author whose estimate of the time needed to complete this book was so laughably wrong.

And Tom Doherty may just be the most creative publisher in the business. There's no idea too wacky for him to at least consider it; and when he decides to do something unusual—like a series of "parallel novels"—he puts everything behind it and makes it happen.

Barbara Bova's creativity and dedication as my agent have blessed my family for most of my career. And I haven't forgotten that the Ender saga first reached the public because, even before she became an agent, her husband, Ben Bova, found a novella called "Ender's Game" on his slush-pile and, with a few small changes, agreed to publish it in the August 1977 *Analog* magazine. That one decision (and it wasn't a no-brainer—other editors turned it down cold) has been putting bread on my table and opening the door for readers to find my other work ever since.

But when the writing day is done and I come down out of my garret room, it's finding my wife, Kristine, and my daughter Zina there that makes it all worth doing. Thanks for the love and joy in my life each day. And to my other kids as well, for leading lives that I'm proud to be connected with.

Praise for *SHADOW OF THE HEGEMON*

"This fine follow-up to *Ender's Shadow* features that novel's hero, Bean (now a young man), wrestling with Card's trademark: superbly real moral and ethical dilemmas. . . . The complexity and serious treatment of the book's young protagonists will attract many sophisticated YA readers, while Card's impeccable prose, fast pacing, and political intrigue will appeal to adult fans of spy novels, thrillers, and science fiction."   —*Publishers Weekly* (starred review)

"As are all Card's books, this one is strangely moving. Although *Shadow of the Hegemon* has the bones of a simple thriller, Card's ability to evoke character—especially the character of children essentially raised by each other while continually under siege—makes these books seem not like fiction but like family stories, tales of what our relatives endured in a world too close to our own."
—*San Jose Mercury News*

"The author's graceful storytelling and engaging cast of youthful characters add an extra dimension to an already gripping story of children caught up in world-shaking events."   —*Library Journal*

"The characterizations are first class, and the fast-paced action features one hair-raising episode after another. . . . *Shadow of the Hegemon* is so nicely integrated into the rest of the Ender canon that readers will be completely enthralled and left anxiously awaiting the next installment."   —*Booklist*

"*Shadow of the Hegemon* is an ideal book with which to start your science fiction year."   —*Rocky Mountain News*

BY ORSON SCOTT CARD
FROM TOM DOHERTY ASSOCIATES

ENDER UNIVERSE

ENDER SERIES
Ender's Game
Ender in Exile
Speaker for the Dead
Xenocide
Children of the Mind

ENDER'S SHADOW SERIES
Ender's Shadow
Shadow of the Hegemon
Shadow Puppets
Shadow of the Giant
Shadows in Flight

THE FIRST FORMIC WAR
(WITH AARON JOHNSTON)
Earth Unaware
Earth Afire
Earth Awakens

THE SECOND FORMIC WAR
(WITH AARON JOHNSTON)
The Swarm
The Hive

Children of the Fleet

ENDER NOVELLAS
A War of Gifts
First Meetings

THE MITHERMAGES
The Lost Gate
The Gate Thief
Gatefather

THE TALES OF ALVIN
MAKER
Seventh Son
Red Prophet

Prentice Alvin
Alvin Journeyman
Heartfire
The Crystal City

HOMECOMING
The Memory of Earth
The Call of Earth
The Ships of Earth
Earthfall
Earthborn

WOMEN OF GENESIS
Sarah
Rebekah
Rachel & Leah

THE COLLECTED
SHORT FICTION OF
ORSON SCOTT CARD
*Maps in a Mirror: The Short
    Fiction of Orson Scott Card*
Keeper of Dreams

STAND-ALONE FICTION
Invasive Procedures (with
    Aaron Johnston)
Empire
Hidden Empire
The Folk of the Fringe
Hart's Hope
Lovelock (with Kathryn H. Kidd)
*Pastwatch: The Redemption of
    Christopher Columbus*
Saints
Songmaster
Treason
The Worthing Saga
Wyrms
Zanna's Gift

SHADOW PUPPETS

Orson Scott Card

TOR®

A TOM DOHERTY ASSOCIATES BOOK
NEW YORK

This is a work of fiction. All of the characters, organizations, and events portrayed in this novel are either products of the author's imagination or are used fictitiously.

SHADOW PUPPETS

Edited by Beth Meacham

A Tor Book
Published by Tom Doherty Associates
120 Broadway
New York, NY 10271

www.tor-forge.com

Tor® is a registered trademark of Macmillan Publishing Group, LLC.

ISBN 978-0-7653-4005-4

Our books may be purchased in bulk for promotional, educational, or business use. Please contact your local bookseller or the Macmillan Corporate and Premium Sales Department at 1-800-221-7945, extension 5442, or by email at MacmillanSpecialMarkets@macmillan.com.

First Edition: August 2002
First International Mass Market Edition: April 2003
First U.S. Mass Market Edition: June 2003

Printed in the United States of America

20 19 18 17 16 15 14

CONTENTS

1

GROWN

From: NoAddress@Untraceable.com#14h9cc0/
SIGN UP NOW AND STAY ANONYMOUS!
To: Trireme%Salamis@Attica-vs-Sparta.hst
Re: Final decision

Wiggin:

Subj not to be killed. Subj will be transported according to plan 2, route 1. Dep Tue. 0400, checkpoint #3 @ 0600, which is first light. Please be smart enough to remember the international dateline. He is yours if you want him.

If your intelligence outweighs your ambition you will kill him. If vice versa, you will try to use him. You did not ask my advice, but I have seen him in action: Kill him.

True, without an antagonist to frighten the world you will never retrieve the power the office of Hegemon once had. It would be the end of your career.

Let him live, and it is the end of your life, and you will leave the world in his power when you die. Who is the monster? Or at least monster #2?

And I have told you how to get him. Am I monster #3?
Or merely fool #1?

Your faithful servant in motley.

Bean kind of liked being tall, even though it was going to kill him.

And at the rate he was growing, it would be sooner rather than later. How long did he have? A year? Three? Five? The ends of his bones were still like a child's, blossoming, lengthening; even his head was growing, so that like a baby he had a soft patch of cartilage and new bone along the crest of his skull.

It meant constant adjustment, as week by week his arms reached farther when he flung them out, his feet were longer and caught on stairs and sills, his legs were longer so that as he walked he covered ground more quickly, and companions had to hurry to keep up. When he trained with his soldiers, the elite company of men that constituted the entire military force of the Hegemony, he could now run ahead of them, his stride longer than theirs.

He had long since earned the respect of his men. But now, thanks to his height, they finally, literally, looked up to him.

Bean stood on the grass where two assault choppers were waiting for his men to board. Today the mission was a dangerous one—to penetrate Chinese air space and intercept a small convoy transporting a prisoner from Beijing toward the interior. Everything depended on secrecy, surprise, and the extraordinarily accurate information the Hegemon, Peter Wiggin, had been receiving from inside China in the past few months.

Bean wished he knew the source of the intelligence, because his life and the lives of his men depended on it. The accuracy up to now could easily have been a setup. Even though "Hegemon" was essentially an empty title now, since most of the world's population resided in countries that had withdrawn their recognition of the authority of the office, Peter Wiggin had been using Bean's soldiers well. They were a constant irritant to the newly expansionist China, inserting themselves here and there at exactly the moment most calculated to disrupt the confidence of the Chinese leadership.

The patrol boat that suddenly disappears, the helicopter that goes down, the spy operation that is abruptly rolled up, blinding the Chinese intelligence service in yet another country—officially the Chinese hadn't even accused the Hegemon of any involvement in such incidents, but that only meant that they didn't want to give any publicity to the Hegemon, didn't want to boost his reputation or prestige among those who feared China in these years since the conquest of India and Indochina. They almost certainly knew who was the source of their woes.

Indeed, they probably gave Bean's little force the credit for problems that were actually the ordinary accidents of life. The death of the foreign minister of a heart attack in Washington, D.C. only minutes before meeting with the U.S. president—they might really think Peter Wiggin's reach was that long, or that he thought the Chinese foreign minister, a party hack, was worth assassinating.

And the fact that a devastating drought was in its second year in India, forcing the Chinese either to buy food on the open market or allow relief workers from Europe and the Americas into the newly captured and still rebellious subcontinent—maybe they even imagined that Peter Wiggin could control the monsoon rains.

Bean had no such illusions. Peter Wiggin had all kinds of contacts throughout the world, a collection of informants that was gradually turning into a serious network of spies, but as far as Bean could tell, Peter was still just playing a game. Oh, Peter thought it was real enough, but he had never seen what happened in the real world. He had never seen people die as a result of his orders.

Bean had, and it was not a game.

He heard his men approaching. He knew without looking that they were very close, for even here, in supposedly safe territory—an advance staging area in the mountains of Mindanao in the Philippines—they moved as silently as possible. But he also knew that he had heard them before they expected him to, for his senses had always been unusually keen. Not the physical sense organs—his ears were quite ordinary—but the ability of his brain to recognize even the slightest variation from the ambient sound. That's why he raised a hand in greeting to men who were only just emerging from the forest behind him.

He could hear the changes in their breathing—sighs, almost-silent chuckles—that told him they recognized that he had caught them again. As if it were a grown-up game of Mother-May-I, and Bean always seemed to have eyes in the back of his head.

Suriyawong came up beside him as the men filed by in two columns to board the choppers, heavily laden for the mission ahead.

"Sir," said Suriyawong.

That made Bean turn. Suriyawong never called him "sir."

His second-in-command, a Thai only a few years older than Bean, was now half a head shorter. He saluted Bean, and then turned toward the forest he had just come from.

When Bean turned to face the same direction, he saw Peter Wiggin, the Hegemon of Earth, the brother of Ender Wiggin who saved the world from the Formic invasion only a few years before—Peter Wiggin, the conniver and gamesman. What was he playing at now?

"I hope you aren't insane enough to be coming along on this mission," said Bean.

"What a cheery greeting," said Peter. "That *is* a gun in your pocket, so I guess you aren't happy to see me."

Bean hated Peter most when Peter tried to banter. So he said nothing. Waited.

"Julian Delphiki, there's been a change of plans," said Peter.

Calling him by his full name, as if he were Bean's father. Well, Bean had a father—even if he didn't know he had one until after the war was over, and they told him that Nikolai Delphiki wasn't just his friend, he was his brother. But having a father and mother show up when you're eleven isn't the same as growing up with them. No one had called Bean "Julian Delphiki" when he was little. No one had called him anything at all, until they tauntingly called him Bean on the streets of Rotterdam.

Peter never seemed to see the absurdity of it, talking down to Bean. I fought in the war against the Buggers, Bean wanted to say. I fought beside your brother Ender, while you were playing your little games with rabble-rousing on the nets. And while you've been filling your empty little role as Hegemon,

I've been leading these men into combat that actually made a difference in the world. And *you* tell *me* there's been a change of plans?

"Let's scrub the mission," said Bean. "Last-minute changes in plan lead to unnecessary losses in battle."

"Actually, this one won't," said Peter. "Because the only change is that you're not going."

"And you're going in my place?" Bean did not have to show scorn in his voice or on his face. Peter was bright enough to know that the idea was a joke. Peter was trained for nothing except writing essays, shmoozing with politicians, playing at geopolitics.

"Suriyawong will command this mission," said Peter.

Suriyawong took the sealed envelope that Peter handed him, but then turned to Bean for confirmation.

Peter no doubt noticed that Suriyawong did not intend to follow Peter's orders unless Bean said he should. Being mostly human, Peter could not resist the temptation to jab back. "Unless," said Peter, "you don't think Suriyawong is ready to lead the mission."

Bean looked at Suriyawong, who smiled back at him.

"Your Excellency, the troops are yours to command," said Bean. "Suriyawong always leads the men in battle, so nothing important will be different."

Which was not quite true—Bean and Suriyawong often had to change plans at the last minute, and Bean ended up commanding all or part of a mission as often as not, depending on which of them had to deal with the emergency. Still, difficult as this operation was, it was not too complicated. Either the convoy would be where it was supposed to be, or it would not. If it was there, the mission would probably succeed. If it was not there, or if it was an ambush, the mission would be aborted and they would return home. Suriyawong and the other officers and soldiers could deal with any minor changes routinely.

Unless, of course, the change in mission was because Peter Wiggin knew that it would fail and he didn't want to risk losing Bean. Or because Peter was betraying them for some arcane reason of his own.

"Please don't open that," said Peter, "until you're airborne."

Suriyawong saluted. "Time to leave," he said.

"This mission," said Peter, "will bring us significantly closer to breaking the back of Chinese expansionism."

Bean did not even sigh. But this tendency of Peter's to make claims about what *would* happen always made him a little tired.

"Godspeed," said Bean to Suriyawong. Sometimes when he said this, Bean remembered Sister Carlotta and wondered if she was actually with God now, and perhaps heard Bean say the closest thing to a prayer that ever passed his lips.

Suriyawong jogged to the chopper. Unlike the men, he carried no equipment beyond a small daypack and his sidearm. He had no need of heavy weaponry, because he expected to remain with the choppers during this operation. There were times when the commander had to lead in combat, but not on a mission like this, where communication was everything and he had to be able to make instant decisions that would be communicated to everyone at once. So he would stay with the e-maps that monitored the positions of every soldier, and talk with them by scrambled satellite uplink.

He would not be safe, there in the chopper. Quite the contrary. If the Chinese were aware of what was coming, or if they were able to respond in time, Suriyawong would be sitting inside one of the two biggest and easiest targets to hit.

That's my place, thought Bean as he watched Suriyawong bound up into the chopper, helped by the outstretched hand of one of the men.

The door of the chopper closed. The two aircraft rose from the ground in a storm of wind and dust and leaves, flattening the grass below them.

Only then did another figure emerge from the forest. A young woman. Petra.

Bean saw her and immediately erupted with anger.

"What are you thinking?" he shouted at Peter over the diminishing sound of the rising choppers. "Where are her bodyguards? Don't you know she's in danger whenever she leaves the safety of the compound?"

"Actually," said Peter—and now the choppers were high enough up that normal voices could be heard— "she's probably never been safer in her life."

"If you think that," said Bean, "you're an idiot."

"Actually, I do think that, and I'm not an idiot." Peter grinned. "You always underestimate me."

"You always overestimate yourself."

"Ho, Bean."

Bean turned to Petra. "Ho, Petra." He had seen her only three days ago, just before they left on this mission. She had helped him plan it; she knew it backward and forward as well as he did. "What's this eemo doing to our mission?" Bean asked her.

Petra shrugged. "Haven't you figured it out?"

Bean thought for a moment. As usual, his unconscious mind had been processing information in the background, well behind what he was aware of. On the surface, he was thinking about Peter and Petra and the mission that had just left. But underneath, his mind had already noticed the anomalies and was ready to list them.

Peter had taken Bean off the mission and given sealed orders to Suriyawong. Obviously, then, there was some change in the mission that he didn't want Bean to know about. Peter had also brought Petra out of hiding and yet claimed she had never been safer. That must mean that for some reason he was sure Achilles was not able to reach her here.

Achilles was the only person on earth whose personal network rivaled Peter's for its ability to stretch across national boundaries. The only way Peter could be sure that Achilles could not reach Petra, even here, was if Achilles was not free to act.

Achilles was a prisoner, and had been for some time.

Which meant that the Chinese, having used him to set up their conquest of India, Burma, Thailand, Vietnam, Laos, and Cambodia, and to arrange their alliance with Russia and the Warsaw Pact, finally noticed that he was a psychopath and locked him up.

Achilles was a prisoner in China. The message contained in Suriyawong's envelope undoubtedly told him the identity of the prisoner that they were supposed to rescue from Chinese custody. That information could not have been communicated before the mission departed, because Bean would not have allowed the mission to go forward if he had known it would lead to Achilles's release.

Bean turned to Peter. "You're as stupid as the German politicians who conspired to bring Hitler to power, thinking they could use him."

"I knew you'd be upset," said Peter calmly.

"Unless the new orders you gave Suriyawong were to kill the prisoner after all."

"You realize that you're way too predictable when it comes to this guy. Just mentioning his name sets you off. It's your Achilles heel. Pardon the jest."

Bean ignored him. Instead he reached out and took Petra's hand. "If you already knew what he was doing, why did you come with him?"

"Because I wouldn't be safe in Brazil anymore," said Petra, "and so I'd rather be with you."

"Both of us together only gives Achilles twice the motivation," said Bean.

"But you're the one who survives no matter what Achilles throws at you," said Petra. "That's where I want to be."

Bean shook his head. "People close to me die."

"On the contrary," said Petra. "People only die when they *aren't* with you."

Well, that was true enough, but irrelevant. In the long run, Poke and Sister Carlotta both died because of Bean. Because they made the mistake of loving him and being loyal to him.

"I'm not leaving your side," said Petra.

"Ever?" asked Bean.

Before she could answer, Peter interrupted. "All this is very touching, but we need to go over what we're doing with Achilles after we get him back."

Petra looked at him as if he were an annoying child. "You really are dim," she said.

"I know he's dangerous," said Peter. "That's why we have to be very careful how we handle this."

"Listen to him," said Petra. "Saying 'we.'"

"There's no 'we,'" said Bean. "Good luck." Still holding Petra's hand, Bean started for the forest. Petra had only a moment to wave cheerily at Peter and then she was beside Bean, jogging toward the trees.

"You're going to *quit*?" shouted Peter after them.

"Just like that? When we're finally close to being able to get things moving our way?"

They didn't stop to argue.

Later, on the private plane Bean chartered to get them from Mindanao to Celebes, Petra mocked Peter's words. " 'When we're finally close to being able to get things moving our way?' "

Bean laughed.

"When was it ever *our* way?" she went on, not laughing now. "It's all about increasing Peter's influence, boosting *his* power and prestige. *Our* way."

"I don't want him dead," said Bean.

"Who, Achilles?"

"No!" said Bean. "*Him* I want dead. It's Peter we have to keep alive. He's the only balance."

"He's lost his balance now," said Petra. "How long before Achilles arranges to have him killed?"

"What worries me is, how long before Achilles penetrates and coopts his entire network?"

"Maybe we're assigning Achilles supernatural powers," said Petra. "He isn't a god. Not even a hero. Just a sick kid."

"No," said Bean. "*I'm* a sick kid. He's the devil."

"Well, so," said Petra, "maybe the devil's a sick kid."

"So you're saying we should still try to help Peter."

"I'm saying that if Peter lives through his little brush with Achilles, he might be more prone to listen to us."

"Not likely," said Bean. "Because if he survives, he'll think it proves he's smarter than we are, so he'll be even less likely to hear us."

"Yeah," said Petra. "It's not like he's going to learn anything."

"First thing we need to do," said Bean, "is split up."

"No," said Petra.

"I've done this before, Petra. Going into hiding. Keeping from getting caught."

"And if we're together we're too identifiable, la la la," she said.

"Saying 'la la la' doesn't mean it isn't true."

"But I don't care," said Petra. "That's the part you're leaving out of your calculations."

"And I *do* care," said Bean, "which is the part you're leaving out of yours."

"Let me put it this way," said Petra. "If we separate, and Achilles finds me and kills me first, then you'll just have one more female you love deeply who is dead because you didn't protect her."

"You fight dirty."

"I fight like a girl."

"And if you stay with me, we'll probably end up dying together."

"No we won't," said Petra.

"I'm not immortal, as you well know."

"But you *are* smarter than Achilles. And luckier. And taller. And nicer."

"The new improved human."

She looked at him thoughtfully. "You know, now that you're tall, we could probably travel as man and wife."

Bean sighed. "I'm not going to marry you."

"Just as camouflage."

It had begun as hints but now it was quite open, her desire to marry him. "I'm not going to have children," he said. "My species ends with me."

"I think that's pretty selfish of you. What if the first homo sapiens had felt that way? We'd all still be neanderthals, and when the Buggers came they would have blasted us all to bits and that would be that."

"We didn't evolve from neanderthals," said Bean.

"Well, it's a good thing we have *that* little fact squared away," said Petra.

"And I didn't evolve at all. I was manufactured. Genetically created."

"Still in the image of God," said Petra.

"Sister Carlotta could say those things, but it's not funny coming from you."

"Yes it is," said Petra.

"Not to me."

"I don't think I *want* to have your babies, if they might inherit your sense of humor."

"That's a relief." Only it wasn't. Because he was attracted to her and she knew it. More than that. He truly cared about her, liked being with her. She was his friend. If he weren't going to die, if he wanted to have a family, if he had any interest in marrying, she was the only female human that he would even consider. But that was the trouble—she was human, and he was not.

After a few moments of silence, she leaned her head on his shoulder and held his hand. "Thank you," she murmured.

"For what I don't know."

"For letting me save your life."

"When did that happen?" asked Bean.

"As long as you have to look out for me," said Petra, "you won't die."

"So you're coming along with me, increasing our risk of being identified and allowing Achilles to get his two worst nemeses with one well-placed bomb, in order to save my life?"

"That's right, genius boy," said Petra.

"I don't even like you, you know." At this moment, he was annoyed enough that the statement was almost true.

"As long as you love me, I don't mind."

And he suspected that her lie, too, was almost true.

2

SURIYAWONG'S KNIFE

From: Salaam%Spaceboy@Inshallah.com
To: Watcher%OnDuty@International.net
Re: What you asked

My Dear Mr. Wiggin/Locke,

Philosophically speaking, all guests in a Muslim home are treated as sacred visitors sent by God and under his care. In practice, for two extremely talented, famous, and unpredictable persons who are hated by one powerful non-Muslim figure and aided by another, this is a very dangerous part of the world, particularly if they seek to remain both hidden and free. I do not believe they will be foolish enough to seek refuge in a Muslim country.

I regret to tell you, however, that your interest and mine do not coincide on this matter, so despite our occasional cooperation in the past, I most certainly will not tell you whether I encounter them or hear news of them.

Your accomplishments are many, and I have helped you in the past and will in the future. But when Ender led us in fighting the Formics these friends were beside me. Where were you?

Respectfully yours,
Alai

Suriyawong opened his orders and was not surprised. He had led missions inside China before, but always for the purpose of sabotage or intelligence gathering, or "involuntary high officer force reduction," Peter's mostly-ironic euphemism for assassination. The fact that this assignment had been to capture rather than kill suggested that it was a person who was not Chinese. Suriyawong had rather hoped it might be one of the leaders of a conquered country—the deposed prime minister of India, for instance, or the captive prime minister of Suriyawong's native Thailand.

He had even entertained, briefly, the thought that it might be one of his own family.

But it made sense that Peter was taking this risk, not for someone of mere political or symbolic value, but for the enemy who had put the world into this strange and desperate situation.

Achilles. Erstwhile gimp-legged cripple, frequent murderer, fulltime psychotic, and warmonger extraordinaire, Achilles had a knack for finding out just what the leaders of nations aspired for and promising them a way to get it. So far he had convinced a faction in the Russian government, the heads of the Indian and Pakistani governments, and various leaders in other lands to do his bidding. When Russia found him a liability, he had fled to India where he already had friends waiting for him. When India and Pakistan were both doing exactly what he had arranged for them to do, he betrayed them using his connections inside China.

The next move, of course, would have been to betray his friends in China and jump ahead of them to a position of even greater power. But the ruling coterie in China was every bit as cynical as Achilles and recognized his pattern of behavior, so not all that long after he had made China the world's only effective superpower, they arrested him.

If the Chinese were so smart, why wasn't Peter? Hadn't Peter himself said, "When Achilles is most useful and loyal to you, that is when he has most certainly betrayed you"? So why was he thinking he could use this monstrous boy?

Or had Achilles managed to convince Peter, despite all the proof that Achilles kept no promises, that this time he would remain loyal to an ally?

I should kill him, thought Suriyawong. In fact, I will. I will report to Peter that Achilles died in the chaos of the rescue. Then the world will be a safer place.

It's not as if Suriyawong hadn't killed dangerous enemies before. And from what Bean and Petra had told him, Achilles was by definition a dangerous enemy, especially to anyone who had ever been kind to him.

"If you've ever seen him in a condition of weakness or helplessness or defeat," Bean had said, "he can't bear for you to stay alive. I don't think it's personal. He doesn't have to kill you with his own hands or watch you die or anything like that. He just has to know that you no longer live in the same world with him."

"So the most dangerous thing you can do," Petra had said, "is to save him, because the very fact that you saw that he needed saving is your death sentence in his mind."

Had they never explained this to Peter?

Of course they had. So in sending Suriyawong to rescue Achilles, Peter knew that he was, in effect, signing Suriyawong's death warrant.

No doubt Peter imagined that he was going to control Achilles, and therefore Suriyawong would be in no danger.

But Achilles had killed the surgeon who repaired his gimp leg, and the girl who had once declined to kill him when he was at her mercy. He had killed the nun who found him on the streets of Rotterdam and got him an education and a chance at Battle School.

To have Achilles's gratitude was clearly a terminal disease. Peter had no power to make Suriyawong immune. Achilles never left a good deed unpunished, however long it might take, however convoluted the path to vengeance might be.

I should kill him, thought Suriyawong, or he will surely kill me.

He's not a soldier, he's a prisoner. To kill him would be murder, even in a war.

But if I don't kill him, he's bound to kill me. May a man not defend himself?

Besides, he's the one who masterminded the plan that put my people into subjugation to the Chinese, destroying a nation that had never been conquered, not by the Burmese, not by colonizing Europeans, not by the Japanese in the Second World War, not by the Communists in their day. For Thailand alone he deserves to die, not to mention all his other murders and betrayals.

But if a soldier does not obey orders, killing only as he is ordered to kill, then what is he worth to his commander? What cause does he serve? Not even his own survival, for in such an army no officer would be able to count on his men, no soldier on his companions.

Maybe I'll be lucky, and his vehicle will blow up with him inside.

Those were the thoughts he wrestled with as they flew below radar, brushing the crests of the waves of the China Sea.

They skimmed over the beach so quickly there was barely time to register the fact, as the onboard computers made the assault craft jog left and right, jerk upward and then drift down again, avoiding obstacles on the ground while trying to stay below radar. Their choppers were thoroughly masked, and the onboard disinfo pretended to all watching satellites that they were anything other than what they actually were. Before long they reached a certain road and turned north, then west, zipping over what Peter's intelligence sources had tagged as checkpoint number three. The men at that checkpoint would radio a warning to the convoy transporting Achilles, of course, but they wouldn't have finished the first sentence before . . .

Suriyawong's pilot spotted the convoy.

"Armor and troop transport fore and aft," he said.

"Take out all support vehicles."

"What if the prisoner has been put in one of the support vehicles?"

"Then there will be a tragic death by friendly fire," said Suriyawong.

The soldiers understood, or at least thought they understood—Suriyawong was going through the motions of rescuing the prisoner, but if the prisoner died he would not mind.

This was not, strictly speaking, true, or at least not at this moment. Suriyawong simply trusted the Chinese soldiers to go absolutely by the book. The convoy was merely a show of force to keep any local crowds or rebels or rogue military groups from attempting to interfere. They had not contemplated the possibility of—or even a motive for—a rescue from some outside force. Certainly not from the tiny commando force of the Hegemon.

Only a half dozen Chinese soldiers were able to get out of the vehicles before the Hegemony missiles blew them up. Suriyawong's soldiers were already firing before they leapt from the settling choppers, and he knew that in moments all resistance would be over.

But the prison van carrying Achilles was undisturbed. No one had emerged from it, not even the drivers.

Violating protocol, Suriyawong jumped down from the command chopper and walked toward the back of the prison van. He stood close as the soldier assigned to blow the door slapped on the unlocking charge and detonated it. There was a loud pop, but no backblast at all as the explosive tore open the latch.

The door jogged open a couple of centimeters.

Suriyawong extended an arm to stop the other soldiers from going into the van to rescue the prisoner.

Instead he opened the door only far enough to toss his own combat knife onto the floor of the van. Then he pushed the door back into place and stood back, waving his men back also.

The van rocked and lurched from some violent activity inside it. Two guns went off. The door flew open as a body collapsed backward into the dirt at their feet.

Be Achilles, thought Suriyawong, looking down at the Chinese officer who was trying to gather his entrails with his hands. Suriyawong had the irrational thought that the man ought really to wash his organs before jamming them back into his abdomen. It was so unsanitary.

A tall young man in prison pajamas appeared in the van door, holding a bloody combat knife in his hand.

You don't look like much, Achilles, thought Suriyawong. But then, you don't have to look all that impressive when you've just killed your guards with a knife you didn't expect someone to throw on the floor at your feet.

"All dead inside?" asked Suriyawong.

A soldier would have answered yes or no, along with a count of the living and dead. But Achilles hadn't been a soldier in Battle School for more than a few days. He didn't have the reflexes of military discipline.

"Very nearly," said Achilles. "Whose stupid idea was it to throw me a knife instead of opening the mossin' door and blasting the hell out of those guys?"

"Check to see if they're dead," Suriyawong said to his nearby men. Moments later they reported that all convoy personnel had been killed. That was essential if the Hegemon was to be able to preserve the fiction that it was not a Hegemony force that had carried out this raid.

"Choppers, in twenty," said Suriyawong.

At once his men scrambled to the choppers.

Suriyawong turned to Achilles. "My commander respectfully invites you to allow us to transport you out of China."

"And if I refuse?"

"If you have your own resources in country, then I will bid you good-bye with my commander's compliments."

This was not at all what Peter's orders said, but Suriyawong knew what he was doing.

"Very well," said Achilles. "Go away and leave me here."

Suriyawong immediately jogged toward his command chopper.

"Wait," called Achilles.

"Ten seconds," Suriyawong called over his shoulder. He jumped inside and turned around. Sure enough, Achilles was close behind, reaching out a hand to be taken up into the bird.

"I'm glad you chose to come with us," said Suriyawong.

Achilles found a seat and strapped himself into it. "I assume your commander is Bean and you're Suriyawong," said Achilles.

The chopper lifted off and began to fly by a different route toward the coast.

"My commander is the Hegemon," said Suriyawong. "You are his guest."

Achilles smiled placidly and silently looked around at the soldiers who had just carried out his rescue.

"What if I had been in one of the other vehicles?" said Achilles. "If I had been in charge of this convoy, there's no chance the prisoner would have been in the obvious place."

"But you were not commanding the convoy," said Suriyawong.

Achilles's smile broadened a little. "So what was that business with tossing in a knife? How did you know my hands would even be free to get the thing?"

"I assumed that you would have arranged to have free hands," said Suriyawong.

"Why? I didn't know you were coming."

"Begging your pardon, sir," said Suriyawong. "But

whatever was or wasn't coming, you would have had your hands free."

"Those were your orders from Peter Wiggin?"

"No sir, that was my judgment in battle," said Suriyawong. It galled him to address Achilles as "sir," but if this little play was to have a happy ending, this was Suriyawong's role for the moment.

"What kind of rescue is this, where you toss the prisoner a knife and stand and wait to see what happens?"

"There were too many variables if we flung open the door," said Suriyawong. "Too great a danger of your being killed in the crossfire."

Achilles said nothing, just looked at the opposite wall of the chopper.

"Besides," said Suriyawong. "This was not a rescue operation."

"What was it, target practice? Chinese skeet?"

"An offer of transportation to an invited guest of the Hegemon," said Suriyawong. "And the loan of a knife."

Achilles held up the bloody thing, dangling it from the point. "Yours?" he asked.

"Unless *you* want to clean it," said Suriyawong.

Achilles handed it to him. Suriyawong took out his cleaning kit and wiped down the blade, then began to polish it.

"You wanted me to die," said Achilles quietly.

"I expected you to solve your own problems," said Suriyawong, "without getting any of my men killed. And since you accomplished it, I believe my decision has proven to be, if not the best course of action, at least a valid one."

"I never thought I'd be rescued by Thais," said Achilles. "Killed by them, yes, but not *saved*."

"You saved yourself," said Suriyawong coldly. "No one here saved you. We opened the door for you and I lent you my knife. I assumed you might not have a knife, and the loan of mine might speed up your victory so you would not delay our return flight."

"You're a strange kind of boy," said Achilles.

"I was not tested for normality before I was entrusted with this mission," said Suriyawong. "But I have no doubt that I would fail such a test."

Achilles laughed. Suriyawong allowed himself a slight smile.

He tried not to guess what thoughts the inscrutable faces of his soldiers might be hiding. Their families, too, had been caught up in the Chinese conquest of Thailand. They, too, had cause to hate Achilles, and it had to gall them to watch Suriyawong sucking up to him.

For a good cause, men—I'm saving our lives as best I can by keeping Achilles from thinking of us as his rescuers, by making sure he believes that none of us ever saw him or even thought of him as helpless.

"Well?" said Achilles. "Don't you have any questions?"

"Yes," said Suriyawong. "Did you already have breakfast or are you hungry?"

"I never eat breakfast," said Achilles.

"Killing people makes me hungry," said Suriyawong. "I thought you might want a snack of some kind."

Now he caught a couple of the men glancing at him, only their eyes barely moving, but it was enough that Suriyawong knew they were reacting to what he said. Killing makes him hungry? Absurd. Now they must know that he was lying to Achilles. It was important to Suriyawong that his men know he was ly-

ing without him having to tell them. Otherwise he
might lose their trust. They might believe he had really given himself to the service of this monster.

Achilles did eat, after a while. Then he slept.

Suriyawong did not trust his sleep. Achilles no
doubt had mastered the art of seeming to be asleep
so he could hear the conversations of others. So Suriyawong talked no more than was necessary to de-
brief his men and get a full count of the personnel
from the convoy that they had killed.

Only when Achilles got off the chopper to pee at
the airfield on Guam did Suriyawong risk sending a
quick message to Ribeirão Preto. There was one person who had to know that Achilles was coming to
stay with the Hegemon: Virlomi, the Indian Battle-
Schooler who had escaped from Achilles in Hyderabad and had become the goddess guarding a bridge
in eastern India until Suriyawong had rescued her. If
she was in Ribeirão Preto when Achilles got there,
her life would be in danger.

And that was very sad for Suriyawong, because it
would mean he would not see Virlomi for a long time,
and he had recently decided that he loved her and
wanted to marry her when they both grew up.

3

MOMMIES AND DADDIES

encrypt key ********
decrypt key *****
To: Graff%pilgrimage@colmin.gov
From: Locke%erasmus@polnet.gov
Re: Unofficial request

I appreciate your warning, but I assure you that I do not underestimate the danger of having X in RP. In fact, that is a matter with which I could use your help, if you are inclined to give it. With JD and PA in hiding, and S compromised by having rescued X, persons close to them are in danger, either directly or through being used as hostages by X. We need to have them out of X's reach, and you are uniquely able to accomplish this. JD's parents are used to being in hiding, and have had some near misses; PA's parents, having already suffered one kidnapping, will also be inclined to cooperate.

The difficulty will come from my parents. There is no chance they will accept protective concealment if I propose it. If it comes from you, they might. I do not need to have my parents here, exposed to danger, where they might be used for leverage or to distract me from what must be accomplished.

Can you come yourself to RP to gather them up before I
return with X? You would have about 30 hours to accomplish this. I apologize for the inconvenience, but you
would once again have my gratitude and continue to
have my support, both of which, I hope, will someday
be more valuable than they are under present circumstances.

PW

Theresa Wiggin knew Graff was coming, since Elena
Delphiki gave her a hurried call as soon as he had
left her house. But she did not change her plans in
the slightest. Not because she hoped to deceive him,
but because there were papayas on the trees in the
backyard that had to be harvested before they dropped
to the ground. She had no intention of letting Graff
interfere with something really important.

So when she heard Graff politely clapping his
hands at the front gate, she was up on a ladder clip-
ping off papayas and laying them into the bag at her
side. Aparecida, the maid, had her instructions, and
so Theresa soon heard Graff's footsteps coming
across the tiles of the terrace.

"Mrs. Wiggin," he said.

"You've already taken two of my children," said
Theresa without looking at him. "I suppose you want
my firstborn, now."

"No," said Graff. "It's you and your husband I'm
after this time."

"Taking us to join Ender and Valentine?" Even
though she was being deliberately obtuse, the idea
nevertheless had a momentary appeal. Ender and Valentine had left all this business behind.

"I'm afraid we can't spare a followup ship to visit their colony for several years yet," said Graff.

"Then I'm afraid you have nothing to offer us that we want," said Theresa.

"I'm sure that's true," said Graff. "It's what Peter needs. A free hand."

"We don't interfere in his work."

"He's bringing a dangerous person here," said Graff. "But I think you know that."

"Gossip flies around here, since there's nothing else for the parents of geniuses to do but twitter to each other about the doings of their brilliant boys and girls. The Arkanians and Delphikis have their children all but married off. And we get such fascinating visitors from outer space. Like you."

"My, but we're testy today," said Graff.

"I'm sure Bean's and Petra's families have agreed to leave Ribeirão Preto so that their children don't have to worry about Achilles taking them hostage. And someday Nikolai Delphiki and Stefan Arkanian will recover from having been mere bit players in their siblings' lives. But John Paul's and my situation is not at all the same. *Our* son is the idiot who decided to bring Achilles here."

"Yes, it must hurt you to have the one child who simply isn't at the same intellectual level as the others," said Graff.

Theresa looked at him, saw the twinkle in his eye, and laughed in spite of herself. "All right, he isn't stupid, he's so cocky he can't conceive of any of his plans failing. But the result is the same. And I have no intention of hearing about his death through some awful little email message. Or—worse—from a news report talking about how 'the brother of the great Ender Wiggin has failed in his bid to revive the office of Hegemon' and then watch how even in death Peter's obituary is accompanied by more footage of Ender after his victory over the Formics."

"You seem to have a very clear view of all the future possibilities," said Graff.

"No, just the unbearable ones. I'm staying, Mr. Colonization Minister. You'll have to find your completely inappropriate middle-aged recruits somewhere else."

"Actually, you're not inappropriate. You're still of childbearing age."

"Having children has brought me such joy," said Theresa, "that it's really marvelous to contemplate having more of them."

"I know perfectly well how much you've sacrificed for your children, and how much you love them. And I knew coming here that you wouldn't want to go."

"So you have soldiers waiting to take me with you by force? You already have my husband in custody?"

"No, no," said Graff. "I think you're right not to go."

"Oh."

"But Peter asked me to protect you, so I had to offer. No, I think it's a good thing for you to stay."

"And why is that?"

"Peter has many allies," said Graff. "But no friends."

"Not even you?"

"I'm afraid I studied him too closely in his childhood to take any of his present charisma at face value."

"He does have that, doesn't he. Charisma. Or at least charm."

"At least as much as Ender, when he chooses to use it."

Hearing Graff speak of Ender—of the kind of young man Ender had become before he was pitched out of the solar system in a colony ship after saving the human race—filled Theresa with familiar, but no less bitter, regrets. Graff knew Ender Wiggin at age seven and ten and twelve, years when Theresa's only links to her youngest, most vulnerable child were a few photographs and fading memories and the ache in her arms where she could remember holding him, and the last lingering sensation of his little arms flung around her neck.

"Even when you brought him back to Earth," said Theresa to Graff, "you didn't let us see him. You took Val to him, but not his father, not me."

"I'm sorry," said Graff. "I didn't know he would never come home at war's end. Seeing you would have reminded him that there was someone in the world who was supposed to protect him and take care of him."

"And that would have been a bad thing?"

"The toughness we needed from Ender was not the person he wanted to be. We had to protect it. Letting him see Valentine was dangerous enough."

"Are you so sure that you were right?"

"Not sure at all. But Ender won the war, and we can never go back and try it another way to see if it would have worked as well."

"And I can never go back and try to find some way through all of this that doesn't end up filling me with resentment and grief whenever I see you or even think of you."

Graff said nothing for the longest time.

"If you're waiting for me to apologize," began Theresa.

"No, no," said Graff. "I was trying to think of any

apology I could make that wouldn't be laughably in-adequate. I never fired a gun in the war, but I still caused casualties, and if it's any consolation, when-ever I think of you and your husband I am also filled with regret."

"Not enough."

"No, I'm sure not," said Graff. "But I'm afraid my deepest regrets are for the parents of Bonzo Madrid, who put their son into my hands and got him back in a box."

Theresa wanted to fling a papaya at him and smear it all over his face. "Reminding me that I'm the mother of a killer?"

"Bonzo was the killer, ma'am," said Graff. "Ender defended himself. You entirely mistook my meaning. I'm the one who allowed Bonzo to be alone with Ender. I, not Ender, am the one responsible for his death. That's why I feel more regret toward the Ma-drid family than toward you. I've made a lot of mis-takes. And I can never be sure which ones were necessary or harmless or even left us better off than if I hadn't made them."

"How do you know you're not making a mistake now, letting me and John Paul stay?"

"As I said, Peter needs friends."

"But does the world need Peter?" asked Theresa.

"We don't always get the leader that we want," said Graff. "But sometimes we get to choose among the leaders that we have."

"And how will the choice be made?" asked Theresa. "On the battlefield or the ballot box?"

"Maybe," said Graff, "by the poisoned fig or the sabotaged car."

Theresa took his meaning at once. "You may be

sure we'll keep an eye on Peter's food and his transportation."

"What," said Graff, "you'll carry all his food on your person, buying it from different grocers every day, and your husband will live in his car, never sleeping?"

"We retired young. One has to fill the empty hours."

Graff laughed. "Good luck, then. I'm sure you'll do all that needs doing. Thanks for talking with me."

"Let's do it again in another ten or twenty years," said Theresa.

"I'll mark it on my calendar."

And with a salute—which was rather more solemn than she would have expected—he walked back into the house and, presumably, on out through the front garden and into the street.

Theresa seethed for a while at what Graff and the International Fleet and the Formics and fate and God had done to her and her family. And then she thought of Ender and Valentine and wept a few tears onto the papayas. And then she thought of herself and John Paul, waiting and watching, trying to protect Peter. Graff was right. They could never watch him perfectly.

They would sleep. They would miss something. Achilles would have an opportunity—many opportunities—and just when they were most complacent he would strike and Peter would be dead and the world would be at Achilles's mercy because who else was clever and ruthless enough to fight him? Bean? Petra? Suriyawong? Nikolai? One of the other Battle School children scattered over the surface of Earth? If there was any who was ambitious enough to stop Achilles, he would have surfaced by now.

She was carrying the heavy bag of papayas into the house—sidling through the door, trying not to bump and bruise the fruit—when it dawned on her what Graff's errand had really been about.

Peter needs a friend, he said. The issue between Peter and Achilles might be resolved by poison or sabotage, he said. But she and John Paul could not possibly watch over Peter well enough to protect him from assassination, he said. Therefore, in what way could she and John Paul possibly be the friends that Peter needed?

The contest between Achilles and Peter would be just as easily resolved by Achilles's death as by Peter's.

At once there flashed into her memory the stories of some of the great poisoners of history, by rumor if not by proof. Lucretia Borgia. Cleopatra. What's-her-name who poisoned everybody around the Emperor Claudius and probably got him in the end, as well.

In olden days, there were no chemical tests to determine conclusively whether poison had been used. Poisoners gathered their own herbs, leaving no trail of purchases, no co-conspirators who might confess or accuse. If anything happened to Achilles before Peter had decided the monster boy had to go, Peter would launch an investigation . . . and when the trail led to his parents, as it inevitably would, how would Peter respond? Make an example of them, letting them go on trial? Or would he protect them, trying to cover up the result of the investigation, leaving his reign as Hegemon to be tainted by the rumors about Achilles's untimely death. No doubt every opponent of Peter's would resurrect Achilles as a martyr, a much-slandered boy who offered the brightest hope to mankind, slain in his youth by the crawlingly vile Peter Wiggin, or his mother the witch or his father the snake.

It was not enough to kill Achilles. It had to be done properly, in a way that would not harm Peter in the long run.

Though it would be better for Peter to endure the rumors and legends about Achilles's death than for Peter himself to be the slain one. She dare not wait too long.

My assignment from Graff, thought Theresa, is to become an assassin in order to protect my son.

And the truly horrifying thing is that I'm not questioning whether to do it, but how. And when.

4

CHOPIN

encrypt key * * * * * * * *
decrypt key * * * * *
To: Pythian%legume@nowyouseeitnowyou.com
From: Graff%pilgrimage@colmin.gov
Re: Aren't we cute

I suppose you can be allowed to indulge your adolescent humor by using obvious pseudonyms like pythian%legume, and I know this is a use-once identity, but really, it smacks of a careless insouciance that worries me. We can't afford to lose you or your traveling companion because you had to make a joke.

Enough of imagining I could possibly influence your decisions. The first few weeks since the Belgian arrived in RP have been eventless. Your and your companion's parents are in training and quarantine, preparatory to going up to one of the colony ships. I will not actually take them off planet without your approval unless some emergency comes up. However, the moment I keep them past their training group's embarkation date, they become unusual and rumors will start to travel. It's dangerous to keep them Earthside for too long. And yet once we get them off-world, it will be even more difficult to get them back. I don't wish to pressure you, but your families' futures are at stake, and so far you haven't even consulted with them directly.

As for the Belgian, PW has given him a job—Assistant to the Hegemon. He has his own letterhead and email identity, a sort of minister without portfolio, with no bureaucracy to command and no money to disburse. Yet he keeps busy all day long. I wonder what he does.

I should have said that the Belgian has no official staff. Unofficially, Suri seems to be at his beck and call. I've heard from several observers that the change in him is quite astonishing. He never showed such exaggerated respect to you or PW as he does to the Belgian. They dine together often, and while the Belgian has never actually visited the barracks and training ground or gone on assignments or maneuvers with your little army, the inference that the Belgian is cultivating some degree of influence or even control over the Hegemony's small fighting force is inescapable. Are you in contact with Suri? When I tried to broach the subject with him, he never so much as answered.

As for you, my brilliant young friend, I hope you realize that all of Sister Carlotta's false identities were provided by the Vatican, and your use of them blares like a trumpet within Vatican walls. They have asked me to assure you that Achilles has no support within their ranks, and never did have, even before he murdered Carlotta, but if they can track you so easily, perhaps someone else can as well. As they say, a word to the wise is sufficient. And here I've gone and written five paragraphs.

—Graff

Petra and Bean traveled together for a month before things came to a head. At first Petra was content to let Bean make all the decisions. After all, she had never gone underground like this, traveling with false identities. He seemed to have all sorts of papers, some of which had been with him in the Philippines, and the rest in various hiding places scattered throughout the world.

The trouble was, all *her* identities were designed for a sixty-year-old woman who spoke languages that Petra had never learned. "This is absurd," she told Bean when he handed her the fourth such identity. "No one will believe this for an instant."

"And yet they do," said Bean.

"And I'd like to know why," she retorted. "I think there's more to this than the paperwork. I think we're getting help every time we pass through an identity check."

"Sometimes yes, sometimes no," said Bean.

"But every time you use some connection of yours to get a security guard to ignore the fact that I do *not* look old enough to be this person—"

"Sometimes, when you haven't had enough sleep—"

"You're too tall to be cute. So give it up."

"Petra, I agree with you," said Bean at last. "These were all for Sister Carlotta, and you don't look like her, and we *are* leaving a trail of favors asked for and favors done. So we need to separate."

"Two reasons why that won't happen," said Petra.

"You mean besides the fact that traveling together was your idea from the beginning? Which you black-mailed me into because we both know you'd get killed without me?—which hasn't stopped you from criticizing the *way* I go about keeping you alive, I notice."

"The second reason," Petra said, ignoring his effort to pick a fight, "is that while we're on the run you can't do anything. And it drives you crazy not to do anything."

"I'm doing a lot of things," said Bean.

"Besides arranging for us to get past stupid security guards with bad ID?"

"Already I've started two wars, cured three diseases, and written an epic poem. If you weren't so self-centered you would have noticed."

"You're such a jack of all trades, Julian."

"Staying alive isn't doing nothing."

"But it isn't doing what you want to do with your life," said Petra.

"Staying alive is all I've ever wanted to do with my life, dear child."

"But in the end, you're going to fail at that," said Petra.

"Most of us do. All of us, actually, unless Sister Carlotta and the Christians turn out to be right."

"You want to accomplish something before you die."

Bean sighed. "Because *you* want that, you think everyone does."

"The human need to leave something of yourself behind is universal."

"But I'm not human."

"No, you're superhuman," she said in disgust. "There's no talking to you, Bean."

"And yet you persist."

But Petra knew perfectly well that Bean felt just as she did—that it wasn't enough to stay in hiding, going from place to place, taking a bus here, a train there, a plane to some far-off city, only to start over again in a few days.

The only reason it mattered that they stay alive was so they could keep their independence long enough to work against Achilles. Except Bean kept denying that he had any such motive, and so they did nothing.

Bean had been maddening ever since Petra first met him in Battle School. He was the most incredibly tiny little runt then, so precocious he seemed snotty even when he said good morning, and even after they had all worked with him for years and had got the true measure of him at Command School, Petra was still the only one of Ender's jeesh that actually liked Bean.

She *did* like him, and not in the patronizing way that older kids take younger ones under their wing. There was never any illusion that Bean needed protection anyway. He arrived at Battle School as a consummate survivor, and within days—perhaps within hours—he knew more about the inner workings of the school than anyone else. The same was true at Tactical School and Command School, and during those crucial weeks before Ender joined them on Eros, when Bean commanded the jeesh in their practice maneuvers.

The others resented Bean then, for the fact that the youngest of them had been chosen to lead in Ender's place and because they feared that he would be their commander always. They were so relieved when Ender arrived, and didn't try to hide it. It had to hurt Bean, but Petra seemed to be the only one who even thought about his feelings. Much good that it did him. The person who seemed to think about Bean's feelings least of them all was Bean himself.

Yet he did value her friendship, though he only rarely showed it. And when she was overtaken by exhaustion during a battle, he was the one who covered for her, and he was the only one who showed that he still believed in her as firmly as ever. Even Ender never quite trusted her with the same level of assignment that she had had before. But Bean remained her friend, even as he obeyed Ender's orders and watched over her in all the remaining battles, ready to cover for her if she collapsed again.

Bean was the one she counted on when the Russians kidnapped her, the one she knew would get the message she hid in an email graphic. And when she was in Achilles's power, it was Bean who was her only hope of rescue. And he got her message, and he saved her from the beast.

Bean might pretend, even to himself, that all he cared about was his own survival, but in fact he was the most perfectly loyal of friends. Far from acting selfishly, he was reckless with his own life when he had a cause he believed in. But he didn't understand this about himself. Since he thought himself completely unworthy of love, it took him the longest time to know that someone loved him. He had finally caught on about Sister Carlotta, long before she died. But he gave little sign that he recognized Petra's feelings toward him. Indeed, now that he was taller than her, he acted as though he thought of her as an annoying little sister.

And that really pissed her off.

Yet she was determined not to leave him—and not because she depended on him for her own survival, either. She feared that the moment he was completely on his own, he would embark on some reckless plan to sacrifice his own life to put an end to Achilles's, and that would be an unbearable outcome, at least to Petra.

Because she had already decided that Bean was wrong in his belief that he should never have children, that the genetic alterations that had made him such a genius should die with him when his uncontrolled growth finally killed him.

On the contrary, Petra had every intention of bearing his children herself.

Being in a holding pattern like this, watching him drive himself crazy with his constant busyness that accomplished nothing important while making him irritable and irritating, Petra was not so self-controlled as not to snap back at him. They genuinely liked each other, and so far they had kept their sniping at a level that both could pretend was "only joking," but something had to change, and soon, or they really would have a fight that made it impossible to stay together—and what would happen to her plans for making Bean's babies then?

What finally got Bean to make a change was when Petra brought up Ender Wiggin.

"What did he save the human race *for?*" she said in exasperation one day in the airport at Darwin.

"So he could stop playing the stupid game."

"It wasn't so Achilles could rule."

"Someday Achilles will die. Caligula did."

"With help from his friends," Petra pointed out.

"And when he dies, maybe somebody better will succeed him. After Stalin, there was Khrushchev. After Caligula, there was Marcus Aurelius."

"Not *right* after. And thirty million died while Stalin ruled."

"So that made thirty million he didn't rule over any more," said Bean.

Sometimes he could say the most terrible things. But she knew him well enough by now to know that he spoke with such callousness only when he was feeling depressed. At times like that he brooded about how he was not a member of the human species and the difference was killing him. It was not how he truly felt. "You're not that cold," she said.

He used to argue when she tried to reassure him about his humanity. She liked to think maybe she was accomplishing something, but she feared that he had stopped answering because he no longer cared what she thought.

"If I settle into one place," he said, "my chance of staying alive is nil."

It irked her that he still spoke of "my chance" instead of "ours."

"You hate Achilles and you don't want him to rule the world and if you're going to have any chance of stopping him, you have to settle in one place and get to work."

"All right, you're so smart, tell me where I'd be safe."

"The Vatican," said Petra.

"How many acres in that particular kingdom? How eager are all those cardinals to listen to an altar boy?"

"All right then, somewhere within the borders of the Muslim League."

"We're infidels," said Bean.

"And they're people who are determined not to fall under the domination of the Chinese or the Hegemon or anybody else."

"My point is that they won't want us."

"My point is that whether they want us or not, we're the enemy of their enemy."

"We're two children, with no army and no information to sell, no leverage at all."

That was so laughable that Petra didn't bother answering. Besides, she had finally won—he was finally talking about where, not whether, he'd settle down and get to work.

———

They found themselves in Poland, and after taking the train from Katowice to Warsaw, they walked together through the Lazienki, one of the great parks of Europe, with centuries-old paths winding among giant trees and the saplings already planted to someday replace them.

"Did you come here with Sister Carlotta?" Petra asked him.

"Once," said Bean. "Ender is part Polish, did you know that?"

"Must be on his mother's side," said Petra. "Wiggin isn't a Polish name."

"It is when you change it from Wieczorek," said Bean. "Don't you think Mr. Wiggin looks Polish? Wouldn't he fit in here? Not that nationality means that much any more."

Petra laughed at that. "Nationality? The thing people die for and kill for and have for centuries?"

"No, I meant ancestry, I suppose. So many people are part this and part that. Supposedly I'm Greek, but my mother's mother was an Ibo diplomat, so . . . when I go to Africa I look quite Greek, and when I go to Greece I look rather African. In my heart I couldn't care less about either."

"You're a special case, Bean," said Petra. "You never had a homeland."

"Or a childhood, I suppose," said Bean.

"None of us in Battle School actually had much experience of either," said Petra.

"Which is, perhaps, why so many Battle School kids are so desperate to prove their loyalty to their birth nation."

That made sense. "Since we have few roots, the ones we have, we cling to." She thought of Vlad, who was so fanatically Russian, and Hot Soup—Han Tzu—so fanatically Chinese, that both of them had willingly helped Achilles when he seemed to be working for their nation's cause.

"And no one completely trusts us," said Bean, "because they know our real nationality is up in space. Our strongest loyalties are to our fellow soldiers."

"Or to ourselves," said Petra, thinking of Achilles.

"But I've never pretended otherwise," said Bean. Apparently he thought she had meant him.

"You're so proud of being completely self-centered," said Petra. "And it isn't even true."

He just laughed at her and walked on.

Families and businessmen and old people and young couples in love all strolled through the park on this unusually sunny autumn afternoon, and in the concert stand a pianist played a work of Chopin, as had been going on every day for centuries. As they walked, Petra boldly reached out and took hold of Bean's hand as if they, too, were lovers, or at least friends who liked to stay close enough to touch. To her surprise, he did not pull his hand away. Indeed, he gripped her hand in return, but if she harbored any notion that Bean was capable of romance, he instantly dispelled it. "Race you around the pond," he said, and so they did.

But what kind of race is it, when the racers never

let go of each other's hands, and the winner pulls the loser laughing over the finish line?

No, Bean was being childish because he had no idea how to go about being manly, and so it was Petra's job to help him figure it out. She reached out and caught his other hand and pulled his arms around her, then stood on tiptoe and kissed him. Mostly on the chin, because he recoiled a little, but it was a kiss nonetheless, and after a moment of consternation, Bean's arms pulled her a little closer and his lips managed to find hers while suffering only a few minor nose collisions.

Neither of them being particularly experienced at this, it wasn't as though Petra could say whether they kissed particularly well. The only other kiss she'd known was with Achilles, and that kiss had taken place with a gun pressed into her abdomen. All she could say with certainty was that any kiss from Bean was better than any kiss from Achilles.

"So you love me," said Petra softly when the kiss ended.

"I'm a raging mass of hormones that I'm too young to understand," said Bean. "You're a female of a closely related species. According to all the best primatologists, I really have no choice."

"That's nice," she said, reaching her arms around his back.

"It's not nice at all," said Bean. "I have no business kissing anybody."

"I asked for it," she said.

"I'm not having children."

"That's the best plan," she said. "I'll have them for you."

"You know what I meant," said Bean.

"It isn't done by kissing, so you're safe so far."

He groaned impatiently and pulled away from her, paced irritably in a circle, and then came right back to her and kissed her again. "I've wanted to do that practically the whole time we've been traveling together."

"I could tell," she said. "From the way you never gave even the tiniest sign that you knew I existed, except as an annoyance."

"I've always had a problem with being too emotionally demonstrative." He held her again. An elderly couple passed by. The man looked disapproving, as if he thought these foolish young people should find a more private place for their kissing and hugging. But the old woman, her white hair held severely by a head scarf, gave him a wink, as if to say, Good for you, young fellow, young girls should be kissed thoroughly and often.

In fact, he was so sure that was what she meant to say that he quoted the words to Petra.

"So you're actually performing a public service," said Petra.

"To the great amusement of the public," said Bean.

A voice came from behind them. "And I assure you the public is amused."

Petra and Bean both turned to see who it was.

A young man, but most definitely not Polish. From the look of him, he should be Burmese or perhaps Thai, certainly from somewhere around the South China Sea. He had to be younger than Petra, even taking into account the way that people from Southeast Asia seemed always to look far younger than their years. Yet he wore the suit and tie of an old-fashioned businessman.

There was something about him—something in the cockiness of his stance, the amused way that he took for granted that he had a right to stand within the circle of their companionship and tease them about something as private as a public kiss—that told Petra that he had to be from Battle School.

But Bean knew more about him than that. "Ambul," he said.

Ambul saluted in that half-sloppy, half-exaggerated style of a Battle School brat, and answered, "Sir."

"I gave you an assignment once," said Bean. "To take a certain launchie and help him figure out how to use his flash suit."

"Which I carried out perfectly," said Ambul. "He was so funny the first time I froze him in the battle room, I had to laugh."

"I can't believe he hasn't killed you by now," said Bean.

"My uselessness to the Thai government saved me."

"My fault, I fear," said Bean.

"Saved my life, I think," said Ambul.

"Hi, I'm Petra," said Petra irritably.

Ambul laughed and shook her hand. "Sorry," he said. "Ambul. I know who you are, and I assumed Bean would have told you who I was."

"I didn't think you were coming," said Bean.

"I don't answer emails," said Ambul. "Except by showing up and seeing if the email was really from the person it's supposed to be from."

"Oh," said Petra, putting things together. "You must be the soldier in Bean's army who was assigned to show Achilles around."

"Only he didn't have the foresight to push Achilles out an airlock without a suit," said Bean. "Which I think shows a shameful lack of initiative on his part."

"Bean notified me as soon as he found out Achilles

was on the loose. He figured there was no chance I wasn't on Achilles's hit list. Saved my life."

"So Achilles made a try?" asked Bean.

They were away from the path now, out in the open, standing on the broad lawn stretching away from the lake where the pianist played. Only the faintest sound of the amplified Chopin reached them here.

"Let's just say that I've had to keep moving," said Ambul.

"Is that why you weren't in Thailand when the Chinese invaded?" asked Petra.

"No," said Ambul. "No, I left Thailand almost as soon as I came home. You see, I was not like most Battle School graduates. I was in the worst army in the history of the battle room."

"My army," said Bean.

"Oh, come on," said Petra. "You only played, what, five games?"

"We never won a single one," said Bean. "I was working on training my men and experimenting with combat techniques and—oh, yes, staying alive with Achilles in Battle School with us."

"So they discontinued Battle School, Bean got promoted to Ender's jeesh, and his soldiers got sent back to Earth with the only perfect no-win record in the history of Battle School. All the other Thais from Battle School were given important places in the military establishment. But, oddly enough, they just couldn't find a thing for me to do except go to public school."

"But that's simply stupid," said Petra. "What were they thinking?"

"It kept me nice and obscure," said Ambul. "It gave my family the freedom to travel out of the country and take me with them—there are advantages to not being perceived as a valuable national resource."

"So you weren't in Thailand when it fell."

"Studying in London," said Ambul. "Which made it almost convenient to hop over the North Sea and zip over to Warsaw for a clandestine meeting."

"Sorry," said Bean. "I offered to pay your way."

"The letter might not have been from you," said Ambul. "And whoever sent it, if I let them buy my tickets, they'd know which planes I was on."

"He sounds as paranoid as we are," said Petra.

"Same enemy," said Ambul. "So, Bean, *sir,* you sent for me, and here I am. Need a witness for your wedding? Or an adult to sign permission forms for you?"

"What I need," said Bean, "is a secure base of operations, independent of any nation or bloc or alliance."

"I suggest you find a nice asteroid somewhere," said Ambul. "The world is pretty well divvied up these days."

"I need people I can trust absolutely," said Bean. "Because at any time we may find ourselves fighting against the Hegemony."

Ambul looked at him in surprise. "I thought you were commander of Peter Wiggin's little army."

"I was. Now I don't even command a decent hand of pinochle," said Bean.

"He does have a first-rate executive officer," said Petra. "Me."

"Ah," said Ambul. "Now I understand why you called on me. You two officers need somebody who'll salute you."

Bean sighed. "I'd appoint you king of Caledonia if I could, but the only position I can actually offer anybody is friend. And I'm a dangerous friend to have, these days."

"So the rumors are true," said Ambul. Petra figured it was about time he put together the information he was gleaning from this conversation. "Achilles is with the Hegemony."

"Peter hoisted him out of China, on his way to prison camp," said Bean.

"Got to give the Chinese credit, they're no eemos, they knew when to get rid of him."

"Not really," said Petra. "They were only sending him into internal exile, and in a low-security caravan at that. Practically invited rescue."

"And you wouldn't do it?" asked Ambul. "That's how you got fired?"

"No," said Bean. "Wiggin pulled me off the mission at the last minute. Gave sealed orders to Suri-yawong and didn't tell me what they were till he had already left. Whereupon I resigned and went into hiding."

"Taking your girltoy with you," said Ambul.

"Actually, Peter sent me along to keep him under very close surveillance," said Petra.

"You seem to be the right person for the job," said Ambul.

"She's not that good," said Bean. "I've come close to noticing her several times."

"So," said Ambul. "Suri went ahead and hoisted Achilles out of China."

"Of all the missions to execute flawlessly," said Bean, "Suri had to pick that one."

"I, on the other hand," said Ambul, "was never one to obey an order if I thought it was stupid."

"That's why I want you to join my completely hopeless operation," said Bean. "If you get killed, I'll know it's your own fault, and not because you were obeying my orders."

"I'll need fedda," said Ambul. "My family isn't rich. And technically I'm still a kid. Speaking of which, how the hell did you get so much taller than me?"

"Steroids," said Bean.

"And I stretch him on a rack every night," said Petra.

"For his own good, I'm sure," said Ambul.

"My mother told me," said Petra, "that Bean is the kind of boy who has to grow on you."

Bean playfully covered her mouth. "Pay no attention to the girl, she's besotted with love."

"You two should get married," said Ambul.

"When I turn thirty," said Bean.

Which, Petra knew, meant never.

They had already been out in the open longer than Bean had ever allowed since they'd gone into hiding. As Bean started telling Ambul what he wanted him to do, they began to walk toward the nearest exit from the park.

It was a simple enough assignment—go to Damascus, the headquarters of the Muslim League, and get a meeting with Alai, one of Ender's closest friends and a member of Ender's jeesh.

"Oh," said Ambul. "I thought you wanted me to do something *possible*."

"I can't get any email to him," said Bean.

"Because as far as I know he's been completely incommunicado ever since the Russians released him, that time when Achilles kidnapped everybody," said Ambul.

Bean seemed surprised. "You know this because . . ."

"Since my parents took me into hiding," said Ambul, "I've been tapping every connection I could get, trying to get information about what was happening. I'm good at networking, aboon. Making and keeping friends. I would have been a good commander, if they hadn't canceled Battle School out from under me."

"So you already know Alai?" said Petra. "Toguro."

"But like I said," Ambul repeated, "he's *completely* incommunicado."

"Ambul, I need his help," said Bean. "I need the shelter of the Muslim League. It's one of the few places on Earth that isn't susceptible to either Chinese pressure or Hegemony wheedling."

"É," said Ambul, "and they achieve that by not letting *any* non-Muslims within the circle."

"I don't want to be in the circle. I don't want to know their secrets."

"Yes you do," said Ambul. "Because if you aren't, if you don't have their complete trust, you'll have no power to do anything at all within their borders. Non-Muslims are officially completely free, but in practical terms, they can't do anything but shop and play tourist."

"Then I'll convert," said Bean.

"Don't even joke about it," said Ambul. "They take their religion very seriously, and to speak of converting as a joke—"

"Ambul, we know that," said Petra. "I'm a friend of Alai's, too, but you notice Bean didn't send me."

Ambul laughed. "You can't mean that the Muslims would lose respect for Alai if he let a woman influence him! The full equality of the sexes is one of the six points that ended the Third Great Jihad."

"You mean the Fifth World War?" asked Bean.

"The War for Universal Liberty," said Petra.

"That's what they called it in Armenian schools."

"That's because Armenia is bigoted against Muslims," said Ambul.

"The only nation of bigots left on Earth," said Petra ruefully.

"Listen, Ambul, if it's impossible to get to Alai," said Bean, "I'll just find something else."

"I didn't say it was impossible," said Ambul.

"Actually, that's exactly what you said," Petra said.

"But I'm a Battle Schooler," said Ambul. "We had classes in doing the impossible. I got A's."

Bean grinned. "Yes, but you didn't graduate from Battle School, did you, so what chance do you have?"

"Who knew that being assigned to your army in school would ruin my entire life?" said Ambul.

"Oh, stop whining," said Petra. "If you'd been a top graduate, now you'd be in a Chinese reeducation camp."

"See?" said Ambul. "I'm missing out on all the character-building experiences."

Bean handed him a slip of paper. "Go there and you'll find the identity stuff you need."

"Complete with holographic ID?" asked Ambul doubtfully.

"It'll adjust to you the first time you use it. Instructions are with it. I've used these before."

"Who does stuff like that?" asked Ambul. "The Hegemony?"

"The Vatican," said Bean. "These are leftovers from my days with one of their operatives."

"All right," said Ambul.

"It'll get you to Damascus, but it won't get you to Alai. You'll need your real identity for that."

"No, I'll need an angel walking before me and a letter of introduction from Mohammed himself."

"The Vatican has those," said Petra. "But they only give them to their top people."

Ambul laughed, and so did Bean, but the air was thick with tension.

"I'm asking you for a lot," said Bean.

"And I don't owe you much," said Ambul.

"You don't owe me anything," said Bean, "and if you did, I wouldn't try to collect it. You know why I asked you, and I know why you're doing it."

Petra knew, too. Bean asked him because he knew Ambul could do it if anyone could. And Ambul was doing it because he knew that if there was to be any hope of stopping Achilles from uniting the world under his rule, it would probably depend on Bean.

"I'm so glad we came to this park," said Petra to Bean. "So romantic."

"Bean knows how to show a girl a good time," said Ambul. He spread his arms wide. "Take a good look. I'm it."

And then he was gone.

Petra reached out and took Bean's hand again.

"Satisfied?" asked Bean.

"More or less," said Petra. "At least you did *something*."

"I've been doing something all along."

"I know," said Petra.

"In fact," said Bean, "you're the one who just goes online to shop."

She chuckled. "Here we are in this beautiful park. Where they keep alive the memory of a great man. A man who gave unforgettable music to the world. What will your memorial be?"

"Maybe two statues. Before and after. Little Bean who fought in Ender's jeesh. Big Julian who brought down Achilles."

"I like that," said Petra. "But I have a better idea."

"Name a colony planet after me?"

"How about this—they have a whole planet populated by your descendants."

Bean's expression soured and he shook his head. "Why? To make war against them? A race of brilliant people who breed as fast as they can because they're going to die before they're twenty. And every one of them curses the name of their ancestor because he didn't end this travesty with his own death."

"It's not a travesty," said Petra. "And what makes you think your . . . difference will breed true?"

"You're right," said Bean, "if I marry a long-lived stupid short girl like you, my progeny should average out to a bunch of average minds who live to be seventy and grow to be six feet tall."

"Do you want to know what I've been doing?" said Petra.

"Not shopping."

"I've been talking to Sister Carlotta."

He stiffened, looked away from her.

"I've been walking down the paths of her life," said Petra. "Talking to people she knew. Seeing what she saw. Learning what she learned."

"I don't want to know," said Bean.

"Why not? She loved you. Once she found you, she lived for you."

"I know that," said Bean. "And she died for me. Because I was stupid and careless. I didn't even need her to come, I just thought I did for a little while and by the time I found out I didn't, she was already in the air, already heading for the missile that killed her."

"There's somewhere I want us to go," said Petra.

"While we're waiting for Ambul to pull off his miracle."

"Listen," said Bean, "Sister Carlotta already told me how to get in touch with the scientists who were studying me. Every now and then I write to them and they tell me how soon they estimate my death will come and how exciting it is, all the progress they're making in understanding human development and all kinds of other kuso because of my body and all the little cultures they've got, keeping my tissues alive. Petra, when you think about it, I'm immortal. Those tissues will be alive in labs all over the world for a thousand years after I'm dead. That's one of the benefits of being completely weird."

"I'm not talking about them," said Petra.

"What, then? Where do you want to go?"

"Anton," she said. "The one who found the key, Anton's Key. The genetic change that resulted in you."

"He's still alive?"

"He's not only alive, he's free. War's over. Not that he's able to do serious research now. The psychological blocks aren't really removable. He has a hard time talking about . . . well, at least *writing* about what happened to you."

"So why bother him?"

"Got anything better to do?"

"I've always got something better to do than go to Romania."

"But he doesn't live there," said Petra. "He's in Catalunya."

"You're kidding."

"Sister Carlotta's homeland. The town of Mataró."

"Why did he go there?" asked Bean.

"Excellent weather," said Petra. "Nights on the

rambla. Tapas with friends. The gentle sea lapping the shore. The hot African wind. The breakers of the winter sea. The memory of Columbus coming to visit the king of Aragon."

"That was Barcelona."

"Well, he talked about seeing the place. And a garden designed by Gaudi. Things he loves to look at. I think he goes from place to place. I think he's very curious about you."

"So is Achilles," said Bean.

"I think that even though he's no longer on the cutting edge of science, there are things he knows that he was never able to tell."

"And still can't."

"It hurts him to say it. But that doesn't mean he couldn't say it, once, to the person who most needs to know."

"And that is?"

"Me," said Petra.

Bean laughed. "Not me?"

"You don't need to know," said Petra. "You've decided to die. But I need to know, because I want our children to live."

"Petra," said Bean. "I'm not going to have any children. Ever."

"Fortunately," said Petra, "the man never does."

She doubted she could ever persuade Bean to change his mind. With luck, though, the uncontrollable desires of the adolescent male might accomplish what reasonable discussion never could. Despite what he thought, Bean was human; and no matter what species he belonged to, he was definitely a mammal. His mind might say no, but his body would shout yes much louder.

Of course, if there was any adolescent male who

could resist his need to mate, it was Bean. It was one of the reasons she loved him, because he was the strongest man she had ever known. With the possible exception of Ender Wiggin, and Ender Wiggin was gone forever.

She kissed Bean again, and this time they were both somewhat better at it.

5

STONES IN THE ROAD

From: PW
To: TW
Re: What are you doing?

What is this housekeeper thing about? I'm not letting you
take a job in the Hegemony, certainly not as a housekeeper. Are you trying to shame me, making it look like
(a) I have my mother on the payroll and (b) I have my
mother working for me as a menial? You already refused
the opportunity I wanted you to take.

From: TW
To: PW
Re: a serpent's tooth

You are always so thoughtful, giving me such interesting
things to do. Touring the colony worlds. Staring at the
walls of my nicely air-conditioned apartment. You do remember that your birth was not parthenogenetic. You are
the only person on God's green earth who thinks I'm too
stupid to be anything but a burden around your neck. But
please don't imagine that I'm criticizing you. I am the
image of a perfect, doting mother. I *know* how well that
plays on the vids.

When Virlomi got Suriyawong's message, she understood at once the danger she was in. But she was almost glad of having a reason to leave the Hegemon's compound.

She had been thinking about going for some time, and Suriyawong himself was the reason. His infatuation with her had become too sad for her to stay much longer.

She liked him, of course, and was grateful to him— he was the one who had truly understood, without being told, how to play the scene so that she could escape from India under the guns of soldiers who would most certainly have shot down the Hegemony helicopters. He was smart and funny and good, and she admired the way he worked with Bean in commanding their fiercely loyal troops, conducting raid after raid with few casualties and, so far, no loss of life.

Suriyawong had everything Battle School was designed to give its students. He was bold, resourceful, quick, brave, smart, ruthless and yet compassionate. And he saw the world through similar eyes, compared to the westerners who otherwise seemed to have the Hegemon's ear.

But somehow he had also fallen in love with her. She liked him too well to shame him by rebuffing advances he had never made, yet she could not love him. He was too young for her, too . . . what? Too intense about his tasks. Too eager to please. Too . . .

Annoying.

There it was. His devotion irritated her. His constant attention. His eyes on her every move. His praise for her mostly trivial achievements.

No, she had to be fair. She was annoyed at everyone, and not because they did anything wrong, but because she was out of her place. She was not a soldier. A strategist, yes, even a leader, but not in combat. There was no one in Ribeirão Preto who was likely to follow her, and nowhere that she wanted to lead them.

How could she fall in love with Suriyawong? He was happy in the life he had, and she was miserable. Anything that made her happier would make him less happy. What future was there in that?

He loved her, and so he thought of her on the way back from China with Achilles and warned her to be gone before he returned. It was a noble gesture on his part, and so she was grateful to him all over again. Grateful that he had quite possibly saved her life.

And grateful that she wouldn't have to see him again.

By the time Graff arrived to pull people out of Ribeirão Preto, she was gone. She never heard the offer to go into the protection of the Ministry of Colonization. But even if she had, she would not have gone.

There was, in fact, only one place she would even think of going. It was where she had been longing to go for months. The Hegemony was fighting China from the outside, but had no use for her. So she would go to India, and do what she could from inside her occupied country.

Her path was a fairly direct one. From Brazil to Indonesia, where she connected with Indian expatriates and obtained a new identity and Sri Lankan papers. Then to Sri Lanka itself, where she persuaded a fishing boat captain to put her ashore on the southeastern coast of India. The Chinese simply didn't have enough of a fleet to patrol the shores of India, so the coasts leaked in both directions.

Virlomi was of Dravidian ancestry, darker-skinned than the Aryans of the north. She fit in well in this countryside. She wore clothing that was simple and poor, because everyone's was; but she also kept it clean, so she would not look like a vagabond or beggar. In fact, however, she was a beggar, for she had no vast reserves of funds and they would not have helped her anyway. In the great cities of India there were millions of connections to the nets, thousands of kiosks where bank accounts could be accessed. But in the countryside, in the villages—in other words, in *India*—such things were rare. For this simple-looking girl to use them would call attention to her, and soon there would be Chinese soldiers looking for her, full of questions.

So she went to the well or the market of each village she entered, struck up conversations with other women, and soon found herself befriended and taken in. In the cities, she would have had to be wary of quislings and informers, but she freely trusted the common people, for they knew nothing of strategic importance, and therefore the Chinese did not bother to scatter bribes among them.

Nor, however, did they have the kind of hatred of the Chinese that Virlomi had expected. Here in the south of India, at least, the Chinese ruled lightly over the common people. It was not like Tibet, where the Chinese had tried to expunge a national identity and the persecutions had reached down to every level of society. India was simply too large to digest all at once, and like the British before them, the Chinese found it easier to rule India by dominating the bureaucratic class and leaving the common folk alone.

Within a few days, Virlomi realized that this was precisely the situation she had to change.

In Thailand, in Burma, in Vietnam, the Chinese were dealing ruthlessly with insurgent groups, and still the guerrilla warfare continued. But India slumbered, as if the people didn't care who ruled them. In fact, of course, the Chinese were even more ruthless in India than elsewhere—but since all their victims were of the urban elite, the rural areas felt only the ordinary pain of corrupt government, unreliable weather, untrustworthy markets, and too much labor for too little reward.

There were guerrillas and insurgents, of course, and the people did not betray them. But they also did not join them, and did not willingly feed them out of their scant food supply, and the insurgents remained timid and ineffective. And those that resorted to brigandage found that the people grew instantly hostile and turned them in to the Chinese at once.

There was no solidarity. As always before, the conquerors were able to rule India because most Indians did not know what it meant to live in "India." They thought they lived in this village or that one, and cared little about the great issues that kept the cities in turmoil.

I have no army, thought Virlomi. But I had no army when I fled Hyderabad to escape Achilles and wandered eastward. I had no plan, except a need to get word to Petra's friends about where Petra was. Yet when I came to a place where there was an opportunity, I saw it, I took it, and I won. That is the plan I have now. To watch, to notice, to act.

For days, for weeks she wandered, watching everything, loving the people in every village she stopped at, for they were kind to this stranger, generous with the next-to-nothing that they had. How can I plot to bring the war to their level, to disrupt their lives? Is it not enough that they're content? If the Chinese are leaving them alone, why can't I?

Because she knew the Chinese would not leave them alone forever. The Middle Kingdom did not believe in tolerance. Whatever they possessed, they made it Chinese or they destroyed it. Right now they were too busy to bother with the common people. But if the Chinese were victorious everywhere, then they would be free to turn their attention to India. Then the boot would press heavily upon the necks of the common folk. Then there would be revolt after revolt, riot after riot, but none of them would succeed. Gandhi's peaceful resistance only worked against an oppressor with a free press. No, India would revolt with blood and terror, and with blood and horror China would suppress the revolts, one at a time.

The Indian people had to be roused from their slumber now, while there were still allies outside their borders who might help them, while the Chinese were still overextended and dared not devote too many resources to the occupation.

I will bring war down on their heads to save them as a nation, as a people, as a culture. I will bring war upon them while there is a chance of victory, to save them from war when there is no possible outcome but despair.

It was pointless, though, to wonder about the morality of what she intended to do, when she had not yet thought of a way to do it.

It was a child who gave her the idea.

She saw him with a bunch of other children, playing at dusk in the bed of a dry stream. During monsoon season, this stream would be a torrent; now it was just a streak of stones in a ditch.

This one child, this boy of perhaps seven or eight,

though he might have been older, his growth stunted by hunger, was not like the other children. He did not join them in running and shouting, shoving and chasing, and tossing back and forth whatever came to hand. Virlomi thought at first he must be crippled, but no, his staggering gait was because he was walking right among the stones of the streambed, and had to adjust his steps to keep his footing.

Every now and then he bent over and picked up something. A little later, he would set it back down.

She came closer, and saw that what he picked up was a stone, and when he set it back down it was only a stone among stones.

What was the meaning of his task, on which he worked so intently, and which had so little result?

She walked to the stream, but well behind his path, and watched his back as he receded into the gathering gloom, bending and rising, bending and rising.

He is acting out my life, she thought. He works at his task, concentrating, giving his all, missing out on the games of his playmates. And yet he makes no difference in the world at all.

Then, as she looked at the streambed where he had already walked, she saw that she could easily find his path, not because he left footprints, but because the stones he picked up were lighter than the others, and by leaving them on the top, he was marking a wavering line of light through the middle of the streambed.

It did not really change her view of his work as meaningless—if anything, it was further proof. What could such a line possibly accomplish? The fact that there was a visible result made his labor all the more pathetic, because when the rains came it would all be swept away, the stones retumbled upon each other, and what difference would it make that for a while, at least, there was a dotted line of lighter stones along the middle of the streambed?

Then, suddenly, her view of it changed. He was not marking a line. He was building a stone wall.

No, that was absurd. A wall whose stones were as much as a meter apart? A wall that was never more than one stone high?

A wall, made of the stones of India. Picked up and set down almost where they had been found. But the stream was different because the wall had been built.

Is this how the Great Wall of China had begun? A child marking off the boundaries of his world?

She walked back to the village and returned to the house where she had been fed and where she would be spending the night. She did not speak of the child and the stones to anyone; indeed, she soon thought of other things and did not think to ask anyone about the strange boy. Nor did she dream of stones that night.

But in the morning, when she awoke with the mother and took her two water pitchers to the public spigot, so she did not have to do that task today, she saw the stones that had been brushed to the sides of the road and remembered the boy.

She set down the pitchers at the side of the road, picked up a few stones, and carried them to the middle of the road. There she set them and returned for more, arranging them in broken a line right across the road.

Only a few dozen stones, when she was done. Not a barrier of any kind. And yet it was a wall. It was as obvious as a monument.

She picked up her pitchers and walked on to the spigot.

As she waited her turn, she talked with the other women, and a few men, who had come for the day's water. "I added to your wall," she said after a while.

"What wall?" they asked her.

"Across the road," she said.

"Who would build a wall across a road?" they asked.

"Like the ones I've seen in other towns. Not a *real* wall. Just a line of stones. Haven't you seen it?"

"I saw *you* putting stones out into the road. Do you know how hard we work to keep it clear?" said one of the men.

"Of course. If you didn't keep it clear everywhere else," said Virlomi, "no one would see where the wall was." She spoke as though what she said were obvious, as though he had surely had this explained to him before.

"Walls keep things out," said a woman. "Or they keep things in. Roads let things pass. If you build a wall across, it isn't a road anymore."

"Yes, *you* at least understand," said Virlomi, though she knew perfectly well that the woman understood nothing. Virlomi barely understood it herself, though she knew that it felt right to her, that at some level below sense it made perfect sense.

"I do?" said the woman.

Virlomi looked around at the others. "It's what they told me in the other towns that had a wall. It's the Great Wall of India. Too late to keep the barbarian invaders out. But in every village, they drop stones, one or two at a time, to make the wall that says, We don't want you here, this is our land, we are free. Because we can still build our wall."

"But . . . it's only a few stones!" cried the exasperated man who had seen her building it. "I kicked a few out of my way, but even if I hadn't, the wall wouldn't have stopped a beetle, let alone one of the Chinese trucks!"

"It's not the wall," said Virlomi. "It's not the stones. It's who dropped them, who built it, and why. It's a message. It's . . . it's the new flag of India."

She was seeing comprehension in some of the eyes around her.

"Who can build such a wall?" asked one of the women.

"Don't all of you add to it? It's built a stone or two at a time. Every time you pass, you bring a stone, you drop it there." She was filling her pitchers now. "Before I carry these pitchers back, I pick up a small stone in each hand. When I pass over the wall, I drop the stones. That's how I've seen it done in the other villages with walls."

"Which other villages?" demanded the man.

"I don't remember their names," said Virlomi. "I only know that they had Walls of India. But I can see that none of you knew about it, so perhaps it was only some child playing a prank, and not a wall after all."

"No," said one of the women. "I've seen people add to it before." She nodded firmly. Even though Virlomi had made up this wall only this morning, and no one but her had ever added to one, she understood what the woman meant by the lie. She wanted to be part of it. She wanted to help create this new flag of India.

"It's all right, then, for women to do it?" asked one of the women doubtfully.

"Oh, of course," said Virlomi. "Men are fighters. Women build the walls."

She picked up her stones and gripped them between

her palms and the jar handles. She did not look back to see if any of the others also picked up stones. She knew, from their footfalls, that many of them—perhaps all—were following her, but she did not look back. When she reached what was left of her wall, she did not try to restore any of the stones the man had kicked away. Instead she simply dropped her two stones in the middle of the largest gap in the line. Then she walked on, still without looking back.

But she heard a few plunks of stones being dropped into the dusty road.

She found occasion twice more during the day to walk back for more water, and each time found more women at the well, and went through the same little drama.

The next day, when she left the town, she saw that the wall was no longer a few stones making a broken line. It crossed the road solidly from side to side, and it was as much as two hands high in places. People made a point of stepping over it, never walking around, never kicking it. And most dropped a stone or two as they passed.

Virlomi went from village to village, each time pretending that she was only passing along a custom she had seen in other places. In a few places, angry men swept away the stones, too proud of their well-kept road to catch the vision she offered. But in those places she simply made, not a wall, but a pile of stones on both sides of the road, and soon the village women began to add to her piles so they grew into sizable heaps of stone, narrowing the road, the stones too numerous to be kicked or swept out of the way. Eventually they, too, would become walls.

In the third week she came for the first time to a village that really did already have a wall. She did not explain anything to them, for they already knew— the word was spreading without her intervention. She only added to the wall and moved quickly on.

It was still only one small corner of southern India, she knew. But it was spreading. It had a life of its own. Soon the Chinese would notice. Soon they would begin tearing down the walls, sending bulldozers to clear the road—or conscripting Indians to move the stones themselves.

And when their walls were torn down, or the people were forced to remove their walls, the real struggle would begin. For now the Chinese would be reaching down into every village, destroying something that the people wanted to have. Something that meant "India" to them. That's what the secret meaning of the wall had been from the moment she started dropping stones to make the first one.

The wall existed precisely so that the Chinese would tear it down. And she named the wall the "flag of India" precisely so that when the people saw their walls destroyed, they would see and feel the destruction of India. Their nation. A nation of wallbuilders.

And so, as soon as the Chinese turned their backs, the Indians walking from place to place would carry stones and drop them in the road, and the wall would grow again.

What would the Chinese do about it? Arrest everyone who carried stones? Make stones illegal? Stones were not a riot. Stones did not threaten soldiers. Stones were not sabotage. Stones were not a boycott. The walls were easily bypassed or pushed aside. It caused the Chinese no harm at all.

Yet it would provoke them into making the Indian people feel the boot of the oppressor.

The walls were like a mosquito bite, making the

Chinese itch but never bleed. Not an injury, just an annoyance. But it infected the new Chinese Empire with a disease. A fatal one, Virlomi hoped.

On she walked through the heat of the dry season, working her way back and forth, avoiding big cities and major highways, zig-zagging her way northward. Nowhere did anyone identify her as the inventor of the walls. She did not even hear rumors of her existence. All the stories spoke of the wall-building as having begun somewhere else.

They were called by many names, these walls. The Flag of India. The Great Indian Wall. The Wall of Women. Even names that Virlomi had never imagined. The Wall of Peace. The Taj Mahal. The Children of India. The Indian Harvest.

All the names were poetry to her. All the names said freedom.

6

HOSPITALITY

From: Flandres%A-Heg@idl.gov
To: mpp%administrator@prison.hs.ru
Re: Funds for idl prisoners

The office of the Hegemon appreciates your continuing to hold prisoners for crimes against the International Defense League, despite the lack of funding. Dangerous persons need to continue in detention for the full term of their sentences. Since IDL policy was to allocate prisoners according to the size and means of the guardian countries, as well as the national origin of the prisoners, you may be sure that Romania does not have more than its fair share of such prisoners. As funds become available, the costs incurred in prisoner maintenance will be reimbursed on a pro rata basis.

However, given that the original international emergency is over, each guardian nation's courts or prison supervisors may determine whether the international law(s) which each IDL prisoner violated is still in force and conforms with local laws. Prisoners should not be held for crimes which are no longer crimes, even if the original sentence has not been fully served.

Categories of laws that may not apply include research restrictions whose purpose was political rather than defensive. In particular, the restriction against genetic modification of human embryos was devised to hold the league together in the face of opposition from Muslim, Catholic, and other "respect-for-life" nations, and as quid pro quo for accepting the restrictions on family size. Prisoners convicted under such laws should be released without prejudice. However, they are not entitled to compensation for time served, since they were lawfully found guilty of crimes and their conviction is not being overturned.

If you have any questions, feel free to ask.

Sincerely,
Achilles de Flandres, Assistant to the Hegemon

When Suriyawong brought Achilles out of China, Peter knew exactly what he meant to do with Achilles.

He would study him for as long as he considered him harmless, and then turn him over to, say, Pakistan for trial.

Peter had prepared very carefully for Achilles's arrival. Every computer terminal in the Hegemony already had shepherds installed, recording every keystroke and taking snapshots of every text page and picture displayed. Most of this was discarded after a fairly short time, but anything Achilles did would be kept and studied, as a way of tracing all his connections and identifying his networks.

Meanwhile, Peter would offer him assignments and see what he did with them. There was no chance that Achilles would, even for a moment, act in the interest of the Hegemony, but he might be useful if Peter kept him on a short enough tether. The trick would be to get as much use out of him as possible, learn as much as possible, but then neutralize him before he could dish up the betrayal he would, without question, be cooking up.

Peter had toyed with the idea of keeping Achilles locked up for a while before actually letting him take part in the operations of the Hegemony. But that sort of thing was only effective if the subject was susceptible to such human emotions as fear or gratitude. It would be wasted on Achilles.

So as soon as Achilles had had a chance to clean up after his flights across the Pacific and over the Andes, Peter invited him to lunch.

Achilles came, of course, and rather surprised Peter by not seeming to do anything at all. He thanked him for rescuing him and for lunch in virtually the same tone—sincerely but not extravagantly grateful. His conversation was informal, pleasant, sometimes funny but never seeming to try for humor. He did not bring up anything about world affairs, the recent wars, why he had been arrested in China, or even a single question about why Peter had rescued him or what he planned to do with him now.

He did not ask Peter if there was going to be a war crimes trial.

And yet he did not seem to be evading anything at all. It seemed as though Peter had only to ask what it had been like, betraying India and subverting Thailand so all of south Asia dropped into his hands like a ripe papaya, and Achilles would tell several interesting anecdotes about it and then move on to discuss the kidnapping of the children from Ender's group at Command School.

But because Peter did not bring it up, Achilles modestly refrained from talking about his achievements.

"I wondered," said Peter, "if you wanted to take a break from working for world peace, or if you'd like to lend a hand around here."

Achilles did not bat an eye at the bitter irony, but instead he seemed to take Peter's words at face value. "I don't know that I'd be much use," he said. "I've been something of an orientalist lately, but I'd have to say that the position your soldiers found me in shows that I wasn't a very good one."

"Nonsense," said Peter, "everyone makes an error now and then. I suspect your only error was too much success. Is it Buddhism, Taoism, or Confucianism that teaches that it is a mistake to do something perfectly? Because it would provoke resentment, and therefore wouldn't be perfect after all?"

"I think it was the Greeks," said Achilles. "Perfection arouses the envy of the gods."

"Or the Communists," said Peter. "Snick off the heads of any blades of grass that rise higher than the rest of the lawn."

"If you think I have any value," said Achilles, "I'd be glad to do whatever is within my abilities."

"Thank you for not saying 'my poor abilities,' " said Peter. "We both know you're a master of the great game, and I, for one, never intend to try to play head-to-head against you."

"I'm sure you'd win handily," said Achilles.

"Why would you think that?" said Peter, disappointed at what seemed, for the first time, like flattery.

"Because," said Achilles, "it's hard to win when your opponent holds all the cards."

Not flattery, then, but a realistic assessment of the situation.

Or ... maybe flattery after all, because of course Peter did not hold all the cards. Achilles almost certainly had plenty of them left, once he was in a position to get to them.

Peter found that Achilles could be very charming. He had a sort of reticence about him. He walked rather slowly—perhaps a habit that originated before the surgery that fixed his gimp leg—and made no effort to dominate a conversation, though he was not uncomfortably silent, either. He was almost nondescript. Charmingly nondescript—was such a thing possible?

Peter had lunch with him three times a week and each time gave him various assignments. Peter gave him letterhead and a net identity that anointed him "Assistant to the Hegemon," but of course that only meant that, in a world where the Hegemon's power consisted of the fading remnants of the unity that had been forced on the world during the Formic Wars, Achilles had been granted the shadow of a shadow of power.

"Our authority," Peter remarked to him at their second lunch, "lies very lightly on the reins of world government."

"The horses seem so comfortable it's almost as though they were not being guided at all," said Achilles, entering into the joke without a smile.

"We govern so skillfully that we never need to use spurs."

"Which is a good thing," said Achilles. "Spurs being in short supply around here these days."

But just because the Hegemony was very nearly an empty shell in terms of actual power did not mean there was no real work to do. Quite the contrary. When one has no power, Peter knew, then the only influence one has comes, not from fear, but from the perception that one has useful favors to offer. There were plenty of institutions and customs left over from the decades when the Triumvirate of Hegemon, Polemarch, and Strategos had governed the human race.

Newly formed governments in various countries were formed on shaky legal ground; a visit from Peter was often quite helpful in giving the illusion of legitimacy. There were countries that owed money to the Hegemony, and since there was no chance of collecting it, the Hegemon could win favor by making a big deal of forgiving the accruing interest because of various noble actions on the part of a government. Thus when Slovenia, Croatia, and Bosnia rushed aid to Italy, sending a fleet when Venice was plagued with a flood and an earthquake at the same time, they were all given amnesty on interest. "Your generous assistance helps bind the world together, which is all that the Hegemony hopes to achieve." It was a chance for the heads of government to get their positive coverage and face time in the vids.

And they also knew that as long as it didn't cost them much, keeping the Hegemony in play was a good idea, since it and the Muslims were the only groups openly opposing China's expansionism. What if China turned out to have ambitions beyond the empire it had already conquered? What if the world beyond the Great Wall suddenly had to unite just to survive? Wouldn't it be good to have a viable Hegemon ready to assume leadership? And the Hegemon, young as he might be, *was* the brother of the great Ender Wiggin, wasn't he?

There were lesser tasks to be accomplished, too.

Hegemony libraries that needed to try to secure local funding. Hegemony police stations all over the world whose archives from the old days needed to stay under Hegemony control even though all the funding came from local sources. Some nasty things had been done as part of the war effort, and there were still plenty of people alive who wanted those archives sealed. Yet there were also powerful people who wanted to make sure the archives were not destroyed. Peter was very careful not to let anything uncomfortable come to light from any of the archives—but was not above letting an uncooperative government know that even if they seized the archive within their own boundaries, there were other archives with duplicate records that were under the control of rival nations.

Ah, the balancing act. And each negotiation, each trade-off, each favor done and favor asked for, Peter treated very carefully, for it was vital that he always get more than he gave, creating the illusion in other nations of more influence and power than he actually had.

For the more influence and power they believed he had, the more influence and power he actually had. The reality lagged far behind the illusion, but that's why it became all the more important to maintain the illusion perfectly.

Achilles could be very helpful at that.

And because he would almost certainly use his opportunities for his own advantage, letting him have a broad range of action would invite him to expose his plans in ways that Peter's spy systems would surely catch. "You won't catch a fish if you hold the hook in one hand and the bait in the other. You need to put them together, and give them a lot of string." Peter's father had said this, and more than once, too, which implied that the poor fellow thought it was clever rather than obvious. But it was obvious because it was true. To get Achilles to reveal his secrets, Peter had to give him the ability to communicate with the outside world at will.

But he couldn't make it too easy, either, or Achilles would guess what Peter really wanted. Therefore Peter, with a great show of embarrassment, put severe restrictions on Achilles's access to the nets. "I hope you realize that there's too much history for me simply to give you carte blanche," he explained. "In time, of course, these restrictions might be lifted, but for now you may write only messages that pertain directly to your assigned tasks, and all your requests to send emails will need to be cleared by my office."

Achilles smiled. "I'm sure your added sense of safety will more than compensate for the delays in what I accomplish."

"I hope we'll all stay safe," said Peter.

This was about as close as Peter and Achilles came to admitting that their relationship was that of jailer to prisoner, or perhaps that of a monarch to a thrice-traitorous courtier.

But to Peter's chagrin, his spy systems turned up . . . nothing. If Achilles sent coded messages to old confederates, Peter could not detect how. The Hegemony compound was in a broadcast bubble, so that no electronic transmissions could enter or leave except through the instruments controlled and monitored by Peter.

Was it possible that Achilles was not even attempting to contact the network of contacts he had been using during his astonishing (and, with luck, permanently terminated) career?

Maybe all his contacts had been burned by one

betrayal or another. Certainly Achilles's Russian network had to have given up on him in disgust. His Indian and Thai contacts were obviously useless now. But wouldn't he still have some kind of network in place in Europe and the Americas?

Did he already have someone within the Hegemony who was his ally? Someone who was sending messages for him, bringing him information, carrying out his errands?

At that point Peter could not help but remember his mother's actions back when Achilles first arrived. It began during Peter's first meeting with him, when the head custodian of all the compound buildings reported to him that Mrs. Wiggin had attempted at first simply to take a key to Achilles's room, and when she was caught at it, to ask for and finally demand it. Her excuse, she said, was that she had to make sure the empregadas had done a better job cleaning the room of such an important guest than they did on her house.

When Peter emailed her a query about her behavior, she got snippy. Mother had long been frustrated by the fact that she was unable to do any meaningful work. In vain did he point out that she could continue her researches and writing, and consult with colleagues by email, as many in her field did by preference. She kept insisting that she wanted to be involved in Hegemony affairs. "Everyone else is," she said. Peter had interpreted this housekeeping venture as more of the same.

Now her actions offered a different possible meaning. Was she trying to leave a message for Achilles? Was she on a more definite errand, like sweeping the room for bugs? That was absurd—what did Mother know of electronic surveillance?

Peter watched the vid of Mother's attempt to steal the key, and her attitude during the confrontation with the empregada who caught her and, after a short time, the housekeeper. Mother was imperious, demanding, impatient.

He had never seen this side of her.

The second time he watched the scene, though, he realized that from the beginning she was tense. Upset. Whatever she was doing, she wasn't used to it. Was reluctant to do it. And when she was confronted, she was not reacting honestly, as Mother normally would. She instead seemed to become someone else. The cliche of the mother of a ruler, vain about her close association with his power.

She was acting.

And acting quite well, since the housekeeper and empregada believed the performance, and Peter had believed it, too, on the first viewing.

It had never occurred to him that Mother might be good at acting.

So good that the only way he knew that it *was* an act was because she had never shown him the slightest sign of being impressed by his power, or of enjoying it in any way. She had always been irritated by the things that his position required her and Father to do.

What if the Theresa Wiggin on this vid was the real Theresa Wiggin, and the one he had seen at home for all these years was the act—the performance, literally, of a lifetime?

Was it possible that Mother was somehow involved with Achilles? Had he corrupted her somehow? It might have happened a year ago, or even earlier. It certainly wouldn't have been a bribe. But perhaps it was extortion that turned her. A threat from Achilles: I can kill your son at any time, so you'd better cooperate with me.

But that was absurd, too. Now that Achilles was in Peter's power, why would she continue to fear such a threat? It was something else.

Or nothing else. It was unthinkable that Mother could be betraying him for any reason. She would have told him. Mother was like a child that way, showing everything—excitement, dismay, anger, disappointment, surprise—the moment she felt it, saying whatever came to mind. She could never sustain a secret like that. Peter and Valentine used to laugh about how obvious Mother was in everything she did—they had never yet been surprised by their birthday and Christmas gifts, not by the main gift, anyway, because Mother just couldn't keep a secret, she kept letting hints slip out.

Or was that, too, an act?

No, no, that would be madness, that would imply that Mother had been acting his whole life, and why would she do that?

It made no sense, and he had to make sense of it. So he invited his father to his office.

"What did you want to see me about, Peter?" asked Father, standing near the door.

"Sit down, Dad, for heaven's sake, you're standing there like a junior employee expecting to be sacked."

"Laid off, anyway," said Father with a thin smile. "Your budget shrinks month by month."

"I thought we'd solve that by printing our own money," said Peter.

"Good idea," said Father. "A sort of international money that could be equally worthless in every country, so that it becomes the benchmark against which all other currencies are weighed. The dollar is worth a hundred billion 'hedges'—that's a good name for it, don't you think? The 'hedge'?—and the yen is worth twenty trillion, and so on."

"That's assuming that we could keep the value just above zero," said Peter. "The computers would all crash if it ever became truly worthless."

"But here's the danger," said Father. "What if it accidentally became worth something? It might cause a depression as other currencies actually *fell* against the hedge."

Peter laughed.

"We're both busy," said Father. "What did you want to see me about?"

Peter showed him the vid.

Father shook his head through most of it. "Theresa, Theresa," he murmured at the end.

"What is she trying to do?" asked Peter.

"Well, obviously, she's figured out a way to kill Achilles and it requires getting into his room. Now she'll have to think of another way."

Peter was astounded. "Kill Achilles? You can't be serious."

"Well, I can't think of any other reason for her to be doing this. You don't think she actually cares if his room is clean, do you? More likely she'd carry a basketful of roaches and disease-carrying lice into the room."

"She hates him? She never said anything about that."

"To you," said Father.

"So she's told you she wants to kill him?"

"Of course not. If she had, I wouldn't have mentioned it to you. I don't betray her confidences. But since she hasn't seen fit to tell me what's going on, I'm perfectly free to give you my best guess, and my best guess is that Theresa has decided that Achilles poses a danger to you—not to mention the whole human race—and so she's decided to kill him. It really makes sense, once you know how your mother thinks."

"Mother doesn't even kill spiders."

"Oh, she kills them just fine when you and I aren't there. You don't think she stands in the middle of the room and goes eek-eek-eek until we come home, do you?"

"You're telling me that my mother is capable of murder?"

"Preemptive assassination," said Father. "And no, I don't think she's capable of it. But I think *she* thinks she's capable of it." He thought for a moment. "And she might be right. The female of the species is more deadly than the male, as they say."

"That makes no sense," said Peter.

"Well, then, I guess you wasted your time and mine bringing me down here. I'm probably wrong anyway. There's probably a much more rational explanation. Like . . . she really cares how well the maids do their work. Or . . . she's hoping to have a love affair with a serial killer who wants to rule the world."

"Thanks, Father," said Peter. "You've been very helpful. Now I know that I was raised by an insane woman and I never knew it."

"Peter, my boy, you don't know either of us."

"What's that supposed to mean?"

"You study everybody else, but your mother and I are like air to you: you just breathe us without noticing we're there. But that's all right, that's how parents are supposed to be in their children's lives. Unconditional love, right? Don't you suppose that's the difference between Achilles and you? That you had parents who loved you, and he didn't?"

"You loved Ender and Valentine," said Peter. It slipped out before he realized what he was saying.

"And not you?" said Father. "Oh. My mistake. I guess there *is* no difference between your upbringing and Achilles's. Too bad, really. Have a nice day, son!"

Peter tried to call him back, but Father pretended not to have heard him and went on his way, whistling the Marseillaise, of all things.

All right, so his suspicions of Mother *were* absurd, though Father had a twisted way of saying so. What a clever family he had, everybody always making a puzzle or a drama out of everything. Or a comedy. That's what he'd just played out with his father, wasn't it? A farce. An absurdity.

If Achilles had a collaborator here, it was probably not Peter's parents. Who else, then? Should he make something of the way Achilles and Suriyawong consulted? But he'd watched the vids of their occasional lunches and they said nothing beyond ordinary chat about the things they were working on. If there was a code it was a very subtle one. It's not even like they were friends—the conversation was always rather stiff and formal, and if anything bothered Peter about them, it was the way Suriyawong always seemed to phrase things in a subservient way.

He certainly never acted subservient to Bean or to Peter.

That was something to think about, too. What had really passed between Suri and Achilles during the rescue and the return to Brazil?

What silliness, Peter told himself. If Achilles has a confederate, they doubtless communicate through dead drops and coded messages in emails or some-thing like that. Spy stuff.

Not dumb attempts to break into Achilles's room—Achilles surely would not stake his life on confeder-ates as dumb as that. And Suriyawong—how could Achilles possibly hope to corrupt *him*? It's not as if Achilles had influence in the Chinese empire now, so he could use Suri's family as hostages.

No, Peter would have to keep looking, keep the electronic surveillance going, until he found out what Achilles was doing to subvert Peter's work—or take it over.

What was not possible was that Achilles had sim-ply given up on his ambitions and was now trying to make a place for himself in the bright future of a world united under the rule of Peter Wiggin.

But wouldn't it be nice if he had.

Maybe it was time to give up on learning anything from Achilles, and start setting him up for destruction.

7

THE HUMAN RACE

From: unready%cincinnatus@anon.set
To: Demosthenes%Tecumseh@freeamerica.org
Re: If I help you

So, Mr. Wonderboy Hegemon, now that you're no longer Demosthenes of "freeamerica.org", is there any good reason why my telling you what I see from the sky wouldn't be treason?

From: Demosthenes%Tecumseh@freeamerica.org
To: unready%cincinnatus@anon.set
Re: Because . . .

Because only the Hegemony is actually doing anything about China, or actively trying to get Russia and the Warsaw Pact out of bed with Beijing.

From: unready%cincinnatus@anon.set
To: Demosthenes%Tecumseh@freeamerica.org
Re: Bullshit

We saw your little army pull somebody out of a prisoner convoy on a highway in China. If that was who we think it was, no way are you ever seeing anything from me again. My info doesn't go to psycho megalomaniacs. Except you, of course.

From: Demosthenes%Tecumseh@freeamerica.org
To: unready%cincinnatus@anon.set
Re: Good call

Good call. Not safe. Here's what. If there's something I should know because you can't act and I can, deaddrop it to my former cinc at a weblink that will come to you from IComeAnon. He'll know what to do with it. He isn't working for me any more for the same reason you're not helping. But he's still on our side—and, fyi, I'M still on our side, too.

Professor Anton had no laboratory and no library. There was no professional journal in his house, nothing to show he had ever been a scientist. Bean was not surprised. Back when the IDL was hunting down anyone doing research into altering the human genome, Anton was considered the most dangerous of men. He had been served with an order of inhibition, which meant that for many years he bore within his brain a device that, when he tried to concentrate on his area of study, he would have a panic attack. He had the strength, once, to hint to Sister Carlotta more than he should have about Bean's condition. But otherwise, he had been shut down in the prime of his career.

Now the order of inhibition had been lifted, but too late. His brain had been trained to avoid thinking deeply about his area of specialization. There was no going back for him.

"Not a problem," said Anton. "Science goes on without me. For instance, there's a new bacterium in my lung that undoes my cancer, bit by bit. I can't smoke any more, or the cancer grows faster than the bacteria can undo it. But I'm getting better, and they didn't have to take out my lungs to do it. Walk with me—I actually enjoy walking now."

They followed him through the garden to the front gate. In Brazil, the gardens were in the front of the house, so passersby could see over the front wall and the greenery and flowers could decorate the street. In Catalunya, as in Italy, the gardens were hidden away in a central courtyard, and the street got no gift but plaster walls and heavy wooden doors. Bean had not realized how much he had come to regard Ribeirão Preto as his home, but he missed it now, walking down the charming yet unrelentingly lifeless street.

Soon they reached the rambla, the broad central avenue that in all the coastal towns led down the slope of the city toward the sea. It was nearing noon, and the rambla was busy with people on errands. Anton pointed out shops and other buildings, telling them about the people who owned them or who worked there or lived there.

"I see you've become quite involved in the life of this city," said Petra.

"Superficially," said Anton. "An old Russian, long exiled in Romania, I'm a curiosity. They talk to me, but not about things that matter in their soul."

"So why not go back to Russia?" asked Bean.

"Ah, Russia. So many things about Russia. Just to remember them brings back the glorious days of my career, when I was gamboling about inside the nucleus of the human cell like a happy little lamb. But you see, those thoughts make me start to panic a little.

So . . . I don't go where I get reminded."

"You're thinking about it now," said Bean.

"No, I'm saying words about it," said Anton. "And besides, if I didn't intend to think about it, I wouldn't have consented to see you."

"And yet," said Bean, "you seem unwilling to look at me."

"Ah, well," said Anton. "If I keep you in my peripheral vision, if I don't think about thinking about you . . . you are the one fruit that my tree of theory bore."

"There were more than a score of us," said Bean. "But the others were murdered."

"You survived," said Anton. "The others didn't. Why was that, do you think?"

"I hid in a toilet tank."

"Yes, yes," said Anton, "so I gleaned from Sister Carlotta, God rest her soul. But why did you, and you alone, sneak out of your bed and go into the bathroom and hide in such a dangerous and difficult place? Scarcely a year old, too. So precocious. So desperate to survive. Yet genetically identical to all your brothers, da?"

"Cloned," said Bean, "so . . . yes."

"It is not all genetics, is it?" said Anton. "It is not all *anything*. So much left to learn. And you are the only teacher."

"I don't know anything about that. I'm a soldier."

"It is your body that would teach us. And every cell inside it."

"Sorry, but I'm still using them," said Bean.

"As I'm still using my mind," said Anton, "even though it won't go where I most want it to take me."

Bean turned to Petra. "Is that why you brought me

here? So Professor Anton could see what a big boy I've become?"

"No," said Petra.

"She brought you here," said Anton, "so I can persuade you that you are human."

Bean sighed, though what he wanted to do was walk away, get a cab to the airport, fly to another country, and be alone. Be away from Petra and her demands on him.

"Professor Anton," said Bean, "I'm quite aware that the genetic alteration that produced my talents and my defects is well within the range of normal variation of the human species. I know that there is no reason to suppose that I could not produce viable offspring if I mated with a human woman. Nor is my trait necessarily dominant—I might have children with it, I might have children without. Now can we simply enjoy our walk down to the sea?"

"Ignorance is not a tragedy," said Anton, "merely an opportunity. But to know and refuse to know what you know, that is foolishness."

Bean looked at Petra. She was not meeting his gaze. Yes, she certainly knew how annoyed he was, and yet she refused to cooperate with him in exiting the situation.

I must love her, thought Bean. Otherwise I would have nothing to do with her, the way she thinks she knows better than I do what's good for me. We have it on record—I'm the smartest person in the world. So why are so many other people eager to give me advice?

"Your life is going to be short," said Anton. "And at the end, there will be pain, physical and emotional. You will grow too large for this world, too large for your heart. But you have always been too large of mind for an ordinary life, da? You have always been apart. A stranger. Human by name, but not truly a member of the species, excluded from all clubs."

Till now, Anton's words had been mere irritants, floating past him like falling leaves. Now they struck him hard, with a sudden rush of grief and regret that left him almost gasping. He could not help the hesitation, the change of stride that showed the others that these words had suddenly begun to affect him. What line had Anton crossed? Yet he *had* crossed it.

"You are lonely," said Anton. "And humans are not designed to be alone. It's in our genes. We're social beings. Even the most introverted person alive is constantly hungry for human association. You are no exception, Bean."

There were tears in his eyes, but Bean refused to acknowledge them. He hated emotions. They took control of him, weakened him.

"Let me tell you what I know," said Anton. "Not as a scientist—that road may not be utterly closed to me, but it's mostly washed out, and full of ruts, and I don't use it. But my life as a man, that door is still open."

"I'm listening," said Bean.

"I have always been as lonely as you," he said. "Never as intelligent, but not a fool, either. I followed my mind into my work, and let it be my life. I was content with that, partly because I was so successful that my work brought great satisfaction, and partly because I was of a disposition not to look upon women with desire." He smiled wanly. "In that era, of my youth, the governments of most countries were actively encouraging those of us whose mating instinct had been short-circuited to indulge those desires and take no mate, have no children. Part of the effort to funnel all of human endeavor into the great struggle with the alien enemy. So it was almost patriotic of me to indulge myself in fleeting affairs that meant nothing, that led nowhere. Where could they lead?"

This is more than I want to know about you, thought Bean. It has nothing to do with me.

"I tell you this," said Anton, "so you understand that I know something of loneliness, too. Because all of a sudden my work was taken away from me. From my *mind*, not just from my daily activities. I could not even think about it. And I quickly discovered that my friendships were not . . . transcendent. They were all tied to my work, and when my work went away, so did these friends. They were not unkind, they still inquired after me, they made overtures, but there was nothing to say, our minds and hearts did not really touch at any point. I discovered that I did not know anybody, and nobody knew me."

Again, that stab of anguish in Bean's heart. This time, though, he was not unprepared, and he breathed a little more deeply and took it in stride.

"I was angry, of course, as who would not be?" said Anton. "And do you know what I wanted?"

Bean did not want to say what he immediately thought of: death.

"Not suicide, never that. My life wish is too strong, and I was not depressed, I was furious. Well, no, I *was* depressed, but I knew that killing myself would only help my enemies—the government—accomplish their real purpose without having had to dirty their hands. No, I did not wish to die. What I wanted, with all my heart, was . . . to begin to live."

"Why do I feel a song coming on?" said Bean. The sarcastic words slipped out of him unbidden.

To his surprise, Anton laughed. "Yes, yes, it's such

a cliché that it should be followed by a love song, shouldn't it? A sentimental tune that tells of how I was not alive until I met my beloved, and now the moon is new, the sea is blue, the month is June, our love is true."

Petra burst out laughing. "You missed your calling. The Russian Cole Porter."

"But my point was serious," said Anton. "When a man's life is bent so that his desire is not toward women, it does not change his longing for meaning in his life. A man searches for something that will outlast his life. For immortality of a kind. For a way to change the world, to have his life matter. But it is all in vain. I was swept away until I existed only in footnotes in other men's articles. It all came down to this, as it always does. You can change the world— as *you* have, Bean, Julian Delphiki—you and Petra Arkanian, both of you, all those children who fought, and the ones who did not fight, all of you—you changed the world. You *saved* the world. All of humanity is your progeny. And yet . . . it is empty, isn't it? They didn't take it away from you the way they took my work from me. But time has taken it away. It's in the past, and yet you are still alive, so what is your life for?"

They were at the stone steps leading down into the water. Bean wanted simply to keep going, to walk into the Mediterranean, down and down, until he found old Poseidon at the bottom of the sea, and deeper, to the throne of Hades. What is my life for?

"You found purpose in Thailand," said Anton. "And then saving Petra, that was a purpose. But what did you save her for? You have gone to the lair of the dragon and carried off the dragon's daughter— for that is what the myth always means, when it doesn't mean the dragon's wife—and now you have her, and . . . you refuse to see what you must do, not *to* her, but *with* her."

Bean turned to Petra with weary resignation. "Petra, how many letters did it take to make clear to Anton precisely what you wanted him to say to me?"

"Don't leap to conclusions, foolish boy," said Anton. "She only wanted to find out if there was any way to correct your genetic problem. She did not speak to me of your personal dilemma. Some of it I learned from my old friend Hyrum Graff. Some of it I knew from Sister Carlotta. And some of it I saw simply by looking at the two of you together. You both give off enough pheromones to fertilize the eggs of passing birds."

"I really don't tell our business to others," said Petra.

"Listen to me, both of you. Here is the meaning of life: for a man to find a woman, for a woman to find a man, the creature most unlike you, and then to make babies with her, with him, or to find them some other way, but then to raise them up, and watch them do the same thing, generation after generation, so that when you die you know you are permanently a part of the great web of life. That you are not a loose thread, snipped off."

"That's not the only meaning of life," said Petra, sounding a little annoyed. Well, thought Bean, you brought us here, so take *your* medicine, too.

"Yes it is," said Anton. "Do you think I haven't had time to think about this? I am the same man, with the same mind, I am the man who found Anton's Key. I have found many other keys as well, but they took away my work, and I had to find another. Well, here it is. I give it to you, the result of all my . . . study.

Shallow as it had to be, it is still the truest thing I ever found. Even men who do not desire women, even women who do not desire men, this does not exempt them from the deepest desire of all, the desire to be an inextricable part of the human race."

"We're all part of it no matter what we do," said Bean. "Even those of us who aren't actually human."

"It's hardwired into all of us. Not just sexual desire—that can be twisted any which way, and it often is. And not just a desire to have children, because many people never get that, and yet they can still be woven into the fabric. No, it's a deep hunger to find a person from that strange, terrifyingly other sex and make a life together. Even old people beyond mating, even people who know they can't have children, there's still a hunger for *this*. For actual marriage, two unlike creatures becoming, as best they can, one."

"I know a few exceptions," said Petra wryly. "I've known a few people of the 'never-again' persuasion."

"I'm not talking about politics or hurt feelings," said Anton. "I'm talking about a trait that the human race absolutely needed to succeed. The thing that makes us neither herd animals nor solitaries, but something in between. The thing that makes us civilized or at least civilizable. And those who are cut off from it by their own desires, by those twists and bends that turn them in another way—like you, Bean, so determined are you that no more children will be born with your defect, and that there will be no children orphaned by your death—those who are cut off because they think they *want* to be cut off, they are still hungry for it, hungrier than ever, especially if they deny it. It makes them angry, bitter, sad, and they don't know why, or if they know, they can't bear to face the knowledge."

Bean did not know or care whether Anton was right, that this desire was inescapable for all human beings, though he suspected that he was—that this life wish had to be present in all living things for any species to continue as they all desperately struggled to do. It isn't a will to survive—that is selfish, and such selfishness would be meaningless, would lead to nothing. It is a will for the species to survive with the self inside it, part of it, tied to it, forever one of the strands in the web—Bean could see that now.

"Even if you're right," Bean said, "that only makes me more determined to overcome that desire and never have a child. For the reasons you just named. I grew up among orphans. I'm not going to leave any behind me."

"They wouldn't be orphans," said Petra. "They'd still have me."

"And when Achilles finds you and kills you?" said Bean harshly. "Are you counting on him being merciful enough to do what Volescu did for my brothers? What I cheated myself out of by being so damned smart?"

Tears leapt to Petra's eyes and she turned away.

"You're a liar when you speak like that," said Anton softly. "And a cruel one, to say such things to her."

"I told the truth," said Bean.

"You're a liar," said Anton, "but you think you need the lie so you won't let go of it. I know what these lies are—I kept my sanity by fencing myself about with lies, and believing them. But you know the truth. If you leave this world without your children in it, without having made that bond with such an alien creature as a woman, then your life will have meant nothing to you, and you'll die in bitterness and alone."

"Like you," said Bean.

"No," said Anton. "Not like me."

"What, you're not going to die? Just because they reversed the cancer doesn't mean something else won't get you in the end."

"No, you mistake me," he said. "I'm getting married."

Bean laughed. "Oh, I see. You're so happy that you want everyone to share your happiness."

"The woman I'm going to marry is a good woman, a kind one. With small children who have no father. I have a pension now—a generous one—and with my help these children will have a home. My proclivities have not changed, but she is still young enough, and perhaps we will find a way for her to bear a child that is truly my own. But if not, then I will adopt her children into my heart. I will rejoin the web. My loose thread will be woven in, knotted to the human race. I will not die alone."

"I'm happy for you," said Bean, surprised at how bitter and insincere he sounded.

"Yes," said Anton, "I'm happy for myself. This will make me miserable, of course. I will be worried about the children all the time—I already am. And getting along with a woman is hard even for men who desire them. Or perhaps especially for them. But you see, it will all mean something."

"I have work of my own to do," said Bean. "The human race faces an enemy almost as terrible, in his own way, as the Formics ever were. And I don't think Peter Wiggin is up to stopping him. In fact it looks to me as if Peter Wiggin is on the verge of losing everything to him, and then who will be left to oppose

him? That's my work. And if I were selfish and stupid
enough to marry my widow and father orphans on
her, it would only distract me from that work. If I
fail, well, how many millions of humans have already
been born and died as loose threads with their lives
snipped off? Given the historical rates of infant mor-
tality, it might be as many as half, certainly at least
a quarter of all humans born. All those meaningless
lives. I'll be one of them. I'll just be one who did his
best to save the world before he died."

To Bean's surprise—and horror—Anton flung his
arms around him in one of those terrifying Russian
hugs from which the unsuspecting westerner thinks
he may never emerge alive. "My boy, you are so noble!" Anton let go of him, laughing. "Listen to yourself! So full of the romance of youth! You will save
the world!"

"I didn't mock your dream," said Bean.

"But I'm not mocking you!" cried Anton. "I celebrate you! Because you are, in a way, a small way,
my son. Or at least my nephew. And look at you!
Living a life entirely for others!"

"I'm completely selfish!" cried Bean in protest.

"Then sleep with this girl, you know she'll let you!
Or marry her and then sleep with anybody else, father
children or not, why should you care? Nothing that
happens outside your body matters. Your children
don't matter to you! You're completely selfish!"

Bean was left with nothing to say.

"Self-delusion dies hard," said Petra softly, slipping
her hand into his.

"I don't love anybody," said Bean.

"You keep breaking your heart with the people you
love," said Petra. "You just can't ever admit it until
they're dead."

Bean thought of Poke. Of Sister Carlotta.

He thought of the children he never meant to have. The children that he would make with Petra, this girl who had been such a wise and loyal friend to him, this woman whom, when he thought he might lose her to Achilles, he realized that he loved more than anyone else on Earth. The children he kept denying, refusing to let them exist because . . .

Because he loved them too much, even now, when they did not exist, he loved them too much to cause them the pain of losing their father, to risk them suffering the pain of dying young when there was no one who could save them.

The pain he could bear himself, he refused to let them bear, he loved them so much.

And now he had to stare the truth in the face: What good would it do to love his children as much as he already did, if he never had those children?

He was crying, and for a moment he let himself go, shedding tears for the dead women he had loved so much, and for his own death, so that he would never see his children grow up, so he would never see Petra grow old beside him, as women and men were meant to do.

Then he got control of himself, and said what he had decided, not with his mind, but with his heart. "If there's some way to be sure that they don't have—that they won't have Anton's Key." Then I'll have children. Then I'll marry Petra.

She felt her hand tighten in his. She understood. She had won.

"Easy," said Anton. "Still just the tiniest bit illegal, but it can be done."

Petra had won, but Bean understood that he had not lost. No, her victory was his as well.

"It will hurt," said Petra. "But let's make the most of what we have, and not let future pain ruin present happiness."

"You're such a poet," murmured Bean. But then he flung one arm over Anton's shoulders, and another around Petra's back, and held to both of them as his blurring eyes looked out over the sparkling sea.

———

Hours later, after dinner in a little Italian restaurant with an ancient garden, after a walk along the rambla in the noisy frolicking crowds of townspeople enjoying their membership in the human race and celebrating or searching for their mates, Bean and Petra sat in the parlor of Anton's old-fashioned home, his fiancée shyly sitting beside him, her children asleep in the back bedrooms.

"You said it would be easy," said Bean. "To be sure my children wouldn't be like me."

Anton looked at him thoughtfully. "Yes," he finally said. "There is one man who not only knows the theory, but has done the work. Nondestructive tests in newly formed embryos. It would mean fertilization in vitro."

"Oh good," said Petra. "A virgin birth."

"It would mean embryos that could be implanted even after the father is dead," said Anton.

"You thought of everything, how sweet," said Bean.

"I'm not sure you want to meet him," said Anton.

"We do," said Petra. "Soon."

"You have a bit of history with him, Julian Delphiki," said Anton.

"I do?" asked Bean.

"He kidnapped you once," said Anton. "Along with

nearly two dozen of your twins. He's the one who turned that little genetic key they named for me. He's the one who would have killed you if you hadn't hid in a toilet."

"Volescu," said Petra, as if the name were a bullet to be pried out of her body.

Bean laughed grimly. "He's still alive?"

"Just released from prison," said Anton. "The laws have changed. Genetic alteration is no longer a crime against humanity."

"Infanticide still is," said Bean. "Isn't it?"

"Technically," said Anton, "under the law it can't be murder when the victims had no legal right to exist. I believe the charge was 'tampering with evidence.' Because the bodies were burned."

"Please tell me," said Petra, "that it isn't perfectly legal to murder Bean."

"You helped save the world between then and now," said Anton. "I think the politics of the situation would be a little different now."

"What a relief," said Bean.

"So this non-murderer, this tamperer with evidence," said Petra, "I didn't know you knew him."

"I didn't—I don't," said Anton. "I've never met him, but he's written to me. Just a day before Petra did, as a matter of fact. I don't know where he is. But I can put you in touch with him. You'll have to take it from there."

"So I finally get to meet the legendary Uncle Constantine," said Bean. "Or, as Father calls him—when he wants to irritate Mother—'My bastard brother.' "

"How did he get out of jail, really?" asked Petra.

"I only know what he told me. But as Sister Carlotta said, the man's a liar to the core. He believes his own lies. In which case, Bean, he might think he's your father. He told *her* that he cloned you and your brothers from himself."

"And you think *he* should help us have children?" asked Petra.

"I think if you want to have children without Bean's little problem, he's the only one who can help you. Of course, many doctors can destroy the embryos and tell you whether they would have had your talents and your curse. But since my little key has never been turned by nature, there's no nondestructive test for it. And in order to get anyone to develop a test, you would have to subject yourself to examination by doctors who would regard you as a career-making opportunity. Volescu's biggest advantage is he already knows about you, and he's in no position to brag about finding you."

"Then give us his email," said Bean. "We'll go from there."

8

TARGETS

From: Betterman%CroMagnon@HomeAddress.com
[FREE email! *Sign up a friend!*]
To: Humble%Assistant@HomeAddress.com   [JESUS
loves you! *ChosenOnes.Org*]
Re: Thanks for your help

Dear Anonymous Benefactor,

I may have been in prison but I wasn't hiding under a
rock. I know who you are, and I know what you've done.
So when you offer to help me continue the research that
was interrupted by my life sentence, and imply that you
are responsible for having my charges reduced and my
sentence commuted, I must suspect an ulterior motive.

I think you plan to use my supposed rendezvous with
these supposed people as a means of killing them. Sort
of like Herod asking the Wise Men to tell him where the
newborn king was, so he could go and worship him also.

From: Humble%Assistant@HomeAddress.com   [Don't
go home ALONE! *LonelyHearts*]

To: Betterman%CroMagnon@HomeAddress.com
[Your ADS get seen! *Free Email!*]
Re: You have misjudged me

Dear Doctor,

You have misjudged me. I have no interest in anyone's death. I want you to help them make babies that don't have any of the father's gifts or problems. Make a dozen for them.

But along the way, if you happen to get any nice little embryos that do have the father's gifts, don't discard them, please. Keep them nice and safe. For me. For us. There are people who would very much like to raise a little garden full of beans.

John Paul Wiggin had noticed some years ago that the whole child-rearing thing wasn't really all it was cracked up to be. Supposedly somewhere there was such a thing as a normal child, but none of them had come anywhere near his house.

Not that he didn't love his kids. He did. More than they would ever know; more, he suspected, than he knew himself. After all, you never know how much you love somebody until the real test comes. Would you die for this person? Would you throw yourself on the grenade, step in front of the speeding car, keep a secret under torture, to save his life? Most people never know the answer to that question. And even those who do know are still not sure whether it was love or duty or self-respect or cultural conditioning or any number of other possible explanations.

John Paul Wiggin loved his kids. But either he didn't have enough of them, or he had too many. If he had more, then having two of them take off for some faraway colony from which they could never return in his lifetime, that might not have been so bad, because there'd still be several left at home for him to enjoy, to help, to admire as parents wanted to admire their children.

And if there had been one fewer. If the government had not requisitioned a third child from them. If Andrew had never been born, had never been accepted into a program for which Peter was rejected, then perhaps Peter's pathological ambition might have stayed within normal bounds. Perhaps his envy and resentment, his need to prove himself worthy after all, would not have tainted his life, darkening even his brightest moments.

Of course, if Andrew hadn't been born, the world might now be honeycombed with Formic hives, and the human race nothing but a few ragged bands surviving in some hostile environment like Tierra del Fuego or Greenland or the Moon.

It wasn't the government requisition, either. Little known fact: Andrew had almost certainly been conceived before the requisition came. John Paul Wiggin wasn't all that good a Catholic, until he realized that the population control laws forbade him to be. Then, because he was a stubborn Pole or a rebellious American or simply because he was that peculiar mix of genes and memory called John Paul Wiggin, there was nothing more important to him than being a good Catholic, particularly when it came to disobeying the population laws.

It was the basis of his marriage with Theresa. She wasn't Catholic herself—which showed that John

Paul wasn't *that* strict about following all the rules—but she came from a big-family tradition and she agreed with him before they got married that they would have more than two children, no matter what it cost them.

In the end, it cost them nothing. No loss of job. No loss of prestige. In fact, they ended up greatly honored as the parents of the savior of the human race.

Only they would never get to see Valentine or Andrew get married, would never see their children. Would probably not live long enough to know when they arrived at their colony world.

And now they were mere fixtures attached to the life of the child they liked the least.

Though truth to tell, John Paul didn't dislike Peter as much as his mother did. Peter didn't get under his skin the way he irritated Theresa. Perhaps that was because John Paul was a good counterbalance to Peter—John Paul could be useful to him. Where Peter kept a hundred things going at once, juggling all his projects and doing none of them perfectly, John Paul was a man who had to dot every *i*, cross every *t*. So without exactly telling anyone what his job was, John Paul kept close watch on everything Peter was doing and followed through on things so they actually got done. Where Peter assumed that underlings would understand his purpose and adapt, John Paul knew that they would misunderstand everything, and spelled it out for them, followed through to make sure things happened just right.

Of course, in order to do this, John Paul had to pretend that he was acting as Peter's eyes and ears. Fortunately, the people he straightened out had no reason to go to Peter and explain the dumb things they had been doing before John Paul showed up with his questions, his checklists, his cheerful chats that didn't quite come right out and admit to being tutorials.

But what could John Paul do when the project Peter was advancing was so deeply dangerous and, yes, stupid that the last thing John Paul wanted to do was help him with it?

John Paul's position in this little community of Hegemoniacs did not allow him to obstruct what Peter was doing. He was a facilitator, not a bureaucrat; he cut the red tape, he didn't spin it out like a spider web.

In the past, the most obstructive thing John Paul could do was not to do anything at all. Without him there, nudging, correcting, things slowed down, and often a project died without his help.

But with Achilles, there was no chance of that. The Beast, as Theresa and John Paul called him, was as methodical as Peter wasn't. He seemed to leave nothing to chance. So if John Paul simply left him alone, he would accomplish everything he wanted.

"Peter, you're not in a position to see what the Beast is doing," John Paul said to him.

"Father, I know what I'm doing."

"He's got time for everybody," said John Paul. "He's friends with every clerk, every janitor, every secretary, every bureaucrat. People you breeze past with a wave or with nothing at all, he sits and chats with them, makes them feel important."

"Yes, he's a charmer, all right."

"Peter—"

"It's not a popularity contest, Father."

"No, it's a loyalty contest. You accomplish exactly as much as the people who serve you decide you'll accomplish, and nothing more. They *are* your power, these public servants you employ, and he's winning their loyalty away from you."

"Superficially, perhaps," said Peter.

"For most people, the superficial is all there is. They act on the feelings of the moment. They like him better than you."

"There's always somebody that people like better," said Peter with a vicious little smile.

John Paul restrained himself from making the obvious one-word retort, because it would devastate Peter. The single crushing word would have been "yes."

"Peter," said John Paul, "when the Beast leaves here, who knows how many people he'll leave behind who like him well enough to slip him a bit of gossip now and then? Or a secret document?"

"Father, I appreciate your concern. And once again, I can only tell you that I have things under control."

"You seem to think that anything you don't know isn't worth knowing," said John Paul, not for the first time.

"And you seem to think that anything I'm doing is not being done well enough," said Peter for at least the hundredth time.

That's how these discussions always went. John Paul did not push it farther than that—he knew that if he became too annoying, if Peter felt too oppressed by having his parents around, they'd be moved out of any position of influence.

That would be unbearable. It would mean losing the last of their children.

"We really ought to have another child or two," said Theresa one day. "I'm still young enough, and we always meant to have more than the three the government allotted us."

"Not likely," said John Paul.

"Why not? Aren't you still a good Catholic, or did that last only as long as being a Catholic meant being a rebel?"

John Paul didn't like the implications of that, particularly because it might have some truth in it. "No, Theresa, darling. We can't have more children because they'd never let us keep them."

"Who? The government doesn't care how many children we have now. They're all future taxpayers or baby makers or cannon fodder to them."

"We're the parents of Ender Wiggin, of Demosthenes, of Locke. Our having another child would be international news. I feared it even before Andrew's battle companions were all kidnapped, but after that there was no doubt."

"Do you seriously think people would assume that because our first three children were so—"

"Darling," said John Paul—knowing that she hated it when he called her darling because he couldn't keep the sarcasm out of the term, "they'd have the babies out of the cradle, that's how fast they'd strike. They'd be targets from the moment of conception, just waiting for somebody to come along and turn them into puppets of one regime or another. And even if we were able to protect them, every moment of their lives would be deformed by the press of public curiosity. If we thought Peter was messed up by being in Andrew's shadow, think what it would be like for them."

"It might be easier for them," said Theresa. "They would never remember *not* being in the shadow of their brothers."

"That only makes it worse," said John Paul. "They'll have no idea of who they are, apart from being somebody's sib."

"It was just a thought."

"I wish we could do it," said John Paul. It was easy to be generous after she had given in.

"I just . . . miss having children around."

"So do I. And if I thought they could *be* children . . ."

"None of our kids was ever really a *child*," said Theresa sadly. "Never really carefree."

John Paul laughed. "The only people who think children are carefree are the ones who've forgotten their own childhood."

Theresa thought for a moment and then laughed. "You're right. Everything is either heaven on earth or the end of the world."

That conversation had been back in Greensboro, after Peter went public with his real identity and before he was given the nearly empty title of Hegemon. They rarely referred back to it.

But the idea was looking more attractive now. There were days when John Paul wanted to go home, sweep Theresa into his arms and say, "Darling"—and he wouldn't be even the tiniest bit sarcastic—"I have our tickets to space. We're joining a colony. We're leaving this world and all its cares behind, and we'll make new babies up in space where they can't save the world or take it over, either."

Then Theresa did this business with trying to get into Achilles's room and John Paul honestly wondered if the stress she was under had affected her mental processes.

———

Precisely because he was so concerned about what she did, he deliberately did not discuss it with her for a couple of days, waiting to see if she brought it up.

She did not. But he didn't really expect her to.

When he judged that the first blush of embarrassment was over and she could discuss things without trying to protect herself, he broached the subject over dessert one night.

"So you want to be a housekeeper," he said.

"I wondered how long it would take you to bring that up," said Theresa with a grin.

"And I wondered how long before you would," said John Paul—with a grin as laced with irony as her own.

"Now you'll never know," she said.

"I think," said John Paul, "that you were planning to kill him."

Theresa laughed. "Oh, definitely, I was under assignment from my controller."

"I assumed as much."

"I was joking," said Theresa at once.

"I'm not. Was it something Graff said? Or just a spy novel?"

"I don't read spy novels."

"I know."

"It wasn't an assignment," said Theresa. "But yes, he did put the thought into my mind. That the best thing for everybody would be for the Beast not to leave Brazil alive."

"Actually, I don't think that's so," said John Paul.

"Why not? Surely you don't think he has any value to the world."

"He brought everybody out of hiding, didn't he?" said John Paul. "Everybody showed their true colors."

"Not everybody. Not yet."

"Things are out in the open. The world is divided into camps. The ambitions are exposed. The traitors are revealed."

"So the job is done," said Theresa, "and there's no more use for him."

"I never really thought of you as a murderer."

"I'm not."

"But you had a plan, right?"

"I was testing to see if any plan was possible—if I *could* get into his room. The answer was no."

"Ah. So the objective remains the same. Only the method has been changed."

"I probably won't do it," said Theresa.

"I wonder how many assassins have told themselves that—right up to the moment when they fired the gun or plunged in the knife or served the poisoned dates?"

"You can stop teasing me now," said Theresa. "I don't care about politics or the repercussions. If killing the Beast cost Peter the Hegemony, I wouldn't care. I'm just not going to sit back and watch the Beast devour my son."

"But there's a better way," said John Paul.

"Besides killing him?"

"To get him away from where he can kill Peter. That's our real goal, isn't it? Not to save the world from the Beast, but to save Peter. If we kill Achilles—"

"I don't recall inviting you into my evil conspiracy."

"Then yes, the Beast is dead, but so is Peter's credibility as Hegemon. He's forever after as tainted as Macbeth."

"I know, I know."

"What we need is to taint the Beast, not Peter."

"Killing is more final."

"Killing makes a martyr, a legend, a victim. Killing

gives you St. Thomas à Becket. The Canterbury pilgrims."

"So what's your better plan?"

"We get the Beast to try to kill *us*."

Theresa looked at him dumbfounded.

"We don't let him *succeed*," said John Paul.

"And I thought Peter was the one who loved brinksmanship. Good heavens, Johnny P, you've just explained where his madness comes from. How in the world can you arrange for someone to *try* to kill you in such a public way that it becomes discovered—and at the same time be absolutely sure that he won't succeed."

"We don't actually let him fire a bullet," said John Paul, a little impatiently. "All we do is gather evidence that he's preparing the attempt. Peter will have no choice but to send him away—and then *we* can make sure people know why. I may be resented a bit here, but people really like you. They won't like the Beast after he plotted to harm their 'Dóce Teresa.'"

"But nobody likes *you*," said Theresa. "What if it's you he goes for first?"

"Whichever," said John Paul.

"And how will we know what he's plotting?"

"Because I put keyboard-reading programs into all the computers on the system and software to analyze his actions and give me reports on everything he does. There's no way for him to make a plan without emailing somebody about something."

"I can think of a hundred ways, one of which is— he does it himself, without telling anybody."

"He'll have to look up our schedule then, won't he? Or something. Something that will be suspicious. Something that I can show to Peter and force him to get rid of the boy."

"So the way to shoot down the Beast is to paint big targets on our own foreheads," said Theresa.

"Isn't that a marvelous plan?" said John Paul, laughing at the absurdity of it. "But I can't think of a better one. And it's nowhere near as bad as yours. Do you actually believe you *could* kill somebody?"

"Mother bear protects the cub," said Theresa.

"Are you with me? Promise not to slip a fatal laxative into his soup?"

"I'll see what your plan is, when you actually come up with one that sounds like it might succeed."

"We'll get the beast thrown out of here," said John Paul. "One way or another."

———

That was the plan—which, John Paul knew, was no plan at all, since Theresa hadn't actually promised him she'd give up on her plot to become a killer-by-stealth.

The trouble was that when he accessed the programs that were monitoring Achilles's computer use, the report said, "No computer use."

This was absurd. John Paul knew the boy had used a computer because he had received a few messages himself—innocent inquiries, but they bore the screen name that Peter had given to the Beast.

But he couldn't ask anybody outright to help him figure out why his spy programs weren't catching Achilles's sign-ons and reading his keystrokes. The word would get around, and then John Paul wouldn't seem quite such an innocent victim when Achilles's plot—whatever it was—came to light.

Even when he actually saw Achilles with his own eyes, logging in and typing away on a message, the report that night—which affirmed that the keystroke monitor was at work on that very machine—still showed no activity from Achilles.

John Paul thought about this for a good long while, trying to imagine how Achilles could have circumvented his software without logging on at least once.

Until it finally dawned on him to ask his software a different question.

"List all log-ons from that computer today," he typed into his desk.

After a few moments, the report came up: "No logons."

No log-ons from any of the nearby computers. No log-ons from any of the faraway computers. No logons, apparently, in the entire Hegemony computer system.

And since people were logging on all the time, including John Paul himself, this result was impossible.

He found Peter in a meeting with Ferreira, the Brazilian computer expert who was in charge of system security. "I'm sorry to interrupt," he said, "but it's even better to tell you this when both of you are together."

Peter was irritated, but answered politely enough. "Go ahead."

John Paul had tried to think of some benign explanation for his having tried to mount a spy operation throughout the Hegemony computer network, but he couldn't. So he told the truth, that he was trying to spy on Achilles—but said nothing about what he intended to do with the information.

By the time he was done, Peter and Ferreira were laughing—bitterly, ironically, but laughing.

"What's funny?"

"Father," said Peter. "Didn't it occur to you that

we had software on the system doing exactly the same job?"

"Which software did you use?" asked Ferreira.

John Paul told him and Ferreira sighed. "Ordinarily my software would have detected his and wiped it out," he said. "But your father has a very privileged access to the net. So privileged that my snoopware had to let it by."

"But didn't your software at least *tell* you?" asked Peter, annoyed.

"His is interrupt-driven, mine is native in the operating system," said Ferreira. "Once his snoopware got past the initial barrier and was resident in the system, there was nothing to report. Both programs do the same job, just at different times in the machine's cycle. They read the keypress and pass the information on to the operating system, which passes it on to the program. They also pass it on to their own keystroke log. But both programs *clear the buffer* so that the keystroke doesn't get read twice."

Peter and John Paul both made the same gesture— hands to the forehead, covering the eyes. They understood at once, of course.

Keystrokes came in and got processed by Ferreira's snoopware or by John Paul's—but never by both. So both keystroke logs would show nothing but random letters, none of which would amount to anything meaningful. None of which would ever look like a log-on—even though there were log-ons all over the system all the time.

"Can we combine the logs?" asked John Paul. "We have all the keystrokes, after all."

"We have the alphabet, too," said Ferreira, "and if we just find the right order to arrange them in, those letters will spell out everything that was ever written."

"It's not as bad as that," said Peter. At least the letters are in order. It shouldn't be that hard to meld them together in a way that makes sense."

"But we have to meld *all* of them in order to find Achilles's log-ons."

"Write a program," said Peter. "One that will find everything that might be a log-on by him, and then you can work on the material immediately following those possibles."

"Write a program," murmured Ferreira.

"Or I will," said Peter. "I don't have anything else to do."

That sarcasm doesn't make people love you, Peter, said John Paul silently.

Then again, there was no chance, given Peter's parents, that such sarcasm would not come readily to his lips.

"I'll sort it out," said Ferreira.

"I'm sorry," said John Paul.

Ferreira only sighed. "Didn't it at least cross your mind that we would have software already in place to do the same job?"

"You mean you had snoopware that would give *me* regular reports on what Achilles was writing?" asked John Paul. Oops. Peter's not the only sarcastic one. But then, I'm not trying to unite the world.

"There's no reason for you to know," said Peter.

Time to bite the bullet. "I think Achilles is planning to kill your mother."

"Father," said Peter impatiently. "He doesn't even know her."

"Do you think there's any chance that he *didn't* hear that she tried to get into his room?"

"But . . . *kill* her?" asked Ferreira.

"Achilles doesn't do things by half-measures," said

John Paul. "And nobody is more loyal to Peter than she is."

"Not even you, Father?" asked Peter sweetly.

"She doesn't see your faults," lied John Paul. "Her motherly instincts blind her."

"But you have no such handicap."

"Not being your mother," said John Paul.

"My snoopware should have caught this anyway," said Ferreira. "I blame only myself. The system shouldn't have had that kind of back door."

"Systems always do," said John Paul.

After Ferreira left, Peter said a few cold words. "I know how to keep Mother completely safe," he said. "Take her away from here. Go to a colony world. Go somewhere and do something, but *stop* trying to protect me."

"Protect you?"

"Do you think I'm so stupid that I'll believe this cockamamy story about Achilles wanting to kill *Mother*?"

"Ah. You're the only person here worth killing."

"I'm the only one whose death would remove a major obstacle from Achilles's path."

John Paul could only shake his head.

"Who else, then?" Peter demanded.

"Nobody else, Peter," said John Paul. "Not a soul. Everybody's safe, because, after all, Achilles has shown himself to be a perfectly rational boy who would never, ever kill somebody without a perfectly rational purpose in view."

"Well, yes, of course, he's psychotic," said Peter. "I didn't mean he wasn't psychotic."

"So many psychotics, so few really effective drugs," said John Paul as he left the room.

———

That night when he told Theresa, she groaned. "So he's been getting a free ride."

"We'll put it all together soon enough, I'm sure," said John Paul.

"No, Johnny P. We *aren't* sure that it will be soon enough. For all we know, it's already too late."

9

CONCEPTION

To: Stone%Cold@IComeAnon.com
From: Third%Party@MysteriousEast.org
Re: Definitely not vichyssoise

I don't know who you are, I don't know what this message means. He is in China. I was a tourist there, walking along a public sidewalk. He gave me a folded slip of paper and asked me to post a message to this remailing site, with the subject line above. So here it is:

"He thinks I told him where Caligula would be but I did not."

I hope this means something to you and that you get it, because he seemed very intense about this. As for me, you don't know who I am, neither does he, and that's the way I like it.

"It's not the same city," said Bean.

"Well, of course not," said Petra. "You're taller."

It was Bean's first return to Rotterdam since he left as a very young child to go into space and learn to be a soldier. In all his wanderings with Sister Carlotta after the war, she never once suggested coming here, and he never thought of it himself.

But this was where Volescu was—he had had the chutzpah to reestablish himself in the city where he had been arrested. Now, of course, he was not calling his work research—even though it had been illegal for many years, other scientists had pursued it quietly and when, after the war, they were able to publish again, they left all of Volescu's achievements in the dust.

So his offices, in an old but lovely building in the heart of the city, were modestly labeled, in Common, REPRODUCTIVE SAFETY SERVICES.

"Safety," said Petra. "An odd name, considering how many babies he killed."

"Not babies," said Bean mildly. "Illegal experiments were terminated, but no actual legal babies were ever involved."

"That really slops your hogs, doesn't it," she said.

"You watch too many vids. You're beginning to pick up American slang."

"What else can I do, with you spending all your time online, saving the world?"

"I'm about to meet my maker," said Bean. "And you're complaining to me about my spending too much time on pure altruism."

"He's not your maker," said Petra.

"Who is, then? My biological parents? They made Nikolai. I was leftovers in the fridge."

"I was referring to God," said Petra.

"I know you were," said Bean, smiling. "Me, I can't help but think that I exist because God blinked. If he'd been paying attention, I could never have happened."

"Don't goad me about religion," said Petra. "I won't play."

"You started it," said Bean.

"I'm not Sister Carlotta."

"I couldn't have married you if you were. Was that your choice? Me or the nunnery?"

Petra laughed and gave him a little shove. But it wasn't much of a shove. Mostly it was just an excuse to touch him. To prove to herself that he was hers, that she could touch him when she liked, and it was all right. Even with God, since they were legally married now. A necessity before in vitro fertilization, so that there could be no question about paternity or joint ownership of the embryos.

A necessity, but also what she wanted.

When had she started wanting this? In Battle School, if anyone had asked her whom she would eventually marry, she would have said, "A fool, since no one smarter would have me," but if pressed, and if she trusted her inquisitor not to blab, she would have said, "Dink Meeker." He was her closest friend in Battle School.

Dink was even Dutch. He wasn't in the Netherlands these days, however. The Netherlands had no military. Dink had been lent to England, rather like a prize football player, and he was cooperating in joint Anglo-American planning, which was such a waste of his talent, since on neither side of the Atlantic was there the slightest desire to get involved in the turmoil that was rocking the rest of the world.

She didn't even regret his absence. She still cared about him, had fond memories of him—even, perhaps, loved him in a vaguely-more-than-platonic way. But after Battle School, where he had been a brave rebel challenging the system, refusing to command an army in the battle room and joining her in helping Ender in his struggle against the teachers—after Battle School, they had worked together almost continuously, and perhaps came to know each other too well. The rebel pose was gone, and he stood revealed as a brilliant but cocky commander. And when she was shamed in front of Dink, when she was overcome by fatigue during a game that turned out to be real, it became a barrier between her and the others, but it was an unvaultable wall between her and Dink.

Even when Ender's jeesh was kidnapped and confined together in Russia, she and Dink bantered with each other just like old times, but she felt no spark.

Through all that time, she would have laughed if anyone suggested that she would fall in love with Bean, and a scant three years later would be married to him. Because if Dink had been the most likely candidate for her heart in Battle School, Bean had to be the least likely. She had helped him a bit, yes, as she had helped Ender when he first started out, but it was a patronizing kind of help, giving a hand up to an underdog.

In Command School, she had come to respect Bean, to see something of his struggle, how he never did anything to win the approval of others, but always gave whatever it took to help his friends. She came to understand him as one of the most deeply altruistic and loyal people she had ever seen—even though he did not see either of these traits in himself, but always found some reason why everything he did was entirely for his own benefit.

When Bean was the only one not kidnapped, she knew at once that he would try anything to save them. The others talked about trying to contact him on the outside, but gave up at once when they heard that he had been killed. Petra never gave up on him. She knew that Achilles could not possibly have killed him so easily. She knew that he would find a way to set her free.

And he had done it.

She didn't love him because he had saved her. She loved him because, during all her months in captivity, constantly having to bear Achilles's looming presence with his leering threat of death entwined with his lust to own her, Bean was her dream of freedom. When she imagined life outside of captivity, she kept thinking of it as life with him. Not as man and wife, but simply: When I'm free, then we'll find some way to fight Achilles. We. We'll. And the "we" was always her and Bean.

Then she learned about his genetic difference. About the death that awaited him from overgrowing his body's ability to nurture itself. And she knew at once that she wanted to bear his children. Not because she wanted to have children who suffered from some freakish affliction that made them brilliant ephemera, butterflies catching the sunlight only for a single day, but because she did not want Bean's life to leave no child behind. She could not bear to lose him, and desperately wanted something of him to stay with her when he was gone.

She could never explain this to him. She could hardly explain it to herself.

But somehow things had come together better than she hoped. Her gambit of getting him to see Anton had persuaded him far more quickly than she had thought would be possible.

It led her to believe that he, too, without even realizing it, had come to love her in return. That just as she wanted him to live on in his children, he now wanted her to be the mother who cared for them after he died.

If that wasn't love, it would do.

They married in Spain, with Anton and his new bride looking on. It had been dangerous to stay there as long as they did, though they tried to take the curse off it by leaving frequently with all their bags and then returning to stay in a different town each time. Their favorite city was Barcelona, which was a fairyland of buildings that looked as if they had all been designed by Gaudi—or, perhaps, had sprung from Gaudi's dreams. They were married in the Cathedral of the Sagrada Familia. It was one of the few genuine Gaudis still standing, and the name made it the perfect place for a wedding. Of course the "sagrada familia" referred officially to the sacred family of Jesus. But that didn't mean it couldn't also apply to all families. Besides, weren't her children going to be immaculately conceived?

The honeymoon, such as it was—a week together, island-hopping through the Balearics, enjoying the Mediterranean Sea and the African breezes—was still a week longer than she had hoped for. After knowing Bean's character about as well as one person ever gets to know another person, Petra had been rather shy about getting to know his body, and letting him know hers. But here Darwin helped them, for the passions that made species survive helped them to forgive each other's awkwardness and foolishness and ignorance and hunger.

She was already taking pills to regulate her ovulation and more pills to stimulate as many eggs as possible to come to maturity. There was no possibility of their conceiving a baby naturally before they began the in vitro fertilization process. But she wished for it all the same, and twice she woke from dreams in which a kindly doctor told them, "I'm sorry, I can't implant embryos, because you're already pregnant."

But she refused to let it trouble her. She would have his baby soon enough.

Now they were here in Rotterdam, getting down to business. Looking, not for the kindly doctor of her dream, but for the mass murderer who only spared Bean's life by accident to provide them with a child who would not die as a giant by the age of twenty.

"If we wait long enough," said Bean, "they'll close the office."

"No," said Petra. "Volescu will wait all night to see you. You're his experiment that succeeded despite his cowardice."

"I thought it was *my* success, not his."

She pressed herself against his arm. "It was *my* success," she said.

"Yours? How?"

"It must have been. I'm the one who ended up with all the prizes."

"If you had ever said things like that in Battle School, you would have been the laughingstock of all the armies."

"That's because the armies were all composed of prepubescent children. Grownups don't think such things are embarrassing."

"Actually, they do," said Bean. "There's only this brief window of adolescence where extravagantly romantic remarks are taken for poetry."

"Such is the power of hormones that we absolutely understand the biological causes of our feelings, and yet we still feel them."

"Let's not go inside," said Bean. "Let's go back to the inn and have some more feelings."

She kissed him. "Let's go inside and make a baby."

"*Try* for a baby," said Bean. "Because I won't let you have one in which Anton's Key is turned."

"I know," she said.

"And I have your promise that embryos with Anton's Key will all be discarded."

"Of course," she said. That satisfied him, though she was sure that he would notice that she had never actually said the words. Maybe he did, unconsciously, and that was why he kept asking.

It was hypocritical and dishonest of her, of course, and she almost felt bad about it sometimes, but what happened after he died would be none of his business.

"All right then," he said.

"All right then," she answered. "Time to go meet the baby killer, né?"

"I don't suppose we should call him that to his face, though, right?"

"Since when are *you* the one who worries about good manners?"

———

Volescu was a weasel, just as Petra knew he would be. He was all business, playing the role of Mr. Scientist, but Petra knew well what lay behind the mask. She could see the way he couldn't keep his eyes off Bean, the mental measurements he was making. She wanted to make some snide remark about how prison seemed to have done him good, he was carrying some extra weight, needed to walk that off . . . but they were here to have the man choose them a baby, and it would serve no purpose to irritate him.

"I couldn't believe I was going to meet you," said Volescu. "I knew from that nun who visited me that one of you had lived, and I was glad. I was already in prison by then, the very thing that destroying the evidence had been designed to prevent. So I didn't need to destroy it after all. I wished I hadn't. Then here she comes and tells me the lost one lived. It was the one ray of hope in a long night of despair. And here you are."

Again he eyed Bean from head to toe.

"Yes," said Bean, "here I am, and very tall for my age, too, as you seem to keep trying to verify."

"I'm sorry," said Volescu. "I know that other business has brought you here. Very important business."

"You're sure," said Bean, "that your test for Anton's Key is absolutely accurate and nondestructive?"

"You exist, don't you? You are what you are, yes? We would not have kept any in which the gene did not take. We had a safe, reliable test."

"Every one of the cloned embryos was brought to life," said Bean. "It worked in every one of them?"

"I was very good with planter viruses in those days. A skill that even now isn't much called for in procedures with humans, since alterations are still illegal." He chuckled, because everyone knew that there was a lively business in tailored human babies in various places around the world, and that skill in gene alteration was in more demand than ever. That was almost certainly Volescu's real business, and the Netherlands was one of the safest places to practice it.

But as Petra listened to him, she became more and more uneasy. Volescu was lying about something. The change in his manner had been slight, but after spending months observing every tiny nuance in Achilles's demeanor, simply as a matter of survival, she had turned herself into a very precise observer of other people. The signs of deception were there. En-

ergized speech, overly rhythmic, too jovial. Eyes that
kept darting away from theirs. Hands that wouldn't
stop touching his coat, his pencil.

What would he be lying about?

It was obvious, once she thought about it.

There was no test. Back when he created Bean,
Volescu had simply introduced the planter virus that
was supposed to alter all the cells of the embryos, and
then waited to see if any embryos lived, and which
of the survivors had been successfully altered. It happened that they all survived. But not all of them necessarily had Anton's Key.

Maybe that was why, of all the nearly two dozen
babies, only Bean escaped.

Maybe Bean was the only one in whom the alteration was successful. The only one with Anton's Key.
The only one who was so preternaturally intelligent
that he was able, at one year of age, to realize there
was danger, climb out of his bassinet, get himself inside a toilet tank, and actually stay alive there until
the danger passed.

That had to be Volescu's lie. Maybe he had developed a test since then, but that was unlikely. Why
would he imagine he'd need it? But he said that he
had such a test so he could . . . could do what?

Start his experiment again. Take their leftover embryos, and instead of discarding the ones with Anton's Key, he'd keep them all and raise them and
study them. This time it wouldn't be just one out of
two dozen who had the enhanced intelligence and the
shortened lifespan. This time, the genetic odds suggested a fifty-fifty distribution of Anton's Key among
the embryos.

So now Petra had a decision to make. If she said
out loud what she was so certain of in her mind, Bean

would probably realize she was right and the entire deal would be off. If Volescu had no way to test, it was certain nobody else did. Bean would refuse to have children at all.

So if she was to have Bean's child, Volescu had to be the one to do it, not because he had a test for Anton's Key, but because Bean believed he did.

But what about the other embryos? They would be her children, too, growing up as the slaves, the experimental subjects of a man like this, completely without morals.

"Of course you know," said Petra, "that you won't do the actual implantation."

Since Bean had never heard this wrinkle in their plans, he was no doubt surprised—but, being Bean, he showed nothing, merely smiled a bit to show that she was speaking for both of them. Such trust. She didn't even feel guilty that he trusted her so much at a moment when she was working so hard to deceive him. She may not be doing what he thought that he wanted, but she knew she was doing what he really desired, deep down in his genes.

Volescu showed surprise, however. "But . . . what do you mean?"

"Forgive me," said Petra, "but we will stay with you through the entire fertilization process, and we will watch as every fertilized embryo is taken to the Women's Hospital, where they will be under hospital security until the implantation takes place."

Volescu's face reddened. "What do you accuse me of?"

"Of being the man you have already proven yourself to be."

"Many years ago, and I paid my debt."

Bean understood now—enough, at least, to join in,

his tone of voice as light and cheerful as Petra's. "We have no doubt of that, but of course we want to make sure we don't have any of our little embryos with Anton's Key waking up to some unpleasant surprises in a room full of children, as I did once."

Volescu rose to his feet. "This interview is over."

Petra's heart sank. She shouldn't have said anything at all. Now there would be no implantation and Bean would discover . . .

"So we proceed to extract the eggs?" asked Bean. "The time is right, I believe. That's why we made the appointment for this day."

Volescu looked at him sharply. "After you insulted me?"

"Come now, Doctor," said Bean. "You take the eggs from her, and then I make my donation. That's how salmon do it. It's really quite natural. Though I'd like to skip the swim upstream, if I can."

Volescu eyed him for a long moment, then smiled his tight little smile. "My little half-nephew Julian has such a sense of humor."

Petra waited, hardly wanting to breathe, definitely not wishing to speak, though a thousand words raced through her head.

"All right, yes, of course you can protect the fertilized embryos however you want. I understand your . . . lack of trust. Even though I know it is misplaced."

"Then while you and Petra do whatever it is you're going to do," said Bean, "I'll call for a couple of couriers from the fertility center at Women's Hospital to come and await the embryos and take them to be frozen."

"It will be hours before we reach that stage," said Volescu.

"We can afford to pay for their time," said Petra.

"And we don't want any chance of slipups or delays."

"I will have to have access to the embryos again for several hours, of course," said Volescu. "In order to separate them and test them."

"In our presence," said Petra. "And the fertility specialist who is going to implant the first one."

"Of course," said Volescu with a tight smile. "I will sort them out for you, and discard the—"

"*We* will discard and destroy any that have Anton's Key," said Bean.

"That goes without saying," said Volescu stiffly.

He hates these rules we've sprung on him, thought Petra. She could see it in his eyes, despite the calm demeanor. He's furious. He's even . . . embarrassed, yes. Well, since that's probably as close as he's ever come to feeling shame, it's good for him.

———

While Petra was examined by the staff doctor who would do the implantation, Bean saw to hiring a security service. A guard would be on duty at the embryo "nursery," as the hospital staff charmingly called it, all day, every day. "Since you're the one who first started being paranoid," Bean told Petra, "I have no choice but to out-paranoid you."

It was a relief, actually. During the days before the embryos were ready for implantation, while Volescu was no doubt trying frantically to devise some non-destructive procedure that he could pretend was a genetic test, Petra was glad not to have to stay in the hospital personally watching over the embryos the whole time.

It gave her a chance to explore the city of Bean's childhood. Bean, however, seemed determined to visit only the tourist sites and then get back to his computer. She knew that it made him nervous to stay in one city for so long, especially because for the first time, their whereabouts were known to another person whom they did not trust. It was doubtful Volescu knew any of their enemies. But Bean insisted on changing hotels every day, and walking blocks from their hotel in order to hail a taxi, so that no enemy could set an easy trap for them.

He was evading more than his enemies, though. He was also evading his past in this city. She scanned a city map and found the area that Bean was clearly avoiding. And the next morning, after Bean had chosen the first cab of the day, she leaned forward and gave the taxi driver directions.

It took Bean only a few moments to realize where the cab was going. She saw him tense up. But he did not refuse to go or even complain about her having compelled him. How could he? It would be an admission that he was avoiding the places he had known as a child. A confession of pain and fear.

She was not going to let him pass the day in silence, however. "I remember the stories you've told me," she said to him, gently. "There aren't many of them, but still I wanted to see for myself. I hope it's not too painful for you. But even if it is, I hope you'll bear it. Because someday I'll want to tell our children about their father. And how can I tell the stories if I don't know where they took place?"

After the briefest pause, Bean nodded.

They left the cab and he took her through the streets of his childhood, which had been old and shabby even then. "It's changed very little," said Bean. "Really just the one difference. There aren't thousands of abandoned children everywhere. Apparently somebody found the budget to deal with the orphans."

She kept asking questions, paying close attention to the answers, and finally he understood how serious she was, how much it meant to her. Bean began taking her off the main streets. "I lived in the alleys," he explained. "In the shadows. Like a vulture, waiting for things to die. I had to watch for scraps that other children didn't see. Things discarded at night. Spills from garbage bins. Anything that might have a few calories in it."

He walked up to one dumpster and laid his hand against it. "This one," he said. "This one saved my life. There was a restaurant then, where that music shop is. I think the restaurant employee who dumped their garbage knew I was lurking. He always took out most of the cooking garbage in the late afternoon, in daylight. The older kids took everything. And then the scraps from the night's meals, those got dumped in the morning, in daylight again, and the other kids got that, too. But he usually came outside once in the darkness. To smoke right here by the garbage bin. And after his smoke, in the darkness, there'd be a scrap of something, right here."

Bean put his hand on a narrow shelf formed by the frame that allowed the garbage truck to lift the bin.

"Such a tiny dinner table," said Petra.

"I think he must have been a survivor of the street himself," said Bean, "because it was never something so large as to attract attention. It was always something I could slip into my mouth all at once, so no one ever saw me holding food in my hand. I would have died without him. It was only a couple of months and then he stopped—probably lost his job or moved on to something else—and I have no idea who he was. But it kept me alive."

"What a lovely thing, to think such a person could have come out of the streets," said Petra.

"Well, yes, now I see that," said Bean. "But at the time I didn't think of that sort of thing at all. I was . . . focused. I knew he was doing it deliberately, but I didn't bother to imagine why, except to eliminate the possibility that it was a trap, or that he had drugged it or poisoned it somehow."

"How did you eliminate *that* possibility?"

"I ate the first thing he put there and I didn't die, and I didn't keel over and then wake up in a child whorehouse somewhere."

"They had such places?"

"There were rumors that that's what happened to children who disappeared from the street. Along with the rumors that they were cooked into spicy stews in the immigrants' section of town. Those I don't believe."

She wrapped her arms around his chest. "Oh, Bean, what a hellish place."

"Achilles came from here, too," he said.

"He was never as small as you were."

"But he was crippled. That bad leg. He had to be smart to stay alive. He had to keep everyone else from crushing him for no better reason than because they could. Maybe his thing about having to eliminate anyone who sees his helplessness—maybe that was a survival mechanism for him, under these circumstances."

"You're such a Christian," said Petra. "So full of charity."

"Speaking of which," said Bean. "I assume you're going to raise our child Armenian Catholic, right?"

"It would make Sister Carlotta happy, don't you think?"

"She was happy no matter what I did," said Bean. "God made her happy. She's happy now, if she's anything at all. She was a happy person."

"You make her sound—what?—mentally deficient?"

"Yes. She was incapable of holding on to malice. A serious defect."

"I wonder if there's a genetic test for it," said Petra. Then she regretted it immediately. The last thing she wanted was for Bean to think too much about genetic tests, and realize what seemed so obvious to her, that Volescu had no test.

They visited many other places, and more and more of them made him tell her little stories. Here's where Poke used to hide a stash of food to reward kids who did well. Here's where Sister Carlotta first sat down with us to teach us to read. This was our best sleeping place during the winter, until some bigger kids found us and drove us out.

"Here's where Poke stood over Achilles with a cinderblock in her hands," said Bean, "ready to dash his brains out."

"If only she had," said Petra.

"She was too good a person," said Bean. "She couldn't imagine the evil that might be in him. I didn't, either, until I saw him lying there, what was in his eyes when he looked up at that cinderblock. I've never seen so much hate. That was all—no fear. I saw her death in his eyes right then. I told her she had to do it. Had to kill him. She couldn't. But it happened just the way I warned her. If you let him live, he'll kill you, I said, and he did."

"Where was it?" asked Petra. "The place where

Achilles killed her? Can you take me there?"

He thought about it for a few moments, then walked her to the waterfront among the docks. They found a clear place where they could see between the boats and ships and barges out to where the great Rhine swept past on its way to the North Sea.

"What a powerful place," said Petra.

"What do you mean?"

"It just—the river, so strong. And yet human beings were able to build this along its banks. This harbor. Nature is strong but the human mind is stronger."

"Except when it isn't," said Bean.

"He gave her body to the river, didn't he?"

"He dumped her into the water, yes."

"But the way Achilles saw what he did. Giving her to the water. Maybe he romanticized it."

"He stabbed her in the eye," said Bean. "I don't care what he thought while he did it, or afterward. He kissed her and then he killed her."

"You didn't see the murder, I hope!" said Petra. It would be too terrible if Bean had been carrying such an image in his mind all these years.

"I saw the kiss," said Bean. "I was too selfish and stupid to see what it meant."

Petra remembered her own kiss from Achilles, and shuddered. "You thought what anyone would have thought," said Petra. "You thought his kiss meant what mine does."

And she kissed him.

He kissed her back. Hungrily.

But when the kiss ended, his face grew wistful again. "I would undo everything, all that I've done with my life since then," said Bean, "if I could only go back and undo that one moment."

"What, you think you could have fought him? Have

you forgotten how small you were then?"

"If I'd been there, if he'd known I was watching, he wouldn't have done it. Achilles never risks discovery if he can help it."

"Or he might have killed you, too."

"He couldn't kill us both at once. Not with that gimp leg. Whichever one he went for, the other would scream bloody murder and go for help."

"Or hit him over the head with a cinderblock."

"Yes, well, Poke could have done that, but I couldn't have lifted it higher than his head. And I don't think dropping a stone on his toe would have done the job."

They stayed by the dock for a little longer, and then made the walk back to the hospital.

The security guard was on duty. All was right with the world.

All. Bean had gone back to his childhood range and he hadn't cried much, hadn't turned away, hadn't fled back to some safe place.

Or so she thought, until they left the hospital, returned to their hotel, and he lay in the bed, gasping for breath until she realized that he was sobbing. Great dry wracking sobs that shook his whole body.

She lay beside him and held him until he slept.

———

Volescu's fakery was so good that for a few moments Petra wondered if he might really have the ability to test the embryos. But no, it was flimflam—he was simply smart enough, scientist enough, to find convincing flimflam that was realistic enough to fool extremely intelligent laypeople like them, and even the fertility doctor they brought with them. He must have made it look like the tests these doctors performed to test for a child's sex or for major genetic defects.

Or else the doctor knew perfectly well it was a scam, but said nothing because all the baby-fixers played the same game, pretending to check for defects that couldn't actually be checked for, knowing that by the time the fakery was discovered, the parents would already have bonded with the child—and even if they hadn't, how could they sue for failing to perform an illegal procedure like sorting for athletic prowess or intellect? Maybe all these baby boutiques were fakers.

The only reason Petra wasn't fooled is that she didn't watch the procedure, she watched Volescu, and by the end of the procedure she knew that he was way too relaxed. He knew that nothing he was doing would make the slightest difference. There was nothing at stake. The test meant nothing.

There were nine embryos. He pretended to identify three of them as having Anton's Key. He tried to hand the containers to one of his assistants to dispose of, but Bean insisted that he give them to their doctor for disposal.

"I don't want any of these embryos to accidentally become a baby," said Bean with a smile.

But to Petra, they already were babies, and it hurt her to watch as Bean supervised the pouring out of the three embryos into a sink, the scouring of the containers to make sure an embryo hadn't managed to thrive in some remaining droplet.

I'm imagining this, thought Petra. For all she knew, the containers he flushed had never contained embryos at all. Why would Volescu sacrifice any of them, when all he had to do was lie and merely *say* that these three had contained embryos with Anton's Key?

So, self-persuaded that no actual harm to a child of hers was being done, she thanked Volescu for his help and they waited for him to leave before anything else was done. Volescu carried nothing from the room that he hadn't come in with.

Then Bean and Petra both watched as the six remaining embryos were frozen, their containers tagged, and all of them secured against tampering.

———

The morning of the implantation, they both awoke almost at first light, too excited, too nervous to sleep. She lay in bed reading, trying to calm herself; he sat at the table in the hotel room, working on email, scanning the nets.

But his mind was obviously on the morning's procedure. "It's going to be expensive," he said. "Keeping guard over the ones we don't implant."

She knew what he was driving at. "You know we've got to keep them frozen until we know if the first implant works. They don't always take."

Bean nodded. "But I'm not an idiot, you know. I'm perfectly aware that you intend to keep all the embryos and implant them one by one until you have as many of my children as possible."

"Well of course," said Petra. "What if our firstborn is as nasty as Peter Wiggin?"

"Impossible," said Bean. "How could a child of mine have any but the sweetest disposition?"

"Unthinkable, I know," said Petra. "And yet somehow I thought of it."

"So this security, it has to continue for years."

"Why?" said Petra. "No one wants the babies that are left. We destroyed the ones with Anton's Key."

"*We* know that," said Bean. "But they're still the

children of two members of Ender's jeesh. Even without my particular curse, they'll still be worth stealing."

"But they won't be old enough to be of any value for years and years," said Petra.

"Not all that many years," said Bean. "How old were we? How old are we even now? There are plenty of people willing to take the children and invest not that many years of training and then put them to work. Playing games and winning wars."

"I'll never let any of them anywhere near military training," said Petra.

"You won't be able to stop them," said Bean.

"We have plenty of money, thanks to the pensions Graff got for us," said Petra. "I'll make sure the security is intense."

"No, I mean you'll never be able to stop the children. From seeking out military service."

He was right, of course. The testing for Battle School included a child's predilection for military command, for the contest of battle. For war. Bean and Petra had proven how strong that passion was in them. It would be unlikely that any child of theirs would be happy without ever having a taste of the military life.

"At least," said Petra, "they won't have to destroy an alien invader before they turn fifteen."

But Bean wasn't listening. His body had suddenly grown alert as he scanned a message on his desk.

"What is it?" she asked.

"I think it's from Hot Soup," said Bean.

She got up and came over to look.

It was an email through one of the anonymous services, this one an Asian-based company called Mysterious East. The subject line was "definitely not vichyssoise." Not cold soup, then. Hot Soup. The Battle School nickname of Han Tzu, who had been in Ender's jeesh and was now assumed to be deeply involved in the highest levels of strategy in China.

A message from him to Bean, until recently the military commander of the Hegemon's forces, would be high treason. This message had been handed to a stranger on a street in China. Probably a European- or African-looking tourist. And the message wasn't hard to understand:

He thinks I told him where Caligula would be but I did not.

"Caligula" could only refer to Achilles. "He" had to refer to Peter.

Han Tzu was saying that Peter thought he was the source of the information about where the prison convoy would be on the day Suriyawong liberated Achilles.

No wonder Peter was sure his source was reliable— Han Tzu himself! Since Han Tzu had been one of the group Achilles kidnapped, he would have plenty of reason to hate him. Motive enough for Peter to believe that Han Tzu would tell him where Achilles would be.

But it wasn't Han Tzu.

And if it wasn't Han Tzu, then who else would send such a message, pretending that it came from him? A message that turned out to be correct?

"We should have known it wasn't from Han Tzu all along," said Bean.

"We didn't know Han Tzu was supposed to be the source," said Petra reasonably.

"Han Tzu would never give information that would

lead to innocent Chinese soldiers getting killed. Peter should have known that."

"*We* would have known it," said Petra, "but Peter doesn't know Hot Soup. And he didn't tell us Hot Soup was his source."

"So of course we know who the source was," said Bean.

"We've got to get word to him at once," said Petra.

Bean was already typing.

"Only this has to mean that Achilles went in there completely prepared," said Petra. "I'd be surprised if he hasn't found a way to read Peter's mail."

"I'm not writing to Peter," said Bean.

"Who, then?"

"Mr. and Mrs. Wiggin," said Bean. "Two separate messages. Pieces of a puzzle. Chances are that Achilles won't be watching their mail, or at least not closely enough to realize he should put these together."

"No," said Petra. "No puzzles. Whether he's watching or not, there's no time to lose. He's been there for months now."

"If he sees an open message it might precipitate action on his part. It might be Peter's death warrant."

"Then notify Graff, send him in."

"Achilles undoubtedly knows Graff already came once to get our parents out," said Bean. "Again, his arrival might trigger things."

"OK," said Petra, thinking. "OK. Here's what. Suriyawong."

"No," said Bean.

"He'll get a coded message instantly. He thinks that way."

"But I don't know if he can be trusted," said Bean.

"Of course he can," said Petra. "He's only pretending to be Achilles's man."

"Of course he is," said Bean. "But what if he isn't just pretending?"

"But he's Suriyawong!"

"I know," said Bean. "But I can't be sure."

"All right," said Petra. "Peter's parents, then. Only don't be too subtle."

"They're not stupid," said Bean. "I don't know Mr. Wiggin that well, but Mrs. Wiggin is—well, she's very subtle. She knows more than she lets on."

"That doesn't mean she's wary. That doesn't mean she'll get the code or talk it over with her husband right away so they can put the messages together."

"Trust me," said Bean.

"No, I'll proofread before you send it," said Petra. "First rule of survival, right? Just because you trust someone's motives doesn't mean you can trust them to do it right."

"You're a cold, cold woman," said Bean.

"It's one of my best features."

A half hour later, they both agreed that the messages should work. Bean sent them. It was a few hours earlier in Ribeirão Preto. Nothing would happen till the Wiggins woke up.

"We'll have to be ready to leave immediately after the implantation," said Petra. If Achilles had been in control of things from the start, then chances were good that his whole network was still in place and he knew exactly where they were and what they were doing.

"I won't be with you," said Bean. "I'll be getting our tickets. Have the guards right in the room with you."

"No," said Petra. "But just outside."

Petra showered first, and she was completely packed when Bean came out of the bathroom. "One thing," said Petra.

"What?" asked Bean as he put his few belongings into the one bag he carried.

"Our tickets—should be to separate destinations."

He stopped packing and looked at her. "I see," he said. "You get what you want from me, and then you walk away."

She laughed nervously. "Well, yes," she said. "You've been telling me this whole time that it's more dangerous for us to travel together."

"And now that you'll have my baby in you, you don't need to be with me any more," said Bean. He was still smiling, but she knew that beneath the jest there was true suspicion.

"Whatever the Wiggins do, all hell is going to break loose," said Petra. "I've memorized all your dead drops and you've memorized all of mine."

"I *gave* you all of yours," said Bean.

"Let's get back together in a week or so," said Petra. "If I'm like my mother, I'll be puking my guts out by then."

"If the implantation is successful."

"I'll miss you every moment," said Petra.

"God help me, but I'll miss you too."

She knew what a painful, frightening thing that was for Bean. To allow himself to love someone so much that he would actually miss her, that was no small matter for him. And the two other women he had allowed himself to love with all his heart had been murdered.

"I won't let anybody hurt our baby," she said.

He thought for a moment, and then his face softened. "That baby is probably the best protection you could have."

She understood and smiled. "No, they won't kill me till they see what our baby turns out like," she said. "But that's no protection from being kidnapped and held until the child is born."

"As long as you and the baby are alive, I'll come and get you."

"That's the thing that frightens me," said Petra. "That we might be the bait they use to set a trap for you."

"We're looking too far ahead," said Bean. "They aren't going to catch us. You or me. And if they do, well, we'll deal with that."

They were packed. They both went over the room one more time to make sure they were leaving nothing behind, no sign they had ever been there. Then they left for Women's Hospital and the child who waited for them there, a bundle of genes wrapped in a few undifferentiated cells, eager to implant themselves in a womb, to start to draw nutrients from a mother's blood, to begin to divide and distinguish themselves into heart and bowel, hands and feet, eyes and ears, mouth and brain.

10

LEFT AND RIGHT

From: PW
To: TW, JPW
Re: Reconciliation of keyboard logs

You'll be happy to learn that we were able to sort out all the logs. We have tracked every computer entry by the person in question. All his entries dealt with official business and assignments he was carrying out for me. Nothing that was in any way improper was done.

Personally, I find this disturbing. Either he found a way to fool both our programs (not likely), or he is actually doing nothing but what he should (even less likely), or he is playing a very deep game about which we have no idea (extremely likely).

Let's talk tomorrow.

Theresa woke up when John Paul got out of bed to pee at four A.M. It worried her that he couldn't make it through the night anymore. He was still a little young to be having prostate problems.

But it wasn't her husband's slackening bladder capacity that kept her awake. It was the memo from Peter informing them that Achilles had done absolutely nothing but what he was supposed to do.

This was impossible. Nobody does exactly what they're supposed to and nothing else. Achilles should have had some friend, some ally, some contact whom he needed to notify that he was out of China and safe. He had a network of informants and agents, and as he showed when he hopped from Russia to India to China, he was always one step ahead of everybody. The Chinese finally wised up to his pattern and short-circuited it, but that didn't mean Achilles didn't have his next move planned. So why hadn't he done anything to set it in motion?

There were more possibilities than the ones Peter listed, of course. Maybe Achilles had a means of bypassing the electromagnetic shield that surrounded the Ribeirão Preto compound. Of course, he couldn't have brought such a device with him when he was rescued, or it would have shown up in the search that was conducted during his first bath in Ribeirão. So someone would have to have brought it to him. And Peter was convinced that no such device could exist. Maybe he was right.

Maybe Achilles's next move was something he planned to do entirely alone.

Maybe there was something he had that he was able to smuggle into Brazil inside his body. Did the surveillance cameras show him, perhaps, combing through his bowel movements? Peter must surely have checked for that.

While she lay there thinking, John Paul had come back from the bathroom. But now she noticed that he had not resumed snoring.

"You're awake?" she asked.

"Sorry I woke you."

"I can't sleep anyway," she said.

"The Beast?"

"We're missing something," said Theresa. "He hasn't suddenly become a loyal servant of the Hegemony."

"I'm not going to get back to sleep either," said John Paul. He got up and padded in bare feet to his computer. She heard him typing and knew that he was checking his mail first.

Busy work, but it was better than lying here staring at the dark ceiling. She got up also, took her desk from the table, and brought it back to bed, where she began checking her own email.

One of the benefits of being the mother of the Hegemon was that she didn't actually have to answer the tedious mail—she could forward it on to one of Peter's secretaries to deal with, since it consisted mostly of tedious attempts of people trying to get her to use her supposed influence with Peter to get him to do something that was not within his power to do, was illegal even if he could do it, and which he would certainly not do even if it were legal.

It left her with very few pieces of mail that she needed to deal with personally.

Most of it could be answered with a few sentences and she dealt with it quickly, if a bit sleepily.

She was about to shut down her desk and try again to get back to sleep when a new piece of mail came in.

To: T%Hegmom@Hegemony.gov
From: Rock%HardPlace@IComeAnon.com

Re: And when thou doest alms, let not thy left hand know what thy right hand doeth.

What was this? Some religious fanatic? But the address was her most private one, used only by John Paul, Peter, and a handful of people she actually liked and knew well.

So who sent it?

She skipped to the bottom. No signature. The message was short.

You'll never guess. There I was at a party-the boring but dangerous kind, with fine china that you know you're going to break, and a tablecloth you're bound to spill India ink on-and do you know what happens? Along comes the very man with whom I wanted to tie the knot. He thinks he's rescuing me from the party! But in fact, he was the very reason I came to the party in the first place. Not that I'll ever tell him! He would BLOW UP if he knew. And then, of course, I'm so nervous I bump into the tureen and hot soup spills all over everything. But . . . you know me! Just a big oaf.

That was the complete text of the message. It was really annoying, because it didn't sound like anyone she knew. She didn't *have* friends who sent letters as empty and pointless as this one. Gossip about a party. Somebody hoping to marry somebody else.

But before she could make any progress on figuring it out, another piece of mail came in.

To: T%Hegmom@Hegemony.gov
From: Sheep%NotGoats@IComeAnon.com
Re: Even as ye have done it unto the least of these . . .

Another biblical quote. Same person? Bound to be. But the message was not chatty at all. In fact, it continued the scriptural motif from the subject line. It had nothing to do with the previous message.

Ye took me in, but I was not naked. I took you in, because you were foolish. Ye never knew me, but I knew you.

 When does the judgment day come? Like a thief in the night. In an hour when ye look not for me. The fool says, He is not coming. Let us eat drink and be merry for he is not coming. Behold I stand at the door and knock

In sorrow shall ye bear children. I will have the power to crush your head, but ye will have the power to bite my heel.

A time to sow, and a time to reap. A time to gather stones together, a time to run like hell.

She who has ears to hear. How beautiful upon the mountains are the feet. I come to bring not peace but a sword.

Theresa got out of bed. John Paul had to see these letters. They meant something, she knew that, especially arriving together like this. The number of people who knew this address was very, very small. And not one of them would write either of these letters.

Therefore either this address had been compromised—but who would bother? She was only the mother of the Hegemon—or these letters were meant to convey a message. And it was from someone who thought that even at this address, her mail might be intercepted by someone else.

Who was that paranoid, but Bean?

Big oaf, that's who he said he was. Bean, definitely.

"John Paul," she said as she padded up behind him.

"This is so strange," he said.

She assumed he was going to tell her about a similar pair of messages, so she waited.

"The Chinese have imposed a completely absurd law in India. About rocks! People aren't allowed to carry rocks without a permit! Anyone caught with rocks is subject to arrest—and they're actually enforcing it. Have they lost their minds?"

She found it impossible to be interested in the idiocies of China's policies in India. "John Paul, I have to show you something."

"Sure," he said, turning to look at the desk she set down on the table next to his computer.

"Read these letters," she said.

He glanced at one, and before she could imagine he had actually read the whole thing, he flipped to the next one. "Yeah, I got them too," he said. "A dullbob and a crenchee. You shouldn't let these things get to you."

"No," she said. "Look at them closer. They came to my private address. I think they're from Bean."

He looked up at her, then turned to his own computer and called up his own copies of the letters. "Me too," he said. "I didn't notice that. Just looked like junk mail, but nobody uses this address."

"The subject lines—"

"Yes," said John Paul. "Both scriptures, even though the first one—"

"Yes, and the first one is about left and right hands, and the second one is from the parable or whatever it is when Jesus speaks to the people on his right hand and the people on his left hand."

"So they both have left and right hands," said John Paul.

"Two parts to the same message."

"Could be," he said.

"The scriptures are all twisted," said Theresa.

"You Mormons learn your scriptures," said John Paul. "We Catholics regard that as a really Protestant thing to do."

"The real scripture says, I was naked, and you clothed me, I was homeless or something like that and you took me in."

"I was a stranger and you took me in," said John Paul.

"So you did read scripture."

"I woke up once during the homily."

"It's word games," said Theresa. "I think the second 'took you in' means 'fooled you,' not 'provided shelter for you.' "

By now John Paul was studying the other letter. "This one's geopolitical. Fine China. India ink. And it ends with 'blow up' in all caps."

" 'Tie the knot,' " said Theresa, looking at the first letter. "The 'tie' could mean somebody from Thailand.' "

"That's stretching it a little," said John Paul, chuckling.

"It's all word games," said Theresa. " 'Power to bite my heel'—that has to refer to the Beast, don't you think? Achilles, who could only be hurt in the heel."

"And Achilles was rescued by a Thai—Suriyawong."

"So now you think 'tie' might be 'Thai'?"

"Yes, you told me so."

"The Thai *thinks* he's rescuing this person from a

party. Suri rescues Achilles, but Achilles is keeping a secret. He would blow up if he knew."

Now John Paul was looking at the second letter. "A time to run like hell. Is this a warning?"

"That's what the last line has to be. She who has ears, let her hear. Use your feet. Because he comes to bring not peace but the sword."

"Mine says 'He who has ears to hear.' "

"You're right, they weren't identical."

"Who's the 'I' in these scriptures?"

"Jesus."

"No, no, I mean, what does the message mean by 'I'? I think it's Achilles. I think it's written as if Achilles were talking. I took you in because you were foolish. Thief in the night, when we aren't looking for him. We're stupid because we think he's not coming but he's here at the door."

"A time to run like hell," said Theresa.

John Paul leaned back and closed his eyes. "A warning from Bean, maybe. Suri thought he was rescuing Achilles but it was exactly what Achilles wanted him to do. And the other letter—that reference to stones, that has to be Petra. They sent us a pair of messages that fit together."

And now it all fell into place. "This is what's been bothering me," said Theresa. "This is why I couldn't sleep."

"You didn't get these letters till just now," said John Paul.

"No, the thing that was keeping me awake, it was how Achilles has done nothing since he got here except his official duties. I was thinking that even though he was short-circuited by the Chinese arresting him, it made no sense for him not to make contact with his network. But what if the Chinese didn't arrest him at all? What if that was a setup? 'You took me in but I was not naked.' "

John Paul nodded. "And I took *you* in, because you were foolish."

"So the whole point of this was to get Achilles inside the compound."

"But so what?" said John Paul. "We've been suspicious of him anyway."

"But this is more than suspicion," said Theresa. "Or they wouldn't have sent it."

"There's no evidence here. Nothing that would persuade Peter."

"Yes there is," said Theresa. "Hot soup."

He looked at her blankly.

"From Ender's jeesh. Han Tzu. Inside China. He would know. He's the authority. He 'spilled everything.' Definitely a setup."

"OK," said John Paul, "so we have the evidence. We know Achilles wasn't really a prisoner, he wanted to be taken."

"Don't you see? This means he really understands Peter. He knew that Peter couldn't resist rescuing him. Maybe he even knew that Bean and Petra would leave. Think about it—we all knew how dangerous Achilles could be, so maybe he was counting on that."

"Everybody closest to Peter left, except us—"

"And Peter *tried* to get us to go."

"And Suriyawong."

"And Achilles has coopted him."

"Or Suri has Achilles convinced he has."

They'd been back and forth on that one before. "Whatever," said Theresa. "Simply by arriving here, Achilles has succeeded in isolating Peter. Then he's spent his whole time being Mr. Nice Guy, doing everything right—and making friends with everybody while he's at it. Everything's going smoothly. Except—"

"Except that he's in a position to kill Peter."

"If he can do it in a way that doesn't implicate him."

"Ready to step in, as Peter's assistant, and say, 'Everything's going smoothly at the Hegemony, we'll just keep things going till a new Hegemon is chosen,' and long before they can choose one, he's compromised all the codes, he's neutralized the army, and China is completely rid of the Hegemony once and for all. They'll get advance word of one of Suri's missions and they wipe out our brave little army and—"

"Why wipe it out, if it already obeys you?" said Theresa.

"We don't know that Suri—"

"What do you think would happen if Peter tried to leave?" she asked.

John Paul thought about that. "Achilles would take over while he was gone. There's a long tradition of *that* maneuver."

"And just as long a tradition of declaring him sick and keeping anyone from having access to him."

"Well, he can't restrict access to Peter as long as *we're* here," said John Paul.

They looked at each other for a long moment.

"Get your passport," said Theresa.

"We can't pack anything."

"Wipe the computers."

"What do you think he'll use? Poison? Some bio-agent?"

"Bio-agent is likeliest. He could have smuggled that in."

"Does it matter?"

"Peter's not going to believe us."

"He's stubborn and self-willed and he thinks we're idiots," said John Paul. "But that doesn't mean he's stupid."

"But he might think he can handle it."

John Paul nodded. "You're right. He is exactly that stupid."

"Wipe all your files on the system and—"

"It doesn't matter," said John Paul. "There are backups."

"Not of these letters, at least."

John Paul printed them out and then destroyed them in the computer's memory, while Theresa wiped them from her desk.

Carrying the paper copies of the letters, they headed for Peter's room.

———

Peter was sleepy, surly, and impatient with them. He kept dismissing their concerns and insisting they wait till morning until finally John Paul lost his temper and dragged Peter out of bed like a teenager. He was so shocked at being treated in such a way that he actually fell silent.

"Stop thinking this is between you and your parents," John Paul said. "These letters are from Bean and Petra, and they're relaying a message from Han-Tzu in China. These are three of the smartest military minds alive, and all three of them have been proven to be smarter than you."

Peter's face reddened with anger.

"Have I got your attention now?" said John Paul. "Will you actually listen?"

"What does it matter if I listen?" said Peter. "Let

one of *them* be Hegemon, they're so much smarter than me."

Theresa bent down and got right in his face. "You're acting like a rebellious teenager while we're trying to tell you the house is on fire."

"Process this information," said John Paul, "as if we were a couple of your informants. Pretend that you think we actually know something. And while you're at it, take a quick poll and see how effectively Achilles has driven away everybody around you who was completely trustworthy—except us."

"I know you mean well," said Peter, but his voice betrayed his anger.

"Shut up," said Theresa. "Just shut up with your patronizing tone. You saw the letters. We didn't make that up. Hot Soup found a way to tell Bean and Petra that the whole rescue was a setup. You were *had*, smart boy. Achilles has this whole place sussed by now. Every move you make, somebody tells him."

"For all we know," said John Paul, "the Chinese have an operation ready to roll."

"Or you're going to be arrested by Suri's soldiers," said Theresa.

"In other words, you have no idea what I'm even supposed to be afraid of."

"That's right," said Theresa. "That's exactly right. Because you played into his hands as if he handed you a script and you read your lines like a robot."

"You're the puppet right now, Peter," said John Paul. "You thought you held the strings, but you're the puppet."

"And you have to leave now," said Theresa.

"What's the emergency?" said Peter impatiently. "You don't know what he's going to do or when."

"Sooner or later you're going to have to go," said

Theresa. "Or do you plan to wait until he kills you? Or us? And when you *do* go, it has to be sudden, unexpected, unplanned. There's no better opportunity than now. While the three of us are still alive. Can you guarantee that will still be true tomorrow? This afternoon? I didn't think so."

"Before dawn," said John Paul. "Out of the compound, into the city, onto a plane, out of Brazil."

Peter just sat there, looking from one to the other.

But the irritated look was gone from his face. Was it possible? Could he have actually heard something that they said?

"If I leave," said Peter, "they'll say I abdicated."

"You can say that you didn't."

"I'll look like a fool. I'll be completely discredited."

"You *were* a fool," said Theresa. "If you say it first, nobody else gets any points for saying it. Cover up nothing. Get a press release out while you're in the air. You're Locke. You're Demosthenes. You can spin anything."

Peter stood up, started pulling clothes out of his dresser drawers. "I think you're right," he said. "I think your analysis is absolutely right."

Theresa looked at John Paul.

John Paul looked at Theresa.

Was this Peter talking?

"Thank you for not giving up on me," he said. "But this Hegemon thing is done. I've lost any chance of making it work. I had my chance, and I blew it. Everybody told me not to bring Achilles here. I had all these plans on how to lead him into a trap. But I was already caught in *his*."

"I've already told you to shut up once this morning," said Theresa. "Don't make me do it again."

Peter didn't bother buttoning his shirt. "Let's go," he said.

Theresa was glad to see that he didn't try to take anything with him. He only stopped at his computer and typed in a single command.

Then he headed for the door.

"Aren't you going to wipe out your files?" asked John Paul. "Alert your head of security?"

"I just did," said Peter.

So he had been prepared for such a day as this. He already had the program in place that would automatically destroy everything that needed destroying. And it would alert those who needed to be alerted.

"We have ten minutes before the people I used to trust get warned to evacuate," said Peter. "Since we don't know which of them we can still trust, we have to be out of here by then."

His plan included looking after those who were still loyal to him, whose lives would be in danger when Achilles took over. Theresa had not imagined Peter would think of such a thing. It was a good thing to know about him.

They didn't skulk or run, just walked through the grounds toward the nearest gate, engaged in animated conversation. It might be early in the morning, but who would imagine that the Hegemon and his parents were making a getaway? No luggage, no hurry, no stealth. Arguing. A perfectly normal scene.

And the argument was real enough. They spoke softly, because in the stillness of dawn they might be overheard even at a distance. But there was plenty of intensity in their hushed voices.

"Skip the melodrama," said John Paul. "Your life isn't over. You made a huge mistake, and there are people who are going to say that running out like this is an even bigger one. But your mother and I know that it isn't. As long as you're alive, there's hope."

"The hope is Bean," said Peter. "*He* hasn't shot himself in the foot. I'll throw my support behind Bean. Or maybe I shouldn't. Maybe my support would just be the kiss of death."

"Peter," said John Paul, "you're the Hegemon. You were elected. You, not this compound. In fact, you're the one who moved the Hegemony offices here. Now you're going to move them somewhere else. Wherever you are, that's the Hegemony. Don't you ever say one thing to imply otherwise. Even if your entire power in the world consists of you and me and your mother, *that's not nothing*. Because you are Peter Wiggin, and dammit, we're John Paul Wiggin and Theresa Wiggin and underneath our charming and civilized exteriors, we're some pretty tough bunducks."

Peter said nothing.

"Well, actually," said Theresa to John Paul, "*we're* the bunducks. Peter's the big sabeek."

Peter shook his head.

"You are," Theresa insisted. "And do you know how I know you are? Because you were smart enough to listen to us and get out in time."

"I was just thinking," said Peter quietly.

"What?" prompted Theresa, before John Paul could give his standard joking reply: It's about time. It would be the wrong joke for this moment, but John Paul was never very good about knowing when it was the wrong time for his standard jokes. They came out by reflex, without being processed through his brain first.

"I've underestimated you two," he said.

"Well, yes," said Theresa.

"In fact, I've been a little shit to you for a long time."

"Not so little," said John Paul.

Theresa cocked a warning eyebrow at him.

"But I still never did anything as dumb as trying to get into his bedroom to kill him," said Peter.

Theresa looked at him sharply. He was grinning at her.

John Paul laughed. She couldn't blame him. He couldn't help retaliating. After all, she had just given him the dreaded eyebrow.

"OK, well, you're right," said Theresa. "That was pretty stupid. But I didn't know what else to do to save you."

"Maybe saving me isn't such a great idea."

"You're the only copy of our DNA left on Earth," said John Paul. "We really don't want to have to start all over, making babies. That's for younger people now."

"Besides," said Theresa. "Saving you means saving the world."

"Right," said Peter derisively.

"You're the only hope," said Theresa.

"Then good luck, world."

"I do believe," said John Paul, "that that was almost a prayer. Don't you think so, Theresa? I think Peter said a prayer."

Peter chuckled. "Yeah, why not. Good luck, world. Amen."

They got to the gate well before the ten minutes were up. There was a cab driver asleep at a cab stand in front of the biggest hotel outside the compound. John Paul woke him and handed him a very large sum of money.

"Take us to the airport," said Theresa.

"But not this one," said John Paul. "I think we want to fly out of Araraquara."

"That's an hour away," said Theresa.

"And we have an hour till the earliest flight anywhere," said John Paul. "Do you want to spend that hour just sitting in an airport that's fifteen minutes away from the compound?"

Peter laughed. "That is so paranoid," he said. "Just like Bean."

"Bean's alive," said John Paul.

"I'm OK with that," said Peter. "Being alive is good."

———

Peter had his press release out from one of the computers in the Araraquara airport. But Achilles didn't waste any time, either.

Peter's story was all true, though he left a few things out. He admitted that he had been fooled into thinking that he was rescuing Achilles when in fact he was bringing the Trojan Horse inside the walls of Troy. It was a terrible mistake because Achilles was serving the Chinese Empire all along, and Hegemony headquarters was completely compromised. Peter declared that he was moving Hegemony headquarters to another location and urged all Hegemony employees who were still loyal to him to wait for word about where to reassemble.

Achilles's press release declared that he, General Suriyawong, and Ferreira, the head of Hegemony computer security, had discovered that Peter was embezzling Hegemony funds and hiding them in secret accounts—money that should have gone to paying Hegemony debts and feeding the poor and trying to achieve world peace. He declared that the office of the

Hegemon would continue to function under the control of Suriyawong as the ranking military leader of Hegemony forces, and that he would help Suriyawong only if he was asked. Meanwhile, a warrant had been issued for Peter Wiggin's arrest to answer charges of embezzlement, malfeasance in office, and high treason against the International Defense League.

In a press release later that day he announced that Hyrum Graff had been removed as Minister of Colonization and was to be arrested for complicity with Peter Wiggin in the conspiracy to defraud the Hegemony.

"The son of a bitch," said John Paul.

"Graff won't obey him," said Theresa. "He'll simply declare that you're still Hegemon and that he answers only to you and Admiral Chamrajnagar."

"But it'll dry up a lot of his funds," said Peter. "He'll have a lot less freedom of movement. Because now there's a price on his head, and in some countries they'd just love to arrest him and turn him over to the Chinese."

"Do you really think Achilles is serving the Chinese interest?" asked Theresa.

"Every bit as loyally as he served mine," said Peter.

Before the plane landed in Miami, Peter had his safe haven. In, of all places, the USA.

"I thought America was determined not to get involved," said John Paul.

"It's just temporary," said Peter.

"But it puts them clearly on our team," said Theresa.

" 'Them'?" said Peter. "*You're* Americans. So am I. The U.S. isn't 'them,' it's *us*."

"Wrong," said Theresa. "You're the Hegemon. You're above nationality. And so, I might add, are we."

11

BABIES

From: Chamrajnagar%sacredriver@ifcom.gov
To: Flandres%A-Heg@idl.gov
Re: MinCol

Mr. Flandres:

The position of Hegemon is not and never was vacant. Peter Wiggin continues to hold that office. Therefore your dismissal of the Hon. Hyrum Graff as Minister of Colonization is void. Graff continues to exercise all previous authority in regard to MinCol affairs off the surface of Earth.

Furthermore, IFCom will regard any interference with his operations on Earth, or with his person as he carries out his duties, as obstruction of a vital operation of the International Fleet, and we will take all appropriate steps.

From: Flandres%A-Heg@idl.gov
To: Chamrajnagar%sacredriver@ifcom.gov
Re: MinCol

Admiral Chamrajnagar, sir:

I cannot imagine why you would write to me about this matter. I am not acting Hegemon, I am Assistant Hegemon. I have forwarded your letter to General Suriyawong, and I hope all future correspondence about such matters will be directed to him.

Your humble servant,
Achilles Flandres

> From: Chamrajnagar%sacredriver@ifcom.gov
> To: Flandres%A-Heg@idl.gov
> Re: MinCol

Forward my letters wherever you like. I know the game you are playing. I am playing a different one. In my game, I hold all the cards. Your game, on the other hand, will only last until people notice that you have no actual cards at all.

The events in Brazil were already all over the nets and the vids when the implantation procedure was complete and Petra was wheeled out into the waiting room of the fertility clinic at Women's Hospital. Bean was waiting for her. With balloons.

They wheeled her out into the reception area. At first she didn't notice him, because she was busy talking with the doctor. Which was fine with him. He wanted to look at her, this woman who might be carrying his child now.

She looked so small.

He remembered looking up at her when they first met in Battle School. This girl—rare in a place that tested for aggressiveness and a certain degree of ruth-

lessness. To him, a newcomer, the youngest child
ever admitted to the school, she seemed so cool, so
tough, like the quintessential bullyboy, smart-
mouthed and belligerent. It was all an act, but a necessary one.

Bean had seen at once that she noticed things. Noticed *him,* for starters, not with amusement or amaze-
ment like the other kids, who could only see how
small he was. No, she clearly gave him some thought,
found him intriguing. Realized, perhaps, that his presence at Battle School when he was clearly underage
implied something interesting about him.

It was partly that trait of hers that led Bean to turn
to her—that and the fact that as a girl she was almost
as much of a misfit as he was bound to be.

She had grown since those days, of course, but
Bean had grown far more, and was now quite a bit
taller than her. It wasn't just height, either. He had
felt her rib cage under his hands, so small and brittle,
or so it seemed. He felt as though he always had to
be gentle with her, or he might inadvertently break
her between his hands.

Did all men feel this way? Probably not. For one
thing, most women were not as light-bodied as Petra,
and for another thing, most men stopped growing
when they reached a certain point. But Bean's hands
and feet were still misproportioned to his body, like
an adolescent's, so that even though he was a tallish
man, it was clear his body meant to grow taller still.
His hands felt like paws. Hers seemed as lost within
his as a baby's.

How, then, will the baby she carries inside her now
seem to me when it is born? Will I be able to cradle
the child in one hand? Will there be a genuine danger

of my hurting the baby? I'm not so good with my hands these days.

And by the time the baby is big enough, robust enough for me to handle safely, I'll be dead.

Why did I consent to do this?

Oh, yes. Because I love Petra. Because she wants my child so badly. Because Anton had some cock-and-bull story about how all men crave marriage and family even if they don't care about sex.

Now she noticed him, and noticed the balloons, and laughed.

He laughed back and went to her, handed her the balloons.

"Husbands don't usually give their wives balloons," she said.

"I thought having a baby implanted was a special occasion."

"I suppose so," she said, "when it's professionally done. Most babies are implanted at home by amateurs, and the wives don't get balloons."

"I'll remember that and try always to have a few on hand."

He walked beside her as an attendant pushed her wheelchair down the hallway toward the entrance.

"So where is my ticket to?" she asked.

"I got you two," said Bean. "Different airlines, different destinations. Plus this train ticket. If either of the flights gives you a bad feeling, even if you can't decide why you have misgivings, don't get on it. Just go to the other airline. Or leave the airport and take the train. The train ticket is an EU pass so you can go anywhere."

"You spoil me," said Petra.

"What do you think?" asked Bean. "Did the baby hook itself onto the uterine wall?"

"I'm not equipped with an internal camera," said Petra, "and I lack the pertinent nerves to be able to feel microscopically small fetuses implant and start to grow a placenta."

"That's a very poor design," said Bean. "When I'm dead, I'll have a few words with God about that."

Petra winced. "Please don't joke about death."

"Please don't ask me to be somber about it."

"I'm pregnant. Or might be. I'm supposed to get my way about everything."

The attendant pushing Petra's wheelchair started to take her toward the front cab in a line of three. Bean stopped him.

"The driver's smoking," said Bean.

"He'll put it out," said the attendant.

"My wife will not get into a car with a driver whose clothing is giving off cigarette smoke residue."

Petra looked at him oddly. He raised an eyebrow, hoping she'd realize that this was not about tobacco.

"He's the first taxi in line," said the attendant, as if it were an incontrovertible law of physics that the first cab in line had to be the one to get the next passengers.

Bean looked at the other two cabs. The second driver looked at him impassively. The third driver smiled. He looked Indonesian or Malay, and Bean knew that in their culture, a smile was pure reflex when facing someone bigger or richer than you.

Yet for some reason he did not feel the mistrust about the Indonesian driver that he felt about the two Dutch drivers ahead of him.

So he pushed her wheelchair toward the third cab. Bean asked, and the driver said yes, he was from Jakarta. The attendant, truly irritated at this breach of protocol, insisted on helping Petra into the cab. Bean

had her bag and put it in the back seat beside her—
he never put anything in the trunks of cabs, in case
he had to run for it.

Then he had to stand there as she drove off. No
time for elaborate good-byes. He had just put everything that mattered in his life into a cab driven by a
smiling stranger, and he had to let it drive away.

Then he went to the first cab in line. The driver
was showing his outrage at the way Bean had violated
the line. The Netherlands was back to being a civilized place, now that it was self-governing again, and
lines were respected. Apparently the Dutch now
prided themselves on being better at queues than the
English, which was absurd, because standing cheerfully in line was the English national sport.

Bean handed the driver a twenty-five-dollar coin,
which he looked at with disdain. "It's stronger than
the Euro right now," said Bean. "And I'm paying you
a fare, so you didn't lose anything because I put my
wife in another cab."

"What is your destination?" said the driver curtly,
his English laced with a prim BBC accent. The Dutch
really needed to have better programming in their
own language so their citizens didn't have to watch
English vids and listen to English radio all the time.

Bean did not answer him until he was inside the
cab, the door closed.

"Drive me to Amsterdam," said Bean.

"What?"

"You heard me," said Bean.

"That's eight hundred dollars," said the driver.

Bean peeled a thousand-dollar bill off his roll and
gave it to him. "Does the video unit in this car actually work?" he asked.

The driver made a show of scanning the bill to see

if it was counterfeit. Bean wished he had used a Hegemony note. You don't like dollars? Well see how you like *this!* But it was unlikely that anybody would take Hegemony money for any purpose these days, what with Achilles's and Peter's faces on every vid in the city and all the talk about how Peter had embezzled Hegemony funds.

Their faces were on the video in the cab, too, when the driver finally got it working. Poor Peter, thought Bean. Now he knows how the popes and anti-popes felt when there were two with a claim to St. Peter's throne. What a lovely taste of history for him. What a mess for the world.

And to Bean's surprise, he found that he didn't actually care that much whether the world was in a mess—not when the messiness wasn't going to affect his own little family.

I'm actually a civilian now, he realized. All I care about is how these world events will affect my family.

Then he remembered: I used to care about world events only insofar as they affected *me*. I used to laugh at Sister Carlotta because she was so concerned.

But he did care. He kept track. He paid attention. He told himself it was so he'd know where he'd be safe. Now, though, with far more reason to worry about safety, he found the whole business of Peter and Achilles fundamentally boring. Peter was a fool to think he could control Achilles, a fool to trust a Chinese source on such a matter. How well Achilles must understand Peter, to know that he would rescue Achilles instead of killing him. But why shouldn't Achilles understand Peter? All he had to do was think of what *he* would do, if he were in Peter's position, but dumber.

Still, even though he was bored, the story from the

newspeople began to make sense, when combined with the things Bean knew. The embezzling story was ludicrous, of course, obviously disinformation from Achilles, though all the predictable nations were in an uproar about it, demanding inquiries: China, Russia, France. What seemed to be true was that Peter and his parents slipped out of the Hegemon's compound in Ribeirão Preto just before dawn this morning, drove to Araraquara, then flew to Montevideo, where they got official permission to fly to the United States as guests of the U.S. government.

It was possible, of course, that their sudden flight was precipitated by something Achilles did or some information they learned about Achilles's immediate plans. But Bean was reasonably sure that these events were triggered by the emails he and Petra had sent early this morning when they got Han Tzu's message.

Apparently the Wiggins had been up either very late or very early, because they must have got the letters almost as soon as they were sent. Got them, deciphered the message, realized the implication of Han Tzu's tip, and then, incredibly enough, persuaded Peter to pay attention and get out without a moment's delay.

Bean had assumed it would take days before Peter would realize the significance of what he had been told. Part of the problem would be his relationship with his parents. Bean and Petra knew how smart the Wiggins were, but most people in the Hegemony didn't have a clue, least of all Peter. Bean tried to imagine the scene when they explained to him that he had been fooled by Achilles. Peter, believing his parents when they told him he had made a mistake? Unthinkable.

And yet he must have believed them right away.

Or they drugged him.

Bean laughed a little at the thought, and then looked up from the vid because the cab was turning sharply.

They were pulling off the main road into a side street. They shouldn't be.

By reflex Bean had the door open and was flinging himself out the door by the time the cab driver could get his gun up from the seat and aim it at him. The bullet zipped over his head as Bean hit the ground and rolled. The cab came to a stop and the driver leapt out to finish the job. Abandoning his bag, Bean scrambled to get around the corner. But he'd never get far enough down the street—which had no pedestrians on it, here in the warehouse district—to get out of the range of a bullet once the cabbie followed him onto the main street.

Another shot came just as he made it past the edge of the building. He thought of pressing himself against the side of the building, in the hopes that the gunman was really stupid and would barrel around the corner without looking.

But that wouldn't work, because the cab that had been second in line was pulling to the curb right in front of him, and the driver was raising his own gun to point it at Bean.

He dived for the ground and two bullets hit the wall where he had been standing. By sheer chance, his leap took him directly in front of the first driver, who was indeed stupid enough to be running around the corner at top speed. He fell over Bean and when he hit the ground, his gun flew out of his hand.

Bean might have gone for the gun, but the second driver was already partly out of his door and would be able to shoot Bean before he could get to it. So

Bean scrambled back to the first cab, which was idling in the side street. Could he get the cab between him and either of the gunmen before they could shoot at him again?

He knew he couldn't. But there was nothing to do but try, and hope that, like bad guys in the vids, these two would be terrible shots and miss him every time. And when he got in the cab to drive it away, it would be very nice if the upholstery of the driver's seat were made of that miracle fabric that stops bullets fired through the back window.

Pop. Pop-pop. And then . . . the ratatat of an automatic weapon.

The two cab drivers didn't have automatic weapons.

Bean was around the front of the cab now, keeping low. To his surprise, neither driver was standing at the corner, pointing a gun at him. Perhaps they had been, a moment ago, but now they were lying there on the ground, filled with bullets and seeping copious amounts of blood all over the pavement.

And around the corner charged two Indonesian-looking men, one with a pistol and the other with a small plastic automatic weapon. Bean recognized the Israeli design, because that was the weapon his own little army had used on missions where they had to be able to conceal their weapons as long as possible.

"Come with us!" shouted one of the Indonesians.

Bean thought this was probably a good idea. Since the assassination attempt had included one backup, it might include more, and the sooner he got out of there the better.

Of course, he didn't know anything about these Indonesians, or why they would have been there at this moment to save his life, but the fact that they had guns and weren't firing them at him implied that for the moment, at least, they were his dearest friends.

He grabbed his suitcase and ran. The front right door of a nondescript German car was open, waiting for him. The moment he dived in, he said, "My wife—she's in another cab."

"She safe," said the man in the back seat, the one with the automatic weapon. "Her driver one of us. Very good choice of cab for her. Very bad choice for you."

"Who *are* you?"

"Indonesian immigrant," said the driver with a grin.

"Muslim," said Bean. "Alai sent you?"

"No, not a lie. True," said the man.

Bean didn't bother correcting him. If the name *Alai* meant nothing to him, what was the point in pursuing the matter? "Where's Petra? My wife?"

"Going to airport. She not using ticket you giving her." The man in the back seat handed him an airline ticket. "She going here."

Bean looked at his ticket. Damascus.

Apparently Ambul's mission had gone well. Damascus was, for all intents and purposes, the capital of the Muslim world. Even though Alai had dropped out of sight, it was unlikely that he was anywhere else.

"Are we going there as guests?" asked Bean.

"Tourists," said the man in the back.

"Good," said Bean. "Because we left something in the hospital here that we might have to come back for." Though it was obvious that Achilles's people— or whoever it was—knew everything about what they were doing at Women's Hospital. In fact . . . there was almost no chance that anything of theirs remained in Women's Hospital.

He looked back at the man in the back seat. He was shaking his head. "Sorry, they telling me when we stop here and shoot guys for you, security guard in hospital stealing what you left there."

Of course. You don't fight your way past a security guard. You just hire him.

And now it was all clear to him. If Petra had gotten in the first cab, it wouldn't have been an assassination, it would have been a kidnapping. This wasn't about killing Bean—that was just a bonus. It was about getting Bean's babies.

Bean knew they hadn't been followed here. They had been betrayed since arriving. Volescu. And if Volescu was in on it, then the embryos that were stolen probably had Anton's Key after all. There was no particular reason for anyone to want his babies if there wasn't at least a chance that they would be prodigies of the kind Bean was.

Volescu's screening test was probably a fraud. Volescu probably had no idea which of the embryos had Anton's Key and which didn't. They'd implant them in surrogates and then see what happened when they were born.

Bean had been taken in by Volescu as surely as Peter had been by Achilles. But it wasn't as if they had trusted Volescu. They had simply trusted him not to be in league with Achilles.

Though it didn't have to be him. Just because he had kidnapped Ender's jeesh didn't mean that he was the only would-be kidnapper in the world. Bean's children, if they had his gifts, would be coveted by any ambitious nation or would-be military leader. Raise them up knowing nothing about their real parents, train them here on Earth as intensely as Bean and the other kids had been trained in Battle School, and by the age of nine or ten you can put them in command of strategy and tactics.

It might even be an entrepreneurial scheme. Maybe Volescu did this alone, hiring gunmen, bribing the security guard, so that he could sell the babies later to the highest bidder.

"Bad news, sorry," said the man in the back seat. "But you still got one baby, yes? In wife, yes?"

"Still the one," said Bean. If they had the ordinary amount of good luck.

Which didn't seem to be the trend at the moment.

Still, going to Damascus. . . . If Alai was really taking them into his protection, Petra would be safe there. Petra and perhaps one child—who might have Anton's Key after all, might be doomed to die without ever seeing the age of twenty. At least those two would be safe.

But the others were out there, children of Bean's and Petra's who would be raised by strangers, as tools, as slaves.

There had been nine embryos. One had been implanted, and three were discarded. That would leave five in the possession of Volescu or Achilles or whoever it was who took them.

Unless Volescu had actually found a way to switch the three that were supposedly discarded, switching containers somehow. There might be eight embryos unaccounted for.

But probably not, probably only the five they knew about. Bean and Petra had both been watching Volescu too carefully for him to get away with the first three, hadn't they?

By force of will, Bean turned his thoughts away from worries he could do nothing about at this moment, and took stock of his situation.

"Thank you," said Bean to the men in the car. "I was careless. Without you, I'd be dead."

"Not careless," said the man in the back. "Young man in love. Wife has baby in her. Time of hope."

Followed immediately, Bean realized, by a time of near despair. He should never have agreed to father children, no matter how much Petra wanted to, no matter how much he loved Petra, no matter how much he too yearned for offspring, for a family. He should have stood firm, because then this would not have been possible. There would have been nothing for his enemies to steal from him. He and Petra would still have been in hiding, undetected, because they would never have had to go to a snake like Volescu.

"Babies good," said the man in the back. "Make you scared, make you crazy. Somebody take away babies, somebody hurt babies, make you crazy. But good anyway. Babies good."

Yeah. Well. Maybe Bean would live long enough to know about that, and maybe he wouldn't.

Because now he knew his life's work, for whatever time he had left before he died of giantism.

He had to get his babies back. Whether they should ever have existed or not, they existed now, each with its own separate genetic identity, each very much alive. Until they were taken, they had been nothing to him but cells in a solution—all that mattered was the one that would be implanted in Petra, the one that would grow and become part of their family. But now they all mattered. Now they were all alive to him, because someone else had them, meant to use them.

He even regretted the ones that had been disposed of. Even if the test had been real, even if they had had Anton's Key, what right did he have to snuff out their genetic identity, just because he oh-soaltruistically wanted to spare them the sorrow of a life as short as his?

Suddenly he realized what he was thinking. What it meant.

Sister Carlotta, you always wanted me to turn Christian—and not just Christian, Catholic. Well, here I am, thinking that as soon as sperm and egg combine, they're a human life, and it's wrong to harm them.

Well, I'm not Catholic, and it wasn't wrong to want children to grow up to have a full life instead of this fifth-of-a-life that I'm headed for.

But how was I different, flushing three of those embryos, from Volescu? He flushed twenty-two of them, I flushed three. He waited till they were nearly two years further along in development—gestation plus a year—but in the end, is it really all that different?

Would Sister Carlotta condemn him for that? Had he committed a mortal sin? Was he only getting what he deserved now, losing five because he willingly threw away three?

No, he could not imagine her saying that to him. Or even thinking it to herself. She would rejoice that he had decided to have a child at all. She would be glad if Petra really was pregnant.

But she would also agree with him that the five that were now in someone else's hands, the five that might be implanted in someone else and turned into babies, he couldn't just let them go. He had to find them and save them and bring them home.

12

PUTTING OUT FIRES

From: Han Tzu
To: Snow Tiger
Re: stones

I am pleased and honored to have the chance once
again to offer my poor counsel to your bright magnifi-
cence. My previous advice to ignore the piles of stones
in the road was obviously foolish, and you saw that a
much wiser course was to declare stone-carrying to be
illegal.

Now I once again have the glorious privilege of giving
bad advice to him who does not need counsel.

Here is the problem as I see it:

1. Having declared a law against stone-carrying, you
cannot back down and repeal the law without showing
weakness.
2. The law against stone-carrying puts you in the position of arresting and punishing women and small children, which is filmed and smuggled out of India to the
great embarrassment of the Universal People's State.

3. The coastline of India being so extensive and our navy so small, we cannot stop the smuggling of these vids.

4. The stones block the roads, making transportation of troops and supplies unpredictable and dangerous, disrupting schedules.

5. The stone piles are being called "The Great Wall of India" and other names which make them a symbol of revolutionary defiance of the Universal People's State.

You tested me by suggesting that there were only two possibilities, which in your wisdom you knew would lead to disastrous consequences. Repealing the law or ceasing to enforce it would encourage further lawlessness. Stricter enforcement will only make martyrs, inflame the opposition, shame us among the ignorant barbarian nations, and encourage further lawlessness.

Through unbelievable luck, I have not failed your clever test. I have found the third alternative that you already saw:

I see now that your plan is to fill trucks with fine gravel and huge stones. Your soldiers will go to villages which have built these new, higher barricades. They will back the trucks up to the barricades and dump the gravel and the boulders in front of their pile, but not on top of it.

1. The rebellious, ungrateful Indian people will reflect upon the difference in size between the Great Wall of India and the Gravel and Boulders of China.

2. Because you will have blocked all roads into and out of each village, they will not get any trucks or buses into or out of their village until they have moved not only

the Great Wall of India but also the Gravel and Boulders of China.

3. They will find that the gravel is too small and the boulders are too large to be moved easily. The great exertion that they must use to clear the roads will be a sufficient teacher without any further punishment of any person.

4. Any vids smuggled out of India will show that we have only done to their roads what they voluntarily did themselves, only more. And the only punishment foreigners will see is Indians picking up rocks and moving them, which is the very thing they chose to do themselves in the first place.

5. Because there are not enough trucks in India to pile gravel and boulders in more than a small fraction of the villages which have built a Great Wall of India, the villages which receive this treatment should be chosen with care to make sure that the maximum number of roads are blocked, disrupting trade and food supplies throughout India.

6. You will also make sure sufficient roads are kept open for *our* supplies, but checkpoints will be set up far from villages and in places that cannot be filmed from a distance. No civilian trucks will be allowed to pass.

7. Certain villages that are starving will be supplied with small amounts of food airlifted by the Chinese military, who will come as saviors bringing food to those who innocently suffer because of the actions of the rebellious and disobedient blockers of roads. We will provide film of these humanitarian operations by our military to all foreign news media.

I applaud your wisdom in thinking of this plan, and thank you for allowing one so foolish as myself to have this chance to examine your way of thinking and see how

you will turn embarrassment to a great lesson for the ungrateful Indian people. Unless, like last time, you have a
plan that is even more subtle and wise, which I have been
unable to anticipate.

From this child who prostrates himself at your feet to learn
wisdom,

Han Tzu

Peter did not want to get out of bed.

This had never happened to him before in his life.

No, not strictly true. He had often wanted not to
get out of bed, but he had always gone ahead and
gotten out of bed anyway. What was different today
was that he was still in bed at nine-thirty in the morning, even though he had a press conference scheduled
for less than half an hour from now in a conference
room in the O. Henry Hotel in his home town of
Greensboro, North Carolina.

He could not plead jet lag. There was only an
hour's time difference between Ribeirão Preto and
Greensboro. It would be a great embarrassment if he
did not get up. So he *would* get up. Very soon now.

Not that it would make any difference. He might,
for the moment, still have the title of Hegemon, but
there were people in many countries with titles like
"king" and "duke" and "marquis," who nevertheless
cooked or took pictures or fixed automobiles for a
living. Perhaps he could go back to college under another name and train himself for a career like his father's, a quiet one working for a company
somewhere.

Or he could go into the bathroom and fill the tub

with water and lie down in it and breathe the water in. A few moments of panic and flailing around, and then the whole problem would go away. In fact, if he hit himself very hard in various places on his body, it might look as though he struggled with an assailant and was murdered. He might even be considered a martyr. At least people might think that he was important enough to have an enemy who thought he was worth killing.

Any minute now, thought Peter, I will get up and shower so I don't look so bedraggled to the media.

I ought to prepare a statement, he thought. Something to the effect of, "Why I am not as pathetic and stupid as my recent actions prove me to be." Or perhaps the direct approach: "Why I am even more pathetic and stupid than my recent actions might indicate."

Given his recent track record, he would probably be saved from the bathtub, given CPR, and then someone would notice the bruises on his body and the lack of an assailant and the story would get out about his pathetic effort to make his suicide attempt look like a brutal murder, thus making his life even more worthless than it already was.

Another knock on the door. Couldn't the maid read the do-not-disturb sign? It was written in four languages. Could she possibly be illiterate in all four of them? No doubt she was also illiterate in a fifth.

Twenty-five minutes until the press conference. Did I doze off? That would be nice. Just . . . doze . . . off. Sorry, I overslept. I've been so very busy. It's exhausting work to turn over—to a megalomaniac killer—everything I built up through my entire life.

Knock knock knock. It's a good thing I didn't kill myself, all this knocking would have ruined my concentration and entirely spoiled my death scene. I should die like Seneca, with fine last speeches. Or Socrates, though that would be harder, since I don't have hemlock but I do have a bathtub. No razor blades, though. I don't grow enough of a beard to need any. Just another sign that I'm only a stupid kid who should never have been permitted to take a role in the grownup world.

The door to his room opened and jammed against the locking bar.

How outrageous! Who dare to use a passkey on *his* room?

And not just a passkey! Someone had the tool that opened the locking bar and now his door was wide open.

Assassins! Well, let them kill me here in the bed, facing them, not cowering in a corner begging them not to shoot.

"Poor baby," said Mother.

"He's depressed," said Father. "Don't make fun of him."

"I can't help but think of what Ender went through, fighting the Formics almost every day for weeks, completely exhausted, and yet he always got up and fought again."

Peter wanted to scream at her. How dare she compare what he had just gone through with Ender's legendary "suffering." Ender never lost a battle, did she think of that? And he had just lost the war! He was entitled to sleep!

"Ready? One, two, three."

Peter felt the whole mattress slide down the bed until he was awkwardly dumped onto the floor, banging his head against the frame of the bedsprings.

"Ow!" he cried.

Wouldn't that make a noble last word to be recorded by posterity?

How did the great Peter Wiggin, Hegemon of Earth (and, of course, brother of Ender Wiggin, sainted savior), meet his end?

He sustained a terrible head injury when his parents dragged him out of a hotel bed the morning after his ignominious escape from his own compound where not one person had threatened him in any way and he had no evidence of any impending threat against his person.

And what were his last words?

A one-word sentence, fit to be engraved on his monument. Ow.

"I don't think we can get him into the shower without actually touching his sacred person," said Mother.

"I think you're right," said Father.

"And if we touch him," said Mother, "there's a real possibility that we will be struck dead on the spot."

Other people had mothers who were compassionate, tender, comforting, understanding. *His* mother was a sarcastic hag who clearly hated him and always had.

"Ice bucket," said Father.

"No ice."

"But it holds water."

This was too stupid. The old throw-water-on-the-sleeping-teenager trick.

"Just go away, I'm getting up in a couple of minutes."

"No," said Mother. "You're getting up now. Your father is filling the ice bucket. You can hear the water running."

"OK, OK, leave the room so I can take my clothes off and get in the shower. Or is this just a subterfuge so you can see me naked again? You've never let me forget how you used to change my diapers, so apparently that was a very important stage in your life."

He was answered by having water dashed in his face. Not a whole bucketful, but enough to soak his head and shoulders.

"Sorry I didn't have time to fill it," said Father. "But when you started making crude sexual innuendos to my wife, I had to use whatever amount of water was at hand to shut you up before you said enough that I would have to beat your bratty little face in."

Peter got up from the mattress on the floor and pulled off the shorts he slept in. "Is this what you came in to see?"

"Absolutely," said Father. "You were wrong, Theresa: he *does* have balls."

"Not enough of them, apparently."

Peter stalked between them and slammed the bathroom door behind him.

———

Half an hour later, after keeping the press waiting only ten minutes past the appointed time, Peter walked alone onto the platform at one end of a packed conference room. All the reporters were holding up their little steadycams, the lenses peering out between the fingers of their clenched fists. It was the best turnout he had ever had at a press conference—though to be fair he had never actually held one in the United States. Maybe here they would all have been like this.

"I'm as surprised as you are to find myself here today," said Peter with a smile. "But I must say I'm grateful to the source that provided me with information that allowed me to make my exit, along with my family, from a place that had once been a safe haven, but which had become the most dangerous place in the world to me.

"I am also grateful to the government of the United States, which not only invited me to bring the office of Hegemon here, on a temporary basis, of course, but also provided me with a generous contingent of the Secret Service to secure the area. I don't believe they're necessary, at least not in such numbers, but then, until recently I didn't think I needed any protection inside the Hegemony compound in Ribeirão Preto."

His smile invited a laugh, and he got one. More of a release of tension than real amusement, but it would do. Father had stressed that—make them laugh now and then, so everybody feels relaxed. That will make them think *you're* relaxed and confident, too.

"My information suggests that the many loyal employees of the Office of Hegemon are in no danger whatsoever, and when a new permanent headquarters is established, I invite all those who want to, to resume their jobs. The disloyal employees, of course, already have other employment."

Another laugh—but a couple of audible groans, too. The press smelled blood, and it didn't help that Peter looked—and was—so very young. Humor, yes, but don't look like a wise-cracking kid. Especially don't look like a wise-cracking kid whose parents had to drag him out of bed this morning.

"I will not give you any information that would compromise my recent benefactor. What I *can* tell you is this: My inconveniently sudden journey—this disruption in the Office of Hegemon—is entirely my fault."

There. That wasn't what a kid would say. That

wasn't even what adult politicians usually said.

"Against the advice of my military commander and others, I brought the notorious Achilles Flandres, at his own request and with his assurances of loyalty to me, into my compound. I was warned that he could not be trusted, and I believed those warnings.

"However, I thought I was clever enough and careful enough to detect any betrayal on his part in plenty of time. That was a miscalculation on my part. Thanks to the help of others, it was not a fatal one.

"The disinformation now coming from Achilles Flandres in the former Hegemony compound about my alleged embezzlement is, of course, false. I have always maintained the financial records of the Hegemony in public. The broad categories of income and disbursement have been published every year on the nets, and this morning I have opened up the entire set of financial records of the Hegemony, and my own personal records, on a secure site with the address 'Hegemon Financial Disclosure.' Except for a few secret items in the budget, which any military analyst can tell you is barely enough to account for the very few military actions of my office over the past few years, every dollar is accounted for. And, yes, we do keep those records in dollars, since the Hegemony currency has fluctuated widely in value, but with a distinctly downward trend, in recent years."

Another laugh. But everyone was writing like crazy, too, and he could see that this policy of full disclosure was working.

"Besides seeing that nothing has been embezzled from the Hegemony," Peter went on, "you will also see that the Hegemony has been working with extremely limited funds. It has been a challenge, with so little money, to marshal the nations of the world to oppose the imperialistic designs of the so-called 'Universal People's State'—otherwise known as the Chinese Empire. We have been extremely grateful to those nations who have continued to support the Hegemony at one level or another. In deference to some of them who prefer their contribution remain secret, we have withheld some twenty names. You are free to speculate about their identity but I will say neither yes or no, except to tell you candidly that China is not one of them."

The biggest laugh yet, and a couple of people even clapped their hands a few times.

"I am outraged that the usurper Achilles Flandres has called into question the credentials of the Minister of Colonization. But if there were any doubts about Flandres's plans, the fact that this was his first act should tell you a great deal about the future he plans for us all. Achilles Flandres will not rest until every human being is under his complete control. Or, of course, dead."

Peter paused, looked down at the rostrum as if he had notes there, though of course he didn't.

"One thing I do not regret, however, about bringing Achilles Flandres to Ribeirão Preto, is that I have had a chance now to take his measure as a human being—though it is only by the broadest definition that I include him in that category. Achilles Flandres has achieved his power in the world, not by his own intelligence or courage, but by exploiting the intelligence and courage of others. He engineered the kidnapping of the children who helped my brother, Ender Wiggin, save humanity from the alien invaders. Why? Because he knew that he himself did not have any hope of ruling the world if any of them were working against him.

"Achilles Flandres's power comes from the willingness of others to believe his lies. But his lies will no longer bring him new allies as they have in the past. He has hitched his little wagon to China and drives China like an ox. But I have heard him laughing at the poor fools in the Chinese government who believed him, mocking them for their petty ambitions, as he told me how unworthy they were to have him guiding their affairs.

"No doubt much of this was merely part of his attempt to convince me that he was no longer working with them. But his ridicule was by name and very specific. His contempt for them was genuine. I almost feel sorry for them—because if his power is ever solidified and he has no further use for them, then they will see what I saw.

"Of course, he has scorn for me as well, and if he's laughing at me right now, I can only agree with him. I was snookered, ladies and gentlemen. In that, I join a distinguished company, some of whom fell from power in Russia after the kidnappings, some of whom are now suffering as political prisoners after China's conquest of India, and some of whom even now are arresting people in India for . . . carrying stones.

"I only hope that I will turn out to be the last person so vain and foolish as to think that Achilles Flandres can be controlled or exploited to serve some higher purpose. Achilles Flandres serves only one purpose— his own pleasure. And what pleases him . . . would be to rule over every man, woman, and child in the human race.

"I was not a fool when I committed the Hegemony to opposing the imperialistic acts of the Chinese government. Now, because of my own mistakes, the prestige of the Hegemony is temporarily diminished. But my opposition to the Chinese Empire's oppression of more than half the people of the world is not diminished. I am the implacable enemy of emperors."

That was as good a stopping point as any.

Peter bowed his head briefly to acknowledge their polite applause. Some in the crowd applauded more than politely—but he was also aware of those who did not clap at all.

The questions began then, but because he had accused himself from the start, he fielded them easily. Two questioners tried to get more information on the source who tipped him off and what it was he tipped Peter off about, but Peter only said, "If I say anything more on this subject, someone who has been kind to me will certainly die. I am surprised you would even ask." After the second time he said this—word for word—no one asked such a question again.

As to those whose questions were merely veiled accusations, he agreed with all those who implied that he had been foolish. When he was asked if he had proven himself too foolish to hold the office of Hegemon, his first reply was a joke: "I was told when I took the job in the first place that accepting it proved I was too dimwitted to serve." Laughter, of course. And then he said, "But I have tried to use that office to serve the cause of peace and self-government for all of humanity, and I challenge anyone to show that I did anything other than advance that cause as much as was possible with the resources I had."

Fifteen minutes later, he apologized for having no further time. "But please email me any further questions you might have, and my staff and I will try to get answers back to you in time for your deadlines. One final word before I go."

They fell silent, waiting.

"The future happiness of the human race depends on good people who want to live at peace with their neighbors, and who are willing to protect their neighbors from those who don't want peace. I'm only one of those people. I'm probably not the best of them, and I hope to God I'm not the smartest. But I happen to be the one who was entrusted with the office of Hegemon. Until my term expires or I am lawfully replaced by the nations that have supported the Hegemony, I will continue to serve in that office."

More applause—and this time he allowed himself to believe that there might be some real enthusiasm in it.

———

He came back to his room exhausted.

Mother and Father were there, waiting. They had refused to go downstairs with him. "If your mother and father are with you," Father had said, "then this better be the press conference where you resign. But if you intend to stay in office, then you go down there alone. Just you. No staff. No parents. No friends. No notes. Just you."

Father had been right. Mother had been right, too. Ender, bless his little heart, was the example he had to follow. If you lose, you lose, but you don't give up.

"How did it go?" asked Mother.

"Well enough, I think," said Peter. "I took questions for fifteen minutes, but they were starting to repeat themselves or get off on wild tangents so I told them to email me any further questions. Was it carried on the vid?"

"We polled thirty news stations," said Father, "and

the top twenty or so newswebs, and most of them had it live."

"So you watched?" said Peter.

"No, we flipped through," said Mother. "But what we saw looked and sounded good. You didn't bat an eye. I think you brought it off."

"We'll see."

"Long term," said Father. "You're going to have a bumpy couple of months. Especially because you can count on it that Achilles hasn't emptied his quiver yet."

"Bow and arrow analogies?" said Peter. "You are so old."

They chuckled at his joke.

"Mom. Dad. Thanks."

"All we did," said Father, "was what we knew that tomorrow you would have wished we had done today."

Peter nodded. Then he sat down on the edge of the bed. "Man, I can't believe I was so dumb. I can't believe I didn't listen to Bean and Petra and Suri and—"

"And us," said Mother helpfully.

"And you and Graff," said Peter.

"You trusted your own judgment," said Father, "and that's exactly what you have to do. You were wrong this time, but you haven't been wrong often, and I doubt you'll ever be this wrong again."

"For heaven's sake don't start taking a vote on your decisions," said Mother. "Or looking at opinion polls or trying to guess how your actions will play with the press."

"I won't," said Peter.

"Because, you see, you're Locke," said Mother. "You already ended one war. After a few days or weeks, the press will start remembering that. And you're Demosthenes—you have quite a fervent following."

"Had," said Peter.

"They saw what they expected from Demosthenes," said Mother. "You didn't weasel, you didn't make excuses, you took the blame you deserved and refused the accusations that were false. You put out your evidence—"

"That was good advice, Dad, thanks," said Peter.

"And," said Mother, "you showed courage."

"By running away from Ribeirão Preto before anyone so much as glared at me?"

"By getting out of bed," she answered.

Peter shook his head. "Then my courage is nothing but borrowed courage."

"Not borrowed," said Mother. "Stored up. In us. Like a bank. We've seen your courage and we saved some for you when you temporarily ran out and needed some of it back."

"Cash flow problem, that's all it was," said Father.

"How many times are you two going to have to save me from myself before this whole drama runs its course?" asked Peter.

"I think . . . six times," said Father.

"No, eight," said Mother.

"You two think you're so cute," said Peter.

"Mm-hm."

"Yep."

A knock at the door. "Room service!" called a voice from outside.

Father was at the door in two quick strides. "Three tomato juices?" he asked.

"No, no, nothing like that. Lunch. Sandwiches. Bowl of ice cream."

Even with that reassurance, Father stepped to the side of the door and pulled it open as far as the lock bar allowed. Nobody fired a weapon, and the guy with the food laughed. "Oh, everybody forgets to undo that thing, happens all the time."

Father opened the door and stepped outside long enough to make sure nobody else was in the hall waiting to follow room service inside.

When the waiter was coming through the door Peter turned around to get out of his way, just in time to see Mother slipping a pistol back into her purse.

"Since when did you start packing?" he asked her.

"Since your chief of computer security turned out to be Achilles's good friend," she said.

"Ferreira?" asked Peter.

"He's been telling the press that he installed snoopware to find out who was embezzling funds, and was shocked to discover it was you."

"Oh," said Peter. "Of course they ran a press conference opposite mine."

"But almost everybody carried yours live and his was just excerpted. And they all followed the Ferreira clip with a repeat of you announcing that you were posting the Hegemony financial records on the nets."

"Bet we crash the server."

"No, all the news organizations cloned it first thing."

Father had finished signing off on the meal and the waiter was gone, the door relocked.

"Let's eat," said Father. "If I recall, this place always has great lunches."

"It's good to be home," said Mother. "Well, not *home,* but in town, anyway."

Peter took a bite and it was good.

They had ordered exactly the sandwich he would

have ordered, that's how well they knew him. Their lives really were focused on their children. He couldn't have ordered *their* sandwiches.

Three place settings on the little rolling cart the waiter had wheeled in.

There should have been five.

"I'm sorry," he said.

"For what?" asked Father, his mouth full.

"That I'm the only kid you've got on Earth."

"Could be worse," said Father. "Could have been none."

And Mother reached over and patted his hand.

13

CALIPH

From: Graff%pilgrimage@colmin.gov
To: Locke%erasmus@polnet.gov
Re: The better part of valor

I know you don't want to hear from me. But given that you are no longer in a secure situation, and our mutual foe is playing again on the world stage, I offer you and your parents sanctuary. I am not suggesting that you go into the colony program. Quite the contrary—I regard you as the only hope of rallying worldwide opposition to our foe. That is why your physical protection is of the utmost importance to us.

For that reason, I have been authorized to invite you to a facility off planet for a few days, a few weeks, a few months. It has full connections to the nets and you will be returned to Earth within forty-eight hours of your request. No one will even know you are gone. But it will put you out of reach of any attempt either to kill or capture you or your parents.

Please take this seriously. Now that we know our enemy has not severed his connections with his previous host, certain intelligence already obtained now makes a different kind of sense. Our best interpretation of this data is that an attempt on your life is imminent.

A temporary disappearance from the surface of the Earth would be very useful to you right now. Think of it as the equivalent of Lincoln's secret journey through Baltimore in order to assume the presidency. Or, if you prefer a less lofty precedent, Lenin's journey to Russia in a sealed railroad car.

Petra assumed that she had been taken to Damascus because Ambul had succeeded in making contact with Alai, but neither of them met her at the airport. Nor was there anyone waiting for her at the security gates. Not that she wanted someone carrying a sign that said "Petra Arkanian"—she might as well send Achilles an email telling him where she was.

She had felt nauseated through the entire flight, but she knew it could not possibly be from pregnancy, not this quickly. It took at least a few hours for the hormones to start to flow. It had to be the stark fear that started when she realized that if Alai's people could find exactly where she was, and have a cab waiting for her, so could Achilles's.

How did Bean know to choose the cab he chose for her? Was it some predilection for Indonesians? Did he reason from evidence she didn't even notice? Or did he choose the third cab simply because he didn't trust the concept of "next in line"?

What cab had he got into, and who was driving it?

Someone bumped into her from behind, and for a moment she had a rush of adrenaline as she thought: This is it! I'm being killed by an assassin who approached me from behind because I was too stupid to look around!

After the momentary panic—and the momentary self-blame—she realized that of course it was not an assassin, it was simply a passenger from her flight, hurrying to get out of the airport, while she, uncertain and lost in her own thoughts, had been walking too slowly and obstructing traffic.

I'll go to a hotel, she thought. But not one that Europeans always go to. But wait, if I go to a hotel where everybody but me is Arab-looking, I'll stand out. Too obvious. Bean would tease me for not having developed any useful survival habits. Though at least I thought twice before checking into an Arab hotel.

The only luggage she had was the bag she was carrying over her shoulder, and at customs she went through the usual questions. "This is all your luggage?" "Yes." "How long do you plan to stay?" "A couple of weeks, I expect." "Two weeks, and no more clothing than this?" "I plan to shop."

It always aroused suspicions to enter a country with too little luggage, but as Bean said, it's better to have a few more questions at customs or passport control than to have to go to the baggage claim area and stand around where bad people have plenty of time to find you.

The only thing worse, in Bean's view, was to use the first restroom in the airline terminal. "Everybody knows women have to pee incessantly," said Bean.

"Actually, it's not incessant, and most men don't notice even if it is," said Petra. But considering that Bean seemed never to need to pee at all, she supposed that her normal human needs seemed excessive to him.

She was well trained now, however. She didn't

even glance at the first restroom she passed, or the second. She probably wouldn't use a bathroom until she got to her hotel room.

Bean, when are you coming? Did they get you onto the next flight? How will we find each other in this city?

She knew he would be furious, however, if she lingered in the airport hoping to meet his flight. For one thing, she would have no idea where his flight would be coming from—he was wont to choose very odd itineraries, so that he could very easily be on a flight from Cairo, Moscow, Algiers, Rome, or Jerusalem. No, it was better to go to a hotel, check in under an alias that he knew about, and—

"Mrs. Delphiki?"

She turned at once at the sound of Bean's mother's name, and then realized that the tall, white-haired gentleman was addressing her.

"Yes." She laughed. "I'm still not used to the idea of being called by my husband's name."

"Forgive me," said the man. "Do you prefer your birth name?"

"I haven't used my own name in many months," said Petra. "Who sent you to meet me?"

"Your host," said the man.

"I have had many hosts in my life," said Petra. "Some of whom I do not wish to visit again."

"But such people as that would not live in Damascus." There was a twinkle in his eye. Then he leaned in close. "There are names that it is not good to say aloud."

"Mine apparently not being one of them," she said with a smile.

"In this time and place," he said, "you are safe while others might not be."

"I'm safe because you're with me?"

"You are safe because I and my . . . what is your Battle School slang? . . . my jeesh and I are here watching over you."

"I didn't see anybody watching over me."

"You didn't even see *me*," said the man. "This is because we're very good at what we do."

"I *did* see you. I just didn't realize you had taken any notice of me."

"As I said."

She smiled. "Very well, I will not name our host. And since you won't either, I'm afraid I can't go with you anywhere."

"Oh, so suspicious," he said with a rueful smile. "Very well, then. Perhaps I can facilitate matters by placing you under arrest." He showed her a very official-looking badge inside a wallet. Though she had no idea what organization had issued the badge, since she had never learned the Arabic alphabet, let alone the language itself.

But Bean had taught her: Listen to your fear, and listen to your trust. She trusted this man, and so she believed his badge without being able to read it. "So you're with Syrian law enforcement," she said.

"As often as not," he replied, smiling again as he put his wallet away.

"Let's walk outside," she said.

"Let's not," he said. "Let's go into a little room here at the airport."

"A toilet stall?" she asked. "Or an interrogation room?"

"My office," he said.

If it was an office, it was certainly well disguised. They got to it by stepping behind the El Al ticket counter and going into the employees' back room.

"El Al?" she asked. "You're Israeli?"

"Israel and Syria are very close friends for the past hundred years. You should keep up on your history."

They walked down a corridor lined with employee lockers, a drinking fountain, and a couple of restroom doors.

"I didn't think the friendship was close enough to allow Syrian law enforcement to use Israel's national airline," said Petra.

"I lied about being with Syrian law enforcement," he said.

"And did they lie out front about being El Al?"

He palmed open an unmarked door, but when she made as if to follow him through it, he shook his head. "No no, first you must place the palm of your hand . . ."

She complied, but wondered how they could possibly have her palm print and sweat signature here in Syria.

No. They didn't, of course. They were getting them right now, so that wherever else she went, she would be recognized by their computer security systems.

The door led to a stairway that went down.

And farther down, and farther yet, until they had to be well underground.

"I don't think this complies with international handicapped access regulations," said Petra.

"What the regulators don't see won't hurt us," said the man.

"A theory that has gotten so many people into so much trouble," said Petra.

They came to an underground tunnel, where a small electric car was waiting for them. No driver. Apparently her companion was going to drive.

Not so. He got into the backseat beside her, and the car took off by itself.

"Let me guess," said Petra. "You don't take most of your VIPs through the El Al ticket counter."

"There are other ways to get to this little street," said the man. "But the people looking for you would not have staked out El Al."

"You'd be surprised at how often my enemy is two steps ahead."

"But what if your friends are three steps ahead?" Then he laughed as if it had been a joke, and not a boast.

"We're alone in a car," said Petra. "Let's have some names now."

"I am Ivan Lankowski," he said.

She laughed in spite of herself. But when he did not smile, she stopped. "I'm sorry," she said. "You don't look Russian, and this is Damascus."

"My paternal grandfather was ethnic Russian, my grandmother was ethnic Kazakh, both were Muslims. My mother's parents are still living, thanks be to Allah, and they are both Jordanian."

"And you never changed the name?"

"It is the heart that makes the Muslim. The heart and the life. My name contains part of my genealogy. Since Allah willed me to be born in this family, who am I to try to deny his gift?"

"Ivan Lankowski," said Petra. "The name I'd like to hear is the name of the one who sent you."

"One's superior officer is never named. It is a basic rule of security."

Petra sighed. "I suppose this proves I'm not in Kansas anymore."

"I don't believe," said Lankowski, "that you have ever been in Kansas, Mrs. Delphiki."

"It was a reference to—"

"I have seen *The Wizard of Oz*," said Lankowski. "I am, after all, an educated man. And . . . I *have* been in Kansas."

"Then you have found wisdom I can only dream of."

He chuckled. "It is an unforgettable place. Just like Jordan was right after the Ice Age, covered with tall grasses, stretching forever in every direction, with the sky everywhere, instead of being confined to a small patch above the trees."

"You are a poet," said Petra. "And also a very old man, to remember the Ice Age."

"The Ice Age was my father's time. I only remember the rainy times right after it."

"I had no idea there were tunnels under Damascus."

"In our wars with the west," said Lankowski, "we learned to bury everything that we did not want blown up. Individually-targeted bombs were first tested on Arabs, did you know that? The archives are full of pictures of exploding Arabs."

"I've seen some of the pictures," said Petra. "I also recall that during those wars, some of the individuals targeted themselves by strapping on their own bombs and blowing them up in public places."

"Yes, we did not have guided missiles, but we did have feet."

"And the bitterness remains?"

"No, no bitterness," said Lankowski. "We once ruled the known world, from Spain to India. Muslims ruled in Moscow, and our soldiers reached into France, and to the gates of Vienna. Our dogs were better educated than the scholars of the West. Then one day we woke up and we were poor and ignorant, and somebody else had all the guns. We knew this could not be the will of Allah, so we fought."

"And discovered that the will of Allah was . . . ?"

"The will of Allah was for many of our people to die, and for the West to occupy our countries again and again until we stopped fighting. We learned our lesson. We are very well behaved now. We abide by all the treaty terms. We have freedom of the press, freedom of religion, liberated women, and democratic elections."

"And tunnels under Damascus."

"And memories." He smiled at her. "And cars without drivers."

"Israeli technology, I believe."

"For a long time we thought of Israel as the enemy's toehold in our holy land. Then one day we remembered that Israel was a member of our family who had gone away into exile, learned everything our enemies knew, and then came home again. We stopped fighting our brother, and our brother gave us all the gifts of the West, but without destroying our souls. How sad it would have been if we had killed all the Jews and driven them out. Who would have taught us then? The Armenians?"

She laughed at his joke, but also listened to his lecture. So this was how they lived with their history—they assigned meanings to everything that allowed them to see God's hand in everything. Purpose. Even power and hope.

But they also still remembered that Muslims had once ruled the world. And they still regarded democracy as something they adopted in order to placate the West.

I really should read the Q'uran, she thought. To see

what lies underneath the façade of western-style sophistication.

This man was sent to meet me, she thought, because this is the face they want visitors to Syria to see. He told me these stories, because this is the attitude they want me to believe that they have.

But this is the pretty version. The one that has been tailored to fit Western ears. The bones of the stories, the blood and the sinews of it, were defeat, humiliation, incomprehension of the will of God, loss of greatness as a people, and a sense of ongoing defeat. These are people with something to prove and with lost status to retrieve. A people who want, not vengeance, but vindication.

Very dangerous people.

Perhaps also very useful people, to a point.

She took her observations to the next step, but couched her words in the same kind of euphemistic story that he had told. "From what you tell me," said Petra, "the Muslim world sees this dangerous time in world history as the moment Allah has prepared you for. You were humbled before, so you would be submissive to Allah and ready for him to lead you to victory."

He said nothing at all for a long time.

"I did not say that."

"Of course you did," said Petra. "It was the premise underlying everything else you said. But you don't seem to realize that you have told this, not to an enemy, but to a friend."

"If you are a friend of God," said Lankowski, "why do you not obey his law?"

"But I did not say I was a friend of God," said Petra. "Only that I was a friend of yours. Some of us cannot live your law, but we can still admire those who do, and wish them well, and help them when we can."

"And come to us for safety because in our world there is safety to be had, while in your world there is none."

"Fair enough," said Petra.

"You are an interesting girl," said Lankowski.

"I've commanded soldiers in war," said Petra, "and I'm married, and I might very well be pregnant. When do I stop being just a girl? Under Islamic law, I mean."

"You are a girl because you are at least forty years younger than I am. It has nothing to do with Islamic law. When you are sixty and I am a hundred, inshallah, you will still be a girl to me."

"Bean is dead, isn't he?" asked Petra.

Lankowski looked startled. "No," he said at once. It was a blurt, unprepared for, and Petra believed him.

"Then something terrible has happened that you can't bear to tell me. My parents—have they been hurt?"

"Why do you think such a thing?"

"Because you're a courteous man. Because your people changed my ticket and brought me here and promised I'd be reunited with my husband. And in all this time we've been walking and riding together, you have never so much as hinted about when or whether I would see Bean."

"I apologize for being remiss," said Lankowski. "Your husband boarded a later flight that came by a different route, but he is coming. And your family is fine, or at least we have no reason to think they're not."

"And yet you are still hesitant," said Petra.

"There was an incident," said Lankowski. "Your

husband is safe. Uninjured. But there was an attempt to kill him. We think if you had been the one who got into the first cab, it would not have been a murder attempt. It would have been a kidnapping."

"And why do you think that? The one who wants my husband dead wants me dead as well."

"Ah, but he wants what you have inside you even more," said Lankowski.

It took only a moment for her to make the logical assumption about why he would know that. "They've taken the embryos," she said.

"The security guard received a rise in salary from a third party, and in return he allowed someone to remove your frozen embryos."

Petra had known Volescu was lying about being able to tell which babies had Anton's Key. But now Bean would know it, too. They both knew the value of Bean's babies on the open market, and that the highest price would come if the babies had Anton's Key in their DNA, or the would-be buyers believed they did.

She found herself breathing too rapidly. It would do no good to hyperventilate. She forced herself to calm down.

Lankowski reached out and patted her hand lightly. Yes, he sees that I'm upset. I don't yet have Bean's skill at hiding what I feel. Though of course his skill might be the simple result of not feeling anything.

Bean would know that Volescu had deceived them. For all they knew, the baby in her womb might be afflicted with Bean's condition. And Bean had vowed that he would never have children with Anton's Key.

"Have there been any ransom demands?" she asked Lankowski.

"Alas, no," he replied. "We do not think they wish

to trouble themselves with the near impossibility of trying to obtain money from you. The risk of being outsmarted and arrested in the process of trying to exchange items of value is too high, perhaps, when compared with the risk involved in selling your babies to third parties."

"I think the risks involved in that are very nearly zero," said Petra.

"Then we agree on the assessment. Your babies will be safe, if that's any consolation."

"Safe to be raised by monsters," said Petra.

"Perhaps they don't see themselves that way."

"Are you confessing that you people are in the market for one of them to raise to be your boy or girl genius?"

"We do not traffic in stolen flesh," said Lankowski. "We long had a problem with a slave trade that would not die. Now if someone is caught owning or selling or buying or transporting a slave, or being in an official position and tolerating slavery, the penalty is death. And the trials are swift, the appeals never granted. No, Mrs. Delphiki, we are not a good place for someone to bring stolen embryos to try to sell them."

Even in her concern about her children—her potential children—she realized what he had just confessed: That the "we" he spoke of was not Syria, but rather some kind of pan-Islamic shadow government that did not, officially at least, exist. An authority that transcended nations.

That was what Lankowski meant when he said that he worked for the Syrian government "as often as not." Because as often as not he worked for a government higher than that of Syria.

They already have their own rival to the Hegemon.

"Perhaps someday," she said, "my children will be trained and used to help defend some nation from Muslim conquest."

"Since Muslims do not invade other nations anymore, I wonder how such a thing could happen?"

"You have Alai sequestered here somewhere. What is he doing, making baskets or pottery to sell at the fair?"

"Are those the only choices you see? Pottery-making or aggressive war?"

But his denials did not interest her. She knew her analysis was as correct as it could be without more data—his denial was not a disproof, it was more likely to be an inadvertent confirmation.

What interested her now was Bean. Where was he? When would he get to Damascus? What would he do about the missing embryos?

Or at least that was what she tried to pretend to herself that she was interested in.

Because all she could really think, in an undercurrent monologue that kept shouting at her from deep inside her mind, was:

He has my babies.

Not the Pied Piper, prancing them away from town. Not Baba Yaga, luring them into her house on chicken legs. Not the witch in the gingerbread cottage, keeping them in cages and fattening them up. None of those grey fantasies. Nothing of fog and mist. Only the absolute black of a place where no light shines, where light is not even remembered.

That's where her babies were.

In the belly of the Beast.

———

The car came to a stop at a simple platform. The underground road went on, to destinations Petra did not bother trying to guess. For all she knew, the tunnel ran to Baghdad, to Amman, under the mountains to Ankara, maybe even under the radioactive desert to arise in the place where the ancient stone waits for the half-life of the half-life of the half-life of death to pass, so pilgrims can come again on haj.

Lankowski reached out a hand and helped her from the car, though she was young and he was old. His attitude toward her was strange, as if he had to treat her very carefully. As if she was not robust, as if she could easily break.

And it was true. She was the one who could break. Who broke.

Only I can't break now. Because maybe I still have one child. Maybe putting this one inside me did not kill it, but gave it life. Maybe it has taken root in my garden and will blossom and bear fruit, a baby on a short twisted stem. And when the fruit is plucked, out will come stem and root as well, leaving the garden empty. And where will the others be then? They have been taken to grow in someone else's plot. Yet I will not break now, because I have this one, perhaps this one.

"Thank you," she said to Lankowski. "But I'm not so fragile as to need help getting out of a car."

He smiled at her, but said nothing. She followed him into the elevator and they rose up into . . .

A garden. As lush as the Philippine jungle clearing where Peter gave the order that would bring the Beast into their house, driving them out.

She saw that the courtyard was glassed over. That's why it was so humid here. That's how it stayed so moist. Nothing was given up to the dry desert air.

Sitting quietly on a stone chair in the middle of the garden was a tall, slender man, his skin the deep cacao brown of the upper Niger where he had been born.

She did not walk up to him at once, but stood admiring what she saw. The long legs, clad not in the business suit that had been the uniform of westerners for centuries now, but in the robes of a sheik. His head was not covered, however. And there was no beard on his chin. Still young, and yet also now a man.

"Alai," she murmured. So softly that she doubted he could hear.

And perhaps he did not hear, but chose that moment only by coincidence, to turn and see her. His brooding expression softened into a smile. But it was not the boyish grin that she had known when he bounded along the low-gravity inner corridors of Battle School. This smile had weariness in it, and old fears long mastered but still present. It was the smile of wisdom.

She realized then why Alai had disappeared from view.

He is Caliph. They have chosen a Caliph again, all the Muslim world under the authority of one man, and it is Alai.

She could not know this, not just from his place here in a garden. Yet she knew from the way he sat in it that this was a throne. She knew from the way she was brought here, with no trappings of power, no guards, no passwords, just a simple man of elegant courtesy leading her to the boy-man seated on the ancient throne. Alai's power was spiritual. In all of Damascus there was no safer place than here. No one would bother him. Millions would die before letting an uninvited stranger set foot here.

He beckoned to her, and it was the gentle invitation of a holy man. She did not have to obey him, and he would not mind if she did not come. But she came.

"Salaam," said Alai.

"Salaam," said Petra.

"Stone girl," he said.

"Hi," she said. The old joke between them, him punning on the meaning of her name in the original Greek, her punning on the *jai* of *jai alai*.

"I'm glad you're safe," he said.

"Your life has changed since you regained your freedom."

"And yours, too," said Alai. "Married now."

"A good Catholic wedding."

"You should have invited me," he said.

"You couldn't have come," she said.

"No," he agreed. "But I would have wished you well."

"Instead you have done well by us when we needed it most."

"I'm sorry that I did nothing to protect the other . . . children. But I didn't know about them in time. And I assumed that Bean and you would have had enough security . . . no, no, please, I'm sorry, I'm re-minding you of pain instead of soothing you."

She sank down and sat on the ground before his throne, and he leaned over to gather her into his arms. She rested her head and arms on his lap, and he stroked her hair. "When we were children, playing the greatest computer game in the world, we had no idea."

"We were saving the world."

"And now we're creating the world we saved."

"Not me," said Petra. "I'm no longer a player."

"Are any of us players?" said Alai. "Or are we only the pieces moved in someone else's game?"

"Inshallah," said Petra.

She had rather expected Alai to chuckle, but he only nodded. "Yes, that is our belief, that all that happens comes from the will of God. But I think it is not your belief."

"No, we Christians have to guess the will of God and try to bring it to pass."

"It feels the same, when things are happening," said Alai. "Sometimes you think that you're in control, because you make things change by your own choices. And then something happens that sweeps all your plans away as if they were nothing, just pieces on a chessboard."

"Shadows that children make on the wall," said Petra, "and someone turns the light off."

"Or turns a brighter one on," said Alai, "and the shadows disappear."

"Alai," said Petra, "will you let us go again? I know your secret."

"Yes, I'll let you go," said Alai. "The secret can't be kept for long. Too many people know it already."

"We would never tell."

"I know," said Alai. "Because we were once in Ender's jeesh. But I'm in another jeesh now. I stand at the head of it, because they asked me to do it, because they said God had chosen me. I don't know about that. I don't hear the voice of God, I don't feel his power inside me. But they come to me with their plans, their questions, the conflicts between nations, and I offer suggestions. And they take them. And things work out. So far at least, they've always worked. So perhaps I am chosen by God."

"Or you're very clever."

"Or very lucky." Alai looked at his hands. "Still, it's better to believe that some high purpose guides our steps than to think that nothing matters except our own small miseries and happinesses."

"Unless our happiness *is* the high purpose."

"If our happiness is the purpose of God," said Alai, "why are so few of us happy?"

"Perhaps he wants us to have the happiness that we can only find for ourselves."

Alai nodded and chuckled. "We Battle School brats, we all have a bit of the imam in us, don't you think?"

"The Jesuit. The rabbi. The lama."

"Do you know how I find my answers? Sometimes, when it's very hard? I ask myself, 'What would Ender do?' "

Petra shook her head. "It's the old joke. 'I ask myself, What would a person smarter than me do in this circumstance, and then I do it.' "

"But Ender isn't imaginary. He was with us, and we knew him. We saw how he built us into an army, how he knew us all, found the best in us, pushed us as hard as we could bear, and sometimes harder, but himself hardest of all."

Petra felt once again the old sting, that she was the only one he had pushed harder than she could bear.

It made her sad and angry, and even though she knew that Alai had not even been thinking of her when he said it, she wanted to lash back at him.

But he had been kind to her and Bean. Had saved them, and brought them here, even though he did not need or want non-Muslims helping him, since his new role as the leader of the world's Muslims required a certain purity, if not in his soul, then certainly in his companionship.

Still, she had to offer.

"We'll help you if you let us," said Petra.

"Help me what?" asked Alai.

"Help you make war against China," she said.

"But we have no plans to make war against China," said Alai. "We have renounced military jihad. The only purification and redemption we attempt is of the soul."

"Do all wars have to be holy wars?"

"No, but unholy wars damn all those who take part in them."

"Who else but you can stand against China?"

"The Europeans. The North Americans."

"It's hard to stand when you have no spine."

"They're an old and tired civilization. We were, too, once. It took centuries of decline and a series of bitter defeats and humiliations before we made the changes that would allow us to serve Allah in unity and hope."

"And yet you maintain armies. You have a network of operatives who shoot their guns when they need to."

Alai nodded gravely. "We're prepared to use force to defend ourselves if we're attacked."

Petra shook her head. For a moment she had felt frustrated because the world needed rescuing, and it sounded as though Alai and his people were renouncing war. Now she was just as disappointed to realize that nothing had really changed. Alai was planning war—but intended to wait until some attack made his war "defensive." Not that she disagreed with the justness of defensive war. It was the falseness of pretending that he had renounced war when he was in fact planning for it.

Or maybe he meant exactly what he said.

It seemed so unlikely.

"You're tired," said Alai. "Even though the jet lag from the Netherlands is not so bad, you should rest. I understand you were ill on your flight."

She laughed. "You had someone on the plane, watching me?"

"Of course," he said. "You're a very important person."

Why should she be important to the Muslims? They didn't want to use her military talents, and she had no political influence in the world. It had to be her baby that made her valuable—but how would her child, if she even had one, have any value to the Islamic world?

"My child," she said, "will not be raised to be a soldier."

Alai raised a hand. "You leap to conclusions, Petra," he said. "We are led, we hope, by Allah. We have no wish to take your child, and while we hope that there will someday be a world in which all children will be raised to know Allah and serve him, we have no desire to take your child from you or keep him here with us."

"Or her," said Petra, unreassured. "If you don't want our baby, why am I an important person?"

"Think like a soldier," said Alai. "You have in your womb what our worst enemy wants most. And, even if you don't have a baby, your death is something that he has to have, for reasons deep in the evil of his heart. His need to reach for you makes you important to those of us who fear him and want to block his path."

Petra shook her head. "Alai," she said, "I and my child could die and it would be a mere blip on the rangefinder to you and your people."

"It's useful for us to keep you alive," said Alai.

"How pragmatic of you. But there's more to it than that."

"Yes," said Alai. "There is."

"Are you going to tell me?"

"It will sound very mystical to you," said Alai.

"But that's hardly a surprise, coming from the Caliph."

"Allah has brought something new into the world—I speak of Bean, the genetic difference between him and the rest of humanity. There are imams who declare him to be an abomination, conceived in evil. There are others who say he is an innocent victim, a child who was conceived as a normal embryo but was altered by evil and can't help what was done to him. But there are others—and the number is by far larger—who say that this could not have been done except by the will of Allah. That Bean's abilities were a key part of our victory over the Formics, so it must have been God's will that brought him into existence at the time we needed him. And since God has chosen to bring this new thing into the world, now we must watch and see whether God allows this genetic change to breed true."

"He's dying, Alai," said Petra.

"I know," said Alai. "But aren't we all?"

"He didn't want to have children at all."

"And yet he changed his mind," said Alai. "The will of God blossoms in all hearts."

"So maybe if the Beast kills us, that's the will of God as well. Why did you bother to prevent it?"

"Because my friends asked me to," said Alai. "Why

are you making this so complicated? The things I want are simple. To do good wherever it's within my power, and where I can't do good, at least do no harm."

"How . . . Hippocratic of you."

"Petra, go to bed, sleep, you're becoming bitchy."

It was true. She was out of sorts, fretting about things she could do nothing to change, wanting Bean to be with her, wanting Alai not to have changed into this regal figure, this holy man.

"You're not happy with what I've become," said Alai.

"You can read minds?" asked Petra.

"Faces," said Alai. "Unlike Achilles and Peter Wiggin, I didn't seek this. I came home from space with no ambition other than to lead a normal life and perhaps serve my country or my God in one way or another. Nor did some party or faction choose me and set me in my place."

"How could you end up in this garden, on that chair, if neither you nor anyone else put you there?" asked Petra. It annoyed her when people lied—even to themselves—about things that simply didn't need to be lied about.

"I came home from my Russian captivity and was put to work planning joint military maneuvers of a pan-Arab force that was being trained to join in the defense of Pakistan."

Petra knew that this pan-Arab force probably began as an army designed to help defend *against* Pakistan, since right up to the moment of the Chinese invasion of India, the Pakistani government had been planning to launch a war against other Muslim nations to unite the Muslim world under their rule.

"Or whatever," said Alai, laughing at her consternation when, once again, he had seemed to read her mind. "It *became* a force for the defense of Pakistan. It put me in contact with military planners from a dozen nations, and more and more they began to come to me with questions well beyond those of military strategy. It was nobody's plan, least of all mine. I didn't think my answers were particularly wise, I simply said whatever seemed obvious to me, or when nothing was clear, I asked questions until clarity emerged."

"And they became dependent on you."

"I don't think so," said Alai. "They simply . . . respected me. They began to want me in meetings with the politicians and diplomats, not just the soldiers. And the politicians and diplomats began asking me questions, seeking my support for their views or plans, and finally choosing me as the mediator between the parties in various disputes."

"A judge," said Petra.

"A Battle School graduate," said Alai, "at a time when my people wanted more than a judge. They wanted to be great again, and to do that they needed a leader that they believed had the favor of Allah. I try to live and act in such a way as to give them the leader they need. Petra, I am still the same boy I was in Battle School. And, like Ender, I may be a leader, but I am also the tool my people created to accomplish their collective purpose."

"Maybe," said Petra, "I'm just jealous. Because Armenia has no great purpose, except to stay alive and free. And no power to accomplish that without the help of great nations."

"Armenia is in no danger from us," said Alai.

"Unless, of course, we provoke the Azerbaijanis,"

said Petra. "Which we do by breathing, I must point out."

"We will not conquer our way to greatness, Petra," said Alai.

"What, then, you'll wait for the whole world to convert to Islam and beg to be admitted to your new world order?"

"Yes," said Alai. "That's just what we'll do."

"As plans go," said Petra, "that's about the most self-delusional one I've ever heard of."

He laughed. "Definitely you need a nap, my beloved sister. You don't want *that* to be the mouth Bean has to listen to when he arrives."

"When will he arrive?"

"Well after dark," said Alai. "Now you see Mr. Lankowski waiting for you at that gate. He'll lead you to your room."

"I sleep in the palace of the Caliph tonight?" asked Petra.

"It's not much, as palaces go," said Alai. "Most of the rooms are public spaces, offices, things like that. I have a very simple bedroom and . . . this garden. Your room will also be very simple—but perhaps it will make it seem luxurious if you think of it as being identical with the one where the Caliph sleeps."

"I feel as if I've been swept away into one of Scheherazade's stories."

"We keep a sturdy roof. You have nothing to fear from rocs."

"You think of everything," said Petra.

"We have an excellent doctor on call, should you wish for medical attention of any kind."

"It's still too soon for a pregnancy test to mean anything," said Petra. "If that's what you meant."

"I meant," said Alai, "that we have an excellent

doctor on call, should you wish for medical attention of *any* kind."

"In that case," said Petra, "my answer is, 'You think of everything.' "

———

She thought she couldn't sleep, but she had nothing better to do than lie on the bed in a room that was downright spartan—with no television and no book but an Armenian translation of the Q'uran. She knew what the presence of this book in her room implied. For many centuries, translations of the Q'uran were regarded as false by definition, since only the original Arabic actually conveyed the words of the Prophet. But in the great opening of Islam that followed their abject defeat in a series of desperate wars with the West, this was one of the first things that was changed.

Every translated copy of the Q'uran contained, on the title page, a quotation from the great imam Zuqaq—the very one who brought about the reconciliation of Israel and the Muslim world. "Allah is above language. Even in Arabic, the Q'uran is translated from the mind of God into the words of men. Everyone should be able to hear the words of God in the language he speaks in his own heart."

So the presence of the Q'uran in Armenian told her, first, that in the palace of the Caliph, there was no recidivism, no return to the days of fanatical Islam, when foreigners were forced to live by Islamic law, women were veiled and barred from the schools and the roads, and young Muslim soldiers strapped bombs to their bodies to blow up the children of their enemies.

And it also told her that her coming was anticipated

and someone had taken great pains to prepare this room for her, simple as it seemed. To have the Q'uran in Common Speech, the more-or-less phonetically spelled English that had been adopted as the language of the International Fleet, would have been sufficient. They wanted to make the point, though, that here in the heart—no, the head—of the Muslim world, they had regard for all nations, all languages. They knew who she was, and they had the holy words for her in the language she spoke in her heart.

She appreciated the gesture and was annoyed by it, both at once. She did not open the book. She rummaged through her bag, then unpacked everything. She showered to clear the must of travel from her hair and skin, and then lay down on the bed because in this room there was nowhere else to sit.

No wonder he spends his time in the garden, she thought. He has to go out there just to turn around.

She woke because someone was at the door. Not knocking. Just standing there, pressing a palm against the reader. What could she possibly have heard that woke her? Footsteps in the corridor?

"I'm not dressed," she called out as the door opened.

"That's what I was hoping," said Bean.

He came in carrying his own bag and set it down beside the one dresser.

"Did you meet Alai?" asked Petra.

"Yes, but we'll talk of that later," said Bean.

"You know he's Caliph," she insisted.

"Later," he said. He pulled his shoes off.

"I think they're planning a war, but pretending that they're not," said Petra.

"They can plan what they like," said Bean. "You're safe here, that's what I care about."

Still in his traveling clothes, Bean lay down on the bed beside her, snaking one arm under her, drawing her close to him. He stroked her back, kissed her forehead.

"They told me about the other embryos," she said. "How Achilles stole them."

He kissed her again and said, "Shhhh."

"I don't know if I'm pregnant yet," said Petra.

"You will be," said Bean.

"I knew that he hadn't checked for Anton's Key," said Petra. "I knew he was lying about that."

"All right," said Bean.

"I knew but I didn't tell you," said Petra.

"Now you've told me."

"I want your child, no matter what."

"Well," said Bean, "in that case we can start the next one the regular way."

She kissed him. "I love you," she said.

"I'm glad to hear that."

"We have to get the others back," said Petra. "They're our children and I don't want somebody else to raise them."

"We'll get them back," said Bean. "That's one thing I know."

"He'll destroy them before he lets us have them."

"Not so," said Bean. "He wants them alive more than he wants us dead."

"How can you possibly know what the Beast is thinking?"

Bean rolled onto his back and lay there facing the ceiling. "On the plane I did a lot of thinking. About something Ender said. How he thought. You have to know your enemy, he said. That's why he studied the Formics constantly. All the footage of the First War, the anatomies of the corpses of the dead Bugger soldiers, and what he couldn't find in the books and vids, he imagined. Extrapolated. Tried to think of who they were."

"You're nothing like Achilles," said Petra. "You're the opposite of him. If you want to know him, think of whatever you're not, and that'll be him."

"Not true," said Bean. "In his sad, twisted way, he loves you, and so, in my own sad twisted way, do I."

"Not the same twists, and that makes all the difference."

"Ender said that you can't defeat a powerful enemy unless you understand him completely, and you can't understand him unless you know the desires of his heart, and you can't know the desires of his heart until you truly love him."

"Please don't tell me that you've decided to love the Beast," said Petra.

"I think," said Bean, "that I always have."

"No, no, no," said Petra in revulsion and she rolled away from him, turned her back on him.

"Ever since I saw him limping up to us, the one bully we thought we could overpower, we little children. His twisted foot, the dangerous hate he felt toward anyone who saw his weakness. The genuine kindness and love he showed to everyone but me and Poke—Petra, that's what nobody understands about Achilles, they see him as a murderer, and a monster—"

"Because he is one."

"A monster who keeps winning the love and trust of people who should know better. I know that man, the one whose eyes look into your soul and judge you and find you *worthy*. I saw how the other children loved him, turned their loyalty from Poke to Achilles, made him their father, truly, in their hearts. And even

though he always kept me at a distance, the fact is
. . . I loved him too."

"I didn't," said Petra. The memory of Achilles's
arms around her as he kissed her—it was unbearable
to her, and she wept.

She felt Bean's hand on her shoulder, then stroking
her side, gently soothing her. "I'm going to destroy
him, Petra," said Bean. "But I'll never do it the way
I've been going about it up till now. I've been avoiding him, reacting to him. Peter had the right idea after
all. He was dumb about it, but the idea was right, to
get close to him. You can't treat him as something
faraway and unintelligible. A force of nature, like a
storm or earthquake, where you have no hope but to
run for shelter. You have to understand him. Get inside his head."

"I've been there," said Petra. "It's a filthy place."

"Yes, I know," said Bean. "A place of fear and fire.
But remember—he lives there all the time."

"Don't tell me I'm supposed to pity him because
he has to live with himself!"

"Petra, I spent the whole flight trying to be Achilles, trying to think of what he yearns for, what he
hopes for, to think of how he thinks."

"And you threw up? Because I did, twice on my
flight, and I didn't have to get inside the Beast to do
it."

"Maybe because you have a little beast inside *you*."

She shuddered. "Don't call him that. Her. It. I'm
not even pregnant yet, probably. It was only this
morning. My baby is not a beast."

"Bad joke, I'm sorry," said Bean. "But listen, Petra,
on the flight I realized something. Achilles is not a
mysterious force. I know exactly what he wants."

"What does he want? Besides us, dead?"

"He wants us to know that the babies are alive. He won't even implant them yet. He'll leave little clues for us to follow—nothing too obvious, because he wants us to think we discovered something he's trying to keep hidden. But we'll find out where they are because he wants us to. They'll all be in one place. Because he wants us to come for them."

"Bait," she said.

"No, not just bait," said Bean. "He could send us a note right now if he wanted that. No, it's more than that. He wants us to think we're very smart to have found out where they are. He wants us to be full of hope that we might rescue them. To be excited, so we'll hurtle into a situation completely unprepared for the fact that he's waiting for us. That way he can see us fall from triumphant hope to utter despair. Before he kills us."

Bean was right, she knew it. "But how can you even pretend to love someone so evil?"

"No, you still don't understand," said Bean. "It's not our despair he wants. It's our hope. He has none. He doesn't understand it."

"Oh, please," said Petra. "An ambitious person *lives* on hope."

"He has no hope. No dream. He tries everything to find one. He goes through the motions of love and kindness, or anything else that might work, and still nothing means anything. Each new conquest only leaves him hungry for another. He's hungry to find something that really matters in life. He knows we have it. Both of us, before we even found each other, we had it."

"I thought you were famous for having no faith," said Petra.

"But you see," said Bean, "Achilles knew me better

than I knew myself. *He* saw it in me. The same thing Sister Carlotta saw."

"Intelligence?" asked Petra.

"Hope," said Bean. "Relentless hope. It never crosses my mind that there's no solution, no chance of survival. Oh, I can conceive of that intellectually, but never are my actions based on despair, because I never really believe it. Achilles knows that I have a reason to live. That's why he wants me so badly. And you, Petra. You more than me. And our babies—they *are* our hope. A completely insane kind of hope, yes, but we made them, didn't we?"

"So," said Petra, grasping the picture now, "he doesn't just want us to die, the way he was perfectly content to let Sister Carlotta die in an airplane, when he was far away. He wants us to see him with our babies."

"And when we realize we can't have them back, that we're going to die after all, the hope that drains out of us, he thinks it'll become his own. He thinks that because he has our babies, he has our hope."

"And he does," said Petra.

"But the hope can never be his. He's incapable of it."

"This is all very interesting," said Petra, "but completely useless."

"But don't you see?" said Bean. "This is how we can destroy him."

"What do you mean?"

"He's going to fall into the pit he dug for us."

"We don't have *his* babies."

"He *hopes* we'll come and give him what he wants. But instead, we'll come prepared to destroy him."

"He's going to be laying an ambush for us. If we come in force, he'll either slip away or—as soon as it's clear he's doomed—he'll kill our babies."

"No, no, we'll let him spring his trap. We'll walk right into it. So that when we face him, we see *him* in *his* moment of triumph. Which is always the moment when somebody is at their stupidest."

"You don't have to be smart when you have all the guns."

"Relax, Petra," said Bean. "I'm going to get our babies back. And kill Achilles while I'm at it. And I'll do it soon, my love. Before I die."

"That's good," said Petra. "It will be so much harder for you to do it afterward."

And then she wept, because, contrary to what Bean had just said, she had no hope. She was going to lose her husband, her children were going to lose their father. No victory over Achilles could change the fact that in the end, she was going to lose him.

He reached out for her again, held her close, kissed her brow, her cheek. "Have our baby," he said. "I'll bring home its brothers and sisters before it's born."

14

SPACE STATION

To: Locke%erasmus@polnet.gov
From: SitePostAlert
Re: Girl on bridge

Now you are not in cesspool, can communicate again.
Have no e-mail here. Stones are mine. Back on bridge
soon. War in earnest. Post to me only, this site, pickup
name BridgeGirl password not stepstool.

Peter found spaceflight boring, just as he'd suspected
he would. Like air travel, only longer and with less
scenery.

Thank heaven Mother and Father had the good
sense not to get all sentimental about the shuttle flight
to the Ministry of Colonization. After all, it was the
same space station that had been Battle School. They
were going to set foot at last where precious little
Ender had had his first triumphs—and, oh yes, killed
a boy.

But there were no footprints here. Nothing to tell
them what it was like for Ender to ride a shuttle to
this place. They were not small children taken away

from their homes. They were adults, and the fate of the world just might rest in their hands.

Come to think of it, that *was* like Ender, wasn't it.

The whole human race was united when Ender came here. The enemy was clear, the danger real, and Ender didn't even have to know what he was doing to win the war.

By comparison, Peter's task was much more difficult. It might seem simpler—find a really good assassin and kill Achilles.

But it wasn't that simple. First, Achilles, being an assassin and a user of assassins, would be ready for such a plot. Second, it wasn't enough to kill Achilles. He was not the army that conquered India and Indochina. He was not the government that ruled more than half the people of the world. Destroy Achilles, and you still have to roll back all the things he did.

It was like Hitler back in World War II. Without Hitler, Germany would never have had the nerve to conquer France and sweep to the gates of Moscow. But if Hitler had been assassinated just before the invasion of Russia, then in all likelihood the common language of the International Fleet would have been German. Because it was Hitler's mistakes, his weaknesses, his fears, his hatreds, that lost the back half of the war, just as it was his drive, his decisions, that won the front half.

Killing Achilles might do nothing more than guarantee a world governed by China.

Still, with him out of the way, Peter would face a rational enemy. And his own assets would not be so superstitiously terrified. The way Bean and Petra and Virlomi fled at the mere thought of Achilles coming to Ribeirão Preto . . . though of course in the long run they weren't wrong, still, it complicated things enormously that he kept having to work alone, unless you counted Mother and Father.

And since they were the only assets he had that he could rely on to serve his interests, he definitely counted them.

Counted them, but was angry at them all the same. He knew it was irrational, but the whole way up to MinCol, he kept coming back to the same seething memory of the way his parents had always judged him as a child and found him wanting, while Ender and Valentine could do no wrong. Being a fundamentally reasonable person, he took due notice of the fact that since Val and Ender left in a colony ship, his parents had been completely supportive of him. Had saved him more than once. He could not have asked any more from them even if they had actually loved him. They did their duty as parents, and more than their duty.

But it didn't erase the pain of those earlier years when everything he did seemed to be wrong, every natural instinct an offense against one of their versions of God or the other. Well, in all your judging, remember this—it was Ender who turned out to be Cain, wasn't it! And you always thought it was going to be me.

Stupid stupid stupid, Peter told himself. Ender didn't kill his brother, Ender defended himself against his enemies. As I have done.

I have to get over this, he told himself again and again during the voyage.

I wish there were something to look at besides the stupid vids. Or Dad snoring. Or Mother looking at me now and then, sizing me up, and then winking. Does she have any idea how awful that is? How demeaning? To wink at me! What about smiling? What about looking at me with that dreamy fond expression she used to have for Val and Ender? Of course she *liked* them.

Stop it. Think about what you have to do, fool.

Think about what you have to write and publish, as Locke and as Demosthenes, to rouse the people in the free countries, to goad the governments of the nations ruled from above. There could be no business as usual, he couldn't allow that. But it was hard to keep the people's attention on a war in which no shots were being fired. A war that took place in a faraway land. What did they care, in Argentina, that the people of India had a government not of their choosing? Why should it matter to a light farmer tending his photovoltaic screens in the Kalahari Desert whether the people of Thailand were having dirt kicked in their faces?

China had no designs on Namibia or Argentina. The war was over. Why wouldn't people just shut up about it and go back to making money?

That was Peter's enemy. Not Achilles, ultimately. Not even China. It was the apathy of the rest of the world that played into their hands.

And here I am in space, no longer free to move about, far more dependent than I've ever been before. Because if Graff decides not to send me back to Earth, then I can't go. There's no alternative transport. He *seems* to be entirely on my side. But it's his former Battle School brats that have his true loyalty. He thinks he can use me as I thought I could use Achilles. I was wrong. But probably he is right.

After all the voyaging, it was so frustrating to *be* there and still have to wait while the shuttle did its little dance of lining up with the station dock. There was nothing to watch. They blanked the "windows" because it was too nauseating in zero-G to watch the Earth spin madly as the shuttle matched the rotation of the great wheel.

My career might already be over. I might already have earned whatever mention I'll have in history. I might already be nothing but a footnote in other people's biographies, a paragraph in the history books.

Really, at this point my best strategy for beefing up my reputation is probably to be assassinated in some colorful way.

But the way things are going, I'll probably die in some tragic airlock accident while doing a routine docking at the MinCol space station.

"Stop wallowing," said Mother.

He looked at her sharply. "I'm not," he said.

"Good," she said. "Be angry at me. That's better than feeling sorry for yourself."

He wanted to snap back angrily, but he realized the futility of denying what they all knew was true. He was depressed, definitely, and yet he still had to work. Like the day of his press conference when they dragged him out of bed. He didn't want a repeat of that humiliation. He'd do his work without having to have his parents prod him like some adolescent. And he wouldn't get snippy at them when they merely told him the truth.

So he smiled at her. "Come on, Mother, you know that if I were on fire, nobody would so much as pee on me to put it out."

"Be honest, son," said his father. "There are hundreds of thousands of people back on Earth who have only to be asked. And some dozens who would do it without waiting for an invitation, if they saw an opportunity."

"There *are* some good points about fame," Peter

observed. "And those with empty bladders would probably chip in with a little spit."

"This is getting quite disgusting," said Mother.

"You say that because it's your job to say it," said Peter.

"I'm underpaid, then," said Mother. "Because it's nearly a fulltime position."

"Your role in life. So womanly. Men need civilizing, and you're just the one to do it."

"I'm obviously not very good at it."

At that moment the IF sergeant who was their flight steward came into the main cabin and told them it was time to go.

Because they docked at the center of the station, there was no gravity. They floated along, gripping handrails as the steward flipped their bags so they sailed through the airlock just under them. They were caught by a couple of orderlies who had obviously done this a hundred times, and were not the least bit impressed by having the Hegemon himself come to MinCol.

Though in all probability nobody knew who they were. They were traveling under false papers, of course, but Graff had undoubtedly let someone in the station know who they really were.

Probably not the orderlies, though.

Not until they were down one spoke of the wheel to a level where there was a definite floor to walk on did they meet anyone of real status in the station. A man in the grey suit that served MinCol as a uniform waited at the foot of the elevator, his hand outstretched. "Mr. and Mrs. Raymond," he said. "I'm Underminister Dimak. And this must be your son, Dick."

Peter smiled wanly at the faint humor in the pseudonym Graff had arbitrarily assigned to him.

"Please tell me that you know who we really are so we don't have to keep up this charade," said Peter.

"*I* know," said Dimak softly, "but nobody else on this station does, and I'd like to keep it that way for now."

"Graff isn't here?"

"The Minister of Colonization is returning from his inspection of the outfitting of the newest colony ship. We're two weeks away from first leg on that one, and starting next week you won't believe the traffic that'll come through here, sixteen shuttles a day, and that's just for the colonists. The freighters go directly to the dry dock."

"Is there," said Father innocently, "a wet dock?"

Dimak grinned. "Nautical terminology dies hard."

Dimak led them along a corridor to a down tube. They slid down the pole after him. The gravity wasn't so intense yet as to make this a problem, even for Peter's parents, who were, after all, in their forties. He helped them step out of the shaft into a lower—and therefore "heavier"—corridor.

There were old-fashioned directional stripes along the walls. "Your palm prints have already been keyed," said Dimak. "Just touch here, and it will lead you to your room."

"This is left over from the old days, isn't it?" said Father. "Though I don't imagine you were here when this was still—"

"But I *was* here," said Dimak. "I was mother to groups of new kids. Not your son, I'm afraid. But an acquaintance of yours, I believe."

Peter did not want to put himself in the pathetic position of naming off Battle School graduates he knew. Mother had no such qualms.

"Petra?" she said. "Suriyawong?"

Dimak leaned in close, so his voice would not have to be pitched loud enough that it might be overheard. "Bean," he said.

"He must have been a remarkable boy," said Mother.

"Looked like a three-year-old when he got here," said Dimak. "Nobody could believe he was old enough for this place."

"He doesn't look like that now," said Peter dryly.

"No, I . . . I know about his condition. It's not public knowledge, but Colonel Graff—the minister, I mean—he knows that I still care what happens to— well, to all my kids, of course—but this one was . . . I imagine your son's first trainer felt much the same way about him."

"I hope so," said Mother.

The sentimentality was getting so sweet Peter wanted to brush his teeth. He palmed the pad by the entrance and three strips lit up. "Green green brown," said Dimak. "But soon you won't be needing this. It's not as if there's miles of open country here to get lost in. The stripe system always assumes that you want to go back to your room, except when you touch the pad just outside the door of your room, and then it thinks you want to go to the bathroom—none inside the rooms, I'm afraid, it wasn't built that way. But if you want to go to the mess hall, just slap the pad twice and it'll know."

He showed them to their quarters, which consisted of a single long room with bunks in rows along both sides of a narrow aisle. "I'm afraid you'll have company for the week we're loading up the ship, but nobody'll be here very long, and then you'll have the place to yourself for three more weeks."

"You're doing a launch a month?" said Peter. "How, exactly, are you funding a pace like that?"

Dimak looked at him blankly. "I don't actually know," he said.

Peter leaned in close and imitated the voice Dimak used for secrets. "I'm the Hegemon," he said. "Officially, your boss works for me."

Dimak whispered back, "You save the world, we'll finance the colony program."

"I could have used a little more money for my operations, I can tell you," said Peter.

"Every Hegemon feels that way," said Dimak. "Which is why our funding doesn't come through you."

Peter laughed. "Smart move. If you think the colonization program is very very important."

"It's the future of the human race," said Dimak simply. "The Buggers—pardon me, the Formics—had the right idea. Spread out as far as you can, so you can't be wiped out in a single disastrous war. Not that it saved them, but . . . we aren't hive creatures."

"Aren't we?" said Father.

"Well, if we are, then who's the queen?" asked Dimak.

"In this place," said Father, "I suspect it's Graff."

"And we're all just his little arms and legs?"

"And mouths and . . . well, yes, of course. A little more independent and a little less obedient than the individual Formics, of course, but that's how a species comes to dominate a world the way we did, and they did. Because you know how to get a large number of individuals to give up their personal will and subject themselves to a group mind."

"So this is philosophy we're doing here," said Dimak.

"Or very cutting-edge science," said Father. "The behavior of humans in groups. Degrees of allegiance. I think about it a lot."

"How interesting."

"I see that you're not interested at all," said Father. "And that I'm now in your book as an eccentric who brings up his theories. But I never do, actually. I don't know why I did just now. I just . . . it's the first time I've been in Graff's house, so to speak. And meeting you was very much like visiting with him."

"I'm . . . flattered," said Dimak.

"John Paul," said Mother, "I do believe you're making Mr. Dimak uncomfortable."

"When people feel great allegiance to their community, they start to take on the mannerisms as well as the morals of their leader," said Father, refusing to give up.

"If their leader *has* a personality," said Peter.

"How do you get to be a leader without one?" asked Father.

"Ask Achilles," said Peter. "He's the opposite. He takes on the mannerisms of the people he wants to have follow him."

"I don't remember that one," said Dimak. "He was only here a few days before he—before we discovered he had a track record of murder back on Earth."

"Someday you have to tell me how Bean got him to confess. He won't tell."

"If he won't tell, neither will I," said Dimak.

"How loyal," said Father.

"Not really," said Dimak. "I just don't know myself. I know it had something to do with a ventilation shaft."

"That confession," said Peter. "The recordings wouldn't still be here, would they?"

"No, they wouldn't," said Dimak. "And even if they were, they're part of a sealed juvenile record."

"Of a mass murderer."

"We only notice laws when they act against our interest," said Dimak.

"See?" said Father. "We've traded philosophies."

"Like tribesmen swapping at a potlatch," said Dimak. "If you don't mind, I'd like to have you talk with Security Chief Uphanad before dinner."

"What about?"

"The colonists aren't a problem—they have a one-way flow and they can't easily communicate planet-side. But you're probably going to be recognized here. And even if you're not, it's hard to maintain a false story for long."

"Then let's not have a false story," said Peter.

"No, let's have a really good one," said Mother.

"Let's just not talk to anybody," said Father.

"Those are precisely the issues that Major Uphanad wants to discuss with you."

Once Dimak had left, they chose bunks at the back of the long room. Peter took a top bunk, of course, but while he was unloading his bags into the locker in the wall behind the bunk, Father discovered that each set of six bunks—three on each side—could be separated from the others by a privacy curtain.

"It has to be a retrofit," said Father. "I can't believe they would let the kids seal themselves off from each other."

"How soundproof is this material?" asked Mother.

Father pulled it around in a circular motion, so it irised shut with him on the other side. They heard nothing from him. Then he dilated it open.

"Well?" he asked.

"Pretty effective sound barrier," said Mother.

"You *did* try to talk to us, didn't you?" asked Peter.

"No, I was listening for you," said Father.

"Well we were listening for *you*, John Paul," said Mother.

"No, I spoke. I didn't shout, but you couldn't hear me, right?"

"Peter," said Mother, "you just got moved to the next compartment over."

"That won't work when the colonists come through."

"You can come back and sleep in Mommy's and Daddy's room when the visitors come," said Mother.

"You'll have to walk through my room in order to get to the bathroom," said Peter.

"That's right," said Father. "I know you're Hegemon and should have the best room, but then, we're not likely to walk in on you making love."

"Don't count on it," said Peter sourly.

"We'll open the door just a little and say 'knock knock' before we come through," said Mother. "It'll give you time to smuggle your best pal out of sight."

It made him faintly nauseated to be having this discussion with his parents. "You two are so cute. I'm really glad to change rooms here, believe me."

It *was* good to have solitude, once the door was closed, even if the price of it was moving all his stuff out of the locker he had just loaded and putting it in a locker in the next section. Now he got a lower bunk, for one thing. And for another thing, he didn't have to put up with listening to his parents try to cheer him up.

He had to have thinking time.

So of course he promptly fell asleep.

Dimak woke him by speaking to him over the intercom. "Mr. Raymond, are you there?"

It took Peter a split second to remember that he was supposed to be Dick Raymond. "Yes. Unless you want my father."

"Already spoke to him," said Dimak. "I've keyed the guidebars to lead you to the security department."

It was on the top level, with the lowest gravity—which made sense, because if security action were required, officers dispersing from the main office would have a downhill trip to wherever they were going.

When they stepped inside the office, Major Uphanad was there to greet them. He offered his hand to all of them.

"Are you from India?" asked Mother, "or Pakistan?"

"India," said Uphanad, not breaking his smile at all.

"I'm so sorry for your country," said Mother.

"I haven't been back there since—in a long time."

"I hope your family is faring well under the Chinese occupation."

"Thank you for your concern," said Uphanad, in a tone of voice that made it clear this topic was finished.

He offered them chairs and sat down himself—behind his desk, taking full advantage of his official position. Peter resented it a little, since he had spent a good while now as the man who was always in the dominant place. He might not have had much actual power, as Hegemon, but protocol always gave him the highest place.

But he was not supposed to be known here. So he could hardly be treated differently from any civilian visitor.

"I know that you are particular guests of the Minister," said Uphanad, "and that you wish your privacy to be undisturbed. What we need to discuss is the boundary of your privacy. Are your faces likely to be recognized?"

"Possibly," said Peter. "Especially his." He pointed to his father. This was a lie, of course, and probably futile, but . . .

"Ah," said Uphanad. "And I assume your real names would be recognized."

"Likely," said Father.

"Certainly," said Mother, as if she were proud of the fact and rather miffed that he had cast any doubt on it at all.

"So . . . should meals be brought to you? Do we need to clear the corridors when you go to the bathroom?"

Sounded like a nightmare to Peter.

"Major Uphanad, we don't want to advertise our presence here, but I'm sure your staff can be trusted to be discreet."

"On the contrary," said Uphanad. "Discreet people make it a point not to take the staff's loyalty for granted."

"Including yours?" asked Mother sweetly.

"Since you have already lied to me repeatedly," said Uphanad, "I think it safe to say that you are taking no one's loyalty for granted."

"Nevertheless," said Peter, "I'm not going to stay cooped up in that tube. I'd like to be able to use your library—I'm assuming you have one—and we can take our meals in the mess hall and use the toilet without inconveniencing others."

"There, you see?" said Uphanad. "You are simply not security minded."

"We can't live here as prisoners," said Peter.

"He didn't mean that," said Father. "He was talking

about the way you simply announced the decision for the three of us. So much for *me* being the one most likely to be recognized."

Uphanad smiled. "The recognition problem is a real one," he said. "I knew you at once, from the vids, Mr. Hegemon."

Peter sighed and leaned back.

"Your face is not as recognizable as if you were an actual politician," said Uphanad. "They thrive on putting their faces before the public. Your career began, if I remember correctly, in anonymity."

"But I've been on the vids," said Peter.

"Listen," said Uphanad. "Few on our staff even watch the vids. I happen to be a news addict, but most people here have rather cut their ties with the gossip of Earth. I think your best way to remain under cover here is to behave as if you had nothing to hide. Be a bit standoffish—don't get into conversations with people that lead to mutual explanations of what you do and who you are, for instance. But if you're cheerful and don't act mysterious, you should be fine. People won't expect to see the Hegemon living with his parents in one of the bunk rooms here." Uphanad grinned. "It will be our little secret, the six of us."

Peter did the count. Him, his parents, Uphanad, Dimak, and . . . oh, Graff, of course.

"I think there will be no assassination attempt here," said Uphanad, "because there are very few weapons on board, all are kept under lock and key, and everybody coming up here is scanned for weaponry. So I suggest you not attempt to carry sidearms. You are trained in hand-to-hand combat?"

"No," said Peter.

"There is a gym on the bottom level, very well equipped. And not just with childsize devices, either.

The adults also need to stay fit. You should use the facility to maintain your bone mass, and so forth, but also we can arrange martial arts classes for you, if you're interested."

"I'm not interested," said Peter. "But it sounds like a good idea."

"Anyone they send against us, though," said Mother, "will be very much better trained in it than we will."

"Perhaps so, perhaps not," said Uphanad. "If your enemies attempt to get to you here, they will have to rely on someone they can get through our screening. People who seem particularly athletic are subjected to special scrutiny. We are, you see, paranoid about one of the anti-colonization groups getting someone up here just to perform an act of sabotage or terrorism."

"Or assassination."

"You see?" said Uphanad. "But I assure you I and my staff are very thorough. We never leave anything unchecked."

"In other words, you knew who we were before we walked in the door."

"Before your shuttle took off, actually," said Uphanad. "Or at least I had a fairly good guess."

They said their good-byes, then settled into the routine of life in a space station.

Day and night were kept on Florida time, for no particular reason but that it was at zero longitude and they had to pick *some* time. Peter found that his parents were not so awfully intrusive as he had feared, and he was relieved that he could not hear their love-making *or* their conversations about him through the divider.

What he did, mostly, was go to the library and write.

Essays, of course, on everything, for every conceivable forum. There were plenty of publications that were happy to have pieces from Locke or Demosthenes, especially now that everyone knew these identities belonged to the Hegemon. With most serious work appearing first on the nets, there was no way to target particular audiences. But he still talked about subjects that would have particular interest in various regions.

The aim of everything he wrote was to fan the flames of suspicion of China and Chinese ambitions. As Demosthenes, he wrote quite directly about the danger of allowing the conquest of India and Indochina to stand, with a lot of who's-next rhetoric. Of course he couldn't stoop to any serious rabble-rousing, because every word he said would be held against the Hegemon.

Life was so much easier when he was anonymous on the nets.

As Locke, however, he wrote statesmanlike, impartial essays about problems that different nations and regions were facing. "Locke" almost never wrote against China directly, but rather took it for granted that there would be another invasion, and that long-term investments in probable target countries might be unwise, that sort of thing.

It was hard work, because every essay had to be made interesting, original, important, or no one would pay attention to it. He had to make sure he never sounded like someone riding a hobby horse—rather the way Father had sounded when he started spouting off about his theories of group loyalty and character to Dimak. Though, to be fair, he'd never heard Father do that before, it still gave him pause and made him realize how easily Locke and Demosthenes—and therefore Peter Wiggin himself—could become at first an irritant, at last a laughingstock.

Father called this process stassenization and made various suggestions for essay topics, some of which Peter used. As to what Father and Mother did with their days, when they weren't reading his essays and commenting on them, catching errors, that sort of thing—well, Peter had no idea.

Maybe Mother had found somebody's room to clean.

———

Graff stopped in for a brief visit on their first morning there, but then was off again—returned to Earth, in fact, on the shuttle that had brought them. He did not return for three weeks, by which time Peter had written nearly forty essays, all of which had been published in various places. Most of them were Locke's essays. And, as usual, most of the attention went to Demosthenes.

When Graff returned, he invited them to dine with him in the Minister's quarters, and they had a convivial dinner during which nothing important was discussed. Whenever the subject seemed to be turning to a matter of real moment, Graff would interrupt with the pouring of water or a joke of some kind—only rarely the funny kind.

This puzzled Peter, because surely Graff could count on his own quarters being secure. But apparently not, because after dinner he invited them on a walk, leading them quickly out of the regular corridors and into some of the service passages. They were lost almost at once, and when Graff finally opened a door and took them onto a wide ledge overlooking a ventilation shaft, they had lost all sense of direction except, of course, where "down" was.

The ventilation shaft led "down" . . . a very long way.

"This is a place of some historical importance," said Graff. "Though few of us know it."

"Ah," said Father knowingly.

And because he had guessed it, Peter realized it should be guessable, and so he guessed. "Achilles was here," he said.

"This," said Graff, "is where Bean and his friends tricked Achilles. Achilles thought he was going to be able to kill Bean here, but instead Bean got him in chains, hanging in the shaft. He could have killed Achilles. His friends recommended it."

"Who were the friends?" asked Mother.

"He never told me, but that's not surprising—I never asked. I thought it would be wiser if there were never any kind of record, even inside my head, of which other children were there to witness Achilles's humiliation and helplessness."

"It wouldn't have mattered, if he had simply killed Achilles. There would have been no murders."

"But, you see," said Graff, "if Achilles had died, then I *would* have had to ask those names, and Bean could not have been allowed to remain in Battle School. We might have lost the war because of that, because Ender relied on Bean quite heavily."

"You let Ender stay after he killed a boy," said Peter.

"The boy died accidentally," said Graff, "as Ender defended himself."

"Defended himself because you left him alone," said Mother.

"I've already faced trial on those charges, and I was acquitted."

"But you were asked to resign your commission," said Mother.

"But I was then given this much higher position as Minister of Colonization. Let's not quibble over the past. Bean got Achilles here, not to kill him, but to induce him to confess. He did confess, very convincingly, and because I heard him do it, I'm on his death list, too."

"Then why are you still alive?" asked Peter.

"Because, contrary to widespread belief, Achilles is not a genius and he makes mistakes. His reach is not infinite and his power can be blocked. He doesn't know everything. He doesn't have everything planned. I think half the time he's winging it, putting himself in the way of opportunity and seizing it when he sees it."

"If he's not a genius, then why does he keep beating geniuses?" asked Peter.

"Because he does the unexpected," said Graff. "He doesn't actually do things remarkably well, he simply does things that no one thought he would do. He stays a jump ahead. And our finest minds were not even thinking about him when he brought off his most spectacular successes. They thought they were civilians again when he had them kidnapped. Bean wasn't trying to oppose Achilles's plans during the war, he was trying to find and rescue Petra. You see? I have Achilles's test scores. He's a champion suckup, and he's very smart or he wouldn't have got here. He knew how to ace a psych test, for instance, so that his violent tendencies remained hidden from us when we chose him to come in the last group we brought to Battle School. He's dangerous, in other words. But he's never had to face an opponent, not really. What the Formics faced, he's never had to face."

"So you're confident," said Peter.

"Not at all," said Graff. "But I'm hopeful."

"You brought us here just to show us this place?" said Father.

"Actually, no. I brought you here because I came up earlier in the day and swept it personally for eavesdropping devices. Plus, I installed a sound damper here, so that our voices are not carrying down the ventilation shaft."

"You think MinCol has been penetrated," said Peter.

"I know it has," said Graff. "Uphanad was doing his routine scan of the logs of outgoing messages, and he found an odd one that was sent within hours of your arrival here. The entire message consisted of the single word *on.* Uphanad's routine scan, of course, is more thorough than most people's desperate search. He found this one simply by looking for anomalies in message length, language patterns, etc. To find codes, you see."

"And this was in code?" asked Father.

"Not a cipher, no. And impossible to decode for that reason. It could simply mean 'affirmative,' as in 'the mission is on.' It might be a foreign word—there are several dozen common languages in which 'on' has meaning by itself. It might be 'no' backward. You see the problem? What alerted Uphanad, besides its brevity, was the fact that it was sent within hours of your arrival—*after* your arrival—and both the sender and the receiver of the message were anonymous."

"How could the sender be anonymous from a secure military-designed facility?" asked Peter.

"Oh, it's quite simple, really," said Graff. "The sender used someone else's sign-on."

"Whose?"

"Uphanad was quite embarrassed when he showed me the printout of the message. Because as far as the computer was concerned, it was sent by Uphanad himself."

"Someone got the log-on of the head of security?" said Father.

"Humiliating, you may be sure," said Graff.

"You've fired him?" asked Mother.

"That would not make us *more* secure, to lose the man who is our best defense against whatever operation that message triggered."

"So you think it *is* the English word 'on' and it means somebody is preparing to move against us."

"I think that's not unlikely. I think the message was sent in the clear. It's only undecipherable because we don't know *what* is 'on.'"

"And you've taken into account," said Mother, "the possibility that Uphanad actually sent this message himself, and is using the fact that he told you about it as cover for the fact that he's the perpetrator."

Graff looked at her a long time, blinked, and then smiled. "I was telling myself, 'suspect everybody,' but now I know what a truly suspicious person is."

Peter hadn't thought of it either. But now it made perfect sense.

"Still, let's not leap to conclusions, either," said Graff. "The real sender of the message might have used Major Uphanad's sign-on precisely so that the chief of security would be our prime suspect."

"How long ago did he find this message?" asked Father.

"A couple of days," said Graff. "I was already

scheduled to come, so I stuck to my schedule."

"No warnings?"

"No," said Graff. "Any departure from routine would let the sender know his signal was discovered and perhaps interpreted. It would lead him to change his plans."

"So what do we do?" asked Peter.

"First," said Graff, "I apologize for thinking you'd be perfectly safe here. Apparently Achilles's reach— or perhaps China's—is longer than we thought."

"So do we go home?" asked Father.

"Second," said Graff, "we can't do anything that would play into their hands. Going home right now, before the threat can be identified and neutralized, would expose you to greater danger. Our betrayer could give another signal that would tell them when and where you were going to arrive on Earth. What your trajectory of descent is going to be. That sort of thing."

"Who would risk killing the Hegemon by downing a shuttle?" said Peter. "The world would be outraged, even the people who'd be happy to see me dead."

"Anything we do that changes our pattern would let the traitor know his signal was intercepted. It might rush the project, whatever it is, before we're ready. No, I'm sorry to say this, but . . . our best course of action is to wait."

"And what if we disagree?" said Peter.

"Then I'll send you home on the shuttle of your choosing, and pray for you all the way down."

"You'd let us go?"

"You're my guest," said Graff. "Not my prisoner."

"Then let's test it," said Peter. "We're leaving on the next shuttle. The one that brought you—when it goes back, we'll be on it."

"Too soon," said Graff. "We have no time to prepare."

"And neither does he. I suggest," said Peter, "that you go to Uphanad and make sure he knows that he has to put a complete blanket of secrecy on our imminent departure. He's not even to tell Dimak."

"But if he's the one," said Mother, "then—"

"Then he can't send a signal," said Peter. "Unless he can find a way to let the information slip out and become public knowledge on the station. That's why it's vital, Minister Graff, that you remain with him at all times after you tell him. So if it's him, he *can't* send the signal."

"But it's probably not him," said Graff, "and now you've let everybody know."

"But now we'll be watching for the outgoing message."

"Unless they simply kill you as you're boarding the shuttle."

"Then our worries will be over," said Peter. "But I think they won't kill us here, because this agent of theirs is too useful to them—or to Achilles, depending on whose man he is—for them to use him up completely on this operation."

Graff pondered this. "So we watch to see who might be sending the message—"

"And you have agents stationed at the landing point on Earth to see if they can spot a would-be assassin."

"I can do that," said Graff. "One tiny problem, though."

"What's that?" said Peter.

"You can't go."

"Why can't I?" said Peter.

"Because your one-man propaganda campaign is working. The people who read your stuff have drifted more strongly into the anti-China camp. It's still a fairly slight movement, but it's real."

"I can write my essays there," said Peter.

"In danger of being killed at any moment," said Graff.

"That could happen here, too," said Peter.

"Well—but you yourself said it was unlikely."

"Let's catch the mole who's working your station," said Peter, "and send him home. Meanwhile, we're heading for Earth. It's been great being here, Minister Graff. But we've got to go."

He looked at his mother and father.

"Absolutely," said Father.

"Do you think," said Mother, "that when we get back to Earth we can find a place with little tiny beds like these?" She clung more tightly to Father's arms. "It's made us so much closer as a family."

15

WAR PLANS

From: Demosthenes%Tecumseh@freeamerica.org
To: DropBox%Feijoada@IComeAnon.net
Re: *******************
    Encrypted using code ********
    Decrypted using code ***********

I spend half my memory capacity just holding on to whatever online identity you're using from week to week. Why not rely on encryption? Nobody's broken hyperprime encryption yet.

Here it is, Bean: Those stones in India? Virlomi started it, of course. Got a message from her: >Now you are not in cesspool, can communicate again. Have no email here. Stones are >mine. Back on bridge soon. War in earnest. Post to me only, this site, pickup name >BridgeGirl password not stepstool.

At least I think that's what "stones are mine" means. And what does "password not stepstool" mean? That the password is "not stepstool"? Or that the password is not "stepstool," in which case it's probably not "aardvark," either, but how does that help?

Anyway, I think she's offering to begin war in earnest inside India. She can't possibly have a nationwide network, but then, maybe she doesn't need one. She was certainly enough in tune with the Indian people to get them all piling stones in the road. And now the whole stone wall business has taken off. Lots of skirmishes between angry hungry citizens and Chinese soldiers. Trucks hijacked. Sabotage of Chinese offices proceeding apace. What can she do more than is already happening?

Given where you are, you may have more need of her information and/or help than I do. But I'd appreciate your help understanding the parts of the message that are opaque to me.

    From: LostIboBoy%Navy@IComeAnon.net
    To: Demosthenes%Tecumseh@freeamerica.org
    Re: >blank<
      Encrypted using code * * * * * * * *
      Decrypted using code * * * * * * * * * *

Here's why I keep changing identities. First, they don't have to decrypt the message to get information if they see patterns in our correspondence—it would be useful for them to know the frequency and timing of our correspondence and the length of our messages. Second, they don't have to decrypt the whole message, they only have to guess our encrypt and decrypt codes. Which I bet you have written down somewhere because you don't actually care whether I get killed because you're too lazy to memorize.

Of course I mean that in the nicest possible way, O right honorable Mr. Hegemon.

Here's what Virlomi meant. Obviously she intended that you not be able to understand the message and correspond with her properly unless you talked to me or Suri. That means she doesn't trust you completely. My guess is that if you wrote to her and left a message using the password "not stepstool," she'd know that you hadn't talked to me. (You don't know how tempting it was just to leave you with that guess.)

When we picked her up from that bridge near the Burmese border, she boarded the chopper by stepping on Suriyawong's back as he lay prostrate before her. The password is not stepstool, it's the real name of her stepstool. And she's going to be back at that bridge, which means she's made her way across India to the Burmese border, where she'll be in a position to disrupt Chinese supply of their troops in India—or, conversely, Chinese attempts to move their troops out of India and back into China or Indochina.

Of course she's only going to be at one bridge. But my guess is that she's already setting up guerrilla groups that are getting ready to disrupt traffic on the other roads between Burma and India, with a strong possibility that she's set up something along the Himalayan border as well. I doubt she can seal the borders, but she can slow and harass their passage, tying up troops trying to protect supply lines and making the Chinese less able to mount offensives or keep their troops supplied with ammunition— always a problem for them.

Personally, I think you should tell her not to tip her hand too soon. I may be able to tell you when to post a reply asking her to start in earnest on a particular date. And no, I won't post myself because I am most certainly watched here, and I don't want them to know about her directly. I've already caught two snoopware intrusions on my desk, which cost me twenty minutes each time, scrambling them so they send back false information to the snoops. Encrypted email like this I can send, but messages posted to dead drops can be picked up by snoopware on the local net.

And yes, these are indeed my friends. But they'd be fools not to keep track of what I'm sending out—if they can.

Bean measured himself in the mirror. He still looked like himself, more or less. But he didn't like the way his head was growing. Larger in proportion to his body. Growing faster.

I should be getting smarter, shouldn't I? More brain space and all?

Instead I'm worrying about what will happen when my head gets too big, my skull and brains too heavy for my neck to hold the whole assemblage in a vertical position.

He measured himself against the coat closet, too. Not all that long ago, he had to stand on tiptoe to reach coat hangers. Then it became easy. Now he was reaching a bit downward from shoulder height.

Door frames were not a problem yet. But he was beginning to feel as though he should duck.

Why should his growth be accelerating now? He already hit the puberty rush.

Petra staggered past him, went into the bathroom, and puked up nothing for about five agonizing minutes.

"They should have drugs for that," he told her afterward.

"They do," said Petra. "But nobody knows how they might affect the baby."

"There've been no studies? Impossible."

"No studies on how they might affect *your* children."

"Anton's Key is just a couple of code spots on the genome."

"Genes often do double and triple duty, or more."

"And the baby probably doesn't even have Anton's Key. And it's not healthy for the baby if you can't keep any food down."

"This won't last forever," said Petra. "And I'll get fed intravenously if I have to. I'm not doing anything to endanger this baby, Bean. Sorry if my puking ruins your appetite for breakfast."

"Nothing ruins my appetite for breakfast," said Bean. "I'm a growing boy."

She retched again.

"Sorry," said Bean.

"I don't do this," she whispered miserably, "because your jokes are so bad."

"No," said Bean. "It's cause my genes are."

She retched again and he left the room, feeling guilty about leaving, but knowing he'd be useless if he stayed. She wasn't one of those people who need petting when they're sick. She preferred to be left alone in her misery. It was one of the ways they were alike. Sort of like injured animals that slink off into the woods to get better—or die—alone.

Alai was waiting for him in the large conference room. Chairs were gathered around a large holo on the floor, where a map was being projected of the terrain and militarily significant roads of India and western China.

By now the others were used to seeing Bean there,

though there were some who still didn't like it. But the Caliph wanted him there, the Caliph trusted him.

They watched as the known locations of Chinese garrison troops were brought up in blue, and then the probable locations of mobile forces and reserves in green. When he first saw this map, Bean made the faux pas of asking where they were getting their information. He was informed, quite coldly, that both Persia and the Israeli-Egyptian consortium had active satellite placement programs, and their spy satellites were the best in orbit. "We can get the blood type of individual enemy soldiers," said Alai with a smile. An exaggeration, of course. But then Bean wondered—some kind of spectroanalysis of their sweat?

Not possible. Alai was joking, not boasting.

Now, Bean trusted their information as much as they did—because of course he had made discreet inquiries through Peter and through some of his own connections. Putting together what Vlad could tell him from Russian intelligence and what Crazy Tom was giving him from England, plus Peter's American sources, it was clear that the Muslims—the Crescent League—had everything the others had. And more.

The plan was simple. Massive troop movements along the border between India and Pakistan, bringing Iranian troops up to the front. This should draw a strong Chinese response, with their troops also concentrated along that border.

Meanwhile, Turkic forces were already in place on, and sometimes inside, China's western border, having traveled over the past few months in disguise as nomads. On paper, the western region of China looked like ideal country for tanks and trucks, but in reality, fuel supply lines would be a recurring nightmare. So the first wave of Turks would enter as cavalry, switching to mechanized transport only when they were in a position to steal and use Chinese equipment.

This was the most dangerous aspect of the plan, Bean knew. The Turkic armies, combining forces from the Hellespont to the Aral Sea and the foothills of the Himalayas, were equipped like raiders, yet had to do the job of an invading army. They had a couple of advantages that might compensate for their lack of armor and air support. Having no supply lines meant the Chinese wouldn't have anything to bomb at first. The native people of the western China province of Xinjiang were Turkic too, and like the Tibetans, they had never stopped seething under the rule of Han China.

Above all, the Turks would have surprise and numbers on their side during the crucial first days. The Chinese garrison troops were all massed on the border with Russia. Until those forces could be moved, the Turks should have an easy time, striking anywhere they wanted, taking out police and supply stations—and, with luck, every airfield in Xinjiang.

By the time Chinese troops moved off the Russian border and into the interior to deal with the Turks, the fully mechanized Turkish troops would be entering China from the west. Now there would be supply lines to attack, but deprived of their forward air bases, and forced to face Turkish fighters which would now be using them, China would not have clear air superiority.

Taking underdefended air bases with cavalry was just the sort of touch Bean would have expected from Alai. They could only hope that Han Tzu would not anticipate Alai having complete authority over the inevitable Muslim move, for the Chinese would have to be crazy not to be planning to defend against a Muslim invasion.

At some point, it was hoped that the Turks would do well enough that the Chinese would be forced to begin shifting troops from India north into Xinjiang. Here the terrain favored Alai's plan, for while some Chinese troops could be airlifted over the Tibetan Himalayas, the Tibetan roads would be disrupted by Turkic demolition teams, and the Chinese troops would all have to be moved eastward from India, around the Himalayas, and into western China from the east rather than the south.

It would take days, and when the Muslims believed that the maximum number of Chinese troops were in transit, where they could not fight anybody, they would launch the massive invasion over the border between Pakistan and India.

So much depended on what the Chinese believed. At first, the Chinese had to believe that the real assault would come from Pakistan, so that the main Chinese force would remain tied up on that frontier. Then, at a crucial point several days into the Turkic operation, the Chinese had to be convinced that the Turkic front was, in fact, the real invasion. They had to be so convinced of this that they would withdraw troops from India, weakening their forces there.

How else does an inexperienced three-million-man army defeat an army of ten million veterans?

They went through contingency plans for the several days following the commitment of Muslim troops in Pakistan, but Bean knew, as did Alai, that nothing that happened after the Muslim troops began crossing the Indian border could be predicted. They had plans in case the invasion failed utterly, and Pakistan had to be protected at fallback positions well inside the

Pakistani border. They had plans for dealing with a complete rout of the Chinese forces—not likely, as they knew. But in the most likely scenario—a difficult back-and-forth battle across a thousand-mile front—plans would have to be improvised to take advantage of every turn of events.

"So," said Alai. "That is the plan. Any comments?"

Around the circle, one officer after another voiced his measured confidence. This was not because they were all yes-men, but because Alai had already listened carefully to the objections they raised before and had altered the plans to deal with those he thought were serious problems.

Only one of the Muslims offered any objection today, and it was the one nonmilitary man, Lankowski, whose role, as best Bean could tell, was halfway between minister-without-portfolio and chaplain. "I think it is a shame," he said, "that our plans are so dependent upon what Russia chooses to do."

Bean knew what he meant. Russia was completely unpredictable in this situation. On the one hand, the Warsaw Pact had a treaty with China that had secured China's long northern border with Russia, freeing them to conquer India in the first place. On the other hand, the Russians and Chinese had been rivals in this region for centuries, and each believed the other held territory that was rightfully theirs.

And there were unpredictable personal issues as well. How many loyal servants of Achilles were still in positions of trust and authority in Russia? At the same time, many Russians were furious at how they had been used by him before he went to India and then China.

Yet Achilles brokered the secret treaty between

Russia and China, so he couldn't be all that detested, could he?

But what was that treaty really worth? Every Russian schoolchild knew that the stupidest Russian tsar of them all had been Stalin, because he made a treaty with Hitler's Germany and then expected it to be kept. Surely the Russians did not really believe China would stay at peace with them forever.

So there was always the chance that Russia, seeing China at a disadvantage, would join the fray. The Russians would see it as a chance to seize territory and to preempt the inevitable Chinese betrayal of them.

That would be a good thing, if the Russians attacked in force but were not terribly successful. It would bleed Chinese troops from the battle against the Muslims. But it would be a very bad thing if Russia did too well or too badly. Too well, and they might slice down through Mongolia and seize Beijing. Then the Muslim victory would become a Russian one. Alai did not want to have Russia in a dominant role in the peace negotiations.

And if Russia entered the war but lost quickly, Chinese troops would not have to watch the Russian border. Free to move, those garrison troops might be hurled against the Turks, or they might be sent through Russian territory to strike into Kazakhstan, threatening to cut off Turkish supply lines.

That was why Alai had expressed his hope that the Russians would be too surprised to do anything at all.

"There's no helping it," said Alai. "We have done all we can do. What Russia does is in the hands of God."

"May I speak?" said Bean.

Alai nodded. All eyes turned to him. At previous

meetings, Bean had said nothing, preferring to talk
with Alai in private, where he did not risk committing
an error in the way he spoke to the Caliph.

"When you have committed to battle," said Bean,
"I believe I can use my own contacts, and persuade
the Hegemon to use his, to urge Russia to pursue
whatever course you think most advisable."

Several of the men shifted uncomfortably in their
chairs.

"Please reassure my worried friends here," said
Alai, "that you have not already been in discussion
with the Hegemon or anyone else about our plans."

"The opposite is true," said Bean. "You are the
ones who are preparing to take action. I have been
providing you with all the information I learned from
them. But I know these people, and what they can
do. The Hegemon has no armies, but he does have
great influence on world opinion. Of course he will
speak in favor of your action. But he also has influence inside Russia, which he could use either to urge
intervention, or to argue against it. My friends, also."

Bean knew that Alai knew that the only friend
worth mentioning was Vlad, and Vlad had been the
only one of the kidnapped members of Ender's jeesh
to join with Achilles and take his side. Whether that
had been because he had truly become a follower of
Achilles or because he thought Achilles was acting in
the interest of Mother Russia, Bean still had not figured out. Vlad provided him with information sometimes, but Bean always looked for a second source
before he fully trusted it.

"Then I will tell you this," said Alai. "Today I
don't know what would be more useful, for Russia to
join in the attack or for Russia to stand by doing
nothing. As long as they don't attack *us*, I'll be con-

tent. But as events unfold, the picture may become clearer."

Bean did not need to point out to Alai that Russia would not enter the war to rescue a failing Muslim invasion—only if the Russians scented victory would they put their own forces at risk. So if Alai waited too long to ask for help, it would not come.

They took a break for the noon meal, but it was very brief, and when they returned to the conference room, the map had changed. There was a third part of the plan, and Bean knew that this was the one that Alai was least certain about.

For months now, Arab armies from Egypt, Iraq, and every other Arab nation had been transported on oil tankers from Arab ports to Indonesia. The Indonesian navy was one of the most formidable in the world, and its carrier-based air force was the only one in the region that rivaled the Chinese in equipment and armament. Everyone knew that it was because of the Indonesian umbrella that the Chinese had not taken Singapore or ventured into the Philippines.

Now it was proposed that the Indonesian navy be used to transport a combined Arab-Indonesian army to effect a landing in Thailand or Vietnam. Both nations were filled with people who longed for deliverance from the Chinese conquerors.

When the plans for the two possible landing sites had been fully laid out, Alai did not ask for criticisms—he had his own. "I think in both cases, our plans for the landing are excellent. My misgiving is the same one I've had all along. There is no serious military objective there to be achieved. The Chinese can afford to lose battle after battle there, using only their available forces, retreating farther and farther, while waiting to see the outcome of the real war. I think the soldiers we sent there would risk dying for no good purpose. It's too much like the Italian campaign in World War II. Long, slow, costly, and ineffective, even if we win every battle."

The Indonesian commander bowed his head. "I am grateful for the Caliph's concern for the lives of our soldiers. But the Muslims of Indonesia could not bear to stand by while their brothers fight. If these objectives are meaningless, find us something meaningful to do."

One of the Arab officers added his agreement. "We've committed our troops to this operation. Is it too late, then, to bring them back and let them join with the Pakistanis and Iranians in the liberation of India? Their numbers might make a crucial difference there."

"The time draws close for the weather to be at its best for our purposes," said Alai. "There's no time to bring back the Arab armies. But I can see no value in sending soldiers into battle for no better reason than solidarity, or delaying the invasion in order to bring the Arab armies into a different theater of war. If it was a mistake to send them to Indonesia, the mistake is my own."

They murmured their disagreement. They could not agree with blaming the Caliph for any mistakes. At the same time, Bean knew that they appreciated knowing they were led by a man who did not blame others. It was part of the reason they loved him.

Alai spoke over their objections. "I have not decided yet whether to launch the third front. But if we do launch it, then the objective we should plan for is Thailand, not Vietnam. I realize the risks of leaving the fleet exposed for a longer time at sea—we will have to count on the Indonesian pilots to protect their ships. I choose Thailand because it is a more coherent country, with terrain more suitable for a swift conquest. In Vietnam, we would have to fight for every inch of territory, and our progress would look slow on the map—the Chinese would feel safe. In Thailand, our progress will look very quick and dangerous. As long as they forget that Thailand is not important to them in the overall war, it might cause them to send troops there to oppose us."

After a few more niceties, the meeting ended. One thing that no one mentioned was the actual date of the invasion. Bean was sure that one had been chosen and that everyone in the room but him knew what it was. He accepted that—it was the one piece of information which he had no need to know, and the most crucial one to withhold from him if he could not be trusted after all.

Back in their room, Bean found Petra asleep. He sat down and used his desk to access his email and check a few sites on the nets. He was interrupted by a light knock on the door. Petra was instantly awake— pregnant or not, she still slept like a soldier—and she was at the door before Bean could shut down his connection and step away from the table.

Lankowski stood there, looking apologetic and regal, a combination that only he could have mastered. "If you will forgive me," he said, "our mutual friend wishes to speak with you in the garden."

"Both of us?" asked Petra.

"Please, unless you are too ill."

Soon they were seated on the bench beside Alai's garden throne—though of course he never called it that, referring to it only as a chair.

"I'm sorry, Petra, that I couldn't bring you into the meeting. Our Crescent League is not recidivist, but it would make some of them too uncomfortable to have a woman present at such meetings."

"Alai, do you think I don't know that?" she said. "You have to deal with the culture around you."

"I assume that Bean has acquainted you with our plans?"

"I was asleep when he returned to the room," said Petra, "so anything that's changed since last time, I don't know."

"I'm sorry, then, but perhaps you can pick up what's happening from the context. Because I know Bean has something to say and he didn't say it yet."

"I saw no flaw in your plans," said Bean. "I think you've done everything that could possibly be done, including being smart enough not to think you can plan what will happen once battle has been joined in India."

"But such praise is not what I saw on your face," said Alai.

"I didn't think my face was readable," said Bean.

"It isn't," said Alai. "That's why I'm asking you."

"We've received an offer that I think you'll be glad of," said Bean.

"From?"

"I don't know if you ever knew Virlomi," said Bean.

"Battle School?"

"Yes."

"Before my time, I think. I was a young boy and paid no attention to girls anyway." He smiled at Petra.

"Weren't we all," said Bean. "Virlomi was the one who made it possible for me and Suriyawong to retrieve Petra from Hyderabad and save the Indian Battle School graduates from being slaughtered by Achilles."

"She has my admiration, then," said Alai.

"She's back in India. All that building of stone obstacles, the so-called Great Wall of India—apparently she's the one who started that."

Now Alai's interest looked like more than mere politeness.

"Peter received a message from her. She has no idea about you and what you're doing, and neither does Peter, but she sent the message in language that he couldn't understand without conferring with me— a very careful and wise thing for her to do, I think."

They exchanged smiles.

"She is in place in the area of a bridge spanning one of the roads between India and Burma. She may be able to disrupt one, many, or even all of the major roads leading between India and China."

Alai nodded.

"It would be a disaster, of course," said Bean, "if she acted on her own and cut the roads before the Chinese are able to move any troops out of India. In other words, if she thinks the real invasion is the Turkish one, then she might think her most helpful role would be to keep Chinese troops *in* India. Ideally, what she would do is wait until they start trying to move troops *back* into India, and *then* cut the roads, keeping them out."

"But if we tell her," said Alai, "and the message is . . . intercepted, then the Chinese will know that the Turkic operation is not the main effort."

"Well, that's why I didn't want to bring this up in front of the others. I can tell you that I believe communication between her and Peter, and between Peter and me, is secure. I believe that Peter is desperate for your invasion to succeed, and Virlomi will be too, and they will not tell anyone anything that would compromise it. But it's your call."

"Peter is desperate for our invasion to succeed?" asked Alai.

"Alai, the man's not stupid. I didn't have to tell him about your plans or even that you *had* plans. He knows that you're here, in seclusion, and he has satellite reports of the troop movements to the Indian frontier. He hasn't discussed it with me, but I wouldn't be at all surprised if he also knew about the Arab presence in Indonesia—that's the kind of thing he always finds out about because he has contacts everywhere."

"Sorry to suspect you," said Alai, "but I'd be remiss if I didn't."

"Think about Virlomi, anyway," said Bean. "It would be tragic if, in her effort to help, she actually hindered your plan."

"But that's not all you wanted to say," said Alai.

"No," said Bean, and he hesitated.

"Go on."

"Your reason for not wanting to open the third front was a sound one," said Bean. "Not wanting to waste lives taking militarily unimportant objectives."

"So you think I shouldn't use that force at all," said Alai.

"No," said Bean. "I think you need to be bolder with them. I think you need to waste more lives on an even more spectacular nonmilitary objective."

Alai turned away. "I was afraid you'd see that."

"I was sure you'd already thought of it."

"I was hoping one of the Arabs or the Indonesians themselves would propose it," said Alai.

"Propose what?" asked Petra.

"The military goal," said Bean, "is to destroy their

armies, which is done by attacking them with superior force, achieving surprise, and cutting off their supply and escape routes. Nothing you do with the third front can achieve any of those objectives."

"I know," said Alai.

"China isn't a democracy. The government doesn't have to win elections. But they need the support of their people all the more because of that."

Petra sighed her understanding. "Invade China itself."

"There is no hope of success in such an invasion," said Alai. "On the other fronts, we will have a citizenry that welcomes us and cooperates with us, while obstructing them. In China, the opposite would be true. Their air force would be working from nearby airfields and could fly sortie after sortie between each wave of our planes. The potential for disaster would be very great."

"Plan for disaster," said Bean. "Begin with disaster."

"You're too subtle for me," said Alai.

"What's disaster in this case? Besides actually getting stopped at the beach—not likely, since China has one of the most invisible shorelines in the world—a disaster is for your force to be dispersed, cut off from supply, and operating without coordinating central control."

"Land them," said Alai, "and have them immediately begin a guerrilla campaign? But they won't have the support of the people."

"I thought about this a lot," said Bean. "The Chinese people are used to oppression—when have they not been oppressed?—but they've never become reconciled to it. Think how many peasant revolts there've been—and against governments far more benign than this one. Now, if your soldiers go into China like Sherman's march to the sea, they'll be opposed at every step."

"But they have to live off the land, if they're cut off from supply," said Alai.

"Strictly disciplined troops can make this work," said Bean. "But this will be hard for the Indonesians, given the way the Chinese have always been regarded within Indonesia itself."

"Trust me to control my troops."

"Then here's what they do. In every village they come to, they take half the food—but only half. They make a big point of leaving the rest, and you tell them it's because Allah did not send you to make war against the Chinese people. If you had to kill anybody to get control of the village, apologize to the family or to the whole village, if it was a soldier who died. Be the nicest invaders they've ever imagined."

"Oh," said Alai. "That's asking a lot, from mere discipline."

Petra was getting the vision of this. "Maybe if you quote to your soldiers that passage from The Elevated Places, where it says, 'Maybe your Lord will destroy your enemy and make you rulers in the land. Then He will see how you act.' "

Alai looked at her in genuine consternation. "*You* quote the Q'uran to *me?*"

"I thought the verse was appropriate," she said. "Isn't that why you had them put it in my room? So I'd read it?"

Alai shook his head. "Lankowski gave you the Q'uran."

"And she read it," added Bean. "We're both surprised."

"It's a good passage to use," said Alai. "Maybe

God will make us rulers in China. Let's show from the start that we can do it justly and righteously."

"The best part of the plan," said Bean, "is that the Chinese soldiers will come right afterward, and fearing that their own armies will be left without supplies, or in the effort to deprive your army of further provender, *they* will probably seize all the rest of the food."

Alai nodded, smiled, then laughed. "Our invading army leaves the Chinese people enough to eat, but the Chinese army makes them starve."

"The likelihood of a public relations victory is very high," said Bean.

"And meanwhile," said Petra, "the Chinese soldiers in India and Xinjiang are going crazy because they don't know what's going on with their families back home."

"The invasion fleet doesn't mass for the attack," said Bean. "It's done in Filipino and Indonesian fishing boats, small forces up and down the coast. The Indonesian fleet, with its carriers, waits far offshore, until they're called in on air strikes against identified military targets. Every time they try to find your army, you melt away. No pitched battles. At first the people will help them; soon enough, the people will help you. You resupply with ammunition and demolition equipment by air drops at night. Food they find for themselves. And all the time they move farther and farther inland, destroying communications, blowing up bridges. No dams, though. Leave the dams alone."

"Of course," said Alai darkly. "We remember Aswan."

"Anyway, that was my suggestion," said Bean. "Militarily, it does nothing for you during the first weeks. The attrition rate will be high at first, until the teams get in from the coast and get used to this kind of combat. But if even a quarter of your contingents are able to remain free and effective, operating inside China, it will force the Chinese to bring more and more troops home from the Indian front."

"Until they sue for peace," said Alai. "We don't actually want to rule over China. We want to liberate India and Indochina, bring back all the captives taken into China, and restore the rightful governments, but with a treaty allowing complete privileges to Muslims within their borders."

"So much bloodshed, for such a modest goal," said Petra.

"And, of course, the liberation of Turkic China," said Alai.

"They'll like *that*," said Bean.

"And Tibet," said Alai.

"Humiliate them enough," said Petra, "and you've merely set the stage for the next war."

"And complete freedom of religion in China as well."

Petra laughed. "It's going to be a long war, Alai. The new empire they'd probably give up—they haven't held it that long, and it's not as if it brought them great wealth and honor. But they've held Tibet and Turkic China for centuries. There are Han Chinese all over both territories."

"Those are problems to be solved later," said Alai, "and not by you. Probably not by me, either. But we know what the West keeps forgetting. If you win, win."

"I think that approach was proven a disaster at Versailles."

"No," said Alai. "It was only proven a disaster *after* Versailles, when France and England didn't have the spine, didn't have the will, to compel obedience to the treaty. After World War II, the Allies were wiser. They left their troops on German soil for nearly a century. In some cases benignly, in some cases brutally, but always definitely there."

"As you said," Bean answered, "you and your successors will find out how well this works, and how to solve the new problems that are bound to come up. But I warn you now, that if liberators turn out to be oppressors, the people they liberated will feel even more betrayed and hate them worse."

"I'm aware of that," said Alai. "And I know what you're warning me of."

"I think," said Bean, "that you won't know whether the Muslim people have actually changed from the bad old days of religious intolerance until you put power in their hands."

"What the Caliph can do," said Alai, "I will do."

"I know you will," said Petra. "I don't envy you your responsibility."

Alai smiled. "Your friend Peter does. In fact, he wants more."

"And your people," said Bean, "will want more on your behalf. You may not want to rule the world, but if you win in China, they'll want you to, in their name. And at that point, Alai, how can you tell them no?"

"With these lips," said Alai. "And this heart."

16

TRAPS

To: Locke%erasmus@polnet.gov
From: Sand%Water@ArabNet.net
Re: Invitation to a party

You don't want to miss this one. Kemal upstairs thinks he's
the whole show, but when Shaw and Pack get started in
the basement, that's when the fireworks start! I say wait
for the downstairs party before you pop any corks.

"John Paul," said Theresa Wiggin quietly, "I don't
understand what Peter's doing here."

John Paul closed his suitcase. "That's the way he
likes it."

"We're supposed to be doing this secretly, but
he—"

"Asked us not to talk about it in here." John Paul
put his finger to his lips, then picked up her suitcase
as well as his and started on the long walk to the
bunkroom door.

Theresa could do nothing but sigh and follow him.
After all they'd been through with Peter, you'd think
he could confide in them. But he still had to play these

games where nobody knew everything that was going on but him. It was only a few hours since he had decided they were going to leave on the next shuttle, and supposedly they were supposed to keep it an absolute secret.

So what does Peter do? Asks practically every member of the permanent station crew to do some favor for him, run some errand, "and you've got to get it to me by 1800."

They weren't idiots. They all knew that 1800 was when everyone going on the next flight had to board for a 1900 departure.

So this great secret had been leaked, by implication, to everybody on the crew.

And yet he still insisted that they not talk about it, and John Paul was going along with him! What kind of madness was this? Peter was clearly not being careless, he was too systematic for it to be an accident. Was he hoping to catch someone in the act of transmitting a warning to Achilles? Well, what if, instead of a warning, they just blew up the shuttle? Maybe that was the operation—to sabotage whatever shuttle they were going home on. Did Peter think of *that*?

Of course he did. It was in Peter's nature to think of everything.

Or at least it was in Peter's nature to *think* he had thought of everything.

Out in the corridor, John Paul kept walking too quickly for her to converse with him, and when she tried anyway, he put his fingers to his lips.

"It's OK," he murmured.

At the elevator to the hub of the station, where the shuttles docked, Dimak was waiting for them. He had to be there, because their palms would not activate the elevator.

"I'm sorry we'll be losing you so soon," said Dimak.

"You never did tell us," said John Paul, "which bunk room was Dragon Army's."

"Ender never slept there anyway," said Dimak. "He had a private room. Commanders always did. Before that he was in several armies, but . . ."

"Too late now, anyway," said John Paul.

The elevator door opened. Dimak stepped inside, held the door for them, palmed the controls, and entered the code for the right flight deck.

Then he stepped back out of the elevator. "Sorry I can't see you off, but Colonel—the Minister suggested I shouldn't know about this."

John Paul shrugged.

The elevator doors closed and they began their ascent.

"Johnny P.," said Theresa, "if we're so worried about being bugged, what was *that* about, talking so openly with him?"

"He carries a damper," said John Paul. "His conversations can't be listened to. Ours can, and this elevator is definitely bugged."

"What, Uphanad told you that?"

"It would be insane to set up security in a tube like this station without bugging the funnel through which everybody has to pass to get inside."

"Well excuse me for not thinking like a paranoid spy."

"I think that's one of your best traits."

She realized that she couldn't say anything she was thinking. And not just because it might be overheard by Uphanad's security system. "I hate it when you 'deal' with me."

"OK, what if I 'handle' you instead?" suggested John Paul, leering just a little.

"If you weren't carrying my bag for me," said Theresa, "I'd . . ."

"Tickle me?"

"You aren't in on this any more than I am," said Theresa. "But you act as if you know everything." Gravity had quickly faded, and now she was holding onto the side rail as she hooked her feet under the floor rail.

"I've guessed some things," said John Paul. "For the rest, all I can do is trust. He really is a very smart boy."

"Not as smart as he thinks," said Theresa.

"But a lot smarter than *you* think," said John Paul.

"I suppose *your* evaluation of his intelligence is just right."

"Such a Goldilocks line. Makes me feel so . . . ursine."

"Why can't you just say 'bearlike'?"

"Because I know the word 'ursine,' and so do you, and it's fun to say."

The elevator doors opened.

"Carry your bag for you, Ma'am?" said John Paul.

"If you want," she said, "but I'm not going to tip you."

"Oh, you really are upset," he murmured.

She pulled herself past him as he started tossing bags to the orderlies.

Peter was waiting at the shuttle entrance. "Cut it rather fine, didn't we?" he said.

"Is it eighteen hundred?" asked Theresa.

"A minute before," said Peter.

"Then we're early," said Theresa. She sailed past him, too, and on into the airlock.

Behind her, she could hear Peter saying, "What's got into *her?*" and John Paul answering, "Later."

It took a moment to reorient herself, once she was inside the shuttle. She couldn't shake the sensation that the floor was in the wrong place—down was left and in was out, or some such thing. But she pulled herself by the handholds on the seat backs until she had found a seat. An aisle seat, to invite other passengers to sit somewhere else.

But there were no other passengers. Not even John Paul and Peter.

After waiting a good five minutes, she became too impatient to sit there any longer.

She found them standing in midair near the airlock, laughing about something.

"Are you laughing at me?" she asked, daring them to say yes.

"No," said Peter at once.

"Only a little," said John Paul. "We can talk now. The pilot has cut all the links to the station, and . . . Peter's wearing a damper, too."

"How nice," said Theresa. "Too bad they didn't have one for me or your father to use."

"They didn't," said Peter. "I've got Graff's. It's not like they keep them in stock."

"Why did you tell everybody you met here that we were leaving on this shuttle? Are you trying to get us killed?"

"Ah, what tangled webs we weave, when we practice to deceive," said Peter.

"So you're playing spider," said Theresa. "What are we, threads? Or flies?"

"Passengers," said John Paul.

And Peter laughed.

"Let me in on the joke," said Theresa, "or I'll space you, I swear I will."

"As soon as Graff knew he had an informer here at the station, he brought his own security team here. Unbeknownst to anyone but him, no messages are actually going into or out of the station. But it looks to anyone on the station as if they are."

"So you're hoping to catch someone sending a message about what shuttle we're on," said Theresa.

"Actually, we expect that no one will send a message at all."

"Then what is this for?" said Theresa.

"What matters is, *who* doesn't send the message." And Peter grinned at her.

"I won't ask anything more," said Theresa, "since you're so smug about how clever you are. I suppose whatever your clever plan is, my dear clever boy thought it up."

"And people say Demosthenes has a sarcastic streak," said Peter.

A moment ago she didn't get it. And now she did. Something clicked, apparently. The right mental gear had shifted, the right synapse had sizzled with electricity for a moment. "You wanted everybody to think they had accidentally discovered we were leaving. And gave them all a chance to send a message," said Theresa. "Except one person. So if he's the one . . ."

John Paul finished her sentence. "Then the message won't get sent."

"Unless he's really clever," said Theresa.

"Smarter than us?" said Peter.

He and John Paul looked at each other. Then both of them shook their heads, said, "Naw," and then burst out laughing.

"I'm glad you too are bonding so well," she said.

"Oh, Mom, don't be a butt about this," said Peter. "I couldn't tell you because if he knew it was a trap it wouldn't work, and he's the one person who might be listening to everything. And for your information I only just got the damper."

"I understand all that," said Theresa. "It's the fact that your father guessed it and I didn't."

"Mom," said Peter, "nobody thinks you're a lackwit, if that's what you're worried about."

"*Lackwit?* In what musty drawer of some dead English professor's dust-covered desk did you find *that* word? I assure you that never in my worst nightmares did I ever suppose that I was a *lackwit*."

"Good," said Peter. "Because if you did, you'd be wrong."

"Shouldn't we be strapping in for takeoff?" asked Theresa.

"No," said Peter. "We're not going anywhere."

"Why not?"

"The station computers are busily running a simulation program saying that the shuttle is in its launch routine. Just to make it look right, we'll be cut loose and drift away from the station. As soon as the only people in the dock are Graff's team from outside, we'll come back and get out of this can."

"This seems like a pretty elaborate shade to catch one informer."

"You raised me with such a keen sense of style, Mom," said Peter. "I can't overcome my childhood at your knee."

———

Lankowski knocked at the door at nearly midnight. Petra had already been asleep for an hour. Bean logged off, disconnected his desk, and opened the door.

"Is there something wrong?" he asked Lankowski.

"Our mutual friend wishes to see the two of you."

"Petra's already asleep," said Bean. But he could see from the coldness of Lankowski's demeanor that something was very wrong. "Is Alai all right?"

"He's very well, thank you," said Lankowski. "Please wake your wife and bring her along as quickly as possible."

Fifteen minutes later, adrenaline making sure that neither he nor Petra was the least bit groggy, they stood before Alai, not in the garden, but in an office, and Alai was sitting behind a desk.

He had a single sheet of paper on the desk and slid it across to Bean.

Bean picked it up and read it.

"You think I sent this," said Bean.

"Or Petra did," said Alai. "I tried to tell myself that perhaps you hadn't impressed upon her the importance of keeping this information from the Hegemon. But then I realized that I was thinking like a very old-fashioned Muslim. She is responsible for her own actions. And she understood as well as you did that maintaining secrecy on this matter was vital."

Bean sighed.

"I didn't send it," said Bean. "Petra didn't send it. We not only understood your desire to keep this secret, we agreed with it. There is zero chance we would have sent information about what you're doing to anyone, period."

"And yet here is this message, sent from our own netbase. From this building!"

"Alai," said Bean, "we're three of the smartest people on Earth. We've been through a war together, and the two of you survived Achilles's kidnapping. And yet when something like this happens, you absolutely know that *we're* the ones who betrayed your trust."

"Who else from outside our circle knew this?"

"Well, let's see. All the men at that meeting have staffs. Their staffs are not made up of idiots. Even if no one explicitly told them, they'll see memos, they'll hear comments. Some of these men might even think it's not a breach of security to tell a deeply trusted aide. And a few of them might actually be only figureheads, so they *have* to tell the people who'll be doing the real work or nothing will get done."

"I know all these men," said Alai.

"Not as well as you know us," said Petra. "Just because they're good Muslims and loyal to you doesn't mean they're all equally *careful*."

"Peter has been building up a network of informants and correspondents since he was . . . well, since he was a kid. Long before any of them knew he was just a kid. It would be shocking if he *didn't* have an informant in your palace."

Alai sat staring at the paper on the desk. "This is a very clumsy sort of disguise for the message," said Alai. "I suppose you would have done a better job of it."

"I would have encrypted it," said Bean, "and Petra probably would have put it inside a graphic."

"I think the very clumsiness of the message should tell you something," said Petra. "The person who wrote this is someone who thinks he only needs to hide this information from somebody outside the inner circle. He would have to know that if *you* saw it, you'd recognize instantly that 'Shaw' refers to the old rulers of Iran, and 'Pack' refers to Pakistan, while 'Kemal' is a transparent reference to the founder of post-Ottoman Turkey. How could you *not* get it?"

Alai nodded. "So he's only coding it like this to keep outsiders from understanding it, in case it gets intercepted by an enemy."

"He doesn't think anybody here would search his outgoing messages," said Petra. "Whereas Bean and I know for a fact that we've been bugged since we got here."

"Not terribly successfully," said Alai with a tight little smile.

"Well, you need better snoopware, to start with," said Bean.

"And if we had sent a message to Peter," said Petra, "we would have told him explicitly to warn our Indian friend not to block the Chinese exit from India, only their return."

"We would have had no other reason to tell Peter about this at all," said Bean. "We don't work for him. We don't really like him all that much."

"He's not," said Petra firmly, "one of us."

Alai nodded, sighed, leaned back in his chair. "Please, sit down," he said.

"Thank you," said Petra.

Bean walked to the window and looked out over lawns sprinkled by purified water from the Mediterranean. Where the favor of Allah was, the desert blossomed. "I don't think there'll be any harm from this," said Bean. "Aside from our losing a bit of sleep tonight."

"You must see that it's hard for me to suspect my closest colleagues here."

"You're the Caliph," said Petra, "but you're also still a very young man, and they see that. They know your plan is brilliant, they love you, they follow you in all the great things you plan for your people. But when you tell them, Keep this an absolute secret, they say yes, they even mean it, but they don't take it really quite seriously because, you see, you're . . ."

"Still a boy," said Alai.

"That will fade with time," said Petra. "You have many years ahead of you. Eventually all these older men will be replaced."

"By younger men that I trust even less," said Alai ruefully.

"Telling Peter is not the same thing as telling an enemy," said Bean. "He shouldn't have had this information in advance of the invasion. But you notice that the informer didn't tell him *when* the invasion would start."

"Yes he did," said Alai.

"Then I don't see it," said Bean.

Petra got up again and looked at the printed-out email. "The message doesn't say anything about the date of the invasion."

"It was sent," said Alai, "on the day of the invasion."

Bean and Petra looked at each other. "Today?" said Bean.

"The Turkic campaign has already begun," said Alai. "As soon as it was dark in Xinjiang. By now we have received confirmation via email messages that three airfields and a significant part of the power grid are in our hands. And so far, at least, there is no sign that the Chinese know anything is happening. It's going better than we could have hoped."

"It's begun," said Bean. "So it was already too late to change the plans for the third front."

"No, it wasn't," said Alai. "Our new orders have been sent. The Indonesian and Arab commanders are very proud to be entrusted with the mission that will take the war home to the enemy."

Bean was appalled. "But the logistics of it . . . there's no time to plan."

"Bean," said Alai with amusement. "We already had the plans for a complicated beach landing. *That* was a logistical nightmare. Putting three hundred separate forces ashore at different points on the Chinese coast, under cover of darkness, three days from today, and supporting them with air raids and air drops— my people can do that in their sleep. That was the best thing about your idea, Bean, my friend. It wasn't a plan at all, it was a situation, and the whole plan is for every individual commander to improvise ways to fulfil the mission objectives. I told them, in my orders, that as long as they keep moving inland, protect their men, and cause maximum annoyance to the Chinese government and military, they can't fail."

"It's begun," said Petra.

"Yes," said Bean. "It's begun, and Achilles is not in China."

Petra looked at Bean and grinned. "Let's see what we can do about keeping him away."

"More to the point," said Bean. "Since we have *not* given Peter the specific message he needs to convey to Virlomi in India, may we do so now, with your permission?"

Alai squinted at him. "Tomorrow. After news of the fighting in Xinjiang has started to come out. I will tell you when."

———

In Uphanad's office, Graff sat with his feet on the desk as Uphanad worked at the security console.

"Well, sir, that's it," said Uphanad. "They're off."

"And they'll arrive when?" said Graff.

"I don't know," said Uphanad. "That's all about trajectories and very complicated equations balancing velocity, mass, speed—I wasn't the astrophysics teacher in Battle School, you recall."

"You were small-force tactics, if I remember," said Graff.

"And when you tried that experiment with military music—having the boys learn to sing together—"

Graff groaned. "Please. Don't remind me. What a deeply stupid idea that was."

"But you saw that at once and let us mercifully drop the whole thing."

"Esprit de corps my ass," said Graff.

Uphanad hit a group of keys on the console keyboard and the screen showed that he had just logged off. "All done here. I'm glad you found out about the informer here in MinCol. Having the Wiggins leave was the only safe option."

"Do you remember," said Graff, "the time I accused you of letting Bean see your log-on?"

"Like yesterday," said Uphanad. "I don't think you were going to believe me until Dimak vouched for me and suggested Bean was crawling around the duct system and peeking through vents."

"Yes, Dimak was sure that you were so methodical you could not possibly have broken your habits in a moment of carelessness. He was right, wasn't he?"

"Yes," said Uphanad.

"I learned my lesson," said Graff. "I trusted you ever since."

"I hope I have earned that trust."

"Many times over. I didn't keep all the faculty from Battle School. Of course, there were some who thought the Ministry of Colonization too tame for their talents. But it isn't really a matter of personal loyalty, is it?"

"What isn't, sir?"

"Our loyalty should be to something larger than a particular person, don't you think? To a cause, perhaps. I'm loyal to the human race—that's a pretentious one, don't you think?—but to a particular project, spreading the human genome throughout as many star systems as possible. So our very existence can never be threatened again. And for that, I'd sacrifice many personal loyalties. It makes me completely predictable, but also someone unreliable, if you get what I mean."

"I think I do, sir."

"So my question, my good friend, is this: What are you loyal to?"

"To this cause, sir. And to you."

"This informant who used your log-on. Did he peer at you through the vents again, do you think?"

"Very unlikely, sir. I think it much more probable that he penetrated the system and chose me at random, sir."

"Yes, of course. But you must understand that because your name was on that email, we had to eliminate you as a possibility first."

"That is only logical, sir."

"So as we sent the Wiggins home on the shuttle, we made sure that every member of the permanent staff found out that they were leaving and had every opportunity to send a message. Except you."

"Except me, sir?"

"I have been with you continuously since they decided to go. That way, if a message was sent, even if it used your log-on, we would know it wasn't you who sent it. But if a message wasn't sent, well . . . it was you who didn't send it."

"This is not likely to be foolproof, sir," said Uphanad. "Someone else might have *not* sent the message for reasons of his or her own, sir. It might be that their departure was not something for which a message was necessary."

"True," said Graff. "But we would not convict you of a crime on the basis of a message not sent. Merely assign you to a less critical responsibility. Or give you the opportunity to resign with pension."

"That is very kind of you, sir."

"Please don't think of *me* as kind, I—"

The door opened. Uphanad turned, obviously surprised. "You can't come in here," he said to the Vietnamese woman who stood in the doorway.

"Oh, I invited her," said Graff. "I don't think you know Colonel Nguyen of the IF Digital Security Force."

"No," said Uphanad, rising to offer his hand. "I didn't even know your office existed. Per se."

She ignored his hand and gave a paper to Graff.

"Oh," he said, not reading it yet. "So we're in the clear in this room."

"The message did not use his log-on," she said.

Graff read the message. It consisted of a single word: "Off." The log-on was that of one of the orderlies from the docks.

The time in the message header showed it had been sent only a couple of minutes before. "So my friend is in the clear," said Graff.

"No sir," said Nguyen.

Uphanad, who had been looking relieved, now seemed baffled. "But I did not send it. How could I?"

Nguyen did not answer him, but spoke only to Graff. "It was sent from this console."

She walked over to the console and started to log back on.

"Let me do that," said Uphanad.

She turned around and there was a stun gun in her hand. "Stand against the wall," she said. "Hands in plain view."

Graff got up and opened the door. "Come on in," he said. Two more IF soldiers entered. "Please inspect Mr. Uphanad for weapons or other lethal items. And under no circumstances is he to be allowed to touch a computer. We wouldn't want him to activate a program wiping out critical materials."

"I don't know how this thing was done," said Uphanad, "but you're wrong about me."

Graff pointed to the console. "Nguyen is never wrong," he said. "She's even more methodical than you."

Uphanad watched. "She's signing on as me." And then, "She used my password. That's illegal!"

Nguyen called Graff over to look at the screen. "Normally, to log off, you press these two keys, you see? But he also pressed *this* one. With his little finger, so you wouldn't actually notice it had been pressed. That key sequence activated a resident program that sent the email, using a random selection from among the staff identities. It *also* launched the ordinary log-off sequence, so to you, it looked like you had just watched somebody log off in a perfectly normal way."

"So he had this ready to send at any time," said Graff.

"But when he *did* send it, it was within five minutes of the actual launch."

Graff and Nguyen turned around to look at Uphanad. Graff could see in his eyes that he saw he had been caught.

"So," said Graff, "how did Achilles get to you? You've never met him, I don't think. Surely he didn't form some attachment with you when he was here for a few days as a student."

"He has my family," said Uphanad, and he burst into tears.

"No no," said Graff. "Control yourself, act like a soldier, we have very little time here in which to correct your failure of judgment. Next time you'll know, if someone comes to you with a threat like this, you come to me."

"They said they'd know if I told you."

"Then you would tell me that, too," said Graff. "But, now you *have* told me. So let's make this thing work to our advantage. What happens when you send this second message?"

"I don't know," said Uphanad. "It doesn't matter anyway. She just sent it again. When they get the same message twice, they'll know something is wrong."

"Oh, they didn't get the message either time," said Graff. "We cut this console off. We cut off the whole station from earthside contact. Just as the shuttle never actually left."

The door opened yet again, and in came Peter, John Paul, and Theresa.

Uphanad turned his face to the wall. The soldiers would have turned him back around, but Graff gave them a gesture: Let be. He knew how proud Uphanad was. This shame in front of the people he had tried to betray was unbearable. Give him time to compose himself.

Only when the Wiggins were sitting did Graff invite Uphanad also to take a seat. He obeyed, hanging his head like a caricature of a whipped dog.

"Sit up, Uphanad, and face this like a man. These are good people, they understand that you did what you thought you must for your family. You were unwise not to trust me more, but even that is understandable."

From Theresa's face, Graff could see that she, at least, was not half so understanding as he seemed to assume. But he won her silence with a gesture.

"I'll tell you what," said Graff. "Let's make this work to our advantage. I actually have a couple of shuttles at my disposal for this operation—compliments of Admiral Chamrajnagar, by the way—so the real quandary is deciding which of them to send when we actually allow your email to go out."

"Two shuttles?" asked Peter.

"We have to make a guess about what Achilles planned to do with this information. If he means to attack you upon landing, well, we have a very heavily armed shuttle that should be able to deal with anything he can throw against it from the ground or the air. I think what he's planning is probably a missile as you're overflying some region where he can get a portable launch platform."

"And your heavily armed shuttle can deal with that?" asked Peter.

"Easily. The trouble is, this shuttle is not supposed to exist. The IF charter specifically forbids any weaponization of atmospheric craft. It's designed to go along with colony ships, in case the extermination of the Formics was not complete and we run into resistance. But if such a shuttle enters Earth's atmosphere and proves its capabilities by shooting down a missile, we could never tell anyone about it without compromising the IF. So we could use this shuttle to get you safely to Earth, but could never tell anyone about the attempt on your life."

"I could live with that," said Peter.

"Except that you don't actually have to get to Earth at this time."

"No, I don't."

"So we can send a different shuttle. Again, one whose existence is not known, but this time it is not illegal. Because it hasn't been weaponized at all. In fact, while it's quite expensive compared to, say, a bazooka, it's very, very cheap compared with a real shuttle. This one's a dummy. It is carefully designed to match the velocity and radar signature of a real shuttle, but it lacks a few things—like any place to put a human being, or any capability of a soft landing."

"So you send this one down," said John Paul, "draw their fire, and then have a propaganda field day."

"We'll have IF observers watching for the boost and we'll be on that launch platform before it can be dismantled, or at least before the perpetrators can get away. Whether it ends up pointing to Achilles or China, either way we can demonstrate that someone on Earth fired at an IF shuttle."

"Puts them in a very bad position," said Peter. "Do we announce that I was the target?"

"We can decide that based on their response, and on who is getting the blame. If it's China, I think we gain more by making it an attack on the International Fleet. If it's Achilles, we gain more by making him out to be an assassin."

"You seem to have been quite free about discussing

these things in front of us," said Theresa. "I suppose now you have to kill us."

"Just me," whispered Uphanad.

"Well, I do have to fire you," said Graff. "And I do have to send you back to Earth, because it just wouldn't do to have you stay on here. You'd just depress everyone else, slinking around looking guilty and unworthy."

Graff's tone was light enough to help keep Uphanad from bursting into tears again.

"I've heard," Graff went on, "that the Indian people need to have loyal men who'll fight for their freedom. That's the loyalty that transcends your loyalty to the Ministry of Colonization, and I understand it. So you must go where your loyalty leads you."

"This is . . . unbelievable mercy, sir," said Uphanad.

"It wasn't my idea," said Graff. "My plan was to have you tried in secret by the IF and executed. But Peter told me that, if you were guilty and it turned out you were protecting family members in Chinese custody, it would be wrong to punish you for the crime of imperfect loyalty."

Uphanad turned to look at Peter. "My betrayal might have killed you and your family."

"But it didn't," said Peter.

"I like to think," said Graff, "that God sometimes shows mercy to us by letting some accident prevent us from actually carrying out our worst plans."

"I don't believe that," said Theresa coldly. "I believe if you point a gun at a man's head and the bullet was a dud, you're still a murderer in the eyes of God."

"Well then," said Graff, "when we're all dead, if we find that we still exist in some form or other, we'll just have to ask God to tell us which of us is right."

PROPHETS

SecureSite.net
From: Locke%erasmus@polnet.gov
PASSWORD: Suriyawong
Re: girl on bridge

Reliable source begs: Do not interfere with Chinese egress from India. But when they need to return or supply, block all possible routes.

The Chinese thought at first that the incidents in Xinjiang province were the work of the insurgents who had been forming and reforming guerrilla groups for centuries. In the protocol-burdened Chinese army, it was not until late afternoon in Beijing that Han Tzu was finally able to get enough information together to prove this was a major offensive originating outside China.

For the fiftieth time since taking a place in the high command in Beijing, Han Tzu despaired of getting anything done. It was always more important to show respect for one's superiors' high status than to tell them the truth and make things happen. Even now, holding in his hands evidence of a level of training, discipline, coordination, and supply that made it impossible for these incidents in Xinjiang to be the work of local rebels, Han Tzu had to wait hours for his request for a meeting to be processed through all the oh-so-important aides, flunkies, functionaries, and poobahs whose sole duty was to look as important and busy as possible while making sure that as little as possible actually got done.

It was fully dark in Beijing when Han Tzu crossed the square separating the Strategy and Planning section from the Administrative section—another bit of mindlessly bad structure, to separate these two sections by a long walk in the open air. They should have been across a low divider from each other, constantly shouting back and forth. Instead, Strategy and Planning were constantly making plans that Administrative couldn't carry out, and Administrative was constantly misunderstanding the purpose of plans and fighting against the very ideas that would make them effective.

How did we ever conquer India? thought Han Tzu.

He kicked at the pigeons scurrying around his feet. They fluttered a few meters away, then came back for more, as if they thought his feet might have shed something edible with each step.

The only reason this government stays in power is that the people of China are pigeons. You can kick them and kick them, and they come back for more. And the worst of them are the bureaucrats. China invented bureaucracy, and with a thousand-year head start on the rest of the world, they'd kept advancing the arts of obfuscation, kingdom-building, and tempests-in-teapots to a level unknown anywhere else. Byzantine bureaucracy was, by comparison, a forthright system.

How did Achilles do it? An outsider, a criminal, a madman—and all of this was well known to the Chinese government—yet he was able to cut through the layers of fawning backstabbers and get straight to the decision-making level. Most people didn't even know where the decision-making level was, since it was certainly *not* the famous leaders at the top, who were too old to think of anything new and too frightened of losing their perks or getting caught out in their decades of criminal acts ever to do anything but say, "Do as you think wise," to their underlings.

It was two levels down that decisions were made, by aides to the top generals. It had taken Han Tzu six months to realize that a meeting with the top man was useless, because he would confer with his aides and follow their recommendations every time. Now he never bothered to meet with anyone else. But to set up such a meeting, of course, required that an elaborate request be made to each general, acknowledging that while the subject of the meeting was so vital it must be held immediately, it was so trivial that each general only needed to send his aide to the meeting in his place.

Han Tzu was never sure whether all this elaborate charade was merely to show proper respect for tradition and form, or whether the generals actually were fooled by all this and made the decision, each time, whether to attend in person or send their aide.

Of course, it was also possible that the general never saw the messages, and the aides made the decision for him. Most likely, though, his memo went to each general with a commentary: "Noble and worthy general would be slighted if not in attendance," for instance, or "Tedious waste of heroic leader's time, unworthy aide will be glad to take notes and report if anything important is said."

Han Tzu had no loyalty to any of these buffoons. Whenever they made decisions on their own, they were hopelessly wrong. The ones that weren't completely bound by tradition were just as controlled by their own egos.

Yet Han Tzu was completely loyal to China. He had always acted in China's best interest, and always would.

The trouble was, he often defined "China's best interest" in a way that might easily get him shot.

Like that message he sent to Bean and Petra, hoping they'd realize the danger to the Hegemon if he really believed Han Tzu had been the source of his information. Sending such a bit of information was definitely treason, since Achilles's adventure had been approved at the highest levels and therefore represented official Chinese policy. And yet it would be a disaster for China's prestige in the world at large if it became known that China had sent an assassin to kill the Hegemon.

Nobody seemed to understand that sort of thing, mostly because they refused to see China as anything other than the center of the universe, around which all other nations orbited. What did it matter if China was regarded as a nation of tyrants and assassins? If someone doesn't like what China does, then that someone can go home and cry in his beer.

But no nation was invincible, not even China. Han Tzu understood that, even if the others did not.

It didn't help that the conquest of India had been so easy. Han Tzu had insisted on devising all sorts of contingency plans when things went wrong with the surprise attack on the Indian, Thai, and Vietnamese armies. But Achilles's campaign of deception had been so successful, and the Thai strategy of defense had been so effective, that the Indians were fully committed, their supplies exhausted, and their morale at rock bottom when the Chinese armies began pouring across the borders, cutting the Indian army to pieces, and swallowing up each piece within days—sometimes within hours.

All the glory went to Achilles, of course, though it had been Han Tzu's careful planning with his staff of nearly eighty Battle School graduates that put the Chinese armies exactly where they needed to be at exactly the time they needed to be there. No, even though Han Tzu's team had written up the orders, they had actually been issued by Administrative, and therefore it was Administrative that won the medals, while Strategy and Planning got a single group commendation that had about the same effect on morale as if some lieutenant colonel had come in and said, "Nice try, boys, we know you meant well."

Well, Achilles was welcome to the glory, because in Han Tzu's opinion, invading India had been pointless and self-defeating—not to mention evil. China did not have the resources to take on India's problems. When Indians governed India, the suffering people could only blame their fellow Indians. But now when things went wrong—which they always did in India—it would all be blamed on the Chinese.

The Chinese administrators who were sent in to govern India stayed surprisingly free of corruption and they worked hard—but the fact is that no nation is governable except by overwhelming force or complete cooperation. And since there was no way conquering Chinese officials would get complete cooperation, and there was no hope of being able to pay for overwhelming force, the only question was when the resistance would become a problem.

It became a problem not long after Achilles left for the Hegemony, when the Indians started piling up stones. Han Tzu had to hand it to them, when it came to truly annoying but symbolically powerful civil disobedience, the Indians were truly the daughters and sons of Gandhi. Even then, the bureaucrats hadn't listened to Han Tzu's advice and ended up getting themselves into a steadily worsening cycle of reprisals.

So . . . it doesn't matter what the outside world thinks, right? We can do whatever we want because no one else has the power or the will to challenge us, is that the story?

What I have in my hands is the answer to *that* theory.

"What does it mean that they've done nothing to acknowledge our offensive?" said Alai.

Bean and Petra sat with him, looking at the holomap that showed every single objective in Xinjiang taken on schedule, as if the Chinese had been handed a script and were doing their part exactly as the Crescent League had asked them to.

"I think things are going very well," said Petra.

"Ridiculously well," said Alai.

"Don't be impatient," said Bean. "Things move slowly in China. And they don't like making public pronouncements about their problems. Maybe they still see this as a group of local insurgents. Maybe they're waiting to announce what's going on until they can tell about their devastating counterattack."

"That's just it," said Alai. "Our satintel says they're

doing nothing. Even the nearest garrison troops are still in place."

"The garrison commanders don't have the authority to send them into battle," said Bean. "Besides, they probably don't even know anything's wrong. Your forces have the land-based communications grid under control, right?"

"That was a secondary objective. That's what they're doing now, just to keep busy."

Petra began to laugh. "I get it," she said.

"What's so funny?" asked Alai.

"The public announcement," said Petra. "You can't announce that a Caliph has been named unanimously by all the Muslim nations."

"We *can* announce it any time," said Alai, irritated.

"But you're waiting. Until the Chinese make their announcement that some unknown nation has attacked them. Only when they've either admitted their ignorance or committed to some theory that's completely false do you come out and tell what's really happening. That the Muslim world is fully united under a Caliph, and that you have taken responsibility for liberating the captive nations from the godless imperialist Chinese."

"You have to admit the story plays better that way," said Alai.

"Absolutely," said Petra. "I'm not laughing because you're wrong to do it that way, I'm simply laughing at the irony that you are so *successful* and the Chinese so completely unprepared that it's actually delaying your announcement! But . . . have patience, dear friend. Somebody in the Chinese high command knows what's happening, and eventually the rest of them will listen to him and they'll mobilize their forces and make some kind of announcement."

"They have to," said Bean. "Or the Russians will deliberately misunderstand their troop movements."

"All right," said Alai. "But unfortunately, all the vids of my announcement were shot during daylight hours. It never crossed our minds that they would take this long to respond."

"You know what?" said Bean. "No one will mind a bit if the vids are clearly prerecorded. But even better would be for you to go on camera, live, to declare yourself and to announce what your armies are doing in Xinjiang."

"The danger with doing it live is that I might let something slip, telling them that the Xinjiang invasion is not the main offensive."

"Alai, you could announce outright that this was not the main offensive, and half the Chinese would think that was disinformation designed to keep their troops in India pinned down along the Pakistani border. In fact, I advise you to do that. Because then you'll have a reputation as a truthteller. It will make your later lies that much more effective."

Alai laughed. "You've eased my mind."

"You're suffering," said Petra, "from the problem that plagues all the top commanders in this age of rapid communications. In the old days, Alexander and Caesar were right there on the field of battle. They could watch, issue orders, deal with things. They were needed. But you're stuck here in Damascus because here is where all the communications come together. If you're needed, you'll be needed here. So instead of having a thousand things to keep your mind busy, you have all this adrenaline flowing and nowhere for it to go."

"I recommend pacing," said Bean.

"Do you play handball?" asked Petra.

"I get the picture," said Alai. "Thank you. I'll be patient."

"And think about my advice," said Bean. "To go on live and tell the truth. Your people will love you better if they see you as being so bold you can simply tell the enemy what you're going to do, and they can't stop you from doing it."

"Go away now," said Alai. "You're repeating yourself."

Laughing, Bean got up. So did Petra.

"I won't have time for you after this, you know," said Alai.

They paused, turned.

"Once it's announced, once everybody knows, I'll have to start holding court. Meeting people. Judging disputes. Showing myself to be the true Caliph."

"Thank you for the time you've spent with us till now," said Petra.

"I hope we never have to oppose each other on the field of battle," said Bean. "The way we've had to oppose Han Tzu in this war."

"Just remember," said Alai. "Han Tzu's loyalties are divided. Mine are not."

"I'll remember that," said Bean.

"Salaam," said Alai. "Peace be in you."

"And in you," said Petra, "peace."

———

When the meeting ended, Han Tzu did not know whether his warning had been believed. Well, even if they didn't believe him now, in a few more hours they'd have no choice. The major force in the Xinjiang invasion would undoubtedly start their assault just before dawn tomorrow. Satellite intelligence would confirm what he'd told them today. But at the cost of twelve more hours of inaction.

The most frustrating moment, however, had come near the end of the meeting, when the senior aide to the senior general had asked, "So if this is the beginning of a major offensive, what do you recommend?"

"Send all available troops in the north—I would recommend fifty percent of all the garrison troops on the Russian border. Prepare them not only to deal with these horse-borne guerrillas but also with a major mechanized army that will probably invade tomorrow."

"What about the concentration of troops in India?" asked the aide. "These are our best soldiers, the most highly trained, and the most mobile."

"Leave them where they are," said Han Tzu.

"But if we strip the garrisons along the Russian border, the Russians will attack."

Another aide spoke up. "The Russians never fight well outside their own borders. Invade them and they'll destroy you, but if they invade you, their soldiers won't fight."

Han Tzu tried not to show his contempt for such ludicrous judgments. "The Russians will do what they do, and if they attack, we'll do what we need to do in response. However, you don't keep your troops from defending against a present enemy because they might be needed for a hypothetical enemy."

All well and good. Until the senior aide to the senior general said, "Very well. I will recommend the immediate removal of troops from India as quickly as possible to meet this current threat."

"That's not what I meant," said Han Tzu.

"But it is what *I* mean," said the aide.

"I believe this is a Muslim offensive," said Han

Tzu. "The enemy across the border in Pakistan is the same enemy attacking us in Xinjiang. They are certainly hoping we'll do exactly what you suggest, so their main offensive will have a better chance of success."

The aide only laughed, and the others laughed with him. "You spent too many years out of China during your childhood, Han Tzu. India is a faraway place. What does it matter what happens there? We can take it again whenever we want. But these invaders in Xinjiang, they are inside China. The Russians are poised on the Chinese border. No matter what the enemy thinks, *that* is the real threat."

"Why?" said Han Tzu, throwing caution to the winds as he directly challenged the senior aide. "Because foreign troops on Chinese soil would mean the present government has lost the mandate of heaven?"

From around the table came the hiss of air suddenly gasped between clenched teeth. To refer to the old idea of the mandate of heaven was poisonously out of step with government policy.

Well, as long as he was irritating people, why stop with that? "Everyone knows that Xinjiang and Tibet are not part of Han China," said Han Tzu. "They are no more important to us than India—conquests that have never become fully Chinese. We once owned Vietnam before, long ago, and lost it, and the loss meant nothing to us. But the Chinese army, that is precious. And if you take troops out of India, you run the grave risk of losing millions of our men to these Muslim fanatics. Then we won't have the mandate of heaven to worry about. We'll have foreign troops in Han China before we know it—and no way to defend against them."

The silence around the table was deadly. They

hated him now, because he had spoken to them of defeat—and told them, disrespectfully, that their ideas were wrong.

"I hope none of you will forget this meeting," said Han Tzu.

"You can be sure that we will not," said the senior aide.

"If I am wrong, then I will bear the consequences of my mistake, and rejoice that your ideas were not stupid after all. What is good for China is good for me, even if I am punished for my mistakes. But if I am right, then we'll see what kind of men you are. Because if you're true Chinese, who love your country more than your careers, you'll remember that I was right and you'll bring me back and listen to me as you should have listened to me today. But if you're the disloyal selfish garden-pigs I think you are, you'll make sure that I'm killed, so that no one outside this room will ever know that you heard a true warning and didn't listen to it when there was still time to save China from the most dangerous enemy we have faced since Genghis Khan."

What a glorious speech. And how refreshing actually to say it with his lips to the people who most needed to hear it, instead of playing the speech over and over in his mind, ever more frustrated because not a word of it had been said aloud.

Of course he would be arrested tonight, and quite possibly shot before morning. Though the more likely pattern would be to arrest him and charge him with passing information to the enemy, blaming him for the defeat that only he actually tried to prevent. There was something about irony that had a special appeal to Chinese people who got a little power. There was a special pleasure in punishing a virtuous man for the powerful man's own crimes.

But Han Tzu would not hide. It might be possible, at this moment, for him to leave China and go into exile. But he would not do it.

Why not?

He could not leave his country in its hour of need. Even though he might be killed for staying, there would be many other Chinese soldiers his age who would die in the next days and weeks. Why shouldn't he be one of them? And there was always the chance, however small and remote, that there were enough decent men among those at that meeting that Han Tzu would be kept alive until it was clear that he was right. Perhaps then—contrary to all expectation— they would bring him back and ask him how to save themselves from this disaster they had brought upon China.

Meanwhile, Han Tzu was hungry, and there was a little restaurant he liked, where the manager and his wife treated him like one of the family. They did not care about his lofty rank or his status as one of the heroes of Ender's jeesh. They liked him for his company. They loved the way he devoured their food as if it were the finest cuisine in the world—which, to him, it was. If these were his last hours of freedom, or even of life, why not spend them with people he liked, eating food he enjoyed?

———

As night fell in Damascus, Bean and Petra walked freely along the streets, looking into shop windows. Damascus still had the traditional markets, where most fresh food and local handwork were sold. But supermarkets, boutiques, and chain stores had reached

Damascus, like almost every other place on earth. Only the wares for sale reflected local taste. There was no shortage of items of European and American design for sale, but what Bean and Petra enjoyed was the strangeness of items that would never find a market in the West, but which apparently were much in demand here.

They traded guesses about what each item was for.

They stopped at an outdoor restaurant with good music played softly enough that they could still converse. They had a strange combination of local food and international cuisine that had even the waiter shaking his head, but they were in the mood to please themselves.

"I'll probably just throw it up tomorrow," said Petra.

"Probably," said Bean. "But it'll be a better grade of—"

"Please!" said Petra. "I'm trying to eat."

"But you brought it up," said Bean.

"I know it's unfair, but when I discuss it, it doesn't make me sick. It's like tickling. You can't really nauseate yourself."

"I can," said Bean.

"I have no doubt of it. Probably one of the attributes of Anton's Key."

They continued talking about nothing much, until they heard some explosions, at first far away, then nearby.

"There can't possibly be an attack on Damascus," said Petra under her voice.

"No, I think it's fireworks," said Bean. "I think it's a celebration."

One of the cooks ran into the restaurant and shouted out a stream of Arabic, which was of course completely unintelligible to Bean and Petra. All at once the local customers jumped up from the table. Some of them ran out of the restaurant—without paying, and nobody made to stop them. Others ran into the kitchen.

The few non-Arabiphones in the restaurant were left to wonder what was going on.

Until a merciful waiter came out and announced in Common Speech, "Food will be delay, I very sorry to tell you. But happy to say why. Caliph will speak in a minute."

"The Caliph?" asked an Englishman. "Isn't he in Baghdad?"

"I thought Istanbul," said a Frenchwoman.

"There has been no Caliph in many centuries," said a professorial-looking Japanese.

"Apparently they have one now," said Petra reasonably. "I wonder if they'll let us into the kitchen to watch with them."

"Oh, I don't know if I *want* to," said the Englishman. "If they've got themselves a new Caliph, they're going to be feeling quite chauvinistic for a while. What if they decide to start hanging foreigners to celebrate?"

The Japanese scholar was outraged at this suggestion. While he and the Englishman politely went for each other's throats, Bean, Petra, the Frenchwoman, and several other westerners went through the swinging door into the kitchen, where the kitchen help barely noticed they were there. Someone had brought a nice-sized flat vid in from one of the offices and set it on a shelf, leaning it against the wall.

Alai was already on the screen.

Not that it did them any good to watch. They couldn't understand a word of it. They'd have to wait for the full translation on one of the newsnets later.

But the map of western China was pretty self-explanatory. No doubt he was telling them that the Muslim people had united to liberate long-captive brothers in Xinjiang. The waiters and cooks punctuated almost every sentence with cheers—Alai seemed to know this would happen, because he left pauses after each declaration.

Unable to understand his words, Bean and Petra concentrated on other things. Bean tried to determine whether this speech was going out live. The clock on the wall was no indicator—of course they would insert it digitally into a prerecorded vid during the broadcast so that no matter when it was first aired, the clock would show the current time. Finally he got his answer when Alai stood up and walked to the window. The camera followed him, and there spread out below him were the lights of Damascus, twinkling in the darkness. He was doing it live. And whatever he said while pointing to the city, it was apparently very effective, because at once the cheering cooks and waiters were weeping openly, without shame, their eyes still glued to the screen.

Petra, meanwhile, was trying to guess how Alai must look to the Muslim people watching him. She knew his face so well, so that she had to try to separate the boy she had known from the man he now was. The compassion she had noticed before was more visible than ever. His eyes were full of love. But there was fire in him, too, and dignity. He did not smile—which was proper for the leader of nations which were now at war, and whose sons were dying in combat, and killing, too. Nor did he rant, whipping them up into some kind of dangerous enthusiasm.

Will these people follow him into battle? Yes, of

course, at first, when he has a tale of easy victories to tell them. But later, when times are hard and fortune does not favor them, will they still follow him?

Perhaps yes. Because what Petra saw in him was not so much a great general—though yes, she could imagine Alexander might have looked like this, or Caesar—as a prophet-king. Saul or David, both young men when first called by prophecy to lead their people into war in God's name. Joan of Arc.

Of course, Joan of Arc ended up dying at the stake, and Saul fell on his own sword—or no, that was Brutus or Cassius, Saul commanded one of his own soldiers to kill him, didn't he? A bad end for both of them. And David died in disgrace, forbidden by God to build the holy temple because he had murdered Uriah to get Bathsheba into a state of marriageable widowhood.

Not a good list of precedents, that.

But they had their glory, didn't they, before they fell.

18

THE WAR ON THE GROUND

To: Chamrajnagar%Jawaharlal@ifcom.gov
From: AncientFire%Embers@han.gov
Re: Official statement coming

My esteemed friend and colleague,

It grieves me that you would even suppose that in this time of trouble, when China is assailed by unprovoked assaults from religious fanatics, we would have either the desire or the resources to provoke the International Fleet. We have nothing but the highest esteem for your institution, which so recently saved all humankind from the onslaught of the stardragons.

Our official statement, which will be released forthwith, does not include our speculations on who is in fact responsible for the tragic shooting down of the IF shuttle while it overflew Brazilian territory. While we do not admit to having any participation in or foreknowledge of the event, we have performed our own preliminary investigation and we believe you will find that the equipment in question may in fact have originated with the Chinese military.

This causes us excruciating embarrassment, and we beg you not to publicize this information. Instead, we provide you with the attached documentation showing that our one missile launcher which is not accounted for, and which therefore may have been used to commit this crime, was released into the control of a certain Achilles de Flandres, ostensibly for military operations in connection with our preemptive defensive action against the Indian aggressor as it ravaged Burma. We believed this materiel had been returned to us, but we discover upon investigation that it was not.

Achilles de Flandres at one time was under our protection, having rendered us a service in connection with forewarning us of the danger that India posed to peace in Southeast Asia. However, certain crimes he committed prior to this service came to our attention, and we arrested him (see documentation). As he was being conveyed to his place of reeducation, unknown forces raided the convoy and released Achilles de Flandres, killing all of the escorting soldiers.

Since Achilles de Flandres ended up almost immediately in the Hegemony compound in Ribeirao Preto, Brazil, and he has been in a position to do much mischief there since the hasty departure of Peter Wiggin, and since the missile was fired from Brazilian territory and the shuttle was shot down over Brazil, we suggest that the place to look for responsibility for this attack on the IF is in Brazil, specifically the Hegemony compound.

Ultimate responsibility for all of de Flandres's actions after his abscondment from our custody must lie with those who took him, namely, Hegemon Peter Wiggin and his military forces, headed by Julian Delphiki and, more recently, the Thai national, Suriyawong, who is regarded by the Chinese government as a terrorist.

I hope that this information, provided to you off the record, will prove useful to you in your investigation. If we can be of any other service that is not inconsistent with our desperate struggle for survival against the onslaught of the barbarian hordes from Asia, we will be glad to provide it.

Your humble and unworthy colleague,

Ancient Fire

    From: Chamrajnagar%Jawaharlal@ifcom.gov
    To: Graff%pilgrimage@colmin.gov
    Re: Who will take the blame?

Dear Hyrum,

You see from the attached message from the esteemed head of the Chinese government that they have decided to offer up Achilles as the sacrificial lamb. I think they'd be glad if we got rid of him for them. Our investigators will officially report that the launcher is of Chinese manufacture and has been traced back to Achilles de Flandres without mentioning that it was originally provided to him by the Chinese government. When asked, we will refuse to speculate. That's the best they can hope for from us.

Meanwhile, we now have the legal basis firmly established for an Earthside intervention—and from evidence provided by the nation most likely to complain about such an intervention. We will do nothing to affect the outcome or progress of the war in Asia. We will first seek the cooperation of the Brazilian government but will make it clear that such cooperation is not required, legally or militarily. We will ask them to isolate the Hegemony compound so that no one can get in or out, pending the arrival of our forces.

I ask that you inform the Hegemon and that you make your plans accordingly. Whether Mr. Wiggin should be present at the taking of the compound is a matter on which I have no opinion.

Virlomi never went into town herself. Those days were over. When she had been free to wander, a pilgrim in a land where people either lived their whole lives in one village or cut themselves loose and spent their whole lives on the road, she had loved coming to villages, each one an adventure, filled with its own tapestry of gossip, tragedy, humor, romance, and irony.

In the college she had briefly attended, between coming home from space and being brought into Indian military headquarters in Hyderabad, she had quickly realized that intellectuals seemed to think that their life—the life of the mind, the endless self-examination, the continuous autobiography afflicted upon all comers—was somehow higher than the repetitive, meaningless lives of the common people.

Virlomi knew the opposite to be true. The intellectuals in the university were all the same. They had precisely the same deep thoughts about exactly the same shallow emotions and trivial dilemmas. They knew this, unconsciously, themselves. When a real event happened, something that shook them to the heart, they withdrew from the game of university life, for reality had to be played out on a different stage.

In the villages, life was about life, not about one-upmanship and display. Smart people were valued because they could solve problems, not because they could speak pleasingly about them. Everywhere she went in India, she constantly heard herself thinking, I could live here. I could stay among these people and marry one of these gentle peasant men and work beside him all my life.

And then another part of her answered, No you couldn't. Because like it or not, you are one of those university people after all. You can visit in the real world, but you don't belong there. You need to live in Plato's foolish dream, where ideas are real and reality is shadow. That is the place you were born for, and as you move from village to village, it is only to learn from them, to teach them, to manipulate them, to use them to achieve your own ends.

But my own ends, she thought, are to give them gifts they need: wise government, or at least self-government.

And then she laughed at herself, because the two were usually opposites. Even if an Indian ruled over Indians, it was not self-government, for the ruler governed the people, and the people governed the ruler. It was mutual government. That's the best that could be aspired to.

Now, though, her pilgrim days were over. She had returned to the bridge where the soldiers stationed to protect it and the nearby villagers had made a kind of god of her.

She came back without fanfare, walking into the village that had taken her most to heart and falling into conversation with women at the well and in the market. She went to the washing stream and lent a hand with the washing of clothes; someone offered to share clothing with her so she could wash her dirty traveling rags, but she laughed and said that one more washing would rub them into dust, but she would like to earn some new clothing by helping a family that had a bit they could spare for her.

"Mistress," said one shy woman, "did we not feed you at the bridge, for nothing?"

So she *was* recognized.

"But I wish to earn the kindness you showed me there."

"You have blessed us many times, lady," said another.

"And now you bless us by coming among us."

"And washing clothes."

So she was still a god.

"I'm not what you think I am," she said. "I am more terrible than your worst fear."

"To our enemies, we pray, lady," said a woman.

"Terrible to them, indeed," said Virlomi. "But I will use your sons and husbands to fight them, and some of them will die."

"Half our sons and husbands were already taken in the war against the Chinese."

"Killed in battle."

"Lost and could not find their way home."

"Carried off into captivity by the Chinese devils."

Virlomi raised a hand to still them. "I will not waste their lives, if they obey me."

"You shouldn't go to war, lady," said one old crone. "There's no good in it. Look at you, young, beautiful. Lie down with one of our young men, or one of our old ones if you want, and make babies."

"Someday," said Virlomi, "I'll choose a husband

and make babies with him. But today my husband is India, and he has been swallowed by a tiger. I must make the tiger sick, so he will throw my husband up."

They giggled, some of them, at this image. But others were very grave.

"How will you do this?"

"I will prepare the men so they don't die because of mistakes. I will assemble all the weapons we need, so no man is wasted because he is unarmed. I will bide my time, so we don't bring down the wrath of the tiger upon us, until we're ready to hurt them so badly that they never recover from the blow."

"You didn't happen to bring a nuclear weapon with you, lady?" asked the crone. Clearly something of an unbeliever.

"It's an offense against God to use such things," said Virlomi. "The Muslim God was burned out of his house and turned his face against them because they used such weapons against each other."

"I was joking," said the crone, ashamed.

"I am not," said Virlomi. "If you don't want me to use your men in the way I have described, tell me, and I'll go away and find another place that wants me. Perhaps your hatred of the Chinese is not so fierce as mine. Perhaps you are content with the way things are in this land."

But they were not content, and their hatred was hot enough, it seemed.

There wasn't much time for training, despite her promise, but then, she wasn't going to use these men for firefights. They were to be saboteurs, thieves, demolition experts. They conspired with construction workers to steal explosives; they learned how to use them; they built dry storage pits in the jungles that clung to the steep hills.

And they went to nearby towns and recruited more men, and then went farther and farther afield, building a network of saboteurs near every key bridge that could be blown up to block the Chinese from the use of the roads they would need to bring troops and supplies back and forth, in and out of India.

There could be no rehearsals. No dry runs. Nothing was done to arouse suspicion of any kind. She forbade her men to make any gestures of defiance, or do anything to interfere with the smooth running of the Chinese transportation network through their hills and mountains.

Some of them chafed at this, but Virlomi said, "I gave my word to your wives and mothers that I would not waste your lives. There will be plenty of dying ahead, but only when your deaths will accomplish something, so that those who live can bear witness: We did this thing, it was not done for us."

Now she never went to town, but lived where she had lived before, in a cave near the bridge that she would blow up herself, when the time came.

But she could not afford to be cut off from the outside world. So three times a day, one of her people would sign on to the nets and check her dead drop sites, print out the messages there, and bring them to her. She made sure they knew how to wipe the information out of the computer's memory, so no one else could see what the computer had shown, and after she read the messages they brought, she burned them.

She got Peter Wiggin's message in good time. So she was ready when her people started coming to her, running, out of breath, excited. "The war with the Turks is going badly for the Chinese," they said. "We have it on the nets, the Turks have taken so many airfields that they can put more planes in the sky in Xinjiang than the Chinese can. They have dropped bombs on Beijing itself, lady!"

"Then you should weep for the children who are dying there," said Virlomi. "But the time for us to fight is not yet."

And the next day, when the trucks began to rumble across the bridges, and line up bumper to bumper along the narrow mountain roads, they begged her, "Let us blow up just one bridge, to show them that India is not sleeping while the Turks fight our enemy for us!"

She only answered them, "Why should we blow up bridges that our enemy is using to leave our land?"

"But we could kill many if we timed the explosion just right!"

"Even if we could kill five thousand by blowing up all the bridges at exactly the right moment, they have five million. We will wait. Not one of you will do anything to warn them that they have enemies in these mountains. The time is soon, but you must wait for my word."

Again and again she said it, all day long, to everyone who came, and they obeyed. She sent them to telephone their comrades in faraway towns near other bridges, and they also obeyed.

For three days. The Chinese-controlled news talked about how devastating armies were about to be brought to bear against the Turkic hordes, ready to punish them for their treachery. The traffic across the bridges and along the mountain roads was unrelenting.

Then came the message she was waiting for.

Now.

No signature, but it was in a dead drop that she had given to Peter Wiggin. She knew that it meant that the main offensive had been launched in the west, and the Chinese would soon begin sending troops and equipment back from China into India.

She did not burn the message. She handed it to the child who had brought it to her and said, "Keep this forever. It is the beginning of our war."

"Is it from a god?" asked the child.

"Perhaps the shadow of the nephew of a god," she answered with a smile. "Perhaps only a man in a dream of a sleeping god."

Taking the child by the hand, she walked down into the village. The people swarmed around her. She smiled at them, patted the children's heads, hugged the women and kissed them.

Then she led this parade of citizens to the office of the local Chinese administrator and walked inside the building. Only a few of the women came with her. She walked right past the desk of the protesting officer on duty and into the office of the Chinese official, who was on the telephone.

He looked up at her and shouted, first in Chinese, then in Common. "What are you doing! Get out of here."

But Virlomi paid no attention to his words. She walked up to him, smiling, reached out her arms as if to embrace him.

He raised his hands in protest, to fend her off with a gesture.

She took his arms, pulled him off balance, and while he staggered to regain his footing, she flung her arms around him, gripped his head, and twisted it sharply.

He fell dead to the floor.

She opened a drawer in his desk, took out his pistol, and shot both of the Chinese soldiers who were rushing into the office. They, too, fell dead to the floor.

She looked calmly at the women. "It is time. Please get on the telephones and call the others in every city. It is one hour till dark. At nightfall, they are to carry out their tasks. With a short fuse. And if anyone tries to stop them, even if it's an Indian, they should kill them as quietly and quickly as possible and proceed with their work."

They repeated the message to her, then set to work at the telephones.

Virlomi went outside with the pistol hidden in the folds of her skirt. When the other two Chinese soldiers in this village came running, having heard the shots, she started jabbering to them in her native dialect. They did not realize that it was not the local language at all, but a completely unrelated tongue from the Dravidian south. They stopped and demanded that she tell them in Common what had happened. She answered with a bullet into each man's belly before they even saw that she had a gun. Then she made sure of them with a bullet to each head as they lay on the ground.

"Can you help me clean the street?" she asked the people who were gawking.

At once they came out into the road and carried the bodies back inside the office.

When the telephoning was done, she gathered them all together at the door of the office. "When the Chinese authorities come and demand that you tell them what happened, you must tell them the truth. A man came walking down the road, an Indian man but not from this village. He looked like a woman, and you thought he must be a god, because he walked right into this office and broke the neck of the magistrate. Then he took the magistrate's pistol and shot the two guards in the office, and then the two who came running up from the village. Not one of you had time to do anything but scream. Then this stranger made you carry the bodies of the dead soldiers into the office and then ordered you to leave while he made telephone calls."

"They will ask us to describe this man."

"Then describe me. Dark. From the south of India."

"They will say, if he looked like a woman, how do you know she was not a woman?"

"Because he killed a man with his bare hands. What woman could do that?"

They laughed.

"But you must not laugh," she said. "They will be very angry. And even if you do not give them any cause, they may punish you very harshly for what happened here. They may think you are lying and torture you to try to get you to tell the truth. And let me tell you right now, you are perfectly free to tell them that you think it may have been the same person who lived in that little cave near the bridge. You may lead them to that place."

She turned to the child who had brought her Peter Wiggin's message. "Bury that paper in the ground until the war is over. It will still be there when you want it."

She spoke to them all once more. "None of you did anything except carry the bodies of the dead to the places I told you to carry them. You would have told the authorities, but the only authorities you know are dead."

She stretched out her arms. "Oh, my beloved peo-

ple, I told you I would bring terrible days to you."
She did not have to pretend to be sad, and her tears
were real as she walked among them, touching hands,
cheeks, shoulders one more time. Then she strode out
along the road and out of the village. The men who
were assigned to do it would blow up the nearby
bridge an hour from now. She would not be there.
She would be walking along paths in the woods,
heading for the command post from which she would
run this campaign of sabotage.

For it would not be enough to blow up these
bridges. They had to be ready to kill the engineers
who would come to repair them, and kill the soldiers
who would come to protect them, and then, when they
brought enough soldiers and enough engineers that
they could not be stopped from rebuilding the bridges,
they would have to cause rockfalls and mudslides to
block the narrow canyons.

If they could seal this border for three days, the
advancing Muslim armies would have time, if they
were competently led, to break through and cut off
the huge Chinese army that still faced them, so that
the reinforcements, when they finally made it through,
would be far, far too late. They, too, would be cut off
in their turn.

———

Ambul had asked for only one favor from Alai, after
setting up the meeting between him and Bean and
Petra. "Let me fight as if I were a Muslim, against
the enemy of my people."

Alai had assigned him, because of his race, to serve
among the Indonesians, where he would not look so
very different.

So it was that Ambul went ashore on a stretch of

marshy coast somewhere south of Shanghai. They went as near as they could on fishing boats, and then clambered into flatbottomed marsh skimmers, which they rowed among the reeds, searching for firm ground.

In the end, though, as they knew they would, they had to leave the boats behind and trudge through miles of mud. They carried their boots in their backpacks, because the mud would have sucked them off if they had tried to wear them.

By the time the sun came up, they were exhausted, filthy, insect-bitten, and famished.

So they rubbed the mud off their feet and ankles, pulled on their socks, put on their boots, and set off at a trot along a trace that soon became a trail, and then a path along the low dike between rice paddies. They jogged past Chinese peasants and said nothing to them.

Let them think we're conscripts or volunteers from the newly conquered south, on a training mission. We don't want to kill civilians. Get in from the coast as far as you can. That's what their officers had said to them, over and over.

Most of the peasants might have ignored them. Certainly they saw no one take off at a run to spread the alarm. But it was not yet noon when they spotted the dust plume of a fast-moving vehicle on a road not far off.

"Down," said their commander in Common.

Without hesitation they flopped down in the water and then frogged their way to the edge of the dike, where they remained hidden. Only their officer raised his head high enough to see what was happening, and his whispered commentary was passed quietly along the line so all fifty men would know.

"Military truck," he said.

Then, "Reservists. No discipline."

Ambul thought: This is a dilemma. Reservists are probably local troops. Old men, unfit men, who treated their military service like a social club, until now, when somebody trotted them out because they were the only soldiers in the area. Killing them would be like killing peasants.

But of course they were armed, so not killing them might be committing suicide.

They could hear the Chinese commander yelling at his part-time soldiers. He was very angry—and very stupid, thought Ambul. What did he think was happening here? If it was a training exercise by some portion of the Chinese army, why would he bring along a contingent of reservists? But if he thought it was a genuine threat, why was he yelling? Why wasn't he trying to reconnoiter with stealth so he could assess the danger and make a report?

Well, not every officer had been to Battle School. It wasn't second nature to them, to think like a true soldier. This fellow had undoubtedly spent most of his military service behind a desk.

The whispered command came down the line. Do not shoot anybody, but take careful aim at somebody when you are ordered to stand up.

The voice of the Chinese officer was coming nearer.

"Maybe they won't notice us," whispered the soldier beside Ambul.

"It's time to make them notice us," Ambul whispered back.

The soldier had been a waiter in a fine restaurant in Jakarta before volunteering for the army after the

Chinese conquest of Indochina. Like most of these men, he had never been under fire.

For that matter, neither have I, thought Ambul. Unless you count combat in the battle room.

Surely that did count. There was no blood, but the tension, the unbearable suspense of combat had been there. The adrenaline, the courage, the terrible disappointment when you knew you had been shot and your suit froze around you, locking you out of the battle. The sense of failure when you let down the buddy you were supposed to protect. The sense of triumph when you felt like you couldn't miss.

I've been here before. Only instead of a dike, I was hiding behind a three-meter cube, waiting for the order to fling myself out, firing at whatever enemies might be there.

The man next to him elbowed him. Like all the others, he obeyed the signal and watched their commander for the order to stand up.

The commander gave the sign, and they all rose up out of the water.

The Chinese reservists and their officer were nicely lined up along a dike that ran perpendicular to the one the Indonesian platoon had been hiding behind. Not one of them had his weapon at the ready.

The Chinese officer had been interrupted in mid-yell. He stopped and turned stupidly to look at the line of forty soldiers, all pointing their weapons at him.

Ambul's commander walked up to the officer and shot him in the head.

At once the reservists threw down their weapons and surrendered.

Every Indonesian platoon had at least one Chinese-speaker, and usually several. Ethnic Chinese in Indonesia had been eager to show their patriotism, and their best interpreter was very efficient in conveying their commander's orders. Of course it was impossible to take prisoners. But they did not want to kill these men.

So they were told to remove all their clothing and carry it to the truck they had arrived in. While they were undressing, the order was passed along the line in Indonesian: Do not laugh at them or show any sign of ridicule. Treat them with great honor and respect.

Ambul understood the wisdom of this order. The purpose of stripping them naked was to make them look ridiculous, of course. But the first people to ridicule them would be Chinese, not Indonesians. When people asked them, they would have to say that the Indonesians treated them with nothing but respect. The public relations campaign was already under way.

Half an hour later, Ambul was with the sixteen men who rode into town in the captured Chinese truck, with one naked and terrified old reservist showing them the way. Just before reaching the small military headquarters, they slowed down and pushed him out of the truck.

It was quick and bloodless. They drove right into the small compound and disarmed everyone there at the point of a gun. The Chinese soldiers were all herded naked into a room without a telephone, and they stayed there in utter silence while the sixteen Indonesians commandeered two more trucks, clean underwear and socks, and a couple of Chinese military radios.

Then they piled all the remaining ammunition and explosives, weapons and radios in the middle of the courtyard, surrounded them with the remaining military vehicles, and set a small amount of plastique in the middle of the pile with a five-minute fuse.

The Chinese interpreter ran to the door of the room where the prisoners were being held, shouted to them that they had five minutes to evacuate this place before everything blew up, and they should warn the townspeople to get away from here.

Then he unlocked the door and ran out to one of the waiting trucks.

Four minutes out of town, they heard the fireworks begin. It was like a war back there—bullets going off, explosions, and a plume of smoke.

Ambul imagined the naked soldiers running from door to door, warning people. He hoped that no one would die because they stopped to laugh at the naked men instead of obeying them.

Ambul was assigned to sit up front beside the driver of one of the captured trucks. He knew they would not have these vehicles for long—they would be too easy to spot—but they would carry them away from this place and give some of the soldiers a chance to catch a quick nap in the back of the truck.

Of course, it was also possible that they would return to the rest of the platoon to find them slaughtered, with a large contingent of Chinese veterans waiting to blow them to bits.

Well, if that happened, it would happen. Nothing he could do in this truck would affect such an outcome in any way. All he could do was keep his eyes open and help the driver stay awake.

There was no ambush. When they got back to the other men, they found most of them asleep, but all the sentries awake and watchful.

Everyone piled into the trucks. The men who had slept a little were assigned to the front seats to drive;

the men who had not slept were put in the backs of the trucks to sleep as best they could while the truck jolted along on back roads.

Ambul was one of those who discovered that if you're tired enough, you can indeed sleep sitting up on a hard bench in a truck with no springs on a rough road. You just can't sleep for very long at a time.

He woke up once to find them moving smoothly along a well-paved road. He stayed awake just long enough to think, Is our commander an idiot, using a highway like this? But he didn't care enough about it to stay awake.

The trucks stopped after only three hours of driving. Everyone was still exhausted, but they had much to do before they could get a real meal, and genuine sleep. The commander had called a halt beside a bridge. He had the men unload everything from the trucks. Then they pushed them off the bridge into the stream.

Ambul thought: That was a foolish mistake. They should have left them neatly parked, and not together, so that air surveillance would not recognize them.

But no, speed was more important than concealment. Besides, the Chinese air force was otherwise engaged. Ambul doubted there'd be many planes available for surveillance any time soon.

While the noncoms were distributing captured supplies among the men, they were told some of what their commander had learned from listening to the captured radios during the drive. The enemy kept speaking of them as paratroopers and assumed they were heading for a major military objective or some rendezvous point. "They don't know who we are or what we're doing, and they're looking for us in all the wrong places," said the commander. "That won't last long, but it's the reason we weren't blown while we were driving along. Plus, they think we're at least a thousand men."

They had made good progress inland, those hours on the road. The terrain was almost hilly here, and despite the fact that every arable inch of China had been under cultivation for millennia, there was some fairly wild country here. They might actually get far enough from this road before night that they could get a decent sleep before taking off again.

Of course, they would do most of their movement by night, most of their sleeping by day.

If they lived through the night. If they survived another day.

Carrying more now than they had when they first came ashore the previous night, they staggered off the road and into the woods alongside the stream. Heading west. Upstream. Inland.

FAREWELLS

To: Porto%Aberto@BatePapo.Org
From: Locke%erasmus@polnet.gov
Re: Ripe

Encryption seed: * * * * * * * * *
Decryption key: * * * * * * * * * * * * * * * *

Is this Bean or Petra? Or both?

After all his subtle strategies and big surprises, it was a petty murder attempt that tagged him. I don't know if the news of the shooting down of an IF shuttle even penetrated the war coverage where you are, but he thought I was aboard. I wasn't, but the Chinese named him as the smoke, and suddenly the IF has legal basis for an Earthside operation. The Brazilian government is cooperating, has the compound on lockdown.

The only trouble is, the compound seems to be defended by your little army. We want to do this without loss of life, but you trained your soldiers very well, and Suri doesn't respond to my feeble attempts to contact him. Before I left, he seemed to be in Achilles's pocket. That might have been protective coloration, but who knows what happened on that return trip from China?

Achilles has a way of getting to people. An Indian officer at MinCol who had known Graff for years was the one who fingered me for the shuttle, because the fact that his family was in a camp in China was used to control him. Does Achilles have a way to control Suri? If Suri commands the soldiers to protect Achilles, will they?

Would it make a difference if you were there? I will be there, but I'm afraid I never quite trusted your assurance that the soldiers would absolutely obey me. I have a feeling that I lost face when I fled the compound. But you know them, I don't.

Your advice would be appreciated. Your presence would be very helpful. I will understand if you choose to provide neither. You owe nothing to me—you were right when I was wrong, and I jeopardized everybody. But at this point, I'd like to do this without killing any of your soldiers, and especially without being killed myself—I wouldn't want to pretend my motives are entirely altruistic. I have no choice but to be there myself. If I'm not on the ground for the penetration of the compound, I can kiss my future as Hegemon good-bye.

Meanwhile, the Chinese don't seem to be doing so well, do they? My congratulations to the Caliph. I hope he will be more generous to his conquered foes than the Chinese were.

Petra found it hard to concentrate on her search of the nets. It was too tempting to switch to the news stories about the war. It was the genetic disease that the doctors had found in her as a child, the disease that sent her into space to spend her formative years in Battle School. She just couldn't leave war alone. Appalling as it was, combat still held irresistible allure. The contest of two armies, each striving for mastery, with no rules except those forced on them by the limitations of their forces and their fear of reprisal in kind.

Bean had insisted that they search for some signal from Achilles. It seemed absurd to her, but Bean was positive that Achilles wanted them to come to him.

"He's on his last legs," said Bean. "Everything's turned against him. He thought he'd positioned himself to take my place. Then he reached too far in shooting down that shuttle, just at the moment that the Crescent League pulled China out from under him. He can't go back there, can't even leave Ribeirão. So he's going to make whatever plays he has left to make. We're loose ends. He doesn't want to leave us dangling. So . . . he's going to call us in."

"Let's not go," Petra had said then, but Bean only laughed. "If I thought you meant that," he said, "I might consider it. But I know you don't. He has our babies. He knows we'll come."

Maybe they would and maybe they wouldn't. What good would it do those embryos if their parents walked into a trap and died?

And it would be a trap. Not a fair trade, not a bargain, my freedom for your babies. No, Achilles was not capable of that, not even to save his own life. Bean had trapped him once before, forced a confession out of him, which led to his being put in a mental institution. He'd never go back there again. Like Napoleon, he'd escaped from one captivity, but from the next there'd be no more escaping. So he wouldn't go. That much both Bean and Petra agreed on. He would only summon them to kill them.

Yet still she searched, wondering how they'd even know when they found what they were looking for.

And while she searched, the war kept drawing her. The campaign in Xinjiang had already moved eastward into the fringes of Han China. The Persians and Pakistanis were on the verge of encircling both halves of the Chinese army in western India.

The news about the Indonesians and Arabs operating inside China was a little more oblique. The Chinese were complaining loudly about Muslim paratroopers performing terrorist attacks inside China, and threatening that they would be treated as spies and war criminals when they were caught. The caliph responded immediately by declaring that these were regular troops, in uniform, and the only thing that bothered the Chinese was that the war they had been so willing to inflict on others had finally come home. "We will hold every level of the Chinese military and the Chinese government personally and individually responsible for each crime against our captured soldiers."

That was the language that only the presumed victors could afford to use, but the Chinese clearly took it to heart, immediately announcing that they had been completely misunderstood, and any soldiers found to be in uniform would be treated as prisoners.

To Petra, though, the most entertaining aspect of the Chinese posturing was that they kept referring to the Indonesian and Arab troops as paratroopers. They simply could not believe that troops landed on the coasts had got so far inland so quickly.

And one other little bit of information. One of the

American newsnets had a commentary by a retired general who almost certainly was being given briefings about what American spy satellites were showing. What caught Petra's attention was when he said, "What I can't understand is why the Chinese troops that were moved out of India a few days ago, to meet the threat in Xinjiang, are not being used in Xinjiang or being sent back into India. Fully a quarter of the Chinese military is just sitting there not being used."

Petra showed this to Bean, who smiled. "Virlomi is very good. She's pinned them down for three days. How long before the Chinese army inside India simply runs out of ammunition?"

"You can't really start a betting pool with just the two of us," said Petra.

"Stop watching the war and get back to work."

"Why wait for Achilles to send this signal that I still don't think he's going to send?" asked Petra. "Why not just accept Peter's invitation and join him for the storming of the compound?

"Because if Achilles thinks he's luring us into a trap, he'll let us get inside without firing a shot. Nobody dies."

"Except us."

"First, Petra, there's no us. You're a pregnant woman, and I don't care how brilliant you are at military affairs, I can't possibly deal with Achilles if the woman who's carrying my baby is standing there in jeopardy."

"So I'm supposed to sit outside watching, not knowing what's going on, whether you're alive or dead?"

"Do we have to have the argument about how I'm going to die in a few years anyway, and you're not, and if I'm dead but we rescue the embryos you can still have babies, but if you're dead, we can't even have the baby you've already got inside you?"

"No, we don't have to have that argument," said Petra angrily.

"And second, you won't be sitting outside watching, because you'll be here in Damascus, following the war news and reading the Q'uran."

"Or clawing my own eyes out in the agony of not knowing. You'd really leave me here?"

"Achilles himself may be trapped inside the Hegemony compound, but he has people to run his errands everywhere. I doubt that many of them were lost when the China connection dried up. *If* it dried up. I don't want you leaving here because it would be just like Achilles to kill you long before you came anywhere near the compound."

"So why don't you think he'll kill *you?*"

"Because he wants me to watch the babies die."

Petra couldn't help it. She burst into tears and bowed over her desk.

"I'm sorry," said Bean. "I didn't mean to make you—"

"Of course you didn't mean to make me cry," said Petra. "I didn't mean to cry, either. Just ignore this."

"I can't ignore it," said Bean. "I can barely understand what you're saying, and you're about to drip snot on your desk."

"It's not snot!" Petra shouted at him, then touched her nose and discovered that it was. She sniffed and then laughed and ran into the bathroom and blew her nose and finished crying by herself.

When she came out, Bean was lying on the bed, his eyes closed.

"I'm sorry," said Petra.

"I'm sorrier," said Bean softly.

"I know you have to go alone. I know I have to stay here. I know all of that, but I hate it, that's all."

Bean nodded.

"So why aren't you searching the nets?"

"Because the message just came."

She walked over to his desk and looked into the display. Bean had connected to an auction site, and there it was:

Wanted: A good womb.

Five human embryos ready for implantation. Battle-School-graduate parents, died in tragic accident. Estate needs to dispose of them immediately. Likely to be extraordinarily brilliant children. Trust fund will be set up for each child successfully implanted and brought to term. Applicants must prove they do not need the money. Top five bidders will have their funds held in escrow by certified accounting firm, pending evaluation.

"Did you reply?" asked Petra. "Or bid?"

"I sent an inquiry in which I suggested that I'd like to have all five, and I'll pick them up in person. I told him to reply to one of my dead drop sites."

"And you're not checking your mail to see if your dead drop has forwarded anything yet?"

"Petra, I'm scared."

"That's a relief. It suggests you aren't insane."

"He's the best survivor I've ever known. He'll have a way out of this."

"No," said Petra. "You're a survivor. He's a killer."

"He's not dead," said Bean. "That makes him a survivor."

"Nobody's been trying to kill him for half his life," said Petra. "His survival is no big deal. You've had a pathological killer on your trail for years, and yet here you are."

"It's not so much that I'm afraid of him killing me," said Bean, "though I don't find it an appealing way to go. I still plan to die by growing so tall I'm hit by a low-flying plane."

"I'm not playing your macabre little how-I'd-like-to-die game."

"But if he does kill me, and then gets out of there alive somehow, what will happen to you?"

"He won't get out of there alive."

"So maybe not. But what if I'm dead, and all the babies are dead?"

"I'll have this one."

"You'll wish you hadn't loved me. I still haven't figured out why you do."

"I'll never wish I hadn't loved you, and I'll always be glad that after I pestered you long enough, you finally decided you loved me too."

"Don't let anybody call the kid by some stupid nickname based on how small she is."

"No legume names?"

The incoming-mail icon flashed on his desk.

"You've got mail," said Petra.

Bean sighed, sat up, slid over onto the chair, and opened the letter.

My oldest friend. I have five little presents with your name written all over them, and not much time left in which to give them to you. I wish you trusted me more, because I've never meant you any harm, but I know you don't, and so you are free to bring an armed escort with you. We'll meet in the open air, the east garden. The east gate will be open. You and the first five with you can come in; any more than that try to come in and you'll all be shot.

I don't know where you are, so I don't know how long it will take for you to get here. When you come, I'll have your property in a refrigerated container, good for six hours at the right temperature. If one of your escort is a specialist with a microscope, you are free to examine the specimens on the spot, and then have the specialist carry them out.

But I hope you and I can chat for a while about old times. Reminisce about the good old days, when we brought civilization to the streets of Rotterdam. We've been down a good long road since then. Changed the world, both of us. Me more than you, kid. Eat your heart out.

Of course, you married the only woman I ever loved, so maybe things balance out in the end.

Naturally, our conversation will be more pleasant if it ends with you taking me out of the compound and giving me safe passage to a place of my own choosing. But I realize that may not be within your power. We really are limited creatures, we geniuses. We know what's best for everybody, but we still don't get our way until we can persuade the lesser creatures to do our bidding. They just don't understand how much happier they'd be if they stopped thinking for themselves. They're so unequipped for it.

Relax, Bean. That was a joke. Or an indecorous truth. Often the same thing.

Give Petra a kiss for me. Let me know when to open the gate.

"Does he really expect you to believe that he'll just let you take the babies?"

"Well, he does imply a swap for his freedom," said Bean.

"The only swap he implies is your life for theirs," said Petra.

"Oh," said Bean. "Is that how you read it?"

"That's what he's saying and you know it. He expects the two of you to die together, right there."

"The real question," said Bean, "is whether he'll really have the embryos there."

"For all we know," said Petra, "they're in a lab in Moscow or Johannesburg or already in the garbage somewhere in Ribeirão."

"Now who's the grim one?"

"It's obvious that he wasn't able to place them out for implantation. So to him they represent failure. They have no value now. Why should he give them to you?"

"I didn't say I'd accept his terms," said Bean.

"But you will."

"The hardest thing about a kidnapping is always the swap, ransom for hostage. Somebody always has to trust somebody, and give up their piece before they've received what the other one has. But this case is really weird, because he's not really asking for anything from me."

"Except your death."

"But he knows I'm dying anyway. It all seems so pointless."

"He's insane, Julian. Haven't you heard?"

"Yes, but his thinking makes sense inside his own head. I mean, he's not schizophrenic, he sees the same reality as the rest of us. He's not delusional. He's just pathologically conscience-free. So how does he see this playing out? Will he just shoot me as I come in? Or will he let me win, maybe even let me kill him, only the joke's on me because the embryos he gives me aren't ours, they're from the tragic mating of two really dumb people. Perhaps two journalists."

"You're joking about this, Bean, and I—"

"I have to catch the next flight. If you think of anything else that I should know, email me, I'll check in at least once before I go in and see the lad."

"He doesn't have them," said Petra. "He already gave them out to his cronies."

"Quite possible."

"Don't go."

"Not possible."

"Bean, you're smarter than he is, but his advantage is, he's more brutal than you are."

"Don't count on it," said Bean.

"Don't you realize that I know both of you better than anyone else in the world?"

"And no matter how well we think we know people, the fact is we're all strangers in the end."

"Oh, Bean, tell me you don't believe that."

"It's self-evident truth."

"I know you!" she insisted.

"No. You don't. But that's all right, because I don't really know me either, let alone you. We never understand anybody, not even ourselves. But Petra, shh, listen. What we've done is, we've created something else. This marriage. It consists of the two of us, and we've become something else together. That's what we know. Not me, not you, but what we are, *who* we are together. Sister Carlotta quoted somebody in the Bible about how a man and a woman marry and they become one flesh. Very mystical and borderline weird. But in a way it's true. And when I die, you won't have Bean, but you'll still have Petra-with-Bean, Bean-with-Petra, whatever we call this new creature that we've made."

"So all those months I spent with Achilles, did we build some disgusting monstrous Petra-with-Achilles thing? Is that what you're saying?"

"No," said Bean. "Achilles doesn't build things. He just finds them, admires them, and tears them apart. There is no Achilles-with-anybody. He's just . . . empty."

"So what happened to that theory of Ender's, that you have to know your enemy in order to beat him?"

"Still true."

"But if you can't know anybody . . ."

"It's imaginary," said Bean. "Ender wasn't crazy, so he knew it was just imaginary. You try to see the world through your enemy's eyes, so you can see what it all means to him. The better you do at it, the more time you spend in the world as he sees it, the more you understand how he views things, how he explains to himself the things he does."

"And you've done that with Achilles."

"Yes."

"So you think you know what he's going to do."

"I have a short list of things I expect."

"And what if you're wrong? Because that's the one certainty in all of this—that whatever you think Achilles is going to do, you're wrong."

"That's his specialty."

"So your short list . . ."

"Well, see, the way I made my list, I thought of all the things I thought he might do, and then I didn't put any of those on my list, I only put on the things I didn't think he'd do."

"That'll work," said Petra.

"Might," said Bean.

"Hold me before you go," she said.

He did.

"Petra, you think you aren't going to see me again. But I'm pretty sure you are."

"Do you realize how it scares me that you're only *pretty* sure?"

"I could die of appendicitis in the plane on the way to Ribeirão. I'm never more than pretty sure of anything."

"Except that I love you."

"Except that we love each other."

———

Bean's flight was the normal misery of hours in a confined space. But at least he was flying west, so the jet lag wasn't as debilitating. He thought he might just go directly in as soon as he arrived, but thought better of it. He needed to think clearly. To be able to improvise and act quickly on impulse. He needed to sleep.

Peter was waiting for him at the doorway of the airplane. Being Hegemon gives you a few privileges denied to other people in airports.

Peter led him down the stairs instead of out the jetway, and they got in a car that drove them directly to the hotel that had been set up as the IF command post. IF soldiers were at every entrance, and Peter assured him there were sharpshooters in every surrounding building, and in this one, too.

"So," said Peter, when they were alone in Bean's room, "what's the plan?"

"You sound as if you think I have one," said Bean.

"Not even a goal?"

"Oh, I have two goals," said Bean. "I promised

Petra right after he stole our embryos that I'd get them back for her, and that I'd kill Achilles in the process."

"And you have no idea how you'll do that."

"Some. But nothing I plan will work anyway, so I don't let myself get too attached to any of them."

"Achilles really isn't that important now," said Peter. "I mean, he's important because in essence everyone inside that compound is his hostage, but on the world stage—he's lost all his influence. Went up in smoke when he shot down that shuttle and the Chinese disavowed him."

Bean shook his head. "Do you really think, if he gets out of this alive, he won't be back at his old games? You think he won't have any takers for his medicine show?"

"I suppose there's no shortage of government people with dreams of power he can seduce them with, or fears that he can exploit."

"Peter, I'm here so he can torment me and then kill me. That's why I'm here. *His* purpose. *His* goal."

"Well, if his is the only plan, then . . ."

"That's right, Peter. *He's* the one with the plan this time. And I'm the one who can surprise him by not doing what he expects."

"All right," said Peter. "I'm in."

"What?"

"You've convinced me. I'm in."

"You're in what?"

"I'm going in the gate with you."

"No you're not."

"I'm Hegemon. I'm not standing outside while you go in and save my people."

"He'll be very happy to kill you along with me."

"You first."

"No, *you* first."

"Whatever," said Peter. "You're not getting through that gate unless I'm one of your five."

"Look, Peter," said Bean. "The reason we're in this predicament is that you think you're smarter than everybody else, so no matter what advice you get, you go off half-cocked and do something astonishingly dumb."

"But I stay around to pick up the pieces."

"I give you credit for that."

"I won't do anything you don't tell me to," said Peter. "It's your show."

"I need to have all five of my escort be highly trained soldiers."

"No you don't," said Peter. "Because if there's any shooting, five won't be enough anyway. So you have to count on there being no shooting. So I might as well be one of the five."

"But I don't want to die with you beside me," said Bean.

"Fine with me, I don't want to die beside you, either."

"You have another seventy or eighty years ahead of you. You're going to gamble with that? Me, I'm just playing with house money."

"You're the best, Bean," said Peter.

"That was in school. What armies have I commanded since then? Other people are doing all the fighting now. I'm not the best, I'm retired."

"You don't retire from your own mind."

"People retire from their minds all the time. What won't let you alone is your reputation."

"Well, I love arguing philosophy with you," said Peter abruptly, "but you need your sleep and I need mine. See you at the east gate in the morning."

In a moment he was out the door.

So what was that sudden departure about?

Bean had the sneaking suspicion that maybe Peter finally believed him that he didn't have a plan and had no guarantee of winning. Not even, in fact, a decent chance of winning, if by winning he meant an outcome in which Bean was alive, Achilles was dead, and Bean had the babies. No doubt Peter had to run and get a life insurance policy. Or drum up some last minute emergency that would absolutely prevent him from going through the gate with Bean after all. "So sorry, I *wish* I were going with you, but you'll do fine, I know it."

Bean thought he'd have trouble getting to sleep, what with the catnaps he got on the plane and the tension of tomorrow's events preying on his mind.

So naturally he fell asleep so fast he didn't even remember turning off the light.

———

In the morning, Bean got up and posted a message to Achilles, naming a time about an hour later for their meeting. Then he wrote a brief note to Petra, just so she'd know he was thinking of her in case this was the last day of his life. Then another note to his parents, and one to Nikolai. At least if he managed to bring Achilles down with him, they'd be safe. That was something.

He walked downstairs to find Peter already waiting beside the IF car that would take them to the perimeter that had been established around the compound. They rode in near silence, because there was really nothing more to say.

At the perimeter, near the east gate, Bean found out very quickly that Peter hadn't lied—the IF was standing behind his determination to go in with

Bean's group. Well, that was fine. Bean didn't really need his companions to do much.

As he had requested before leaving Damascus, the IF had a uniformed doctor, two highly trained sharp-shooters, and a fully equipped hazard squad, one of whom was to come in with Bean's party.

"Achilles will have a container that purports to be a transport refrigerator for a half dozen frozen embryos," Bean said to the hazardist. "If I have you carry it outside, then that means I'm sure it's a bomb or contains some toxin, and I want it treated that way—even if I say something different inside there. If it turns out to have been embryos after all, well, that's my own mistake, and I'll explain it to my wife. If I have the doctor here carry it, that means I'm sure it's the embryos, and the package is to be treated that way."

"And what if you're not sure?" asked Peter.

"I'll be sure," said Bean, "or I won't give it to anybody."

"Why don't you just carry it yourself?" asked the hazardist, "and tell us what to do when it gets out-side?"

Peter answered for him. "Mr. Delphiki doesn't ex-pect to get back out alive."

"My goal for all four of you," said Bean, "is for you to walk out of there uninjured. There's no chance of that if you start shooting, for any reason. That's why none of you is going to carry a loaded weapon."

They looked at him as if he were insane.

"I'm not going in there unarmed," said one of the other men.

"Fine," said Bean. "Then there'll be one less. He didn't say I had to bring five."

"Technically," said Peter to the other sharpshooter,

"you won't be unarmed. Just unloaded. So they'll treat you as if you *did* have bullets, because they won't know you don't."

"I'm a soldier, not a sap," said the man, and he walked away.

"Anybody else?" said Bean.

In answer, the other sharpshooter took the full clip out of his weapon, popped out the bullets one by one, and then ejected the first bullet from the chamber.

"I don't carry a weapon anyway," said the doctor.

"Don't need a loaded pistol to carry a bomb," said the hazardist.

With a slim plastic .22-caliber pistol already tucked into the back of his pants, Bean was now the only person in his party with a loaded gun.

"I guess we're ready to go," said Bean.

———

It was a dazzling tropical morning as they stepped through the gate into the east garden. Birds in all the trees ranted their calls as if they were trying to memorize something and just couldn't get it to stick. There was not a soul in sight.

Bean wasn't going to wander around searching for Achilles. He definitely wasn't going to get far from the gate. So, about ten paces in, he stopped. So did the others.

And they waited.

It didn't take long. A soldier in the Hegemony uniform stepped out into the open. Then another, and another, until the fifth soldier appeared.

Suriyawong.

He gave no sign of recognition. Rather he looked right past both Bean and Peter as if they were nothing to him.

Achilles stepped out behind them—but stayed close to the trees, so he wouldn't be too easy a target for sharpshooters. He was carrying, as promised, a small transport fridge.

"Bean," he said with a smile. "My how you've grown."

Bean said nothing.

"Oh, we aren't in a jesting mood," he said. "I'm not either, really. It's almost a sentimental moment for me, to see you again. To see you as a man. Considering I knew you when you were this high."

He held out the transport fridge. "Here they are, Bean."

"You're just going to give them to me?"

"I don't really have a use for them. There weren't any takers in the auction."

"Volescu went to a lot of trouble to get these for you," said Bean.

"What trouble? He bribed a guard. Using my money."

"How did you get Volescu to help you, anyway?" asked Bean.

"He owed me," said Achilles. "I'm the one who got him out of jail. I got our brilliant Hegemon here to give me authority to authorize the release of prisoners whose crimes had ceased to be crimes. He didn't make the connection that I'd be releasing your creator into the wild." Achilles grinned at Peter.

Peter said nothing.

"You trained these men well, Bean," said Achilles. "Being with them is like . . . well, it's like being with my family again. Like on the streets, you know?"

Bean said nothing.

"Well, all right, you don't want to chat, so take the embryos."

Bean remembered one very important fact. Achilles didn't care about killing his victims with his own hands. It was enough for him that they die, whether he was present or not.

Bean turned to the hazardist. "Would you do me a favor and take this just outside the gate? I want to stay and talk with Achilles for a couple of minutes."

The hazardist walked up to Achilles and took the transport fridge from him. "Is it fragile?" he asked.

Achilles answered, "It's very securely packed and padded, but don't play football with it."

In only a few steps, he was out the gate.

"So what did you want to talk about?" asked Achilles.

"A couple of little questions I'm curious about."

"I'll listen. Maybe I'll answer."

"Back in Hyderabad. There was a Chinese officer who knocked you unconscious to break our stalemate."

"Oh, is that who did it?"

"Whatever happened to him?"

"I'm not sure. I think his chopper was shot down in combat only a few days later."

"Oh," said Bean. "Too bad. I wanted to ask him what it felt like to hit you."

"Really, Bean, aren't we both too old for that sort of gibe?"

Outside the gate there was a muffled explosion.

Achilles looked around, startled. "What was that?"

"I'm pretty sure," said Bean, "that it was an explosion."

"Of what?"

"Of the bomb you just tried to give me," said Bean. "Inside a containment chamber."

Achilles tried, for a moment, to look innocent. "I don't know what you . . ."

Then he apparently realized there was no point in feigning ignorance when the thing had just exploded. He pulled the remote detonator out of his pocket, pressed the button a couple of times. "Damn all this modern technology, nothing ever works right." He grinned at Bean. "Got to give me credit for trying."

"So . . . do you have the embryos or not?" asked Bean.

"They're inside, safe," said Achilles.

Bean knew that was a lie. In fact, he had decided yesterday that it was most likely the embryos had never been brought here at all.

But he'd get more mileage out of this by pretending to believe Achilles. And there was always the chance that it wasn't a lie.

"Show me," Bean said.

"You have to come inside, then," said Achilles.

"OK."

"That'll take us outside the range of the sharp-shooters you no doubt have all around the compound, waiting to shoot me down."

"And inside the range of whoever you have waiting for me there."

"Bean. Be realistic. You're dead whenever I want you dead."

"Well, that's not strictly true," said Bean. "You've wanted me dead a lot more often than I've died."

Achilles grinned. "Do you know what Poke was saying just before she had that accident and fell into the Rhine?"

Bean said nothing.

"She was saying that I shouldn't hold a grudge against you for telling her to kill me when we first met. He's just a little kid, she said. He didn't know what he was saying."

Still, Bean said nothing.

"I wish I could tell you Sister Carlotta's last words, but . . . you know how collateral damage is in wartime. You just don't get any warning."

"The embryos," said Bean. "You said you were going to show me where they are."

"All right then," said Achilles. "Follow me."

As soon as Achilles's back was turned, the doctor looked at Bean and frantically shook his head.

"It's all right," Bean told the doctor and the other soldier. "You can go on out. You won't be needed any more."

Achilles turned back around. "You're letting your escort go?"

"Except for Peter," said Bean. "He insists on staying with me."

"I didn't hear him say that," said Achilles. "I mean, he seemed so eager to get away when he left this place, I thought for sure he didn't want to see it again."

"I'm trying to figure out how you were able to fool so many people," said Peter.

"But I'm not trying to fool you," said Achilles. "Though I can see how someone like you would long to find a really masterful liar to study with." Laughing, Achilles turned his back again, and led the way toward the main office building.

Peter came closer to Bean as they followed him inside. "Are you sure you know what you're doing?" he asked quietly.

"I told you before, I have no idea."

Once inside, they were indeed confronted by another dozen soldiers. Bean knew them all by name.

But he said nothing to them, and none of them met his gaze or showed any sign that they knew him.

What does Achilles want? thought Bean. His first plan was to send me out of the compound with a remote-controlled bomb, so it's not as if he planned to keep me alive. Now he's got me surrounded by soldiers, and doesn't tell them to shoot.

Achilles turned around and faced him. "Bean," he said. "I can't believe you didn't make some kind of arrangement for me to get out of here."

"Is that why you tried to blow me up?" asked Bean.

"That was when I believed you'd try to kill me as soon as you thought you had the embryos. Why didn't you?"

"Because I knew I didn't have the embryos."

"Do you and Petra already think of them as your children? Have you named them yet?"

"There's no arrangement to get you out of here, Achilles, because there's no place for you to go. The only people that still had any use for you are busy getting their butts kicked by a bunch of pissed-off Muslims. You saw to it that you couldn't go anywhere in space when you shot down that shuttle."

"In all fairness, Bean, you have to remember that nobody was supposed to know it was me who did it. But someone really should tell me—why wasn't Peter on that shuttle? I suppose somebody caught my informant." He looked back and forth from Peter to Bean, looking for an answer.

Bean did not confirm or deny. Peter, too, kept his silence. What if Achilles lived through this somehow? Why bring down Achilles's wrath on a man who already had enough trouble in his life?

"But if you caught my informant," said Achilles, "why in the world would Chamrajnagar—or Graff, if it was him—launch the shuttle anyway? Was catching me doing something naughty so important they'd risk a shuttle and its crew just to catch me? I find that quite . . . flattering. Sort of like winning the Nobel Prize for scariest villain."

"I think," said Bean, "that you don't have the embryos at all. I think you dispersed them as soon as you got them. I think you already had them implanted in surrogates."

"Wrong," said Achilles. He reached inside his pants pocket and took out a small container. Exactly like the ones in which the embryos had been frozen. "I brought one along, just to show you. Of course, he's probably thawed quite a bit. My body heat and all that. What do you think? Do we still have time to get this little sucker implanted in somebody? Petra's already pregnant, I hear, so you can't use her. I know! Peter's mother! She always likes to be so helpful, and she's used to giving birth to geniuses. Here, Peter, catch!"

He tossed the container toward Peter, but too hard, so it sailed over Peter's upstretched hands and hit the floor. It didn't break, but instead rolled and rolled.

"Aren't you going to get it?" Achilles asked Bean.

Bean shrugged. He walked over to where the container had come to rest. The liquid inside it sloshed. Fully thawed.

He stepped on it, broke it, ground it under his foot.

Achilles whistled. "Wow. You are some disciplinarian. Your kids can't get away with *anything* with you."

Bean walked toward Achilles.

"Now, Bean, I can see how you might be irritated at me, but I never claimed to be an athlete. When did I have a chance to play ball, will you tell me that?

You grew up where I did. I can't help it that I don't know how to throw accurately."

He was still affecting his ironic tone of voice, but Bean could see that Achilles was afraid now. He had been expecting Bean to beg, or grieve—something that would keep him off balance and give control to Achilles. But Bean was seeing things through Achilles's eyes now, and he understood: You do whatever your enemy can't believe that you would even think of doing. You just do it.

Bean reached into the butt holster that rode inside his pants, hanging from the waistband, and pulled out the flat .22-caliber pistol concealed there. He pointed it at Achilles's right eye, then the left.

Achilles took a couple of steps backward. "You can't kill me," he said. "You don't know where the embryos are."

"I know you don't have them," said Bean, "and that I'm not going to get them without letting you go. And I'm not letting you go. So I guess that means the embryos are forever lost to me. Why should you go on living?"

"Suri," said Achilles. "Are you asleep?"

Suriyawong pulled his long knife from its sheath.

"That's not what's needed here," said Achilles. "He has a gun."

"Hold still, Achilles," said Bean. "Take it like a man. Besides, if I miss, you might live through it and spend the rest of your days as a brain-damaged shell of a man. We want this to be nice and clean and final, don't we?"

Achilles pulled another vial out of his pockets. "This is the real thing, Bean." He reached out his hand, offering it. "You killed one, but there are still the other four."

Bean slapped it out of his hand. This one broke when it hit the floor.

"Those are your children you're killing!" cried Achilles.

"I know you," said Bean. "I know that you would never promise me something you could actually deliver."

"Suriyawong!" shouted Achilles. "Shoot him!"

"Sir," said Suriyawong.

It was the first sound he'd made since Bean came through the east gate.

Suriyawong knelt down, laid his knife on the smooth floor, and slid it toward Achilles until it rested at his feet.

"What's this supposed to be?" demanded Achilles.

"The loan of a knife," said Suriyawong.

"But he has a gun!" cried Achilles.

"I expect you to solve your own problems," said Suriyawong, "without getting any of my men killed."

"Shoot him!" cried Achilles. "I thought you were my friend."

"I told you from the start," said Suriyawong. "I serve the Hegemon." And with that, Suriyawong turned his back on Achilles.

So did all the other soldiers.

Now Bean understood why Suriyawong had worked so hard to earn Achilles's trust: so that at this moment of crisis, Suri was in a position to betray him.

Achilles laughed nervously. "Come on now, Bean. We've known each other a long time." He had backed up against a wall. He tried to lean against it. But his legs were a little wobbly and he started to slide down the wall. "I know you, Bean," he said. "You can't just kill a man in cold blood, no matter how much you hate him. It's not in you to do that."

"Yes it is," said Bean.

He aimed the pistol down at Achilles's right eye and pulled the trigger. The eye snapped shut from the wind of the bullet passing between the eyelids and from the obliteration of the eye itself. His head rocked just a little from the force of the little bullet entering, but not leaving.

Then he slumped over and sprawled out on the floor. Dead.

It didn't bring back Poke, or Sister Carlotta, or any of the other people he had killed. It didn't change the nations of the world back to the way they were before Achilles started making them his building blocks, to break apart and put together however he wanted. It didn't end the wars Achilles had started. It didn't make Bean feel any better. There was no joy in vengeance, and precious little in justice, either.

But there was this: Achilles would never kill again.

That was all Bean could ask of a little .22.

20

HOME

From: YourFresh%Vegetable@Freebie.net
To: MyStone%Maiden@Freebie.net
Re: Come home

He's dead..

I'm not.

He didn't have them.

We'll find them, one way or another, before I die.

Come home. There's nobody trying to kill you any more.

Petra flew on a commercial jet, in a reserved seat, under her own name, using her own passport.

Damascus was full of excitement, for it was now the capital of a Muslim world united for the first time in nearly two thousand years. Sunni and Shi'ite leaders alike had been declaring for the Caliph. And Damascus was the center of it all.

But her excitement was of a different kind. It was

partly the baby that was maturing inside her, and the changes already happening to her body. It was partly the relief at being free of the death sentence Achilles had passed on her so long ago.

Mostly, though, it was that giddy sense of having been on the edge of losing everything, and winning after all. It swept over her as she was walking down the aisle of the plane, and her knees went rubbery under her and she almost fell.

The man behind her took her elbow and helped her regain her legs. "Are you all right?" he asked.

"I'm just a little bit pregnant," she said.

"You must get over this business of falling down before the baby gets too big."

She laughed and thanked him, then put her own bag in the overhead—without needing help, thank you—and took her seat.

On the one hand, it was sad flying without her husband beside her.

On the other hand, it was wonderful to be flying home to him.

———

He met her at the airport and gathered her into a huge hug. His arms were so long. Had they grown in the few days since he left her?

She refused to think about that.

"I hear you saved the world," she said to him when the embrace finally ended.

"Don't believe those rumors."

"My hero," she said.

"I'd rather be your lover," he whispered.

"My giant," she whispered back.

In answer, he embraced her again, and then leaned

back, lifting her off her feet. She laughed as he whirled her around like a child.

The way her father had done when she was little.

The way he would never do with their children.

"Why are you crying?" he asked her.

"It's just tears in my eyes," she said. "It's not *crying*. You've *seen* crying, and this isn't it. These are happy-to-see-you tears."

"You're just happy to be in a place where trees grow without waiting around to be planted and irrigated."

They walked out of the airport a few minutes later and he was right, she *was* happy to be out of the desert. In the years they had lived in Ribeirão she had discovered an affinity for lush places. She needed the Earth to be alive around her, everything green, all that photosynthesis going on in public, without a speck of modesty. Things that ate sunlight and drank rain. "It's good to be home," she said.

"Now I'm home, too," said Bean.

"You were here already," she said.

"But you weren't, till now."

She sighed and clung to him a little.

They took the first cab.

———

They went to the Hegemony compound, of course, but instead of going to their house—if, indeed, it *was* their house, since they had given it up when they resigned from the Hegemon's service that day back in the Philippines—Bean took her right to the Hegemon's office.

Peter was waiting there for her, along with Graff and the Wiggins. There were hugs that became kisses and handshakes that became hugs.

Peter told all about what happened up in space. Then they made Petra tell about Damascus, though she protested that it was nothing at all, just a city happy with victory.

"The war's not over yet," said Peter.

"They're full of Muslim unity," said Petra.

"Next thing you know," said Graff, "the Christians and Jews will get back together. The only thing standing between them, after all, is that business with Jesus."

"It's a good thing," said Theresa, "to have a little less division in the world."

"I think it's going to take a lot of divisions," said John Paul, "to bring about less division."

"I told you they were happy in Damascus, not that I thought they were right to be," said Petra. "There are signs of trouble ahead. There's an imam preaching that India and Pakistan should be reunited under a single government again."

"Let me guess," said Peter. "A Muslim one."

"If they liked what Virlomi did to the Chinese," said Bean, "they'll love what she can get the Hindus to do to get free of the Pakistanis."

"And Peter will love this one," said Petra. "An Iraqi politician made a speech in Baghdad in which he very pointedly said, 'In a world where Allah has chosen a Caliph, why do we need a Hegemon?' "

They laughed, but their faces were serious when the laughing stopped.

"Maybe he's right," said Peter. "Maybe when this war is over, the Caliph will *be* the Hegemon, in fact if not in name. Is that a bad thing? The goal was to unite the world in peace. I volunteered to do it, but if somebody else gets it done, I'm not going to get anybody killed just to take the job away from him."

Theresa took hold of his wrist, and Graff chuckled. "Keep talking like that, and I'll understand why I've been supporting you all these years."

"The Caliph is not going to replace the Hegemon," said Bean, "or erase the need for one."

"No?" asked Peter.

"Because a leader can't take his people to a place where they don't want to go."

"But they want him to rule the world," said Petra.

"But to rule the world, he has to keep the whole world content with his rule," said Bean. "And how can he keep non-Muslims content without making orthodox Muslims extremely discontented? It's what the Chinese found in India. You can't swallow a nation. It finds a way to get itself vomited out. Begging your pardon, Petra."

"So your friend Alai will realize this, and not try to rule over non-Muslim people?" asked Theresa.

"Our friend Alai would have no problem with that idea," said Petra. "The question is whether the Caliph will."

"I hope we won't remember this day," said Graff, "as the time when we first started fighting the next war."

Peter spoke up. "As I said before, this war's not over yet."

"Both of the frontline Chinese armies in India have been surrounded and the noose is tightening," said Graff. "I don't think they have a Stalingrad-style defense in them, do you? The Turkic armies have reached the Hwang He and Tibet just declared its independence and is slaughtering the Chinese troops there. The Indonesians and Arabs are impossible to catch and they're already making a serious dent in internal communications in China. It's just a matter of time before they realize it's pointless to keep killing people when the outcome is inevitable."

"It takes a lot of dead soldiers before governments ever catch on to that," said Theresa.

"Mother always takes the cheerful view," said Peter, and they laughed.

Finally, though, it was time for Petra to hear the story of what happened inside the compound. Peter ended up telling most of it, because Bean kept skipping all the details and rushing straight to the end.

"Do you think Achilles believed Suriyawong would really kill Bean for him?" asked Petra.

"I think," said Bean, "that Suriyawong told him that he would."

"You mean he intended to do it, and changed his mind?"

"I think," said Bean, "that Suri planned that moment from the start. He made himself indispensable to Achilles. He won his trust. The cost of it was losing the trust of everyone else."

"Except you," said Petra.

"Well, you see, I *know* Suri. Even though you can't ever really know anybody—don't throw my own words back up to me, Petra—"

"I didn't! I wasn't!"

"I walked into the compound without a plan, and with only one real advantage. I knew two things that Achilles didn't know. I knew that Suri would never give himself to the service of a man like Achilles, so if he seemed to be doing so, it was a lie. And I knew something about myself. I knew that I could, in fact, kill a man in cold blood if that's what it took to make my wife and children safe."

"Yes," said Peter, "I think that's the one thing he just didn't believe, not even at the end."

"It wasn't cold blood," said Theresa.

"Yes it was," said Bean.

"It was, Mother," said Peter. "It was the right thing to do, and he chose to do it, and it was done. Without having to work himself up into a frenzy to do it."

"That's what heroes do," said Petra. "Whatever's necessary for the good of their people."

"When we start saying words like 'hero,' " said Bean, "it's time to go home."

"Already?" said Theresa. "I mean, Petra just got here. And I have to tell her all my horrible stories about how hard each of my deliveries was. It's my duty to terrify the mother-to-be. It's a tradition."

"Don't worry, Mrs. Wiggin," said Bean. "I'll bring her back every few days, at least. It's not that far."

"Bring me back?" said Petra.

"We left the Hegemon's employ, remember?" said Bean. "We only worked for him so we'd have a legal pretext for fighting Achilles and the Chinese, so there'd be nothing for us to do. We have enough money from our Battle School pensions. So we aren't going to live in Ribeirão Preto."

"But I like it here," said Petra.

"Uh-oh, a fight, a fight," said John Paul.

"Only because you haven't lived in Araraquara yet. It's a better place to raise children."

"I know Araraquara," said Petra. "You lived there with Sister Carlotta, didn't you?"

"I lived everywhere with Sister Carlotta," said Bean. "But it's a good place to raise children."

"You're Greek and I'm Armenian. Of course we need to raise our children to speak Portuguese."

———

The house Bean had rented was small, but it had a second bedroom for the baby, and a lovely little garden, and monkeys that lived in the tall trees on the property behind them. Petra imagined her little girl or boy coming out to play and hearing the chatter of the monkeys and delighting in the show they put on for all comers.

"But there's no furniture," said Petra.

"I knew I was taking my life in my hands picking out the house without you," said Bean. "The furniture is up to you."

"Good," said Petra. "I'll make you sleep in a frilly pink room."

"Will you be sleeping there with me?"

"Of course."

"Then frilly pink is fine with me, if that's what it takes."

———

Peter, unsentimental as he was, saw no reason to hold a funeral for Achilles. But Bean insisted on at least a graveside service, and he paid for the carving of the monument. Under the name "Achilles de Flandres," the year of his birth, and the date of his death, the inscription said:

> Born crippled in body and spirit,
> He changed the face of the world.
> Among all the hearts he broke
> And lives he ended far too young
> Were his own heart
> And his own life.
> May he find peace.

It was a small group gathered there in the cemetery in Ribeirão Preto. Bean and Petra, the Wiggins, Peter.

Graff had gone back to space. Suriyawong had led his little army back to Thailand, to help their homeland drive out the conquerors and restore itself.

No one had anything much to say over Achilles's grave. They could not pretend that they weren't all glad that he was dead. Bean read the inscription he had written, and everyone agreed that it wasn't just fair to Achilles, it was generous.

In the end it was only Peter who had something he could say from the heart.

"Am I the only one here who sees something of himself in the man who's lying in this box?"

No one had an answer for him, either yes or no.

———

Three bloody weeks later, the war ended. If the Chinese had accepted the terms the Caliph had offered in the first place, they would have lost only their new conquests, plus Xinjiang and Tibet. Instead, they waited until Canton had fallen, Shanghai was besieged, and the Turkic troops were surrounding Beijing.

So when the Caliph drew the new map, the province of Inner Mongolia was given to the nation of Mongolia, and Manchuria and Taiwan were given their independence. And China had to guarantee the safety of teachers of religion. The door had been opened to Muslim proselytizing.

The Chinese government promptly fell. The new government repudiated the ceasefire terms, and the Caliph declared martial law until new elections could be held.

And somewhere in the rugged terrain of easternmost India, the goddess of the bridge lived among her worshipers, biding her time, watching to see whether

India was going to be free or had merely changed one tyranny for another.

———

In the aftermath of war, while Indians, Thais, Burmese, Vietnamese, Cambodians and Laotians searched their onetime conquerors' land for family members who had been carried off, Bean and Petra also searched as best they could by computer, hoping to find some record of what Volescu and Achilles had done with their lost children.

ACKNOWLEDGMENTS

In writing this sequel to *Ender's Shadow* and *Shadow of the Hegemon,* I faced two new problems. First, I was expanding the roles of several minor characters from earlier books, and ran the serious risk of inventing aspects of their appearance or their past that would contradict some long-forgotten detail in a previous volume. To avoid this as much as possible, I relied on two online communities.

The Philotic Web (http://www.philoticweb.net) carries a timeline combining the story flows of *Ender's Game* and *Ender's Shadow*, which proved invaluable to me. It was created by Nathan M. Taylor with the help of Adam Spieckermann.

On my own website, Hatrack River (http://www.hatrack.com), I posted the first five chapters of the manuscript of this novel, in the hope that readers who had read the other books in the series more recently than I might be able to catch inadvertent inconsistencies and other problems. The Hatrack River community did not disappoint me. Among the many who responded—and I thank them all—I found particular value in the suggestions of Keiko A. Haun ("accio"), Justin Pullen, Chris Bridges, Josh Galvez ("Zevlag"), David Tayman ("Taalcon"), Alison Purnell ("Eaquae Legit"), Vicki Norris ("CKDexter-Haven"), Michael Sloan ("Papa Moose"), and Oliver Withstandley.

In addition, I had the help, chapter by chapter

through the whole book, of my regular crew of first readers—Phillip and Erin Absher, Kathryn H. Kidd, and my son Geoffrey. My wife, Kristine A. Card, as usual read each chapter while the pages were still warm from the LaserJet. Without them I could not have proceeded with this book.

The second problem posed by this novel was that I wrote it during the war in Afghanistan between the U.S. and its allies and the Taliban and Al Qaeda forces. Since in *Shadow Puppets* I had to show the future state of relations between the Muslim and Western worlds, and between Israel and its Muslim neighbors, I had to make a prediction about how the current hate-filled situation might someday be resolved. Since I take quite seriously my responsibility to the nations and peoples I write about, I was dependent for much of my understanding of the causes of the present situation on Bernard Lewis's *What Went Wrong?: Western Impact and Middle Eastern Response* (Oxford University Press, 2001).

This book is dedicated to my wife's parents. Besides the fact that much of the peace and joy in Kristine's and my lives comes from our close and harmonious relationship with both our extended families, I owe an additional debt to James B. Allen, for his excellent work as a historian, yes, but more personally for having taught me to approach history fearlessly, going wherever the evidence leads, assuming neither the best nor the worst about people of the past, and adapting my personal worldview wherever it needs adjustment, but never carelessly throwing out previous ideas that remain valid.

To my assistants, Kathleen Bellamy and Scott Allen, I owe much more than I pay them. As for my children, Geoffrey, Emily, and Zina, and my wife, Kristine, they are the reason it's worth getting out of bed each day.

Praise for *Shadow of the Hegemon*

"This fine follow-up to *Ender's Shadow* features that novel's hero, Bean (now a young man), wrestling with Card's trademark: superbly real moral and ethical dilemmas. . . . The complexity and serious treatment of the book's young protagonists will attract many sophisticated YA readers, while Card's impeccable prose, fast pacing, and political intrigue will appeal to adult fans of spy novels, thrillers, and science fiction."
—*Publishers Weekly* (starred review)

"As are all Card's books, this one is strangely moving. Although *Shadow of the Hegemon* has the bones of a simple thriller, Card's ability to evoke character—especially the character of children essentially raised by each other while continually under siege—makes these books seem not like fiction but like family stories, tales of what our relatives endured in a world too close to our own."   —*San Jose Mercury News*

"The author's graceful storytelling and engaging cast of youthful characters add an extra dimension to an already gripping story of children caught up in world-shaking events."   —*Library Journal*

"The novels of Orson Scott Card's Ender series are an intriguing combination of action, military and political strategy, elaborate war games, and psychology."
—*USA Today*

"Bean comes out mostly, though not entirely, from Ender's shadow in this fast-paced, stand-alone sequel to *Ender's Shadow*, which picks up a year later after the Battle School kids have all been returned to Earth."
—*Locus*

Praise for *Ender's Shadow*

"Card is always at his best, as here, when he's writing about children: an absorbing, near-flawless performance that, while fully intelligible, should send everyone scurrying to reread the original."
—*Kirkus Reviews*

"As always, everyone will be struck by the power of Card's children, always more and less than human, perfect yet struggling, tragic yet hopeful, wondrous and strange." —*Publishers Weekly* (starred review)

"The author's superb storytelling and his genuine insight into the moral dilemmas that lead good people to commit questionable actions make this title a priority for most libraries." —*Library Journal*

"[*Ender's Shadow* is] a strong, encouraging, enlightening story that reads as brave and as bright as the young adult novels since Heinlein, but with enough depth, breadth, and Dickensian squalor to stand proudly alongside any mainstream novel on your shelf."
—*The San Diego Union-Tribune*

"An excellent addition to the series, which will leave readers panting for the next installment." —*Kliatt*

Praise for Orson Scott Card

"Card's prose is powerful here, as is his consideration of mystical and quasi-religious themes. Though billed as the final Ender novel, this story leaves enough mysteries unexplored to justify another entry; and Card fans should find that possibility, like this novel, very welcome indeed."

—*Publishers Weekly* (starred review) on
Children of the Mind

"Orson Scott Card, one of our best writers, understands that to imagine the Other is one of the best ways to explore our hidden selves."

—*The Columbus Dispatch*

"An undeniable heavyweight . . . This book combines Card's quirky style with his hard ethical dilemmas and sharply drawn portraits."

—New York *Daily News* on *Ender's Game*

"Card has taken the venerable SF concepts of a superman and an interstellar war against aliens, and, with superb characterization, pacing, and language, combines them into a seamless story of compelling power."

—*Booklist* on *Ender's Game*

"This book provides a harrowing look at the price we pay for trying to mold our posterity in our own aggressive image of what we believe is right."

—*The Christian Science Monitor* on *Ender's Game*

BY ORSON SCOTT CARD
FROM TOM DOHERTY ASSOCIATES

ENDER UNIVERSE

ENDER SAGA
Ender's Game
Ender in Exile
Speaker for the Dead
Xenocide
Children of the Mind

SHADOW SERIES
Ender's Shadow
Shadow of the Hegemon
Shadow Puppets
Shadow of the Giant
Shadows in Flight

THE FIRST FORMIC WAR
(WITH AARON JOHNSTON)
Earth Unaware
Earth Afire
Earth Awakens

THE SECOND FORMIC WAR
(WITH AARON JOHNSTON)
The Swarm
The Hive

Children of the Fleet

ENDER NOVELLAS
A War of Gifts
First Meetings

THE MITHERMAGES
The Lost Gate
The Gate Thief
Gatefather

THE TALES OF ALVIN
MAKER
Seventh Son
Red Prophet

Prentice Alvin
Alvin Journeyman
Heartfire
The Crystal City

HOMECOMING
The Memory of Earth
The Call of Earth
The Ships of Earth
Earthfall
Earthborn

WOMEN OF GENESIS
Sarah
Rebekah
Rachel & Leah

THE COLLECTED
SHORT FICTION OF
ORSON SCOTT CARD
*Maps in a Mirror: The Short
Fiction of Orson Scott Card*
Keeper of Dreams

STANDALONE FICTION
Invasive Procedures (with
Aaron Johnston)
Empire
Hidden Empire
The Folk of the Fringe
Hart's Hope
Lovelock (with Kathryn H. Kidd)
*Pastwatch: The Redemption of
Christopher Columbus*
Saints
Songmaster
Treason
The Worthing Saga
Wyrms
Zanna's Gift

SHADOW
OF THE
HEGEMON

ORSON SCOTT CARD

TOR®

A TOM DOHERTY ASSOCIATES BOOK
NEW YORK

This is a work of fiction. All of the characters, organizations, and events portrayed in this novel are either products of the author's imagination or are used fictitiously.

SHADOW OF THE HEGEMON

Copyright © 2000 by Orson Scott Card

A Tor Book
Published by Tom Doherty Associates
120 Broadway
New York, NY 10271

www.tor-forge.com

Tor® is a registered trademark of Macmillan Publishing Group, LLC.

ISBN 978-0-8125-6595-9

Our books may be purchased in bulk for promotional, educational, or business use. Please contact your local bookseller or the Macmillan Corporate and Premium Sales Department at 1-800-221-7945, extension 5442, or by email at MacmillanSpecialMarkets@macmillan.com.

First Edition: January 2001
First Mass Market Edition: December 2001

Printed in the United States of America

18 17 16 15

TO CHARLES BENJAMIN CARD
YOU ARE ALWAYS LIGHT TO US,
YOU SEE THROUGH ALL THE SHADOWS,
AND WE HEAR YOUR STRONG VOICE
SINGING IN OUR DREAMS.

CONTENTS

Part One

VOLUNTEERS

I

Petra

To: Chamrajnagar%sacredriver@ifcom.gov
From: Locke%espinoza@polnet.gov
Re: What are you doing to protect the children?

Dear Admiral Chamrajnagar,
I was given your idname by a mutual friend who once worked for you but now is a glorified dispatcher—I'm sure you know whom I mean. I realize that your primary responsibility now is not so much military as logistical, and your thoughts are turned to space rather than the political situation on Earth. After all, you decisively defeated the nationalist forces led by your predecessor in the League War, and that issue seems settled. The I.F. remains

independent and for that we are all grateful.

What no one seems to understand is that peace on Earth is merely a temporary illusion. Not only is Russia's long-pent expansionism still a driving force, but also many other nations have aggressive designs on their neighbors. The forces of the Strategos are being disbanded, the Hegemony is rapidly losing all authority, and Earth is poised on the edge of cataclysm.

The most powerful resource of any nation in the wars to come will be the children trained in Battle, Tactical, and Command School. While it is perfectly appropriate for these children to serve their native countries in future wars, it is inevitable that at least some nations that lack such I.F.-certified geniuses or who believe that rivals have more-gifted commanders will inevitably take preemptive action, either to secure that enemy resource for their own use or, in any event, to deny the enemy the use of that resource. In short, these children are in grave danger of being kidnapped or killed.

I recognize that you have a hands-off policy toward events on Earth, but it was the I.F. that identified these chil-

dren and trained them, thus making them
targets. Whatever happens to these
children, the I.F. has ultimate responsibility. It would go a long way toward
protecting them if you were to issue an
order placing these children under
Fleet protection, warning any nation or
group attempting to harm or interfere
with them that they would face swift
and harsh military retribution. Far
from regarding this as interference in
Earthside affairs, most nations would
welcome this action, and, for whatever
it is worth, you would have my complete
support in all public forums.

I hope you will act immediately. There
is no time to waste.

Respectfully,
Locke

Nothing looked right in Armenia when Petra Arkanian
returned home. The mountains were dramatic, of
course, but they had not really been part of her childhood experience. It was not until she got to Maralik
that she began to see things that should mean something to her. Her father had met her in Yerevan while
her mother remained at home with her eleven-year-old
brother and the new baby—obviously conceived even
before the population restrictions were relaxed when
the war ended. They had no doubt watched Petra on
television. Now, as the flivver took Petra and her father
along the narrow streets, he began apologizing. "It
won't seem much to you, Pet, after seeing the world."

"They didn't show us the world much, Papa. There were no windows in Battle School."

"I mean, the spaceport, and the capital, all the important people and wonderful buildings . . ."

"I'm not disappointed, Papa." She had to lie in order to reassure him. It was as if he had given her Maralik as a gift, and now was unsure whether she liked it. She didn't know yet whether she would like it or not. She hadn't liked Battle School, but she got used to it. There was no getting used to Eros, but she had endured it. How could she dislike a place like this, with open sky and people wandering wherever they wanted?

Yet she *was* disappointed. For all her memories of Maralik were the memories of a five-year-old, looking up at tall buildings, across wide streets where large vehicles loomed and fled at alarming speeds. Now she was much older, beginning to come into her womanly height, and the cars were smaller, the streets downright narrow, and the buildings—designed to survive the next earthquake, as the old buildings had not—were squat. Not ugly—there was grace in them, given the eclectic styles that were somehow blended here, Turkish and Russian, Spanish and Riviera, and, most incredibly, Japanese. It was a marvel to see how they were still unified by the choice of colors, the closeness to the street, the almost uniform height as all strained against the legal maximums.

She knew of all this because she had read about it on Eros as she and the other children sat out the League War. She had seen pictures on the nets. But nothing had prepared her for the fact that she had left here as a five-year-old and now was returning at fourteen.

"What?" she said. For Father had spoken and she hadn't understood him.

"I asked if you wanted to stop for a candy before we went home, the way we used to."

Candy. How could she have forgotten the word for candy?

Easily, that's how. The only other Armenian in Battle School had been three years ahead of her and graduated to Tactical School, so they overlapped only for a few months. She had been seven when she got from Ground School to Battle School, and he was ten, leaving without ever having commanded an army. Was it any wonder that he didn't want to jabber in Armenian to a little kid from home? So in effect she had gone without speaking Armenian for nine years. And the Armenian she had spoken then was a five-year-old's language. It was so hard to speak it now, and harder still to understand it.

How could she tell Father that it would help her greatly if he would speak to her in Fleet Common—English, in effect? He spoke it, of course—he and Mother had made a point of speaking English at home when she was little, so she would not be handicapped linguistically if she was taken into Battle School. In fact, as she thought about it, that was part of her problem. How often had Father actually called candy by the Armenian word? Whenever he let her walk with him through town and they stopped for candy, he would make her ask for it in English, and call each piece by its English name. It was absurd, really—why would she need to know, in Battle School, the English names of Armenian candies?

"What are you laughing for?"

"I seem to have lost my taste for candy while I was in space, Father. Though for old times' sake, I hope you'll have time to walk through town with me again. You won't be as tall as you were the last time."

"No, nor will your hand be as small in mine." He laughed, too. "We've been robbed of years that would be precious now, to have in memory."

"Yes," said Petra. "But I was where I needed to be."

Or was I? I'm the one who broke first. I passed all the tests, until the test that mattered, and there I broke first. Ender comforted me by telling me he relied on me most and pushed me hardest, but he pushed us all and relied upon us all and I'm the one who broke. No one ever spoke of it; perhaps here on Earth not one living soul knew of it. But the others who had fought with her knew it. Until that moment when she fell asleep in the midst of combat, she had been one of the best. After that, though she never broke again, Ender also never trusted her again. The others watched over her, so that if she suddenly stopped commanding her ships, they could step in. She was sure that one of them had been designated, but never asked who. Dink? Bean? Bean, yes—whether Ender assigned him to do it or not, she knew Bean would be watching, ready to take over. She was not reliable. They did not trust her. She did not trust herself.

Yet she would keep that secret from her family, as she kept it in talking to the prime minister and the press, to the Armenian military and the schoolchildren who had been assembled to meet the great Armenian hero of the Formic War. Armenia needed a hero. She was the only candidate out of this war. They had shown her how the online textbooks already listed her among the ten greatest Armenians of all time. Her picture, her biography, and quotations from Colonel Graff, from Major Anderson, from Mazer Rackham.

And from Ender Wiggin. "It was Petra who first stood up for me at risk to herself. It was Petra who trained me when no one else would. I owe everything

I accomplished to her. And in the final campaign, in battle after battle she was the commander I relied upon."

Ender could not have known how those words would hurt. No doubt he meant to reassure her that he did rely upon her. But because she knew the truth, his words sounded like pity to her. They sounded like a kindly lie.

And now she was home. Nowhere on Earth was she so much a stranger as here, because she ought to feel at home here, but she could not, for no one knew her here. They knew a bright little girl who was sent off amid tearful good-byes and brave words of love. They knew a hero who returned with the halo of victory around her every word and gesture. But they did not know and would never know the girl who broke under the strain and in the midst of battle simply . . . fell asleep. While her ships were lost, while real men died, she slept because her body could stay awake no more. That girl would remain hidden from all eyes.

And from all eyes would be hidden also the girl who watched every move of the boys around her, evaluating their abilities, guessing at their intentions, determined to take any advantage she could get, refusing to bow to any of them. Here she was supposed to become a child again—an older one, but a child nonetheless. A dependent.

After nine years of fierce watchfulness, it would be restful to turn over her life to others, wouldn't it?

"Your mother wanted to come. But she was afraid to come." He chuckled as if this were amusing. "Do you understand?"

"No," said Petra.

"Not afraid of you," said Father. "Of her firstborn daughter she could never be afraid. But the cameras.

The politicians. The crowds. She is a woman of the kitchen. Not a woman of the market. Do you understand?"

She understood the Armenian easily enough, if that's what he was asking, because he had caught on, he was speaking in simple language and separating his words a little so she would not get lost in the stream of conversation. She was grateful for this, but also embarrassed that it was so obvious she needed such help.

What she did not understand was a fear of crowds that could keep a mother from coming to meet her daughter after nine years.

Petra knew that it was not the crowds or the cameras that Mother was afraid of. It was Petra herself. The lost five-year-old who would never be five again, who had had her first period with the help of a Fleet nurse, whose mother had never bent over her homework with her, or taught her how to cook. No, wait. She had baked pies with her mother. She had helped roll out the dough. Thinking back, she could see that her mother had not actually let her do anything that mattered. But to Petra it had seemed that she was the one baking. That her mother trusted her.

That turned her thoughts to the way Ender had coddled her at the end, pretending to trust her as before but actually keeping control.

And because that was an unbearable thought, Petra looked out the window of the flivver. "Are we in the part of town where I used to play?"

"Not yet," said Father. "But nearly. Maralik is still not such a large town."

"It all seems new to me," said Petra.

"But it isn't. It never changes. Only the architecture. There are Armenians all over the world, but only because they were forced to leave to save their lives. By nature, Armenians stay at home. The hills are the womb, and we have no desire to be born." He chuckled at his joke.

Had he always chuckled like that? It sounded to Petra less like amusement than like nervousness. Mother was not the only one afraid of her.

At last the flivver reached home. And here at last she recognized where she was. It was small and shabby compared to what she had remembered, but in truth she had not even thought of the place in many years. It stopped haunting her dreams by the time she was ten. But now, coming home again, it all returned to her, the tears she had shed in those first weeks and months in Ground School, and again when she left Earth and went up to Battle School. This was what she had yearned for, and at last she was here again, she had it back . . . and knew that she no longer needed it, no longer really wanted it. The nervous man in the car beside her was not the tall god who had led her through the streets of Maralik so proudly. And the woman waiting inside the house would not be the goddess from whom came warm food and a cool hand on her forehead when she was sick.

But she had nowhere else to go.

Her mother was standing at the window as Petra emerged from the flivver. Father palmed the scanner to accept the charges. Petra raised a hand and gave a small wave to her mother, a shy smile that quickly grew into a grin. Her mother smiled back and gave her own small wave in reply. Petra took her father's hand and walked with him to the house.

The door opened as they approached. It was Stefan, her brother. She would not have known him from her memories of a two-year-old, still creased with baby fat. And he, of course, did not know her at all. He beamed the way the children from the school group had beamed at her, thrilled to meet a celebrity but not really aware of her as a person. He was her brother, though, and so she hugged him and he hugged her back. "You're really Petra!" he said.

"You're really Stefan!" she answered. Then she turned to her mother. She was still standing at the window, looking out.

"Mother?"

The woman turned, tears streaking her cheeks. "I'm so glad to see you, Petra," she said.

But she made no move to come to Petra, or even to reach out to her.

"But you're still looking for the little girl who left nine years ago," said Petra.

Mother burst into tears, and now she reached out her arms and Petra strode to her, to be enfolded in her embrace. "You're a woman now," said Mother. "I don't know you, but I love you."

"I love you too, Mother," said Petra. And was pleased to realize that it was true.

They had about an hour, the four of them—five, once the baby woke up. Petra shunted aside their questions—"Oh, everything about me has already been published or broadcast. It's *you* that I want to hear about"—and learned that her father was still editing textbooks and supervising translations, and her mother was still the shepherd of the neighborhood, watching out for everyone, bringing food when someone was sick, taking care of children while parents ran errands, and providing lunch for any child who showed up. "I remember once that Mother and I had lunch alone, just the two of us," Stefan joked. "We didn't know what to say, and there was so much food left over."

"It was already that way when I was little," Petra said. "I remember being so proud of how the other kids loved my mother. And so jealous of the way she loved them!"

"Never as much as I loved my own girl and boy," said Mother. "But I do love children, I admit it, every one of them is precious in the sight of God, every one of them is welcome in my house."

"Oh, I've known a few you wouldn't love," said Petra.

"Maybe," said Mother, not wishing to argue, but plainly not believing that there could be such a child.

The baby gurgled and Mother lifted her shirt to tuck the baby to her breast.

"Did I slurp so noisily?" asked Petra.

"Not really," said Mother.

"Oh, tell the truth," said Father. "She woke the neighbors."

"So I was a glutton."

"No, merely a barbarian," said Father. "No table manners."

Petra decided to ask the delicate question boldly and have done with it. "The baby was born only a month after the population restrictions were lifted."

Father and Mother looked at each other, Mother with a beatific expression, Father with a wince. "Yes, well, we missed you. We wanted another little girl."

"You would have lost your job," said Petra.

"Not right away," said Father.

"Armenian officials have always been a little slow about enforcing those laws," said Mother.

"But eventually, you could have lost everything."

"No," said Mother. "When you left, we lost half of everything. Children are everything. The rest is . . . nothing."

Stefan laughed. "Except when I'm hungry. Food is something!"

"You're always hungry," said Father.

"Food is always something," said Stefan.

They laughed, but Petra could see that Stefan had had no illusions about what the birth of this child would have meant. "It's a good thing we won the war."

"Better than losing it," said Stefan.

"It's nice to have the baby and obey the law, too," said Mother.

"But you didn't get your little girl."

"No," said Father. "We got our David."

"We didn't need a little girl after all," said Mother. "We got you back."

Not really, thought Petra. And not for long. Four years, maybe fewer, and I'll be off to university. And you won't miss me by then, because you'll know that I'm not the little girl you love, just this bloody-handed veteran of a nasty military school that turned out to have real battles to fight.

After the first hour, neighbors and cousins and friends from Father's work began dropping by, and it was not until after midnight that Father had to announce that tomorrow was not a national holiday and he needed to have *some* sleep before work. It took yet another hour to shoo everyone out of the house, and by then all Petra wanted was to curl up in bed and hide from the world for at least a week.

But by the end of the next day, she knew she had to get out of the house. She didn't fit into the routines. Mother loved her, yes, but her life centered around the baby and the neighborhood, and while she kept trying to engage Petra in conversation, Petra could see that she was a distraction, that it would be a relief for Mother when Petra went to school during the day as Stefan did, returning only at the scheduled time. Petra understood, and that night announced that she wanted to register for school and begin class the next day.

"Actually," said Father, "the people from the I.F. said that you could probably go right on to university."

"I'm fourteen," said Petra. "And there are serious gaps in my education."

"She never even heard of Dog," said Stefan.

"What?" said Father. "What dog?"

"Dog," said Stefan. "The zip orchestra. You know."

"Very famous group," said Mother. "If you heard them, you'd take the car in for major repairs."

"Oh, *that* Dog," said Father. "I hardly think that's the education Petra was talking about."

"Actually, it is," said Petra.

"It's like she's from another planet," said Stefan. "Last night I realized she never heard of *anybody*."

"I *am* from another planet. Or, properly speaking, asteroid."

"Of course," said Mother. "You need to join your generation."

Petra smiled, but inwardly she winced. Her generation? She had no generation, except the few thousand kids who had once been in Battle School, and now were scattered over the surface of the Earth, trying to find out where they belonged in a world at peace.

School would not be easy, Petra soon discovered. There were no courses in military history and military strategy. The mathematics was pathetic compared to what she had mastered in Battle School, but with literature and grammar she was downright backward: Her knowledge of Armenian was indeed childish, and while she was fluent in the version of English spoken in Battle School—including the slang that the kids used there—she had little knowledge of the rules of grammar and no understanding at all of the mixed Armenian and English slang that the kids used with each other at school.

Everyone was very nice to her, of course—the most popular girls immediately took possession of her, and the teachers treated her like a celebrity. Petra allowed herself to be led around and shown everything, and studied the chatter of her new friends very carefully, so she could learn the slang and hear how school English and Armenian were nuanced. She knew that soon enough the popular girls would tire of her—especially when they realized how bluntly outspoken Petra was, a trait that she had no intention of changing. Petra was quite used to the fact that people who cared about the social hierarchy usually ended up hating her and, if they were wise, fearing her, since pretensions didn't last long in her presence. She would find her real friends over the next few weeks—if, in fact, there were any here who would value her for what she was. It didn't matter. All the friendships here, all the social concerns, seemed so trivial to her. There was nothing at stake here, except each student's own social life and academic future, and what did that matter? Petra's previous schooling had all been conducted in the shadow of war, with the fate of humanity riding on the outcome of her studies and the quality of her skills. Now, what did it matter? She would read Armenian literature because she wanted to learn Armenian, not because she thought it actually mattered what some expatriate like Saroyan thought about the lives of children in a long-lost era of a far-off country.

The only part of school that she truly loved was physical education. To have sky over her head as she ran, to have the track lie flat before her, to be able to run and run for the sheer joy of it and without a clock ticking out her allotted time for aerobic exercise— such a luxury. She could not compete, physically, with most of the other girls. It would take time for her body to reconstruct itself for high gravity, for despite the great pains that the I.F. went to to make sure that soldiers' bodies did not deteriorate too much during long months and years in space, nothing trained you for living on a planet's surface except living there. But Petra didn't care that she was one of the last to complete every race, that she couldn't leap even the lowest hurdle. It felt good simply to run freely, and her weakness gave her goals to meet. She would be competitive soon enough. That was one of the aspects of her innate personality that had taken her to Battle School in the first place—that she had no particular interest in competition because she always started from the assumption that, if it mattered, she would find a way to win.

And so she settled in to her new life. Within weeks she was fluent in Armenian and had mastered the local slang. As she had expected, the popular girls dropped her in about the same amount of time, and a few weeks later, the brainy girls had cooled toward her as well. It was among the rebels and misfits that she found her friends, and soon she had a circle of confidants and co-conspirators that she called her "jeesh," Battle School slang for close friends, a private army. Not that she was the commander or anything, but they were all loyal to each other and amused at the antics of the teachers and the other students, and when a school counselor called her in to tell her that the administration was growing concerned about the fact that Petra seemed to be associating with an antisocial element in school, she knew that she was truly at home in Maralik.

Then one day she came home from school to find the front door locked. She carried no house key—no one did in their neighborhood because no one locked up, or even, in good weather, closed their doors. She could hear the baby crying inside the house, so instead of making her mother come to the front door to let her in, she walked around back and came into the kitchen to find that her mother was tied to a chair, gagged, her eyes wide and frantic with fear.

Before Petra had time to react, a hypostick was slapped against her arm and, without ever seeing who had done it, she slipped into darkness.

2

Bean

To: Locke%espinoza@polnet.gov
From: Chamrajnagar%%@ifcom.gov
Re: Do not write to me again

Mr. Peter Wiggin,
Did you really think I would not have
the resources to know who you are? You
may be the author of the "Locke Proposal," giving you a reputation as a
peacemaker, but you are also partly responsible for the world's present in-
stability by your jingoist use of your
sister's identity as Demosthenes. I
have no illusions about your motives.

It is outrageous of you to suggest that
I jeopardize the neutrality of the International Fleet in order to take control of children who have completed

```
their military service with the I.F. If
you attempt to manipulate public opin-
ion to force me to do so, I will expose
your identity as both Locke and Demos-
thenes.

I have changed my idname and have in-
formed our mutual friend that he is not
to attempt to relay communication be-
tween you and me again. The only com-
fort you are entitled to take from my
letter is this: The I.F. will not in-
terfere with those trying to assert
hegemony over other nations and peo-
ples—not even you.

Chamrajnagar
```

The disappearance of Petra Arkanian from her home in Armenia was worldwide news. The headlines were full of accusations hurled by Armenia against Turkey, Azerbaijan, and every other Turkish-speaking nation, and the stiff or fiery denials and counter-accusations that came in reply. There were the tearful interviews with her mother, the only witness, who was sure the kidnappers were Azerbaijani. "I know the language, I know the accent, and that's who took my little girl!"

Bean was with his family on the second day of their vacation at the beach on the island of Ithaca, but this was Petra, and he read the nets and watched the vids avidly, along with his brother, Nikolai. They both reached the same conclusion right away. "It wasn't any of the Turkish nations," Nikolai announced to their parents. "That's obvious."

Father, who had been working in government for many years, agreed. "Real Turks would have made sure to speak only Russian."

"Or Armenian," said Nikolai.

"No Turk speaks Armenian," said Mother. She was right, of course, since real Turks would never deign to learn it, and those in Turkish countries who did speak Armenian were, by definition, not really Turks and would never be trusted with a delicate assignment like kidnapping a military genius.

"So who was it?" said Father. "Agents provocateurs, trying to start a war?"

"My bet is on the Armenian government," said Nikolai. "Put her in charge of their military."

"Why kidnap her when they could employ her openly?" asked Father.

"Taking her out of school openly," said Nikolai, "would be an announcement of Armenia's military intentions. It might provoke preemptive actions by surrounding Turkey or Azerbaijan."

There was superficial plausibility in what Nikolai was saying, but Bean knew better. He had already foreseen this possibility back when all the militarily gifted children were still in space. At that time the main danger had come from the Polemarch, and Bean wrote an anonymous letter to a couple of opinion leaders on Earth, Locke and Demosthenes, urging them to get all the Battle School children back to Earth so they couldn't be seized or killed by the Polemarch's forces in the League War. The warning had worked, but now that the League War was over, too many governments had begun to think and act complacently, as if the world now had peace instead of a fragile ceasefire. Bean's original analysis still held. It was Russia that was behind the Polemarch's coup attempt in the League War, and it was likely to be Russia that was behind the kidnapping of Petra Arkanian.

Still, he didn't have any hard evidence of this and knew of no way to get it—now that he wasn't inside a Fleet installation, he had no access to military computer systems. So he kept his skepticism to himself, and made a joke out of it. "I don't know, Nikolai," he said. "Since staging this kidnapping is having an even more destabilizing effect, I'd have to say that *if* she was taken by her own government, it proves they really *really* need her, because it was a deeply dumb thing to do."

"If they're *not* dumb," said Father, "who did it?"

"Somebody who's ambitious to fight and win wars and smart enough to know they need a brilliant commander," said Bean. "And either big enough or invisible enough or far enough away from Armenia not to care about the consequences of kidnapping her. In fact, I'll bet that whoever took her would be perfectly delighted if war broke out in the Caucasus."

"So you think it's some large and powerful nation close by?" asked Father. Of course, there was only one large and powerful nation close to Armenia.

"Could be, but there's no telling," said Bean. "Anybody who needs a commander like Petra wants a world in turmoil. Enough turmoil, and anybody might emerge on top. Plenty of sides to play off against each other." And now that Bean had said it, he began to believe it. Just because Russia was the most aggressive nation before the League War didn't mean that other nations weren't going to get into the game.

"In a world in chaos," said Nikolai, "the army with the best commander wins."

"If you want to find the kidnapper, look for the

country that talks most about peace and conciliation," said Bean, playing with the idea and saying whatever came to mind.

"You're too cynical," said Nikolai. "Some who talk about peace and conciliation merely want peace and conciliation."

"You watch—the nations that offer to arbitrate are the ones that think they should rule the world, and this is just one more move in the game."

Father laughed. "Don't read too much into *that*," he said. "Most of the nations that are always offering to arbitrate are trying to recover lost status, not gain new power. France. America. Japan. They're always meddling just because they used to have the power to back it up and they haven't caught on yet that they don't anymore."

Bean smiled. "You never know, do you, Papa. The very fact that you dismiss the possibility that they could be the kidnappers makes me regard them as all the more likely candidates."

Nikolai laughed and agreed.

"That's the problem with having two Battle School graduates in the house," said Father. "You think because you understand military thinking that you understand political thinking, too."

"It's all maneuver and avoiding battle until you have overwhelming superiority," said Bean.

"But it's also about the will to power," said Father. "And even if individuals in America and France and Japan have the will to power, the people don't. Their leaders will never get them moving. You have to look at nations on the make. Aggressive peoples who think they have a grievance, who think they're undervalued. Belligerent, snappish."

"A whole nation of belligerent, snappish people?" asked Nikolai.

"Sounds like Athens," said Bean.

"A nation that takes that attitude toward other nations," said Father. "Several self-consciously Islamic nations have the character to make such a play, but they'd never kidnap a Christian girl to lead their armies."

"They might kidnap her to prevent her own nation from using her," said Nikolai. "Which brings us back to Armenia's neighbors."

"It's an interesting puzzle," said Bean, "which we can figure out later, after we get to wherever we're going."

Father and Nikolai looked at him as if he were crazy. "Going?" asked Father.

It was Mother who understood. "They're kidnapping Battle School graduates. Not just that, but a member of Ender's team from the actual battles."

"And one of the best," said Bean.

Father was skeptical. "One incident doesn't make a pattern."

"Let's not wait to see who's next," said Mother. "I'd rather feel silly later for overreacting than grieve because we dismissed the possibility."

"Give it a few days," said Father. "It will all blow over."

"We've already given it six hours," said Bean. "If the kidnappers are patient, they won't strike again for months. But if they're impatient, they're already in motion against all their other targets. For all we know, the only reason Nikolai and I aren't in the bag already is because we threw off their plans by going on vacation."

"Or else," said Nikolai, "our being here on this island gives them the perfect opportunity."

"Father," said Mother, "why don't you call for some protection?"

Father hesitated.

Bean understood why. The political game was a delicate one, and anything Father did right now could have repercussions throughout his career. "You won't be perceived as asking for special privileges for yourself," said Bean. "Nikolai and I are a precious national resource. I believe the prime minister is on record as saying that several times. Letting Athens know where we are and suggesting they protect us and get us out of here is a good idea."

Father got on the cellphone.

He got only a System Busy response.

"That's it," said Bean. "There's no way the phone system can be too busy here on Ithaca. We need a boat."

"An airplane," said Mother.

"A boat," said Nikolai. "And not a rental. They're probably waiting for us to put ourselves in their hands, so there won't be a struggle."

"Several of the nearby houses have boats," said Father. "But we don't know these people."

"They know *us*," said Nikolai. "Especially Bean. We *are* war heroes, you know."

"But any house around here could be the very one from which they're watching us," said Father. "*If* they're watching us. We can't trust anybody."

"Let's get in our bathing suits," said Bean, "and walk to the beach and then wander as far as we can before we cut inland and find somebody with a boat."

Since no one had a better plan, they put it into action at once. Within two minutes they were out the door, carrying no wallets or purses, though Father and Mother slipped a few identification papers and credit cards into their suits. Bean and Nikolai laughed and teased each other as usual, and Mother and Father held hands and talked quietly, smiling at their sons . . . as usual. No sign of alarm. Nothing to cause anyone watching to spring into action.

They were only about a quarter mile up the beach when they heard an explosion—loud, as if it were close, and the shockwave made them stumble. Mother fell. Father helped her up as Bean and Nikolai looked back.

"Maybe it's not our house," said Nikolai.

"Let's not go back and check," said Bean.

They began to jog up the beach, matching their speed to Mother, who was limping a little from having skinned one knee and twisted the other when she fell. "Go on ahead," she said.

"Mother," said Nikolai, "taking you is the same as taking us, because we'd do whatever they wanted to get you back."

"They don't want to take us," said Bean. "Petra they wanted to use. Me they want dead."

"No," said Mother.

"He's right," said Father. "You don't blow up a house in order to kidnap the occupants."

"But we don't know it was our house!" Mother insisted.

"Mother," said Bean. "It's basic strategy. Any resource you can't get control of, you destroy so your enemy can't have it."

"What enemy?" Mother said. "Greece has no enemies!"

"When somebody wants to rule the world," said Nikolai, "eventually everyone is his enemy."

"I think we should run faster," said Mother.

They did.

As they ran, Bean thought through what Mother had said. Nikolai's answer was right, of course, but Bean couldn't help but wonder: Greece might have no enemies, but *I* have. Somewhere in this world, Achilles is alive. Supposedly he's in custody, a prisoner because he is mentally ill, because he has murdered again and again. Graff promised that he would never be set free. But Graff was court-martialed—exonerated, yes, but retired from the military. He's now Minister of Colonization, no longer in a position to keep his promise about Achilles. And if there's one thing Achilles wants, it's me, dead.

Kidnapping Petra, that's something Achilles would think of. And if he was in a position to cause *that* to happen—if some government or group was listening to him—then it would have been a simple enough matter for him to get the same people to kill Bean.

Or would Achilles insist on being there in person?

Probably not. Achilles was not a sadist. He killed with his own hands when he needed to, but would never put himself at risk. Killing from a distance would actually be preferable. Using other hands to do his work.

Who else would want Bean dead? Any other enemy would seek to capture him. His test scores from Battle School were a matter of public record since Graff's trial. The military in every nation knew that he was the kid who in many ways had topped Ender himself. He would be the one most desired. He would also be the one most feared, if he were on the other side in a war. Any of them might kill him if they knew they couldn't take him. But they would try to take him first. Only Achilles would prefer his death.

But he said nothing of this to his family. His fears about Achilles would sound too paranoid. He wasn't sure whether he believed them himself. And yet, as he ran along the beach with his family, he grew more certain with every step that whoever had kidnapped Petra was in some way under Achilles' influence.

They heard the rotors of helicopters before they saw them, and Nikolai's reaction was instantaneous. "Inland now!" he shouted. They scrambled for the nearest wooden stairway leading up the cliff from the beach.

They were only halfway up before the choppers came into view. There was no point in trying to hide. One of the choppers set down on the beach below them, the other on the bluff above.

"Down is easier than up," said Father. "And the choppers do have Greek military insignia."

What Bean didn't point out, because everyone knew it, was that Greece was part of the New Warsaw Pact, and it was quite possible that Greek military craft might be acting under Russian command.

In silence they walked back down the stairs. Hope and despair and fear tugged at them by turns.

The soldiers who spilled out of the chopper were wearing Greek Army uniforms.

"At least they're not trying to pretend they're Turks," said Nikolai.

"But how would the Greek Army know to come rescue us?" said Mother. "The explosion was only a few minutes ago."

The answer came quickly enough, once they got to the beach. A colonel who Father knew slightly came to meet them, saluting them. No, saluting Bean, with the respect due to a veteran of the Formic War.

"I bring you greetings from General Thrakos," said the colonel. "He would have come himself, but there was no time to waste when the warning came."

"Colonel Dekanos, we think our sons might be in danger," said Father.

"We realized that the moment word came of the kidnapping of Petra Arkanian," said Dekanos. "But you weren't at home and it took a few hours to find out where you were."

"We heard an explosion," said Mother.

"If you had been inside the house," said Dekanos, "you'd be as dead as the people in the surrounding houses. The army is securing the area. Fifteen choppers were sent up to search for you—we hoped—or, if you were dead, the perpetrators. I have already reported to Athens that you are alive and well."

"They were jamming the cellphone," said Father.

"Whoever did this has a very effective organization," said Dekanos. "Nine other children, it turns out, were taken within hours of Petra Arkanian."

"Who?" demanded Bean.

"I don't know the names yet," said Dekanos. "Only the count."

"Were any of the others simply killed?" asked Bean.

"No," said Dekanos. "Not that I've heard, anyway."

"Then why did they blow up our house?" Mother demanded.

"If we knew why," said Dekanos, "we'd know who. And vice versa."

They were belted into their seats. The chopper rose from the beach—but not very high. By now the other choppers were ranged around them and above them. Flying escort.

"Ground troops are continuing the search for the perpetrators," said Dekanos. "But your survival is our highest priority."

"We appreciate that," said Mother.

But Bean was not all that appreciative. The Greek military would, of course, put them in hiding and protect them carefully. But no matter what they did, the one thing they could not do was conceal the knowledge of his location from the Greek government itself. And the Greek government had been part of the Russia-dominated Warsaw Pact for generations now, since before the Formic War. Therefore Achilles—if it was Achilles, if it was Russia he worked for, if, if—would be able to find out where they were. Bean knew that it was not enough for him to be in protection. He had to be in true concealment, where no government could find him, where no one but himself would know who he was.

The trouble was, he was not only still a child, he was a famous child. Between his youth and his celebrity, it would be almost impossible for him to move unnoticed through the world. He would have to have help. So for the time being, he had to remain in military custody and simply hope that it would take him less time to get away than it would take Achilles to get to him.

If it was Achilles.

3

Message in a Bottle

```
To: Carlotta%agape@vatican.net/orders/
sisters/ind
From: Graff%pilgrimage@colmin.gov
Re: Danger
```

I have no idea where you are and that's
good, because I believe you are in
grave danger, and the harder it is to
find you, the better.

Since I'm no longer with the I.F., I'm
not kept abreast of things there. But
the news is full of the kidnapping of
most of the children who served with
Ender in Command School. That could
have been done by anybody, there is no
shortage of nations or groups that

might conceive and carry out such a project. What you may not know is that there was no attempt to kidnap one of them. From a friend of mine I have learned that the beach house in Ithaca where Bean and his family were vacationing was simply blown up—with so much force that the neighboring houses were also flattened and everyone in them killed. Bean and his family had already escaped and are under the protection of the Greek military. Supposedly this is a secret, in hopes that the assassins will think they succeeded, but in fact, like most governments, Greece leaks like a colander, and the assassins probably already know more than I do about where Bean is.

There is only one person on Earth who would prefer Bean dead.

That means that the people who got Achilles out of that mental hospital are not just using him—he is making, or at least influencing, their decisions to fit his private agenda. The danger to you is grave. The danger to Bean, more so. He must go into deep hiding, and he cannot go alone. To save his life and yours, the only thing I can think of is to get both of you off planet. We are within months of launching our first colony ships. If I am the only one to know your real identities, we can keep

```
you safe until launch. But we must get
Bean out of Greece as quickly as possi-
ble. Are you with me?

Do not tell me where you are. We will
work out how to meet.
```

How stupid did they think she was?

It took Petra only about half an hour to realize that these people weren't Turkish. Not that she was some kind of expert on language, but they'd be babbling along and every now and then out would pop a word of Russian. She didn't understand Russian either, except for a few loan words in Armenian, and Azerbaijani had loan words like that, too, but the thing is, when you say a Russian loan word in Armenian, you give it an Armenian pronunciation. These clowns would switch to an easy, native-sounding Russian accent when they hit those words. She would have to have been a gibbon in the slow-learner class not to realize that the Turkish pose was just that, a pose.

So when she decided she'd learned all she could with her eyes closed, listening, she spoke up in Fleet Common. "Aren't we across the Caucasus yet? When do I get to pee?"

Someone said an expletive.

"No, pee," she answered. She opened her eyes and blinked. She was on the floor of some ground vehicle. She started to sit up.

A man pushed her back down with his foot.

"Oh, that's clever. Keep me out of sight as we coast along the tarmac, but how will you get me into the airplane without anyone seeing? You want me to come out walking and acting normal so nobody gets all excited, right?"

"You'll act that way when we tell you to or we'll kill you," said the man with the heavy foot.

"If you had the authority to kill me, I'd be dead back in Maralik." She started to rise again. Again the foot pushed her back down.

"Listen carefully," she said. "I've been kidnapped because somebody wants me to plan a war for them. That means I'm going to be meeting with the top brass. They're not stupid enough to think they'll get anything decent from me without my willing cooperation. That's why they wouldn't let you kill my mother. So when I tell them that I won't do anything for them until I have your balls in a paper bag, how long do you think it will take them to decide what's more important to them? My brain or your balls?"

"We *do* have the authority to kill you."

It took her only moments to decide why such authority might have been given to morons like these. "Only if I'm in imminent danger of being rescued. Then they'd rather have me dead than let somebody else get the use of me. Let's see you make a case for *that* here on the runway at the Gyuniri airport."

A different rude word this time.

Somebody spurted out a sentence of Russian. She caught the gist of it from the intonation and the bitter laughter afterward. "They warned you she was a genius."

Genius, hell. If she was so smart, why hadn't she anticipated the possibility that somebody would make a grab for the kids who won the war? And it had to be kids, not just her, because she was too far down the list for somebody outside Armenia to make her their only choice. When the front door was locked, she should have run for the cops instead of puttering around to the back door. And that was another stupid thing they did, locking the front door. In Russia you had to lock your doors, they probably thought that was normal. They should have done better research. Not that it helped her now, of course. Except that she knew they weren't all that careful and they weren't all that bright. Anybody can kidnap someone who's taking no precautions.

"So Russia makes her play for world domination, is that it?" she asked.

"Shut up," said the man in the seat in front of her.

"I don't speak Russian, you know, and I won't learn."

"You don't have to," said a woman.

"Isn't that ironic?" said Petra. "Russia plans to take over the world, but they have to speak English to do it."

The foot on her belly pressed down harder.

"Remember your balls in a bag," she said.

A moment, and then the foot let up.

She sat up, and this time no one pushed her down.

"Untape me so I can get myself up on the seat. Come on! My arms hurt in this position! Haven't you learned anything since the days of the KGB? Unconscious people don't have to have their circulation cut off. Fourteen-year-old Armenian girls can probably be overpowered quite easily by big strong Russian goons."

By now the tape was off and she was sitting beside Heavy-foot and a guy who never looked at her, just kept watching out the left window, then the right, then the left again. "So this is Gyuniri airport?"

"What, you don't recognize it?"

"I've never been here before. When would I? I've only taken two airplane trips in my life, one out of Yerevan when I was five, and the other coming back, nine years later."

"She knew it was Gyuniri because it's the closest

airport that doesn't fly commercial jets," said the
woman. She spoke without any tone in her voice—not
contempt, not deference. Just . . . flat.

"Whose bright idea was this? Because captive generals don't strategize all that well."

"First, why in the world do you think anyone would
tell us?" said the woman. "Second, why don't you shut
up and find things out when they matter?"

"Because I'm a cheerful, talkative extrovert who
likes to make friends," said Petra.

"You're a bossy, nosy introvert who likes to piss
people off," said the woman.

"Oh, you actually did some research."

"No, just observation." So she did have a sense of
humor. Maybe.

"You'd better just pray you can get over the Caucasus before you have to answer to the Armenian Air
Force."

Heavy-foot made a derisory noise, proving that he
didn't recognize irony when he heard it.

"Of course, you'll probably have only a small
plane, and we'll probably fly out over the Black Sea.
Which means that I.F. satellites will know exactly
where I am."

"You're not I.F. personnel anymore," said the
woman.

"Meaning they don't care what happens to you,"
said Heavy-foot.

By now they had pulled to a stop beside a small
plane. "A jet, I'm impressed," said Petra. "Does it
have any weaponry? Or is it just wired with explosives
so that if the Armenian Air Force does start to force
you down, you can blow me up and the whole plane
with me?"

"Do we have to tie you again?" asked the woman.

"That would look really good to the people in the control tower."

"Get her out," said the woman.

Stupidly, the men on both sides of her opened their doors and got out, leaving her a choice of exits. So she chose Heavy-foot because she knew he was stupid, whereas the other man was anyone's guess. And, yes, he truly was stupid, because he held her by only one arm as he used his other hand to close the door. So she lurched to one side as if she had stumbled, drawing him off balance, and then, still using his grip to support her weight, she did a double kick, one in the groin and one in the knee. She landed solidly both times, and he let go of her very nicely before falling to the ground, writhing, one hand clutching his crotch and the other trying to slide his kneecap back around to the front of his knee.

Did they think she'd forgotten all her hand-to-hand unarmed combat training? Hadn't she warned him that she'd have his balls in a bag?

She made a good run for it, and she was feeling pretty good about how much speed she had picked up during her months of running at school, until she realized that they weren't following her. And that meant they knew they didn't have to.

No sooner had she noticed this than she felt something sharp pierce the skin over her right shoulder blade. She had time to slow down but not to stop before she collapsed into unconsciousness again.

———

This time they kept her drugged until they reached their destination, and since she never saw any scenery except the walls of what seemed to be an underground bunker, she had no guesses about where they might have taken her. Somewhere in Russia, that's all. And from the soreness of the bruises on her arms and legs and neck and the scrapes on her knees and palms and nose, she guessed that they hadn't been too careful with her. The price she paid for being a bossy, nosy introvert. Or maybe it was the part about pissing people off.

She lay on her bunk until a doctor came in and treated her scrapes with a special no-anesthetic blend of alcohol and acid, or so it seemed. "Was that just in case it didn't hurt enough?" she asked.

The doctor didn't answer. Apparently they had warned the woman what happened to those who spoke to her.

"The guy I kicked in the balls, did they have to amputate them?"

Still no answer. Not even a trace of amusement. Could this possibly be the one educated person in Russia who didn't speak Common?

Meals were brought to her, lights went on and off, but no one came to speak to her and she was not allowed out of her room. She heard nothing through the heavy doors, and it became clear that her punishment for her misbehavior on the trip was going to be solitary confinement for a while.

She resolved not to beg for mercy. Indeed, once it became clear to her that she was in isolation, she accepted it and isolated herself still further, neither speaking nor responding to the people who came and went. They never tried to speak to her, either, so the silence of her world was complete.

They did not understand how self-contained she was. How her mind could show her more than mere reality ever could. She could recall memories by the sheaf, by the bale. Whole conversations. And then new versions of those conversations, in which she was actually able to say the clever things that she only really thought of later.

She could even relive every moment of the battles on Eros. Especially the battle where she fell asleep in the middle. How tired she was. How she struggled frantically to stay awake. How she could feel her mind being so sluggish that she began to forget where she was, and why, and even who she was.

To escape from this endlessly repeating scene, she tried to think of other things. Her parents, her little brother. She could remember everything they had said and done since she returned, but after a while the only memories that mattered to her were the early ones from before Battle School. Memories she had suppressed for nine years, as best she could. All the promises of the family life that was lost to her. The good-bye when her mother wept and let her go. Her father's hand as he led her to the car. That hand had always meant that she was safe, before. But this time that hand led her to a place where she never felt safe again. She knew she had chosen to go—but she was only a child, and she knew that this was what was expected of her. That she should not succumb to the temptation to run to her weeping mother and cling to her and say no, I won't do it, let someone else become a soldier, I want to stay here and bake with Mama and play mother to my own little dolls. Not go off into space where I can learn how to kill strange and terrible creatures—and, by the way, humans as well, who trusted me and then I fell . . . a . . . sleep.

Being alone with her memories was not all that happy for her.

She tried fasting, simply ignoring the food they brought her, the liquids too, nothing by mouth. She expected someone to speak to her then, to cajole. But no. The doctor came in, slapped an injection into her arm, and when she woke up her hand was sore where the IV had been and she realized that there was no point in refusing to eat.

She hadn't thought to keep a calendar at first, but after the IV she did keep a calendar on her own body, pressing a fingernail into her wrist until it bled. Seven days on the left wrist, then switch to the right, and all she had to remember in her head was the number of weeks.

Except she didn't bother going for three. She realized that they were going to outwait her because, after all, they had the others they had kidnapped, and no doubt some of them were cooperating, so it was perfectly all right with them if she stayed in her cell and got farther and farther behind so that when she finally did emerge, she'd be the worst of them at whatever it was they were doing.

Fine, what did she care? She was never going to help them anyway.

But if she was to have any chance to get free of these people and this place, she had to be out of this room and into a place where she could earn enough trust to be able to get free.

Trust. They'd expect her to lie, they'd expect her to plot. Therefore she had to be as convincing as possible. Her long time in solitary was a help, of course—everyone knew that isolation caused untold mental pressures. Another thing that helped was that it was undoubtedly known to them by now, from the other children, that she was the first one who broke under pressure during the battles on Eros. So they would be predisposed to believe a breakdown now.

She began to cry. It wasn't hard. There were plenty of real tears pent up in her. But she shaped those emotions, made it into a whimpering cry that went on and on and on. Her nose filled with mucus, but she did not blow it. Her eyes streamed with tears but she did not wipe them. Her pillow got soaked with tears and covered with snot but she did not evade the wet place. Instead she rolled her hair right through it as she turned over, did it again and again until her hair was matted with mucus and her face stiff with it. She made sure her crying did not get more desperate—let no one think she was trying to get attention. She toyed with the idea of falling silent when anyone came into the room, but decided against it—she figured it would be more convincing to be oblivious to other people's coming and going.

It worked. Someone came in after a day of this and slapped her with another injection. And this time when she woke up, she was in a hospital bed with a window that showed a cloudless northern sky. And sitting by her bed was Dink Meeker.

"Ho Dink," she said.

"Ho Petra. You pasted these conchos over real good."

"One does what one can for the cause," she said. "Who else?"

"You're the last to come out of solitary. They got the whole team from Eros, Petra. Except Ender, of course. And Bean."

"He's not in solitary?"

"No, they didn't keep it a secret who was still in the box. We thought you made a pretty fine showing."

"Who was second-longest?"

"Nobody cares. We were all out in the first week. You lasted five."

So it had been two and a half weeks before she started her calendar.

"Because I'm the stupid one."

" 'Stubborn' is the right word."

"Know where we are?"

"Russia."

"I meant where in Russia."

"Far from any borders, they assure us."

"What are our resources?"

"Very thick walls. No tools. Constant observation. They weigh our bodily wastes, I'm not kidding."

"What have they got us doing?"

"Like a really dumbed-down Battle School. We put up with it for a long time till Fly Molo finally gave up and when one of the teachers was quoting one of Von Clausewitz's stupider generalizations, Fly continued the quotation, sentence after sentence, paragraph after paragraph, and the rest of us joined in as best we could—I mean, nobody has a memory like Fly, but we do OK—and they finally got the idea that we could teach the stupid classes to them. So now it's just . . . war games."

"Again? You think they're going to spring it on us later that the games are real?"

"No, this is just planning stuff. Strategy for a war between Russia and Turkmenistan. Russia and an alliance between Turkmenistan, Kazakhstan, Azerbaijan, and Turkey. War with the United States and Canada. War with the old NATO alliance except Germany. War with Germany. On and on. China. India. Really stupid stuff, too, like between Brazil and Peru, which makes no sense but maybe they were testing our compliance or something."

"All this in five weeks?"

"Three weeks of kuso classes, and then two weeks of war games. When we finish our plan, see, they run it on the computer to show us how it went. Someday they're going to catch on that the only way to do this that isn't a waste of time is to have one of us making the plan for the opponent as well."

"My guess is you just told them."

"I've told them before but they're hard to persuade. Typical military types. Makes you understand why the whole concept of Battle School was developed in the first place. If the war had been up to adults, there'd be Buggers at every breakfast table in the world by now."

"But they *are* listening?"

"I think they record it all and play it back at slow speeds to see if we're passing messages subvocally."

Petra smiled.

"So why did you finally decide to cooperate?" he asked.

She shrugged. "I don't think I decided."

"Hey, they don't pull you out of the room until you express really sincere interest in being a good, compliant little kid."

She shook her head. "I don't think I did that."

"Yeah, well, whatever you did, you were the last of Ender's jeesh to break, kid."

A short buzzer sounded.

"Time's up," said Dink. He got up, leaned over, kissed her brow, and left the room.

———

Six weeks later, Petra was actually enjoying the life. By complying with the kids' demands, their captors had finally come up with some decent equipment.

Software that allowed them very realistic head-to-head strategic and tactical wargaming. Access to the nets so they could do decent research into terrains and capabilities so their wargaming had some realism—though they knew every message they sent was censored, because of the number of messages that were rejected for one obscure reason or another. They enjoyed each other's company, exercised together, and by all appearances seemed to be completely happy and compliant Russian commanders.

Yet Petra knew, as they all knew, that every one of them was faking. Holding back. Making dumb mistakes which, if they were made in combat, would lead to gaps that a clever enemy could exploit. Maybe their captors realized this, and maybe they didn't. At least it made them all feel better, though they never spoke of it. But since they were all doing it, and cooperating by not exposing those weaknesses by exploiting them in the games, they could only assume that everyone felt the same about it.

They chatted comfortably about a lot of things— their disdain for their captors, memories of Ground School, Battle School, Command School. And, of course, Ender. He was out of the reach of these bastards, so they made sure to mention him a lot, to talk about how the I.F. was bound to use him to counter all these foolish plans the Russians were making. They knew they were blowing smoke, that the I.F. wouldn't do anything, they even said so. But still, Ender was there, the ultimate trump card.

Till the day one of the erstwhile teachers told them that a colony ship had gone, with Ender and his sister Valentine aboard.

"I didn't even know he had a sister," said Hot Soup.

No one said anything, but they all knew that this was impossible. They had all known Ender had a sister. But . . . whatever Hot Soup was doing, they'd play along and see what the game was.

"No matter what they tell us, one thing we know," said Hot Soup. "Wiggin is still with us."

Again, they weren't sure what he meant by this. After the briefest pause, though, Shen clapped his hand to his chest and cried out, "In our hearts forever."

"Yes," said Hot Soup. "Ender is in our hearts."

Just the tiniest extra emphasis on the name "Ender."

But he had said Wiggin before.

And before that, he had called attention to the fact that they all knew Ender had a sister. They also knew that Ender had a brother. Back on Eros, while Ender was in bed recovering from his breakdown after finding out the battles had been real, Mazer Rackham had told them some things about Ender. And Bean had told them more, as they were trapped together while the League War played itself out. They had listened as Bean expounded on what Ender's brother and sister meant to him, that the reason Ender had been born at all during the days of the two-child law was because his brother and sister were so brilliant, but the brother was too dangerously aggressive and the sister too passively compliant. How Bean knew all this he wouldn't tell, but the information was indelibly planted in their memories, tied as it was with those tense days after their victory over the Formics and before the defeat of the Polemarch in his attempt to take over the I.F.

So when Hot Soup said "Wiggin is still with us," he had not been referring to Ender or Valentine, because they most assuredly were not "with us."

Peter, that was the brother's name. Peter Wiggin.

Hot Soup was telling them that he was one whose mind was perhaps as brilliant as Ender's, and he was still on Earth. Maybe, if they could somehow contact him on the outside, he would ally himself with his brother's battle companions. Maybe he could find a way to get them free.

The game now was to find some way to communicate with him.

Sending email would be pointless—the last thing they needed to do was have their captors see a bunch of email addressed to every possible variant of Peter Wiggin's name at every single mailnet that they could think of. And sure enough, by that evening Alai was telling them some tall tale about a genie in a bottle that had washed up on the shore. Everyone listened with feigned interest, but they knew the real story had been stated right at the beginning, when Alai said, "The fisherman thought maybe the bottle had a message from some castaway, but when he popped the cork, a cloud of smoke came out and . . ." and they got it. What they had to do was send a message in a bottle, a message that would go indiscriminately to everyone everywhere, but which could only be understood by Ender's brother, Peter.

But as she thought about it, Petra realized that with all these other brilliant brains working to reach Peter Wiggin, she might as well work on an alternative plan. Peter Wiggin was not the only one outside who might help them. There was Bean. And while Bean was almost certainly in hiding, so that he would have far less freedom of action than Peter Wiggin, that didn't mean they couldn't still find him.

She thought about it for a week in every spare moment, rejecting idea after idea.

Then she thought of one that might get past the censors.

She worked out the text of her message very carefully in her head, making sure that it was phrased and worded exactly right. Then, with that memorized, she figured the binary code of each letter in standard two-byte format, and memorized that. Then she started the really hard stuff. All done in her head, so nothing was ever committed to paper or typed into the computer, where a keystroke monitor could report to their captors whatever she wrote.

In the meantime, she found a complex black-and-white drawing of a dragon on a netsite somewhere in Japan and saved it as a small file. When she finally had the message fully encoded in her mind, it took only a few minutes of fiddling with the drawing and she was done. She added it as part of her signature on every letter she sent. She spent so little time on it that she did not think it would look to her captors like anything more than a harmless whim. If they asked, she could say she added the picture in memory of Ender's Dragon Army in Battle School.

Of course, it wasn't just a picture of a dragon anymore. Now there was a little poem under it.

```
Share this dragon.
If you do,
lucky end for
them and you.
```

She would tell them, if they asked, that the words were just an ironic joke. If they didn't believe her, they would strip off the picture and she'd have to find another way.

She sent it on every letter from then on. Including to the other kids. She got it back from them on messages after that, so they had picked up on what she was doing and were helping. Whether their captors were actually letting it leave the building or not, she had no way of knowing—at first. Finally, though, she started getting it back on messages from outside. A single glance told her that she had succeeded—her coded message was still embedded in the picture. It hadn't been stripped out.

Now it was just a question of whether Bean would see it and look at it closely enough to realize that there was a mystery to solve.

4

Custody

To: Graff%pilgrimage@colmin.gov
From: Chamrajnagar%Jawaharlal@ifcom.gov
Re: Quandary

You know better than anyone how vital
it is to maintain the independence of
the Fleet from the machinations of
politicians. That was my reason for rejecting "Locke's" suggestion. But in
the event I was wrong. Nothing jeopar-
dizes Fleet independence more than the
prospect of one nation becoming dominant, especially if, as seems likely,
the particular nation is one that has
already shown a disposition to take
over the I.F. and use it for nationalist purposes.

I'm afraid I was rather harsh with
Locke. I dare not write to him directly, because, while Locke would be
reliable, one can never know what
Demosthenes would do with an official
letter of apology from the Polemarch.
Therefore please arrange for him to be
notified that my threat is rescinded and
I wish him well.

I do learn from my mistakes. Since one
of Wiggin's companions remains outside
the control of the aggressor, prudence
dictates that young Delphiki be protected. Since you are Earthside and I am
not, I give you brevet command over an
IFM contingent and any other resources
you need, orders forthcoming through
level 6 backchannels (of course). I
give you specific instructions not to
tell me or anyone else of the steps
you have taken to protect Delphiki or
his family. There is to be no record in
the I.F. system or that of any government.

By the way, trust no one in the Hegemony. I always knew they were a nest of
careerists, but recent experience shows
that the careerist is now being replaced by worse: the ideologue rampant.

Act swiftly. It appears that we are either on the verge of a new war, or the
League War never quite ended after all.

How many days can you stay closed in, surrounded by guards, before you start to feel like a prisoner? Bean never felt claustrophobic in Battle School. Not even on Eros, where the low ceilings of the Buggers' tunnels teetered over them like a car slipping off its jack. Not like this, closed up with his family, pacing the four-room apartment. Well, not actually pacing it. He just *felt* like pacing it, and instead sat still, controlling himself, trying to think of some way to get control of his own life.

Being under someone else's protection was bad enough—he had never liked that, though it had happened before, when Poke protected him on the streets of Rotterdam, and then when Sister Carlotta saved him from certain death by taking him in and sending him to Battle School. But both those times, there were things he could do to make sure everything went right. This was different. He knew something was going to go wrong, and there was nothing he could do about it.

The soldiers guarding this apartment, surrounding the building, they were all good, loyal men, Bean had no reason to doubt that. They weren't going to betray him. Probably. And the bureaucracy that was keeping his location a secret—no doubt it would just be an honest oversight, not a conscious betrayal, that would give his address to his enemies.

And in the meantime, Bean could only wait, pinned down by his protectors. They were the web, holding him in place for the spider. And there wasn't a thing he could say to change this situation. If Greece were fighting a war, they'd set Bean and Nikolai to work, making plans, charting strategies. But when it came to a matter of security, they were just children, to be protected and taken care of. It would do no good for Bean to explain that his best protection was to get out of here, get off completely on his own, make a life for himself on the streets of some city where he could be nameless and faceless and lost and safe. Because they looked at him and saw nothing but a little kid. And who listens to little kids?

Little kids have to be taken care of.

By adults who don't have it in their power to keep those little kids safe.

He wanted to throw something through the window and jump down after it.

Instead he sat still. He read books. He signed on to the nets using one of his many names and cruised around, looking for whatever dribbles of information oozed through the military security systems of every nation, hoping for something to tell him where Petra and Fly Molo and Vlad and Dumper were being held. Some country that was showing signs of a little more cockiness because they thought they had the winning hand now. Or a country that was acting more cautious and methodical because finally somebody with a brain was running their strategy.

But it was pointless, because he knew he wasn't going to find it this way. The real information never got onto the net until it was too late to do anything about it. Somebody knew. The facts he needed to find his way to his friends were available in a dozen sites—he knew that, *knew* it, because that's the way it always was, the historians would find it and wonder for a thousand pages at a time: Why didn't anybody notice? Why didn't anybody put it together? Because the people who had the information were too dim to know what they had, and the people who could have understood it were locked in an apartment in an abandoned resort that even tourists didn't want to come to anymore.

The worst thing was that even Mother and Father were getting on his nerves. After a childhood with no parents, the best thing that had ever happened to him was when Sister Carlotta's research found his biological parents. The war ended, and when all the other kids got to go home to their families, Bean wasn't left over. He got to go home to his family, too. He had no childhood memories of them, of course. But Nikolai had, and Nikolai let Bean borrow them as if they were his own.

They were good people, his mother and his father. They never made him feel as if he were an intruder, a stranger, even a visitor. It was as if he had always belonged with them. They liked him. They loved him. It was a strange, exhilarating feeling to be with people who didn't want anything from you except your happiness, who were glad just to have you around.

But when you're already going crazy from confinement, it doesn't matter how much you like somebody, how much you love them, how grateful you are for their kindness to you. They will make you nuts. Everything they do grates on you like a bad song that won't get out of your head. You just want to scream at them to *shut. Up.* But you don't, because you love them and you know that you're probably driving them crazy too and as long as there's no hope of release you've got to keep things calm . . .

And then finally there comes a knock on the door and you open it up and you realize that something different is finally going to happen.

It was Colonel Graff and Sister Carlotta at the door. Graff in a suit now, and Sister Carlotta in an extravagant auburn wig that made her look really stupid but also kind of pretty. The whole family recognized them at once, except that Nikolai had never met Sister Carlotta. But when Bean and his family got up to greet them, Graff held up a hand to stop them and Carlotta put her finger to her lips. They came inside and closed the door after them and beckoned the family to gather in the bathroom.

It was a tight fit, the six of them in there. Father and Mother ended up standing in the shower while Graff hung a tiny machine from the overhead light. Once it was in place and the red light began blinking, Graff spoke softly.

"Hi," he said. "We came to get you out of this place."

"Why all the precautions in here?" asked Father.

"Because part of the security system here is to listen in on everything said in this apartment."

"To protect us, they spy on us?" asked Mother.

"Of course they do," said Father.

"Since anything we say here might leak into the system," said Graff, "and would most certainly leak right back out of the system, I brought this little machine, which hears every sound we make and produces countersounds that nullify them so we pretty much can't be heard."

"Pretty much?" asked Bean.

"That's why we won't go into any details," said Graff. "I'll tell you only this much. I'm the Minister of Colonization, and we have a ship that leaves in a few months. Just time enough to get you off Earth, up to the ISL, and over to Eros for the launch."

But even as he said it, he was shaking his head, and Sister Carlotta was grinning and shaking *her* head, too, so that they would know that this was all a lie. A cover story.

"Bean and I have been in space before, Mother," said Nikolai, playing along. "It's not so bad."

"It's what we fought the war for," Bean chimed in. "The Formics wanted Earth because it was just like the worlds they already lived on. So now that they're gone, we get *their* worlds, which should be good for us. It's only fair, don't you think?"

Of course their parents both understood what was happening, but Bean knew Mother well enough by now that he wasn't surprised that she had to ask a completely useless and dangerous question just to be sure.

"But we're not really . . ." she began. Then Father's hand gently covered her mouth.

"It's the only way to keep us safe," Father said. "Once we're going at lightspeed, it'll seem like a couple of years to us, while decades pass on Earth. By the time we reach the other planet, everybody who wants us dead will be dead themselves."

"Like Joseph and Mary taking Jesus into Egypt," said Mother.

"Exactly," said Father.

"Except they got to go back to Nazareth."

"If Earth destroys itself in some stupid war," said Father, "it won't matter to us anymore, because we'll be part of a new world. Be happy about this, Elena. It means we can stay together." Then he kissed her.

"Time to go, Mr. and Mrs. Delphiki. Bring the boys, please." Graff reached up and yanked the damper from the ceiling light.

The soldiers who waited for them in the hall wore the uniform of the I.F. Not a Greek uniform was in sight. And these young men were armed to the teeth. As they walked briskly to the stairs—no elevators, no doors that might suddenly open to leave them trapped in a box for an enemy to toss in a grenade or a few thousand projectiles—Bean watched the way the soldier in the lead watched everything, checked every corner, the light under every door in the hall, so that nothing could surprise him. Bean also saw how the man's body moved inside his clothes, with a kind of contained strength that made his clothes seem like Kleenex, he could rip through the fabric just by tugging at it a little, because nothing could hold him in except his own self-control. It was like his sweat was pure testosterone. This was what a man was supposed to be. This was a *soldier.*

I was never a soldier, thought Bean. He tried to imagine himself the way he had been in Battle School, strapping on cut-down flash-suit pieces that never fit him right. He always looked like somebody's pet monkey dressed up as a human for the joke of it. Like a toddler who got clothes out of his big brother's dresser. The man in front of him, that's what Bean wanted to be when he grew up. But try as he might, he could never imagine himself actually being big. No, not even being full size. He would always be looking up at the world. He might be male, he might be human, or at least humanesque, but he would never be manly. No one would ever look at him and say, Now, *that's* a man.

Then again, this soldier had never given orders that changed the course of history. Looking great in a uniform wasn't the only way to earn your place in the world.

Down the stairs, three flights, and then a pause for just a moment well back from the emergency exit while two of the soldiers came out and watched for the signal from the men in the I.F. chopper waiting thirty meters away. The signal came. Graff and Sister Carlotta led the way, still at a brisk walk. They looked neither left nor right, just focused on the helicopter. They got in, sat down, buckled up, and the chopper tilted and rose from the grass and flew low out over the water.

Mother was all for demanding to know the real plan, but again Graff cut off all discussion with a cheerful bellow of "Let's wait to discuss this until we can do it without shouting!"

Mother didn't like it. None of them did. But there was Sister Carlotta smiling her best nun smile, like a sort of Virgin-in-training. How could they help but trust her?

Five minutes in the air and then they set down on the deck of a submarine. It was a big one, with the stars and stripes of the United States, and it occurred to Bean that since they didn't know what country had kidnapped the other kids, how could they be sure they weren't just walking into the hands of their enemies?

But once they got down inside the ship, they could see that while the crew was in U.S. uniforms, the only people carrying weapons were the I.F. soldiers who had brought them and a half-dozen more who had been waiting for them with the sub. Since power came from the barrel of a gun, and the only guns on the ship were under Graff's command, Bean's mind was eased a little.

"If you try to tell us that we can't talk *here,*" Mother began—but to her consternation Graff again held up a hand, and Sister Carlotta again made a shushing gesture as Graff beckoned them to follow their lead soldier through the narrow corridors of the sub.

Finally the six of them were packed once more into a tiny space—this time the executive officer's cabin—and once again they waited while Graff hung his noise damper and turned it on. When the light started blinking, Mother was the first to speak.

"I'm trying to figure out how we can tell we aren't being kidnapped just like the others," she said dryly.

"You got it," said Graff. "They were all taken by a group of terrorist nuns, aided by fat old bureaucrats."

"He's joking," said Father, trying to soothe Mother's immediate wrath.

"I know he's joking. I just don't think it's funny. After all we've been through, and then we're supposed to go along without a word, without a question, just . . . *trusting*."

"Sorry," said Graff. "But you were already trusting the Greek government back where you were. You've got to trust somebody, so why not us?"

"At least the Greek Army explained things to us and pretended we had a right to make some decisions," said Mother.

They didn't explain things to me and Nikolai, Bean wanted to say.

"Come, children, no bickering," said Sister Carlotta. "The plan is very simple. The Greek Army continues to guard that apartment building as if you were still inside it, taking meals in and doing laundry. This fools no one, probably, but it makes the Greek government feel like they're part of the program. In the meantime, four passengers answering your description but flying under assumed names are taken to Eros, where they embark on the first colony ship, and only then, when the ship is launched, is an announcement made that for their protection, the Delphiki family have opted for permanent emigration and a new life in a new world."

"And where are we really?" asked Father.

"I don't know," said Graff very simply.

"And neither do I," said Sister Carlotta.

Bean's family looked at them in disbelief.

"I guess that means we won't be staying in the sub,"

said Nikolai, "because then you'd absolutely know where we are."

"It's a double blind," said Bean. "They're splitting us up. I'll go one way, you'll go another."

"Absolutely not," said Father.

"We've had enough of a divided family," said Mother.

"It's the only way," said Bean. "I knew it already. I . . . want it that way."

"You want to leave us?" said Mother.

"It's me they want to kill," said Bean.

"We don't know that!" said Mother.

"But we're pretty sure," said Bean. "If I'm not with you, then even if you're found, they'll probably leave you alone."

"And if we're divided," said Nikolai, "it changes the profile of what they're looking for. Not a mother and father and two boys. Now it's a mother and father and one boy. And a grandma and her grandchild." Nikolai grinned at Sister Carlotta.

"I was rather hoping to be taken for an aunt," she said.

"You talk as if you already know the plan!" said Mother.

"It was obvious," said Nikolai. "From the moment they told us the cover story in the bathroom. Why else would Colonel Graff bring Sister Carlotta?"

"It wasn't obvious to me," said Mother.

"Or to me," said Father. "But that's what happens when your sons are both brilliant military minds."

"How long?" Mother demanded. "When will it end? When do we get to have Bean back with us?"

"I don't know," said Graff.

"He can't know, Mother," said Bean. "Not until we know who did the kidnappings and why. When we know what the threat actually is, then we can judge when we've taken sufficient countermeasures to make it safe for us to come partway out of hiding."

Mother suddenly burst into tears. "And you *want* this, Julian?"

Bean put his arms around her. Not because he felt any personal need to do it, but because he knew she needed that gesture from him. Living with a family for a year had not given him the full complement of normal human emotional responses, but at least it had made him more aware of what they ought to be. And he did have one normal reaction—he felt a little guilty that he could only fake what Mother needed, instead of having it come from the heart. But such gestures never came from the heart, for Bean. It was a language he had learned too late for it to come naturally to him. He would always speak the language of the heart with an awkward foreign accent.

The truth was that even though he loved his family, he was eager to get to a place where he could get to work making the contacts he needed to get the information that would let him find his friends. Except for Ender, he was the only one from Ender's jeesh who was outside and free. They needed him, and he'd wasted enough time already.

So he held his mother, and she clung to him, and she shed many tears. He also embraced his father, but more briefly; and he and Nikolai only punched each other's arms. All foreign gestures to Bean, but they knew he meant to mean them, and took them as if they were real.

The sub was fast. They weren't very long at sea before they reached a crowded port—Salonika, Bean assumed, though it could have been any other cargo port on the Aegean. The sub never actually entered the harbor. Instead, it surfaced between two ships moving in a parallel track toward the harbor. Mother, Father, Nikolai, and Graff were transferred to a freighter along with two of the soldiers, who were now in civilian clothes, as if that could conceal the soldierly way they acted. Bean and Carlotta stayed behind. Neither group would know where the other was. There would be no effort to contact each other. That had been another hard realization for Mother. "Why can't we write?"

"Nothing is easier to track than email," said Father. "Even if we use disguised online identities, if someone finds us, and we're writing regularly to Julian, then they'll see the pattern and track him down."

Mother understood it then. With her head, if not her heart.

Down inside the sub, Bean and Sister Carlotta sat down at a tiny table in the mess.

"Well?" said Bean.

"Well," said Sister Carlotta.

"Where are *we* going?" asked Bean.

"I have no idea," said Sister Carlotta. "They'll transfer us to another ship at another port, and we'll get off, and I have these false identities that we're supposed to use, but I really have no idea where we should go from there."

"We have to keep moving. No more than a few weeks in any one place," said Bean. "And I have to get on the nets with new identities every time we move, so no one can track the pattern."

"Do you seriously think someone will catalogue all the email in the entire world and follow up on all the ones that move around?" asked Sister Carlotta.

"Yes," said Bean. "They probably already do, so it's just a matter of running a search."

"But that's billions of e-mails a day."

"That's why it takes so many clerks to check all the email addresses on the file cards in the central switchboard," said Bean. He grinned at Sister Carlotta.

She did not grin back. "You really are a snotty and disrespectful little boy," she said.

"You're really leaving it up to me to decide where we go?"

"Not at all. I'm merely waiting to make a decision until we both agree."

"Oh, now, *that's* a cheap excuse to stay down here in this sub with all these great-looking men."

"Your level of banter has become even more crude than it was when you lived on the streets of Rotterdam," she said, coolly analytical.

"It's the war," said Bean. "It . . . it changes a man."

She couldn't keep a straight face any longer. Even though her laugh was only a single bark, and her smile lasted only a moment longer, it was enough. She still liked him. And he, to his surprise, still liked her, even though it had been years since he lived with her while she educated him to a level where Battle School would take him. He was surprised because, at the time he lived with her, he had never let himself realize that he liked her. After Poke's death, he hadn't been willing to admit to himself that he liked anybody. But now he knew the truth. He liked Sister Carlotta just fine.

Of course, she would probably get on his nerves after a while, too, just like his parents had. But at least when that happened, they could pick up and move. There wouldn't be soldiers keeping them indoors and away from the windows.

And if it ever became truly annoying, Bean could leave and strike out on his own. He'd never say that to

Sister Carlotta, because it would only worry her. Besides, she was bound to know it already. She had all the test data. And those tests had been designed to tell everything about a person. Why, she probably knew him better than he knew himself.

Of course, *he* knew that back when he took the tests, there was hardly an honest answer on any of the psychological tests. He had already read enough psychology by the time he took them that he knew exactly what answers were needed to show the profile that would probably get him into Battle School. So in fact she didn't know him from those tests at all.

But then, he didn't have any idea what his real answers would have been, then or now. So it isn't as if he knew himself any better.

And because she had observed him, and she was wise in her own way, she probably *did* know him better than he knew himself.

What a laugh, though. To think that one human being could ever really know another. You could get used to each other, get so habituated that you could speak their words right along with them, but you never knew why other people said what they said or did what they did, because they never even knew themselves. Nobody understands anybody.

And yet somehow we live together, mostly in peace, and get things done with a high enough success rate that people keep trying. Human beings get married and a lot of the marriages work, and they have children and most of them grow up to be decent people, and they have schools and businesses and factories and farms that have results at some level of acceptability—all without having a clue what's going on inside any-body's head.

Muddling through, that's what human beings do.

That was the part of being human that Bean hated the most.

5

Ambition

To: Locke%espinoza@polnet.gov
From: Graff%%@colmin.gov
Re: Correction

I have been asked to relay a message
that a threat of exposure has been rescinded, with apologies. Nor should you
be alarmed that your identity is widely
known. Your identity was penetrated at
my direction several years ago, and
while multiple persons then under my
command were made aware of who you are,
it is a group that has neither reason
nor disposition to violate confidential-
ity. The only exception has now been
chastened by circumstance. On a personal level, let me say that I have no

doubt of your capacity to achieve your
ambition. I can only hope that, in the
event of success, you will choose to
emulate Washington, MacArthur, or Augustus rather than Napoleon, Alexander,
or Hitler.

Colmin

Now and then Peter was almost overwhelmed by a desire to tell somebody what was actually happening in
his life. He never succumbed to the desire, of course,
since to tell it would be to undo it. But especially now
that Valentine had gone, it was almost unbearable to sit
there reading a personal letter from the Minister of
Colonization and not shout for the other students in the
library to come and see.

When he and Valentine had first broken through and
placed essays or, in Valentine's case, diatribes on some
of the major political nets, they had done a little hugging and laughing and jumping around. But it never
took long for Valentine to remember how much she
loathed half the positions she was forced to espouse in
her Demosthenes persona, and her resulting gloom
would calm him down as well. Peter missed her, of
course, but he did not miss the arguments, the whining
about having to be the bad guy. She could never see
how the Demosthenes persona was the interesting one,
the most fun to work with. Well, when he was done
with it he'd give it back to her—long before she got to
whatever planet it was that she and Ender were heading for. She'd know by then that even at his most outrageous, Demosthenes was a catalyst, making things
happen.

Valentine. Stupid to choose Ender and exile over Peter and *life*. Stupid to get so angry over the obvious necessity of keeping Ender off planet. For his own protection, Peter told her, and hadn't events proven it? If he'd come home as Valentine originally wanted, he'd be a captive somewhere, or dead, depending on whether his captors had been able to get him to cooperate. I was right, Valentine, as I've always been right about everything. But you'd rather be nice than right, you'd rather be liked than powerful, and you'd rather be in exile with the brother who worships you than share power with the brother who made you influential.

Ender was already gone, Valentine. When they took him away to Battle School, he was never coming home—not the precious little Enderpoo that you adored and petted and watched over like a little mommy playing with a doll. They were going to make a soldier out of him, a killer—did you even *look* at the video they showed during Graff's court-martial?—and if something named Andrew Wiggin came home, it would *not* be the Ender you sentimentalized to the point of nausea. He'd be a damaged, broken, useless soldier whose war was finished. Pushing to have him sent off to a colony was the kindest thing I could have done for our erstwhile brother. Nothing would have been sadder than having his biography include the ruin that his life would have become here on Earth, even if nobody bothered to kidnap him. Like Alexander, he'll go out with a flash of brilliant light and live forever in glory, instead of withering away and dying in miserable obscurity, getting trotted out for parades now and then. I was the kind one!

Good riddance to both of you. You would have been drags on my boat, thorns in my side, pains in my ass.

But it would have been fun to show Valentine the letter from Graff—Graff himself! Even though he hid his private access code, even though he was condescending in his urging Peter to emulate the nice guys of history—as if anybody ever *planned* to create an ephemeral empire like Napoleon's or Hitler's—the fact was that even knowing that Locke, far from being some elder statesman speaking anonymously from retirement, was just an underage college student, Graff still thought Peter was worth talking to. Still worth giving advice to, because Graff knew that Peter Wiggin mattered now and would matter in the future. Damn right, Graff!

Damn right, everybody! Ender Wiggin may have saved your asses against the Buggers, but I'm the one who's going to save humanity's collective rectum from its own colostomy. Because human beings have always been more dangerous to the survival of the human race than anything else except the complete destruction of planet Earth, and now we're taking steps to evade even that by spreading our seed—including little Enderseed himself—to other worlds. Does Graff have any idea how hard I worked to make his little Ministry of Colonization come into existence in the first place? Has anybody bothered to track the history of the good ideas that have actually become law to see how many times the trail leads back to Locke?

They actually consulted with me when they were deciding whether to offer you the title of Colmin with which you so affectedly sign your emails. Bet you didn't know *that*, Mr. Minister. Without *me*, you might have been signing your letters with stupid good-luck dragon pictures like half the morons on the net these days.

And for a few minutes it just about killed him that nobody could know about this letter except himself and Graff.

And then . . .

The moment passed. His breathing returned to normal. His wiser self prevailed. It's better not to be distracted by the interference of personal fame. In due course his name would be revealed, he'd take his place in a position of authority instead of mere influence. For now, anonymity would do.

He saved the message from Graff, and then sat there staring at the display.

His hand was trembling.

He looked at it as if it were someone else's hand. What in the world is *that* about, he wondered. Am I such a celebrity hound that getting a letter from a top Hegemony official makes me shake like a teenager at a pop concert?

No. The cool realist took over. He was not trembling out of excitement. That, as always, was transitory, already gone.

He was trembling out of fear.

Because somebody was assembling a team of strategists. The top kids from the Battle School program. The ones they chose to fight the final battle to save humanity. Somebody had them and meant to use them. And sooner or later, that somebody would be Peter's rival, head to head with him, and Peter would have to outthink not only that rival, but also the kids he had managed to bend to his will.

Peter hadn't made it into Battle School. He didn't have what it took. For one reason or another, he was cut from the program without ever leaving home. So *every* kid who went to Battle School was more likely to make a good strategist and tactician than Peter Wiggin, and Peter's principal rival for hegemony had collected around himself the very best of them all.

Except for Ender, of course. Ender, whom I *could* have brought home if I had pulled the right strings and manipulated public opinion the other way. Ender, who was the best of all and might have been standing by my side. But no, I sent him away. For his own damn good. For his own *safety*. And now here I am, facing the struggle that my whole life has been devoted to, and all I've got to face the best of the Battle School is . . . me.

His hand trembled. So what? He'd be crazy *not* to be just a little bit afraid.

But when that moron Chamrajnagar threatened to expose him and bring the whole thing crashing down, just because he was too stupid to see how Demosthenes was necessary in order to bring about results that Locke's persona could never reach for—he had spent weeks in hell over that. Watching as the Battle School kids were kidnapped. Unable to do anything, to say anything pertinent. Oh, he answered letters that some people sent, he did enough investigating to satisfy himself that only Russia had the resources to bring it off. But he dared not use Demosthenes to demand that the I.F. be investigated for its failure to protect these children. Demosthenes could only make some routine suppositions about how it was bound to be the Warsaw Pact that had taken the kids—but of course everyone expected Demosthenes to say that, he was a well-known russophobe, it meant nothing. All because some shortsighted, stupid, self-serving admiral had decided to interfere with the one person on Earth who seemed to care about trying to keep the world from another visit from Attila the Hun. He wanted to scream at

Chamrajnagar: I'm the one who writes essays while the other guy kidnaps children, but because you know who I am and you have no clue who *he* is, you reach out to stop *me*? That was about as bright as the pinheads who handed the government of Germany to Hitler because they thought he would be "useful" to them.

Now Chamrajnagar had relented. Sent a cowardly apology through someone else so he could avoid letting Peter have a letter with his signature on it. Too late anyway. The damage was done. Chamrajnagar had not only done nothing, he had kept Peter from doing anything, and now Peter faced a chess game where his side of the board had nothing but pawns, and the other player had a double complement of knights, rooks, and bishops.

So Peter's hand trembled. And he sometimes caught himself wishing that he weren't in this thing so utterly, absolutely alone. Did Napoleon, in his tent alone, wonder what the hell he was doing, betting everything, over and over again, on the ability of his army to do the impossible? Didn't Alexander, once in a while, wish there were someone else he could trust to make a decision or two?

Peter's lip curled in self-contempt. Napoleon? Alexander? It was the other guy who had a stableful of steeds like that to ride. While I have had it certified by the Battle School testing program that I am about as militarily talented as, say, John F. Kennedy, that U.S. President who lost his PT boat through carelessness and got a medal for it because his father had money and political pull, and then became President and made an unbroken string of stupid moves that never hurt him much politically because the press loved him so much.

That's me. I can manipulate the press. I can paint public opinion, nudge and pull and poke and inject things into it, but when it comes to war—and it will come to war—I'm going to look about as clever as the French when the blitzkrieg rolled through.

Peter looked around the reading room. Not much of a library. Not much of a school. But because he entered college early, being a certifiably gifted pupil, and not caring a whit about his formal education, he had gone to the hometown branch of the state university. For the first time he found himself envying the other students who were studying there. All they had to worry about was the next test, or keeping their scholarship, or their dating life.

I could have a life like theirs.

Right. He'd have to kill himself if he ever came to care what some teacher thought of an essay he wrote, or what some girl thought about the clothes he wore, or whether one soccer team could beat another.

He closed his eyes and leaned back in his chair. All this self-doubt was pointless. He knew he would never stop until he was forced to stop. From childhood on, he knew that the world was his to change, if he found the right levers to pull. Other children bought the stupid idea that they had to wait until they grew up to do anything important. Peter knew better from the start. *He* could never have been fooled the way Ender was into thinking he was playing a game. For Peter, the only game worth playing was the real world. The only reason Ender was fooled was because he let other people shape reality for him. That had never been Peter's problem.

Except that all Peter's influence on the real world had been possible only because he could hide behind the anonymity of the net. He had created a persona—

two personas—that could change the world because nobody knew they were children and therefore ignorable. But when it came to armies and navies clashing in the real world, the influence of political thinkers receded. Unless, like Winston Churchill, they were recognized as being so wise and so right that when the crisis came, the reins of real power were put in their hands. That was fine for Winston—old, fat, and full of booze as he was, people still took him seriously. But as far as anyone who saw Peter Wiggin could know, he was still a kid.

Still, Winston Churchill had been the inspiration for Peter's plan. Make Locke seem so prescient, so right about everything, that when war began, public fear of the enemy and public trust in Locke would overwhelm their disdain for youth and allow Peter to reveal the face behind the mask and, like Winston, take his place as leader of the good guys.

Well, he had miscalculated. He had not guessed that Chamrajnagar already knew who he was. Peter wrote to him as the first step in a public campaign to get the Battle School children under the protection of the Fleet. Not so that they would actually be removed from their home countries—he never expected any government to allow *that*—but so that, when someone moved against them, it would be widely known that Locke had sounded the warning. But Chamrajnagar had forced Peter to keep Locke silent, so no one knew that Locke had foreseen the kidnappings but Chamrajnagar and Graff. The opportunity had been missed.

Peter wouldn't give up. There was some way to get back on track. And sitting there in the library in Greensboro, North Carolina, leaning back in a chair with his eyes closed like any other weary student, he'd think of it.

———

They rousted Ender's jeesh out of bed at 0400 and assembled them in the dining room. No one explained anything, and they were forbidden to talk. So they waited for five minutes, ten, twenty. Petra knew that the others were bound to be thinking the same things she was thinking: The Russians had caught on that they were sabotaging their own battle plans. Or maybe somebody had noticed the coded message in the dragon picture. Whatever it was, it wasn't going to be nice.

Thirty minutes after they were rousted, the door opened. Two soldiers came in and stood at attention. And then, to Petra's utter surprise, in walked . . . a kid. No older than they were. Twelve? Thirteen? Yet the soldiers were treating him with respect. And the kid himself moved with the easy confidence of authority. He was in charge here. And he loved it.

Had Petra seen him before? She didn't think so. Yet he looked at them as if he knew them. Well, of course he did—if he had authority here, he had no doubt been observing them for the weeks they'd been in captivity.

A child in charge. Had to be a Battle School kid— why else would a government give such power to somebody so young? From his age they had to be contemporaries. But she couldn't place him. And her memory was very, very good.

"Don't worry," said the boy. "The reason you don't know me is that I came to Battle School late, and I was only there a little while before you all left for Tactical. But I know *you*." He grinned. "Or is there someone here who *did* know me when I came in? Don't worry, I'll be studying the vid later. Looking for that little shock of recognition. Because if any of you did know me, well, then I'll know something more about you. I'll know that I saw you once before, silhouetted in the dark, walking away from me, leaving me for dead."

With that, Petra knew who he was. Knew because Crazy Tom had told them about it—how Bean had set a trap for this boy that he knew in Rotterdam, and with the help of four other kids had hung him up in an air shaft until he confessed to a dozen murders or so. They left him there, gave the recording to the teachers, and told them where he was. Achilles.

The only member of Ender's jeesh who had been with Bean that day was Crazy Tom. Bean had never talked about it, and no one asked. It made Bean a figure of mystery, that he had come from a life so dark and frightening that it was peopled with monsters like Achilles. What none of them had ever expected was to find Achilles, not in a mental institution or a prison, but here in Russia with soldiers under his command and themselves as his prisoners.

When Achilles studied the vids, it was possible that Crazy Tom would show recognition. And when he told his story, he would no doubt see recognition on all their faces. She had no idea what this meant, but she knew it couldn't be good. One thing was certain—she wasn't going to let Crazy Tom face the consequences alone.

"We all know who you are," said Petra. "You're Achilles. And nobody left you for dead, the way Bean told it. They left you for the teachers. To arrest and send you back to Earth. To a mental institution, no doubt. Bean even showed us your picture. If anybody recognized you, it was from that."

Achilles turned to her and smiled. "Bean would never tell that story. He would never show my picture."

"Then you don't know Bean," said Petra. She hoped the others would realize that admitting they heard it from Crazy Tom would be dangerous to him. Probably fatal, with this oomay in charge of the triggers. Bean wasn't here, so naming him as the source made sense.

"Oh, yes, you're quite the team," said Achilles. "Passing signals to each other, sabotaging the plans you submit, thinking we'll be too stupid to notice. Did you really think we'd set you to work on *real* plans before we turned you?"

As usual, Petra couldn't shut up. But she didn't really want to, either. "Trying to see which of us felt like outsiders, so you could turn them?" she said. "What a joke—there *were* no outsiders in Ender's jeesh. The only outsider here is you."

In fact, though, she knew perfectly well that Carn Carby, Shen, Vlad, and Fly Molo felt like outsiders, for various reasons. She felt like one herself. Her words were designed only to urge them all to maintain solidarity.

"So now you divide us up and start working on us," said Petra. "Achilles, we know your moves before you make them."

"You really can't hurt my pride," said Achilles. "Because I don't have any. All I care about is uniting humanity under one government. Russia is the only nation, the only *people* who have the will to greatness and the power to back it up. You're here because some of you might be useful in that effort. If we think you have what it takes, we'll invite you to join us. The rest of you, we'll just keep on ice till the war is over. The real losers, well, we'll send you home and hope your home government uses you against us." He grinned. "Come on, don't look so grim. You know you were going crazy back home. You didn't even know those people. You left them when you were so little you still got shit on your fingers when you wiped your ass. What did they know about you? What did you know about them? That they let you go. Me, I didn't have any families, Battle School just meant three meals a day. But you, they took away everything from you. You don't owe them anything. What you've got is your mind. Your talent. You've been tagged for greatness. You won their war with the Buggers for them. And they sent you home so your parents could go back to *raising* you?"

Nobody said anything. Petra was sure they all had as much contempt for his spiel as she did. He knew nothing about them. He'd never be able to divide them. He'd never win their loyalty. They knew too much about him. And they didn't like being held against their will.

He knew it, too. Petra saw it in his eyes, the rage dancing there as he realized that they had nothing but contempt for him.

At least he could see *her* contempt, because he zeroed in on her, took a few steps closer, smiling ever more kindly.

"Petra, it's so nice to meet you," he said. "The girl who tested so aggressive they had to check your DNA to make sure you weren't really a boy."

Petra felt the blood drain from her face. Nobody was supposed to know about that. It was a test the psychiatrists in Ground School had ordered when they decided her contempt for them was a symptom of dysfunction instead of what they deserved for asking her such stupid questions. It wasn't even supposed to be in her file. But apparently a record existed somewhere. Which was, of course, the message Achilles intended to get across to them: He knew everything. And, as a side benefit, it would start the others wondering just how piffed up she was.

"Ten of you. Only two missing from the glorious victory. Ender, the great one, the genius, the keeper of the holy grail—he's off founding a colony somewhere. We'll all be in our fifties by the time he gets there, and he'll still be a little kid. We're going to make history. He *is* history." Achilles smirked at his pun.

But Petra knew that mocking Ender wasn't going to play with this group. Achilles no doubt assumed that the ten of them were also-rans, runners-up, the ones who wanted to have Ender's job and had to sit there and watch him do it. He assumed that they were all burning with envy—because he would have been eaten alive with it. But he was wrong. He didn't understand them at all. They *missed* Ender. They were Ender's jeesh. And this yelda actually thought that he could forge them into a team the way Ender had.

"And then there's Bean," Achilles went on. "The youngest of you, the one whose test scores made you all look like halfwits. He could teach the rest of you classes in how to lead armies—except you probably wouldn't understand him, he's such a genius. Where *could* he be? Anybody miss him?"

Nobody answered. This time, though, Petra knew that the silence hid a different set of feelings. There had been some resentment of Bean. Not because of his brilliance, or at least no one admitted resenting him for that. What annoyed them was the way he just assumed he knew better than anyone. And that awkward time before Ender arrived on Eros, when Bean was the acting commander of the jeesh, that was hard on some of them, taking orders from the youngest of them. So maybe Achilles had guessed right about that.

Except that nobody was proud of those feelings, and bringing them out in the open didn't exactly make them love Achilles. Of course, it might be shame he was trying to provoke. Achilles might be smarter than they thought.

Probably not. He was so out of his league in trying to scope this group of military prodigies that he might as well be wearing a clown suit and throwing water balloons for all the respect he was going to get.

"Ah, yes, Bean," said Achilles. "I'm sorry to inform you that he's dead."

This was apparently too much for Crazy Tom, who yawned and said, "No he's not."

Achilles looked amused. "You think you know more about it than I do?"

"We've been on the nets," said Shen. "We'd know."

"You've been away from your desks since 2200. How do you know what's been happening while you slept?" Achilles glanced at his watch. "Oops, you're right. Bean *is* still alive right now. And for another fifteen minutes or so. Then . . . whoosh! A nice little rocket straight to his little bedroom to blow him up right on his little bed. We didn't even have to buy his location from the Greek military. Our friends there gave us the information for free."

Petra's heart sank. If Achilles could arrange for them to be kidnapped, he could certainly arrange for Bean to be killed. Killing was always easier than taking someone alive.

Did Bean already notice the message in the dragon, decode it, and pass along the information? Because if he's dead, there's no one else who'll be able to do it.

Immediately she was ashamed that the news of Bean's death made her think first of herself. But it didn't mean she didn't care about the kid. It meant that she trusted him so much that she had pinned all her hopes on him. If he died, those hopes died with him. It was not indecent of her to think of that.

To say it out loud, *that* would be indecent. But you can't help the thoughts that come to mind.

Maybe Achilles was lying. Or maybe Bean would survive, or get away. And if he died, maybe he'd already decoded the message. Maybe he hadn't. There was nothing Petra could do to change the outcome.

"What, no tears?" said Achilles. "And here I thought you were such close friends. I guess that was all hero-hype." He chuckled. "Well, I'm done with you for now." He turned to a soldier by the door. "Travel time."

The soldier left. They heard a few words of Russian and at once sixteen soldiers came in and divided up, one pair to each of the kids.

"You're being separated now," said Achilles. "Wouldn't want anyone to start thinking of a rescue operation. You can still email each other. We want your creative synergy to continue. After all, you're the finest little military minds that humanity was able to squeeze out in its hour of need. We're all really proud of you, and we look forward to seeing your finest work in the near future."

One of the kids farted loudly.

Achilles only grinned, winked at Petra, and left.

Ten minutes later they were all in separate vehicles, being driven away to points unknown, somewhere in the vast reaches of the largest country on the face of the Earth.

Part Two
ALLIANCES

6

Code

To: Graff%pilgrimage@colmin.gov
From: Konstan%Briseis@helstrat.gov
Re: Leak

Your Excellency, I write to you myself
because I was most vociferously opposing to your plan to take young Julian
Delphiki from our protection. I was
wrong as we learnt from the missile assault on former apartment today leaving
two soldiers dead. We are follow your
previous advice by public release that
Julian was killed in attack. His room
was target in late night and he would
die instead of soldiers sleeping there.
Penetration of our system very deep,
obviously. We trust no one now. You

were just in time and I regret my making of delay. My pride in Hellene military made me blind. You see I speak
Common a little after all, no more
bluffing between me and true friend to
Greece. Because of you and not me a
great national resource is not destroy.

If Bean had to be in hiding, there were worse places he
could be than Araraquara. The town, named for a
species of parrot, had been kept as something of a mu-
seum piece, with cobbled streets and old buildings.
They weren't particularly beautiful old buildings or
picturesque houses—even the cathedral was rather
dull, and not particularly ancient, having been finished
in the twentieth century. Still, there was the sense of a
quieter way of life that had once been common in
Brasil. The growth that had turned nearby Ribeirão
Preto into a sprawling metropolis had pretty much
passed Araraquara by. And even though the people
were modern enough—you heard as much Common
on the streets as Portuguese these days—Bean felt at
home here in a way that he had never felt in Greece,
where the desire to be fully European and fully Greek
at the same time distorted public life and public
spaces.

"It won't do to feel too much at home," said Sister
Carlotta. "We can't stay anywhere for long."

"Achilles is the devil," said Bean. "Not God. He
can't reach everywhere. He can't find us without some
kind of evidence."

"He doesn't have to reach everywhere," said Sister
Carlotta. "Only where we are."

"His hate for us makes him blind," said Bean.

"His fear makes him unnaturally alert."

Bean grinned—it was an old game between them. "It might not be Achilles who took the other kids."

"It might not be gravity that holds us to Earth," said Sister Carlotta, "but rather an unknown force with identical properties."

Then she grinned, too.

Sister Carlotta was a good traveling companion. She had a sense of humor. She understood his jokes and he enjoyed hers. But most of all, she liked to spend hours and hours without saying a thing, doing her work while he did his own. When they did talk, they were evolving a kind of oblique language where they both already knew everything that mattered so they only had to refer to it and the other would understand. Not that this implied they were kindred spirits or deeply attuned. It's just that their lives only touched at a few key points—they were in hiding, they were cut off from friends and family, and the same enemy wanted them dead. There was no one to gossip about because they knew no one. There was no chat because they had no interests beyond the projects at hand: trying to figure out where the other kids were being held, trying to determine what nation Achilles was serving (which would no doubt soon be serving him), and trying to understand the shape the world was taking so they could interfere with it, perhaps bending the course of history to a better end.

That was Sister Carlotta's goal, at least, and Bean was willing to take part in it, given that the same research required for the first two projects was identical to the research required for the last. He wasn't sure that he cared about the shape of history in the future.

He said that to Sister Carlotta once, and she only

smiled. "Is it the world outside yourself you don't care about," she said, "or the future as a whole, including your own?"

"Why should I care about narrowing down which things in particular I don't care about?"

"Because if you didn't care about your own future, you wouldn't care whether you were alive to see it, and you wouldn't be going through all this nonsense to stay alive."

"I'm a mammal," said Bean. "I try to live forever whether I actually want to or not."

"You're a child of God, so you care what happens to his children whether you admit it to yourself or not."

It was not her glib response that bothered him, because he expected it—he had provoked it, really, no doubt (he told himself) because he liked the reassurance that *if* there was a God, then Bean mattered to him. No, what bothered him was the momentary darkness that passed across her face. A fleeting expression, barely revealed, which he would not have noticed had he not known her face so well, and had darkness so rarely been expressed on it.

Something that I said made her feel sad. And yet it was a sadness that she wants to conceal from me. What did I say? That I'm a mammal? She's used to my gibes about her religion. That I might not want to live forever? Perhaps she worries that I'm depressed. That I try to live forever, despite my desires? Perhaps she fears that I'll die young. Well, that was why they were in Araraquara—to prevent his early death. And hers, too, for that matter. He had no doubt, though, that if a gun were pointed at him, she would leap in front of him to take the bullet. He did not understand why. He would not do the same for her, or for anyone. He would try to warn her, or pull her out of the way, or interfere with the shooter, whatever he could do that left them both a reasonable chance of survival. But he would not deliberately die to save her.

Maybe it was a thing that women did. Or maybe that grown-ups did for children. To give your life to save someone else. To weigh your own survival and decide that it mattered less to you than the survival of another. Bean could not fathom how anyone could feel that way. Shouldn't the irrational mammal take over, and force them to act for their own survival? Bean had never tried to suppress his own survival instinct, but he doubted that he could even if he tried. But then, maybe older people were more willing to part with their lives, having already spent the bulk of their starting capital. Of course, it made sense for parents to sacrifice themselves for the sake of their children, particularly parents too old to make more babies. But Sister Carlotta had never had children. And Bean was not the only one that she would die for. She would leap out to take a bullet for a stranger. She valued her own life less than anyone's. And that made her utterly alien to him.

Survival, not of the fittest, but of myself—that is the purpose at the core of my being. That is the reason, ultimately, that I do all the things that I've done. There have been moments when I felt compassion—when, alone of Ender's jeesh, I knowingly sent men to their certain deaths, I felt a deep sorrow for them. But I sent them, and they went. Would I, in their place, have gone as they did, obeying an order? Dying to save unknown future generations who would never know their names?

Bean doubted it.

He would gladly serve humanity if it happened also to serve himself. Fighting the Formics alongside Ender and the other kids, that made sense because saving humanity included saving Bean. And if by managing to stay alive somewhere in the world, he was also a thorn in the side of Achilles, making him less cautious, less wise, and therefore easier to defeat—well, it was a pleasant bonus that Bean's pursuit of his own survival happened also to give the human race a chance to defeat the monster. And since the best way to survive would be to find Achilles and kill him first, he might turn out to be one of the great benefactors of human history. Though now that he thought about it, he couldn't remember a single assassin who was remembered as a hero. Brutus, perhaps. His reputation had had its ups and downs. Most assassins, though, were despised by history. Probably because successful assassins tended to be those whose target was not particularly dangerous to anyone. By the time everyone agreed that a particular monster was well worth assassinating, the monster had far too much power and paranoia to leave any possibility of an assassination actually being carried out.

He got nowhere when he tried to discuss it with Sister Carlotta.

"I can't argue with you so I don't know why you bother. I only know that I won't help you plot his assassination."

"You don't consider it self-defense?" said Bean. "What is this, one of those stupid vids where the hero can never actually kill a bad guy who isn't actually pointing a gun at him right that very moment?"

"It's my faith in Christ," said Carlotta. "Love your enemy, do good to those who hate you."

"Well, where does that leave us? The nicest thing we could do for Achilles would be to post our address on the nets and wait for him to send someone to kill us."

"Don't be absurd," said Carlotta. "Christ said be

good to your enemies. It wouldn't be good for Achilles to find us, because then he'd kill us and have even more murders to answer for before the judgment bar of God. The best thing we can do for Achilles is to keep him from killing us. And if we love him, we'll stop him from ruling the world while we're at it, since power like that would only compound his opportunities to sin."

"Why don't we love the hundreds and thousands and millions of people who'll die in the wars he's planning to launch?"

"We do love them," said Carlotta. "But you're confused the way so many people are, who don't understand the perspective of God. You keep thinking that death is the most terrible thing that can happen to a person, but to God, death just means you're coming home a few moments ahead of schedule. To God, the dreadful outcome of a human life is when that person embraces sin and rejects the joy that God offers. So of all the millions who might die in a war, each individual life is tragic only if it ends in sin."

"So why are you going to such trouble to keep *me* alive?" asked Bean, thinking he knew the answer.

"You want me to say something that will weaken my case," said Carlotta. "Like telling you that I'm human and so I want to prevent your death right now because I love you. And that's true, I have no children but you're as close as I come to having any, and I would be stricken to the soul if you died at the hands of that twisted boy. But in truth, Julian Delphiki, the reason I work so hard to prevent your death is because, if you died today, you would probably go to hell."

To his surprise, Bean was stung by this. He understood enough of what Carlotta believed that he could have predicted this attitude, but the fact that she put it into words still hurt. "I'm not going to repent and get baptized, so I'm bound to go to hell, therefore no matter when I die I'm doomed," he said.

"Nonsense. Our understanding of doctrine is not perfect, and no matter what the popes have said, I don't believe for a moment that God is going to damn for eternity the billions of children he allowed to be born and die without baptism. No, I think you're likely to go to hell because, despite all your brilliance, you are still quite amoral. Sometime before you die, I pray most earnestly that you will learn that there are higher laws that transcend mere survival, and higher causes to serve. When you give yourself to such a great cause, my dear boy, *then* I will not fear your death, because I know that a just God will forgive you for the oversight of not having recognized the truth of Christianity during your lifetime."

"You really are a heretic," said Bean. "None of those doctrines would pass muster with any priest."

"They don't even pass muster with me," said Carlotta. "But I don't know a soul who doesn't maintain two separate lists of doctrines—the ones that they *believe* that they believe; and the ones that they actually try to live by. I'm simply one of the rare ones who knows the difference. You, my boy, are not."

"Because I don't believe in any doctrines."

"That," said Carlotta with exaggerated smugness, "is proof positive of my assertion. You are so convinced that you believe only what you believe that you believe, that you remain utterly blind to what you *really* believe without believing you believe it."

"You were born in the wrong century," said Bean. "You could make Thomas Aquinas tear out his hair. Nietzsche and Derrida would accuse you of obfuscation. Only the Inquisition would know what to do with you—toast you nice and brown."

"Don't tell me you've actually read Nietzsche and Derrida. Or Aquinas, for that matter."

"You don't have to eat the entire turd to know that it's not a crab cake."

"You arrogant impossible boy."

"But Geppetta, I'm *not* a real boy."

"You're certainly not a puppet, or not *my* puppet, anyway. Go outside and play now, I'm busy."

Sending him outside was not a punishment, however. Sister Carlotta knew that. From the moment they got their desks linked to the nets, they had both spent most of every day indoors, gathering information. Carlotta, whose identity was shielded by the firewalls in the Vatican computer system, was able to continue all her old relationships and thus had access to all her best sources, taking care only to avoid saying where she was or even what time zone she was in. Bean, however, had to create a new identity from scratch, hiding behind a double blind of mail servers specializing in anonymity, and even then he kept no identity for longer than a week. He formed no relationships and therefore could develop no sources. When he needed specific information, he had to ask Carlotta to help him find it, and then she had to determine whether it was something she might legitimately ask, or whether it was something that might be a clue that she had Bean with her. Most of the time she decided she dared not ask. So Bean was crippled in his research. Still, they shared what information they could, and despite his disadvantages, there was one advantage that remained to him: The mind looking at his data was his own. The mind that had scored higher than anyone else on the Battle School tests.

Unfortunately, Truth did not care much about such credentials. It refused to give up and reveal itself just because it realized you were bound to find it eventually.

Bean could only take so many hours of frustration before he had to get up and go outside. It wasn't just to get away from his work, however. "The climate agrees with me," he told Sister Carlotta on their second day, when, dripping with sweat, he headed for his third shower since waking. "I was born to live with heat and humidity."

At first she had insisted on going everywhere with him. But after a few days he was able to persuade her of several things. First, he looked old enough not to be accompanied by his grandmother everywhere he went—"Avó Carlotta" was what he called her here, their cover story. Second, she would be no protection for him anyway, since she had no weapons and no defensive skills. Third, he was the one who knew how to live on the streets, and even though Araraquara was hardly the kind of dangerous place that Rotterdam had been when he was younger, he had already mapped in his mind a hundred different escape routes and hiding places, just by reflex. When Carlotta realized that she would need his protection a lot more than he would need hers, she relented and allowed him to go out alone, as long as he did his best to remain inconspicuous.

"I can't stop people from noticing the foreign boy."

"You don't look that foreign," she said. "Mediterranean body types are common here. Just try not to speak a lot. Always look like you have an errand but never like you're in a hurry. But then, it was you who taught *me* that that was how to avoid attracting attention."

And so here he was today, weeks after they arrived in Brasil, wandering the streets of Araraquara and wondering what great cause might make his life worthwhile in Carlotta's eyes. For despite all her faith, it was *her* approval, not God's, that seemed like it might be worth striving for, as long as it didn't interfere with his project of staying alive. Was it enough to be a thorn in Achilles' side? Enough to look for ways to oppose him? Or was there something else he should be doing?

At the crest of one of Araraquara's many hills there was a sorvete shop run by a Japanese-Brazilian family. The family had been in business there for centuries, as their sign proclaimed, and Bean was both amused and moved by this, in light of what Carlotta had said. For this family, making flavored frozen desserts to eat from a cone or cup was the great cause that gave them continuity through the ages. What could be more trivial than that? And yet Bean came here, again and again, because their recipes were, in fact, delicious, and when he thought about how many other people for these past two or three hundred years must have paused and taken a moment's pleasure in the sweet and delicate flavors, in the feel of the smooth sorvete in their mouths, he could not disdain that cause. They offered something that was genuinely good, and people's lives were better because they offered it. It was not a noble cause that would get written up in the histories. But it was not nothing, either. A person could do worse than spend some large percentage of his life in a cause like that.

Bean wasn't even sure what it meant to give himself to a cause. Did that mean turning over his decision-making to someone else? What an absurd idea. In all likelihood there was no one smarter than him on Earth, and though that did not mean he was incapable of error, it certainly meant he'd have to be a fool to turn over his decisions to someone even *more* likely to be wrong.

Why he was wasting time on Carlotta's sentiment-ridden philosophy of life he didn't know. Doubtless that was one of his mistakes—the emotional human aspect of his mentality overriding the inhumanly aloof brilliance that, to his chagrin, only sometimes controlled his thinking.

The sorvete cup was empty. Apparently he had eaten it all without noticing. He hoped his mouth had enjoyed every taste of it, because the eating was done by reflex while he thought his thoughts.

Bean discarded the cup and went his way. A bicyclist passed him. Bean saw how the cyclist's whole body bounced and rattled and vibrated from the cobblestones. *That* is human life, thought Bean. So bounced around that we can never see anything straight.

Supper was beans and rice and stringy beef in the pensão's public dining room. He and Carlotta ate together in near silence, listening to other people's conversations and the clanking and clinking of dishes and silverware. Any real conversation between them would doubtless leak some memorable bit of information that might raise questions and attract attention. Like, why did a woman who talked like a nun have a grandson? Why did this child who looked to be six talk like a philosophy professor half the time? So they ate in silence except for conversations about the weather.

After supper, as always, they each signed on to the nets to check their mail. Carlotta's mail was interesting and real. All of Bean's correspondents, this week anyway, thought he was a woman named Lettie who was working on her dissertation and needed information, but who had no time for a personal life and so rebuffed with alacrity any attempt at friendly and personal conversation. But so far, there was no way to find Achilles' signature in any nation's behavior. While most countries simply did not have the resources to kidnap Ender's jeesh in such a short time, of those that did have the resources, there was not one that Bean could rule out because they lacked the arrogance or aggressiveness or contempt for law to do it. Why, it could even have been done by Brasil itself—for all he knew, his former companions from the Formic War might be imprisoned somewhere in Araraquara. They might hear in the early morning the rumble of the very garbage truck that picked up the sorvete cup that he threw away today.

"I don't know why people spread these things," said Carlotta.

"What?" asked Bean, grateful for the break from the eye-blearing work he was doing.

"Oh, these stupid superstitious good-luck dragons. There must be a dozen different dragon pictures now."

"Oh, é," said Bean. "They're everywhere, I just don't notice them anymore. Why dragons, anyway?"

"I think this is the oldest of them. At least it's the one I saw first, with the little poem," said Carlotta. "If Dante were writing today, I'm sure there'd be a special place in his hell for people who start these things."

"What poem?"

" 'Share this dragon,' " Carlotta recited. " 'If you do, lucky end for them and you.' "

"Oh, yeah, dragons always bring a lucky end. I mean, what does that poem actually *say*? That you'll die lucky? That it'll be lucky for you to end?"

Carlotta chuckled.

Bored with his correspondence, Bean kept the nonsense going. "Dragons aren't always lucky. They had to discontinue Dragon Army in Battle School, it was so unlucky. Till they revived it for Ender, and no doubt they gave it to him because people thought it was bad luck and they were trying to stack everything against him."

Then a thought passed through his mind, ever so briefly, but it woke him from his lethargy.

"Forward me that picture."

"I bet you already have it on a dozen letters."

"I don't want to search. Send me that one."

"You're still that Lettie person? Haven't you been that one for two weeks now?"

"Five days."

It took a few minutes for the message to be routed to him, but when it finally showed up in his mail, he looked closely at the image.

"Why in the world are you paying attention to this?" asked Carlotta.

He looked up to see her watching him.

"I don't know. Why are you paying attention to the way I'm paying attention to it?" He grinned at her.

"Because you think it matters. I may not be as smart as you are about most things, but I'm very much smarter than you are about you. I know when you're intrigued."

"Just the juxtaposition of the image of a dragon with the word 'end.' Endings really aren't considered all that lucky. Why wouldn't the person write 'luck will come' or 'lucky fate' or something else? Why 'lucky end'?"

"Why not?"

"End. Ender. Ender's army was Dragon."

"Now, that's a little far-fetched."

"Look at the drawing," said Bean. "Right in the middle, where the bitmap is so complicated—there's one line that's damaged. The dots don't line up at all. It's virtually random."

"It just looks like noise to me."

"If you were being held captive but you had computer access, only every bit of mail you sent out was scrutinized, how would you send a message?" asked Bean.

"You don't think this could be a message from—do you?"

"I have no idea. But now that I've thought of it, it's worth looking at, don't you think?"

By now Bean had pasted the dragon image into a graphics program and was studying that line of pixels. "Yes, this is random, the whole line. Doesn't belong here, and it's not just noise because the rest of the image is still completely intact except for this other line that's partly broken. Noise would be randomly distributed."

"See what it is, then," said Carlotta. "You're the genius, I'm the nun."

Soon Bean had the two lines isolated in a separate file and was studying the information as raw code. Viewed as one-byte or two-byte text code, there was nothing that remotely resembled language, but of course it couldn't, could it, or it would never have got out. So *if* it was a message, then it had to be in some kind of code.

For the next few hours Bean wrote programs to help him manipulate the data contained in those lines. He tried mathematical schemes and graphic reinterpretations, but in truth he knew all along that it wouldn't be anything that complex. Because whoever created it would have had to do it without the aid of a computer. It had to be something relatively simple, designed only to keep a cursory examination from revealing what it was.

And so he kept coming back to ways of reinterpreting the binary code as text. Soon enough he came upon a scheme that seemed promising. Two-byte text code, but shifted right by one position for each character, except when the right shift would make it correspond with two actual bytes in memory, in which case double shift. That way a real character would never show up if someone looked at the file with an ordinary view program.

When he used that method on the one line, it came up as text characters only, which was not likely to happen by chance. But the other line came up random-seeming garbage.

So he left-shifted the other line, and it, too, became nothing but text characters.

"I'm in," he said. "And it *is* a message."

"What does it say?"

"I haven't the faintest idea."

Carlotta got up and came to look over his shoulder. "It's not even language. It doesn't divide into words."

"That's deliberate," said Bean. "If it divided into words it would look like a message and invite decoding. The easy way that any amateur can decode language is by checking word lengths and the frequency of appearance of certain letter patterns. In Common, you look for letter groupings that could be 'a' and 'the' and 'and,' that sort of thing."

"And you don't even know what language it's in."

"No, but it's bound to be Common, because they know they're sending it to somebody who doesn't have a key. So it has to be decodable, and that means Common."

"So they're making it easy and hard at the same time?"

"Yes. Easy for me, hard for everyone else."

"Oh, come now. You think this was written to you?"

"Ender. Dragon. I was *in* Dragon Army, unlike most of them. And whom else would they be writing to? I'm outside, they're in. They know that everyone is there but me. And I'm the only person that they'd know they could reach without tipping their hand to everybody else."

"What, did you have some private code?"

"Not really, but what we have is common experience, the slang of Battle School, things like that. You'll see. When I crack it, it'll be because I recognize a word that nobody else would recognize."

"*If* it's from them."

"It is," said Bean. "It's what I'd do. Get word out. This picture is like a virus. It goes everywhere and gets its code into a million places, but nobody knows it's a code because it looks like something that most people think they already understand. It's a fad, not a message. Except to me."

"Almost thou persuadest me," said Carlotta.

"I'll crack it before I go to bed."

"You're too little to drink that much coffee. It'll give you an aneurysm."

She went back to her own mail.

Since the words weren't separated, Bean had to look for other patterns that might give things away. There were no obvious repeated two-letter or three-letter patterns that didn't lead to obvious dead ends. That didn't surprise him. If he had been composing such a message, he would have dropped out all the articles and conjunctions and prepositions and pronouns that he possibly could. Not only that, but most of the words were probably deliberately misspelled to avoid repetitive patterns. But some words would be spelled correctly, and they would be designed to be unrecognizable to most people who weren't from the Battle School culture.

There were only two places where the same character was apparently doubled, one in each line. That might just be the result of one word ending with the same letter that began another, but Bean doubted it. Nothing would be left to chance in this message. So he wrote a little program that would take the doubled letters in one word and, beginning with "aa," show him what the surrounding letters might be to see if anything looked plausible to him. And he started with the doubled letters in the shorter line, because that pair was surrounded by another pair, in a 1221 pattern.

The obvious failures, like "xddx" and "pffp," took no time, but he had to investigate all the variants on "abba" and "adda" and "deed" and "effe" to see what they did to the message. Some were promising and he saved them for later exploration.

"Why is it in Greek now?" asked Carlotta.

She was looking over his shoulder again. He hadn't heard her get up and come over behind him.

"I converted the original message to Greek characters so that I wouldn't get distracted by trying to read meanings into letters I hadn't decoded yet. The ones I'm actually working on are in Roman letters."

At that moment, his program showed the letters "iggi."

"Piggies," said Sister Carlotta.

"Maybe, but it doesn't flag anything for me." He started cycling through the dictionary matches with "iggi," but none of them did any better than "piggies" had.

"Does it have to be a word?" said Carlotta.

"Well, if it's a number, then this is a dead end," said Bean.

"No, I mean, why not a name?"

Bean saw it at once. "How blind can I be." He plugged the letters *w* and *n* to the positions before and after "iggi" and then spread the results through the whole message, making the program show hyphens for the undeciphered letters. The two lines now read

```
--n----g--n--n--n--i--n--g
-n-n-wiggin-
```

"That doesn't look right for Common," said Carlotta. "There should be a lot more *i*'s than that."

"I'm assuming that the message deliberately leaves out letters as much as possible, especially vowels, so it won't look like Common."

"So how will you know when you've decoded it?"

"When it makes sense."

"It's bedtime. I know, you're not sleeping till you've solved it." He barely noticed that she moved away from behind him. He was busy trying the other doubled letter. This time he had a more complicated job, because the letters before and after the double pair were different. It meant far more combinations to try, and being able to eliminate *g, i, n,* and *w* didn't speed up the process all that much.

Again, there were quite a few readings that he saved—more than before—but nothing rang a bell until he got to "jees." The word that Ender's companions in the final battle used for themselves. "Jeesh."

Could it be? It was definitely a word that might be used as a flag.

```
h—n—jeesh—g—en—s—ns—n——si——n——s—g
            —n—n—wiggin——
```

If those twenty-seven letters were right, then he had only thirty left to solve. He rubbed his eyes, sighed, and set to work.

———

It was noon when the smell of oranges woke him. Sister Carlotta was peeling a mexerica orange. "People are eating these things on the street and spitting the pulp on the sidewalk. You can't chew it up enough to swallow it. But the juice is the best orange you'll ever taste in your life."

Bean got out of bed and took the segment she offered him. She was right. She handed him a bowl to spit the pulp into. "Good breakfast," said Bean.

"Lunch," she said. She held up a paper. "I take it you consider this to be a solution?"

It was what he had printed out before going to bed.

```
hlpndrjeeshtgdrenrusbnstun6rmysiz40ntrys-
               btg
         bnfndwigginptr
```

"Oh," said Bean. "I didn't print out the one with the word breaks." Putting another mexerica segment in his mouth, Bean padded on bare feet to the computer, called up the right file, and printed it. He brought it back, handed it to Carlotta, spat out pulp, and took his own mexerica from her shopping bag and began peeling.

"Bean," she said. "I'm a normal mortal. I get 'help' and is this 'Ender'?"

Bean took the paper from her.

```
hlp ndr jeesh tgdr en rus bns tun 6 rmy
            siz 40 n try sbtg
            bn fnd wiggin ptr
```

"The vowels are left out as much as possible, and there are other misspellings. But what the first line says is, 'Help. Ender's jeesh is together in Russia—'"

"T-g-d-r is 'together'? And 'in' is spelled like French?"

"Exactly," said Bean. "I understood it and it doesn't look like Common." He went on interpreting. "The next part was confusing for a long time, until I realized that the 6 and the 40 were numbers. I got almost all the other letters before I realized that. The thing is, the numbers matter, but there's no way to guess them from context. So the next few words are designed to give a context to the numbers. It says 'Bean's toon was 6'—that's because Ender divided Dragon Army into five toons instead of the normal four, but then he gave me a sort of ad hoc toon, and if you added it to the count, it was number six. Only who would know that except for somebody from Battle School? So only somebody like me would get the number. Same thing with the next one. 'Army size 40.' Everyone in Battle School knew that there were forty soldiers in every army. Unless you counted the commander, in which case it was forty-one, but see, it doesn't matter, because that digit is trivial."

"How do you know that?"

"Because the next letter is *n*. For 'north.' The message is telling their location. They know they're in

Russia. And because they can apparently see the sun or at least shadows on the wall, and they know the date, they can calculate their latitude, more or less. Six-four-zero north. Sixty-four north."

"Unless it means something else."

"No, the message is meant to be obvious."

"To you."

"Yes, to me. The rest of that line is 'try sabotage.' I think that means that they're trying to screw up whatever the Russians are trying to make them do. So they're pretending to go along but really gumming up the works. Very smart to get that on record. The fact that Graff was court-martialed after winning the Formic War suggests that they'd better get it on record that they were *not* collaborating with the enemy—in case the other side wins."

"But Russia isn't at war with anybody."

"The Polemarch was Russian, and Warsaw Pact troops were at the heart of his side in the League War. You've got to remember, Russia was the country that was most on the make before the Formics came and started tearing up real estate and forced humanity to unite under the Hegemon and create the International Fleet. They have always felt cheated out of their destiny, and now that the Formics are gone, it makes sense that they'd be eager to get back on the fast track. They don't think of themselves as bad guys, they think of themselves as the only people with the will and the resources to unite the world for real, permanently. They think they're doing a good thing."

"People always do."

"Not always. But yes, to wage war you have to be able to sell your own people on the idea that either you're fighting in self-defense, or you're fighting because you deserve to win, or you're fighting in order to save other people. The Russian people respond to an altruistic sales pitch as easily as anybody else."

"So what about the second line?"

" 'Bean find Wiggin Peter.' They're suggesting that I look for Ender's older brother. He didn't go off on the colony ship with Ender and Valentine. And he's been a player, under the net identity of Locke. And I suppose he's running Demosthenes, too, now that Valentine is gone."

"You knew about that?"

"I knew a lot of things," said Bean. "But the main thing is that they're right. Achilles is hunting for me and he's hunting for you, and he's got all the rest of Ender's jeesh, but he doesn't even know Ender's brother exists and he wouldn't care if he did. But you know and I know that Peter Wiggin would have been in Battle School except for a little character flaw. And for all we know, that character flaw may be exactly what he needs to be a good match against Achilles."

"Or it may be exactly the flaw that makes it so a victory for Peter is no better than a victory for Achilles, in terms of the amount of suffering in the world."

"Well, we won't know until we find him, will we?" said Bean.

"To find him, Bean, you'd have to reveal who you are."

"Yes," said Bean. "Isn't this exciting?" He did an exaggerated wriggle like a little kid being taken to the zoo.

"This is your life you're playing with."

"You're the one who wanted me to find a cause."

"Peter Wiggin isn't a cause, he's dangerous. You haven't heard what Graff had to say about him."

"On the contrary," said Bean. "How do you think I learned about him?"

"But he might be no better than Achilles!"

"I know of several ways already that he's better than Achilles. First, he's not trying to kill us. Second, he's already got a huge network of contacts with people all over the world, some of whom know he's as young as he is but most of whom have no idea. Third, he's ambitious just like Achilles is, only Achilles has already assembled almost all of the children who were tagged as the most brilliant military commanders in the world, while Peter Wiggin will have only one. Me. Do you think he's dumb enough not to use me?"

"*Use* you. That's the operative word here, Bean."

"Well, aren't *you* being used in *your* cause?"

"By God, not by Peter Wiggin."

"I'll bet Peter Wiggin sends a lot clearer messages than God does," said Bean. "And if I don't like what he's doing, I can always quit."

"With someone like Peter, you can't always quit."

"He can't make me think of what I don't want to think about. Unless he's a remarkably stupid genius, he'll know that."

"I wonder if Achilles knows that, as he's trying to squeeze brilliance out of the other children."

"Exactly. Between Peter Wiggin and Achilles, what are the odds that Wiggin could be worse?"

"Oh, it's hard to imagine how that could be."

"So let's start thinking of a way to contact Locke without giving away our identity and our location."

"I'm going to need more mexerica oranges before we leave Brasil," said Carlotta.

Only then did he notice that the two of them had already blown through the whole bagful. "Me too," he said.

As she left, the empty bag in hand, she paused at the door. "You did very well with that message, Julian Delphiki."

"Thanks, Grandma Carlotta."

She left smiling.

Bean held up the message and scanned it again. The only part of the message that he hadn't fully interpreted for her was the last word. He didn't think "ptr" meant Peter. That would have been redundant. "Wiggin" was enough to identify him. No, the "ptr" at the end was a signature. This message was from Petra. She could have tried to write directly to Peter Wiggin. But she had written to Bean, coding it in a way that Peter would never have understood.

She's relying on me.

Bean knew how the others in Ender's jeesh had resented him. Not a lot, but a little. When they were all in Command School on Eros, before Ender arrived, the military had made Bean the acting commander in all their test battles, even though he was the youngest of them all, even younger than Ender. He knew he'd done a good job, and won their respect. But they never liked taking orders from him and were undisguisedly happy when Ender arrived and Bean was dropped back to be one of them. Nobody ever said, "Good job, Bean," or "Hey, you did OK." Except Petra.

She had done for him on Eros the same thing that Nikolai had done for him in Battle School—provided him with a kind word now and then. He was sure that neither Nikolai nor Petra ever realized how important their casual generosity had been to him. But he remembered that when he needed a friend, the two of them had been there for him. Nikolai had turned out, by the workings of not-entirely-coincidental fate, to be his brother. Did that make Petra his sister?

It was Petra who reached out to him now. She trusted him to recognize the message, decode it, and act on it.

There were files in the Battle School record system that said that Bean was not human, and he knew that Graff at least sometimes felt that way because he had overheard those words from his own lips. He knew that Carlotta loved him but she loved Jesus more and anyway, she was old and thought of him as a child. He could rely on her, but she did not rely on him.

In his Earthside life before Battle School, the only friend Bean had ever had was a girl named Poke, and Achilles had murdered her long before. Murdered her only moments after Bean left her, and moments before he realized his mistake and rushed back to warn her and instead found her body floating in the Rhine. She died trying to save Bean, and she died because Bean couldn't be relied upon to take as much care to save her.

Petra's message meant that maybe he had another friend who needed him after all. And this time, he would not turn his back. This time it was his turn to save his friend, or die trying. How's that for a cause, Sister Carlotta?

7

Going Public

To: Demosthenes%Tecumseh@free
america.org, Locke%erasmus@polnet.gov
From: dontbother@firewall.set
Re: Achilles heel

Dear Peter Wiggin,
A message smuggled to me from the kidnapped children confirms they are (or
were, at the time of sending) together,
in Russia near the sixty-fourth parallel, doing their best to sabotage those
trying to exploit their military talents. Since they will doubtless be separated and moved frequently, the exact
location is unimportant, and I am quite
sure you already knew Russia was the
only country with both the ambition and

the means to acquire all the members of
Ender's jeesh.

I'm sure you recognize the impossibility of releasing these children through
military intervention—at the slightest
sign of a plausible effort to extract
them, they will be killed in order to
deprive an enemy of such assets. But it
might be possible to persuade either
the Russian government or some if not
all of those holding the individual
children that releasing them is in Russia's best interest. This might be accomplished by exposing the individual
who is almost certainly behind this
audacious action, and your two identities are uniquely situated to accuse
him in a way that will be taken seriously.

Therefore I suggest that you do a bit
of research into a break-in at a high-
security institution for the crimi-
nally insane in Belgium during the
League War. Three guards were killed
and the inmates were released. All but
one were recaptured quickly. The one
who got away was once a student at Battle School. He is behind the kidnapping. When it is revealed that this
psychopath has control of these children, it will cause grave misgivings
inside the Russian command system. It

```
will also give them a scapegoat if they
decide to return the children.

Don't bother trying to trace this email
identity. It already never existed. If
you can't figure out who I am and how to
contact me from the research you're
about to do, then we don't have much to
talk about anyway.
```

Peter's heart sank when he opened the letter to Demosthenes and saw that it had also been sent to Locke. The salutation "Dear Peter Wiggin" only confirmed it—someone besides the office of the Polemarch had broken his identities. He expected the worst—some kind of blackmail or a demand that he support this or that cause.

To his surprise, the message was nothing of the kind. It came from someone who claimed to have received a message from the kidnapped kids—and gave him a tantalizing path to follow. Of course he immediately searched the news archives and found the break-in at a high-security mental hospital near Genk. Finding the name of the inmate who got away was much harder, requiring that, as Demosthenes, he ask for help from a law enforcement contact in Germany, and then, as Locke, for additional help from a friend in the Anti-Sabotage Committee in the Office of the Hegemon.

It yielded a name that made Peter laugh, since it was in the subject line of the email that prompted this search. Achilles, pronounced "ah-SHEEL" in the French manner. An orphan rescued from the streets of Rotterdam by, of all things, a Catholic nun working for the procurement section of the Battle School. He was given surgery to correct a crippled leg, then taken up to Battle School, where he lasted only a few days before being exposed as a serial killer by some of the other students, though in fact he had not killed anyone in the Battle School.

The list of his victims was interesting. He had a pattern of killing anyone who had ever made him feel or seem helpless or vulnerable. Including the doctor who had repaired his leg. Apparently he wasn't much for gratitude.

Putting together the information, Peter could see that his unknown correspondent was right. If in fact this sicko was running the operation that was using these kids for military planning, it was almost certain that the Russian officers working with him did not know his criminal record. Whatever agency liberated Achilles from the mental hospital would not have shared that information with the military who were expected to work with him. There would be outrage that would be heard at the highest levels of the Russian government.

And even if the government did not act to get rid of Achilles and release the kids, the Russian Army jealously guarded its independence from the rest of the government, especially the intelligence-and-dirty-jobs agencies. There was a good chance that some of these children might "escape" before the government acted—indeed, such unauthorized actions might force the government to make it official and pretend that the "early releases" had been authorized.

It was always possible, of course, that Achilles would kill one or more of the kids as soon as he was exposed. At least Peter would not have to face those particular children in battle. And now that he knew something about Achilles, Peter was in a much better position to face him in a head-to-head struggle.

Achilles killed with his own hands. Since that was a very stupid thing to do, and Achilles did not test stupid, it had to be an irresistible compulsion. People with irresistible compulsions could be terrifying enemies—but they could also be beaten.

For the first time in weeks, Peter felt a glimmer of hope. This was how his work as Locke and Demosthenes paid off—people with certain kinds of secret information that they wanted to make public found ways to hand it to Peter without his even having to ask for it. Much of his power came from this disorganized network of informants. It never bothered his pride that he was being "used" by this anonymous correspondent. As far as Peter was concerned, they were using each other. And besides, Peter had earned the right to get such helpful gifts.

Still, Peter always looked gift horses in the mouth. As either Locke or Demosthenes, he emailed friends and contacts in various government agencies, trying to get confirmation of various aspects of the story he was preparing to write. Could the break-in at the mental institution have been carried out by Russian agents? Did satellite surveillance show any kind of activity near the sixty-fourth parallel that might correspond with the arrival or departure of the ten kidnapped kids? Was anything known about the whereabouts of Achilles that would contradict the idea of his being in control of the whole kidnap operation?

It took a couple of days to get the story right. He tried it first as a column by Demosthenes, but he soon realized that since Demosthenes was constantly putting out warnings about Russian plots, he might not be taken very seriously. It had to be Locke who published this. And that would be dangerous, because up to now Locke had been scrupulous about not seeming to take sides against Russia. That would now make it more likely that his exposure of Achilles would be taken seriously—but it ran a grave risk of costing Locke some of his best contacts in Russia. No matter how much a Russian might despise what his government was doing, the devotion to Mother Russia ran deep. There was a line you couldn't cross. For more than a few of his contacts there, publishing this piece would cross that line.

Until he hit upon the obvious solution. Before submitting the piece to *International Aspects,* he would send copies to his Russian contacts to give a heads-up on what was coming. Of course the exposé would fly through the Russian military. It was possible that the repercussions would begin even before his column officially appeared. And his contacts would know he wasn't trying to hurt Russia—he was giving them a chance to clean house, or at least put a spin on the story before it ran.

It wasn't a long story, but it named names and opened doors that other reporters could follow up on. And they *would* follow up. From the first paragraph, it was dynamite.

> The mastermind behind the kidnapping of Ender's "jeesh" is a serial killer named Achilles. He was taken from a mental institution during the League War in order to bring his dark genius to bear on Russian military strategy. He has repeatedly murdered with his own hands, and now ten brilliant children who once saved the world are completely at his mercy. What were the Russians thinking when they gave power to this psychopath? Or was Achilles' bloody record concealed even from them?

There it was—in the first paragraph, right along with the accusation, Locke was generously providing the spin that would allow the Russian government and military to extricate themselves from this mess.

It took twenty minutes to send the individual messages to all his Russian contacts. In each message, he warned them that they had only about six hours before he had to turn in his column to the editor at *International Aspects. IA*'s fact-checkers would add another hour or two to the delay, but they would find complete confirmation of everything.

Peter pushed SEND, SEND, SEND.

Then he settled down to pore over the data to figure out how it revealed to him the identity of his correspondent. Another mental patient? Hardly likely— they were all brought back into confinement. An employee of the mental hospital? Impossible for someone like that to find out who was behind Locke and Demosthenes. Someone in law enforcement? More likely—but few names of investigators were offered in the news stories. Besides, how could he know *which* of the investigators had tipped him off? No, his correspondent had promised, in effect, a unique solution. Something in the data would tell him *exactly* who his informant was, and exactly how to reach him. Emailing investigators indiscriminately would serve only to risk exposing Peter with no guarantee that any of the people he contacted would be the right one.

The one thing that did not happen as he searched for his correspondent's identity was any kind of response from any of his Russian friends. If the story had been wrong, or if the Russian military had already known about Achilles' history and wanted to cover it up, he would have been getting constant emails urging him not to run the story, then demanding, and finally threatening him. So the fact that no one wrote him at all served as all the confirmation he needed from the Russian end.

As Demosthenes, he was anti-Russian. As Locke, he was reasonable and fair to all nations. As Peter, though, he was envious of the Russian sense of national identity, the cohesiveness of Russians when they felt their country was in danger. If Americans had ever had such powerful bonds, they had expired long before Peter was born. To be Russian was the most powerful part of a person's identity. To be American was about as important as being a Rotarian—very important if you were elected to high office, but barely noticeable in most citizens' sense of who they were. That was why Peter never planned his future with America in mind. Americans expected to get their way, but they had no passion for anything. Demosthenes could stir up anger and resentment, but it amounted to spitefulness, not purpose. Peter would have to root himself elsewhere. Too bad Russia wasn't available to him. It was a nation that had a vast will to greatness, coupled with the most extraordinary run of stupid leadership in history, with the possible exception of the kings of Spain. And Achilles had got there first.

Six hours after sending the article to his Russian contacts, he pushed SEND once more, submitting it to his editor. As he expected, three minutes later he got a response.

You're sure?

To which Peter replied, "Check it. My sources confirm."

Then he went to bed.

And woke up almost before he had gone to sleep. He couldn't have closed his book, and then his eyes, for more than a couple of minutes before he realized that he had been looking in the wrong direction for his informant. It wasn't one of the investigators who tipped him off. It was someone connected to the I.F. at the highest level, someone who knew that Peter Wiggin was Locke and Demosthenes. But not Graff or Chamrajnagar—they would not have left hints about who they really were. Someone else, someone in whom they confided, perhaps.

But no one from the I.F. had turned up in the information about Achilles' escape. Except for the nun who found Achilles in the first place.

He reread the message. Could this have come from a nun? Possibly, but why would she be sending the information so anonymously? And why would the kidnapped children smuggle a message to her?

Had she recruited one of them?

Peter got out of bed and padded to his desk, where he called up the information on all the kidnapped children. Every one of them came to Battle School through the normal testing process; none had been found by the nun, and so none of them would have any reason to smuggle a message to her.

What other connection could there be? Achilles was an orphan on the streets of Rotterdam when Sister Carlotta identified him as having military talent—he couldn't have had any family connections. Unless he was like that Greek kid from Ender's jeesh who was killed in a missile attack a few weeks ago, the supposed orphan whose real family was identified while he was in Battle School.

Orphan. Killed in a missile attack. What was his name? Julian Delphiki. Called Bean. A name he picked up when he was an orphan . . . where?

Rotterdam. Just like Achilles.

It was not a stretch to imagine that Sister Carlotta found both Bean and Achilles. Bean was one of Ender's companions on Eros during the last battle. He was the only one who, instead of being kidnapped, had been killed. Everyone assumed it was because he was so heavily protected by the Greek military that the would-be kidnappers gave up and settled for keeping rival powers from using him. But what if there was never any intention to kidnap him, because Achilles already knew him and, more to the point, Bean knew too much about Achilles?

And what if Bean was not dead at all? What if he was living in hiding, protected by the widespread belief that he was dead? It was absolutely believable that the captive kids would choose him to receive their smuggled message, since he was the only one of their group, besides Ender himself, who wasn't in captivity with them. And who else would have such a powerful motive to work to get them out, along with the proven mental ability to think of a strategy like the one the informant had laid out in his letter?

A house of cards, that's what he was building, one leap after another—but each intuitive jump felt absolutely right. That letter was written by Bean. Julian Delphiki. And how would Peter contact him? Bean could be anywhere, and there was no hope of contacting him since anybody who knew he was alive would be all the more certain to pretend that he was dead and refuse to accept a message for him.

Again, the solution should be obvious from the data, and it was. Sister Carlotta.

Peter had a contact in the Vatican—a sparring partner in the wars of ideas that flared up now and then among those who frequented the discussions of international relations on the nets. It was already morning in Rome, though barely. But if anyone was at his desk early in Italy, it would be a hardworking monk attached to the Vatican foreign-affairs office.

Sure enough, an answer came back within fifteen minutes.

```
Sister Carlotta's location is pro-
tected. Messages can be forwarded. I
will not read what you send via me. (You
can't work here if you don't know how to
keep your eyes closed.)
```

Peter composed his message to Bean and sent it—to Sister Carlotta. If anyone knew how to reach Julian Delphiki in hiding, it would be the nun who had first found him. It was the only possible solution to the challenge his informant had given him.

Finally he went back to bed, knowing that he wouldn't sleep long—he'd undoubtedly keep waking through the night and checking the nets to see the reaction to his column.

What if no one cared? What if nothing happened? What if he had fatally compromised the Locke persona, and for no gain?

As he lay in bed, pretending to himself that he might sleep, he could hear his parents snoring in their room across the hall. It was both strange and comforting to hear them. Strange that he could be worrying about whether something he had written might *not* cause an international incident, and yet he was still living in his parents' house, their only child left at home. Comforting because it was a sound he had known since infancy, that comforting assurance that they were alive, they were close by, and the fact that he could hear them meant that when monsters leapt from the dark corners of the room, they would hear him screaming.

The monsters had taken on different faces over the years, and hid in corners of rooms far from his own, but that noise from his parents' bedroom was proof that the world had not ended yet.

Peter wasn't sure why, but he knew that the letter he had just sent to Julian Delphiki, via Sister Carlotta, via his friend in the Vatican, would put an end to his long idyll, playing at world affairs while having his mother do his laundry. He was finally putting himself into play, not as the cool and distant commentator Locke or the hot-blooded demagogue Demosthenes, both of them electronic constructs, but as Peter Wiggin, a young man of flesh and blood, who could be caught, who could be harmed, who could be killed.

If anything should have kept him awake, it was that thought. But instead he felt relieved. Relaxed. The long waiting was almost over. He fell asleep and did not wake until his mother called him to breakfast.

His father was reading a newsprint at breakfast. "What's the headline, Dad?" asked Peter.

"They're saying that the Russians kidnapped those kids. And put them under the control of a known murderer. Hard to believe, but they seem to know all about this Achilles guy. Got busted out of a mental hospital in Belgium. Crazy world we live in. Could have been Ender." He shook his head.

Peter could see how his mother froze for just a moment at the mention of Ender's name. Yes, yes, Mother, I know he's the child of your heart and you grieve every time you hear his name. And you ache for your beloved daughter Valentine who has left Earth and will never return, not in your lifetime. But you still have your firstborn with you, your brilliant and good-looking son Peter, who is bound to produce brilliant and beautiful grandchildren for you someday, along with a few other things like, oh, who knows, maybe bringing peace to Earth by unifying it under one government? Will that console you just a little bit?

Not likely.

"The killer's name is . . . Achilles?"

"No last name. Like some kind of pop singer or something."

Peter cringed inside. Not because of what his father had said, but because Peter had come *this* close to correcting his father's pronunciation of "Achilles." Since Peter couldn't be sure that any of the rags mentioned the French pronunciation of Achilles' name, how would he explain knowing the correct pronunciation to Father?

"Has Russia denied it, of course?" asked Peter.

Father scanned the newsprint again. "Nothing about it in this story," he said.

"Cool," said Peter. "Maybe that means it's true."

"If it was true," said Father, "they *would* deny it. That's the way Russians are."

As if Father knew anything at all about the "way Russians are."

Got to move out, thought Peter, and live on my own. I'm in college. I'm trying to spring ten prisoners from custody a third of the way around the world. Maybe I should use some of the money I've been earning as a columnist to pay rent.

Maybe I should do it right away, so that if Achilles finds out who I am and comes to kill me, I won't bring danger down on my family.

Only Peter knew even as he formed this thought that there was another, darker thought hidden deep inside himself: Maybe if I get out of here, they'll blow up the house when I'm not there, the way they must have done with Julian Delphiki. Then they'll think I'm dead and I'll be safe for a while.

No, I don't wish for my parents to die! What kind of monster would wish for that? I don't want that.

But one thing Peter never did was lie to himself, or at least not for long. He didn't wish for his parents to die, certainly not violently in an attack aimed at him. But he knew that if it did happen, he'd prefer not to be with them at the time. Better, of course, if no one was home. But . . . me first.

Ah yes. *That* was what Valentine hated about him. Peter had almost forgotten. *That's* why Ender was the son that everyone loved. Sure, Ender wiped out a whole species of aliens, not to mention offing a kid in a bathroom in Battle School. But he wasn't *selfish* like Peter.

"You aren't eating, Peter," said Mother.

"Sorry," said Peter. "I'm getting some test results back today, and I was brooding I guess."

"What subject?" asked Mother.

"World history," said Peter.

"Isn't it strange to realize that when they write history books in the future, your brother's name will always be mentioned?" said Mother.

"Not strange," said Peter. "That's just one of the perks you get when you save the world."

Behind his jocularity, though, he made a much grimmer promise to his mother. Before you die, Mother, you'll see that while Ender's name shows up in a chapter or two, it will be impossible to discuss this century or the next without mentioning my name on almost every page.

"Got to run," said Father. "Good luck with the test."

"Already took the test, Dad. I'm just getting the grade today."

"That's what I meant. Good luck on the grade."

"Thanks," said Peter.

He went back to eating while Mother walked Father to the door so they could kiss good-bye.

I'll have that someday, thought Peter. Someone who'll kiss me good-bye at the door. Or maybe just someone to put a blindfold over my head before they shoot me. Depending on how things turn out.

8

Bread Van

To:Demosthenes%Tecumseh@freeamerica
.org
From: unready%cincinnatus@anon.set
Re: satrep

Satellite reports from date Delphiki
family killed: Nine vehicles simultaneous departure from northern Russia
location, 64 latitude. Encrypted destination list attached. Genuine dispersal? Decoy? What's our best
strategy, my friend? Eliminate or rescue? Are they children or weapons of
mass destruction? Hard to know. Why did
that bastard Locke get Ender Wiggin
sent away? We could use that boy now I
think. As for why only nine, not ten

```
vehicles: Maybe one is dead or sick.
Maybe one has turned. Maybe two have
turned and were sent together. All
guesswork. I only see raw satdat, not
intelnetcom reports. If you have other
sources on that, feed some back to me?


Custer
```

Petra knew that loneliness was the tool they were using against her. Don't let the girl talk to any human at all, then when one shows up she'll be so grateful she'll blurt confessions, she'll believe lies, she'll make friends with her worst enemy.

Weird how you can know exactly what the enemy is doing to you and it still works. Like a play her parents took her to her second week back home after the war. It had a four-year-old girl on the stage asking her mother why her father wasn't home yet. The mother is trying to find a way to tell her that the father was killed by an Azerbaijani terrorist bomb—a secondary bomb that went off to kill people trying to rescue survivors of the first, smaller blast. Her father died as a hero, trying to save a child trapped in the wreckage even after the police shouted at him to stay away, there was probably going to be a second blast. The mother finally tells the child.

The little girl stamps her foot angrily and says, "He's *my* papa! Not that little boy's papa!" And the mother says, "That little boy's mama and papa weren't there to help him. Your father did what he hoped somebody else would do for you, if he couldn't be there for you." And the little girl starts to cry and says, "Now he isn't ever going to be there for me. And I don't want somebody else. I want my papa."

Petra sat there watching this play, knowing exactly how cynical it was. Use a child, play on the yearning for family, tie it to nobility and heroism, make the villains the ancestral enemy, and make the child say childishly innocent things while crying. A computer could have written it. But it still worked. Petra cried like a baby, just like the rest of the audience.

That's what isolation was doing to her and she knew it. Whatever they were hoping for, it would probably work. Because human beings are just machines, Petra knew that, machines that do what you want them to do, if you only know the levers to pull. And no matter how complex people might seem, if you just cut them off from the network of people who give shape to their personality, the communities that form their identity, they'll be reduced to that set of levers. Doesn't matter how hard they resist, or how well they know they're being manipulated. Eventually, if you take the time, you can play them like a piano, every note right where you expect it.

Even me, thought Petra.

All alone, day after day. Working on the computer, getting assignments by mail from people who gave no hint of personality. Sending messages to the others in Ender's jeesh, but knowing that their letters, too, were being censored of all personal references. Just data getting transferred back and forth. No netsearches now. She had to file her request and wait for an answer filtered through the people who controlled her. All alone.

She tried sleeping too much, but apparently they drugged her water—they got her so hopped up she couldn't sleep at all. So she stopped trying to play passive resistance games. Just went along, becoming the machine they wanted her to be, pretending to herself that by only pretending to be a machine, she wouldn't actually become one, but knowing at the same time that whatever people pretend to be, they become.

And then comes the day when the door opens and somebody walks in.

Vlad.

He was from Dragon Army. Younger than Petra, and a good guy, but she didn't know him all that well. The bond between them, though, was a big one: Vlad was the only other kid in Ender's jeesh who broke the way Petra did, had to be pulled out of the battles for a day. Everybody was kind to them but they both knew—it made them the weak ones. Objects of pity. They all got the same medals and commendations, but Petra knew that their medals meant less than the others, their commendations were empty, because they were the ones who hadn't cut it while the others did. Not that Petra had ever talked about it with Vlad. She just knew that he knew the same things she knew, because he had been down the same long dark tunnel.

And here he was.

"Ho, Petra," he said.

"Ho, Vlad," she answered. She liked hearing her own voice. It still worked. Liked hearing his, too.

"I guess I'm the new instrument of torture they're using on you," said Vlad.

He said it with a smile. That told Petra that he wanted it to seem like a joke. Which told her that it wasn't really a joke at all.

"Really?" she said. "Traditionally, you're simply supposed to kiss me and let someone else do the torture."

"It's not really torture. It's the way out."

"Out of what?"

"Out of prison. It's not what you think, Petra. The hegemony is breaking up, there's going to be war. The question is whether it drives the world down into chaos or leads to one nation ruling all the others. And if it's one nation, which nation should it be?"

"Let me guess. Paraguay."

"Close," said Vlad. He grinned. "I know, it's easier for me. I'm from Belarus, we make a big deal about being a separate country, but in our hearts, we don't mind the thought of Russia being the country that comes out on top. Nobody outside of Belarus gives a lobster tit about how we're not really Russians. So sure, I wasn't hard to talk into it. And you're Armenian, and they spent a lot of years being oppressed by Russia in the old Communist days. But Petra, just how Armenian are you? What's really good for Armenia anyway? That's what I'm supposed to say to you, anyway. To get you to see that Armenia benefits if Russia comes out on top. No more sabotage. Really help us get ready for the real war. You cooperate, and Armenia gets a special place in the new order. You get to bring in your whole country. That's not nothing, Petra. And if you don't help, that doesn't do a thing for anybody. Doesn't help you. Doesn't help Armenia. Nobody ever knows what a hero you were."

"Sounds like a death threat."

"Sounds like a threat of loneliness and obscurity. You weren't born to be nobody, Petra. You were born to shine. This is a chance to be a hero again. I know you think you don't care, but come on, admit it—it was great being Ender's jeesh."

"And now we're what's-his-name's jeesh. He'll really share the glory with us," said Petra.

"Why not? He's still the boss, he doesn't mind having heroes serve under him."

"Vlad, he'll make sure nobody knows any of us existed, and he'll kill us when he's done with us." She hadn't meant to speak so honestly. She knew it would get back to Achilles. She knew it would guarantee that her prophecy would come true. But there it was—the lever worked. She was so grateful to have a friend there, even one who had obviously been coopted, that she couldn't help but blurt.

"Well, Petra, what can I say? I told them, you're the tough one. I told you what's on offer. Think about it. There's no hurry. You've got plenty of time to decide."

"You're going?"

"That's the rule," said Vlad. "You say no, I go. Sorry."

He got up.

She watched him go out the door. She wanted to say something clever and brave. She wanted some name to call him to make him feel bad for throwing in his lot with Achilles. But she knew that anything she said would be used against her one way or another. Anything she said would reveal another lever to the lever-pullers. What she'd already said was bad enough.

So she kept her silence and watched the door close and lay there on her bed until her computer beeped and she went to it and there was another assignment and she went to work and solved it and sabotaged it just like usual and thought, This is going rather well after all, I didn't break or anything.

And then she went to bed and cried herself to sleep. For a few minutes, though, just before she slept, she felt that Vlad was her truest, dearest friend and she would have done anything for him, just to have him back in the room with her.

Then that feeling passed and she had one last fleeting thought: If they were really all that smart, they would have known that I'd feel like that, right that moment; and Vlad would have come in and I would have leapt from my bed and thrown my arms around him and told him yes, I'll do it, I'll work with you, thank you for coming to me like that, Vlad, thank you.

Only they missed their chance.

As Ender had once said, most victories came from instantly exploiting your enemy's stupid mistakes, and not from any particular brilliance in your own plan. Achilles was very clever. But not perfect. Not all-knowing. He may not win. I may even get out of here without dying.

Peaceful at last, she fell asleep.

———

They woke her in darkness.

"Get up."

No greeting. She couldn't see who it was. She could hear footsteps outside her door. Boots. Soldiers?

She remembered talking to Vlad. Rejecting his offer. He said there was no hurry; she had plenty of time to decide. But here they were, rousting her in the middle of the night. To do what?

Nobody was laying a hand on her. She dressed in darkness—they didn't hurry her. If this was supposed to be some sort of torture session or interrogation they wouldn't wait for her to dress, they'd make sure she was as uncomfortable, as off-balance as possible.

She didn't want to ask questions, because that would seem weak. But then, *not* asking questions was passive.

"Where are we going now?"

No answer. That was a bad sign. Or was it? All she knew about these things was from the few fictional war vids she'd seen in Battle School and a few spy movies in Armenia. None of it ever seemed believable to her, yet here she was in a real spy-movie situation and her only source of information about what to expect was those stupid fictional vids and movies. What happened to her superior reasoning ability? The talents that got her into Battle School in the first place? Apparently those only worked when you thought you were playing games in school. In the real world, fear sets in and you fall back on lame made-up stories written by people who had no idea how things like this really worked.

Except that the people doing these things to her had also seen the same dumb vids and movies, so how did she know they weren't modeling *their* actions and attitudes and even their words on what they'd seen in the movies? It's not like anybody had a training course on how to look tough and mean when you were rousting a pubescent girl in the middle of the night. She tried to imagine the instruction manual. *If she is going to be transported to another location, tell her to hurry, she's keeping everyone waiting. If she's going to be tortured, make snide comments about how you hope she got plenty of rest. If she is going to be drugged, tell her that it won't hurt a bit, but laugh snidely so she'll think you're lying. If she is going to be executed, say nothing.*

Oh, this is good, she told herself. Talk yourself into fearing the absolute worst. Make sure you're as close to a state of panic as possible.

"I've got to pee," she said.

No answer.

"I can do it here. I can do it in my clothes. I can do it naked. I can do it in my clothes or naked wherever we're going. I can dribble it along the way. I can write my name in the snow. It's harder for girls, it requires a lot more athletic activity, but we can do it."

Still no answer.

"Or you can let me go to the bathroom."

"All right," he said.

"Which?"

"Bathroom." He walked out the door.

She followed him. Sure enough, there were soldiers out there. Ten of them. She stopped in front of one burly soldier and looked up at his face. "It's a good thing they brought *you*. If it had just been those other guys, I would have made my stand and fought to the death. But with you here, I had no choice but to give myself up. Good work, soldier."

She turned and walked on toward the bathroom. Wondering if she had seen just the faintest hint of a smile on that soldier's face. *That* wasn't in the movie script, was it? Oh, wait. The hero was supposed to have a smart mouth. She was right in character. Only now she understood that all those clever remarks that heroes made were designed to conceal their raw fear. Insouciant heroes aren't brave or relaxed. They're just trying not to embarrass themselves in the moments before they die.

She got to the bathroom and of course he came right in with her. But she'd been in Battle School and if she'd had a shy bladder she would have died of urea poisoning long ago. She dropped trou, sat on the john, and let go. The guy was out the door long before she was ready to flush.

There was a window. There were ceiling air ducts. But she was in the middle of nowhere and it's not like she had anywhere she could run. How did they do this in the vids? Oh, yeah. A friend would have already placed a weapon in some concealed location and the hero would find it, assemble it, and come out firing. That's what was wrong with this whole situation. No friends.

She flushed, rearranged her clothing, washed her hands, and walked back out to her friendly escorts.

They walked her outside to a convoy, of sorts. There were two black limousines and four escort vehicles. She saw two girls about her size and hair color get into the back of each of the limos. Petra, by contrast, was kept close to the building, under the eaves, until she was at the back of a bakery van. She climbed in. None of her guards came with her. There were two men in the back of the van, but they were in civilian clothes. "What am I, bread?" she asked.

"We understand your need to feel that you're in control of the situation through humor," said one of the men.

"What, a psychiatrist? This is worse than torture. What happened to the Geneva convention?"

The psychiatrist smiled. "You're going home, Petra."

"To God? Or Armenia?"

"At this moment, neither. The situation is still . . . flexible."

"I'd say it's flexible, if I'm going home to a place where I've never been before."

"Loyalties have not yet been sorted out. The branch of government that kidnapped you and the other children was acting without the knowledge of the army or the elected government—"

"Or so they say," said Petra.

"You understand my situation perfectly."

"So who are you loyal to?"

"Russia."

"Isn't that what they'll all say?"

"Not the ones who turned our foreign policy and military strategy over to a homicidal maniac child."

"Are those three equal accusations?" asked Petra. "Because *I'm* guilty of being a child. And homicide, too, in some people's opinion."

"Killing Buggers was not homicide."

"I suppose it was insecticide."

The psychiatrist looked baffled. Apparently he didn't know Common well enough to understand a wordplay that nine-year-olds thought was endlessly funny in Battle School.

The van began to move.

"Where are we going, since it's not home?"

"We're going into hiding to keep you out of the hands of this monster child until the breadth of this conspiracy can be discovered and the conspirators arrested."

"Or vice versa," said Petra.

The psychiatrist looked baffled again. But then he understood. "I suppose that's possible. But then, I'm not an important man. How would they know to look for me?"

"You're important enough that you have soldiers who obey you."

"They're not obeying me. We're all obeying someone else."

"And who is that?"

"If, through some misfortune, you were retaken by Achilles and his sponsors, you won't be able to answer that question."

"Besides, you'd all be dead before they could get to me, so your names wouldn't matter anyway, right?"

He looked at her searchingly. "You seem cynical about this. We *are* risking our lives to save you."

"You're risking *my* life, too."

He nodded slowly. "Do you want to return to your prison?"

"I just want you to be aware that being kidnapped a second time isn't exactly the same thing as being set free. You're so sure that you're smart enough and your people are loyal enough to bring this off. But if you're wrong, I could get killed. So yes, you're taking risks— but so am I, and nobody asked me."

"I ask you now."

"Let me out of the van right here," said Petra. "I'll take my chances alone."

"No," said the psychiatrist.

"I see. So I *am* still a prisoner."

"You are in protective custody."

"But I am a certified strategic and tactical genius," said Petra, "and you're not. So why are you in charge of *me*?"

He had no answer.

"I'll tell you why," said Petra. "Because this is not about saving the little children who were stolen away by the evil wicked child. This is about saving Mother Russia a lot of embarrassment. So it isn't enough for me to be safe. You have to return me to Armenia under just the right circumstances, with just the right spin, that the faction of the Russian government that you serve will be exonerated of all guilt."

"We are not guilty."

"My point is not that you're lying about that, but that you regard that as a much higher priority than saving me. Because I assure you, riding along in this van, I fully expect to be retaken by Achilles and his . . . what did you call them? Sponsors."

"And why do you suppose that this will happen?"

"Does it matter why?"

"You're the genius," said the psychiatrist. "Apparently you have already seen some flaw in our plan."

"The flaw is obvious. Far too many people know about it. The decoy limousines, and soldiers, the escorts. You're sure that not one of those people is a plant? Because if *any* of them is reporting to Achilles' sponsors, then they already know which vehicle really has me in it, and where it's going."

"They don't know where it's going."

"They do if the driver is the one who was planted by the other side."

"The driver doesn't know where we're going."

"He's just going around in circles?"

"He knows the first rendezvous point, that's all."

Petra shook her head. "I knew you were stupid, because you became a talk-therapy shrink, which is like being a minister of a religion in which you get to be God."

The psychiatrist turned red. Petra liked that. He was stupid, and he didn't like hearing it, but he definitely needed to hear it because he clearly had built his whole life around the idea that he was smart, and now that he was playing with live ammunition, thinking he was smart was going to get him killed.

"I suppose you're right, that the driver *does* know where we're going *first,* even if he doesn't know where we plan to go from the first rendezvous." The psychiatrist shrugged elaborately. "But that can't be helped. You have to trust *someone.*"

"And you decided to trust this driver because . . . ?"

The psychiatrist looked away.

Petra looked at the other man. "You're talkative."

"I am think," said the man in halting Common, "you make Battle School teachers crazy with talk."

"Ah," said Petra. "*You're* the brains of the outfit."

The man looked puzzled, but also offended—he wasn't sure how he had been insulted, since he probably didn't know the word *outfit,* but he knew an insult had been intended.

"Petra Arkanian," said the psychiatrist, "since you're right that I don't know the driver all that well, tell me what I should have done. You have a better plan than trusting him?"

"Of course," said Petra. "You tell him the rendezvous point, plan with him very carefully how he'll drive there."

"I did that," said the psychiatrist.

"I know," said Petra. "Then, at the last minute, just as you're loading me into the van, you take the wheel and make him ride in one of the limousines. And then you drive to a different place entirely. Or better yet, you take me to the nearest town and turn me loose and let me take care of myself."

Again, the psychiatrist looked away. Petra was amused at how transparent his body language was. You'd think a shrink would know how to conceal his own tells.

"These people who kidnapped you," said the psychiatrist, "they are a tiny minority, even within the intelligence organizations they work for. They can't be everywhere."

Petra shook her head. "You're a Russian, you were taught Russian history, and you actually believe that the intelligence service can't be everywhere and hear everything? What, did you spend your entire childhood watching American vids?"

The psychiatrist had had enough. Putting on his finest medical airs, he delivered his ultimate put-down. "And you're a child who never learned decent respect. You may be brilliant in your native abilities, but that doesn't mean you understand a political situation you know nothing about."

"Ah," said Petra. "The you're-just-a-child, you-don't-have-as-much-experience argument."

"Naming it doesn't mean it's untrue."

"I'm sure you understand the nuances of political speeches and maneuvers. But this is a military operation."

"It is a political operation," the psychiatrist corrected her. "No shooting."

Again, Petra was stunned at the man's ignorance. "Shooting is what happens when military operations fail to achieve their purposes through maneuver. *Any* operation that's intended to physically deprive the enemy of a valued asset is military."

"This operation is about freeing an ungrateful little girl and sending her home to her mama and papa," said the psychiatrist.

"You want me to be grateful? Open the door and let me out."

"The discussion is over," said the psychiatrist. "You can shut up now."

"Is that how you end your sessions with your patients?"

"I never said I was a psychiatrist," said the psychiatrist.

"Psychiatry was your education," said Petra. "And I know you had a practice for a while, because *real* people don't talk like shrinks when they're trying to reassure a frightened child. Just because you got involved in politics and changed careers doesn't mean you aren't still the kind of bonehead who goes to witch-doctor school and thinks he's a scientist."

The man's fury was barely contained. Petra enjoyed the momentary thrill of fear that ran through her. Would he slap her? Not likely. As a psychiatrist, he would probably fall back on his one limitless resource—professional arrogance.

"Laymen usually sneer at sciences they don't understand," said the psychiatrist.

"That," said Petra, "is precisely my point. When it comes to military operations, you're a complete novice. A layman. A bonehead. And I'm the expert. And you're too stupid to listen to me even now."

"Everything is going smoothly," said the psychiatrist. "And you'll feel very foolish and apologize as you thank me when you get on the plane to return to Armenia."

Petra only smiled tightly. "You didn't even look in the cab of this delivery van to make sure it was the same driver before we drove off."

"Someone else would have noticed if the driver changed," said the psychiatrist. But Petra could tell she had finally made him uneasy.

"Oh, yes, I forgot, we trust your fellow conspirators to see all and miss nothing, because, after all, *they* aren't psychiatrists."

"I'm a psychologist," he said.

"Ouch," said Petra. "That must have hurt, to admit you're only half-educated."

The psychologist turned away from her. What was the term the shrinks in Ground School used for that behavior—avoidance? Denial? She almost asked him, but decided to leave well enough alone.

And people thought she couldn't control her tongue.

They rode for a while in bristling silence.

But the things she said must have been working on him, nagging at him. Because after a while he got up and walked to the front and opened the door between the cargo area and the cab.

A deafening gunshot rang through the closed interior, and the psychiatrist fell back. Petra felt hot brains and stinging bits of bone spatter her face and arms. The man across from her started reaching for a weapon under his coat, but he was shot twice and slumped over dead without touching it.

The door from the cab opened the rest of the way. It was Achilles standing there, holding the gun in his hand. He said something.

"I can't hear you," said Petra. "I can't even hear my own voice."

Achilles shrugged. Speaking louder and mouthing the words carefully, he tried again. She refused to look at him.

"I'm not going to try to listen to you," she said, "while I still have his blood all over me."

Achilles set down the gun—far out of her reach—and pulled off his shirt. Bare-chested, he handed it to her, and when she refused to take it, he started wiping her face with it until she snatched it out of his hands and did the job herself.

The ringing in her ears was fading, too. "I'm surprised you didn't wait to kill them until you'd had a chance to tell them how smart you are," said Petra.

"I didn't need to," said Achilles. "You already told them how dumb they were."

"Oh, you were listening?"

"Of course the compartment back here was wired for sound," said Achilles. "And video."

"You didn't have to kill them," said Petra.

"That guy was going for his gun," said Achilles.

"Only after his friend was dead."

"Come now," said Achilles. "I thought Ender's whole method was the preemptive use of ultimate force. I only do what I learned from your hero."

"I'm surprised you did this one yourself," said Petra.

"What do you mean, 'this one'?" said Achilles.

"I assumed you were stopping the other rescues, too."

"You forget," said Achilles, "I've already had months to evaluate you. Why keep the others, when I can have the best?"

"Are you flirting with me?" She said it with as much disdain as she could muster. Those words usually worked to shut down a boy who was being smug. But he only laughed.

"I don't flirt," he said.

"I forgot," said Petra. "You shoot first, and then flirting isn't necessary."

That got to him a little—made him pause a moment, brought the slightest hint of a quickening of breath. It occurred to Petra that her mouth was indeed going to get her killed. She had never actually seen someone get shot before, except in movies and vids. Just because she thought of herself as the protagonist of this biographical vid she was trapped in didn't mean she was safe. For all she knew, Achilles meant to kill her, too.

Or did he? Could he have really meant that she was the only one of the team he was keeping? Vlad would be so disappointed.

"How did you happen to choose me?" she asked, changing the subject.

"Like I said, you're the best."

"That is such kuso," said Petra. "The exercises I did for you weren't any better than anyone else's."

"Oh, those battle plans, those were just to keep you

busy while the real tests were going on. Or rather, to make you think you were keeping *us* busy."

"What was this real test, then, since I supposedly succeeded at it better than anyone else?"

"Your little dragon drawing," said Achilles.

She could feel the blood drain from her face. He saw it and laughed.

"Don't worry," said Achilles. "You won't be punished. That was the test, to see which of you would succeed in getting a message outside."

"And my prize is staying with you?" She said it with all the disgust she could put in her voice.

"Your prize," said Achilles, "is staying alive."

She felt sick at heart. "Even you wouldn't kill all the others, for no reason."

"If they're killed, there's a reason. If there's a reason, they'll be killed. No, we suspected that your dragon drawing would have *some* meaning to someone. But we couldn't find a code in it."

"There wasn't a code in it," said Petra.

"Oh yes there was," said Achilles. "You somehow encoded it in such a way that someone was able to recognize it and decode it. I know this because the news stories that suddenly appeared, triggering this whole crisis, had some specific information that was more or less correct. One of the messages you guys tried to send must have gotten through. So we went back over every email sent by every one of you, and the only thing that couldn't be accounted for was your dragon clip art."

"If you can read a message in that," said Petra, "then you're smarter than I am."

"On the contrary," said Achilles. "You're smarter than I am, at least about strategy and tactics—like evading the enemy while keeping in close communication with allies. Well, not all *that* close, since it took them so long to publish the information you sent."

"You bet on the wrong horse," said Petra. "It wasn't a message, and therefore however they got the news it must have come from one of the other guys."

Achilles only laughed. "You're a stubborn liar, aren't you?"

"I'm not lying when I tell you that if I have to keep riding with these corpses in this compartment, I'm going to get sick."

He smiled. "Vomit away."

"So your pathology includes a weird need to hang around with the dead," said Petra. "You'd better be careful—you know where that leads. First you'll start dating them, and then one day you'll bring a dead person home to meet your mother and father. Oops. I forgot, you're an orphan."

"So I brought them to show *you*."

"Why did you wait so long to shoot them?" asked Petra.

"I wanted it set up just right. So I could shoot the one while he was standing in the doorway. So his body would block any returning fire from the other guy. And besides, I was also enjoying the way you took them apart. You know, arguing with them like you did. Sounded like you hate shrinks almost as much as I do. And you were never even committed to a mental institution. I would have applauded several of your best bon mots, only I might have been overheard."

"Who's driving this van?" asked Petra, ignoring his flattery.

"Not me," said Achilles. "Are you?"

"How long are you planning to keep me imprisoned?" asked Petra.

"As long as it takes."

"As long as it takes to do what?"

"Conquer the world together, you and I. Isn't that romantic? Or, well, it *will* be romantic, when it happens."

"It will never be romantic," said Petra. "Nor will I help you conquer your dandruff problem, let alone the world."

"Oh, you'll cooperate," said Achilles. "I'll kill the other members of Ender's jeesh, one by one, until you give in."

"You don't have them," said Petra. "And you don't know where they are. They're safe from you."

Achilles grinned mock-sheepishly. "There's just no fooling Genius Girl, is there? But, you see, they're bound to surface somewhere, and when they do, they'll die. I don't forget."

"That's one way to conquer the world," said Petra. "Kill everybody one by one until you're the only one left."

"Your first job," said Achilles, "is to decode that message you sent out."

"What message?"

Achilles picked up his gun and pointed it at her.

"Kill me and you'll always wonder if I really sent out a message at all," said Petra.

"But at least I won't have to listen to your smug voice lying to me," said Achilles. "That would almost be a consolation."

"You seem to be forgetting that I wasn't a volunteer on this expedition. If you don't like listening to me, let me go."

"You're so sure of yourself," said Achilles. "But I know you better than you know yourself."

"And what is it you think you know about me?" asked Petra.

"I know that you'll eventually give in and help me,"

"Well, I know *you* better than you know yourself, too," said Petra.

"Oh, really?"

"I know that eventually you'll kill me. Because you always do. So let's just skip all the boring stuff in between. Kill me now. End the suspense."

"No," said Achilles. "Things like that are much better as a surprise. Don't you think? At least, that's the way God always did it."

"Why am I even talking to you?" asked Petra.

"Because you're so lonely after being in solitary for all these months that you'd do anything for human company. Even talk to *me*."

She hated that he was probably right. "Human company—apparently you're under the delusion that you qualify."

"Oh, you're mean," said Achilles, laughing. "Look, I'm bleeding."

"You've got blood on your hands, all right."

"And you've got it all over your face," said Achilles. "Come on, it'll be fun."

"And here I thought nothing would ever be more tedious than solitary confinement."

"You're the best, Petra," said Achilles. "Except for one."

"Bean," said Petra.

"Ender," said Achilles. "Bean is nothing. Bean is dead."

Petra said nothing.

Achilles looked at her searchingly. "No smart remarks?"

"Bean is dead and you're alive," said Petra. "There's no justice."

The van slowed down and stopped.

"There," said Achilles. "Our lively conversation made the time *fly* by."

Fly. She heard an airplane overhead. Landing or taking off?

"Where are we flying?" she asked.

"Who says we're flying anywhere?"

"I think we're flying out of the country," said Petra, speaking the ideas as they came to her. "I think you realized that you were going to lose your cushy job here in Russia, and you're sneaking out of the country."

"You're really very good. You keep setting a new standard for cleverness," said Achilles.

"And you keep setting a new standard for failure."

He hesitated a moment, then went on as if she hadn't spoken. "They're going to pit the other kids against me," he said. "You already know them. You know their weaknesses. Whoever I'm up against, you're going to advise me."

"Never."

"We're in this together," said Achilles. "I'm a nice guy. You'll like me, eventually."

"Oh, I know," said Petra. "What's not to like?"

"Your message," said Achilles. "You wrote it to Bean, didn't you?"

"What message?" said Petra.

"That's why you don't believe he's dead."

"I believe he's dead," said Petra. But she knew her earlier hesitation had given her away.

"Or else you wonder—if he got your message before I had him killed, why did it take so long after he died to have it hit the news? And here's the obvious answer, Pet. Somebody else figured it out. Somebody else decoded it. And that really pisses me off. So don't tell me what the message said. I'm going to decode it myself. It can't be that hard."

"Downright easy," said Petra. "After all, I'm dumb enough to end up as your prisoner. So dumb, in fact, that I never sent anybody a message."

"When I do decode it, though, I hope it won't say anything disparaging about me. Because then I'd have to beat the shit out of you."

"You're right," said Petra. "You *are* a charmer."

Fifteen minutes later, they were on a small private jet, flying south by southeast. It was a luxurious vehicle, for its size, and Petra wondered if it belonged to one of the intelligence services or to some faction in the military or maybe to some crime lord. Or maybe all three at once.

She wanted to study Achilles, watch his face, his body language. But she didn't want him to see her showing interest in him. So she looked out the window, wondering as she did so whether she wasn't just doing the same thing the dead psychologist had done—looking away to avoid facing bitter truth.

When the chime announced that they could unbelt themselves, Petra got up and headed for the bathroom. It was small, but compared to commercial airplane toilets it was downright commodious. And it had cloth towels and real soap.

She did her best with a damp towel to wipe blood and body matter from her clothes. She had to keep wearing the dirty clothing but she could at least get rid of the visible chunks. The towel was so foul by the time she finished the job that she tossed it and got a fresh one to start in on her face and hands. She scrubbed until her face was red and raw, but she got it all off. She even soaped her hair and washed it as best she could in the tiny sink. It was hard to rinse, pouring one cup of water at a time over her head.

The whole time, she kept thinking of the fact that

the psychiatrist's last minutes were spent listening to her tell him how stupid he was and point out the worthlessness of his life's work. And yes, she was right, as his death proved, but that didn't change the fact that however impure his motives might have been, he *was* trying to save her from Achilles. He had given his life in that effort, however badly planned it might have been. All the other rescues went off smoothly, and they were probably just as badly planned as hers. So much depended on chance. Everybody was stupid about some things. Petra was stupid about the things she said to people who had power over her. Goading them. Daring them to punish her. She did it even though she knew it was stupid. And wasn't it even stupider to do something stupid that you *know* is stupid?

What did he call her? An ungrateful little girl.

He tagged me, all right.

As bad as she felt about his death, as horrified over what she had seen, as frightened as she was to be in Achilles' control, as lonely as she had been for these past weeks, she still couldn't figure out a way to cry about it. Because deeper than all these feelings was something even stronger. Her mind kept thinking of ways to get word to someone about where she was. She had done it once, she could do it again, right? She might feel bad, she might be a miserable specimen of human life, she might be in the midst of a traumatic childhood experience, but she was *not* going to submit to Achilles for one moment longer than she had to.

The plane lurched suddenly, throwing her against the toilet. She half-fell onto it—there wasn't room to fall down all the way—but she couldn't get up because the plane had gone into a steep dive, and for a few moments she found herself gasping as the oxygen-rich air was replaced by cold upper-level air that left her dizzy.

The hull was breached. They've shot us down.

And for all that she had an indomitable will to live, she couldn't help but think: Good for them. Kill Achilles now, and no matter who else is on the plane, it'll be a great day for humanity.

But the plane soon leveled out, and the air was breathable before she blacked out. They must not have been very high when it happened.

She opened the bathroom door and stepped back into the main cabin.

The side door was partway open. And standing a couple of meters back from it was Achilles, the wind whipping at his hair and clothes. He was posing, as if he knew just how fine a figure he cut, standing there on the brink of death.

She approached him, glancing at the door to make sure she stayed well back from it, and to see how high they were. Not very, compared to cruising altitude, but higher than any building or bridge or dam. Anyone who fell from this plane would die.

Could she get behind him and push?

He smiled broadly when she got near.

"What happened?" she shouted over the noise of the wind.

"It occurred to me," he yelled back, "that I made a mistake bringing you with me."

He opened the door on purpose. He opened it for her.

Just as she began to step back, his hand lashed out and seized her by the wrist.

The intensity of his eyes was startling. He didn't look crazy. He looked . . . fascinated. Almost as if he found her amazingly beautiful. But of course it wasn't *her*. It was his power over her that fascinated him. It was himself that he loved so intensely.

She didn't try to pull away. Instead, she twisted her wrist so that she also gripped him.

"Come on, let's jump together," she shouted. "That would be the most romantic thing we could do."

He leaned close. "And miss out on all the history we're going to make together?" he said. Then he laughed. "Oh, I see, you thought I was going to throw you out of the plane. No, Pet, I took hold of you so that I could anchor you while you close the door. Wouldn't want the wind to suck you out, would we?"

"I have a better idea," said Petra. "I'll be the anchor, you close the door."

"But the anchor has to be the stronger, heavier one," said Achilles. "And that's me."

"Let's just leave it open, then," said Petra.

"Can't fly all the way to Kabul with the door open."

What did it mean, his telling her their destination? Did it mean that he trusted her a little? Or that it didn't matter what she knew, since he had decided she was going to die?

Then it occurred to her that if he wanted her dead, she would die. It was that simple. So why worry about it? If he wanted to kill her by pushing her out the door, how was that different from a bullet in the brain? Dead was dead. And if he didn't plan to kill her, the door needed to be closed, and having him serve as anchor was the second-best plan.

"Isn't there somebody in the crew who can do this?" she asked.

"There's just the pilot," said Achilles. "Can *you* land a plane?"

She shook her head.

"So he stays in the cockpit, and we close the door."

"I don't mean to be a nag," said Petra, "but opening the door was a really stupid thing to do."

He grinned at her.

Holding tight to his wrist, she slid along the wall toward the door. It was only partially open, the kind of door that worked by sliding up. So she didn't have to reach very far out of the plane. Still, the cold wind snatched at her arm and made it very hard to get a grip on the door handle to pull it down into place. And even when she got it down into position, she simply didn't have the strength to overcome the wind resistance and pull it snug.

Achilles saw this, and now that the door wasn't open enough for anyone to fall out and the wind could no longer suck anybody out, he let go of her and of the bulkhead and joined her in pulling at the handle.

If I push instead of pulling, thought Petra, the wind will help me, and maybe we'll both get sucked right out.

Do it, she told herself. Do it. Kill him. Even if you die doing it, it's worth it. This is Hitler, Stalin, Genghis, Attila all rolled into one.

But it might not work. He might not get sucked out. She might die alone, pointlessly. No, she would have to find a way to destroy him later, when she could be sure it would work.

At another level, she knew that she simply wasn't ready to die. No matter how convenient it might be for the rest of humanity, no matter how richly Achilles deserved to die, she would not be his executioner, not now, not if she had to give her own life to kill him. If that made her a selfish coward, so be it.

They pulled and pulled and finally, with a whoosh, the door passed the threshold of wind resistance and locked nicely into place. Achilles pulled the lever that locked it.

"Traveling with you is always such an adventure," said Petra.

"No need to shout," said Achilles. "I can hear you just fine."

"Why can't you just run with the bulls at Pamplona, like any normal self-destructive person?" asked Petra.

He ignored her gibe. "I must value you more than I thought." He said it as if it took him rather by surprise.

"You mean you still have a spark of humility? You might actually need someone else?"

Again he ignored her words. "You look better without blood all over your face."

"But I'll never be as pretty as you."

"Here's my rule about guns," said Achilles. "When people are getting shot, always stand behind the shooter. It's a lot less messy there."

"Unless people are shooting back."

Achilles laughed. "Pet, I *never* use a gun when someone might shoot back."

"And you're so well-mannered, you always open a door for a lady."

His smile faded. "Sometimes I get these impulses," he said. "But they're not irresistible."

"Too bad. And here you had such a good insanity defense going."

His eyes blazed for a moment. Then he went back to his seat.

She cursed herself. Goading him like this, how is it different from jumping out of the airplane?

Then again, maybe it was the fact that she spoke to him without cringing that made him value her.

Fool, she said to herself. You are not equipped to understand this boy—you're not insane enough. Don't try to guess why he does what he does, or how he feels about you or anybody or anything. Study him so you can learn how he makes his plans, what he's likely to do, so that someday you can defeat him. But don't ever try to understand. If you can't even understand yourself, what hope do you have of comprehending somebody as deformed as Achilles?

They did not land in Kabul. They landed in Tashkent, refueled, and then went over the Himalayas to New Delhi.

So he lied to her about their destination. He hadn't trusted her after all. But as long as he refrained from killing her, she could endure a little mistrust.

9

Communing with the Dead

```
To: Carlotta%agape@vatican.net/orders/
sisters/ind
From: Locke%erasmus@polnet.gov
Re: An answer for your dead friend
```

```
If you know who I really am, and you
have contact with a certain person pur-
ported to be dead, please inform that
person that I have done my best to ful-
fill expectations. I believe further
collaboration is possible, but not
through intermediaries. If you have no
idea what I'm talking about, then
please inform me of that, as well, so I
can begin my search again.
```

Bean came home to find that Sister Carlotta had
packed their bags.

"Moving day?" he asked.

They had agreed that either one of them could decide that it was time to move on, without having to defend the decision. It was the only way to be sure of acting on any unconscious cues that someone was closing in on them. They didn't want to spend their last moments of life listening to each other say, "I knew we should have left three days ago!" "Well why didn't you say so?" "Because I didn't have a *reason*."

"We have two hours till the flight."

"Wait a minute," said Bean. "You decide we're going, I decide the destination." That was how they'd decided to keep their movements random.

She handed him the printout of an email. It was from Locke. "Greensboro, North Carolina, in the U.S.," she said.

"Perhaps I'm not decoding this right," said Bean, "but I don't see an invitation to visit him."

"He doesn't want intermediaries," said Carlotta. "We can't trust his email to be untraced."

Bean took a match and burned the email in the sink. Then he crumbled the ashes and washed them down the drain. "What about Petra?"

"Still no word. Nine of Ender's jeesh released. The Russians are simply saying that Petra's place of captivity has not yet been discovered."

"Kuso," said Bean.

"I know," said Carlotta, "but what can we do if they won't tell us? I'm afraid she's dead, Bean. You've got to realize that's the likeliest reason for them to stonewall."

Bean knew it, but didn't believe it. "You don't know Petra," he said.

"You don't know Russia," said Carlotta.

"Most people are decent in every country," said Bean.

"Achilles is enough to tip the balance wherever he goes."

Bean nodded. "Rationally, I have to agree with you. Irrationally, I expect to see her again someday."

"If I didn't know you so well, I might interpret that as a sign of your faith in the resurrection."

Bean picked up his suitcase. "Am I bigger, or is this smaller?"

"The case is the same size," said Carlotta.

"I think I'm growing."

"Of course you're growing. Look at your pants."

"I'm still wearing them," said Bean.

"More to the point, look at your ankles."

"Oh." There was more ankle showing than when he bought them.

Bean had never seen a child grow up, but it bothered him that in the weeks they had been in Araraquara, he had grown at least five centimeters. If this was puberty, where were the other changes that were supposed to go along with it?

"We'll buy you new clothes in Greensboro," said Sister Carlotta.

Greensboro. "Ender's home town."

"He only visited there once. His family moved there after he left for Battle School."

"Oh, é. He grew up in the big city, like me."

Sister Carlotta gave one bark of a laugh. "Not at all like you."

"Because he didn't have to fight off other children just to eat?"

"Plenty to eat," said Sister Carlotta. "Yet he did his first killing there all the same."

"You just won't let go of that, will you?" said Bean.

"When you had Achilles in your power, *you* didn't kill him."

Bean didn't like hearing himself compared to Ender that way. Not when it showed Ender at a disadvantage. "Sister Carlotta, we'd have a whole lot less difficulty right now if I *had* killed him."

"You showed mercy. You turned the other cheek. You gave him a chance to make something worthwhile out of his life."

"I made sure he'd get committed to a mental institution."

"Are you so determined to believe in your own lack of virtue?"

"Yes," said Bean. "I prefer truth to lies."

"There," said Carlotta. "Yet another virtue to add to my list."

Bean laughed in spite of himself. "I'm glad you like me," he said.

"Are you afraid to meet him?"

"Who?"

"Ender's brother."

"Not afraid," said Bean.

"How *do* you feel, then?"

"Skeptical," said Bean.

"He showed humility in that email," said Sister Carlotta. "He wasn't sure that he'd figured things out exactly right."

"Oh, there's a thought. The humble Hegemon."

"He's not Hegemon yet," said Carlotta.

"He got nine of Ender's jeesh released, just by publishing a column. He has influence. He has ambition. And now to learn he has humility—well, it's just too much for me."

"Laugh all you want. Let's go out and find a cab."

There was no last-minute business to take care of. They had paid cash for everything, owed nothing. They could walk away.

They lived on money drawn from accounts Graff had set up for them. There was nothing about the account Bean was using now to tag it as belonging to Julian Delphiki. It held his military salary, including his combat and retirement bonuses. The I.F. had given all of Ender's jeesh very large trust funds that they couldn't touch till they came of age. The saved-up pay and bonuses were just to tide them over during their childhood. Graff had assured him that he would not run out of money while he was in hiding.

Sister Carlotta's money came from the Vatican. One person there knew what she was doing. She, too, would have money enough for her needs. Neither of them had the temperament to exploit the situation. They spent little, Sister Carlotta because she wanted nothing more, Bean because he knew that any kind of flamboyance or excess would mark him in people's memories. He always had to seem to be a child running errands for his grandmother, not an undersized war hero cashing in on his back pay.

Their passports caused them no problems, either. Again, Graff had been able to pull strings for them. Given the way they looked—both of Mediterranean ancestry—they carried passports from Catalonia. Carlotta knew Barcelona well, and Catalan was her childhood language. She barely spoke it now, but no matter—hardly anyone did. And no one would be surprised that her grandson couldn't speak the language at all. Besides, how many Catalans would they meet in their travels? Who would try to test their story? If someone got too nosy, they'd simply move on to some other city, some other country.

They landed in Miami, then Atlanta, then Greensboro. They were exhausted and slept the night at an
airport hotel. The next day, they logged in and printed
out guides to the county bus system. It was a fairly
modern system, enclosed and electric, but the map
made no sense to Bean.

"Why don't any of the buses go through here?" he
asked.

"That's where the rich people live," said Sister Carlotta.

"They make them all live together in one place?"

"They feel safer," said Carlotta. "And by living
close together, they have a better chance of their children marrying into other rich families."

"But why don't they want buses?"

"They ride in individual vehicles. They can afford
the fees. It gives them more freedom to choose their
own schedule. And it shows everyone just how rich
they are."

"It's still stupid," said Bean. "Look how far the
buses have to go out of their way."

"The rich people didn't want their streets to be enclosed in order to hold a bus system."

"So what?" asked Bean.

Sister Carlotta laughed. "Bean, isn't there plenty of
stupidity in the military, too?"

"But in the long run, the guy who wins battles gets
to make the decisions."

"Well, these rich people won the economic battles.
Or their grandparents did. So now they get their way
most of the time."

"Sometimes I feel like I don't know anything."

"You've lived half your life in a tube in space, and
before that you lived on the streets of Rotterdam."

"I've lived in Greece with my family and in Araraquara, too. I should have figured this out."

"That was Greece. And Brazil. This is America."

"So money rules in America, but not those other places?"

"No, Bean. Money rules almost everywhere. But different cultures have different ways of displaying it. In Araraquara, for instance, they made sure that the tram lines ran out to the rich neighborhoods. Why? So the servants could come to work. In America, they're more afraid of criminals coming to steal, so the sign of wealth is to make sure that the only way to reach them is by private car or on foot."

"Sometimes I miss Battle School."

"That's because in Battle School, you were one of the very richest in the only coin that mattered there."

Bean thought about that. As soon as the other kids realized that, young and small as he was, he could outperform them in every class, it gave him a kind of power. Everyone knew who he was. Even those who mocked him had to give him a grudging respect. But . . . "I didn't always get my way."

"Graff told me some of the outrageous things you did," said Carlotta. "Climbing through the air ducts to eavesdrop. Breaking into the computer system."

"But they caught me."

"Not as soon as they'd like to have caught you. And were you punished? No. Why? Because you were rich."

"Money and talent aren't the same thing."

"That's because you can inherit money that was earned by your ancestors," said Sister Carlotta. "And everybody recognizes the value of money, while only select groups recognize the value of talent."

"So where does Peter live?"

She had the addresses of all the Wiggin families. There weren't many—the more common spelling had an *s* at the end. "But I don't think this will help us," said Carlotta. "We don't want to meet him at home."

"Why not?"

"Because we don't know whether his parents are aware of what he's doing or not. Graff was pretty sure they don't know. If two foreigners come calling, they're going to start to wonder what their son is doing on the nets."

"Where, then?"

"He could be in secondary school. But given his intelligence, I'd bet on his being in college." She was accessing more information as she spoke. "Colleges colleges colleges. Lots of them in town. The biggest first, the better for him to disappear in . . ."

"Why would he need to disappear? Nobody knows who he is."

"But he doesn't want anyone to realize that he spends no time on his schoolwork. He has to look like an ordinary kid his age. He should be spending all his free time with friends. Or with girls. Or with friends looking for girls. Or with friends trying to distract themselves from the fact that they can't find any girls."

"For a nun, you seem to know a lot about this."

"I wasn't born a nun."

"But you were born a girl."

"And no one is a better observer of the folkways of the adolescent male than the adolescent female."

"What makes you think he doesn't do all those things?"

"Being Locke and Demosthenes is a fulltime job."

"So why do you think he's in college at all?"

"Because his parents would be upset if he stayed home all day, reading and writing email."

Bean wouldn't know about what might make parents upset. He'd only known his parents since the end of the war, and they'd never found anything serious to criticize about him. Or maybe they never felt like he was really theirs. They didn't criticize Nikolai much, either. But . . . more than they did Bean. There simply hadn't been enough time together for them to feel as comfortable, as parental, with their new son Julian.

"I wonder how my parents are doing."

"If anything was wrong, we would have heard," said Carlotta.

"I know," said Bean. "That doesn't mean I can't wonder."

She didn't answer, just kept working her desk, bringing new pages into the display. "Here he is," she said. "A nonresident student. No address. Just email and a campus box."

"What about his class schedule?" asked Bean.

"They don't post that."

Bean laughed. "And that's supposed to be a problem?"

"No, Bean, you aren't going to crack their system. I can't think of a better way for you to attract attention than to trip some trap and get a mole to follow you home."

"I don't get followed by moles."

"You never see the ones that follow you."

"It's just a college, not some intelligence service."

"Sometimes people with the least that is worth stealing are the most concerned with giving the appearance of having great treasures hidden away."

"Is that from the Bible?"

"No, it's from observation."

"So what do we do?"

"Your voice is too young," said Sister Carlotta. "I'll work the phone."

She talked her way to the head registrar of the university. "He was a very nice boy to carry all my things after the wheel broke on my cart, and if these keys are his I want to get them back to him right away, before he worries. . . . No I will not drop them in the mail, how would that be 'right away'? Nor will I leave them with you, they might not be his, and *then* what would I do? If they *are* his keys, he will be very glad you told me where his classes are, and if they aren't his keys, then what harm will it cause? . . . All right, I'll wait."

Sister Carlotta lay back on the bed. Bean laughed at her. "How did a nun get so good at lying?"

She held down the MUTE button. "It isn't lying to tell a bureaucrat whatever story it takes to get him to do his job properly."

"But if he does his job properly, he won't give you any information about Peter."

"If he does his job properly, he'll understand the purpose of the rules and therefore know when it is appropriate to make exceptions."

"People who understand the purpose of the rules don't become bureaucrats," said Bean. "That's something we learned really fast in Battle School."

"Exactly," said Carlotta. "So I have to tell him the story that will help him overcome his handicap." Abruptly she refocused her attention on the phone. "Oh, how very nice. Well, that's fine. I'll see him there."

She hung up the phone and laughed. "Well, after all that, the registrar emailed him. His desk was connected, he admitted that he *had* lost his keys, and he wants to meet the nice old lady at Yum-Yum."

"What is *that*?" asked Bean.

"I haven't the slightest idea, but the way she said it, I figured that if I were an old lady living near campus, I'd already know." She was already deep in the city directory. "Oh, it's a restaurant near campus. Well, this is it. Let's go meet the boy who would be king."

"Wait a minute," said Bean. "We can't go straight there."

"Why not?"

"We have to get some keys."

Sister Carlotta looked at him like he was crazy. "I made up the bit about the keys, Bean."

"The registrar knows that you're meeting Peter Wiggin to give him back his keys. What if he happens to be going to Yum-Yum right now for lunch? And he sees us meet Peter, and nobody gives anybody any keys?"

"We don't have a lot of time."

"OK, I have a better idea. Just act flustered and tell him that in your hurry to get there to meet him, you forgot to *bring* the keys, so he should come back to the house with you."

"You have a talent for this, Bean."

"Deception is second nature to me."

The bus was on time and moved briskly, this being an off-peak time, and soon they were on campus. Bean was better at translating maps into real terrain, so he led the way to Yum-Yum.

The place looked like a dive. Or rather, it was trying to look like a dive from an earlier era. Only it really *was* rundown and under-maintained, so it was a dive trying to look like a nice restaurant decorated to look like a dive. Very complicated and ironic, Bean decided, remembering what Father used to say about a neighborhood restaurant near their house on Crete: Abandon lunch, all ye who enter here.

The food looked like common-people's restaurant food everywhere—more about delivering fats and sweets than about flavor or nutrition. Bean wasn't picky, though. There were foods he liked better than others, and he knew something of the difference between fine cuisine and plain fare, but after the streets of Rotterdam and years of dried and processed food in space, anything that delivered the calories and nutrients was fine with him. But he made the mistake of going for the ice cream. He had just come from Araraquara, where the sorvete was memorable, and the American stuff was too fatty, the flavors too syrupy. "Mmmm, deliciosa," said Bean.

"Fecha a boquinha, menino," she answered. "E não fala português aqui."

"I didn't want to critique the ice cream in a language they'd understand."

"Doesn't the memory of starvation make you more patient?"

"Does everything have to be a moral question?"

"I wrote my dissertation on Aquinas and Tillich," said Sister Carlotta. "All questions are philosophical."

"In which case, all answers are unintelligible."

"And you're not even in grad school yet."

A tall young man slid onto the bench beside Bean. "Sorry I'm late," he said. "You got my keys?"

"I feel so foolish," said Sister Carlotta. "I came all the way here and then I realized I left them back home. Let me buy you some ice cream and then you can walk home with me and get them."

Bean looked up at Peter's face in profile. The resemblance to Ender was plain, but not close enough that anyone could ever mistake one for the other.

So this is the kid who brokered the ceasefire that ended the League War. The kid who wants to be Hege-

mon. Good looking, but not movie-star handsome—
people would like him, but still trust him. Bean had
studied the vids of Hitler and Stalin. The difference
was palpable—Stalin never had to get elected; Hitler
did. Even with that stupid mustache, you could see it in
Hitler's eyes, that ability to see into you, that sense that
whatever he said, wherever he looked, he was speaking
to you, looking at you, that he cared about you. But
Stalin, he looked like the liar that he was. Peter was
definitely in the charismatic category. Like Hitler.

Perhaps an unfair comparison, but those who coveted power invited such thoughts. And the worst was
seeing the way Sister Carlotta played to him. True, she
was acting a part, but when she spoke to him, when
that gaze was fixed on her, she preened a little, she
warmed to him. Not so much that she'd behave foolishly, but she was aware of him with a heightened intensity that Bean didn't like. Peter had the seducer's
gift. Dangerous.

"I'll walk home with you," said Peter. "I'm not hungry. Have you already paid?"

"Of course," said Sister Carlotta. "This is my grandson, by the way. Delfino."

Peter turned to notice Bean for the first time—
though Bean was quite sure Peter had sized him up
thoroughly before he sat down. "Cute kid," he said.
"How old is he? Does he go to school yet?"

"I'm little," said Bean cheerfully, "but at least I'm
not a yelda."

"All those vids of Battle School life," said Peter.
"Even little kids are picking up that stupid polyglot
slang."

"Now, children, you must get along, I insist on it."
Sister Carlotta led the way to the door. "My grandson

is visiting this country for the first time, young man, so he doesn't understand American banter."

"Yes I do," said Bean, trying to sound like a petulant child and finding it quite easy, since he really was annoyed.

"He speaks English pretty well. But you better hold his hand crossing this street, the campus trams zoom through here like Daytona."

Bean rolled his eyes and submitted to having Carlotta hold his hand across the street. Peter was obviously trying to provoke him, but why? Surely he wasn't so shallow as to think humiliating Bean would give him some advantage. Maybe he took pleasure in making other people feel small.

Finally, though, they were away from campus and had taken enough twists and turns to make sure they weren't being followed.

"So you're the great Julian Delphiki," said Peter.

"And you're Locke. They're touting you for Hegemon when Sakata's term is over. Too bad you're only virtual."

"I'm thinking of going public soon," said Peter.

"Ah, that's why you got the plastic surgery to make you so pretty," said Bean.

"This old face?" said Peter. "I only wear it when I don't care how I look."

"Boys," said Sister Carlotta. "*Must* you display like baby chimps?"

Peter laughed easily. "Come on, Mom, we was just playin'. Can't we still go to the movies?"

"Off to bed without supper, the lot of you," said Sister Carlotta.

Bean had had enough of this. "Where's Petra?" he demanded.

Peter looked at him as if he were insane. "*I* don't have her."

"You have sources," said Bean. "You know more than you're telling me."

"You know more than you're telling me, too," said Peter. "I thought we were working on trusting each other, and *then* we open the floodgates of wisdom."

"Is she dead?" said Bean, not willing to be deflected.

Peter looked at his watch. "At this moment. I don't know."

Bean stopped walking. Disgusted, he turned to Sister Carlotta. "We wasted a trip," he said. "And risked our lives for nothing."

"Are you sure?" said Sister Carlotta.

Bean looked back at Peter, who seemed genuinely bemused. "He wants to be Hegemon," said Bean, "but he's nothing." Bean walked away. He had memorized the route, of course, and knew how to get to the bus station without Sister Carlotta's help. Figuring out the bus route would distract him from the bitter disappointment of finding out that Peter was a game-playing fool.

No one called after him, and he did not look back.

———

Bean took, not the bus to the hotel, but the one that passed nearest the neighborhood school that Peter and Valentine probably attended. What if Ender had actually grown up here, had attended schools in this town instead of the city? His whole life might have been shaped differently. Maybe Ender's first killing would never have happened—maybe there would have been no bully like the boy Stilson, who ambushed Ender with his gang and paid for it with his life. And if Ender had not proved his brutal efficiency in combat, his determination to win without scruple or hesitation, would he have been taken into the Battle School program?

Bean had been there for Ender's second killing, which was pretty much the same situation as the first. Ender—alone, outnumbered, surrounded—talking his way into single combat and then destroying his enemy so no will to fight would remain. There were military strategists who taught that principle of warfare. But Ender had known it instinctively, at the age of five.

I knew things at that age, thought Bean. And younger, too. Not how to kill—that was beyond me, I was too small. But how to live. That was hard.

For me it was hard, but not for Ender. Bean walked through the neighborhoods of modest old houses and even more modest new ones—but to him they were all miracles. Not that he hadn't had plenty of chances, living with his family in Greece after the war, to see how most children grew up. How much of a child's character came from the place he grew up, the people, the family, the friends? How much was born in him? Could a harsh place like Rotterdam make a military genius out of a child? Could a gentler place like Greensboro keep a child's genius from surfacing?

I had more native talent for war than Ender had. But he was still the better commander. Was it because Ender grew up where he never worried about finding another meal, where people praised him and protected him? I grew up where if I found a scrap of food I had to worry that another street kid might kill me for it. Shouldn't that have made me the one who fought most desperately, and Ender the one who held back?

It wasn't the place. Two people in identical situations would never make exactly the same choices. Ender is who he is, and I am who I am. It was in him to destroy the Formics. It was in me to stay alive.

So what's in me now? I'm a commander without an army. I have a mission to perform, but no knowledge of how to perform it. Petra, if she's still alive, is in desperate peril, and she counts on me to free her. The others are all free. She alone remains hidden. What has Achilles done to her? I will not have Petra end like Poke.

There it was. The difference between Ender and Bean. Ender came out of his bitterest battle of childhood undefeated. He had done what was required. But Bean had not even realized the danger his friend Poke was in until too late. If he had seen in time how immediate her peril was, he could have warned her, helped her. Saved her. Instead, her body was tossed into the Rhine, to be found bobbing like so much garbage among the wharves.

And it was happening again.

Bean stood in front of the Wiggin house. Ender had never seen it, and no pictures of it had been shown at the court of inquiry. But it was exactly what Bean had expected. A tree in the front yard, with wooden slats nailed into the trunk to form a ladder to the platform in a high crotch of the tree. A tidy, well-tended garden. A place of peace and refuge. Something Ender never had. Peter and Valentine lived here, though.

Where is Petra's garden? For that matter, where is mine?

Bean knew he was being unreasonable. If Ender had come back to Earth, he too would no doubt be in hiding—if Achilles or someone else hadn't simply killed him straight off. And even as things stood, he couldn't help but wonder if Ender might not prefer to be living as Bean was, on Earth, in hiding, than where he was now, in space, bound for another world and a life of permanent exile from the world of his birth.

A woman came out of the front door of the house. Mrs. Wiggin?

"Are you lost?" she asked.

Bean realized that in his disappointment—no, call it despair—he had forgotten his vigilance. This house might be watched. Even if it was not, Mrs. Wiggin herself might remember him, this young boy who appeared in front of her house during school hours.

"Is this where Ender Wiggin's family lives?"

A cloud passed across her face, just momentarily, but Bean saw how her expression saddened before her smile could be put back. "Yes, it is," she said. "But he didn't grow up here and we don't give tours."

For reasons Bean could not understand, on impulse he said, "I was with him. In the last battle. I fought under him."

Her smile changed again, away from mere courtesy and kindness, toward something like warmth and pain. "Ah," she said. "A veteran." And then the warmth faded and was replaced by worry. "I know all the faces of Ender's companions in that last battle. You're the one who's dead. Julian Delphiki."

Just like that, his cover was blown—and he had done it to himself, by telling her that he was in Ender's jeesh. What was he thinking? There were only eleven of them. "Obviously, there's someone who wants to kill me," he said. "If you tell anyone I came here, it will help him do it."

"I won't tell. But it was careless of you to come here."

"I had to see," said Bean, wondering if that was anything like a true explanation.

She didn't wonder. "That's absurd," she said. "You wouldn't risk your life to come here without a reason." And then it came together in her mind. "Peter's not home right now."

"I know," Bean said. "I was just with him at the university." And then he realized—there was no reason for her to think he was coming to see Peter, unless she had some idea of what Peter was doing. "You know," he said.

She closed her eyes, realizing now what she had confessed. "Either we are both very great fools," she said, "or we must have trusted each other at once, to let our guard down so readily."

"We're only fools if the other can't be trusted," said Bean.

"We'll find out, won't we?" Then she smiled. "No use leaving you standing out here on the street, for people to wonder why a child your size is not in school."

He followed her up the walkway to the front door. Bean was walking up to a door that Ender must have longed to see. But he never came home. Like Bonzo, the other casualty of the war. Bonzo, killed; Ender, missing in action; and now Bean coming up the walk to Ender's home. Only this was no sentimental visit with a grieving family. It was a different war now, but war it was, and she had another son at risk these days.

She was not supposed to know what he was doing. Wasn't that the whole point of Peter's having to camouflage his activities by pretending to be a student?

She made him a sandwich without even asking, as if she simply assumed that a child would be hungry. It was, of all things, that plain American cliché, peanut butter on white bread. Had she made such sandwiches for Ender?

"I miss him," said Bean, because he knew that would make her like him.

"If he had been here," said Mrs. Wiggin, "he probably would have been killed. When I read what . . . *Locke* . . . wrote about that boy from Rotterdam, I couldn't imagine he would have let Ender live. You knew him, too, didn't you. What's his name?"

"Achilles," said Bean.

"You're in hiding," she said. "But you seem so young."

"I travel with a nun named Sister Carlotta," said Bean. "We claim we're grandmother and grandson."

"I'm glad you're not alone."

"Neither is Ender."

Tears came to her eyes. "I suppose he needed Valentine more than we did."

On impulse—again, an instinctive act instead of a calculated decision—Bean reached out and set his hand in hers. She smiled at him.

The moment passed. Bean realized again how dangerous it was to be here. What if this house was under surveillance? The I.F. knew about Peter—what if they were observing the house?

"I should go," said Bean.

"I'm glad you came by," she said. "I must have wanted very much to talk to someone who knew Ender without being envious of him."

"We were all envious," said Bean. "But we also knew he was the best of us."

"Why else would you envy him, if you didn't think he was better?"

Bean laughed. "Well, when you envy somebody, you tell yourself he isn't really better after all."

"So . . . did the other children envy his abilities?" asked Mrs. Wiggin. "Or only the recognition he received?"

Bean didn't like the question, but then remembered who it was that was asking. "I should turn that question back on you. Did Peter envy his abilities? Or only the recognition?"

She stood there, considering whether to answer or not. Bean knew that family loyalty worked against her saying anything. "I'm not just idly asking," Bean said. "I don't know how much you know about what Peter's doing . . ."

"We read everything he publishes," said Mrs. Wiggin. "And then we're very careful to act as if we hadn't a clue what's going on in the world."

"I'm trying to decide whether to throw in with Peter," said Bean. "And I have no way of knowing what to make of him. How much to trust him."

"I wish I could help you," said Mrs. Wiggin. "Peter marches to a different drummer. I've never really caught the rhythm."

"Don't you like him?" asked Bean, knowing he was too blunt, but knowing also that he wasn't going to get many chances like this, to talk to the mother of a potential ally—or rival.

"I love him," said Mrs. Wiggin. "He doesn't show us much of himself. But that's only fair—we never showed our children much of ourselves, either."

"Why not?" asked Bean. He was thinking of the openness of his mother and father, the way they knew Nikolai, and Nikolai knew them. It had left him almost gasping, the unguardedness of their conversations with each other. Clearly the Wiggin household did not have that custom.

"It's very complicated," said Mrs. Wiggin.

"Meaning that you think it's none of my business."

"On the contrary, I know it's very much your business." She sighed and sat back down. "Come on, let's not pretend this is only a doorstep conversation. You came here to find out about Peter. The easy answer is simply to tell you that we don't know a thing. He never tells anyone anything they want to know, unless it would be useful to him for them to know it."

"But the hard answer?"

"We've been hiding from our children, almost from the start," said Mrs. Wiggin. "We can hardly be surprised or resentful when they learned at a very early age to be secretive."

"What were you hiding?"

"We don't tell our children, and I should tell you?" But she answered her own question at once. "If Valentine and Ender were here, I think we *would* talk to them. I even tried to explain some of this to Valentine before she left to join Ender in . . . space. I did a very bad job, because I had never put it in words before. Let me just . . . let me start by saying . . . we were going to have a third child anyway, even if the I.F. hadn't asked us to."

Where Bean had grown up, the population laws hadn't meant much—the street children of Rotterdam were all extra people and knew perfectly well that by law not one of them should have been born, but when you're starving, it's hard to care much about whether you're going to get into the finest schools. Still, when the laws were repealed, he read about them and knew the significance of their decision to have a third child. "Why would you do that?" asked Bean. "It would hurt all your children. It would end your careers."

"We were very careful not to *have* careers," said Mrs. Wiggin. "Not careers that we'd hate to give up.

What we had was only jobs. You see, we're religious people."

"There are lots of religious people in the world."

"But not in America," said Mrs. Wiggin. "Not the kind of fanatic that does something so selfish and anti-social as to have more than two children, just because of some misguided religious ideas. And when Peter tested so high as a toddler, and they started monitoring him—well, that was a disaster for us. We had hoped to be . . . unobtrusive. To disappear. We're very bright people, you know."

"I wondered why the parents of such geniuses didn't have noted careers of their own," said Bean. "Or at least some kind of standing in the intellectual community."

"Intellectual community," said Mrs. Wiggin scornfully. "America's intellectual community has never been very bright. Or honest. They're all sheep, following whatever the intellectual fashion of the decade happens to be. Demanding that everyone follow their dicta in lockstep. Everyone has to be open-minded and tolerant of the things they believe, but God forbid they should ever concede, even for a moment, that someone who disagrees with them might have some fingerhold on truth."

She sounded bitter.

"I sound bitter," she said.

"You've lived your life," said Bean. "So you think you're smarter than the smart people."

She recoiled a bit. "Well, that's the kind of comment that explains why we never discuss our faith with anyone."

"I didn't mean it as an attack," said Bean. "I think I'm smarter than anybody I've ever met, because I am.

I'd have to be dumber than I am not to know it. You really believe in your religion, and you resent the fact that you had to hide it from others. That's all I was saying."

"Not religion, reli*gions,*" she said. "My husband and I don't even share the same doctrine. Having a large family in obedience to God, that was about the only thing we agreed on. And even at that, we both had elaborate intellectual justifications for our decision to defy the law. For one thing, we didn't think it would hurt our children at all. We meant to raise them in faith, as believers."

"So why didn't you?"

"Because we're cowards after all," said Mrs. Wiggin. "With the I.F. watching, we would have had constant interference. They would have intervened to make sure we didn't teach our children anything that would prevent them from fulfilling the role that Ender and you ended up fulfilling. That's when we started hiding our faith. Not really from our children, just from the Battle School people. We were so relieved when Peter's monitor was taken away. And then Valentine's. We thought we were done. We were going to move to a place where we wouldn't be so badly treated, and have a third child, and a fourth, as many as we could have before they arrested us. But then they came to us and requisitioned a third child. So we didn't have to move. You see? We were lazy and frightened. If the Battle School was going to give us a cover to allow us to have one more child, then why not?"

"But then they took Ender."

"And by the time they took him, it was too late. To raise Peter and Valentine in our faith. If you don't teach children when they're little, it's never really inside them. You have to hope they'll come to it later, on their own. It can't come from the parents, if you don't begin when they're little."

"Indoctrinating them."

"That's what parenting is," said Mrs. Wiggin. "Indoctrinating your children in the social patterns that you want them to live by. The intellectuals have no qualms about using the schools to indoctrinate our children in *their* foolishness."

"I wasn't trying to provoke you," said Bean.

"And yet you use words that imply criticism."

"Sorry," said Bean.

"You're still a child," said Mrs. Wiggin. "No matter how bright you are, you still absorb a lot of the attitudes of the ruling class. I don't like it, but there you are. When they took Ender away, and we finally could live without constant scrutiny of every word that we said to our children, we realized that Peter was already completely indoctrinated in the foolishness of the schools. He would never have gone along with our earlier plan. He would have denounced us. We would have lost him. So do you cast off your firstborn child in order to give birth to a fourth or fifth or sixth? Peter seemed sometimes not to have any conscience at all. If ever anyone needed to believe in God, it was Peter, and he didn't."

"He probably wouldn't have anyway," said Bean.

"You don't know him," said Mrs. Wiggin. "He lives by pride. If we had made him proud of being a secret believer, he would have been valiant in that struggle. Instead he's . . . not."

"So you never even tried to convert him to your beliefs?" asked Bean.

"Which ones?" asked Mrs. Wiggin. "*We* had always thought that the big struggle in our family would be over which religion to teach them, his or mine. Instead we had to watch over Peter and find ways to help him find . . . decency. No, something much more important than that. Integrity. Honor. We monitored him the way that the Battle School had monitored all three of them. It took all our patience to keep our hands off when he forced Valentine to become Demosthenes. It was so contrary to her spirit. But we soon saw that it was not changing her—that her nobility of heart was, if anything, stronger through resistance to Peter's control."

"You didn't try to simply block him from what he was doing?"

She laughed harshly. "Oh, now, you're supposed to be the smart one. Could someone have blocked *you*? And Peter failed to get into Battle School because he was *too* ambitious, too rebellious, too unlikely to fulfill assignments and follow orders. *We* were supposed to influence him by forbidding him or blocking him?"

"No, I can see you couldn't," said Bean. "But you did nothing at all?"

"We taught him as best we could," said Mrs. Wiggin. "Comments at meals. We could see how he tuned us out, how he despised our opinions. It didn't help that we were trying so hard to conceal that we knew everything he'd written as Locke; our conversations really were . . . abstract. Boring, I suppose. And we didn't have those intellectual credentials. Why should he respect us? But he *heard* our ideas. Of what nobility is. Goodness and honor. And whether he believed us at some level or simply found such things within himself, we've seen him grow. So . . . you ask me if you can trust him, and I can't answer, because . . . trust him to do what? To act as you want him to? Never. To act according to some predictable pattern? I should laugh. But we've seen signs of honor. We've seen him do things that were very hard, but that seemed to be not just for show, but because he really believed in what he was doing. Of course, he might have simply been doing things that would make Locke seem virtuous and admirable. How can we know, when we can't ask him?"

"So you can't talk to him about what matters to you, because you know he'll despise you, and he can't talk to you about what matters to him, because you've never shown him that you actually have the understanding to grasp what he's thinking."

Tears sprang to her eyes and glistened there. "Sometimes I miss Valentine so much. She was so breathtakingly honest and good."

"So she told you she was Demosthenes?"

"No," said Mrs. Wiggin. "She was wise enough to know that if she didn't keep Peter's secret, it would split the family apart forever. No, she kept that hidden from us. But she made sure we knew just what kind of person Peter was. And about everything else in her life, everything Peter left for her to decide for herself, she told us that, and she listened to us, too, she cared what we thought."

"So you told her what you believe?"

"We didn't tell her about our faith," said Mrs. Wiggin. "But we taught her the results of that faith. We did the best we could."

"I'm sure you did," said Bean.

"I'm not stupid," said Mrs. Wiggin. "I know you despise us, just as we know Peter despises us."

"I don't," said Bean.

"I've been lied to enough to recognize it when you do it."

"I don't despise you for . . . I don't despise you at all," said Bean. "But you have to see that the way you all hide from each other, Peter growing up in a family where nobody tells anybody anything that matters— that doesn't make me really optimistic about ever being able to trust him. I'm about to put my life in his hands. And now I find out that in his whole life, he's never had an honest relationship with anybody."

Her eyes grew cold and distant then. "I see that I've provided you with useful information. Perhaps you should go now."

"I'm not judging you," said Bean.

"Don't be absurd, of course you are," said Mrs. Wiggin.

"I'm not condemning you, then."

"Don't make me laugh. You condemn us, and you know what? I agree with you. I condemn us too. We set out to do God's will, and we've ended up damaging the one child we have left to us. He's grimly determined to make his mark in the world. But what sort of mark will it be?"

"An indelible one," said Bean. "If Achilles doesn't destroy him first."

"We did some things right," said Mrs. Wiggin. "We gave him the freedom to test his own abilities. We could have stopped him from publishing, you know. He thinks he outsmarted us, but only because we played incredibly dumb. How many parents would have let their teenage son meddle in world affairs? When he wrote against . . . against letting Ender come home—you don't know how hard it was for me not to claw his arrogant little eyes out. . . ."

For the first time, he saw something of the rage and frustration she must have been going through. He thought: This is how Peter's mother feels about him. Maybe orphanhood wasn't such a drawback.

"But I didn't, did I?" said Mrs. Wiggin.

"Didn't what?"

"Didn't stop him. And he turned out to be right. Because if Ender were here on Earth, he'd either be dead, or he would have been one of the kidnapped children, or he'd be in hiding like you. But I still . . . Ender is his brother, and he exiled him from Earth forever. And I couldn't help but remember the terrible threats he made when Ender was still little, and lived with us. He told Ender and Valentine then that someday he would kill Ender, and pretend that it was an accident."

"Ender's not dead."

"My husband and I have wondered, in the dark nights when we try to make sense of what has happened to our family, to all our dreams, we've wondered if Peter got Ender exiled because he loved him and knew the dangers he'd face if he returned to Earth. Or if he exiled him because he feared that if Ender came home Peter would kill him, just as he threatened to—so then, exiling Ender could be viewed as a sort of, I don't know, an elementary kind of self-control. Still, a very selfish thing, but still showing a sort of vague respect for decency. That would be progress."

"Or maybe none of the above."

"Or maybe we're all guided by God in this, and God has brought you here."

"So Sister Carlotta says."

"She might be right."

"I don't much care either way," said Bean. "If there is a God, I think he's pretty lousy at his job."

"Or you don't understand what his job is."

"Believe me, Sister Carlotta is the nunnish equivalent of a Jesuit. Let's not even get into trading sophistries, I've been trained by an expert and, as you say, you're not in practice."

"Julian Delphiki," said Mrs. Wiggin, "I knew when I saw you out on the front sidewalk that I not only could, I *must* tell you things that I have spoken of to no one but my husband, and I've even said things that I've never said to him. I've told you things that Peter never imagined that I knew or thought or saw or felt. If you have a low opinion of my mothering, please keep in mind that whatever you know, you know because I told you, and I told you because I think that someday Peter's future may depend on your knowing what he's going to do, or how to help him. Or—Peter's future as a decent human being might depend on his helping *you.* So I bared my heart to you. For Peter's sake. And I face your scorn, Julian Delphiki, for Peter's sake as well. So don't fault my love for my son. Whether he thinks he cares or not, he grew up with parents who love him and have done everything we could for him. Including lie to him about what we believe, what we know, so that he can move through his world like Alexander, boldly reaching for the ends of the earth, with the complete freedom that comes from having parents who are too stupid to stop you. Until you've had a child of your own and sacrificed for that child and twisted your life into a pretzel, into a knot for him, don't you dare to judge me and what I've done."

"I'm not judging you," said Bean. "Truly I'm not. As you said, I'm just trying to understand Peter."

"Well, do you know what I think?" said Mrs. Wiggin. "I think you've been asking all the wrong questions. 'Can I trust him?'" She mimicked him scornfully. "Whether you trust somebody or distrust him has a lot more to do with the kind of person *you* are than the kind of person he is. The real question you ought to be asking is, Do you really want Peter Wiggin to rule the world? Because if you help him, and he somehow lives through all this, that's where it will lead. He won't stop until he achieves that. And he'll burn up your future along with anybody else's, if it will help him reach that goal. So ask yourself, will the world be a better place with Peter Wiggin as Hegemon? And not some benign ceremonial figurehead like the ineffectual toad who holds that office now. I mean Peter Wiggin as the Hegemon who reshapes this world into whatever form he wants it to have."

"But you're assuming that I care whether the world is a better place," said Bean. "What if all I care about is my own survival or advancement? Then the only question that would matter is, Can I use Peter to advance my own plans?"

She laughed and shook her head. "Do *you* believe that about yourself? Well, you *are* a child."

"Pardon me, but did I ever pretend to be anything else?"

"You pretend," said Mrs. Wiggin, "to be a person of such enormous value that you can speak of 'allying' with Peter Wiggin as if you brought armies with you."

"I don't bring armies," said Bean, "but I bring victory for whatever army he gives me."

"Would Ender have been like you, if he had come home? Arrogant? Aloof?"

"Not at all," said Bean. "But I never killed anybody."

"Except Buggers," said Mrs. Wiggin.

"Why are we at war with each other?" said Bean.

"I've told you everything about my son, about my family, and you've given me nothing back. Except your . . . sneer."

"I'm not sneering," said Bean. "I like you."

"Oh, thank you very much."

"I can see in you the mother of Ender Wiggin," said Bean. "You understand Peter the way Ender under-

stood his soldiers. The way Ender understood his enemies. And you're bold enough to act instantly when
the opportunity presents itself. I show up on your
doorstep, and you give me all this. No, ma'am, I don't
despise you at all. And you know what I think? I think
that, perhaps without even realizing it yourself, you
believe in Peter completely. You want him to succeed.
You think he should rule the world. And you've told
me all this, not because I'm such a nice little boy, but
because you think that by telling me, you'll help Peter
move that much closer toward ultimate victory."

She shook her head. "Not everybody thinks like a
soldier."

"Hardly anyone does," said Bean. "Precious few
soldiers, for that matter."

"Let me tell you something, Julian Delphiki. You
didn't have a mother and father, so you need to be told.
You know what I dread most? That Peter will pursue
these ambitions of his so relentlessly that he'll never
have a life."

"Conquering the world isn't a life?" asked Bean.

"Alexander the Great," said Mrs. Wiggin. "He
haunts my nightmares for Peter. All his conquests, his
victories, his grand achievements—they were the acts
of an adolescent boy. By the time he got around to
marrying, to having a child, it was too late. He died in
the midst of it. And he probably wouldn't have done a
very good job of it either. He was already too powerful
before he even tried to find love. That's what I fear for
Peter."

"Love? That's what this all comes down to?"

"No, not just love. I'm talking about the cycle of
life. I'm talking about finding some alien creature and
deciding to marry her and stay with her forever, no
matter whether you even like each other or not a few

years down the road. And why will you do this? So you can make babies together, and try to keep them alive and teach them what they need to know so that someday *they'll* have babies, and keep the whole thing going. And you'll never draw a secure breath until you have grandchildren, a double handful of them, because then you know that your line won't die out, your influence will continue. Selfish, isn't it? Only it's not selfish, it's what life is for. It's the only thing that brings happiness, ever, to anyone. All the other things—victories, achievements, honors, causes—they bring only momentary flashes of pleasure. But binding yourself to another person and to the children you make together, that's life. And you can't do it if your life is centered on your ambitions. You'll never be happy. It will never be enough, even if you rule the world."

"Are you telling me? Or telling Peter?" asked Bean.

"I'm telling you what I truly want for Peter," said Mrs. Wiggin. "But if you're a tenth as smart as you think you are, you'll get that for yourself. Or you'll never have real joy in this life."

"Excuse me if I'm missing something here," said Bean, "but as far as I can tell, marrying and having children has brought you nothing but grief. You've lost Ender, you've lost Valentine, and you spent your life pissed off at Peter or fretting about him."

"Yes," she said. "Now you're getting it."

"Where's the joy? That's what I'm not getting."

"The grief *is* the joy," said Mrs. Wiggin. "I have someone to grieve for. Whom do you have?"

Such was the intensity of their conversation that Bean had no barrier in place to block what she said. It stirred something inside him. All the memories of people that he'd loved—despite the fact that he refused to love anyone. Poke. Nikolai. Sister Carlotta. Ender. His parents, when he finally met them. "I have someone to grieve for," said Bean.

"You think you do," said Mrs. Wiggin. "Everyone thinks they do, until they take a child into their heart. Only then do you know what it is to be a hostage to love. To have someone else's life matter more than your own."

"Maybe I know more than you think," said Bean.

"Maybe you know nothing at all," said Mrs. Wiggin.

They faced each other across the table, a loud silence between them. Bean wasn't even sure they'd been quarreling. Despite the heat of their exchange, he couldn't help but feel that he'd just been given a strong dose of the faith that she and her husband shared with each other.

Or maybe it really was objective truth, and he simply couldn't grasp it because he wasn't married.

And never would be. If there was ever anyone whose life virtually guaranteed that he'd be a terrible father, it was Bean. Without ever exactly saying it aloud, he'd always known that he would never marry, never have children.

But her words had this much effect: For the first time in his life, he found himself almost wishing that it were not so.

In that silence, Bean heard the front door open, and Peter's and Sister Carlotta's voices. At once Bean and Mrs. Wiggin rose to their feet, feeling and looking guilty, as if they had been caught in some kind of clandestine rendezvous. Which, in a way, they had.

"Mother, I've met a traveler," said Peter when he came into the room.

Bean heard the beginning of Peter's lie like a blow

to the face—for Bean knew that the person Peter was lying to knew his story was false, and yet would lie in return by pretending to believe.

This time, though, the lie could be nipped in the bud.

"Sister Carlotta," said Mrs. Wiggin. "I've heard so much about you from young Julian here. He says you are the world's only Jesuit nun."

Peter and Sister Carlotta looked at Bean in bafflement. What was he doing there? He almost laughed at their consternation, in part because he couldn't have answered that question himself.

"He came here like a pilgrim to a shrine," said Mrs. Wiggin. "And he very bravely told me who he really is. Peter, you must be very careful not to tell anyone that this is one of Ender's companions. Julian Delphiki. He wasn't killed in that explosion, after all. Isn't that wonderful? We must make him welcome here, for Ender's sake, but he's still in danger, so it has to be our secret who he is."

"Of course, Mother," said Peter. He looked at Bean, but his eyes betrayed nothing of what he was feeling. Like the cold eyes of a rhinoceros, unreadable, yet with enormous danger behind them all the same.

Sister Carlotta, though, was obviously appalled. "After all our security precautions," she said, "and you just blurt it out? And this house is bound to be watched."

"We had a good conversation," said Bean. "That's not possible in the midst of lies."

"It's my life you were risking here, too, you know," said Carlotta.

Mrs. Wiggin touched her arm. "Do stay here with us, won't you? We have room in our house for visitors."

"We can't," said Bean. "She's right. Coming here at

all has compromised us both. We'll probably want to fly out of Greensboro first thing in the morning."

He glanced at Sister Carlotta, knowing that she would understand that he was really saying they should leave by train that night. Or by bus the day after tomorrow. Or rent an apartment under assumed names and stay here for a week. The lying had begun again, for safety's sake.

"At least stay for dinner?" asked Mrs. Wiggin. "And meet my husband? I think he'll be just as intrigued as I was to meet a boy who is so famously dead."

Bean saw Peter's eyes glaze over. He understood why—to Peter, a dinner with his parents would be an excruciating social exercise during which nothing important could be said. Wouldn't all your lives be simpler if you could just tell each other the truth? But Mrs. Wiggin had said that Peter needed to feel that he was on his own. If he knew that his parents knew of his secret activities, that would infantilize him, apparently. Though if he were really the sort of man that could rule the world, surely he could deal with knowing that his parents were in on his secrets.

Not my decision. I gave my word.

"We'd be glad to," said Bean. "Though there's a danger of having your house blown up because we're in it."

"Then we'll eat out," said Mrs. Wiggin. "See how simple things can be? If something's going to be blown up, let it be a restaurant. They carry insurance for that sort of thing."

Bean laughed. But Peter didn't. Because, Bean realized, Peter doesn't know how much she knows, and therefore he thinks her comment was idiocy instead of irony.

"Not Italian food," said Sister Carlotta.

"Oh, of course not," said Mrs. Wiggin. "I don't know of a decent Italian restaurant in Greensboro."

With that, the conversation turned to safe and meaningless topics. Bean took a certain relish in watching how Peter squirmed at the utter waste of time that such chitchat represented. I know more about your mother than you do, thought Bean. I have more respect for her.

But you're the one she loves.

Bean was annoyed to notice the envy in his own heart. Nobody's immune from those petty human emotions, he knew that. But somehow he had to learn how to distinguish between true observations and what his envy told him. Peter had to learn the same. The trust that Bean had given so easily to Mrs. Wiggin would have to be earned step by step between him and Peter. Why?

Because he and Peter were so alike. Because he and Peter were natural rivals. Because he and Peter could so easily be deadly enemies.

As I am a second Ender in his eyes, is he a second Achilles in mine? If there were no Achilles in the world, would I think of Peter as the evil I must destroy?

And if we do defeat Achilles together, will we then have to turn and fight each other, undoing all our triumphs, destroying everything we've built?

10

Brothers in Arms

```
To: RusFriend%BabaYaga@MosPub.net
From: VladDragon%slavnet.com
Re: allegiance
```

Let's make one thing clear. I never
"joined" with Achilles. From all I
could see, Achilles was speaking for
Mother Russia. It was Mother Russia
that I agreed to serve, and that is a
decision I did not and do not regret. I
believe the artificial divisions among
the peoples of Greater Slavia serve
only to keep any of us from achieving
our potential in the world. In the
chaos that has resulted from the exposure of Achilles' true nature, I would
be glad of any opportunity to serve.

> The things I learned in Battle School
> could well make a difference to the fu-
> ture of our people. If my link with
> Achilles makes it impossible for me to
> be of service, so be it. But it would
> be a shame if we all suffered from that
> last act of sabotage by a psychopath.
> It is precisely now that I am most
> needed. Mother Russia will find no more
> loyal son than this one.

For Peter, the dinner at Leblon with his parents and Bean and Carlotta consisted of long periods of excruciating boredom interrupted by short passages of sheer panic. Nothing that anyone was saying mattered in the slightest. Because Bean was passing himself off as little more than a tourist visiting Ender's shrine, all anyone could talk about was Ender Ender Ender. But inevitably the conversation would skirt topics that were highly sensitive, things that might give away what Peter was really doing and the role that Bean might end up playing.

The worst was when Sister Carlotta—who, nun or not, clearly knew how to be a malicious bitch when she wanted to—began probing Peter about his studies at UNCG, even though she knew perfectly well that his schoolwork there was merely a cover for far more important matters. "I'm just surprised, I suppose, that you spend your time on a regular course of study when clearly you have abilities that should be used on a broader stage," she said.

"I need the degree, just like anyone else," said Peter, writhing inside.

"But why not study things that will prepare you to play a role on the great stage of world affairs?"

Ironically, it was Bean who rescued him. "Come now, Grandmother," he said. "A man of Peter Wiggin's ability is ready to do anything he wants, whenever he wants. Formal study is just busywork to him anyway. He's only doing it to prove to other people that he's able to live by the rules when he needs to. Right, Peter?"

"Close enough," Peter said. "I'm even less interested in my studies than you all are, and you shouldn't be interested in them at all."

"Well, if you hate it so much, why are we paying for tuition?" asked Father.

"We're not," Mother reminded him. "Peter has such a nice scholarship that they're paying *him* to attend there."

"Not getting their money's worth, though, are they?" said Father.

"They're getting what they want," said Bean. "For the rest of his life, whatever Peter here accomplishes, it will be mentioned that he studied at UNCG. He'll be a walking advertisement for them. I'd call that a pretty good return on investment, wouldn't you?"

The kid had mastered the kind of language Father understood—Peter had to credit Bean with knowing his audience when he spoke. Still, it annoyed Peter that Bean had so easily sussed what kind of idiots his parents were, and how easily they could be pandered to. It was as if, by pulling Peter's conversational irons out of the fire, Bean was rubbing it in about Peter's still being a child living at home, while Bean was out dealing with life more directly. It made Peter chafe all the more.

Only at the end of the dinner, as they left the Brazilian restaurant and headed for the Market/Holden station, did Bean drop his bombshell. "You know that since we've compromised ourselves here, we have to go back into hiding at once." Peter's parents made little noises of sympathy, and then Bean said, "What I was wondering was, why doesn't Peter go with us? Get out of Greensboro for a while? Would you like to, Peter? Do you have a passport?"

"No, he doesn't," said Mother, at exactly the same moment that Peter said, "Of course I do."

"You do?" asked Mother.

"Just in case," said Peter. He didn't add: I have six passports from four countries, as a matter of fact, and ten different bank identities with funds from my writing gigs socked away.

"But you're in the middle of a semester," said Father.

"I can take a leave whenever I want," said Peter. "It sounds interesting. Where are you going?"

"We don't know," said Bean. "We don't decide until the last minute. But we can email you and tell you where we are."

"Campus email addresses aren't secure," said Father helpfully.

"No email is really secure, is it?" asked Mother.

"It will be a coded message," said Bean. "Of course."

"It doesn't sound very sensible to me," said Father. "Peter may think his studies are just busywork, but in fact you have to have that degree just to get started in life. You need to stick to something long term and finish it, Peter. If your transcript shows that you did your education in fits and starts, that won't look good to the best companies."

"What career do you think I'm going to pursue?" Peter asked, annoyed. "Some kind of corporate dull bob?"

"I really hate it when you use that ersatz Battle School slang," said Father. "You didn't go there, and it makes you sound like some kind of teenage wannabe."

"I don't know about that," said Bean, before Peter could blow up. "I *was* there, and I think that stuff is just part of the language. I mean, the word 'wannabe' was once slang, wasn't it? It can grow into the language just by people using it."

"It makes him sound like a kid," said Father, but it was just a parting shot, Father's pathetic need to have the last word.

Peter said nothing. But he wasn't grateful to Bean for taking his side. On the contrary, the kid really pissed him off. It's like Bean thought he could come into Peter's life and intervene between him and his parents like some kind of savior. It diminished Peter in his own eyes. None of the people who wrote to him or read his work as Locke or Demosthenes ever condescended to him, because they didn't know he was a kid. But the way Bean was acting was a warning of things to come. If Peter did come out under his real name, he would immediately have to start dealing with condescension. People who had once trembled at the idea of coming under Demosthenes' scrutiny, people who had once eagerly sought Locke's imprimatur, would now poo-poo anything Peter wrote, saying, Of course a child would think that way, or, more kindly but no less devastatingly, When he has more experience, he'll come to see that. . . . Adults were always saying things like that. As if experience actually had some correlation with increased wisdom; as if most of the stupidity in the world were not propounded by adults.

Besides, Peter couldn't help but feel that Bean was

enjoying it, that he loved having Peter at such a disadvantage. Why *had* the little weasel gone to his house? To come home and find Bean sitting there talking to his mother, that was like catching a burglar in the act. He hadn't liked Bean from the beginning—especially not after the petulant way he walked off just because Peter didn't immediately answer the question he was asking. Admittedly, Peter *had* been teasing him a little, and there was an element of condescension about it— toying with the little kid before telling him what he wanted to know. But Bean's retaliation had gone way overboard. Especially this miserable dinner.

And yet . . .

Bean was the real thing. The best that Battle School had produced. Peter could use him. Peter might actually even need him, precisely because he could not yet afford to come out publicly as himself. Bean had the credibility despite his size and age, because he'd fought the fight. He could actually do things instead of having to pull strings in the background or try to manipulate government decisions by influencing public opinion. If Peter could secure some kind of working alliance with him, it might go a long way toward compensating for his impotence. If only Bean weren't so insufferably smug.

Can't let my personal feelings interfere with the work at hand.

"Tell you what," Peter said. "Mom and Dad, you've got stuff to do tomorrow, but my first class isn't till noon. Why don't I go with these two wherever they're spending the night and talk through the possibility of maybe taking a field trip with them."

"I don't want you just taking off and leaving your mother to worry about what's happening to you," said Father. "I think it's very clear to all of us that young

Mr. Delphiki here is a trouble magnet, and I think your mother has lost enough children without having to worry about something even worse happening to you."

It made Peter cringe the way Father always talked as if it were only Mother who would be worried, only Mother who cared what happened to him. And if it was true—who could tell, with Father?—that was even worse. Either Father didn't care what happened to Peter, or he did care but was such a git that he couldn't admit it.

"I won't leave town without checking in with Mommy," said Peter.

"You don't need to be sarcastic," said Father.

"Dear," said Mother, "Peter isn't five, to be rebuked in front of company." Which, of course, made him seem to be maybe six years old. Thanks so much for helping, Mom.

"Aren't families complicated?" said Sister Carlotta.

Oh, thanks, thou holy bitch, said Peter silently. You and Bean are the ones who complicated the situation, and now you make smug little comments about how much better it is for unconnected people like you. Well, these parents are my *cover*. I didn't pick them, but I have to use them. And for you to mock my situation only shows your ignorance. And, probably, your envy, seeing how you are never going to have children or even get laid in your whole life, Mrs. Jesus.

"Poor Peter has the worst of both worlds," said Mother. "He's the oldest, so he was always held to a higher standard, and yet he's the last of our children left at home, which means he also gets babied more than he can bear. It's so awful, the fact that parents are mere human beings and constantly make mistakes. I think sometimes Peter wishes he had been raised by robots."

Which made Peter want to slide right down into the

sidewalk and spend the rest of his life as an invisible patch of concrete. I converse with spies and military officers, with political leaders and power brokers—and my mother still has the power to humiliate me at will!

"Do what you want," said Father. "It's not like you're a minor. We can't stop you."

"We could never stop him from doing what he wanted even when he *was* a minor," said Mother.

Damn right, thought Peter.

"The curse of having children who are smarter than you," said Father, "is that they think their superior rational process is enough to compensate for their lack of experience."

If I were a little brat like Bean, that comment would have been the last straw. I would have walked away and not come home for a week, if ever. But I'm not a child and I can control my personal resentments and do what's expedient. I'm not going to throw off my camouflage out of pique.

At the same time, I can't be faulted, can I, for wondering if there's any chance that my father might have a stroke and go permanently mute.

They were at the station. With a round of goodbyes, Father and Mother took the bus north toward home, and Peter got on an eastbound bus with Bean and Carlotta.

And, as Peter expected, they got off at the first stop and crossed over to catch the westbound bus. They really made a religion out of paranoia.

Even when they got back to the airport hotel, they did not enter the building. Instead they walked through the shopping mall that had once been a parking garage back when people drove cars to the airport. "Even if they bug the mall," said Bean, "I doubt they can afford the manpower to listen to everything people say."

"If they're bugging your room," said Peter, "that means they're already on to you."

"Hotels routinely bug their rooms," said Bean. "To catch vandals and criminals in the act. It's a computer scan, but nothing stops the employees from listening in."

"This is America," said Peter.

"You spend way too much time thinking about global affairs," said Bean. "If you ever do have to go underground, you won't have a clue how to survive."

"You're the one who invited me to join you in hiding," said Peter. "What was that nonsense about? I'm not going anywhere. I have too much work to do."

"Ah, yes," said Bean. "Pulling the world's strings from behind a curtain. The trouble is, the world is about to move from politics to war, and your strings are going to be snipped."

"It's still politics."

"But the decisions are made on the battlefield, not in the conference rooms."

"I know," said Peter. "That's why we should work together."

"I can't think why," said Bean. "The one thing I asked you for—information about where Petra is— you tried to sell me instead of just giving it to me. Doesn't sound like you want an ally. Sounds like you want a customer."

"Boys," said Sister Carlotta. "Bickering isn't how this is going to work."

"If it's going to work," said Peter, "it's going to work however Bean and I make it work. Between us."

Sister Carlotta stopped cold, grabbed Peter's shoulder, and drew him close. "Get this straight right now, you arrogant twit. You're not the only brilliant person in the world, and you're far from being the only one who thinks he pulls all the strings. Until you have the courage to come out from behind the veil of these ersatz personalities, you don't have much to offer those of us who are working in the real world."

"Don't ever touch me like that again," said Peter.

"Oh, the personage is sacred?" said Sister Carlotta. "You really do live on Planet Peter, don't you?"

Bean interrupted before Peter could answer the bitch. "Look, we gave you everything we had on Ender's jeesh, no strings attached."

"And I used it. I got most of them out, and pretty damn fast, too."

"But not the one who sent the message," said Bean. "I want Petra."

"And I want world peace," said Peter. "You think too small."

"I may think too small for you," said Bean, "but you think too small for me. Playing your little computer games, juggling stories back and forth—well, my friend trusted me and asked me for help. She was trapped with a psychopathic killer and she doesn't have anyone but me who cares a rat's ass what happens to her."

"She has her family," murmured Sister Carlotta. Peter was pleased to learn that she corrected Bean, too. An all-purpose bitch.

"You want to save the world, but you're going to have to do it one battle at a time, one country at a time. And you need people like me, who get our hands dirty," said Bean.

"Oh, spare me your delusions," said Peter. "You're a little boy in hiding."

"I'm a general who's between armies," said Bean. "If I weren't, you wouldn't be talking to me."

"And you want an army so you can go rescue Petra," said Peter.

"So she's alive?"

"How would I know?"

"I don't know how you'd know. But you know more than you're telling me, and if you don't give me what you have, right now, you arrogant oomay, I'm done with you, I'll leave you here playing your little net games, and go find somebody who's not afraid to come out of Mama's house and take some risks."

Peter was almost blind with rage.

For a moment.

And then he calmed himself, forced himself to stand outside the situation. What was Bean showing him? That he cared more for personal loyalty than for longterm strategy. That was dangerous, but not fatal. And it gave Peter leverage, knowing what Bean cared about more than personal advancement.

"What I know about Petra," said Peter, "is that when Achilles disappeared, so did she. My sources inside Russia tell me that the only liberation team that was interfered with was the one rescuing her. The driver, a bodyguard, and the team leader were shot dead. There was no evidence that Petra was injured, though they know she was present for one of the killings."

"How do they know?" asked Bean.

"The spatter pattern from a head shot had been blocked in a silhouette about her size on the inside wall of the van. She was covered with the man's blood. But there was no blood from her body."

"They know more than that."

"A small private jet, which once belonged to a crimelord but was confiscated and used by the intelligence service that sponsored Achilles, took off from a nearby airfield and flew, after a refueling stop, to India. One of the airport maintenance personnel said that it looked to him like a honeymoon trip. Just the pilot and the young couple. But no luggage."

"So he has her with him," said Bean.

"In India," said Sister Carlotta.

"And my sources in India have gone silent," said Peter.

"Dead?" asked Bean.

"No, just careful," said Peter. "The most populous country on Earth. Ancient enmities. A chip on the national shoulder from being treated like a second-class country by everyone."

"The Polemarch is an Indian," said Bean.

"And there's reason to believe he's been passing I.F. data to the Indian military," said Peter. "Nothing that can be proved, but Chamrajnagar is not as disinterested as he pretends to be."

"So you think Achilles may be just what India wants to help them launch a war."

"No," said Peter. "I think India may be just what Achilles wants to help him launch an empire. Petra is what *they* want to help them launch a war."

"So Petra is the passport Achilles used to get into a position of power in India."

"That would be my guess," said Peter. "That's all I know, and all I guess. But I can also tell you that your chance of getting in and rescuing her is nil."

"Pardon me," said Bean, "but you don't know what I'm capable of doing."

"When it comes to intelligence-gathering," said Peter, "the Indians aren't in the same league as the Russians. I don't think your paranoia is needed anymore.

Achilles isn't in a position to do anything to you right now."

"Just because Achilles is in India," said Bean, "doesn't mean that he's limited to knowing only what the Indian intelligence service can find out for him."

"The agency that's been helping him in Russia is being taken over and probably will be shut down," said Peter.

"I know Achilles," said Bean, "and I can promise you—if he really is in India, working for them, then it is absolutely certain that he has already betrayed them and has connections and fallback positions in at least three other places. And at least one of them will have an intelligence service with excellent world-wide reach. If you make the mistake of thinking Achilles is limited by borders and loyalties, he'll destroy you."

Peter looked down at Bean. He wanted to say, I already knew all that. But it would be a lie if he said that. He hadn't known that about Achilles, except in the abstract sense that he tried never to underestimate an opponent. Bean's knowledge of Achilles was better than his. "Thank you," said Peter. "I wasn't taking that into account."

"I know," said Bean ungraciously. "It's one of the reasons I think you're headed for failure. You think you know more than you actually know."

"But I listen," said Peter. "And I learn. Do you?"

Sister Carlotta laughed. "I do believe that the two most arrogant boys in the world have finally met, and they don't much like what they see."

Peter did not even glance at her, and neither did Bean. "Actually," said Peter, "I *do* like what I see."

"I wish I could say the same," said Bean.

"Let's keep walking," said Peter. "We've been standing in one place too long."

"At least he's picking up on our paranoia," said Sister Carlotta.

"Where will India make its move?" asked Peter. "The obvious thing would be war with Pakistan."

"Again?" said Bean. "Pakistan would be an indigestible lump. It would block India from further expansion, just trying to get the Muslims under control. A terrorist war that would make the old struggle with the Sikhs look like a child's birthday party."

"But they can't move anywhere else as long as they have Pakistan poised to plunge a dagger in their back," said Peter.

Bean grinned. "Burma? But is it worth taking?"

"It's on the way to more valuable prizes, if China doesn't object," said Peter. "But are you just ignoring the Pakistan problem?"

"Molotov and Ribbentrop," said Bean.

The men who negotiated the nonaggression pact between Russia and Germany in the 1930s that divided Poland between them and freed Germany to launch World War II. "I think it will have to be deeper than that," said Peter. "I think, at some level, an alliance."

"What if India offers Pakistan a free hand against Iran? It can go for the oil. India is free to move east. To scoop up the countries that have long been under her cultural influence. Burma. Thailand. Not Muslim countries, so Pakistan's conscience is clear."

"Is China going to sit and watch?" asked Peter.

"They might if India tosses them Vietnam," said Bean. "The world is ripe to be divided up among the great powers. India wants to be one. With Achilles directing their strategy, with Chamrajnagar feeding them information, with Petra to command their armies, they can play on the big stage. And then, when Pakistan has exhausted itself fighting Iran . . ."

The inevitable betrayal. If Pakistan didn't strike first. "That's too far down the line to predict now," said Peter.

"But it's the way Achilles thinks," said Bean. "Two betrayals ahead. He was using Russia, but maybe he already had this deal with India in place. Why not? In the long run, the whole world is the tail, and India is the dog."

More important than Bean's particular conclusions was the fact that Bean had a good eye. He lacked detailed intelligence, of course—how would he get that?—but he saw the big picture. He thought the way a global strategist had to think.

He was worth talking to.

"Well, Bean," said Peter, "here's my problem. I think I can get you in position to help block Achilles. But I can't trust you not to do something stupid."

"I won't mount a rescue operation for Petra until I know it will succeed."

"That's a foolish thing to say. You never *know* a military operation will succeed. And that's not what worries me. I'm sure if you mounted a rescue, it would be a well-planned and well-executed one."

"So what worries you about me?" asked Bean.

"That you're making the assumption that Petra wants to be rescued."

"She does," said Bean.

"Achilles seduces people," said Peter. "I've read his files, his history. This kid has a golden voice, apparently. He makes people trust him—even people who know he's a snake. They think, He won't betray *me*, because we have such a special closeness."

"And then he kills them. I know that," said Bean.

"But does Petra? *She* hasn't read his file. *She* didn't know him on the streets of Rotterdam. She didn't even know him in the brief time he was in Battle School."

"She knows him now," said Bean.

"You're sure of that?" asked Peter.

"But I'll promise you—I won't try to rescue her until I've been in communication with her."

Peter mulled this over for a moment. "She might betray you."

"No," said Bean.

"Trusting people will get you killed," said Peter. "I don't want you to bring me down with you."

"You have it backward," said Bean. "I don't trust anybody, except to do what they think is necessary. What they think they have to do. But I know Petra, and I know the kind of thing she'll think she has to do. It's *me* I'm trusting, not her."

"And he can't bring you down," said Sister Carlotta, "because you're not up."

Peter looked at her, making little effort to conceal his contempt. "I am where I am," he said. "And it's not down."

"Locke is where Locke is," said Carlotta. "And Demosthenes. But Peter Wiggin is nowhere. Peter Wiggin is nothing."

"What's your problem?" Peter demanded. "Is it bothering you that your little puppet here might actually be cutting a few of the strings you pull?"

"There are no strings," said Carlotta. "And you're too stupid, apparently, to realize that *I'm* the one who believes in what you're doing, not Bean. He couldn't care less who rules the world. But I do. Arrogant and condescending as you are, I've already made up my mind that if anybody's going to stop Achilles, it's you.

But you're fatally weakened by the fact that you are ripe to be blackmailed by the threat of exposure. Chamrajnagar knows who you are. He's feeding information to India. Do you really think for one moment that Achilles won't find out—and soon, if not already—exactly who is behind Locke? The one who got him booted out of Russia? Do you really think he isn't already working on plans to kill you?"

Peter blushed with shame. To have this nun tell him what he should have realized by himself was humiliating. But she was right—he wasn't used to thinking of physical danger.

"That's why we wanted you to come with us," said Bean.

"Your cover is already blown," said Sister Carlotta.

"The moment I go public as a kid," said Peter Wiggin, "most of my sources will dry up."

"No," said Sister Carlotta. "It all depends on *how* you come out."

"Do you think I haven't thought this through a thousand times?" said Peter. "Until I'm old enough . . ."

"No," said Sister Carlotta. "Think for a minute, Peter. National governments have just gone through a nasty little scuffle over ten *children* that they want to have command their armies. You're the older brother of the greatest of them all. Your youth is an asset. And if you control the way the information comes out, instead of having somebody else expose you . . ."

"It will be a momentary scandal," said Peter. "No matter how my identity comes out, there'll be a flurry of commentary on it, and then I'll be old news—only I'll have been fired from most of my writing gigs. People won't return my calls or answer my mail. I really *will* be a college student then."

"That sounds like something you decided years

ago," said Sister Carlotta, "and haven't looked at with fresh eyes since then."

"Since this seems to be tell-Peter-he's-stupid day, let's hear *your* plan."

Sister Carlotta grinned at Bean. "Well, I was wrong. He actually *can* listen to other people."

"I told you," said Bean.

Peter suspected that this little exchange was designed merely to make him think Bean was on his side. "Just tell me your plan and skip the sucking-up phase."

"The term of the current Hegemon will end in about eight months," said Sister Carlotta. "Let's get several influential people to start floating the name of Locke as the replacement."

"That's your plan? The office of Hegemon is worthless."

"Wrong," said Sister Carlotta, "and wrong. The office is not worthless—eventually you'll have to have it in order to make you the legitimate leader of the world against the threat posed by Achilles. But that's later. Right now, we float the name of Locke, not so you'll get the office, but so that you can have an excuse to publicly announce, as Locke, that you can't be considered for such an office because you are, after all, merely a teenager. *You* tell people that you're Ender Wiggin's older brother, that you and Valentine worked for years to try to hold the League together and to prepare for the League War so that your little brother's victory didn't lead to the self-destruction of humanity. But you are still too young to take an actual office of public trust. See how it works? Now your announcement won't be a confession or a scandal. It will be one more example of how nobly you place the interest of world peace and good order ahead of your own personal ambition."

"I'll still lose some of my contacts," said Peter.

"But not many. The news will be positive. It will have the right spin. All these years, Locke has been the brother of the genius Ender Wiggin. A prodigy."

"And there's no time to waste," said Bean. "You have to do it before Achilles can strike. Because you *will* be exposed within a few months."

"Weeks," said Sister Carlotta.

Peter was furious with himself. "Why didn't I see this? It's obvious."

"You've been doing this for years," said Bean. "You had a pattern that worked. But Achilles has changed everything. You've never had anybody gunning for you before. What matters to me is not that you failed to see it on your own. What matters is that when we pointed it out to you, you were willing to hear it."

"So I've passed your little test?" said Peter nastily.

"Just as I hope I'll pass yours," said Bean. "If we're going to work together, we have to be able to tell each other the truth. Now I know you'll listen to me. You just have to take my word for it that I'll listen to you. But I listen to *her,* don't I?"

Peter was churning with dread. They were right, the time had come, the old pattern was over. And it was frightening. Because now he had to put everything on the line, and he might fail.

But if he didn't act now, if he didn't risk everything, he would certainly fail. Achilles' presence in the equation made it inevitable.

"So how," said Peter, "will we get this groundswell started so I can decline the honor of being a candidate for the Hegemony?"

"Oh, that's easy," said Carlotta. "If you give the OK, then by tomorrow there can be news stories about how a highly placed source at the Vatican confirms that Locke's name is being floated as a possible successor when the current Hegemon's term expires."

"And then," said Bean, "a highly placed officer in the Hegemony—the Minister of Colonization, to be exact, though no one will say that—will be quoted as saying that Locke is not just a good candidate, he's the best candidate, and may be the only candidate, and with the support of the Vatican he thinks Locke is the frontrunner."

"You've planned this all out," said Peter.

"No," said Sister Carlotta. "It's just that the only two people we know are my highly placed friend in the Vatican and our good friend ex-Colonel Graff."

"We're committing all our assets," said Bean, "but they'll be enough. The moment those stories run—tomorrow—you be ready to reply for the next morning's nets. At the same time that everybody's giving their first reactions to your brand-new frontrunner status, the world will be reading your announcement that you refuse to be considered for such an office because your youth would make it too difficult for you to wield the authority that the office of Hegemon requires."

"And that," said Sister Carlotta, "is the very thing that gives you the moral authority to be accepted as Hegemon when the time comes."

"By declining the office," said Peter, "I make it more likely that I'll get it."

"Not in peacetime," said Carlotta. "Declining an office in peacetime takes you out of the running. But there's going to be war. And then the fellow who sacrificed his own ambition for the good of the world will look better and better. Especially when his last name is Wiggin."

Do they have to keep bringing up the fact that my relationship to Ender is more important than my years of work?

"You aren't against using that family connection, are you?" asked Bean.

"I'll do what it takes," said Peter, "and I'll use whatever works. But . . . tomorrow?"

"Achilles got to India yesterday, right?" said Bean. "Every day we delay this is a day that he has a chance to expose you. Do you think he'll wait? You exposed *him*—he'll crave the turnabout, and Chamrajnagar won't be shy about telling him, will he?"

"No," said Peter. "Chamrajnagar has already shown me how he feels about me. He'll do nothing to protect me."

"So here we are once again," said Bean. "We're giving you something, and you're going to use it. Are you going to help me? How can I get into a position where I have troops to train and command? Besides going back to Greece, I mean."

"No, not Greece," said Peter. "They're useless to you, and they'll end up doing only what Russia permits. No freedom of action."

"Where, then?" said Sister Carlotta. "Where do you have influence?"

"In all modesty," said Peter, "at this moment, I have influence everywhere. Day after tomorrow, I may have influence nowhere."

"So let's act now," said Bean. "Where?"

"Thailand," said Peter. "Burma has no hope of resisting an Indian attack, or of putting together an alliance that might have a chance. But Thailand is historically the leader of southeast Asia. The one nation that was never colonized. The natural leader of the

Tai-speaking peoples in the surrounding nations. And they have a strong military."

"But I don't speak the language," said Bean.

"Not a problem," said Peter. "The Thai have been multilingual for centuries, and they have a long history of allowing foreigners to take positions of power and influence in their government, as long as they're loyal to Thailand's interests. You have to throw in your lot with them. They have to trust you. But it seems plain enough that you know how to be loyal."

"Not at all," said Bean. "I'm completely selfish. I survive. That's all I do."

"But you survive," said Peter, "by being absolutely loyal to the few people you depend on. I read just as much about you as I did about Achilles."

"What was written about me reflects the fantasies of the newspeople," said Bean.

"I'm not talking about the news," said Peter. "I read Carlotta's memos to the I.F. about your childhood in Rotterdam."

They both stopped walking. Ah, have I surprised you? Peter couldn't help but take pleasure in knowing that he had shown that he, too, knew some things about *them*.

"Those memos were eyes only," said Carlotta. "There should have been no copies."

"Ah, but whose eyes?" said Peter. "There are no secrets to people with the right friends."

"*I* haven't read those memos," said Bean.

Carlotta looked searchingly at Peter. "Some information is worthless except to destroy," she said.

And now Peter wondered what secrets she had about Bean. Because when he spoke of "memos," he in fact was thinking of a report that had been in Achilles' file, which had drawn on a couple of those memos as a source about life on the streets of Rotterdam. The comments about Bean had been merely ancillary matters. He really hadn't read the actual memos. But now he wanted to, because there was clearly something that she didn't want Bean to know.

And Bean knew it, too.

"What's in those memos that you don't want Peter to tell me?" Bean demanded.

"I had to convince the Battle School people that I was being impartial about you," said Sister Carlotta. "So I had to make negative statements about you in order to get them to believe the positive ones."

"Do you think that would hurt my feelings?" said Bean.

"Yes, I do," said Carlotta. "Because even if you understand the reason why I said some of those things, you'll never forget that I said them."

"They can't be worse than what I imagine," said Bean.

"It's not a matter of being bad or worse. They can't be *too* bad or you wouldn't have got into Battle School, would you? You were too young and they didn't believe your test scores and they knew there wouldn't be time to train you unless you really were . . . what I said. I just don't want you to have my words in your memory. And if you have any sense, Bean, you'll never read them."

"Toguro," said Bean. "I've been gossiped about by the person I trust most, and it's so bad she begs me not to try to find out."

"Enough of this nonsense," said Peter. "We've all faced some nasty blows today. But we've got an alliance started here, haven't we? You're acting in my interest tonight, getting that groundswell started so I can reveal myself on the world's stage. And I've got to get you into Thailand, in a position of trust and influence, before I expose myself as a teenager. Which of us gets to sleep first, do you think?"

"Me," said Sister Carlotta. "Because I don't have any sins on my conscience."

"Kuso," said Bean. "You have all the sins of the world on your mind."

"You're confusing me with somebody else," said Sister Carlotta.

To Peter their banter sounded like family chatter— old jokes, repeated because they're comfortable.

Why didn't his own family have any of that? Peter had bantered with Valentine, but she had never really opened up to him and played that way. She always resented him, even feared him. And their parents were hopeless. There was no clever banter there, there were no shared jokes and memories.

Maybe I really was raised by robots, Peter thought.

"Tell your parents we really appreciated the dinner," said Bean.

"Home to bed," said Sister Carlotta.

"You won't be sleeping in your hotel tonight, will you?" said Peter. "You'll be leaving."

"We'll email you how to contact us," said Bean.

"You'll have to leave Greensboro yourself, you know," said Sister Carlotta. "Once you reveal your identity, Achilles will know where you are. And even though India has no reason to kill you, Achilles does. He kills anyone who has even *seen* him in a position of helplessness. You actually *put* him in that position. You're a dead man, as soon as he can reach you."

Peter thought of the attempt that had been made on Bean's life. "He was perfectly happy to kill your parents right along with you, wasn't he?" Peter asked.

"Maybe," said Bean, "you should tell your mom and dad who you are before they read about it on the nets. And then help them get out of town."

"At some point we have to stop hiding from Achilles and face him openly."

"Not until you have a government committed to keeping you alive," said Bean. "Until then, you stay in hiding. And your parents, too."

"I don't think they'll even believe me," said Peter. "My parents, I mean. When I tell them that I'm really Locke. What parents would? They'll probably try to commit me as delusional."

"Trust them," said Bean. "I think you think they're stupid. But I can assure you that they're not. Or at least your mother isn't. You got your brains from somebody. They'll deal with this."

So it was that when Peter got home at ten o'clock, he went to his parents' room and knocked on their door.

"What is it?" asked Father.

"Are you awake?" Peter asked.

"Come in," said Mother.

They chatted mindlessly for a few minutes about dinner and Sister Carlotta and that delightful little Julian Delphiki, so hard to believe that a child that young could possibly have done all that he had done in his short life. And on and on, until Peter interrupted them.

"I have something to tell you," said Peter. "Tomorrow, some friends of Bean's and Carlotta's will be starting a phony movement to get Locke nominated as Hegemon. You know who Locke is? The political commentator?"

They nodded.

"And the next morning," Peter went on, "Locke is going to come out with a statement that he has to decline such an honor because he's just a teenage boy living in Greensboro, North Carolina."

"Yes?" said Father.

Did they really not get it? "It's me, Dad," said Peter. "I'm Locke."

They looked at each other. Peter waited for them to say something stupid.

"Are you going to tell them that Valentine was Demosthenes, too?" asked Mother.

For a moment he thought she was saying that as a joke, that she thought that the only thing more absurd than Peter being Locke would be Valentine being Demosthenes.

Then he realized that there was no irony in her question at all. It was an important point, and one he needed to address—the contradiction between Locke and Demosthenes had to be resolved, or there *would* still be something for Chamrajnagar and Achilles to expose. And blaming Valentine for Demosthenes right from the start was an important thing to do.

But not as important to him as the fact that Mother knew it. "How long have you known?" he asked.

"We've been very proud of what you've accomplished," said Father.

"As proud as we've ever been of Ender," Mother added.

Peter almost staggered under the emotional blow. They had just told him the thing that he had wanted most to hear his entire life, without ever quite admitting it to himself. Tears sprang to his eyes.

"Thanks," he murmured. Then he closed the door and fled to his room. Somehow, fifteen minutes later, he got enough control of his emotions that he could write the letters he had to write to Thailand, and begin writing his self-exposure essay.

They knew. And far from thinking him a second-rater, a disappointment, they were as proud of him as they had ever been of Ender.

His whole world was about to change, his life would be transformed, he might lose everything, he might win everything. But all he could feel that night, as he finally went to bed and drifted off to sleep, was utter, foolish happiness.

Part Three

MANEUVERS

11

Bangkok

Posted on Military History Forum by HectorVictorious@firewall.net
Topic: Who Remembers Briseis?

When I read the Iliad, I see the same things everyone else does—the poetry, of course, and the information about heroic bronze-age warfare. But I see something else, too. It might have been Helen whose face launched a thousand ships, but it was Briseis who almost wrecked them. She was a powerless captive, a slave, and yet Achilles almost tore the Greek alliance apart because he wanted her.

The mystery that intrigues me is: Was she extraordinarily beautiful? Or was it her mind that Achilles coveted? No, seriously: Would she have been happy for long as Achilles' captive? Would she, perhaps, have gone to him willingly? Or remained a surly, resistant slave?

Not that it would have mattered to Achilles—he would have used his captive the same way, regardless of her feelings. But one imagines Briseis taking note of the tale about Achilles' heel and slipping that information to someone within the walls of Troy . . .

Briseis, if only I could have heard from you!

—Hector Victorious

Bean amused himself by leaving messages for Petra scattered all over the forums that she might visit—if she was alive, if Achilles allowed her to browse the nets, if she realized that a topic heading like "Who Remembers Briseis?" was a reference to her, and if she was free to reply as his message covertly begged her to do. He wooed her under other names of women loved by military leaders: Guinevere, Josephine, Roxane— even Barsine, the Persian wife of Alexander that Roxane murdered soon after his death. And he signed himself with the name of a nemesis or chief rival or successor: Mordred, Hector, Wellington, Cassander.

He took the dangerous step of allowing these identities to continue to exist, each consisting only of a for-

warding order to another anonymous net identity that
held all mail it received as encrypted postings on an
open board with no-tracks protocols. He could visit
and read the postings without leaving a trace. But firewalls could be pierced, protocols broken.

He could afford to be a little more careless now about
his online identities, if only because his real-world location was now known to people whose trustworthiness
he could not assess. Do you worry about the fifth lock
on the back door, when the front door is open?

They had welcomed him generously in Bangkok.
General Naresuan promised him that no one would
know his real identity, that he would be given soldiers
to train and intelligence to analyze and his advice
would be sought constantly as the Thai military prepared for all kinds of future contingencies. "We are
taking seriously Locke's assessment that India will
soon pose a threat to Thai security, and we will of
course want your help in preparing contingency
plans." All so warm and courteous. Bean and Carlotta
were installed in a general-officer-level apartment on a
military base, given unlimited privileges concerning
meals and purchases, and then . . . ignored.

No one called. No one consulted. The promised intelligence did not flow. The promised soldiers were
never assigned.

Bean knew better than to even inquire. The promises were not forgotten. If he asked about them, Naresuan would be embarrassed, would feel challenged.
That would never do. Something had happened. Bean
could only imagine what.

At first, of course, he feared that Achilles had gotten to the Thai government somehow, that his agents
now knew exactly where Bean was, that his death was
imminent.

That was when he sent Carlotta away.

It was not a pleasant scene. "You should come with me," she said. "They won't stop you. Walk away."

"I'm not leaving," said Bean. "Whatever has gone wrong is probably local politics. Somebody here doesn't like having me around—maybe Naresuan himself, maybe someone else."

"If you feel safe enough to stay," said Sister Carlotta, "then there's no reason for me to go."

"You can't pass yourself off as my grandmother here," said Bean. "The fact that I have a guardian weakens me."

"Spare me the scene you're trying to play," said Carlotta. "I know there are reasons why you'd be better off without me, and I know there are ways that I could help you greatly."

"If Achilles knows where I am already, then his penetration of Bangkok is deep enough that I'll never get away," said Bean. "You might. The information that an older woman is with me might not have reached him yet. But it will soon, and he wants you dead as much as he wants to kill me. I don't want to have to worry about you here."

"I'll go," said Carlotta. "But how do I write to you, since you never keep the same address?"

He gave her the name of his folder on the no-tracks board he was using, and the encryption key. She memorized it.

"One more thing," said Bean. "In Greensboro, Peter said something about reading your memos."

"I think he was lying," said Carlotta.

"I think the way you reacted proved that whether he read them or not, there *were* memos, and you don't want me to read them."

"There were, and I don't," said Carlotta.

"And that's the other reason I want you to leave," said Bean.

The expression on her face turned fierce. "You can't trust me when I tell you that there is nothing in those memos that you need to know right now?"

"I need to know everything about myself. My strengths, my weaknesses. You know things about me that you told Graff and you didn't tell me. You're still not telling me. You think of yourself as my master, able to decide things for me. That means we're not partners after all."

"Very well," said Carlotta. "I am acting in your best interest, but I understand that you don't see it that way." Her manner was cold, but Bean knew her well enough to recognize that it was not anger she was controlling, but grief and frustration. It was a cold thing to do, but for her own sake he had to send her away and keep her from being in close contact with him until he understood what was going on here in Bangkok. The contretemps about the memos made her willing to go. And he really was annoyed.

She was out the door in fifteen minutes and on her way to the airport. Nine hours later he found a posting from her on his encrypted board: She was in Manila, where she could disappear within the Catholic establishment there. Not a word about their quarrel, if that's what it had been. Only a brief reference to "Locke's confession," as the newspeople were calling it. "Poor Peter," wrote Carlotta. "He's been hiding for so long, it's going to be hard for him to get used to having to face the consequences of his words."

To her secure address at the Vatican, Bean replied, "I just hope Peter has the brains to get out of Greensboro. What he needs right now is a small country to run, so he can get some administrative and political experience. Or at least a city water department."

And what I need, thought Bean, is soldiers to command. That's why I came here.

For weeks after Carlotta left, the silence continued. It became obvious, soon enough, that whatever was going on had nothing to do with Achilles, or Bean would be dead by now. Nor could it have had anything to do with Locke being revealed as Peter Wiggin—the freeze-out had already begun before Peter published his declaration.

Bean busied himself with whatever tasks seemed meaningful. Though he had no access to military-level maps, he could still access the publicly available satellite maps of the terrain between India and the heart of Thailand—the rough mountain country of northern and eastern Burma, the Indian Ocean coastal approaches. India had a substantial fleet, by Indian Ocean standards—might they attempt to run the Strait of Malacca and strike at the heart of Thailand from the gulf? All possibilities had to be prepared for.

Some basic intelligence about the makeup of the Indian and Thai military was available on the nets. Thailand had a powerful air force—there was a chance of achieving air dominance, if they could protect their bases. Therefore it would be essential to have the capability of laying down emergency airstrips in a thousand different places, an engineering feat well within the reach of the Thai military—if they trained for it now and dispersed crews and fuel and spare parts throughout the country. That, along with mines, would be the best protection against a coastal landing.

The other Indian vulnerability would be supply lines and lanes of advance. Since India's military strat-

egy would inevitably depend on throwing vast, irresistible armies against the enemy, the defense was to
keep those vast armies hungry and harry them constantly from the air and from raiding parties. And if, as
was likely, the Indian Army reached the fertile plain of
the Chao Phraya or the Aoray Plateau, they had to find
the land utterly stripped, the food supplies dispersed
and hidden—those that weren't destroyed.

It was a brutal strategy, because the Thai people
would suffer along with the Indian Army—indeed,
they would suffer more. So the destruction had to be
set up so it would only take place at the last minute.
And, as much as possible, they had to be able to evacuate women and children to remote areas or even to
camps in Laos and Cambodia. Not that borders would
stop the Indian army, but terrain might. Having many
isolated targets for the Indians would force them to divide their forces. Then—and only then—would it
make sense for the Thai military to take on smaller
portions of the Indian army in hit-and-run engage-
ments or, where possible, in pitched battles where the
Thai side would have temporary numerical parity and
superior air support.

Of course, for all Bean knew this was already the
longstanding Thai military doctrine and if he made
these suggestions he would only annoy them—or
make them feel that he had contempt for them.

So he worded his memo very carefully. Lots of
phrases like, "No doubt you already have this in
place," and "as I'm sure you have long expected." Of
course, even those phrases could backfire, if they
hadn't thought of these things—it would sound patronizing. But he had to do something to break this
stalemate of silence.

He read the memo over and over, revising each time.

He waited days to send it, so he could see it in new perspectives. Finally, certain that it was as rhetorically inoffensive as he could make it, he put it into an email and sent it to the Office of the Chakri—the supreme military commander. It was the most public and potentially embarrassing way he could deliver the memo, since mail to that address was inevitably sorted and read by aides. Even printing it out and carrying it by hand would have been more subtle. But the idea was to stir things up; if Naresuan wanted him to be subtle, he would have given him a private email address to write to.

Fifteen minutes after he sent the memo, his door unceremoniously opened and four military police came in. "Come with us, sir," said the sergeant in charge.

Bean knew better than to delay or to ask questions. These men knew nothing but the instructions they had been given, and Bean would find out what those were by waiting to see what they did.

They did not take him to the office of the Chakri. Instead he was taken to one of the temporary buildings that had been set up on the old parade grounds—the Thai military had only recently given up marching as part of the training of soldiers and the display of military might. Only three hundred years after the American Civil War had proven that the days of marching in formation into battle were over. For military organizations, that was about the normal time lag. Sometimes Bean half-expected to find some army somewhere that was still training its soldiers to fight with sabers from horseback.

There was no label, not even a number, on the door they led him to. And when he came inside, none of the soldier-clerks even looked up at him. His arrival was both expected and unimportant, their attitude said. Which meant, of course, that it was *very* important, or they would not be so studiously perfect about not noticing him.

He was led to an office door, which the sergeant opened for him. He went in; the military police did not. The door closed behind him.

Seated at the desk was a major. This was an awfully high rank to have manning a reception desk, but today, at least, that seemed to be the man's duty. He depressed the button on an intercom. "The package is here," he said.

"Send it in." The voice that came back sounded young. So young that Bean understood the situation at once.

Of course. Thailand had contributed its share of military geniuses to Battle School. And even though none of Ender's jeesh had been of Thai parentage, Thailand, like many east and south Asian countries, was overrepresented in the population of Battle School as a whole.

There had even been three Thai soldiers who served with Bean in Dragon Army. Bean remembered every kid in that army very well, along with his complete dossier, since he was the one who had drawn up the list of soldiers who should make up Ender's army. Since most countries seemed to value their returning Battle School graduates in proportion to their closeness to Ender Wiggin, it was most likely one of those three who had been given a position of such influence here that he would be able to intercept a memo to the Chakri so quickly. And of the three, the one Bean would expect to see in the most prominent position, taking the most aggressive role, was . . .

Surrey. Suriyawong. "Surly," as they called him behind his back, since he always seemed to be pissed off about something.

And there he was, standing behind a table covered with maps.

Bean saw, to his surprise, that he was actually almost as tall as Suriyawong. Surrey had not been very big, but everyone towered over Bean in Battle School. Bean was catching up. He might not spend his whole life hopelessly undersized. It was a promising thought.

There was nothing promising about Surrey's attitude, though. "So the colonial powers have decided to use India and Thailand to fight their surrogate wars," he said.

Bean knew at once what had gotten under Suriyawong's skin. Achilles was a Belgian Walloon by birth, and Bean, of course, was Greek. "Yes, of course," said Bean. "Belgium and Greece are bound to fight out their ancient differences on bloody battlefields in Burma."

"Just because you were in Ender's jeesh," said Suriyawong, "does not mean that you have any understanding of the military situation of Thailand."

"My memo was designed to show how limited my knowledge was, because Chakri Naresuan has not provided me with the access to intelligence that he indicated I would receive when I arrived."

"If we ever need your advice, we'll provide you with intelligence."

"If you only provide me with the intelligence you think I need," said Bean, "then my advice will only consist of telling you what you already know, and I might as well go home now."

"Yes," said Suriyawong. "That would be best."

"Suriyawong," said Bean, "you don't really know me."

"I know you were always an emossin' little showoff who always had to be smarter than everybody else."

"I *was* smarter than everybody else," said Bean. "I've got the test scores to prove it. So what? That didn't mean they made me commander of Dragon Army. It didn't mean Ender made me a toon leader. I know just how worthless being smart is, compared with being good at command. I also know just how ignorant I am here in Thailand. I didn't come here because I thought Thailand would be prostrate without my brilliant mind to lead you into battle. I came here because the most dangerous human on this planet is running the show in India and by my best calculations, Thailand is going to be his primary target. I came here because if Achilles is going to be stopped from setting up his tyranny over the world, this is where it has to be done. And I thought, like George Washington in the American revolution, you might actually welcome a Lafayette or a Steuben to help in the cause."

"If your foolish memo was an example of your 'help,' you can leave now."

"So you already have the capability of making temporary airstrips within the amount of time that a fighter is in the air? So they can land at an airstrip that didn't exist when they took off?"

"That *is* an interesting idea and we're having the engineers look at it and evaluate the feasibility."

Bean nodded. "Good. That tells me all I needed to know. I'll stay."

"No, you will not!"

"I'll stay because, despite the fact that you're pissed off that I'm here, you still recognized a good idea when you heard it and put it into play. You're not an idiot, and therefore you're worth working with."

Suriyawong slapped the table and leaned over it, furious. "You condescending little oomay, I'm not your moose."

Bean answered him calmly. "Suriyawong, I don't want your job. I don't want to run things here. I just want to be useful. Why not use me the way Ender did? Give me a few soldiers to train. Let me think of weird things to do and figure out how to do them. Let me be ready so that when the war comes, and there's some impossible thing you need done, you can call me in and say, Bean, I need you to do something to slow down this army for a day, and I've got no troops anywhere near there. And I'll say, Are they drawing water from a river? Good, then let's give their whole army dysentery for a week. That should slow them down. And I'll get in there, get a bioagent into the water, bypass their water purification system, and get out. Or do you already have a water-drugging diarrhea team?"

Suriyawong held his expression of cold anger for a few moments, and then it broke. He laughed. "Come on, Bean, did you make that up on the spot, or have you really planned an operation like that?"

"Made it up just now," said Bean. "But it's kind of a fun idea, don't you think? Dysentery has changed the course of history more than once."

"Everybody immunizes their soldiers against the known bioagents. And there's no way of stopping downstream collateral damage."

"But Thailand is bound to have some pretty hot and heavy bioresearch, right?"

"Purely defensive," said Suriyawong. Then he smiled and sat down. "Sit, sit. You really are content to take a background position?"

"Not only content, but eager," said Bean. "If Achilles knew I was here, he'd find a way to kill me. The last thing I need is to be prominent—until we actually get into combat, at which time it might be a nice psychological blow to give Achilles the idea that I'm running things. It won't be true, but it might make him even crazier to think it's me he's facing. I've outmaneuvered him before. He's afraid of me."

"It's not my own position I was trying to protect," said Suriyawong. Bean understood this to mean that of course it *was* his position he was protecting. "But Thailand kept its independence when every other country in this area was ruled by Europeans. We're very proud of keeping foreigners out."

"And yet," said Bean, "Thailand also has a history of letting foreigners in—and using them effectively."

"As long as they know their place," said Suriyawong.

"Give me a place, and I'll remember to stay in it," said Bean.

"What kind of contingent do you want to work with?"

What Bean asked for wasn't a large number of men, but he wanted to draw them from every branch of service. Only two fighter-bombers, two patrol boats, a handful of engineers, a couple of light armored vehicles to go along with a couple of hundred soldiers and enough choppers to carry everything but the boats and planes. "And the power to requisition odd things that we think of. Rowboats, for instance. High explosives so we can train in making cliffs fall and bridges collapse. Whatever I think of."

"But you don't actually commit to combat without permission."

"Permission," said Bean, "from whom?"

"Me," said Suriyawong.

"But you're not Chakri," said Bean.

"The Chakri," said Suriyawong, "exists to provide me with everything I ask for. The planning is entirely in my hands."

"Glad to know who's aboon here." Bean stood up. "For what it's worth, I was most help to Ender when I had access to everything he knew."

"In your dreams," said Suriyawong.

Bean grinned. "I'm dreaming of good maps," said Bean. "And an accurate assessment of the current situation of the Thai military."

Suriyawong thought about that for a long moment.

"How many of your soldiers are you sending into battle blindfolded?" asked Bean. "I hope I'm the only one."

"Until I'm sure you really are my soldier," said Suriyawong, "the blindfold stays on. But . . . you can have the maps."

"Thank you," said Bean.

He knew what Suriyawong feared: that Bean would use any information he got to come up with alternate strategies and persuade the Chakri that he would do a better job as chief strategist than Suriyawong. For it was patently untrue that Suriyawong was the aboon here. Chakri Naresuan might trust him and had obviously delegated great responsibility to him. But the authority remained in Naresuan's hands, and Suriyawong served at his pleasure. That's why Suriyawong feared Bean—he could be replaced.

He'd find out soon enough that Bean was not interested in palace politics. If he remembered correctly, Suriyawong was of the royal family—though the last few polygynist kings of Siam had had so many children that it was hard to imagine that there were many Thais who were not royal to one degree or another. Chulalongkorn had established the principle, centuries ago, that princes had a duty to serve, but not a right to high office. Suriyawong's life belonged to Thailand as a matter of honor, but he would hold his position in the military only as long as his superiors considered him the best for the job.

Now that Bean knew who it was who had been keeping him down, it would be easy enough to destroy Surrey and take his place. After all, Suriyawong had been given the responsibility to carry out Naresuan's promises to Bean. He had deliberately disobeyed the Chakri's orders. All Bean really needed to do was use a back door—some connection of Peter's, probably— to get word to Naresuan that Suriyawong had blocked Bean from getting what he needed, and there would be an inquiry and the first seeds of doubt about Suriya-wong would be planted.

But Bean did not want Suriyawong's job.

He wanted a fighting force that he could train to work together so smoothly, so resourcefully, so brilliantly that when he made contact with Petra and found out where she was, he could go in and get her out alive. With or without Surly's permission. He'd help the Thai military as best he could, but Bean had his own objectives, and they had nothing to do with building a career in Bangkok.

"One last thing," said Bean. "I have to have a name here, something that won't alert anyone outside Thailand that I'm a child and a foreigner—that might be enough to tip off Achilles about who I am."

"What name do you have in mind? How about Süa—it means tiger."

"I have a better name," said Bean. "Borommakot."

Suriyawong looked puzzled for a moment, till he remembered the name from the history of Ayudhya, the ancient Tai city-state of which Siam was the successor. "That was the nickname of the uparat who stole the throne from Aphai, the rightful successor."

"I was just thinking of what the name means," said Bean. " 'In the urn. Awaiting cremation.' " He grinned. "As far as Achilles is concerned, I'm just a walking dead man."

Suriyawong relaxed. "Whatever. I thought as a foreigner you might appreciate having a shorter name."

"Why? I don't have to say it."

"You have to sign it."

"I'm not issuing written orders, and the only person I'll be reporting to is you. Besides, Borommakot is fun to say."

"You know your Thai history," said Suriyawong.

"Back in Battle School," said Bean. "I got fascinated with Thailand. A nation of survivors. The ancient Tai people managed to take over vast reaches of the Cambodian Empire and spread throughout southeast Asia, all without anybody noticing. They were conquered by Burma and emerged stronger than ever. When other countries were falling under European domination, Thailand managed to expand its borders for a surprisingly long time, and even when it lost Cambodia and Laos, it held its core. I think Achilles is going to find what everybody else has found—the Thai are not easily conquered, and, once conquered, not easily ruled."

"Then you have some idea of the soul of the Thai," said Suriyawong. "But no matter how long you study us, you will never be one of us."

"You're mistaken," said Bean. "I already am one of you. A survivor, a free man, no matter what."

Suriyawong took this seriously. "Then as one free

man to another, welcome to the service of Thailand."

They parted amicably, and by the end of the day, Bean saw that Suriyawong intended to keep his word. He was provided with a list of soldiers—four preexisting fifty-man companies with fair records, so they weren't giving him the dregs. And he would have his helicopters, his jets, his patrol boats to train with.

He should have been nervous, preparing to face soldiers who were bound to be skeptical about having him as their commander. But he had been in that situation before, in Battle School. He would win over these soldiers by the simplest expedient of all. Not flattery, not favors, not folksy friendliness. He would win their loyalty by showing them that he knew what to do with an army, so they would have the confidence that when they went into battle, their lives would not be wasted in some doomed enterprise. He would tell them, from the start, "I will never lead you into an action unless I know we can win it. Your job is to become such a brilliant fighting force that there is no action I can't lead you into. We're not in this for glory. We're in this to destroy the enemies of Thailand any way we can."

They'd get used to being led by a little Greek boy soon enough.

12

Islamabad

To: GuillaumeLeBon%Egalite@Haiti.gov
From: Locke%erasmus@polnet.gov
Re: Terms for Consultation

M. LeBon, I appreciate how difficult it
was for you to approach me. I believe
that I could offer you worthwhile views
and suggestions, and, more to the
point, I believe you are committed to
acting courageously on behalf of the
people you govern and therefore any
suggestions I made would have an excellent chance of being put into effect.

But the terms you suggest are unac-
ceptable to me. I will not come to
Haiti by dark of night or masked as a
tourist or student, lest anyone find
out that you are consulting a teenage

boy from America. I am still the author of every word written by Locke,
and it is as that widely known figure,
whose name is on the proposals that
ended the League War, that I will come
openly to consult with you. If my previous reputation were not reason
enough for you to be able to invite me
openly, then the fact that I am the
brother of Ender Wiggin, on whose
shoulders the fate of all humanity so
recently was placed, should set a
precedent you can follow without embarrassment. Not to mention the presence of children from Battle School in
almost every military headquarters on
Earth. The sum you offered is a
princely one. But it will never be
paid, for under the terms you suggested, I will not come, and if you
invite me openly, I will certainly
come but will accept no payment—not
even for my expenses while I am in
your country. As a foreigner, I could
not possibly match your deep and abiding love for the people of Haiti, but
I care very much that every nation and
people on Earth share in the prosperity and freedom that are their
birthright, and I will accept no fee
for helping in that cause.

By bringing me openly, you decrease
your personal risk, for if my suggestions are unpopular, you can lay the

blame on me. And the personal risk I
take by coming openly is far greater,
for if the world judges my proposals
to be unsound or if, in implementing
them, you discover them to be unwork-
able, I will publicly bear the discredit. I speak candidly, because
these are realities we both must face:
Such is my confidence that my suggestions will be excellent and that you
will be able to implement them effectively. When we have finished our work,
you can play Cincinnatus and retire to
your farm, while I will play Solon and
leave the shores of Haiti, both of us
confident that we have given your people a fair chance to take their proper
place in the world.

Sincerely,
Peter Wiggin

Petra never forgot for an instant that she was a captive
and a slave. But, like most captives, like most slaves,
as she lived from day to day she became accustomed
to her captivity and found ways to be herself within the
tight boundaries around her.

She was guarded every moment, and her desk was
crippled so she could send no outgoing messages.
There would be no repetition of her message to Bean.
And even when she saw that someone—could it be
Bean, not killed after all?—was trying to speak to her,
leaving messages on every military, historical, and ge-
ographic forum that spoke about women held in
bondage to some warrior or other, she did not let it fret

her. She could not answer, so she would waste no time trying.

Eventually the work that was forced on her became a challenge that she found interesting for its own sake. How to mount a campaign against Burma and Thailand and, eventually, Vietnam that would sweep all resistance before it, yet never provoke China to intervene. She saw at once that the vast size of the Indian Army was its greatest weakness, for the supply lines would be impossible to defend. So, unlike the other strategists Achilles was using—mostly Indian Battle School graduates—Petra did not bother with the logistics of a sledgehammer campaign. Eventually the Indian forces would have to divide anyway, unless the Burmese and Thai armies simply lined up to be slaughtered. So she planned an unpredictable campaign—dazzling thrusts by small, mobile forces that could live off the land. The few pieces of mobile armor would race forward, supplied with petrol by air tankers.

She knew her plan was the only one that made sense, and not just because of the intrinsic problems it solved. Any plan that involved putting ten million soldiers so near to the border with China would provoke Chinese intervention. Her plan would never put enough soldiers near China to constitute a threat. Nor would her plan lead to a war of attrition that would leave both sides exhausted and weak. Most of India's strength would remain in reserve, ready to strike wherever the enemy showed weakness.

Achilles gave copies of her plan to the others, of course—he called it "cooperation," but it functioned as an exercise in one-upmanship. All the others had quickly climbed into Achilles' pocket, and now were eager to please him. They sensed, of course, that Achilles wanted Petra humiliated, and duly gave him what he wanted. They mocked her plan as if any fool could see it was hopeless, even though their criticisms were specious and her main points were never even addressed. She bore it, because she was a slave, and because she knew that eventually, some of them were bound to catch on to the way Achilles manipulated them and used them. But she knew that she had done a brilliant job, and it would be a delicious irony if the Indian Army—no, be honest, if Achilles—did not use her plan, and marched head-on to destruction.

It did not bother her conscience to have come up with an effective strategy for Indian expansion in southeast Asia. She knew it would never be used. Even her strategy of small, quick strike forces did not change the fact that India could not afford a two-front war. Pakistan would not let the opportunity pass if India committed itself to an eastern war.

Achilles had simply chosen the wrong country to try to lead into war. Tikal Chapekar, the Indian prime minister, was an ambitious man with delusions of the nobility of his cause. He might very well believe in Achilles' persuasions and long to begin an attempt to "unify" southeast Asia. A war might even begin. But it would founder quickly as Pakistan prepared to attack in the west. Indian adventurism would evaporate as it always had.

She even said as much to Achilles when he visited her one morning after her plans had been so resoundingly rejected by her fellow strategists. "Follow whatever plan you like, nothing will ever work as you think it will."

Achilles simply changed the subject—when he visited her, he preferred to reminisce with her as if they were a couple of old people remembering their childhoods together. Remember this about Battle School? Remember that? She wanted to scream in his face that he had only been there for a few days before Bean had him chained up in an air shaft, confessing to his crimes. He had no right to be nostalgic for Battle School. All he was accomplishing was to poison her own memories of the place, for now when Battle School came up, she just wanted to change the subject, to forget it completely.

Who would have imagined that she would ever think of Battle School as her era of freedom and happiness? It certainly hadn't seemed that way at the time.

To be fair, her captivity was not painful. As long as Achilles was in Hyderabad, she had the run of the base, though she was never unobserved. She could go to the library and do research—though one of her guards had to thumb the ID pad, verifying that she had logged on as herself, with all the restrictions that implied, before she could access the nets. She could run through the dusty countryside that was used for military maneuvers—and sometimes could almost forget the other footfalls keeping syncopated rhythm with her own. She could eat what she wanted, sleep when she wanted. There were times when she almost forgot she wasn't free. There were far more times when, knowing she was not free, she almost decided to stop hoping that her captivity would ever end.

It was Bean's messages that kept her hope alive. She could not answer him, and therefore stopped thinking of his messages as actual communications. Instead they were something deeper than mere attempts at making contact. They were proof that she had not been forgotten. They were proof that Petra Arkanian, Battle

School brat, still had a friend who respected her and cared for her enough to refuse to give up. Each message was a cool kiss to her fevered brow.

And then one day Achilles came to her and told her he was going on a trip.

She assumed at once that this meant she would be confined to her room, locked down and under guard, until Achilles returned.

"No locks this time," said Achilles. "You're coming with me."

"So it's someplace inside India?"

"In one sense yes," said Achilles. "In another, no."

"I'm not interested in your games," she said, yawning. "I'm not going."

"Oh, you won't want to miss this," said Achilles. "And even if you did, it wouldn't matter, because I need you, so you'll be there."

"What can you possibly need me for?"

"Oh, well, when you put it that way, I suppose I should be more precise. I need you to see what takes place at the meeting."

"Why? Unless there's a successful assassination attempt, there's nothing I want to see you do."

"The meeting," said Achilles, "is in Islamabad."

Petra had no smart reply to that. The capital of Pakistan. It was unthinkable. What possible business could Achilles have there? And why would he bring her?

They flew—which of course reminded her of the eventful flight that had brought her to India as Achilles' prisoner. The open door—should I have pulled him out with me and brought him brutally down to earth?

During the flight Achilles showed her the letter he had sent to Ghaffar Wahabi, the "prime minister" of Pakistan—actually, of course, the military dictator . . .

or Sword of Islam, if you preferred it that way. The letter was a marvel of deft manipulation. It would never have attracted any attention in Islamabad, however, if it had not come from Hyderabad, the headquarters of the Indian Army. Even though Achilles' letter never actually said so, it would be assumed in Pakistan that Achilles came as an unofficial envoy of the Indian government.

How many times had an Indian military plane landed at this military airbase near Islamabad? How many times had Indian soldiers in uniform been allowed to set foot on Pakistani soil—bearing their sidearms, no less? And all to carry a Belgian boy and an Armenian girl to talk to whatever lower-level official the Pakistanis decided to fob off on them.

A bevy of stone-faced Pakistani officials led them to a building a short distance from where their plane was being refueled. Inside, on the second floor, the leading official said, "Your escort must remain outside."

"Of course," said Achilles. "But my assistant comes in with me. I must have a witness to remind me in case my memory flags."

The Indian soldiers stood near the wall at full attention. Achilles and Petra walked through the open door.

There were only two people in the room, and she recognized one of them immediately from his pictures. With a gesture, he indicated where they should sit.

Petra walked to her chair in silence, never taking her eyes off Ghaffar Wahabi, the prime minister of Pakistan. She sat beside and slightly behind Achilles, as a lone Pakistani aide sat just at Wahabi's right hand. This was no lower-level official. Somehow, Achilles' letter had opened all the doors, right to the very top.

They needed no interpreter, for Common was, though not their birth language, a childhood acquisition for both of them, and they spoke without accent. Wahabi seemed skeptical and distant, but at least he did not play any humiliation games—he did not keep them waiting, he ushered them into the room himself, and he did not challenge Achilles in any way.

"I have invited you because I wish to hear what you have to say," said Wahabi. "So please begin."

Petra wanted so badly for Achilles to do something horribly wrong—to simper and beam, or to try to strut and show off his intelligence.

"Sir, I'm afraid that it may sound at first as if I am trying to teach Indian history to you, a scholar in that field. It is from your book that I learned everything I'm about to say."

"It is easy to read my book," said Wahabi. "What did you learn from it that I do not already know?"

"The next step," said Achilles. "The step so obvious that I was stunned when you did not take it."

"So this is a book review?" asked Wahabi. But with those words he smiled faintly, to take away the edge of hostility.

"Over and over again, you show the great achievements of the Indian people, and how they are overshadowed, swallowed up, ignored, despised. The civilization of the Indus is treated as a poor also-ran to Mesopotamia and Egypt and even that latecomer China. The Aryan invaders brought their language and religion and imposed it on the people of India. The Moguls, the British, each with their overlay of beliefs and institutions. I must tell you that your book is regarded with great respect in the highest circles of the Indian government, because of the impartial way you treated the religions brought to India by invaders."

Petra knew that this was not idle flattery. For a Pakistani scholar, especially one with political ambitions, to write a history of the subcontinent without praising the Muslim influence and condemning the Hindu religion as primitive and destructive was brave indeed.

Wahabi raised a hand. "I wrote then as a scholar. Now I am the voice of the people. I hope my book has not led you into a quixotic quest for reunification of India. Pakistan is determined to remain pure."

"Please do not leap to conclusions," said Achilles. "I agree with you that reunification is impossible. Indeed, it is a meaningless term. Hindu and Muslim were never united except under an oppressor, so how could they be reunited?"

Wahabi nodded, and waited for Achilles to go on.

"What I saw throughout your account," said Achilles, "was a profound sense of the greatness inherent in the Indian people. Great religions have been born here. Great thinkers have arisen who have changed the world. And yet for two hundred years, when people think of the great powers, India and Pakistan are never on the list. And they never have been. And this makes you angry, and it makes you sad."

"More sad than angry," said Wahabi, "but then, I'm an old man, and my temper has abated."

"China rattles its swords, and the world shivers, but India is barely glanced at. The Islamic world trembles when Iraq or Turkey or Iran or Egypt swings one way or another, and yet Pakistan, stalwart for its entire history, is never treated as a leader. Why?"

"If I knew the answer," said Wahabi, "I would have written a different book."

"There are many reasons in the distant past," said Achilles, "but they all come down to one thing. The Indian people could never act together."

"Again, the language of unity," said Wahabi.

"Not at all," said Achilles. "Pakistan cannot take his rightful place of leadership in the Muslim world, because whenever he looks to the west, Pakistan hears the heavy steps of India behind him. And India cannot take her rightful place as the leader of the east, because the threat of Pakistan looms behind her."

Petra admired the deft way Achilles made his choice of pronouns seem casual, uncalculated—India the woman, Pakistan the man.

"The spirit of God is more at home in India and Pakistan than any other place. It is no accident that great religions have been born here, or have found their purest form. But Pakistan keeps India from being great in the east, and India keeps Pakistan from being great in the west."

"True, but insoluble," said Wahabi.

"Not so," said Achilles. "Let me remind you of another bit of history, from only a few years before Pakistan's creation as a state. In Europe, two great nations faced each other—Stalin's Russia and Hitler's Germany. These two leaders were great monsters. But they saw that their enmity had chained them to each other. Neither could accomplish anything as long as the other threatened to take advantage of the slightest opening."

"You compare India and Pakistan to Hitler and Stalin?"

"Not at all," said Achilles, "because so far, India and Pakistan have shown less sense and less self-control than either of those monsters."

Wahabi turned to his aide. "As usual, India has found a new way to insult us." The aide arose to help him to his feet.

"Sir, I thought you were a wise man," said Achilles.

"There is no one here to see you posture. No one to quote what I have said. You have nothing to lose by hearing me out, and everything to lose by leaving."

Petra was stunned to hear Achilles speak so sharply. Wasn't this taking his non-flatterer approach a little far? Any normal person would have apologized for the unfortunate comparison with Hitler and Stalin. But not Achilles. Well, this time he had surely gone too far. If this meeting failed, his whole strategy would come to nothing, and the tension he was under had led to this misstep.

Wahabi did not sit back down. "Say what you have to say, and be quick," he said.

"Hitler and Stalin sent their foreign ministers, Ribbentrop and Molotov, and despite the hideous denunciations that each had made against the other, they signed a nonaggression pact and divided Poland between them. It's true that a couple of years later, Hitler abrogated this pact, which led to millions of deaths and Hitler's eventual downfall, but that is irrelevant to your situation, because unlike Hitler and Stalin, you and Chapekar are men of honor—you are of India, and you both serve God faithfully."

"To say that Chapekar and I both serve God is blasphemy to one or the other of us, or both," said Wahabi.

"God loves this land and has given the Indian people greatness," said Achilles—so passionately that if Petra had not known better, she might have believed he had some kind of faith. "Do you really believe it is the will of God that both Pakistan and India remain in obscurity and weakness, solely because the people of India have not yet awakened to the will of Allah?"

"I do not care what atheists and madmen say about the will of Allah."

Good for you, thought Petra.

"Nor do I," said Achilles. "But I can tell you this. If you and Chapekar signed an agreement, not of unity, but of nonaggression, you could divide Asia between you. And if the decades pass and there is peace between these two great Indian nations, then will the Hindu not be proud of the Muslim, and the Muslim proud of the Hindu? Will it not be possible then for Hindus to hear the teachings of the Quran, not as the book of their deadly enemy, but rather as the book of their fellow Indians, who share with India the leadership of Asia? If you don't like the example of Hitler and Stalin, then look at Portugal and Spain, ambitious colonizers who shared the Iberian Peninsula. Portugal, to the west, was smaller and weaker—but it was also the bold explorer that opened up the seas. Spain sent one explorer, and he was Italian—but he discovered a new world."

Petra again saw the subtle flattery at work. Without saying so directly, Achilles had linked Portugal—the weaker but braver nation—to Pakistan, and the nation that prevailed through dumb luck to India.

"They might have gone to war and destroyed each other, or weakened each other hopelessly. Instead they listened to the Pope, who drew a line on the earth and gave everything east of it to Portugal and everything west of it to Spain. Draw your line across the Earth, Ghaffar Wahabi. Declare that you will not make war against the great Indian people who have not yet heard the word of Allah, but will instead show to all the world the shining example of the purity of Pakistan. While in the meantime, Tikal Chapekar will unite eastern Asia under Indian leadership, which they have long hungered for. Then, in the happy day when the Hindu people heed the Book, Islam will spread in one breath from New Delhi to Hanoi."

Wahabi slowly sat back down.

Achilles said nothing.

Petra knew then that his boldness had succeeded.

"Hanoi," said Wahabi. "Why not Beijing?"

"On the day that the Indian Muslims of Pakistan are made guardians of the sacred city, on that day the Hindus may imagine entering the forbidden city."

Wahabi laughed. "You are outrageous."

"I am," said Achilles. "But I'm right. About everything. About the fact that this is what your book was pointing to. That this is the obvious conclusion, if only India and Pakistan are blessed to have, at the same time, leaders with such vision and courage."

"And why does this matter to you?" said Wahabi.

"I dream of peace on Earth," said Achilles.

"And so you encourage Pakistan and India to go to war?"

"I encourage you to agree *not* to go to war with each other."

"Do you think Iran will peacefully accept Pakistan's leadership? Do you think the Turks will embrace us? It will have to be by conquest that we create this unity."

"But you *will* create it," said Achilles. "And when Islam is united under Indian leadership, it will no longer be humiliated by other nations. One great Muslim nation, one great Hindu nation, at peace with each other and too powerful for any other nation to dare to attack. That is how peace comes to Earth. God willing."

"Inshallah," echoed Wahabi. "But now it is time for me to know by what authority you say these things. You hold no office in India. How do I know you have not been sent to lull me while Indian armies amass for yet another unprovoked assault?"

Petra wondered if Achilles had planned to get Wahabi to say something so precisely calculated to give him the perfect dramatic moment, or if it was just chance. For Achilles' only answer to Wahabi was to draw from his portfolio a single sheet of paper, bearing a small signature at the bottom in blue ink.

"What is that?" said Wahabi.

"My authority," said Achilles. He handed the paper to Petra. She arose and carried it to the middle of the room, where Wahabi's aide took it from her hand.

Wahabi perused it, shaking his head. "And this is what he signed?"

"He more than signed it," said Achilles. "Ask your satellite team to tell you what the Indian Army is doing even as we speak."

"They are withdrawing from the border?"

"Someone has to be the first to offer trust. It's the opportunity you've been waiting for, you and all your predecessors. The Indian Army is withdrawing. You could send your troops forward. You could turn this gesture of peace into a bloodbath. Or you could give the orders to move your troops west and north. Iran is waiting for you to show them the purity of Islam. The Caliphate of Istanbul is waiting for you to unshackle it from the chains of the secular government of Turkey. Behind you, you will have only your brother Indians, wishing you well as you show the greatness of this land that God has chosen, and that finally is ready to rise."

"Save the speech," said Wahabi. "You understand that I have to verify that this signature is genuine, and that the Indian troops are moving in the direction that you say."

"You will do what you have to do," said Achilles. "I will return to India now."

"Without waiting for my answer?"

"I haven't asked you a question," said Achilles.

"Tikal Chapekar has asked that question, and it is to him you must give your answer. I am only the messenger."

With that, Achilles rose to his feet. Petra did, too. Achilles strode boldly to Wahabi and offered his hand. "I hope you will forgive me, but I could not bear to return to India without being able to say that the hand of Ghaffar Wahabi touched mine."

Wahabi reached out and took Achilles' hand. "Foreign meddler," said Wahabi, but his eyes twinkled, and Achilles smiled in reply.

Could this possibly have *worked*? Petra wondered. Molotov and Ribbentrop had to negotiate for weeks, didn't they? Achilles did this in a single meeting.

What were the magic words?

But as they walked out of the room, escorted again by the four Indian soldiers who had come with them—her guards—Petra realized there had been no magic words. Achilles had simply studied both men and recognized their ambitions, their yearning for greatness. He had told them what they most wanted to hear. He gave them the peace that they had secretly longed for.

She had not been there for the meeting with Chapekar that led to Achilles' getting that signed nonaggression pact and the promise to withdraw, but she could imagine it. "You must make the first gesture," Achilles must have said. "It's true that the Muslims might take advantage of it, might attack. But you have the largest army in the world, and govern the greatest people. Let them attack, and you will absorb the blow and then return to roll over them like water bursting from a dam. And no one will criticize you for taking a chance on peace."

And now it finally struck home. The plans she had

been drawing up for the invasion of Burma and Thailand were not mere foolery. They would be used. Hers or someone else's. The blood would begin to flow. Achilles would get his war.

I didn't sabotage my plans, she realized. I was so sure they could not be used that I didn't bother to build weaknesses into them. They might actually work.

What have I done?

And now she understood why Achilles had brought her along. He wanted to strut in front of her, of course—for some reason, he felt the need to have someone witness his triumphs. But it was more than that. He also wanted to rub her face in the fact that he was actually going to do what she had so often said could not be done.

Worst of all, she found herself hoping that her plan would be used, not because she wanted Achilles to win his war, but because she wanted to stick it to the other Battle School brats who had mocked her plan so mercilessly.

I have to get word to Bean somehow. I have to warn him, so he can get word to the governments of Burma and Thailand. I have to do something to subvert my own plan of attack, or their destruction will be on my shoulders.

She looked at Achilles, who was dozing in his seat, oblivious to the miles racing by beneath him, returning him to the place where his wars of conquest would begin. If she could only remove his murders from the equation, on balance he would be quite a remarkable boy. He was a Battle School discard with the label "psychopath" attached to him, and yet somehow he had gotten not one but three major world governments to do his bidding.

I was a witness to this most recent triumph, and I'm still not sure how he brought it off.

She remembered the story from her childhood, about Adam and Eve in the garden, and the talking snake. Even as a little girl she had said—to the consternation of her family—What kind of idiot was Eve, to believe a snake? But now she understood, for she had heard the voice of the snake and had watched as a wise and powerful man had fallen under its spell.

Eat the fruit and you can have the desires of your heart. It's not evil, it's noble and good. You'll be praised for it.

And it's delicious.

13

Warnings

To: Carlotta%agape@vatican.net/orders/
sisters/ind
From: Graff%bonpassage@colmin.gov
Re: Found?

I think we've found Petra. A good
friend in Islamabad who is aware of my
interest in finding her tells me that a
strange envoy from New Delhi came for a
brief meeting with Wahabi yesterday—a
teenage boy who could only be Achilles;
and a teenage girl of the right description who said nothing. Petra? I
think it likely.

Bean needs to know what I've learned.
First, my friend tells me that this
meeting was almost immediately followed

by orders to the Pakistani military to move back from the border with India. Couple that with the already-noted Indian removal from that frontier, and I think we're witnessing the impossible—after two centuries of intermittent but chronic warfare, a real attempt at peace. And it seems to have been done by or with the help of Achilles. (Since so many of our colonists are Indian, there are those in my ministry who fear that an outbreak of peace on the subcontinent might jeopardize our work!)

Second, for Achilles to bring Petra along on this sensitive mission implies that she is not an unwilling participant in his projects. Given that in Russia Vlad also was seduced into working with Achilles, however briefly, it is not unthinkable that even as confirmed a skeptic as Petra might have become a true believer while in captivity. Bean must be made aware of this possibility, for he may be hoping to rescue someone who does not wish to be rescued.

Third, tell Bean that I can make contacts in Hyderabad, among former Battle School students working in the Indian high command. I will not ask them to compromise their loyalty to their country, but I will ask about Petra and find out what, if anything, they have seen or heard. I think old school loyalty

```
may  trump  patriotic  secrecy  on  this
point.
```

Bean's little strike force was all that he could have hoped for. These were not elite soldiers the way Battle School students had been—they were not selected for the ability to command. But in some ways this made them easier to train. They weren't constantly analyzing and second-guessing. In Battle School, too, many soldiers kept trying to show off to everyone, so they could enhance their reputation in the school—commanders constantly had to struggle to keep their soldiers focused on the overall goal of the army.

Bean knew from his studies that in real-world armies, the opposite was more usually the problem—that soldiers tried *not* to do brilliantly at anything, or learn too quickly, for fear of being thought a suckup or show-off by their fellow soldiers. But the cure for both problems was the same. Bean worked hard to earn a reputation for tough, fair judgment.

He played no favorites, made no friends, but always noticed excellence and commented on it. His praise, however, was not effusive. Usually he would simply make a note about it in front of others. "Sergeant, your team made no mistakes." Only when an accomplishment was exceptional did he praise it explicitly, and then only with a terse "Good."

As he expected, the rarity of his praise as well as its fairness soon made it the most valued coin in his strike force. Soldiers who did good work did not have special privileges and were given no special authority, so they were not resented by the others. The praise was not effusive, so it never embarrassed them. Instead, they were admired by the others, and emulated. And the focus of the soldiers became the earning of Bean's recognition.

That was true power. Frederick the Great's dictum that soldiers had to fear their officers more than they feared the enemy was stupid. Soldiers needed to believe they had the respect of their officers, and to value that respect more than they valued life itself. Moreover, they had to know that their officers' respect was justified—that they really were the good soldiers their officers believed them to be.

In Battle School, Bean had used his brief time in command of an army to teach himself—he led his men to defeat every time, because he was more interested in learning what he could learn than in racking up points. This was demoralizing to his soldiers, but he didn't care—he knew that he would not be with them long, and that the time of the Battle School was nearly over. Here in Thailand, though, he knew that the battles coming up were real, the stakes high, and his soldiers' lives would be on the line. Victory, not information, was the goal.

And, behind that obvious motive, there lay an even deeper one. Sometime in the coming war—or even before, if he was lucky—he would be using a portion of this strike force to make a daring rescue attempt, probably deep inside India. There would be zero tolerance for error. He *would* bring Petra out. He *would* succeed.

He drove himself as hard as he drove any of his men. He made it a point to train alongside them—a child going through all the exercises the men went through. He ran with them, and if his pack was lighter it was only because he needed to carry fewer calories in order to survive. He had to carry smaller, lighter weapons, but no one begrudged him that—besides, they saw that his bullets went to the mark as often as theirs. There was nothing he asked them to do that he did not do himself. And when he was not as good as his men, he had no qualms about going to one of the best of them and asking him for criticism and advice— which he then followed.

This was unheard of, for a commander to risk allowing himself to appear unskilled or weak in front of his men. And Bean would not have done it, either, because the benefits did not usually outweigh the risks. However, he was planning to go along with them on difficult maneuvers, and his training had been theoretical and game-centered. He had to become a soldier, so he could be there to deal with problems and emergencies during operations, so he could keep up with them, and so that, in a pinch, he could join effectively in a fight.

At first, because of his youth and small stature, some of the soldiers had tried to make things easier for him. His refusal had been quiet but firm. "I have to learn this too," he would say, and that was the end of the discussion. Naturally, the soldiers watched him all the more intensely, to see how he measured up to the high standard he set for them. They saw him tax his body to the utmost. They saw that he shrank from nothing, that he came out of mudwork slimier than anyone, that he went over obstacles just as high as anyone's, that he ate no better food and slept on no better a patch of ground on maneuvers.

They did not see how much he modeled this strike force on the Battle School armies. With two hundred men, he divided them into five companies of forty. Each company, like Ender's Battle School army, was divided into five toons of eight men each. Every toon was expected to be able to carry out operations entirely on its own; every company was expected to be able to deal with complete independence. At the same time, he made sure that they became skilled observers, and trained them to see the kinds of things he needed them to see.

"You are my eyes," he said. "You need to see what I would look for *and* what you would see. I will always tell you what I am planning and why, so you will know if you see a problem I didn't anticipate, which might change my plan. Then you will make sure I know. My best chance of keeping you all alive is to know everything that is in your heads during battle, just as your best chance of staying alive is to know everything that is in my head."

Of course, he knew that he could not tell them everything. No doubt they understood this as well. But he spent an inordinate amount of time, by standard military doctrine, telling his men the reasoning behind his orders, and he expected his company and toon commanders to do the same with their men. "That way, when we give you an order without any reasons, you will know that it's because there's no time for explanation, that you must act now—but that there *is* a good reason, which we *would* tell you if we could."

Once when Suriyawong came to observe his training of his troops, he asked Bean if this was how he recommended training soldiers throughout the whole army.

"Not a chance," said Bean.

"If it works for you, why wouldn't it work everywhere?"

"Usually you don't need it and can't afford the time," said Bean.

"But you can?"

"These soldiers are going to be called on to do the impossible. They aren't going to be sent to hold a position or advance against an enemy posting. They're going to be sent to do difficult, complicated things right under the eyes of the enemy, under circumstances where they can't go back for new instructions but have to adapt and succeed. That is impossible if they don't understand the purpose behind all their orders. And they have to know exactly how their commanders think so that trust is perfect—and so they can compensate for their commanders' inevitable weaknesses."

"*Your* weaknesses?" asked Suriyawong.

"Hard to believe, Suriyawong, but yes, I have weaknesses."

That earned a faint smile from Surly—a rare prize. "Growing pains?" asked Suriyawong.

Bean looked down at his ankles. He had already had new uniforms made twice, and it was time for a third go. He was almost as tall now as Suriyawong had been when Bean first arrived in Bangkok half a year before. Growing caused him no pain. But it worried him, since it seemed unconnected with any other sign of puberty. Why, after all these years of being undersized, was his body now so determined to catch up?

He experienced none of the problems of adolescence—not the clumsiness that comes from having limbs that swing farther than they used to, not the rush of hormones that clouded judgment and distracted attention. So if he grew enough to carry better weapons, that could only be a plus.

"Someday I hope to be as fine a man as you," said Bean.

Suriyawong grunted. He knew that Surly would

take it as a joke. He also knew that, somewhere deeper than consciousness, Suriyawong would also take it at face value, for people always did. And it was important for Suriyawong to have the constant reassurance that Bean respected his position and would do nothing to undermine him.

That had been months ago, and Bean was able to report to Suriyawong a long list of possible missions that his men had been trained for and could perform at any time. It was his declaration of readiness.

Then came the letter from Graff. Carlotta forwarded it to him as soon as she got it. Petra was alive. She was probably with Achilles in Hyderabad.

Bean immediately notified Suriyawong that an intelligence source of a friend of his verified an apparent nonaggression pact between India and Pakistan, and a movement of troops away from the shared border— along with his opinion that this guaranteed an invasion of Burma within three weeks.

As to the other matters in the letter, Graff's assertion that Petra might have gone over to Achilles' cause was, of course, absurd—if Graff believed that, he didn't know Petra. What alarmed Bean was that she had been so thoroughly neutralized that she could *seem* to be on Achilles' side. This was the girl who always spoke her mind no matter how much abuse it caused to come down on her head. If she had fallen silent, it meant she was in despair.

Isn't she getting my messages? Has Achilles cut her off from information so thoroughly that she doesn't even roam the nets? That would explain her failure to answer. But still, Petra was used to standing alone. That wouldn't explain her silence.

It had to be her own strategy for mastery. Silence, so

that Achilles would forget how much she hated him. Though surely she knew him well enough by now to know that he never forgot anything. Silence, so that she could avoid even deeper isolation—that was possible. Even Petra could keep her mouth shut if every time she spoke up it cut her off from more and more information and opportunities.

Finally, though, Bean had to entertain the possibility that Graff was right. Petra was human. She feared death like anyone else. And if she had, in fact, witnessed the death of her two guardians in Russia, and if Achilles had committed the killings with his own hands—which Bean believed likely—then Petra was facing something she had never faced before. She could speak up to idiotic commanders and teachers in Battle School because the worst that could happen was reprimands. With Achilles, what she had to fear was death.

And the fear of death changed the way a person saw the world, Bean knew that. He had lived his first years of life under the constant pressure of that fear. Moreover, he had spent a considerable time specifically under Achilles' power. Even though he never forgot the danger Achilles posed, even Bean had come to think Achilles wasn't such a bad guy, that in fact he was a good leader, doing brave and bold things for his "family" of street urchins. Bean had admired him and learned from him—right up to the moment when Achilles murdered Poke.

Petra, fearing Achilles, submitting to his power, had to watch him closely just to stay alive. And, watching him, she would come to admire him. It's a common trait of primates to become submissive and even worshipful toward one who has the power to kill them.

Even if she fought off those feelings, they would still be there.

But she'll awaken from it, when she's out from under that power. I did. She will. So even if Graff is right, and Petra has become something of a disciple to Achilles, she will turn heretic once I get her out.

Still, the fact remained—he had to be prepared to bring her out even if she resisted rescue or tried to betray them.

He added dartguns and will-bending drugs to his army's arsenal and training.

Naturally, he would need more hard data than he had if he was to mount an operation to rescue her. He wrote to Peter, asking him to use some of his old Demosthenes contacts in the U.S. to get what intelligence data they had on Hyderabad. Beyond that, Bean really had no resources to tap without giving away his location. Because it was a sure thing that he couldn't ask Suriyawong for information about Hyderabad. Even if Suriyawong was feeling favorably disposed— and he *had* been sharing more information with Bean lately—there was no way to explain why he could possibly need information about the Indian high command base at Hyderabad.

Only after days of waiting for Peter, while training his men and himself in the use of darts and drugs, did Bean realize another important implication of discovering that Petra might actually be cooperating with Achilles. Because none of their strategy was geared to the kind of campaign Petra might design.

He requested a meeting with both Suriyawong and the Chakri. After all these months of never seeing the Chakri's face, he was surprised that the meeting was granted—and without delay. He sent his request when he got up at five in the morning. At seven, he was in the Chakri's office, with Suriyawong beside him.

Suriyawong only had time to mouth, with annoyance, the words "What is this?" before the Chakri started the meeting.

"What is this?" said the Chakri. He smiled at Suriyawong; he knew he was echoing Suriyawong's question. But Bean also knew that it was a smile of mockery. You couldn't control this Greek boy after all.

"I just found out information that you both need to know," said Bean. Of course, this implied that Suriyawong might not have recognized the importance of the information, so that Bean had to bring it to Chakri Naresuan directly. "I meant no lack of respect. Only that you must be aware of this immediately."

"What possible information can you have," said Chakri Naresuan, "that we don't already know?"

"Something that I learned from a well-connected friend," said Bean. "All our assumptions were based on the idea of the Indian Army using the obvious strategy—to overwhelm Burmese and Thai defenses with huge armies. But I just learned that Petra Arkanian, one of Ender Wiggin's jeesh, may be working with the Indian Army. I never thought she would collaborate with Achilles, but the possibility exists. And if she's directing the campaign, it won't be a flood of soldiers at all."

"Interesting," said the Chakri. "What strategy would she use?"

"She would still overwhelm you with numbers, but not with massed armies. Instead there would be probing raids, incursions by smaller forces, each one designed to strike, draw your attention, and then fade. They don't even have to retreat. They just live off the land until they can re-form later. Each one is easily beaten, except that there's nothing to beat. By the time we get there, they're gone. No supply lines. No vulnerabilities, just probe after probe until we can't respond to them all. Then the probes start getting bigger. When we get there, with our thinly stretched forces, the enemy is waiting. One of our groups destroyed, then another."

The Chakri looked at Suriyawong. "What Borommakot says is possible," said Suriyawong. "They can keep up such a strategy forever. We never damage them, because they have an infinite supply of troops, and they risk little on each attack. But every loss we suffer is irreplaceable, and every retreat gives them ground."

"So why wouldn't this Achilles think of such a strategy on his own?" asked the Chakri. "He's a very bright boy, they say."

"It's a cautious strategy," said Bean. "One that is very frugal with the lives of the soldiers. And it's slow."

"And Achilles is never careful with the lives of his soldiers?"

Bean thought back to his days in Achilles' "family" on the streets of Rotterdam. Achilles was, in fact, careful of the lives of the other children. He took great pains to make sure they were not exposed to risk. But that was because his power base absolutely depended on losing none of them. If any of the children had been hurt, the others would have melted away. That would not be the case with the Indian Army. Achilles would spend them like autumn leaves.

Except that Achilles' goal was not to rule India. It was to rule the world. So it did matter that he earn a reputation as a beneficent leader. That he seem to value the lives of his people.

"Sometimes he is, when it suits him," said Bean. "That's why he would follow such a plan if Petra outlined it for him."

"So what would it mean," said the Chakri, "if I told you that the attack on Burma has just been launched, and it is a massive frontal assault by huge Indian forces, just as you originally outlined in your first memo to us?"

Bean was stunned. Already? The apparent nonaggression pact between India and Pakistan was only a few days old. They could not possibly have amassed troops that quickly.

Bean was surprised to see that Suriyawong also had been unaware that war had begun.

"It was an extremely well-planned campaign," said the Chakri. "The Burmese only had a day's warning. The Indian troops moved like smoke. Whether it is your evil friend Achilles or your brilliant friend Petra or the mere simpletons of the Indian high command, they managed it superbly."

"What it means," said Bean, "is that Petra is not being listened to. Or that she is deliberately sabotaging the Indian Army's strategy. I'm relieved to know this, and I apologize for raising a warning that was not needed. May I ask, sir, if Thailand is coming into the war now?"

"Burma has not asked for help," said the Chakri.

"By the time Burma asks Thailand for help," said Bean, "the Indian Army will be at our borders."

"At that point," said the Chakri, "we will not wait for them to ask."

"What about China?" asked Bean.

The Chakri blinked twice before answering. "What about China?"

"Have they warned India? Have they responded in any way?"

"Matters with China are handled by a different branch of government," said the Chakri.

"India may have twice the population of China," said Bean, "but the Chinese Army is better equipped. India would think twice before provoking Chinese intervention."

"Better equipped," said the Chakri. "But is it deployed in a usable way? Their troops are kept along the Russian border. It would take weeks to bring them down here. If India plans a lightning strike, they have nothing to fear from China."

"As long as the I.F. keeps missiles from flying," said Suriyawong. "And with Chamrajnagar as Polemarch, you can be sure no missiles will attack India."

"Oh, that's another new development," said the Chakri. "Chamrajnagar submitted his resignation from the I.F. ten minutes after the attack on Burma was launched. He will return to Earth—to India—to accept his new appointment as leader of a coalition government that will guide the newly enlarged Indian empire. For of course, by the time a ship can bring him back to Earth, the war will be over, one way or another."

"Who is the new Polemarch?" asked Bean.

"That is the dilemma," said the Chakri. "There are those who wonder whom the Hegemon can nominate, considering that no one can quite trust anyone now. Some are wondering why the Hegemon should name a Polemarch at all. We've done without a Strategos since the League War. Why do we need the I.F. at all?"

"To keep the missiles from flying," said Suriyawong.

"That is the only serious argument in favor of keeping the I.F.," said the Chakri. "But many governments believe that the I.F. should be reduced to the role of policing above the atmosphere. There is no reason for any but a tiny fraction of the I.F.'s strength to be retained. And as for the colonization program, many are saying it is a waste of money, when war is erupting here on Earth. Well, enough of this little school class. There is grown-up work to be done. You will be consulted if we find that you are needed."

The Chakri's dismissive air was surprising. It revealed a high level of hostility to both of these Battle School graduates, not just the foreign one.

It was Suriyawong who challenged the Chakri on this. "Under what circumstances would we be called upon?" he asked. "Either the plans I drew up will work or they won't. If they work, you won't call on me. If they don't, you'll regard that as proof that I didn't know what I was doing, and you still won't call on me."

The Chakri pondered this for a few moments. "Why, I'd never thought of it that way. I believe you're right."

"No, you're wrong," said Suriyawong. "Nothing ever goes as planned during a war. We have to be able to adapt. I and the other Battle School graduates are trained for that. We should be kept informed of every development. Instead, you have cut me off from the intelligence that is flowing in. I should have seen this information the moment I woke up and looked at my desk. Why are you cutting me off?"

For the same reason you cut *me* off, Bean thought. So that when victory comes, all the credit can flow to the Chakri. "The Battle School children advised in the planning stages, but of course during the actual war, we did not leave it up to the children." And if things went badly, "We faithfully executed the plans drawn up by the Battle School children, but apparently schoolwork did not prepare them for the real world." The Chakri was covering his ass.

Suriyawong seemed to understand this also, for he gave no more argument. He arose. "Permission to leave, sir," he said.

"Granted. To you, too, Borommakot. Oh, and we'll probably be taking back the soldiers Suriyawong gave you to play with. Restoring them to their original units. Please prepare them to leave at once."

Bean also rose to his feet. "So Thailand is entering the war?"

"You will be informed of anything you need to know, when you need to know it."

As soon as they were outside the Chakri's office, Suriyawong sped up his pace. Bean had to run to catch up.

"I don't want to talk to you," said Suriyawong.

"Don't be a big baby about it," said Bean scornfully. "He's only doing to you what you already did to me. Did I run off and pout?"

Suriyawong stopped and whirled on Bean. "You and your stupid meeting!"

"He already cut you off," said Bean. "Already. Before I even asked to meet."

Suriyawong knew that Bean was right. "So I'm stripped of influence."

"And I never had any," said Bean. "What are we going to do about it?"

"Do?" said Suriyawong. "If the Chakri forbids it, no one will obey my orders. Without authority, I'm just a boy, still too young to enlist in the army."

"What we'll do first," said Bean, "is figure out what this all means."

"It means the Chakri is an oomay careerist," said Suriyawong.

"Come, let's walk out of the building."

"They can draw our words out of the open air, too, if they want," said Suriyawong.

"They have to *try* to do that. Here, anything we say is automatically recorded."

So Suriyawong walked with Bean out of the building that housed the highest of the Thai high command, and together they wandered toward the married officers' housing, to a park with playground equipment for the children of junior officers. When they sat on the swings, Bean realized that he was actually getting a little too big for them.

"Your strike force," said Suriyawong. "Just when it might have been most needed, it'll be dispersed."

"No it won't," said Bean.

"And why not?"

"Because you drew it from the garrison protecting the capital. Those troops won't be sent away. So they'll remain in Bangkok. The important thing is to keep all our matériel together and within easy reach. Do you think you still have authority for that?"

"As long as I call it routine cycling into storage," said Suriyawong, "I suppose so."

"And you'll know where these men are assigned, so when we need to, we can call them back to us."

"If I try that, I'll be cut off from the net," said Suriyawong.

"If we try that," said Bean, "it will be because the net doesn't matter."

"Because the war is lost."

"Think about it," said Bean. "Only a stupid careerist would openly disdain you like this. He *wanted* to shame and discourage you. Have you given him some offense?"

"I always give offense," said Suriyawong. "That's

why everyone called me Surly behind my back in Battle School. The only person I know who *is* more arrogant than I *seem* is you."

"Is Naresuan a fool?" asked Bean.

"I had not thought so," said Suriyawong.

"So this is a day for people who are not fools to act like fools."

"Are you saying I am also a fool?"

"I was saying that Achilles is apparently a fool."

"Because he is attacking with massed forces? You told us that was what we should expect. Apparently Petra did not give him the better plan."

"Or he's not using it."

"But he'd have to be a fool not to use it," said Suriyawong.

"So *if* Petra gave him the better plan, and he declined to use it, then he *and* the Chakri are both fools today. As when the Chakri pretended that he has no influence over foreign policy."

"About China, you mean?" Suriyawong thought about this for a moment. "You're right, of course he has influence. But perhaps he simply didn't want us to know what the Chinese were doing. Perhaps that was why he was so sure he didn't need us, that he didn't need to enter Burma. Because he *knows* the Chinese are coming in."

"So," said Bean. "While we sit here, watching the war, we will learn much from the plain events as they unfold. If China intervenes to stop the Indians before Achilles ever gets to Thailand, then we know Chakri Naresuan is a smart careerist, not a stupid one. But if China does not intervene, then we have to wonder why Naresuan, who is not a foolish man, has chosen to act like one."

"What do you suspect him of?" asked Suriyawong.

"As for Achilles," said Bean, "no matter how we construe these events, he has been a fool."

"No, he's only a fool if Petra actually gave him the better plan and he's ignoring it."

"On the contrary," said Bean. "He's a fool no matter what. To enter into this war with even the possibility that China will intervene, that is foolish in the extreme."

"So perhaps he knows that China will not intervene, and then the Chakri would be the only fool," said Suriyawong.

"Let's watch and see."

"I'll watch and grind my teeth," said Suriyawong.

"Watch with me," said Bean. "Let's drop this stupid competition between us. You care about Thailand. I care about figuring out what Achilles is doing and stopping him. At this moment, those two concerns coincide almost perfectly. Let's share everything we know."

"But you know nothing."

"I know nothing that *you* know," said Bean. "And you know nothing that I know."

"What can you possibly know?" said Suriyawong. "I'm the eemo who cut you off from the intelligence net."

"I knew about the deal between India and Pakistan."

"So did we."

"But you didn't tell me," said Bean. "And yet I knew."

Suriyawong nodded. "Even if the sharing is mostly one way, from me to you, it's long overdue, don't you think?"

"I'm not interested in what's early or late," said Bean. "Only what happens next."

They went to the officers' mess and had lunch, then walked back to Suriyawong's building, dismissed his staff for the rest of the day, and, with the building to themselves, sat in Suriyawong's office and watched the progress of the war on Worldnet. Burmese resistance was brave but futile.

"Poland in 1939," said Bean.

"And here in Thailand," said Suriyawong, "we're being as timid as France and England."

"At least China isn't invading Burma from the north, the way Russia invaded Poland from the east," said Bean.

"Small mercies," said Suriyawong.

But Bean wondered. Why *doesn't* China step in? Beijing wasn't saying anything to the press. No comment, about a war on their doorstep? What does China have up its sleeve?

"Maybe Pakistan wasn't the only country to sign a nonaggression pact with India," said Bean.

"Why? What would China gain?" asked Suriyawong.

"Vietnam?" said Bean.

"Worthless, compared to the menace of having India poised with a vast army at the underbelly of China."

Soon, to distract themselves from the news—and from their loss of any kind of influence—they stopped paying attention to the vids and reminisced about Battle School. Neither of them brought up the really bad experiences, only the funny things, the ridiculous things, and they laughed their way into the evening, until it was dark outside.

This afternoon with Suriyawong, now that they were friends, reminded Bean of home—in Crete, with his parents, with Nikolai. He tried to keep from thinking about them most of the time, but now, laughing with Suriyawong, he was filled with a bittersweet longing. He had that one year of something like a normal life, and now it was over. Blown to bits like the house they had been vacationing in. Like the government-protected apartment Graff and Sister Carlotta had taken them away from in the nick of time.

Suddenly a thrill of fear ran through Bean. He knew something, though he could not say how. His mind had made some connection and he didn't understand how, but he had no doubt that he was right.

"Is there any way out of this building that can't be seen from the outside?" asked Bean, in a whisper so faint he could hardly hear himself.

Suriyawong, who had been in the middle of a story about Major Anderson's penchant for nose-picking when he thought nobody was watching, looked at him like he was crazy. "What, you want to play hide-and-seek?"

Bean continued to whisper. "A way out."

Suriyawong took the hint and whispered back. "I don't know. I always use the doors. Like most doors, they're visible from both sides."

"A sewer line? A heating duct?"

"This is Bangkok. We don't have heating ducts."

"*Any* way out."

Suriyawong's whisper changed back to voice. "I'll look at the blueprints. But tomorrow, man, tomorrow. It's getting late and we talked right through dinner."

Bean grabbed his shoulder, forced him to look into his eyes. "Suriyawong," he whispered, even more softly, "I'm not joking. Right now, out of this building unobserved."

Finally Suriyawong got it: Bean was genuinely

afraid. His whisper was quiet again. "Why, what's happening?"

"Just tell me how."

Suriyawong closed his eyes. "Flood drainage," he whispered. "Old ditches. They just laid these temporary buildings down on top of the old parade ground. There's a shallow ditch that runs right under the building. You can hardly tell it's there, but there's a gap."

"Where can we get under the building from inside?"

Suriyawang rolled his eyes. "These temporary buildings are made of lint." To prove his point, he pulled away the corner of the large rug in the middle of the room, rolled it back, and then, quite easily, pried up a floor section.

Underneath it was sod that had died from lack of sunlight. There were no gaps between floor and sod.

"Where's the ditch?" asked Bean.

Suriyawong thought again. "I think it crosses the hall. But the carpet is tacked down there."

Bean turned up the volume of the vid and went out the door of Suriyawong's office and through the anteroom to the hall. He pried up a corner of the carpet and ripped. Carpet fluff flew, and Bean kept pulling until Suriyawong stopped him. "I think about here," he said.

They pulled up another floor section. This time there was a depression in the yellowed sod.

"Can you get through that?" asked Bean.

"Hey, you're the one with the big head," said Suriyawong.

Bean threw himself down. The ground was damp— this *was* Bangkok—and he was clammy and filthy in moments as he wriggled along. Every floor joist was a challenge, and a couple of times he had to dig with his army-issue knife to make way for his head. But he made good progress anyway, and wriggled out into the darkness only a few minutes later. He stayed down, though, and saw that Suriyawong, despite not knowing what was going on, did not raise his head when he emerged from under the building, but continued to creep along just as Bean was doing.

They kept going until they reached the next point where the old eroded ditch went under another temporary building.

"Please tell me we're not going under another building."

Bean looked at the pattern of lights from the moon, from nearby porches and area lights. He had to count on his enemies being at least a little careless. If they were using infrared, this escape was meaningless. But if they were just eyeballing the place, watching the doors, he and Surly were already where slow, easy movement wouldn't be seen.

Bean started to roll himself up the incline.

Suriyawong grabbed him by the boot. Bean looked at him. Suriyawong pantomimed rubbing his cheeks, his forehead, his ears.

Bean had forgotten. His Greek skin was lighter than Suriyawong's. He would catch more light.

He rubbed his face, his ears, his hands with damp soil from under the grass. Suriyawong nodded.

They rolled—at a deliberate pace—up out of the ditch and wriggled slowly along the base of the building until they were around the corner. Here there were bushes to offer some shelter. They stood in the shadows for a moment, then walked, casually, away from the building as if they had just emerged from the door. Bean hoped not to be visible to anyone watching Suriyawong's building, but even if they could be seen, they shouldn't attract any attention, as long as no one noticed that they seemed to be just a little undersized.

Not until they were a quarter mile away did Suriya-wong finally speak. "Do you mind telling me the name of this game?"

"Staying alive," said Bean.

"I never knew paranoid schizophrenia could strike so fast."

"They've tried twice," said Bean. "And they had no qualms about killing my family along with me."

"But we were just talking," said Suriyawong. "What did you see?"

"Nothing."

"Or hear?"

"Nothing," said Bean. "I had a feeling."

"Please don't tell me that you're a psychic."

"No, I'm not. But something about the events of the past few hours must have made some unconscious connection. I listen to my fears. I act on them."

"And this works?"

"I'm still alive," said Bean. "I need a public computer. Can we get off the base?"

"It depends on how all-pervasive this plot against you is," said Suriyawong. "You need a bath, by the way."

"What about some place with ordinary public computer access?"

"Sure, there are visitor facilities near the tram station entrance. But would it be ironic if your assassins were using it?"

"My assassins aren't visitors," said Bean.

This bothered Suriyawong. "You don't even know if anybody's really out to kill you, but you're sure it's somebody in the Thai Army?"

"It's Achilles," said Bean. "And Achilles isn't in Russia. India doesn't have any intelligence service that could carry out an operation like this inside the high command. So it has to be somebody that Achilles has corrupted."

"Nobody here is in the pay of India," said Suriyawong.

"Probably not," said Bean. "But India isn't the only place Achilles has friends by now. He was in Russia for a while. He has to have made other connections."

"It's so hard to take this seriously, Bean," said Suriyawong. "If you suddenly start laughing and say Gotcha that time, I *will* kill you."

"I might be wrong," said Bean, "but I'm not joking."

They got to the visitor facility and found no one using any of the computers. Bean logged on using one of his many false identities and wrote a message to Graff and Sister Carlotta.

```
You know who this is. I believe an at-
tempt is about to be made on my life.
Would you send immediate messages to
contacts within the Thai government,
warning them that such an attempt is
coming and tell them that it involves
conspirators inside the Chakri's inner
circle. No one else could have the ac-
cess. And I believe the Chakri had
prior knowledge. Any Indians suppos-
edly involved are fall guys.
```

"You can't write that," said Suriyawong. "You have no evidence to accuse Naresuan. I'm annoyed with him, but he's a loyal Thai."

"He's a loyal Thai," said Bean, "but you can be loyal and still want me dead."

"But not *me*," said Suriyawong.

"If you want it to look like the evil action of out-siders," said Bean, "then a brave Thai has to die along with me. What if they make our deaths look as if an In-dian strike force did it? That would be provocation for a declaration of war, wouldn't it?"

"The Chakri doesn't need a provocation."

"He does if he wants the Burmese to believe that Thailand isn't just grabbing for a piece of Burma." Bean went back to his note.

```
Please tell them that Suriyawong and I
are alive. We will come out of hiding
when we see Sister Carlotta with at
least one high government official who
Suriyawong would recognize on sight.
Please act immediately. If I am wrong,
you will be embarrassed. If I am right,
you will have saved my life.
```

"I'm sick to my stomach thinking of how humili-ated I'm going to be. Who are these people you're writing to?"

"People I trust. Like you."

Then, before sending the message, he added Peter's "Locke" address to the destination box.

"You know Ender Wiggin's brother?" asked Suriya-wong.

"We've met."

Bean logged off.

"What now?" asked Suriyawong.

"We hide somewhere, I guess," said Bean.

Then they heard an explosion. Windows rattled. The floor trembled. The power flickered. The computers began to reboot.

"Got that done just in time," said Bean.

"Was that it?" asked Suriyawong.

"É," said Bean. "I think we're dead."

"Where do we hide?"

"If they did the deed, it's because they think we were still in there. So they won't be watching for us now. We can go to my barracks. My men will hide me."

"You're willing to bet my life on that?" asked Suriyawong.

"Yes," said Bean. "My track record of keeping you alive is pretty good so far."

As they walked out of the building, they saw military vehicles rushing toward where gray smoke was billowing up into the moonlit night. Others were heading for the entrances to the base. No one would be getting in or out.

By the time they reached the barracks where Bean's strike force was quartered, they could hear bursts of gunfire. "Now they're killing all the fake Indian spies this will be blamed on," said Bean. "The Chakri will regretfully inform the government that they all resisted capture and none were taken alive."

"Again you accuse him," said Suriyawong. "Why? How did you know this would happen?"

"I think I knew because there were too many smart people acting stupidly," said Bean. "Achilles *and* the Chakri. And he treated us angrily. Why? Because killing us bothered him. So he had to convince himself that we were disloyal children who had been corrupted by the I.F. We were a danger to Thailand. Once he hated us and feared us, killing us was justified."

"That's a long stretch from there to knowing they were about to kill us."

"They were probably set to do it at my quarters. But I stayed with you. It was quite possible they were planning for another opportunity—the Chakri would summon us to meet him somewhere, and we'd be killed instead. But when we stayed for hours and hours in your quarters, they realized *this* was the perfect opportunity. They had to check with the Chakri and get his consent to do it ahead of schedule. They probably had to rush to get the Indian stooges into place—they might even be genuine captured spies. Or they might be drugged Thai criminals who will have incriminating documents found on them."

"I don't care who they are," said Suriyawong. "I still don't understand how you knew."

"Neither do I," said Bean. "Most of the time, I analyze things very quickly and understand exactly why I know what I know. But sometimes my unconscious mind runs ahead of my conscious mind. It happened that way in the last battle, with Ender. We were doomed to defeat. I couldn't see a solution. And yet I said something, an ironic statement, a bitter joke—and it contained within it exactly the solution Ender needed. From then on, I've been trying to heed those unconscious processes that give me answers. I've thought back over my life and seen other times when I said things that were not really justified by my conscious analysis. Like the time when we stood over Achilles as he lay on the ground, and I told Poke to kill him. She wouldn't do it, and I couldn't persuade her, because I truly didn't understand why. Yet I understood what he was. I knew he had to die, or he would kill her."

"You know what I think?" said Suriyawong. "I think you heard something outside. Or noticed something subliminally on the way in. Somebody watching. And that's what triggered you."

Bean could only shrug. "You may well be right. As I said, I don't know."

It was after hours, but Bean could still palm his way through the locks to get in without setting off alarms. They hadn't bothered to deauthorize him. His entry into the building would show up on a computer somewhere, but it was a drone program and by the time any human looked at it, Bean's friends should have things well in motion.

Bean was glad to see that even though his men were in their home barracks on the grounds of the Thai high command base, they had not slacked in their discipline. No sooner were they inside the door than both Bean and Suriyawong were seized and pressed against the wall while they were checked for weapons.

"Good work," said Bean.

"Sir!" said the surprised soldier.

"And Suriyawong," said Bean.

"Sir!" said both the sentries.

A few others had been wakened by the scuffle.

"No lights," Bean said quickly. "And no loud talking. Weapons loaded. Prepare to move out on a moment's notice."

"Move out?" said Suriyawong.

"If they realize we're in here and decide to finish the job," said Bean, "this place is indefensible."

While some soldiers quietly woke the sleepers and all were busy dressing and loading their weapons, Bean had one of the sentries lead them to a computer. "You sign on," he said to the soldier.

As soon as he had logged on, Bean took his place and wrote, using the soldier's identity, to Graff, Carlotta, and Peter.

```
Both packages safe and awaiting pickup.
Please come right away before packages
are returned to sender.
```

Bean sent out one toon, divided into four pairs, to reconnoiter. When each pair returned another pair from another toon replaced them. Bean wanted to have enough warning to get these men out of the barracks before any kind of assault could be mounted.

In the meanwhile, they turned on a vid and watched the news. Sure enough, here came the first report. Indian agents had apparently penetrated the Thai command base and blown up a temporary building, killing Suriyawong, Thailand's most distinguished Battle School graduate, who had headed military doctrine and strategic planning for the past year and a half, since returning from space. It was a great national tragedy. There was no confirmation yet, but preliminary reports indicated that some of the Indian agents had been killed by the heroic soldiers defending Suriyawong. A visiting Battle School graduate had also been killed.

Some of Bean's soldiers chuckled, but soon enough they were all grim-faced. The fact that the reporters had been told Bean and Suriyawong were dead meant that whoever made the report believed they were both inside the offices at an hour when the only way anyone could know that was if the bodies had been found, or the building had been under observation. Since the bodies had obviously not been found, whoever was writing the official reports from the Chakri's office must have been part of the plot.

"I can understand someone wanting to kill Borommakot," said Suriyawong. "But why would anyone want to kill *me*?"

The soldiers laughed. Bean smiled.

Patrols returned and went out, again, again. No movement toward the barracks. The news carried the initial response from various commentators. India apparently wanted to cripple the Thai military by eliminating the nation's finest military mind. This was intolerable. The government would have no choice now but to declare war and join Burma in the struggle against Indian aggression.

Then new information came. The Prime Minister had declared that he would take personal control of this disaster. Someone in the military had obviously slipped badly to allow a foreign penetration of the high command's own base. Therefore, to protect the Chakri's reputation and make sure there was no hint of a cover-up of military errors, Bangkok city police would be supervising the investigation, and Bangkok city fire officials would investigate the wreckage of the exploded building.

"Good job," said Suriyawong. "The Prime Minister's cover story is strong and the Chakri won't resist letting police onto the base."

"If the fire investigators arrive soon enough," said Bean, "they might even prevent the Chakri's men from entering the building as soon as it cools enough from the fire. So they won't even know we weren't there."

Sirens moving through the base announced the arrival of the police and fire department. Bean kept waiting for the sound of gunfire. But it never came.

Instead, two of the patrols came rushing back.

"Someone is coming, but not soldiers. Bangkok police, sixteen of them, with a civilian."

"Just one?" asked Bean. "Is one of them a woman?"

"Not a woman, and just one. I believe, sir, that it is the Prime Minister himself."

Bean sent out more patrols to see if any military forces were within range.

"How did they know we were here?" asked Suriyawong.

"Once they took control of the Chakri's office," said Bean, "they could use the military personnel files to find out that the soldier who sent that last email was in this barracks when he sent it."

"So it's safe to come out?"

"Not yet," said Bean.

A patrol returned. "The Prime Minister wishes to enter this barracks alone, sir."

"Please," said Bean. "Invite him in."

"So you're sure he's not wired up with explosives to kill us all?" asked Suriyawong. "I mean, your paranoia has kept us alive so far."

As if in answer, the vid showed Chakri driving away from the main entrance to the base, under police escort. The reporter was explaining that Naresuan had resigned as Chakri, but the Prime Minister insisted that he merely take a leave of absence. In the meantime, the Minister of Defense was taking direct personal control of the Chakri's office, and generals from the field were being brought in to staff other positions of trust. Until then, the police had control of the command system. "Until we know how these Indian agents penetrated our most sensitive base," the Minister of Defense said, "we cannot be sure of our security."

The Prime Minister entered the barracks.

"Suriyawong," he said. He bowed deeply.

"Mr. Prime Minister," said Suriyawong, bowing noticeably less deeply. Ah, the vanity of a Battle School graduate, thought Bean.

"A certain nun is flying here as quickly as she can," said the Prime Minister, "but we hoped that you might trust me enough to come out without waiting for her arrival. She was on the opposite side of the world, you see."

Bean strode forward and spoke in his not-bad Thai. "Sir," he said, "I believe Suriyawong and I are safer here with these loyal troops than we would be anywhere else in Bangkok."

The Prime Minister looked at the soldiers standing, fully armed, at attention. "So someone has a private army right in the middle of this base," he said.

"I did not make my meaning clear," said Bean. "These soldiers are absolutely loyal to *you*. They are yours to command, because you are Thailand at this moment, sir."

The Prime Minister bowed, very slightly, and turned to the soldiers. "Then I order you to arrest this foreigner."

Immediately Bean's arms were gripped by the soldiers nearest to him, as another soldier patted him down for weapons.

Suriyawong's eyes widened, but he gave no other sign of surprise.

The Prime Minister smiled. "You may release him now," he said. "The Chakri warned me, before he took his voluntary leave of absence, that these soldiers had been corrupted and were no longer loyal to Thailand. I see now that he was misinformed. And since that is the case, I believe you are right. You are safer here, under their protection, until we explore the limits of the con-

spiracy. In fact, I would appreciate it if I could depu-
tize a hundred of your men to serve with my police
force as it takes control of this base."

"I urge you to take all but eight of them," said Bean.

"Which eight?" asked the Prime Minister.

"Any of these toons of eight, sir, could stand for a
day against the Indian Army."

This was, of course, absurd, but it had a fine ring to
it, and the men loved hearing him say it.

"Then, Suriyawong," said the Prime Minister, "I
would appreciate your taking command of all but eight
of these men and leading them in taking control of this
base in my name. I will assign one policeman to each
group, so that they can clearly be identified as acting
under my authority. And one group of eight will, of
course, remain with you for your protection at all
times."

"Yes sir," said Suriyawong.

"I remember saying in my last campaign," said the
Prime Minister, "that the children of Thailand held the
keys to our national survival. I had no idea at the time
how literally and how quickly that would be fulfilled."

"When Sister Carlotta arrives," said Bean, "you can
tell her that she is no longer needed, but I would be
glad to see her if she has the time."

"I'll tell her that," said the Prime Minister. "Now
let's get to work. We have a long night ahead of us."

Everyone was quite solemn as Suriyawong called
out the toon leaders. Bean was impressed that he knew
who they were by name and face. Suriyawong might
not have sought out Bean's company very much, but
he had done an excellent job of keeping track of what
Bean was doing. Only when everyone had moved out
on their assignments, each toon with its own cop like a

battle flag, did Suriyawong and the Prime Minister allow themselves to smile. "Good work," said the Prime Minister.

"Thank you for believing our message," said Bean.

"I wasn't sure I could believe Locke," said the Prime Minister, "and the Hegemon's Minister of Colonization is, after all, just a politician now. But when the Pope telephoned me personally, I had no choice but to believe. Now I must go out and tell the people the absolute truth about what happened here."

"That Indian agents did indeed attempt to kill me and an unnamed foreign visitor," asked Suriyawong, "but we survived because of quick action by heroic soldiers of the Thai Army? Or did the unnamed foreign visitor die?"

"I fear that he died," Bean suggested. "Blown to bits in the explosion."

"In any event," said Suriyawong, "you will assure the people, the enemies of Thailand have learned tonight that the Thai military may be challenged, but we cannot be defeated."

"I'm glad you were trained for the military, Suriyawong," said the Prime Minister. "I would not want to face you as an opponent in a political campaign."

"It is unthinkable that we would be opponents," said Suriyawong, "since we could not possibly disagree on any subject."

Everyone got the irony, but no one laughed. Suriyawong left with the Prime Minister and eight soldiers. Bean remained in the barracks with the last toon, and together they watched as the lies unfolded on the vid.

And as the news droned on, Bean thought of Achilles. Somehow he had found out Bean was alive—but that would be the Chakri, of course. But if the Chakri had turned to Achilles' side, why was he

spinning the story of Suriyawong's death as a pretext
for war with India? It made no sense. Having Thailand
in the war from the beginning could only work against
India. Add that to India's use of the clunky, obvious,
life-wasting strategy of mass attack, and it began to
look as though Achilles were some kind of idiot.

He was not an idiot. Therefore he was playing some
sort of deeper game, and despite the much-vaunted
cleverness of his unconscious mind, Bean did not yet
know what it was. And Achilles would know soon
enough, if he did not know already, that Bean was not
dead.

He's in a killing mood, thought Bean.

Petra, thought Bean. Help me find a way to save you.

14

Hyderabad

Posted on the International Politics
Forum by EnsiRaknor@TurkMilNet.gov
Topic: Where is Locke when we need him?

Am I the only one who wishes we had
Locke's take on the recent developments
in India? With India across the Burmese
border and Pakistani troops massing in
Baluchistan, threatening Iran and the
gulf, we need a new way of looking at
south Asia. The old models clearly
don't work.

What I want to know is, did IntPolFor
drop Locke's column when Peter Wiggin
came forward as the author, or did Wiggin resign? Because if it was IPF's decision, it was, to put it bluntly, a

stupid one. We never knew who Locke was—we listened to him because he made sense, and time after time he was the only one who made sense out of problematical situations, or at least was the first to see clearly what was going on. What does it matter if he's a teenager, an embryo, or a talking pig?

For that matter, as the Hegemon's term is near expiration, I am more and more uneasy with the current Hegemon-designate. Whoever suggested Locke almost a year ago had the right idea. Only now let's put him in office under his own name. What Ender Wiggin did in the Formic War, Peter Wiggin might be able to do in the conflagration that looms—put an end to it.

Reply 14, by Talleyrandophile@polnet.gov

I don't mean to be suspicious, but how do we know you're not Peter Wiggin, trying to put his name into play again?

Reply 14.1, by EnsiRaknor@TurkMilNet.gov

I don't mean to get personal, but Turkish Military Network IDs aren't given out to American teenagers doing consultation work in Haiti. I realize that international politics can make paranoids seem sane, but if Peter Wiggin could write under this ID, he must al-

ready run the world. But perhaps who I
am does make a difference. I'm in my
twenties now, but I'm a Battle School
grad. So maybe that's why the idea of
putting a kid in charge of things
doesn't sound so crazy to me.

Virlomi knew who Petra was the moment she first
showed up in Hyderabad—they had met before. Even
though she was considerably older, so her time in Battle School overlapped Petra's by only a year, in those
days Virlomi took notice of every girl in the place. An
easy task, since Petra's arrival brought the total number
of girls to nine—five of whom graduated at the same
time as Virlomi. It seemed as though having girls in the
school were regarded as an experiment that had failed.

Back in Battle School, Petra had been a tough
launchy with a smart mouth, who proudly refused all
offers of advice. She seemed determined to make it as
a girl among boys, meeting the same standards, taking
their guff without help. Virlomi understood. She had
had the same attitude herself, at first. She just hoped
that Petra would not have to have such painful experiences as those Virlomi had had before finally realizing
that the hostility of boys was, in most cases, insuperable, and a girl needed all the friends she could get.

Petra was memorable enough that of course Virlomi
recognized her name when the stories of Ender's jeesh
came out after the war. The one girl among them, the
Armenian Joan of Arc. Virlomi read the articles and
smiled. So Petra had been as tough as she thought
she'd be. Good for her.

Then Ender's jeesh was kidnapped or killed, and
when the kidnapped ones were returned from Russia,

Virlomi was heartsick to see that the only one whose fate remained unknown was Petra Arkanian.

Only she didn't have long to grieve. For suddenly the team of Indian Battle School graduates had a new commander, whom they immediately recognized as the same Achilles that Locke had accused of being a psychopathic killer. And soon they found that he was frequently shadowed by a silent, tired-looking girl whose name was never spoken.

But Virlomi knew her. Petra Arkanian.

Whatever Achilles' motive in keeping her name to himself, Virlomi didn't like it and so she made sure that everyone on the strategy team knew that this was the missing member of Ender's jeesh. They said nothing about Petra to Achilles, of course—merely responded to his instructions and reported to him as required. And soon enough Petra's silent presence was treated as if it were ordinary. The others hadn't known her.

But Virlomi knew that if Petra was silent, it meant something quite dreadful. It meant Achilles had some hold over her. A hostage—some kidnapped family member? Threats? Or something else? Had Achilles somehow overmastered Petra's will, which had once seemed so indomitable?

Virlomi took great pains to make sure that Achilles did not notice her paying special attention to Petra. But she watched the younger girl, learning all she could. Petra used her desk as the others did, and took part in reading intelligence reports and everything else that was sent to all of them. But something was wrong, and it took a while for Virlomi to realize what it was—Petra never typed anything at all while she was logged on to the system. There were a lot of netsites that required passwords or at least registration to sign on. But after typing her password to simply log on in the morning, Petra never typed again.

She's been blocked, Virlomi realized. That's why she never emails any of us. She's a prisoner here. She can't pass messages outside. And she doesn't talk to any of us because she's been forbidden to.

When she wasn't logged on, though, she must have been working furiously, because now and then Achilles would send a message to all of them, detailing new directions their planning should go. The language in these messages was not Achilles'—it was easy to spot the shift in style. He was getting these strategic insights—and they were good ones—from Petra, who was one of the nine who were chosen to save humanity from the Formics. One of the finest minds on Earth. And she was enslaved by this psychopathic Belgian.

So, while the others admired the brilliant strategies they were developing for aggressive war against Burma and Thailand, as Achilles' memos whipped up their enthusiasm for "India finally rising to take her rightful place among the nations," Virlomi grew more and more skeptical. Achilles cared nothing for India, no matter how good his rhetoric sounded. And when she found herself tempted to believe in him, she had only to look at Petra to remember what he was.

Because the others all seemed to buy into Achilles' version of India's future, Virlomi kept her opinions to herself. And she watched and waited for Petra to look at her, so she could give her a wink or a smile.

The day came. Petra looked. Virlomi smiled.

Petra looked away as casually as if Virlomi had been a chair and not a person trying to make contact.

Virlomi was not discouraged. She kept trying for eye contact until finally one day Petra passed near her on the way to a water fountain and slipped and caught herself on Virlomi's chair. In the midst of the noise of Petra's scuffling feet, Virlomi clearly heard her words: "Stop it. He's watching."

And that was it. Confirmation of what Virlomi had suspected about Achilles, proof that Petra had noticed her, and a warning that her help was not needed.

Well, that was nothing new. Petra never needed help, did she?

Then came the day, only a month ago, when Achilles sent a memo around ordering that they needed to update the old plans—the original strategy of mass assault, throwing huge armies with their huge supply lines against the Burmese. They were all stunned. Achilles gave no explanation, but he seemed unusually taciturn, and they all got the message. The brilliant strategy had been set aside by the adults. Some of the finest military minds in the world had come up with the strategy, and the adults were going to ignore them.

Everyone was outraged, but they soon settled back into the routine of work, trying to get the old plans into shape for the coming war. Troops had moved, supplies had been replenished in one area or fallen short in another. But they worked out the logistics. And when they received Achilles'—or, as Virlomi assumed, Petra's—plan for moving the bulk of the army from the Pakistani border to face the Burmese, they admired the brilliance of it, fitting the needs of the army into the existing rail and air traffic so that from satellites, no unusual movements would be visible until suddenly the armies were on the border, forming up. At most the enemy would have two days' notice; if they were careless, only a single day before it became obvious.

Achilles left on one of his frequent trips, only this

time Petra disappeared too. Virlomi feared for her. Had
she served her purpose, and now that he was done with
her, would he kill her?

But no. She came back the same night, when
Achilles did.

And the next morning, word came to begin the
movement of troops. Following Petra's deft plan to get
them to the Burmese border. And then, ignoring Petra's equally deft plan, they would launch their clumsy
mass attack.

It makes no sense, thought Virlomi.

Then she got the email from the Hegemony Minister of Colonization—Colonel Graff, that old sabeek.

```
I'm sure you're aware that one of our
Battle School graduates, Petra Arkan-
ian, was not returned with the others
who took part with Ender Wiggin in the
final battle. I am very interested in
locating her, and believe she may have
been transported against her will to a
place within the borders of India. If
you know anything about her whereabouts
and present condition, could you let
someone know? I'm sure you'd want some-
one to do the same for you.
```

Almost immediately there came an e-mail from
Achilles.

```
I'm sure you understand that because
this is wartime, any attempt to convey
information to someone outside the In-
dian military will be regarded as espi-
```

onage and treason, and you will be
killed forthwith.

So Achilles was definitely keeping Petra incommunicado, and cared very much that she remain hidden to outsiders.

Virlomi did not even have to think about what she would do. This had nothing to do with Indian military security. So, while she took his death threat seriously, she did not believe there was anything morally wrong with attempting to circumvent it.

She could not write directly to Colonel Graff. Nor could she send any kind of message containing any reference, however oblique, to Petra. Any email going out from Hyderabad was going to be scrutinized. And, now that Virlomi thought about it, she and the other Battle School graduates ensconced here in the Planning and Doctrine Division were only slightly more free than Petra. She could not leave the grounds. She could not have contact with anyone who was not military with a high-level security clearance.

Spies have radio equipment or dead drops, thought Virlomi. But how do you go about becoming a spy when you have no way to reach outside but writing letters, yet there's no one you can write a letter to and no way to say what you need to say without getting caught?

She might have thought of a solution on her own. But Petra simplified the process for her by coming up behind her at the drinking fountain. As Virlomi straightened up from drinking and Petra slipped in to take her place, Petra said, "I am Briseis."

And that was all.

The reference was obvious—everyone in Battle

School knew the Iliad. And with Achilles being their overseer at the moment, the Briseis reference was obvious. And yet it was not. Briseis had been held by someone else, and Achilles—the original one—had been furious because he felt slighted that he didn't have her. So what could she mean by saying she was Briseis?

It had to do with the letter from Graff and Achilles' warning. So it must be a key, a way to get word out about Petra. And to get word out required the net. So *Briseis* must mean something to someone out on the net. Perhaps there was some kind of coded electronic dead drop, keyed on the name Briseis. Perhaps Petra had already found someone to contact, but could not do it because she was cut off from the nets.

Virlomi didn't bother doing a general search. If someone out there was looking for Petra, the message would have to be at a site that Petra would be able to find without deviating from legitimate military research. Which meant that Virlomi probably already knew the site where the message was waiting.

The problem she was officially working on at the moment was to determine the most efficient way to minimize risk to supply helicopters while not consuming too much fuel. The problem was so technical that there was no way she could explain doing historical or theoretical research.

But Sayagi, a Battle School graduate five years her senior, was working on problems of pacifying and winning the allegiance of local populations in occupied countries. So Virlomi went to him. "I've gone greeyaz on my algorithms."

"You want my help?" he asked.

"No, no, I just need to set it aside for a couple of

hours so I can come back to it fresh. Anything I can help you look for?"

Of course Sayagi had received the same messages as Virlomi, and he was sharp enough not to take Virlomi's offer at face value.

"I don't know, what kind of thing could you do?"

"Any historical research? Or theoretical? On the nets?" She was tipping him to what she needed. And he understood.

"Toguro. I hate that stuff. I need data on failed approaches to pacification and conciliation. Besides killing or deporting everybody and moving in a new population."

"What do you already have?"

"You're wide open, I've been avoiding it."

"Thanks. You want a report or just links?"

"Paste-ups are enough. No links, though. That's too much like doing the work myself."

A perfectly innocent exchange. Virlomi had her cover now.

She went back to her desk and began browsing the historical and theoretical sites. She never actually ran a search on the name "Briseis"—that would be too obvious, the monitoring software would pick that right up and Achilles, if he saw it, would make the connection. Instead, Virlomi browsed through the sites, looking at subject headings.

Briseis showed up on the second site she tried.

It was a posting from someone calling himself HectorVictorious. Hector was not exactly an auspicious name—he was a hero, and the only person who was any kind of match for Achilles, but in the end Hector was killed and Achilles dragged his corpse around the walls of Troy.

Still, the message was clear, if you knew to think of Briseis as a codename for Petra.

Virlomi worked her way through several other postings, pretending to read them while actually composing her reply to HectorVictorious. When she was ready, she went back and typed it in, knowing as she did it that it might well be the cause of her own immediate execution.

```
I vote for her remaining a resistant
slave. Even if she was forced into si-
lence, she would find a way to hold on
to her soul. As for slipping a message
to someone inside Troy, how do you know
she didn't? And what good would it have
done? It wasn't that long afterward
that everyone in Troy was dead. Or
didn't you ever hear of the Trojan
horse? I know—Briseis should have
warned the Trojans to beware of Greeks
bearing gifts. Or found a friendly na-
tive to do it for her.
```

She signed it with her own name and email address. After all, this was supposed to be a perfectly innocent posting. Indeed, she worried that it might be *too* innocent. What if the person who was looking for Petra didn't realize that her references to Briseis resisting and being forced into silence were actually eyewitness reports? Or that the "friendly native" reference was to Virlomi herself?

But her address inside the Indian military network should alert whoever this was to pay special attention.

Now, of course, with the message posted, Virlomi

had to continue going through the motions of doing the useless research that Sayagi had "asked" her to do. It would be a couple of tedious hours—wasted time, if no one got the message.

———

Petra tried not to be obvious about watching what Virlomi was doing. After all, if Virlomi was as smart as she needed to be in order to bring this off, she wouldn't do anything that was worth watching. But Petra saw when Virlomi went over to Sayagi and talked for a while. And Petra noticed that Virlomi seemed to be browsing when she got back to her desk, mousing through online pages instead of writing or calculating. Was she going to spot those Hector Victorious postings?

Either she would or she wouldn't. Petra couldn't allow herself to think about it anymore. Because in a way it would be better for everyone if Virlomi simply didn't get it. Who knew how subtle Achilles was? For all Petra knew, those postings might be traps designed to catch her getting someone else to help her. That could be fatal all the way around.

But Achilles couldn't be everywhere. He was bright, he was suspicious, he played a deep game. But he was only one person and he couldn't think of everything. Besides, how important was Petra to him, really? He hadn't even used her campaign strategy. Surely he kept her around as a vanity, nothing more.

The reports coming back from the front were just what one might expect—Burmese resistance was only token, since they were massing their main forces in places where the terrain favored them. Canyons. River crossings.

All futile, of course. No matter where the Burmese made their stand, the Indian Army would simply flow around them. There weren't enough Burmese soldiers to make serious efforts at more than a handful of places, while there were so many Indians that they could press forward at every point, leaving only enough men at the Burmese strong points to keep them pinned down while the bulk of the Indian Army completed the takeover of Burma and moved on toward the mountain passes into Thailand.

That's where the challenge would begin, of course. For Indian supply lines would stretch all the way across Burma by then, and the Thai Air Force was formidable, especially since they had been observed testing a new temporary airfield system that could be built in many cases during the time a bomber was airborne. Not really worth it, bombing airfields when they could be replaced in two or three hours.

So even though the intelligence reports from inside Thailand were very good—detailed, accurate, and recent—on the most important points they didn't matter. There were few meaningful targets, given the strategy the Thai were using.

Petra knew Suriyawong, the Battle School grad who was running strategy and doctrine in Bangkok. He was good. But to Petra it looked a little suspicious that the new Thai strategy began, abruptly, only a few weeks after Petra and Achilles arrived in India from Russia. Suriyawong had already been in place in Bangkok for a year. Why the sudden change? It might be that someone had tipped them off about Achilles' presence in Hyderabad and what that might mean. Or it might be that someone else had joined Suriyawong and influenced his thinking.

Bean.

Petra refused to believe that he was dead. Those messages had to be from him. And even though Suriyawong was perfectly capable of thinking of the new Thai strategy himself, it was such a comprehensive set of changes, without any sign of gradual development, that it cried out for the obvious explanation—it came from a fresh set of eyes. Who else but Bean?

The trouble was, if it *was* Bean, Achilles' intelligence sources inside Thailand were so good that it was quite possible Bean would be spotted. And if Achilles' earlier attempt to kill Bean had failed, there was no chance that Achilles would refrain from trying again.

She couldn't think about that. If he had saved himself once, he could do it again. After all, maybe someone had excellent intelligence sources inside India, too.

And it might not be Bean leaving those Briseis messages. It might be Dink Meeker, for instance. Only that really wasn't Dink's style. Bean had always been something of a sneak. Dink was confrontational. He would go on the nets proclaiming that he knew Petra was in Hyderabad and demanding that she be released at once. Bean was the one who had figured out that the Battle School kept track of where students were by monitoring transmitters in their clothing. Take off all your clothes and go around buck naked, and the Battle School administrators wouldn't have a clue where you were. Not only had Bean thought of it, he had done it, climbing around in airshafts in the middle of the night. When he told her about it, as they waited around on Eros for the League War to settle down so they could go home, Petra hadn't really believed him at first. Not until he looked her coldly in the eye and said, "I don't joke, and if I did, this isn't particularly funny."

"I didn't think you were joking," said Petra. "I thought you were bragging."

"I was," said Bean. "But I wouldn't waste my time bragging about things I hadn't actually done."

That was Bean—admitting his faults right along with his virtues. No false modesty, and no vanity, either. If he bothered to talk to you at all, he never shaped his words to make himself look better or worse than he was.

She hadn't really known him in Battle School. How could she? She was older, and even though she noticed him and spoke to him a few times—she always made a point of speaking to new kids who were getting the pariah treatment, since she knew they needed friends, even if it was only a girl—she simply hadn't had much reason to talk to him.

And then there was the disastrous time when Petra had been suckered into trying to give Ender a warning—which turned out to be bogus, and in fact Ender's enemies were using Petra's attempt to warn Ender as the opportunity to jump him and beat him up. Bean was the one who saw through it and broke it up. And, quite naturally, he leapt to the conclusion that Petra was part of the conspiracy against Ender. He had continued to suspect her for quite a while. Petra wasn't really sure when he finally believed in her innocence. But it had been a barrier between them for a long time on Eros. So it wasn't until after the war ended that they even had a chance to get to know each other.

That was when Petra realized what Bean really was. It was hard to see past his small size and think of him as anything other than a preschooler or launchy or something. Even though everyone knew that he was the one that would have been chosen to take Ender's place, if Ender had broken under the strain of battle. A lot of them resented the fact. But Petra didn't. She knew Bean was the best of Ender's jeesh. It didn't bother her.

What was Bean, really? A dwarf. That's what she had to realize. With adult dwarfs, you could see in their faces that they were older than their size would indicate. But because Bean was still a child, and had none of the short-limbed deformations of dwarfism, he looked like the age his size implied. If you talked to him like a child, though, he tuned you out. Petra never had done that, so except when he thought she was a traitor to Ender, Bean always treated her with respect.

The funny thing was, it was all based on a misunderstanding. Bean thought Petra talked to him like a regular human being because she was so mature and wise that she didn't treat him like a little kid. But the truth was, she *did* treat him exactly the way she treated little kids. It's just that she always treated little kids like adults. So she got credit for being understanding, when in fact she was just lucky.

By the time the war was over, though, it didn't matter. They knew they were going home—all of them, it turned out, but Ender—and once they got back to Earth, they expected they wouldn't see each other again. So there was a kind of freedom, caution tossed to the wind. You could say what you wanted. You didn't have to take offense at anything because it wouldn't matter in a few months. It was the first time they could actually have fun.

And the person Petra enjoyed the most was Bean.

Dink, who had been close to Petra for a while in Battle School, was a little miffed by the way Petra was always with Bean. He even accused her—obliquely, because he didn't want to get frozen out completely— of having something romantic going on with Bean.

Well, of course he thought that way—puberty had already struck Dink Meeker, and like all boys that age, he thought everybody's mental processes were infused with testosterone.

It was something else, though, between Petra and Bean. Not brother and sister, either. Not mother-son or any other weird psychofake analogy she could think of. She just . . . liked him. She had spent so long having to prove to prickly, envious, and frightened boys that she was, in fact, smarter and better at everything than they were, that it took her quite by surprise to be with someone so arrogant, so absolutely sure of his own brilliance, that he didn't feel at all threatened by her. If she knew something that he didn't know, he listened, he watched, he learned. The only other person she'd known who was like that with her was Ender.

Ender. She missed him terribly sometimes. She had tutored him—and taken a lot of heat from Bonzo Madrid, their commander at the time, for doing it. And as it became clear what Ender was, and she joined gladly with those who followed him, obeyed him, gave themselves to him, she nevertheless had a secret place in her memory where she kept the knowledge that she had been Ender's friend at a time when no one else had the courage. She had made a difference in his life, and even when others thought she had betrayed him, Ender never thought that.

She loved Ender with a helpless mixture of worship and longing that led to foolish dreams of impossible futures, tying her life with his until they died. She fantasized about raising children together, the most brilliant children in the world. About being able to stand beside the greatest human being in the world—for so she thought he was—and having everybody recognize that he had chosen her to stand with him forever.

Dreams. After the war, Ender was beaten down. Broken. Finding out that he had actually caused the extermination of the Formics was more than he could bear. And because she, too, had broken during the war, her shame kept her away from him until it was too late, until they had divided Ender from the rest of them.

Which is why she knew that her feelings toward Bean were completely different. No such dreams and fantasies. Just a sense of complete acceptance. She belonged with Bean, not the way a wife belonged with a husband or, God forbid, a girlfriend with a boyfriend, but rather the way a left hand belonged with the right. They simply fit. Nothing exciting about it, nothing to write home about. But it could be counted on. She imagined that, of all the Battle School kids, of all the members of Ender's jeesh, it would be Bean that she would remain close to.

Then they got off the shuttle and were dispersed throughout the world. And even though Armenia and Greece were relatively close together—compared to, say, Shen in Japan or Hot Soup in China—they never saw each other, they never even wrote. She knew that Bean was going home to meet a family that he had never known, and she was busy trying to get involved with her own family again. She didn't exactly pine for him, or he for her. And besides, they didn't need to hang out together or chat all the time for her to know that, left hand with right hand, they were still friends, still belonged together. That when she needed someone, the first person she should call on was Bean.

In a world that didn't have Ender Wiggin in it, that

meant he was the person she loved most. That she would miss most if anything happened to him.

Which is why she could pretend that she wasn't going to worry about Bean getting folded by Achilles, but it wasn't true. She worried all the time. Of course, she worried about herself, too—and maybe a little more about herself than about him. But she'd already lost one love in her life, and even though she told herself that these childhood friendships wouldn't matter in twenty years, she didn't want to lose the other.

Her desk beeped at her.

There was a message in the display.

```
When did I designate this as naptime?
Come see me.
```

Only Achilles wrote with such peremptory rudeness. She hadn't been napping. She had been thinking. But it wasn't worth arguing with him about it.

She logged off and got up from her desk.

It was evening, getting dark outside. Her mind really had wandered. Most of the others on the day shift in Planning and Doctrine had already left, and the night response team was coming in. A couple of the day shift were still at their desks, though.

She caught a glance from Virlomi, one of the late ones. The girl looked worried. That meant she probably *had* done something in response to the Briseis posting, and now feared repercussions. Well, she was right to worry. Who knew how Achilles would speak or write or act if he was planning to kill somebody? Petra's personal opinion was that he was always planning to kill someone, so there was no difference in his behavior to warn you if you were next. Go home and try to get some sleep, Virlomi. Even if Achilles has caught you trying to help me and has decided to have you killed, you won't be able to do anything about it, so you might as well sleep the sleep of a child.

Petra left the big barn of a room they all worked in and moved through the corridors as if in a trance. Had she been asleep when Achilles wrote to her? Who cared.

As far as Petra knew, she was the only one in Planning and Doctrine who even knew where Achilles' office was. She had been in it often, but was not impressed by the privilege. She had the freedom of a slave or a captive. Achilles let her intrude on his privacy because he didn't think of her as a person.

One wall of his office was a 2D computer display, now showing a detailed map of the India-Burma border region. As reports came in from troops in the field and from satellites, it was updated by clerks, so Achilles could glance at it any time and see the best available intelligence on placement. Apart from that, the room was spartan. Two chairs—not comfortable ones—a table, a bookcase, and a cot. Petra suspected that somewhere on the base there was a comfortable suite of rooms with a soft bed that was never used. Whatever else Achilles was, he wasn't a hedonist. He never cared much about personal comfort, not that she had seen, anyway.

He didn't take his eyes off the map when she came in—but she was used to that. When he made a point of ignoring her, she took it as his perverse way of paying attention to her. It was when he looked right at her without seeing her that she felt truly invisible.

"The campaign's going very well," said Achilles.

"It's a stupid plan, and the Thai are going to cut it to shreds."

"They had a sort of coup a few minutes ago," said

Achilles. "The commander of the Thai military blew up young Suriyawong. Terrible case of professional jealousy, apparently."

Petra tried to keep from showing her sadness at Suriyawong's death and her disgust at Achilles. "You're not seriously expecting me to believe you had nothing to do with it?"

"Well, *they're* blaming it on Indian spies, of course. But there were no Indian spies involved."

"Not even the Chakri?"

"Definitely not spying for India," said Achilles.

"For whom, then?"

Achilles laughed. "You're so untrusting. My Briseis."

She had to work at staying relaxed, at not betraying anything when he called her that.

"Ah, Pet, you *are* my Briseis, don't you realize?"

"Not really," said Petra. "Briseis was in somebody else's tent."

"Oh, I have your *body* with me, and I get the product of your brain, but your heart still belongs to someone else."

"It belongs to me," said Petra.

"It belongs to Hector," said Achilles. "But . . . how can I bear to tell you this? Suriyawong was not alone in his office when the building was blown to bits. Another person contributed scraps of flesh and bone and a fine aerosol of blood to the general gore. Unfortunately, this means I can't drag his body around the walls of Troy."

Petra was sick inside. Had he heard her tell Virlomi, "I am Briseis"? And whom was he talking about, saying those things about Hector?

"Just tell me what you're talking about or don't," said Petra.

"Oh, don't tell me you haven't seen those little

messages all over the forums," said Achilles. "About Briseis, and Guinevere, and every other tragic romantic heroine who got trapped with some overbearing bunduck."

"What about them?"

"You know who wrote them," said Achilles.

"Do I?"

"I forgot. You refuse to play guessing games. All right, it was Bean, and you knew that."

Petra felt unwanted emotions welling up—she suppressed them. If those messages were posted by Bean, then he *had* lived through the previous assassination attempt. But that would mean Bean was "Hector Victorious," and Achilles' little allegory meant that Bean was indeed in Bangkok, and Achilles had spotted him and tried again to kill him. He had died along with Suriyawong.

"I'm glad to have you to tell me what I know. It saves my having to actually use my own memory."

"I know it's tearing you up, my poor Pet. The funny thing is, dear Briseis, Bean was just a bonus. It was Suriyawong that we targeted from the start."

"Fine. Congratulations. You're a genius. Whatever it is you want me to say so you'll shut up and let me get some dinner."

Talking rudely to Achilles was the only illusion of freedom Petra was able to retain. She figured it amused him. And she wasn't dumb enough to talk to him that way in front of anyone else.

"You had your heart set on Bean saving you, didn't you?" said Achilles. "That's why when old Graff sent that stupid request for information, you tipped that Virlomi kid to try responding to Bean."

Petra tasted despair. Achilles really did monitor everything.

"Come on, the water fountain's the most obvious place to bug," said Achilles.

"I thought you had important things to do."

"Nothing's more important in my life than you, Pet," said Achilles. "If I could just get you to come into my tent."

"You've kidnapped me twice. You watch me wherever I go. I don't know how I could be farther in your tent than I am."

"In . . . my . . . tent," said Achilles. "You're still my enemy."

"Oh, I forgot, I'm supposed to be so eager to please my captor that I surrender my volition to you."

"If I wanted that, I'd have you tortured, Pet," said Achilles. "But I don't want you that way."

"How kind of you."

"No, if I can't have you freely with me, as my friend and ally, then I'll just kill you. I'm not into torture."

"After you've used my work."

"But I'm not using your work," said Achilles.

"Oh, that's right. Because Suriyawong is dead, so you don't need to worry now about having any real opposition."

Achilles laughed. "Sure. That's it."

Which meant, of course, that she hadn't understood at all.

"It's easy to fool a person you keep living in a box. I only know what you tell me."

"But I tell you everything," said Achilles, "if only you were bright enough to get it."

Petra closed her eyes. She kept thinking of poor Suriyawong. So serious all the time. He had done his best for his country, and then it was his own commander-in-chief who killed him. Did he know? I hope not.

If she kept thinking of poor Suriyawong, she wouldn't have to think of Bean at all.

"You're not listening," said Achilles.

"Oh, thanks for telling me that," said Petra. "I thought I was."

Achilles was about to say something else, but then he cocked his head. The hearing aid he wore was a radio receiver tied to his desk. Somebody had just started talking to him.

Achilles turned from her to his desk. He typed a few things, read a few things. His face showed no emotion—but that was a real change, since he had been smiling and pleasant until the voice came. Something had gone wrong. Indeed, Petra knew him well enough now that she thought she recognized the signs of anger. Or maybe—she wondered, she hoped—fear.

"They aren't dead," Petra said.

"I'm busy," he said.

She laughed. "That's the message, isn't it? Once again, your assassins have piffed it. If you want a job done right, Achilles, you've got to do it yourself."

He turned away from the desk display and looked her in the eye. "He sent out a message from the barracks of his strike force there in Thailand. Of course the Chakri saw it."

"Not dead," said Petra. "He just keeps beating you."

"Narrowly escaping with his life while my plans are never interfered with at all . . ."

"Come on, you know he got you booted out of Russia."

Achilles raised his eyebrows. "So you admit you sent a coded message."

"Bean doesn't need coded messages to beat you," she said.

Achilles rose from his chair and walked over to her. She braced herself for a slap. But he planted a hand in her chest and shoved the chair over backward.

Her head hit the floor. It left her dazed, lights flashing through her peripheral vision. And then a wave of pain and nausea.

"He sent for dear old Sister Carlotta," said Achilles. His voice betrayed no emotion. "She's flying around the world to help him. Isn't that nice of her?"

Petra could barely comprehend what he was saying. The only thought she could hold on to was: Don't let there be any permanent brain damage. That was her whole self. She'd rather die than lose the brilliance that made her who she was.

"But that gives me time to set up a little surprise," said Achilles. "I think I'll make Bean very sorry that he's alive."

Petra wanted to say something to that, but she couldn't remember what. Then she couldn't remember what he had said. "What?"

"Oh, is your poor little head swimming, my Pet? You should be more careful with the way you lean back on that chair."

Now she remembered what he had said. A surprise. For Sister Carlotta. To make Bean sorry he's alive.

"Sister Carlotta is the one who got you off the streets of Rotterdam," said Petra. "You owe her everything. Your leg operation. Going to Battle School."

"I owe her nothing," said Achilles. "You see, she chose Bean. She sent him. Me, she passed over. I'm the one who brought civilization to the streets. I'm the one who kept her precious little Bean alive. But him she sends up into space, and me she leaves in the dirt."

"Poor baby," said Petra.

He kicked her, hard, in the ribs. She gasped.

"And as for Virlomi," he said, "I think I can use her to teach you a lesson about disloyalty to me."

"That's the way to bring me into your tent," said Petra.

Again he kicked her. She tried not to groan, but it came out anyway. This passive resistance strategy was not working.

He acted as if he hadn't done it. "Come on, why are you lying there? Get up."

"Just kill me and have done with it," she said. "Virlomi was just trying to be a decent human being."

"Virlomi was warned what would happen."

"Virlomi is nothing to you but a way to hurt me."

"You're not that important. And if I want to hurt you, I know how." He made as if to kick her again. She stiffened, curled away from the blow. But it didn't come.

Instead he reached down a hand to her. "Get up, my Pet. The floor is no place to nap."

She reached up and took his hand. She let him bear most of her weight as she rose up, so he was pulling hard.

Fool, she thought. I was trained for personal combat. You weren't in Battle School long enough to get that training.

As soon as her legs were under her, she shoved upward. Since that was the direction he had been pulling, he lost his balance and went over backward, falling over the legs of her chair.

He did not hit his head. He immediately tried to scramble to his feet. But she knew how to respond to his movements, kicking sharply at him with her heavy army-issue shoes, shifting her weight so that her kicks never came at the place he was protecting. Every kick hurt him. He tried to scramble backward, but she pressed on, relentless, and because he was using his arms to help him scuttle across the floor, she was able to kick him in the head, a solid blow that rocked him back and laid him out.

Not unconscious, but a little dizzy. Well, see how you like it.

He tried to do some kind of street-fighting move, kicking out with his legs while his eyes were looking elsewhere, but it was pathetic. She easily jumped over his legs and landed a scuffing kick right up between his legs.

He cried out in pain.

"Come on, get up," she said. "You're going to kill Virlomi, so kill me first. Do it. You're the killer. Get your gun. Come on."

And then, without her quite seeing how he did it, there was indeed a gun in his hand.

"Kick me again," he said through gritted teeth. "Kick me faster than this bullet."

She didn't move.

"I thought you wanted to die," he said.

She could see it now. He wouldn't shoot her. Not till he had shot Virlomi in front of her.

She had missed her chance. While he was down, before he got the gun—from the back of his waistband? from under the furniture?—she should have snapped his neck. This wasn't a wrestling match, this was her chance to put an end to him. But her instinct had taken over, and her instinct was not to kill, only to disable her opponent, because that's what she had practiced in Battle School.

Of all the things I could have learned from Ender,

the killer instinct, going for the final blow from the start, why was that the one I overlooked?

Something Bean had explained about Achilles. Something Graff had told him, after Bean had gotten him shipped back to Earth. That Achilles had to kill anyone who had ever seen him helpless. Even the doctor who had repaired his gimp leg, because she'd seen him laid out under anaesthetic and taken a knife to him.

Petra had just destroyed whatever feeling it was that had made him keep her alive. Whatever he had wanted from her, he wouldn't want it now. He wouldn't be able to bear having her around. She was dead.

Yet, no matter what else was going on, she was still a tactician. Thick headed as she was, her mind could still do this dance. The enemy saw things this way; so change it so he sees them another way.

Petra laughed. "I never thought you'd let me do that," she said.

He slowly, painfully, was getting to his feet, the gun trained on her.

She went on. "You always had to be el supremo, like the bunducks in Battle School. I never thought you had the guts to be like Ender or Bean, till now."

Still he said nothing. But he was standing there. He was listening.

"Crazy, isn't it? But Bean and Ender, they were so little. And they didn't care. Everybody looking down at them, *me* towering over them, they were the only guys in Battle School who weren't terrified of having somebody see a girl be better than them, bigger than them." Keep it going, keep spinning it. "They put Ender in Bonzo's army too early, he hadn't been trained. Didn't know how to do anything. And Bonzo gave orders, nobody was to work with him. So here I had this little kid, helpless, didn't know anything. That's what I like, Achilles. Smarter than me, but smaller. So I taught him. Chisel Bonzo, I didn't care. He was like *you've* always been, constantly showing me who's boss. But Ender knew how to let me run it. I taught him everything. I would have died for him."

"You're sick," said Achilles.

"Oh, you're going to tell me you didn't know that? You had the gun the whole time, why did you let me do that, if it wasn't—if you weren't trying to . . ."

"Trying to what?" he said. He was keeping his voice steady, but the craziness was plainly visible, and his voice trembled just a little. She had pushed him past the borders of sanity, deep into his madness. It was Caligula she was seeing now. But he was listening. If she found the right story to put on what just happened, maybe he would settle for . . . something else. Making his horse consul. Making Petra . . .

"Weren't you trying to seduce me?" she said.

"You don't even have your tits yet," he said.

"I don't think it's tits you're looking for," she said. "Or you would never have dragged me around with you in the first place. What was all that talk about wanting me in your tent? Loyal? You wanted me to belong to you. And all the time you did that sabeek stuff, pushing me around—that just made me feel contempt for you. I was looking down on you the whole time. You were nothing, just another sack of testosterone, another chimp hooting and beating his chest. But then you let me—you *did* let me, didn't you? You don't expect me to believe I really could have done that?"

A faint smile touched the corners of his lips.

"Doesn't that spoil it, if you think I did it on purpose?" he said.

She strode to him, right to the barrel of the gun, and, letting it press into her abdomen, she reached up, grabbed him by the neck, and pulled his head down to where she could kiss him.

She had no idea how to do it, except what she'd seen in movies. But she was apparently doing it well enough. The gun stayed in her belly, but his other arm wrapped around her, pulled her closer.

In the back of her mind, she remembered what Bean told her—that the last thing he had seen Achilles do before killing Bean's friend Poke was kiss her. Bean had had nightmares about it. Achilles kissing her, and then in the middle of the kiss, strangling her. Not that Bean actually saw that part. Maybe it didn't happen that way at all.

But no matter how you cut it, Achilles was a dangerous boy to kiss. And there was that gun in her belly. Maybe this was the moment he longed for. Maybe his dreams were about this—kissing a girl, and blowing a hole in her body while he did.

Well, blow away, she thought. Before I watch you kill Virlomi for the crime of having compassion for me and courage enough to act, I'd rather be dead myself. I'd rather kiss you than watch you kill her, and there's nothing in the world that could disgust me more than having to pretend that you're the . . . thing . . . I love.

The kiss ended. But she did not let go of him. She would not step back, she would not break this embrace. He had to believe that she wanted him. That she was in his emossin' tent.

He was breathing lightly, quickly. His heartbeat was rapid. Prelude to a kill? Or just the aftermath of a kiss.

"I said I'd kill anyone who tried to answer Graff," he said. "I have to."

"She didn't answer Graff, did she?" said Petra. "I know you have to keep control of things, but you don't have to be a strutting yelda about it. She doesn't know you know what she did."

"She'll think she got away with it."

"But *I'll* know," said Petra, "that you weren't afraid to give me what I want."

"What, you think you've found some way to make me do what you want?" he said.

Now she could back away from him. "I thought I'd found a man who didn't have to prove he was big by pushing people around. I guess I was wrong. Do what you want. Men like you disgust me." She put as much contempt into her voice, onto her face, as she could. "Here, prove you're a man. Shoot me. Shoot everybody. I've known *real* men. I thought you were one of them."

He lowered the gun. She did not show her relief. Just kept her eyes looking into his.

"Don't ever think you've got me figured out," he said.

"I don't care whether I figure you out or not," she said. "All I care about is, you're the first man since Ender and Bean who had guts enough to let me stand over him."

"Is that what you're going to say?" he asked.

"Say? Who to? I don't have any friends out there. The only person worth talking to in this whole place is you."

He stood there, breathing heavily again, a bit of the craziness back in his eyes.

What am I saying wrong?

"You're going to bring this off," she said. "I don't know how you're going to do it, but I can taste it. You're going to run the whole show. They're all going to be under you, Achilles. Governments, universities, corporations, all eager to please you. But when we're alone, where nobody else can see, we'll both know that you're strong enough to keep a strong woman with you."

"You?" said Achilles. "A woman?"

"If I'm not a woman, what were you doing with me in here?"

"Take off your clothes," he said.

The craziness was still there. He was testing her somehow. Waiting for her to show . . .

To show that she was faking. That she was really afraid of him, after all. That her story was all a lie, designed to trick him.

"No," she said. "You take off yours."

And the craziness faded.

He smiled.

He tucked the gun into the back of his pants.

"Get out of here," he said. "I've got a war to run."

"It's night," she said. "Nobody's moving."

"There's a lot more to this war than the armies," said Achilles.

"When do I get to stay in your tent?" she asked. "What do I have to do?" She could hardly believe she was saying this, when all she wanted was to get out.

"You have to be the thing I need," he said. "And right now, you're not."

He walked to his desk, sat down.

"And pick up your chair on the way out."

He started typing. Orders? For what? To kill whom? She didn't ask. She picked up the chair. She walked out.

And kept walking, through the corridors to the room where she slept alone. Knowing, with every step, that she was monitored. There would be vids. He would check them, to see how she acted. To see if she meant what she'd said. So she couldn't stop and press her face against the wall and cry. She had to be . . . what? How would this play in a movie or a vid if she were a woman who was frustrated because she wanted to be with her man?

I don't know! she screamed inside. I'm not an actress!

And then, a much quieter voice in her head answered. Yes you are. And a pretty good one. Because for another few minutes, maybe another hour, maybe another night, you're alive.

No triumph, either. She couldn't seem to gloat, couldn't show relief. Frustration, annoyance—and some pain where he kicked her, where her head hit the floor—that's all she could show.

Even alone in her bed, the lights off, she lay there, pretending, lying. Hoping that whatever she did in her sleep would not provoke him. Would not bring that crazy frightened searching look into his eyes.

Not that it would be any guarantee, of course. There was no sign of craziness when he shot those men in the bread van back in Russia. Don't ever think you've got me figured out, he said.

You win, Achilles. I don't think I've got you figured out. But I've learned how to play one lousy string. That's something.

I also knocked you onto the floor, beat the goffno out of you, kicked you in your little kintamas, and made you think you liked it. Kill me tomorrow or whenever you want—my shoe going into your face, you can't take that away from me.

———

In the morning, Petra was pleased to find that she was still alive, considering what she had done the night before. Her head ached, her ribs were sore, but nothing was broken.

And she was starving. She had missed dinner the night before, and perhaps there was something about beating up her jailer that made her especially hungry. She didn't usually eat breakfast, so she had no accustomed place to sit. At other meals, she sat by herself, and others, respecting her solitude or fearing Achilles' displeasure, did not sit with her.

But today, on impulse, she took her tray to a table that had only a couple of empty spots. The conversation grew quiet when she first sat down, and a few people greeted her. She smiled back at them, but then concentrated on her food. Their conversation resumed.

"There's no way she got off the base."

"So she's still here."

"Unless someone *took* her."

"Maybe it's a special assignment or something."

"Sayagi says he thinks she's dead."

A chill ran through Petra's body.

"Who?" she asked.

The others glanced at her, but then glanced away. Finally one of them said, "Virlomi."

Virlomi was gone. And no one knew where she was.

He killed her. He said he would, and he did. The only thing I gained by what I did last night was that he didn't do it in front of me.

I can't stand this. I'm done. My life is not worth living. To be his captive, to have him kill anyone who tries to help me in any way . . .

No one was looking at her. Nor were they talking.

They know Virlomi tried to answer Graff, because she must have said something to Sayagi when she walked over to him yesterday. And now she's gone.

Petra knew she had to eat, no matter how sick at

heart she felt, no matter how much she wanted to cry, to run screaming from the room, to fall on the floor and beg their forgiveness for . . . for what? For being alive when Virlomi was dead.

She finished all she could bear to eat, and left the mess hall.

But as she walked through the corridors to the room where they all worked, she realized: Achilles would not have killed her like this. There was no point in killing her if the others didn't get to see her arrested and taken away. It wouldn't do what he needed it to do, if she just disappeared in the night.

At the same time, if she had escaped, he couldn't announce it. That would be even worse. So he would simply remain silent, and leave the impression with everyone that she was probably dead.

Petra imagined Virlomi walking boldly out of the building, her sheer bravado carrying the day. Or perhaps, dressed as one of the women who cleaned floors and windows, she had slipped out unnoticed. Or had she climbed a wall, or run a minefield? Petra didn't even know what the perimeter looked like, or how closely guarded it might be. She had never been given a tour.

Wishful thinking, that's all this is, she told herself as she sat down to the day's work. Virlomi is dead, and Achilles is simply waiting to announce it, to make us all suffer from not knowing.

But as the day wore on, and Achilles did not appear, Petra began to believe that perhaps she had gotten away. Maybe Achilles was staying away because he didn't want anyone speculating about any visible bruises he might have. Or maybe he's having some scrotal problems and he's having some doctor check him out—though heaven help him if Achilles decided that having a doctor handle his injured testes was worthy of the death penalty.

Maybe he was staying away because Virlomi was gone and Achilles did not want them to see him frustrated and helpless. When he caught her and could drag her into the room and shoot her dead in front of them, *then* he could face them.

And as long as that didn't happen, there was a chance Virlomi was alive.

Stay that way, my friend. Run far and don't pause for anything. Cross some border, find some refuge, swim to Sri Lanka, fly to the moon. Find some miracle, Virlomi, and live.

15

Murder

To:Graff%pilgrimage@colmin.gov
From:Carlotta%agape@vatican.net/or-
ders/sisters/ind
Re: Please forward

The attached file is encrypted. Please
wait twelve hours after the time of
sending and if you don't hear from me,
forward it to Bean. He'll know the key.

It took less than four hours to secure and inspect the entire high command base in Bangkok. Computer experts would be probing to try to find out whom it was that Naresuan had been communicating with outside, and whether he was in fact involved with a foreign power or this gambit was a private venture. When Suriyawong's work with the Prime Minister was finished, he came alone to the barracks where Bean was waiting.

Most of Bean's soldiers had already returned, and Bean had sent most of them to bed. He still watched the news in a desultory fashion—nothing new was being said, so he was interested only in seeing how the talking heads were spinning it. In Thailand, everything was charged with patriotic fervor. Abroad, of course, it was a different story. All the Common broadcasts were taking a more skeptical view that Indian operatives had really made the assassination attempt.

"Why would India want to provoke Thai entry into the war?"

"They know Thailand will come in eventually whether Burma asks them or not. So they felt they had to deprive Thailand of its best Battle School graduate."

"Is one child so dangerous?"

"Maybe you should ask the Formics. If you can find any."

And on and on, everyone trying to appear smart—or at least smarter than the Indian and Thai governments, which was the game the media always played. What mattered to Bean was how this would affect Peter. Was there any mention of the possibility that Achilles was running the show in India? Not a breath. Anything yet about Pakistani troop movements near Iran? The "Bangkok bombing" had driven that slow-moving story off the air. Nobody was giving this any global implications. As long as the I.F. was there to keep the nukes from flying, it was still just politics as usual in south Asia.

Except it wasn't. Everybody was so busy trying to look wise and unsurprised that nobody was standing up and screaming that this whole set of events was completely different from anything that had gone before. The most populous nation in the world has dared to turn its back on a two-hundred-year-old enemy and invade the small, weak country to its east. Now India was attacking Thailand. What did that mean? What was India's goal? What possible benefit could there be?

Why weren't they talking about these things?

"Well," said Suriyawong, "I don't think I'm going to go to sleep very soon."

"Everything all cleaned up?"

"More like everybody who worked closely with the Chakri has been sent home and put under house arrest while the investigation continues."

"That means the entire high command."

"Not really," said Suriyawong. "The best field commanders are out in the field. Commanding. One of them will be brought in as acting Chakri."

"They should give it to you."

"They should, but they won't. Aren't you just a little hungry?"

"It's late."

"This is Bangkok."

"Well, not really," said Bean. "This is a military base."

"When is your friend's flight due in?"

"Morning. Just after dawn."

"Ouch. She's going to be out of sorts. You going to meet her at the airport?"

"I didn't think about it."

"Let's go get dinner," said Suriyawong. "Officers do it all the time. We can take a couple of strike force soldiers with us to make sure we don't get hassled for being children."

"Achilles isn't going to give up on killing me."

"Us. He aimed at *us* this time."

"He might have a backup."

"Bean, I'm hungry. Are you hungry?" Suriyawong turned to the members of the toon that had been with him. "Any of you hungry?"

"Not really," said one of them. "We ate at the regular time."

"Sleepy," said another.

"Anybody awake enough to go into the city with us?"

Immediately all of them stepped forward.

"Don't ask perfect soldiers whether they want to protect their CO," said Bean.

"Designate a couple to go with us and let the others sleep," said Suriyawong.

"Yes sir," said Bean. He turned to the men. "Honest assessment. Which of you will be least impaired by failing to get enough sleep tonight?"

"Will we be allowed sleep tomorrow?" asked one.

"Yes," said Bean. "So it's a matter of how much it affects you to get off your rhythm."

"I'll be fine." Four others felt the same way. So Bean chose the two nearest. "Two of you keep watch for two more hours, then go back to the normal watch rotation."

Outside the building, with their two bodyguards walking five meters behind them, Bean and Suriyawong finally had a chance to talk candidly. First, though, Suriyawong had to know. "You really keep a regular watch rotation even here at the base?"

"Was I wrong?" asked Bean.

"Obviously not, but . . . you really are paranoid."

"I know I have an enemy who wants me dead. An

enemy who happens to be hopping from one powerful position to another."

"More powerful each time," said Suriyawong. "In Russia, he didn't have the power to start a war."

"He might not in India, either," said Bean.

"There's a war," said Suriyawong. "You're saying it isn't his?"

"It's his," said Bean. "But he's probably still having to persuade adults to go along with him."

"Win a few, and they hand you your own army," said Suriyawong.

"Win a few more, and they hand you the country," said Bean. "As Napoleon and Washington showed."

"How many do you have to win to get the world?"

Bean let the question hang.

"Why did he go after us?" asked Suriyawong. "I think you're right, that this operation at least was entirely Achilles'. It's not the kind of thing the Indian government goes for. India is a democracy. Folding children doesn't play well. No way he got approval."

"It might not even be India," said Bean. "We don't really know anything."

"Except that it's Achilles," said Suriyawong. "Think about the stuff that doesn't make sense. A second-rate, obvious campaign strategy that we're probably going to be able to take apart. A nasty bit of business like this that can only soil India's reputation in the rest of the world."

"Obviously he's not acting in India's best interest," said Bean. "But they think he is, if he's really the one who brought off this deal with Pakistan. He's acting for himself. And I can see what he gains by kidnapping Ender's jeesh and by trying to kill you."

"Fewer rivals?"

"No," said Bean. "He makes Battle School grads look like the most important weapons in the war."

"But he's not a Battle School grad."

"He was *in* Battle School, and he's that age. He doesn't want to have to wait till he grows up to be king of the world. He wants everyone to believe that a child should lead them. If you're worth killing, if Ender's jeesh is worth stealing . . ." It also helps Peter Wiggin, Bean realized. He didn't go to Battle School, but if children are plausible world leaders, his own track record as Locke raises him above any other contenders. Military ability is one thing. Ending the League War was a much stronger qualification. It trumped "psychopathic Battle School expulsee" hands down.

"Do you think that's all?" asked Suriyawong.

"What's all?" asked Bean. He had lost the thread. "Oh, you mean is that enough to explain why Achilles would want you dead?" Bean thought about it. "I don't know. Maybe. But it doesn't tell us why he's setting up India for a much bloodier war than it has to fight."

"What about this," said Suriyawong. "Make everybody fear what war will bring, so they want to strengthen the Hegemony to keep the war from spreading."

"That's fine, except nobody's going to nominate Achilles as Hegemon."

"Good point. Are we ruling out the possibility that Achilles is just stupid?"

"Yes, that's not a possibility."

"What about Petra, could she have fooled him into sticking with this obvious but somewhat dumb and wasteful strategy?"

"That *is* possible, except that Achilles is very sharp

at reading people. I don't know if Petra could lie to him. I never saw her lie to anybody. I don't know if she can."

"Never saw her lie to *anybody*?" asked Suriyawong.

Bean shrugged. "We became very good friends, at the end of the war. She speaks her mind. She may hold something back sometimes, but she tells you she's doing it. No smoke, no mirrors. The door's either open or it's shut."

"Lying takes practice," observed Suriyawong.

"Like the Chakri?"

"You don't get to that position by pure military ability. You have to make yourself look very good to a lot of people. And hide a lot of things you're doing."

"You're not suggesting Thailand's government is corrupt," said Bean.

"I'm suggesting Thailand's government is political. I hope this doesn't surprise you. Because I'd heard that you were bright."

They got a car to take them into town—Suriyawong had always had the authority to requisition a car and a driver, he just never used it till now.

"So where do we eat?" asked Bean. "It's not like I have a restaurant guide with me."

"I grew up in families with better chefs than any restaurant," said Suriyawong.

"So we go to your house?"

"My family lives near Chiang Mai."

"That's going to be a battle zone."

"Which is why I think they're actually in Vientiane, though security rules would keep them from telling me. My father is running a network of dispersed munitions factories." Suriyawong grinned. "I had to make sure I siphoned off some of these defense jobs for my family."

"In other words, he was best man for the task."

"My mother was best for the task, but this *is* Thailand. Our love affair with Western culture ended a century ago."

They ended up having to ask the soldiers, and they only knew the kind of place they could afford to eat. So they found themselves eating at a tiny all-night diner in a part of town that wasn't the worst, but wasn't the nicest, either. And the whole thing was so cheap it felt practically free.

Suriyawong and the soldiers went down on the food as if it were the best meal they'd ever had. "Isn't this *great*?" asked Suriyawong. "When my parents had company, and they were eating all the fancy stuff in the dining room with visitors, we kids would eat in the kitchen, the stuff the servants ate. *This* stuff. *Real* food."

No doubt that's why the Americans at Yum-Yum in Greensboro loved what they got there, too. Childhood memories. Food that tasted like safety and love and getting rewarded for good behavior. A treat—we're going out. Bean didn't have any such memories, of course. He had no nostalgia for picking up food wrappers and licking the sugar off the plastic and then trying to get at any of it that rubbed off on his nose.

What was he nostalgic for? Life in Achilles' "family"? Battle School? Not likely. And his time with his family in Greece had come too late to be part of his early childhood memories. He liked being in Crete, he loved his family, but no, the only good memories of his childhood were in Sister Carlotta's apartment when she took him off the street and fed him and kept him safe and helped him prepare to take the Battle School tests—his ticket off Earth, to where he'd be safe from Achilles.

It was the only time in his childhood when he felt safe. And even though he didn't believe it or understand it at the time, he felt loved, too. If he could sit down in some restaurant and eat a meal like the ones Sister Carlotta prepared there in Rotterdam, he'd probably feel the way those Americans felt about Yum-Yum, or these Thais felt about this place.

"Our friend Borommakot doesn't really like the food," said Suriyawong. He spoke in Thai, because Bean had picked up the language quite readily, and the soldiers weren't as comfortable in Common.

"He may not like it," said one soldier, "but it's making him grow."

"Soon he'll be as tall as you," said the other.

"How tall do Greeks get?" asked the first.

Bean froze.

So did Suriyawong.

The two soldiers looked at them with some alarm. "What, did you see something?"

"How did you know he was Greek?" asked Suriyawong.

The soldiers glanced at each other and then suppressed their smiles.

"I guess they're not stupid," said Bean.

"We saw all the vids on the Bugger War, we saw your face, you think you're not famous? Don't you know?"

"But you never said anything," said Bean.

"That would have been rude."

Bean wondered how many people made him in Araraquara and Greensboro, but were too polite to say anything.

It was three in the morning when they got to the airport. The plane was due in about six. Bean was too keyed up to sleep. He assigned himself to keep watch, and let the soldiers and Suriyawong doze.

So it was Bean who noticed when a flurry of activity began around the podium about forty-five minutes before the flight was supposed to arrive. He got up and went to ask what was going on.

"Please wait, we'll make an announcement," said the ticket agent. "Where are your parents? Are they here?"

Bean sighed. So much for fame. Suriyawong, at least, should have been recognized. Then again, everyone here had been on duty all night and probably hadn't heard any of the news about the assassination attempt, so they wouldn't have seen Suriyawong's face flashed in the vids again and again. He went back to waken one of the soldiers so he could find out, adult to adult, what was going on.

His uniform probably got him information that a civilian wouldn't have been told. He came back looking grim. "The plane went down," he said.

Bean felt his heart plummet. Achilles? Had he found a way to get to Sister Carlotta?

It couldn't be. How could he know? He couldn't be monitoring every airplane flight in the world.

The message Bean had sent via the computer in the barracks. The Chakri might have seen it. If he hadn't been arrested by then. He might have had time to relay the information to Achilles, or whatever intermediary they used. How else could Achilles have known that Carlotta would be coming?

"It's not him this time," said Suriyawong, when Bean told him what he was thinking. "There are plenty of reasons a plane can drop out of radar."

"She didn't say it disappeared," said the soldier. "She said it went down."

Suriyawong looked genuinely stricken. "Borom-makot, I'm sorry." Then Suriyawong went to a telephone and contacted the Prime Minister's office. Being Thailand's pride and joy, who had just survived an assassination attempt, had its benefits. In a very few minutes they were escorted into the meeting room at the airport where officials from the government and the military were conferring, linked to aviation authorities and investigating agencies worldwide.

The plane had gone down over southern China. It was an Air Shanghai flight, and China was treating it as an internal matter, refusing to allow outside investigators to come to the crash site. But air traffic satellites had the story—there was an explosion, a big one, and the plane was in small fragments before any part of it reached the ground. No chance of survivors.

Only one faint hope remained. Maybe she hadn't made a connection somewhere. Maybe she wasn't on board.

But she was.

I could have stopped her, thought Bean. When I agreed to trust the Prime Minister without waiting for Carlotta to arrive, I could have sent word at once to have her go home. But instead he waited around and watched the vids and then went out for a night on the town. Because he wanted to see her. Because he had been frightened and he needed to have her with him.

Because he was too selfish even to think of the danger he was exposing her to. She flew under her own name—she had never done that when they were together. Was that his fault?

Yes. Because he had summoned her with such urgency that she didn't have time to do things covertly.

She just had the Vatican arrange her flights, and that was it. The end of her life.

The end of her ministry, that's how she'd think about it. The jobs left undone. The work that someone else would have to do.

All he'd done, ever since she met him, was steal time from her, keep her from the things that really mattered in her life. Having to do her work on the run, in hiding, for his sake. Whenever he needed her, she dropped everything. What had he ever done to deserve it? What had he ever given her in return? And now he had interrupted her work permanently. She would be so annoyed. But even now, if he could talk to her, he knew what she'd say.

It was always my choice, she'd say. You're part of the work God gave me. Life ends, and I'm not afraid to return to God. I'm only afraid for you, because you keep yourself such a stranger to him.

If only he could believe that she was still alive somehow. That she was there with Poke, maybe, taking her in now the way she took Bean in so many years ago. And the two of them laughing and reminiscing about clumsy old Bean, who just had a way of getting people killed.

Someone touched his arm. "Bean," whispered Suriyawong. "Bean, let's get you out of here."

Bean focused and realized that there were tears running down his cheeks. "I'm staying," he said.

"No," said Suriyawong. "Nothing's going to happen here. I mean let's go to the official residence. That's where the diplomatic greeyaz is flying."

Bean wiped his eyes on his sleeves, feeling like a little kid as he did it. What a thing to be seen doing in front of his men. But that was just too bad—it would be a far worse sign of weakness to try to conceal it or pathetically ask them not to tell. He did what he did, they saw what they saw, so be it. If Sister Carlotta wasn't worth some tears from someone who owed her as much as Bean did, then what were tears for, and when should they be shed?

There was a police escort waiting for them. Suriyawong thanked their bodyguards and ordered them back to the barracks. "No need to get up till you feel like it," he said.

They saluted Suriyawong. Then they turned to Bean and saluted him. Sharply. In best military fashion. No pity. Just honor. He returned their salute the same way—no gratitude, just respect.

———

The morning in the official residence was infuriating and boring by turns. China was being intransigent. Even though most of the passengers were Thai businessmen and tourists, it was a Chinese plane over Chinese airspace, and because there were indications that it might have been a ground-to-air missile attack rather than a planted bomb, it was being kept under tight military security.

Definitely Achilles, Bean and Suriyawong agreed. But they had talked enough about Achilles that Bean agreed to let Suriyawong brief the Thai military and state department leaders who needed to have all the information that might make sense of this.

Why would India want to blow up a passenger plane flying over China? Could it really have been solely to kill a nun who was coming to visit a Greek boy in Bangkok? That was simply too far-fetched to believe. Yet, bit by bit, and with the help of the Minister of Colonization, who could take them through details about Achilles' psychopathology that hadn't even been in Locke's reporting on him, they began to understand that yes, indeed, this might well have been a kind of defiant message from Achilles to Bean, telling him that he might have gotten away this time, but Achilles could still kill whomever he wanted.

While Suriyawong was briefing them, however, Bean was taken upstairs to the private residence, where the Prime Minister's wife very kindly led him to a guest bedroom and asked him if he had a friend or family member she should send for, or if he wanted a minister or priest of some religion or other. He thanked her and said that all he really needed was some time alone.

She closed the door behind her, and Bean cried silently until he was exhausted, and then, curled up on a mat on the floor, he went to sleep.

When he awoke it was still bright daylight beyond the louvered shutters. His eyes were still sore from crying. He was still exhausted. He must have woken up because his bladder was full. And he was thirsty. That was life. Pump it in, pump it out. Sleep and wake, sleep and wake. Oh, and a little reproduction here and there. But he was too young, and Sister Carlotta had opted out of that side of life. So for them the cycle had been pretty much the same. Find some meaning in life. But what? Bean was famous. His name would live in history books forever. Probably just as part of a list in the chapter on Ender Wiggin, but that was fine, that was more than most people got. When he was dead he wouldn't care.

Carlotta wouldn't be in any history books. Not even a footnote. Well, no, that wasn't true. Achilles was going to be famous, and she was the one who found him.

More than a footnote after all. Her name would be remembered, but always because it was linked with the koncho who killed her because she had seen how helpless he was and saved him from the life of the street.

Achilles killed her, but of course, he had my help.

Bean forced himself to think of something else. He could already feel that burning in his eyelids that meant tears were about to flow. That was done. He needed to keep his wits about him. Very important to keep thinking.

There was a courtesy computer in the room, with standard netlinks and some of Thailand's leading connection software. Soon Bean was signed on in one of his less-used identities. Graff would know things that the Thai government wasn't getting. So would Peter. And they would write to him.

Sure enough, there were messages from both of them encrypted on one of his dropsites. He pulled them both off.

They were the same. An email forwarded from Sister Carlotta herself.

Both of them said the same thing. The message had arrived at nine in the morning, Thailand time. They were supposed to wait twelve hours in case Sister Carlotta herself contacted them to retract the message. But when they learned with independent confirmation that there was no chance she was alive, they decided not to wait. Whatever the message was, Sister Carlotta had set it up so that if she didn't take an active step to block it, every day, it would automatically go to Graff and to Peter to send on to him.

Which meant that every day of her life, she had

thought of him, had done something to keep him from seeing this, and yet had also made sure that he would see whatever it was that this message contained.

Her farewell. He didn't want to read it. He had cried himself out. There was nothing left.

And yet she wanted him to read it. And after all she had done for him, he could surely do this for her.

The file was double-encrypted. Once he had opened it with his own decoding, it remained encoded by her. He had no idea what the password would be, and therefore it had to be something that she would expect him to think of.

And because he would only be trying to find the key after she was dead, the choice was obvious. He entered the name *Poke* and the decryption proceeded at once.

It was, as he expected, a letter to him.

```
Dear Julian, Dear Bean, Dear Friend,

Maybe Achilles killed me, maybe he
didn't. You know how I feel about
vengeance. Punishment belongs to God,
and besides, anger makes people stupid,
even people as bright as you. Achilles
must be stopped because of what he is,
not because of anything he did to me.
My manner of death is meaningless to
me. Only my manner of life mattered,
and that is for my Redeemer to judge.

But you already know these things, and
that is not why I wrote this letter.
```

There is information about you that you have a right to know. It's not pleasant information, and I was going to wait to tell you until you already had some inkling. I was not about to let my death keep you in ignorance, however. That would be giving either Achilles or the random chances of life—whichever caused my sudden death—too much power over you.

You know that you were born as part of an illegal scientific experiment using embryos stolen from your parents. You have preternatural memories of your own astonishing escape from the slaughter of your siblings when the experiment was terminated. What you did at that age tells anyone who knows the story that you are extraordinarily intelligent. What you have not known, until now, is why you are so intelligent, and what it implies about your future.

The person who stole your frozen embryo was a scientist, of sorts. He was working on the genetic enhancement of human intelligence. He based his experiment on the theoretical work of a Russian scientist named Anton. Though Anton was under an order of intervention and could not tell me directly, he courageously found a way to circumvent the programming and tell me of the genetic change that was made in you. (Though Anton was under the impression that the change could only be made in an unfertilized egg, this was really only a technical problem, not a theoretical one.)

There is a double key in the human genome. One of the keys deals with human intelligence. If turned one way, it places a block on the ability of the brain to function at peak capacity. In you, Anton's key has been turned. Your brain was not frozen in its growth. It did not stop making new neurons at an early age. Your brain continues to grow and make new connections. Instead of having a limited capacity, with patterns formed during early development, your brain adds new capacities and new patterns as they are needed. You are mentally like a one-year-old, but with experience. The mental feats that infants routinely perform, which are far greater than anything that adults manage, will always remain within your reach. For your entire life, for instance, you will be able to master new languages like a native speaker. You will be able to make and maintain connections with your own memory that are unlike those of anyone else. You are, in other words, uncharted—or perhaps self-charted—territory.

But there is a price for that unfettering of your brain. You have probably already guessed it. If your brain keeps growing, what happens to your head? How does all that brain matter stay inside?

Your head continues to grow, of course. Your skull has never fully closed. I have had your skull measurements tracked, naturally. The growth is slow, and much of the growth of your brain has involved the creation of more but smaller neurons. Also, there has been some thinning of your skull, so you may or may not have noticed the growth in the circumferences of your head—but it is real.

You see, the other side of Anton's key involves human growth. If we did not stop growing, we would die very young. Yet to live long requires that we give up more and more of our intelligence, because our brains must lock down and stop growing earlier in our life cycle. Most human beings fluctuate within a fairly narrow range. You are not even on the charts.

Bean, Julian, my child, you will die very young. Your body will continue to grow, not the way puberty would do it,

with one growth spurt and then an adult
height. As one scientist put it, you
will never reach adult height, because
there is no adult height. There is only
height at time of death. You will
steadily grow taller and larger until
your heart gives out or your spine collapses. I tell you this bluntly, because there is no way to soften this
blow.

No one knows what course your growth
will take. At first I took great encouragement from the fact that you seemed
to be growing more slowly than originally estimated. I was told that by the
age of puberty, you would have caught
up with other children your age—but you
did not. You remained far behind them.
So I hoped that perhaps he was wrong,
that you might live to age forty or
fifty, or even thirty. But in the year
you were with your family, and in the
time we have been together, you have
been measured and your growth rate is
accelerating. All indications are that
it will continue to accelerate. If you
live to be twenty, you will have defied
all rational expectations. If you die
before the age of fifteen, it will be
only a mild surprise. I shed tears as I
write these words, because if ever
there was a child who could serve humanity by having a long adult life, it
is you. No, I will be honest, my tears

are because I think of you as being, in so many ways, my own son, and the only thing that makes me glad about the fact that you are learning of your future through this letter is that it means I have died before you. The worst fear of every loving parent, you see, is that they will have to bury a child. We nuns and priests are spared that grief. Except when we take it upon ourselves, as I so foolishly and gladly have done with you.

I have full documentation of all the findings of the team that has been studying you. They will continue to study you, if you allow them. The netlink is at the end of this letter. They can be trusted, because they are decent people, and because they also know that if the existence of their project becomes known, they will be in grave danger, for research into the genetic enhancement of human intelligence remains against the law. It is entirely your choice whether you cooperate. They already have valuable data. You may live your life without reference to them, or you may continue to provide them with information. I am not terribly interested in the science of it. I worked with them because I needed to know what would happen to you.

Forgive me for keeping this information from you. I know that you think
you would have preferred to know it
all along. I can only say, in my defense, that it is good for human beings to have a period of innocence and
hope in their lives. I was afraid that
if you knew this too soon, it would
rob you of that hope. And yet to deprive you of this knowledge robbed you
of the freedom to decide how to spend
the years you have. I was going to
tell you soon.

There are those who have said that because of this small genetic difference,
you are not human. That because Anton's
key requires two changes in the genome,
not one, it could never have happened
randomly, and therefore you represent a
new species, created in the laboratory.
But I tell you, you and Nikolai are
twins, not separate species, and I, who
have known you as well as any other
person, have never seen anything from
you but the best and purest of humanity. I know you will not accept my religious terminology, but you know what
it means to me. You have a soul, my
child. The Savior died for you as for
every other human being ever born. Your
life is of infinite worth to a loving
God. And to me, my son.

You will find your own purpose for the
time you have left to live. Do not be
reckless with your life, just because
it will not be long. But do not guard
it overzealously, either. Death is not
a tragedy to the one who dies. To have
wasted the life before that death, that
is the tragedy. Already you have used
your years better than most. You will
yet find many new purposes, and you will
accomplish them. And if anyone in
heaven heeds the voice of this old nun,
you will be well watched over by angels
and prayed for by many saints.

With love, Carlotta

Bean erased the letter. He could pull it from his
dropsite and decode it again, if he needed to refer back
to it. But it was burned into his memory. And not just
as text on a desk display. He had heard it in Carlotta's
voice, even as his eyes moved across the words that the
desk put up before him.

He turned off the desk. He walked to the window
and opened it. He looked out over the garden of the official residence. In the distance he could see airplanes
making their approach to the airport, as others, having
just taken off, rose up into the sky. He tried to picture
Sister Carlotta's soul rising up like one of those airplanes. But the picture kept changing to an Air Shanghai flight coming in to land, and Sister Carlotta
walking off the plane and looking him up and down
and saying, "You need to buy new pants."

He went back inside and lay down on his mat, but

not to sleep. He did not close his eyes. He stared at the ceiling and thought about death and life and love and loss. And as he did, he thought he could feel his bones grow.

Part Four

DECISIONS

16

Treachery

To: Demosthenes%Tecumseh@freeamerica
.org
From: Unready%cincinnatus@anon.set
Re: Air Shanghai

The pinheads running this show have decided not to share satellite info on
Air Shanghai with anyone outside the
military, claiming that it involves vital interests of the United States. The
only other countries with satellites
capable of seeing what ours can see are
China, Japan, and Brazil, and of these
only China has a satellite in position
to see it. So the Chinese know. And
when I'm done with this letter, you'll
know, and you'll know how to use the

information. I don't like seeing big countries beat up on little ones, except when the big country is mine. So sue me.

The Air Shanghai flight was brought down by a ground-to-air missile, which was fired from INSIDE THAILAND. However, computer time-lapse tracking of movements in that area of Thailand show that the only serious candidate for how the ground-to-air missile got to its launch site is a utility truck whose movements originated in, get this, China.

Details: The truck (little white Vietnamese-made "Ho"-type vehicle) originated at a warehouse in Gejiu (which has already been tagged as a munitions clearinghouse) and crossed the Vietnamese border between Jinping, China, and Sinh Ho, Vietnam. It then crossed the Laotian border via the Ded Tay Chang pass. It traversed the widest part of Laos and entered Thailand near Tha Li, but at this point moved off the main roads. It passed near enough to the point from which the missile was launched for it to have been offloaded and transported manually to the site. And get this: All this movement happened MORE THAN A MONTH AGO.

I don't know about you, but to me and
everybody else here, that looks like
China wants a "provocation" to go to
war against Thailand. Bangkok-bound Air
Shanghai jet, carrying mostly Thai passengers, is shot down, over China, by a
g-to-a launched from Thailand. China
can make it look as though the Thai
Army was trying to create a fake provocation against them, when in fact the
reverse is the case. Very complicated,
but the Chinese know they can show
satellite proof that the missile was
launched from inside Thailand. They can
also prove that it had to have radar
assistance from sophisticated military
tracking systems—which will imply, in
the Chinese version, that the Thai military was behind it, though WE know it
means the Chinese military was in control. And when the Chinese ask for independent corroboration, you can count
on it: Our beloved government, since it
loves business better than honor, will
back up the Chinese story, never mentioning the movements of that little
truck. Thus America will stay in the
good graces of its trading partner. And
Thailand gets chiseled.

Do your thing, Demosthenes. Get this
out into the public domain before our
government can play toady. Just try to
find a way to do it that doesn't point

at me. This isn't just job-losing territory. I could go to jail.

When Suriyawong came to see if Bean wanted any
dinner—a nine o'clock repast for the officers on duty,
not an official meal with the P.M.—Bean almost followed him right down. He needed to eat, and now was
as good a time as any. But he realized that he had not
read any of his email after getting Sister Carlotta's last
letter, so he told Suriyawong to start without him but
save him a place.

He checked the dropsite that Peter had used to forward Carlotta's message, and found a more recent letter from Peter. This one included the text of a letter
from one of Demosthenes' contacts inside the U.S.
satellite intelligence service, and combined with Peter's own analysis of the situation, it made everything
clear to Bean. He fired off a quick response, taking Peter's suspicions a step further, and then headed down
to dinner.

Suriyawong and the adult officers—several of them
field generals who had been summoned to Bangkok
because of the crisis in the high command—were
laughing. They fell silent when Bean entered the
room. Ordinarily, he might have tried to put them at
ease. Just because he was grieving did not change the
fact that in the midst of crises, humor was needed to
break the tension. But at this moment their silence was
useful, and he used it.

"I just received information from one of my best
sources of intelligence," Bean said. "You in this room
are those who most need to hear it. But if the Prime
Minister could also join us, it would save time."

One of the generals started to protest that a foreign
child did not summon the Prime Minister of Thailand,

but Suriyawong stood and bowed deeply to him. The man stopped talking. "Forgive me, sir," said Suriyawong, "but this foreign boy is Julian Delphiki, whose analysis of the final battle with the Formics led directly to Ender's victory."

Of course the general knew that already, but Suriyawong, by allowing him to pretend that he had not known, gave him a way to backpedal without losing face.

"I see," said the general. "Then perhaps the Prime Minister will not be offended at this summons."

Bean helped Suriyawong smooth things over as best he could. "Forgive me for having spoken with such rudeness. You were right to rebuke me. I can only hope you will excuse me for being forgetful of proper manners. The woman who raised me was on the Air Shanghai flight."

Again, the general certainly knew this; again, it allowed him to bow and murmur his commiseration. Proper respect had been shown to everyone. Now things could proceed.

The Prime Minister left his dinner with various high officials of the Chinese government, and stood against the wall, listening, as Bean relayed what he had learned from Peter about the source of the missile that brought down the jet.

"I have been in consultation off and on all day with the foreign minister of China," said the Prime Minister. "He has said nothing about the missile being launched from inside Thailand."

"When the Chinese government is ready to act on this provocation," said Bean, "they will pretend to have just discovered it."

The Prime Minister looked pained. "Could it not have been Indian operatives trying to make it seem that it was a Chinese venture?"

"It could have been anyone," said Bean. "But it was Chinese."

The prickly general spoke up. "How do you know this, if the satellite does not confirm it?"

"It would make little sense for it to be Indian," said Bean. "The only countries that could possibly detect the truck would be China and the U.S., which is well known to be in China's pocket. But China would know that they had not fired the missile, and they would know that Thailand had not fired it, so what would be the point?"

"It makes no sense for China to do it, either," said the Prime Minister.

"Sir," said Bean, "nothing makes sense in any of the things that have happened in the last few days. India has made a nonaggression pact with Pakistan and both nations have moved their troops away from their shared border. Pakistan is moving against Iran. India has invaded Burma, not because Burma is a prize, but because it stands between India and Thailand, which *is*. But India's attack makes no sense—right, Suriyawong?"

Suriyawong instantly understood that Bean was asking him to share in this, so that it would not all come from a European. "As Bean and I told the Chakri yesterday, the Indian attack on Burma is not just stupidly designed, it was *deliberately* stupidly designed. India has commanders wise enough and well-enough trained to know that sending masses of soldiers across the border, with the huge supply problem they represent, creates an easy target for our strategy of harassment. It also leaves them fully committed. And yet they have launched precisely such an attack."

"So much the better for us," said the prickly general.

"Sir," said Suriyawong, "it is important for you to

understand that they have the services of Petra Arkanian, and both Bean and I know that Petra would never
sign off on the strategy they're using. So that is obviously *not* their strategy."

"What does this have to do with the Air Shanghai
flight?" asked the Prime Minister.

"Everything," said Bean. "And with the attempt on
Suriyawong's and my life last night. The Chakri's little
game was meant to provoke Thailand into an immediate entry into the war with India. And even though the
ploy did not work, and the Chakri was exposed, we are
still maintaining the fiction that it was an Indian provocation. Your meetings with the Chinese foreign minister are part of your effort to involve the Chinese in the
war against India—no, don't tell me that you can't
confirm or deny it, it's obvious that's what such meetings would have to be about. And I'll bet the Chinese
are telling you that they are massing troops on the
Burmese border in order to attack the Indians suddenly, when they are most exposed."

The Prime Minister, who had indeed been opening
his mouth to speak, held his silence.

"Yes, of course they are telling you this. But the Indians also know that the Chinese are massing on the
Burmese border, and yet they proceed with their attack
on Burma, and their forces are almost fully committed,
making no provision for defense against a Chinese attack from the north. Why? Are we going to pretend
that the Indians are *that* stupid?"

It was Suriyawong who answered as it dawned on
him. "The Indians also have a nonaggression pact with
China. They think the Chinese troops are massing at
the border in order to attack *us*. They and the Indians
have divided up southeast Asia."

"So this missile that the Chinese launched from

Thailand to shoot down their own airliner over their own territory," said the Prime Minister, "that will be their excuse to break off negotiations and attack us by surprise?"

"No one is surprised by Chinese treachery," said one of the generals.

"But that's not the whole picture," said Bean. "Because we have not yet accounted for Achilles."

"He's in India," said Suriyawong. "He planned the attempt to kill us last night."

"And we know he planned that attempt," said Bean, "because I was there. He wanted you dead as a provocation, but he gave approval for it to happen last night because we would both be killed in the same explosion. And we know that he is behind the downing of the Air Shanghai jet, because even though the missile was in place for a month, ready to be fired, this was not yet the right moment to create the provocation. The Chinese foreign minister is still in Bangkok. Thailand has not yet had several days to commit its troops to battle, depleting our supplies and sending most of our forces on missions far to the northwest. Chinese troops have not yet fully deployed to the north of us. That missile should not have been fired for several days, at least. But it was fired this morning because Achilles knew Sister Carlotta was on that airplane, and he could not pass up the opportunity to kill her."

"But you said the missile was a Chinese operation," said the Prime Minister. "Achilles is in India."

"Achilles is in India, but is Achilles working for India?"

"Are you saying he's working for China?" asked the Prime Minister.

"Achilles is working for Achilles," said Suriyawong. "But yes, now the picture is clear."

"Not to me," said the prickly general.

Suriyawong eagerly explained. "Achilles has been setting India up from the beginning. While Achilles was still in Russia, he doubtless used the Russian intelligence service to make contacts inside China. He promised he could hand them all of south and southeast Asia in a single blow. Then he goes to India and sets up a war in which India's army is fully committed in Burma. Until now, China has never been able to move against India, because the Indian Army was concentrated in the west and northwest, so that as Chinese troops came over the passes of the Himalayas, they were easily fought off by Indian troops. Now, though, the entire Indian Army is exposed, far from the heartland of India. If the Chinese can achieve a surprise attack and destroy that army, India will be defenseless. They will have no choice but to surrender. We're just a sideshow to them. They will attack us in order to lull the Indians into complacency."

"So they don't intend to invade Thailand?" asked the Prime Minister.

"Of course they do," said Bean. "They intend to rule from the Indus to the Mekong. But the Indian army is the main objective. Once that is destroyed, there is nothing in their way."

"And all this," said the prickly general, "we deduce from the fact that a certain Catholic nun was on the airplane?"

"We deduce this," said Bean, "from the fact that Achilles is controlling events in China, Thailand, and India. Achilles knew Sister Carlotta was on that plane because the Chakri intercepted my message to the Prime Minister. Achilles is running this show. He's betraying everybody to everybody else. And in the end, he stands at the top of a new empire that contains more than half the population of the world. China, India, Burma, Thailand, Vietnam. Everyone will have to accommodate this new superpower."

"But Achilles does not run China," said the Prime Minister. "As far as we know, he has never been *in* China."

"The Chinese no doubt think they're using him," said Bean. "But I know Achilles, and my guess is that within a year, the Chinese leaders will find themselves either dead or taking their orders from him."

"Perhaps," said the Prime Minister, "I should go warn the Chinese foreign minister of the great danger he is in."

The prickly general stood up. "This is what comes of allowing children to play at world affairs. They think that real life is like a computer game, a few mouse clicks and nations rise and fall."

"This is precisely how nations rise and fall," said Bean. "France in 1940. Napoleon remaking the map of Europe in the early 1800s, creating kingdoms so his brothers would have someplace to rule. The victors in World War I, cutting up kingdoms and drawing insane lines on the map that would lead to war again and again. The Japanese conquest of most of the western Pacific in December of 1941. The collapse of the Soviet Empire in 1989. Events can be sudden indeed."

"But those were great forces at work," said the general.

"Napoleon's whims were not a great force. Nor was Alexander, toppling empires wherever he went. There was nothing inevitable about Greeks reaching the Indus."

"I don't need history lessons from you."

Bean was about to retort that yes, apparently he

did—but Suriyawong shook his head. Bean got the message.

Suriyawong was right. The Prime Minister was not convinced, and the only generals who were speaking up were the ones who were downright hostile to Bean's and Suriyawong's ideas. If Bean continued to push, he would merely find himself marginalized in the coming war. And he needed to be in the thick of things, if he was to be able to use the strike force he had so laboriously created.

"Sir," said Bean to the general, "I did not mean to teach you anything. You have nothing to learn from me. I have merely offered you the information I received, and the conclusions I drew from it. If these conclusions are incorrect, I apologize for wasting your time. And if we proceed with the war against India, I ask only for the chance to serve Thailand honorably, in order to repay your kindness to me."

Before the general could say anything—and it was plain he was going to make a haughty reply—the Prime Minister intervened. "Thank you for giving us your best—Thailand survives in this difficult place because our people and our friends offer everything they have in the service of our small but beautiful land. Of course we will want to use you in the coming war. I believe you have a small strike force of highly trained and versatile Thai soldiers. I will see to it that your force is assigned to a commander who will find good use for that force, and for you."

It was a deft announcement to the generals at that table that Bean and Suriyawong were under his protection. Any general who attempted to quash their participation would simply find that they were assigned to another command. Bean could not have hoped for more.

"And now," said the Prime Minister, "while I am happy to have spent this quarter hour in your company, gentlemen, I have the foreign minister of China no doubt wondering why I am so rude as to stay away for all this time."

The Prime Minister bowed and left.

At once the prickly general and the others who were most skeptical returned to the joking conversation that Bean's arrival had interrupted, as if nothing had happened.

But General Phet Noi, who was field commander of all Thai forces in the Malay Peninsula, beckoned to Suriyawong and Bean. Suriyawong picked up his plate and moved to a place beside Phet Noi, while Bean paused only to fill his own plate from the pots on the serving table before joining them.

"So you have a strike force," said Phet Noi.

"Air, sea, and land," said Bean.

"The main Indian offensive," said Phet Noi, "is in the north. My army will be watching for Indian landings on the coast, but our role will be vigilance, not combat. Still, I think that if your strike force launched its missions from the south, you would be less likely to become tangled up in raids originating in the much more important northern commands."

Phet Noi obviously knew that his own command was the one least important to the conduct of the war—but he was as determined to get involved as Bean and Suriyawong were. They could help each other. For the rest of the meal, Bean and Suriyawong conversed earnestly with Phet Noi, discussing where in the Malay panhandle of Thailand the strike force might best be stationed. Finally, they were the last three at table.

"Sir," said Bean, "now that we're alone, the three of us, there is something I must tell you."

"Yes?"

"I will serve you loyally, and I will obey your orders. But if the opportunity comes, I will use my strike force to accomplish an objective that is not, strictly speaking, important to Thailand."

"And that is?"

"My friend Petra Arkanian is the hostage—no, I believe she is the virtual slave—of Achilles. Every day she lives in constant danger. When I have the information necessary to make success likely, I will use my strike force to bring her out of Hyderabad."

Phet Noi thought about this, his face showing nothing. "You know that Achilles may be holding on to her precisely because she is the bait that will lure you into a trap."

"That is possible," said Bean, "but I don't believe that it's what Achilles is doing. He believes he is able to kill anyone, anywhere. He doesn't need to set traps for me. To lie in wait is a sign of weakness. I believe he's holding on to Petra for his own reasons."

"You know him," said Phet Noi, "and I do not." He reflected for a moment. "As I listened to what you said about Achilles and his plans and treacheries, I believed that events might unfold exactly as you said. What I could not see was how Thailand could possibly turn this into victory. Even with advance warning, we can't prevail against China in the field of battle. China's supply lines into Thailand would be short. Almost a quarter of the population of Thailand is Chinese in origin, and while most of them are loyal Thai citizens, a large fraction of them still regard China as their homeland. China would not lack for saboteurs and collaborators within our country, while India has no such connection. How can we prevail?"

"There is only one way," said Bean. "Surrender at once."

"What?" said Suriyawong.

"Prime Minister Paribatra should go to the Chinese foreign minister, declare that Thailand wishes to be an ally of China. We will put most of our military temporarily under Chinese command to be used against the Indian aggressors as needed, and will supply not only our own armies, but the Chinese armies as well, to the limit of our abilities. Chinese merchants will have unrestricted access to Thai markets and manufacturing."

"But that would be shameful," said Suriyawong.

"It was shameful," said Bean, "when Thailand allied itself with Japan during World War II, but Thailand survived and Japanese troops did not occupy Thailand. It was shameful when Thailand bowed to the Europeans and surrendered Laos and Cambodia to France, but the heart of Thailand remained free. If Thailand doesn't preemptively ally itself to China and give China a free hand, then China will rule here anyway, but Thailand itself will utterly lose its freedom and its national existence, for many years at least, and perhaps forever."

"Am I listening to an oracle?" asked Phet Noi.

"You are listening to the fears of your own heart," said Bean. "Sometimes you have to feed the tiger so it won't devour you."

"Thailand will never do this," said Phet Noi.

"Then I suggest you make arrangements for your escape and life in exile," said Bean, "because when the Chinese take over, the ruling class is destroyed."

They all knew Bean was talking about the conquest

of Taiwan. All government officials and their families, all professors, all journalists, all writers, all politicians and their families were taken from Taiwan to reeducation camps in the western desert, where they were set to work performing manual labor, they and their children, for the rest of their lives. None of them ever returned to Taiwan. None of their children ever received approval for education beyond the age of fourteen. The method had been so effective in pacifying Taiwan that there was no chance they would not use the same method in their conquests now.

"Would I be a traitor, to plan for defeat by creating my own escape route?" Phet Noi wondered aloud.

"Or would you be a patriot, keeping at least one Thai general and his family out of the hands of the conquering enemy?" asked Bean.

"Is our defeat certain, then?" asked Suriyawong.

"You can read a map," said Bean. "But miracles happen."

Bean left them to their silent thoughts and returned to his room, to report to Peter on the likely Thai response.

17

On a Bridge

To: Chamrajnagar%sacredriver@ifcom.gov
From: Wiggin%resistance@haiti.gov
Re: For the sake of India, please do
not set foot on Earth

Esteemed Polemarch Chamrajnagar,

For reasons that will be made clear by
the attached essay, which I will soon
publish, I fully expect that you will
return to Earth just in time to be
caught up in India's complete subjugation by China.

If your return to India had any chance
of preserving her independence, you
would bear any risk and return, regard-

less of any advice. And if your estab-
lishing a government in exile could accomplish anything for your native land,
who would try to persuade you to do
otherwise?

But India's strategic position is so
exposed, and China's relentlessness in
conquest is so well known, that you
must know both courses of action are
futile.

Your resignation as Polemarch does not
take effect until you reach Earth. If
you do not board the shuttle, but instead return to IFCom, you remain Polemarch. You are the only possible
Polemarch who could secure the International Fleet. A new commander could not
distinguish between Chinese who are
loyal to the Fleet and those whose first
allegiance is to their now-dominant
homeland. The I.F. must not fall under
the sway of Achilles. You, as Polemarch, could reassign suspect Chinese
to innocuous postings, preventing any
Chinese grab for control. If you return
to Earth, and Achilles has influence
over your successor as Polemarch, the
I.F. will become a tool of conquest.

If you remain as Polemarch, you will be
accused, as an Indian, of planning to
pursue vengeance against China. Therefore, to prove your impartiality and

avoid suspicion, you will have to remain utterly aloof from all Earthside
wars and struggles. You can trust me
and my allies to maintain the resistance to Achilles regardless of the apparent odds, if for no other reason
than this: His ultimate triumph means
our immediate death.

Stay in space and, by doing so, allow
the possibility of humanity escaping
the domination of a madman. In return,
I vow to do all in my power to free India from Chinese rule and return it to
self-rule.

Sincerely, Peter Wiggin

The soldiers around her knew perfectly well who Virlomi was. They also knew the reward that had been offered for her capture—or her dead body. The charge
was treason and espionage. But from the start, as she
passed through the checkpoint at the entrance of the
base at Hyderabad, the common soldiers had believed
in her and befriended her.

"You will hear me accused of spying or worse," she
said, "but it isn't true. A treacherous foreign monster
rules in Hyderabad, and he wants me dead for personal
reasons. Help me."

Without a word, the soldiers walked her away from
where the cameras might spot her, and waited. When
an empty supply truck came up, they stopped it and
while some of them talked to the driver, the others
helped her get in. The truck drove through, and she
was out.

Ever since, she had turned to the footsoldiers for help. Officers might or might not let compassion or righteousness interfere with obedience or ambition— the common soldiers had no such qualms. She was transported in the midst of a crush of soldiers on a crowded train, offered so much food smuggled out of mess halls that she could not eat it all, and given bunk space while weary men slept on the floor. No one laid a hand on her except to help her, and none betrayed her.

She moved across India to the east, toward the war zone, for she knew that her only hope, and the only hope for Petra Arkanian, was for her to find, or be found by, Bean.

Virlomi knew where Bean would be: making trouble for Achilles wherever and however he could. Since the Indian Army had chosen the dangerous and foolish strategy of committing all its manpower to battle, she knew that the effective counterstrategy would be harassment and disruption of supply lines. And Bean would come to whatever point on the supply line was most crucial and yet most difficult to disrupt.

So, as she neared the front, Virlomi went over in her mind the map she had memorized. To move large amounts of supplies and munitions quickly from India to the troops sweeping through the great plain where the Irrawaddy flowed, there were two general routes. The northern route was easier, but far more exposed to raids. The southern route was harder, but more protected. Bean would be working on disrupting the southern route.

Where? There were two roads over the mountains from Imphal in India to Kalemyo in Burma. They both passed through narrow canyons and crossed deep gorges. Where would it be hardest to rebuild a blown bridge or a collapsed highway? On both routes, there were candidate locations. But the hardest to rebuild was on the western route, a long stretch of road carved out of rock along the edge of a steep defile, leading to a bridge over a deep gorge. Bean would not just blow up this bridge, Virlomi thought, because it would not be that hard to span. He would also collapse the road in several places, so the engineers wouldn't be able to get to the place where the bridge must be anchored without first blasting and shaping a new road.

So that is where Virlomi went, and waited.

Water she found flowing cleanly through the side ravines. She was given food by passing soldiers, and soon learned that they were looking for her. Word had spread that the Woman-in-hiding needed food. And still no officer knew to look for her, and still no assassin from Achilles came to kill her. Poor as the soldiers were, apparently the reward did not tempt them. She was proud of her people even as she mourned for them, to have such a man as Achilles rule over them.

She heard of daring raids at easier spots on the eastern road, and traffic on the western road grew heavier, the roads trembling day and night as India burned up her fuel reserves supplying an army far larger than the war required. She asked the soldiers if they had heard of Thai raiders led by a child, and they laughed bitterly. "Two children," they said. "One white, one brown. They come in their helicopters, they destroy, they leave. Whomever they touch, they kill. Whatever they see, they destroy."

Now she began to worry. What if the one that came to take this bridge was not Bean, but the other one? No doubt another Battle School grad—Suriyawong came to mind—but would Bean have told him about her letter? Would he have any idea that she held within her head the plan of the base at Hyderabad? That she knew where Petra was?

Yet she had no choice. She would have to show herself, and hope.

So the days passed, waiting for the sound of the helicopters coming, bringing the strike force that would destroy this road.

———

Suriyawong had never been a commander in Battle School. They closed down the program before he rose to that position. But he had dreamed of command, studied it, planned it, and now, working with Bean in command of this or that configuration of their strike force, he finally understood the terror and exhilaration of having men listen to you, obey you, throw themselves into action and risk death because they trust you. Each time, because these men were so well-trained and resourceful and their tactics so effective, he brought back his whole complement. Injuries, but no deaths. Aborted missions, sometimes—but no deaths.

"It's the aborted missions," said Bean, "that earn you their trust. When you see that it's more dangerous than we anticipated, that it requires attrition to get the objective, then show the men you value their lives more than the objective of the moment. Later, when you have no choice but to commit them to grave risk, they'll know it's because this time it's worth dying. They know you won't spend them like a child, on candy and trash."

Bean was right, which hardly surprised Suriyawong. Bean was not just the smartest, he had also watched

Ender close at hand, had been Ender's secret weapon in Dragon Army, had been his backup commander on Eros. Of course he knew what leadership was.

What surprised Suriyawong was Bean's generosity. Bean had created this strike force, and trained these men, had earned their trust. Throughout that time, Suriyawong had been of little help, and had shown outright hostility at times. Yet Bean included Suriyawong, entrusted him with command, encouraged the men to help Suriyawong learn what they could do. Through it all, Bean had never treated Suriyawong as a subordinate or inferior, but rather had deferred to him as his superior officer.

In return, Suriyawong never commanded Bean to do anything. Rather, they reached a consensus on most things, and when they could not agree, Suriyawong deferred to Bean's decision and supported him in it.

Bean has no ambition, Suriyawong realized. He has no wish to be better than anyone else, or to rule over anyone, or to have more honor.

Then, on the missions where they worked together, Suriyawong saw something else: Bean had no fear of death.

Bullets could be flying, explosives could be near detonation, and Bean would move without fear and with only token concealment. It was as if he dared the enemy to shoot him, dared their own explosives to defy him and go off before he was ready.

Was this courage? Or did he wish for death? Had Sister Carlotta's death taken away some of his will to live? To hear him talk, Suriyawong would not have supposed it. Bean was too grimly determined to rescue Petra for Suriyawong to believe that he wanted to die. He had something urgent to live for. And yet he showed no fear of battle.

It was as if he knew the day that he would die, and this was not that day.

He certainly hadn't stopped caring about anything. Indeed, the quiet, icy, controlled, arrogant Bean that Suriyawong had known before had become, since the day Carlotta died, impatient and agitated. The calm he showed in battle, in front of the men, was certainly not there when he was alone with Suriyawong and Phet Noi. And the favorite object of his curses was not Achilles—he almost never spoke of Achilles—but Peter Wiggin.

"He's had everything for a month! And he does these little things—persuading Chamrajnagar not to return to Earth yet, persuading Ghaffar Wahabi not to invade Iran—and he tells me about them, but the big thing, publishing Achilles' whole treacherous strategy, he won't do that—and he tells *me* not to do it myself! Why not? If the Indian government could be forced to see how Achilles plans to betray them, they might be able to pull enough of their army out of Burma to make a stand against the Chinese. Russia might be able to intervene. The Japanese fleet might threaten Chinese trade. At the very least, the Chinese themselves might see Achilles for what he is, and jettison him even as they follow his plan! And all he says is, It's not the right moment, it's too soon, not yet, you have to trust me, I'm with you on this, right to the end."

He was scarcely kinder in his execrations of the Thai generals running the war—or ruining it, as he said. Suriyawong had to agree with him—the whole plan depended on keeping Thai forces dispersed, but now that the Thai Air Force had control of the air over Burma, they had concentrated their armies and airbases in forward positions. "I told them what the danger was," said Bean, "and they still gather their forces into one convenient place."

Phet Noi listened patiently; Suriyawong, too, gave up trying to argue with him. Bean was right. People were behaving foolishly, and not out of ignorance. Though of course they would say, later, "But we didn't *know* Bean was right."

To which Bean already had his answer: "You didn't know I was wrong! So you should have been prudent!"

The only thing different in Bean's diatribes was that he went hoarse for a week, and when his voice came back, it was lower. For a kid who had always been so tiny, even for his age, puberty—if that's what this was—certainly had struck him young. Or maybe he had just stretched out his vocal cords with all his ranting.

But now, on a mission, Bean was silent, the calm of battle already on him. Suriyawong and Bean boarded their choppers last, making sure all their men were aboard; one last salute to each other, and then they ducked inside and the door closed and the choppers rose into the air. They jetted along near the surface of the Indian Ocean, the chopper blades folded and enclosed until they got near Cheduba Island, today's staging area. Then the choppers dispersed, rose into the air, cut the jets, and opened their blades for vertical landing.

Now they would leave behind their reserves—the men and choppers that could bring out anyone stranded by a mechanical problem or unforeseen complication. Bean and Suriyawong never rode together—one chopper failure should not behead the mission. And each of them had redundant equipment, so that either could complete the whole mission. More than once, the redundancy had saved lives and missions—

Phet Noi made sure they were always equipped because, as he said, "You give the matériel to the commanders who know how to use it."

Bean and Suriyawong were too busy to chat in the staging area, but they did come together for a few moments, as they watched the reserve team camouflage their choppers and scrim their solar collectors. "You know what I wish?" said Bean.

"You mean besides wanting to be an astronaut when you grow up?" said Suriyawong.

"That we could scrub this mission and take off for Hyderabad."

"And get ourselves killed without ever seeing a sign of Petra, who has probably already been moved to someplace in the Himalayas."

"That's the genius of my plan," said Bean. "I take a herd of cattle hostage and threaten to shoot a cow a day till they bring her back."

"Too risky. The cows always make a break for it." But Suriyawong knew that to Bean, the inability to do anything for Petra was a constant ache. "We'll do it. Peter's looking for someone who'll give him current information about Hyderabad."

"Like he's working on publishing Achilles' plans." The favorite diatribe. Only because they were on a mission, Bean remained calm, ironic rather than furious.

"All done," said Suriyawong.

"See you in the mountains."

It was a dangerous mission. The enemy couldn't watch every kilometer of highway, but they had learned to converge quickly when the Thai choppers were spotted, and their strike force was having to finish their missions with less and less time to spare. And this spot was likely to be defended. That was why Bean's contingent—four of the five companies—

would be deployed to clear away any defenders and protect Suriyawong's group while they laid the charges and blew up the road and the bridge.

All was going according to plan—indeed, better than expected, because the enemy seemed not to know they were there—when one of the men pointed out, "There's a woman on the bridge."

"A civilian?"

"You need to see," said the soldier.

Suriyawong left the spot where the explosives were being placed and climbed back up to the bridge. Sure enough, a young Indian woman was standing there, her arms stretched out toward either side of the ravine.

"Has anyone mentioned to her that the bridge is going to explode, and we don't actually care if anyone's on it?"

"Sir," said the soldier, "she's asking for Bean."

"By name?"

He nodded.

Suriyawong looked at the woman again. A very young woman. Her clothing was filthy, tattered. Had it once been a military uniform? It certainly wasn't the way local women dressed.

She looked at him. "Suriyawong," she called.

Behind him, he could hear several soldiers exhale or gasp in surprise or wonder. How did this Indian woman know? It worried Suriyawong a little. The soldiers were reliable in almost everything, but if they once got god-stuff into their heads, it could complicate everything.

"I'm Suriyawong," he said.

"You were in Dragon Army," she said. "And you work with Bean."

"What do you want?" he demanded.

"I want to talk with you privately, here on the bridge."

"Sir, don't go," said the soldier. "Nobody's shooting, but we've spotted a half-dozen Indian soldiers. You're dead if you go out there."

What would Bean do?

Suriyawong stepped out onto the bridge, boldly but not in any hurry. He waited for the gunshot, wondering if he would feel the pain of impact before he heard the sound. Would the nerves of his ears report to his brain faster than the nerves of whatever body part the bullet tore into? Or would the sniper hit him in the head, mooting the point?

No bullet. He came near her, and stopped when she said, "This is as close as you should come, or they'll worry and shoot you."

"You control those soldiers?" asked Suriyawong.

"Don't you know me yet?" she said. "I'm Virlomi. I was ahead of you in Battle School."

He knew the name. He would never have recognized her face. "You left before I got there."

"Not many girls in Battle School. I thought the legend would live on."

"I heard of you."

"I'm a legend here, too. My people aren't firing because they think I know what I'm doing out here. And I thought you recognized me, because your soldiers on both sides of this ravine have refrained from shooting any of the Indian soldiers, even though I know they've spotted them."

"Maybe Bean recognized you," said Sirayawong. "In fact, I've heard your name more recently. You're the one who wrote back to him, aren't you? You were in Hyderabad."

"I know where Petra is."

"Unless they've moved her."

"Do you have any better sources? I tried to think of any way I could to get a message to Bean without getting caught. Finally I realized there was no computer solution. I had to bring the message in my head."

"So come with us."

"Not that simple," she said. "If they think I'm a captive, you'll never get out of here. Handheld g-to-a."

"Ouch," said Suriyawong. "Ambush. They knew we were coming?"

"No," said Virlomi. "They knew I was here. I didn't say anything, but they all knew that the Woman-in-hiding was at this bridge, so they figured that the gods were protecting this place."

"And the gods needed g-to-a missiles?"

"No, *I'm* the one they're protecting. The gods have the bridge, the men have me. So here's the deal. You pull your explosives off the bridge. Abort the mission. They see that I have the power to make the enemy go away without harming anything. And then they watch me call one of your departing choppers down to me, and I get on of my own free will. That's the only way you're getting out of here. Not really anything I designed, but I don't see any other way out."

"I always hate aborting missions," said Suriyawong. But before she could argue, he laughed and said, "No, don't worry, it's fine. It's a good plan. If Bean were down here on this bridge, he'd agree in a heartbeat."

Suriyawong walked back to his men. "No, it's not a god or a holy woman. She's Virlomi, a Battle School grad, and she has intelligence that's more valuable than this bridge. We're aborting the mission."

The soldier took this in, and Suriyawong could see

him trying to factor the magical element in with the orders.

"Soldier," said Suriyawong, "I have not been be-witched. This woman knows the groundplan of the Indian Army high command base in Hyderabad."

"Why would an Indian give that to us?" the soldier asked.

"Because the bunduck who's running the Indian side of the war has a prisoner there who's vital to the war."

Now it was making sense to the soldier. The magic element receded. He pulled his satrad off his belt and punched in the abort code. All the other satrads immediately vibrated in the preset pattern.

At once the explosives teams began dismantling. If they were to evacuate without dismantling, a second code, for urgency, would be sent. Suriyawong did not want any part of their matériel to fall into Indian hands. And he thought a more leisurely pace might be better.

"Soldier, I need to *seem* to be hypnotized by this woman," he said. "I am *not* hypnotized, but I'm faking it so the Indian soldiers all around us will think she's controlling me. Got that?"

"Yes sir."

"So while I walk back toward her, you call Bean and tell him that I need all the choppers but mine to evacuate, so the Indians can see they're gone. Then say 'Petra.' Got that? Tell him *nothing* else, no matter what he asks. We may be monitored, if not here, then in Hyderabad." Or Beijing, but he didn't want to complicate things by saying that.

"Yes sir."

Suriyawong turned his back on the soldier, walked three paces closer to Virlomi, and then prostrated himself before her.

Behind him, he could hear the soldier saying exactly what he had been told to say.

And after a very little while, choppers began to rise into the air from both sides of the ravine. Bean's troops were on the way out.

Suriyawong got up and returned to his men. His company had come in two choppers. "All of you get in the chopper with the explosives," he said. "Only the pilot and co-pilot stay in the other chopper."

The men obeyed immediately, and within three minutes Suriyawong was alone at his end of the bridge. He turned and bowed once again to Virlomi, then walked calmly to his chopper and climbed aboard.

"Rise slowly," he told the pilot, "and then pass slowly near the woman in the middle of the bridge, doorside toward her. At no point is any weapon to be trained on her. Nothing remotely threatening."

Suriyawong watched through the window. Virlomi was not signaling.

"Rise higher, as if we were leaving," said Suriyawong.

The pilot obeyed.

Finally, Virlomi began waving her arms, beckoning with both of them, slowly, as if she were reeling them back in with each movement of her arms.

"Slow down and then begin to descend toward her. I want no chance of error. The last thing we need is some downdraft to get her caught in the blades."

The pilot laughed grimly and brought the chopper like a dancer down onto the bridge, far enough away that Virlomi wasn't actually under the blades, but close enough that it would be only a few steps for her to come aboard.

Suriyawong ran to the door and opened it.

Virlomi did not just walk to the chopper. She danced to it, making ritual-like circling movements with each step.

On impulse, he got out of the chopper and prostrated himself again. When she got near enough, he said—loud enough to be heard over the chopper blades—"Walk on me!"

She did, planting her bare feet on his shoulders and walking down his back. Suriyawong didn't know how they could have communicated more clearly to the Indian soldiers that not only had Virlomi saved their bridge, she had also taken control of this chopper.

She was inside.

He got up, turned slowly, and sauntered onto the chopper.

The sauntering ended the moment he was inside. He rammed the door lever up into place and shouted, "I want jets as fast as you can!"

The chopper rose dizzily. "Strap down," Suriyawong ordered Virlomi. Then, seeing she wasn't familiar with the inside of this craft, he pushed her into place and put the ends of her harness into her hands. She got it at once and finished the job while he hurled himself into his place and got his straps in place just as the chopper cut the blades and plummeted for a moment before the jets kicked in. Then they rocketed down the ravine and out of range of the handheld g-to-a missiles.

"You just made my day," said Suriyawong.

"Took you long enough," said Virlomi. "I thought this bridge was one of the first places you'd hit."

"We figured that's what people would think, so we kept not coming here."

"Greeyaz," she said. "I should have remembered to

think completely ass-backward in order to predict what Battle School brats would do."

———

Bean had known the moment he saw her on the bridge that she had to be Virlomi, the Indian Battle Schooler who had answered his Briseis posting. He could only trust that Suriyawong would realize what was happening before he found the need to shoot somebody. And Surly had not let him down.

When they got back to the staging area, Bean barely greeted Virlomi before he started giving orders. "I want the whole staging area dismantled. Everybody's coming with us." While the company commanders saw to that, Bean ordered one of the chopper communications team to set up a net connection for him.

"That's satellite," the soldier said. "We'll be located right away."

"We'll be gone before anyone can react," said Bean.

Only then did he start explaining to Suriyawong and Virlomi. "We're fully equipped, right?"

"But not fully fueled."

"I'll take care of that," he said. "We're going to Hyderabad right now."

"But I haven't even drawn up the plans."

"Time for that in the air," he said. "This time we ride together, Suriyawong. Can't be helped—we both have to know the whole plan."

"We've waited this long," said Suriyawong. "What's the hurry now?"

"Two things," said Bean. "How long do you think it'll be before word reaches Achilles that our strike force picked up an Indian woman who was waiting for us on a bridge? Second thing—I'm going to force Peter Wiggin's hand. All hell is going to break loose, and we're riding the wave."

"What's the objective?" asked Virlomi. "To save Petra? To kill Achilles?"

"To bring out every Battle School kid who'll come with us."

"They'll never leave India," she said. "I may decide to stay myself."

"Wrong on both counts," said Bean. "I give India less than a week before Chinese troops have control of New Delhi and Hyderabad and any other city they want."

"Chinese?" asked Virlomi. "But there's some kind of—"

"Nonaggression pact?" said Bean. "Arranged by Achilles?"

"He's been working for China all along," said Suriyawong. "The Indian Army is exposed, undersupplied, exhausted, demoralized."

"But . . . if China comes in on the side of the Thai, isn't that what you want?"

Suriyawong gave a sharp, bitter laugh. "China comes in on the side of China. We tried to warn our own people, but they're sure *they* have a deal with Beijing."

Virlomi understood at once. Battle School–trained, she knew how to think the way Bean and Suriyawong did. "So that's why Achilles didn't use Petra's plan."

Bean and Suriyawong laughed and gave short little bows to each other.

"You knew about Petra's plan?"

"We assumed there'd be a better plan than the one India's using."

"So you have a plan to stop China?" said Virlomi.

"Not a chance," said Bean. "China might have been stopped a month ago, but nobody listened." He thought of Peter and barely stanched the fury. "Achilles himself may still be stopped, or at least weakened. But our goal is to keep the Indian Battle School team from falling into Chinese hands. Our Thai friends already have escape routes planned. So when we get to Hyderabad, we not only need to find Petra, we need to offer escape to anyone who'll come. Will they listen to you?"

"We'll see, won't we?" said Virlomi.

"The connection's ready," said a soldier. "I didn't actually link yet, because that's when the clock starts ticking."

"Do it," said Bean. "I've got some things to say to Peter Wiggin."

I'm coming, Petra. I'm getting you out.

As for Achilles, if he happens to come within my reach, there'll be no mercy this time, no relying on someone else to keep him out of circulation. I'll kill him without discussion. And my men will have orders to do the same.

18

Satyagraha

```
encrypt key ********
decrypt key *****
To: Locke%erasmus@polnet.gov
From: Borommakot@chakri.thai.gov/scom
Re: Now, or I will
```

I'm in a battlefield situation and I
need two things from you, now.

First, I need permission from the Sri
Lankan government to land at the base
at Kilinochchi to refuel, ETA less than
an hour. This is a nonmilitary rescue
mission to retrieve Battle School graduates in imminent danger of capture,
torture, enslavement, or at the very
least imprisonment.

Second, to justify this and all other actions I'm about to take; to persuade those Battle Schoolers to come with me; and to create confusion in Hyderabad, I need you to publish now. Repeat, NOW. Or I will publish my own article, here attached, which specifically names you as a coconspirator with the Chinese, as proven by your failure to publish what you know in a timely manner. Even though I don't have Locke's worldwide reach, I have a nice little email list of my own, and my article will get attention. Yours, however, would have far faster results, and I would prefer it to come from you.

Pardon my threat. I can't afford to play any more of your "wait for the right time" games. I'm getting Petra out.

encrypt key *****
decrypt key ********
To: Borommakot@chakri.thai.gov/scom
From: Locke%erasmus@polnet.gov
Re: Done

Confirmed: Sri Lanka grants landing permission/refueling privileges at Kilinochchi for aircraft on humanitarian mission. Thai markings?

Confirmed: my essay released as of now, worldwide push distribution. This in-

```
cludes urgent fyi push into the systems
at Hyderabad and Bangkok.
```

```
Your threat was sweetly loyal to your
friend, but not necessary. This was the
time I was waiting for. Apparently you
didn't realize that the moment I pub-
lished, Achilles would have to move his
operations, and would probably take Pe-
tra with him. How would you have found
her, if I had published a month ago?
```

```
encrypt key ********
decrypt key *****
To: Locke%erasmus@polnet.gov
From: Borommakot@chakri.thai.gov/scom
Re: Done
```

```
Confirm: Thai markings
```

```
As to your excuse: Kuso. If that had
been your reason for delay, you would
have told me a month ago. I know the
real reason, even if you don't, and it
makes me sick.
```

For two weeks after Virlomi disappeared, Achilles had not once come into the planning room—which no one minded, especially after the reward was issued for Virlomi's return. No one dared speak of it openly, but all were glad she had escaped Achilles' vengeance. They were all aware, of course, of the heightened security around them—for their "protection." But it didn't change their lives much. It wasn't as if any of them had ever had time to go frolicking in downtown Hyderabad, or fraternizing with officers twice or three times their age on the base.

Petra was skeptical of the reward offer, though. She knew Achilles well enough to know that he was perfectly capable of offering a reward for the capture of someone he had already killed. What safer cover could he have? Still, if that were the case it would imply that he did not have carte blanche from Tikal Chapekar—if he had to hide things from the Indian government, it meant Achilles was not yet running everything.

When he did return, there was no sign of a bruise on his face. Either Petra's kick had not left a mark, or it took two weeks for it to heal completely. Her own bruises were not yet gone, but no one could see them, since they were under her shirt. She wondered if he had any testicular pain. She wondered if he had had to see a urologist. She did not allow any trace of her gloating to appear on her face.

Achilles was full of talk about how well the war was going and what a good job they were doing in Planning. The army was well supplied and despite the harassment of the cowardly Thai military, the campaign was moving forward on schedule. The revised schedule, of course.

Which was such greeyaz. He was talking to the *planners*. They knew perfectly well that the army was bogged down, that they were still fighting the Burmese in the Irrawaddy plain because the Thai Army's harassment tactics made it impossible to mount the crushing offensive that would have driven the Burmese into the mountains and allowed the Indian Army to proceed into Thailand. Schedule? There was no schedule now.

What Achilles was telling them was: This is the party line. Make sure no memo or email from this room gives anyone even the slightest hint that events are not going according to plan.

It did not change the fact that everyone in Planning could smell defeat. Supplying a huge army on the move was taxing enough to India's limited resources. Supplying it when half the supplies were likely to disappear due to enemy action was chewing through India's resources faster than they could hope to replenish them.

At current rates of manufacture and consumption, the army would run out of munitions in seven weeks. But that would hardly matter—unless some miracle happened, they would run out of nonrenewable fuel in four.

Everyone knew that if Petra's plan had been followed, India would have been able to continue such an offensive indefinitely, and attrition would already have destroyed Burmese resistance. The war would already be on Thai soil, and the Indian Army would not be limping along with a relentless deadline looming up behind them.

They did not talk in the planning room, but at meals they carefully, obliquely discussed things. Was it too late to revert to the other strategy? Not really—but it would require a strategic withdrawal of the bulk of India's army, which would be impossible to conceal from the people and the media. Politically, it would be a disaster. But then, running out of bullets or fuel would be even more disastrous.

"We have to draw up plans for withdrawal anyway," said Sayagi. "Unless some miracle happens in the field—some brilliance in a field commander that has hitherto been invisible, some political collapse in Burma or Thailand—we're going to need a plan to extricate our people."

"I don't think we'll get permission to spend time on that," someone answered.

Petra rarely said anything at meals, despite her new custom of sitting at table with one or another group from Planning. This time, though, she spoke up. "Do it in your heads," she said.

They paused for a moment, and then Sayagi nodded. "Good plan. No confrontation."

From then on, part of mealtime consisted of cryptic reports from each member of the team on the status of every portion of the withdrawal plan.

Another time that Petra spoke had nothing to do with military planning, per se. Someone had jokingly said that this would be a good time for Bose to return. Petra knew the story of Subhas Chandra Bose, the Netaji of the Japanese-backed anti-British-rule Indian National Army during World War II. When he died in a plane crash on the way to Japan at the end of the war, the legend among the Indian people was that he was not really dead, but lived on, planning to return someday to lead the people to freedom. In the centuries since then, invoking the return of Bose was both a joke and a serious comment—that the current leadership was as illegitimate as the British Raj had been.

From the mention of Bose, the conversation turned to a discussion of Gandhi. Someone started talking about "peaceful resistance"—never implying that anyone in Planning might contemplate such a thing, of course—and someone else said, "No, that's *passive* resistance."

That was when Petra spoke up. "This is India, and you know the word. It's satyagraha, and it doesn't mean peaceful or passive resistance at all."

"Not everyone here speaks Hindi," said a Tamil planner.

"But everyone here should know Gandhi," said Petra.

Sayagi agreed with her. "Satyagraha is something else. The willingness to endure great personal suffering in order to do what's right."

"What's the difference, really?"

"Sometimes," said Petra, "what's right is not peaceful or passive. What matters is that you do not hide from the consequences. You bear what must be borne."

"That sounds more like courage than anything else," said the Tamil.

"Courage to do right," said Sayagi. "Courage even when you can't win."

"What happened to 'discretion is the better part of valor'?"

"A quotation from a cowardly character in Shakespeare," someone else pointed out.

"Not contradictory anyway," said Sayagi. "Completely different circumstances. If there's a chance of victory later through withdrawal now, you keep your forces intact. But personally, as an individual, if you know that the price of doing right is terrible loss or suffering or even death, satyagraha means that you are all the more determined to do right, for fear that fear might make you unrighteous."

"Oh, paradoxes within paradoxes."

But Petra turned it from superficial philosophy to something else entirely. "I am trying," she said, "to achieve satyagraha."

And in the silence that followed, she knew that some, at least, understood. She was alive right now because she had *not* achieved satyagraha, because she had *not* always done the right thing, but had done only what was necessary to survive. And she was preparing to change that. To do the right thing regardless of whether she lived through it or not. And for whatever reason—respect for her, uncomfortableness with the intensity of it, or serious contemplation—they remained silent until the meal ended and they spoke again of quotidian things.

Now the war had been going for a month, and Achilles was giving them daily pep talks about how victory was imminent even as they wrestled privately with the growing problems of extricating the army. There *had* been some victories, and at two points the Indian Army was now in Thai territory—but that only lengthened the supply lines and put the army into mountainous country again, where their large numbers could not be brought to bear against the enemy, yet still had to be supplied. And these offensives had chewed through fuel and munitions. In a few days, they would have to choose between fueling tanks and fueling supply trucks. They were about to become a very hungry all-infantry army.

As soon as Achilles left, Sayagi stood up. "It is time to write down our plan for withdrawal and submit it. We must declare victory and withdraw."

There was no dissent. Even though the vids and the nets were full of stories of the great Indian victories, the advance into Thailand, these plans had to be written down, the orders drawn up, while there was still time and fuel enough to carry them out.

So they spent that morning writing each component of the plan. Sayagi, as their de facto leader, assembled them into a single, fairly coherent set of documents. In the meantime, Petra browsed the net and worked on the project she had been assigned by Achilles, taking no part in what they were doing. They didn't need her for this, and it was her desk that was most closely monitored by Achilles. As long as she was being obedient, Achilles might not notice that the others were not.

When they were almost done, she spoke up, even though she knew that Achilles would be notified quickly of what she said—that he might even be listening through that hearing aid in his ear. "Before you email it," she said, "post it."

At first they probably thought she meant the internal posting, where they could all read it. But then they saw that, using her fingernail on a piece of rough tan toilet paper, she had scratched a net address and was now holding it out.

It was Peter Wiggin's "Locke" forum.

They looked at her like she was crazy. To post military plans in a public place?

But then Sayagi began to nod. "They intercept all our emails," he said. "This is the only way it will get to Chapekar himself."

"To make military secrets public," someone said. He did not need to finish. They knew the penalty.

"Satyagraha," said Sayagi. He took the toilet paper with the address and sat down to go to that netsite. "I am the one doing this, and no one else," he said. "The rest of you warned me not to. There is no reason for more than one person to risk the consequences." Moments later, the data was flowing to Peter Wiggin's forum.

Only then did he send it as email to the general command—which would be routed through Achilles' computer.

"Sayagi," someone said. "Did you see what else is posted here? On this netsite?"

Petra also moved to the Locke forum and discovered that the lead essay on Locke's site was headed,

"Chinese treachery and the fall of India." The subhead said, "Will China, too, fall victim to a psychopath's twisted plans?"

Even as they were reading Locke's essay detailing how China had made promises to both Thailand and India, and would attack now that both armies were fully exposed and, in India's case, overextended, they received emails that contained the same essay, pushed into the system on an urgent basis. That meant it had already been cleared at the top—Chapekar knew what Locke was alleging.

Therefore, their emailed plans for immediate withdrawal of Indian troops from Burma had reached Chapekar at exactly the time when he knew they would be necessary.

"Toguro," breathed Sayagi. "We look like geniuses."

"We *are* geniuses," someone grumbled, and everyone laughed.

"Does anyone think," asked the Tamil, "we'll hear another pep talk from our Belgian friend about how well the war is going?"

Almost as an answer, they heard gunfire outside.

Petra felt a thrill of hope run through her: Achilles tried to make a run for it, and he was shot.

But then a more practical idea replaced her hope: Achilles foresaw this possibility, and has his own forces already in place to cover his escape.

And finally, despair: When he comes for me, will it be to kill me, or take me with him?

More gunfire.

"Maybe," said Sayagi, "we ought to disperse."

He was walking toward the door when it opened and Achilles came in, followed by six Sikhs carrying automatic weapons. "Have a seat, Sayagi," said Achilles. "I'm afraid we have a hostage situation here. Someone made some libelous assertions about me on the nets, and when I declined to be detained during the inquiry, shooting began. Fortunately, I have some friends, and while we're waiting for them to provide me with transportation to a neutral location, you are my guarantors of safety."

Immediately, the two Battle School grads who were Sikhs stood up and said, to Achilles' soldiers, "Are we under threat of death from you?"

"As long as you serve the oppressor," one of them answered.

"*He* is the oppressor!" one of the Sikh Battle Schoolers said, pointing to Achilles.

"Do you think the Chinese will be any kinder to our people than New Delhi has?" said the other.

"Remember how the Chinese treated Tibet and Taiwan! That is our future, because of *him*!"

The Sikh soldiers were obviously wavering.

Achilles drew a pistol from his back and shot the soldiers dead, one after another. The last two had time to try to rush at him, but every shot he fired struck home.

The pistol shots still rang in the room when Sayagi said, "Why didn't they shoot you?"

"I had them unload their weapons before entering the room," Achilles said. "I told them we didn't want any accidents. But don't think you can overpower me because I'm alone with a half-empty clip. This room has long been wired with explosives, and they go off when my heart stops beating or when I activate the controller implanted under the skin of my chest."

A pocket phone beeped and, without lowering his gun, Achilles answered it. "No, I'm afraid one of my soldiers went out of control, and in order to keep the children safe, I had to shoot some of my own men.

The situation is unchanged. I am monitoring the perimeter. Keep back, and these children will be safe."

Petra wanted to laugh. Most of the Battle Schoolers here were older than Achilles himself.

Achilles clicked off the phone and pocketed it. "I'm afraid I told them that I had you as my hostages before it was actually true."

"Caught you with your pants down, né?" said Sayagi. "You had no way of knowing you'd need hostages, or that we'd all be here. There are no explosives in this room."

Achilles turned to him and calmly shot him in the head. Sayagi crumpled and fell. Several of the others cried out. Achilles calmly changed clips.

No one charged him while he was reloading.

Not even, thought Petra, me.

There's nothing like casual murder to turn the onlookers into vegetables.

"Satyagraha," said Petra.

Achilles whirled on her. "What was that? What language?"

"Hindi," she said. "It means, 'One bears what one must.'"

"No more Hindi," said Achilles. "From anyone. Or any other language but Common. And if you talk, it had better be to me, and it had better not be something stupid and defiant like the words that got Sayagi killed. If all goes well, my relief should be here in only a few hours. And then Petra and I will go away and leave you to your new government. A Chinese government."

Many of them looked at Petra then. She smiled at Achilles. "So your tent door is still open?"

He smiled back. Warmly. Lovingly. Like a kiss.

But she knew that he was taking her away solely in order to relish the time in which she would have false hopes, before he pushed her from a helicopter or strangled her on the tarmac or, if he grew too impatient, simply shot her as she prepared to follow him out of this room. His time with her was over. His triumph was near—the architect of China's conquest of India, returning to China as a hero. Already plotting how he would take control of the Chinese government and then set out to conquer the other half of the world's population.

For now, though, she was alive, and so were the other Battle Schoolers, except Sayagi. The reason Sayagi died, of course, was not what he said to Achilles. He died because he was the one who posted the withdrawal plans on Locke's forum. Being plans for a retreat under unpredictable fire, they were still usable even with Chinese troops pouring down into Burma, even with Chinese planes bombing the retreating soldiers. The Indian commanders would be able to make a stand. The Chinese would have to fight hard before they won.

But they would win. The Indian defense could last no more than a few days, no matter how bravely they fought. That was when the trucks would stop rolling and food and munitions would run out. The war was already lost. There was only a little time for the Indian elite to attempt to flee before the Chinese swept in, unresisted, with their behead-the-society method of controlling an occupied country.

While these events unfolded, the Battle School graduates who would have kept India out of this dangerous situation in the first place, and whose planning was the only thing keeping the Chinese temporarily at bay, sat in a large room with seven corpses, one gun, and the young man who had betrayed them all.

More than three hours later, gunfire began again, in the distance. The booming sound of anti-aircraft guns.

Achilles was on the phone in an instant. "Don't fire at the incoming aircraft," he said, "or these geniuses start dying."

He clicked off before they could say anything in reply.

The shooting stopped.

They heard the rotors—choppers landing on the roof.

What a stupid place for them to land, thought Petra. Just because the roof is marked as a heliport doesn't mean they have to obey the signs. Up there, the Indian soldiers surrounding this place will have an easy target, and they'll see everything that happens. They'll know when Achilles is on the roof. They'll know which chopper to shoot down first, because he's in it. If this is the best plan the Chinese can come up with, Achilles is going to have a harder time using China as a base to take over the world than he thinks.

More choppers. Now that the roof was full, a few of them were landing on the grounds.

The door burst open, and a dozen Chinese soldiers fanned out through the room. A Chinese officer followed them in and saluted Achilles. "We came at once, sir."

"Good work," said Achilles. "Let's get them all up on the roof."

"You said you'd let us go!" said one of the Battle Schoolers.

"One way or another," said Achilles, "you're all going to end up in China anyway. Now get up and form into a line against that wall."

More choppers. And then the whoosh, whump of an explosion.

"Those stupid eemos," said the Tamil, "they're going to get us all killed."

"Such a shame," said Achilles, pointing his pistol at the Tamil's head.

The Chinese officer was already talking into his satrad. "Wait," he said. "It's not the Indians. They've got Thai markings."

Bean, thought Petra. You've come at last. Either that or death. Because if Bean wasn't running this Thai raid, the Thai could have no other objective than to kill everything that moved in Hyderabad.

Another whoosh-whump. Another. "They've taken out everything on the roof," the Chinese officer said. "The building's on fire, we've got to get out."

"Whose stupid idea was it to land up there anyway?" asked Achilles.

"It was the closest point to evacuate them from!" answered the officer angrily. "There aren't enough choppers left to take all these."

"They're coming," said Achilles, "even if we have to leave soldiers behind."

"We'll get them in a few days anyway. I don't leave my men behind!"

Not a bad commander, even if he's a little dim about tactics, thought Petra.

"They won't let us take off unless we've got their Indian geniuses with us."

"The Thai won't let us take off at all!"

"Of course they will," said Achilles. "They're here to kill me and rescue *her*." He pointed at Petra.

So Achilles knew it was Bean that was coming.

Petra showed nothing on her face.

If Achilles decided to leave without the hostages, there was a good chance he would kill them all. Deprive the enemy of a resource. And, more important, take away their hope.

"Achilles," she said, walking toward him. "Let's leave these others and get out. We'll be taking off from the ground. They won't know who's in what chopper. As long as we go *now.*"

As she approached him, he swung his pistol to point at her chest. She did not even pause, merely walked toward him, past him, to the door. She opened it. "Now, Achilles. You don't have to die in flames today, but that's where you're headed, the longer you wait."

"She's right," said the Chinese officer.

Achilles grinned and looked from Petra to the officer and back again. We've shamed you in front of the others, thought Petra. We've shown that we knew what to do, and you didn't. Now you have to kill us both. This officer doesn't know he's dead, but I do. Then again, I was dead anyway. So now let's get out of here without killing anybody else.

"Nothing in this room matters but you," said Petra. She grinned back at him. "Soak a noky, boy."

Achilles turned back to point the gun, first at one Battle Schooler, then another. They recoiled or flinched, but he did not fire. He dropped his gun hand to his side and walked from the room, grabbing Petra by the arm as he passed her. "Come on, Pet," he said. "The future is calling."

Bean is coming, thought Petra, and Achilles is not going to let me get even a meter away from him. He knows Bean is here for me, so I'm the one person he'll make sure Bean never rescues.

Maybe we'll all kill each other today.

She thought back to the airplane ride that brought her and Achilles to India. The two of them standing at the open door. Maybe there would be another chance today—to die, taking Achilles with her. She wondered if Bean would understand that it was more important for Achilles to die than for her to live. More important, would he know that *she* understood that? It was the right thing to do, and now that she really knew Achilles, the kind of man he was, she would gladly pay that price and call it cheap.

19

Rescue

To:Wahabi%inshallah@Pakistan.gov
From:Chapekar%hope@India.gov
Re:For the Indian people

My Dear Friend Ghaffar,
I honor you because when I came to you
with an offer of peace between our two
families within the Indian people, you
accepted and kept your word in every
particular.

I honor you because you have lived a
life that places the good of your people above your own ambition.

I honor you because in you rests the
hope for my people's future.

I make this letter public even as I
send it to you, not knowing what your
response will be, for my people must
know now, while I can still speak to
them all, what I am asking of you and
giving to you.

As the treacherous Chinese violate
their promises and threaten to destroy
our army, which has been weakened by
the treachery of the one called
Achilles, whom we treated as a guest
and a friend, it is clear to me that
without a miracle, the vast expanse of
the nation of India will be defenseless
against the invaders pouring into our
country from the north. Soon the ruthless conqueror will work his will from
Bengal to Punjab. Of all the Indian
people, only those in Pakistan, led by
you, will be free.

I ask you now to take upon yourself all
the hopes of the Indian people. Our
struggle over the next few days will
give you time, I hope, to bring your
armies back to our border, where you
will be prepared to stand against the
Chinese enemy.

I now give you permission to cross that
border at any point where it is necessary, so you can establish stronger defensive positions. I order all Indian

soldiers remaining at the Pakistani border to offer no resistance whatsoever to Pakistani forces entering our country, and to cooperate by providing full maps of all our defenses, and all codes and codebooks. All our matériel at the border is to be turned over to Pakistan as well.

I ask you that any citizens of India who come under the rule of the Pakistani government be treated as generously as you would wish us, were our situations reversed, to treat your people. Whatever past offenses have been committed between our families, let us forgive each other and commit no new offenses, but treat each other as brothers and sisters who have been faithful to different faces of the same God, and who must now stand shoulder to shoulder to defend India against the invader whose only god is power and whose worship is cruelty.

Many members of the Indian government, military, and educational system will flee to Pakistan. I beg you to open your borders to them, for if they remain in India, only death or captivity will be in their future. All other Indians have no reason to fear individual persecution from the Chinese, and I beg you not to flee to Pakistan, but rather to

remain inside India, where, God willing, you will soon be liberated.

I myself will remain in India, to bear
whatever burden is placed upon my people by the conqueror. I would rather be
Mandela than de Gaulle. There is to be
no government-in-exile. Pakistan is
the government of the Indian people
now. I say this with the full authority
of Congress.

May God bless all honorable people, and
keep them free.

Your brother and friend,
Tikal Chapekar

Jetting over the dry southern reaches of India felt to
Bean like a strange dream, where the landscape never
changed. Or no, it was a vidgame, with a computer
making up scenery on the fly, recycling the same algorithms to create the same type of scenery in general,
but never quite the same in detail.

Like human beings. DNA that differed by only the
tiniest amounts from person to person, and yet those
differences giving rise to saints and monsters, fools
and geniuses, builders and wreckers, lovers and takers.
More people live in this one country, India, than lived
in the whole world only three or four centuries ago.
More people live here today than lived in the entire
history of the world up to the time of Christ. All the
history of the Bible and the Iliad and Herodotus and
Gilgamesh and everything that had been pieced to-

gether by archaeologists and anthropologists, all of those human relationships, all those achievements, could all have been played out by the people we're flying over right now, with people left over to live through new stories that no one would ever hear.

In these few days, China would conquer enough people to make five thousand years of human history, and they would treat them like grass, to be mown till all were the same level, with anything that rose above that level discarded to be mere compost.

And what am I doing? Riding along on a machine that would have given that old prophet Ezekiel a heart attack before he could even write about seeing a shark in the sky. Sister Carlotta used to joke that Battle School was the wheel in the sky that Ezekiel saw in his vision. So here I am, like a figure out of some ancient vision, and what am I doing? That's right, out of the billions of people I might have saved, I'm choosing the one I happen to know and like the best, and risking the lives of a couple of hundred good soldiers in order to do it. And if we get out of this alive, what will I do then? Spend the few years of life remaining to me, helping Peter Wiggin defeat Achilles so he can do exactly what Achilles is already so close to doing—unite humanity under the rule of one sick, ambitious marubo?

Sister Carlotta liked to quote from another biblical git—vanity, vanity, all is vanity. There is nothing new under the sun. A time to scatter rocks and a time to gather rocks together.

Well, as long as God didn't tell anybody what the rocks were for, I might as well leave the rocks and go get my friend, if I can.

As they approached Hyderabad, they picked up a lot of radio chatter. Tactical stuff from satrads, not just the net traffic you'd expect because of the Chinese surprise attack in Burma that had been triggered by Peter's essay. As they got closer, the onboard computers were able to distinguish the radio signatures of Chinese troops as well as Indian.

"Looks like Achilles' retrieval crew got here ahead of us," said Suriyawong.

"But no shooting," said Bean. "Which means they've already got to the planning room and they're holding the Battle Schoolers as hostages."

"You got it," said Suriyawong. "Three choppers on the roof."

"There'll be more on the ground, but let's complicate their lives and take out those three."

Virlomi had misgivings. "What if they think it's the Indian Army attacking and they kill the hostages?"

"Achilles is not so stupid he won't make sure who's doing the shooting before he starts using up his ticket home."

It was like target practice, and three missiles took out three choppers, just like that.

"Now get us onto blades and show the Thai markings," said Suriyawong.

It was, as usual, a sickening climb and drop before the blades took over. But Bean was used to the sense of clawing nausea and was able to notice, out the windows, that the Indian troops were cheering and waving.

"Oh, suddenly now we're the good guys," said Bean.

"I think we're just the not-quite-so-evil guys," said Suriyawong.

"I think you're taking irresponsible risks with the lives of my friends," said Virlomi.

Bean sobered at once. "Virlomi, I know Achilles, and the only way to keep him from killing your friends, just for spite, is to keep him worried and off balance. To give him no time to display his malice."

"I meant that if one of those missiles had gone astray," she said, "it could have hit the room they're in and killed them all."

"Oh, is that all you're worried about?" Bean said. "Virlomi, I *trained* these men. There are situations in which they might miss, but this was not one of them."

Virlomi nodded. "I understand. The confidence of the field commander. It's been a long time since I had a toon of my own."

A few choppers stayed aloft, watching the perimeter; most set down in front of the building where the planning room was located. Suriyawong had already briefed the company commanders he was taking into the building by satrad as they flew. Now he jumped from the chopper as soon as the door opened and, with Virlomi running behind him, he got his group moving, executing the plan.

At once, Bean's chopper lifted back up and, with another chopper, hopped the building to come down on the other side. This was where they found the two remaining Chinese helicopters, blades spinning. Bean had his pilot set down so the chopper's weapons were pointed at the sides of the two Chinese machines. Then he and the thirty men with him went out both doors as Chinese troops across the open space between them did the same.

Bean's other chopper remained airborne, waiting to see whether its missiles or the troops inside would be needed first.

The Chinese had Bean's troops outnumbered, but that wasn't really the issue. Nobody was shooting, because the Chinese wanted to get away alive, and there was no hope of that if shooting broke out, because the airborne chopper would simply destroy both the remaining Chinese machines and then it wouldn't matter

what happened on the ground, they'd never get home
and their mission would be a failure.

So the two little armies formed up just like regiments in the Napoleonic wars, neat little lines. Bean
wanted to shout something like "fix bayonets" or
"load"—but nobody was using muskets and besides,
what interested him would be coming out the door of
the building. . . .

And there he was, rushing straight for the nearest
chopper, gripping Petra by the arm and half-dragging
her along. Achilles held a pistol down at his side. Bean
wanted to have one of his sharpshooters take him out,
but he knew that then the Chinese would open fire and
Petra would certainly be killed. So he called out to
Achilles.

Achilles ignored him. Bean knew what he was
thinking—get inside the chopper while everybody's
holding their fire, and then Bean would be helpless,
unable to do anything to Achilles without also harming
Petra.

So Bean spoke into his satrad and the hovering
chopper did what the gunner was trained to do—fired
a missile that blew up just beyond the nearer Chinese
chopper. The machine itself blocked the blast so Petra
and Achilles weren't hurt—but the chopper was
rocked over onto its side and then, as the blades
chewed to bits against the ground, it flipped over and
over and smashed up against a barracks. A few soldiers
slithered out, trying to drag out others with broken
limbs or other injuries before the machine went up in
flames.

Achilles and Petra now stood in the middle of the
open space. The only remaining Chinese chopper was
too far for him to run to. He did the only thing he could
do, under the circumstances. He held Petra in front of

him with a gun pointed to her head. It wasn't a move they taught you in Battle School. It was straight from the vids.

In the meantime, the Chinese officer in charge—a colonel, if Bean remembered correctly how to translate the rank insignia, which was a very high rank for a small-scale operation like this one—strode out with his men. Bean did not have to instruct him to stay far away from Achilles and Petra. The colonel would know that any move to get between Achilles and Bean's men would lead to shooting, since there was only a stalemate as long as Bean had the ability to kill Achilles the moment he harmed Petra.

Without looking at the soldiers near him, Bean said, "Who has a trank pistol?"

One was slapped into his open hand. Someone murmured, "Keep your hand on a real gun, too."

And someone else said, "I hope the Indian Army doesn't realize that Achilles doesn't have *any* Indian kids with him. They couldn't care less about an Armenian." Bean appreciated it when his men thought through the whole situation. No time for praise now, though.

He stepped away from his men and walked toward Achilles and Petra. As he did, he saw Suriyawong and Virlomi come out the door through which the Chinese colonel had just come. Suriyawong called out, "All secure. Loading. Achilles murdered only one of ours."

"One of 'ours'?" said Achilles. "When did Sayagi become one of *yours*? You mean that I can kill anybody else and you don't care, but touch a Battle School brat and I'm a murderer?"

"You're never taking off in that chopper with Petra," said Bean.

"I know I'm never taking off *without* her," said

Achilles. "If I don't have her with me, you'll blow that chopper into bits so small they'd have to use a comb to gather them up."

"Then I guess I'll just have one of my sharpshooters kill you."

Petra smiled.

She was telling him yes, do it.

"Colonel Yuan-xi will then regard his mission as a failure, and he will kill as many of you as he can. Petra first."

Bean saw that the colonel had gotten his men on board the chopper—those who had come with him from the building and those who had deployed from the choppers when Bean first landed. Only he, Achilles, and Petra remained outside.

"Colonel," said Bean, "the only way this doesn't end in blood is if we can trust each other's word. I promise you that as long as Petra is alive, uninjured, and with me, you can take off safely with no interference from me or my strike force. Whether you have Achilles with you is of no importance to me."

Petra's smile vanished, replaced with a face that was an obvious mask of anger. She did not want Achilles to get away.

But she still hoped to live—that was why she was saying nothing, so Achilles wouldn't know that she was demanding his death, even at the cost of her own.

What she was ignoring was the fact that the Chinese commander had to meet the minimum conditions for mission success—he had to have Achilles with him when he left. If he didn't, a lot of people here would die, and for what? Achilles' worst deeds were already done. From here on, no one would ever trust his word on anything. Whatever power he got now would be by force and fear, not by deception. Which meant that he would be making enemies every day, driving people into the arms of his opponents.

He might still win more battles and more wars and he might even seem to triumph completely, but, like Caligula, he would make assassins out of the people closest to him. And when he died, men just as evil but perhaps not as crazy would take his place. Killing him now would not make that much difference to the world.

Keeping Petra alive, however, would make all the difference in the world to Bean. He had made the mistakes that killed Poke and Sister Carlotta. But he was going to make no mistakes today. Petra would live because Bean couldn't bear any other outcome. She didn't even get a vote on the matter.

The colonel was weighing the situation.

Achilles was not. "I'm moving to the chopper now. My fingers are pretty tight on this trigger. Don't make me flinch, Bean."

Bean knew what Achilles was thinking: Can I kill Bean at the last moment and still get away, or should I leave that pleasure for another time?

And that was an advantage for Bean, because his thinking was not clouded by thoughts of personal vengeance.

Except, he realized, that it was. Because he, too, was trying to think of some way to save Petra and still kill Achilles.

The colonel walked up closer behind Achilles before calling out his answer to Bean. "Achilles is the architect of a great Chinese victory, and he must come to

Beijing to be received in honor. My orders say nothing about the Armenian."

"They'll never let us take off without her, you fool," said Achilles.

"Sir, I give you my word, my parole. Even though Achilles has already murdered a woman and a girl who did nothing but good for him, and deserves to die for his crimes, I will let him go and let you go."

"Then our missions do not conflict," said the colonel. "I agree to your terms, provided you also agree to care for any of my men who remain behind according to the rules of war."

"I agree," said Bean.

"I'm in charge of our mission," said Achilles, "and I don't agree."

"You are not in charge of our mission, sir," said the colonel.

Bean knew exactly what Achilles would do. He would take the gun away from Petra's head long enough to shoot the colonel. Achilles would expect this move to surprise people, but Bean was not surprised at all. His hand with the trank gun was already rising before Achilles even started to turn to the colonel.

But Bean was not the only one who knew what to expect from Achilles. The colonel had deliberately moved close enough to Achilles that as he swung the gun around, the colonel slapped the weapon out of Achilles' hand. At the same moment, with his other hand the colonel slapped Achilles' arm close to the elbow, and even though there seemed to be almost no force behind the blow, Achilles' arm bent sickeningly backward. Achilles cried out in pain and dropped to his knees, letting go of Petra. She immediately launched herself to the side, out of the way, and at that moment Bean fired the trank gun. He was able to adjust the aim at the last split second, and the tiny pellet struck Achilles' shirt with such force that even though the casing collapsed against the cloth, the tranquilizer blew right through the fabric and penetrated Achilles' skin. He collapsed immediately.

"It's only a tranquilizer," said Bean. "He'll be awake in six hours or so, with a headache."

The colonel stood there, not bending yet to even notice Achilles, his eyes still fixed on Bean. "Now there is no hostage. Your enemy is on the ground. How good is your word, sir, when the circumstance in which it was given goes away?"

"Men of honor," said Bean, "are brothers no matter what uniform they wear. You may put him aboard, and take off. I recommend that you fly in formation with us until we are south of the defenses around Hyderabad. Then you may fly your own course, and we'll fly ours."

"That is a wise plan," said the colonel.

He knelt and started to pick up Achilles' limp body. It was tricky work, and so Bean, small as he was, stepped forward to help by taking Achilles' legs.

Petra was on her feet by then, and when Bean glanced at her he could see that she was eyeing Achilles' pistol, which lay on the ground near her. Bean could almost read her mind. To kill Achilles with his own gun had to be tempting—and Petra had not given her word.

But before she could even move toward the pistol, Bean had his trank gun pointed at her. "You could also wake up in six hours with a headache," he said.

"No need," she said. "I know that I'm also bound by your word." And, without stooping for the gun, she came and helped Bean carry his end of Achilles' body.

They rolled Achilles through the wide door of the chopper. Soldiers inside the machine took him and carried him back, presumably to a place where he could be secured during flight maneuvers. The chopper was grossly overcrowded, but only with men— there were no supplies or heavy munitions, so it would fly as well as normal. It would simply be uncomfortable for the passengers.

"You don't want to ride home on that chopper," said Bean. "I invite you to ride with us."

"But you're not going where I'm going," said the colonel.

"I know this boy you have just taken aboard," said Bean. "Even if he doesn't remember what you did when he wakes up, someone will tell him someday, and once he knows, you'll be marked. He never forgets. He will certainly kill you."

"Then I will have died obeying my orders and fulfilling my mission," said the colonel.

"Full asylum," said Bean, "and a life spent helping liberate China and all other nations from the kind of evil he represents."

"I know that you mean to be kind," said the colonel, "but it hurts my soul to be offered such rewards for betraying my country."

"Your country is led by men without honor," said Bean. "And yet they are sustained in power by the honor of men like you. Who, then, betrays his country? No, we have no time for arguments. I only plant the idea so it will fester in your soul." Bean smiled.

The colonel smiled back. "Then you are a devil, sir, as we Chinese always knew you Europeans to be."

Bean saluted him. He returned the salute and got on board.

The chopper door closed.

Bean and Petra ran out of the downdraft as the Chinese machine rose up into the air. There it hovered as Bean ordered everyone into the one chopper that remained on the ground. Less than two minutes later, his chopper, too, rose up, and the Thai and Chinese machines flew together over the building, where they were joined by the other helijets of Bean's strike force as they rose up from the ground or converged from their watching points at the perimeter.

They flew together toward the south, slowly, on blades. No Indian weapon was fired at them. For the Indian officers no doubt knew that their best young military minds were being taken to far more safety than they could possibly have in Hyderabad, or anywhere in India, once the Chinese came in force.

Then Bean gave the order, and all his choppers rose up, cut the blades, and dropped as the jets came on and the blades folded back for the quick ride back to Sri Lanka.

Inside the chopper, Petra sat glumly in her straps. Virlomi was beside her, but they did not speak to each other.

"Petra," said Bean.

She did not look up.

"Virlomi found us, we did not find her. Because of her, we were able to come for you."

Petra still did not look up, but she reached out a hand and laid it on Virlomi's hands, which were clasped in her lap. "You were brave and good," said Petra. "Thank you for having compassion for me."

Then she looked up to meet Bean's gaze. "But I don't thank *you,* Bean. I was ready to kill him. I would have done it. I would have found a way."

"He's going to kill himself in the end," said Bean. "He's going to overreach himself, like Robespierre, like Stalin. Others will see his pattern and when they realize he's finally about to put them to the guillotine, they'll decide they've had enough and he will, most certainly, die."

"But how many will he kill along the way? And now your hands are stained with all their blood, because you loaded him onto that chopper alive. Mine, too."

"You're wrong," said Bean. "He is the only one responsible for his killings. And you're wrong about what would have happened if we had let him take you along. You would not have lived through that ride."

"You don't know that."

"I know Achilles. When that chopper rose to about twenty stories up, you would have been pushed out the door. And do you know why?"

"So you could watch," she said.

"No, he would have waited till I was gone," said Bean. "He's not stupid. He regards his own survival as far more important than your death."

"Then why would he kill me now? Why are you so sure?"

"Because he had his arm around you like a lover," said Bean. "Standing there with the gun to your head, he held you with affection. I think he meant to kiss you before he took you on board. He'd want me to see that."

"She would never let him kiss her," said Virlomi with disgust.

But Petra met Bean's gaze, and the tears in her eyes were a truer answer than Virlomi's brave words. She had already let Achilles kiss her. Just like Poke.

"He marked you," said Bean. "He loved you. You had power over him. After he didn't need you anymore as the hostage to keep me from killing him, you could not go on living."

Suriyawong shuddered. "What made him that way?"

"Nothing *made* him that way," said Bean. "No matter what terrible things happened in his life, no matter what dreadful hungers rose up from his soul, he chose to act on those desires, he chose to do the things he did. *He's* responsible for his own actions, and no one else. Not even those who saved his life."

"Like you and me today," said Petra.

"Sister Carlotta saved his life today," said Bean. "The last thing she asked me was to leave vengeance up to God."

"Do you believe in God?" asked Suriyawong, surprised.

"More and more," said Bean. "And less and less."

Virlomi took Petra's hands between hers and said, "Enough of blame and enough of Achilles. You're free of him. You can have whole minutes and hours and days in which you don't have to think of what he'll do to you if he hears what you say, and how you have to act when he might be watching. The only way he can hurt you now is if you keep watching *him* in your own heart."

"Listen to her, Petra," said Suriyawong. "She's a goddess, you know."

Virlomi laughed. "I save bridges and summon choppers."

"And you blessed me," said Suriyawong.

"I never did," said Virlomi.

"When you walked on my back," said Suriyawong. "My whole body is now the path of a goddess."

"Only the back part," said Virlomi. "You'll have to find someone else to bless the front."

While they bantered, half-drunk with success and liberty and the overwhelming tragedy they were leaving behind them, Bean watched Petra, saw the tears drop from her eyes onto her lap, longed to be able to reach out and touch them away from her eyes. But what good would that do? Those tears had risen up from deep wells of pain, and his mere touch would do nothing to dry them at their source. It would take time to do that, and time was the one thing that he did not have. If Petra knew happiness in her life—happiness, that precious thing that Mrs. Wiggin talked about—it would come when she shared her life with someone else. Bean had saved her, had freed her, not so he could have her or be part of her life, but so that he did not have to bear the guilt of her death as he bore the deaths of Poke and Carlotta. It was a selfish thing he did, in a way. But in another way, there would be nothing for himself at all from this day's work.

Except that when his death came, sooner rather than later, he might well look back on this day's work with more pride than anything else in his life. Because today he won. In the midst of all this terrible defeat, he had found a victory. He had cheated Achilles out of one of his favorite murders. He had saved the life of his dearest friend, even though she wasn't quite grateful yet. His army had done what he needed it to do, and not one life had been lost out of the two hundred men he had first been given. Always before he had been part of someone else's victory. But today, today *he* won.

20

Hegemon

To: Chamrajnagar%Jawaharlal@ifcom.gov
From:PeterWiggin%freeworld@hegemon.gov
Re: Confirmation

Dear Polemarch Chamrajnagar,
Thank you for allowing me to reconfirm
your appointment as Polemarch as my
first official act. We both know that I
was giving you only what you already
had, while you, by accepting that re-
confirmation as if it actually meant
something, restored to the office of
Hegemon some of the luster that has
been torn from it by the events of recent months. There are many who feel
that it is an empty gesture to appoint
a Hegemon who leads only about a third

of the human race and has no particular influence over the third that officially supports him. Many nations are racing to find some accommodation with the Chinese and their allies, and I live under the constant threat of having my office abolished as one of the first gestures they can make to win the favor of the new superpower. I am, in short, a Hegemon without hegemony.

And it is all the more remarkable that you would make this generous gesture toward the very individual that you once regarded as the worst of all possible Hegemons. The weaknesses in my character that you saw then have not magically vanished. It is only by comparison with Achilles, and only in a world where your homeland groans under the Chinese lash, that I begin to look like an attractive alternative or a source of hope instead of despair. But regardless of my weaknesses, I also have strengths, and I make you a promise:

Even though you are bound by your oath of office never to use the International Fleet to influence the course of events on Earth, except to intercept nuclear weapons or punish those who use them, I know that you are still a man of Earth, a man of India, and you care deeply

```
what happens to all people, and partic-
ularly to your people. Therefore I
promise you that I will devote the rest
of my life to reshaping this world into
one that you would be glad of, for your
people, and for all people. And I hope
that I succeed well enough, before one
or the other of us dies, that you will
be glad of the support you gave to me
today.

Sincerely,
Peter Wiggin, Hegemon
```

Over a million Indians made it out of India before the Chinese sealed the borders. Out of a population of a billion and a half, that was far too few. At least ten times that million were transported over the next year, from India to the cold lands of Manchuria and the high deserts of Sinkiang. Among the transported ones was Tikal Chapekar. The Chinese gave no report to outsiders about the fate of him or any of the other "former oppressors of the Indian people." The same, on a far smaller scale, happened to the governing elites of Burma, Thailand, Vietnam, Cambodia, and Laos.

As if this vast redrawing of the world's map were not enough, Russia announced that it had joined China as its ally, and that it considered the nations of eastern Europe that were not loyal members of the New Warsaw Pact to be provinces in rebellion. Without firing a shot, Russia was able, simply by promising not to be as dreadful an overlord as China, to rewrite the Warsaw Pact until it was more or less the constitution of an empire that included all of Europe east of Germany,

Austria, and Italy in the south, and east of Sweden and Norway in the north.

The weary nations of western Europe were quick to "welcome" the "discipline" that Russia would bring to Europe, and Russia was immediately given full membership in the European Community. Because Russia now controlled the votes of more than half the members of that community, it would require a constant tug of war to keep some semblance of independence, and rather than play that game, Great Britain, Ireland, Iceland, and Portugal left the European Community. But even they took great pains to assure the Russian bear that this was purely over economic issues and they really welcomed this renewed Russian interest in the West.

America, which had long since become the tail to China's dog in matters of trade, made a few grumpy noises about human rights and then went back to business as usual, using satellite cartography to redraw the map of the world to fit the new reality and then sell the atlases that resulted. In sub-Saharan Africa, where India had once been their greatest single trading partner and cultural influence, the loss of India was much more devastating, and they loyally denounced the Chinese conquest even as they scrambled to find new markets for their goods. Latin America was even louder in their condemnation of all the aggressors, but lacking serious military forces, their bluster could do no harm. In the Pacific, Japan, with its dominant fleet, could afford to stand firm; the other island nations that faced China across various not-so-wide bodies of water had no such luxury.

Indeed, the only force that stood firm against China and Russia while facing them across heavily defended borders were the Muslim nations. Iran generously forgot how threateningly Pakistani troops had loomed along their borders in the month before India's fall, and Arabs joined with Turks in Muslim solidarity against any Russian encroachment across the Caucasus or into the vast steppes of central Asia. No one seriously thought that Muslim military might could stand for long against a serious attack from China, and Russia was only scarcely less dangerous, but the Muslims laid aside their grievances, trusted in Allah, and kept their borders bristling with the warning that this nettle would be hard to grasp.

This was the world as it was the day that Peter "Locke" Wiggin was named as the new Hegemon. China let it be known that choosing any Hegemon at all was an affront, but Russia was a bit more tolerant, especially because many governments that cast their vote for Wiggin did so with the public declaration that the office was more ceremonial than practical, a gesture toward world unity and peace, and not at all an attempt to roll back the conquests that had brought "peace" to an unstable world.

But privately, many leaders of the very same governments assured Peter that they expected him to do all he could to bring about diplomatic "transformations" in the occupied countries. Peter listened to them politely and said reassuring things, but he felt nothing but scorn for them—for without military might, he had no way of negotiating with anyone about anything.

His first official act was to reconfirm the appointment of Polemarch Chamrajnagar—an action which China officially protested as illegal because the office of Hegemon no longer existed, and while they would do nothing to interfere with Chamrajnagar's continued leadership of the Fleet, they would no longer contribute financially either to the Hegemony or the Fleet.

Peter then confirmed Graff as Hegemony Minister of Colonization—and, again, because his work was off-world, China could do nothing more than cut off its contribution of funds.

But the lack of money forced Peter's next decision. He moved the Hegemony capital out of the former Netherlands and returned the Low Countries to self-government, which immediately put a stop to unrestricted immigration into those nations. He closed down most Hegemony services worldwide except for medical and agricultural research and assistance programs. He moved the main Hegemony offices to Brazil, which had several important assets:

First, it was a large enough and powerful enough country that the enemies of the Hegemony would not be quick to provoke it by assassinating the Hegemon within its borders.

Second, it was in the southern hemisphere, with strong economic ties to Africa, the Americas, and the Pacific, so that being there kept Peter within the mainstream of international commerce and politics.

And third, Brazil invited Peter Wiggin to come there. No one else did.

———

Peter had no delusions about what the office of Hegemon had become. He did not expect anyone to come to him. He went to them.

Which is why he left Haiti and crossed the Pacific to Manila, where Bean and his Thai army and the Indians they rescued had found temporary refuge. Peter knew that Bean was still angry at him, so he was relieved that Bean not only agreed to see him, but treated him with open respect when he arrived. His two hundred soldiers were crisply turned out to greet him, and when

Bean introduced him to Petra, Suriyawong, and Virlomi and the other Indian Battle Schoolers, he phrased everything as if he were presenting his friends to a man of higher rank.

In front of all of them, Bean then made a little speech. "To His Excellency the Hegemon, I offer the service of this band of soldiers—veterans of war, former opponents, and now, because of treachery, exiles from their homeland and brothers- and sisters-at-arms. This was not my decision, nor the decision of the majority. Each individual here was given the choice, and chose to make this offer of our service. We are few, but nations have found our service valuable before. We hope that we now can serve a cause that is higher than any nation, and whose end will be the establishment of a new and honorable order in the world."

Peter was surprised only by the formality of the offer, and the fact that it was made without any sort of negotiation beforehand. He also noticed that Bean had arranged to have cameras present. This would be news. So Peter made a brief, soundbite-oriented reply accepting their offer, praising their achievements, and expressing regret at the suffering of their people. It would play well—twenty seconds on the vids, and in full on the nets.

When the ceremonies were done, there was an inspection of their inventory—all the equipment they had been able to rescue from Thailand. Even their fighter-bomber pilots and patrol boat crews had managed to make their way from southern Thailand to the Philippines, so the Hegemon had an air force and a fleet. Peter nodded and commented gravely as he saw each item in the inventory—the cameras were still running.

Later, though, when they were alone, Peter finally

allowed himself a rueful, self-mocking laugh. "If it weren't for you I'd have nothing at all," he said. "But to compare this to the vast fleets and air forces and armies that the Hegemon once commanded . . ."

Bean looked at him coldly. "The office had to be greatly diminished," he said, "before they'd have given it to you."

The honeymoon, apparently, was over. "Yes," Peter said, "that's true, of course."

"And the world had to be in a desperate condition, with the existence of the office of Hegemon in doubt."

"That, too, is true," said Peter. "And for some reason you seem to be angry about this."

"That's because, apart from the not-trivial matter of Achilles' penchant for killing people now and then, I fail to see much difference between you and him. You're both content to let any number of people suffer needlessly in order to advance your personal ambitions."

Peter sighed. "If that's all the difference that you see, I don't understand how you could offer your service to me."

"I see other differences, of course," said Bean. "But they're matters of degree, not of kind. Achilles makes treaties he never intends to keep. You merely write essays that might have saved nations, but you delay publishing them so that those nations will fall, putting the world in a position desperate enough that they would make you Hegemon."

"Your statement is true," said Peter, "*only* if you believe that earlier publication would have saved India and Thailand."

"Early in the war," said Bean, "India still had the supplies and equipment to resist Chinese attack. Thailand's forces were still fully dispersed and hard to find."

"But if I had published early in the war," said Peter, "India and Thailand would not have seen their peril, and they wouldn't have believed me. After all, the Thai government didn't believe *you,* and you warned them of everything."

"You're Locke," said Bean.

"Ah yes. Because I had so much credibility and prestige, nations would tremble and believe my words. Aren't you forgetting something? At your insistence, I had declared myself to be a teenage college student. I was still recovering from that, trying to prove in Haiti that I could actually govern. I might have had the prestige left to be taken seriously in India and Thailand— but I might not. And if I published too soon, before China was ready to act, China would simply have denied everything to both sides, the war would have proceeded, and then there would have been no shock value at all to my publication. I wouldn't have been able to trigger the invasion at exactly the moment you needed me to."

"Don't pretend that this was your plan all along."

"It was my plan," said Peter, "to withhold publication until it could be an act of power instead of an act of futility. Yes, I was thinking of my prestige, because right now the only power I have is that prestige and the influence it gives me with the governments of the world. It's a coin that is minted very slowly, and if spent ineffectively, disappears. So yes, I protect that power very carefully, and use it sparingly, so that later, when I need to have it, it will still exist."

Bean was silent.

"You hate what happened in the war," said Peter. "So

do I. It's possible—not likely, but possible—that if I had published earlier, India might have been able to mount a real resistance. They might still have been fighting now. Millions of soldiers might have been dying even as we speak. Instead, there was a clean, almost bloodless victory for China. And now the Chinese have to govern a population almost twice the size of their own, with a culture every bit as old and all-absorbing as their own. The snake has swallowed a crocodile, and the question is going to arise again and again—who is digesting whom? Thailand and Vietnam will be just as hard to govern, and even the Burmese have never managed to govern Burma. What I did saved lives. It left the world with a clear moral picture of who did the stabbing in the back, and who was stabbed. And it leaves China victorious and Russia triumphant—but with captive, angry populations to govern who will not stand with them when the final struggle comes. Why do you think China made a quick peace with Pakistan? Because they knew they could not fight a war against the Muslim world with Indian revolt and sabotage a constant threat. And that alliance between China and Russia—what a joke! Within a year they'll be quarreling, and they'll be back to weakening each other across that long Siberian border. To people who think superficially, China and Russia look triumphant. But I never thought you were a superficial thinker."

"I see all that," said Bean.

"But you don't care. You're still angry at me."

Bean said nothing.

"It's hard," said Peter, "to see how all of this seems to work to my advantage, and not blame me for profiteering from the suffering of others. But the real issue is, What am I going to be able to do, and what will I actually do, now that I'm nominally the leader of the world, and actually the administrator of a small tax base, a few international service agencies, and this military force you gave to me today? I did the few things that were in my power to shape events so that when I got this office, it would still be worth having."

"But above all, to get that office."

"Yes, Bean. I'm arrogant. I think I'm the only person who understands what to do and has what it takes to do it. I think the world needs me. In fact, I'm even more arrogant than you. Is that what this comes down to? I should have been humbler? Only you are allowed to assess your own abilities candidly and decide that you're the best man for a particular job?"

"I don't want the job."

"I don't want *this* job, either," said Peter. "What I want is the job where the Hegemon speaks, and wars stop, where the Hegemon can redraw borders and strike down bad laws and break up international cartels and bring all of humanity a chance for a decent life in peace and whatever freedom their culture will allow. And I'm going to get that job, by creating it step by step. Not only that, I'm going to do it with your help, because you want somebody to do that job, and you know, just as surely as I do, that I'm the only one who can do it."

Bean nodded, saying nothing.

"You know all that, and you're still angry with me."

"I'm angry with Achilles," said Bean. "I'm angry with the stupidity of those who refused to listen to me. But you're here, and they're not."

"It's more than that," said Peter. "If that's all it was, you would have talked yourself out of your wrath long before we had this conversation."

"I know," said Bean. "But you don't want to hear it."

"Because it will hurt my feelings? Let me make a stab at it, then. You're angry because every word from my mouth, every gesture, every expression on my face reminds you of Ender Wiggin. Only I'm not Ender, I'll never be Ender, you think Ender should be doing what I'm doing, and you hate me for being the one who made sure Ender got sent away."

"It's irrational," said Bean. "I know that. I know that by sending him away you saved his life. The people who helped Achilles try to kill me would have worked day and night to kill Ender without any prompting from Achilles at all. They would have feared him far more than they feared you or me. I know that. But you look and talk so much like him. And I keep thinking, if Ender had been here, he wouldn't have botched things the way I did."

"The way I read it, it's the other way around. If *you* hadn't been there with Ender, *he* would have botched it at the end. No, don't argue, it doesn't matter. What *does* matter is, the world's the way it is right now, and we're in a position where, if we move carefully, if we think through and plan everything just right, we can fix this. We make it better. No regrets. No wishing we could undo the past. We just look to the future and work our zhupas off."

"I'll look to the future," said Bean, "and I'll help you all I can. But I'll regret whatever I want to regret."

"Fair enough," said Peter. "Now that we've agreed on that, I think you should know. I've decided to revive the office of Strategos."

Bean gave one hoot of derision. "You're putting *that* title on the commander of a force of two hundred soldiers, a couple of planes, a couple of boats, and an overheated company of strategic planners?"

"Hey, if I can be called Hegemon, you can take on a title like that."

"I notice you didn't want any vids of me getting that title."

"No, I didn't," said Peter. "I don't want people to hear the news while looking at vids of a kid. I want them to learn of your appointment as Strategos while seeing stock footage of the victory over the Formics and hearing voice-overs about your rescue of the Indian Battle Schoolers."

"Well, fine," said Bean. "I accept. Do I get a fancy uniform?"

"No," said Peter. "At the rate you're growing lately, we'd have to pay for new ones too often, and you'd bankrupt us."

A thoughtful expression passed across Bean's face.

"What," said Peter, "did I offend again?"

"No," said Bean. "I was just wondering what your parents said, when you declared yourself to be Locke."

Peter laughed. "Oh, they pretended that they'd known it all along. Parents."

———

At Bean's suggestion, Peter located the headquarters of the Hegemony in a compound just outside the city of Ribeirão Preto in the state of São Paulo. There they would have excellent air connections anywhere in the world, while being surrounded by small towns and agricultural land. They'd be far from any government body. It was a pleasant place to live as they planned and trained to achieve the modest goal of freeing the captive nations while holding the line against any new aggressions.

The Delphiki family came out of hiding and joined

Bean in the safety of the Hegemony compound. Greece was part of the Warsaw Pact now, and there was no going home for them. Peter's parents also came, because they understood that they would become targets for anyone wanting to get to Peter. He gave them both jobs in the Hegemony, and if they minded the disruption of their lives, they never gave a sign of it.

The Arkanians left their homeland, too, and came gladly to live in a place where their children would not be stolen from them. Suriyawong's parents had made it out of Thailand, and they moved the family fortune and the family business to Ribeirão Preto. Other Thai and Indian families with ties to Bean's army or the Battle School graduates came as well, and soon there were thriving neighborhoods where Portuguese was rarely heard.

As for Achilles, month after month they heard nothing about him. Presumably he got back to Beijing. Presumably, he was worming his way into power one way or another. But they allowed themselves, as the silence about him continued, to hope that perhaps the Chinese, having made use of him, now knew him well enough to keep him away from the reins of power.

———

On a cloudy winter afternoon in June, Petra walked through the cemetery in the town of Araraquara, only twenty minutes by train from Ribeirão Preto. She took care to make sure she approached Bean from a direction where he could see her coming. Soon she stood beside him, looking at a marker.

"Who is buried here?" she asked.

"No one," said Bean, who showed no surprise at seeing her. "It's a cenotaph."

Petra read the names that were on it.

Poke.

Carlotta.

There was nothing else.

"There's a marker for Sister Carlotta somewhere in Vatican City," said Bean. "But there was no body recovered that could actually be buried anywhere. And Poke was cremated by people who didn't even know who she was. I got the idea for this from Virlomi."

Virlomi had set up a cenotaph for Sayagi in the small Hindu cemetery that already existed in Ribeirão Preto. It was a bit more elaborate—it included the dates of his birth and death, and called him "a man of satyagraha."

"Bean," said Petra, "it's quite insane of you to come here. No bodyguard. This marker standing here so that assassins can set their sights before you show up."

"I know," said Bean.

"At least you could have invited me along."

He turned to her, tears in his eyes. "This is my place of shame," he said. "I worked very hard to make sure your name would not be here."

"Is that what you tell yourself? There's no shame here, Bean. There's only love. And that's why I belong here—with the other lonely girls who gave their hearts to you."

Bean turned to her, put his arms around her, and wept into her shoulder. He had grown, to stand tall enough for that. "They saved my life," he said. "They *gave* me life."

"That's what good people do," said Petra. "And then they die, every one of them. It's a damned shame."

He gave one short laugh—whether at her small levity or at himself, for weeping, she did not know. "Nothing lasts long, does it," said Bean.

"They're still alive in you."

"Who am I alive in?" said Bean. "And don't say you."

"I will if I want. You saved *my* life."

"They never had children, either one of them," said Bean. "No one ever held either Poke or Carlotta the way a man does with a woman, or had a baby with them. They never got to see their children grow up and have children of their own."

"By Sister Carlotta's choice," said Petra.

"Not Poke's."

"They both had you."

"That's the futility of it," said Bean. "The only child they had was me."

"So . . . you owe it to them to carry on, to marry, to have more children who'll remember them both for your sake."

Bean stared off into space. "I have a better idea. Let me tell *you* about them. And you tell *your* children. Will you do that? If you could promise me that, then I think that I could bear all this, because they wouldn't just disappear from memory when I die."

"Of course I'll do that, Bean, but you're talking as if your life were already over, and it's just beginning. Look at you, you're getting along, you'll have a man's height before long, you'll—"

He touched her lips, gently, to silence her. "I'll have no wife, Petra. No babies."

"Why not? If you tell me you've decided to become a priest I'll kidnap you myself and get you out of this Catholic country."

"I'm not human, Petra," Bean replied. "And my species dies with me."

She laughed at his joke.

But as she looked into his eyes, she saw that it

wasn't a joke at all. Whatever he meant by that, he really thought that it was true. Not human. But how could he think that? Of all the people Petra knew, who was more human than Bean?

"Let's go back home," Bean finally said, "before somebody comes along and shoots us just for loitering."

"Home," said Petra.

Bean only halfway understood. "Sorry it's not Armenia."

"No, I don't think Armenia is home either," she said. "And Battle School sure wasn't, nor Eros. This *is* home, though. I mean, Ribeirão Preto. But here, too. Because . . . my family's here, of course, but . . ."

And then she realized what she was trying to say.

"It's because *you're* here. Because you're the one who went through it all with me. You're the one who knows what I'm talking about. What I'm remembering. Ender. That terrible day with Bonzo. And the day I fell asleep in the middle of a battle on Eros. You think *you* have shame." She laughed. "But it's OK to remember even *that* with you. Because you knew about that, and you still came to get me out."

"Took me long enough," said Bean.

They walked out of the cemetery toward the train station, holding hands because neither of them wanted to feel separate right now.

"I have an idea," said Petra.

"What?"

"If you ever change your mind—you know, about marrying and having babies—hang on to my address. Look me up."

Bean was silent for a long moment. "Ah," he finally said, "I get it. I rescued the princess, so now I can marry her if I want."

"That's the deal."

"Yeah, well, I notice you didn't mention it until after you heard my vow of celibacy."

"I suppose that was perverse of me."

"Besides, it's a cheat. Aren't I supposed to get half the kingdom, too?"

"I've got a better idea," she answered. "You can have it all."

Afterword

Just as *Speaker for the Dead* was a different kind of novel from *Ender's Game,* so also is *Shadow of the Hegemon* a different kind of book from *Ender's Shadow*. No longer are we in the close confines of Battle School or the asteroid Eros, fighting a war against insectoid aliens. Now, with *Hegemon,* we are on Earth, playing what amounts to a huge game of *Risk*—only you have to play politics and diplomacy as well in order to get power, hold onto it, and give yourself a place to land if you lose it.

Indeed, the game that this novel most resembles is the computer classic *Romance of the Three Kingdoms,* which is itself based on a Chinese historical novel, thus affirming the ties between history, fiction, and gaming. While history responds to irresistible forces and conditions (*pace* the extraordinarily illuminating book *Guns, Germs, and Steel,* which should be required reading by everyone who writes history or historical fiction, just so they understand the ground rules), in the specifics, history happens as it happens for highly personal reasons. The reasons European civilization prevailed over indigenous civilizations of the Americas consist of the implacable laws of history; but the reason why it was Cortez and Pizarro who prevailed over the Aztec and Inca empires by winning particular battles on particular days, instead of being cut down and destroyed as they might have been, had everything to do with their own character and the character and recent history of the emperors opposing them. And it happens that it is the novelist, not the historian, who has the freer hand at imagining what causes individual human beings to do the things they do.

Which is hardly a surprise. Human motivation cannot be documented, at least not with any kind of finality. After all, we rarely understand our own motivations, and so, even when we write down what we honestly believe to be our reasons for making the choices we make, our explanation is likely to be wrong or partly wrong or at least incomplete. So even when a historian or biographer has a wealth of information at hand, in the end he still has to make that uncomfortable leap into the abyss of ignorance before he can declare why a person did the things he did. The French Revolution inexorably led to anarchy and then tyranny for comprehensible reasons, following predictable paths. But nothing could have predicted Napoleon himself, or even that a single dictator of such gifts would emerge.

Novelists who write about Great Leaders, however, too often fall into the opposite trap. Able to imagine personal motivations, the people who write novels rarely have the grounding in historical fact or the grasp of historical forces to set their plausible characters into an equally plausible society. Most such attempts are laughably wrong, even when written by people who have actually been involved in the society of movers and shakers, for even those caught up in the maelstrom of politics are rarely able to see through the trees well enough to comprehend the forest. (Besides, most political or military novels by political or military leaders tend to be self-serving and self-justifying, which makes them almost as unreliable as books written by the ignorant.) How likely is it that someone who took part in the Clinton administration's immoral decision to launch unprovoked attacks on Afghanistan and the Sudan in the late summer of 1998 would be able to write a novel in which the political exigencies that led to these criminal acts are accurately recounted? Anyone in a position to know or guess the real interplay of human desires among the major players will also be so culpable that it will be impossible for him to tell the truth, even if he is honest enough to attempt it, simply because the people involved were so busy lying to themselves and to each other throughout the process that everyone involved is bound to be snow-blind.

In *Shadow of the Hegemon,* I have the advantage of writing a history that hasn't happened, because it is in the future. Not thirty million years in the future, as with my Homecoming books, or even three thousand years in the future, as with the trilogy of *Speaker for the Dead, Xenocide,* and *Children of the Mind,* but rather only a couple of centuries in the future, after nearly a century of international stasis caused by the Formic War. In the future history posited by *Hegemon,* nations and peoples of today are still recognizable, though the relative balance among them has changed. And I have both the perilous freedom and the solemn obligation to attempt to tell my characters' highly personal stories as they move (or are moved) amid the highest circles of power in the governing and military classes of the world.

If there is anything that can be called my "life study," it is precisely this subject area: great leaders and great forces shaping the interplay of nations and peoples throughout history. As a child, I would put myself to sleep at night imagining a map of the world as it existed in the late fifties, just as the great colonial empires were beginning to grant independence, one by one, to the colonies that had once made up those great swathes of British pink and French blue across Africa and southern Asia. I imagined all those colonies as free countries, and, choosing one of them or some other relatively small nation, I would imagine alliance, unifications, invasions, conquests, until all the world was united under one magnanimous, democratic government. Cincinnatus and George Washington, not Caesar or Napoleon, were my models. I read Machiavelli's *The Prince* and Shirer's *Rise and Fall of the Third Reich,* but I also read Mormon scripture (most notably the Book of Mormon stories of the generals Gideon, Moroni, Helaman, and Gidgiddoni, and Doctrine and Covenants section 121) and the Old and New Testaments, all the while trying to imagine how one might govern well when law gives way to exigency, and the circumstances under which war becomes righteous.

I don't pretend that the imaginings and studies of my life have brought me to great answers, and you will find no such answers in *Shadow of the Hegemon*. But I do believe I understand something of the workings of the world of government, politics, and war, both at their best and at their worst. I have sought the borderline between strength and ruthlessness, between ruthlessness and cruelty, and at the other extreme, between goodness and weakness, between weakness and betrayal. I have pondered how it is that some societies are able to get young men to kill and die with fervor trumping fear, and yet others seem to lose their will to survive or at least their will to do the things that make survival possible. And *Shadow of the Hegemon* and the two remaining books in this long tale of Bean, Petra, and Peter are my best attempt to use what I have learned in a tale in which great forces, large populations, and individuals of heroic if not always virtuous character combine to give shape to an imaginary, but I hope believable, history.

I am crippled in this effort by the factor that real life is rarely plausible—we believe that people would or could do these things only because we have documentation. Fiction, lacking that documentation, dares not be half so implausible. On the other hand, we can do what history never can—we can assign motive to human behavior, which cannot be refuted by any witness or evidence. So, despite doing my utmost to be truthful about how history happens, in the end I must depend on the novelist's tools. Do you care about this person, or that one? Do you believe such a person would do the things I say they do, for the reasons I assign?

History, when told as epic, often has the thrilling grandeur of Dvorak or Smetana, Borodin or Mussorgsky, but historical fiction must also find the intimacies and dissonances of the delicate little piano pieces of Satie and Debussy. For it is in the millions of small melodies that the truth of history is always found, for history only matters because of the effects we see or imagine in the lives of the ordinary people who are caught up in, or give shape to, the great events. Tchaikowsky can carry me away, but I tire quickly of the large effect, which feels so hollow and false on the second hearing. Of Satie I never tire, for his music is endlessly surprising and yet perfectly satisfying. If I can bring off this novel in Tchaikowsky's terms, that is well and good; but if I can also give you moments of Satie, I am far happier, for that is the harder and, ultimately, more rewarding task.

Besides my lifelong study of history in general, two books particularly influenced me during the writing of *Shadow of the Hegemon.* When I saw *Anna and the King,* I became impatient with my own ignorance of real Thai history, and so found David K. Wyatt's *Thailand: A Short History* (Yale, 1982, 1984). Wyatt writes clearly and convincingly, making the history of the Thai people both intelligible and fascinating. It is hard to imagine a nation that has been more lucky in the quality of its leaders as Thailand and its predecessor kingdoms, which managed to survive invasions from every direction and European and Japanese ambitions in Southeast Asia, all the while maintaining its own national character and remaining, more than many kingdoms and oligarchies, responsive to the needs of the Thai people. (I followed Wyatt's lead in calling the pre-Siamese language and the people who spoke it, in lands from Laos to upper Burma and southern China, "Tai," reserving "Thai" for the modern language and kingdom that bear that name.)

My own country once had leaders comparable to Siam's Mongkut and Chulalongkorn, and public servants as gifted and selfless as many of Chulalongkorn's brothers and nephews, but unlike Thailand, America is now a nation in decline, and my people have little will to be well led. America's past and its resources make it a major player for the nonce, but nations of small resources but strong will can change the course of world history, as the Huns, the Mongols, and the Arabs have shown, sometimes to devastating effect, and as the people of the Ganges have shown far more pacifically.

Which brings me to the second book, Lawrence James's *Raj: The Making and Unmaking of British India* (Little, Brown, 1997). Modern Indian history reads like one long tragedy of good, or at least bold, intentions leading to disaster, and in *Shadow of the Hegemon* I consciously echoed some of the themes I found in James's book.

As always, I relied on others to help me with this book by reading the first draft of each chapter to give me some idea whether I had wrought what I intended. My wife, Kristine; my son Geoffrey; and Kathy H. Kidd and Erin and Phillip Absher were my most immediate readers, and I thank them for helping prevent many a moment of inclarity or ineffectiveness.

The person most influential in giving this book the shape it has, however, is the aforementioned Phillip Absher, for when he read the first version of a chapter in which Petra was rescued from Russian captivity and united with Bean, he commented that I had built up her kidnapping so much that it was rather disappointing how easily the problem turned out to be resolved. I had not realized how high I had raised expectations, but I could see that he was right—that her easy release was not only a breaking of an implied promise with the reader, but also implausible under the circumstances. So instead of her kidnapping being an early event in a very involved story, I realized that it could and should provide the overarching structure of the entire novel, thus splitting what was to be one novel into two. As the story of Han Qing-jao took over *Xenocide* and caused it to become two books, so also the story of Petra took over this, Bean's second book, and caused there to be a third, *Shadow of Death* (which I may extend to the longer phrase from the Twenty-third Psalm, *The Valley of the Shadow of Death*; it would never do to become tied to a title too early). The book originally planned to be third will now be the fourth, *Shadow of the Giant.* All because Phillip felt a bit disappointed and, just as importantly, said so, causing me to think again about the structure I had unconsciously created in subversion of my conscious plans.

At the last minute, Ami Chopine of philoticweb.net found a real howler of an inconsistency between this book and *Ender's Game.* Ami, I owe you big time! (And thanks to Terry Jude, Matthew Schwartz, and Joshua Smith, too.)

I rarely write two novels at once, but I did this time, going back and forth between *Shadow of the Hegemon* and *Sarah,* my historical novel about the wife of Abraham (Shadow Mountain, 2000). The novels sustained each other in odd ways, each of them dealing with history during times of chaos and transformation—like the one the world is embarking upon at the time of this writing. In both stories, personal loyalties, ambitions, and passions sometimes shape the course of the history and sometimes surf upon history's wave, trying merely to stay just ahead of the breaking crest. May all who read these books find their own ways to do the same. It is in the turmoil of chaos that we discover what, if anything, we are.

As always, I have relied upon Kathleen Bellamy and Scott Allen to help keep communications open between me and my readers, and many who visited and took part in my online communities at *http://www.hat-rack.com, http://www.frescopix.com,* and *http://www.-nauvoo.com*) helped me, often in ways they did not realize.

Many writers produce their art from a maelstrom of domestic chaos and tragedy. I am fortunate enough to write from within an island of peace and love, created by my wife, Kristine, my children, Geoffrey, Emily, Charlie Ben, and Zina, and good and dear friends and family who surround us and enrich our lives with their good will, kind help, and happy company. Perhaps I would write better were my life more miserable, but I have no interest in performing the experiment.

In particular, though, I write this book for my second son, Charlie Ben, who wordlessly has given great gifts to all who know him. Within the small community of his family, of school friends at Gateway Education Center, and of church friends in the Greensboro Summit Ward, Charlie Ben has given and received much friendship and love without uttering a word, as he patiently endures his pain and limitations, gladly receives the kindness of others, and generously shares his love and joy with all who care to receive it. Twisted by cerebral palsy, his body movements may look strange and disturbing to strangers, but to those willing to look more closely, a young man of beauty, humor, kindness, and joy can be found. May we all learn to see past such outward signs, and show our true selves through all barriers, however opaque they seem. And Charlie, who will never hold this book in his own hands or read it with his own eyes, will nevertheless hear it read to him by loving friends and family members. So to you, Charlie, I say: I am proud of all you do with your life, and glad to be your father; though you deserved a better one, you have been generous enough to love the one you have.

The next morning, Bean, Nikolai, and three other kids in their launch group had their assignments to Dragon Army. Months before they should have been promoted to soldiers. The unchosen kids were envious, furious by turn. Especially when they realized Bean was one of the chosen. "Do they *make* uniform flash suits that size?"

It was a good question. And the answer was no, they didn't. The colors of Dragon Army were grey, orange, grey. Because soldiers were usually a lot older than Bean when they came in, they had to cut a flash suit down for Bean, and they didn't do it all that well. Flash suits weren't manufactured in space, and nobody had the tools to do a first-rate job of alteration.

When they finally got it to fit him, Bean wore his flash suit to the Dragon Army barracks. Because it had taken him so long to be fitted, he was the last to arrive. Wiggin arrived at the door just as Bean was entering. "Go ahead," said Wiggin.

It was the first time Wiggin had ever spoken to him— for all Bean knew, the first time Wiggin had even noticed him. So thoroughly had Bean concealed his fascination with Wiggin that he had made himself effectively invisible.

Wiggin followed him into the room. Bean started down the corridor between the bunks, heading for the back of the room where the younger soldiers always had to sleep. He glanced at the other kids, who were all looking at him as he passed with a mixture of horror and amusement. They were in an army so lame that *this* little kid was part of it?

Behind him, Wiggin was starting his first speech. Voice confident, loud enough but not shouting, not nervous. "I'm Ender Wiggin. I'm your commander."

ENDER'S SHADOW

ORSON SCOTT CARD

TOR®

A TOM DOHERTY ASSOCIATES BOOK
NEW YORK

This is a work of fiction. All of the characters, organizations, and events portrayed in this novel are either products of the authors' imaginations or are used fictitiously.

ENDER'S SHADOW

Copyright © 1999 by Orson Scott Card

Edited by Beth Meacham

A Tor Book
Published by Tom Doherty Associates
120 Broadway
New York, NY 10271

www.tor-forge.com

Tor® is a registered trademark of Macmillan Publishing Group, LLC.

ISBN 978-0-8125-7571-2

Our books may be purchased in bulk for promotional, educational, or business use. Please contact your local bookseller or the Macmillan Corporate and Premium Sales Department at 1-800-221-7945, extension 5442, or by e-mail at MacmillanSpecialMarkets@macmillan.com.

First Edition: September 1999
First International Mass Market Edition: August 2000
First U.S. Mass Market Edition: December 2000

Printed in the United States of America

29 28 27 26 25 24 23 22

TO DICK AND HAZIE BROWN
IN WHOSE HOME NO ONE IS HUNGRY
AND IN WHOSE HEARTS
NO ONE IS A STRANGER

CONTENTS

ENDER'S
SHADOW

Foreword

This book is, strictly speaking, not a sequel, because it begins about where *Ender's Game* begins, and also ends, very nearly, at the same place. In fact, it is another telling of the same tale, with many of the same characters and settings, only from the perspective of another character. It's hard to know what to call it. A companion novel? A parallel novel? Perhaps a "parallax," if I can move that scientific term into literature.

Ideally, this novel should work as well for readers who have never read *Ender's Game* as for those who have read it several times. Because it is not a sequel, there is nothing you need to know from the novel *Ender's Game* that is not contained here. And yet, if I have achieved my literary goal, these two books complement and fulfill each other. Whichever one you read first, the other novel should still work on its own merits.

For many years, I have gratefully watched as *Ender's Game* has grown in popularity, especially among school-age readers. Though it was never intended as a young-adult novel, it has been embraced by many in that age group and by many teachers who find ways to use the book in their classrooms.

I have never found it surprising that the existing sequels—*Speaker for the Dead, Xenocide,* and *Children of the Mind*—never appealed as strongly to those younger readers. The obvious reason is that *Ender's Game* is centered around a child, while the sequels are about adults; perhaps more important, *Ender's Game* is, at least on the surface, a heroic, adventurous novel, while the sequels are a completely different kind of fiction, slower paced, more contemplative and idea-centered, and dealing with themes of less immediate import to younger readers.

Recently, however, I have come to realize that the 3,000-year gap between *Ender's Game* and its sequels leaves plenty of room for other sequels that are more closely tied to the original. In fact, in one sense *Ender's Game* has no sequels, for the other three books make one continuous story in themselves, while *Ender's Game* stands alone.

For a brief time I flirted seriously with the idea of opening up the *Ender's Game* universe to other writers, and went so far as to invite a writer whose work I greatly admire, Neal Shusterman, to consider working with me to create novels about Ender Wiggin's companions in Battle School. As we talked, it became clear that the most obvious character to begin with would be Bean, the child-soldier whom Ender treated as he had been treated by his adult teachers.

And then something else happened. The more we talked, the more jealous I became that Neal might be the one to write such a book, and not me. It finally dawned on me that, far from being finished with writing about "kids in space," as I cynically described the project, I actually had more to say, having actually learned something in the intervening dozen years since *Ender's Game* first appeared in 1985. And so, while still hoping that Neal and I can work together on something, I deftly swiped the project back.

I soon found that it's harder than it looks, to tell the same story twice, but differently. I was hindered by the fact that even though the viewpoint characters were different, the author was the same, with the same core beliefs about the world. I was helped by the fact that in the intervening years, I have learned a few things, and was able to bring different concerns and a deeper understanding to the project. Both books come from the same mind, but not the same; they draw on the same memories of childhood, but from a different perspective. For the reader, the parallax is created by Ender and Bean, standing a little ways apart as they move through the same events. For the writer, the parallax was created by a dozen years in which my older children grew up, and younger ones were born, and the world changed around me, and I learned a few things about human nature and about art that I had not known before.

Now you hold this book in your hands. Whether the literary experiment succeeds for you is entirely up to you to judge. For me it was worth dipping again into the same well, for the water was greatly changed this time, and if it has not been turned exactly into wine, at least it has a different flavor because of the different vessel that it was carried in, and I hope that you will enjoy it as much, or even more.

—*Greensboro, North Carolina, January 1999*

Part One
URCHIN

I

Poke

"You think you've found somebody, so suddenly my program gets the ax?"

"It's not about this kid that Graff found. It's about the low quality of what you've been finding."

"We knew it was long odds. But the kids I'm working with are actually fighting a war just to stay alive."

"Your kids are so malnourished that they suffer serious mental degradation before you even begin testing them. Most of them haven't formed any normal human bonds, they're so messed up they can't get through a day without finding something they can steal, break, or disrupt."

"They also represent possibility, as all children do."

"That's just the kind of sentimentality that discredits your whole project in the eyes of the I.F."

Poke kept her eyes open all the time. The younger children were supposed to be on watch, too, and sometimes they could be quite observant, but they just didn't notice all the things they needed to notice, and that meant that

Poke could only depend on herself to see danger.

There was plenty of danger to watch for. The cops, for instance. They didn't show up often, but when they did, they seemed especially bent on clearing the streets of children. They would flail about them with their magnetic whips, landing cruel stinging blows on even the smallest children, haranguing them as vermin, thieves, pestilence, a plague on the fair city of Rotterdam. It was Poke's job to notice when a disturbance in the distance suggested that the cops might be running a sweep. Then she would give the alarm whistle and the little ones would rush to their hiding places till the danger was past.

But the cops didn't come by that often. The real danger was much more immediate—big kids. Poke, at age nine, was the matriarch of her little crew (not that any of them knew for sure that she was a girl), but that cut no ice with the eleven- and twelve- and thirteen-year-old boys and girls who bullied their way around the streets. The adult-size beggars and thieves and whores of the street paid no attention to the little kids except to kick them out of the way. But the older children, who were among the kicked, turned around and preyed on the younger ones. Any time Poke's crew found something to eat—especially if they located a dependable source of garbage or an easy mark for a coin or a bit of food—they had to watch jealously and hide their winnings, for the bullies liked nothing better than to take away whatever scraps of food the little ones might have. Stealing from younger children was much safer than stealing from shops or passersby. And they enjoyed it, Poke could see that. They liked how the little kids cowered and obeyed and whimpered and gave them whatever they demanded.

So when the scrawny little two-year-old took up a perch on a garbage can across the street, Poke, being observant, saw him at once. The kid was on the edge of starvation. No, the kid was starving. Thin arms and legs, joints that looked ridiculously oversized, a distended belly. And if hunger didn't kill him soon, the onset of autumn would, because his clothing was thin and there wasn't much of it even at that.

Normally she wouldn't have paid him more than passing attention. But this one had eyes. He was still looking around with intelligence. None of that stupor of the walking dead, no longer searching for food or even caring to find a comfortable place to lie while breathing their last taste of the stinking air of Rotterdam. After all, death would not be such a change for them. Everyone knew that Rotterdam was, if not the capital, then the main seaport of Hell. The only difference between Rotterdam and death was that with Rotterdam, the damnation wasn't eternal.

This little boy—what was he doing? Not looking for food. He wasn't eyeing the pedestrians. Which was just as well—there was no chance that anyone would leave anything for a child that small. Anything he might get would be taken away by any other child, so why should he bother? If he wanted to survive, he should be following older scavengers and licking food wrappers behind them, getting the last sheen of sugar or dusting of flour clinging to the packaging, whatever the first comer hadn't licked off. There was nothing for this child out here on the street, not unless he got taken in by a crew, and Poke wouldn't have him. He'd be nothing but a drain, and her kids were already having a hard enough time without adding another useless mouth.

He's going to ask, she thought. He's going to whine and beg. But that only works on the rich people. I've got my crew to think of. He's not one of them, so I don't care about him. Even if he is small. He's nothing to me.

A couple of twelve-year-old hookers who didn't usually work this strip rounded a corner, heading toward Poke's base. She gave a low whistle. The kids immediately drifted apart, staying on the street but trying not to look like a crew.

It didn't help. The hookers knew already that Poke was a crew boss, and sure enough, they caught her by the arms and slammed her against a wall and demanded their "permission" fee. Poke knew better than to claim she had nothing to share—she always tried to keep a reserve in order to placate hungry bullies. These hookers, Poke could see why they were hungry. They didn't look like what the pedophiles wanted, when they came cruising through. They were too gaunt, too old-looking. So until they grew bodies and started attracting the slightly-less-perverted trade, they had to resort to scavenging. It made Poke's blood boil, to have them steal from her and her crew, but it was smarter to pay them off. If they beat her up, she couldn't look out for her crew now, could she? So she took them to one of her stashes and came up with a little bakery bag that still had half a pastry in it.

It was stale, since she'd been holding it for a couple of days for just such an occasion, but the two hookers grabbed it, tore open the bag, and one of them bit off more than half before offering the remainder to her friend. Or rather, her former friend, for of such predatory acts are feuds born. The two of them started fighting, screaming at each other, slapping, raking at each other with clawed hands. Poke watched closely, hoping that they'd drop the remaining fragment of pastry, but no such luck. It went into the mouth of the same girl who had already eaten the first bite—and it was that first girl who won the fight too, sending the other one running for refuge.

Poke turned around, and there was the little boy right behind her. She nearly tripped over him. Angry as she was at having had to give up food to those street-whores, she gave him a knee and knocked him to the ground. "Don't stand behind people if you don't want to land on your butt," she snarled.

He simply got up and looked at her, expectant, demanding.

"No, you little bastard, you're not getting nothing from me," said Poke. "I'm not taking one bean out of the mouths of my crew, you aren't *worth* a bean."

Her crew was starting to reassemble, now that the bullies had passed.

"Why you give your food to them?" said the boy. "You need that food."

"Oh, excuse me!" said Poke. She raised her voice, so her crew could hear her. "I guess you ought to be the crew boss here, is that it? You being so big, you got no trouble keeping the food."

"Not me," said the boy. "I'm not worth a bean, remember?"

"Yeah, I remember. Maybe *you* ought to remember and shut up."

Her crew laughed.

But the little boy didn't. "You got to get your own bully," he said.

"I don't *get* bullies, I get rid of them," Poke answered. She didn't like the way he kept talking, standing up to her. In a minute she was going to have to hurt him.

"You give food to bullies every day. Give that to *one* bully and get him to keep the others away from you."

"You think I never thought of that, stupid?" she said. "Only once he's bought, how I keep him? He won't fight for us."

"If he won't, then kill him," said the boy.

That made Poke mad, the stupid impossibility of it, the power of the idea that she knew she could never lay hands on. She gave him a knee again, and this time kicked him when he went down. "Maybe I start by killing you."

"I'm not worth a bean, remember?" said the boy. "You kill one bully, get another to fight for you, he want your food, he scared of you too."

She didn't know what to say to such a preposterous idea.

"They eating you up," said the boy. "Eating you up. So you got to kill one. Get him down, everybody as small as me. Stones crack any size head."

"You make me sick," she said.

"Cause you didn't think of it," he said.

He was flirting with death, talking to her that way. If

she injured him at all, he'd be finished, he must know that.

But then, he had death living with him inside his flimsy little shirt already. Hard to see how it would matter if death came any closer.

Poke looked around at her crew. She couldn't read their faces.

"I don't need no baby telling me to kill what we can't kill."

"Little kid come up behind him, you shove, he fall over," said the boy. "Already got you some big stones, bricks. Hit him in the head. When you see brains you done."

"He no good to me dead," she said. "I want my own bully, he keep us safe, I don't want no dead one."

The boy grinned. "So now you like my idea," he said.

"Can't trust no bully," she answered.

"He watch out for you at the charity kitchen," said the boy. "You get in at the kitchen." He kept looking her in the eye, but he was talking for the others to hear. "He get you *all* in at the kitchen."

"Little kid get into the kitchen, the big kids, they beat him," said Sergeant. He was eight, and mostly acted like he thought he was Poke's second-in-command, though truth was she didn't have a second.

"You get you a bully, he make them go away."

"How he stop two bullies? Three bullies?" asked Sergeant.

"Like I said," the boy answered. "You push him down, he not so big. You get your rocks. You be ready. Ben't you a soldier? Don't they call you Sergeant?"

"Stop talking to him, Sarge," said Poke. "I don't know why any of us is talking to some two-year-old."

"I'm four," said the boy.

"What your name?" asked Poke.

"Nobody ever said no name for me," he said.

"You mean you so stupid you can't remember your own name?"

"Nobody ever said no name," he said again. Still he looked her in the eye, lying there on the ground, the crew around him.

"Ain't worth a bean," she said.

"Am so," he said.

"Yeah," said Sergeant. "One damn bean."

"So now you got a name," said Poke. "You go back and sit on that garbage can, I think about what you said."

"I need something to eat," said Bean.

"If I get me a bully, if what you said works, then maybe I give you something."

"I need something now," said Bean.

She knew it was true.

She reached into her pocket and took out six peanuts she had been saving. He sat up and took just one from her hand, put it in his mouth and slowly chewed.

"Take them all," she said impatiently.

He held out his little hand. It was weak. He couldn't make a fist. "Can't hold them all," he said. "Don't hold so good."

Damn. She was wasting perfectly good peanuts on a kid who was going to die anyway.

But she was going to try his idea. It was audacious, but it was the first plan she'd ever heard that offered any hope of making things better, of changing something about their miserable life without her having to put on girl clothes and going into business. And since it was his idea, the crew had to see that she treated him fair. That's how you stay crew boss, they always see you be fair.

So she kept holding her hand out while he ate all six peanuts, one at a time.

After he swallowed the last one, he looked her in the eye for another long moment, and then said, "You better be ready to kill him."

"I want him alive."

"Be ready to kill him if he ain't the right one." With that, Bean toddled back across the street to his garbage can and laboriously climbed on top again to watch.

"You ain't no four years old!" Sergeant shouted over to him.

"I'm four but I'm just little," he shouted back.

Poke hushed Sergeant up and they went looking for stones and bricks and cinderblocks. If they were going to have a little war, they'd best be armed.

———

Bean didn't like his new name, but it was a name, and having a name meant that somebody else knew who he was and needed something to call him, and that was a good thing. So were the six peanuts. His mouth hardly knew what to do with them. Chewing hurt.

So did watching as Poke screwed up the plan he gave her. Bean didn't choose her because she was the smartest crew boss in Rotterdam. Quite the opposite. Her crew barely survived because her judgment wasn't that good. And she was too compassionate. Didn't have the brains to make sure she got enough food herself to look well fed, so while her own crew knew she was nice and liked her, to strangers she didn't look prosperous. Didn't look good at her job.

But if she really *was* good at her job, she would never have listened to him. He never would have got close. Or if she did listen, and did like his idea, she would have got rid of him. That's the way it worked on the street. Nice kids died. Poke was almost too nice to stay alive. That's what Bean was counting on. But that's what he now feared.

All this time he invested in watching people while his body ate itself up, it would be wasted if she couldn't bring it off. Not that Bean hadn't wasted a lot of time himself. At first when he watched the way kids did things on the street, the way they were stealing from each other, at each other's throats, in each other's pockets, selling every part of themselves that they could sell, he saw how things could be better if somebody had any brains, but he didn't trust his own insight. He was sure there must be something else that he just didn't get. He struggled to learn more—of everything. To learn to read so he'd know what the signs said on trucks and stores and wagons and bins. To learn enough Dutch and enough I.F. Common to understand everything that was said around him. It didn't help that hunger constantly distracted him. He probably could have found more to eat if he hadn't spent so much time studying the people. But finally he realized: He already understood it. He had understood it from the start. There was no secret that Bean just didn't get yet because he was only little. The reason all these kids handled everything so stupidly was because they were stupid.

They were stupid and he was smart. So why was he starving to death while these kids were still alive? That was when he decided to act. That was when he picked Poke as his crew boss. And now he sat on a garbage can watching her blow it.

She chose the wrong bully, that's the first thing she did. She needed a guy who made it on size alone, intimidating people. She needed somebody big and dumb, brutal but controllable. Instead, she thinks she needs somebody *small*. No, stupid! Stupid! Bean wanted to scream at her as she saw her target coming, a bully who called himself Achilles after the comics hero. He was little and mean and smart and quick, but he had a gimp leg. So she thought she could take him down more easily. Stupid! The idea isn't just to take him down—you can take *anybody* down the first time because they won't expect it. You need somebody who will *stay* down.

But he said nothing. Couldn't get her mad at him. See what happens. See what Achilles is like when he's beat. She'll see—it won't work and she'll have to kill him and hide the body and try again with another bully before word gets out that there's a crew of little kids taking down bullies.

So up comes Achilles, swaggering—or maybe that was just the rolling gait that his bent leg forced on him—and Poke makes an exaggerated show of cowering and trying to get away. Bad job, thought Bean. Achilles gets it already. Something's wrong. You were supposed to act like you normally do! Stupid! So Achilles looks around a lot more. Wary. She tells him she's got something stashed—that part's normal—and she leads him into the trap in the alley. But look, he's holding back. Being careful. It isn't going to work.

But it does work, because of the gimp leg. Achilles can see the trap being sprung but he can't get away, a couple of little kids pile into the backs of his legs while Poke and Sergeant push him from the front and down he goes. Then there's a couple of bricks hitting his body and his bad leg and they're thrown hard—the little kids get it, they do their job, even if Poke is stupid—and yeah, that's good, Achilles *is* scared, he thinks he's going to die.

Bean was off his perch by now. Down the alley, watching, closer. Hard to see past the crowd. He pushes his way in, and the little kids—who are all bigger than he is—recognize him, they know he earned a view of this, they let him in. He stands right at Achilles' head. Poke stands above him, holding a big cinderblock, and she's talking.

"You get us into the food line at the shelter."

"Sure, right, I will, I promise."

Don't believe him. Look at his eyes, checking for weakness.

"You get more food this way, too, Achilles. You get my crew. We get enough to eat, we have more strength, we bring more to you. You need a crew. The other bullies shove you out of the way—we've seen them!—but with us, you don't got to take no shit. See how we do it? An army, that's what we are."

OK, now he was getting it. It *was* a good idea, and he wasn't stupid, so it made sense to him.

"If this is so smart, Poke, how come you didn't do this before now?"

She had nothing to say to that. Instead, she glanced at Bean.

Just a momentary glance, but Achilles saw it. And Bean

knew what he was thinking. It was so obvious.

"Kill him," said Bean.

"Don't be stupid," said Poke. "He's in."

"That's right," said Achilles. "I'm in. It's a good idea."

"Kill him," said Bean. "If you don't kill him now, he's going to kill *you*."

"You let this little walking turd get away with talking shit like this?" said Achilles.

"It's your life or his," said Bean. "Kill him and take the next guy."

"The next guy won't have my bad leg," said Achilles. "The next guy won't think he needs you. I know I do. I'm in. I'm the one you want. It makes sense."

Maybe Bean's warning made her more cautious. She didn't cave in quite yet. "You won't decide later that you're embarrassed to have a bunch of little kids in your crew?"

"It's *your* crew, not mine," said Achilles.

Liar, thought Bean. Don't you see that he's lying to you?

"What this is to me," said Achilles, "this is my family. These are my kid brothers and sisters. I got to look after my family, don't I?"

Bean saw at once that Achilles had won. Powerful bully, and he had called these kids his sisters, his brothers. Bean could see the hunger in their eyes. Not the regular hunger, for food, but the real hunger, the deep hunger, for family, for love, for belonging. They got a little of that by being in Poke's crew. But Achilles was promising more. He had just beaten Poke's best offer. Now it was too late to kill him.

Too late, but for a moment it looked as if Poke was so stupid she was going to go ahead and kill him after all. She raised the cinderblock higher, to crash it down.

"No," said Bean. "You can't. He's family now."

She lowered the cinderblock to her waist. Slowly she turned to look at Bean. "You get the hell out of here," she said. "You no part of my crew. You get *nothing* here."

"No," said Achilles. "You better go ahead and kill me, you plan to treat him that way."

Oh, that sounded brave. But Bean knew Achilles wasn't brave. Just smart. He had already won. It meant nothing that he was lying there on the ground and Poke still had the cinderblock. It was his crew now. Poke was finished. It would be a while before anybody but Bean and Achilles understood that, but the test of authority was here and now, and Achilles was going to win it.

"This little kid," said Achilles, "he may not be part of your crew, but he's part of my family. You don't go telling my brother to get lost."

Poke hesitated. A moment. A moment longer.

Long enough.

Achilles sat up. He rubbed his bruises, he checked out his contusions. He looked in joking admiration to the little kids who had bricked him. "Damn, you bad!" They laughed—nervously, at first. Would he hurt them because they hurt him? "Don't worry," he said. "You showed me what you can do. We have to do this to more than a couple of bullies, you'll see. I had to know you could do it right. Good job. What's your name?"

One by one he learned their names. Learned them and remembered them, or when he missed one he'd make a big deal about it, apologize, visibly work at remembering. Fifteen minutes later, they loved him.

If he could do this, thought Bean, if he's this good at making people love him, why didn't he do it before?

Because these fools always look up for power. People above you, they never want to share power with you. Why you look to them? They give you nothing. People below you, you give them hope, you give them respect, *they* give you power, cause they don't think they have any, so they don't mind giving it up.

Achilles got to his feet, a little shaky, his bad leg more sore than usual. Everybody stood back, gave him some space. He could leave now, if he wanted. Get away, never come back. Or go get some more bullies, come back and punish the crew. But he stood there, then smiled, reached into his pocket, took out the most incredible thing. A bunch of raisins. A whole handful of them. They looked at his hand as if it bore the mark of a nail in the palm.

"Little brothers and sisters first," he said. "Littlest first." He looked at Bean. "You."

"Not him!" said the next littlest. "We don't even know him."

"Bean was the one wanted us to *kill* you," said another.

"Bean," said Achilles. "Bean, you were just looking out for my family, weren't you?"

"Yes," said Bean.

"You want a raisin?"

Bean nodded.

"You first. You the one brought us all together, OK?"

Either Achilles would kill him or he wouldn't. At this moment, all that mattered was the raisin. Bean took it. Put it in his mouth. Did not even bite down on it. Just let his saliva soak it, bringing out the flavor of it.

"You know," said Achilles, "no matter how long you hold it in your mouth, it never turns back into a grape."

"What's a grape?"

Achilles laughed at him, still not chewing. Then he gave out raisins to the other kids. Poke had never shared out so many raisins, because she had never had so many to share. But the little kids wouldn't understand that. They'd think, Poke gave us garbage, and Achilles gave us raisins. That's because they were stupid.

2

Kitchen

"I know you've already looked through this area, and you're probably almost done with Rotterdam, but something's been happening lately, since you visited, that . . . oh, I don't know if it's really anything, I shouldn't have called."

"Tell me, I'm listening."

"There's always been fighting in the line. We try to stop them, but we only have a few volunteers, and they're needed to keep order inside the dining room, that and serve the food. So we know that a lot of kids who should get a turn can't even get in the line, because they're pushed out. And if we do manage to stop the bullies and let one of the little ones in, then they get beaten up afterward. We never see them again. It's ugly."

"Survival of the fittest."

"Of the cruelest. Civilization is supposed to be the opposite of that."

"*You're* civilized. They're not."

"Anyway, it's changed. All of a sudden. Just in the past few days. I don't know why. But I just—you said that any-

thing unusual—and whoever's behind it—I mean, can civilization suddenly evolve all over again, in the middle of a
jungle of children?"

"That's the only place it ever evolves. I'm through in
Delft. There was nothing for us here. I already have enough
blue plates."

Bean kept to the background during the weeks that followed. He had nothing to offer now—they already had
his best idea. And he knew that gratitude wouldn't last
long. He wasn't big and he didn't eat much, but if he was
constantly underfoot, annoying people and chattering at
them, it would soon become not only fun but popular to
deny him food in hopes that he'd die or go away.

Even so, he often felt Achilles' eyes on him. He noticed
this without fear. If Achilles killed him, so be it. He had
been a few days from death anyway. It would just mean
his plan didn't work so well after all, but since it was his
only plan, it didn't matter if it turned out not to have been
good. If Achilles remembered how Bean urged Poke to
kill him—and of course he did remember—and if Achilles was planning how and when he would die, there was
nothing Bean could do to prevent it.

Sucking up wouldn't help. That would just look like
weakness, and Bean had seen for a long time how bullies—and Achilles was still a bully at heart—thrived on
the terror of other children, how they treated people even
worse when they showed their weakness. Nor would offering more clever ideas, first because Bean didn't have
any, and second because Achilles would think it was an
affront to his authority. And the other kids would resent
it if Bean kept acting like he thought he was the only one
with a brain. They already resented him for having
thought of this plan that had changed their lives.

For the change was immediate. The very first morning,
Achilles had Sergeant go stand in the line at Helga's
Kitchen on Aert Van Nes Straat, because, he said, as long
as we're going to get the crap beaten out of us anyway,

we might as well try for the best free food in Rotterdam in case we get to eat before we die. He talked like that, but he had made them practice their moves till the last light of day the night before, so they worked together better and they didn't give themselves away so soon, the way they did when they were going after him. The practice gave them confidence. Achilles kept saying, "They'll expect this," and "They'll try that," and because he was a bully himself, they trusted him in a way they had never trusted Poke.

Poke, being stupid, kept trying to act as if she was in charge, as if she had only delegated their training to Achilles. Bean admired the way that Achilles did not argue with her, and did not change his plans or instructions in any way because of what she said. If she urged him to do what he was already doing, he'd keep doing it. There was no show of defiance. No struggle for power. Achilles acted as if he had already won, and because the other kids followed him, he had.

The line formed in front of Helga's early, and Achilles watched carefully as bullies who arrived later inserted themselves in line in a kind of hierarchy—the bullies knew which ones got pride of place. Bean tried to understand the principle Achilles used to pick which bully Sergeant should pick a fight with. It wasn't the weakest, but that was smart, since beating the weakest bully would only set them up for more fights every day. Nor was it the strongest. As Sergeant walked across the street, Bean tried to see what it was about the target bully that made Achilles pick him. And then Bean realized—this was the strongest bully who had no friends with him.

The target was big and he looked mean, so beating him would look like an important victory. But he talked to no one, greeted no one. He was out of his territory, and several of the other bullies were casting resentful glances at him, sizing him up. There might have been a fight here today even if Achilles hadn't picked this soup line, this stranger.

Sergeant was cool as you please, slipping into place directly in front of the target. For a moment, the target just stood there looking at him, as if he couldn't believe what he was seeing. Surely this little kid would realize his deadly mistake and run away. But Sergeant didn't even act as if he noticed the target was there.

"Hey!" said the target. He shoved Sergeant hard, and from the angle of the push, Sergeant should have been propelled away from the line. But, as Achilles had told him, he planted a foot right away and launched himself forward, hitting the bully in front of the target in line, even though that was not the direction in which the target had pushed him.

The bully in front turned around and snarled at Sergeant, who pleaded, "He pushed me."

"He hit you himself," said the target.

"Do I look that stupid?" said Sergeant.

The bully-in-front sized up the target. A stranger. Tough, but not unbeatable. "Watch yourself, skinny boy."

That was a dire insult among bullies, since it implied incompetence and weakness.

"Watch your own self."

During this exchange, Achilles led a picked group of younger kids toward Sergeant, who was risking life and limb by staying right up between the two bullies. Just before reaching them, two of the younger kids darted through the line to the other side, taking up posts against the wall just beyond the target's range of vision. Then Achilles started screaming.

"What the hell do you think you're doing, you turd-stained piece of toilet paper! I send my boy to hold my place in line and you *shove* him? You *shove* him into my *friend* here?"

Of course they weren't friends at all—Achilles was the lowest-status bully in this part of Rotterdam and he always took his place as the last of the bullies in line. But the target didn't know that, and he wouldn't have time to find out. For by the time the target was turned to face

Achilles, the boys behind him were already leaping against his calves. There was no waiting for the usual exchange of shoves and brags before the fight began. Achilles began it and ended it with brutal swiftness. He pushed hard just as the younger boys hit, and the target hit the cobbled street hard. He lay there dazed, blinking. But already two other little kids were handing big loose cobblestones to Achilles, who smashed them down, one, two, on the target's chest. Bean could hear the ribs as they popped like twigs.

Achilles pulled him by his shirt and flopped him right back down on the street. He groaned, struggled to move, groaned again, lay still.

The others in line had backed away from the fight. This was a violation of protocol. When bullies fought each other, they took it into the alleys, and they didn't try for serious injury, they fought until supremacy was clear and it was over. This was a new thing, using cobblestones, breaking bones. It scared them, not because Achilles was so fearsome to look at, but because he had done the forbidden thing, and he had done it right out in the open.

At once Achilles signaled Poke to bring the rest of the crew and fill in the gap in the line. Meanwhile, Achilles strutted up and down the line, ranting at the top of his voice. "You can disrespect me, I don't care, I'm just a cripple, I'm just a guy with a gimp leg! But don't you go shoving my family! Don't you go shoving one of my children out of line! You hear me? Because if you do that some truck's going to come down this street and knock you down and break your bones, just like happened to this little pinprick, and next time maybe your head's going to be what breaks till your brains fall out on the street. You got to watch out for speeding trucks like the one that knocked down this fart-for-brains right here in front of my soup kitchen!"

There it was, the challenge. *My* kitchen. And Achilles didn't hold back, didn't show a spark of timidity about it. He kept the rant going, limping up and down the line, staring each bully in the face, daring him to argue. Shadowing his movements on the other side of the line were the two younger boys who had helped take down the stranger, and Sergeant strutted at Achilles' side, looking happy and smug. They reeked of confidence, while the other bullies kept glancing over their shoulders to see what those leg-grabbers behind them were doing.

And it wasn't just talk and brag, either. When one of the bullies started looking belligerent, Achilles went right up into his face. However, as he had planned beforehand, he didn't actually go after the belligerent one—he was ready for trouble, asking for it. Instead, the boys launched themselves at the bully directly after him in line. Just as they leapt, Achilles turned and shoved the new target, screaming, "What do you think is so damn funny!" He had another cobblestone in his hands at once, standing over the fallen one, but he did not strike. "Go to the end of the line, you moron! You're lucky I'm letting you eat in my kitchen!"

It completely deflated the belligerent one, for the bully Achilles knocked down and obviously could have smashed was the one next *lower* in status. So the belligerent one hadn't been threatened or harmed, and yet Achilles had scored a victory right in his face and he hadn't been a part of it.

The door to the soup kitchen opened. At once Achilles was with the woman who opened it, smiling, greeting her like an old friend. "Thank you for feeding us today," he said. "I'm eating last today. Thank you for bringing in my friends. Thank you for feeding my family."

The woman at the door knew how the street worked. She knew Achilles, too, and that something very strange was going on here. Achilles always ate last of the bigger boys, and rather shamefacedly. But his new patronizing attitude hardly had time to get annoying before the first of Poke's crew came to the door. "My family," Achilles announced proudly, passing each of the little kids into the hall. "You take good care of my children."

Even Poke he called his child. If she noticed the humiliation of it, though, she didn't show it. All she cared about was the miracle of getting into the soup kitchen. The plan had worked.

And whether she thought of it as her plan or Bean's didn't matter to Bean in the least, at least not till he had the first soup in his mouth. He drank it as slowly as he could, but it was still gone so fast that he could hardly believe it. Was this all? And how had he managed to spill so much of the precious stuff on his shirt?

Quickly he stuffed his bread inside his clothing and headed for the door. Stashing the bread and leaving, that was Achilles' idea and it was a good one. Some of the bullies inside the kitchen were bound to plan retribution. The sight of little kids eating would be galling to them. They'd get used to it soon enough, Achilles promised, but this first day it was important that all the little kids get out while the bullies were still eating.

When Bean got to the door, the line was still coming in, and Achilles stood by the door, chatting with the woman about the tragic accident there in the line. Paramedics must have been summoned to carry the injured boy away—he was no longer groaning in the street. "It could have been one of the little kids," he said. "We need a policeman out here to watch the traffic. That driver would never have been so careless if there was a cop here."

The woman agreed. "It could have been awful. They said half his ribs were broken and his lung was punctured." She looked mournful, her hands fretting.

"This line forms up when it's still dark. It's dangerous. Can't we have a light out here? I've got my children to think about," said Achilles. "Don't you want my little kids to be safe? Or am I the only one who cares about them?"

The woman murmured something about money and how the soup kitchen didn't have much of a budget.

Poke was counting children at the door while Sergeant ushered them out into the street.

Bean, seeing that Achilles was trying to get the adults to protect them in line, decided the time was right for him to be useful. Because this woman was compassionate and Bean was by far the smallest child, he knew he had the most power over her. He came up to her, tugged on her woollen skirt. "Thank you for watching over us," he said. "It's the first time I ever got into a real kitchen. Papa Achilles told us that *you* would keep us safe so we little ones could eat here every day."

"Oh, you poor thing! Oh, look at you." Tears streamed down the woman's face. "Oh, oh, you poor darling." She embraced him.

Achilles looked on, beaming. "I got to watch out for them," he said quietly. "I got to keep them safe."

Then he led his family—it was no longer in any sense Poke's crew—away from Helga's kitchen, all marching in a line. Till they rounded the corner of a building and then they ran like hell, joining hands and putting as much distance between them and Helga's kitchen as they could. For the rest of the day they were going to have to lie low. In twos and threes the bullies would be looking for them.

But they *could* lie low, because they didn't need to forage for food today. The soup already gave them more calories than they normally got, and they had the bread.

Of course, the first tax on that bread belonged to Achilles, who had eaten no soup. Each child reverently offered his bread to their new papa, and he took a bite from each one and slowly chewed it and swallowed it before reaching for the next offered bread. It was quite a lengthy ritual. Achilles took a mouthful of every piece of bread except two: Poke's and Bean's.

"Thanks," said Poke.

She was so stupid, she thought it was a gesture of respect. Bean knew better. By not eating their bread, Achilles was putting them outside the family. We are dead, thought Bean.

That's why Bean hung back, why he held his tongue and remained unobtrusive during the next few weeks.

That was also why he endeavored never to be alone. Always he was within arm's reach of one of the other kids.

But he didn't linger near Poke. That was a picture he didn't want to get locked in anyone's memory, him tagging along with Poke.

From the second morning, Helga's soup kitchen had an adult outside watching, and a new light fixture on the third day. By the end of a week the adult guardian was a cop. Even so, Achilles never brought his group out of hiding until the adult was there, and then he would march the whole family right to the front of the line, and loudly thank the bully in first position for helping him look out for his children by saving them a place in line.

It was hard on all of them, though, seeing how the bullies looked at them. They had to be on their best behavior while the doorkeeper was watching, but murder was on their minds.

And it didn't get better; the bullies didn't "get used to it," despite Achilles' bland assurances that they would. So even though Bean was determined to be unobtrusive, he knew that something had to be done to turn the bullies away from their hatred, and Achilles, who thought the war was over and victory achieved, wasn't going to do it.

So as Bean took his place in line one morning, he deliberately hung back to be last of the family. Usually Poke brought up the rear—it was her way of trying to pretend that she was somehow involved in ushering the little ones in. But this time Bean deliberately got in place behind her, with the hate-filled stare of the bully who should have had first position burning on his head.

Right at the door, where the woman was standing with Achilles, both of them looking proud of his family, Bean turned to face the bully behind him and asked, in his loudest voice, "Where's *your* children? How come you don't bring *your* children to the kitchen?"

The bully would have snarled something vicious, but the woman at the door was watching with raised eyebrows. "You look after little children, too?" she asked. It was obvious she was delighted about the idea and wanted the answer to be yes. And stupid as this bully was, he knew that it was good to please adults who gave out food. So he said, "Of course I do."

"Well, you can bring them, you know. Just like Papa Achilles here. We're always glad to see the little children."

Again Bean piped up. "They let people with little children come inside *first!*"

"You know, that's such a good idea," said the woman. "I think we'll make that a rule. Now, let's move along, we're holding up the hungry children."

Bean did not even glance at Achilles as he went inside.

Later, after breakfast, as they were performing the ritual of giving bread to Achilles, Bean made it a point to offer his bread yet again, though there was danger in reminding everyone that Achilles never took a share from him. Today, though, he had to see how Achilles regarded him, for being so bold and intrusive.

"If they all bring little kids, they'll run out of soup faster," said Achilles coldly. His eyes said nothing at all—but that, too, was a message.

"If they all become papas," said Bean, "they won't be trying to kill us."

At that, Achilles' eyes came to life a little. He reached down and took the bread from Bean's hand. He bit down on the crust, tore away a huge piece of it. More than half. He jammed it into his mouth and chewed it slowly, then handed the remnant of the bread back to Bean.

It left Bean hungry that day, but it was worth it. It didn't mean that Achilles wasn't going to kill him someday, but at least he wasn't separating him from the rest of the family anymore. And that remnant of bread was far more food than he used to get in a day. Or a week, for that matter.

He was filling out. Muscles grew in his arms and legs again. He didn't get exhausted just crossing a street. He could keep up easily now, when the others jogged along.

They all had more energy. They were healthy, compared to street urchins who didn't have a papa. Everyone could see it. The other bullies would have no trouble recruiting families of their own.

———

Sister Carlotta was a recruiter for the International Fleet's training program for children. It had caused a lot of criticism in her order, and finally she won the right to do it by pointedly mentioning the Earth Defense Treaty, which was a veiled threat. If she reported the order for obstructing her work on behalf of the I.F., the order could lose its tax-exempt and draft-exempt status. She knew, however, that when the war ended and the treaty expired, she would no doubt be a nun in search of a home, for there would be no place for her among the Sisters of St. Nicholas.

But her mission in life, she knew, was to care for little children, and the way she saw it, if the Buggers won the next round of the war, all the little children of the Earth would die. Surely God did not mean that to happen—but in her judgment, at least, God did not want his servants to sit around waiting for God to work miracles to save them. He wanted his servants to labor as best they could to bring about righteousness. So it was her business, as a Sister of St. Nicholas, to use her training in child development in order to serve the war effort. As long as the I.F. thought it worthwhile to recruit extraordinarily gifted children to train them for command roles in the battles to come, then she would help them by finding the children that would otherwise be overlooked. They would never pay anyone to do something as fruitless as scouring the filthy streets of every overcrowded city in the world, searching among the malnourished savage children who begged and stole and starved there; for the chance of finding a child with the intelligence and ability and character to make a go of it in Battle School was remote.

To God, however, all things were possible. Did he not

say that the weak would be made strong, and the strong weak? Was Jesus not born to a humble carpenter and his bride in the country province of Galilee? The brilliance of children born to privilege and bounty, or even to bare sufficiency, would hardly show forth the miraculous power of God. And it was the miracle she was searching for. God had made humankind in his own image, male and female he created them. No Buggers from another planet were going to blow down what God had created.

Over the years, though, her enthusiasm, if not her faith, had flagged a little. Not one child had done better than a marginal success on the tests. Those children were indeed taken from the streets and trained, but it wasn't Battle School. They weren't on the course that might lead them to save the world. So she began to think that her real work was a different kind of miracle—giving the children hope, finding even a few to be lifted out of the morass, to be given special attention by the local authorities. She made it a point to indicate the most promising children, and then follow up on them with email to the authorities. Some of her early successes had already graduated from college; they said they owed their lives to Sister Carlotta, but she knew they owed their lives to God.

Then came the call from Helga Braun in Rotterdam, telling her of certain changes in the children who came to her charity kitchen. Civilization, she had called it. The children, all by themselves, were becoming civilized.

Sister Carlotta came at once, to see a thing that sounded like a miracle. And indeed, when she beheld it with her own eyes, she could hardly believe it. The line for breakfast was now flooded with little children. Instead of the bigger ones shoving them out of the way or intimidating them into not even bothering to try, they were shepherding them, protecting them, making sure each got his share. Helga had panicked at first, fearful that she would run out of food—but she found that when potential benefactors saw how these children were acting, donations increased.

There was always plenty now—not to mention an increase in volunteers helping.

"I was at the point of despair," she told Sister Carlotta. "On the day when they told me that a truck had hit one of the boys and broken his ribs. Of course that was a lie, but there he lay, right in the line. They didn't even try to conceal him from me. I was going to give up. I was going to leave the children to God and move in with my oldest boy in Frankfurt, where the government is not required by treaty to admit every refugee from any part of the globe."

"I'm glad you didn't," said Sister Carlotta. "You can't leave them to God, when God has left them to us."

"Well, that's the funny thing. Perhaps that fight in the line woke up these children to the horror of the life they were living, for that very day one of the big boys—but the weakest of them, with a bad leg, they call him Achilles—well, I suppose *I* gave him that name years ago, because Achilles had a weak heel, you know—Achilles, anyway—he showed up in the line with a group of little children. He as much as asked me for protection, warning me that what happened to that poor boy with the broken ribs—he was the one I call Ulysses, because he wanders from kitchen to kitchen—he's still in hospital, his ribs were completely smashed in, can you believe the brutality?—Achilles, anyway, he warned me that the same thing might happen to his little ones, so I made the special effort, I came early to watch over the line, and badgered the police to finally give me a man, off-duty volunteers at first, on part pay, but now regulars—you'd think I would have been watching over the line all along, but don't you see? It didn't make any difference because they didn't do their intimidation in the line, they did it where I couldn't see, so no matter how I watched over them, it was only the bigger, meaner boys who ended up in the line, and yes, I know they're God's children too and I fed them and tried to preach the gospel to them as they ate, but I was losing heart, they were so heartless themselves, so devoid of compassion, but Achilles, anyway, he had taken on a whole group of them, including the littlest child I ever saw on the streets, it just broke my heart, they call him Bean, so *small*, he looked to be two years old, though I've learned since that he thinks he's four, and he *talks* like he's ten at least, very precocious, I suppose that's why he lived long enough to get under Achilles' protection, but he was skin and bone, people say that when somebody's skinny, but in the case of this little Bean, it was true, I didn't know how he had muscles enough to walk, to *stand,* his arms and legs were as thin as an ant— oh, isn't that awful? To compare him to the Buggers? Or I should say, the Formics, since they're saying now that *Buggers* is a bad word in English, even though I.F. Common is *not* English, even though it began that way, don't you think?"

"So, Helga, you're telling me it began with this Achilles."

"Do call me Hazie. We're friends now, aren't we?" She gripped Sister Carlotta's hand. "You must meet this boy. Courage! Vision! Test him, Sister Carlotta. He is a leader of men! He is a civilizer!"

Sister Carlotta did not point out that civilizers often didn't make good soldiers. It was enough that the boy was interesting, and she had missed him the first time around. It was a reminder to her that she must be thorough.

In the dark of early morning, Sister Carlotta arrived at the door where the line had already formed. Helga beckoned to her, then pointed ostentatiously at a rather good-looking young man surrounded by smaller children. Only when she got closer and saw him take a couple of steps did she realize just how bad his right leg was. She tried to diagnose the condition. Was it an early case of rickets? A clubfoot, left uncorrected? A break that healed wrong?

It hardly mattered. Battle School would not take him with such an injury.

Then she saw the adoration in the eyes of the children,

the way they called him Papa and looked to him for approval. Few adult men were good fathers. This boy of—what, eleven? twelve?—had already learned to be an extraordinarily good father. Protector, provider, king, god to his little ones. Even as ye do it unto the least of these, ye have done it unto me. Christ had a special place deep in his heart for this boy Achilles. So she *would* test him, and maybe the leg could be corrected; or, failing that, she could surely find a place for him in some good school in one of the cities of the Netherlands—pardon, the International Territory—that was not completely overwhelmed by the desperate poverty of refugees.

He refused.

"I can't leave my children," he said.

"But surely one of the others can look after them."

A girl who dressed as a boy spoke up. "I can!"

But it was obvious she could not—she was too small herself. Achilles was right. His children depended on him, and to leave them would be irresponsible. The reason she was here was because he was civilized; civilized men do not leave their children.

"Then I will come to you," she said. "After you eat, take me where you spend your days, and let me teach you all in a little school. Only for a few days, but that would be good, wouldn't it?"

It *would* be good. It had been a long time since Sister Carlotta had actually taught a group of children. And never had she been given such a class as this. Just when her work had begun to seem futile even to her, God gave her such a chance. It might even be a miracle. Wasn't it the business of Christ to make the lame walk? If Achilles did well on the tests, then surely God would let the leg also be fixed, would let it be within the reach of medicine.

"School's good," said Achilles. "None of these little ones can read."

Sister Carlotta knew, of course, that if Achilles could read, he certainly couldn't do it well.

But for some reason, perhaps some almost unnoticeable

movement, when Achilles said that none of the little ones could read, the smallest of them all, the one called Bean, caught her eye. She looked at him, into eyes with sparks in them like distant campfires in the darkest night, and she knew that *he* knew how to read. She knew, without knowing how, that it was not Achilles at all, that it was this little one that God had brought her here to find.

She shook off the feeling. It was Achilles who was the civilizer, doing the work of Christ. It was the leader that the I.F. would want, not the weakest and smallest of the disciples.

———

Bean stayed as quiet as possible during the school sessions, never speaking up and never giving an answer even when Sister Carlotta tried to insist. He knew that it wouldn't be good for him to let anyone know that he could already read and do numbers, nor that he could understand every language spoken in the street, picking up new languages the way other children picked up stones. Whatever Sister Carlotta was doing, whatever gifts she had to bestow, if it ever seemed to the other children that Bean was trying to show them up, trying to get ahead of them, he knew that he would not be back for another day of school. And even though she mostly taught things he already knew how to do, in her conversation there were many hints of a wider world, of great knowledge and wisdom. No adult had ever taken the time to speak to them like this, and he luxuriated in the sound of high language well spoken. When she taught it was in I.F. Common, of course, that being the language of the street, but since many of the children had also learned Dutch and some were even native Dutch speakers, she would often explain hard points in that language. When she was frustrated though, and muttered under her breath, that was in Spanish, the language of the merchants of Jonker Frans Straat, and he tried to piece together the meanings of new words from her muttering. Her knowledge was a banquet, and if he remained quiet enough, he would be able to stay and feast.

School had only been going for a week, however, when he made a mistake. She passed out papers to them, and they had writing on them. Bean read his paper at once. It was a "Pre-Test" and the instructions said to circle the right answers to each question. So he began circling answers and was halfway down the page when he realized that the entire group had fallen silent.

They were all looking at him, because Sister Carlotta was looking at him.

"What are you doing, Bean?" she asked. "I haven't even told you what to do yet. Please give me your paper."

Stupid, inattentive, careless—if you die for this, Bean, you deserve it.

He handed her the paper.

She looked at it, then looked back at him very closely. "Finish it," she said.

He took the paper back from her hand. His pencil hovered over the page. He pretended to be struggling with the answer.

"You did the first fifteen in about a minute and a half," said Sister Carlotta. "Please don't expect me to believe that you're suddenly having a hard time with the next question." Her voice was dry and sarcastic.

"I can't do it," he said. "I was just playing anyway."

"Don't lie to me," said Carlotta. "Do the rest."

He gave up and did them all. It didn't take long. They were easy. He handed her the paper.

She glanced over it and said nothing. "I hope the rest of you will wait until I finish the instructions and read you the questions. If you try to guess at what the hard words are, you'll get all the answers wrong."

Then she proceeded to read each question and all the possible answers out loud. Only then could the other children set their marks on the papers.

Sister Carlotta didn't say another thing to call attention to Bean after that, but the damage was done. As soon as school was over, Sergeant came over to Bean. "So you can read," he said.

Bean shrugged.

"You been lying to us," said Sergeant.

"Never said I couldn't."

"Showed us all up. How come *you* didn't teach us?"

Because I was trying to survive, Bean said silently. Because I didn't want to remind Achilles that I was the smart one who thought up the original plan that got him this family. If he remembers that, he'll also remember who it was who told Poke to kill him.

The only answer he actually gave was a shrug.

"Don't like it when somebody holds out on us."

Sergeant nudged him with a foot.

Bean did not have to be given a map. He got up and jogged away from the group. School was out for him. Maybe breakfast, too. He'd have to wait till morning to find that out.

He spent the afternoon alone on the streets. He had to be careful. As the smallest and least important of Achilles' family, he might be overlooked. But it was more likely that those who hated Achilles would have taken special notice of Bean as one of the most memorable. They might take it into their heads that killing Bean or beating him to paste and leaving him would make a dandy warning to Achilles that he was still resented, even though life was better for everybody.

Bean knew there were plenty of bullies who felt that way. Especially the ones who weren't able to maintain a family, because they kept being too mean with the little children. The little ones learned quickly that when a papa got too nasty, they could punish him by leaving him alone at breakfast and attaching themselves to some other family. They would eat before him. They would have someone else's protection from him. He would eat last. If they ran out of food, he would get nothing, and Helga wouldn't even mind, because *he* wasn't a papa, *he* wasn't watching out for little ones. So those bullies, those marginal ones,

they hated the way things worked these days, and they
didn't forget that it was Achilles who had changed it all.
Nor could they go to some other kitchen—the word had
spread among the adults who gave out food, and now all
the kitchens had a rule that groups with little children got
to be first in line. If you couldn't hold on to a family, you
could get pretty hungry. And nobody looked up to you.

Still, Bean couldn't resist trying to get close enough to
some of the other families to hear their talk. Find out how
the other groups worked.

The answer was easy to learn: They didn't work all that
well. Achilles really was a good leader. That sharing of
bread—none of the other groups did that. But there was
a lot of punishing, the bully smacking kids who didn't do
what he wanted. Taking their bread away from them because they didn't do something, or didn't do it quickly
enough.

Poke had chosen right, after all. By dumb luck, or
maybe she wasn't all that stupid. Because she had picked,
not just the weakest bully, the easiest to beat, but also the
smartest, the one who understood how to win and hold
the loyalty of others. All Achilles had ever needed was
the chance.

Except that Achilles still didn't share her bread, and
now she was beginning to realize that this was a bad thing,
not a good one. Bean could see it in her face when she
watched the others do the ritual of sharing with Achilles.
Because he got soup now—Helga brought it to him at the
door—he took much smaller pieces, and instead of biting
them off he tore them and ate them with a smile. Poke
never got that smile from him. Achilles was never going
to forgive her, and Bean could see that she was beginning
to feel the pain of that. For she loved Achilles now, too,
the way the other children did, and the way he kept her
apart from the others was a kind of cruelty.

Maybe that's enough for him, thought Bean. Maybe
that's his whole vengeance.

Bean happened to be curled up behind a newsstand

when several bullies began a conversation near him. "He's full of brag about how Achilles is going to pay for what he did."

"Oh, right, Ulysses is going to punish him, right."

"Well, maybe not directly."

"Achilles and his stupid family will just take him apart. And this time they won't aim for his chest. He said so, didn't he? Break open his head and put his brains on the street, that's what Achilles'll do."

"He's still just a cripple."

"Achilles gets away with everything. Give it up."

"I'm hoping Ulysses does it. Kills him, flat out. And then none of us take in any of his bastards. You got that? Nobody takes them in. Let them all die. Put them all in the river."

The talk went on that way until the boys drifted away from the newsstand.

Then Bean got up and went in search of Achilles.

3

Payback

"I think I have someone for you."

"You've thought that before."

"He's a born leader. But he does not meet your physical specifications."

"Then you'll pardon me if I don't waste time on him."

"If he passes your exacting intellectual and personality requirements, it is quite possible that for a minuscule portion of the brass button or toilet paper budget of the I.F., his physical limitations might be repaired."

"I never knew nuns could be sarcastic."

"I can't reach you with a ruler. Sarcasm is my last resort."

"Let me see the tests."

"I'll let you see the boy. And while we're at it, I'll let you see another."

"Also physically limited?"

"Small. Young. But so was the Wiggin boy, I hear. And this one—somehow on the streets he taught himself to read."

"Ah, Sister Carlotta, you help me fill the empty hours of my life."

"Keeping you out of mischief is how I serve God."

Bean went straight to Achilles with what he heard. It was too dangerous, to have Ulysses out of the hospital and word going around that he meant to get even for his humiliation.

"I thought that was all behind us," said Poke sadly. "The fighting I mean."

"Ulysses has been in bed for all this time," said Achilles. "Even if he knows about the changes, he hasn't had time to get how it works yet."

"So we stick together," said Sergeant. "Keep you safe."

"It might be safer for all," said Achilles, "if I disappear for a few days. To keep *you* safe."

"Then how will we get in to eat?" asked one of the younger ones. "They'll never let us in without you."

"Follow Poke," said Achilles. "Helga at the door will let you in just the same."

"What if Ulysses gets you?" asked one of the young ones. He rubbed the tears out of his eyes, lest he be shamed.

"Then I'll be dead," said Achilles. "I don't think he'll be content to put me in the hospital."

The child broke down crying, which set another to wailing, and soon it was a choir of boo-hoos, with Achilles shaking his head and laughing. "I'm not going to die. You'll be safe if I'm out of the way, and I'll come back after Ulysses has time to cool down and get used to the system."

Bean watched and listened in silence. He didn't think Achilles was handling it right, but he had given the warning and his responsibility was over. For Achilles to go into hiding was begging for trouble—it would be taken as a sign of weakness.

Achilles slipped away that night to go somewhere that he couldn't tell them so that nobody could accidentally let it slip. Bean toyed with the idea of following him to see what he really did, but realized he would be more useful with the main group. After all, Poke would be their leader now, and Poke was only an ordinary leader. In other words, stupid. She needed Bean, even if she didn't know it.

That night Bean tried to keep watch, for what he did not know. At last he did sleep, and dreamed of school, only it wasn't the sidewalk or alley school with Sister Carlotta, it was a real school, with tables and chairs. But in the dream Bean couldn't sit at a desk. Instead he hovered in the air over it, and when he wanted to he flew anywhere in the room. Up to the ceiling. Into a crevice in the wall, into a secret dark place, flying upward and upward as it got warmer and warmer and . . .

He woke in darkness. A cold breeze stirred. He needed to pee. He also wanted to fly. Having the dream end almost made him cry out with the pain of it. He couldn't remember ever dreaming of flying before. Why did he have to be little, with these stubby legs to carry him from place to place? When he was flying he could look down at everyone and see the tops of their silly heads. He could pee or poop on them like a bird. He wouldn't have to be afraid of them because if they got mad he could fly away and they could never catch him.

Of course, if I *could* fly, everyone else could fly too and I'd still be the smallest and slowest and they'd poop and pee on me anyway.

There was no going back to sleep. Bean could feel that in himself. He was too frightened, and he didn't know why. He got up and went into the alley to pee.

Poke was already there. She looked up and saw him.

"Leave me alone for a minute," she said.

"No," he said.

"Don't give me any crap, little boy," she said.

"I know you squat to pee," he said, "and I'm not looking anyway."

Glaring, she waited until he turned his back to urinate

against the wall. "I guess if you were going to tell about me you already would have," she said.

"They all know you're a girl, Poke. When you're not there, Papa Achilles talks about you as 'she' and 'her.'"

"He's not my papa."

"So I figured," said Bean. He waited, facing the wall.

"You can turn around now." She was up and fastening her pants again.

"I'm scared of something, Poke," said Bean.

"What?"

"I don't know."

"You don't know what you're scared of?"

"That's why it's so scary."

She gave a soft, sharp laugh. "Bean, all that means is that you're four years old. Little kids see shapes in the night. Or they don't see shapes. Either way they're scared."

"Not me," said Bean. "When I'm scared, it's because something's wrong."

"Ulysses is looking to hurt Achilles, that's what."

"That wouldn't make you sad, would it?"

She glared at him. "We're eating better than ever. Everybody's happy. It was your plan. And I never cared about being the boss."

"But you hate him," said Bean.

She hesitated. "It feels like he's always laughing at me."

"How do *you* know what little kids are scared of?"

"Cause I used to be one," said Poke. "And I remember."

"Ulysses isn't going to hurt Achilles," said Bean.

"I know that," said Poke.

"Because you're planning to find Achilles and protect him."

"I'm planning to stay right here and watch out for the children."

"Or else maybe you're planning to find Ulysses first and kill him."

"How? He's bigger than me. By a lot."

"You didn't come out here to pee," said Bean. "Or else your bladder's the size of a gumball."

"You *listened?*"

Bean shrugged. "You wouldn't let me watch."

"You think too much, but you don't know enough to make sense of what's going on."

"I think Achilles was lying to us about what he's going to do," said Bean, "and I think you're lying to me right now."

"Get used to it," said Poke. "The world is full of liars."

"Ulysses doesn't care who he kills," said Bean. "He'd be just as happy to kill you as Achilles."

Poke shook her head impatiently. "Ulysses is nothing. He isn't going to hurt anybody. He's all brag."

"So why are you up?" asked Bean.

Poke shrugged.

"*You're* going to try to kill Achilles, aren't you," said Bean. "And make it look like Ulysses did it."

She rolled her eyes. "Did you drink a big glass of stupid juice tonight?"

"I'm smart enough to know you're lying!"

"Go back to sleep," she said. "Go back to the other children."

He regarded her for a while, and then obeyed.

Or rather, seemed to obey. He went back into the crawl space where they slept these days, but immediately crept out the back way and clambered up crates, drums, low walls, high walls, and finally got up onto a low-hanging roof. He walked to the edge in time to see Poke slip out of the alley into the street. She *was* going somewhere. To meet someone.

Bean slid down a pipe onto a rainbarrel, and scurried along Korte Hoog Straat after her. He tried to be quiet, but she wasn't trying, and there were other noises of the city, so she never heard his footfalls. He clung to the shadows of walls, but didn't dodge around too much. It was pretty straightforward, following her—she only turned twice. Headed for the river. Meeting someone.

Bean had two guesses. It was either Ulysses or Achilles. Who else did she know, that wasn't already asleep in the nest? But then, why meet either of them? To plead with Ulysses for Achilles' life? To heroically offer herself in his place? Or to try to persuade Achilles to come back and face down Ulysses instead of hiding? No, these were all things that Bean might have thought of doing—but Poke didn't think that far ahead.

Poke stopped in the middle of an open space on the dock at Scheepmakershaven and looked around. Then she saw what she was looking for. Bean strained to see. Someone waiting in a deep shadow. Bean climbed up on a big packing crate, trying to get a better view. He heard the two voices—both children—but he couldn't make out what they were saying. Whoever it was, he was taller than Poke. But that could be either Achilles or Ulysses.

The boy wrapped his arms around Poke and kissed her.

This was really weird. Bean had seen grownups do that plenty of times, but what would kids do it for? Poke was nine years old. Of course there were whores that age, but everybody knew that the johns who bought them were perverts.

Bean had to get closer, to hear what they were saying. He dropped down the back of the packing crate and slowly walked into the shadow of a kiosk. They, as if to oblige him, turned to face him; in the deep shadow he was invisible, at least if he kept still. He couldn't see them any better than they could see him, but he could hear snatches of their conversation now.

"You promised," Poke was saying. The guy mumbled in return.

A boat passing on the river scanned a spotlight across the riverside and showed the face of the boy Poke was with. It was Achilles.

Bean didn't want to see any more. To think he had once believed Achilles would someday kill Poke. This thing between girls and boys was something he just didn't get.

In the midst of hate, this happens. Just when Bean was beginning to make sense of the world.

He slipped away and ran up Posthoornstraat.

But he did not head back to their nest in the crawlspace, not yet. For even though he had all the answers, his heart was still jumping; something is wrong, it was saying to him, something is wrong.

And then he remembered that Poke wasn't the only one hiding something from him. Achilles had also been lying. Hiding something. Some plan. Was it just this meeting with Poke? Then why all this business about hiding from Ulysses? To take Poke as his girl, he didn't have to hide to do that. He could do that right out in the open. Some bullies did that, the older ones. They usually didn't take nine-year-olds, though. Was that what Achilles was hiding?

"You promised," Poke said to Achilles there on the dock.

What did Achilles promise? That was why Poke came to him—to pay him for his promise. But what could Achilles be promising her that he wasn't already giving her as part of his family? Achilles didn't have anything.

So he must have been promising *not* to do something. Not to kill her? Then that would be too stupid even for Poke, to go off alone with Achilles.

Not to kill *me*, thought Bean. That's the promise. Not to kill *me*.

Only I'm not the one in danger, or not the most danger. I might have said to kill him, but Poke was the one who knocked him down, who stood over him. That picture must still be in Achilles' mind, all the time he must remember it, must dream about it, him lying on the ground, a nine-year-old girl standing over him with a cinderblock, threatening to kill him. A cripple like him, somehow he had made it into the ranks of the bullies. So he was tough—but always mocked by the boys with two good legs, the lowest-status bully. And the lowest moment of his life had to be then, when a nine-year-old girl knocked him down and a bunch of little kids stood over him.

Poke, he blames you most. You're the one he has to smash in order to wipe out the agony of that memory.

Now it was clear. Everything Achilles had said today was a lie. He wasn't hiding from Ulysses. He would face Ulysses down—probably still would, tomorrow. But when he faced Ulysses, Achilles would have a much bigger grievance. You killed Poke! He would scream the accusation. Ulysses would look so stupid and weak, denying it after all the bragging he'd done about how he'd get even. He might even admit to killing her, just for the brag of it. And then Achilles would strike at Ulysses and nobody would blame him for killing the boy. It wouldn't be mere self-defense, it would be defense of his family.

Achilles was just too damn smart. And patient. Waiting to kill Poke until there was somebody else who could be blamed for it.

Bean ran back to warn her. As fast as his little legs would move, the longest strides he could take. He ran forever.

There was nobody there on the dock where Poke had met Achilles.

Bean looked around helplessly. He thought of calling out, but that would be stupid. Just because it was Poke that Achilles hated most didn't mean that he had forgiven Bean, even if he did let Bean give him bread.

Or maybe I've gone crazy over nothing. He was hugging her, wasn't he? She came willingly, didn't she? There are things between boys and girls that I just don't understand. Achilles is a provider, a protector, not a murderer. It's *my* mind that works that way, *my* mind that thinks of killing someone who is helpless, just because he might pose a danger later. Achilles is the good one. I'm the bad one, the criminal.

Achilles is the one who knows how to love. I'm the one who doesn't.

Bean walked to the edge of the dock and looked across the channel. The water was covered with a low-flowing

mist. On the far bank, the lights of Boompjes Straat twinkled like Sinterklaas Day. The waves lapped like tiny
kisses against the pilings.

He looked down into the river at his feet. Something
was bobbing in the water, bumped up against the wharf.

Bean looked at it for a while, uncomprehending. But
then he understood that he had known all along what it
was, he just didn't want to believe it. It was Poke. She
was dead. It was just as Bean had feared. Everybody on
the street would believe that Ulysses was guilty of the
murder, even if nothing could be proved. Bean had been
right about everything. Whatever it was that passed between boys and girls, it didn't have the power to block
hatred, vengeance for humiliation.

And as Bean stood there, looking down into the water,
he realized: I either have to tell what happened, right now,
this minute, to everybody, or I have to decide never to
tell anybody, because if Achilles gets any hint that I saw
what I saw tonight, he'll kill me and not give it a second
thought. Achilles would simply say: Ulysses strikes again.
Then he can pretend to be avenging two deaths, not one,
when he kills Ulysses.

No, all Bean could do was keep silence. Pretend that
he hadn't seen Poke's body floating in the river, her up-
turned face clearly recognizable in the moonlight.

She was stupid. Stupid not to see through Achilles'
plans, stupid to trust him in any way, stupid not to listen
to me. As stupid as I was, to walk away instead of calling
out a warning, maybe saving her life by giving her a witness that Achilles could not hope to catch and therefore
could not silence.

She was the reason Bean was alive. She was the one
who gave him a name. She was the one who listened to
his plan. And now she had died for it, and he could have
saved her. Sure, he told her at the start to kill Achilles,
but in the end she had been right to choose him—he was
the only one of the bullies who could have figured it all
out and brought it off with such style. But Bean had also

been right. Achilles was a champion liar, and when he decided that Poke would die, he began building up the lies that would surround the murder—lies that would get Poke off by herself where he could kill her without witnesses; lies to alibi himself in the eyes of the younger kids.

I trusted him, thought Bean. I knew what he was from the start, and yet I trusted him.

Aw, Poke, you poor, stupid, kind, decent girl. You saved me and I let you down.

It's not *just* my fault. *She's* the one who went off alone with him.

Alone with him, trying to save my life? What a mistake, Poke, to think of anyone but yourself!

Am I going to die from her mistakes, too?

No. I'll die from my own damn mistakes.

Not tonight, though. Achilles had not set any plan in motion to get Bean off by himself. But from now on, when he lay awake at night, unable to drift off, he would think about how Achilles was just waiting. Biding his time. Till the day when Bean, too, would find himself in the river.

———

Sister Carlotta tried to be sensitive to the pain these children were suffering, so soon after one of their own was strangled and thrown in the river. But Poke's death was all the more reason to push forward on the testing. Achilles had not been found yet—with this Ulysses boy having already struck once, it was unlikely that Achilles would come out of hiding for some time. So Sister Carlotta had no choice but to proceed with Bean.

At first the boy was distracted, and did poorly. Sister Carlotta could not understand how he could fail even the elementary parts of the test, when he was so bright he had taught himself to read on the street. It had to be the death of Poke. So she interrupted the test and talked to him about death, about how Poke was caught up in spirit into the presence of God and the saints, who would care for her and make her happier than she had ever been in life. He did not seem interested. If anything, he did worse as they began the next phase of the test.

Well, if compassion didn't work, sternness might.

"Don't you understand what this test is for, Bean?" she asked.

"No," he said. The tone of his voice added the unmistakable idea "and I don't care."

"All you know about is the life of the street. But the streets of Rotterdam are only a part of a great city, and Rotterdam is only one city in a world of thousands of such cities. The whole human race, Bean, that's what this test is about. Because the Formics—"

"The Buggers," said Bean. Like most street urchins, he sneered at euphemism.

"They will be back, scouring the Earth, killing every living soul. This test is to see if you are one of the children who will be taken to Battle School and trained to be a commander of the forces that will try to stop them. This test is about saving the world, Bean."

For the first time since the test began, Bean turned his full attention to her. "Where is Battle School?"

"In an orbiting platform in space," she said. "If you do well enough on this test, you get to be a spaceman!"

There was no childlike eagerness in his face. Only hard calculation.

"I've been doing real bad so far, haven't I," he said.

"The test results so far show that you're too stupid to walk and breathe at the same time."

"Can I start over?"

"I have another version of the tests, yes," said Sister Carlotta.

"Do it."

As she brought out the alternate set, she smiled at him, tried to relax him again. "So you want to be a spaceman, is that it? Or is it the idea of being part of the International Fleet?"

He ignored her.

This time through the test, he finished everything, even though the tests were designed not to be finished in the allotted time. His scores were not perfect, but they were close. So close that nobody would believe the results.

So she gave him yet another battery of tests, this one designed for older children—the standard tests, in fact, that six-year-olds took when being considered for Battle School at the normal age. He did not do as well on these; there were too many experiences he had not had yet, to be able to understand the content of some of the questions. But he still did remarkably well. Better than any student she had ever tested.

And to think she had thought it was Achilles who had the real potential. This little one, this infant, really—he was astonishing. No one would believe she had found him on the streets, living at the starvation level.

A suspicion crept into her mind, and when the second test ended and she recorded the scores and set them aside, she leaned back in her chair and smiled at bleary-eyed little Bean and asked him, "Whose idea was it, this family thing that the street children have come up with?"

"Achilles' idea," said Bean.

Sister Carlotta waited.

"His idea to call it a family, anyway," said Bean.

She still waited. Pride would bring more to the surface, if she gave him time.

"But having a bully protect the little ones, that was my plan," said Bean. "I told it to Poke and she thought about it and decided to try it and she only made one mistake."

"What mistake was that?"

"She chose the wrong bully to protect us."

"You mean because he couldn't protect her from Ulysses?"

Bean laughed bitterly as tears slid down his cheeks.

"Ulysses is off somewhere bragging about what he's going to do."

Sister Carlotta knew but did not want to know. "Do you know who killed her, then?"

"I told her to kill him. I told her he was the wrong one. I saw it in his face, lying there on the ground, that he would never forgive her. But he's cold. He waited so long. But he never took bread from her. That should have told her. She shouldn't have gone off alone with him." He began crying in earnest now. "I think she was protecting *me*. Because I told her to kill him that first day. I think she was trying to get him not to kill me."

Sister Carlotta tried to keep emotion out of her voice. "Do you believe you might be in danger from Achilles?"

"I am now that I told you," he said. And then, after a moment's thought. "I was already. He doesn't forgive. He pays back, always."

"You realize that this isn't the way Achilles seems to me, or to Hazie. Helga, that is. To us, he seems—civilized."

Bean looked at her like she was crazy. "Isn't that what it *means* to be civilized? That you can *wait* to get what you want?"

"You want to get out of Rotterdam and go to Battle School so you can get away from Achilles."

Bean nodded.

"What about the other children. Do you think they're in danger from him?"

"No," said Bean. "He's their papa."

"But not yours. Even though he took bread from you."

"He hugged her and kissed her," said Bean. "I saw them on the dock, and she let him kiss her and then she said something about how he promised, and so I left, but then I realized and I ran back and it couldn't have been long, just running for maybe six blocks, and she was dead with her eye stabbed out, floating in the water, bumping up against the dock. He can kiss you and kill you, if he hates you enough."

Sister Carlotta drummed her fingers on the desk. "What a quandary."

"What's a quandary?"

"I was going to test Achilles, too. I think he could get into Battle School."

Bean's whole body tightened. "Then don't send me. Him or me."

"Do you really think . . ." Her voice trailed off. "You think he'd try to kill you there?"

"*Try?*" His voice was scornful. "Achilles doesn't just *try.*"

Sister Carlotta knew that the trait Bean was speaking of, that ruthless determination, was one of the things that they looked for in Battle School. It might make Achilles more attractive to them than Bean. And they could channel such murderous violence up there. Put it to good use.

But civilizing the bullies of the street had not been Achilles' idea. It had been Bean who thought of it. Incredible, for a child so young to conceive of it and bring it about. This child was the prize, not the one who lived for cold vengeance. But one thing was certain. It would be wrong of her to take them both. Though she could certainly take the other one and get him into a school here on Earth, get him off the street. Surely Achilles would become truly civilized then, where the desperation of the street no longer drove children to do such hideous things to each other.

Then she realized what nonsense she had been thinking. It wasn't the desperation of the street that drove Achilles to murder Poke. It was pride. It was Cain, who thought that being shamed was reason enough to take his brother's life. It was Judas, who did not shrink to kiss before killing. What was she thinking, to treat evil as if it were a mere mechanical product of deprivation? All the children of the street suffered fear and hunger, helplessness and desperation. But they didn't all become cold-blooded, calculating murderers.

If, that is, Bean was right.

But she had no doubt that Bean was telling her the truth. If Bean was lying, she would give up on herself as a judge of children's character. Now that she thought about it, Achilles was slick. A flatterer. Everything he said was calculated to impress. But Bean said little, and spoke plainly when he did speak. And he was young, and his fear and grief here in this room were real.

Of course, he also had urged that a child be killed.

But only because he posed a danger to others. It wasn't pride.

How can I judge? Isn't Christ supposed to be the judge of quick and dead? Why is this in my hands, when I am not fit to do it?

"Would you like to stay here, Bean, while I transmit your test results to the people who make the decisions about Battle School? You'll be safe here."

He looked down at his hands, nodded, then laid his head on his arms and sobbed.

———

Achilles came back to the nest that morning. "I couldn't stay away," he said. "Too much could go wrong." He took them to breakfast, just like always. But Poke and Bean weren't there.

Then Sergeant did his rounds, listening here and there, talking to other kids, talking to an adult here and there, finding out what was happening, anything that might be useful. It was along the Wijnhaven dock that he heard some of the longshoremen talking about the body found in the river that morning. A little girl. Sergeant found out where her body was being held till the authorities arrived. He didn't shy away, he walked right up to the body under a tarpaulin, and without asking permission from any of the others standing there, he pulled it back and looked at her.

"What are you doing, boy!"

"Her name is Poke," he said.

"You know her? Do you know who might have killed her?"

"A boy named Ulysses, that's who killed her," said

Sergeant. Then he dropped the tarp and his rounds were over. Achilles had to know that his fears had been justified, that Ulysses was taking out anybody he could from the family.

"We've got no choice but to kill him," said Sergeant.

"There's been enough bloodshed," said Achilles. "But I'm afraid you're right."

Some of the younger children were crying. One of them explained, "Poke fed me when I was going to die."

"Shut up," said Sergeant. "We're eating better now than we ever did when Poke was boss."

Achilles put a hand on Sergeant's arm, to still him. "Poke did the best a crew boss could do. And she's the one who got me into the family. So in a way, anything I get for you, she got for you."

Everyone nodded solemnly at that.

A kid asked, "You think Ulysses got Bean, too?"

"Big loss if he did," said Sergeant.

"Any loss to my family is a big loss," said Achilles. "But there'll be no more. Ulysses will either leave the city, now, or he's dead. Put the word out, Sergeant. Let it be known on the street that the challenge stands. Ulysses doesn't eat in any kitchen in town, until he faces me. That's what he decided for himself, when he chose to put a knife in Poke's eye."

Sergeant saluted him and took off at a run. The picture of businesslike obedience.

Except that as he ran, he, too, was crying. For he had not told anyone how Poke died, how her eye was a bloody wound. Maybe Achilles knew some other way, maybe he had already heard but didn't mention it till Sergeant came back with the news. Maybe maybe. Sergeant knew the truth. Ulysses didn't raise his hand against anybody. Achilles did it. Just as Bean warned in the beginning. Achilles would never forgive Poke for beating him. He killed her now because Ulysses would get blamed for it. And then sat there talking about how good she was and how they should all be grateful to her and everything

Achilles got for them, it was really Poke who got it.

So Bean was right all along. About everything. Achilles might be a good papa to the family, but he was also a killer, and he never forgives.

Poke knew that, though. Bean warned her, and she knew it, but she chose Achilles for their papa anyway. Chose him and then died for it. She was like Jesus that Helga preached about in her kitchen while they ate. She died for her people. And Achilles, he was like God. He made people pay for their sins no matter what they did.

The important thing is, stay on the good side of God. That's what Helga teaches, isn't it? Stay right with God.

I'll stay right with Achilles. I'll honor my papa, that's for sure, so I can stay alive until I'm old enough to go out on my own.

As for Bean, well, he was smart, but not smart enough to stay alive, and if you're not smart enough to stay alive, then you're better off dead.

By the time Sergeant got to his first corner to spread the word about Achilles' ban on Ulysses from any kitchen in town, he was through crying. Grief was done. This was about survival now. Even though Sergeant knew Ulysses hadn't killed anybody, he meant to, and it was still important for the family's safety that he die. Poke's death provided a good excuse to demand that the rest of the papas stand back and let Achilles deal with him. When it was all over, Achilles would be the leader among all the papas of Rotterdam. And Sergeant would stand beside him, knowing the secret of his vengeance and telling no one, because that's how Sergeant, that's how the family, that's how all the urchins of Rotterdam would survive.

4

Memories

"I was mistaken about the first one. He tests well, but his character is not well suited to Battle School."

"I don't see that on the tests you've shown me."

"He's very sharp. He gives the right answers, but they aren't true."

"And what test did you use to determine this?"

"He committed murder."

"Well, that is a drawback. And the other one? What am I supposed to do with so young a child? A fish this small I would generally throw back into the stream."

"Teach him. Feed him. He'll grow."

"He doesn't even have a name."

"Yes he does."

"Bean? That isn't a name, it's a joke."

"It won't be when he's done with it."

"Keep him until he's five. Make of him what you can and show me your results then."

"I have other children to find."

"No, Sister Carlotta, you don't. In all your years of

searching, this one is the best you've found. And there isn't time to find another. Bring this one up to snuff, and all your work will be worth it, as far as the I.F. is concerned."

"You frighten me, when you say there isn't time."

"I don't see why. Christians have been expecting the imminent end of the world for millennia."

"But it keeps not ending."

"So far, so good."

At first all Bean cared about was the food. There was enough of it. He ate everything they put before him. He ate until he was full—that most miraculous of words, which till now had had no meaning for him. He ate until he was stuffed. He ate until he was sick. He ate so often that he had bowel movements every day, sometimes twice a day. He laughed about it to Sister Carlotta. "All I do is eat and poop!" he said.

"Like any beast of the forest," said the nun. "It's time for you to begin to earn that food."

She was already teaching him, of course, daily lessons in reading and arithmetic, bringing him "up to level," though what level she had in mind, she never specified. She also gave him time to draw, and there were sessions where she had him sit there and try to remember every detail about his earliest memories. The clean place in particular fascinated her. But there were limits to memory. He was very small then, and had very little language. Everything was a mystery. He did remember climbing over the railing around his bed and falling to the floor. He didn't walk well at the time. Crawling was easier, but he liked walking because that's what the big people did. He clung to objects and leaned on walls and made good progress on two feet, only crawling when he had to cross an open space.

"You must have been eight or nine months old," Sister Carlotta said. "Most people don't remember that far back."

"I remember that everybody was upset. That's why I

climbed out of bed. All the children were in trouble."

"All the children?"

"The little ones like me. And the bigger ones. Some of the grownups came in and looked at us and cried."

"Why?"

"Bad things, that's all. I knew it was a bad thing coming and I knew it would happen to all of us who were in the beds. So I climbed out. I wasn't the first. I don't know what happened to the others. I heard the grownups yelling and getting all upset when they found the empty beds. I hid from them. They didn't find me. Maybe they found the others, maybe they didn't. All I know is when I came out all the beds were empty and the room was very dark except a lighted sign that said *exit*."

"You could read then?" She sounded skeptical.

"When I *could* read, I remembered that those were the letters on the sign," said Bean. "They were the only letters I saw back then. Of course I remembered them."

"So you were alone and the beds were empty and the room was dark."

"They came back. I heard them talking. I didn't understand most of the words. I hid again. And this time when I came out, even the beds were gone. Instead, there were desks and cabinets. An office. And no, I didn't know what an office was then, either, but now I do know what an office is and I remember that's what the rooms had all become. Offices. People came in during the day and worked there, only a few at first but my hiding place turned out not to be so good, when people were working there. And I was hungry."

"Where did you hide?"

"Come on, you know. Don't you?"

"If I knew, I wouldn't ask."

"You saw the way I acted when you showed me the toilet."

"You hid inside the toilet?"

"The tank on the back. It was hard to get the lid up. And it wasn't comfortable in there. I didn't know what it was for. But people started using it and the water rose and fell and the pieces moved and it scared me. And like I said, I was hungry. Plenty to drink, except that I peed in it myself. My diaper was so waterlogged it fell off my butt. I was naked."

"Bean, do you understand what you're telling me? That you were doing all this before you were a year old?"

"You're the one who said how old I was," said Bean. "I didn't know about ages then. You told me to remember. The more I tell you, the more comes back to me. But if you don't believe me . . ."

"I just . . . I do believe you. But who were the other children? What was the place where you lived, that clean place? Who were those grown-ups? Why did they take away the other children? Something illegal was going on, that's certain."

"Whatever," said Bean. "I was just glad to get out of the toilet."

"But you were naked, you said. And you left the place?"

"No, I got found. I came out of the toilet and a grownup found me."

"What happened?"

"He took me home. That's how I got clothing. I called them clothings then."

"You were talking."

"Some."

"And this grownup took you home and bought you clothing."

"I think he was a janitor. I know more about jobs now and I think that's what he was. It was night when he worked, and he didn't wear a uniform like a guard."

"What happened?"

"That's when I first found out about legal and illegal. It wasn't legal for him to have a child. I heard him yelling at this woman about me and most of it I didn't understand, but at the end I knew he had lost and she had won, and he started talking to me about how I had to go away, and so I went."

"He just turned you loose in the streets?"

"No, I left. I think now he was going to have to give me to somebody else, and it sounded scary, so I left before he could do it. But I wasn't naked or hungry anymore. He was nice. After I left I bet he didn't have any more trouble."

"And that's when you started living on the streets."

"Sort of. A couple of places I found, they fed me. But every time, other kids, big ones, would see that I was getting fed and they'd come shouting and begging and the people would stop feeding me or the bigger kids would shove me out of the way or take the food right out of my hands. I was scared. One time a big kid got so mad at me for eating that he put a stick down my throat and made me throw up what I just ate, right on the street. He even tried to eat it but he couldn't, it made him try to throw up, too. That was the scariest time. I hided all the time after that. Hid. All the time."

"And starved."

"And watched," said Bean. "I ate some. Now and then. I didn't die."

"No, you didn't."

"I saw plenty who did. Lots of dead children. Big ones and little ones. I kept wondering how many of them were from the clean place."

"Did you recognize any of them?"

"No. Nobody looked like they ever lived in the clean place. Everybody looked hungry."

"Bean, thank you for telling me all this."

"You asked."

"Do you realize that there is no way you could have survived for three years as an infant?"

"I guess that means I'm dead."

"I just . . . I'm saying that God must have been watching over you."

"Yeah. Well, sure. So why didn't he watch over all those dead kids?"

"He took them to his heart and loved them."

"So then he *didn't* love me?"

"No, he loved you too, he—"

" 'Cause if he was watching so careful, he could have given me something to eat now and then."

"He brought me to you. He has some great purpose in mind for you, Bean. You may not know what it is, but God didn't keep you alive so miraculously for no reason."

Bean was tired of talking about this. She looked so happy when she talked about God, but he hadn't figured it out yet, what God even was. It was like, she wanted to give God credit for every good thing, but when it was bad, then she either didn't mention God or had some reason why it was a good thing after all. As far as Bean could see, though, the dead kids would rather have been alive, just with more food. If God loved them so much, and he could do whatever he wanted, then why wasn't there more food for these kids? And if God just wanted them dead, why didn't he let them die sooner or not even be born at all, so they didn't have to go to so much trouble and get all excited about trying to be alive when he was just going to take them to his heart. None of it made any sense to Bean, and the more Sister Carlotta explained it, the less he understood it. Because if there was somebody in charge, then he ought to be fair, and if he wasn't fair, then why should Sister Carlotta be so happy that he was in charge?

But when he tried to say things like that to her, she got really upset and talked even more about God and used words he didn't know and it was better just to let her say what she wanted and not argue.

It was the reading that fascinated him. And the numbers. He loved that. Having paper and pencil so he could actually write things, that was really good.

And maps. She didn't teach him maps at first, but there were some on the walls and the shapes of them fascinated him. He would go up to them and read the little words written on them and one day he saw the name of the river and realized that the blue was rivers and even bigger blue areas were places with even more water than the river, and then he realized that some of the other words were the same names that had been written on the street signs and so he figured out that somehow this thing was a picture of Rotterdam, and then it all made sense. Rotterdam the way it would look to a bird, if the buildings were all invisible and the streets were all empty. He found where the nest was, and where Poke had died, and all kinds of other places.

When Sister Carlotta found out that he understood the map, she got very excited. She showed him maps where Rotterdam was just a little patch of lines, and one where it was just a dot, and one where it was too small even to be seen, but she knew where it *would* be. Bean had never realized the world was so big. Or that there were so many people.

But Sister Carlotta kept coming back to the Rotterdam map, trying to get him to remember where things from his earliest memories were. Nothing looked the same, though, on the map, so it wasn't easy, and it took a long time for him to figure out where some of the places were where people had fed him. He showed these to Sister Carlotta, and she made a mark right on the map, showing each place. And after a while he realized—all those places were grouped in one area, but kind of strung out, as if they marked a path from where he found Poke leading back through time to . . .

To the clean place.

Only that was too hard. He had been too scared, coming out of the clean place with the janitor. He didn't know where it was. And the truth was, as Sister Carlotta herself said, the janitor might have lived anywhere compared to the clean place. So all she was going to find by following Bean's path backward was maybe the janitor's flat, or at least where he lived three years ago. And even then, what would the janitor know?

He would know where the clean place was, that's what he'd know. And now Bean understood: It was very important to Sister Carlotta to find out where Bean came from.

To find out who he really was.

Only . . . he already knew who he really was. He tried to say this to her. "I'm right here. This is who I really am. I'm not pretending."

"I know that," she said, laughing, and she hugged him, which was all right. It felt good. Back when she first started doing it, he didn't know what to do with his hands. She had to show him how to hug her back. He had seen some little kids—the ones with mamas or papas—doing that but he always thought they were holding on tight so they wouldn't drop off onto the street and get lost. He didn't know that you did it just because it felt good. Sister Carlotta's body had hard places and squishy places and it was very strange to hug her. He thought of Poke and Achilles hugging and kissing, but he didn't want to kiss Sister Carlotta and after he got used to what hugging was, he didn't really want to do that either. He let her hug him. But he didn't ever think of hugging her himself. It just didn't come into his mind.

He knew that sometimes she hugged him instead of explaining things to him, and he didn't like that. She didn't want to tell him why it mattered that she find the clean place, so she hugged him and said, "Oh, you dear thing," or "Oh, you poor boy." But that only meant that it was even more important than she was saying, and she thought he was too stupid or ignorant to understand if she tried to explain.

He kept trying to remember more and more, if he could, only now he didn't tell her everything because she didn't tell *him* everything and fair was fair. He would find the clean room himself. Without her. And then tell her if he decided it would be good for him to have her know. Because what if she found the wrong answer? Would she put him back on the street? Would she keep him from going to school in the sky? Because that's what she promised at first, only after the tests she said he did very well only he would *not* go in the sky until he was five and maybe not even then because it was not entirely her decision and that's when he knew that she didn't have the power to keep her own promises. So if she found out the wrong thing about him, she might not be able to keep *any* of her promises. Not even the one about keeping him safe from Achilles. That's why he had to find out on his own.

He studied the map. He pictured things in his mind. He talked to himself as he was falling asleep, talked and thought and remembered, trying to get the janitor's face back into his mind, and the room he lived in, and the stairs outside where the mean lady stood to scream at him.

And one day, when he thought he had remembered enough, Bean went to the toilet—he liked the toilets, he liked to make them flush even though it scared him to see things disappear like that—and instead of coming back to Sister Carlotta's teaching place, he went the other way down the corridor and went right out the door onto the street and no one tried to stop him.

That's when he realized his mistake, though. He had been so busy trying to remember the janitor's place that it never occurred to him that he had no idea where *this* place was on the map. And it wasn't in a part of town that he knew. In fact, it hardly seemed like the same world. Instead of the street being full of people walking and pushing carts and riding bikes or skating to get from one place to another, the streets were almost empty, and there were cars parked everywhere. Not a single store, either. All houses and offices, or houses made into offices with little signs out front. The only building that was different was the very one he had just come out of. It was blocky and square and bigger than the others, but it had no sign out in front of it at all.

He knew where he was going, but he didn't know how

to get there from here. And Sister Carlotta would start looking for him soon.

His first thought was to hide, but then he remembered that she knew all about his story of hiding in the clean place, so she would also think of hiding and she would look for him in a hiding place close to the big building.

So he ran. It surprised him how strong he was now. It felt like he could run as fast as a bird flying, and he didn't get tired, he could run forever. All the way to the corner and around it onto another street.

Then down another street, and another, until he would have been lost except he started out lost and when you start out completely lost, it's hard to get loster. As he walked and trotted and jogged and ran up and down streets and alleys, he realized that all he had to do was find a canal or a stream and it would lead him to the river or to a place that he recognized. So the first bridge that went over water, he saw which way the water flowed and chose streets that would keep him close. It wasn't as if he knew where he was yet, but at least he was following a plan.

It worked. He came to the river and walked along it until he recognized, off in the distance and partly around a bend in the river, Maasboulevard, which led to the place where Poke was killed.

The bend in the river—he knew it from the map. He knew where all of Sister Carlotta's marks had been. He knew that he had to go through the place where he used to live on the streets in order to get past them and closer to the area where the janitor might have lived. And that wouldn't be easy, because he would be known there, and Sister Carlotta might even have the cops looking for him and *they* would look there because that's where all the street urchins were and they would expect him to become a street urchin again.

What they were forgetting was that Bean wasn't hungry anymore. And since he wasn't hungry, he wasn't in a hurry.

He walked the long way around. Far from the river, far from the busy part of town where the urchins were. Whenever the streets started looking crowded he would widen his circle and stay away from the busy places. He took the rest of that day and most of the next making such a wide circle that for a while he was not in Rotterdam anymore at all, and he saw some of the countryside, just like the pictures—farmland and the roads built up higher than the land around them. Sister Carlotta had explained to him once that most of the farmland was lower than the level of the sea, and great dikes were the only thing keeping the sea from rushing back onto the land and covering it. But Bean knew that he would never get close to any of the big dikes. Not by walking, anyway.

He drifted back into town now, into the Schiebroek district, and late in the afternoon of the second day he recognized the name of Rindijk Straat and soon found a cross street whose name he knew, Erasmus Singel, and then it was easy to get to the earliest place he could remember, the back door of a restaurant where he had been fed when he was still a baby and didn't talk right and grownups rushed to feed him and help him instead of kicking him out of the way.

He stood there in the dusk. Nothing had changed. He could almost picture the woman with the little bowl of food, holding it out to him and waving a spoon in her hand and saying something in a language he didn't understand. Now he could read the sign above the restaurant and realized that it was Armenian and that's probably what the woman had been speaking.

Which way had he walked to come here? He had smelled the food when he was walking along . . . here? He walked a little way up, a little way down the street, turning and turning to reorient himself.

"What are you doing here, fatso?"

It was two kids, maybe eight years old. Belligerent but not bullies. Probably part of a crew. No, part of a family, now that Achilles had changed everything. If the changes had spread to this part of town.

"I'm supposed to meet my papa here," said Bean.

"And who's your papa?"

Bean wasn't sure whether they took the word "papa" to mean his father or the papa of his "family." He took the chance, though, of saying "Achilles."

They scoffed at the idea. "He's way down by the river, why would he meet a fatso like you clear up here?"

But their derision was not important—what mattered was that Achilles' reputation had spread this far through the city.

"I don't have to explain his business to you," said Bean. "And all the kids in Achilles' family are fat like me. That's how well we eat."

"Are they all short like you?"

"I used to be taller, but I asked too many questions," said Bean, pushing past them and walking across Rozenlaan toward the area where the janitor's flat seemed likeliest to be.

They didn't follow him. Such was the magic of Achilles' name—or perhaps it was just Bean's utter confidence, paying them no notice as if he had nothing to fear from them.

Nothing looked familiar. He kept turning around and checking to see if he recognized things when looking in the direction he might have been going after leaving the janitor's flat. It didn't help. He wandered until it was dark, and kept wandering even then.

Until, quite by chance, he found himself standing at the foot of a street lamp, trying to read a sign, when a set of initials carved on the pole caught his attention. P♡DVM, it said. He had no idea what it meant; he had never thought of it during all his attempts to remember; but he knew that he had seen it before. And not just once. He had seen it several times. The janitor's flat was very close.

He turned slowly, scanning the area, and there it was:

A small apartment building with both an inside and an outside stairway.

The janitor lived on the top floor. Ground floor, first floor, second floor, third. Bean went to the mailboxes and tried to read the names, but they were set too high on the wall and the names were all faded, and some of the tags were missing entirely.

Not that he ever knew the janitor's name, truth to tell. There was no reason to think he would have recognized it even if he had been able to read it on the mailbox.

The outside stairway did not go all the way up to the top floor. It must have been built for a doctor's office on the first floor. And because it was dark, the door at the top of the stairs was locked.

There was nothing to do but wait. Either he would wait all night and get into the building through one entrance or another in the morning, or someone would come back in the night and Bean would slip through a door behind him.

He fell asleep and woke up, slept and woke again. He worried that a policeman would see him and shove him away, so when he woke the second time he abandoned all pretense of being on watch and crept under the stairs and curled up there for the night.

He was awakened by drunken laughter. It was still dark, and beginning to rain just a little—not enough to start dripping off the stairs, though, so Bean was dry. He stuck his head out to see who was laughing. It was a man and a woman, both merry with alcohol, the man furtively pawing and poking and pinching, the woman fending him off with halfhearted slaps. "Can't you wait?" she said.

"No," he said.

"You're just going to fall asleep without doing anything," she said.

"Not this time," he said. Then he threw up.

She looked disgusted and walked on without him. He staggered after her. "I feel better now," he said. "It'll be better."

"The price just went up," she said coldly. "And you brush your teeth first."

" 'Course I brush my teeth."

They were right at the front of the building now. Bean was waiting to slip in after them.

Then he realized that he didn't have to wait. The man *was* the janitor from all those years before.

Bean stepped out of the shadows. "Thanks for bringing him home," he said to the woman.

They both looked at him in surprise.

"Who are you?" asked the janitor.

Bean looked at the woman and rolled his eyes. "He's not *that* drunk, I hope," said Bean. To the janitor he said, "Mama will not be happy to see you come home like this again."

"Mama!" said the janitor. "Who the hell are you talking about?"

The woman gave the janitor a shove. He was so off balance that he lurched against the wall, then slid down it to land on his buttocks on the sidewalk. "I should have known," she said. "You bring me home to your *wife?*"

"I'm not married," said the janitor. "This kid isn't mine."

"I'm sure you're telling the truth on both points," said the woman. "But you better let him help you up the stairs anyway. Mama's waiting." She started to walk away.

"What about my forty gilders?" he asked plaintively, knowing the answer even as he asked.

She made an obscene gesture and walked on into the night.

"You little bastard," said the janitor.

"I had to talk to you alone," said Bean.

"Who the hell are you? Who's your mama?"

"That's what I'm here to find out," said Bean. "I'm the baby you found and brought home. Three years ago."

The man looked at him in stupefaction.

Suddenly a light went on, then another. Bean and the

janitor were bathed in overlapping flashlight beams. Four policemen converged on them.

"Don't bother running, kid," said a cop. "Nor you, Mr. Fun Time."

Bean recognized Sister Carlotta's voice. "They aren't criminals," she said. "I just need to talk to them. Up in his apartment."

"You followed me?" Bean asked her.

"I knew you were searching for him," she said. "I didn't want to interfere until you found him. Just in case you think you were really smart, young man, we intercepted four street thugs and two known sex offenders who were after you."

Bean rolled his eyes. "You think I've forgotten how to deal with them?"

Sister Carlotta shrugged. "I didn't want this to be the first time you ever made a mistake in your life." She did have a sarcastic streak.

———

"So as I told you, there was nothing to learn from this Pablo de Noches. He's an immigrant who lives to pay for prostitutes. Just another of the worthless people who have gravitated here ever since the Netherlands became international territory."

Sister Carlotta had sat patiently, waiting for the inspector to wind down his I-told-you-so speech. But when he spoke of a man's worthlessness, she could not let the remark go unchallenged. "He took in that baby," she said. "And fed the child and cared for him."

The inspector waved off the objection. "We needed one more street urchin? Because that's all that people like this ever produce."

"You didn't learn *nothing* from him," Sister Carlotta said. "You learned the location where the boy was found."

"And the people renting the building during that time are untraceable. A company name that never existed. Nothing to go on. No way to track them down."

"But that nothing *is* something," said Sister Carlotta. "I tell you that these people had many children in this place, which they closed down in a hurry, with all the children but one taken away. You tell me that the company was a false name and can't be traced. So now, in your experience, doesn't that tell you a great deal about what was going on in that building?"

The inspector shrugged. "Of course. It was obviously an organ farm."

Tears came to Sister Carlotta's eyes. "And that is the only possibility?"

"A lot of defective babies are born to rich families," said the inspector. "There is an illegal market in infant and toddler organs. We close down the organ farms whenever we find out where they are. Perhaps we were getting close to this organ farm and they got wind of it and closed up shop. But there is no paper in the department on any organ farm that we actually found at that time. So perhaps they closed down for another reason. Still, nothing."

Patiently, Sister Carlotta ignored his inability to realize how valuable this information was. "Where do the babies come from?"

The inspector looked at her blankly. As if he thought she was asking him to explain the facts of life.

"The organ farm," she said. "Where do they get the babies?"

The inspector shrugged. "Late-term abortions, usually. Some arrangement with the clinics, a kickback. That sort of thing."

"And that's the only source?"

"Well, I don't know. Kidnappings? I don't think that could be much of a factor, there aren't *that* many babies leaking through the security systems in the hospitals. People selling babies? It's been heard of, yes. Poor refugees arrive with eight children, and then a few years later they have only six, and they cry about the ones who died but who can prove anything? But nothing you can trace."

"The reason I'm asking," said Sister Carlotta, "is that this child is unusual. *Extremely* unusual."

"Three arms?" asked the inspector.

"Brilliant. Precocious. He escaped from this place before he was a year old. Before he could walk."

The inspector thought about that for a few moments. "He *crawled* away?"

"He hid in a toilet tank."

"He got the lid up before he was a year old?"

"He said it was hard to lift."

"No, it was probably cheap plastic, not porcelain. You know how these institutional plumbing fixtures are."

"You can see, though, why I want to know about the child's parentage. Some miraculous combination of parents."

The inspector shrugged. "Some children are born smart."

"But there is a hereditary component in this, inspector. A child like this must have . . . remarkable parents. Parents likely to be prominent because of the brilliance of their own minds."

"Maybe. Maybe not," said the inspector. "I mean, some of these refugees, they might be brilliant, but they're caught up in desperate times. To save the other children, maybe they sell a baby. That's even a *smart* thing to do. It doesn't rule out refugees as the parents of this brilliant boy you have."

"I suppose that's possible," said Sister Carlotta.

"It's the most information you'll ever have. Because this Pablo de Noches, he knows nothing. He barely could tell me the name of the town he came from in Spain."

"He was drunk when he was questioned," said Sister Carlotta.

"We'll question him again when he's sober," said the inspector. "We'll let you know if we learn anything more. In the meantime, though, you'll have to make do with what I've already told you, because there isn't anything more."

"I know all I need to know for now," said Sister Carlotta. "Enough to know that this child truly is a miracle, raised up by God for some great purpose."

"I'm not Catholic," said the inspector.

"God loves you all the same," said Sister Carlotta cheerfully.

Part Two

LAUNCHY

5

Ready or not

"Why are you giving me a five-year-old street urchin to tend?"

"You've seen the scores."

"Am I supposed to take those seriously?"

"Since the whole Battle School program is based on the reliability of our juvenile testing program, yes, I think you should take his scores seriously. I did a little research. No child has ever done better. Not even your star pupil."

"It's not the validity of the tests that I doubt. It's the tester."

"Sister Carlotta is a nun. You'll never find a more honest person."

"Honest people have been known to deceive themselves. To want so desperately, after all these years of searching, to find one—just one—child whose value will be worth all that work."

"And she's found him."

"Look at the *way* she found him. Her first report touts this Achilles child, and this—this Bean, this Legume—he's just an afterthought. Then Achilles is gone, not another mention of him—did he die? Wasn't she trying to get a leg operation for him?—and it's Haricot Vert who is now her candidate."

" 'Bean' is the name he calls himself. Rather as your Andrew Wiggin calls himself 'Ender.' "

"He's not *my* Andrew Wiggin."

"And Bean is not Sister Carlotta's child, either. If she were inclined to fudge the scores or administer tests unfairly, she would have pushed other students into the program long before now, and we'd already know how unreliable she was. She has never done that. She washes out her most hopeful children herself, then finds some place for them on Earth or in a non-command program. I think you're merely annoyed because you've already decided to focus all your attention and energy on the Wiggin boy, and you don't want any distraction."

"When did I lie down on your couch?"

"If my analysis is wrong, do forgive me."

"Of course I'll give this little one a chance. Even if I don't for one second believe these scores."

"Not just a chance. Advance him. Test him. Challenge him. Don't let him languish."

"You underestimate our program. We advance and test and challenge all our students."

"But some are more equal than others."

"Some take better advantage of the program than others."

"I'll look forward to telling Sister Carlotta about your enthusiasm."

Sister Carlotta shed tears when she told Bean that it was time for him to leave. Bean shed none.

"I understand that you're afraid, Bean, but don't be," she said. "You'll be safe there, and there's so much to learn. The way you drink down knowledge, you'll be very happy there in no time. So you won't really miss me at all."

Bean blinked. What sign had he given that made her think he was afraid? Or that he would miss her?

He felt none of those things. When he first met her, he might have been prepared to feel something for her. She was kind. She fed him. She was keeping him safe, giving him a life.

But then he found Pablo the janitor, and there was Sister Carlotta, stopping Bean from talking to the man who had saved him long before she did. Nor would she tell him anything that Pablo had said, or anything she had learned about the clean place.

From that moment, trust was gone. Bean knew that whatever Sister Carlotta was doing, it wasn't for him. She was using him. He didn't know what for. It might even be something he would have chosen to do himself. But she wasn't telling him the truth. She had secrets from him. The way Achilles kept secrets.

So during the months that she was his teacher, he had grown more and more distant from her. Everything she taught, he learned—and much that she didn't teach as well. He took every test she gave him, and did well; but he showed her nothing he had learned that she hadn't taught him.

Of course life with Sister Carlotta was better than life on the street—he had no intention of going back. But he did not trust her. He was on guard all the time. He was as careful as he had ever been back in Achilles' family. Those brief days at the beginning, when he wept in front of her, when he let go of himself and spoke freely—that had been a mistake that he would not repeat. Life was better, but he wasn't safe, and this wasn't home.

Her tears were real enough, he knew. She really did love him, and would really miss him when he left. After all, he had been a perfect child, compliant, quick, obedient. To her, that meant he was "good." To him, it was only a way of keeping his access to food and learning. He wasn't stupid.

Why did she assume he was afraid? Because she was

afraid *for* him. Therefore there might indeed be something to fear. He would be careful.

And why did she assume that he would miss her? Because she would miss him, and she could not imagine that what she was feeling, he might not feel as well. She had created an imaginary version of him. Like the games of Let's Pretend that she tried to play with him a couple of times. Harking back to her own childhood, no doubt, growing up in a house where there was always enough food. Bean didn't have to pretend things in order to exercise his imagination when he was on the street. Instead he had to imagine his plans for how to get food, for how to insinuate himself into a crew, for how to survive when he knew he seemed useless to everyone. He had to imagine how and when Achilles would decide to act against him for having advocated that Poke kill him. He had to imagine danger around every corner, a bully ready to seize every scrap of food. Oh, he had plenty of imagination. But he had no interest at all in playing Let's Pretend.

That was *her* game. She played it all the time. Let's pretend that Bean is a good little boy. Let's pretend that Bean is the son that this nun can never have for real. Let's pretend that when Bean leaves, he'll cry—that he's not crying now because he's too afraid of this new school, this journey into space, to let his emotions show. Let's pretend that Bean loves me.

And when he understood this, he made a decision: It will do no harm to me if she believes all this. And she wants very much to believe it. So why not give it to her? After all, Poke let me stay with the crew even though she didn't need me, because it would do no harm. It's the kind of thing Poke would do.

So Bean slid off his chair, walked around the table to Sister Carlotta, and put his arms as far around her as they would reach. She gathered him up onto her lap and held him tight, her tears flowing into his hair. He hoped her nose wasn't running. But he clung to her as long as she clung to him, letting go only when she let go of him. It was what she wanted from him, the only payment that she had ever asked of him. For all the meals, the lessons, the books, the language, for his future, he owed her no less than to join her in this game of Let's Pretend.

Then the moment passed. He slid off her lap. She dabbed at her eyes. Then she rose, took his hand, and led him out to the waiting soldiers, to the waiting car.

As he approached the car, the uniformed men loomed over him. It was not the grey uniform of the I.T. police, those kickers of children, those wielders of sticks. Rather it was the sky blue of the International Fleet that they wore, a cleaner look, and the people who gathered around to watch showed no fear, but rather admiration. This was the uniform of distant power, of safety for humanity, the uniform on which all hope depended. This was the service he was about to join.

But he was so small, and as they looked down at him he *was* afraid after all, and clung more tightly to Sister Carlotta's hand. Was he going to become one of them? Was he going to be a man in such a uniform, with such admiration directed at him? Then why was he afraid?

I'm afraid, Bean thought, because I don't see how I can ever be so tall.

One of the soldiers bent down to him, to lift him into the car. Bean glared up at him, defying him to dare such a thing. "I can do it," he said.

The soldier nodded slightly, and stood upright again. Bean hooked his leg up onto the running board of the car and hoisted himself in. It was high off the ground, and the seat he held to was slick and offered scant purchase to his hands. But he made it, and positioned himself in the middle of the back seat, the only position where he could see between the front seats and have some idea of where the car would be going.

One of the soldiers got into the driver's seat. Bean expected the other to get into the back seat beside Bean, and anticipated an argument about whether Bean could sit in the middle or not. Instead, he got into the front on the other side. Bean was alone in back.

He looked out the side window at Sister Carlotta. She was still dabbing at her eyes with a handkerchief. She gave him a little wave. He waved back. She sobbed a little. The car glided forward along the magnetic track in the road. Soon they were outside the city, gliding through the countryside at a hundred and fifty kilometers an hour. Ahead was the Amsterdam airport, one of only three in Europe that could launch one of the shuttles that could fly into orbit. Bean was through with Rotterdam. For the time being, at least, he was through with Earth.

———

Since Bean had never flown on an airplane, he did not understand how different the shuttle was, though that seemed to be all that the other boys could talk about at first. I thought it would be bigger. Doesn't it take off straight up? That was the old shuttle, stupid. There aren't any tray tables! That's cause in null-G you can't set anything down anyway, bonehead.

To Bean, the sky was the sky, and all he'd ever cared about was whether it was going to rain or snow or blow or burn. Going up into space did not seem any more strange to him than going up to the clouds.

What fascinated him were the other children. Boys, most of them, and all older than him. Definitely all larger. Some of them looked at him oddly, and behind him he heard one whisper, "Is he a kid or a doll?" But snide remarks about his size and his age were nothing new to him. In fact, what surprised him was that there was only the one remark, and it was whispered.

The kids themselves fascinated him. They were all so fat, so soft. Their bodies were like pillows, their cheeks full, their hair thick, their clothes well fitted. Bean knew, of course, that he had more fat on him now than at any time since he left the clean place, but he didn't see himself, he only saw them, and couldn't help comparing them to the kids on the street. Sergeant could take any of them apart. Achilles could . . . well, no use thinking about Achilles.

Bean tried to imagine them lining up outside a charity kitchen. Or scrounging for candy wrappers to lick. What a joke. They had never missed a meal in their lives. Bean wanted to punch them all so hard in the stomach that they would puke up everything they ate that day. Let them feel some pain there in their gut, that gnawing hunger. And then let them feel it again the next day, and the next hour, morning and night, waking and sleeping, the constant weakness fluttering just inside your throat, the faintness behind your eyes, the headache, the dizziness, the swelling of your joints, the distension of your belly, the thinning of your muscles until you barely have strength to stand. These children had never looked death in the face and then chosen to live anyway. They were confident. They were unwary.

These children are no match for me.

And, with just as much certainty: I will never catch up to them. They'll always be bigger, stronger, quicker, healthier. Happier. They talked to each other boastfully, spoke wistfully of home, mocked the children who had failed to qualify to come with them, pretended to have inside knowledge about how things really were in Battle School. Bean said nothing. Just listened, watched them maneuver, some of them determined to assert their place in the hierarchy, others quieter because they knew their place would be lower down; a handful relaxed, unworried, because they had never had to worry about the pecking order, having been always at the top of it. A part of Bean wanted to engage in the contest and win it, clawing his way to the top of the hill. Another part of him disdained the whole group of them. What would it mean, really, to be top dog in this mangy pack?

Then he glanced down at his small hands, and at the hands of the boy sitting next to him.

I really do look like a doll compared to the rest of them.

Some of the kids were complaining about how hungry they were. There was a strict rule against eating for twenty-four hours before the shuttle flight, and most of these kids had never gone so long without eating. For Bean, twenty-four hours without food was barely noticeable. In his crew, you didn't worry about hunger until the second week.

The shuttle took off, just like any airplane, though it had a long, long runway to get it up to speed, it was so heavy. Bean was surprised at the motion of the plane, the way it charged forward yet seemed to hold still, the way it rocked a little and sometimes bumped, as if it were rolling over irregularities in an invisible road.

When they got up to a high altitude, they rendezvoused with two fuel planes, in order to take on the rest of the rocket fuel needed to achieve escape velocity. The plane could never have lifted off the ground with that much fuel on board.

During the refueling, a man emerged from the control cabin and stood at the front of the rows of seats. His sky blue uniform was crisp and perfect, and his smile looked every bit as starched and pressed and unstainable as his clothes.

"My dear darling little children," he said. "Some of you apparently can't read yet. Your seat harnesses are to remain in place throughout the entire flight. Why are so many of them unfastened? Are you going somewhere?"

Lots of little clicks answered him like scattered applause.

"And let me also warn you that no matter how annoying or enticing some other child might be, keep your hands to yourself. You should keep in mind that the children around you scored every bit as high as you did on every test you took, and some of them scored higher."

Bean thought: That's impossible. Somebody here had to have the highest score.

A boy across the aisle apparently had the same thought. "Right," he said sarcastically.

"I was making a point, but I'm willing to digress," said the man. "Please, share with us the thought that so enthralled you that you could not contain it silently within you."

The boy knew he had made a mistake, but decided to tough it out. "Somebody here has the highest score."

The man continued looking at him, as if inviting him to continue.

Inviting him to dig himself a deeper grave, thought Bean.

"I mean, you said that everybody scored as high as everybody else, and some scored higher, and that's just obviously not true."

The man waited some more.

"That's all I had to say."

"Feel better?" said the man.

The boy sullenly kept his silence.

Without disturbing his perfect smile, the man's tone changed, and instead of bright sarcasm, there was now a sharp whiff of menace. "I asked you a question, boy."

"No, I don't feel better."

"What's your name?" asked the man.

"Nero."

A couple of children who knew a little bit about history laughed at the name. Bean knew about the emperor Nero. He did not laugh, however. He knew that a child named Bean was wise not to laugh at other kids' names. Besides, a name like that could be a real burden to bear. It said something about the boy's strength or at least his defiance that he didn't give some nickname.

Or maybe Nero *was* his nickname.

"Just . . . Nero?" asked the man.

"Nero Boulanger."

"French? Or just hungry?"

Bean did not get the joke. Was Boulanger a name that had something to do with food?

"Algerian."

"Nero, you are an example to all the children on this

shuttle. Because most of them are so foolish, they think it is better to keep their stupidest thoughts to themselves. You, however, understand the profound truth that you must reveal your stupidity openly. To hold your stupidity inside you is to embrace it, to cling to it, to protect it. But when you expose your stupidity, you give yourself the chance to have it caught, corrected, and replaced with wisdom. Be brave, all of you, like Nero Boulanger, and when you have a thought of such surpassing ignorance that you think it's actually smart, make sure to make some noise, to let your mental limitations squeak out some whimpering fart of a thought, so that you have a chance to learn."

Nero grumbled something.

"Listen—another flatulence, but this time even less articulate than before. Tell us, Nero. Speak up. You are teaching us all by the example of your courage, however half-assed it might be."

A couple of students laughed.

"And listen—your fart has drawn out other farts, from people equally stupid, for they think they are somehow superior to you, and that they could not just as easily have been chosen to be examples of superior intellect."

There would be no more laughter.

Bean felt a kind of dread, for he knew that somehow, this verbal sparring, or rather this one-sided verbal assault, this torture, this public exposure, was going to find some twisted path that led to him. He did not know how he sensed this, for the uniformed man had not so much as glanced at Bean, and Bean had made no sound, had done nothing to call attention to himself. Yet he knew that he, not Nero, would end up receiving the cruelest thrust from this man's dagger.

Then Bean realized why he was sure it would turn against him. This had turned into a nasty little argument about whether someone had higher test scores than anyone else on the shuttle. And Bean had assumed, for no reason whatsoever, that he was the child with the highest scores.

Now that he had seen his own belief, he knew it was

absurd. These children were all older and had grown up with far more advantages. He had had only Sister Carlotta as a teacher—Sister Carlotta and, of course, the street, though few of the things he learned *there* had shown up on the tests. There was no way that Bean had the highest score.

Yet he still knew, with absolute certainty, that this discussion was full of danger for him.

"I told you to speak up, Nero. I'm waiting."

"I still don't see how anything I said was stupid," said Nero.

"First, it was stupid because I have all the authority here, and you have none, so I have the power to make your life miserable, and you have no power to protect yourself. So how much intelligence does it take just to keep your mouth shut and avoid calling attention to yourself? What could be a more obvious decision to make when confronted with such a lopsided distribution of power?"

Nero withered in his seat.

"Second, you seemed to be listening to me, not to find out useful information, but to try to catch me in a logical fallacy. This tells us all that you are used to being smarter than your teachers, and that you listen to them in order to catch them making mistakes and prove how smart you are to the other students. This is such a pointless, stupid way of listening to teachers that it is clear you are going to waste months of our time before you finally catch on that the only transaction that matters is a transfer of useful information from adults who possess it to children who do not, and that catching mistakes is a criminal misuse of time."

Bean silently disagreed. The criminal misuse of time was *pointing out* the mistakes. Catching them—noticing them—that was essential. If you did not in your own mind distinguish between useful and erroneous information, then you were not *learning* at all, you were merely replacing ignorance with false belief, which was no improvement.

The part of the man's statement that was true, however, was about the uselessness of speaking up. If I know that the teacher is wrong, and say nothing, then I remain the only one who knows, and that gives me an advantage over those who believe the teacher.

"Third," said the man, "my statement only seems to be self-contradictory and impossible because you did not think beneath the surface of the situation. In fact it is not necessarily true that one person has the highest scores of everyone on this shuttle. That's because there were many tests, physical, mental, social, and psychological, and many ways to define 'highest' as well, since there are many ways to be physically or socially or psychologically fit for command. Children who tested highest on stamina may not have tested highest on strength; children who tested highest on memory may not have tested highest on anticipatory analysis. Children with remarkable social skills might be weaker in delay of gratification. Are you beginning to grasp the shallowness of your thinking that led you to your stupid and useless conclusion?"

Nero nodded.

"Let us hear the sound of your flatulence again, Nero. Be just as loud in acknowledging your errors as you were in making them."

"I was wrong."

There was not a boy on that shuttle who would not have avowed a preference for death to being in Nero's place at that moment. And yet Bean felt a kind of envy as well, though he did not understand why he would envy the victim of such torture.

"And yet," said the man, "you happen to be less wrong on this particular shuttle flight than you would have been in any other shuttle filled with launchies heading for Battle School. And do you know why?"

He did not choose to speak.

"Does anyone know why? Can anyone guess? I am inviting speculation."

No one accepted the invitation.

"Then let me choose a volunteer. There is a child here named—improbable as it might sound—'Bean.' Would that child please speak?"

Here it comes, thought Bean. He was filled with dread; but he was also filled with excitement, because this was what he wanted, though he did not know why. Look at me. Talk to me, you with the power, you with the authority.

"I'm here, sir," said Bean.

The man made a show of looking and looking, unable to see where Bean was. Of course it was a sham—he knew exactly where Bean was sitting before he ever spoke. "I can't see where your voice came from. Would you raise a hand?"

Bean immediately raised his hand. He realized, to his shame, that his hand did not even reach to the top of the high-backed seat.

"I still can't see you," said the man, though of course he could. "I give you permission to unstrap and stand on your seat."

Bean immediately complied, peeling off the harness and bounding to his feet. He was barely taller than the back of the seat in front of him.

"Ah, there you are," said the man. "Bean, would you be so kind as to speculate about why, in this shuttle, Nero comes closer to being correct than on any other?"

"Maybe somebody here scored highest on a lot of tests."

"Not just a lot of tests, Bean. All the tests of intellect. All the psychological tests. All the tests pertinent to command. Every one of them. Higher than anyone else on this shuttle."

"So I *was* right," said the newly defiant Nero.

"No you were not," said the man. "Because that remarkable child, the one who scored highest on all the tests related to command, happens to have scored the very lowest on the physical tests. And do you know why?"

No one answered.

"Bean, as long as you're standing, can you speculate about why this one child might have scored lowest on the physical tests?"

Bean knew how he had been set up. And he refused to try to hide from the obvious answer. He would say it, even though the question was designed to make the others detest him for answering it. After all, they would detest him anyway, no matter who said the answer.

"Maybe he scored lowest on the physical tests because he's very, very small."

Groans from many boys showed their disgust at his answer. At the arrogance and vanity that it suggested. But the man in uniform only nodded gravely.

"As should be expected from a boy of such remarkable ability, you are exactly correct. Only this boy's unusually small stature prevented Nero from being correct about there being one child with higher scores than everybody else." He turned to Nero. "So close to not being a complete fool," he said. "And yet . . . even if you had been right, it would only have been by accident. A broken clock is right two times a day. Sit down now, Bean, and put on your harness. The refueling is over and we're about to boost."

Bean sat down. He could feel the hostility of the other children. There was nothing he could do about that right now, and he wasn't sure that it was a disadvantage, anyway. What mattered was the much more puzzling question: Why did the man set him up like that? If the point was to get the kids competing with each other, they could have passed around a list with everyone's scores on all the tests, so they all could see where they stood. Instead, Bean had been singled out. He was already the smallest, and knew from experience that he was therefore a target for every mean-spirited impulse in a bully's heart. So why did they draw this big circle around him and all these arrows pointing at him, practically demanding that he be the main target of everyone's fear and hate?

Draw your targets, aim your darts. I'm going to do well enough in this school that someday I'll be the one with the authority, and then it won't matter who likes *me*. What will matter is who *I* like.

"As you may remember," said the man, "before the first fart from the mouthhole of Nero Bakerboy here, I was starting to make a point. I was telling you that even though some child here may seem like a prime target for your pathetic need to assert supremacy in a situation where you are unsure of being recognized for the hero that you want people to think you are, you must control yourself, and refrain from poking or pinching, jabbing or hitting, or even making snidely provocative remarks or sniggering like warthogs just because you think somebody is an easy target. And the reason why you should refrain from doing this is because you don't know who in this group is going to end up being *your* commander in the future, the admiral when you're a mere captain. And if you think for one moment that they will forget how you treated them now, today, then you really are a fool. If they're good commanders, they'll use you effectively in combat no matter how they despise you. But they don't have to be helpful to you in advancing your career. They don't have to nurture you and bring you along. They don't have to be kind and forgiving. Just think about that. The people you see around you will someday be giving you orders that will decide whether you live or die. I'd suggest you work on earning their respect, not trying to put them down so you can show off like some schoolyard punk."

The man turned his icy smile on Bean one more time.

"And I'll bet that Bean, here, is already planning to be the admiral who gives you all orders someday. He's even planning how he'll order *me* to stand solitary watch on some asteroid observatory till my bones melt from osteoporosis and I ooze around the station like an amoeba."

Bean hadn't given a moment's thought to some future

contest between him and this particular officer. He had no desire for vengeance. He wasn't Achilles. Achilles was stupid. And this officer was stupid for thinking that Bean would think that way. No doubt, however, the man thought Bean would be grateful because he had just warned the others not to pick on him. But Bean had been picked on by tougher bastards than these could possibly be; this officer's "protection" was not needed, and it made the gulf between Bean and the other children wider than before. If Bean could have lost a couple of tussles, he would have been humanized, accepted perhaps. But now there would be no tussles. No easy way to build bridges.

That was the reason for the annoyance that the man apparently saw on Bean's face. "I've got a word for you, Bean. I don't care what you do to me. Because there's only one enemy that matters. The Buggers. And if you can grow up to be the admiral who can give us victory over the Buggers and keep Earth safe for humanity, then make me eat my own guts, ass-first, and I'll still say, Thank you, sir. The Buggers are the enemy. Not Nero. Not Bean. Not even me. So keep your hands off each other."

He grinned again, mirthlessly.

"Besides, the last time somebody tried picking on another kid, he ended up flying through the shuttle in null-G and got his arm broken. It's one of the laws of strategy. Until you know that you're tougher than the enemy, you maneuver, you don't commit to battle. Consider that your first lesson in Battle School."

First lesson? No wonder they used this guy to tend children on the shuttle flights instead of having him teach. If you followed *that* little piece of wisdom, you'd be paralyzed against a vigorous enemy. Sometimes you *have* to commit to a fight even when you're weak. You don't *wait* till you *know* you're tougher. You *make* yourself tougher by whatever means you can, and then you strike by surprise, you sneak up, you backstab, you blindside, you cheat, you lie, you do whatever it takes to make sure that you come out on top.

This guy might be real tough as the only adult on a shuttle full of kids, but if he were a kid on the streets of Rotterdam, he'd "maneuver" himself into starvation in a month. If he wasn't killed before that just for talking like he thought his piss was perfume.

The man turned to head back to the control cabin.

Bean called out to him.

"What's your name?"

The man turned and fixed him with a withering stare. "Already drafting the orders to have my balls ground to powder, Bean?"

Bean didn't answer. Just looked him in the eye.

"I'm Captain Dimak. Anything else you want to know?"

Might as well find out now as later. "Do you teach at Battle School?"

"Yes," he said. "Coming down to pick up shuttle-loads of little boys and girls is how we get Earthside leave. Just as with you, my being on this shuttle means my vacation is over."

The refueling planes peeled away and rose above them. No, it was their own craft that was sinking. And the tail was sinking lower than the nose of the shuttle.

Metal covers came down over the windows. It felt like they were falling faster, faster . . . until, with a bone-shaking roar, the rockets fired and the shuttle began to rise again, higher, faster, faster, until Bean felt like he was going to be pushed right through the back of his chair. It seemed to go on forever, unchanging.

Then . . . silence.

Silence, and then a wave of panic. They were falling again, but this time there was no downward direction, just nausea and fear.

Bean closed his eyes. It didn't help. He opened them again, tried to reorient himself. No direction provided equilibrium. But he had schooled himself on the street not to succumb to nausea—a lot of the food he had to eat had already gone a little bad, and he couldn't afford to throw it up. So he went into his anti-nausea routine—deep breaths, distracting himself by concentrating on wiggling his toes. And, after a surprisingly short time, he was used to the null-G. As long as he didn't expect any direction to be down, he was fine.

The other kids didn't have his routine, or perhaps they were more susceptible to the sudden, relentless loss of balance. Now the reason for the prohibition against eating before the launch became clear. There was plenty of retching going on, but with nothing to throw up, there was no mess, no smell.

Dimak came back into the shuttle cabin, this time standing on the ceiling. Very cute, thought Bean. Another lecture began, this time about how to get rid of planetside assumptions about directions and gravity. Could these kids possibly be so stupid they needed to be told such obvious stuff?

Bean occupied the time of the lecture by seeing how much pressure it took to move himself around within his loosely-fitting harness. Everybody else was big enough that the harnesses fit snugly and prevented movement. Bean alone had room for a little maneuvering. He made the most of it. By the time they arrived at Battle School, he was determined to have at least a little skill at movement in null-G. He figured that in space, his survival might someday depend on knowing just how much force it would take to move his body, and then how much force it would take to stop. Knowing it in his mind wasn't half so important as knowing it with his body. Analyzing things was fine, but good reflexes could save your life.

6

Ender's shadow

"Normally your reports on a launch group are brief. A few troublemakers, an incident report, or—best of all— nothing."

"You're free to disregard any portion of my report, sir."

"Sir? My, but aren't we the prickly martinet today."

"What part of my report did you think was excessive?"

"I think this report is a love song."

"I realize that it might seem like sucking up, to use with every launch the technique you used with Ender Wiggin—"

"You use it with *every* launch?"

"As you noticed yourself, sir, it has interesting results. It causes an immediate sorting out."

"A sorting out into categories that might not otherwise exist. Nevertheless, I accept the compliment implied by your action. But seven pages about Bean—really, did you actually learn that much from a response that was primarily silent compliance?"

"That is just my point, sir. It was not compliance at all.

It was—I was performing the experiment, but it felt as though his were the big eye looking down the microscope, and I were the specimen on the slide."

"So he unnerved you."

"He would unnerve anyone. He's cold, sir. And yet—"

"And yet hot. Yes, I read your report. Every scintillating page of it."

"Yes sir."

"I think you know that it is considered good advice for us *not* to get crushes on our students."

"Sir?"

"In this case, however, I am delighted that you are so interested in Bean. Because, you see, I am not. I already have the boy I think gives us our best chance. Yet there is considerable pressure, because of Bean's damnable faked-up test scores, to give him special attention. Very well, he shall have it. And you shall give it to him."

"But sir . . ."

"Perhaps you are unable to distinguish an order from an invitation."

"I'm only concerned that . . . I think he already has a low opinion of me."

"Good. Then he'll underestimate you. Unless you think his low opinion might be correct."

"Compared to him, sir, we might all be a little dim."

"Close attention is your assignment. Try not to worship him."

All that Bean had on his mind was survival, that first day in Battle School. No one would help him—that had been made clear by Dimak's little charade in the shuttle. They were setting him up to be surrounded by . . . what? Rivals at best, enemies at worst. So it was the street again. Well, that was fine. Bean had survived on the street. And would have kept on surviving, even if Sister Carlotta hadn't found him. Even Pablo—Bean might have made it even without Pablo the janitor finding him in the toilet of the clean place.

So he watched. He listened. Everything the others learned, he had to learn just as well, maybe better. And on top of that, he had to learn what the others were oblivious to—the workings of the group, the systems of the Battle School. How teachers got on with each other. Where the power was. Who was afraid of whom. Every group had its bosses, its suckups, its rebels, its sheep. Every group had its strong bonds and its weak ones, friendships and hypocrisies. Lies within lies within lies. And Bean had to find them all, as quickly as possible, in order to learn the spaces in which he could survive.

They were taken to their barracks, given beds, lockers, little portable desks that were much more sophisticated than the one he had used when studying with Sister Carlotta. Some of the kids immediately began to play with them, trying to program them or exploring the games built into them, but Bean had no interest in that. The computer system of Battle School was not a person; mastering it might be helpful in the long run, but for today it was irrelevant. What Bean needed to find out was all outside the launchy barracks.

Which is where, soon enough, they went. They arrived in the "morning" according to space time—which, to the annoyance of many in Europe and Asia, meant Florida time, since the earliest stations had been controlled from there. For the kids, having launched from Europe, it was late afternoon, and that meant they would have a serious time-lag problem. Dimak explained that the cure for this was to get vigorous physical exercise and then take a short nap—no more than three hours—in the early afternoon, following which they would again have plenty of physical exercise so they could fall asleep that night at the regular bedtime for students.

They piled out to form a line in the corridor. "Green Brown Green," said Dimak, and showed them how those lines on the corridor walls would always lead them back to their barracks. Bean found himself jostled out of line several times, and ended up right at the back. He didn't care—mere jostling drew no blood and left no bruise, and last in line was the best place from which to observe.

Other kids passed them in the corridor, sometimes individuals, sometimes pairs or trios, most with brightly-colored uniforms in many different designs. Once they passed an entire group dressed alike and wearing helmets and carrying extravagant sidearms, jogging along with an intensity of purpose that Bean found intriguing. They're a crew, he thought. And they're heading off for a fight.

They weren't too intense to notice the new kids walking along the corridor, looking up at them in awe. Immediately there were catcalls. "Launchies!" "Fresh meat!" "Who make cocó in the hall and don't clean it up!" "They even smell stupid!" But it was all harmless banter, older kids asserting their supremacy. It meant nothing more than that. No real hostility. In fact it was almost affectionate. They remembered being launchies themselves.

Some of the launchies ahead of Bean in line were resentful and called back some vague, pathetic insults, which only caused more hooting and derision from the older kids. Bean had seen older, bigger kids who hated younger ones because they were competition for food, and drove them away, not caring if they caused the little ones to die. He had felt real blows, meant to hurt. He had seen cruelty, exploitation, molestation, murder. These other kids didn't know love when they saw it.

What Bean wanted to know was how that crew was organized, who led it, how he was chosen, what the crew was *for*. The fact that they had their own uniform meant that it had official status. So that meant that the adults were ultimately in control—the opposite of the way crews were organized in Rotterdam, where adults tried to break them up, where newspapers wrote about them as criminal conspiracies instead of pathetic little leagues for survival.

That, really, was the key. Everything the children did here was shaped by adults. In Rotterdam, the adults were either hostile, unconcerned, or, like Helga with her charity kitchen, ultimately powerless. So the children could shape their own society without interference. Everything was based on survival—on getting enough food without getting killed or injured or sick. Here, there were cooks and doctors, clothing and beds. Power wasn't about access to food—it was about getting the approval of adults.

That's what those uniforms meant. Adults chose them, and children wore them because adults somehow made it worth their while.

So the key to everything was understanding the teachers.

All this passed through Bean's mind, not so much verbally as with a clear and almost instantaneous understanding that within that crew there was no power at all, compared to the power of the teachers, before the uniformed catcallers reached him. When they saw Bean, so much smaller than any of the other kids, they broke out laughing, hooting, howling. "That one isn't big enough to be a turd!" "I can't believe he can *walk!*" "Did'ums wose um's mama?" "Is it even *human?*"

Bean tuned them out immediately. But he could feel the enjoyment of the kids ahead of him in line. They had been humiliated in the shuttle; now it was Bean's turn to be mocked. They loved it. And so did Bean—because it meant that he was seen as less of a rival. By diminishing him, the passing soldiers had made him just that much safer from . . .

From what? What was the *danger* here?

For there would be danger. That he knew. There was always danger. And since the teachers had all the power, the danger would come from them. But Dimak had started things out by turning the other kids against him. So the children themselves were the weapons of choice. Bean had to get to know the other kids, not because they themselves were going to be his problem, but because their weaknesses, their desires could be used against him by the teachers. And, to protect himself, Bean would have to work to undercut their hold on the other children. The only safety here was to subvert the teachers' influence.

And yet that was the greatest danger—if he was caught doing it.

They palmed in on a wall-mounted pad, then slid down a pole—the first time Bean had ever done it with a smooth shaft. In Rotterdam, all his sliding had been on rainspouts, signposts, and lightpoles. They ended up in a section of Battle School with higher gravity. Bean did not realize how light they must have been on the barracks level until he felt how heavy he was down in the gym.

"This is just a little heavier than Earth normal gravity," said Dimak. "You have to spend at least a half-hour a day here, or your bones start to dissolve. And you have to spend the time exercising, so you keep at peak endurance. And that's the key—endurance exercise, not bulking up. You're too small for your bodies to endure that kind of training, and it fights you here. Stamina, that's what we want."

The words meant almost nothing to the kids, but soon the trainer had made it clear. Lots of running on treadmills, riding on cycles, stair-stepping, pushups, situps, chinups, backups, but no weights. Some weight equipment was there, but it was all for the use of teachers. "Your heart rate is monitored from the moment you enter here," said the trainer. "If you don't have your heart rate elevated within five minutes of arrival and you don't keep it elevated for the next twenty-five minutes, it goes on your record *and* I see it on my control board here."

"I get a report on it too," said Dimak. "And you go on the pig list for everyone to see you've been lazy."

Pig list. So that's the tool they used—shaming them in front of the others. Stupid. As if Bean cared.

It was the monitoring board that Bean was interested in. How could they possibly monitor their heart rates and know what they were doing, automatically, from the moment they arrived? He almost asked the question, until he realized the only possible answer: The uniform. It was in the clothing. Some system of sensors. It probably told them a lot more than heart rate. For one thing, they could certainly track every kid wherever he was in the station, all the time. There must be hundreds and hundreds of kids here, and there would be computers reporting the whereabouts, the heart rates, and who could guess what other information about them. Was there a room somewhere with teachers watching every step they took?

Or maybe it wasn't the clothes. After all, they had to palm in before coming down here, presumably to identify themselves. So maybe there were special sensors in this room.

Time to find out. Bean raised his hand. "Sir," he said.

"Yes?" The trainer did a doubletake on seeing Bean's size, and a smile played around the corners of his mouth. He glanced at Dimak. Dimak did not crack a smile or show any understanding of what the trainer was thinking.

"Is the heart rate monitor in our clothing? If we take off any part of our clothes while we're exercising, does it—"

"You are not authorized to be out of uniform in the gym," said the trainer. "The room is kept cold on purpose so that you will not need to remove clothing. You will be monitored at all times."

Not really an answer, but it told him what he needed to know. The monitoring depended on the clothes. Maybe there was an identifier in the clothing and by palming in, they told the gym sensors which kid was wearing which set of clothing. That would make sense.

So clothing was probably anonymous from the time you put on a clean set until you palmed in somewhere. That was important—it meant that it might be possible to be untagged without being naked. Naked, Bean figured, would probably be conspicuous around here.

They all exercised and the trainer told them which of them were not up to the right heart rate and which of them were pushing too hard and would fatigue themselves too soon. Bean quickly got an idea of the level he had to work at, and then forgot about it. He'd remember by reflex, now that he knew.

It was mealtime, then. They were alone in the mess hall—as fresh arrivals, they were on a separate schedule that day. The food was good and there was a lot of it. Bean was stunned when some of the kids looked at their portion and complained about how little there was. It was a feast! Bean couldn't finish it. The whiners were informed by the cooks that the quantities were all adapted to their individual dietary needs—each kid's portion size came up on a computer display when he palmed in upon entering the mess hall.

So you don't eat without your palm on a pad. Important to know.

Bean soon found out that his size was going to get official attention. When he brought his half-finished tray to the disposal unit, an electronic chiming sound brought the on-duty nutritionist to speak to him. "It's your first day, so we aren't going to be rigid about it. But your portions are scientifically calibrated to meet your dietary needs, and in the future you will finish every bit of what you are served."

Bean looked at him without a word. He had already made his decision. If his exercise program made him hungrier, then he'd eat more. But if they were expecting him to gorge himself, they could forget it. It would be a simple enough matter to dump excess food onto the trays of the whiners. They'd be happy with it, and Bean would eat only as much as his body wanted. He remembered hunger very well, but he had lived with Sister Carlotta for many months, and he knew to trust his own appetite. For a while he had let her goad him into eating more than he actually was hungry for. The result had been a sense of loginess, a harder time sleeping and a harder time staying awake. He went back to eating only as much as his body wanted, letting his hunger be his guide, and it kept him sharp and quick. That was the only nutritionist he trusted. Let the whiners get sluggish.

Dimak stood after several of them had finished eating. "When you're through, go back to the barracks. If you think you can find it. If you have any doubt, wait for me and I'll bring the last group back myself."

The corridors were empty when Bean went out into the corridor. The other kids palmed the wall and their green-brown-green strip turned on. Bean watched them go. One of them turned back. "Aren't you coming?" Bean said nothing. There was nothing to say. He was obviously standing still. It was a stupid question. The kid turned around and jogged on down the corridor toward the barracks.

Bean went the other way. No stripes on the wall. He knew that there was no better time to explore than now. If he was caught out of the area he was supposed to be in, they'd believe him if he claimed to have got lost.

The corridor sloped up both behind him and in front of him. To his eyes it looked like he was always going up-hill, and when he looked back, it was uphill to go back the way he had come. Strange. But Dimak had already explained that the station was a huge wheel, spinning in space so that centrifugal force would replace gravity. That meant the main corridor on each level was a big circle, so you'd always come back to where you started, and "down" was always toward the outside of the circle. Bean made the mental adjustment. It was dizzying at first, to picture himself on his side as he walked along, but then he mentally changed the orientation so that he imagined the station as a wheel on a cart, with him at the bottom of it no matter how much it turned. That put the people above him upside down, but he didn't care. Wherever he was was the bottom, and that way down stayed down and up stayed up.

The launchies were on the mess hall level, but the older kids must not be, because after the mess halls and the kitchens, there were only classrooms and unmarked doors with palmpads high enough that they were clearly not meant for children to enter. Other kids could probably reach those pads, but not even by jumping could Bean hope to palm one. It didn't matter. They wouldn't respond to any child's handprint, except to bring some adult to find out what the kid thought he was doing, trying to enter a room where he had no business.

By long habit—or was it instinct?—Bean regarded such barriers as only temporary blocks. He knew how to climb over walls in Rotterdam, how to get up on roofs. Short as he was, he still found ways to get wherever he needed to go. Those doors would not stop him if he decided he needed to get beyond them. He had no idea right now how he'd do it, but he had no doubt that he would find a way. So he wasn't annoyed. He simply tucked the information away, waiting until he thought of some way to use it.

Every few meters there was a pole for downward passage or a ladderway for going up. To get down the pole to the gym, he had had to palm a pad. But there seemed to be no pad on most of these. Which made sense. Most poles and ladderways would merely let you pass between floors—no, they called them decks; this was the International Fleet and so everything pretended to be a ship—while only one pole led down to the gym, to which they needed to control access so that it didn't get overcrowded with people coming when they weren't scheduled. As soon as he had made sense of it, Bean didn't have to think of it anymore. He scrambled up a ladder.

The next floor up had to be the barracks level for the older kids. Doors were more widely spaced, and each door had an insignia on it. Using the colors of some uniform— no doubt based on their stripe colors, though he doubted the older kids ever had to palm the wall to find their way around—there was also the silhouette of an animal. Some of them he didn't recognize, but he recognized a couple of birds, some cats, a dog, a lion. Whatever was in use symbolically on signs in Rotterdam. No pigeon. No fly. Only noble animals, or animals noted for courage. The dog silhouette looked like some kind of hunting animal, very thin around the hips. Not a mongrel.

So this is where the crews meet, and they have animal

symbols, which means they probably call themselves by animal names. Cat Crew. Or maybe Lion Crew. And probably not Crew. Bean would soon learn what they called themselves. He closed his eyes and tried to remember the colors and insignia on the crew that passed and mocked him in the corridor earlier. He could see the shape in his mind, but didn't see it on any of the doors he passed. It didn't matter—not worth traveling the whole corridor in search of it, when that would only increase his risk of getting caught.

Up again. More barracks, more classrooms. How many kids in a barracks? This place was bigger than he thought.

A soft chime sounded. Immediately, several doors opened and kids began to pour out into the corridor. A changeover time.

At first Bean felt more secure among the big kids, because he thought he could get lost in the crowd, the way he always did in Rotterdam. But that habit was useless here. This wasn't a random crowd of people on their own errands. These might be kids but they were military. They knew where everybody was supposed to be, and Bean, in his launchy uniform, was way out of place. Almost at once a couple of older kids stopped him.

"You don't belong on this deck," said one. At once several others stopped to look at Bean as if he were an object washed into the street by a storm.

"Look at the size of this one."

"Poor kid gots to sniff everybody's butt, neh?"

"Eh!"

"You're out of area, launchy."

Bean said nothing, just looked at each one as he spoke. Or she.

"What are your colors?" asked a girl.

Bean said nothing. Best excuse would be that he didn't remember, so he couldn't very well name them now.

"He's so small he could walk between my legs without touching my—"

"Oh, shut up, Dink, that's what you said when Ender—"

"Yeah, Ender, right."

"You don't think this is the kid they—"

"Was Ender *this* small when he arrived?"

"—been saying, he another Ender?"

"Right, like this one's going to shoot to the top of the standings."

"It wasn't Ender's fault that Bonzo wouldn't let him fire his weapon."

"But it's a fluke, that's all I'm saying—"

"This the one they talking about? One like Ender? Top scores?"

"Just get him down to the launchy level."

"Come with me," said the girl, taking him firmly by the hand.

Bean came along meekly.

"My name is Petra Arkanian," she said.

Bean said nothing.

"Come on, you may be little and you may be scared, but they don't let you in here if you're deaf or stupid."

Bean shrugged.

"Tell me your name before I break your stubby little fingers."

"Bean," he said.

"That's not a name, that's a lousy meal."

He said nothing.

"You don't fool me," she said. "This mute thing, it's just a cover. You came up here on purpose."

He kept his silence but it stabbed at him, that she had figured him out so easily.

"Kids for this school, they're chosen because they're smart and they've got initiative. So of course you wanted to explore. The thing is, they expect it. They probably know you're doing it. So there's no point in hiding it. What are they going to do, give you some big bad piggy points?"

So that's what the older kids thought about the pig list.

"This stubborn silence thing, it'll just piss people off. I'd forget about it if I were you. Maybe it worked with Mommy and Daddy, but it just makes you look stubborn and ridiculous because anything that matters, you're going to tell anyway, so why not just talk?"

"OK," said Bean.

Now that he was complying, she didn't crow about it. The lecture worked, so the lecture was over. "Colors?" she asked.

"Green brown green."

"Those launchy colors sound like something you'd find in a dirty toilet, don't you think?"

So she was just another one of the stupid kids who thought it was cute to make fun of launchies.

"It's like they designed everything to get the older kids to make fun of the younger ones."

Or maybe she wasn't. Maybe she was just talking. She was a talker. There weren't a lot of talkers on the streets. Not among the kids, anyway. Plenty of them among the drunks.

"The system around here is screwed. It's like they want us to act like little kids. Not that that's going to bother *you*. Hell, you're already doing some dumb lost-little-kid act."

"Not now," he said.

"Just remember this. No matter what you do, the teachers know about it and they already have some stupid theory about what this means about your personality or whatever. They *always* find a way to use it against you, if they want to, so you might as well not try. No doubt it's already in your report that you took this little jaunt when you were supposed to be having beddy-bye time and that probably tells them that you 'respond to insecurity by seeking to be alone while exploring the limits of your new environment.' " She used a fancy voice for the last part.

And maybe she had more voices to show off to him, but he wasn't going to stick around to find out. Apparently she was a take-charge person and didn't have anybody to take charge of until he came along. He wasn't interested in becoming her project. It was all right being Sister Carlotta's project because she could get him out of the street and into Battle School. But what did this Petra Arkanian have to offer him?

He slid down a pole, stopped in front of the first opening, pushed out into the corridor, ran to the next ladderway, and scooted up two decks before emerging into another corridor and running full out. She was probably right in what she said, but one thing was certain—he was not going to have her hold his hand all the way back to green-brown-green. The last thing he needed, if he was going to hold his own in this place, was to show up with some older kid holding his hand.

Bean was four decks above the mess level where he was supposed to be right now. There were kids moving through here, but nowhere near as many as the deck below. Most of the doors were unmarked, but a few stood open, including one wide arch that opened into a game room.

Bean had seen computer games in some of the bars in Rotterdam, but only from a distance, through the doors and between the legs of men and women going in and out in their endless search for oblivion. He had never seen a child playing a computer game, except on the vids in store windows. Here it was real, with only a few players catching quick games between classes so that each game's sounds stood out. A few kids playing solo games, and then four of them playing a four-sided space game with a holographic display. Bean stood back far enough not to intrude in their sightlines and watched them play. Each of them controlled a squadron of four tiny ships, with the goal of either wiping out all the other fleets or capturing— but not destroying—each player's slow-moving mothership. He learned the rules and the terminology by listening to the four boys chatter as they played.

The game ended by attrition, not by any cleverness—

the last boy simply happened to be the least stupid in his use of his ships. Bean watched as they reset the game. No one put in a coin. The games here were free.

Bean watched another game. It was just as quick as the first, as each boy committed his ships clumsily, forgetting about whichever one was not actively engaged. It was as if they thought of their force as one active ship and three reserves.

Maybe the controls didn't allow anything different. Bean moved closer. No, it was possible to set the course for one, flip to control another ship, and another, then return to the first ship to change its course at any time.

How did these boys get into Battle School if this was all they could think of? Bean had never played a computer game before, but he saw at once that any competent player could quickly win if this was the best competition available.

"Hey, dwarf, want to play?"

One of them had noticed him. Of course the others did, too.

"Yes," said Bean.

"Well Bugger that," said the one who invited him. "Who do you think you are, Ender Wiggin?"

They laughed and then all four of them walked away from the game, heading for their next class. The room was empty. Class time.

Ender Wiggin. The kids in the corridor talked about him, too. Something about Bean made these kids think of Ender Wiggin. Sometimes with admiration, sometimes with resentment. This Ender must have beaten some older kids at a computer game or something. And he was at the top of the standings, that's what somebody said. Standings in what?

The kids in the same uniform, running like one crew, heading for a fight—that was the central fact of life here. There was one core game that everyone played. They lived in barracks according to what team they were on. Every kid's standings were reported so everybody else knew them. And whatever the game was, the adults ran it.

So this was the shape of life here. And this Ender Wiggin, whoever he was, he was at the top of it all, he led the standings.

Bean reminded people of him.

That made him a little proud, yes, but it also annoyed him. It was safer not to be noticed. But because this other small kid had done brilliantly, everybody who saw Bean thought of Ender and that made Bean memorable. That would limit his freedom considerably. There was no way to disappear here, as he had been able to disappear in crowds in Rotterdam.

Well, who cared? He couldn't be hurt now, not really. No matter what happened, as long as he was here at Battle School he would never be hungry. He'd always have shelter. He had made it to heaven. All he had to do was the minimum required to not get sent home early. So who cared if people noticed him or not? It made no difference. Let them worry about their standings. Bean had already won the battle for survival, and after that, no other competition mattered.

But even as he had that thought, he knew it wasn't true. Because he did care. It wasn't enough just to survive. It never had been. Deeper than his need for food had been his hunger for order, for finding out how things worked, getting a grasp on the world around him. When he was starving, of course he used what he learned in order to get himself into Poke's crew and get her crew enough food that there would be enough to trickle some down to him at the bottom of the pecking order. But even when Achilles had turned them into his family and they had something to eat every day, Bean hadn't stopped being alert, trying to understand the changes, the dynamics in the group. Even with Sister Carlotta, he had spent a lot of effort trying to understand why and how she had the power to do for him what she was doing, and the basis on which she had chosen him. He had to know. He had to have the picture of everything in his mind.

Here, too. He could have gone back to the barracks and napped. Instead, he risked getting in trouble just to find out things that no doubt he would have learned in the ordinary course of events.

Why did I come up here? What was I looking for?

The key. The world was full of locked doors, and he had to get his hands on every key.

He stood still and listened. The room was nearly silent. But there was white noise, background rumble and hiss that made it so sounds didn't carry throughout the entire station.

With his eyes closed, he located the source of the faint rushing sound. Eyes open, he then walked to where the vent was. An out-flowing vent with slightly warmer air making a very slight breeze. The rushing sound was not the hiss of air here at the vent, but rather a much louder, more distant sound of the machinery that pumped air throughout the Battle School.

Sister Carlotta had told him that in space, there was no air, so wherever people lived, they had to keep their ships and stations closed tight, holding in every bit of air. And they also had to keep changing the air, because the oxygen, she said, got used up and had to be replenished. That's what this air system was about. It must go everywhere through the ship.

Bean sat before the vent screen, feeling around the edges. There were no visible screws or nails holding it on. He got his fingernails under the rim and carefully slid his fingers around it, prying it out a little, then a little more. His fingers now fit under the edges. He pulled straight forward. The vent came free, and Bean toppled over backward.

Only for a moment. He set aside the screen and tried to see into the vent. The vent duct was only about fifteen centimeters deep from front to back. The top was solid, but the bottom was open, leading down into the duct system.

Bean sized up the vent opening just the way he had, years before, stood on the seat of a toilet and studied the inside of the toilet tank, deciding whether he could fit in it. And the conclusion was the same—it would be cramped, it would be painful, but he could do it.

He reached an arm inside and down. He couldn't feel the bottom. But with arms as short as his, that didn't mean much. There was no way to tell by looking which way the duct went when it got down to the floor level. Bean could imagine a duct leading under the floor, but that felt wrong to him. Sister Carlotta had said that every scrap of material used to build the station had to be hauled up from Earth or the manufacturing plants on the moon. They wouldn't have big gaps between the decks and the ceilings below because that would be wasted space into which precious air would have to be pumped without anyone breathing it. No, the ductwork would be in the outside walls. It was probably no more than fifteen centimeters deep anywhere.

He closed his eyes and imagined an air system. Machinery making a warm wind blow through the narrow ducts, flowing into every room, carrying fresh breathable air everywhere.

No, that wouldn't work. There had to be a place where the air was getting sucked in and drawn back. And if the air blew in at the outside walls, then the intake would be . . . in the corridors.

Bean got up and ran to the door of the game room. Sure enough, the corridor's ceiling was at least twenty centimeters lower than the ceiling inside the room. But no vents. Just light fixtures.

He stepped back into the room and looked up. All along the top of the wall that bordered on the corridor there was a narrow vent that looked more decorative than practical. The opening was about three centimeters. Not even Bean could fit through the intake system.

He ran back to the open vent and took off his shoes.

No reason to get hung up because his feet were so much bigger than they needed to be.

He faced the vent and swung his feet down into the opening. Then he wriggled until his legs were entirely down the hole and his buttocks rested on the rim of the vent. His feet still hadn't found bottom. Not a good sign. What if the vent dropped straight down into the machinery?

He wriggled back out, then went in the other way. It was harder and more painful, but now his arms were more usable, giving him a good grip on the floor as he slid chest-deep into the hole.

His feet touched bottom.

Using his toes, he probed. Yes, the ductwork ran to the left and the right, along the outside wall of the room. And the opening was tall enough that he could slide down into it, then wriggle—always on his side—along from room to room.

That was all he needed to know at present. He gave a little jump so his arms reached farther out onto the floor, meaning to use friction to let him pull himself up. Instead, he just slid back down into the vent.

Oh, this was excellent. Someone would come looking for him, eventually, or he'd be found by the next batch of kids who came in to play games, but he did not want to be found like this. More to the point, the ductwork would only give him an alternate route through the station if he could climb out of the vents. He had a mental image of somebody opening a vent and seeing his skull looking out at them, his dead body completely dried up in the warm wind of the air ducts where he starved to death or died of thirst trying to get out of the vents.

As long as he was just standing there, though, he might as well find out if he could cover the vent opening from the inside.

He reached over and, with difficulty, got a finger on the screen and was able to pull it toward him. Once he got a hand solidly on it, it wasn't hard at all to get it over the opening. He could even pull it in, tightly enough that it probably wouldn't be noticeably different to casual observers on the other side. With the vent closed, though, he had to keep his head turned to one side. There wasn't room enough for him to turn it. So once he got in the duct system, his head would either stay turned to the left or to the right. Great.

He pushed the vent back out, but carefully, so that it didn't fall to the floor. Now it was time to climb out in earnest.

After a couple more failures, he finally realized that the screen was exactly the tool he needed. Laying it down on the floor in front of the vent, he hooked his fingers under the far end. Pulling back on the screen provided him with the leverage to lift his body far enough to get his chest over the rim of the vent opening. It hurt, to hang the weight of his body on such a sharp edge, but now he could get up on his elbows and then on his hands, lifting his whole body up through the opening and back into the room.

He thought carefully through the sequence of muscles he had used and then thought about the equipment in the gym. Yes, he could strengthen those muscles.

He put the vent screen back into place. Then he pulled up his shirt and looked at the red marks on his skin where the rim of the vent opening had scraped him mercilessly. There was some blood. Interesting. How would he explain it, if anyone asked? He'd have to see if he could reinjure the same spot by climbing around on the bunks later.

He jogged out of the game room and down the corridor to the nearest pole, then dropped to the mess hall level. All the way, he wondered why he had felt such urgency about getting into the ducts. Whenever he got like that in the past, doing some task without knowing why it even mattered, it had turned out that there was a danger that he had sensed but that hadn't yet risen to his conscious mind. What was the danger here?

Then he realized—in Rotterdam, out on the street, he

had always made sure he knew a back way out of everything, an alternate path to get from one place to another. If he was running from someone, he never dodged into a cul-de-sac to hide unless he knew another way out. In truth, he never really *hid* at all—he evaded pursuit by keeping on the move, always. No matter how awful the danger following him might be, he could not hold still. It felt terrible to be cornered. It hurt.

It hurt and was wet and cold and he was hungry and there wasn't enough air to breathe and people walked by and if they just lifted the lid they would find him and he had no way to run if they did that, he just had to sit there waiting for them to pass without noticing him. If they used the toilet and flushed it, the equipment wouldn't work right because the whole weight of his body was pressing down on the float. A lot of the water had spilled out of the tank when he climbed in. They'd notice something was wrong and they'd find him.

It was the worst experience of his life, and he couldn't stand the idea of ever hiding like that again. It wasn't the small space that bothered him, or that it was wet, or that he was hungry or alone. It was the fact that the only way out was into the arms of his pursuers.

Now that he understood that about himself, he could relax. He hadn't found the ductwork because he sensed some danger that hadn't yet risen to his conscious mind. He found the ductwork because he remembered how bad it felt to hide in the toilet tank as a toddler. So whatever danger there might be, he hadn't sensed it yet. It was just a childhood memory coming to the surface. Sister Carlotta had told him that a lot of human behavior was really acting out our responses to dangers long past. It hadn't sounded sensible to Bean at the time, but he didn't argue, and now he could see that she was right.

And how could he know there would never be a time when that narrow, dangerous highway through the ductwork might not be exactly the route he needed to save his life?

He never did palm the wall to light up green-brown-green. He knew exactly where his barracks was. How could he not? He had been there before, and knew every step between the barracks and every other place he had visited in the station.

And when he got there, Dimak had not yet returned with the slow eaters. His whole exploration hadn't taken more than twenty minutes, including his conversation with Petra and watching two quick computer games during the class break.

He awkwardly hoisted himself up from the lower bunk, dangling for a while from his chest on the rim of the second bunk. Long enough that it hurt in pretty much the same spot he had injured climbing out of the vent. "What are you doing?" asked one of the launchies near him.

Since the truth wouldn't be understood, he answered truthfully. "Injuring my chest," he said.

"I'm trying to sleep," said the other boy. "You're supposed to sleep, too."

"Naptime," said another boy. "I feel like I'm some stupid four-year-old."

Bean wondered vaguely what these boys' lives had been like, when taking a nap made them think of being four years old.

———

Sister Carlotta stood beside Pablo de Noches, looking at the toilet tank. "Old-fashioned kind," said Pablo. "Norteamericano. Very popular for a while back when the Netherlands first became international."

She lifted the lid on the toilet tank. Very light. Plastic.

As they came out of the lavatory, the office manager who had been showing them around looked at her curiously. "There's not any kind of danger from using the toilets, is there?" she asked.

"No," said Sister Carlotta. "I just had to see it, that's all. It's Fleet business. I'd appreciate it if you didn't talk about our visit here."

Of course, that almost guaranteed that she would talk about nothing else. But Sister Carlotta counted on it sounding like nothing more than strange gossip.

Whoever had run an organ farm in this building would not want to be discovered, and there was a lot of money in such evil businesses. That was how the devil rewarded his friends—lots of money, up to the moment he betrayed them and left them to face the agony of hell alone.

Outside the building, she spoke again to Pablo. "He really hid in there?"

"He was very tiny," said Pablo de Noches. "He was crawling when I found him, but he was soaking wet up to his shoulder on one side, and his chest. I thought he peed himself, but he said no. Then he showed me the toilet. And he was red here, here, where he pressed against the mechanism."

"He was talking," she said.

"Not a lot. A few words. So *tiny*. I could not believe a child so small could talk."

"How long was he in there?"

Pablo shrugged. "Shriveled up skin like old lady. All over. Cold. I was thinking, he will die. Not warm water like a swimming pool. Cold. He shivered all night."

"I can't understand why he *didn't* die," said Sister Carlotta.

Pablo smiled. "No hay nada que Dios no puede hacer."

"True," she answered. "But that doesn't mean we can't figure out *how* God works his miracles. Or why."

Pablo shrugged. "God does what he does. I do my work and live, the best man I can be."

She squeezed his arm. "You took in a lost child and saved him from people who meant to kill him. God saw you do that and he loves you."

Pablo said nothing, but Sister Carlotta could guess what he was thinking—how many sins, exactly, were washed away by that good act, and would it be enough to keep him out of hell?

"Good deeds do not wash away sins," said Sister Carlotta. "Solo el redentor puede limpiar su alma."

Pablo shrugged. Theology was not his skill.

"You don't do good deeds for yourself," said Sister Carlotta. "You do them because God is in you, and for those moments you are his hands and his feet, his eyes and his lips."

"I thought God was the baby. Jesus say, if you do it to this little one, you do it to me."

Sister Carlotta laughed. "God will sort out all the fine points in his own due time. It is enough that we try to serve him."

"He was so small," said Pablo. "But God was in him."

She bade him good-bye as he got out of the taxi in front of his apartment building.

Why did I have to see that toilet with my own eyes? My work with Bean is done. He left on the shuttle yesterday. Why can't I leave the matter alone?

Because he should have been dead, that's why. And after starving on the streets for all those years, even if he lived he was so malnourished he should have suffered serious mental damage. He should have been permanently retarded.

That was why she could not abandon the question of Bean's origin. Because maybe he *was* damaged. Maybe he *is* retarded. Maybe he started out so smart that he could lose half his intellect and still be the miraculous boy he is.

She thought of how St. Matthew kept saying that all the things that happened in Jesus' childhood, his mother treasured them in her heart. Bean is not Jesus, and I am not the Holy Mother. But he is a boy, and I have loved him as my son. What he did, no child of that age could do.

No child of less than a year, not yet walking by himself, could have such clear understanding of his danger that he would know to do the things that Bean did. Children that age often climbed out of their cribs, but they did not hide in a toilet tank for hours and then come out alive and ask for help. I can call it a miracle all I want, but I have to understand it. They use the dregs of the Earth in those organ farms. Bean has such extraordinary gifts that he could only have come from extraordinary parents.

And yet for all her research during the months that Bean lived with her, she had never found a single kidnapping that could possibly have been Bean. No abducted child. Not even an accident from which someone might have taken a surviving infant whose body was therefore never found. That wasn't proof—not every baby that disappeared left a trace of his life in the newspapers, and not every newspaper was archived and available for a search on the nets. But Bean had to be the child of parents so brilliant that the world took note of them—didn't he? Could a mind like his come from ordinary parents? Was that the miracle from which all other miracles flowed?

No matter how much Sister Carlotta tried to believe it, she could not. Bean was not what he seemed to be. He was in Battle School now, and there was a good chance he would end up someday as the commander of a great fleet. But what did anyone know about him? Was it possible that he was not a natural human being at all? That his extraordinary intelligence had been given him, not by God, but by someone or something else?

There was the question: If not God, then who could make such a child?

Sister Carlotta buried her face in her hands. Where did such thoughts come from? After all these years of searching, why did she have to keep doubting the one great success she had?

We have seen the beast of Revelation, she said silently. The Bugger, the Formic monster bringing destruction to the Earth, just as prophesied. We have seen the beast, and long ago Mazer Rackham and the human fleet, on the brink of defeat, slew that great dragon. But it will come again, and St. John the Revelator said that when it did, there would be a prophet who came with him.

No, no. Bean is good, a good-hearted boy. He is not

any kind of devil, not the servant of the beast, just a boy of great gifts that God may have raised up to bless this world in the hour of its greatest peril. I know him as a mother knows her child. I am not wrong.

Yet when she got back to her room, she set her computer to work, searching now for something new. For reports from or about scientists who had been working, at least five years ago, on projects involving alterations in human DNA.

And while the search program was querying all the great indexes on the nets and sorting their replies into useful categories, Sister Carlotta went to the neat little pile of folded clothing waiting to be washed. She would not wash it after all. She put it in a plastic bag along with Bean's sheets and pillowcase, and sealed the bag. Bean had worn this clothing, slept on this bedding. His skin was in it, small bits of it. A few hairs. Maybe enough DNA for a serious analysis.

He was a miracle, yes, but she would find out just what the dimensions of this miracle might be. For her ministry had not been to save the children of the cruel streets of the cities of the world. Her ministry had been to help save the one species made in the image of God. That was still her ministry. And if there was something wrong with the child she had taken into her heart as a beloved son, she would find out about it, and give warning.

7

Exploration

"So this launch group was slow getting back to their barracks."

"There is a twenty-one-minute discrepancy."

"Is that a lot? I didn't even know this sort of thing was tracked."

"For safety. And to have an idea, in the event of emergency, where everyone is. Tracking the uniforms that departed from the mess hall and the uniforms that entered the barracks, we come up with an aggregate of twenty-one minutes. That could be twenty-one children loitering for exactly one minute, or one child for twenty-one minutes."

"That's very helpful. Am I supposed to ask them?"

"No! They aren't supposed to know that we track them by their uniforms. It isn't good for them to know how much we know about them."

"And how little."

"Little?"

"If it was one student, it wouldn't be good for him to know that our tracking methods don't tell us who it was."

"Ah. Good point. And . . . actually, I came to you because I believe that it *was* one student only."

"Even though your data aren't clear?"

"Because of the arrival pattern. Spaced out in groups of two or three, a few solos. Just the way they left the mess hall. A little bit of clumping—three solos become a three-some, two twos arrive as four—but if there had been some kind of major distraction in the corridor, it would have caused major coalescing, a much larger group arriving at once after the disturbance ended."

"So. One student with twenty-one minutes unaccounted for."

"I thought you should at least be aware."

"What would he do with twenty-one minutes?"

"You know who it was?"

"I will, soon enough. Are the toilets tracked? Are we sure it wasn't somebody so nervous he went in to throw up his lunch?"

"Toilet entry and exit patterns were normal. In and out."

"Yes, I'll find out who it was. And keep watching the data for this launch group."

"So I was right to bring this to your attention?"

"Did you have any doubt of it?"

Bean slept lightly, listening, as he always did, waking twice that he remembered. He didn't get up, just lay there listening to the breathing of the others. Both times, there was a little whispering somewhere in the room. Always children's voices, no urgency about them, but the sound was enough to rouse Bean and kindle his attention, just for a moment till he was sure there was no danger.

He woke the third time when Dimak entered the room. Even before sitting up, Bean knew that's who it was, from the weight of his step, the sureness of his movement, the press of authority. Bean's eyes were open before Dimak spoke; he was on all fours, ready to move in any direction, before Dimak finished his first sentence.

"Naptime is over, boys and girls, time for work."

It was not about Bean. If Dimak knew what Bean had done after lunch and before their nap, he gave no sign. No immediate danger.

Bean sat on his bunk as Dimak instructed them in the use of their lockers and desks. Palm the wall beside the locker and it opens. Then turn on the desk and enter your name and a password.

Bean immediately palmed his own locker with his right hand, but did not palm the desk. Instead, he checked on Dimak—busy helping another student near the door— then scrambled to the unoccupied third bunk above his own and palmed *that* locker with his left hand. There was a desk inside that one, too. Quickly he turned on his own desk and typed in his name and a password. Bean. Achilles. Then he pulled out the other desk and turned it on. Name? Poke. Password? Carlotta.

He slipped the second desk back into the locker and closed the door, then tossed his first desk down onto his own bunk and slipped down after it. He did not look around to see if anyone noticed him. If they did, they'd say something soon enough; visibly checking around would merely call attention to him and make people suspect him who would not otherwise have noticed what he did.

Of course the adults would know what he had done. In fact, Dimak was certainly noticing already, when one child complained that his locker wouldn't open. So the station computer knew how many students there were and stopped opening lockers when the right total had been opened. But Dimak did not turn and demand to know who had opened two lockers. Instead, he pressed his own palm against the last student's locker. It popped open. He closed it again, and now it responded to the student's palm.

So they were going to let him have his second locker, his second desk, his second identity. No doubt they would watch him with special interest to see what he did with it. He would have to make a point of fiddling with it now and then, clumsily, so they'd think they knew what he wanted a second identity for. Maybe some kind of prank. Or to write down secret thoughts. That would be fun— Sister Carlotta was always prying after his secret thoughts, and no doubt these teachers would, too. Whatever he wrote, they'd eat it up.

Therefore they wouldn't be looking for his truly private work, which he would perform on his own desk. Or, if it was risky, on the desk of one of the boys across from him, both of whose passwords he had carefully noticed and memorized. Dimak was lecturing them about protecting their desks at all times, but it was inevitable that kids would be careless, and desks would be left lying around.

For now, though, Bean would do nothing riskier than what he had already done. The teachers had their own reasons for letting him do it. What mattered is that they not know his own.

After all, he didn't know himself. It was like the vent— if he thought of something that might get him some advantage later, he did it.

Dimak went on talking about how to submit homework, the directory of teachers' names, and the fantasy game that was on every desk. "You are not to spend study time playing the game," he said. "But when your studies are done, you are permitted a few minutes to explore."

Bean understood at once. The teachers *wanted* the students to play the game, and knew that the best way to encourage it was to put strict limits on it . . . and then not enforce them. A game—Sister Carlotta had used games to try to analyze Bean from time to time. So Bean always turned them into the same game: Try to figure out what Sister Carlotta is trying to learn from the way I play this game.

In this case, though, Bean figured that anything he did with the game would tell them things that he didn't want them to know about him. So he would not play at all, unless they compelled him. And maybe not even then. It was one thing to joust with Sister Carlotta; here, they no doubt had real experts, and Bean was not going to give them a chance to learn more about him than he knew himself.

Dimak took them on the tour, showing them most of what Bean had already seen. The other kids went ape over the game room. Bean did not so much as glance at the vent into which he had climbed, though he did make it a point to fiddle with the game he had watched the bigger boys play, figuring out how the controls worked and verifying that his tactics could, in fact, be carried out.

They did a workout in the gym, in which Bean immediately began working on the exercises that he thought he'd need—one-armed pushups and pullups being the most important, though they had to get a stool for him to stand on in order to reach the lowest chinning bar. No problem. Soon enough he'd be able to jump to reach it. With all the food they were giving him, he could build up strength quickly.

And they seemed grimly determined to pack food into him at an astonishing rate. After the gym they showered, and then it was suppertime. Bean wasn't even hungry yet, and they piled enough food onto his tray to feed his whole crew back in Rotterdam. Bean immediately headed for a couple of the kids who had whined about their small portions and, without even asking permission, scraped his excess onto their trays. When one of them tried to talk to him about it, Bean just put his finger to his lips. In answer, the boy grinned. Bean still ended up with more food than he wanted, but when he turned in his tray, it was scraped clean. The nutritionist would be happy. It remained to be seen if the janitors would report the food Bean left on the floor.

Free time. Bean headed back to the game room, hoping that tonight he'd actually see the famous Ender Wiggin. If he was there, he would no doubt be the center of a group of admirers. But at the center of the groups he saw were only the ordinary prestige-hungry clique-formers who thought they were leaders and so would follow their group anywhere in order to maintain that delusion. No way could any of them be Ender Wiggin. And Bean was not about to ask.

Instead, he tried his hand at several games. Each time, though, the moment he lost for the first time, other kids would push him out of the way. It was an interesting set of social rules. The students knew that even the shortest, greenest launchy was entitled to his turn—but the moment a turn ended, so did the protection of the rule. And they were rougher in shoving him than they needed to be, so the message was clear—you shouldn't have been using that game and making me wait. Just like the food lines at the charity kitchens in Rotterdam—except that absolutely nothing that mattered was at stake.

That was interesting, to find that it wasn't hunger that caused children to become bullies on the street. The bulliness was already in the child, and whatever the stakes were, they would find a way to act as they needed to act. If it was about food, then the children who lost would die; if it was about games, though, the bullies did not hesitate to be just as intrusive and send the same message. Do what I want, or pay for it.

Intelligence and education, which all these children had, apparently didn't make any important difference in human nature. Not that Bean had really thought they would.

Nor did the low stakes make any difference in Bean's response to the bullies. He simply complied without complaint and took note of who the bullies were. Not that he had any intention of punishing them or of avoiding them, either. He would simply remember who acted as a bully and take that into account when he was in a situation where that information might be important.

No point in getting emotional about anything. Being emotional didn't help with survival. What mattered was to learn everything, analyze the situation, choose a course of action, and then move boldly. Know, think, choose, do.

There was no place in that list for "feel." Not that Bean didn't have feelings. He simply refused to think about them or dwell on them or let them influence his decisions, when anything important was at stake.

"He's even smaller than Ender was."

Again, again. Bean was so tired of hearing that.

"Don't talk about that hijo de puta to me, bicho."

Bean perked up. Ender had an enemy. Bean was wondering when he'd spot one, for someone who was first in the standings *had* to have provoked something besides admiration. Who said it? Bean drifted nearer to the group the conversation had come from. The same voice came up again. Again. And then he knew: That one was the boy who had called Ender an hijo de puta.

He had the silhouette of some kind of lizard on his uniform. And a single triangle on his sleeve. None of the boys around him had the triangle. All were focused on him. Captain of the team?

Bean needed more information. He tugged on the sleeve of a boy standing near him.

"What," said the boy, annoyed.

"Who's that boy there?" asked Bean. "The team captain with the lizard."

"It's a salamander, pinhead. Salamander *army*. And he's the *commander*."

Teams are called armies. Commander is the triangle rank. "What's his name?"

"Bonzo Madrid. And he's an even bigger asshole than you." The boy shrugged himself away from Bean.

So Bonzo Madrid was bold enough to declare his hatred for Ender Wiggin, but a kid who was not in Bonzo's army had contempt for *him* in turn and wasn't afraid to say so to a stranger. Good to know. The only enemy Ender had, so far, was contemptible.

But . . . contemptible as Bonzo might be, he *was* a commander. Which meant it was possible to become a commander without being the kind of boy that everybody respected. So what was their standard of judgment, in assigning command in this war game that shaped the life of Battle School?

More to the point, how do I get a command?

That was the first moment that Bean realized that he even had such a goal. Here in Battle School, he had arrived with the highest scores in his launch group—but he was the smallest and youngest and had been isolated even further by the deliberate actions of his teacher, making him a target of resentment. Somehow, in the midst of all this, Bean had made the decision that this would not be like Rotterdam. He was not going to live on the fringes, inserting himself only when it was absolutely essential for his own survival. As rapidly as possible, he was going to put himself in place to command an army.

Achilles had ruled because he was brutal, because he was willing to kill. That would always trump intelligence, when the intelligent one was physically smaller and had no strong allies. But here, the bullies only shoved and spoke rudely. The adults controlled things tightly and so brutality would not prevail, not in the assignment of command. Intelligence, then, had a chance to win out. Eventually, Bean might not have to live under the control of stupid people.

If this was what Bean wanted—and why not try for it, as long as some more important goal didn't come along first?—then he had to learn how the teachers made their decisions about command. Was it solely based on performance in classes? Bean doubted it. The International Fleet had to have smarter people than that running this school. The fact that they had that fantasy game on every desk suggested that they were looking at personality as well. Character. In the end, Bean suspected, character mattered more than intelligence. In Bean's litany of survival— know, think, choose, do—intelligence only mattered in the first three, and was the decisive factor only in the second one. The teachers knew that.

Maybe I *should* play the game, thought Bean.

Then: Not yet. Let's see what happens when I don't play.

At the same time he came to another conclusion he did not even know he had been concerned about. He would talk to Bonzo Madrid.

Bonzo was in the middle of a computer game, and he was obviously the kind of person who thought of anything unexpected as an affront to his dignity. That meant that for Bean to accomplish what he wanted, he could not approach Bonzo in a cringing way, like the suckups who surrounded him as he played, commending him even for his stupid mistakes in gameplay.

Instead, Bean pushed close enough to see when Bonzo's onscreen character died—again. "Señor Madrid, puedo hablar convozco?" The Spanish came to mind easily enough—he had listened to Pablo de Noches talk to fellow immigrants in Rotterdam who visited his apartment, and on the telephone to family members back in Valencia. And using Bonzo's native language had the desired effect. He didn't ignore Bean. He turned and glared at him.

"What do you want, bichinho?" Brazilian slang was common in Battle School, and Bonzo apparently felt no need to assert the purity of his Spanish.

Bean looked him in the eye, even though he was about twice Bean's height, and said, "People keep saying that I remind them of Ender Wiggin, and you're the only person around here who doesn't seem to worship him. I want to know the truth."

The way the other kids fell silent told Bean that he had judged aright—it was dangerous to ask Bonzo about Ender Wiggin. Dangerous, but that's why Bean had phrased his request so carefully.

"Damn right I don't worship the fart-eating insubordinate traitor, but why should I tell *you* about him?"

"Because you won't lie to me," said Bean, though he actually thought it was obvious Bonzo would probably lie outrageously in order to make himself look like the hero of what was obviously a story of his own humiliation at Ender's hands. "And if people are going to keep comparing me to the guy, I've got to know what he really is. I don't want to get iced because I do it all wrong here. You don't owe me nothing, but when you're small like me, you gots to have somebody who can tell you the stuff you gots to know to survive." Bean wasn't quite sure of the slang here yet, but what he knew, he used.

One of the other kids chimed in, as if Bean had written him a script and he was right on cue. "Get lost, launchy, Bonzo Madrid doesn't have time to change diapers."

Bean rounded on him and said fiercely, "I can't ask the teachers, they don't tell the truth. If Bonzo don't talk to me who I ask then? *You?* You don't know zits from zeroes."

It was pure Sergeant, that spiel, and it worked. Everybody laughed at the kid who had tried to brush him off, and Bonzo joined in, then put a hand on Bean's shoulder. "I'll tell you what I know, kid, it's about time somebody wanted to hear the truth about that walking rectum." To the kid that Bean had just fronted, Bonzo said, "Maybe you better finish my game, it's the only way you'll ever get to play at that level."

Bean could hardly believe a commander would say such a pointlessly offensive thing to one of his own subordinates. But the boy swallowed his anger and grinned and nodded and said, "That's right, Bonzo," and turned to the game, as instructed. A real suckup.

By chance Bonzo led him to stand right in front of the wall vent where Bean had been stuck only a few hours before. Bean gave it no more than a glance.

"Let me tell you about Ender. He's all about beating the other guy. Not just winning—he has to beat the other guy into the ground or he isn't happy. No rules for him. You give him a plain order, and he acts like he's going to obey it, but if he sees a way to make himself look good and all he has to do is disobey the order, well, all I can say is, I pity whoever has him in his army."

"He used to be Salamander?"

Bonzo's face reddened. "He wore a uniform with our colors, his name was on my roster, but he was *never* Salamander. The minute I saw him, I knew he was trouble. That cocky look on his face, like he thinks the whole Battle School was made just to give him a place to strut. I wasn't having it. I put in to transfer him the second he showed up and I refused to let him practice with us, I knew he'd learn our whole system and then take it to some other army and use what he learned from me to stick it to my army as fast as he could. I'm not stupid!"

In Bean's experience, that was a sentence never uttered except to prove its own inaccuracy.

"So he didn't follow orders."

"It's more than that. He goes crying like a baby to the teachers about how I don't let him practice, even though they *know* I've put in to transfer him out, but he whines and they let him go in to the battleroom during freetime and practice alone. Only he starts getting kids from his launch group and then kids from other armies, and they go in there as if he was their commander, doing what he tells them. That really pissed off a lot of us. And the teachers always give that little suckup whatever he wants, so when we commanders *demanded* that they bar our soldiers from practicing with him, they just said, 'Freetime is *free*,' but everything is part of the game, sabe? Everything, so they're letting him cheat, and every lousy soldier and sneaky little bastard goes to Ender for those freetime practices so every army's system is compromised, sabe? You plan your strategy for a game and you never know if your plans aren't being told to a soldier in the enemy army the second they come out of your mouth, sabe?"

Sabe sabe sabe. Bean wanted to shout back at him, Sí, yo *sé*, but you couldn't show impatience with Bonzo. Besides, this was all fascinating. Bean was getting a pretty good picture of how this army game shaped the life of Battle School. It gave the teachers a chance to see not only how the kids handled command, but also how they responded to incompetent commanders like Bonzo. Apparently, he had decided to make Ender the goat of his army, only Ender refused to take it. This Ender Wiggin was the kind of kid who got it that the teachers ran everything and used them by getting that practice room. He didn't ask them to get Bonzo to stop picking on him, he asked them for an alternate way to train himself. Smart. The teachers had to love that, and Bonzo couldn't do a thing about it.

Or could he?

"What did you do about it?"

"It's what we're going to do. I'm about fed up. If the teachers won't stop it, somebody else will have to, neh?" Bonzo grinned wickedly. "So I'd stay out of Ender Wiggin's freetime practice if I were you."

"Is he really number one in the standings?"

"Number one is piss," said Bonzo. "He's dead last in loyalty. There's not a commander who wants him in his army."

"Thanks," said Bean. "Only now it kind of pisses me off that people say I'm like him."

"Just because you're small. They made him a soldier when he was still way too young. Don't let them do that to you, and you'll be OK, sabe?"

"Ahora sé," said Bean. He gave Bonzo his biggest grin.

Bonzo smiled back and clapped him on his shoulder. "You'll do OK. When you get big enough, if I haven't graduated yet, maybe you'll be in Salamander."

If they leave you in command of an army for another day, it's just so that the other students can learn how to make the best of taking orders from a higher-ranking idiot. "I'm not going to be a soldier for a *long* time," said Bean.

"Work hard," said Bonzo. "It pays off." He clapped him on the shoulder yet again, then walked off with a big grin on his face. Proud of having helped a little kid. Glad to have convinced somebody of his own twisted version of dealing with Ender Wiggin, who was obviously smarter farting than Bonzo was talking.

And there was a threat of violence against the kids who practiced with Ender Wiggin in freetime. That was good to know. Bean would have to decide now what to do with that information. Get the warning to Ender? Warn the teachers? Say nothing? Be there to watch?

Freetime ended. The game room cleared out as everyone headed to their barracks for the time officially dedicated to independent study. Quiet time, in other words. For most of the kids in Bean's launch group, though, there was nothing to study—they hadn't had any classes yet. So for tonight, study meant playing the fantasy game on their desks and bantering with each other to assert position. Everybody's desk popped up with the suggestion that they could write letters home to their families. Some of the kids chose to do that. And, no doubt, they all assumed that's what Bean was doing.

But he was not. He signed on to his first desk as Poke and discovered that, as he suspected, it didn't matter which desk he used, it was the name and password that determined everything. He would never have to pull that second desk out of its locker. Using the Poke identity, he wrote a journal entry. This was not unexpected—"diary" was one of the options on the desk.

What should he be? A whiner? "Everybody pushed me out of the way in the game room just because I'm little, it isn't fair!" A baby? "I miss Sister Carlotta so so so much, I wish I could be in my own room back in Rotterdam." Ambitious? "I'll get the best scores on everything, they'll see."

In the end, he decided on something a little more subtle.

What would Achilles do if he were me? Of course he's not little, but with his bad leg it's almost the same thing. Achilles always knew how to wait and not show them anything. That's what I've got to do, too. Just wait and see what pops up. Nobody's going to want to be my friend at first. But after a while, they'll get used to me and we'll start sorting ourselves out in the classes. The first ones who'll let me get close will be the weaker ones, but that's not a problem. You build your crew based on loyalty first, that's what Achilles did, build loyalty and train them to obey. You work with what you have, and go from there.

Let them stew on *that*. Let them think he was trying to turn Battle School into the street life that he knew. They'd believe it. And in the meantime, he'd have time to learn as much as he could about how Battle School actually worked, and come up with a strategy that actually fit the situation.

Dimak came in one last time before lights out. "Your desks keep working after lights out," he said, "but if you use it when you're supposed to be sleeping, we'll know about it and we'll know what you're doing. So it better be important, or you go on the pig list."

Most of the kids put their desks away; a couple of them defiantly kept them out. Bean didn't care either way. He had other things to think about. Plenty of time for the desk tomorrow, or the next day.

He lay in the near-darkness—apparently the babies here had to have a little light so they could find their way to the toilet without tripping—and listened to the sounds around him, learning what they meant. A few whispers, a few shushes. The breathing of boys and girls as, one by one, they fell asleep. A few even had light child-snores. But under those human sounds, the windsound from the air system, and random clicking and distant voices, sounds of the flexing of a station rotating into and out of sunlight, the sound of adults working through the night.

This place was so expensive. Huge, to hold thousands of kids and teachers and staff and crew. As expensive as a ship of the fleet, surely. And all of it just to train little children. The adults may keep the kids wrapped up in a game, but it was serious business to *them*. This program of training children for war wasn't just some wacko educational theory gone mad, though Sister Carlotta was probably right when she said that a lot of people thought it was. The I.F. wouldn't maintain it at this level if it weren't expected to give serious results. So these kids snoring and soughing and whispering their way into the darkness, they really mattered.

They expect results from me. It's not just a party up here, where you come for the food and then do what you want. They really do want to make commanders out of us. And since Battle School has been going for a while, they probably have proof that it works—kids who already graduated and went on to compile a decent service record. That's what I've got to keep in mind. Whatever the system is here, it works.

A different sound. Not regular breathing. Jagged little breaths. An occasional gasp. And then . . . a sob.

Crying. Some boy was crying himself to sleep.

In the nest, Bean had heard some of the kids cry in their sleep, or as they neared sleep. Crying because they were hungry or injured or sick or cold. But what did these kids have to cry about here?

Another set of soft sobs joined the first.

They're homesick, Bean realized. They've never been away from mommy and daddy before, and it's getting to them.

Bean just didn't get it. He didn't feel that way about anybody. You just live in the place you're in, you don't worry about where you used to be or where you wish you were, *here* is where you are and here's where you've got to find a way to survive and lying in bed boo-hooing doesn't help much with *that*.

No problem, though. Their weakness just puts me farther ahead. One less rival on my road to becoming a commander.

Is that how Ender Wiggin thought about things? Bean recalled everything he had learned about Ender so far. The kid was resourceful. He didn't openly fight with Bonzo, but he didn't put up with his stupid decisions, either. It was fascinating to Bean, because on the street the one rule he knew for sure was, you don't stick your neck out unless your throat's about to be slit anyway. If you have a stupid crew boss, you don't tell him he's stupid, you don't show him he's stupid, you just go along and keep your head down. That's how kids survived.

When he had to, Bean had taken a bold risk. Got himself onto Poke's crew that way. But that was about food. That was about not dying. Why did Ender take such a risk when there was nothing at stake but his standing in the war game?

Maybe Ender knew something Bean didn't know. Maybe there was some reason why the game was more important than it seemed.

Or maybe Ender was one of those kids who just couldn't stand to lose, ever. The kind of kid who's for the team only as long as the team is taking him where he wants to go, and if it isn't, then it's every man for himself. That's what Bonzo thought. But Bonzo was stupid.

Once again, Bean was reminded that there were things he didn't understand. Ender wasn't doing every man for himself. He didn't practice alone. He opened his free time practice to other kids. Launchies, too, not just kids who could do things for him. Was it possible he did that just because it was a decent thing to do?

The way Poke had offered herself to Achilles in order to save Bean's life?

No, Bean didn't *know* that's what she did, he didn't *know* that's why she died.

But the possibility was there. And in his heart, he believed it. That was the thing he had always despised about her. She acted tough but she was soft at heart. And yet . . . that softness was what saved his life. And try as he might, he couldn't get himself to take the too-bad-for-her attitude that prevailed on the street. She listened to me when I talked to her, she did a hard thing that risked her own life on the chance that it would lead to a better life for all her crew. Then she offered me a place at her table and, in the end, she put herself between me and danger. Why?

What was this great secret? Did Ender know it? How did he learn it? Why couldn't Bean figure it out for himself? Try as he might, though, he couldn't understand Poke. He couldn't understand Sister Carlotta, either. Couldn't understand the arms she held him with, the tears she shed over him. Didn't they understand that no matter how much they loved him, he was still a separate person, and doing good for him didn't improve *their* lives in any way?

If Ender Wiggin has this weakness, then I will not be anything like him. I am not going to sacrifice myself for anybody. And the beginning of that is that I refuse to lie in my bed and cry for Poke floating there in the water with her throat slit, or boo-hoo because Sister Carlotta isn't asleep in the next room.

He wiped his eyes, rolled over, and willed his body to relax and go to sleep. Moments later, he was dozing in that light, easy-to-rouse sleep. Long before morning his pillow would be dry.

———

He dreamed, as human beings always dream—random firings of memory and imagination that the unconscious mind tries to put together into coherent stories. Bean rarely paid attention to his own dreams, rarely even remembered that he dreamed at all. But this morning he awoke with a clear image in his mind.

Ants, swarming from a crack in the sidewalk. Little black ants. And larger red ants, doing battle with them, destroying them. All of them scurrying. None of them looking up to see the human shoe coming down to stamp the life out of them.

When the shoe came back up, what was crushed under it was not ant bodies at all. They were the bodies of children, the urchins from the streets of Rotterdam. All of Achilles' family. Bean himself—he recognized his own face, rising above his flattened body, peering around for one last glimpse at the world before death.

Above him loomed the shoe that killed him. But now it was worn on the end of a bugger's leg, and the bugger laughed and laughed.

Bean remembered the laughing bugger when he awoke, and remembered the sight of all those children crushed flat, of his own body mashed like gum under a shoe. The meaning was obvious: While we children play at war, the buggers are coming to crush us. We must look above the level of our private struggles and keep in mind the greater enemy.

Except that Bean rejected that interpretation of his own dream the moment he thought of it. Dreams have no meaning at all, he reminded himself. And even if they do mean something, it's a meaning that reveals what I feel, what I fear, not some deep abiding truth. So the buggers are coming. So they might crush us all like ants under their feet. What's that to me? My business right now is to keep Bean alive, to advance myself to a position where I might be useful in the war against the buggers. There's nothing I can do to stop them right now.

Here's the lesson Bean took from his own dream: Don't be one of the scurrying, struggling ants.

Be the shoe.

———

Sister Carlotta had reached a dead end in her search of the nets. Plenty of information on human genetics studies, but nothing like what she was looking for.

So she sat there, doodling with a nuisance game on her desk while trying to think of what to do next and wondering why she was bothering to look into Bean's beginnings at all, when the secure message arrived from the I.F. Since the message would erase itself a minute after arrival, to be re-sent every minute until it was read by the recipient, she opened it at once and keyed in her first and second passwords.

```
FROM: Col.Graff@BattleSchool.IF
TO: Ss.Carlotta@SpecAsn.RemCon.IF
RE: Achilles
```

```
Please report all info on "Achilles" as known to
subject.
```

As usual, a message so cryptic that it didn't actually have
to be encrypted, though of course it had been. This was
a secure message, wasn't it? So why not just use the kid's
name. "Please report on 'Achilles' as known to *Bean*."

Somehow Bean had given them the name Achilles, and
under circumstances such that they didn't want to ask him
directly to explain. So it had to be in something he had
written. A letter to her? She felt a little thrill of hope and
then scoffed at her own feelings. She knew perfectly well
that mail from the kids in Battle School was almost never
passed along, and besides, the chance of Bean actually
writing to her was remote. But they had the name somehow, and wanted to know from her what it meant.

The trouble is, she didn't want to give him that information without knowing what it would mean for Bean.

So she prepared an equally cryptic reply:

```
Will reply by secure conference only.
```

Of course this would infuriate Graff, but that was just a
perk. Graff was so used to having power far beyond his
rank that it would be good for him to have a reminder
that all obedience was voluntary and ultimately depended
on the free choice of the person receiving the orders. And
she *would* obey, in the end. She just wanted to make sure
Bean was not going to suffer from the information. If they
knew he had been so closely involved with both the perpetrator and the victim of a murder, they might drop him
from the program. And even if she was sure it would be

all right to talk about it, she might be able to get a quid pro quo.

It took another hour before the secure conference was set up, and when Graff's head appeared in the display above her computer, he was not happy. "What game are you playing today, Sister Carlotta?"

"You've been putting on weight, Colonel Graff. That's not healthy."

"Achilles," he said.

"Man with a bad heel," she said. "Killed Hector and dragged his body around the gates of Troy. Also had a thing for a captive girl named Briseis."

"You know that's not the context."

"I know more than that. I know you must have got the name from something Bean wrote, because the name is not pronounced uh-KILL-eez, it's pronounced ah-SHEEL. French."

"Someone local there."

"Dutch is the native language here, though Fleet Common has just about driven it out as anything but a curiosity."

"Sister Carlotta, I don't appreciate your wasting the expense of this conference."

"And I'm not going to talk about it until I know why you need to know."

Graff took a few deep breaths. She wondered if his mother taught him to count to ten, or if, perhaps, he had learned to bite his tongue from dealing with nuns in Catholic school.

"We are trying to make sense of something Bean wrote."

"Let me see it and I'll help you as I can."

"He's not your responsibility anymore, Sister Carlotta," said Graff.

"Then why are you asking me about him? He's your responsibility, yes? So I can get back to work, yes?"

Graff sighed and did something with his hands, out of sight in the display. Moments later the text of Bean's diary entry appeared on her display below and in front of Graff's face. She read it, smiling slightly.

"Well?" asked Graff.

"He's doing a number on you, Colonel."

"What do you mean?"

"He knows you're going to read it. He's misleading you."

"You *know* this?"

"Achilles might indeed be providing him with an example, but not a good one. Achilles once betrayed someone that Bean valued highly."

"Don't be vague, Sister Carlotta."

"I wasn't vague. I told you precisely what I wanted you to know. Just as Bean told you what he wanted you to hear. I can promise you that his diary entries will only make sense to you if you recognize that he is writing these things for you, with the intent to deceive."

"Why, because he didn't keep a diary down there?"

"Because his memory is perfect," said Sister Carlotta. "He would never, never commit his real thoughts to a readable form. He keeps his own counsel. Always. You will never find a document written by him that is not meant to be read."

"Would it make a difference if he was writing it under another identity? Which he thinks we don't know about?"

"But you *do* know about it, and so he *knows* you will know about it, so the other identity is there only to confuse you, and it's working."

"I forgot, you think this kid is smarter than God."

"I'm not worried that you don't accept my evaluation. The better you know him, the more you'll realize that I'm right. You'll even come to believe those test scores."

"What will it take to get you to help me with this?" asked Graff.

"Try telling me the truth about what this information will mean to Bean."

"He's got his primary teacher worried. He disappeared for twenty-one minutes on the way back from lunch—we have a witness who talked to him on a deck where he had no business, and that still doesn't account for that last seventeen minutes of his absence. He doesn't play with his desk—"

"You think setting up false identities and writing phony diary entries isn't playing?"

"There's a diagnostic/therapeutic game that all the children play—he hasn't even signed on yet."

"He'll know that the game is psychological, and he won't play it until he knows what it will cost him."

"Did you teach him that attitude of default hostility?"

"No, I learned it from him."

"Tell me straight. Based on this diary entry, it looks as though he plans to set up his own crew here, as if this were the street. We need to know about this Achilles so we'll know what he actually has in mind."

"He plans no such thing," said Sister Carlotta.

"You say it so forcefully, but without giving me a single reason to trust your conclusion."

"You called *me*, remember?"

"That's not enough, Sister Carlotta. Your opinions on this boy are suspect."

"He would never emulate Achilles. He would never write his true plans where you could find them. He does not build crews, he joins them and uses them and moves on without a backward glance."

"So investigating this Achilles won't give us a clue about Bean's future behavior?"

"Bean prides himself on not holding grudges. He thinks they're counterproductive. But at some level, I believe he wrote about Achilles specifically because you would read what he wrote and would want to know more about Achilles, and if you investigated him you would discover a very bad thing that Achilles did."

"To Bean?"

"To a friend of his."

"So he *is* capable of having friendships?"

"The girl who saved his life here on the street."

"And what's *her* name?"

"Poke. But don't bother looking for her. She's dead."

Graff thought about that a moment. "Is that the bad thing Achilles did?"

"Bean has reason to believe so, though I don't think it would be evidence enough to convict in court. And as I said, all these things may be unconscious. I don't think Bean would knowingly try to get even with Achilles, or anybody else, for that matter, but he might hope you'd do it for him."

"You're still holding back, but I have no choice but to trust your judgment, do I?"

"I promise you that Achilles is a dead end."

"And if you think of a reason why it might not be so dead after all?"

"I want your program to succeed, Colonel Graff, even more than I want Bean to succeed. My priorities are not skewed by the fact that I do care about the child. I really have told you everything now. But I hope you'll help me also."

"Information isn't traded in the I.F., Sister Carlotta. It flows from those who have it to those who need it."

"Let me tell you what I want, and you decide if I need it."

"Well?"

"I want to know of any illegal or top secret projects involving the alteration of the human genome in the past ten years."

Graff looked off into the distance. "It's too soon for you to be off on a new project, isn't it. So this is the same old project. This is about Bean."

"He came from somewhere."

"You mean his mind came from somewhere."

"I mean the whole package. I think you're going to end up relying on this boy, betting all our lives on him, and I think you need to know what's going on in his genes. It's a poor second to knowing what's happening in his mind, but that, I suspect, will always be out of reach for you."

"You sent him up here, and then you tell me something like this. Don't you realize that you have just guaranteed that I will never let him move to the top of our selection pool?"

"You say that now, when you've only had him for a day," said Sister Carlotta. "He'll grow on you."

"He damn well better not shrink or he'd get sucked away by the air system."

"Tut-tut, Colonel Graff."

"Sorry, Sister," he answered.

"Give me a high enough clearance and I'll do the search myself."

"No," he said. "But I'll get summaries sent to you."

She knew that they would give her only as much information as they thought she should have. But when he tried to fob her off with useless drivel, she'd deal with that problem, too. Just as she would try to get to Achilles before the I.F. found him. Get him away from the streets and into a school. Under another name. Because if the I.F. found him, in all likelihood they would test him—or find her scores on him. If they tested him, they would fix his foot and bring him up to Battle School. And she had promised Bean that he would never have to face Achilles again.

8

Good Student

"He doesn't play the fantasy game at *all?*"

"He has never so much as chosen a figure, let alone come through the portal."

"It's not possible that he hasn't discovered it."

"He reset the preferences on his desk so that the invitation no longer pops up."

"From which you conclude . . ."

"He knows it isn't a game. He doesn't want us analyzing the workings of his mind."

"And yet he wants us to advance him."

"I don't know that. He buries himself in his studies. For three months he's been getting perfect scores on every test. But he only reads the lesson material once. His study is on other subjects of his own choosing."

"Such as?"

"Vauban."

"Seventeenth-century fortifications? What is he *thinking?*"

"You see the problem?"

"How does he get along with the other children?"

"I think the classic description is 'loner.' He is polite. He volunteers nothing. He asks only what he's interested in. The kids in his launch group think he's strange. They know he scores better than them on everything, but they don't hate him. They treat him like a force of nature. No friends, but no enemies."

"That's important, that they don't hate him. They should, if he stays aloof like that."

"I think it's a skill he learned on the street—to turn away anger. He never gets angry himself. Maybe that's why the teasing about his size stopped."

"Nothing that you're telling me suggests that he has command potential."

"If you think he's trying to show command potential and failing at it, then you're right."

"So . . . what do you *think* he's doing?"

"Analyzing *us*."

"Gathering information without giving any. Do you really think he's that sophisticated?"

"He stayed alive on the street."

"I think it's time for you to probe a little."

"And let him know that his reticence bothers us?"

"If he's as clever as you think, he already knows."

Bean didn't mind being dirty. He had gone years without bathing, after all. A few days didn't bother him. And if other people minded, they kept their opinions to themselves. Let them add it to the gossip about him. Smaller and younger than Ender! Perfect scores on every test! Stinks like a pig!

That shower time was precious. That's when he could sign on to his desk as one of the boys bunking near him—while they were showering. They were naked, wearing only towels to the shower, so their uniforms weren't tracking them. During that time Bean could sign on and explore the system without letting the teachers know that he was learning the tricks of the system. It tipped his hand, just a little, when he altered the preferences so he didn't have to face that stupid invitation to play their mind game every time he changed tasks on his desk. But that wasn't a very difficult hack, and he decided they wouldn't be particularly alarmed that he'd figured it out.

So far, Bean had found only a few really useful things, but he felt as though he was on the verge of breaking through more important walls. He knew that there was a virtual system that the students were meant to hack through. He had heard the legends about how Ender (of course) had hacked the system on his first day and signed on as God, but he knew that while Ender might have been unusually quick about it, he wasn't doing anything that wasn't expected of bright, ambitious students.

Bean's first achievement was to find the way the teachers' system tracked student computer activity. By avoiding the actions that were automatically reported to the teachers, he was able to create a private file area that they wouldn't see unless they were deliberately looking for it. Then, whenever he found something interesting while signed on as someone else, he would remember the location, then go and download the information into his secure area and work on it at his leisure—while his desk reported that he was reading works from the library. He actually read those works, of course, but far more quickly than his desk reported.

With all that preparation, Bean expected to make real progress. But far too quickly he ran into the firewalls— information the system had to have but wouldn't yield. He found several workarounds. For instance, he couldn't find any maps of the whole station, only of the student-accessible areas, and those were always diagrammatic and cute, deliberately out of scale. But he did find a series of emergency maps in a program that would automatically display them on the walls of the corridors in the event of a pressure-loss emergency, showing the nearest safety locks. These maps *were* to scale, and by combining them into a single map in his secure area, he was able to create a schema of the whole station. Nothing was labeled except the locks, of course, but he learned of the existence of a parallel system of corridors on either side of the student area. The station must be not one but three parallel wheels, cross-linked at many points. That's where the teachers and staff lived, where the life support was located, the communications with the Fleet. The bad news was that they had separate air-circulation systems. The ductwork in one would not lead him to either of the others. Which meant that while he could probably spy on anything going on in the student wheel, the other wheels were out of reach.

Even within the student wheel, however, there were plenty of secret places to explore. The students had access to four decks, plus the gym below A-Deck and the battleroom above D-Deck. There were actually nine decks, however, two below A-Deck and three above D. Those spaces had to be used for something. And if they thought it was worth hiding it from the students, Bean figured it was worth exploring.

And he would have to start exploring soon. His exercise was making him stronger, and he was staying lean by not overeating—it was unbelievable how much food they tried to force on him, and they kept increasing his portions, probably because the previous servings hadn't caused him to gain as much weight as they wanted him to gain. But what he could not control was the increase in his height. The ducts would be impassable for him before too long—if they weren't already. Yet using the air system to get him access to the hidden decks was not something he could do during showers. It would mean losing sleep. So he kept putting it off—one day wouldn't make that much difference.

Until the morning when Dimak came into the barracks first thing in the morning and announced that everyone was to change his password immediately, with his back turned to the rest of the room, and was to tell no one what the new password was. "Never type it in where anyone can see," he said.

"Somebody's been using other people's passwords?" asked a kid, his tone suggesting that he thought this an appalling idea. Such dishonor! Bean wanted to laugh.

"It's required of all I.F. personnel, so you might as well develop the habit now," said Dimak. "Anyone found using the same password for more than a week will go on the pig list."

But Bean could only assume that they had caught on to what he was doing. That meant they had probably looked back into his probing for the past months and knew pretty much what he had found out. He signed on and purged his secure file area, on the chance that they hadn't actually found it yet. Everything he really needed there, he had already memorized. He would never rely on the desk again for anything his memory could hold.

Stripping and wrapping his towel around him, Bean headed for the showers with the others. But Dimak stopped him at the door.

"Let's talk," he said.

"What about my shower?" asked Bean.

"Suddenly you care about cleanliness?" asked Dimak.

So Bean expected to be chewed out for stealing passwords. Instead, Dimak sat beside him on a lower bunk near the door and asked him far more general questions. "How are you getting on here?"

"Fine."

"I know your test scores are good, but I'm concerned that you aren't making many friends among the other kids."

"I've got a lot of friends."

"You mean you know a lot of people's names and don't quarrel with anybody."

Bean shrugged. He didn't like this line of questioning any better than he would have liked an inquiry into his computer use.

"Bean, the system here was designed for a reason.

There are a lot of factors that go into our decisions concerning a student's ability to command. The classwork is an important part of that. But so is leadership."

"Everybody here is just full of leadership ability, right?"

Dimak laughed. "Well, that's true, you can't all be leaders at once."

"I'm about as big as a three-year-old," said Bean. "I don't think a lot of kids are eager to start saluting me."

"But you could be building networks of friendship. The other kids are. You don't."

"I guess I don't have what it takes to be a commander."

Dimak raised an eyebrow. "Are you suggesting you *want* to be iced?"

"Do my test scores look like I'm trying to fail?"

"What *do* you want?" asked Dimak. "You don't play the games the other kids play. Your exercise program is weird, even though you know the regular program is designed to strengthen you for the battleroom. Does that mean you don't intend to play that game, either? Because if that's your plan, you really *will* get iced. That's our primary means of assessing command ability. That's why the whole life of the school is centered around the armies."

"I'll do fine in the battleroom," said Bean.

"If you think you can do it without preparation, you're mistaken. A quick mind is no replacement for a strong, agile body. You have no idea how physically demanding the battleroom can be."

"I'll join the regular workouts, sir."

Dimak leaned back and closed his eyes with a small sigh. "My, but you're compliant, aren't you, Bean."

"I try to be, sir."

"That is such complete bullshit," said Dimak.

"Sir?" Here it comes, thought Bean.

"If you devoted the energy to making friends that you devote to hiding things from the teachers, you'd be the most beloved kid in the school."

"That would be Ender Wiggin, sir."

"And don't think we haven't picked up on the way you obsess about Wiggin."

"Obsess?" Bean hadn't asked about him after that first day. Never joined in discussions about the standings. Never visited the battleroom during Ender's practice sessions.

Oh. What an obvious mistake. Stupid.

"You're the only launchy who has completely avoided so much as seeing Ender Wiggin. You track his schedule so thoroughly that you are never in the same room with him. That takes real effort."

"I'm a launchy, sir. He's in an army."

"Don't play dumb, Bean. It's not convincing and it wastes my time."

Tell a useless and obvious truth, that was the rule. "Everyone compares me to Ender all the time 'cause I came here so young and small. I wanted to make my own way."

"I'll accept that for now because there's a limit to how deeply I want to wade into your bullshit," said Dimak.

But in saying what he'd said about Ender, Bean wondered if it might not be true. Why shouldn't I have such a normal emotion as jealousy? I'm not a machine. So he was a little offended that Dimak seemed to assume that something more subtle had to be going on. That Bean was lying no matter what he said.

"Tell me," said Dimak, "why you refuse to play the fantasy game."

"It looks boring and stupid," said Bean. That was certainly true.

"Not good enough," said Dimak. "For one thing, it *isn't* boring and stupid to any other kid in Battle School. In fact, the game adapts itself to your interests."

I have no doubt of *that,* thought Bean. "It's all pretending," said Bean. "None of it's real."

"Stop hiding for one second, can't you?" snapped Dimak. "You know perfectly well that we use the game to analyze personality, and that's why you refuse to play."

"Sounds like you've analyzed my personality anyway," said Bean.

"You just don't let up, do you?"

Bean said nothing. There was nothing to say.

"I've been looking at your reading list," said Dimak. "Vauban?"

"Yes?"

"Fortification engineering from the time of Louis the Fourteenth?"

Bean nodded. He thought back to Vauban and how his strategies had adapted to fit Louis's ever-more-straitened finances. Defense in depth had given way to a thin line of defenses; building new fortresses had largely been abandoned, while razing redundant or poorly placed ones continued. Poverty triumphing over strategy. He started to talk about this, but Dimak cut him off.

"Come on, Bean. Why are you studying a subject that has nothing to do with war in space?"

Bean didn't really have an answer. He had been working through the history of strategy from Xenophon and Alexander to Caesar and Machiavelli. Vauban came in sequence. There was no plan—mostly his readings were a cover for his clandestine computer work. But now that Dimak was asking him, what *did* seventeenth-century fortifications have to do with war in space?

"I'm not the one who put Vauban in the library."

"We have the full set of military writings that are found in every library in the fleet. Nothing more significant than that."

Bean shrugged.

"You spent two hours on Vauban."

"So what? I spent as long on Frederick the Great, and I don't think we're doing field drills, either, or bayoneting anyone who breaks ranks during a march into fire."

"You didn't actually read Vauban, did you," said Dimak. "So I want to know what you *were* doing."

"I *was* reading Vauban."

"You think we don't know how fast you read?"

"And *thinking* about Vauban?"

"All right then, what were you thinking?"

"Like you said. About how it applies to war in space."
Buy some time here. What *does* Vauban have to do with
war in space?

"I'm waiting," said Dimak. "Give me the insights that
occupied you for two hours just yesterday."

"Well of course fortifications are impossible in space,"
said Bean. "In the traditional sense, that is. But there are
things you can do. Like his mini-fortresses, where you
leave a sallying force outside the main fortification. You
can station squads of ships to intercept raiders. And there
are barriers you can put up. Mines. Fields of flotsam to
cause collisions with fast-moving ships, holing them. That
sort of thing."

Dimak nodded, but said nothing.

Bean was beginning to warm to the discussion. "The
real problem is that unlike Vauban, we have only one
strong point worth defending—Earth. And the enemy is
not limited to a primary direction of approach. He could
come from anywhere. From anywhere all at once. So we
run into the classic problem of defense, cubed. The farther
out you deploy your defenses, the more of them you have
to have, and if your resources are limited, you soon have
more fortifications than you can man. What good are
bases on moons Jupiter or Saturn or Neptune, when the
enemy doesn't even have to come in on the plane of the
ecliptic? He can bypass all our fortifications. The way
Nimitz and MacArthur used two-dimensional island-
hopping against the defense in depth of the Japanese in
World War II. Only our enemy can work in three dimensions. Therefore we cannot possibly maintain defense in
depth. Our only defense is early detection and a single
massed force."

Dimak nodded slowly. His face showed no expression.
"Go on."

Go on? That wasn't enough to explain two hours of
reading? "Well, so I thought that even that was a recipe

for disaster, because the enemy is free to divide his forces. So even if we intercept and defeat ninety-nine of a hundred attacking squadrons, he only has to get one squadron through to cause terrible devastation on Earth. We saw how much territory a single ship could scour when they first showed up and started burning over China. Get ten ships to Earth for a single day—and if they spread us out enough, they'd have a lot more than a day!—and they could wipe out most of our main population centers. All our eggs are in that one basket."

"And all this you got from Vauban," said Dimak.

Finally. That was apparently enough to satisfy him. "From thinking about Vauban, and how much harder our defensive problem is."

"So," said Dimak, "what's your solution?"

Solution? What did Dimak think Bean was? I'm thinking about how to get control of the situation here in Battle School, not how to save the world! "I don't think there is a solution," said Bean, buying time again. But then, having said it, he began to believe it. "There's no point in trying to defend Earth at all. In fact, unless they have some defensive device we don't know about, like some way of putting an invisible shield around a planet or something, the enemy is just as vulnerable. So the only strategy that makes any sense at all is an all-out attack. To send our fleet against *their* home world and destroy it."

"What if our fleets pass in the night?" asked Dimak. "We destroy each other's worlds and all we have left are ships?"

"No," said Bean, his mind racing. "Not if we sent out a fleet immediately after the Second Bugger War. After Mazer Rackham's strike force defeated them, it would take time for word of their defeat to come back to them. So we build a fleet as quickly as possible and launch it against their home world immediately. That way the news of their defeat reaches them at the same time as our devastating counterattack."

Dimak closed his eyes. "Now you tell us."

"No," said Bean, as it dawned on him that he was right about everything. "That fleet was already sent. Before anybody on this station was born, that fleet was launched."

"Interesting theory," said Dimak. "Of course you're wrong on every point."

"No I'm not," said Bean. He knew he wasn't wrong, because Dimak's air of calm was not holding. Sweat was standing out on his forehead. Bean had hit on something really important here, and Dimak knew it.

"I mean your theory is right, about the difficulty of defense in space. But hard as it is, we still have to do it, and that's why you're here. As to some fleet we supposedly launched—the Second Bugger War exhausted humanity's resources, Bean. It's taken us this long to get a reasonable-sized fleet again. And to get better weaponry for the next battle. If you learned anything from Vauban, you should have learned that you can't build more than your people have resources to support. Besides which, you're assuming we know where the enemy's home world is. But your analysis is good insofar as you've identified the magnitude of the problem we face."

Dimak got up from the bunk. "It's nice to know that your study time isn't completely wasted on breaking into the computer system," he said.

With that parting shot, he left the barracks.

Bean got up and walked back to his own bunk, where he got dressed. No time for a shower now, and it didn't matter anyway. Because he knew that he had struck a nerve in what he said to Dimak. The Second Bugger War hadn't exhausted humanity's resources, Bean was sure of that. The problems of defending a planet were so obvious that the I.F. couldn't possibly have missed them, especially not in the aftermath of a nearly-lost war. They knew they had to attack. They built the fleet. They launched it. It was gone. It was inconceivable that they had done anything else.

So what was all this nonsense with the Battle School for? Was Dimak right, that Battle School was simply about building up the defensive fleet around Earth to counter any enemy assault that might have passed our invasion fleet on the way?

If that were true, there would be no reason to conceal it. No reason to lie. In fact, all the propaganda on Earth was devoted to telling people how vital it was to prepare for the next Bugger invasion. So Dimak had done nothing more than repeat the story that the I.F. had been telling everybody on Earth for three generations. Yet Dimak was sweating like a fish. Which suggested that the story wasn't true.

The defensive fleet around Earth was already fully manned, that was the problem. The normal process of recruitment would have been enough. Defensive war didn't take brilliance, just alertness. Early detection, cautious interception, protection of an adequate reserve. Success depended not on the quality of command, but on the quantity of available ships and the quality of the weaponry. There was no reason for Battle School—Battle School only made sense in the context of an offensive war, a war where maneuver, strategy, and tactics would play an important role. But the offensive fleet was already gone. For all Bean knew, the battle had already been fought years ago and the I.F. was just waiting for news about whether we had won or lost. It all depended on how many lightyears away the Bugger home planet was.

For all we know, thought Bean, the war is already over, the I.F. knows that we won, and they simply haven't told anybody.

And the reason for that was obvious. The only thing that had ended war on Earth and bound together all of humanity was a common cause—defeating the Buggers. As soon as it was known that the Bugger threat was eliminated, all the pent-up hostilities would be released. Whether it was the Muslim world against the West, or long-restrained Russian imperialism and paranoia against the Atlantic alliance, or Indian adventurism, or . . . or all of them at once. Chaos. The resources of the International Fleet would be co-opted by mutinying commanders from one faction or another. Conceivably it could mean the destruction of Earth—without any help from the Formics at all.

That's what the I.F. was trying to prevent. The terrible cannibalistic war that would follow. Just as Rome tore itself apart in civil war after the final elimination of Carthage—only far worse, because the weapons were more terrible and the hatreds far deeper, national and religious hatreds rather than the mere personal rivalries among leading citizens of Rome.

The I.F. was determined to prevent it.

In that context, Battle School made perfect sense. For many years, almost every child on Earth had been tested, and those with any potential brilliance in military command were taken out of their homeland and put into space. The best of the Battle School graduates, or at least those most loyal to the I.F., might very well be used to command armies when the I.F. finally announced the end of the war and struck preemptively to eliminate national armies and unify the world, finally and permanently, under one government. But the main purpose of the Battle School was to get these kids off Earth so that they could not become commanders of the armies of any one nation or faction.

After all, the invasion of France by the major European powers after the French Revolution led to the desperate French government discovering and promoting Napoleon, even though in the end he seized the reins of power instead of just defending the nation. The I.F. was determined that there would be no Napoleons on Earth to lead the resistance. All the potential Napoleons were here, wearing silly uniforms and battling each other for supremacy in a stupid game. It was all pig lists. By taking us, they have tamed the world.

"If you don't get dressed, you'll be late for class," said

Nikolai, the boy who slept on the bottommost bunk directly across from Bean.

"Thanks," said Bean. He shed his dry towel and hurriedly pulled on his uniform.

"Sorry I had to tell them about your using my password," said Nikolai,

Bean was dumbfounded.

"I mean, I didn't *know* it was you, but they started asking me what I was looking for in the emergency map system, and since I didn't know what they were talking about, it wasn't hard to guess that somebody was signing on as me, and there you are, in the perfect place to see my desk whenever I sign on, and . . . I mean, you're really smart. But it's not like I set out to tell on you."

"That's fine," said Bean. "Not a problem."

"But, I mean, what *did* you find out? From the maps?"

Until this moment, Bean would have blown off the question—and the boy. Nothing much, I was just curious, that's what he would have said. But now his whole world had changed. Now it mattered that he have connections with the other boys, not so he could show his leadership ability to the teachers, but so that when war did break out on Earth, and when the I.F.'s little plan failed, as it was bound to do, he would know who his allies and enemies were among the commanders of the various national and factional armies.

For the I.F.'s plan *would* fail. It was a miracle it hadn't failed already. It depended too heavily on millions of soldiers and commanders being more loyal to the I.F. than to their homeland. It would not happen. The I.F. itself would break up into factions, inevitably.

But the plotters no doubt were aware of that danger. They would have kept the number of plotters as small as possible—perhaps only the triumvirate of Hegemon, Strategos, and Polemarch and maybe a few people here at Battle School. Because this station was the heart of the plan. Here was where every single gifted commander for two generations had been studied intimately. There were records on every one of them—who was most talented, most valuable. What their weaknesses were, both in character and in command. Who their friends were. What their loyalties were. Which of them, therefore, should be approached to command the I.F.'s forces in the intrahuman wars to come, and which should be stripped of command and held incommunicado until hostilities were over.

No wonder they were worried about Bean's lack of participation in their little mind game. It made him an unknown quantity. It made him dangerous.

Now it was even more dangerous for Bean to play than ever. Not playing might make them suspicious and fearful—but in whatever move they planned against him, at least they wouldn't know anything about him. While if he did play, then they might be less suspicious—but if they did move against him, they would do it knowing whatever information the game gave to them. And Bean was not at all confident of his ability to outplay the game. Even if he tried to give them misleading results, that strategy in itself might tell them more about him than he wanted them to know.

And there was another possibility, too. He might be completely wrong. There might be key information that he did not have. Maybe no fleet had been launched. Maybe they hadn't defeated the Buggers at their home world. Maybe there really was a desperate effort to build a defensive fleet. Maybe maybe maybe.

Bean had to get more information in order to have some hope that his analysis was correct and that his choices would be valid.

And Bean's isolation had to end.

"Nikolai," said Bean, "you wouldn't believe what I found out from those maps. Did you know there are nine decks, not just four?"

"Nine?"

"And that's just in this wheel. There are two other wheels they never tell us about."

"But the pictures of the station show only the one wheel."

"Those pictures were all taken when there *was* only one wheel. But in the plans, there are three. Parallel to each other, turning together."

Nikolai looked thoughtful. "But that's just the plans. Maybe they never built those other wheels."

"Then why would they still have maps for them in the emergency system?"

Nikolai laughed. "My father always said, bureaucrats never throw anything away."

Of course. Why hadn't he thought of that? The emergency map system was no doubt programmed before the first wheel was ever brought into service. So all those maps would already be in the system, even if the other wheels were never built, even if two-thirds of the maps would never have a corridor wall to be displayed on. No one would bother to go into the system and clean them out.

"I never thought of that," said Bean. He knew, given his reputation for brilliance, that he could pay Nikolai no higher compliment. As indeed the reaction of the other kids in nearby bunks showed. No one had ever had such a conversation with Bean before. No one had ever thought of something that Bean hadn't obviously thought of first. Nikolai was blushing with pride.

"But the nine decks, that makes sense," said Nikolai.

"Wish I knew what was on them," said Bean.

"Life support," said the girl named Corn Moon. "They got to be making oxygen somewhere here. That takes a lot of plants."

More kids joined in. "And staff. All we ever see are teachers and nutritionists."

"And maybe they *did* build the other wheels. We don't *know* they didn't."

The speculation ran rampant through the group. And at the center of it all: Bean.

Bean and his new friend, Nikolai.

"Come on," said Nikolai, "we'll be late for math."

Part Three

SCHOLAR

9

Garden of Sofia

"So he found out how many decks there are. What can he possibly do with that information?"

"Yes, that's the exact question. What was he planning, that he felt it necessary to find that out? Nobody else even looked for that, in the whole history of this school."

"You think he's plotting revolution?"

"All we know about this kid is that he survived on the streets of Rotterdam. It's a hellish place, from what I hear. The kids are vicious. They make *Lord of the Flies* look like *Pollyanna*."

"When did you read *Pollyanna*?"

"It was a book?"

"How can he plot a revolution? He doesn't have any friends."

"I never said anything about revolution, that's *your* theory."

"I don't have a theory. I don't understand this kid. I never even wanted him up here. I think we should just send him home."

"No."

"No *sir,* I'm sure you meant to say."

"After three months in Battle School, he figured out that defensive war makes no sense and that we must have launched a fleet against the Bugger home worlds right after the end of the last war."

"He knows *that?* And you come telling me he knows how many *decks* there are?"

"He doesn't *know* it. He guessed. I told him he was wrong."

"I'm sure he believed you."

"I'm sure he's in doubt."

"This is all the more reason to send him back to Earth. Or out to some distant base somewhere. Do you realize the nightmare if there's a breach of security on this?"

"Everything depends on how he uses the information."

"Only we don't know anything about him, so we have no way of knowing how he'll use it."

"Sister Carlotta—"

"Do you *hate* me? That woman is even more inscrutable than your little dwarf."

"A mind like Bean's is not to be thrown away just because we fear there might be a security breach."

"Nor is security to be thrown away for the sake of one really smart kid."

"Aren't we smart enough to create new layers of deception for him? Let him find out something that he'll think is the truth. All we have to do is come up with a lie that we think he'll believe."

Sister Carlotta sat in the terrace garden, across the tiny table from the wizened old exile.

"I'm just an old Russian scientist living out the last years of his life on the shores of the Black Sea." Anton took a long drag on his cigarette and blew it out over the railing, adding it to the pollution flowing from Sofia out over the water.

"I'm not here with any law enforcement authority," said Sister Carlotta.

"You have something much more dangerous to me. You are from the Fleet."

"You're in no danger."

"That's true, but only because I'm not going to tell you anything."

"Thank you for your candor."

"You value candor, but I don't think you would appreciate it if I told you the thoughts your body arouses in the mind of this old Russian."

"Trying to shock nuns is not much sport. There is no trophy."

"So you take nunnitude seriously."

Sister Carlotta sighed. "You think I came here because I know something about you and you don't want me to find out more. But I came here because of what I can't find out about you."

"Which is?"

"Anything. Because I was researching a particular matter for the I.F., they gave me a summary of articles on the topic of research into altering the human genome."

"And my name came up?"

"On the contrary, your name was never mentioned."

"How quickly they forget."

"But when I read the few papers available from the people they did mention—always early work, before the I.F. security machine clamped down on them—I noticed a trend. Your name was always cited in their footnotes. Cited constantly. And yet not a word of yours could be found. Not even abstracts of papers. Apparently you have never published."

"And yet they quote me. Almost miraculous, isn't it? You people do collect miracles, don't you? To make saints?"

"No beatification until after you're dead, sorry."

"I have only one lung left as it is," said Anton. "So I don't have that long to wait, as long as I keep smoking."

"You could stop."

"With only one lung, it takes twice as many cigarettes to get the same nicotine. Therefore I have had to increase my smoking, not cut down. This should be obvious, but then, you do not think like a scientist, you think like a woman of faith. You think like an obedient person. When you find out something is bad, you don't do it."

"Your research was into genetic limitations on human intelligence."

"Was it?"

"Because it's in that area that you are always cited. Of course, these papers were never *about* that exact subject, or they too would have been classified. But the titles of the articles mentioned in the footnotes—the ones you never wrote, since you never published anything—are all tied to that area."

"It is so easy in a career to find oneself in a rut."

"So I want to ask you a hypothetical question."

"My favorite kind. Next to rhetorical ones. I can nap equally well through either kind."

"Suppose someone were to break the law and attempt to alter the human genome, specifically to enhance intelligence."

"Then someone would be in serious danger of being caught and punished."

"Suppose that, using the best available research, he found certain genes that he could alter in an embryo that would enhance the intelligence of the person when he was born."

"Embryo! Are you testing me? Such changes can only happen in the egg. A single cell."

"And suppose a child was born with these alterations in place. The child was born and he grew up enough for his great intelligence to be noticed."

"I assume you are not speaking of your own child."

"I'm speaking of no child at all. A hypothetical child. How would someone recognize that this child had been genetically altered? Without actually examining the genes."

Anton shrugged. "What does it matter if you examine the genes? They will be normal."

"Even though you altered them?"

"It is such a little change. Hypothetically speaking."

"Within the normal range of variation?"

"It is two switches, one that you turn on, one that you turn off. The gene is already there, you see."

"What gene?"

"Savants were the key, for me. Autistic, usually. Dysfunctional. They have extraordinary mental powers. Lightning-fast calculations. Phenomenal memories. But they are inept, even retarded in other areas. Square roots of twelve-digit numbers in seconds, but incapable of conducting a simple purchase in a store. How can they be so brilliant, and so stupid?"

"That gene?"

"No, it was another, but it showed me what was possible. The human brain could be far smarter than it is. But is there a, how you say, bargain?"

"Trade-off."

"A terrible bargain. To have this great intellect, you have to give up everything else. That's how the brains of autistic savants accomplish such feats. They do one thing, and the rest is a distraction, an annoyance, beyond the reach of any conceivable interest. Their attention truly is undivided."

"So all hyperintelligent people would be retarded in some other way."

"That is what we all assumed, because that is what we saw. The exceptions seemed to be only mild savants, who were thus able to spare some concentration on ordinary life. Then I thought . . . but I can't tell you what I thought, because I have been served with an order of inhibition."

He smiled helplessly. Sister Carlotta's heart fell. When someone was a proven security risk, they implanted in his brain a device that caused any kind of anxiety to launch a feedback loop, leading to a panic attack. Such people were then given periodic sensitization to make sure that they felt a great deal of anxiety when they contemplated talking about the forbidden subject. Viewed one way, it was a monstrous intrusion on a person's life; but if it was compared to the common practice of imprisoning or killing people who could not be trusted with a vital secret, an order of intervention could look downright humane.

That explained, of course, why Anton was amused by everything. He had to be. If he allowed himself to become agitated or angry—any strong negative emotion, really— then he would have a panic attack even without talking about forbidden subjects. Sister Carlotta had read an article once in which the wife of a man equipped with such a device said that their life together had never been happier, because now he took everything so calmly, with good humor. "The children love him now, instead of dreading his time at home." She said that, according to the article, only hours before he threw himself from a cliff. Life was better, apparently, for everyone but him.

And now she had met a man whose very memories had been rendered inaccessible.

"What a shame," said Sister Carlotta.

"But stay. My life here is a lonely one. You're a sister of mercy, aren't you? Have mercy on a lonely old man, and walk with me."

She wanted to say no, to leave at once. At that moment, however, he leaned back in his chair and began to breathe deeply, regularly, with his eyes closed, as he hummed a little tune to himself.

A ritual of calming. So . . . at the very moment of inviting her to walk with him, he had felt some kind of anxiety that triggered the device. That meant there was something important about his invitation.

"Of course I'll walk with you," she said. "Though technically my order is relatively unconcerned with mercy to individuals. We are far more pretentious than that. Our business is trying to save the world."

He chuckled. "One person at a time would be too slow, is that it?"

"We make our lives of service to the larger causes of humanity. The Savior already died for sin. We work on trying to clean up the consequences of sin on other people."

"An interesting religious quest," said Anton. "I wonder whether my old line of research would have been considered a service to humanity, or just another mess that someone like you would have to clean up."

"I wonder that myself," said Sister Carlotta.

"We will never know." They strolled out of the garden into the alley behind the house, and then to a street, and across it, and onto a path that led through an untended park.

"The trees here are very old," Sister Carlotta observed.

"How old are *you,* Carlotta?"

"Objectively or subjectively?"

"Stick to the Gregorian calendar, please, as most recently revised."

"That switch away from the Julian system still sticks in the Russian craw, does it?"

"It forced us for more than seven decades to commemorate an October Revolution that actually occurred in November."

"You are much too young to remember when there were Communists in Russia."

"On the contrary, I am old enough now to have all the memories of my people locked within my head. I remember things that happened long before I was born. I remember things that never happened at all. I live in memory."

"Is that a pleasant place to dwell?"

"Pleasant?" He shrugged. "I laugh at all of it because I must. Because it is so sweetly sad—all the tragedies, and yet nothing is learned."

"Because human nature never changes," she said.

"I have imagined," he said, "how God might have done

better, when he made man—in his own image, I believe."

"Male and female created he them. Making his image anatomically vague, one must suppose."

He laughed and clapped her rather too forcefully on the back. "I didn't know you could laugh about such things! I am pleasantly surprised!"

"I'm glad I could bring cheer into your bleak existence."

"And then you sink the barb into the flesh." They reached an overlook that had rather less of a view of the sea than Anton's own terrace. "It is not a bleak existence, Carlotta. For I can celebrate God's great compromise in making human beings as we are."

"Compromise?"

"Our bodies could live forever, you know. We don't have to wear out. Our cells are all alive; they can maintain and repair themselves, or be replaced by fresh ones. There are even mechanisms to keep replenishing our bones. Menopause need not stop a woman from bearing children. Our brains need not decay, shedding memories or failing to absorb new ones. But God made us with death inside."

"You are beginning to sound serious about God."

"God made us with death inside, and also with intelligence. We have our seventy years or so—perhaps ninety, with care—in the mountains of Georgia, a hundred and thirty is not unheard of, though I personally believe they are all liars. They would claim to be immortal if they thought they could get away with it. We could live forever, if we were willing to be stupid the whole time."

"Surely you're not saying that God had to choose between long life and intelligence for human beings!"

"It's there in your own Bible, Carlotta. Two trees— knowledge and life. You eat of the tree of knowledge, and you will surely die. You eat of the tree of life, and you remain a child in the garden forever, undying."

"You speak in theological terms, and yet I thought you were an unbeliever."

"Theology is a joke to me. Amusing! I laugh at it. I

can tell amusing stories about theology, to jest with believers. You see? It pleases me and keeps me calm."

At last she understood. How clearly did he have to spell it out? He was telling her the information she asked about, but doing it in code, in a way that fooled not only any eavesdroppers—and there might well be listeners to every word they said—but even his own mind. It was all a jest; therefore he could tell her the truth, as long as he did it in this form.

"Then I don't mind hearing your wild humorous forays into theology."

"Genesis tells of men who lived to be more than nine hundred years old. What it does not tell you is how very stupid these men all were."

Sister Carlotta laughed aloud.

"That's why God had to destroy humanity with his little flood," Anton went on. "Get rid of those stupid people and replace them with quicker ones. Quick quick quick, their minds moved, their metabolism. Rushing onward into the grave."

"From Methuselah at nearly a millennium of life to Moses with his hundred and twenty years, and now to us. But our lives are getting longer."

"I rest my case."

"Are we stupider now?"

"So stupid that we would rather have long life for our children than see them become too much like God, knowing . . . good and evil . . . knowing . . . everything." He clutched at his chest, gasping. "Ah, God! God in heaven!" He sank to his knees. His breath was shallow and rapid now. His eyes rolled back in his head. He fell over.

Apparently he hadn't been able to maintain his self-deception. His body finally caught on to how he had managed to tell his secret to this woman by speaking it in the language of religion.

She rolled him onto his back. Now that he had fainted, his panic attack was subsiding. Not that fainting was trivial in a man of Anton's age. But he would not need any heroism to bring him back, not this time. He would wake up calm.

Where were the people who were supposed to be monitoring him? Where were the spies who were listening in to their conversation?

Pounding feet on the grass, on the leaves.

"A bit slow, weren't you?" she said without looking up.

"Sorry, we didn't expect anything." The man was youngish, but not terribly bright-looking. The implant was supposed to keep him from spilling his tale; it was not necessary for his guards to be clever.

"I think he'll be all right."

"What were you talking about?"

"Religion," she said, knowing that her account would probably be checked against a recording. "He was criticizing God for mis-making human beings. He claimed to be joking, but I think that a man of his age is never really joking when he talks about God, do you?"

"Fear of death gets in them," said the young man sagely—or at least as sagely as he could manage.

"Do you think he accidentally triggered this panic attack by agitating his own anxiety about death?" If she asked it as a question, it wasn't actually a lie, was it?

"I don't know. He's coming around."

"Well, I certainly don't want to cause him any more anxiety about religious matters. When he wakes up, tell him how grateful I am for our conversation. Assure him that he has clarified for me one of the great questions about God's purpose."

"Yes, I'll tell him," said the young man earnestly.

Of course he would garble the message hopelessly.

Sister Carlotta bent over and kissed Anton's cold, sweaty forehead. Then she rose to her feet and walked away.

So that was the secret. The genome that allowed a human being to have extraordinary intelligence acted by speeding up many bodily processes. The mind worked faster. The child developed faster. Bean was indeed the product of an experiment in unlocking the savant gene. He had been given the fruit of the tree of knowledge. But there was a price. He would not be able to taste of the tree of life. Whatever he did with his life, he would have to do it young, because he would not live to be old.

Anton had not done the experiment. He had not played God, bringing forth human beings who would live in an explosion of intelligence, sudden fireworks instead of single, long-burning candles. But he had found a key God had hidden in the human genome. Someone else, some follower, some insatiably curious soul, some would-be visionary longing to take human beings to the next stage of evolution or some other such mad, arrogant cause—this someone had taken the bold step of turning that key, opening that door, putting the killing, brilliant fruit into the hand of Eve. And because of that act—that serpentine, slithering crime—it was Bean who had been expelled from the garden. Bean who would now, surely, die—but die like a god, knowing good and evil.

10

Sneaky

"I can't help you. You didn't give me the information I asked for."

"We gave you the damned summaries."

"You gave me nothing and you know it. And now you come to me asking me to evaluate Bean for you—but you do not tell me why, you give me no context. You expect an answer but you deprive me of the means of providing it."

"Frustrating, isn't it?"

"Not for me. I simply won't give you any answer."

"Then Bean is out of the program."

"If your mind is made up, no answer of mine will change you, especially because you have made certain my answer will be unreliable."

"You know more than you've told me, and I must have it."

"How marvelous. You have achieved perfect empathy with me, for that is the exact statement I have repeatedly made to you."

"An eye for an eye? How Christian of you."

"Unbelievers always want *other* people to act like Christians."

"Perhaps you haven't heard, but there's a war on."

"Again, I could have said the same thing to you. There's a war on, yet you fence me around with foolish secrecy. Since there is no evidence of the Formic enemy spying on us, this secrecy is not about the war. It's about the Triumvirate maintaining their power over humanity. And I am not remotely interested in that."

"You're wrong. That information is secret in order to prevent some terrible experiments from being performed."

"Only a fool closes the door when the wolf is already inside the barn."

"Do you have proof that Bean is the result of a genetic experiment?"

"How can I prove it, when you have cut me off from all evidence? Besides, what matters is not *whether* he has altered genes, but what those genetic changes, if he has them, might lead him to do. Your tests were all designed to allow you to predict the behavior of normal human beings. They may not apply to Bean."

"If he's that unpredictable, then we can't rely on him. He's out."

"What if he's the only one who can win the war? Do you drop him from the program then?"

Bean didn't want to have much food in his body, not tonight, so he gave away almost all his food and turned in a clean tray long before anyone else was done. Let the nutritionist be suspicious—he had to have time alone in the barracks.

The engineers had always located the intake at the top of the wall over the door into the corridor. Therefore the air must flow into the room from the opposite end, where the extra bunks were unoccupied. Since he had not been able to see a vent just glancing around that end of the room, it had to be located under one of the lower bunks. He couldn't search for it when others would see him, because no one could be allowed to know that he was interested in the vents. Now, alone, he dropped to the floor and in moments was jimmying at the vent cover. It came off readily. He tried putting it back on, listening carefully for the level of noise that operation caused. Too much. The vent screen would have to stay off. He laid it on the floor beside the opening, but out of the way so he wouldn't accidentally bump into it in the darkness. Then, to be sure, he took it completely out from under that bunk and slid it under the one directly across.

Done. He then resumed his normal activities.

Until night. Until the breathing of the others told him that most, if not all, were asleep.

Bean slept naked, as many of the boys did—his uniform would not give him away. They were told to wear their towels when going to and from the toilet in the night, so Bean assumed that it, too, could be tracked. So as Bean slid down from his bunk, he pulled his towel from its hook on the bunk frame and wrapped it around himself as he trotted to the door of the barracks.

Nothing unusual. Toilet trips were allowed, if not encouraged, after lights out, and Bean had made it a point to make several such runs during his time in Battle School. No pattern was being violated. And it was a good idea to make his first excursion with an empty bladder.

When he came back, if anyone was awake all they saw was a kid in a towel heading back to his bunk.

But he walked past his bunk and quietly sank down and slid under the last bunk, where the uncovered vent awaited him. His towel remained on the floor under the bunk, so that if anyone woke enough to notice that Bean's bunk was empty, they would see that his towel was missing and assume he had gone to the toilet.

It was no less painful this time, sliding into the vent, but once inside, Bean found that his exercise had paid off. He was able to slide down at an angle, always moving slowly enough to make no noise and to avoid snagging his skin on any protruding metal. He wanted no injuries he'd have to explain.

In the utter darkness of the air duct, he had to keep his mental map of the station constantly in mind. The faint nightlight of each barracks cast only enough light into the air ducts to allow him to make out the location of each vent. But what mattered was not the location of the other barracks on this level. Bean had to get either up or down to a deck where teachers lived and worked. Judging from the amount of time it took Dimak to get to their barracks the rare times that a quarrel demanded his attention, Bean assumed that his quarters were on another deck. And because Dimak always arrived breathing a little heavily, Bean also assumed it was a deck below their own level, not above—Dimak had to climb a ladder, not slide down a pole, to reach them.

Nevertheless, Bean had no intention of going down first. He had to see whether he could successfully climb to a higher deck before getting himself potentially trapped on a lower one.

So when he finally—after passing three barracks— came to a vertical shaft, he did not climb down. Instead, he probed the walls to see how much larger it was than the horizontals. It was much wider—Bean could not reach all the way across it. But it was only slightly deeper, front to back. That was good. As long as Bean didn't work too hard and sweat too much, friction between his skin and the front and back walls of the duct would allow him to inch his way upward. And in the vertical duct, he could face forward, giving his neck a much-needed respite from being perpetually turned to one side.

Downward was almost harder than upward, because once he started sliding it was harder to stop. He was also aware that the lower he went, the heavier he would become. And he had to keep checking the wall beside him, looking for another side duct.

But he didn't have to find it by probing, after all. He

could see the side duct, because there was light in both directions. The teachers didn't have the same lights-out rules as the students, and their quarters were smaller, so that vents came more frequently, spilling more light into the duct.

In the first room, a teacher was awake and working at his desk. The trouble was that Bean, peering out of a vent screen near the floor, could not see a thing he was typing.

It would be that way in all the rooms. The floor vents would not work for him. He had to get into the air-intake system.

Back to the vertical duct. The wind was coming from above, and so that was where he had to go if he was to cross over from one system to another. His only hope was that the duct system would have an access door before he reached the fans, and that he would be able to find it in the dark.

Heading always into the wind, and finding himself noticeably lighter after climbing past seven decks, he finally reached a wider area with a small light strip. The fans were much louder, but he still wasn't near enough to see them. It didn't matter. He would be out of this wind.

The access door was clearly marked. It also might be wired to sound an alarm if it was opened. But he doubted it. That was the kind of thing that was done in Rotterdam to guard against burglars. Burglary wasn't a serious problem on space stations. This door would only have been alarmed if all doors in the station were fitted with alarms. He'd find out soon enough.

He opened the door, slipped out into a faintly lighted space, closed the door behind him.

The structure of the station was visible here, the beams, the sections of metal plating. There were no solid surfaces. The room was also noticeably colder, and not just because he was out of the hot wind. Cold hard space was on the other side of those curved plates. The furnaces might be located here, but the insulation was very good, and they had not bothered to pump much of that hot air into this space, relying instead on seepage to heat it. Bean hadn't been this cold since Rotterdam . . . but compared to wearing thin clothing in the winter streets with the wind off the North Sea, this was still almost balmy. It annoyed Bean that he had become so pampered here that he even cared about such a slight chill. And yet he couldn't keep himself from shivering a couple of times. Even in Rotterdam, he hadn't been naked.

Following the ductwork, he climbed up the workmen's ladderways to the furnaces and then found the air-intake ducts and followed them back down. It was easy to find an access door and enter the main vertical duct.

Because the air in the intake system did not have to be under positive pressure, the ducts did not have to be so narrow. Also, this was the part of the system where dirt had to be caught and removed, so it was more important to maintain access; by the time air got past the furnaces, it was already as clean as it was ever going to get. So instead of shinnying up and down narrow shafts, Bean scrambled easily down a ladder, and in the low light still had no trouble reading the signs telling which deck each side opening led to.

The side passages weren't really ducts at all. Instead, they consisted of the entire space between the ceiling of one corridor and the floor of the one above. All the wiring was here, and the water pipes—hot, cold, sewer. And besides the strips of dim worklights, the space was frequently lighted by the vents on both sides of the space— those same narrow strips of vent openings that Bean had seen from the floor below on his first excursion.

Now he could see easily down into each teacher's quarters. He crept along, making as little noise as possible— a skill he had perfected prowling through Rotterdam. He quickly found what he was looking for—a teacher who was awake, but not working at his desk. The man was not well known to Bean, because he supervised an older group of launchies and did not teach any of the classes Bean was taking. He was heading for a shower. That meant he would come back to the room and, perhaps, would sign in again, allowing Bean to have a chance at getting both his log-in name and his password.

No doubt the teachers changed passwords often, so whatever he got wouldn't last long. Moreover, it was always possible that attempting to use a teacher's password on a student desk might set off some kind of alarm. But Bean doubted it. The whole security system was designed to shut students out, to monitor student behavior. The teachers would not be so closely watched. They frequently worked on their desks at odd hours, and they also frequently signed on to student desks during the day to call on their more powerful tools to help solve a student's problem or give a student more personalized computer resources. Bean was reasonably sure that the risk of discovery was outweighed by the benefits of snagging a teacher's identity.

While he waited, he heard voices a few rooms up. He wasn't quite close enough to make out the words. Did he dare risk missing the bather's return?

Moments later he was looking down into the quarters of . . . Dimak himself. Interesting. He was talking to a man whose holographic image appeared in the air over his desk. Colonel Graff, Bean realized. The commandant of Battle School.

"My strategy was simple enough," Graff was saying. "I gave in and got her access to the stuff she wanted. She was right, I can't get good answers from her unless I let her see the data she's asking for."

"So did she give you any answers?"

"No, too soon. But she gave me a very good question."

"Which is?"

"Whether the boy is actually human."

"Oh, come on. Does she think he's a Bugger larva in a human suit?"

"Nothing to do with the Buggers. Genetically enhanced. It would explain a lot."

"But still human, then."

"Isn't that debatable? The difference between humans and chimpanzees is genetically slight. Between humans and neanderthals it had to be minute. How much difference would it take for him to be a different species?"

"Philosophically interesting, but in practical terms—"

"In practical terms, we don't know what this kid will do. There's no data on his species. He's a primate, which suggests certain regularities, but we can't assume anything about his motivations that—"

"Sir, with all due respect, he's still a kid. He's a human being. He's not some alien—"

"That's precisely what we've got to find out before we determine how much we can rely on him. And that's why you are to watch him even more carefully. If you can't get him into the mind game, then find some other way to figure out what makes him tick. Because we can't use him until we know just how much we can rely on him."

Interesting that they openly call it the mind game among themselves, thought Bean.

Then he realized what they were saying. "Can't get him into the mind game." As far as Bean knew, he was the only kid who didn't play the fantasy game. They were talking about him. New species. Genetically altered. Bean felt his heart pounding in his chest. What am I? Not just smart, but . . . different.

"What about the breach of security?" Dimak asked.

"That's the other thing. You've got to figure out what he knows. Or at least how likely he is to spill it to any other kids. That's the greatest danger right now. Is the possibility of this kid being the commander we need great enough to balance the risk of breaching security and collapsing the program? I thought with Ender we had an all-or-nothing long-odds bet, but this one makes Ender look like a sure thing."

"I didn't think of you as a gambler, sir."

"I'm not. But sometimes you're forced into the game."

"I'm on it, sir."

"Encrypt everything you send me on him. No names.

No discussions with other teachers beyond the normal. Contain this."

"Of course."

"If the only way we can beat the Buggers is to replace ourselves with a new species, Dimak, then have we really saved humanity?"

"One kid is not replacement of a species," said Dimak.

"Foot in the door. Camel's nose in the tent. Give them an inch."

"*Them,* sir?"

"Yes, I'm paranoid and xenophobic. That's how I got this job. Cultivate those virtues and you, too, might rise to my lofty station."

Dimak laughed. Graff didn't. His head disappeared from the display.

Bean had the discipline to remember that he was waiting to get a password. He crept back to the bather's room.

Still not back.

What breach of security were they talking about? It must have been recent, for them to be discussing it with such urgency. That meant it had to be Bean's conversation with Dimak about what was really going on with the Battle School. And yet his guess that the battle had already happened could not be it, or Dimak and Graff would not be talking about how he might be the only way they could beat the Buggers. If the Buggers were still unbeaten, the breach of security had to be something else.

It could still be that his earlier guess was partly right, and Battle School existed as much to strip the Earth of good commanders as to beat the Buggers. Graff and Dimak's fear might be that Bean would let other kids in on the secret. For some of them, at least, it might rekindle their loyalty to the nation or ethnic group or ideology of their parents.

And since Bean had definitely been planning to probe the loyalties of other students over the next months and years, he now would have to be doubly cautious not to let his pattern of conversation attract the attention of the teachers. All he needed to know was which of the best and brightest kids had the strongest home loyalties. Of course, for that Bean would need to figure out just how loyalty worked, so he would have some idea of how to weaken it or strengthen it, how to exploit it or turn it.

But just because this first guess of Bean's could explain their words didn't mean it was right. And just because the final Bugger war had not yet been fought didn't mean his initial guess was completely wrong. They might, for instance, have launched a fleet against the Bugger home world years ago, but were still preparing commanders to fight off an invasion fleet now approaching Earth. In that case, the security breach Graff and Dimak feared was that Bean would frighten others by letting them know how urgent and dire the situation of humanity was.

The irony was that of all the children Bean had ever known, none could keep a secret as well as he did. Not even Achilles, for in refusing his share of Poke's bread, he had tipped his hand.

Bean could keep a secret, but he also knew that sometimes you had to give some hint of what you knew in order to get more information. That was what had prompted Bean's conversation with Dimak. It was dangerous, but in the long run, if he could keep them from removing him from the school entirely in order to silence him—not to mention keeping them from killing him—he had learned more important information than he had given them. In the end, the only things they could learn from him were about himself. And what he learned from them was about everything else—a much larger pool of knowledge.

Himself. That was their puzzle—who he was. Silly to be concerned about whether he was human. What else *could* he be? He had never seen any child show any desire or emotion that he himself had not felt. The only difference was that Bean was stronger, and did not let his fleeting needs and passions control his actions. Did that make him alien? He was human—only better.

The teacher came back into the room. He hung up his damp towel, but even before he dressed he sat back down and logged on. Bean watched his fingers move over the keys. It was so quick. A blur of keystrokes. He would have to replay the memory in his mind many times to make sure. But at least he had seen it; nothing obstructed his view.

Bean crawled back toward the vertical intake shaft. The evening's expedition had already taken as long as he dared—he needed his sleep, and every minute away increased the risk of chance discovery.

In fact, he had been very lucky on this first foray through the ducts. To happen to hear Dimak and Graff conversing about him, to happen to watch a teacher who conveniently gave him a clear view of his log-in. For a moment it crossed Bean's mind that they might know he was in the air system, might even have staged all this for him, to see what he'd do. It might be just one more experiment.

No. It wasn't just luck that this teacher showed him the log-in. Bean had chosen to watch him because he was going to shower, because his desk was sitting on the table in such a way that Bean had a reasonable chance of seeing the log-in. It was an intelligent choice on Bean's part. He had gone with the best odds, and it paid off.

As for Dimak and Graff, it might have been chance that he overheard them talking, but it was his own choice to move closer at once in order to hear. And, come to think of it, he had chosen to go exploring in the ducts because of precisely the same event that had prompted Graff and Dimak to be so concerned. Nor was it a surprise that their conversation happened after lights-out for the children— that's when things would have quieted down, and, with duties done, there would be time for a conversation without Graff calling Dimak in for a special meeting, which might arouse questions in the minds of the other teachers. Not luck, really—Bean had made his own luck. He saw the log-in and overheard the conversation because he had made that quick decision to get into the intake system and acted on it at once.

He had always made his own luck.

Maybe that was something that went along with whatever genetic alteration Graff had found out about.

She, they had said. *She* had raised the question of whether Bean was genetically human. Some woman who was searching for information, and Graff had given in, was letting her have access to facts that had been hidden from her. That meant that he would receive more answers from this woman as she began to use that new data. More answers about Bean's origins.

Could it be Sister Carlotta who had doubted Bean's humanity?

Sister Carlotta, who wept when he left her and went into space? Sister Carlotta, who loved him as a mother loves her child? How could *she* doubt him?

If they wanted to find some inhuman human, some alien in a human suit, they ought to take a good long look at a nun who embraces a child as her own, and then goes around casting doubt about whether he's a real boy. The opposite of Pinocchio's fairy. She touches a real boy and turns him into something awful and fearful.

It could not have been Sister Carlotta they were talking about. Just another woman. His guess that it might be her was simply wrong, just like his guess that the final battle with the Buggers had already happened. That's why Bean never fully trusted his own guesses. He acted on them, but always kept himself open to the possibility that his interpretations might be wrong.

Besides, *his* problem was not figuring out whether he really was human or not. Whatever he was, he was himself and must act in such a way as to not only stay alive but also get as much control over his own future as possible. The only danger to him was that *they* were concerned about the issue of his possible genetic alteration. Bean's task was therefore to appear so normal that their fears on that score would be dispelled.

But how could he pretend to be normal? He hadn't been brought here because he was normal, he was brought here because he was extraordinary. For that matter, so were all the other kids. And the school put so much strain on them that some became downright odd. Like Bonzo Madrid, with his loud vendetta against Ender Wiggin. So in fact, Bean shouldn't appear normal, he should appear weird in the expected ways.

Impossible to fake that. He didn't know yet what signs the teachers were looking for in the behavior of the children here. He could find ten things to do, and do them, never guessing that there were ninety things he hadn't noticed.

No, what he had to do was not to *act* in predictable ways, but to *become* what they hoped their perfect commander would be.

When he got back to his barracks, climbed back up to his bunk, and checked the time on his desk, he found that he had done it all in less than an hour. He put away his desk and lay there replaying in his mind the image in his memory of the teacher's fingers, logging in. When he was reasonably certain of what the log-in and password were, he allowed himself to drift toward sleep.

Only then, as he was beginning to doze, did he realize what his perfect camouflage would be, quelling their fears and bringing him both safety and advancement.

He had to become Ender Wiggin.

11

Daddy

"Sir. I asked for a private interview."

"Dimak is here because your breach of security affects his work."

"Breach of security! This is why you reassign me?"

"There is a child who used your log-in to the master teacher system. He found the log-in record files and re-wrote them to give himself an identity."

"Sir, I have faithfully adhered to all regulations. I never sign on in front of the students."

"Everyone *says* they never sign on, but then it turns out they do."

"Excuse me, sir, but Uphanad does not. He's always on the others when he catches them doing it. Actually, he's kind of anal about it. Drives us all crazy."

"You can check my log-in records. I never sign on during teaching hours. In fact, I never sign on outside my quarters."

"Then how could this child possibly get in using your log-in?"

"My desk sits on my table, like so. If I may use your desk to demonstrate."

"Of course."

"I sit like so. I keep my back to the door so no one can even see in. I never sign on in any other position."

"Well it's not like there's a window he can peek through!"

"Yes there is, sir."

"Dimak?"

"There *is* a window, sir. Look. The vent."

"Are you seriously suggesting that he could—"

"He *is* the smallest child who ever—"

"It was that little *Bean* child who got my log-in?"

"Excellent, Dimak, you've managed to let his name slip out, haven't you."

"I'm sorry, sir."

"Ah. Another security breach. Will you send Dimak home with me?"

"I'm not sending anybody home."

"Sir, I must point out that Bean's intrusion into the master teacher system is an excellent opportunity."

"To have a student romping through the student data files?"

"To study Bean. We don't have him in the fantasy game, but now we have the game *he* chooses to play. We watch where he goes in the system, what he does with this power he has created for himself."

"But the damage he can do is—"

"He won't do any damage, sir. He won't do anything to give himself away. This kid is too street-smart. It's information he wants. He'll look, not touch."

"So you've got him analyzed already, is that it? You know what he's doing at all times?"

"I know that if there's a story we really want him to believe, he has to discover it himself. He has to *steal* it from us. So I think this little security breach is the perfect way to heal a much more important one."

"What I'm wondering is, if he's been crawling through the ducts, what *else* has he heard?"

"If we close off the duct system, he'll know he was caught, and then he won't trust what we set up for him to find."

"So I have to permit a child to crawl around through the ductwork and—"

"He can't do it much longer. He's growing, and the ducts are extremely shallow."

"That's not much comfort right now. And, unfortunately, we'll still have to kill Uphanad for knowing too much."

"Please assure me that you're joking."

"Yes, I'm joking. You'll have him as a student soon enough, Captain Uphanad. Watch him very carefully. Speak of him only with me. He's unpredictable and dangerous."

"Dangerous. Little Bean."

"He cleaned *your* clock, didn't he?"

"Yours too, sir, begging your pardon."

Bean worked his way through every student at Battle School, reading the records of a half dozen or so per day. Their original scores, he found, were the least interesting thing about them. Everyone here had such high scores on all the tests given back on Earth that the differences were almost trivial. Bean's own scores were the highest, and the gap between him and the next highest, Ender Wiggin, was wide—as wide as the gap between Ender and the next child after him. But it was all relative. The difference between Ender and Bean amounted to half of a percentage point; most of the children clustered between 97 and 98 percent.

Of course, Bean knew what they could not know, that for him getting the highest possible score on the tests had been easy. He could have done more, he could have done better, but he had reached the boundary of what the test could discover. The gap between him and Ender was much wider than they supposed.

And yet . . . in reading the records, Bean came to see that the scores were merely a guide to a child's potential. The teachers talked most about things like cleverness, insight, intuition; the ability to develop rapport, to outguess an opponent; the courage to act boldly, the caution to make certain before committing, the wisdom to know which course was the appropriate one. And in considering this, Bean realized that he was not necessarily any better at *these* things than the other students.

Ender Wiggin really did know things that Bean did not know. Bean might have thought to do as Wiggin did, arranging extra practices to make up for being with a commander who wouldn't train him. Bean even might have tried to bring in a few other students to train with him, since many things could not be done alone. But Wiggin had taken all comers, no matter how difficult it became to practice with so many in the battleroom, and according to the teachers' notes, he spent more time now training others than in working on his own technique. Of course, that was partly because he was no longer in Bonzo Madrid's army, so he got to take part in the regular practices. But he still kept working with the other kids, especially the eager launchies who wanted a head start before they were promoted into a regular army. Why?

Is he doing what I'm doing, studying the other students to prepare for a later war on Earth? Is he building some kind of network that reaches out into all the armies? Is he somehow mistraining them, so he can take advantage of their mistakes later?

From what Bean heard about Wiggin from the kids in his launch group who attended those practices, he came to realize that it was something else entirely. Wiggin seemed really to care about the other kids doing their best. Did he need so badly for them to like him? Because it was working, if that's what he was trying for. They worshiped him.

But there had to be more to it than some hunger for love. Bean couldn't get a handle on it.

He found that the teachers' observations, while helpful, didn't really help him get inside Wiggin's head. For one thing, they kept the psychological observations from the mind game somewhere else that Bean didn't have access to. For another, the teachers couldn't really get into Wiggin's mind because they simply didn't think at his level.

Bean did.

But Bean's project wasn't to analyze Wiggin out of scientific curiosity, or to compete with him, or even to understand him. It was to make himself into the kind of child that the teachers would trust, would rely on. Would regard as fully human. For that project, Wiggin was his teacher because Wiggin had already done what Bean needed to do.

And Wiggin had done it without being perfect. Without being, as far as Bean could tell, completely sane. Not that anyone was. But Wiggin's willingness to give up hours every day to training kids who could do nothing for him— the more Bean thought about it, the less sense it made. Wiggin was not building a network of supporters. Unlike Bean, he didn't have a perfect memory, so Bean was quite sure Wiggin was not compiling a mental dossier on every other kid in Battle School. The kids he worked with were not the best, and were often the most fearful and dependent of the launchies and of the losers in the regular armies. They came to him because they thought being in the same room with the soldier who was leading in the standings might bring some luck to them. But why did Wiggin keep giving his time to *them?*

Why did Poke die for me?

That was the same question. Bean knew it. He found several books about ethics in the library and called them up on his desk to read. He soon discovered that the only theories that explained altruism were bogus. The stupidest was the old sociobiological explanation of uncles dying for nephews—there were no blood ties in armies now, and people often died for strangers. Community theory was fine as far as it went—it explained why communities all honored sacrificial heroes in their stories and rituals, but it still didn't explain the heroes themselves.

For that was what Bean saw in Wiggin. This was the hero at his root.

Wiggin really does not care as much about himself as he does about these other kids who aren't worth five minutes of his time.

And yet this may be the very trait that makes everyone focus on him. Maybe this is why in all those stories Sister Carlotta told him, Jesus always had a crowd around him.

Maybe this is why I'm so afraid of Wiggin. Because *he's* the alien, not me. He's the unintelligible one, the unpredictable one. He's the one who doesn't do things for sensible, predictable reasons. I'm going to survive, and once you know that, there's nothing more to know about me. Him, though, he could do anything.

The more he studied Wiggin, the more mysteries Bean uncovered. The more he determined to act like Wiggin until, at some point, he came to see the world as Wiggin saw it.

But even as he tracked Wiggin—still from a distance— what Bean could not let himself do was what the younger kids did, what Wiggin's disciples did. He could not call him Ender. Calling him by his last name kept him at a distance. A microscope's distance, anyway.

What did Wiggin study when he read on his own? Not the books of military history and strategy that Bean had blown through in a rush and was now rereading method-ically, applying everything to both space combat and modern warfare on Earth. Wiggin did his share of reading, too, but when he went into the library he was just as likely to look at combat vids, and the ones he watched most often were of Bugger ships. Those and the clips of Mazer Rackham's strike force in the heroic battle that broke the back of the Second Invasion.

Bean watched them too, though not over and over again—once he saw them, he remembered them perfectly and could replay them in his mind, with enough detail that he could notice things later that he hadn't realized at first. Was Wiggin seeing something new each time he went back to these vids? Or was he looking for something that he hadn't yet found?

Is he trying to understand the way the Buggers think? Why doesn't he realize that the library here simply doesn't have enough of the vids to make it useful? It's all propaganda stuff here. They withheld all the terrible scenes of dead guys, of fighting and killing hand to hand when ships were breached and boarded. They didn't have vids of defeats, where the Buggers blew the human ships out of the sky. All they had here was ships moving around in space, a few minutes of preparation for combat.

War in space? So exciting in the made-up stories, so boring in reality. Occasionally something would light up, mostly it was just dark.

And, of course, the obligatory moment of Mazer Rackham's victory.

What could Wiggin possibly hope to learn?

Bean learned more from the omissions than from what he actually saw. For instance, there was not one picture of Mazer Rackham anywhere in the library. That was odd. The Triumvirates' faces were everywhere, as were those of other commanders and political leaders. Why not Rackham? Had he died in the moment of victory? Or was he, perhaps, a fictitious figure, a deliberately-created legend, so that there could be a name to peg the victory to? But if that were the case, they'd have created a face for him— it was too easy to do that. Was he deformed?

Was he really, really small?

If I grow up to be the commander of the human fleet that defeats the Buggers, will they hide my picture, too, because someone so tiny can never be seen as a hero?

Who cares? I don't want to be a hero.

That's Wiggin's gig.

———

Nikolai, the boy across from him. Bright enough to make some guesses Bean hadn't made first. Confident enough not to get angry when he caught Bean intruding on him. Bean was so hopeful when he came at last to Nikolai's file.

The teacher evaluation was negative. "A place-holder." Cruel—but was it true?

Bean realized: I have been putting too much trust in the teachers' evaluations. Do I have any real evidence that they're right? Or do I believe in their evaluations because I am rated so highly? Have I let them flatter me into complacency?

What if all their evaluations were hopelessly wrong?

I had no teacher files on the streets of Rotterdam. I actually knew the children. Poke—I made my own judgment of her, and I was almost right, just a few surprises here and there. Sergeant—no surprises at all. Achilles— yes, I knew him.

So why have I stayed apart from the other students? Because they isolated me at first, and because I decided that the teachers had the power. But now I see that I was only partly right. The teachers have the power here and now, but someday I will not be in Battle School, and what does it matter then what the teachers think of me? I can learn all the military theory and history that I want, and it will do me no good if they never entrust me with command. And I will never be placed in charge of an army or a fleet unless they have reason to believe that other men would follow me.

Not men today, but boys, most of them, a few girls. Not men, but they *will* be men. How do they choose their leaders? How do I make them follow one who is so small, so resented?

What did Wiggin do?

Bean asked Nikolai which of the kids in their launch group practiced with Wiggin.

"Only a few. And they on the fringes, neh? Suckups and brags."

"But who are they?"

"You trying to get in with Wiggin?"

"Just want to find out about him."

"What you want to know?"

The questions bothered Bean. He didn't like talking so much about what he was doing. But he didn't sense any malice in Nikolai. He just wanted to know.

"History. He the best, neh? How he get that way?" Bean wondered if he sounded quite natural with the soldier slang. He hadn't used it that much. The music of it, he still wasn't quite there.

"You find out, you tell me." He rolled his eyes in self-derision.

"I'll tell you," said Bean.

"I got a chance to be best like Ender?" Nikolai laughed. "*You* got a chance, the way you learn."

"Wiggin's snot ain't honey," said Bean.

"What does that mean?"

"He human like anybody. I find out, I tell you, OK?"

Bean wondered why Nikolai already despaired about his own chances of being one of the best. Could it be that the teachers' negative evaluation was right after all? Or had they unconsciously let him see their disdain for him, and he believed them?

From the boys Nikolai had pointed out—the brags and suckups, which wasn't an inaccurate evaluation as far as it went—Bean learned what he wanted to know. The names of Wiggin's closest friends.

Shen. Alai. Petra—her again! But Shen the longest.

Bean found him in the library during study time. The only reason to go there was for the vids—all the books could be read from the desks. Shen wasn't watching vids, though. He had his desk with him, and he was playing the fantasy game.

Bean sat down beside him to watch. A lion-headed man in chain mail stood before a giant, who seemed to be offering him a choice of drinks—the sound was shaped so that Bean couldn't hear it from beside the desk, though

Shen seemed to be responding; he typed in a few words. His lion-man figure drank one of the substances and promptly died.

Shen muttered something and shoved the desk away.

"That the Giant's Drink?" said Bean. "I heard about that."

"You've never played it?" said Shen. "You can't win it. I *thought*."

"I heard. Didn't sound fun."

"*Sound* fun? You haven't tried it? It's not like it's hard to find."

Bean shrugged, trying to fake the mannerisms he'd seen other boys use. Shen looked amused. Because Bean did the cool-guy shrug wrong? Or because it looked cute to have somebody so small do it?

"Come on, you don't play the fantasy game?"

"What you said," Bean prompted him. "You *thought* nobody ever won it."

"I saw a guy in a place I'd never seen. I asked him where it was, and he said, 'Other side of the Giant's Drink.'"

"He tell you how to get there?"

"I didn't ask."

"Why not?"

Shen grinned, looked away.

"It be Wiggin, neh?" asked Bean.

The grin faded. "I didn't say that."

"I know you're his friend, that's why I came here."

"What is this? You spying on him? You from Bonzo?"

This was not going well. Bean hadn't realized how protective Wiggin's friends might be. "I'm from me. Look, nothing bad, OK? I just—look, I just want to know about—you know him from the start, right? They say you been his friend from launchy days."

"So what?"

"Look, he got friends, right? Like you. Even though he always does better in class, always the best on everything, right? But they don't hate him."

"Plenty bichão hate him."

"I got to make some friends, man." Bean knew that he shouldn't try to sound pitiful. Instead, he should sound like a pitiful kid who was trying really hard *not* to sound pitiful. So he ended his maudlin little plea with a laugh. As if he was trying to make it sound like a joke.

"You're pretty short," said Shen.

"Not on the planet I'm from," said Bean.

For the first time, Shen let a genuine smile come to his face. "The planet of the pygmies."

"Them boys too big for me."

"Look, I know what you're saying," said Shen. "I had this funny walk. Some of the kids were ragging me. Ender stopped them."

"How?"

"Ragged them more."

"I never heard he got a mouth."

"No, he didn't say nada. Did it on the desk. Sent a message from God."

Oh, yeah. Bean had heard about that. "He did that for you?"

"They were making fun of my butt. I had a big butt. Before workouts, you know? Back then. So he make fun of them for looking at my butt. But he signs it God."

"So they didn't know it was him."

"Oh, they knew. Right away. But he didn't *say* anything. Out loud."

"That's how you got to be friends? He the protector of the little guys?" Like Achilles . . .

"*Little* guys?" said Shen. "He was the smallest in our launch group. Not like you, but way small. Younger, see."

"He was youngest, but he became your protector?"

"No. Not like that. No, he kept it from going on, that's all. He went to the group—it was Bernard, he was getting together the biggest guys, the tough guys—"

"The bullies."

"Yeah, I guess. Only Ender, he goes to Bernard's number one, his best friend. Alai. He gets Alai to be his friend, too."

"So he stole away Bernard's support?"

"No, man. No, it's not like that. He made friends with Alai, and then got Alai to help him make friends with Bernard."

"Bernard . . . he's the one, Ender broke his arm in the shuttle."

"That's right. And I think, really, Bernard never forgave him, but he saw how things were."

"How were things?"

"Ender's *good,* man. You just—he doesn't hate anybody. If you're a good person, you're going to like him. You want him to like you. If he likes you, then you're OK, see? But if you're scum, he just makes you mad. Just knowing he exists, see? So Ender, he tries to wake up the good part of you."

"How do you wake up 'good parts'?"

"I don't know, man. You think I know? It just . . . you know Ender long enough, he just makes you want him to be proud of you. That sounds so . . . sounds like I'm a baby, neh?"

Bean shook his head. What it sounded like to him was devotion. Bean hadn't really understood this. Friends were friends, he thought. Like Sergeant and Poke used to be, before Achilles. But it was never love. When Achilles came, they loved him, but it was more like worship, like . . . a god, he got them bread, they gave bread back to him. Like . . . well, like what he called himself. Papa. Was it the same thing? Was Ender Achilles all over again?

"You're smart, kid," said Shen. "I was there, neh? Only I never once thought, How did Ender *do* it? How can I do the same, be like him? It's like that was Ender, he's great, but it's nothing *I* could do. Maybe I should have tried. I just wanted to be . . . *with* him."

"Cause you're good, too," said Bean.

Shen rolled his eyes. "I guess that's what I was saying,

wasn't it? Implying, anyway. Guess that makes me a brag, neh?"

"Big old brag," said Bean, grinning.

"He's just . . . he makes you want to . . . I'd die for him. That sounds like hero talk, neh? But it's true. I'd die for him. I'd kill for him."

"You'd fight for him."

Shen got it at once. "That's right. He's a born commander."

"Alai fight for him too?"

"A lot of us."

"But some not, yes?"

"Like I said, the bad ones, they hate him, he makes them crazy."

"So the whole world divides up—good people love Wiggin, bad people hate Wiggin."

Shen's face went suspicious again. "I don't know why I told you all that merda. You too smart to believe any of it."

"I do believe it," said Bean. "Don't be mad at me." He'd learned that one a long time ago. Little kid says, Don't be mad at me, they feel a little silly.

"I'm not mad," said Shen. "I just thought you were making fun of me."

"I wanted to know how Wiggin makes friends."

"If I knew that, if I really understood that, I'd have more friends than I do, kid. But I got Ender as my friend, and all his friends are my friends too, and I'm their friend, so . . . it's like a family."

A family. Papa. Achilles again.

That old dread returned. That night after Poke died. Seeing her body in the water. Then Achilles in the morning. How he acted. Was that Wiggin? Papa until he got his chance?

Achilles was evil, and Ender was good. Yet they both created a family. Both had people who loved them, who would die for them. Protector, papa, provider, mama. Only parent to a crowd of orphans. We're all street kids up here in Battle School, too. We might not be hungry, but we're all still wishing for a family.

Except me. Last thing I need. Some papa smiling at me, waiting with a knife.

Better to *be* the papa than to have one.

How can I do that? Get somebody to love me the way Shen loves Wiggin?

No chance. I'm too little. Too cute. I got nothing they want. All I can do is protect myself, work the system. Ender's got plenty to teach those that have some hope of doing what he's done. But me, I have to learn my own way.

Even as he made the decision, though, he knew he wasn't done with Wiggin. Whatever Wiggin had, whatever Wiggin knew, Bean *would* learn it.

And so passed the weeks, the months. Bean did all his regular classwork. He attended the regular battleroom classes with Dimak teaching them how to move and shoot, the basic skills. On his own he completed all the enrichment courses you could take at your own desk, certifying in everything. He studied military history, philosophy, strategy. He read ethics, religion, biology. He kept track of every student in the school, from the newly arrived launchies to the students about to graduate. When he saw them in the halls, he knew more about them than they knew about themselves. He knew their nation of origin. He knew how much they missed their families and how important their native country or ethnic or religious group was to them. He knew how valuable they might be to a nationalist or idealist resistance movement.

And he kept reading everything Wiggin read, watching everything Wiggin watched. Hearing about Wiggin from the other kids. Watching Wiggin's standings on the boards. Meeting more of Wiggin's friends, hearing them talk about him. Bean listened to all the things Wiggin was quoted as saying and tried to fit them into some coherent philosophy, some worldview, some attitude, some plan.

And he found out something interesting. Despite Wig-

gin's altruism, despite his willingness to sacrifice, not one
of his friends ever said that Wiggin came and talked over
his problems. They all went to Wiggin, but who did Wiggin
go to? He had no more *real* friends than Bean did.
Wiggin kept his own counsel, just like Bean.

Soon Bean found himself being advanced out of classes
whose work he had already mastered and being plunged
into classwork with older and older groups, who looked
at him with annoyance at first, but later simply with awe,
as he raced past them and was promoted again before they
were half done. Had Wiggin been pushed through his
classwork at an accelerated rate? Yes, but not quite as
fast. Was that because Bean was better? Or because the
deadline was getting closer?

For the sense of urgency in teacher evaluations was
getting greater. The ordinary students—as if any child
here were ordinary—were getting briefer and briefer notations. They weren't being ignored, exactly. But the best
were being identified and lifted out.

The *seeming* best. For Bean began to realize that the
teachers' evaluations were often colored by which students they liked the best. The teachers pretended to be
dispassionate, impartial, but in fact they got sucked in by
the more charismatic children, just as the other students
did. If a kid was likable, they gave him better comments
on leadership, even if he was really just glib and athletic
and needed to surround himself with a team. As often as
not, they tagged the very students who would be the least
effective commanders, while ignoring the ones who, to
Bean, showed real promise. It was frustrating to watch
them make such obvious mistakes. Here they had Wiggin
right before their eyes—Wiggin, who was the real thing—
and they still went on misreading everybody else. Getting
all excited about some of these energetic, self-confident,
ambitious kids even though they weren't actually produc-
ing excellent work.

Wasn't this whole school set up in order to find and
train the best possible commanders? The Earthside testing

did pretty well—there were no real dolts among the students. But the system had overlooked one crucial factor: How were the teachers chosen?

They were career military, all of them. Proven officers with real ability. But in the military you don't get trusted positions just because of your ability. You also have to attract the notice of superior officers. You have to be liked. You have to fit in with the system. You have to look like what the officers above you think that officers should look like. You have to think in ways that they are comfortable with.

The result was that you ended up with a command structure that was top-heavy with guys who looked good in uniform and talked right and did well enough not to embarrass themselves, while the really good ones quietly did all the serious work and bailed out their superiors and got blamed for errors they had advised against until they eventually got out.

That was the military. These teachers were all the kind of people who thrived in that environment. And they were selecting their favorite students based on precisely that same screwed-up sense of priorities.

No wonder a kid like Dink Meeker saw through it and refused to play. He was one of the few kids who was both likable *and* talented. His likability made them try to make him commander of his own army; his talent let him understand why they were doing it and turn them down because he couldn't believe in such a stupid system. And other kids, like Petra Arkanian, who had obnoxious personalities but could handle strategy and tactics in their sleep, who had the confidence to lead others into war, to trust their own decisions and act on them—they didn't care about trying to be one of the guys, and so they got overlooked, every flaw became magnified, every strength belittled.

So Bean began constructing his own anti-army. Kids who weren't getting picked out by the teachers, but were the real talents, the ones with heart and mind, not just face and chat. He began to imagine who among them should be officers, leading their own toons under the command of . . .

Of Ender Wiggin, of course. Bean could not imagine anyone else in that position. Wiggin would know how to use them.

And Bean knew just where he should be. Close to Wiggin. A toon leader, but the most trusted of them. Wiggin's righthand man. So when Wiggin was about to make a mistake, Bean could point out to him the error he was making. And so that Bean could be close enough to maybe understand why Wiggin was human and he himself was not.

———

Sister Carlotta used her new security clearance like a scalpel, most of the time, slicing her way into the information establishment, picking up answers here and new questions there, talking to people who never guessed what her project was, why she knew so much about their top-secret work, and quietly putting it all together in her own mind, in memos to Colonel Graff.

But sometimes she wielded her top security clearance like a meat-ax, using it to get past prison wardens and security officers, who saw her unbelievable level of need-to-know and then, when they checked to make sure her documents weren't a stupid forgery, were screamed at by officers so high-ranked that it made them want to treat Sister Carlotta like God.

That's how, at last, she came face to face with Bean's father. Or at least the closest thing to a father that he had.

"I want to talk to you about your installation in Rotterdam."

He looked at her sourly. "I already reported on everything. That's why I'm not dead, though I wonder if I made the right choice."

"They told me you were quite the whiner," said Sister

Carlotta, utterly devoid of compassion. "I didn't expect it to surface so quickly."

"Go to hell." He turned his back on her.

As if that meant anything. "Dr. Volescu, the records show that you had twenty-three babies in your organ farm in Rotterdam."

He said nothing.

"But of course that's a lie."

Silence.

"And, oddly enough, I know that the lie is not your idea. Because I know that your installation was not an organ farm indeed, and that the reason you aren't dead is because you agreed to plead guilty to running an organ farm in exchange for never discussing what you were *really* doing there."

He slowly turned around again. Enough that he could look up and see her with a sidelong glance. "Let me see that clearance you tried to show me before."

She showed it to him again. He studied it.

"What do you know?" he asked.

"I know your real crime was continuing a research project after it was closed down. Because you had these fertilized eggs that had been meticulously altered. You had turned Anton's key. You wanted them to be born. You wanted to see who they would become."

"If you know all that, why have you come to me? Everything I knew is in the documents you must have read."

"Not at all," said Sister Carlotta. "I don't care about confessions. I don't care about logistics. I want to know about the babies."

"They're all dead," he said. "We killed them when we knew we were about to be discovered." He looked at her with bitter defiance. "Yes, infanticide. Twenty-three murders. But since the government couldn't admit that such children had ever existed, I was never charged with the crimes. God judges me, though. God will press the charges. Is that why you're here? Is that who gave you your clearance?"

You make jokes about this? "All I want to know is what you learned about them."

"I learned nothing, there was no time, they were still babies."

"You had them for almost a year. They developed. All the work done since Anton found his key was theoretical. *You* watched the babies grow."

A slow smile crept across his face. "This is like those Nazi medical crimes all over again. You deplore what I did, but you still want to know the results of my research."

"You monitored their growth. Their health. Their intellectual development."

"We were about to start the tracking of intellectual development. The project wasn't funded, of course, so it's not as if we could provide much more than a clean warm room and basic bodily needs."

"Their bodies, then. Their motor skills."

"Small," he said. "They are born small, they grow slowly. Undersized and underweight, all of them."

"But very bright?"

"Crawling very young. Making pre-speech sounds far earlier than normal. That's all we knew. I didn't see them often myself. I couldn't afford the risk of detection."

"So what was your prognosis?"

"Prognosis?"

"How did you see their future?"

"Dead. That's everyone's future. What are you talking about?"

"If they hadn't been slaughtered, Dr. Volescu, what would have happened?"

"They would have kept on growing, of course."

"And later?"

"There *is* no later. They keep on growing."

She thought for a moment, trying to process the information.

"That's right, Sister. You're getting it. They grow

slowly, but they never stop. That's what Anton's key does. Unlocks the mind because the brain never stops growing. But neither does anything else. The cranium keeps expanding—it's never fully closed. The arms and legs, longer and longer."

"So when they reach adult height . . ."

"There is no adult height. There's just height at time of death. You can't keep growing like that forever. There's a reason why evolution builds a stop-clock into the growth control of long-lived bodies. You can't keep growing without some organ giving out, eventually. Usually the heart."

The implications filled Sister Carlotta with dread. "And the rate of this growth? In the children, I mean? How long until they are at normal height for their age?"

"My guess was that they'd catch up twice," said Volescu. "Once just before puberty, and then the normal kids would leap ahead for a while, but slow and steady wins the race, n'est-ce pas? By twenty, they would be giants. And then they'd die, almost certainly before age twenty-five. Do you have any idea how huge they would be? So my killing them, you see—it was a mercy."

"I doubt any of them would have chosen to miss out on even the mere twenty years you took from them."

"They never knew what happened to them. I'm not a monster. We drugged them all. They died in their sleep and then the bodies were incinerated."

"What about puberty? Would they ever mature sexually?"

"That's the part we'll never know, isn't it?"

Sister Carlotta got up to go.

"He lived, didn't he?" asked Volescu.

"Who?"

"The one we lost. The one whose body wasn't with the others. I counted only twenty-two going into the fire."

"When you worship Moloch, Dr. Volescu, you get no answers but the ones your chosen god provides."

"Tell me what he's like." His eyes were so hungry.

"You know it was a boy?"

"They were all boys," said Volescu.

"What, did you discard the girls?"

"How do you think I got the genes I worked with? I implanted my own altered DNA into denucleated eggs."

"God help us, they were all your own twins?"

"I'm not the monster you think I am," said Volescu. "I brought the frozen embryos to life because I had to know what they would become. Killing them was my greatest sorrow."

"And yet you did it—to save yourself."

"I was afraid. And the thought came to me: They're only copies. It isn't murder to discard the copies."

"Their souls and lives were their own."

"Do you think the government would have let them live? Do you really think they would have survived? Any of them?"

"You don't deserve to have a son," said Sister Carlotta.

"But I have one, don't I?" He laughed. "While you, Miss Carlotta, perpetual bride of the invisible God, how many do *you* have?"

"They may have been copies, Volescu, but even dead they're worth more than the original."

He continued laughing as she walked down the corridor away from him, but it sounded forced. She knew his laughter was a mask for grief. But it wasn't the grief of compassion, or even of remorse. It was the grief of a damned soul.

Bean. God be thanked, she thought, that you do not know your father, and never will. You're nothing like him. You're far more human.

In the back of her mind, though, she had one nagging doubt. Was she sure Bean had more compassion, more humanity? Or was Bean as cold of heart as this man? As incapable of empathy? Was he all mind?

Then she thought of him growing and growing, from this too-tiny child to a giant whose body could no longer sustain life. This was the legacy your father gave you.

This was Anton's key. She thought of David's cry, when he learned of the death of his son. Absalom! Oh Absalom! Would God I could die for thee, Absalom, my son!

But he was not dead yet, was he? Volescu might have been lying, might simply be wrong. There might be some way to prevent it. And even if there was not, there were still many years ahead of Bean. And how he lived those years still mattered.

God raises up the children that he needs, and makes men and women of them, and then takes them from this world at his good pleasure. To him all of life is but a moment. All that matters is what that moment was used for. And Bean *would* use it well. She was sure of that.

Or at least she hoped it with such fervor that it felt like certainty.

12

Roster

"If Wiggin's the one, then let's get him to Eros."

"He's not ready for Command School yet. It's premature."

"Then we have to go with one of the alternates."

"That's your decision."

"*Our* decision! What do we have to go on but what you tell us?"

"I've told you about those older boys, too. You have the same data I have."

"Do we have all of it?"

"Do you *want* all of it?"

"Do we have the data on all the children with scores and evaluations at such a high level?"

"No."

"Why not?"

"Some of them are disqualified for various reasons."

"Disqualified by whom?"

"By me."

"On what grounds?"

"One of them is borderline insane, for instance. We're trying to find some structure in which his abilities will be useful. But he could not possibly bear the weight of complete command."

"That's one."

"Another is undergoing surgery to correct a physical defect."

"Is it a defect that limits his ability to command?"

"It limits his ability to be trained to command."

"But it's being fixed."

"He's about to have his third operation. If it works, he might amount to something. But, as you say, there won't be time."

"How many more children have you concealed from us?"

"I have *concealed* none of them. If you mean how many have I simply not referred to you as potential commanders, the answer is *all* of them. Except the ones whose names you already have."

"Let me be blunt. We hear rumors about a very young one."

"They're all young."

"We hear rumors about a child who makes the Wiggin boy look slow."

"They all have their different strengths."

"There are those who want you relieved of your command."

"If I'm not to be allowed to select and train these kids properly, I'd prefer to be relieved, sir. Consider this a request."

"So it was a stupid threat. Advance them all as quickly as you can. Just keep in mind that they need a certain amount of time in Command School, too. It does us no good to give them all your training if they don't have time to get ours."

Dimak met Graff in the battleroom control center. Graff conducted all his secure meetings here, until they could be sure Bean had grown enough that he couldn't get through the ducts. The battlerooms had their own separate air systems.

Graff had an essay on his desk display. "Have you read this? 'Problems in Campaigning Between Solar Systems Separated by Lightyears.' "

"It's been circulating pretty widely among the faculty."

"But it isn't signed," said Graff. "You don't happen to know who wrote it, do you?"

"No, sir. Did you write it?"

"I'm no scholar, Dimak, you know that. In fact, this was written by a student."

"At Command School?"

"A student here."

At that moment Dimak understood why he had been called in. "Bean."

"Six years old. The paper reads like a work of scholarship!"

"I should have guessed. He picks up the voice of the strategists he's been reading. Or their translators. Though I don't know what will happen now that he's he's been reading Frederick and Bulow in the original—French and German. He inhales languages and breathes them back out."

"What did you think of this paper?"

"You already know it's killing me to keep key information from this boy. If he can write *this* with what he knows, what would happen if we told him everything? Colonel Graff, why can't we promote him right out of Battle School, set him loose as a theorist, and then watch what he spits out?"

"Our job isn't to find theorists here. It's too late for theory anyway."

"I just think . . . look, a kid so small, who'd follow him? He's being wasted here. But when he writes, nobody knows how little he is. Nobody knows how young he is."

"I see your point, but we're not going to breach security, period."

"Isn't he already a grave security risk?"

"The mouse who scutters through the ducts?"

"No. I think he's grown too big for that. He doesn't do those side-arm pushups anymore. I thought the security risk came from the fact that he guessed that an offensive fleet had been launched generations ago, so why were we still training children for command?"

"From analysis of his papers, from his activities when he signs on as a teacher, we think he's got a theory and it's wonderfully wrong. But he believes his false theory *only* because he doesn't know about the ansible. Do you understand? Because that's the main thing we'd have to tell him about, isn't it?"

"Of course."

"So you see, that's the one thing we can't tell him."

"What is his theory?"

"That we're assembling children here in preparation for a war between nations, or between nations and the I.F. A landside war, back on Earth."

"Why would we take the kids into space to prepare for a war on Earth?"

"Think just a minute and you'll get it."

"Because . . . because when we've licked the Formics, there probably *will* be a little landside conflict. And all the talented commanders—the I.F. would already have them."

"You see? We can't have this kid publishing, not even within the I.F. Not everybody has given up loyalty to groups on Earth."

"So why did you call me in?"

"Because I *do* want to use him. We aren't running the war here, but we *are* running a school. Did you read his paper about the ineffectiveness of using officers as teachers?"

"Yes. I felt slapped."

"This time he's mostly wrong, because he has no way of knowing how nontraditional our recruitment of faculty has always been. But he may also be a little bit right.

Because our system of testing for officer potential was designed to produce candidates with the traits identified in the most highly regarded officers in the Second Invasion."

"Hi-ho."

"You see? Some of the highly regarded were officers who performed well in battle, but the war was too short to weed out the deadwood. The officers they tested included just the kind of people he criticized in his paper. So . . ."

"So he had the wrong reason, but the right result."

"Absolutely. It gives us little pricks like Bonzo Madrid. You've known officers like him, haven't you? So why should we be surprised that our tests give him command of an army even though he has no idea what to do with it. All the vanity and all the stupidity of Custer or Hooker or—hell, pick your own vain incompetent, it's the most common kind of general officer."

"May I quote you?"

"I'll deny it. The thing is, Bean has been studying the dossiers of all the other students. We think he's evaluating them for loyalty to their native identity group, and also for their excellence as commanders."

"By *his* standards of excellence."

"We need to get Ender the command of an army. We're under a lot of pressure to get our leading candidates into Command School. But if we bust one of the current commanders in order to make a place for Ender, it'll cause too much resentment."

"So you have to give him a new army."

"Dragon."

"There are still kids here who remember the last Dragon Army."

"Right. I like that. The jinx."

"I see. You want to give Ender a running start."

"It gets worse."

"I thought it would."

"We also aren't going to give him any soldiers that

aren't already on their commanders' transfer list."

"The dregs? What are you *doing* to this kid?"

"If we choose them, by our ordinary standards, then yes, the dregs. But we aren't going to choose Ender's army."

"Bean?"

"Our tests are worthless on this, right? Some of those dregs are the very best students, according to Bean, right? And he's been studying the launchies. So give him an assignment. Tell him to solve a hypothetical problem. Construct an army only out of launchies. Maybe the soldiers on the transfer lists, too."

"I don't think there's any way to do that without telling him that we're on to his fake teacher log-in."

"So tell him."

"Then he won't believe anything he found while searching."

"He didn't find anything," said Graff. "We didn't have to plant anything fake for him to find, because he had his false theory. See? So whether he thinks we planted stuff or not, he'll stay deceived and we're still secure."

"You seem to be counting on your understanding of his psychology."

"Sister Carlotta assures me that he differs from ordinary human DNA in only one small area."

"So now he's human again?"

"I've got to make decisions based on *something,* Dimak!"

"So the jury's still out on the human thing?"

"Get me a roster of the hypothetical army Bean would pick, so we can give it to Ender."

"He'll put himself in it, you know."

"He damn well better, or he's not as smart as we've been thinking."

"What about Ender? Is he ready?"

"Anderson thinks he is." Graff sighed. "To Bean, it's still just a game, because none of the weight has fallen on him yet. But Ender . . . I think he knows, deep down, where this is going to lead. I think he feels it already."

"Sir, just because you're feeling the weight doesn't mean he is."

Graff laughed. "You cut straight to the heart of things, don't you!"

"Bean's hungry for it, sir. If Ender isn't, then why not put the burden where it's wanted?"

"If Bean's hungry for it, it proves he's still too young. Besides, the hungry ones always have something to prove. Look at Napoleon. Look at Hitler. Bold at first, yes, but then *still* bold later on, when they need to cautious, to pull back. Patton. Caesar. Alexander. Always overreaching, never quite putting the finish on it. No, it's Ender, not Bean. Ender doesn't want to do it, so he won't have anything to prove."

"Are you sure you're not just picking the kind of commander you'd want to serve under?"

"That's precisely what I'm doing," said Graff. "Can you think of a better standard?"

"The thing is, you can't pass the buck on this one, can you? Can't say how it was the tests, you just followed the tests. The scores. Whatever."

"Can't run this like a machine."

"That's why you don't want Bean, isn't it? Because he was *made,* like a machine."

"I don't analyze myself. I analyze *them.*"

"So if we win, who really won the war? The commander you picked? Or you, for picking him?"

"The Triumvirate, for trusting me. After their fashion. But if we lose . . ."

"Well *then* it's definitely you."

"We're *all* dead then. What will they do? Kill me first? Or leave me till last so I can contemplate the consequences of my error?"

"Ender, though. I mean if he's the one. *He* won't say it's you. He'll take it all on himself. Not the credit for victory—just the blame for failure."

"Win or lose, the kid I pick is going to have a brutal time of it."

———

Bean got his summons during lunch. He reported at once to Dimak's quarters.

He found his teacher sitting at his desk, reading something. The light was set so that Bean couldn't read it through the dazzle.

"Have a seat," said Dimak.

Bean jumped up and sat on Dimak's bed, his legs dangling.

"Let me read you something," said Dimak. " 'There are no fortifications, no magazines, no strong points. . . . In the enemy solar system, there can be no living off the land, since access to habitable planets will be possible only after complete victory. . . . Supply lines are not a problem, since there are none to protect, but the cost of that is that all supplies and ordnance must be carried with the invading fleet. . . . In effect, all interstellar invasion fleets are suicide attacks, because time dilation means that even if a fleet returns intact, almost no one they knew will still be alive. They can never return, and so must be sure that their force is sufficient to be decisive and therefore is worth the sacrifice. . . . Mixed-sex forces allow the possibility of the army becoming a permanent colony and/or occupying force on the captured enemy planet."

Bean listened complacently. He had left it in his desk for them to find it, and they had done so.

"You wrote this, Bean, but you never submitted it to anybody."

"There was never an assignment that it fit."

"You don't seem surprised that we found it."

"I assume that you routinely scan our desks."

"Just as you routinely scan ours?"

Bean felt his stomach twist with fear. They knew.

"Cute, naming your false log-in 'Graff' with a caret in front of it."

Bean said nothing.

"You've been scanning all the other students' records. Why?"

"I wanted to know them. I've only made friends with a few."

"Close friends with none."

"I'm little and I'm smarter than they are. Nobody's standing in line."

"So you use their records to tell you more about them. Why do you feel the need to understand them?"

"Someday I'll be in command of one of these armies."

"Plenty of time to get to know your soldiers then."

"No sir," said Bean. "No time at all."

"Why do you say that?"

"Because of the way I've been promoted. And Wiggin. We're the two best students in this school, and we're being raced through. I'm not going to have much time when I get an army."

"Bean, be realistic. It's going to be a long time before anybody's going to be willing to follow you into battle."

Bean said nothing. He knew that this was false, even if Dimak didn't.

"Let's see just how good your analysis is. Let me give you an assignment."

"For which class?"

"No class, Bean. I want you to create a hypothetical army. Working only with launchies, construct an entire roster, the full complement of forty-one soldiers."

"*No* veterans?"

Bean meant the question neutrally, just checking to make sure he understood the rules. But Dimak seemed to take it as criticism of the unfairness of it. "No, tell you what, you can include veterans who are posted for transfer at their commanders' request. That'll give you some experienced ones."

The ones the commander couldn't work with. Some really were losers, but some were the opposite. "Fine," said Bean.

"How long do you think it will take you?"

Bean already had a dozen picked out. "I can tell the list to you right now."

"I want you to think about it seriously."

"I already have. But you need to answer a couple of questions first. You said forty-one soldiers, but that would include the commander."

"All right, forty, and leave the commander blank."

"I have another question. Am I to command the army?"

"You can write it up that way, if you want."

But Dimak's very unconcern told Bean that the army was not for him. "This army's for Wiggin, isn't it?"

Dimak glowered. "It's hypothetical."

"Definitely Wiggin," said Bean. "You can't boot somebody else out of command to make room for him, so you're giving Wiggin a whole new army. I bet it's Dragon."

Dimak looked stricken, though he tried to cover it.

"Don't worry," said Bean. "I'll give him the best army you can form, following those rules."

"I *said* this was hypothetical!"

"You think I wouldn't figure it out when I found myself in Wiggin's army and everybody else in it was also on my roster?"

"Nobody's said we're actually going to follow your roster!"

"You will. Because I'll be right and you'll know it," said Bean. "And I can promise you, it'll be a hell of an army. With Wiggin to train us, we'll kick ass."

"Just do the hypothetical assignment, and talk to no one about it. Ever."

That was dismissal, but Bean didn't want to be dismissed yet. They came to *him*. They were having *him* do their work. He wanted to have his say while they were still listening. "The reason this army can be so good is that your system's been promoting a lot of the wrong kids. About half the best kids in this school are launchies or on the transfer lists, because they're the ones who haven't already been beaten into submission by the kiss-ass idiots you put in command of armies or toons. These misfits and little kids are the ones who can win. Wiggin will figure that out. He'll know how to use us."

"Bean, you're not as smart about everything as you think you are!"

"Yes I am, sir," said Bean. "Or you wouldn't have given this assignment to me. May I be dismissed? Or do you want me to tell you the roster now?"

"Dismissed," said Dimak.

I probably shouldn't have provoked him, thought Bean. Now it's possible that he'll fiddle with my roster just to prove he can. But that's not the kind of man he is. If I'm not right about that, then I'm not right about anybody else, either.

Besides, it felt good to speak the truth to someone in power.

———

After working with the list a little while, Bean was just as glad that Dimak hadn't taken him up on his foolish offer to make up the roster on the spot. Because it wasn't just a matter of naming the forty best soldiers among the launchies and the transfer lists.

Wiggin was way early for command, and that would make it harder for older kids to take it—getting put into a kid's army. So he struck off the list all who were older than Wiggin.

That left him with nearly sixty kids who were good enough to be in the army. Bean was ranking them in order of value when he realized that he was about to make another mistake. Quite a few of these kids were in the group of launchies and soldiers that practiced with Wiggin during free time. Wiggin would know these kids best, and naturally he'd look to them to be his toon leaders. The core of his army.

The trouble was, while a couple of them would do fine as toon leaders, relying on that group would mean passing over several who weren't part of that group. Including Bean.

So he doesn't choose me to lead a toon. He isn't going to choose me anyway, right? I'm too little. He won't look at me and see a leader.

Is this just about me, then? Am I corrupting this process just to get myself a chance to show what I can do?

And if I am, what's wrong with that? I know what I can do, and no one else really gets it. The teachers think I'm a scholar, they know I'm smart, they trust my judgment, but they aren't making this army for me, they're making it for him. I still have to prove to them what I can do. And if I really am one of the best, it would be to the benefit of the program to have it revealed as quickly as possible.

And then he thought: Is this how idiots rationalize their stupidity to themselves?

"Ho, Bean," said Nikolai.

"Ho," said Bean. He passed a hand across his desk, blanking the display. "Tell me."

"Nothing to tell. *You* looked grim."

"Just doing an assignment."

Nikolai laughed. "You never look that serious doing classwork. You just read for a while and then you type for a while. Like it was nothing. This is something."

"An extra assignment."

"A hard one, neh?"

"Not very."

"Sorry to break in. Just thought maybe something was wrong. Maybe a letter from home."

They both laughed at that. Letters weren't that common here. Every few months at the most. And the letters were pretty empty when they came. Some never got mail at all. Bean was one of them, and Nikolai knew why. It wasn't a secret, he was just the only one who noticed and the only one who asked about it. "No family at *all?*" he had said. "Some kids' families, maybe I'm the lucky one," Bean answered him, and Nikolai agreed. "But not mine.

I wish you had parents like mine." And then he went on about how he was an only child, but his parents really worked hard to get him. "They did it with surgery, fertilized five or six eggs, then twinned the healthiest ones a few more times, and finally they picked me. I grew up like I was going to be king or the Dalai Lama or something. And then one day the I.F. says, we need him. Hardest thing my parents ever did, saying yes. But I said, What if I'm the next Mazer Rackham? And they let me go."

That was months ago, but it was still between them, that conversation. Kids didn't talk much about home. Nikolai didn't discuss his family with anybody else, either. Just with Bean. And in return, Bean told him a little about life on the street. Not a lot of details, because it would sound like he was asking for pity or trying to look cool. But he mentioned how they were organized into a family. Talked about how it was Poke's crew, and then it became Achilles' family, and how they got into a charity kitchen. Then Bean waited to see how much of this story started circulating.

None of it did. Nikolai never said a word about it to anyone else. That was when Bean was sure that Nikolai was worth having as a friend. He could keep things to himself without even having to be asked to do it.

And now here Bean was, making up the roster for this great army, and here sat Nikolai, asking him what he was doing. Dimak had said to tell no one, but Nikolai could keep a secret. What harm could it do?

Then Bean recovered his senses. Knowing about this wouldn't help Nikolai in any way. Either he'd be in Dragon Army or he wouldn't. If he wasn't, he'd know Bean hadn't put him there. If he was, it would be worse, because he'd wonder if Bean had included him in the roster out of friendship instead of excellence.

Besides, Nikolai shouldn't be in Dragon Army. Bean liked him and trusted him, but Nikolai was not among the best of the launchies. He was smart, he was quick, he was good—but he was nothing special.

Except to me, thought Bean.

"It was a letter from *your* parents," said Bean. "They've stopped writing to you, they like me better."

"Yeah, and the Vatican is moving to Mecca."

"And I'm going to be made Polemarch."

"No jeito," said Nikolai. "You too tall, bicho." Nikolai picked up his desk. "I can't help you with your classwork tonight, Bean, so please don't beg me." He lay back on his bed, started into the fantasy game.

Bean lay back, too. He woke up his display and began wrestling with the names again. If he eliminated every one of the kids who'd been practicing with Wiggin, how many of the good ones would it leave? Fifteen veterans from the transfer lists. Twenty-two launchies, including Bean.

Why *hadn't* these launchies taken part in Wiggin's free-time practices? The veterans, they were already in trouble with their commanders, they weren't about to antagonize them any more, so it made sense for them not to have taken part. But these launchies, weren't they ambitious? Or were they bookish, trying to do it all through classwork instead of catching on that the battleroom was everything? Bean couldn't fault them for that—it had taken him a while to catch on, too. Were they so confident of their own abilities they didn't think they needed the extra prep? Or so arrogant they didn't want anybody to think they owed their success to Ender Wiggin? Or so shy they . . .

No. He couldn't possibly guess their motives. They were all too complex anyway. They were smart, with good evaluations—good by Bean's standards, not necessarily by the teachers'. That was all he needed to know. If he gave Wiggin an army without a single kid he'd worked with in practices, then all the army would start out equal in his eyes. Which meant Bean would have the same chance as any other kid to earn Wiggin's eye and maybe get command of a toon. If they couldn't compete with Bean for that position, then too damn bad for them.

But that left him with thirty-seven names on the roster. Three more slots to fill.

He went back and forth on a couple. Finally decided to include Crazy Tom, a veteran who held the unenviable record of being the most-transferred soldier in the history of the game who wasn't actually iced and sent home. So far. The thing was, Crazy Tom really was good. Sharp mind. But he couldn't stand it when somebody above him was stupid and unfair. And when he got pissed, he really went off. Ranting, throwing things, tearing bedding off every bed in his barracks once, another time writing a message about what an idiot his commander was and mailing it to every other student in the school. A few actually got it before the teachers intercepted it, and they said it was the hottest thing they ever read. Crazy Tom. Could be disruptive. But maybe he was just waiting for the right commander. He was in.

And a girl, Wu, which of course had become Woo and even Woo-*hoo*. Brilliant at her studies, absolutely a killer in the arcade games, but she refused to be a toon leader and as soon as her commanders asked her, she put in for a transfer and refused to fight until they gave it to her. Weird. Bean had no idea why she did that—the teachers were baffled, too. Nothing in her tests to show why. What the hell, thought Bean. She's in.

Last slot.

He typed in Nikolai's name.

Am I doing him a favor? He's not bad, he's just a little slower than these kids, just a little gentler. It'll be hard for him. And if he's left out of it, he won't mind. He'll just do his best with whatever army he gets sent to eventually.

And yet . . . Dragon Army is going to be a legend. Not just here in Battle School, either. These kids are going to go on to be leaders in the I.F. Or somewhere, anyway. And they'll tell stories about when they were in Dragon Army with the great Ender Wiggin. And if I include Nikolai, then even if he isn't the best of the soldiers, even if he's in fact the slowest, he'll still be *in*, he'll still be able to tell those stories someday. And he's not bad. He won't embarrass himself. He won't bring down the army. He'll do OK. So why not?

And I want him with me. He's the only one I've ever talked to. About personal things. The only one who knows the name of Poke. I want him. And there's a slot on the roster.

Bean went down the list one more time. Then he alphabetized it and mailed it to Dimak.

———

The next morning, Bean, Nikolai, and three other kids in their launch group had their assignment to Dragon Army. Months before they should have been promoted to soldiers. The unchosen kids were envious, hurt, furious by turn. Especially when they realized Bean was one of the chosen. "Do they *make* uniform flash suits that size?"

It was a good question. And the answer was no, they didn't. The colors of Dragon Army were grey, orange, grey. Because soldiers were usually a lot older than Bean when they came in, they had to cut a flash suit down for Bean, and they didn't do it all that well. Flash suits weren't manufactured in space, and nobody had the tools to do a first-rate job of alteration.

When they finally got it to fit him, Bean wore his flash suit to the Dragon Army barracks. Because it had taken him so long to be fitted, he was the last to arrive. Wiggin arrived at the door just as Bean was entering. "Go ahead," said Wiggin.

It was the first time Wiggin had ever spoken to him—for all Bean knew, the first time Wiggin had even noticed him. So thoroughly had Bean concealed his fascination with Wiggin that he had made himself effectively invisible.

Wiggin followed him into the room. Bean started down the corridor between the bunks, heading for the back of the room where the younger soldiers always had to sleep. He glanced at the other kids, who were all looking at him as he passed with a mixture of horror and amusement.

They were in an army so lame that *this* little tiny kid was part of it?

Behind him, Wiggin was starting his first speech. Voice confident, loud enough but not shouting, not nervous. "I'm Ender Wiggin. I'm your commander. Bunking will be arranged by seniority."

Some of the launchies groaned.

"Veterans to the back of the room, newest soldiers to the front."

The groaning stopped. That was the opposite of the way things were usually arranged. Wiggin was already shaking things up. Whenever he came into the barracks, the kids closest to him would be the new ones. Instead of getting lost in the shuffle, they'd always have his attention.

Bean turned around and headed back to the front of the room. He was still the youngest kid in Battle School, but five of the soldiers were from more recently arrived launch groups, so they got the positions nearest the door. Bean got an upper bunk directly across from Nikolai, who had the same seniority, being from the same launch group.

Bean clambered up onto his bed, hampered by his flash suit, and put his palm beside the locker. Nothing happened.

"Those of you who are in an army for the first time," said Wiggin, "just pull the locker open by hand. No locks. Nothing private here."

Laboriously Bean pulled off his flash suit to stow it in his locker.

Wiggin walked along between the bunks, making sure that seniority was respected. Then he jogged to the front of the room. "All right, everybody. Put on your flash suits and come to practice."

Bean looked at him in complete exasperation. Wiggin had been looking right at him when he started taking off his flash suit. Why didn't he suggest that Bean not take the damn thing off?

"We're on the morning schedule," Wiggin continued. "Straight to practice after breakfast. Officially you have a free hour between breakfast and practice. We'll see what happens after I find out how good you are."

Truth was, Bean felt like an idiot. Of course Wiggin would head for practice immediately. He shouldn't have needed a warning not to take the suit off. He should have *known*.

He tossed his suit pieces onto the floor and slid down the frame of the bunk. A lot of the other kids were talking, flipping clothes at each other, playing with their weapons. Bean tried to put on the cut-down suit, but couldn't figure out some of the jury-rigged fastenings. He had to take off several pieces and examine them to see how they fit, and finally gave up, took it all off, and started assembling it on the floor.

Wiggin, unconcerned, glanced at his watch. Apparently three minutes was his deadline. "All right, everybody out, now! On your way!"

"But I'm naked!" said one boy—Anwar, from Ecuador, child of Egyptian immigrants. His dossier ran through Bean's mind.

"Dress faster next time," said Wiggin.

Bean was naked, too. Furthermore, Wiggin was standing right there, watching him struggle with his suit. He could have helped. He could have waited. What am I getting myself in for?

"Three minutes from first call to running out the door—that's the rule this week," said Wiggin. "Next week the rule is two minutes. Move!"

Out in the corridor, kids who were in the midst of free time or were heading for class stopped to watch the parade of the unfamiliar uniforms of Dragon Army. And to mock the ones that were even more unusual.

One thing for sure. Bean was going to have to practice getting dressed in his cut-down suit if he was going to avoid running naked through the corridors. And if Wiggin didn't make any exceptions for him the first day, when he'd only just got his nonregulation flash suit, Bean certainly was *not* going to ask for special favors.

I chose to put myself in this army, Bean reminded himself as he jogged along, trying to keep pieces of his flash suit from spilling out of his arms.

Part Four

SOLDIER

13

Dragon Army

"I need access to Bean's genetic information," said Sister Carlotta.

"That's not for you," said Graff.

"And here I thought my clearance level would open *any* door."

"We invented a special new category of security, called 'Not for Sister Carlotta.' We don't want you sharing Bean's genetic information with anyone else. And you were already planning on putting it in other hands, weren't you?"

"Only to perform a test. So . . . you'll have to perform it for me. I want a comparison between Bean's DNA and Volescu's."

"I thought you told me Volescu was the source of the cloned DNA."

"I've been thinking about it since I told you that, Colonel Graff, and you know what? Bean doesn't look anything like Volescu. I couldn't see how he could possibly grow up to be like him, either."

"Maybe the difference in growth patterns makes him look different, too."

"Maybe. But it's also possible Volescu is lying. He's a vain man."

"Lying about everything?"

"Lying about anything. About paternity, quite possibly. And if he's lying about that—"

"Then maybe Bean's prognosis isn't so bleak? Don't you think we've already checked with our genetics people? Volescu wasn't lying about that, anyway. Anton's key will probably behave just the way he described."

"Please. Run the test and tell me the results."

"Because you don't want Bean to be Volescu's son."

"I don't want Bean to be Volescu's twin. And neither, I think, do you."

"Good point. Though I must tell you, the boy does have a vain streak."

"When you're as gifted as Bean, accurate self-assessment looks like vanity to other people."

"Yeah, but he doesn't have to rub it in, does he?"

"Uh-oh. Has someone's ego been hurt?"

"Not mine. Yet. But one of his teachers is feeling a little bruised."

"I notice you aren't telling me I faked his scores anymore."

"Yes, Sister Carlotta, you were right all along. He deserves to be here. And so does . . . Well, let's just say you hit the jackpot after all those years of searching."

"It's humanity's jackpot."

"I said he was worth bringing up here, not that he was the one who'll lead us to victory. The wheel's still spinning on that one. And my money's on another number."

Going up the ladderways while holding a flash suit wasn't practical, so Wiggin made the ones who were dressed run up and down the corridor, working up a sweat, while Bean and the other naked or partially-dressed kids got their suits on. Nikolai helped Bean get his suit fastened; it humiliated Bean to need help, but it would have been worse to be the last one finished—the pesky little teeny brat who slows everyone down. With Nikolai's help, he was not the last one done.

"Thanks."

"No ojjikay."

Moments later, they were streaming up the ladders to the battleroom level. Wiggin took them all the way to the upper door, the one that opened out into the middle of the battleroom wall. The one used for entering when it was an actual battle. There were handholds on the sides, the ceiling, and the floor, so students could swing out and hurl themselves into the null-G environment. The story was that gravity was lower in the battleroom because it was closer to the center of the station, but Bean had already realized that was bogus. There would still be some centrifugal force at the doors and a pronounced Coriolis effect. Instead, the battlerooms were completely null. To Bean, that meant that the I.F. had a device that would either block gravitation or, more likely, produce false gravity that was perfectly balanced to counter Coriolis and centrifugal forces in the battleroom, starting exactly at the door. It was a stunning technology—and it was never discussed inside the I.F., at least not in the literature available to students in Battle School, and completely unknown outside.

Wiggin assembled them in four files along the corridor and ordered them to jump up and use the ceiling handholds to fling their bodies into the room. "Assemble on the far wall, as if you were going for the enemy's gate." To the veterans that meant something. To the launchies, who had never been in a battle and had never, for that matter, entered through the upper door, it meant nothing at all. "Run up and go four at a time when I open the gate, one group per second." Wiggin walked to the back of the group and, using his hook, a controller strapped to the inside of his wrist and curved to conform to his left hand, he made the door, which had seemed quite solid, disappear.

"Go!" The first four kids started running for the gate. "Go!" The next group began to run before the first had even reached it. There would be no hesitation or somebody would crash into you from behind. "Go!" The first group grabbed and swung with varying degrees of clumsiness and heading out in various directions. "Go!" Later groups learned, or tried to, from the awkwardness of the earlier ones. "Go!"

Bean was at the end of the line, in the last group. Wiggin laid a hand on his shoulder. "You can use a side hand-hold if you want."

Right, thought Bean. *Now* you decide to baby me. Not because my meshugga flash suit didn't fit together right, but just because I'm short. "Go suck on it," said Bean.

"Go!"

Bean kept pace with the other three, though it meant pumping his legs half again as fast, and when he got near the gate he took a flying leap, tapped the ceiling handhold with his fingers as he passed, and sailed out into the room with no control at all, spinning in three nauseating directions at once.

But he didn't expect himself to do any better, and instead of fighting the spin, he calmed himself and did his anti-nausea routine, relaxing himself until he neared a wall and had to prepare for impact. He didn't land near one of the recessed handholds and wasn't facing the right way to grab anything even if he had. So he rebounded, but this time was a little more stable as he flew, and he ended up on the ceiling very near the back wall. It took him less time than some to make his way down to where the others were assembling, lined up along the floor under the middle gate on the back wall—the enemy gate.

Wiggin sailed calmly through the air. Because he had a hook, during practice he could maneuver in midair in ways that soldiers couldn't; during battle, though, the hook would be useless, so commanders had to make sure they didn't become dependent on the hook's added control. Bean noted approvingly that Wiggin seemed not to use the hook at all. He sailed in sideways, snagged a handhold on the floor about ten paces out from the back wall, and hung in the air. Upside down.

Fixing his gaze on one of them, Wiggin demanded, "Why are you upside down, soldier?"

Immediately some of the other soldiers started to turn themselves upside down like Wiggin.

"Attention!" Wiggin barked. All movement stopped. "I said why are you upside down!"

Bean was surprised that the soldier didn't answer. Had he forgotten what the teacher did in the shuttle on the way here? The deliberate disorientation? Or was that something that only Dimak did?

"I said why does every one of you have his feet in the air and his head toward the ground!"

Wiggin didn't look at Bean in particular, and this was one question Bean didn't want to answer. There was no assurance of which particular correct answer Wiggin was looking for, so why open his mouth just to get shut down?

It was a kid named Shame—short for Seamus—who finally spoke up. "Sir, this is the direction we were in coming out of the door." Good job, thought Bean. Better than some lame argument that there was no up or down in null-G.

"Well what difference is that supposed to make! What difference does it make what the gravity was back in the corridor! Are we going to fight in the corridor? Is there any gravity here?"

No sir, they all murmured.

"From now on, you forget about gravity before you go through that door. The old gravity is gone, erased. Understand me? Whatever your gravity is when you get to the door, remember—the enemy's gate is *down*. Your feet are toward the enemy gate. Up is toward your own gate. North is that way"—he pointed toward what had been the

ceiling—"south is that way, east is that way, west is—
what way?"

They pointed.

"That's what I expected," said Wiggin. "The only process you've mastered is the process of elimination, and
the only reason you've mastered that is because you can
do it in the toilet."

Bean watched, amused. So Wiggin subscribed to the
you're-so-stupid-you-need-me-to-wipe-your-butts school
of basic training. Well, maybe that was necessary. One of
the rituals of training. Boring till it was over, but . . . commander's choice.

Wiggin glanced at Bean, but his eyes kept moving.

"What was the circus I saw out here! Did you call that
forming up? Did you call that flying? Now everybody,
launch and form up on the ceiling! Right now! Move!"

Bean knew what the trap was and launched for the wall
they had just entered through before Wiggin had even
finished talking. Most of the others also got what the test
was, but a fair number of them launched the wrong way—
toward the direction Wiggin had called *north* instead of
the direction he had identified as *up*. This time Bean happened to arrive near a handhold, and he caught it with
surprising ease. He had done it before in his launch
group's battleroom practices, but he was small enough
that, unlike the others, it was quite possible for him to
land in a place that had no handhold within reach. Short
arms were a definite drawback in the battleroom. On short
bounds he could aim at a handhold and get there with
some accuracy. On a cross-room jump there was little
hope of that. So it felt good that this time, at least, he
didn't look like an oaf. In fact, having launched first, he
arrived first.

Bean turned around and watched as the ones who had
blown it made the long, embarrassing second leap to join
the rest of the army. He was a little surprised at who some
of the bozos were. Inattention can make clowns of us all,
he thought.

Wiggin was watching him again, and this time it was no passing glance.

"You!" Wiggin pointed at him. "Which way is down?"

Didn't we just cover this? "Toward the enemy door."

"Name, kid?"

Come on, Wiggin really didn't know who the short kid with the highest scores in the whole damn school was? Well, if we're playing mean sergeant and hapless recruit, I better follow the script. "This soldier's name is Bean, sir."

"Get that for size or for brains?"

Some of the other soldiers laughed. But not many of them. *They* knew Bean's reputation. To them it was no longer funny that he was so small—it was just embarrassing that a kid that small could make perfect scores on tests that had questions they didn't even understand.

"Well, Bean, you're right onto things." Wiggin now included the whole group as he launched into a lecture on how coming through the door feet first made you a much smaller target for the enemy to shoot at. Harder for him to hit you and freeze you. "Now, what happens when you're frozen?"

"Can't move," somebody said.

"That's what frozen *means*," said Wiggin. "But what *happens* to you?"

Wiggin wasn't phrasing his question very clearly, in Bean's opinion, and there was no use in prolonging the agony while the others figured it out. So Bean spoke up. "You keep going in the direction you started in. At the speed you were going when you were flashed."

"That's true," said Wiggin. "You five, there on the end, move!" He pointed at five soldiers, who spent long enough looking at each other to make sure which five he meant that Wiggin had time to flash them all, freezing them in place. During practice, it took a few minutes for a freeze to wear off, unless the commander used his hook to unfreeze them earlier.

"The next five, move!"

Seven kids moved at once—no time to count. Wiggin flashed them as quickly as he flashed the others, but because they had already launched, they kept moving at a good clip toward the walls they had headed for.

The first five were hovering in the air near where they had been frozen.

"Look at these so-called soldiers. Their commander ordered them to move, and now look at them. Not only are they frozen, they're frozen right here, where they can get in the way. While the others, because they moved when they were ordered, are frozen down there, plugging up the enemy's lanes, blocking the enemy's vision. I imagine that about five of you have understood the point of this."

We all understand it, Wiggin. It's not like they bring stupid people up here to Battle School. It's not like I didn't pick you the best available army.

"And no doubt Bean is one of them. Right, Bean?"

Bean could hardly believe that Wiggin was singling him out *again*.

Just because I'm little, he's using me to embarrass the others. The little guy knows the answers, so why don't you big boys.

But then, Wiggin doesn't realize yet. He thinks he has an army of incompetent launchies and rejects. He hasn't had a chance to see that he actually has a select group. So he thinks of me as the most ludicrous of a sad lot. He's found out I'm not an idiot, but he still assumes the others are.

Wiggin was still looking at him. Oh, yeah, he had asked a question. "Right, sir," said Bean.

"Then what is the point?"

Spit back to him exactly what he just said to us. "When you are ordered to move, move fast, so if you get iced you'll bounce around instead of getting in the way of your own army's operations."

"Excellent. At least I have one soldier who can figure things out."

Bean was disgusted. This was the commander who was

supposed to turn Dragon into a legendary army? Wiggin was supposed to be the alpha and omega of the Battle School, and he's playing the game of singling me out to be the goat. Wiggin didn't even find out our scores, didn't discuss his soldiers with the teachers. If he did, he'd already know that I'm the smartest kid in the school. The others all know it. That's why they're looking at each other in embarrassment. Wiggin is revealing his own ignorance.

Bean saw how Wiggin seemed to be registering the distaste of his own soldiers. It was just an eyeblink, but maybe Wiggin finally got it that his make-fun-of-the-shrimp ploy was backfiring. Because he finally got on with the business of training. He taught them how to kneel in midair—even flashing their own legs to lock them in place—and then fire between their knees as they moved downward toward the enemy, so that their legs became a shield, absorbing fire and allowing them to shoot for longer periods of time out in the open. A good tactic, and Bean finally began to get some idea of why Wiggin might not be a disastrous commander after all. He could sense the others giving respect to their new commander at last.

When they'd got the point, Wiggin thawed himself and all the soldiers he had frozen in the demonstration. "Now," he said, "which way is the enemy's gate?"

"Down!" they all answered.

"And what is our attack position?"

Oh, right, thought Bean, like we can all give an explanation in unison. The only way to answer was to demonstrate—so Bean flipped himself away from the wall, heading for the other side, firing between his knees as he went. He didn't do it perfectly—there was a little rotation as he went—but all in all, he did OK for his first actual attempt at the maneuver.

Above him, he heard Wiggin shout at the others. "Is Bean the only one who knows how?"

By the time Bean had caught himself on the far wall, the whole rest of the army was coming after him, shouting as if they were on the attack. Only Wiggin remained at the ceiling. Bean noticed, with amusement, that Wiggin was standing there oriented the same way he had been in the corridor—his head "north," the old "up." He might have the theory down pat, but in practice, it's hard to shake off the old gravity-based thinking. Bean had made it a point to orient himself sideways, his head to the west. And the soldiers near him did the same, taking their orientation from him. If Wiggin noticed, he gave no sign.

"Now come back at me, all of you, attack *me!*"

Immediately his flash suit lit up with forty weapons firing at him as his entire army converged on him, firing all the way. "Ouch," said Wiggin when they arrived. "You got me."

Most of them laughed.

"Now, what are your legs good for, in combat?"

Nothing, said some boys.

"Bean doesn't think so," said Wiggin.

So he isn't going to let up on me even now. Well, what does he want to hear? Somebody else muttered "shields," but Wiggin didn't key in on that, so he must have something else in mind. "They're the best way to push off walls," Bean guessed.

"Right," said Wiggin.

"Come on, pushing off is movement, not combat," said Crazy Tom. A few others murmured their agreement.

Oh good, now it starts, thought Bean. Crazy Tom picks a meaningless quarrel with his commander, who gets pissed off at him and . . .

But Wiggin didn't take umbrage at Crazy Tom's correction. He just corrected him back, mildly. "There *is* no combat without movement. Now, with your legs frozen like this, can you push off walls?"

Bean had no idea. Neither did anyone else.

"Bean?" asked Wiggin. Of course.

"I've never tried it," said Bean, "but maybe if you faced the wall and doubled over at the waist—"

"Right but wrong. Watch me. My back's to the wall,

legs are frozen. Since I'm kneeling, my feet are against the wall. Usually, when you push off you have to push downward, so you string out your body behind you like a string *bean,* right?"

The group laughed. For the first time, Bean realized that maybe Wiggin wasn't being stupid to get the whole group laughing at the little guy. Maybe Wiggin knew perfectly well that Bean was the smartest kid, and had singled him out like this because he could tap into all the resentment the others felt for him. This whole session was guaranteeing that the other kids would all think it was OK to laugh at Bean, to despise him even though he was smart.

Great system, Wiggin. Destroy the effectiveness of your best soldier, make sure he gets no respect.

However, it was more important to learn what Wiggin was teaching than to feel sullen about the way he was teaching it. So Bean watched intently as Wiggin demonstrated a frozen-leg takeoff from the wall. He noticed that Wiggin gave himself a deliberate spin. It would make it harder for him to shoot as he flew, but it would also make it very hard for a distant enemy to focus enough light on any part of him for long enough to get a kill.

I may be pissed off, but that doesn't mean I can't learn.

It was a long and grueling practice, drilling over and over again on new skills. Bean saw that Wiggin wasn't willing to let them learn each technique separately. They had to do them all at once, integrating them into smooth, continuous movements. Like dancing, Bean thought. You don't learn to shoot and then learn to launch and then learn to do a controlled spin—you learn to launch-shoot-spin.

At the end, all of them dripping with sweat, exhausted, and flushed with the excitement of having learned stuff that they'd never heard of other soldiers doing, Wiggin assembled them at the lower door and announced that they'd have another practice during free time. "And don't tell me that free time is supposed to be free. I know that, and you're perfectly free to do what you want. I'm *invit-*

ing you to come to an extra, *voluntary* practice."

They laughed. This group consisted entirely of kids who had *not* chosen to do extra battleroom practice with Wiggin before, and he was making sure they understood that he expected them to change their priorities now. But they didn't mind. After this morning they knew that when Wiggin ran a practice, every second was effective. They couldn't afford to miss a practice or they'd fall significantly behind. Wiggin would get their free time. Even Crazy Tom wasn't arguing about it.

But Bean knew that he had to change his relationship with Wiggin right now, or there was no chance that he would get a chance for leadership. What Wiggin had done to him in today's practice, feeding on the resentment of the other kids for this little pipsqueak, would make it even less plausible for Bean to be made a leader within the army—if the other kids despised him, who would follow him?

So Bean waited for Wiggin in the corridor after the others had gone on ahead.

"Ho, Bean," said Wiggin.

"Ho, Ender," said Bean. Did Wiggin catch the sarcasm in the way Bean said his name? Was that why he paused a moment before answering?

"*Sir*," said Wiggin softly.

Oh, cut out the merda, I've seen those vids, we all *laugh* at those vids. "I know what you're doing, *Ender,* sir, and I'm warning you."

"Warning me?"

"I can be the best man you've got, but don't play games with me."

"Or what?"

"Or I'll be the worst man you've got. One or the other." Not that Bean expected Wiggin to understand what he meant by that. How Bean could only be effective if he had Wiggin's trust and respect, how otherwise he'd just be the little kid, useful for nothing. Wiggin would probably take it to mean that Bean meant to cause trouble if

Wiggin didn't use him. And maybe he did mean that, a little.

"And what do you want?" asked Wiggin. "Love and kisses?"

Say it flat out, put it in his mind so plainly he can't pretend not to understand. "I want a toon."

Wiggin walked close to Bean, looked down at him. To Bean, though, it was a good sign that Wiggin hadn't just laughed. "Why should you get a toon?"

"Because I'd know what to do with it."

"Knowing what to do with a toon is easy. It's getting them to do it that's hard. Why should any soldier want to follow a little pinprick like you?"

Wiggin had got straight to the crux of the problem. But Bean didn't like the malicious way he said it. "They used to call *you* that, I hear. I hear Bonzo Madrid still does."

Wiggin wasn't taking the bait. "I asked you a question, soldier."

"I'll earn their respect, sir, if you don't stop me."

To his surprise, Wiggin grinned. "I'm helping you."

"Like hell."

"Nobody would notice you, except to feel sorry for the little kid. But I made sure they *all* noticed you today."

You should have done your research, Wiggin. You're the only one who didn't know already who I was.

"They'll be watching every move you make," said Wiggin. "All you have to do to earn their respect now is be perfect."

"So I don't even get a chance to learn before I'm being judged." That's not how you bring along talent.

"Poor kid. Nobody's treatin' him fair."

Wiggin's deliberate obtuseness infuriated Bean. You're smarter than this, Wiggin!

Seeing Bean's rage, Wiggin brought a hand forward and pushed him until his back rested firmly against the wall. "I'll tell you how to get a toon. Prove to me you know what you're doing as a soldier. Prove to me you know how to use other soldiers. And then prove to me that somebody's willing to follow you into battle. Then you'll get your toon. But not bloody well until."

Bean ignored the hand pressing against him. It would take a lot more than that to intimidate him physically. "That's fair," he said. "*If* you actually work that way, I'll be a toon leader in a month."

Now it was Wiggin's turn to be angry. He reached down, grabbed Bean by the front of his flash suit, and slid him up the wall so they stood there eye to eye. "When I say I work a certain way, Bean, then that's the way I work."

Bean just grinned at him. In this low gravity, so high in the station, picking up little kids wasn't any big test of strength. And Wiggin was no bully. There was no serious threat here.

Wiggin let go of him. Bean slid down the wall and landed gently on his feet, rebounded slightly, settled again. Wiggin walked to the pole and slid down. Bean had won this encounter by getting under Wiggin's skin. Besides, Wiggin knew he hadn't handled this situation very well. He wouldn't forget. In fact, it was Wiggin who had lost a little respect, and he knew it, and he'd be trying to earn it back.

Unlike you, Wiggin, I *do* give the other guy a chance to learn what he's doing before I insist on perfection. You screwed up with me today, but I'll give you a chance to do better tomorrow and the next day.

But when Bean got to the pole and reached out to take hold, he realized his hands were trembling and his grip was too weak. He had to pause a moment, leaning on the pole, till he had calmed enough.

That face-to-face encounter with Wiggin, he hadn't won that. It might even have been a stupid thing to do. Wiggin *had* hurt him with those snide comments, that ridicule. Bean had been studying Wiggin as the subject of his private theology, and today he had found out that all this time Wiggin didn't even know Bean existed. Everybody compared Bean to Wiggin—but apparently Wiggin

hadn't heard or didn't care. He had treated Bean like nothing. And after having worked so hard this past year to
earn respect, Bean didn't find it easy to be nothing again.
It brought back feelings he thought he left behind in Rotterdam. The sick fear of imminent death. Even though he
knew that no one here would raise a hand against him, he
still remembered being on the edge of dying when he first
went up to Poke and put his life in her hands.

Is that what I've done, once again? By putting myself
on this roster, I gave my future into this boy's hands. I
counted on him seeing in me what I see. But of course
he couldn't. I have to give him time.

If there *was* time. For the teachers were moving quickly
now, and Bean might not *have* a year in this army to prove
himself to Wiggin.

14

Brothers

"You have results for me?"

"Interesting ones. Volescu *was* lying. Somewhat."

"I hope you're going to be more precise than that."

"Bean's genetic alteration was not based on a clone of Volescu. But they *are* related. Volescu is definitely not Bean's father. But he is almost certainly Volescu's half-uncle or a double cousin. I hope Volescu has a half-brother or double first cousin, because such a man is the only possible father of the fertilized egg that Volescu altered."

"You have a list of Volescu's relatives, I assume?"

"We didn't need any family at the trial. And Volescu's mother was not married. He uses her name."

"So Volescu's father had another child somewhere only you don't even know his name. I thought you knew everything."

"We know everything that we knew was worth knowing. That's a crucial distinction. We simply haven't looked for Volescu's father. He's not guilty of anything important. We can't investigate everybody."

"Another matter. Since you know everything that you know is worth knowing, perhaps you can tell me why a certain crippled boy has been removed from the school where I placed him?"

"Oh. Him. When you suddenly stopped touting him, we got suspicious. So we checked him out. Tested him. He's no Bean, but he definitely belongs here."

"And it never crossed your mind that I had good reason for keeping him out of Battle School?"

"We assumed that you thought that we might choose Achilles over Bean, who was, after all, far too young, so you offered only your favorite."

"You assumed. I've been dealing with you as if you were intelligent, and you've been dealing with me as if I were an idiot. Now I see it should have been the exact reverse."

"I didn't know Christians got so angry."

"Is Achilles already in Battle School?"

"He's still recovering from his fourth surgery. We had to fix the leg on Earth."

"Let me give you a word of advice. Do *not* put him in Battle School while Bean is still there."

"Bean is only six. He's still too young to *enter* Battle School, let alone graduate."

"If you put Achilles in, take Bean out. Period."

"Why?"

"If you're too stupid to believe me after all my other judgments turned out to be correct, why should I give you the ammunition to let you second-guess me? Let me just say that putting them in school together is a probable death sentence for one of them."

"Which one?"

"That rather depends on which one sees the other first."

"Achilles says he owes everything to Bean. He loves Bean."

"Then by all means, believe him and not me. But don't send the body of the loser back to me to deal with. You bury your own mistakes."

"That sounds pretty heartless."

"I'm not going to weep over the grave of either boy. I tried to save both their lives. You apparently seem determined to let them find out which is fittest in the best Darwinian fashion."

"Calm down, Sister Carlotta. We'll consider what you've told us. We won't be foolish."

"You've already been foolish. I have no high expectations for you now."

As days became weeks, the shape of Wiggin's army began to unfold, and Bean was filled with both hope and despair. Hope, because Wiggin was setting up an army that was almost infinitely adaptable. Despair, because he was doing it without any reliance on Bean.

After only a few practices, Wiggin had chosen his toon leaders—every one of them a veteran from the transfer lists. In fact, every veteran was either a toon leader or a second. Not only that, instead of the normal organization— four toons of ten soldiers each—he had created five toons of eight, and then made them practice a lot in half-toons of four men each, one commanded by the toon leader, the other by the second.

No one had ever fragmented an army like that before. And it wasn't just an illusion. Wiggin worked hard to make sure the toon leaders and seconds had plenty of leeway. He'd tell them their objective and let the leader decide how to achieve it. Or he'd group three toons together under the operational command of one of the toon leaders to handle one operation, while Wiggin himself commanded the smaller remaining force. It was an extraordinary amount of delegation.

Some of the soldiers were critical at first. As they were milling around near the entrance to the barracks, the veterans talked about how they'd practiced that day—in ten groups of four. "Everybody knows it's loser strategy to divide your army," said Fly Molo, who commanded A toon.

Bean was a little disgusted that the soldier with the highest rank after Wiggin would say something disparaging about his commander's strategy. Sure, Fly was learning, too. But there's such a thing as insubordination.

"He hasn't divided the army," said Bean. "He's just organized it. And there's no such thing as a rule of strategy that you can't break. The idea is to have your army concentrated at the decisive point. Not to keep it huddled together all the time."

Fly glared at Bean. "Just cause you little guys can hear us doesn't mean you understand what we're talking about."

"If you don't want to believe me, think what you want. My talking isn't going to make you stupider than you already are."

Fly came at him, grabbing him by the arm and dragging him to the edge of his bunk.

At once, Nikolai launched himself from the bunk opposite and landed on Fly's back, bumping his head into the front of Bean's bunk. In moments, the other toon leaders had pulled Fly and Nikolai apart—a ludicrous fight anyway, since Nikolai wasn't that much bigger than Bean.

"Forget it, Fly," said Hot Soup—Han Tzu, leader of D toon. "Nikolai thinks he's Bean's big brother."

"What's the kid doing mouthing off to a toon leader?" demanded Fly.

"You were being insubordinate toward our commander," said Bean. "And you were also completely wrong. By your view, Lee and Jackson were idiots at Chancellorsville."

"He keeps doing it!"

"Are you so stupid you can't recognize the truth just because the person telling it to you is short?" All of Bean's frustration at not being one of the officers was spilling out. He knew it, but he didn't feel like controlling it. They needed to hear the truth. And Wiggin needed to have the support when he was being taken down behind his back.

Nikolai was standing on the lower bunk, so he was as close to Bean as possible, affirming the bond between them. "Come on, Fly," said Nikolai. "This is *Bean,* remember?"

And, to Bean's surprise, that silenced Fly. Until this moment, Bean had not realized the power that his reputation had. He might be just a regular soldier in Dragon Army, but he was still the finest student of strategy and military history in the school, and apparently everybody—or at least everybody but Wiggin—knew it.

"I should have spoken with more respect," said Bean.

"Damn right," said Fly.

"But so should you."

Fly lunged against the grip of the boys holding him.

"Talking about Wiggin," said Bean. "You spoke without respect. 'Everybody knows it's loser strategy to divide your army.' " He got Fly's intonation almost exactly right. Several kids laughed. And, grudgingly, so did Fly.

"OK, right," said Fly. "I was out of line." He turned to Nikolai. "But I'm still an officer."

"Not when you're dragging a little kid off his bunk you're not," said Nikolai. "You're a bully when you do that."

Fly blinked. Wisely, no one else said a thing until Fly had decided how he was going to respond. "You're right, Nikolai. To defend your friend against a bully." He looked from Nikolai to Bean and back again. "Pusha, you guys even look like brothers." He walked past them, heading for his bunk. The other toon leaders followed him. Crisis over.

Nikolai looked at Bean then. "I was never as squished up and ugly as you," he said.

"And if I'm going to grow up to look like you, I'm going to kill myself now," said Bean.

"Do you have to talk to really *big* guys like that?"

"I didn't expect you to attack him like a one-man swarm of bees."

"I guess I wanted to jump on somebody," said Nikolai.

"You? Mr. Nice Guy?"

"I don't feel so nice lately." He climbed up on the bunk beside Bean, so they could talk more softly. "I'm out of my depth here, Bean. I don't belong in this army."

"What do you mean?"

"I wasn't ready to get promoted. I'm just average. Maybe not that good. And even though this army wasn't a bunch of heroes in the standings, these guys are good. Everybody learns faster than me. Everybody *gets* it and I'm still standing there thinking about it."

"So you work harder."

"I *am* working harder. You—you just get it, right away, everything, you see it all. And it's not that I'm stupid. I always get it, too. Just . . . a step behind."

"Sorry," said Bean.

"What are *you* sorry about? It's not *your* fault."

Yes it is, Nikolai. "Come on, you telling me you wish you weren't part of Ender Wiggin's army?"

Nikolai laughed a little. "He's really something, isn't he?"

"You'll do your part. You're a good soldier. You'll see. When we get into the battles, you'll do as well as anybody."

"Eh, probably. They can always freeze me and throw me around. A big lumpy projectile weapon."

"You're not so lumpy."

"Everybody's lumpy compared to you. I've watched you—you give away half your food."

"They feed me too much."

"I've got to study." Nikolai jumped across to his bunk.

Bean felt bad sometimes about having put Nikolai in this situation. But when they started winning, a lot of kids outside of Dragon Army would be wishing they could trade places with him. In fact, it was kind of surprising Nikolai realized he wasn't as qualified as the others. After all, the differences weren't that pronounced. Probably there were a lot of kids who felt just like Nikolai. But

Bean hadn't really reassured him. In fact, he had probably reaffirmed Nikolai's feelings of inferiority.

What a sensitive friend I am.

———

There was no point in interviewing Volescu again, not after getting such lies from him the first time. All that talk of copies, and him the original—there was no mitigation now. He was a murderer, a servant of the Father of Lies. He would do nothing to help Sister Carlotta. And the need to find out what might be expected of the one child who evaded Volescu's little holocaust was too great to rely again on the word of such a man.

Besides, Volescu had made contact with his half-brother or double cousin—how else could he have obtained a fertilized egg containing his DNA? So Sister Carlotta should be able either to follow Volescu's trail or duplicate his research.

She learned quickly that Volescu was the illegitimate child of a Romanian woman in Budapest, Hungary. A little checking—and the judicious use of her security clearance—got her the name of the father, a Greek-born official in the League who had recently been promoted to service on the Hegemon's staff. That might have been a roadblock, but Sister Carlotta did not need to speak to the grandfather. She only needed to know who he was in order to find out the names of his three legitimate children. The daughter was eliminated because the shared parent was a male. And in checking the two sons, she decided to go first to visit the married one.

They lived on the island of Crete, where Julian ran a software company whose only client was the International Defense League. Obviously this was not a coincidence, but nepotism was almost honorable compared to some of the outright graft and favor-trading that was endemic in the League. In the long run such corruption was basically harmless, since the International Fleet had seized control of its own budget early on and never let the League touch it again. Thus the Polemarch and the Strategos had far more money at their disposal than the Hegemon, which made him, though first in title, weakest in actual power and independence of movement.

And just because Julian Delphiki owed his career to his father's political connections did not necessarily mean that his company's product was not adequate and that he himself was not an honest man. By the standards of honesty that prevailed in the world of business, anyway.

Sister Carlotta found that she did not need her security clearance to get a meeting with Julian and his wife, Elena. She called and said she would like to see them on a matter concerning the I.F., and they immediately opened their calendar to her. She arrived in Knossos and was immediately driven to their home on a bluff overlooking the Aegean. They looked nervous—indeed, Elena was almost frantic, wringing a handkerchief.

"Please," she said, after accepting their offer of fruit and cheese. "Please tell me why you are so upset. There's nothing about my business that should alarm you."

The two of them glanced at each other, and Elena became flustered. "Then there's nothing wrong with our boy?"

For a moment, Sister Carlotta wondered if they already knew about Bean—but how could they?

"Your son?"

"Then he's all right!" Elena burst into tears of relief and when her husband knelt beside her, she clung to him and sobbed.

"You see, it was very hard for us to let him go into service," said Julian. "So when a religious person calls to tell us she needs to see us on business pertaining to the I.F., we thought—we leapt to the conclusion—"

"Oh, I'm so sorry. I didn't know you had a son in the military, or I would have been careful to assure you from the start that . . . but now I fear I am here under false pretenses. The matter I need to speak to you about is personal, so personal you may be reluctant to answer. Yet it *is* about a matter that is of some importance to the I.F. Truthful answers cannot possibly expose you to any personal risk, I promise."

Elena got control of herself. Julian seated himself again, and now they looked at Sister Carlotta almost with cheerfulness. "Oh, ask whatever you want," said Julian. "We're just happy that—whatever you want to ask."

"We'll answer if we can," said Elena.

"You say you have a son. This raises the possibility that—there is reason to wonder if you might not at some point have . . . was your son conceived under circumstances that would have allowed a clone of his fertilized egg to be made?"

"Oh yes," said Elena. "That is no secret. A defect in one fallopian tube and an ectopic pregnancy in the other made it impossible for me to conceive in utero. We wanted a child, so they drew out several of my eggs, fertilized them with my husband's sperm, and then cloned the ones we chose. There were four that we cloned, six copies of each. Two girls and two boys. So far, we have implanted only the one. He was such a—such a special boy, we did not want to dilute our attention. Now that his education is out of our hands, however, we have been thinking of bearing one of the girls. It's time." She reached over and took Julian's hand and smiled. He smiled back.

Such a contrast to Volescu. Hard to believe there was any genetic material in common.

"You said six copies of each of the four fertilized eggs," said Sister Carlotta.

"Six including the original," said Julian. "That way we have the best chance of implanting each of the four and carrying them through a full pregnancy."

"A total of twenty-four fertilized eggs. And only one of them was implanted?"

"Yes, we were very fortunate, the first one worked perfectly."

"Leaving twenty-three."

"Yes. Exactly."

"Mr. Delphiki, all twenty-three of those fertilized eggs remain in storage, waiting for implantation?"

"Of course."

Sister Carlotta thought for a moment. "How recently have you checked?"

"Just last week," said Julian. "As we began talking about having another child. The doctor assured us that nothing has happened to the eggs and they can be implanted with only a few hours' notice."

"But did the doctor actually check?"

"I don't know," said Julian.

Elena was starting to tense up a little. "What have you heard?" she asked.

"Nothing," said Sister Carlotta. "What I am looking for is the source of a particular child's genetic material. I simply need to make sure that your fertilized eggs were not the source."

"But of course they were not. Except for our son."

"Please don't be alarmed. But I would like to know the name of your doctor and the facility where the eggs are stored. And then I would be glad if you would call your doctor and have him go, in person, to the facility and insist upon seeing the eggs himself."

"They can't be seen without a microscope," said Julian.

"See that they have not been disturbed," said Sister Carlotta.

They had both become hyperalert again, especially since they had no idea what this was all about—nor could they be told. As soon as Julian gave her the name of doctor and hospital, Sister Carlotta stepped onto the porch and, as she gazed at the sail-specked Aegean, she used her global and got herself put through to the I.F. headquarters in Athens.

It would take several hours, perhaps, for either her call or Julian's to bring in the answer, so she and Julian and Elena made a heroic effort to appear unconcerned. They took her on a walking tour of their neighborhood, which offered views both ancient and modern, and of nature verdant, desert, and marine. The dry air was refreshing as long as the breeze from the sea did not lag, and Sister Carlotta enjoyed hearing Julian talk about his company and Elena talk about her work as a teacher. All thought of their having risen in the world through government corruption faded as she realized that however he got his contract, Julian was a serious, dedicated creator of software, while Elena was a fervent teacher who treated her profession as a crusade. "I knew as soon as I started teaching our son how remarkable he was," Elena told her. "But it wasn't until his pre-tests for school placement that we first learned that his gifts were particularly suited for the I.F."

Alarm bells went off. Sister Carlotta had assumed that their son was an adult. After all, they were not a young couple. "How old is your son?"

"Eight years old now," said Julian. "They sent us a picture. Quite a little man in his uniform. They don't let many letters come through."

Their son was in Battle School. They appeared to be in their forties, but they might not have started to have a family until late, and then tried in vain for a while, going through a tubal pregnancy before finding out that Elena could no longer conceive. Their son was only a couple of years older than Bean.

Which meant that Graff could compare Bean's genetic code with that of the Delphiki boy and find out if they were from the same cloned egg. There would be a control, to compare what Bean was like with Anton's key turned, as opposed to the other, whose genes were unaltered.

Now that she thought about it, of *course* any true sibling of Bean's would have exactly the abilities that would bring the attention of the I.F. Anton's key made a child into a savant in general; the particular mix of skills that the I.F. looked for were not affected. Bean would have had those skills no matter what; the alteration merely allowed him to bring a far sharper intelligence to bear on abilities he already had.

If Bean was in fact their child. Yet the coincidence of twenty-three fertilized eggs and the twenty-three children that Volescu had produced in the "clean room"—what other conclusion could she reach?

And soon the answer came, first to Sister Carlotta, but immediately thereafter to the Delphikis. The I.F. investigators had gone to the clinic with the doctor and together they had discovered that the eggs were missing.

It was hard news for the Delphikis to bear, and Sister Carlotta discreetly waited outside while Elena and Julian took some time alone together. But soon they invited her in. "How much can you tell us?" Julian asked. "You came here because you suspected our babies might have been taken. Tell me, were they born?"

Sister Carlotta wanted to hide behind the veil of military secrecy, but in truth there was no military secret involved—Volescu's crime was a matter of public record. And yet . . . weren't they better off not knowing?

"Julian, Elena, accidents happen in the laboratory. They might have died anyway. Nothing is certain. Isn't it better just to think of this as a terrible accident? Why add to the burden of the loss you already have?"

Elena looked at her fiercely. "You *will* tell me, Sister Carlotta, if you love the God of truth!"

"The eggs were stolen by a criminal who . . . illegally caused them to be brought through gestation. When his crime was about to be discovered, he gave them a painless death by sedative. They did not suffer."

"And this man will be put on trial?"

"He has already been tried and sentenced to life in prison," said Sister Carlotta.

"Already?" asked Julian. "How long ago were our babies stolen?"

"More than seven years ago."

"Oh!" cried Elena. "Then our babies . . . when they died . . ."

"They were infants. Not a year old yet."

"But why *our* babies? Why would he steal them? Was he going to sell them for adoption? Was he . . ."

"Does it matter? None of his plans came to fruition," said Sister Carlotta. The nature of Volescu's experiments *was* a secret.

"What was the murderer's name?" asked Julian. Seeing her hesitation, he insisted. "His name is a matter of public record, is it not?"

"In the criminal courts of Rotterdam," said Sister Carlotta. "Volescu."

Julian reacted as if slapped—but immediately controlled himself. Elena did not see it.

He knows about his father's mistress, thought Sister Carlotta. He understands now what part of the motive had to be. The legitimate son's children were kidnapped by the bastard, experimented on, and eventually killed—and the legitimate son didn't find out about it for seven years. Whatever privations Volescu fancied that his fatherlessness had caused him, he had taken his vengeance. And for Julian, it also meant that his father's lusts had come back to cause this loss, this pain to Julian and his wife. The sins of the fathers are visited upon the children unto the third and fourth generation. . . .

But didn't the scripture say the third and fourth generation of them that hate me? Julian and Elena did not hate God. Nor did their innocent babies.

It makes no more sense than Herod's slaughter of the babes of Bethlehem. The only comfort was the trust that a merciful God caught up the spirits of the slain infants into his bosom, and that he brought comfort, eventually, to the parents' hearts.

"Please," said Sister Carlotta. "I cannot say you should not grieve for the children that you will never hold. But you can still rejoice in the child that you have."

"A million miles away!" cried Elena.

"I don't suppose . . . you don't happen to know if the Battle School ever lets a child come home for a visit," said Julian. "His name is Nikolai Delphiki. Surely under the circumstances . . ."

"I'm so sorry," said Sister Carlotta. Reminding them of the child they had was not such a good idea after all, when they did not, in fact, have him. "I'm sorry that my coming led to such terrible news for you."

"But you learned what you came to learn," said Julian.

"Yes," said Sister Carlotta.

Then Julian realized something, though he said not a word in front of his wife. "Will you want to return to the airport now?"

"Yes, the car is still waiting. Soldiers are much more patient than cab drivers."

"I'll walk you to the car," said Julian.

"No, Julian," said Elena, "don't leave me."

"Just for a few moments, my love. Even now, we don't forget courtesy." He held his wife for a long moment, then led Sister Carlotta to the door and opened it for her.

As they walked to the car, Julian spoke of what he had come to understand. "Since my father's bastard is already in prison, you did not come here because of his crime."

"No," she said.

"One of our children is still alive," he said.

"What I tell you now I should not tell, because it is not within my authority," said Sister Carlotta. "But my first allegiance is to God, not the I.F. If the twenty-two children who died at Volescu's hand were yours, then a twenty-third may be alive. It remains for genetic testing to be done."

"But we will not be told," said Julian.

"Not yet," said Sister Carlotta. "And not soon. Perhaps not ever. But if it is within my power, then a day will come when you will meet your second son."

"Is he . . . do you know him?"

"If it is your son," she said, "then yes, I know him. His life has been hard, but his heart is good, and he is such a boy as to make any father or mother proud. Please don't ask me more. I've already said too much."

"Do I tell this to my wife?" asked Julian. "What will be harder for her, to know or not know?"

"Women are not so different from men. *You* preferred to know."

Julian nodded. "I know that you were only the bearer of news, not the cause of our loss. But your visit here will not be remembered with happiness. Yet I want you to know that I understand how kindly you have done this miserable job."

She nodded. "And you have been unfailingly gracious in a difficult hour."

Julian opened the door of her car. She stooped to the seat, swung her legs inside. But before he could close the door for her, she thought of one last question, a very important one.

"Julian, I know you were planning to have a daughter next. But if you had gone on to bring another son into the world, what would you have named him?"

"Our firstborn was named for my father, Nikolai," he said. "But Elena wanted to name a second son for me."

"Julian Delphiki," said Sister Carlotta. "If this truly is your son, I think he would be proud someday to bear his father's name."

"What name does he use now?" asked Julian.

"Of course I cannot say."

"But . . . not Volescu, surely."

"No. As far as I'm concerned, he'll never hear that name. God bless you, Julian Delphiki. I will pray for you and your wife."

"Pray for our children's souls, too, Sister."

"I already have, and do, and will."

———

Major Anderson looked at the boy sitting across the table from him. "Really, it's not that important a matter, Nikolai."

"I thought maybe I was in trouble."

"No, no. We just noticed that you seemed to be a particular friend of Bean. He doesn't have a lot of friends."

"It didn't help that Dimak painted a target on him in the shuttle. And now Ender's gone and done the same thing. I suppose Bean can take it, but smart as he is, he kind of pisses off a lot of the other kids."

"But not you?"

"Oh, he pisses me off, too."

"And yet you became his friend."

"Well, I didn't mean to. I just had the bunk across from him in launchy barracks."

"You traded for that bunk."

"Did I? Oh. Eh."

"And you did that before you knew how smart Bean was."

"Dimak told us in the shuttle that Bean had the highest scores of any of us."

"Was that why you wanted to be near him?"

Nikolai shrugged.

"It was an act of kindness," said Major Anderson. "Perhaps I'm just an old cynic, but when I see such an inexplicable act I become curious."

"He really does kind of look like my baby pictures. Isn't that dumb? I saw him and I thought, he looks just like cute little baby Nikolai. Which is what my mother always called me in my baby pictures. I never thought of them as *me*. I was big Nikolai. That was cute little baby Nikolai. I used to pretend that he was my little brother and we just happened to have the same name. Big Nikolai and Cute Little Baby Nikolai."

"I see that you're ashamed, but you shouldn't be. It's a natural thing for an only child to do."

"I wanted a brother."

"Many who have a brother wish they didn't."

"But the brother I made up for myself, he and I got along fine." Nikolai laughed at the absurdity of it.

"And you saw Bean and thought of him as the brother you once imagined."

"At first. Now I know who he really is, and it's better.

It's like . . . sometimes he's the little brother and I'm looking out for him, and sometimes he's the big brother and he's looking out for me."

"For instance?"

"What?"

"A boy that small—how does he look out for you?"

"He gives me advice. Helps me with classwork. We do some practice together. He's better at almost everything than I am. Only I'm bigger, and I think I like him more than he likes me."

"That may be true, Nikolai. But as far as we can tell, he likes you more than he likes anybody else. He just . . . so far, he may not have the same capacity for friendship that you have. I hope that my asking you these questions won't change your feelings and actions toward Bean. We don't assign people to be friends, but I hope you'll remain Bean's."

"I'm not his friend," said Nikolai.

"Oh?"

"I told you. I'm his brother." Nikolai grinned. "Once you get a brother, you don't give him up easy."

15

Courage

"Genetically, they're identical twins. The only difference is Anton's key."

"So the Delphikis have two sons."

"The Delphikis have one son, Nikolai, and he's with us for the duration. Bean was an orphan found on the streets of Rotterdam."

"Because he was kidnapped."

"The law is clear. Fertilized eggs are property. I know that this is a matter of religious sensitivity for you, but the I.F. is bound by law, not—"

"The I.F. uses law where possible to achieve its own ends. I know you're fighting a war. I know that some things are outside your power. But the war will not go on forever. All I ask is this: Make this information part of a record— part of many records. So that when the war ends, the proof of these things can and will survive. So the truth won't stay hidden."

"Of course."

"No, not of course. You know that the moment the

Formics are defeated, the I.F. will have no reason to exist. It will try to continue to exist in order to maintain international peace. But the League is not politically strong enough to survive in the nationalist winds that will blow. The I.F. will break into fragments, each following its own leader, and God help us if any part of the fleet ever should use its weapons against the surface of the Earth."

"You've been spending too much time reading the Apocalypse."

"I may not be one of the genius children in your school, but I see how the tides of opinion are flowing here on Earth. On the nets a demagogue named Demosthenes is inflaming the West about illegal and secret maneuvers by the Polemarch to give an advantage to the New Warsaw Pact, and the propaganda is even more virulent from Moscow, Baghdad, Buenos Aires, Beijing. There are a few rational voices, like Locke, but they're given lip service and then ignored. You and I can't do anything about the fact that world war will certainly come. But we *can* do our best to make sure these children don't become pawns in that game."

"The only way they won't be pawns is if they're players."

"You've been raising them. Surely you don't *fear* them. Give them their chance to play."

"Sister Carlotta, all my work is aimed at preparing for the showdown with the Formics. At turning these children into brilliant, reliable commanders. I can't look beyond that mark."

"Don't *look.* Just leave the door open for their families, their nations to claim them."

"I can't think about that right now."

"Right now is the only time you'll have the power to do it."

"You overestimate me."

"You underestimate yourself."

Dragon Army had only been practicing for a month when Wiggin came into the barracks only a few seconds after lights-on, brandishing a slip of paper. Battle orders. They would face Rabbit Army at 0700. And they'd do it without breakfast.

"I don't want anybody throwing up in the battleroom."

"Can we at least take a leak first?" asked Nikolai.

"No more than a decaliter," said Wiggin.

Everybody laughed, but they were also nervous. As a new army, with only a handful of veterans, they didn't actually expect to win, but they didn't want to be humiliated, either. They all had different ways of dealing with nerves—some became silent, others talkative. Some joked and bantered, others turned surly. Some just lay back down on their bunks and closed their eyes.

Bean watched them. He tried to remember if the kids in Poke's crew ever did these things. And then realized: They were *hungry,* not afraid of being shamed. You don't get this kind of fear until you have enough to eat. So it was the bullies who felt like these kids, afraid of humiliation but not of going hungry. And sure enough, the bullies standing around in line showed all these attitudes. They were always performing, always aware of others watching them. Fearful they would have to fight; eager for it, too.

What do I feel?

What's wrong with me that I have to think about it to know?

Oh . . . I'm just sitting here, watching. I'm one of *those*.

Bean pulled out his flash suit, but then realized he had to use the toilet before putting it on. He dropped down onto the deck and pulled his towel from its hook, wrapped it around himself. For a moment he flashed back to that night he had tossed his towel under a bunk and climbed into the ventilation system. He'd never fit now. Too thickly muscled, too tall. He was still the shortest kid in Battle School, and he doubted if anyone else would notice how he'd grown, but he was aware of how his arms and legs were longer. He could reach things more easily.

Didn't have to jump so often just to do normal things like palming his way into the gym.

I've changed, thought Bean. My body, of course. But also the way I think.

Nikolai was still lying in bed with his pillow over his head. Everybody had his own way of coping.

The other kids were all using the toilets and getting drinks of water, but Bean was the only one who thought it was a good idea to shower. They used to tease him by asking if the water was still warm when it got all the way down there, but the joke was old now. What Bean wanted was the steam. The blindness of the fog around him, of the fogged mirrors, everything hidden, so he could be anyone, anywhere, any size.

Someday they'll all see me as I see myself. Larger than any of them. Head and shoulders above the rest, seeing farther, reaching farther, carrying burdens they could only dream of. In Rotterdam all I cared about was staying alive. But here, well fed, I've found out who I am. What I might be. *They* might think I'm an alien or a robot or something, just because I'm not genetically ordinary. But when I've done the great deeds of my life, they'll be proud to claim me as a human, furious at anyone who questions whether I'm truly one of them.

Greater than Wiggin.

He put the thought out of his mind, or tried to. This wasn't a competition. There was room for two great men in the world at the same time. Lee and Grant were contemporaries, fought against each other. Bismarck and Disraeli. Napoleon and Wellington.

No, that's not the comparison. It's *Lincoln* and Grant. Two great men working together.

It was disconcerting, though, to realize how rare that was. Napoleon could never bear to let any of his lieutenants have real authority. All victories had to be his alone. Who was the great man beside Augustus? Alexander? They had friends, they had rivals, but they never had partners.

That's why Wiggin has kept me down, even though he knows by now from the reports they give to army commanders that I've got a mind better than anybody else in Dragon. Because I'm too obviously a rival. Because I made it clear that first day that I intended to rise, and he's letting me know that it won't happen while I'm with his army.

Someone came into the bathroom. Bean couldn't see who it was because of the fog. Nobody greeted him. Everybody else must have finished here and gone back to get ready.

The newcomer walked through the fog past the opening in Bean's shower stall. It was Wiggin.

Bean just stood there, covered with soap. He felt like an idiot. He was in such a daze he had forgotten to rinse, was just standing in the fog, lost in his thoughts. Hurriedly he moved under the water again.

"Bean?"

"Sir?" Bean turned to face him. Wiggin was standing in the shower entrance.

"I thought I ordered everybody to get down to the gym."

Bean thought back. The scene unfolded in his mind. Yes, Wiggin *had* ordered everybody to bring their flash suits to the gym.

"I'm sorry. I . . . was thinking of something else . . ."

"Everybody's nervous before their first battle."

Bean hated that. To have Wiggin see him doing something stupid. Not remembering an order—Bean remembered *everything*. It just hadn't registered. And now he was patronizing him. Everybody's nervous!

"*You* weren't," said Bean.

Wiggin had already stepped away. He came back. "Wasn't I?"

"Bonzo Madrid gave you orders not to take your weapon out. You were supposed to just stay there like a dummy. You weren't nervous about doing *that*."

"No," said Wiggin. "I was pissed."

"Better than nervous."

Wiggin started to leave. Then returned again. "Are *you* pissed?"

"I did that before I showered," said Bean.

Wiggin laughed. Then his smile disappeared. "You're late, Bean, and you're still busy rinsing. I've already got your flash suit down in the gym. All we need now is your ass in it." Wiggin took Bean's towel off its hook. "I'll have this waiting for you down there, too. Now move."

Wiggin left.

Bean turned the water off, furious. That was completely unnecessary, and Wiggin knew it. Making him go through the corridor wet and naked during the time when other armies would be coming back from breakfast. That was low, and it was stupid.

Anything to put me down. Every chance he gets.

Bean, you idiot, you're still standing here. You could have run down to the gym and beaten him there. Instead, you're shooting your stupid self in the stupid foot. And why? None of this makes sense. None of this is going to help you. You want him to make you a toon leader, not think of you with contempt. So why are you doing things to make yourself look stupid and young and scared and unreliable?

And still you're standing here, frozen.

I'm a coward.

The thought ran through Bean's mind and filled him with terror. But it wouldn't go away.

I'm one of those guys who freezes up or does completely irrational things when he's afraid. Who loses control and goes slack-minded and stupid.

But I didn't do that in Rotterdam. If I had, I'd be dead.

Or maybe I *did* do it. Maybe that's why I didn't call out to Poke and Achilles when I saw them there alone on the dock. He wouldn't have killed her if I'd been there to witness what happened. Instead I ran off until I realized the danger she was in. But why didn't I realize it before? Because I *did* realize it, just as I heard Wiggin tell us to meet in the gym. Realized it, understood it completely, but was too cowardly to act. Too afraid that something would go wrong.

And maybe that's what happened when Achilles lay on the ground and I told Poke to kill him. I was wrong and she was right. Because *any* bully she caught that way would probably have held a grudge—and might easily have acted on it immediately, killing her as soon as they let him up. Achilles was the likeliest one, maybe the only one that would agree to the arrangement Bean had thought up. There was no choice. But I got scared. Kill him, I said, because I wanted it to go away.

And still I'm standing here. The water is off. I'm dripping wet and cold. But I can't move.

Nikolai was standing in the bathroom doorway. "Too bad about your diarrhea," he said.

"What?"

"I told Ender about how you were up with diarrhea in the night. That's why you had to go to the bathroom. You were sick, but you didn't want to tell him because you didn't want to miss the first battle."

"I'm so scared I couldn't take a dump if I wanted to," said Bean.

"He gave me your towel. He said it was stupid of him to take it." Nikolai walked in and gave it to him. "He said he needs you in the battle, so he's glad you're toughing it out."

"He doesn't need me. He doesn't even want me."

"Come on, Bean," said Nikolai. "You can do this."

Bean toweled off. It felt good to be moving. Doing something.

"I think you're dry enough," said Nikolai.

Again, Bean realized he was simply drying and drying himself, over and over.

"Nikolai, what's wrong with me?"

"You're afraid that you'll turn out to be just a little kid. Well, here's a clue: You *are* a little kid."

"So are you."

"So it's OK to be really bad. Isn't that what you keep telling me?" Nikolai laughed. "Come on, if I can do it, bad as I am, so can you."

"Nikolai," said Bean.

"What now?"

"I really *do* have to crap."

"I sure hope you don't expect me to wipe your butt."

"If I don't come out in three minutes, come in after me."

Cold and sweating—a combination he wouldn't have thought possible—Bean went into the toilet stall and closed the door. The pain in his abdomen was fierce. But he couldn't get his bowel to loosen up and let go.

What am I so *afraid* of?

Finally, his alimentary system triumphed over his nervous system. It felt like everything he'd ever eaten flooded out of him at once.

"Time's up," said Nikolai. "I'm coming in."

"At peril of your life," said Bean. "I'm done, I'm coming out."

Empty now, clean, and humiliated in front of his only real friend, Bean came out of the stall and wrapped his towel around him.

"Thanks for keeping me from being a liar," said Nikolai.

"What?"

"About your having diarrhea."

"For you I'd get dysentery."

"Now that's friendship."

By the time they got to the gym, everybody was already in their flash suits, ready to go. While Nikolai helped Bean get into his suit, Wiggin had the rest of them lie down on the mats and do relaxation exercises. Bean even had time to lie down for a couple of minutes before Wiggin had them get up. 0656. Four minutes to get to the battleroom. He was cutting it pretty fine.

As they ran along the corridor, Wiggin occasionally jumped up to touch the ceiling. Behind him, the rest of the army would jump up and touch the same spot when they reached it. Except the smaller ones. Bean, his heart still burning with humiliation and resentment and fear, did not try. You do that kind of thing when you belong with the group. And he didn't belong. After all his brilliance in class, the truth was out now. He was a coward. He didn't belong in the military at all. If he couldn't even risk playing a game, what would he be worth in combat? The real generals exposed themselves to enemy fire. Fearless, they had to be, an example of courage to their men.

Me, I freeze up, take long showers, and dump a week's rations into the head. Let's see them follow that example.

At the gate, Wiggin had time to line them up in toons, then remind them, "Which way is the enemy's gate?"

"Down!" they all answered.

Bean only mouthed the word. *Down. Down down down.*

What's the best way to get down off a goose?

What are you doing up on a goose in the first place, you fool!

The grey wall in front of them disappeared, and they could see into the battleroom. It was dim—not dark, but so faintly lighted that the only way they could see the enemy gate was the light of Rabbit Army's flash suits pouring out of it.

Wiggin was in no hurry to get out of the gate. He stood there surveying the room, which was arranged in an open grid, with eight "stars"—large cubes that served as obstacles, cover, and staging platforms—distributed fairly evenly if randomly through the space.

Wiggin's first assignment was to C toon. Crazy Tom's toon. The toon Bean belonged to. Word was whispered down the file. "Ender says slide the wall." And then, "Tom says flash your legs and go in on your knees. South wall."

Silently they swung into the room, using the handholds to propel themselves along the ceiling to the east wall. "They're setting up their battle formation. All we want to do is cut them up a little, make them nervous, confused, because they don't know what to do with us. We're raiders. So we shoot them up, then get behind that star. *Don't* get stuck out in the middle. And *aim.* Make every shot count."

Bean did everything mechanically. It was habit now to get in position, freeze his own legs, and then launch with his body oriented the right way. They'd done it hundreds of times. He did it exactly right; so did the other seven soldiers in the toon. Nobody was looking for anyone to fail. He was right where they expected him to be, doing his job.

They coasted along the wall, always within reach of a handhold. Their frozen legs were dark, blocking the lights of the rest of their flash suits until they were fairly close. Wiggin was doing something up near the gate to distract Rabbit Army's attention, so the surprise was pretty good.

As they got closer, Crazy Tom said, "Split and rebound to the star—me north, you south."

It was a maneuver that Crazy Tom had practiced with his toon. It was the right time for it, too. It would confuse the enemy more to have two groups to shoot at, heading different directions.

They pulled up on handholds. Their bodies, of course, swung against the wall, and suddenly the lights of their flash suits were quite visible. Somebody in Rabbit saw them and gave the alarm.

But C was already moving, half the toon diagonally south, the other half north, and all angling downward toward the floor. Bean began firing; the enemy was also firing at him. He heard the low whine that said somebody's beam was on his suit, but he was twisting slowly, and far enough from the enemy that none of the beams was in one place long enough to do damage. In the meantime, he found that his arm tracked perfectly, not trembling at all. He had practiced this a lot, and he was good at it. A clean kill, not just an arm or leg.

He had time for a second before he hit the wall and

had to rebound up to the rendezvous star. One more enemy hit before he got there, and then he snagged a handhold on the star and said, "Bean here."

"Lost three," said Crazy Tom. "But their formation's all gone to hell."

"What now?" said Dag.

They could tell from the shouting that the main battle was in progress.

Bean was thinking back over what he had seen as he approached the star.

"They sent a dozen guys to this star to wipe us out," said Bean. "They'll come around the east and west sides."

They all looked at him like he was insane. How could he know this?

"We've got about one more second," said Bean.

"All south," said Crazy Tom.

They swung up to the south side of the star. There were no Rabbits on that face, but Crazy Tom immediately led them in an attack around to the west face. Sure enough, there were Rabbits there, caught in the act of attacking what they clearly thought of as the "back" of the star— or, as Dragon Army was trained to think of it, the bottom. So to the Rabbits, the attack seemed to come from below, the direction they were least aware of. In moments, the six Rabbits on that face were frozen and drifting along below the star.

The other half of the attack force would see that and know what had happened.

"Top," said Crazy Tom.

To the enemy, that would be the front of the star—the position most exposed to fire from the main formation. The last place they'd expect Tom's toon to go.

And once they were there, instead of continuing to attempt to engage the strike force coming against them, Crazy Tom had them shoot at the main Rabbit formation, or what was left of it—mostly disorganized groups hiding behind stars and firing at Dragons coming down at them from several directions. The five of them in C toon had time to hit a couple of Rabbits each before the strike force found them again.

Without waiting for orders, Bean immediately launched away from the surface of the star so he could shoot downward at the strike force. This close, he was able to do four quick kills before the whining abruptly stopped and his suit went completely stiff and dark. The Rabbit who got him wasn't one of the strike force—it was somebody from the main force above him. And to his satisfaction, Bean could see that because of his firing, only one soldier from C toon was hit by the strike force sent against them. Then he rotated out of view.

It didn't matter now. He was out. But he had done well. Seven kills that he was sure of, maybe more. And it was more than his personal score. He had come up with the information Crazy Tom needed in order to make a good tactical decision, and then he had taken the bold action that kept the strike force from causing too many casualties. As a result, C toon remained in position to strike at the enemy from behind. Without any place to hide, Rabbit would be wiped out in moments. And Bean was part of it.

I didn't freeze once we got into action. I did what I was trained to do, and I stayed alert, and I thought of things. I can probably do better, move faster, see more. But for a first battle, I did fine. I can do this.

Because C toon was crucial to the victory, Wiggin used the other four toon leaders to press their helmets to the corners of the enemy gate, and gave Crazy Tom the honor of passing through the gate, which is what formally ended the game, bringing the lights on bright.

Major Anderson himself came in to congratulate the winning commander and supervise cleanup. Wiggin quickly unfroze the casualties. Bean was relieved when his suit could move again. Using his hook, Wiggin drew them all together and formed his soldiers into their five toons before he began unfreezing Rabbit Army. They stood at attention in the air, their feet pointed down, their heads up—and as Rabbit unfroze, they gradually oriented themselves in the same direction. They had no way of knowing it, but to Dragon, that was when victory became complete—for the enemy was now oriented as if their *own* gate was down.

———

Bean and Nikolai were already eating breakfast when Crazy Tom came to their table. "Ender says instead of fifteen minutes for breakfast, we have till 0745. And he'll let us out of practice in time to shower."

That was good news. They could slow down their eating.

Not that it mattered to Bean. His tray had little food on it, and he finished it immediately. Once he was in Dragon Army, Crazy Tom had caught him giving away food. Bean told him that he was always given too much, and Tom took the matter to Ender, and Ender got the nutritionists to stop overfeeding Bean. Today was the first time Bean ever wished for more. And that was only because he was so up from the battle.

"Smart," said Nikolai.

"What?"

"Ender tells us we've got fifteen minutes to eat, which feels rushed and we don't like it. Then right away he sends around the toon leaders, telling us we have till 0745. That's only ten minutes longer, but now it feels like forever. And a shower—we're supposed to be able to shower right after the game, but now we're grateful."

"*And* he gave the toon leaders the chance to bring good news," said Bean.

"Is that important?" asked Nikolai. "We know it was Ender's choice."

"Most commanders make sure all good news comes from them," said Bean, "and bad news from the toon leaders. But Wiggin's whole technique is building up his toon leaders. Crazy Tom went in there with nothing more than his training and his brains and a single objective—strike first from the wall and get behind them. All the rest was up to him."

"Yeah, but if his toon leaders screw up, it looks bad on Ender's record," said Nikolai.

Bean shook his head. "The point is that in his very first battle, Wiggin divided his force for tactical effect, and C toon was able to continue attacking even after we ran out of plans, because Crazy Tom was really, truly in charge of us. We didn't sit around wondering what Wiggin wanted us to do."

Nikolai got it, and nodded. "Bacana. That's right."

"Completely right," said Bean. By now everybody at the table was listening. "And that's because Wiggin isn't just thinking about Battle School and standings and merda like that. He keeps watching vids of the Second Invasion, did you know that? He's thinking about how to beat the *Buggers.* And he knows that the way you do that is to have as many commanders ready to fight them as you can get. Wiggin doesn't want to come out of this with Wiggin as the only commander ready to fight the Buggers. He wants to come out of this with him *and* the toon leaders *and* the seconds *and* if he can do it every single one of his soldiers ready to command a fleet against the Buggers if we have to."

Bean knew his enthusiasm was probably giving Wiggin credit for more than he had actually planned, but he was still full of the glow of victory. And besides, what he was saying was true—Wiggin was no Napoleon, holding on to the reins of control so tightly that none of his commanders was capable of brilliant independent command. Crazy Tom had performed well under pressure. He had made the right decisions—including the decision to listen to his smallest, most useless-looking soldier. And Crazy Tom had done that because Wiggin had set the example by listening to his toon leaders. You learn, you analyze, you choose, you act.

After breakfast, as they headed for practice, Nikolai asked him, "Why do you call him Wiggin?"

"Cause we're not friends," said Bean.

"Oh, so it's Mr. Wiggin and Mr. Bean, is that it?"

"No. *Bean* is my first name."

"Oh. So it's Mr. Wiggin and Who The Hell Are You."

"Got it."

———

Everybody expected to have at least a week to strut around and brag about their perfect won-lost record. Instead, the next morning at 0630, Wiggin appeared in the barracks, again brandishing battle orders. "Gentlemen, I hope you learned something yesterday, because today we're going to do it again."

All were surprised, and some were angry—it wasn't fair, they weren't ready. Wiggin just handed the orders to Fly Molo, who had just been heading out for breakfast. "Flash suits!" cried Fly, who clearly thought it was a cool thing to be the first army ever to fight two in a row like this.

But Hot Soup, the leader of D toon, had another attitude. "Why didn't you tell us earlier?"

"I thought you needed the shower," said Wiggin. "Yesterday Rabbit Army claimed we only won because the stink knocked them out."

Everybody within earshot laughed. But Bean was not amused. He knew that the paper hadn't been there first thing, when Wiggin woke up. The teachers planted it late. "Didn't find the paper till you got back from the showers, right?"

Wiggin gave him a blank look. "Of course. I'm not as close to the floor as you."

The contempt in his voice struck Bean like a blow. Only then did he realize that Wiggin had taken his question as a criticism—that Wiggin had been inattentive and hadn't *noticed* the orders. So now there was one more mark against Bean in Wiggin's mental dossier. But Bean couldn't let that upset him. It's not as if Wiggin didn't have him tagged as a coward. Maybe Crazy Tom told

Wiggin about how Bean contributed to the victory yesterday, and maybe not. It wouldn't change what Wiggin had seen with his own eyes—Bean malingering in the shower. And now Bean apparently taunting him for making them all have to rush for their second battle. Maybe I'll be made toon leader on my thirtieth birthday. And then only if everybody else is drowned in a boat accident.

Wiggin was still talking, of course, explaining how they should expect battles any time, the old rules were coming apart. "I can't pretend I like the way they're screwing around with us, but I do like one thing—that I've got an army that can handle it."

As he put on his flash suit, Bean thought through the implications of what the teachers were doing. They were pushing Wiggin faster and also making it harder for him. And this was only the beginning. Just the first few sprinkles of a snotstorm.

Why? Not because Wiggin was so good he needed the testing. On the contrary—Wiggin was training his army well, and the Battle School would only benefit from giving him plenty of time to do it. So it had to be something outside Battle School.

Only one possibility, really. The Bugger invaders were getting close. Only a few years away. They had to get Wiggin through training.

Wiggin. Not all of us, just Wiggin. Because if it were everybody, then everybody's schedule would be stepped up like this. Not just ours.

So it's already too late for me. Wiggin's the one they've chosen to rest their hopes on. Whether I'm toon leader or not will never matter. All that matters is: Will Wiggin be ready?

If Wiggin succeeds, there'll still be room for me to achieve greatness in the aftermath. The League will come apart. There'll be war among humans. Either I'll be used by the I.F. to help keep the peace, or maybe I can get into some army on Earth. I've got plenty of life ahead of me. Unless Wiggin commands our fleet against the invading

Buggers and loses. Then none of us has any life at all.

All I can do right now is my best to help Wiggin learn everything he can learn here. The trouble is, I'm not close enough to him for me to have any effect on him at all.

The battle was with Petra Arkanian, commander of Phoenix Army. Petra was sharper than Carn Carby had been; she also had the advantage of hearing how Wiggin worked entirely without formations and used little raiding parties to disrupt formations ahead of the main combat. Still, Dragon finished with only three soldiers flashed and nine partially disabled. A crushing defeat. Bean could see that Petra didn't like it, either. She probably felt like Wiggin had poured it on, deliberately setting her up for humiliation. But she'd get it, soon enough—Wiggin simply turned his toon leaders loose, and each of them pursued total victory, as he had trained them. Their system worked better, that's all, and the old way of doing battle was doomed.

Soon enough, all the other commanders would start adapting, learning from what Wiggin did. Soon enough, Dragon Army would be facing armies that were divided into five toons, not four, and that moved in a free-ranging style with a lot more discretion given to the toon leaders. The kids didn't get to Battle School because they were idiots. The only reason the techniques worked a second time was because there'd only been a day since the first battle, and nobody expected to have to face Wiggin again so soon. Now they'd know that changes would have to be made fast. Bean guessed that they'd probably never see another formation.

What then? Had Wiggin emptied his magazine, or would he have new tricks up his sleeve? The trouble was, innovation never resulted in victory over the long term. It was too easy for the enemy to imitate and improve on your innovations. The real test for Wiggin would be what he did when he was faced with slugfests between armies using similar tactics.

And the real test for me will be seeing if I can stand it

when Wiggin makes some stupid mistake and I have to sit here as an ordinary soldier and watch him do it.

The third day, another battle. The fourth day, another. Victory. Victory. But each time, the score was closer. Each time, Bean gained more confidence as a soldier—and became more frustrated that the most he could contribute, beyond his own good aim, was occasionally making a suggestion to Crazy Tom, or reminding him of something Bean had noticed and remembered.

Bean wrote to Dimak about it, explaining how he was being underused and suggesting that he would be getting better trained by working with a worse commander, where he'd have a better chance of getting his own toon.

The answer was short. "Who else would want you? Learn from Ender."

Brutal but true. No doubt even Wiggin didn't really want him. Either he was forbidden to transfer any of his soldiers, or he had tried to trade Bean away and no one would take him.

———

It was free time of the evening after their fourth battle. Most of the others were trying to keep up with their classwork—the battles were really taking it out of them, especially because they could all see that they needed to practice hard to stay ahead. Bean, though, coasted through classwork like always, and when Nikolai told him he didn't need any more damned help with his assignments, Bean decided that he should take a walk.

Passing Wiggin's quarters—a space even smaller than the cramped quarters the teachers had, just space for a bunk, one chair, and a tiny table—Bean was tempted to knock on the door and sit down and have it out with Wiggin once and for all. Then common sense prevailed over frustration and vanity, and Bean wandered until he came to the arcade.

It wasn't as full as it used to be. Bean figured that was because everyone was holding extra practices now, trying to implement whatever they thought it was Wiggin was doing before they actually had to face him in battle. Still, a few were still willing to fiddle with the controllers and make things move on screens or in holodisplays.

Bean found a flat-screen game that had, as its hero, a mouse. No one was using it, so Bean started maneuvering it through a maze. Quickly the maze gave way to the wallspaces and crawlspaces of an old house, with traps set here and there, easy stuff. Cats chased him—ho hum. He jumped up onto a table and found himself face to face with a giant.

A giant who offered him a drink.

This was the fantasy game. This was the psychological game that everybody else played on their desks all the time. No wonder no one was playing it here. They all recognized it and that wasn't the game they came here to play.

Bean was well aware that he was the only kid in the school who had never played the fantasy game. They had tricked him into playing this once, but he doubted that anything important could be learned from what he had done so far. So screw 'em. They could trick him into playing up to a point, but he didn't have to go further.

Except that the giant's face had changed. It was Achilles.

Bean stood there in shock for a moment. Frozen, frightened. How did they know? Why did they do it? To put him face-to-face with Achilles, by surprise like that. Those bastards.

He walked away from the game.

Moments later, he turned around and came back. The giant was no longer on the screen. The mouse was running around again, trying to get out of the maze.

No, I won't play. Achilles is far away and he does not have the power to hurt me. Or Poke either, not anymore. I don't have to think about him and I sure as hell don't have to drink anything he offers me.

Bean walked away again, and this time did not come back.

He found himself down by the mess. It had just closed, but Bean had nothing better to do, so he sat down in the corridor beside the mess hall door and rested his forehead on his knees and thought about Rotterdam and sitting on top of a garbage can watching Poke working with her crew and how she was the most decent crew boss he'd seen, the way she listened to the little kids and gave them a fair share and kept them alive even if it meant not eating so much herself and that's why he chose her, because she had mercy—mercy enough that she just might listen to a child.

Her mercy killed her.

I killed her when I chose her.

There better be a God. So he can damn Achilles to hell forever.

Someone kicked at his foot.

"Go away," said Bean, "I'm not bothering you."

Whoever it was kicked again, knocking Bean's feet out from under him. With his hands he caught himself from falling over. He looked up. Bonzo Madrid loomed over him.

"I understand you're the littlest dingleberry clinging to the butt hairs of Dragon Army," said Bonzo.

He had three other guys with him. Big guys. They all had bully faces.

"Hi, Bonzo."

"We need to talk, pinprick."

"What is this, espionage?" asked Bean. "You're not supposed to talk to soldiers in other armies."

"I don't need espionage to find out how to beat Dragon Army," said Bonzo.

"So you're just looking for the littlest Dragon soldiers wherever you can find them, and then you'll push them around a little till they cry?"

Bonzo's face showed his anger. Not that it didn't always show anger.

"Are you begging to eat out of your own asshole, pin-prick?"

Bean didn't like bullies right now. And since, at the moment, he felt guilty of murdering Poke, he didn't really care if Bonzo Madrid ended up being the one to administer the death penalty. It was time to speak his mind.

"You're at least three times my weight," said Bean, "except inside your skull. You're a second-rater who somehow got an army and never could figure out what to do with it. Wiggin is going to grind you into the ground and he isn't even going to have to try. So does it really matter what you do to me? I'm the smallest and weakest soldier in the whole school. Naturally *I'm* the one you choose to kick around."

"Yeah, the smallest and weakest," said one of the other kids.

Bonzo didn't say anything, though. Bean's words had stung. Bonzo had his pride, and he knew now that if he harmed Bean it would be a humiliation, not a pleasure.

"Ender Wiggin isn't going to beat me with that collection of launchies and rejects that he calls an army. He may have psyched out a bunch of dorks like Carn and . . . *Petra.*" He spat her name. "But whenever *we* find crap my army can pound it flat."

Bean affixed him with his most withering glare. "Don't you get it, Bonzo? The teachers have picked Wiggin. He's the best. The best ever. They didn't give him the worst army. They gave him the *best* army. Those veterans you call rejects—they were soldiers so good that the *stupid* commanders couldn't get along with them and tried to transfer them away. Wiggin knows how to use good soldiers, even if you don't. That's why Wiggin is winning. He's smarter than you. And his soldiers are all smarter than your soldiers. The deck is stacked against you, Bonzo. You might as well give up now. When your pathetic little Salamander Army faces us, you'll be so whipped you'll have to pee sitting down."

Bean might have said more—it's not like he had a plan,

and there was certainly a lot more he could have said—
but he was interrupted. Two of Bonzo's friends scooped
him up and held him high against the wall, higher than
their own heads. Bonzo put one hand around his throat,
just under his jaw, and pressed back. The others let go.
Bean was hanging by his neck, and he couldn't breathe.
Reflexively he kicked, struggling to get some purchase
with his feet. But long-armed Bonzo was too far away for
any of Bean's kicking to land on him.

"The game is one thing," Bonzo said quietly. "The
teachers can rig that and give it to their little Wiggin cat-
amite. But there'll come a time when it isn't a game. And
when that time comes, it won't be a frozen flash suit that
makes it so Wiggin can't move. Comprendes?"

What answer was he hoping for? It was a sure thing
Bean couldn't nod or speak.

Bonzo just stood there, smiling maliciously, as Bean
struggled.

Everything started turning black around the edges of
Bean's vision before Bonzo finally let him drop to the
floor. He lay there, coughing and gasping.

What have I done? I goaded Bonzo Madrid. A bully
with none of Achilles' subtlety. When Wiggin beats him,
Bonzo isn't going to take it. He won't stop with a demonstration, either. His hatred for Wiggin runs deep.

As soon as he could breathe again, Bean headed back
to the barracks. Nikolai noticed the marks on his neck at
once. "Who was choking you?"

"I don't know," said Bean.

"Don't give me that," said Nikolai. "He was facing you,
look at the fingermarks."

"I don't remember."

"You remember the pattern of arteries on your own
placenta."

"I'm not going to tell you," said Bean. To that, Nikolai
had no answer, though he didn't like it.

Bean signed on as 'Graff and wrote a note to Dimak,
even though he knew it would do no good.

"Bonzo is insane. He could kill somebody, and Wiggin's the one he hates the most."

The answer came back quickly, almost as if Dimak had been waiting for the message. "Clean up your own messes. Don't go crying to mama."

The words stung. It wasn't Bean's mess, it was Wiggin's. And, ultimately, the teachers', for having put Wiggin in Bonzo's army to begin with. And then to taunt him because he didn't have a mother—when did the teachers become the enemy here? They were supposed to protect us from crazy kids like Bonzo Madrid. How do they think I'm going to clean this mess up?

The only thing that will stop Bonzo Madrid is to kill him.

And then Bean remembered standing there looking down at Achilles, saying, "You got to kill him."

Why couldn't I have kept my mouth shut? Why did I have to goad Bonzo Madrid? Wiggin is going to end up like Poke. And it will be my fault again.

16

Companion

"So you see, Anton, the key you found has been turned, and it may be the salvation of the human race."

"But the poor boy. To live his life so small, and then die as a giant."

"Perhaps he'll be . . . amused at the irony."

"How strange to think that my little key might turn out to be the salvation of the human race. From the invading beasts, anyway. Who will save us when we become our own enemy again?"

"We are not enemies, you and I."

"Not many people are enemies to anyone. But the ones full of greed or hate, pride or fear—their passion is strong enough to lever all the world into war."

"If God can raise up a great soul to save us from one menace, might he not answer our prayers by raising up another when we need him?"

"But Sister Carlotta, you know the boy you speak of was not raised up by God. He was created by a kidnapper, a baby-killer, an outlaw scientist."

"Do you know why Satan is so angry all the time? Because whenever he works a particularly clever bit of mischief, God uses it to serve his own righteous purposes."

"So God uses wicked people as his tools."

"God gives us the freedom to do great evil, if we choose. Then he uses his own freedom to create goodness out of that evil, for that is what he chooses."

"So in the long run, God always wins."

"Yes."

"In the short run, though, it *can* be uncomfortable."

"And when, in the past, would you have preferred to die, instead of being alive here today?"

"There it is. We get used to everything. We find hope in anything."

"That's why I've never understood suicide. Even those suffering from great depression or guilt—don't they feel Christ the Comforter in their hearts, giving them hope?"

"You're asking me?"

"God not being convenient, I ask a fellow mortal."

"In my view, suicide is not really the wish for life to end."

"What is it, then?"

"It is the only way a powerless person can find to make everybody else look away from his shame. The wish is not to die, but to hide."

"As Adam and Eve hid from the Lord."

"Because they were naked."

"If only such sad people could remember: Everyone is naked. Everyone wants to hide. But life is still sweet. Let it go on."

"You don't believe that the Formics are the beast of the Apocalypse, then, Sister?"

"No, Anton. I believe they are also children of God."

"And yet you found this boy specifically so he could grow up to destroy them."

"*Defeat* them. Besides, if God does not want them to die, they will not die."

"And if God wants *us* to die, we will. Why do you work so hard, then?"

"Because these hands of mine, I gave them to God, and I serve him as best I can. If he had not wanted me to find Bean, I would not have found him."

"And if God wants the Formics to prevail?"

"He'll find some other hands to do it. For that job, he can't have mine."

Lately, while the toon leaders drilled the soldiers, Wiggin had taken to disappearing. Bean used his ^Graff logon to find what he was doing. He'd gone back to studying the vids of Mazer Rackham's victory, much more intensely and single-mindedly than ever before. And this time, because Wiggin's army was playing games daily and winning them all, the other commanders and many toon leaders and common soldiers as well began to go to the library and watch the same vids, trying to make sense of them, trying to see what Wiggin saw.

Stupid, thought Bean. Wiggin isn't looking for anything to use here in Battle School—he's created a powerful, versatile army and he'll figure out what to do with them on the spot. He's studying those vids in order to figure out how to beat the Buggers. Because he knows now: He will face them someday. The teachers would not be wrecking the whole system here in Battle School if they were not nearing the crisis, if they did not need Ender Wiggin to save us from the invading Buggers. So Wiggin studies the Buggers, desperate for some idea of what they want, how they fight, how they die.

Why don't the teachers see that Wiggin is done? He's not even thinking about Battle School anymore. They should take him out of here and move him into Tactical School, or whatever the next stage of his training will be. Instead, they're pushing him, making him tired.

Us too. We're tired.

Bean saw it especially in Nikolai, who was working harder than the others just to keep up. If we were an ordinary army, thought Bean, most of us would be like Nikolai. As it is, many of us are—Nikolai was not the first to show his weariness. Soldiers drop silverware or food trays at mealtimes. At least one has wet his bed. We argue more at practice. Our classwork is suffering. Everyone has limits. Even me, even genetically-altered Bean the thinking machine, I need time to relubricate and refuel, and I'm not getting it.

Bean even wrote to Colonel Graff about it, a snippy little note saying only, "It is one thing to train soldiers and quite another to wear them out." He got no reply.

Late afternoon, with a half hour before mess call. They had already won a game that morning and then practiced after class, though the toon leaders, at Wiggin's suggestion, had let their soldiers go early. Most of Dragon Army was now dressing after showers, though some had already gone on to kill time in the game room or the video room . . . or the library. Nobody was paying attention to classwork now, but a few still went through the motions.

Wiggin appeared in the doorway, brandishing the new orders.

A second battle on the *same day.*

"This one's hot and there's no time," said Wiggin. "They gave Bonzo notice about twenty minutes ago, and by the time we get to the door they'll have been inside for a good five minutes at least."

He sent the four soldiers nearest the door—all young, but not launchies anymore, they were veterans now—to bring back the ones who had left. Bean dressed quickly— he had learned how to do it by himself now, but not without hearing plenty of jokes about how he was the only soldier who had to practice getting dressed, and it was still slow.

As they dressed, there was plenty of complaining about how this was getting stupid, Dragon Army should have a break now and then. Fly Molo was the loudest, but even Crazy Tom, who usually laughed at everything, was pissed about it. When Tom said, "Same day nobody ever do two battles!" Wiggin answered, "Nobody ever beat Dragon Army, either. This be your big chance to lose?"

Of course not. Nobody intended to lose. They just wanted to complain about it.

It took a while, but finally they were gathered in the corridor to the battleroom. The gate was already open. A few of the last arrivals were still putting on their flash suits. Bean was right behind Crazy Tom, so he could see down into the room. Bright light. No stars, no grid, no hiding place of any kind. The enemy gate was open, and yet there was not a Salamander soldier to be seen.

"My heart," said Crazy Tom. "They haven't come out yet, either."

Bean rolled his eyes. Of course they were out. But in a room without cover, they had simply formed themselves up on the ceiling, gathered around Dragon Army's gate, ready to destroy everybody as they came out.

Wiggin caught Bean's facial expression and smiled as he covered his own mouth to signal them all to be silent. He pointed all around the gate, to let them know where Salamander was gathered, then motioned for them to move back.

The strategy was simple and obvious. Since Bonzo Madrid had kindly pinned his army against a wall, ready to be slaughtered, it only remained to find the right way to enter the battleroom and carry out the massacre.

Wiggin's solution—which Bean liked—was to transform the larger soldiers into armored vehicles by having them kneel upright and freeze their legs. Then a smaller soldier knelt on each big kid's calves, wrapped one arm around the bigger soldier's waist, and prepared to fire. The largest soldiers were used as launchers, throwing each pair into the battleroom.

For once being small had its advantages. Bean and Crazy Tom were the pair Wiggin used to demonstrate what he wanted them all to do. As a result, when the first two pairs were thrown into the room, Bean got to begin the slaughter. He had three kills almost at once—at such close range, the beam was tight and the kills came fast. And as they began to go out of range, Bean climbed around Crazy Tom and launched off of him, heading east and somewhat up while Tom went even faster toward the far side of the room. When other Dragons saw how Bean had managed to stay within firing range, while moving sideways and therefore remaining hard to hit, many of them did the same. Eventually Bean was disabled, but it hardly mattered—Salamander was wiped out to the last man, and without a single one of them getting off the wall. Even when it was obvious they were easy, stationary targets, Bonzo didn't catch on that he was doomed until he himself was already frozen, and nobody else had the initiative to countermand his original order and start moving so they wouldn't be so easy to hit. Just one more example of why a commander who ruled by fear and made all the decisions himself would always be beaten, sooner or later.

The whole battle had taken less than a full minute from the time Bean rode Crazy Tom through the door until the last Salamander was frozen.

What surprised Bean was that Wiggin, usually so calm, was pissed off and showing it. Major Anderson didn't even have a chance to give the official congratulations to the victor before Wiggin shouted at him, "I thought you were going to put us against an army that could match us in a fair fight."

Why would he think that? Wiggin must have had some kind of conversation with Anderson, must have been promised something that hadn't been delivered.

But Anderson explained nothing. "Congratulations on the victory, commander."

Wiggin wasn't going to have it. It wasn't going to be business as usual. He turned to his army and called out to Bean by name. "If you had commanded Salamander Army, what would you have done?"

Since another Dragon had used him to shove off in midair, Bean was now drifting down near the enemy gate, but he heard the question—Wiggin wasn't being subtle about this. Bean didn't want to answer, because he knew what a serious mistake this was, to speak slightingly of

Salamander and call on the smallest Dragon soldier to correct Bonzo's stupid tactics. Wiggin hadn't had Bonzo's hand around his throat the way Bean had. Still, Wiggin was commander, and Bonzo's tactics had been stupid, and it was fun to say so.

"Keep a shifting pattern of movement going in front of the door," Bean answered, loudly, so every soldier could hear him—even the Salamanders, still clinging to the ceiling. "You never hold still when the enemy knows exactly where you are."

Wiggin turned to Anderson again. "As long as you're cheating, why don't you train the other army to cheat intelligently!"

Anderson was still calm, ignoring Wiggin's outburst. "I suggest that you remobilize your army."

Wiggin wasn't wasting time with rituals today. He pressed the buttons to thaw both armies at once. And instead of forming up to receive formal surrender, he shouted at once, "Dragon Army dismissed!"

Bean was one of those nearest the gate, but he waited till nearly last, so that he and Wiggin left together. "Sir," said Bean. "You just humiliated Bonzo and he's—"

"I know," said Wiggin. He jogged away from Bean, not wanting to hear about it.

"He's dangerous!" Bean called after him. Wasted effort. Either Wiggin already knew he'd provoked the wrong bully, or he didn't care.

Did he do it deliberately? Wiggin was always in control of himself, always carrying out a plan. But Bean couldn't think of any plan that required yelling at Major Anderson and shaming Bonzo Madrid in front of his whole army.

Why would Wiggin do such a stupid thing?

———

It was almost impossible to think of geometry, even though there was a test tomorrow. Classwork was utterly unimportant now, and yet they went on taking the tests and turning in or failing to turn in their assignments. The last few days, Bean had begun to get less-than-perfect scores. Not that he didn't know the answers, or at least how to figure them out. It's that his mind kept wandering to things that mattered more—new tactics that might surprise an enemy; new tricks that the teachers might pull in the way they set things up; what might be, must be going on in the larger war, to cause the system to start breaking apart like this; what would happen on Earth and in the I.F. once the Buggers were defeated. If they were defeated. Hard to care about volumes, areas, faces, and dimensions of solids. On a test yesterday, working out problems of gravity near planetary and stellar masses, Bean finally gave up and wrote:

$$2 + 2 = \pi \sqrt{2 + n}$$

When you know the value of n, I'll finish this test.

He knew that the teachers all knew what was going on, and if they wanted to pretend that classwork still mattered, fine, let them, but *he* didn't have to play.

At the same time, he knew that the problems of gravity mattered to someone whose only likely future was in the International Fleet. He also needed a thorough grounding in geometry, since he had a pretty good idea of what math was yet to come. He wasn't going to be an engineer or artillerist or rocket scientist or even, in all likelihood, a pilot. But he had to know what they knew better than they knew it, or they'd never respect him enough to follow him.

Not tonight, that's all, thought Bean. Tonight I can rest. Tomorrow I'll learn what I need to learn. When I'm not so tired.

He closed his eyes.

He opened them again. He opened his locker and took out his desk.

Back on the streets of Rotterdam he had been tired,

worn out by hunger and malnutrition and despair. But he kept watching. Kept thinking. And therefore he was able to stay alive. In this army everyone was getting tired, which meant that there would be more and more stupid mistakes. Bean, of all of them, could least afford to become stupid. Not being stupid was the only asset he had.

He signed on. A message appeared in his display.

See me at once—Ender

It was only ten minutes before lights out. Maybe Wiggin sent the message three hours ago. But better late than never. He slid off his bunk, not bothering with shoes, and padded out into the corridor in his stocking feet. He knocked at the door marked

COMMANDER

DRAGON ARMY

"Come in," said Wiggin.

Bean opened the door and came inside. Wiggin looked tired in the way that Colonel Graff usually looked tired. Heavy skin around the eyes, face slack, hunched in the shoulders, but eyes still bright and fierce, watching, thinking. "Just saw your message," said Bean.

"Fine."

"It's near lights-out."

"I'll help you find your way in the dark."

The sarcasm surprised Bean. As usual, Wiggin had completely misunderstood the purpose of Bean's comment. "I just didn't know if you knew what time it was—"

"I always know what time it is."

Bean sighed inwardly. It never failed. Whenever he had any conversation with Wiggin, it turned into some kind of pissing contest, which Bean always lost even when it was Wiggin whose deliberate misunderstanding caused the whole thing. Bean hated it. He recognized Wiggin's genius and honored him for it. Why couldn't he see anything good in Bean?

But Bean said nothing. There was nothing he could say that would improve the situation. Wiggin had called him in. Let Wiggin move the meeting forward.

"Remember four weeks ago, Bean? When you told me to make you a toon leader?"

"Eh."

"I've made five toon leaders and five assistants since then. And none of them was you." Wiggin raised his eyebrows. "Was I right?"

"Yes, sir." But only because you didn't bother to give me a chance to prove myself before you made the assignments.

"So tell me how you've done in these eight battles."

Bean wanted to point out how time after time, his suggestions to Crazy Tom had made C toon the most effective in the army. How his tactical innovations and creative responses to flowing situations had been imitated by the other soldiers. But that would be brag and borderline insubordination. It wasn't what a soldier who wanted to be an officer would say. Either Crazy Tom had reported Bean's contribution or he hadn't. It wasn't Bean's place to report on anything about himself that wasn't public record. "Today was the first time they disabled me so early, but the computer listed me as getting eleven hits before I had to stop. I've never had less than five hits in a battle. I've also completed every assignment I've been given."

"Why did they make you a soldier so young, Bean?"

"No younger than you were." Technically not true, but close enough.

"But why?"

What was he getting at? It was the teachers' decision. Had he found out that Bean was the one who composed the roster? Did he know that Bean had chosen himself? "I don't know."

"Yes you do, and so do I."

No, Wiggin wasn't asking specifically about why *Bean* was made a soldier. He was asking why launchies were suddenly getting promoted so young. "I've tried to guess, but they're just guesses." Not that Bean's guesses were ever just guesses—but then, neither were Wiggin's. "You're—very good. They knew that, they pushed you ahead—"

"Tell me *why,* Bean."

And now Bean understood the question he was really asking. "Because they need us, that's why." He sat on the floor and looked, not into Wiggin's face, but at his feet. Bean knew things that he wasn't supposed to know. That the teachers didn't know he knew. And in all likelihood, there were teachers monitoring this conversation. Bean couldn't let his face give away how much he really understood. "Because they need somebody to beat the Buggers. That's the only thing they care about."

"It's important that you know that, Bean."

Bean wanted to demand, Why is it important that *I* know it? Or are you just saying that people in general should know it? Have you finally seen and understood who I am? That I'm *you,* only smarter and less likable, the better strategist but the weaker commander? That if you fail, if you break, if you get sick and die, then I'm the one? Is that why I need to know this?

"Because," Wiggin went on, "most of the boys in this school think the game is important *for itself,* but it isn't. It's only important because it helps them find kids who might grow up to be real commanders, in the real war. But as for the game, screw that. That's what they're doing. Screwing up the game."

"Funny," said Bean. "I thought they were just doing it to us." No, if Wiggin thought Bean needed to have this explained to him, he did *not* understand who Bean really was. Still, it was Bean in Wiggin's quarters, having this conversation with him. That was something.

"A game nine weeks earlier than it should have come. A game every day. And now two games in the same day.

Bean, I don't know what the teachers are doing, but my army is getting tired, and I'm getting tired, and they don't care at all about the rules of the game. I've pulled the old charts up from the computer. No one has ever destroyed so many enemies and kept so many of his own soldiers whole in the history of the game."

What was this, brag? Bean answered as brag was meant to be answered. "You're the best, Ender."

Wiggin shook his head. If he heard the irony in Bean's voice, he didn't respond to it. "Maybe. But it was no accident that I got the soldiers I got. Launchies, rejects from other armies, but put them together and my worst soldier could be a toon leader in another army. They've loaded things my way, but now they're loading it all against me. Bean, they want to break us down."

So Wiggin did understand how his army had been selected, even if he didn't know who had done the selecting. Or maybe he knew everything, and this was all that he cared to show Bean at this time. It was hard to guess how much of what Wiggin did was calculated and how much merely intuitive. "They can't break you."

"You'd be surprised." Wiggin breathed sharply, suddenly, as if there were a stab of pain, or he had to catch a sudden breath in a wind; Bean looked at him and realized that the impossible was happening. Far from baiting him, Ender Wiggin was actually confiding in him. Not much. But a little. Ender was letting Bean see that he was human. Bringing him into the inner circle. Making him . . . what? A counselor? A confidant?

"Maybe you'll be surprised," said Bean.

"There's a limit to how many clever new ideas I can come up with every day. Somebody's going to come up with something to throw at me that I haven't thought of before, and I won't be ready."

"What's the worst that could happen?" asked Bean. "You lose one game."

"Yes. That's the worst that could happen. I can't lose *any* games. Because if I lose *any* . . ."

He didn't complete the thought. Bean wondered what Ender imagined the consequences would be. Merely that the legend of Ender Wiggin, perfect soldier, would be lost? Or that his army would lose confidence in him, or in their own invincibility? Or was this about the larger war, and losing a game here in Battle School might shake the confidence of the teachers that Ender was the commander of the future, the one to lead the fleet, if he could be made ready before the Bugger invasion arrived?

Again, Bean did not know how much the teachers knew about what Bean had guessed about the progress of the wider war. Better to keep silence.

"I need you to be clever, Bean," said Ender. "I need you to think of solutions to problems we haven't seen yet. I want you to try things that no one has ever tried because they're absolutely stupid."

So what is this about, Ender? What have you decided about me, that brings me into your quarters tonight? "Why me?"

"Because even though there are some better soldiers than you in Dragon Army—not many, but some—there's nobody who can think better and faster than you."

He *had* seen. And after a month of frustration, Bean realized that it was better this way. Ender had seen his work in battle, had judged him by what he did, not by his reputation in classes or the rumors about his having the highest scores in the history of the school. Bean had earned this evaluation, and it had been given him by the only person in this school whose high opinion Bean longed for.

Ender held out his desk for Bean to see. On it were twelve names. Two or three soldiers from each toon. Bean immediately knew how Ender had chosen them. They were all good soldiers, confident and reliable. But not the flashy ones, the stunters, the show-offs. They were, in fact, the ones that Bean valued most highly among those who were not toon leaders. "Choose five of these," said Ender. "One from each toon. They're a special squad, and you'll train them. Only during the extra practice sessions. Talk to me about what you're training them to do. Don't spend too long on any one thing. Most of the time you and your squad will be part of the whole army, part of your regular toons. But when I need you. When there's something to be done that only you can do."

There was something else about these twelve. "These are all new. No veterans."

"After last week, Bean, all our soldiers are veterans. Don't you realize that on the individual soldier standings, all forty of our soldiers are in the top fifty? That you have to go down seventeen places to find a soldier who *isn't* a Dragon?"

"What if I can't think of anything?" asked Bean.

"Then I was wrong about you."

Bean grinned. "You weren't wrong."

The lights went out.

"Can you find your way back, Bean?"

"Probably not."

"Then stay here. If you listen very carefully, you can hear the good fairy come in the night and leave our assignment for tomorrow."

"They won't give us another battle tomorrow, will they?" Bean meant it as a joke, but Ender didn't answer.

Bean heard him climb into bed.

Ender was still small for a commander. His feet didn't come near the end of the bunk. There was plenty of room for Bean to curl up at the foot of the bed. So he climbed up and then lay still, so as not to disturb Ender's sleep. If he was sleeping. If he was not lying awake in the silence, trying to make sense of . . . what?

For Bean, the assignment was merely to think of the unthinkable—stupid ploys that might be used against them, and ways to counter them; equally stupid innovations they might introduce in order to sow confusion among the other armies and, Bean suspected, get them sidetracked into imitating completely nonessential strategies. Since few of the other commanders understood why

Dragon Army was winning, they kept imitating the nonce tactics used in a particular battle instead of seeing the underlying method Ender used in training and organizing his army. As Napoleon said, the only thing a commander ever truly controls is his own army—training, morale, trust, initiative, command and, to a lesser degree, supply, placement, movement, loyalty, and courage in battle. What the enemy will do and what chance will bring, those defy all planning. The commander must be able to change his plans abruptly when obstacles or opportunities appear. If his army isn't ready and willing to respond to his will, his cleverness comes to nothing.

The less effective commanders didn't understand this. Failing to recognize that Ender won because he and his army responded fluidly and instantly to change, they could only think to imitate the specific tactics they saw him use. Even if Bean's creative gambits were irrelevant to the outcome of the battle, they would lead other commanders to waste time imitating irrelevancies. Now and then something he came up with might actually be useful. But by and large, he was a sideshow.

That was fine with Bean. If Ender wanted a sideshow, what mattered was that he had chosen Bean to create that show, and Bean would do it as well as it could be done.

But if Ender was lying awake tonight, it was not because he was concerned about Dragon Army's battles tomorrow and the next day and the next. Ender was thinking about the Buggers and how he would fight them when he got through his training and was thrown into war, with the real lives of real men depending on his decisions, with the survival of humanity depending on the outcome.

In *that* scheme, what is my place? thought Bean. I'm glad enough that the burden is on Ender, not because I could not bear it—maybe I could—but because I have more confidence that Ender can bring it off than that I could. Whatever it is that makes men love the commander who decides when they will die, Ender has that, and if I have it no one has yet seen evidence of it. Besides, even without genetic alteration, Ender has abilities that the tests didn't measure for, that run deeper than mere intellect.

But he shouldn't have to bear all this alone. I can help him. I can forget geometry and astronomy and all the other nonsense and concentrate on the problems he faces most directly. I'll do research into the way other animals wage war, especially swarming hive insects, since the Formics resemble ants the way we resemble primates.

And I can watch his back.

Bean thought again of Bonzo Madrid. Of the deadly rage of bullies in Rotterdam.

Why have the teachers put Ender in this position? He's an obvious target for the hatred of the other boys. Kids in Battle School had war in their hearts. They hungered for triumph. They loathed defeat. If they lacked these attributes, they would never have been brought here. Yet from the start, Ender had been set apart from the others—younger but smarter, the leading soldier and now the commander who makes all other commanders look like babies. Some commanders responded to defeat by becoming submissive—Carn Carby, for instance, now praised Ender behind his back and studied his battles to try to learn how to win, never realizing that you had to study Ender's training, not his battles, to understand his victories. But most of the other commanders were resentful, frightened, ashamed, angry, jealous, and it was in their character to translate such feelings into violent action . . . if they were sure of victory.

Just like the streets of Rotterdam. Just like the bullies, struggling for supremacy, for rank, for respect. Ender has stripped Bonzo naked. It cannot be borne. He'll have his revenge, as surely as Achilles avenged his humiliation.

And the teachers understand this. They intend it. Ender has clearly mastered every test they set for him—whatever Battle School usually taught, he was done with. So why didn't they move him on to the next level? Because there was a lesson they were trying to teach, or a test they were trying to get him to pass, which was not within the usual curriculum. Only this particular test could end in death. Bean had felt Bonzo's fingers around his throat. This was a boy who, once he let himself go, would relish the absolute power that the murderer achieves at his victim's moment of death.

They're putting Ender into a street situation. They're testing him to see if he can survive.

They don't know what they're doing, the fools. The street is not a test. The street is a lottery.

I came out a winner—I was alive. But Ender's survival won't depend on his ability. Luck plays too large a role. Plus the skill and resolve and power of the opponent.

Bonzo may be unable to control the emotions that weaken him, but his presence in Battle School means that he is not without skill. He was made a commander because a certain type of soldier will follow him into death and horror. Ender is in mortal danger. And the teachers, who think of us as children, have no idea how quickly death can come. Look away for only a few minutes, step away far enough that you can't get back in time, and your precious Ender Wiggin, on whom all your hopes are pinned, will be quite, quite dead. I saw it on the streets of Rotterdam. It can happen just as easily in your nice clean rooms here in space.

So Bean set aside classwork for good that night, lying at Ender's feet. Instead, he had two new courses of study. He would help Ender prepare for the war he cared about, with the Buggers. But he would also help him in the street fight that was being set up for him.

It wasn't that Ender was oblivious, either. After some kind of fracas in the battleroom during one of Ender's early freetime practices, Ender had taken a course in self-defense, and knew something about fighting man to man. But Bonzo would not come at him man to man. He was too keenly aware of having been beaten. Bonzo's purpose would not be a rematch, it would not be vindication. It would be punishment. It would be elimination. He would bring a gang.

And the teachers would not realize the danger until it was too late. They still didn't think of anything the children did as "real."

So after Bean thought of clever, stupid things to do with his new squad, he also tried to think of ways to set Bonzo up so that, in the crunch, he would have to take on Ender Wiggin alone or not at all. Strip away Bonzo's support. Destroy the morale, the reputation of any bully who might go along with him.

This is one job Ender *can't* do. But it can be done.

Part Five

LEADER

17

Deadline

"I don't even know how to interpret this. The mind game had only one shot at Bean, and it puts up this one kid's face, and he goes off the charts with—what, fear? Rage? Isn't there anybody who knows how this so-called game works? It ran Ender through a wringer, brought in those pictures of his brother that it couldn't possibly have had, only it got them. And this one—was it some deeply insightful gambit that leads to powerful new conclusions about Bean's psyche? Or was it simply the only person Bean knew whose picture was already in the Battle School files?"

"Was that a rant, or is there any particular one of those questions you want answered?"

"What I want you to answer is this question: How the hell can you tell me that something was 'very significant' if you have no idea what it signifies!"

"If someone runs after your car, screaming and waving his arms, you know that something significant is intended, even if you can't hear a word he's saying."

"So that's what this was? Screaming?"

"That was an analogy. The image of Achilles was extraordinarily important to Bean."

"Important positive, or important negative?"

"That's too cut-and-dried. If it was negative, are his negative feelings because Achilles caused some terrible trauma in Bean? Or negative because having been torn away from Achilles was traumatic, and Bean longs to be restored to him?"

"So if we have an independent source of information that tells us to keep them apart . . ."

"Then either that independent source is really really right. . . ."

"Or really really wrong."

"I'd be more specific if I could. We only had a minute with him."

"That's disingenuous. You've had the mind game linked to all his work with his teacher-identity."

"And we've reported to you about that. It's partly his hunger to have control—that's how it began—but it has since become a way of taking responsibility. He has, in a way, *become* a teacher. He has also used his inside information to give himself the illusion of belonging to the community."

"He does belong."

"He has only one close friend, and that's more of a big brother, little brother thing."

"I have to decide whether I can put Achilles into Battle School while Bean is there, or give up one of them in order to keep the other. Now, from Bean's response to Achilles' face, what counsel can you give me."

"You won't like it."

"Try me."

"From that incident, we can tell you that putting them together will be either a really really bad thing, or—"

"I'm going to have to take a long, hard look at your budget."

"Sir, the whole purpose of the program, the way it

works, is that the computer makes connections we would never think of, and gets responses we weren't looking for. It's not actually under our control."

"Just because a program isn't out of control doesn't mean intelligence is present, either in the program or the programmer."

"We don't use the word 'intelligence' with software. We regard that as a naive idea. We say that it's 'complex.' Which means that we don't always understand what it's doing. We don't always get conclusive information."

"Have you *ever* gotten conclusive information about anything?"

"*I* chose the wrong word this time. 'Conclusive' isn't ever the goal when we are studying the human mind."

"Try 'useful.' Anything useful?"

"Sir, I've told you what we know. The decision was yours before we reported to you, and it's still your decision now. Use our information or not, but is it sensible to shoot the messenger?"

"When the messenger won't tell you what the hell the message *is*, my trigger finger gets twitchy. Dismissed."

Nikolai's name was on the list that Ender gave him, but Bean ran into problems immediately.

"I don't want to," said Nikolai.

It had not occurred to Bean that anyone would refuse.

"I'm having a hard enough time keeping up as it is."

"You're a good soldier."

"By the skin of my teeth. With a big helping of luck."

"That's how *all* good soldiers do it."

"Bean, if I lose one practice a day from my regular toon, then I'll fall behind. How can I make it up? And one practice a day with you won't be enough. I'm a smart kid, Bean, but I'm not Ender. I'm not you. That's the thing that I don't think you really get. How it feels *not* to be you. Things just aren't as easy and clear."

"It's not easy for me, either."

"Look, I know that, Bean. And there are some things I

310 ORSON SCOTT CARD

can do for you. This isn't one of them. Please."

It was Bean's first experience with command, and it wasn't working. He found himself getting angry, wanting to say Screw you and go on to someone else. Only he couldn't be angry at the only true friend he had. And he also couldn't easily take no for an answer. "Nikolai, what we're doing won't be hard. Stunts and tricks."

Nikolai closed his eyes. "Bean, you're making me feel bad."

"I don't want you to feel bad, Sinterklaas, but this is the assignment I was given, because Ender thinks Dragon Army needs this. You were on the list, his choice not mine."

"But you don't have to choose me."

"So I ask the next kid, and he says, 'Nikolai's on this squad, right?' and I say, No, he didn't want to. That makes them all feel like they can say no. And they'll *want* to say no, because nobody wants to be taking orders from me."

"A month ago, sure, that would have been true. But they know you're a solid soldier. I've heard people talk about you. They respect you."

Again, it would have been so easy to do what Nikolai wanted and let him off the hook on this. And, as a friend, that would be the *right* thing to do. But Bean couldn't think as a friend. He had to deal with the fact that he had been given a command and he had to make it work.

Did he really need Nikolai?

"I'm just thinking out loud, Nikolai, because you're the only one I can say this to, but see, I'm scared. I wanted to lead a toon, but that's because I didn't know anything about what leaders do. I've had a week of battles to see how Crazy Tom holds the group of us together, the voice he uses for command. To see how Ender trains us and trusts us, and it's a dance, tiptoe, leap, spin, and I'm afraid that I'll fail, and there isn't *time* to fail, I have to make this work, and when you're with me, I know there's at least one person who isn't halfway hoping for this smart little kid to fail."

"Don't kid yourself," said Nikolai. "As long as we're being honest."

That stung. But a leader had to take that, didn't he? "No matter what you feel, Nikolai, you'll give me a chance," said Bean. "And because you're giving me a chance, the others will, too. I need . . . loyalty."

"So do I, Bean."

"You need my loyalty as a friend, in order to let you, personally, be happy," said Bean. "I need loyalty as a leader, in order to fulfil the assignment given to us by our commander."

"That's mean," said Nikolai.

"Eh," said Bean. "Also true."

"You're mean, Bean."

"Help me, Nikolai."

"Looks like our friendship goes only one way."

Bean had never felt like this before—this knife in his heart, just because of the words he was hearing, just because somebody *else* was angry with him. It wasn't just because he wanted Nikolai to think well of him. It was because he knew that Nikolai was at least partly right. Bean was using his friendship against him.

It wasn't because of that pain, however, that Bean decided to back off. It was because a soldier who was with him against his will would not serve him well. Even if he was a friend. "Look, if you won't, you won't. I'm sorry I made you mad. I'll do it without you. And you're right, I'll do fine. Still friends, Nikolai?"

Nikolai took his offered hand, held it. "Thank you," he whispered.

Bean went immediately to Shovel, the only one on Ender's list who was also from C toon. Shovel wasn't Bean's first choice—he had just the slightest tendency to delay, to do things halfheartedly. But because he was in C toon, Shovel had been there when Bean advised Crazy Tom. He had observed Bean in action.

Shovel set aside his desk when Bean asked if they could talk for a minute. As with Nikolai, Bean clambered up onto the bunk to sit beside the larger boy. Shovel was from Cagnes-sur-Mer, a little town on the French Riviera, and he still had that open-faced friendliness of Provence. Bean liked him. Everybody liked him.

Quickly Bean explained what Ender had asked him to do—though he didn't mention that it was just a sideshow. Nobody would give up a daily practice for a something that wouldn't be crucial to victory. "You were on the list Ender gave me, and I'd like you to—"

"Bean, what are you doing?"

Crazy Tom stood in front of Shovel's bunk.

At once Bean realized his mistake. "Sir," said Bean, "I should have talked to you first. I'm new at this and I just didn't think."

"New at what?"

Again Bean laid out what he had been asked to do by Ender.

"And Shovel's on the list?"

"Right."

"So I'm going to lose you *and* Shovel from my practices?"

"Just one practice per day."

"I'm the only toon leader who loses two."

"Ender said one from each toon. Five, plus me. Not my choice."

"Merda," said Crazy Tom. "You and Ender just didn't think of the fact that this is going to hit me harder than any of the other toon leaders. Whatever you're doing, why can't you do it with five instead of six? You and four others—one from each of the other toons?"

Bean wanted to argue, but realized that going head to head wasn't going to get him anywhere. "You're right, I didn't think of that, and you're right that Ender might very well change his mind when he realizes what he's doing to your practices. So when he comes in this morning, why don't you talk to him and let me know what the two of you decide? In the meantime, though, Shovel might tell me no, and then the question doesn't matter anymore, right?"

Crazy Tom thought about it. Bean could see the anger ticking away in him. But leadership had changed Crazy Tom. He no longer blew up the way he used to. He caught himself. He held it in. He waited it out.

"OK, I'll talk to Ender. If Shovel wants to do it."

They both looked at Shovel.

"I think it'd be OK," said Shovel. "To do something weird like this."

"I won't let up on either of you," said Crazy Tom. "And you don't talk about your wacko toon during my practices. You keep it outside."

They both agreed to that. Bean could see that Crazy Tom was wise to insist on that. This special assignment would set the two of them apart from the others in C toon. If they rubbed their noses in it, the others could feel shut out of an elite. That problem wouldn't show up as much in any of the other toons, because there'd only be one kid from each toon in Bean's squad. No chat. Therefore no nose-rubbing.

"Look, I don't have to talk to Ender about this," said Crazy Tom. "Unless it becomes a problem. OK?"

"Thanks," said Bean.

Crazy Tom went back to his own bunk.

I did that OK, thought Bean. I didn't screw up.

"Bean?" said Shovel.

"Eh?"

"One thing."

"Eh."

"Don't call me Shovel."

Bean thought back. Shovel's real name was Ducheval. "You prefer 'Two Horses'? Sounds kind of like a Sioux warrior."

Shovel grinned. "That's better than sounding like the tool you use to clean the stable."

"Ducheval," said Bean. "From now on."

"Thanks. When do we start?"

"Freetime practice today."

"Bacana."

Bean almost danced away from Ducheval's bunk. He had done it. He had handled it. Once, anyway.

And by the time breakfast was over, he had all five on his toon. With the other four, he checked with their toon leaders first. No one turned him down. And he got his squad to promise to call Ducheval by his right name from then on.

———

Graff had Dimak and Dap in his makeshift office in the battleroom bridge when Bean came. It was the usual argument between Dimak and Dap—that is, it was about nothing, some trivial question of one violating some minor protocol or other, which escalated quickly into a flurry of formal complaints. Just another skirmish in their rivalry, as Dap and Dimak tried to gain some advantage for their proteges, Ender and Bean, while at the same time trying to keep Graff from putting them in the physical danger that both saw looming. When the knock came at the door, voices had been raised for some time, and because the knock was not loud, it occurred to Graff to wonder what might have been overheard.

Had names been mentioned? Yes. Both Bean and Ender. And also Bonzo. Had Achilles' name come up? No. He had just been referred to as "another irresponsible decision endangering the future of the human race, all because of some insane theory about games being one thing and genuine life-and-death struggles being another, completely unproven and unprovable except in the blood of some child!" That was Dap, who had a tendency to wax eloquent.

Graff, of course, was already sick at heart, because he agreed with both teachers, not only in their arguments against each other, but also in their arguments against his own policy. Bean was demonstrably the better candidate on all tests; Ender was just as demonstrably the better candidate based on his performance in actual leadership situations. And Graff *was* being irresponsible to expose both boys to physical danger.

But in both cases, the child had serious doubts about his own courage. Ender had his long history of submission to his older brother, Peter, and the mind game had shown that in Ender's unconscious, Peter was linked to the Buggers. Graff knew that Ender had the courage to strike, without restraint, when the time came for it. That he could stand alone against an enemy, without anyone to help him, and destroy the one who would destroy him. But Ender didn't know it, and he had to know.

Bean, for his part, had shown physical symptoms of panic before his first battle, and while he ended up performing well, Graff didn't need any psychological tests to tell him that the doubt was there. The only difference was, in Bean's case Graff shared his doubt. There *was* no proof that Bean would strike.

Self-doubt was the one thing that neither candidate could afford to have. Against an enemy that did not hesitate—that *could* not hesitate—there could be no pause for reflection. The boys had to face their worst fears, knowing that no one would intervene to help. They had to know that when failure would be fatal, they would not fail. They had to pass the test and know that they had passed it. And both boys were so perceptive that the danger could not be faked. It had to *be* real.

Exposing them to that risk was utterly irresponsible of Graff. Yet he knew that it would be just as irresponsible not to. If Graff played it safe, no one would blame him if, in the actual war, Ender or Bean failed. That would be small consolation, though, given the consequences of failure. Whichever way he guessed, if he was wrong, everybody on Earth might pay the ultimate price. The only thing that made it possible was that if either of them was killed, or damaged physically or mentally, the other was still there to carry on as the sole remaining candidate.

If both failed, what then? There were many bright children, but none who were that much better than commanders already in place, who had graduated from Battle School many years ago.

Somebody has to roll the dice. Mine are the hands that hold those dice. I'm not a bureaucrat, placing my career above the larger purpose I was put here to serve. I will not put the dice in someone else's hands, or pretend that I don't have the choice I have.

For now, all Graff could do was listen to both Dap and Dimak, ignore their bureaucratic attacks and maneuvers against him, and try to keep them from each other's throats in their vicarious rivalry.

That small knock at the door—Graff knew before the door opened who it would be.

If he had heard the argument, Bean gave no sign. But then, that was Bean's specialty, giving no sign. Only Ender managed to be more secretive—and he, at least, had played the mind game long enough to give the teachers a map of his psyche.

"Sir," said Bean.

"Come in, Bean." Come in, Julian Delphiki, longed-for child of good and loving parents. Come in, kidnapped child, hostage of fate. Come and talk to the Fates, who are playing such clever little games with your life.

"I can wait," said Bean.

"Captain Dap and Captain Dimak can hear what you have to say, can't they?" asked Graff.

"If you say so, sir. It's not a secret. I would like to have access to station supplies."

"Denied."

"That's not acceptable, sir."

Graff saw how both Dap and Dimak glanced at him. Amused at the audacity of the boy? "Why do you think so?"

"Short notice, games every day, soldiers exhausted and yet still being pressured to perform in class—fine, Ender's dealing with it and so are we. But the only possible reason you could be doing this is to test our resourcefulness. So I want some resources."

"I don't remember your being commander of Dragon Army," said Graff. "I'll listen to a requisition for specific equipment from your commander."

"Not possible," said Bean. "He doesn't have time to waste on foolish bureaucratic procedures."

Foolish bureaucratic procedures. Graff had used that exact phrase in the argument just a few minutes ago. But Graff's voice had *not* been raised. How long *had* Bean been listening outside the door? Graff cursed himself silently. He had moved his office up here specifically because he knew Bean was a sneak and a spy, gathering intelligence however he could. And then he didn't even post a guard to stop the boy from simply walking up and listening at the door.

"And you do?" asked Graff.

"I'm the one he assigned to think of stupid things you might do to rig the game against us, and think of ways to deal with them."

"What do you think you're going to find?"

"I don't know," said Bean. "I just know that the only things *we* ever see are our uniforms and flash suits, our weapons and our desks. There are other supplies here. For instance, there's paper. We never get any except during written tests, when our desks are closed to us."

"What would you do with paper in the battleroom?"

"I don't know," said Bean. "Wad it up and throw it around. Shred it and make a cloud of dust out of it."

"And who would clean this up?"

"Not my problem," said Bean.

"Permission denied."

"That's not acceptable, sir," said Bean.

"I don't mean to hurt your feelings, Bean, but it matters less than a cockroach's fart whether you accept my decision or not."

"I don't mean to hurt *your* feelings, sir, but you clearly have no idea what you're doing. You're improvising.

Screwing with the system. The damage you're doing is going to take years to undo, and you don't care. That means that it doesn't matter what condition this school is in a year from now. That means that everybody who matters is going to be graduated soon. Training is being accelerated because the Buggers are getting too close for delays. So you're pushing. And you're especially pushing Ender Wiggin."

Graff felt sick. He knew that Bean's powers of analysis were extraordinary. So, also, were his powers of deception. Some of Bean's guesses weren't right—but was that because he didn't know the truth, or because he simply didn't want them to know how much he knew, or how much he guessed? *I never wanted you here, Bean, because you're too dangerous.*

Bean was still making his case. "When the day comes that Ender Wiggin is looking for ways to stop the Buggers from getting to Earth and scouring the whole planet the way they started to back in the First Invasion, are you going to give him some bullshit answer about what resources he can or cannot use?"

"As far as you're concerned, the ship's supplies don't exist."

"As far as I'm concerned," said Bean, "Ender is *this* close to telling you to fry up your game and eat it. He's sick of it—if you can't see that, you're not much of a teacher. He doesn't care about the standings. He doesn't care about beating other kids. All he cares about is preparing to fight the Buggers. So how hard do you think it will be for me to persuade him that your program here is crocked, and it's time to quit playing?"

"All right," said Graff. "Dimak, prepare the brig. Bean is to be confined until the shuttle is ready to take him back to Earth. This boy is out of Battle School."

Bean smiled slightly. "Go for it, Colonel Graff. I'm done here anyway. I've got everything *I* wanted here—a first-rate education. I'll never have to live on the street again. I'm home free. Let me out of your game, right now, I'm ready."

"You won't be free on Earth, either. Can't risk having you tell these wild stories about Battle School," said Graff.

"Right. Take the best student you ever had here and put him in jail because he asked for access to the supply closet and you didn't like it. Come on, Colonel Graff. Swallow hard and back down. You need my cooperation more than I need yours."

Dimak could barely conceal his smile.

If only confronting Graff like this were sufficient proof of Bean's courage. And for all that Graff had doubts about Bean, he didn't deny that he was good at maneuver. Graff would have given almost anything not to have Dimak and Dap in the room at this moment.

"It was your decision to have this conversation in front of witnesses," said Bean.

What, was the kid a mind reader?

No, Graff had glanced at the two teachers. Bean simply knew how to read his body language. The kid missed nothing. That's why he was so valuable to the program.

Isn't this why we pin our hopes on these kids? Because they're good at maneuver?

And if I know anything about command, don't I know this—that there are times when you cut your losses and leave the field?

"All right, Bean. One scan through supply inventory."

"With somebody to explain to me what it all is."

"I thought you already knew everything."

Bean was polite in victory; he did not respond to taunting. The sarcasm gave Graff a little compensation for having to back down. He knew that's all it was, but this job didn't have many perks.

"Captain Dimak and Captain Dap will accompany you," said Graff. "One scan, and either one of them can veto anything you request. They will be responsible for the consequences of any injuries resulting from your use of any item they let you have."

"Thank you, sir," said Bean. "In all likelihood I won't find anything useful. But I appreciate your fairminded-ness in letting us search the station's resources to further the educational objectives of the Battle School."

The kid had the jargon down cold. All those months of access to the student data, with all the notations in the files, Bean had clearly learned more than just the factual contents of the dossiers. And now Bean was giving him the spin that he should use in writing up a report about his decision. As if Graff were not perfectly capable of creating his own spin.

The kid is patronizing me. Little bastard thinks that he's in control.

Well, I have some surprises for him, too.

"Dismissed," said Graff. "All of you."

They got up, saluted, left.

Now, thought Graff, I have to second-guess all my future decisions, wondering how much my choices are influenced by the fact that this kid really pisses me off.

———

As Bean scanned the inventory list, he was really searching primarily for something, anything, that might be made into a weapon that Ender or some of his army could carry to protect him from physical attack by Bonzo. But there was nothing that would be both concealable from the teachers and powerful enough to give smaller kids sufficient leverage over larger ones.

It was a disappointment, but he'd find other ways to neutralize the threat. And now, as long as he was scanning the inventory, *was* there anything that he might be able to use in the battleroom? Cleaning supplies weren't very promising. Nor would the hardware stocks make much sense in the battleroom. What, throw a handful of screws?

The safety equipment, though . . .

"What's a deadline?" asked Bean.

Dimak answered. "Very fine, strong cord that's used to secure maintenance and construction workers when they're working outside the station."

"How long?"

"With links, we can assemble several kilometers of secure deadline," said Dimak. "But each coil unspools to a hundred meters."

"I want to see it."

They took him into parts of the station that children never went to. The decor was far more utilitarian here. Screws and rivets were visible in the plates on the walls. The intake ducts were visible instead of being hidden inside the ceiling. There were no friendly lightstripes for a child to touch and get directions to his barracks. All the palm pads were too high for a child to comfortably use. And the staff they passed saw Bean and then looked at Dap and Dimak as if they were crazy.

The coil was amazingly small. Bean hefted it. Light, too. He unspooled a few decameters of it. It was almost invisible. "This will hold?"

"The weight of two adults," said Dimak.

"It's so fine. Will it cut?"

"Rounded so smoothly it can't cut anything. Wouldn't do us any good if it went slicing through things. Like spacesuits."

"Can I cut it into short lengths?"

"With a blowtorch," said Dimak.

"This is what I want."

"Just one?" asked Dap, rather sarcastically.

"And a blowtorch," said Bean.

"Denied," said Dimak.

"I was joking," said Bean. He walked out of the supply room and started jogging down the corridor, retracing the route they had just taken.

They jogged after him. "Slow down!" Dimak called out.

"Keep up!" Bean answered. "I've got a toon waiting for me to train them with this."

"Train them to do what!"

"I don't know!" He got to the pole and slid down. It passed him right through to the student levels. Going this direction, there was no security clearance at all.

His toon was waiting for him in the battleroom. They'd been working hard for him the past few days, trying all kinds of lame things. Formations that could explode in midair. Screens. Attacks without guns, disarming enemies with their feet. Getting into and out of spins, which made them almost impossible to hit but also kept them from shooting at anybody else.

The most encouraging thing was the fact that Ender spent almost the entire practice time watching Bean's squad whenever he wasn't actually responding to questions from leaders and soldiers in the other toons. Whatever they came up with, Ender would know about it and have his own ideas about when to use it. And, knowing that Ender's eyes were on them, Bean's soldiers worked all the harder. It gave Bean more stature in their eyes, that Ender really did care about what they did.

Ender's good at this, Bean realized again for the hundredth time. He knows how to form a group into the shape he wants it to have. He knows how to get people to work together. And he does it by the most minimal means possible.

If Graff were as good at this as Ender, I wouldn't have had to act like such a bully in there today.

The first thing Bean tried with the deadline was to stretch it across the battleroom. It reached, with barely enough slack to allow knots to be tied at both ends. But a few minutes of experimentation showed that it would be completely ineffective as a tripwire. Most enemies would simply miss it; those that did run into it might be disoriented or flipped around, but once it was known that it was there, it could be used like part of a grid, which meant it would work to the advantage of a creative enemy.

The deadline was designed to keep a man from drifting

off into space. What happens when you get to the end of the line?

Bean left one end fastened to a handhold in the wall, but coiled the other end around his waist several times. The line was now shorter than the width of the battle-room's cube. Bean tied a knot in the line, then launched himself toward the opposite wall.

As he sailed through the air, the deadline tautening behind him, he couldn't help thinking: I hope they were right about this wire not being capable of cutting. What a way to end—sliced in half in the battleroom. *That* would be an interesting mess for them to clean up.

When he was a meter from the wall, the line went taut. Bean's forward progress was immediately halted at his waist. His body jacknifed and he felt like he'd been kicked in the gut. But the most surprising thing was the way his inertia was translated from forward movement into a sideways arc that whipped him across the battle-room toward where D toon was practicing. He hit the wall so hard he had what was left of his breath knocked out of him.

"Did you see that!" Bean screamed, as soon as he could breathe. His stomach hurt—he might not have been sliced in half, but he would have a vicious bruise, he knew that at once, and if he hadn't had his flash suit on, he could well believe there would have been internal injuries. But he'd be OK, and the deadline had let him change directions abruptly in midair. "Did you see it! Did you see it!"

"Are you all right!" Ender shouted.

He realized that Ender thought he was injured. Slowing down his speech, Bean called out again, "Did you see how fast I went! Did you see how I changed direction!"

The whole army stopped practice to watch as Bean played more with the deadline. Tying two soldiers together got interesting results when one of them stopped, but it was hard to hold on. More effective was when Bean had Ender use his hook to pull a star out of the wall and put it into the middle of the battleroom. Bean tied himself and launched from the star; when the line went taut, the edge of the star acted as a fulcrum, shortening the length of the line as he changed direction. And as the line wrapped around the star, it shortened even more upon reaching each edge. At the end, Bean was moving so fast that he blacked out for a moment upon hitting the star. But the whole of Dragon Army was stunned at what they had seen. The deadline was completely invisible, so it looked as though this little kid had launched himself and then suddenly started changing direction and speeding up in midflight. It was seriously disturbing to see it.

"Let's do it again, and see if I can shoot while I'm doing it," said Bean.

———

Evening practice didn't end till 2140, leaving little time before bed. But having seen the stunts Bean's squad was preparing, the army was excited instead of weary, fairly scampering through the corridors. Most of them probably understood that what Bean had come up with were stunts, nothing that would be decisive in battle. It was fun anyway. It was new. And it was Dragon.

Bean started out leading the way, having been given that honor by Ender. A time of triumph, and even though he knew he was being manipulated by the system— behavior modification through public honors—it still felt good.

Not so good, though, that he let up his alertness. He hadn't gone far along the corridor until he realized that there were too many Salamander uniforms among the other boys wandering around in this section. By 2140, most armies were in their barracks, with only a few stragglers coming back from the library or the vids or the game room. Too many Salamanders, and the other soldiers were often big kids from armies whose commanders bore no special love toward Ender. It didn't take a genius to recognize a trap.

Bean jogged back and tagged Crazy Tom, Vlad, and

Hot Soup, who were walking together. "Too many Salamanders," Bean said. "Stay back with Ender." They got it at once—it was public knowledge that Bonzo was breathing out threats about what "somebody" ought to do to Ender Wiggin, just to put him in his place. Bean continued his shambling, easygoing run toward the back of the army, ignoring the smaller kids but tagging the other two toon leaders and all the seconds—the older kids, the ones who might have some chance of standing up to Bonzo's crew in a fight. Not *much* of a chance, but all that was needed was to keep them from getting at Ender until the teachers intervened. No way could the teachers stand aloof if an out-and-out riot erupted. Or could they?

Bean passed right by Ender, got behind him. He saw, coming up quickly, Petra Arkanian in her Phoenix Army uniform. She called out. "Ho, Ender!"

To Bean's disgust, Ender stopped and turned around. The boy was too trusting.

Behind Petra, a few Salamanders fell into step. Bean looked the other way, and saw a few more Salamanders and a couple of set-faced boys from other armies, drifting down the corridor past the last of the Dragons. Hot Soup and Crazy Tom were coming quickly, with more toon leaders and the rest of the larger Dragons coming behind them, but they weren't moving fast enough. Bean beckoned, and he saw Crazy Tom pick up his pace. The others followed suit.

"Ender, can I talk to you," said Petra.

Bean was bitterly disappointed. Petra was the Judas. Setting Ender up for Bonzo—who would have guessed? She *hated* Bonzo when she was in his army.

"Walk with me," said Ender.

"It's just for a moment," said Petra.

Either she was a perfect actress or she was oblivious, Bean realized. She only seemed aware of the other Dragon uniforms, never as much as glancing at anybody else. She isn't in on it after all, thought Bean. She's just an idiot.

At last, Ender seemed to be aware of his exposed position. Except for Bean, all the other Dragons were past him now, and that was apparently enough—at last—to make him uncomfortable. He turned his back on Petra and walked away, briskly, quickly closing the gap between him and the older Dragons.

Petra was angry for a moment, then jogged quickly to catch up with him. Bean stood his ground, looking at the oncoming Salamanders. They didn't even glance at him. They just picked up their pace, continuing to gain on Ender almost as fast as Petra was.

Bean took three steps and slapped the door of Rabbit Army barracks. Somebody opened it. Bean had only to say, "Salamander's making a move against Ender," and at once Rabbits started to pour out the door into the corridor. They emerged just as the Salamanders reached them, and started following along.

Witnesses, thought Bean. And helpers, too, if the fight seemed unfair.

Ahead of him, Ender and Petra were talking, and the larger Dragons fell in step around them. The Salamanders continued to follow closely, and the other thugs joined them as they passed. But the danger was dissipating. Rabbit Army and the older Dragons had done the job. Bean breathed a little easier. For the moment, at least, the danger was over.

Bean caught up with Ender in time to hear Petra angrily say, "How can you think I did? Don't you know who your friends are?" She ran off, ducked into a ladderway, scrambled upward.

Carn Carby of Rabbit caught up with Bean. "Everything OK?"

"I hope you don't mind my calling out your army."

"They came and got me. We seeing Ender safely to bed?"

"Eh."

Carn dropped back and walked along with the bulk of his soldiers. The Salamander thugs were now outnumbered about three to one. They backed off even more, and some of them peeled away and disappeared up ladderways or down poles.

When Bean caught up with Ender again, he was surrounded by his toon leaders. There was nothing subtle about it now—they were clearly his bodyguards, and some of the younger Dragons had realized what was happening and were filling out the formation. They got Ender to the door of his quarters and Crazy Tom pointedly entered before him, then allowed him to go in when he certified that no one was lying in wait. As if one of them could palm open a commander's door. But then, the teachers had been changing a lot of the rules lately. Anything could happen.

Bean lay awake for a while, trying to think what he could do. There was no way they could be with Ender every moment. There was classwork—armies were deliberately broken up then. Ender was the only one who could eat in the commanders' mess, so if Bonzo jumped him there . . . but he wouldn't, not with so many other commanders around him. Showers. Toilet stalls. And if Bonzo assembled the right group of thugs, they'd slap Ender's toon leaders aside like balloons.

What Bean had to do was try to peel away Bonzo's support. Before he slept, he had a half-assed little plan that might help a little, or might make things work, but at least it was something, and it would be public, so the teachers couldn't claim after the fact, in their typical bureaucrat cover-my-butt way that they hadn't known anything was going on.

He thought he could do something at breakfast, but of course there was a battle first thing in the morning. Pol Slattery, Badger Army. The teachers had found a new way to mess with the rules, too. When Badgers were flashed, instead of staying frozen till the end of the game they thawed after five minutes, the way it worked in practice. But Dragons, once hit, stayed rigid. Since the battleroom was packed with stars—plenty of hiding places—it took a while to realize that they were having to shoot the same soldiers more than once as they maneuvered through the stars, and Dragon Army came closer to losing than it ever had. It was all hand to hand, with a dozen of the remaining Dragons having to watch batches of frozen Badgers, reshooting them periodically and meanwhile frantically looking around for some other Badger sneaking up from behind.

The battle took so long that by the time they got out of the battleroom, breakfast was over. Dragon Army was pissed off—the ones who had been frozen early on, before they knew the trick, had spent more than an hour, some of them, floating in their rigid suits, growing more and more frustrated as the time wore on. The others, who had been forced to fight outnumbered and with little visibility against enemies who kept reviving, they were exhausted. Including Ender.

Ender gathered his army in the corridor and said, "Today you know everything. No practice. Get some rest. Have some fun. Pass a test."

They were all grateful for the reprieve, but still, they weren't getting any breakfast today and nobody felt like cheering. As they walked back to the barracks, some of them grumbled, "Bet they're serving breakfast to Badger Army right now."

"No, they got them up and served them breakfast before."

"No, they ate breakfast and then five minutes later they get to eat another."

Bean, however, was frustrated because he hadn't had a chance to carry out his plan at breakfast. It would have to wait till lunch.

The good thing was that because Dragon wasn't practicing, Bonzo's guys wouldn't know where to lie in wait for him. The bad thing was that if Ender went off by himself, there'd be nobody to protect him.

So Bean was relieved when he saw Ender go into his quarters. In consultation with the other toon leaders, Bean set up a watch on Ender's door. One Dragon sat outside the barracks for a half-hour shift, then knocked on the door and his replacement came out. No way was Ender going to go wandering off without Dragon Army knowing it.

But Ender never came out and finally it was lunchtime. All the toon leaders sent the soldiers on ahead and then detoured past Ender's door. Fly Molo knocked loudly— actually, he slapped the door hard five times. "Lunch, Ender."

"I'm not hungry." His voice was muffled by the door. "Go on and eat."

"We can wait," said Fly. "Don't want you walking to the commanders' mess alone."

"I'm not going to eat any lunch at all," said Ender. "Go on and I'll see you after."

"You heard him," said Fly to the others. "He'll be safe in here while we eat."

Bean had noticed that Ender did not promise to stay in his room throughout lunch. But at least Bonzo's people wouldn't know where he was. Unpredictability was helpful. And Bean wanted to get the chance to make his speech at lunch.

So he ran to the messroom and did not get in line, but instead bounded up onto a table and clapped his hands loudly to get attention. "Hey, everybody!"

He waited until the group went about as close to silent as it was going to get.

"There's some of you here who need a reminder of a couple of points of I.F. law. If a soldier is ordered to do something illegal or improper by his commanding officer, he has a responsibility to refuse the order and report it. A soldier who obeys an illegal or improper order is fully responsible for the consequences of his actions. Just in case any of you here are too dim to know what that means, the law says that if some commander orders you to commit a crime, that's no excuse. You are forbidden to obey."

Nobody from Salamander would meet Bean's gaze, but

a thug in Rat uniform answered in a surly tone. "You got something in mind, here, pinprick?"

"I've got *you* in mind, Lighter. Your scores are pretty much in the bottom ten percent in the school, so I thought you might need a little extra help."

"You can shut your facehole right now, that's the help I need!"

"Whatever Bonzo had you set to do last night, Lighter, you and about twenty others, what I'm telling you is *if* you'd actually tried something, every single one of you would have been out of Battle School on his ass. Iced. A complete failure, because you listened to Bonehead Madrid. Can I be any more clear than that?"

Lighter laughed—it sounded forced, but then, he wasn't the only one laughing. "You don't even know what's going on, pinprick," one of them said.

"I know Bonehead's trying to turn you into a street crew, you pathetic losers. He can't beat Ender in the battleroom, so he's going to get a dozen tough guys to beat up one little kid. You all hear that? You know what Ender is—the best damn commander ever to come through here. He might be the only one able to do what Mazer Rackham did and beat the Buggers when they come back, did you think of that? And these guys are so *smart* they want to beat his brains out. So when the Buggers come, and we've only got pus-brains like Bonzo Madrid to lead our fleets to defeat, then as the Buggers scour the Earth and kill every last man, woman, and child, the survivors will all know that *these* fools are the ones who got rid of the one guy who could have led us to victory!"

The whole place was dead silent now, and Bean could see, looking at the ones he recognized as having been with Bonzo's group last night, that he was getting through to them.

"Oh, you *forgot* the Buggers, is that it? You *forgot* that this Battle School wasn't put here so you could write home to Mommy about your high standings on the scoreboard. So you go ahead and help Bonzo out, and while you're at it, why not just slit your own throats, too, cause that's what you're doing if you hurt Ender Wiggin. But for the rest of us—well, how many here think that Ender Wiggin is the one commander we would all want to follow into battle? Come on, how many of you!"

Bean began to clap his hands slowly, rhythmically. Immediately, all the Dragons joined in. And very quickly, most of the rest of the soldiers were also clapping. The ones who weren't were conspicuous and could see how the others looked at them with scorn or hate.

Pretty soon, the whole room was clapping. Even the food servers.

Bean thrust both his hands straight up in the air. "The butt-faced Buggers are the only enemy! Humans are all on the same side! Anybody who raises a hand against Ender Wiggin is a Bugger-lover!"

They responded with cheers and applause, leaping to their feet.

It was Bean's first attempt at rabble-rousing. He was pleased to see that, as long as the cause was right, he was pretty damn good at it.

Only later, when he had his food and was sitting with C toon, eating it, did Lighter himself come up to Bean. He came up from behind, and the rest of C toon was on their feet, ready to take him on, before Bean even knew he was there. But Lighter motioned them to sit down, then leaned over and spoke right into Bean's ear. "Listen to this, Queen Stupid. The soldiers who are planning to take Wiggin apart aren't even *here.* So much for your stupid speech."

Then he was gone.

And, a moment later, so was Bean, with C toon gathering the rest of Dragon Army to follow behind him.

Ender wasn't in his quarters, or at least he didn't answer. Fly Molo, as A toon commander, took charge and divided them into groups to search the barracks, the game room, the vid room, the library, the gym.

But Bean called out for his squad to follow him. To

the bathroom. That's the one place that Bonzo and his boys could plan on Ender having to go, eventually.

By the time Bean got there, it was all over. Teachers and medical staff were clattering down the halls. Dink Meeker was walking with Ender, his arm across Ender's shoulder, away from the bathroom. Ender was wearing only his towel. He was wet, and there was blood all over the back of his head and dripping down his back. It took Bean only a moment to realize that it was not his blood. The others from Bean's squad watched as Dink led Ender back to his quarters and helped him inside. But Bean was already on his way to the bathroom.

The teachers ordered him out of the way, out of the corridor. But Bean saw enough. Bonzo lying on the floor, medical staff doing CPR. Bean knew that you don't do that to somebody whose heart is beating. And from the inattentive way the others were standing around, Bean knew it was only a formality. Nobody expected Bonzo's heart to start again. No surprise. His nose had been jammed up inside his head. His face was a mass of blood. Which explained the bloody back of Ender's head.

All our efforts didn't amount to squat. But Ender won anyway. He knew this was coming. He learned self-defense. He used it, and he didn't do a half-assed job of it, either.

If Ender had been Poke's friend, Poke wouldn't have died.

And if Ender had depended on Bean to save him, he'd be just as dead as Poke.

Rough hands dragged Bean off his feet, pushed him against a wall. "What did you see!" demanded Major Anderson.

"Nothing," said Bean. "Is that Bonzo in there? Is he hurt?"

"This is none of your business. Didn't you hear us order you away?"

Colonel Graff arrived then, and Bean could see that the teachers around him were furious at him—yet couldn't say anything, either because of military protocol or because one of the children was present.

"I think Bean has stuck his nose into things once too often," said Anderson.

"Are you going to send Bonzo home?" asked Bean. "Cause he's just going to try it again."

Graff gave him a withering glance. "I heard about your speech in the mess hall," said Graff. "I didn't know we brought you up here to be a politician."

"If you don't ice Bonzo and get him *out* of here, Ender's never going to be safe, and we won't stand for it!"

"Mind your own business, little boy," said Graff. "This is men's work here."

Bean let himself be dragged away by Dimak. Just in case they still wondered whether Bean saw that Bonzo was dead, he kept the act going just a little longer. "He's going to come after me, too," he said. "I don't want Bonzo coming after me."

"He's not coming after you," said Dimak. "He's going home. Count on it. But don't talk about this to anyone else. Let them find out when the official word is given out. Got it?"

"Yes, sir," said Bean.

"And where did you get all that nonsense about not obeying a commander who gives illegal orders?"

"From the Uniform Code of Military Conduct," said Bean.

"Well, here's a little fact for you—nobody has ever been prosecuted for obeying orders."

"That," said Bean, "is because nobody's done anything so outrageous that the general public got involved."

"The Uniform Code doesn't apply to students, at least not that part of it."

"But it applies to teachers," said Bean. "It applies to *you*. Just in case you obeyed any illegal or improper orders today. By . . . what, I don't know . . . standing by while a fight broke out in a bathroom? Just because your commanding officer told you to let a big kid beat up on a little kid."

If that information bothered Dimak, he gave no sign. He stood in the corridor and watched as Bean went into the Dragon Army barracks.

It was crazy inside. Dragon Army felt completely helpless and stupid, furious and ashamed. Bonzo Madrid had outsmarted them! Bonzo had gotten Ender alone! Where were Ender's soldiers when he needed them?

It took a long time for things to calm down. Through it all, Bean just sat on his bunk, thinking his own thoughts. Ender didn't just win his fight. Didn't just protect himself and walk away. Ender killed him. Struck a blow so devastating that his enemy will never, never come after him again.

Ender Wiggin, you're the one who was born to be commander of the fleet that defends Earth from the Third Invasion. Because that's what we need—someone who'll strike the most brutal blow possible, with perfect aim and with no regard for consequences. Total war.

Me, I'm no Ender Wiggin. I'm just a street kid whose only skill was staying alive. Somehow. The only time I was in real danger, I ran like a squirrel and took refuge with Sister Carlotta. Ender went alone into battle. I go alone into my hidey-hole. I'm the guy who makes big brave speeches standing on tables in the mess hall. Ender's the guy who meets the enemy naked and overpowers him against all odds.

Whatever genes they altered to make me, they weren't the ones that mattered.

Ender almost died because of me. Because I goaded Bonzo. Because I failed to keep watch at the crucial time. Because I didn't stop and think like Bonzo and figure out that he'd wait for Ender to be alone in the shower.

If Ender had died today, it would have been my fault all over again.

He wanted to kill somebody.

Couldn't be Bonzo. Bonzo was already dead.

Achilles. That's the one he needed to kill. And if Achilles had been there at that moment, Bean would have tried. Might have succeeded, too, if violent rage and desperate shame were enough to beat down any advantage of size and experience Achilles might have had. And if Achilles killed Bean anyway, it was no worse than Bean deserved, for having failed Ender Wiggin so completely.

He felt his bed bounce. Nikolai had jumped the gap between the upper bunks.

"It's OK," murmured Nikolai, touching Bean's shoulder.

Bean rolled onto his back, to face Nikolai.

"Oh," said Nikolai. "I thought you were crying."

"Ender won," said Bean. "What's to cry about?"

18

Friend

"This boy's death was not necessary."

"This boy's death was not foreseen."

"But it was foreseeable."

"You can always foresee things that already happened. These are children, after all. We did *not* anticipate this level of violence."

"I don't believe you. I believe that this is precisely the level of violence you anticipated. This is what you set up. You think that the experiment succeeded."

"I can't control your opinions. I can merely disagree with them."

"Ender Wiggin is ready to move on to Command School. That is my report."

"I have a separate report from Dap, the teacher assigned to watch him most closely. And that report—for which there are to be *no* sanctions against Captain Dap—tells me that Andrew Wiggin is 'psychologically unfit for duty.'"

"*If* he is, which I doubt, it is only temporary."

"How much time do you think we have? No, Colonel

Graff, for the time being we have to regard your course of action regarding Wiggin as a failure, and the boy as ruined not only for our purposes but quite possibly for any other as well. So, if it can be done without further killings, I want the other one pushed forward. I want him here in Command School as close to immediately as possible."

"Very well, sir. Though I must tell you that I regard Bean as unreliable."

"Why, because you haven't turned him into a killer yet?"

"Because he is not human, sir."

"The genetic difference is well within the range of ordinary variation."

"He was manufactured, and the manufacturer was a criminal, not to mention a certified loon."

"I could see some danger if his *father* were a criminal. Or his mother. But his *doctor*? The boy is exactly what we need, as quickly as we can get him."

"He is unpredictable."

"And the Wiggin boy is not?"

"Less unpredictable, sir."

"Very carefully answered, considering that you just insisted that the murder today was 'not foreseeable.' "

"*Not* murder, sir!"

"Killing, then."

"The mettle of the Wiggin boy is proved, sir, while Bean's is not."

"I have Dimak's report—for which, again, he is not to be—"

"Punished, I know, sir."

"Bean's behavior throughout this set of events has been exemplary."

"Then Captain Dimak's report was incomplete. Didn't he inform you that it was Bean who may have pushed Bonzo over the edge to violence by breaking security and informing him that Ender's army was composed of exceptional students?"

"That *was* an act with unforeseeable consequences."

"Bean was acting to save his own life, and in so doing he

shunted the danger onto Ender Wiggin's shoulders. That he later tried to ameliorate the danger does not change the fact that when Bean is under pressure, he turns traitor."

"Harsh language!"

"This from the man who just called an obvious act of self-defense 'murder'?"

"Enough of this! You are on leave of absence from your position as commander of Battle School for the duration of Ender Wiggin's so-called rest and recuperation. If Wiggin recovers enough to come to Command School, you may come with him and continue to have influence over the education of the children we bring here. If he does not, you may await your court-martial on Earth."

"I am relieved effective when?"

"When you get on the shuttle with Wiggin. Major Anderson will stand in as acting commander."

"Very well, sir. Wiggin *will* return to training, sir."

"*If* we still want him."

"When you are over the dismay we all feel at the unfortunate death of the Madrid boy, you will realize that I am right, and Ender is the only viable candidate, all the more now than before."

"I allow you that Parthian shot. And, if you are right, I wish you Godspeed on your work with the Wiggin boy. Dismissed."

Ender was still wearing only his towel when he stepped into the barracks. Bean saw him standing there, his face a rictus of death, and thought: He knows that Bonzo is dead, and it's killing him.

"Ho, Ender," said Hot Soup, who was standing near the door with the other toon leaders.

"There gonna be a practice tonight?" asked one of the younger soldiers.

Ender handed a slip of paper to Hot Soup.

"I guess that means not," said Nikolai softly.

Hot Soup read it. "Those sons of bitches! Two at once?"

Crazy Tom looked over his shoulder. "Two armies!"

"They'll just trip over each other," said Bean. What appalled him most about the teachers was not the stupidity of trying to combine armies, a ploy whose ineffectiveness had been proved time after time throughout history, but rather the get-back-on-the-horse mentality that led them to put *more* pressure on Ender at this of all times. Couldn't they see the damage they were doing to him? Was their goal to train him or break him? Because he was trained long since. He should have been promoted out of Battle School the week before. And now they give him one more battle, a completely meaningless one, when he's already over the edge of despair?

"I've got to clean up," said Ender. "Get them ready, get everybody together, I'll meet you there, at the gate." In his voice, Bean heard a complete lack of interest. No, something deeper than that. Ender doesn't *want* to win this battle.

Ender turned to leave. Everyone saw the blood on his head, his shoulders, down his back. He left.

They all ignored the blood. They had to. "Two fart-eating armies!" cried Crazy Tom. "We'll whip their butts!"

That seemed to be the general consensus as they got into their flash suits.

Bean tucked the coil of deadline into the waist of his flash suit. If Ender ever needed a stunt, it would be for this battle, when he was no longer interested in winning.

As promised, Ender joined them at the gate before it opened—just barely before. He walked down the corridor lined with his soldiers, who looked at him with love, with awe, with trust. Except Bean, who looked at him with anguish. Ender Wiggin was not larger than life, Bean knew. He was exactly life-sized, and so his larger-than-life burden was too much for him. And yet he was bearing it. So far.

The gate went transparent.

Four stars had been combined directly in front of the gate, completely blocking their view of the battleroom. Ender would have to deploy his forces blind. For all he knew, the enemy had already been let into the room fifteen minutes ago. For all he could possibly know, they were deployed just as Bonzo had deployed *his* army, only this time it would be completely effective, to have the gate ringed with enemy soldiers.

But Ender said nothing. Just stood there looking at the barrier.

Bean had halfway expected this. He was ready. What he did wasn't all that obvious—he only walked forward to stand directly beside Ender at the gate. But he knew that was all it would take. A reminder.

"Bean," said Ender. "Take your boys and tell me what's on the other side of this star."

"Yes *sir*," said Bean. He pulled the coil of deadline from his waist, and with his five soldiers he made the short hop from the gate to the star. Immediately the gate he had just come through became the ceiling, the star their temporary floor. Bean tied the deadline around his waist while the other boys unspooled the line, arranging it in loose coils on the star. When it was about one-third played out, Bean declared it to be sufficient. He was guessing that the four stars were really eight—that they made a perfect cube. If he was wrong, then he had way too much deadline and he'd crash into the ceiling instead of making it back behind the star. Worse things could happen.

He slipped out beyond the edge of the star. He was right, it was a cube. It was too dim in the room to see well what the other armies were doing, but they seemed to be deploying. There had been no head start this time, apparently. He quickly reported this to Ducheval, who would repeat it to Ender while Bean did his stunt. Ender would no doubt start bringing out the rest of the army at once, before the time clicked down to zero.

Bean launched straight down from the ceiling. Above

him, his toon was holding the other end of the deadline secure, making sure it fed out properly and stopped abruptly.

Bean did not enjoy the wrenching of his gut when the deadline went taut, but there was kind of a thrill to the increase of speed as he suddenly moved south. He could see the distant flashing of the enemy firing up at him. Only soldiers from one half of the enemy's area were firing.

When the deadline reached the next edge of the cube, his speed increased again, and now he was headed upward in an arc that, for a moment, looked like it was going to scrape him against the ceiling. Then the last edge bit, and he scooted in behind the star and was caught deftly by his toon. Bean wiggled his arms and legs to show that he was none the worse for his ride. What the enemy was thinking about his magical maneuvers in midair he could only guess. What mattered was that Ender had *not* come through the gate. The timer must be nearly out.

Ender came alone through the gate. Bean made his report as quickly as possible. "It's really dim, but light enough you can't follow people easily by the lights on their suits. Worst possible for seeing. It's all open space from this star to the enemy side of the room. They've got eight stars making a square around their door. I didn't see anybody except the ones peeking around the boxes. They're just sitting there waiting for us."

In the distance, they heard the enemy begin catcalls. "Hey! We be hungry, come and feed us! Your ass is draggin'! Your ass is Dragon!"

Bean continued his report, but had no idea if Ender was even listening. "They fired at me from only one half their space. Which means that the two commanders are *not* agreeing and neither one has been put in supreme command."

"In a real war," said Ender, "any commander with brains at all would retreat and save this army."

"What the hell," said Bean. "It's only a game."

"It stopped being a game when they threw away the rules."

This wasn't good, thought Bean. How much time did they have to get their army through the gate? "So, you throw 'em away, too." He looked Ender in the eye, demanding that he wake up, pay attention, *act*.

The blank look left Ender's face. He grinned. It felt damn good to see that. "OK. Why not. Let's see how they react to a formation."

Ender began calling the rest of the army through the gate. It was going to get crowded on the top of that star, but there was no choice.

As it turned out, Ender's plan was to use another of Bean's stupid ideas, which he had watched Bean practice with his toon. A screen formation of frozen soldiers, controlled by Bean's toon, who remained unfrozen behind them. Having once told Bean what he wanted him to do, Ender joined the formation as a common soldier and left everything up to Bean to organize. "It's your show," he said.

Bean had never expected Ender to do any such thing, but it made a kind of sense. What Ender wanted was not to have this battle; allowing himself to be part of a screen of frozen soldiers, pushed through the battle by someone else, was as close to sleeping through it as he could get.

Bean set to work at once, constructing the screen in four parts consisting of one toon each. Each of toons A through C lined up four and three, arms interlocked with the men beside them, the upper row of three with toes hooked under the arms of the four soldiers below. When everybody was clamped down tight, Bean and his toon froze them. Then each of Bean's men took hold of one section of the screen and, careful to move very slowly so that inertia would not carry the screen out of their control, they maneuvered them out from above the star and slowly moved them down until they were just under it. Then they joined them back together into a single screen, with Bean's squad forming the interlock.

"When did you guys practice this?" asked Dumper, the leader of E toon.

"We've never done this before," Bean answered truthfully. "We've done bursting and linking with one-man screens, but seven men each? It's all new to us."

Dumper laughed. "And there's Ender, plugged into the screen like anybody. That's trust, Bean old boy."

That's despair, thought Bean. But he didn't feel the need to say *that* aloud.

When all was ready, E toon got into place behind the screen and, on Bean's command, pushed off as hard as they could.

The screen drifted down toward the enemy's gate at a pretty good clip. Enemy fire, though it was intense, hit only the already-frozen soldiers in front. E toon and Bean's squad kept moving, very slightly, but enough that no stray shot could freeze them. And they managed to do some return fire, taking out a few of the enemy soldiers and forcing them to stay behind cover.

When Bean figured they were as far as they could get before Griffin or Tiger launched an attack, he gave the word and his squad burst apart, causing the four sections of the screen also to separate and angle slightly so they were drifting now toward the corners of the stars where Griffin and Tiger were gathered. E toon went with the screens, firing like crazy, trying to make up for their tiny numbers.

After a count of three, the four members of Bean's squad who had gone with each screen pushed off again, this time angling to the middle and downward, so that they rejoined Bean and Ducheval, with momentum carrying them straight toward the enemy gate.

They held their bodies rigid, *not* firing a shot, and it worked. They were all small; they were clearly drifting, not moving with any particular purpose; the enemy took them for frozen soldiers if they were noticed at all. A few were partially disabled with stray shots, but even when under fire they never moved, and the enemy soon ignored them.

When they got to the enemy gate, Bean slowly, word-lessly, got four of them with their helmets in place at the corners of the gate. They pressed, just as in the end-of-game ritual, and Bean gave Ducheval a push, sending him through the gate as Bean drifted upward again.

The lights in the battleroom went on. The weapons all went dead. The battle was over.

It took a few moments before Griffin and Tiger realized what had happened. Dragon only had a few soldiers who weren't frozen or disabled, while Griffin and Tiger were mostly unscathed, having played conservative strategies. Bean knew that if either of them had been aggressive, Ender's strategy wouldn't have worked. But having seen Bean fly around the star, doing the impossible, and then watching this weird screen approach so slowly, they were intimidated into inaction. Ender's legend was such that they dared not commit their forces for fear of falling into a trap. Only . . . that *was* the trap.

Major Anderson came into the room through the teacher-gate. "Ender," he called.

Ender was frozen; he could only answer by grunting loudly through clenched jaws. That was a sound that victorious commanders rarely had to make.

Anderson, using the hook, drifted over to Ender and thawed him. Bean was half the battleroom away, but he heard Ender's words, so clear was his speech, so silent was the room. "I beat you again, sir."

Bean's squad members glanced at him, obviously wondering if he was resentful at Ender for claiming credit for a victory that was engineered and executed entirely by Bean. But Bean understood what Ender was saying. He wasn't talking about the victory over Griffin and Tiger armies. He was talking about a victory over the teachers. And *that* victory *was* the decision to turn the army over to Bean and sit it out himself. If they thought they were putting Ender to the ultimate test, making him fight two armies right after a personal fight for survival in the bathroom, he beat them—he sidestepped the test.

Anderson knew what Ender was saying, too. "Nonsense, Ender," said Anderson. He spoke softly, but the room was so silent that his words, too, could be heard. "Your battle was with Griffin and Tiger."

"How stupid do you think I am?" said Ender.

Damn right, said Bean silently.

Anderson spoke to the group at large. "After that little maneuver, the rules are being revised to require that all of the enemy's soldiers must be frozen or disabled before the gate can be reversed."

"Rules?" murmured Ducheval as he came back through the gate. Bean grinned at him.

"It could only work once anyway," said Ender.

Anderson handed the hook to Ender. Instead of thawing his soldiers one at a time, and only then thawing the enemy, Ender entered the command to thaw everyone at once, then handed the hook back to Anderson, who took it and drifted away toward the center, where the end-of-game rituals usually took place.

"Hey!" Ender shouted. "What is it next time? My army in a cage without guns, with the rest of the Battle School against them? How about a little equality?"

So many soldiers murmured their agreement that the sound of it was loud, and not all came from Dragon Army. But Anderson seemed to pay no attention.

It was William Bee of Griffin Army who said what almost everyone was thinking. "Ender, if you're on one side of the battle, it won't be equal no matter what the conditions are."

The armies vocally agreed, many of the soldiers laughing, and Talo Momoe, not to be outclassed by Bee, started clapping his hands rhythmically. "Ender Wiggin!" he shouted. Other boys took up the chant.

But Bean knew the truth—knew, in fact, what Ender knew. That no matter how good a commander was, no matter how resourceful, no matter how well-prepared his army, no matter how excellent his lieutenants, no matter how courageous and spirited the fight, victory almost always went to the side with the greater power to inflict damage. Sometimes David kills Goliath, and people never forget. But there were a lot of little guys Goliath had already mashed into the ground. Nobody sang songs about *those* fights, because they knew that was the likely outcome. No, that was the *inevitable* outcome, except for the miracles.

The Buggers wouldn't know or care how legendary a commander Ender might be to his own men. The human ships wouldn't have any magical tricks like Bean's deadline to dazzle the Buggers with, to put them off their stride. Ender knew that. Bean knew that. What if David hadn't had a sling, a handful of stones, and the time to throw? What good would the excellence of his aim have done him then?

So yes, it was good, it was right for the soldiers of all three armies to cheer Ender, to chant his name as he drifted toward the enemy gate, where Bean and his squad waited for him. But in the end it meant nothing, except that everyone would have too much hope in Ender's ability. It only made the burden on Ender heavier.

I would carry some of it if I could, Bean said silently. Like I did today, you can turn it over to me and I'll do it, if I can. You don't have to do this alone.

Only even as he thought this, Bean knew it wasn't true. If it could be done, Ender was the one who would have to do it. All those months when Bean refused to see Ender, hid from him, it was because he couldn't bear to face the fact that Ender was what Bean only wished to be— the kind of person on whom you could put all your hopes, who could carry all your fears, and he would not let you down, would not betray you.

I want to be the kind of boy you are, thought Bean. But I don't want to go through what you've been through to get there.

And then, as Ender passed through the gate and Bean

followed behind him, Bean remembered falling into line behind Poke or Sergeant or Achilles on the streets of Rotterdam, and he almost laughed as he thought, I don't want to have to go through what *I've* gone through to get here, either.

Out in the corridor, Ender walked away instead of waiting for his soldiers. But not fast, and soon they caught up with him, surrounded him, brought him to a stop through their sheer ebullience. Only his silence, his impassivity, kept them from giving full vent to their excitement.

"Practice tonight?" asked Crazy Tom.

Ender shook his head.

"Tomorrow morning then?"

"No."

"Well, when?"

"Never again, as far as I'm concerned."

Not everyone had heard, but those who did began to murmur to each other.

"Hey, that's not fair," said a soldier from B toon. "It's not our fault the teachers are screwing up the game. You can't just stop teaching us stuff because—"

Ender slammed his hand against the wall and shouted at the kid. "I don't care about the game anymore!" He looked at other soldiers, met their gaze, refused to let them pretend they didn't hear. "Do you understand that?" Then he whispered. "The game is over."

He walked away.

Some of the boys wanted to follow him, took a few steps. But Hot Soup grabbed a couple of them by the neck of their flash suits and said, "Let him be alone. Can't you see he wants to be alone?"

Of course he wants to be alone, thought Bean. He killed a kid today, and even if he doesn't know the outcome, he knows what was at stake. These teachers were willing to let him face death without help. Why should he play along with them anymore? Good for you, Ender.

Not so good for the rest of us, but it's not like you're our father or something. More like a brother, and the thing with brothers is, you're supposed to take turns being the keeper. Sometimes you get to sit down and be the brother who is kept.

Fly Molo led them back to the barracks. Bean followed along, wishing he could go with Ender, talk to him, assure him that he agreed completely, that he understood. But that was pathetic, Bean realized. Why should Ender care whether *I* understand him or not? I'm just a kid, just one of his army. He knows me, he knows how to use me, but what does he care whether I know him?

Bean climbed to his bunk and saw a slip of paper on it.

Transfer

Bean

Rabbit Army

Commander

That was Carn Carby's army. Carn was being removed from command? He was a good guy—not a great commander, but why couldn't they wait till he graduated?

Because they're through with this school, that's why. They're advancing everybody they think needs some experience with command, and they're graduating other students to make room for them. I might have Rabbit Army, but not for long, I bet.

He pulled out his desk, meaning to sign on as ˆGraff and check the rosters. Find out what was happening to everybody. But the ˆGraff log-in didn't work. Apparently they no longer considered it useful to permit Bean to keep his inside access.

From the back of the room, the older boys were raising a hubbub. Bean heard Crazy Tom's voice rising above the rest. "You mean I'm supposed to figure out how to beat Dragon Army?" Word soon filtered to the front. The toon leaders and seconds had all received transfer orders. Every single one of them was being given command of an army. Dragon had been stripped.

After about a minute of chaos, Fly Molo led the other toon leaders along between the bunks, heading toward the door. Of course—they had to go tell Ender what the teachers had done to him now.

But to Bean's surprise, Fly stopped at his bunk and looked up at him, then glanced at the other toon leaders behind him.

"Bean, somebody's got to tell Ender."

Bean nodded.

"We thought . . . since you're his friend . . ."

Bean let nothing show on his face, but he was stunned. Me? Ender's friend? No more than anyone else in this room.

And then he realized. In this army, Ender had everyone's love and admiration. And they all knew they had Ender's trust. But only Bean had been taken inside Ender's confidence, when Ender assigned him his special squad. And when Ender wanted to stop playing the game, it was Bean to whom he had turned over his army. Bean was the closest thing to a friend they had seen Ender have since he got command of Dragon.

Bean looked across at Nikolai, who was grinning his ass off. Nikolai saluted him and mouthed the word *commander*.

Bean saluted Nikolai back, but could not smile, knowing what this would do to Ender. He nodded to Fly Molo, then slid off the bunk and went out the door.

He didn't go straight to Ender's quarters, though. Instead, he went to Carn Carby's room. No one answered. So he went on to Rabbit barracks and knocked. "Where's Carn?" he asked.

"Graduated," said Itú, the leader of Rabbit's A toon. "He found out about half an hour ago."

"We were in a battle."

"I know—two armies at once. You won, right?"

Bean nodded. "I bet Carn wasn't the only one graduated early."

"A lot of commanders," said Itú. "More than half."

"Including Bonzo Madrid? I mean, he graduated?"

"That's what the official notice said." Itú shrugged. "Everybody knows that if anything, Bonzo was probably iced. I mean, they didn't even list his assignment. Just 'Cartagena.' His hometown. Is that iced or what? But let the teachers call it what they want."

"I'll bet the total who graduated was nine," said Bean. "Neh?"

"Eh," said Itú. "Nine. So you know something?"

"Bad news, I think," said Bean. He showed Itú his transfer orders.

"Santa merda," said Itú. Then he saluted. Not sarcastically, but not enthusiastically, either.

"Would you mind breaking it to the others? Give them a chance to get used to the idea before I show up for real? I've got to go talk to Ender. Maybe he already knows they've just taken his entire leadership and given them armies. But if he doesn't, I've got to tell him."

"*Every* Dragon toon leader?"

"And every second." He thought of saying, Sorry Rabbit got stuck with me. But Ender would never have said anything self-belittling like that. And if Bean was going to be a commander, he couldn't start out with an apology. "I think Carn Carby had a good organization," said Bean, "so I don't expect to change any of the toon leadership for the first week, anyway, till I see how things go in practice and decide what shape we're in for the kind of battles we're going to start having now that most of the commanders are kids trained in Dragon."

Itú understood immediately. "Man, that's going to be strange, isn't it? Ender trained all you guys, and now you've got to fight each other."

"One thing's for sure," said Bean. "I have no intention of trying to turn Rabbit into a copy of Ender's Dragon. We're not the same kids and we won't be fighting the same opponents. Rabbit's a good army. We don't have to copy anybody."

Itú grinned. "Even if that's just bullshit, sir, it's first-rate bullshit. I'll pass it on." He saluted.

Bean saluted back. Then he jogged to Ender's quarters.

Ender's mattress and blankets and pillow had been thrown out into the corridor. For a moment Bean wondered why. Then he saw that the sheets and mattress were still damp and bloody. Water from Ender's shower. Blood from Bonzo's face. Apparently Ender didn't want them in his room.

Bean knocked on the door.

"Go away," said Ender softly.

Bean knocked again. Then again.

"Come in," said Ender.

Bean palmed the door open.

"Go away, Bean," said Ender.

Bean nodded. He understood the sentiment. But he had to deliver his message. So he just looked at his shoes and waited for Ender to ask him his business. Or yell at him. Whatever Ender wanted to do. Because the other toon leaders were wrong. Bean didn't have any special relationship with Ender. Not outside the game.

Ender said nothing. And continued to say nothing.

Bean looked up from the ground and saw Ender gazing at him. Not angry. Just . . . watching. What does he see in me, Bean wondered. How well does he know me? What does he think of me? What do I amount to in his eyes?

That was something Bean would probably never know. And he had come here for another purpose. Time to carry it out.

He took a step closer to Ender. He turned his hand so the transfer slip was visible. He didn't offer it to Ender, but he knew Ender would see it.

"You're transferred?" asked Ender. His voice sounded dead. As if he'd been expecting it.

"To Rabbit Army," said Bean.

Ender nodded. "Carn Carby's a good man. I hope he recognizes what you're worth."

The words came to Bean like a longed-for blessing. He swallowed the emotion that welled up inside him. He still had more of his message to deliver.

"Carn Carby was graduated today," said Bean. "He got his notice while we were fighting our battle."

"Well," said Ender. "Who's commanding Rabbit then?" He didn't sound all that interested. The question was expected, so he asked it.

"Me," said Bean. He was embarrassed; a smile came inadvertently to his lips.

Ender looked at the ceiling and nodded. "Of course. After all, you're only four years younger than the regular age."

"It isn't funny," said Bean. "I don't know what's going on here." Except that the system seems to be running on sheer panic. "All the changes in the game. And now this. I wasn't the only one transferred, you know. They graduated half the commanders, and transferred a lot of our guys to command their armies."

"Which guys?" Now Ender did sound interested.

"It looks like—every toon leader and every assistant."

"Of course. If they decide to wreck my army, they'll cut it to the ground. Whatever they're doing, they're thorough."

"You'll still win, Ender. We all know that. Crazy Tom, he said, 'You mean I'm supposed to figure out how to beat Dragon Army?' Everybody knows you're the best." His words sounded empty even to himself. He wanted to be encouraging, but he knew that Ender knew better. Still he babbled on. "They can't break you down, no matter what they—"

"They already have."

They've broken trust, Bean wanted to say. That's not the same thing. *You* aren't broken. *They're* broken. But all that came out of his mouth were empty, limping words. "No, Ender, they can't—"

"I don't care about their game anymore, Bean," said
Ender. "I'm not going to play it anymore. No more practices. No more battles. They can put their little slips of
paper on the floor all they want, but I won't go. I decided
that before I went through the door today. That's why I
had you go for the gate. I didn't think it would work, but
I didn't care. I just wanted to go out in style."

I know that, thought Bean. You think I didn't know
that? But if it comes down to style, you certainly got *that*.
"You should've seen William Bee's face. He just stood
there trying to figure out how he had lost when you only
had seven boys who could wiggle their toes and he only
had three who couldn't."

"Why should I want to see William Bee's face?" said
Ender. "Why should I want to beat anybody?"

Bean felt the heat of embarrassment in his face. He'd
said the wrong thing. Only . . . he didn't know what the
right thing was. Something to make Ender feel better.
Something to make him understand how much he was
loved and honored.

Only that love and honor were part of the burden Ender
bore. There was nothing Bean could say that would not
make it all the heavier on Ender. So he said nothing.

Ender pressed his palms against his eyes. "I hurt Bonzo
really bad today, Bean. I really hurt him bad."

Of course. All this other stuff, that's nothing. What
weighs on Ender is that terrible fight in the bathroom. The
fight that your friends, your army, did nothing to prevent.
And what hurts you is not the danger you were in, but
the harm you did in protecting yourself.

"He had it coming," said Bean. He winced at his own
words. Was that the best he could come up with? But
what else could he say? No problem, Ender. Of course,
he looked dead to *me,* and I'm probably the only kid in
this school who actually knows what death looks like, but
. . . no problem! Nothing to worry about! He had it coming!

"I knocked him out standing up," said Ender. "It was

like he was dead, standing there. And I kept hurting him."

So he did know. And yet . . . he didn't actually *know*. And Bean wasn't about to tell him. There were times for absolute honesty between friends, but this wasn't one of them.

"I just wanted to make sure he never hurt me again."

"He won't," said Bean. "They sent him home."

"Already?"

Bean told him what Itú had said. All the while, he felt like Ender could see that he was concealing something. Surely it was impossible to deceive Ender Wiggin.

"I'm glad they graduated him," said Ender.

Some graduation. They're going to bury him, or cremate him, or whatever they're doing with corpses in Spain this year.

Spain. Pablo de Noches, who saved his life, came from Spain. And now a body was going back there, a boy who turned killer in his heart, and died for it.

I must be losing it, thought Bean. What does it matter that Bonzo was Spanish and Pablo de Noches was Spanish? What does it matter that anybody is anything?

And while these thoughts ran through Bean's mind, he babbled, trying to talk like someone who didn't know anything, trying to reassure Ender but knowing that if Ender believed that he knew nothing, then his words were meaningless, and if Ender realized that Bean was only faking ignorance, then his words were all lies. "Was it true he had a whole bunch of guys gang up on you?" Bean wanted to run from the room, he sounded so lame, even to himself.

"No," said Ender. "It was just him and me. He fought with honor."

Bean was relieved. Ender was turned so deeply inward right now that he didn't even register what Bean was saying, how false it was.

"I didn't fight with honor," said Ender. "I fought to win."

Yes, that's right, thought Bean. Fought the only way

that's worth fighting, the only way that has any point. "And you did. Kicked him right out of orbit." It was as close as Bean could come to telling him the truth.

There was a knock on the door. Then it opened, immediately, without waiting for an answer. Before Bean could turn to see who it was, he knew it was a teacher— Ender looked up too high for it to be a kid.

Major Anderson and Colonel Graff.

"Ender Wiggin," said Graff.

Ender rose to his feet. "Yes sir." The deadness had returned to his voice.

"Your display of temper in the battleroom today was insubordinate and is not to be repeated."

Bean couldn't believe the stupidity of it. After what Ender had been through—what the teachers had *put* him through—and they have to keep playing this oppressive game with him? Making him feel utterly alone even *now?* These guys were relentless.

Ender's only answer was another lifeless "Yes sir." But Bean was fed up. "I think it was about time somebody told a teacher how we felt about what you've been doing."

Anderson and Graff didn't show a sign they'd even heard him. Instead, Anderson handed Ender a full sheet of paper. Not a transfer slip. A full-fledged set of orders. Ender was being transferred out of the school.

"Graduated?" Bean asked.

Ender nodded.

"What took them so long?" asked Bean. "You're only two or three years early. You've already learned how to walk and talk and dress yourself. What will they have left to teach you?" The whole thing was such a joke. Did they really think anybody was fooled? You reprimand Ender for insubordination, but then you graduate him because you've got a war coming and you don't have a lot of time to get him ready. He's your hope of victory, and you treat him like something you scrape off your shoe.

"All I know is, the game's over," said Ender. He folded the paper. "None too soon. Can I tell my army?"

"There isn't time," said Graff. "Your shuttle leaves in twenty minutes. Besides, it's better not to talk to them after you get your orders. It makes it easier."

"For them or for you?" Ender asked.

He turned to Bean, took his hand. To Bean, it was like the touch of the finger of God. It sent light all through him. Maybe I am his friend. Maybe he feels toward me some small part of the . . . feeling I have for him.

And then it was over. Ender let go of his hand. He turned toward the door.

"Wait," said Bean. "Where are you going? Tactical? Navigational? Support?"

"Command School," said Ender.

"*Pre*-command?"

"Command." Ender was out the door.

Straight to Command School. The elite school whose location was even a secret. Adults went to Command School. The battle must be coming very soon, to skip right past all the things they were supposed to learn in Tactical and Pre-Command.

He caught Graff by the sleeve. "Nobody goes to Command School until they're sixteen!" he said.

Graff shook off Bean's hand and left. If he caught Bean's sarcasm, he gave no sign of it.

The door closed. Bean was alone in Ender's quarters.

He looked around. Without Ender in it, the room was nothing. Being here meant nothing. Yet it was only a few days ago, not even a week, when Bean had stood here and Ender told him he was getting a toon after all.

For some reason what came into Bean's mind was the moment when Poke handed him six peanuts. It was life that she handed to him then.

Was it life that Ender gave to Bean? Was it the same thing?

No. Poke gave him life. Ender gave it meaning.

When Ender was here, this was the most important room in Battle School. Now it was no more than a broom closet.

Bean walked back down the corridor to the room that had been Carn Carby's until today. Until an hour ago. He palmed it—it opened. Already programmed in.

The room was empty. Nothing in it.

This room is mine, thought Bean.

Mine, and yet still empty.

He felt powerful emotions welling up inside him. He should be excited, proud to have his own command. But he didn't really care about it. As Ender said, the game was nothing. Bean would do a decent job, but the reason he'd have the respect of his soldiers was because he would carry some of Ender's reflected glory with him, a shrimpy little Napoleon flumping around wearing a man's shoes while he barked commands in a little tiny child's voice. Cute little Caligula, "Little Boot," the pride of Germanicus's army. But when he was wearing his father's boots, those boots were empty, and Caligula knew it, and nothing he ever did could change that. Was that his madness?

It won't drive *me* mad, thought Bean. Because I don't covet what Ender has or what he is. It's enough that *he* is Ender Wiggin. I don't have to be.

He understood what this feeling was, welling up in him, filling his throat, making tears stand out in his eyes, making his face burn, forcing a gasp, a silent sob. He bit on his lip, trying to let pain force the emotion away. It didn't help. Ender was gone.

Now that he knew what the feeling was, he could control it. He lay down on the bunk and went into the relaxing routine until the need to cry had passed. Ender had taken his hand to say good-bye. Ender had said, "I hope he recognizes what you're worth." Bean didn't really have anything left to prove. He'd do his best with Rabbit Army because maybe at some point in the future, when Ender was at the bridge of the flagship of the human fleet, Bean might have some role to play, some way to help. Some stunt that Ender might need him to pull to dazzle the Buggers. So he'd please the teachers, impress the hell out of them, so that they would keep opening doors for him, until one day a door would open and his friend Ender would be on the other side of it, and he could be in Ender's army once again.

19

Rebel

"Putting in Achilles was Graff's last act, and we know there were grave concerns. Why not play it safe and at least change Achilles to another army?"

"This is not necessarily a Bonzo Madrid situation for Bean."

"But we have no assurance that it's not, sir. Colonel Graff kept a lot of information to himself. A lot of conversations with Sister Carlotta, for instance, with no memo of what was said. Graff knows things about Bean and, I can promise you, about Achilles as well. I think he's laid a trap for us."

"Wrong, Captain Dimak. If Graff laid a trap, it was not for us."

"You're sure of that?"

"Graff doesn't play bureaucratic games. He doesn't give a damn about you and me. If he laid a trap, it's for Bean."

"Well, that's my point!"

"I understand your point. But Achilles stays."

"Why?"

"Achilles' tests show him to be of a remarkably even temperament. He is no Bonzo Madrid. Therefore Bean is in no physical danger. The stress seems to be psychological. A test of character. And that is precisely the area where we have the very least data about Bean, given his refusal to play the mind game and the ambiguity of the information we got from his playing with his teacher log-in. Therefore I think this forced relationship with his bugbear is worth pursuing."

"Bugbear or nemesis, sir?"

"We will monitor closely. I will *not* be keeping adults so far removed that we can't get there to intervene in time, the way Graff arranged it with Ender and Bonzo. Every precaution will be taken. I am not playing Russian roulette the way Graff was."

"Yes you are, sir. The only difference is that he knew he had only one empty chamber, and you don't know how many chambers are empty because he loaded the gun."

On his first morning as commander of Rabbit Army, Bean woke to see a paper lying on his floor. For a moment he was stunned at the thought that he would be given a battle before he even met his army, but to his relief the note was about something much more mundane.

Because of the number of new commanders, the tradition of not joining the commanders' mess until after the first victory is abolished. You are to dine in the commanders' mess starting immediately.

It made sense. Since they were going to accelerate the battle schedule for everyone, they wanted to have the commanders in a position to share information right from the start. And to be under social pressure from their peers, as well.

Holding the paper in his hand, Bean remembered how Ender had held his orders, each impossible new permutation of the game. Just because this order made sense did not make it a good thing. There was nothing sacred about the game itself that made Bean resent changes in the rules and customs, but the way the teachers were manipulating them *did* bother him.

Cutting off his access to student information, for instance. The question wasn't why they cut it off, or even why they let him have it for so long. The question was why the other commanders didn't have that much information all along. If they were supposed to be learning to lead, then they should have the tools of leadership.

And as long as they were changing the system, why not get rid of the really pernicious, destructive things they did? For instance, the scoreboards in the mess halls. Standings and scores! Instead of fighting the battle at hand, those scores made soldiers and commanders alike more cautious, less willing to experiment. That's why the ludicrous custom of fighting in formations had lasted so long—Ender can't have been the first commander to see a better way. But nobody wanted to rock the boat, to be the one who innovated and paid the price by dropping in the rankings. Far better to treat each battle as a completely separate problem, and to feel free to engage in battles as if they were *play* rather than work. Creativity and challenge would increase drastically. And commanders wouldn't have to worry when they gave an order to a toon or an individual whether they were causing a particular soldier to sacrifice his standing for the good of the army.

Most important, though, was the challenge inherent in Ender's decision to reject the game. The fact that he graduated before he could really go on strike didn't change the fact that if he had done so, Bean would have supported him in it.

Now that Ender was gone, a boycott of the game didn't make sense. Especially if Bean and the others were to advance to a point where they might be part of Ender's fleet when the real battles came. But they could take charge of the game, use it for their own purposes.

So, dressed in his new—and ill-fitting—Rabbit Army

uniform, Bean soon found himself once again standing on a table, this time in the much smaller officers' mess. Since Bean's speech the day before was already the stuff of legend, there was laughter and some catcalling when he got up.

"Do people where you come from eat with their feet, Bean?"

"Instead of getting up on tables, why don't you just *grow*, Bean?"

"Put some stilts on so we can keep the tables clean!"

But the other new commanders who had, until yesterday, been toon leaders in Dragon Army, made no catcalls and did not laugh. Their respectful attention to Bean soon prevailed, and silence fell over the room.

Bean flung up an arm to point to the scoreboard that showed the standings. "Where's Dragon Army?" he asked.

"They dissolved it," said Petra Arkanian. "The soldiers have been folded into the other armies. Except for you guys who used to be Dragon."

Bean listened, keeping his opinion of her to himself. All he could think of, though, was two nights before, when she was, wittingly or not, the Judas who was supposed to lure Ender into a trap.

"Without Dragon up there," said Bean, "that board means nothing. Whatever standing any of us gets would not be the same if Dragon were still there."

"There's not a hell of a lot we can do about it," said Dink Meeker.

"The problem isn't that Dragon is missing," said Bean. "The problem is that we shouldn't have that board at all. *We're* not each other's enemies. The *Buggers* are the only enemy. *We're* supposed to be allies. We should be learning from each other, sharing information and ideas. We should feel free to experiment, trying new things without being afraid of how it will affect our standings. That board up there, that's the *teachers'* game, getting us to turn against each other. Like Bonzo. Nobody here is as crazy with jealousy as he was, but come on, he was what those standings were bound to create. He was all set to beat in the brains of our best commander, our best hope against the next Bugger invasion, and why? Because Ender humiliated him in the *standings*. Think about that! The standings were more important to him than the war against the Formics!"

"Bonzo was crazy," said William Bee.

"So let's *not* be crazy," said Bean. "Let's get those standings out of the game. Let's take each battle one at a time, a clean slate. Try anything you can think of to win. And when the battle is over, both commanders sit down and explain what they were thinking, why they did what they did, so we can learn from each other. No secrets! Everybody try everything! And screw the standings!"

There were murmurs of assent, and not just from the former Dragons.

"That's easy for you to say," said Shen. "*Your* standing right now is tied for last."

"And there's the problem, right there," said Bean. "You're suspicious of my motives, and why? Because of the standings. But aren't we all supposed to be commanders in the same fleet someday? Working together? Trusting each other? How sick would the I.F. be, if all the ship captains and strike force commanders and fleet admirals spent all their time worrying about their standings instead of working together to try to beat the Formics! I want to learn from you, Shen. I don't want to *compete* with you for some empty rank that the teachers put up on that wall in order to manipulate us."

"I'm sure you guys from Dragon are all concerned about learning from us losers," said Petra.

There it was, out in the open.

"Yes! Yes, I *am* concerned. Precisely because I've been in Dragon Army. There are nine of us here who know pretty much only what we learned from Ender. Well, brilliant as he was, he's not the only one in the fleet or even in the school who knows anything. I need to learn how *you* think. I don't need you keeping secrets from me, and you don't need me keeping secrets from you. Maybe part of what made Ender so good was that he kept all his toon leaders talking to each other, free to try things but only as long as we shared what we were doing."

There was more assent this time. Even the doubters were nodding thoughtfully.

"So what I propose is this. A unanimous rejection of that board up there, not only the one in here but the one in the soldiers' mess, too. We all agree not to pay attention to it, period. We ask the teachers to disconnect the things or leave them blank. If they refuse, we bring in sheets to cover it, or we throw chairs until we break it. We don't have to play *their* game. We can take charge of our own education and get ready to fight the *real* enemy. We have to remember, always, who the real enemy is."

"Yeah, the teachers," said Dink Meeker.

Everybody laughed. But then Dink Meeker stood up on the table beside Bean. "I'm the senior commander here, now they've graduated all the oldest guys. I'm probably the oldest soldier left in Battle School. So I propose that we adopt Bean's proposal right now, and I'll go to the teachers to demand that the boards be shut off. Is there anyone opposed?"

Not a sound.

"That makes it unanimous. If the boards are still on at lunch, let's bring sheets to cover them up. If they're still on at dinner, then forget using chairs to vandalize, let's just refuse to take our armies to any battles until the boards are off."

Alai spoke up from where he stood in the serving line. "*That'll* shoot our standings all to . . ."

Then Alai realized what he was saying, and laughed at himself. "Damn, but they've got us brainwashed, haven't they!"

———

Bean was still flushed with victory when, after break-fast, he made his way to Rabbit barracks in order to meet his soldiers officially for the first time. Rabbit was on a midday practice schedule, so he only had about half an hour between breakfast and the first classes of the morning. Yesterday, when he talked to Itú, his mind had been on other things, with only the most cursory attention to what was going on inside Rabbit barracks. But now he realized that, unlike Dragon Army, the soldiers in Rabbit were all of the regular age. Not one was even close to Bean's height. He looked like somebody's doll, and worse, he felt like that too, walking down the corridor between the bunks, seeing all these huge boys—and a couple of girls—looking down at him.

Halfway down the bunks, he turned to face those he had already passed. Might as well address the problem immediately.

"The first problem I see," said Bean loudly, "is that you're all way too tall."

Nobody laughed. Bean died a little. But he had to go on.

"I'm growing as fast as I can. Beyond that, I don't know what I can do about it."

Only now did he get a chuckle or two. But that was a relief, that even a few were willing to meet him partway.

"Our first practice together is at 1030. As to our first battle together, I can't predict that, but I can promise you this—the teachers are *not* going to give me the traditional three months after my assignment to a new army. Same with all the other new commanders just appointed. They gave Ender Wiggin only a few weeks with Dragon before they went into battle—and Dragon was a new army, constructed out of nothing. Rabbit is a good army with a solid record. The only new person here is me. I expect the battles to begin in a matter of days, a week at most, and I expect battles to come frequently. So for the first couple of practices, you'll really be training me in your existing system. I need to see how you work with your toon leaders, how the toons work with each other, how you respond to orders, what commands you use. I'll have a couple of things to say that are more about attitude than tactics, but by and large, I want to see you doing things as you've always done them under Carn. It would help me, though, if you practiced with intensity, so I can see you at your sharpest. Are there any questions?"

None. Silence.

"One other thing. Day before yesterday, Bonzo and some of his friends were stalking Ender Wiggin in the halls. I saw the danger, but the soldiers in Dragon Army were mostly too small to stand up against the crew Bonzo had assembled. It wasn't an accident that when I needed help for my commander, I came to the door of Rabbit Army. This wasn't the closest barracks. I came to you because I knew that you had a fair-minded commander in Carn Carby, and I believed that his army would have the same attitude. Even if you didn't have any particular love for Ender Wiggin or Dragon Army, I knew that you would not stand by and let a bunch of thugs pound on a smaller kid that they couldn't beat fair and square in battle. And I was right about you. When you poured out of this barracks and stood as witnesses in the corridor, I was proud of what you stood for. I'm proud now to be one of you."

That did it. Flattery rarely fails, and never does if it's sincere. By letting them know they had already earned his respect, he dissipated much of the tension, for of course they were worried that as a former Dragon he would have contempt for the first army that Ender Wiggin beat. Now they knew better, and so he'd have a chance to win their respect as well.

Itú started clapping, and the other boys joined in. It wasn't a long ovation, but it was enough to let him know the door was open, at least a crack.

He raised his hands to silence the applause—just in time, since it was already dying down. "I'd like to speak to the toon leaders for a few minutes in my quarters. The rest of you are dismissed till practice."

Almost at once, Itú was beside him. "Good job," he said. "Only one mistake."

"What was that?"

"You aren't the only new person here."

"They assigned one of the Dragon soldiers to Rabbit?" For a moment, Bean allowed himself to hope that it would be Nikolai. He could use a reliable friend.

No such luck.

"No, a Dragon soldier would be a veteran! I mean this guy is *new*. He just got to Battle School yesterday afternoon and he was assigned here last night, after you came by."

"A launchy? Assigned straight to an army?"

"Oh, we asked him about that, and he's had a lot of the same classwork. He went through a bunch of surgeries down on Earth, and he studied through it all, but—"

"You mean he's recovering from surgery, too?"

"No, he walks fine, he's—look, why don't you just meet him? All I need to know is, do you want to assign him to a toon or what?"

"Eh, let's see him."

Itú led him to the back of the barracks. There he was, standing beside his bunk, several inches taller than Bean remembered, with legs of even length now, both of them straight. The boy he had last seen fondling Poke, minutes before her dead body went into the river.

"Ho, Achilles," said Bean.

"Ho, Bean," said Achilles. He grinned winningly. "Looks like you're the big guy here."

"So to speak," said Bean.

"You two know each other?" said Itú.

"We knew each other in Rotterdam," said Achilles.

They can't have assigned him to me by accident. I never told anybody but Sister Carlotta about what he did, but how can I guess what she told the I.F.? Maybe they put him here because they thought both of us being from the Rotterdam streets, from the same crew—the same family—I might be able to help him get into the mainstream of the school faster. Or maybe they knew that he was a murderer who was able to hold a grudge for a long, long time, and strike when least expected. Maybe they knew that he planned for my death as surely as he planned for Poke's. Maybe he's here to be my Bonzo Madrid.

Except that I haven't taken any personal defense classes. And I'm half his size—I couldn't jump high enough to hit him in the nose. Whatever they were trying to accomplish by putting Ender's life at risk, Ender always had a better chance of surviving than I will.

The only thing in my favor is that Achilles wants to survive and prosper more than he wants vengeance. Since he can hold a grudge forever, he's in no hurry to act on it. And, unlike Bonzo, he'll never allow himself to be goaded into striking under circumstances where he'd be identifiable as the killer. As long as he thinks he needs me and as long as I'm never alone, I'm probably safe.

Safe. He shuddered. Poke felt safe, too.

"Achilles was *my* commander there," said Bean. "He kept a group of us kids alive. Got us into the charity kitchens."

"Bean is too modest," said Achilles. "The whole thing was his idea. He basically taught us the whole idea of working together. I've studied a lot since then, Bean. I've had a year of nothing but books and classes—when they weren't cutting into my legs and pulverizing and regrowing my bones. And I finally know enough to understand just what a leap you helped us make. From barbarism into civilization. Bean here is like a replay of human evolution."

Bean was not so stupid as to fail to recognize when flattery was being used on him. At the same time, it was more than a little useful to have this new boy, straight from Earth, already know who Bean was and show respect for him.

"The evolution of the pygmies, anyway," said Bean.

"Bean was the toughest little bastard you ever saw on the street, I got to tell you."

No, this was not what Bean needed right now. Achilles had just crossed the line from flattery into possession. Stories about Bean as a "tough little bastard" would, of necessity, set Achilles up as Bean's superior, able to evaluate him. The stories might even be to Bean's credit—but they would serve more to validate Achilles, make him an insider far faster than he would otherwise have been. And Bean did not want Achilles to be inside yet.

Achilles was already going on, as more soldiers gathered closer to hear. "The way I got recruited into Bean's crew was—"

"It wasn't my crew," said Bean, cutting him off. "And here in Battle School, we don't tell stories about home and we don't listen to them either. So I'd appreciate it if you never spoke again of anything that happened Rotterdam, not while you're in my army."

He'd done the nice bit during his opening speech. But now was the time for authority.

Achilles didn't show any sign of embarrassment at the reprimand. "I get it. No problem."

"It's time for you to get ready to go to class," said Bean to the soldiers. "I need to confer with my toon leaders only." Bean pointed to Ambul, a Thai soldier who, according to what Bean read in the student reports, would have been a toon leader long ago, except for his tendency to disobey stupid orders. "You, Ambul. I assign you to get Achilles to and from his correct classes and acquaint him with how to wear a flash suit, how it works, and the basics of movement in the battleroom. Achilles, you are to obey Ambul like God until I assign you to a regular toon."

Achilles grinned. "But I don't obey God."

You think I don't know that? "The correct answer to an order from me is 'Yes sir.' "

Achilles' grin faded. "Yes sir."

"I'm glad to have you here," Bean lied.

"Glad to be here, sir," said Achilles. And Bean was reasonably sure that while Achilles was *not* lying, his reason for being glad was very complicated, and certainly included, by now, a renewed desire to see Bean die.

For the first time, Bean understood the reason Ender had almost always acted as if he was oblivious to the danger from Bonzo. It was a simple choice, really. Either he could act to save himself, or he could act to maintain control over his army. In order to hold real authority, Bean had to insist on complete obedience and respect from his soldiers, even if it meant putting Achilles down, even if it meant increasing his personal danger.

And yet another part of him thought: Achilles wouldn't be here if he didn't have the ability to be a leader. He performed extraordinarily well as our papa in Rotterdam. It's my responsibility now to get him up to speed as quickly as possible, for the sake of his potential usefulness to the I.F. I can't let my personal fear interfere with that, or my hatred of him for what he did to Poke. So even if Achilles is evil incarnate, my job is to turn him into a highly effective soldier with a good shot at becoming a commander.

And in the meantime, I'll watch my back.

20

Trial and Error

"You brought him up to Battle School, didn't you?"

"Sister Carlotta, I'm on a leave of absence right now. That means I've been sacked, in case you don't understand how the I.F. handles these things."

"Sacked! A miscarriage of justice. You ought to be shot."

"If the Sisters of St. Nicholas had convents, your abbess would make you do serious penance for that un-Christian thought."

"You took him out of the hospital in Cairo and directly into space. Even though I warned you."

"Didn't you notice that you telephoned me on a regular exchange? I'm on Earth. Someone else is running Battle School."

"He's a serial murderer now, you know. Not just the girl in Rotterdam. There was a boy there, too, the one Helga called Ulysses. They found his body a few weeks ago."

"Achilles has been in medical care for the past year."

"The coroner estimates that the killing took place at

least that long ago. The body was hidden behind some long-term storage near the fish market. It covered the smell, you see. And it goes on. A teacher at the school I put him in."

"Ah. That's right. *You* put him in a school long before I did."

"The teacher fell to his death from an upper story."

"No witnesses. No evidence."

"Exactly."

"You see a trend here?"

"But that's *my* point. Achilles does not kill carelessly. Nor does he choose his victims at random. Anyone who has seen him helpless, crippled, beaten—he can't bear the shame. He has to expunge it by getting absolute power over the person who dared to humiliate him."

"You're a psychologist now?"

"I laid the facts before an expert."

"The supposed facts."

"I'm not in court, Colonel. I'm talking to the man who put this killer in school with the child who came up with the original plan to humiliate him. Who called for his death. My expert assured me that the chance of Achilles *not* striking against Bean is zero."

"It's not as easy as you think, in space. No dock, you see."

"Do you know how I knew you had taken him into space?"

"I'm sure you have your sources, both mortal and heavenly."

"My dear friend, Dr. Vivian Delamar, was the surgeon who reconstructed Achilles' leg."

"As I recall, you recommended her."

"Before I knew what Achilles really was. When I found out, I called her. Warned her to be careful. Because my expert also said that *she* was in danger."

"The one who restored his leg? Why?"

"No one has seen him more helpless than the surgeon who cuts into him as he lies there drugged to the gills.

Rationally, I'm sure he knew it was wrong to harm this woman who did him so much good. But then, the same would apply to Poke, the first time he killed. *If* it was the first time."

"So . . . Dr. Vivian Delamar. You alerted her. What did she see? Did he murmur a confession under anaesthetic?"

"We'll never know. He killed her."

"You're joking."

"I'm in Cairo. Her funeral is tomorrow. They were calling it a heart attack until I urged them to look for a hypodermic insertion mark. Indeed they found one, and now it's on the books as a murder. Achilles *does* know how to read. He learned which drugs would do the job. How he got her to sit still for it, I don't know."

"How can I believe this, Sister Carlotta? The boy is generous, gracious, people are drawn to him, he's a born leader. People like that don't kill."

"Who are the dead? The teacher who mocked him for his ignorance when he first arrived in the school, showed him up in front of the class. The doctor who saw him laid out under anaesthetic. The street girl whose crew took him down. The street boy who vowed to kill him and made him go into hiding. Maybe the coincidence argument would sway a jury, but it shouldn't sway you."

"Yes, you've convinced me that the danger might well be real. But I already alerted the teachers at Battle School that there might be some danger. And now I really am not in charge of Battle School."

"You're still in *touch*. If you give them a more urgent warning, they'll take steps."

"I'll give the appropriate warning."

"You're lying to me."

"You can tell that over the phone?"

"You *want* Bean exposed to danger!"

"Sister . . . yes, I do. But not this much of it. Whatever I can do, I'll do."

"If you let Bean come to harm, God will have an accounting from you."

"He'll have to get in line, Sister Carlotta. The I.F. court-martial takes precedence."

Bean looked down into the air vent in his quarters and marveled that he had ever been small enough to fit in there. What was he then, the size of a rat?

Fortunately, with a room of his own now he wasn't limited to the outflow vents. He put his chair on top of his table and climbed up to the long, thin intake vents along the wall on the corridor side of his room. The vent trim pried out as several long sections. The paneling above it was separate from the riveted wall below. And it, too, came off fairly easily. Now there was room enough for almost any kid in Battle School to shinny in to the crawl space over the corridor ceiling.

Bean stripped off his clothes and once again crawled into the air system.

It was more cramped this time—it was surprising how much he'd grown. He made his way quickly to the maintenance area near the furnaces. He found how the lighting systems worked, and carefully went around removing lightbulbs and wall glow units in the areas he'd be needing. Soon there was a wide vertical shaft that was utterly dark when the door was closed, with deep shadows even when it was open. Carefully he laid his trap.

———

Achilles never ceased to be astonished at how the universe bent to his will. Whatever he wished seemed to come to him. Poke and her crew, raising him above the other bullies. Sister Carlotta, bringing him to the priests' school in Bruxelles. Dr. Delamar, straightening his leg so he could *run*, so he looked no different from any other boy his age. And now here he was in Battle School, and who should be his first commander but little Bean, ready to take him under his wing, help him rise within this school. As if the universe were created to serve him, with all the people in it tuned to resonate with his desires.

The battleroom was cool beyond belief. War in a box. Point the gun, the other kid's suit freezes. Of course, Ambul had made the mistake of demonstrating this by freezing Achilles and then laughing at his consternation at floating in the air, unable to move, unable to change the direction of his drift. People shouldn't do that. It was wrong, and it always gnawed at Achilles until he was able to set things right. There should be more kindness and respect in the world.

Like Bean. It looked so promising at first, but then Bean started putting him down. Making sure the others saw that Achilles *used* to be Bean's papa, but now he was just a soldier in Bean's army. There was no need for that. You don't go putting people down. Bean had changed. Back when Poke first put Achilles on his back, shaming him in front of all those little children, it was Bean who showed him respect. "Kill him," Bean had said. He knew, then, that tiny boy, he knew that even on his back, Achilles was dangerous. But he seemed to have forgotten that now. In fact, Achilles was pretty sure that Bean must have told Ambul to freeze his flash suit and humiliate him in the practice room, setting him up for the others to laugh at him.

I was your friend and protector, Bean, because you showed respect for me. But now I have to weigh that in the balance with your behavior here in Battle School. No respect for me at all.

The trouble was, the students in Battle School were given nothing that could be used as a weapon, and everything was made completely safe. No one was ever alone, either. Except the commanders. Alone in their quarters. That was promising. But Achilles suspected that the teachers had a way of tracking where every student was at any given time. He'd have to learn the system, learn how to evade it, before he could start setting things to rights.

But he knew this: He'd learn what he needed to learn. Opportunities would appear. And he, being Achilles, would see those opportunities and seize them. Nothing could interrupt his rise until he held all the power there was to hold within his hands. Then there would be perfect justice in the world, not this miserable system that left so many children starving and ignorant and crippled on the streets while others lived in privilege and safety and health. All those adults who had run things for thousands of years were fools or failures. But the universe obeyed Achilles. He and he alone could correct the abuses.

On his third day in Battle School, Rabbit Army had its first battle with Bean as commander. They lost. They would not have lost if Achilles had been commander. Bean was doing some stupid touchy-feely thing, leaving things up to the toon leaders. But it was obvious that the toon leaders had been badly chosen by Bean's predecessor. If Bean was to win, he needed to take tighter control. When he tried to suggest this to Bean, the child only smiled knowingly—a maddeningly superior smile—and told him that the key to victory was for each toon leader and, eventually, each soldier to see the whole situation and act independently to bring about victory. It made Achilles want to slap him, it was so stupid, so wrongheaded. The one who knew how to order things did not leave it up to others to create their little messes in the corners of the world. He took the reins and pulled, sharp and hard. He whipped his men into obedience. As Frederick the Great said: The soldier must fear his officers more than he fears the bullets of the enemy. You could not rule without the naked exercise of power. The followers must bow their heads to the leader. They must *surrender* their heads, using only the mind and will of the leader to rule them. No one but Achilles seemed to understand that this was the great strength of the Buggers. They had no individual minds, only the mind of the hive. They submitted perfectly to the queen. We cannot defeat the Buggers until we learn from them, become like them.

But there was no point in explaining this to Bean. He would not listen. Therefore he would never make Rabbit

Army into a hive. He was working to create chaos. It was unbearable.

Unbearable—yet, just when Achilles thought he couldn't bear the stupidity and waste any longer, Bean called him to his quarters.

Achilles was startled, when he entered, to find that Bean had removed the vent cover and part of the wall panel, giving him access to the air-duct system. This was not at all what Achilles had expected.

"Take your clothes off," said Bean.

Achilles smelled an attempt at humiliation.

Bean was taking off his own uniform. "They track us through the uniforms," said Bean. "If you aren't wearing one, they don't know where you are, except in the gym and the battleroom, where they have really expensive equipment to track each warm body. We aren't going to either of those places, so strip."

Bean was naked. As long as Bean went first, Achilles could not be shamed by doing the same.

"Ender and I used to do this," said Bean. "Everybody thought Ender was such a brilliant commander, but the truth is he knew all the plans of the other commanders because we'd go spying through the air ducts. And not just the commanders, either. We found out what the teachers were planning. We always knew it in advance. Not hard to win that way."

Achilles laughed. This was too cool. Bean might be a fool, but this Ender that Achilles had heard so much about, *he* knew what he was doing.

"It takes two people, is that it?"

"To get where I can spy on the teachers, there's a wide shaft, pitch black. I can't climb down. I need somebody to lower me down and haul me back up. I didn't know who in Rabbit Army I could trust, and then . . . there you were. A friend from the old days."

It was happening again. The universe, bending to his will. He and Bean would be alone. No one would be tracking where they were. No one would know what had happened.

"I'm in," said Achilles.

"Boost me up," said Bean. "You're tall enough to climb up alone."

Clearly, Bean had come this way many times before. He scampered through the crawl space, his feet and butt flashing in the spill from the corridor lights. Achilles noted where he put his hands and feet, and soon was as adept at Bean at picking his way through. Every time he used his leg, he marveled at the use of it. It went where he wanted it to go, and had the strength to hold him. Dr. Delamar might be a skilled surgeon, but even she said that she had never seen a body respond to the surgery as Achilles' did. His body knew how to be whole, expected to be strong. All the time before, those crippled years, had been the universe's way of teaching Achilles the unbearability of disorder. And now Achilles was perfect of body, ready to move ahead in setting things to rights.

Achilles very carefully noted the route they took. If the opportunity presented itself, he would be coming back alone. He could not afford to get lost, or give himself away. No one could know that he had ever been in the air system. As long as he gave them no reason, the teachers would never suspect him. All they knew was that he and Bean were friends. And when Achilles grieved for the child, his tears would be real. They always were, for there was a nobility to these tragic deaths. A grandeur as the great universe worked its will through Achilles' adept hands.

The furnaces roared as they came into a room where the framing of the station was visible. Fire was good. It left so little residue. People died when they accidentally fell into fire. It happened all the time. Bean, crawling around alone . . . it would be good if they went near the furnace.

Instead, Bean opened a door into a dark space. The light from the opening showed a black gap not far inside.

"Don't step over the edge of that," Bean said cheerfully. He picked up a loop of very fine cord from the ground. "It's a deadline. Safety equipment. Keeps workmen from drifting off into space when they're working on the outside of the station. Ender and I set it up—it goes over a beam up there and keeps me centered in the shaft. You can't grip it in your hands, it cuts too easily if it slides across your skin. So you loop it tight around your body—no sliding, see?—and brace yourself. The gravity's not that intense, so I just jump off. We measured it out, so I stop right at the level of the vents leading to the teachers' quarters."

"Doesn't it hurt when you stop?"

"Like a bitch," said Bean. "No pain no gain, right? I take off the deadline, I snag it on a flap of metal and it stays there till I get back. I'll tug on it three times when I get it back on. Then you pull me back up. But *not* with your hands. You go out the door and walk out there. When you get to place where we came in, go around the beam there and go till you touch the wall. Just wait there until I can get myself swinging and land back here on this ledge. Then I unloop myself and you come back in and we leave the deadline for next time. Simple, see?"

"Got it," said Achilles.

Instead of walking to the wall, it would be simple enough to just keep walking. Get Bean floating in the air where he couldn't get hold of anything. Plenty of time, then, to find a way to tie it off inside that dark room. With the roar of the furnaces and fans, nobody would hear Bean calling for help. Then Achilles would have time to explore. Figure out how to get into the furnaces. Swing Bean back, strangle him, carry the body to the fire. Drop the deadline down the shaft. Nobody would find it. Quite possibly no one would ever find Bean, or if they did, his soft tissues would be consumed. All evidence of strangulation would be gone. Very neat. There'd be some improvisation, but there always was. Achilles could handle little problems as they came up.

Achilles looped the deadline over his head, then drew it tight under his arms as Bean climbed into the loop at the other end.

"Set," said Achilles.

"Make sure it's tight, so it doesn't have any slack to cut you when I hit bottom."

"Yes, it's tight."

But Bean had to check. He got a finger under the line. "Tighter," said Bean.

Achilles tightened it more.

"Good," said Bean. "That's it. Do it."

Do it? Bean was the one who was supposed to do it.

Then the deadline went taut and Achilles was lifted off his feet. With a few more yanks, he hung in the air in the dark shaft. The deadline dug harshly into his skin.

When Bean said "do it" he was talking to someone else. Someone who was already here, lying in wait. The traitorous little bastard.

Achilles said nothing, however. He reached up to see if he could touch the beam above him, but it was out of reach. Nor could he climb the line, not with bare hands, not with the line drawn taut by his own body weight.

He wriggled on the line, starting himself swinging. But no matter how far he went in any direction, he touched nothing. No wall, no place where he might find purchase.

Time to talk.

"What's this about, Bean?"

"It's about Poke," said Bean.

"She's dead, Bean."

"You kissed her. You killed her. You put her in the river."

Achilles felt the blood run hot into his face. No one saw that. He was guessing. But then . . . how did he know that Achilles had kissed her first, unless he saw?

"You're wrong," said Achilles.

"How sad if I am. Then the wrong man will die for the crime."

"Die? Be serious, Bean. You aren't a killer."

"But the hot dry air of the shaft will do it for me. You'll dehydrate in a day. Your mouth's already a little dry, isn't it? And then you'll just keep hanging here, mummifying. This is the intake system, so the air gets filtered and purified. Even if your body stinks for a while, nobody will smell it. Nobody will see you—you're above where the light shines from the door. And nobody comes in here anyway. No, the disappearance of Achilles will be the mystery of Battle School. They'll tell ghost stories about you to frighten the launchies."

"Bean, I didn't do it."

"I saw you, Achilles, you poor fool. I don't care what you say, I *saw* you. I never thought I'd have the chance to make you pay for what you did to her. Poke did nothing but good to you. I told her to kill you, but she had mercy. She made you king of the streets. And for that you killed her?"

"I didn't kill her."

"Let me lay it out for you, Achilles, since you're clearly too stupid to see where you are. First thing is, you forgot where you were. Back on Earth, you were used to being a lot smarter than everybody around you. But here in Battle School, *everybody* is as smart as you, and most of us are smarter. You think Ambul didn't see the way you looked at him? You think he didn't know he was marked for death after he laughed at you? You think the other soldiers in Rabbit doubted me when I told them about you? They'd already seen that there was something wrong with you. The adults might have missed it, they might buy into the way you suck up to them, but *we* didn't. And since we just had a case of one kid trying to kill another, nobody was going to put up with it again. Nobody was going to wait for you to strike. Because here's the thing— we don't give a shit about fairness here. We're soldiers. Soldiers do not give the other guy a sporting chance. Soldiers shoot in the back, lay traps and ambushes, lie to the enemy and outnumber the other bastard every chance they get. Your kind of murder only works among civilians.

And you were too cocky, too stupid, too insane to realize that."

Achilles knew that Bean was right. He had miscalculated grossly. He had forgotten that when Bean said for Poke to kill him, he had not just been showing respect for Achilles. He had also been trying to get Achilles killed.

This just wasn't working out very well.

"So you have only two ways for this to end. One way, you just hang there, we take turns watching to make sure you don't figure some way out of this, until you're dead and then we leave you and go about our lives. The other way, you confess to everything—and I mean everything, not just what you think I already know—and you keep confessing. Confess to the teachers. Confess to the psychiatrists they send you to. Confess your way into a mental hospital back on Earth. We don't care which you choose. All that matters is that you never again walk freely through the corridors of Battle School. Or anywhere else. So . . . what will it be? Dry out on the line, or let the teachers know just how crazy you are?"

"Bring me a teacher, I'll confess."

"Didn't you hear me explain how stupid we're not? You confess now. Before witnesses. With a recorder. We don't bring some teacher up here to see you hanging there and feel all squishy sorry for you. Any teacher who comes here will know exactly what you are, and there'll be about six marines to keep you subdued and sedated because, Achilles, they don't play around here. They don't give people chances to escape. You've got no rights here. You don't get rights again until you're back on Earth. Here's your last chance. Confession time."

Achilles almost laughed out loud. But it was important for Bean to think that he had won. As, for the moment, he had. Achilles could see now that there was no way for him to remain in Battle School. But Bean wasn't smart enough just to kill him and have done. No, Bean was, completely unnecessarily, allowing him to live. And as long as Achilles was alive, then time would move things his way. The universe would bend until the door was opened and Achilles went free. And it would happen sooner rather than later.

You shouldn't have left a door open for me, Bean. Because I *will* kill you someday. You and everyone else who has seen me helpless here.

"All right," said Achilles. "I killed Poke. I strangled her and put her in the river."

"Go on."

"What more? You want to know how she wet herself and took a shit while she was dying? You want to know how her eyes bugged out?"

"One murder doesn't get you psychiatric confinement, Achilles. You know you've killed before."

"What makes you think so?"

"Because it didn't bother you."

It never bothered, not even the first time. You just don't understand power. If it *bothers* you, you aren't fit to *have* power. "I killed Ulysses, of course, but just because he was a nuisance."

"And?"

"I'm not a mass murderer, Bean."

"You live to kill, Achilles. Spill it all. And then convince me that it really *was* all."

But Achilles had just been playing. He had already decided to tell it all.

"The most recent was Dr. Vivian Delamar," he said. "I told her not to do the operations under total anaesthetic. I told her to leave me alert, I could take it even if there was pain. But she had to be in control. Well, if she really loved control so much, why did she turn her back on me? And why was she so stupid as to think I really had a gun? By pressing hard in her back, I made it so she didn't even feel the needle go in right next to where the tongue depressors were poking her. Died of a heart attack right there in her own office. Nobody even knew I'd been in there. You want more?"

"I want it all, Achilles."

It took twenty minutes, but Achilles gave them the whole chronicle, all seven times he had set things right. He liked it, actually, telling them like this. Nobody had ever had a chance to understand how powerful he was till now. He wanted to see their faces, that's the only thing that was missing. He wanted to see the disgust that would reveal their weakness, their inability to look power in the face. Machiavelli understood. If you intend to rule, you don't shrink from killing. Saddam Hussein knew it—you have to be willing to kill with your own hand. You can't stand back and let others do it for you all the time. And Stalin understood it, too—you can never be loyal to anybody, because that only weakens you. Lenin was good to Stalin, gave him his chance, raised him out of nothing to be the keeper of the gate to power. But that didn't stop Stalin from imprisoning Lenin and then killing him. That's what these fools would never understand. All those military writers were just armchair philosophers. All that military history—most of it was useless. War was just one of the tools that the great men used to get and keep their power. And the only way to stop a great man was the way Brutus did it.

Bean, you're no Brutus.

Turn on the light. Let me see the faces.

But the light did not go on. When he was finished, when they left, there was only the light through the door, silhouetting them as they left. Five of them. All naked, but carrying the recording equipment. They even tested it, to make sure it had picked up Achilles' confession. He heard his own voice, strong and unwavering. Proud of what he'd done. That would prove to the weaklings that he was "insane." They would keep him alive. Until the universe bent things to his will yet again, and set him free to reign with blood and horror on Earth. Since they hadn't let him see their faces, he'd have no choice. When all the power was in his hands, he'd have to kill everyone who was in Battle School at this time. That would be a good idea, anyway. Since all the brilliant military minds of the age had been assembled here at one time or another, it was obvious that in order to rule safely, Achilles would have to get rid of everyone whose name had ever been on a Battle School roster. Then there'd be no rivals. And he'd keep testing children as long as he lived, finding any with the slightest spark of military talent. Herod understood how you stay in power.

Part Six

VICTOR

21

Guesswork

"We're not waiting any longer for Colonel Graff to repair the damage done to Ender Wiggin. Wiggin doesn't need Tactical School for the job he'll be doing. And we need the others to move on at once. *They* have to get the feel of what the old ships can do before we bring them here and put them on the simulators, and that takes time."

"They've only had a few games."

"I shouldn't have allowed them as much time as I have. ISL is two months away from you, and by the time they're done with Tactical, the voyage from there to FleetCom will be four months. That gives them only three months in Tactical before we have to bring them to Command School. Three months in which to compress three years of training."

"I should tell you that Bean seems to have passed Colonel Graff's last test."

"Test? When I relieved Colonel Graff, I thought his sick little testing program ended as well."

"We didn't know how dangerous this Achilles was. We

had been warned of *some* danger, but . . . he seemed so likable . . . I'm not faulting Colonel Graff, you understand, *he* had no way of knowing."

"Knowing what?'

"That Achilles is a serial killer."

"That should make Graff happy. Ender's count is up to two."

"I'm not joking, sir. Achilles has seven murders on his tally."

"And he passed the screening?"

"He knew how to answer the psychological tests."

"Please tell me that none of the seven took place at Battle School."

"Number eight would have. But Bean got him to confess."

"Bean's a priest now?"

"Actually, sir, it was deft strategy. He outmaneuvered Achilles—led him into an ambush, and confession was the only escape."

"So Ender, the nice middle-class American boy, kills the kid who wants to beat him up in the bathroom. And Bean, the hoodlum street kid, turns a serial killer over to law enforcement."

"The more significant thing for our purposes is that Ender was good at building teams, but he beat Bonzo hand to hand, one on one. And then Bean, a loner who had almost no friends after a year in the school, he beats Achilles by assembling a team to be his defense and his witnesses. I have no idea if Graff predicted these outcomes, but the result was that his tests got each boy to act not only against our expectations, but also against his own predilections."

"Predilections. Major Anderson."

"It will all be in my report."

"Try to write the entire thing without using the word *predilection* once."

"Yes, sir."

"I've assigned the destroyer *Condor* to take the group."

"How many do you want, sir?"

"We have need of a maximum of eleven at any one time. We have Carby, Bee, and Momoe on their way to Tactical already, but Graff tells me that of those three, only Carby is likely to work well with Wiggin. We do need to hold a slot for Ender, but it wouldn't hurt to have a spare. So send ten."

"*Which* ten?"

"How the hell should I know? Well . . . Bean, him for sure. And the nine others that you think would work best with either Bean or Ender in command, whichever one it turns out to be."

"One list for both possible commanders?"

"With Ender as the first choice. We want them all to train together. Become a team."

The orders came at 1700. Bean was supposed to board the *Condor* at 1800. It's not as if he had anything to pack. An hour was more time than they gave Ender. So Bean went and told his army what was happening, where he was going.

"We've only had five games," said Itú.

"Got to catch the bus when it comes to the stop, neh?" said Bean.

"Eh," said Itú.

"Who else?" asked Ambul.

"They didn't tell me. Just . . . Tactical School."

"We don't even know where it is."

"Somewhere in space," said Itú.

"No, really?" It was lame, but they laughed. It wasn't all that hard a good-bye. He'd only been with Rabbit for eight days.

"Sorry we didn't win any for you," said Itú.

"We would have won, if I'd wanted to," said Bean.

They looked at him like he was crazy.

"I was the one who proposed that we get rid of the standings, stop caring who wins. How would it look if we do that and I win every time?"

"It would look like you really did care about the standings," said Itú.

"That's not what bothers me," said another toon leader. "Are you telling me you set us up to *lose?*"

"No, I'm telling you I had a different priority. What do we learn from beating each other? Nothing. We're never going to have to fight human children. We're going to have to fight Buggers. So what do we need to learn? How to coordinate our attacks. How to respond to each other. How to feel the course of the battle, and take responsibility for the whole thing even if you don't have command. *That's* what I was working on with you guys. And if we *won,* if we went in and mopped up the walls with them, using *my* strategy, what does that teach *you?* You already worked with a good commander. What you needed to do was work with each other. So I put you in tough situations and by the end you were finding ways to bail each other out. To make it work."

"We never made it work well enough to win."

"That's not how I measured it. You made it work. When the Buggers come again, they're going to make things go wrong. Besides the normal friction of war, they're going to be doing stuff we couldn't think of because they're not human, they don't think like us. So plans of attack, what good are they then? We try, we do what we can, but what really counts is what you do when command breaks down. When it's just you with your squadron, and you with your transport, and you with your beat-up strike force that's got only five weapons among eight ships. How do you help each other? How do you make do? That's what I was working on. And then I went back to the officers' mess and told them what I learned. What you guys showed me. I learned stuff from them, too. I told you all the stuff I learned from them, right?"

"Well, you *could* have told us what you were learning from *us,*" said Itú. They were all still a bit resentful.

"I didn't have to *tell* you. You learned it."

"At least you could have told us it was OK not to win."

"But you were supposed to *try* to win. I didn't tell you because it only works if you think it counts. Like when the Buggers come. It'll count then, for real. That's when you get really smart, when losing means that you and everybody you ever cared about, the whole human race, will die. Look, I didn't think we'd have long together. So I made the best use of the time, for you and for me. You guys are all ready to take command of armies."

"What about you, Bean?" asked Ambul. He was smiling, but there was an edge to it. "You ready to command a fleet?"

"I don't know. It depends on whether they want to win." Bean grinned.

"Here's the thing, Bean," said Ambul. "Soldiers don't like to lose."

"And *that*," said Bean, "is why losing is a much more powerful teacher than winning."

They heard him. They thought about it. Some of them nodded.

"*If* you live," Bean added. And grinned at them.

They smiled back.

"I gave you the best thing I could think of to give you during this week," said Bean. "And learned from you as much as I was smart enough to learn. Thank you." He stood and saluted them.

They saluted back.

He left.

And went to Rat Army barracks.

"Nikolai just got his orders," a toon leader told him.

For a moment Bean wondered if Nikolai would be going to Tactical School with him. His first thought was, No way is he ready. His second thought was, I wish he could come. His third thought was, I'm not much of a friend, to think first how he doesn't deserve to be promoted.

"What orders?" Bean asked.

"He's got him an army. Hell, he wasn't even a toon leader here. Just *got* here last week."

"Which army?"

"Rabbit." The toon leader looked at Bean's uniform again. "Oh. I guess he's replacing *you.*"

Bean laughed and headed for the quarters he had just left.

Nikolai was sitting inside with the door open, looking lost.

"Can I come in?"

Nikolai looked up and grinned. "Tell me you're here to take your army back."

"I've got a hint for you. Try to win. They think that's important."

"I couldn't believe you lost all five."

"You know, for a school that doesn't list standings anymore, everybody sure keeps track."

"I keep track of *you.*"

"Nikolai, I wish you were coming with me."

"What's happening, Bean? Is this it? Are the Buggers here?"

"I don't know."

"Come on, you figure these things out."

"If the Buggers were really coming, would they leave all you guys here in the station? Or send you back to Earth? Or evacuate you to some obscure asteroid? I don't know. Some things point to the end being really close. Other things seem like nothing important's going to happen anywhere around here."

"So maybe they're about to launch this huge fleet against the Bugger world and you guys are supposed to grow up on the voyage."

"Maybe," said Bean. "But the time to launch *that* fleet was right after the Second Invasion."

"Well, what if they didn't find out where the Bugger home world *was* until now?"

That stopped Bean cold. "Never crossed my mind," said Bean. "I mean, they must have been sending signals home. All we had to do was track that direction. Follow the light, you know. That's what it says in the manuals."

"What if they don't communicate by light?"

"Light may take a year to go a lightyear, but it's still faster than anything else."

"Anything else that we know about," said Nikolai.

Bean just looked at him.

"Oh, I know, that's stupid. The laws of physics and all that. I just—you know, I keep thinking, that's all. I don't like to rule things out just because they're impossible."

Bean laughed. "Merda, Nikolai, I should have let you talk more and me talk less back when we slept across from each other."

"Bean, you know I'm not a genius."

"All geniuses here, Nikolai."

"I was scraping by."

"So maybe you're not a Napoleon, Nikolai. Maybe you're just an Eisenhower. Don't expect me to cry for you."

It was Nikolai's turn to laugh.

"I'll miss you, Bean."

"Thanks for coming with me to face Achilles, Nikolai."

"Guy gave me nightmares."

"Me too."

"And I'm glad you brought the others along too. Itú, Ambul, Crazy Tom, I felt like we could've used six more, and Achilles was hanging from a wire. Guys like him, you can understand why they invented hanging."

"Someday," said Bean, "you're going to need me the way I needed you. And I'll be there."

"I'm sorry I didn't join your squad, Bean."

"You were right," said Bean. "I asked you because you were my friend, and I thought I needed a friend, but I should have *been* a friend, too, and seen what *you* needed."

"I'll never let you down again."

Bean threw his arms around Nikolai. Nikolai hugged him back.

Bean remembered when he left Earth. Hugging Sister

Carlotta. Analyzing. This is what she needs. It costs me nothing. Therefore I'll give her the hug.

I'm not that kid anymore.

Maybe because I was able to come through for Poke after all. Too late to help her, but I still got her killer to admit it. I still got him to pay something, even if it can never be enough.

"Go meet your army, Nikolai," said Bean. "I've got a spaceship to catch."

He watched Nikolai go out the door and knew, with a sharp pang of regret, that he would never see his friend again.

———

Dimak stood in Major Anderson's quarters.

"Captain Dimak, I watched Colonel Graff indulge your constant complaints, your resistance to his orders, and I kept thinking, Dimak might be right, but I would never tolerate such lack of respect if *I* were in command. I'd throw him out on his ass and write 'insubordinate' in about forty places in his dossier. I thought I should tell you that before you make your complaint."

Dimak blinked.

"Go ahead, I'm waiting."

"It isn't so much a complaint as a question."

"Then ask your question."

"I thought you were supposed to choose a team that was equally compatible with Ender *and* with Bean."

"The word *equally* was never used, as far as I can recall. But even if it was, did it occur to you that it might be impossible? I could have chosen forty brilliant children who would all have been proud and eager to serve under Andrew Wiggin. How many would be *equally* proud and eager to serve under Bean?"

Dimak had no answer for that.

"The way I analyze it, the soldiers I chose to send on this destroyer are the students who are emotionally closest and most responsive to Ender Wiggin, while also being among the dozen or so best commanders in the school. These soldiers also have no particular animosity toward Bean. So if they find him placed over them, they'll probably do their best for him."

"They'll never forgive him for not being Ender."

"I guess that will be Bean's challenge. Who else should I have sent? Nikolai is Bean's friend, but he'd be out of his depth. Someday he'll be ready for Tactical School, and then Command, but not yet. And what other friends does Bean have?"

"He's won a lot of respect."

"And lost it again when he lost all five of his games."

"I've explained to you why he—"

"Humanity doesn't need explanations, Captain Dimak! It needs winners! Ender Wiggin had the fire to win. Bean is capable of losing five in a row as if they didn't even matter."

"They didn't matter. He learned what he needed to learn from them."

"Captain Dimak, I can see that I'm falling into the same trap that Colonel Graff fell into. You have crossed the line from teaching into advocacy. I would dismiss you as Bean's teacher, were it not for the fact that the question is already moot. I'm sending the soldiers I decided on already. If Bean is really so brilliant, he'll figure out a way to work with them."

"Yes sir," said Dimak.

"If it's any consolation, do remember that Crazy Tom was one of the ones Bean brought along to hear Achilles' confession. Crazy Tom *went*. That suggests that the better they know Bean, the more seriously they take him."

"Thank you, sir."

"Bean is no longer your responsibility, Captain Dimak. You did well with him. I salute you for it. Now . . . get back to work."

Dimak saluted.

Anderson saluted.

Dimak left.

———

On the destroyer *Condor,* the crew had no idea what to do with these children. They all knew about the Battle School, and both the captain and the pilot were Battle School graduates. But after perfunctory conversation— What army were you in? Oh, in my day Rat was the best, Dragon was a complete loser, how things change, how things stay the same—there was nothing more to say.

Without the shared concerns of being army commanders, the children drifted into their natural friendship groups. Dink and Petra had been friends almost from their first beginnings in Battle School, and they were so senior to the others that no one tried to penetrate that closed circle. Alai and Shen had been in Ender Wiggin's original launch group, and Vlad and Dumper, who had commanded B and E toons and were probably the most worshipful of Ender, hung around with them. Crazy Tom, Fly Molo, and Hot Soup had already been a trio back in Dragon Army. On a personal level, Bean did not expect to be included in any of these groups, and he wasn't particularly excluded, either; Crazy Tom, at least, showed real respect for Bean, and often included him in conversation. If Bean belonged to any of these groups, it was Crazy Tom's.

The only reason the division into cliques bothered him was that this group was clearly being assembled, not just randomly chosen. Trust needed to grow between them all, strongly if not equally. But they had been chosen for Ender—any idiot could see that—and it was not Bean's place to suggest that they play the onboard games together, learn together, do anything together. If Bean tried to assert any kind of leadership, it would only build more walls between him and the others than already existed.

There was only one of the group that Bean didn't think belonged there. And he couldn't do anything about that. Apparently the adults did not hold Petra responsible for her near-betrayal of Ender in the corridor the evening before Ender's life-or-death struggle with Bonzo. But Bean was not so sure. Petra was one of the best of the commanders, smart, able to see the big picture. How could she possibly have been fooled by Bonzo? Of course she couldn't have been hoping for Ender's destruction. But she had been careless, at best, and at worst might have been playing some kind of game that Bean did not yet understand. So he remained suspicious of her. Which wasn't good, to have such mistrust, but there it was.

Bean passed the four months of the voyage in the ship's library, mostly. Now that they were out of Battle School, he was reasonably sure that they weren't being spied on so intensely. The destroyer simply wasn't equipped for it. So he no longer had to choose his reading material with an eye to what the teachers would make of his selections.

He read no military history or theory whatsoever. He had already read all the major writers and many of the minor ones and knew the important campaigns backward and forward, from both sides. Those were in his memory to be called upon whenever he needed them. What was missing from his memory was the big picture. How the world worked. Political, social, economic history. What happened in nations when they weren't at war. How they got into and out of wars. How victory and defeat affected them. How alliances were formed and broken.

And, most important of all, but hardest to find: What was going on in the world today. The destroyer library had only the information that had been current when last it docked at Interstellar Launch—ISL—which is where the authorized list of documents was made available for download. Bean could make requests for more information, but that would require the library computer to make requisitions and use communications bandwidth that would have to be justified. It would be noticed, and then they'd wonder why this child was studying matters that could have no possible concern for him.

From what he could find on board, however, it was still possible to piece together the basic situation on Earth, and to reach some conclusions. During the years before the First Invasion, various power blocs had jockeyed for position, using some combination of terrorism, "surgical" strikes, limited military operations, and economic sanctions, boycotts, and embargos to gain the upper hand or give firm warnings or simply express national or ideological rage. When the Buggers showed up, China had just emerged as the dominant world power, economically and militarily, having finally reunited itself as a democracy. The North Americans and Europeans played at being China's "big brothers," but the economic balance had finally shifted.

What Bean saw as the driving force of history, however, was the resurgent Russian Empire. Where the Chinese simply took it for granted that they were and should be the center of the universe, the Russians, led by a series of ambitious demagogues and authoritarian generals, felt that history had cheated them out of their rightful place, century after century, and it was time for that to end. So it was Russia that forced the creation of the New Warsaw Pact, bringing its effective borders back to the peak of Soviet power—and beyond, for this time Greece was its ally, and an intimidated Turkey was neutralized. Europe was on the verge of being neutralized, the Russian dream of hegemony from the Pacific to the Atlantic at last within reach.

And then the Formics came and cut a swath of destruction through China that left a hundred million dead. Suddenly land-based armies seemed trivial, and questions of international competition were put on hold.

But that was only superficial. In fact, the Russians used their domination of the office of the Polemarch to build up a network of officers in key places throughout the fleet. Everything was in place for a vast power play the moment the Buggers were defeated—or before, if they thought it was to their advantage. Oddly, the Russians were rather open about their intentions—they always had been. They had no talent for subtlety, but they made up for it with amazing stubbornness. Negotiations for anything could take decades. And meanwhile, their penetration of the fleet was nearly total. Infantry forces loyal to the Strategos would be isolated, unable to get to the places where they were needed because there would be no ships to carry them.

When the war with the Buggers ended, the Russians clearly planned that within hours they would rule the fleet and therefore the world. It was their destiny. The North Americans were as complacent as ever, sure that destiny would work everything out in their favor. Only a few demagogues saw the danger. The Chinese and the Muslim world were alert to the danger, and even they were unable to make any kind of stand for fear of breaking up the alliance that made resistance to the Buggers possible.

The more he studied, the more Bean wished that he did not have to go to Tactical School. This war would belong to Ender and his friends. And while Bean loved Ender as much as any of them, and would gladly serve with them against the Buggers, the fact was that they didn't need him. It was the next war, the struggle for world domination, that fascinated him. The Russians *could* be stopped, if the right preparations were made.

But then he had to ask himself: *Should* they be stopped? A quick, bloody, but effective coup which would bring the world under a single government—it would mean the end of war among humans, wouldn't it? And in such a climate of peace, wouldn't all nations be better off?

So, even as Bean developed his plan for stopping the Russians, he tried to evaluate what a worldwide Russian Empire would be like.

And what he concluded was that it would not last. For along with their national vigor, the Russians had also nurtured their astonishing talent for misgovernment, that sense of personal entitlement that made corruption a way of life. The institutional tradition of competence that would be essential for a successful world government was nonexistent. It was in China that those institutions and values were most vigorous. But even China would be a poor substitute for a genuine world government that transcended any national interest. The wrong world government would eventually collapse under its own weight.

Bean longed to be able to talk these things over with someone—with Nikolai, or even with one of the teachers. It slowed him down to have his own thoughts move around in circles—without outside stimulation it was hard to break free of his own assumptions. One mind can think only of its own questions; it rarely surprises itself. But he made progress, slowly, during that voyage, and then during the months of Tactical School.

Tactical was a blur of short voyages and detailed tours of various ships. Bean was disgusted that they seemed to concentrate entirely on older designs, which seemed pointless to him—why train your commanders in ships they won't actually be using in battle? But the teachers treated his objection with contempt, pointing out that ships were ships, in the long run, and the newest vessels had to be put into service patrolling the perimeters of the solar system. There were none to spare for training children.

They were taught very little about the art of pilotry, for they were not being trained to fly the ships, only to command them in battle. They had to get a sense of how the weapons worked, how the ships moved, what could be expected of them, what their limitations were. Much of it was rote learning . . . but that was precisely the kind of learning Bean could do almost in his sleep, being able to recall anything that he had read or heard with any degree of attention.

So throughout Tactical School, while he performed as well as anyone, his real concentration was still on the problems of the current political situation on Earth. For Tactical School was at ISL, and so the library there was constantly being updated, and not just with the material authorized for inclusion in finite ships' libraries. For the first time, Bean began to read the writings of current political thinkers on Earth. He read what was coming out of Russia, and once again was astonished at how nakedly they pursued their ambitions. The Chinese writers saw the danger, but being Chinese, made no effort to rally support in other nations for any kind of resistance. To the Chinese, once something was known in China, it was known everywhere that mattered. And the Euro-American nations seemed dominated by a studied ignorance that to Bean appeared to be a death wish. Yet there were some who were awake, struggling to create coalitions.

Two popular commentators in particular came to Bean's attention. Demosthenes at first glance seemed to be a rabble-rouser, playing on prejudice and xenophobia. But he was also having considerable success in leading a popular movement. Bean didn't know if life under a government headed by Demosthenes would be any better than living under the Russians, but Demosthenes would at least make a contest out of it. The other commentator that Bean took note of was Locke, a lofty, high-minded fellow who nattered about world peace and forging alliances—yet amid his apparent complacency, Locke actually seemed to be working from the same set of facts as Demosthenes, taking it for granted that the Russians were vigorous enough to "lead" the world, but unprepared to do so in a "beneficial" way. In a way, it was as if Demosthenes and Locke were doing their research together, reading all the same sources, learning from all the same correspondents, but then appealing to completely different audiences.

For a while, Bean even toyed with the possibility that Locke and Demosthenes were the same person. But no, the writing styles were different, and more importantly, they thought and analyzed differently. Bean didn't think anyone was smart enough to fake that.

Whoever they were, these two commentators were the people who seemed to see the situation most accurately, and so Bean began to conceive of his essay on strategy in the post-Formic world as a letter to both Locke and Demosthenes. A private letter. An anonymous letter. Because his observations should be known, and these two seemed to be in the best position to bring Bean's ideas to fruition.

Resorting to old habits, Bean spent some time in the library watching several officers log on to the net, and soon had six log-ins that he could use. He then wrote his letter in six parts, using a different log-in for each part, and then sent the parts to Locke and Demosthenes within minutes of each other. He did it during an hour when the library was crowded, and made sure that he himself was logged on to the net on his own desk in his barracks, ostensibly playing a game. He doubted they'd be counting his keystrokes and realize that he wasn't actually doing anything with his desk during that time. And if they did trace the letter back to him, well, too bad. In all likelihood, Locke and Demosthenes would not try to trace him—in his letter he asked them not to. They would either believe him or not; they would agree with him or not; beyond that he could not go. He had spelled out for them exactly what the dangers were, what the Russian strategy obviously was, and what steps must be taken to ensure that the Russians did not succeed in their preemptive strike.

One of the most important points he made was that the children from Battle, Tactical, and Command School had to be brought back to Earth as quickly as possible, once the Buggers were defeated. If they remained in space, they would either be taken by the Russians or kept in ineffectual isolation by the I.F. But these children were the finest military minds that humanity had produced in this generation. If the power of one great nation was to be subdued, it would require brilliant commanders in opposition to them.

Within a day, Demosthenes had an essay on the nets calling for the Battle School to be dissolved at once and all those children brought home. "They have kidnapped our most promising children. Our Alexanders and Napoleons, our Rommels and Pattons, our Caesars and Fredericks and Washingtons and Saladins are being kept in a tower where we can't reach them, where they can't help their own people remain free from the threat of Russian domination. And who can doubt that the Russians intend to seize those children and use them? Or, if they can't, they will certainly try, with a single well-placed missile, to blast them all to bits, depriving us of our natural military leadership." Delicious demagoguery, designed to spark fear and outrage. Bean could imagine the consternation in the military as their precious school became a political issue. It was an emotional issue that Demosthenes would not let go of and other nationalists all over the world would fervently echo. And because it was about children, no politician could dare oppose the principle that all the children in Battle School would come home the *moment* the war ended. Not only that, but on this issue, Locke lent his prestigious, moderate voice to the cause, openly supporting the principle of the return of the children. "By all means, pay the piper, rid us of the invading rats—and then bring our children home."

I saw, I wrote, and the world changed a little. It was a heady feeling. It made all the work at Tactical School seem almost meaningless by comparison. He wanted to bound into the classroom and tell the others about his triumph. But they would look at him like he was crazy. They knew nothing about the world at large, and took no responsibility for it. They were closed into the military world.

Three days after Bean sent his letters to Locke and Demosthenes, the children came to class and found that they were to depart immediately for Command School, this time joined by Carn Carby, who had been a class ahead of them in Tactical School. They had spent only three months at ISL, and Bean couldn't help wondering if his letters had not had some influence over the timing. If there was some danger that the children might be sent home prematurely, the I.F. had to make sure their prize specimens were out of reach.

22

Reunion

"I suppose I should congratulate you for undoing the damage you did to Ender Wiggin."

"Sir, I respectfully disagree that I did any damage."

"Ah, good then, I *don't* have to congratulate you. You do realize that your status here will be as observer."

"I hope that I will also have opportunities to offer advice based on my years of experience with these children."

"Command School has worked with children for years."

"Respectfully, sir, Command School has worked with adolescents. Ambitious, testosterone-charged, competitive teenagers. And quite aside from that, we have a lot riding on these particular children, and I know things about them that must be taken into account."

"All those things should be in your reports."

"They are. But with all respect, is there anyone there who has memorized my reports so thoroughly that the appropriate details will come to mind the instant they're needed?"

"I'll listen to you, Colonel Graff. And please stop assur-

ing me of how respectful you are whenever you're about
to tell me I'm an idiot."

"I thought that my leave of absence was designed to
chasten me. I'm trying to show that I've been chastened."

"Are there any of these details about the children that
come to mind right now?"

"An important one, sir. Because so much depends on
what Ender does or does not know, it is vital that you
isolate him from the other children. During actual practices
he can be there, but under no circumstances can you allow
free conversation or sharing of information."

"And why is that?"

"Because if Bean ever comes to know about the ansible,
he'll leap straight to the core situation. He may figure it
out on his own as it is—you have no idea how difficult it
is to conceal information from him. Ender is more trusting—but Ender can't do his job *unless* he knows about the
ansible. You see? He and Bean cannot be allowed to have
any free time together. Any conversation that is not on
point."

"But if this is so, then Bean is not capable of being Ender's backup, because then he would *have* to be told about
the ansible."

"It won't matter then."

"But you yourself were the author of the proposition
that only a child—"

"Sir, none of that applies to Bean."

"Because?"

"Because he's not human."

"Colonel Graff, you make me tired."

The voyage to Command School was four long months,
and this time they were being trained continuously, as
thorough an education in the mathematics of targeting,
explosives, and other weapons-related subjects as could
be managed on board a fast-moving cruiser. Finally, too,
they were being forged again into a team, and it quickly
became clear to everyone that the leading student was

Bean. He mastered everything immediately, and was soon the one whom the others turned to for explanations of concepts they didn't grasp at once. From being the lowest in status on the first voyage, a complete outsider, Bean now became an outcast for the opposite reason—he was alone in the position of highest status.

He struggled with the situation, because he knew that he needed to be able to function as part of the team, not just as a mentor or expert. Now it became vital that he take part in their downtime, relaxing with them, joking, joining in with reminiscences about Battle School. And about even earlier times.

For now, at last, the Battle School tabu against talking about home was gone. They all spoke freely of mothers and fathers who by now were distant memories, but who still played a vital role in their lives.

The fact that Bean had no parents at first made the others a little shy with him, but he seized the opportunity and began to speak openly about his entire experience. Hiding in the toilet tank in the clean room. Going home with the Spanish custodian. Starving on the streets as he scouted for his opportunity. Telling Poke how to beat the bullies at their own game. Watching Achilles, admiring him, fearing him as he created their little street family, marginalized Poke, and finally killed her. When he told them of finding Poke's body, several of them wept. Petra in particular broke down and sobbed.

It was an opportunity, and Bean seized it. Naturally, she soon fled the company of others, taking her emotions into the privacy of her quarters. As soon afterward as he could, Bean followed her.

"Bean, I don't want to talk."

"I do," said Bean. "It's something we have to talk about. For the good of the team."

"Is that what we are?" she asked.

"Petra, you know the worst thing I've ever done. Achilles was dangerous, I knew it, and I still went away and left Poke alone with him. She died for it. That burns in me every day of my life. Every time I start to feel happy, I remember Poke, how I owe my life to her, how I could have saved her. Every time I love somebody, I have that fear that I'll betray them the same way I did her."

"Why are you telling me this, Bean?"

"Because you betrayed Ender and I think it's eating at you."

Her eyes flashed with rage. "I did not! And it's eating at *you,* not me!"

"Petra, whether you admit it to yourself or not, when you tried to slow Ender down in the corridor that day, there's no way you didn't know what you were doing. I've seen you in action, you're sharp, you see everything. In some ways you're the best tactical commander in the whole group. It's absolutely impossible that you didn't see how Bonzo's thugs were all there in the corridor, waiting to beat the crap out of Ender, and what did you do? You tried to slow him down, peel him off from the group."

"And you stopped me," said Petra. "So it's moot, isn't it?"

"I have to know why."

"You don't have to know squat."

"Petra, we have to fight shoulder to shoulder someday. We have to be able to trust each other. I don't trust you because I don't know why you did that. And now you won't trust me because you know I don't trust *you.*"

"Oh what a tangled web we weave."

"What the hell does that mean?"

"My father said it. Oh what a tangled web we weave when first we practice to deceive."

"Exactly. Untangle this for me."

"You're the one who's weaving a web for me, Bean. You know things you don't tell the rest of us. You think I don't see that? So you want me to restore your trust in me, but you don't tell me anything useful."

"I opened my soul to you," said Bean.

"You told me about your *feelings.*" She said it with utter contempt. "So good, it's a relief to know you have them, or at least to know that you think it's worth pretending to have them, nobody's quite sure about that. But what you don't ever tell us is what the hell is actually going on here. We think you know."

"All I have are guesses."

"The teachers told you things back in Battle School that none of the rest of us knew. You knew the name of every kid in the school, you knew things about us, all of us. You knew things you had no business knowing."

Bean was stunned to realize that his special access had been so noticeable to her. Had he been careless? Or was she even more observant than he had thought? "I broke into the student data," said Bean.

"And they didn't catch you?"

"I think they did. Right from the start. Certainly they knew about it later." And he told her about choosing the roster for Dragon Army.

She flopped down on her bunk and addressed the ceiling. "You chose them! All those rejects and those little launchy bastards, *you* chose them!"

"Somebody had to. The teachers weren't competent to do it."

"So Ender had the best. He didn't *make* them the best, they already *were* the best."

"The best that weren't already in armies. I'm the only one who was a launchy when Dragon was formed who's with this team now. You and Shen and Alai and Dink and Carn, you weren't in Dragon, and you're obviously among the best. Dragon won because they were good, yes, but also because Ender knew what to do with them."

"It still turns one little corner of my universe upside down."

"Petra, this was a trade."

"Was it?"

"Explain why you weren't a Judas back in Battle School."

"I was a Judas," said Petra. "How's that for an explanation?"

Bean was sickened. "You can say it like that? Without shame?"

"Are you stupid?" asked Petra. "I was doing the same thing you were doing, trying to save Ender's life. I knew Ender had trained for combat, and those thugs hadn't. I was also trained. Bonzo had been working these guys up into a frenzy, but the fact is, they didn't like Bonzo very much, he had just pissed them off at Ender. So if they got in a few licks against Ender, right there in the corridor where Dragon Army and other soldiers would get into it right away, where Ender would have me beside him in a limited space so only a few of them could come at us at once—I figured that Ender would get bruised, get a bloody nose, but he'd come out of it OK. And all those walking scabies would be satisfied. Bonzo's ranting would be old news. Bonzo would be alone again. Ender would be safe from anything worse."

"You were gambling a lot on your fighting ability."

"And Ender's. We were both damn good then, and in excellent shape. And you know what? I think Ender understood what I was doing, and the only reason he didn't go along with it was you."

"Me?"

"He saw you plunging right into the middle of everything. You'd get your head beaten in, that was obvious. So he had to avoid the violence then. Which means that because of you, he got set up the next day when it really *was* dangerous, when Ender was completely alone with no one for backup."

"So why didn't you explain this before?"

"Because you were the only one besides Ender who knew I was setting him up, and I didn't really care what you thought then, and I'm not that concerned about it now."

"It was a stupid plan," said Bean.

"It was better than yours," said Petra.

"Well, I guess when you look at how it all turned out,

we'll never know how stupid your plan was. But we sure know that mine was shot to hell."

Petra flashed him a brief, insincere grin. "Now, do you trust me again? Can we go back to the intimate friendship we've shared for so long?"

"You know something, Petra? All that hostility is wasted on me. In fact, it's bad aim on your part to even try it. Because I'm the best friend you've got here."

"Oh really?"

"Yes, really. Because I'm the only one of these boys who ever chose to have a girl as his commander."

She paused a moment, staring at him blankly before saying, "I got over the fact that I'm a girl a long time ago."

"But they didn't. And you know they didn't. You know that it bothers them all the time, that you're not really one of the guys. They're your friends, sure, at least Dink is, but they all like you. At the same time, there were what, a dozen girls in the whole school? And except for you, none of them were really topflight soldiers. They didn't take you seriously."

"Ender did," said Petra.

"And I do," said Bean. "The others all know what happened in the corridor, you know. It's not like it was a secret. But you know why they haven't had this conversation with you?"

"Why?"

"Because *they* all figured you were an idiot and didn't realize how close you came to getting Ender pounded into the deck. I'm the only one who had enough respect for you to realize that you would never make such a stupid mistake by accident."

"I'm supposed to be flattered?"

"You're supposed to stop treating me like the enemy. You're almost as much of an outsider in this group as I am. And when it comes down to actual combat, you need someone who'll take you as seriously as you take yourself."

"Do me no favors."

"I'm leaving now."

"About time."

"And when you think about this more and you realize I'm right, you don't have to apologize. You cried for Poke, and that makes us friends. You can trust me, and I can trust you, and that's all."

She was starting some retort as he left, but he didn't stick around long enough to hear what it was. Petra was just that way—she had to act tough. Bean didn't mind. He knew they'd said the things they needed to say.

———

Command School was at FleetCom, and the location of FleetCom was a closely guarded secret. The only way you ever found out where it was to be assigned there, and very few people who had been there ever came back to Earth.

Just before arrival, the kids were briefed. FleetCom was in the wandering asteroid Eros. And as they approached, they realized that it really was *in* the asteroid. Almost nothing showed on the surface except the docking station. They boarded the shuttlebug, which reminded them of schoolbuses, and took the five-minute ride down to the surface. There the shuttlebug slid inside what looked like a cave. A snakelike tube reached out to the bug and enclosed it completely. They got out of the shuttlebug into near-zero gravity, and a strong air current sucked them like a vacuum cleaner up into the bowels of Eros.

Bean knew at once that this place was not shaped by human hands. The tunnels were all too low—and even then, the ceilings had obviously been raised after the initial construction, since the lower walls were smooth and only the top half-meter showed tool marks. The Buggers made this, probably when they were mounting the Second Invasion. What was once their forward base was now the center of the International Fleet. Bean tried to imagine the battle required to take this place. The Buggers scuttering along the tunnels, the infantry coming in with low-power explosives to burn them out. Flashes of light. And then cleanup, dragging the Formic bodies out of the tunnels and bit by bit converting it into a human space.

This is how we got our secret technologies, thought Bean. The Buggers had gravity-generating machines. We learned how they worked and built our own, installing them in the Battle School and wherever else they were needed. But the I.F. never announced the fact, because it would have frightened people to realize how advanced their technology was.

What else did we learn from them?

Bean noticed how even the children hunched a little to walk through the tunnels. The headroom was at least two meters, and not one of the kids was nearly that tall, but the proportions were all wrong for human comfort, so the roof of the tunnels seemed oppressively low, ready to collapse. It must have been even worse when we first arrived, before the roofs were raised.

Ender would thrive here. He'd hate it, of course, because he was human. But he'd also use the place to help him get inside the minds of the Buggers who built it. Not that you could ever really understand an alien mind. But this place gave you a decent chance to try.

The boys were bunked up in two rooms; Petra had a smaller room to herself. It was even more bare here than Battle School, and they could never escape the coldness of the stone around them. On Earth, stone had always seemed solid. But in space, it seemed downright porous. There were bubble holes all through the stone, and Bean couldn't help feeling that air was leaking out all the time. Air leaking out, and cold leaking in, and perhaps something else, the larvae of the Buggers chewing like earthworms through the solid stone, crawling out of the bubble holes at night when the room was dark, crawling over their foreheads and reading their minds and . . .

He woke up, breathing heavily, his hand clutching his

forehead. He hardly dared to move his hand. Had something been crawling on him?

His hand was empty.

He wanted to go back to sleep, but it was too close to reveille for him to hope for that. He lay there thinking. The nightmare was absurd—there could not possibly be any Buggers alive here. But something made him afraid. Something was bothering him, and he wasn't sure what.

He thought back to a conversation with one of the technicians who serviced the simulators. Bean's had malfunctioned during practice, so that suddenly the little points of light that represented his ships moving through three-dimensional space were no longer under his control. To his surprise, they didn't just drift on in the direction of the last orders he gave. Instead, they began to swarm, to gather, and then changed color as they shifted to be under someone else's control.

When the technician arrived to replace the chip that had blown, Bean asked him why the ships didn't just stop or keep drifting. "It's part of the simulation," the technician said. "What's being simulated here is not that you're the pilot or even the captain of these ships. You're the admiral, and so inside each ship there's a simulated captain and a simulated pilot, and so when your contact got cut off, they acted the way the real guys would act if they lost contact. See?"

"That seems like a lot of trouble to go to."

"Look, we've had a lot of time to work on these simulators," said the technician. "They're *exactly* like combat."

"Except," said Bean, "the time-lag."

The technician looked blank for a moment. "Oh, right. The time-lag. Well, that just wasn't worth programming in." And then he was gone.

It was that moment of blankness that was bothering Bean. These simulators were as perfect as they could make them, *exactly* like combat, and yet they didn't include the time-lag that came from lightspeed communications. The distances being simulated were large enough that most of the time there should be at least a slight delay between a command and its execution, and sometimes it should be several seconds. But no such delay was programmed in. All communications were being treated as instantaneous. And when Bean asked about it, his question was blown off by the teacher who first trained them on the simulators. "It's a simulation. Plenty of time to get used to the lightspeed delay when you train with the real thing."

That sounded like typically stupid military thinking even at the time, but now Bean realized it was simply a lie. If they programmed in the behavior of pilots and captains when communications were cut off, they could very easily have included the time-lag. The reason these ships were simulated with instantaneous response was because that *was* an accurate simulation of conditions they would meet in combat.

Lying awake in the darkness, Bean finally made the connection. It was so obvious, once he thought of it. It wasn't just gravity control they got from the Buggers. It was faster-than-light communication. It's a big secret from people on Earth, but our ships can talk to each other instantaneously.

And if the ships can, why not FleetCom here on Eros? What was the range of communication? Was it truly instantaneous regardless of distance, or was it merely faster than light, so that at truly great distances it began to have its own time-lag?

His mind raced through the possibilities, and the implications of those possibilities. Our patrol ships will be able to warn us of the approaching enemy fleet long before it reaches us. They've probably known for years that it was coming, and how fast. That's why we've been rushed through our training like this—they've known for years when the Third Invasion would begin.

And then another thought. If this instantaneous communication works regardless of distance, then we could even be talking to the invasion fleet we sent against the Formic home planet right after the Second Invasion. If our starships were going near lightspeed, the relative time differential would complicate communication, but as long as we're imagining miracles, that would be easy enough to solve. We'll know whether our invasion of their world succeeded or not, moments afterward. Why, if the communication is really powerful, with plenty of bandwidth, FleetCom could even watch the battle unfold, or at least watch a simulation of the battle, and . . .

A simulation of the battle. Each ship in the expeditionary force sending back its position at all times. The communications device receives that data and feeds it into a computer and what comes out is . . . the simulation we've been practicing with.

We are training to command ships in combat, not here in the solar system, but lightyears away. They sent the pilots and the captains, but the admirals who will command them are still back here. At FleetCom. They had generations to find the right commanders, and we're the ones.

It left him gasping, this realization. He hardly dared to believe it, and yet it made far better sense than any of the other more plausible scenarios. For one thing, it explained perfectly why the kids had been trained on older ships. The fleet they would be commanding had launched decades ago, when those older designs were the newest and the best.

They didn't rip us through Battle School and Tactical School because the Bugger fleet is about to reach our solar system. They're in a hurry because *our* fleet is about to reach the Buggers' world.

It was like Nikolai said. You can't rule out the impossible, because you never know which of your assumptions about what was possible might turn out, in the real universe, to be false. Bean hadn't been able to think of this simple, rational explanation because he had been locked in the box of thinking that lightspeed limited both travel *and* communication. But the technician let down just the tiniest part of the veil they had covering the truth, and because Bean finally found a way to open his mind to the possibility, he now knew the secret.

Sometime during their training, anytime at all, without the slightest warning, without ever even telling us they're doing it, they can switch over and we'll be commanding real ships in a real battle. We'll think it's a game, but we'll be fighting a war.

And they don't tell us because we're children. They think we can't handle it. Knowing that our decisions will cause death and destruction. That when we lose a ship, real men die. They're keeping it a secret to protect us from our own compassion.

Except me. Because now I know.

The weight of it suddenly came upon him and he could hardly breathe, except shallowly. Now I know. How will it change the way I play? I can't let it, that's all. I was already doing my best—knowing this won't make me work harder or play better. It might make me do worse. Might make me hesitate, might make me lose concentration. Through their training, they had all learned that winning depended on being able to forget everything but what you were doing at that moment. You could hold all your ships in your mind at once—but only if any ship that no longer matters could be blocked out completely. Thinking about dead men, about torn bodies having the air sucked out of their lungs by the cold vacuum of space, who could still play the game knowing that this was what it really meant?

The teachers were right to keep this secret from us. That technician should be court-martialed for letting me see behind the curtain.

I can't tell anyone. The other kids shouldn't know this. And if the teachers know that I know it, they'll take me out of the game.

So I have to fake it.

No. I have to disbelieve it. I have to forget that it's

true. It *isn't* true. The truth is what they've been telling us. The simulation is simply ignoring lightspeed. They trained us on old ships because the new ones are all deployed and can't be wasted. The fight we're preparing for is to repel invading Formics, not to invade their solar system. This was just a crazy dream, pure self-delusion. Nothing goes faster than light, and therefore information can't be transmitted faster than light.

Besides, if we really did send an invasion fleet that long ago, they don't need little kids to command them. Mazer Rackham must be with that fleet, no way would it have launched without him. Mazer Rackham is still alive, preserved by the relativistic changes of near-lightspeed travel. Maybe it's only been a few years to him. And he's ready. We aren't needed.

Bean calmed his breathing. His heartrate slowed. I can't let myself get carried away with fantasies like that. I would be so embarrassed if anyone knew the stupid theory I came up with in my sleep. I can't even tell this as a dream. The game is as it always was.

Reveille sounded over the intercom. Bean got out of bed—a bottom bunk, this time—and joined in as normally as possible with the banter of Crazy Tom and Hot Soup, while Fly Molo kept his morning surliness to himself and Alai did his prayers. Bean went to mess and ate as he normally ate. Everything was normal. It didn't mean a thing that he couldn't get his bowels to unclench at the normal time. That his belly gnawed at him all day, and at mealtime he was faintly nauseated. That was just lack of sleep.

Near the end of three months on Eros, their work on the simulators changed. There would be ships directly under their control, but they also had others under them to whom they had to give commands out loud, besides using the controls to enter them manually. "Like combat," said their supervisor.

"In combat," said Alai, "we'd know who the officers serving under us were."

"That would matter if you depended on them to give you information. But you do not. All the information you need is conveyed to your simulator and appears in the display. So you give your orders orally as well as manually. Just assume that you will be obeyed. Your teachers will be monitoring the orders you give to help you learn to be explicit and immediate. You will also have to master the technique of switching back and forth between crosstalk among yourselves and giving orders to individual ships. It's quite simple, you see. Turn your heads to the left or right to speak to each other, whichever is more comfortable for you. But when your face is pointing straight at the display, your voice will be carried to whatever ship or squadron you have selected with your controls. And to address all the ships under your control at once, head straight forward and duck your chin, like this."

"What happens if we raise our heads?" asked Shen.

Alai answered before the teacher could. "Then you're talking to God."

After the laughter died down, the teacher said, "Almost right, Alai. When you raise your chin to speak, you'll be talking to *your* commander."

Several spoke at once. "*Our* commander?"

"You did not think we were training all of you to be supreme commander at once, did you? No no. For the moment, we will assign one of you at random to be that commander, just for practice. Let's say . . . the little one. You. Bean."

"I'm supposed to be commander?"

"Just for the practices. Or is he not competent? You others will not obey him in battle?"

The others answered the teacher with scorn. Of course Bean was competent. Of course they'd follow him.

"But then, he never did win a battle when he commanded Rabbit Army," said Fly Molo.

"Excellent. That means that you will all have the challenge of making this little one a winner in spite of himself. If you do not think *that* is a realistic military situation, you have not been reading history carefully enough."

So it was that Bean found himself in command of the ten other kids from Battle School. It was exhilarating, of course, for neither he nor the others believed for one moment that the teacher's choice had been random. They knew that Bean was better at the simulator than anybody. Petra was the one who said it after practice one day. "Hell, Bean, I think you have this all in your head so clear you could close your eyes and still play." It was almost true. He did not have to keep checking to see where everyone was. It was all in his head at once.

It took a couple of days for them to handle it smoothly, taking orders from Bean and giving their own orders orally along with the physical controls. There were constant mistakes at first, heads in the wrong position so that comments and questions and orders went to the wrong destination. But soon enough it became instinctive.

Bean then insisted that others take turns being in the command position. "I need practice taking orders just like they do," he said. "And learning how to change my head position to speak up and sideways." The teacher agreed, and after another day, Bean had mastered the technique as well as any of the others.

Having other kids in the master seat had another good effect as well. Even though no one did so badly as to embarrass himself, it was clear that Bean was sharper and faster than anyone else, with a keener grasp of developing situations and a better ability to sort out what he was hearing and remember what everybody had said.

"You're not *human*," said Petra. "*Nobody* can do what you do!"

"Am so human," said Bean mildly. "And I know somebody who can do it better than me."

"Who's that?" she demanded.

"Ender."

They all fell silent for a moment.

"Yeah, well, he ain't here," said Vlad.

"How do *you* know?" said Bean. "For all we know, he's been here all along."

"That's stupid," said Dink. "Why wouldn't they have him practice with us? Why would they keep it a secret?"

"Because they like secrets," said Bean. "And maybe because they're giving him different training. And maybe because it's like Sinterklaas. They're going to bring him to us as a present."

"And maybe you're full of merda," said Dumper.

Bean just laughed. Of course it would be Ender. This group was assembled for Ender. Ender was the one all their hopes were resting on. The reason they put Bean in that master position was because Bean was the substitute. If Ender got appendicitis in the middle of the war, it was Bean they'd switch the controls to. Bean who'd start giving commands, deciding which ships would be sacrificed, which men would die. But until then, it would be Ender's choice, and for Ender, it would only be a game. No deaths, no suffering, no fear, no guilt. Just . . . a game.

Definitely it's Ender. And the sooner the better.

The next day, their supervisor told them that Ender Wiggin was going to be their commander starting that afternoon. When they didn't act surprised, he asked why. "Because Bean already told us."

———

"They want me to find out how you've been getting your inside information, Bean." Graff looked across the table at the painfully small child who sat there looking at him without expression.

"I don't have any inside information," said Bean.

"You knew that Ender was going to be the commander."

"I *guessed*," said Bean. "Not that it was hard. Look at who we are. Ender's closest friends. Ender's toon leaders. He's the common thread. There were plenty of other kids you could have brought here, probably about as good as us. But these are the ones who'd follow Ender straight into space without a suit, if he told us he needed us to do it."

"Nice speech, but you have a history of sneaking."

"Right. *When* would I be doing this sneaking? When are any of us alone? Our desks are just dumb terminals and we never get to see anybody else log on so it's not like I can capture another identity. I just do what I'm told all day every day. You guys keep assuming that we kids are stupid, even though you chose us because we're really, really smart. And now you sit there and accuse me of having to *steal* information that any idiot could guess."

"Not *any* idiot."

"That was just an expression."

"Bean," said Graff, "I think you're feeding me a line of complete bullshit."

"Colonel Graff, even if that were true, which it isn't, so what? So I found out Ender was coming. I'm secretly monitoring your dreams. So *what?* He'll still come, he'll be in command, he'll be brilliant, and then we'll all graduate and I'll sit in a booster seat in a ship somewhere and give commands to grownups in my little-boy voice until they get sick of hearing me and throw me out into space."

"I don't care about the fact that you knew about Ender. I don't care that it was a guess."

"I know you don't care about those things."

"I need to know what else you've figured out."

"Colonel," said Bean, sounding very tired, "doesn't it occur to you that the very fact that you're asking me this question *tells* me there's something else for me to figure out, and therefore greatly increases the chance that I *will* figure it out?"

Graff's smile grew even broader. "That's just what I told the . . . officer who assigned me to talk to you and ask these questions. I told him that we would end up telling you more, just by having the interview, than you would ever tell us, but he said, 'The kid is *six*, Colonel Graff.' "

"I think I'm seven."

"He was working from an old report and hadn't done the math."

"Just tell me what secret you want to make sure I don't know, and I'll tell you if I already knew it."

"Very helpful."

"Colonel Graff, am I doing a good job?"

"Absurd question. Of course you are."

"If I do know anything that you don't want us kids to know, have I talked about it? Have I told any of the other kids? Has it affected my performance in any way?"

"No."

"To me that sounds like a tree falling in the forest where no one can hear. If I *do* know something, because I figured it out, but I'm not telling anybody else, and it's not affecting my work, then why would you waste time finding out whether I know it? Because after this conversation, you may be sure that I'll be looking very hard for any secret that might be lying around where a seven-year-old might find it. Even if I do find such a secret, though, I *still* won't tell the other kids, so it *still* won't make a difference. So why don't we just drop it?"

Graff reached under the table and pressed something.

"All right," said Graff. "They've got the recording of our conversation and if that doesn't reassure them, nothing will."

"Reassure them of what? And who is 'them'?"

"Bean, this part is not being recorded."

"Yes it is," said Bean.

"I turned it off."

"Puh-leeze."

In fact, Graff was not altogether sure that the recording *was* off. Even if the machine he controlled was off, that didn't mean there wasn't another.

"Let's walk," said Graff.

"I hope not outside."

Graff got up from the table—laboriously, because he'd put on a lot of weight and they kept Eros at full gravity—and led the way out into the tunnels.

As they walked, Graff talked softly. "Let's at least make them work for it," he said.

"Fine," said Bean.

"I thought you'd want to know that the I.F. is going crazy because of an apparent security leak. It seems that someone with access to the most secret archives wrote letters to a couple of net pundits who then started agitating for the children of Battle School to be sent home to their native countries."

"What's a pundit?" asked Bean.

"My turn to say puh-leeze, I think. Look, I'm not accusing you. I just happen to have seen a text of the letters sent to Locke and Demosthenes—they're both being closely watched, as I'm sure you would expect—and when I read those letters—interesting the differences between them, by the way, very cleverly done—I realized that there was not really any top secret information in there, beyond what any child in Battle School knows. No, the thing that's really making them crazy is that the political analysis is dead on, even though it's based on insufficient information. From what is publicly known, in other words, the writer of those letters couldn't have figured out what he figured out. The Russians are claiming that somebody's been spying on them—and lying about what they found, of course. But I accessed the library on the destroyer *Condor* and found out what you were reading. And then I checked your library use on the ISL while you were in Tactical School. You've been a busy boy."

"I try to keep my mind occupied."

"You'll be happy to know that the first group of children has already been sent home."

"But the war's not over."

"You think that when you start a political snowball rolling, it will always go where you wanted it to go? You're smart but you're naive, Bean. Give the universe a push, and you don't know which dominoes will fall. There are always a few you never thought were connected. Someone will always push back a little harder than you expected.

But still, I'm happy that you remembered the other children and set the wheels in motion to free them."

"But not us."

"The I.F. has no obligation to remind the agitators on Earth that Tactical School and Command School are still full of children."

"I'm not going to remind them."

"I know you won't. No, Bean, I got a chance to talk to you because you panicked some of the higher-ups with your educated guess about who would command your team. But I was hoping for a chance to talk to you because there are a couple of things I wanted to tell you. Besides the fact that your letter had pretty much the desired effect."

"I'm listening, though I admit to no letter."

"First, you'll be fascinated to know the identity of Locke and Demosthenes."

"Identity? Just one?"

"One mind, two voices. You see, Bean, Ender Wiggin was born third in his family. A special waiver, not an illegal birth. His older brother and sister are just as gifted as he is, but for various reasons were deemed inappropriate for Battle School. But the brother, Peter Wiggin, is a very ambitious young man. With the military closed off to him, he's gone into politics. Twice."

"He's Locke *and* Demosthenes," said Bean.

"He plans the strategy for both of them, but he only writes Locke. His sister Valentine writes Demosthenes."

Bean laughed. "Now it makes sense."

"So both your letters went to the same people."

"If I wrote them."

"And it's driving poor Peter Wiggin crazy. He's really tapping into all his sources inside the fleet to find out who sent those letters. But nobody in the Fleet knows, either. The six officers whose log-ins you used have been ruled out. And as you can guess, *nobody* is checking to see if the only seven-year-old ever to go to Tactical School might have dabbled in political epistolary in his spare time."

"Except you."

"Because, by God, I'm the only person who understands exactly how brilliant you children actually are."

"How brilliant are we?" Bean grinned.

"Our walk won't last forever, and I won't waste time on flattery. The other thing I wanted to tell you is that Sister Carlotta, being unemployed after you left, devoted a lot of effort to tracking down your parentage. I can see two officers approaching us right now who will put an end to this unrecorded conversation, and so I'll be brief. You have a name, Bean. You are Julian Delphiki."

"That's Nikolai's last name."

"Julian is the name of Nikolai's father. And of your father. Your mother's name is Elena. You are identical twins. Your fertilized eggs were implanted at different times, and your genes were altered in one very small but significant way. So when you look at Nikolai, you see yourself as you would have been, had you not been genetically altered, and had you grown up with parents who loved you and cared for you."

"Julian Delphiki," said Bean.

"Nikolai is among those already heading for Earth. Sister Carlotta will see to it that, when he is repatriated to Greece, he is informed that you are indeed his brother. His parents already know that you exist—Sister Carlotta told them. Your home is a lovely place, a house on the hills of Crete overlooking the Aegean. Sister Carlotta tells me that they are good people, your parents. They wept with joy when they learned that you exist. And now our interview is coming to an end. We were discussing your low opinion of the quality of teaching here at Command School."

"How did you guess."

"You're not the only one who can do that."

The two officers—an admiral and a general, both wearing big false smiles—greeted them and asked how the interview had gone.

"You have the recording," said Graff. "Including the part where Bean insisted that it was still being recorded."

"And yet the interview continued."

"I was telling him," said Bean, "about the incompetence of the teachers here at Command School."

"Incompetence?"

"Our battles are always against exceptionally stupid computer opponents. And then the teachers insist on going through long, tedious analyses of these mock combats, even though no enemy could possibly behave as stupidly and predictably as these simulations do. I was suggesting that the only way for us to get decent competition here is if you divide us into two groups and have us fight each other."

The two officers looked at each other. "Interesting point," said the general.

"Moot," said the admiral. "Ender Wiggin is about to be introduced into your game. We thought you'd want to be there to greet him."

"Yes," said Bean. "I do."

"I'll take you," said the admiral.

"Let's talk," the general said to Graff.

On the way, the admiral said little, and Bean could answer his chat without thought. It was a good thing. For he was in turmoil over the things that Graff had told him. It was almost not a surprise that Locke and Demosthenes were Ender's siblings. If they were as intelligent as Ender, it was inevitable that they would rise into prominence, and the nets allowed them to conceal their identity enough to accomplish it while they were still young. But part of the reason Bean was drawn to them had to be the sheer familiarity of their voices. They must have sounded like Ender, in that subtle way in which people who have lived long together pick up nuances of speech from each other. Bean didn't realize it consciously, but unconsciously it would have made him more alert to those essays. He should have known, and at some level he did know.

But the other, that Nikolai was really his brother—how could he believe that? It was as if Graff had read his heart and found the lie that would penetrate most deeply into his soul and told it to him. I'm Greek? My brother happened to be in my launch group, the boy who became my dearest friend? Twins? Parents who love me?

Julian Delphiki?

No, I can't believe this. Graff has never dealt honestly with us. Graff was the one who did not lift a finger to protect Ender from Bonzo. Graff does nothing except to accomplish some manipulative purpose.

My name is Bean. Poke gave me that name, and I won't give it up in exchange for a lie.

———

They heard his voice, first, talking to a technician in another room. "How can I work with squadron leaders I never see?"

"And why would you need to see them?" asked the technician.

"To know who they are, how they think—"

"You'll learn who they are and how they think from the way they work with the simulator. But even so, I think you won't be concerned. They're listening to you right now. Put on the headset so you can hear them."

They all trembled with excitement, knowing that he would soon hear their voices as they now heard his.

"Somebody say something," said Petra.

"Wait till he gets the headset on," said Dink.

"How will we know?" asked Vlad.

"Me first," said Alai.

A pause. A new faint hiss in their earphones.

"Salaam," Alai whispered.

"Alai," said Ender.

"And me," said Bean. "The dwarf."

"Bean," said Ender.

Yes, thought Bean, as the others talked to him. That's who I am. That's the name that is spoken by the people who know me.

23

Ender's Game

"General, you are the Strategos. You have the authority to do this, and you have the obligation."

"I don't need disgraced former Battle School commandants to tell me my obligations."

"If you do not arrest the Polemarch and his conspirators—"

"Colonel Graff, if I *do* strike first, then I will bear the blame for the war that ensues."

"Yes, you would, sir. Now tell me, which would be the better outcome—everybody blames you, but we win the war, or nobody blames you, because you've been stood up against a wall and shot after the Polemarch's coup results in worldwide Russian hegemony?"

"I will not fire the first shot."

"A military commander not willing to strike preemptively when he has firm intelligence—"

"The politics of the thing—"

"If you let them win it's the end of politics!"

"The Russians stopped being the bad guys back in the twentieth century!"

"Whoever is doing the bad things, that's the bad guy. You're the sheriff, sir, whether people approve of you or not. Do your job."

With Ender there, Bean immediately stepped back into his place among the toon leaders. No one mentioned it to him. He had been the leading commander, he had trained them well, but Ender had always been the natural commander of this group, and now that he was here, Bean was small again.

And rightly so, Bean knew. He had led them well, but Ender made him look like a novice. It wasn't that Ender's strategies were better than Bean's—they weren't, really. Different sometimes, but more often Bean watched Ender do exactly what he would have done.

The important difference was in the way he led the others. He had their fierce devotion instead of the ever-so-slightly-resentful obedience Bean got from them, which helped from the start. But he also earned that devotion by noticing, not just what was going on in the battle, but what was going on in his commanders' minds. He was stern, sometimes even snappish, making it clear that he expected better than their best. And yet he had a way of giving an intonation to innocuous words, showing appreciation, admiration, closeness. They felt known by the one whose honor they needed. Bean simply did not know how to do that. His encouragement was always more obvious, a bit heavy-handed. It meant less to them because it felt more calculated. It *was* more calculated. Ender was just . . . himself. Authority came from him like breath.

They flipped a genetic switch in me and made me an intellectual athlete. I can get the ball into the goal from anywhere on the field. But knowing *when* to kick. Knowing how to forge a team out of a bunch of players. What switch was it that was flipped in Ender Wiggin's genes?

Or is that something deeper than the mechanical genius of the body? Is there a spirit, and is what Ender has a gift from God? We follow him like disciples. We look to him to draw water from the rock.

Can I learn to do what he does? Or am I to be like so many of the military writers I've studied, condemned to be second-raters in the field, remembered only because of their chronicles and explanations of other commanders' genius? Will I write a book after this, telling all about how Ender did it?

Let Ender write that book. Or Graff. I have work to do here, and when it's done, I'll choose my own work and do it as well as I can. If I'm remembered only because I was one of Ender's companions, so be it. Serving with Ender is its own reward.

But ah, how it stung to see how happy the others were, and how they paid no attention to him at all, except to tease him like a little brother, like a mascot. How they must have hated it when he was their leader.

And the worst thing was, that's how Ender treated him, too. Not that any of them were ever allowed to see Ender. But during their long separation, Ender had apparently forgotten how he once relied on Bean. It was Petra that he leaned on most, and Alai, and Dink, and Shen. The ones who had never been in an army with him. Bean and the other toon leaders from Dragon Army were still used, still trusted, but when there was something hard to do, something that required creative flair, Ender never thought of Bean.

Didn't matter. Couldn't think about that. Because Bean knew that along with his primary assignment as one of the squadron chiefs, he had another, deeper work to do. He had to watch the whole flow of each battle, ready to step in at any moment, should Ender falter. Ender seemed not to guess that Bean had that kind of trust from the teachers, but Bean knew it, and if sometimes it made him a little distracted in fulfilling his official assignments, if sometimes Ender grew impatient with him for being a little late, a little inattentive, that was to be expected. For what Ender did not know was that at any moment, if the supervisor signaled him, Bean could take over and continue Ender's plan, watching over all of the squadron leaders, saving the game.

At first, that assignment seemed empty—Ender was healthy, alert. But then came the change.

It was the day after Ender mentioned to them, casually, that he had a different teacher from theirs. He referred to him as "Mazer" once too often, and Crazy Tom said, "He must have gone through hell, growing up with that name."

"When he was growing up," said Ender, "the name wasn't famous."

"Anybody that old is dead," said Shen.

"Not if he was put on a lightspeed ship for a lot of years and then brought back."

That's when it dawned on them. "Your teacher is *the* Mazer Rackham?"

"You know how they say he's a brilliant hero?" said Ender.

Of course they knew.

"What they don't mention is, he's a complete hard-ass."

And then the new simulation began and they got back to work.

Next day, Ender told them that things were changing. "So far we've been playing against the computer or against each other. But starting now, every few days Mazer himself and a team of experienced pilots will control the opposing fleet. Anything goes."

A series of tests, with Mazer Rackham himself as the opponent. It smelled fishy to Bean.

These aren't tests, these are setups, preparations for the conditions that might come when they face the actual Bugger fleet near their home planet. The I.F. is getting preliminary information back from the expeditionary fleet, and they're preparing us for what the Buggers are actually going to throw at us when battle is joined.

The trouble was, no matter how bright Mazer Rackham

and the other officers might be, they were still human. When the real battle came, the Buggers were bound to show them things that humans simply couldn't think of.

Then came the first of these "tests"—and it was embarrassing how juvenile the strategy was. A big globe formation, surrounding a single ship.

In this battle it became clear that Ender knew things that he wasn't telling them. For one thing, he told them to ignore the ship in the center of the globe. It was a decoy. But how could Ender know that? Because he knew that the Buggers would *show* a single ship like that, and it was a lie. Which means that the Buggers expect us to go for that one ship.

Except, of course, that this was not really the Buggers, this was Mazer Rackham. So why would Rackham expect the Buggers to expect humans to strike for a single ship?

Bean thought back to those vids that Ender had watched over and over in Battle School—all the propaganda film of the Second Invasion.

They never showed the battle because there wasn't one. Nor did Mazer Rackham command a strike force with a brilliant strategy. Mazer Rackham hit a single ship and the war was over. That's why there's no video of hand-to-hand combat. Mazer Rackham killed the queen. And now he expects the Buggers to show a central ship as a decoy, because that's how we won last time.

Kill the queen, and all the Buggers are defenseless. Mindless. That's what the vids meant. Ender knows that, but he also knows that the Buggers know that we know it, so he doesn't fall for their sucker bait.

The second thing that Ender knew and they didn't was the use of a weapon that hadn't been in any of their simulations till this first test. Ender called it "Dr. Device" and then said nothing more about it—until he ordered Alai to use it where the enemy fleet was most concentrated. To their surprise, the thing set off a chain reaction that leapt from ship to ship, until all but the most outlying Formic ships were destroyed. And it was an easy matter to mop up those stragglers. The playing field was clear when they finished.

"Why was their strategy so stupid?" asked Bean.

"That's what I was wondering," said Ender. "But we didn't lose a ship, so that's OK."

Later, Ender told them what Mazer said—they were simulating a whole invasion sequence, and so he was taking the simulated enemy through a learning curve. "Next time they'll have learned. It won't be so easy."

Bean heard that and it filled him with alarm. An invasion sequence? Why a scenario like that? Why not warm-ups before a single battle?

Because the Buggers have more than one world, thought Bean. Of course they do. They found Earth and expected to turn it into yet another colony, just as they've done before.

We have more than one fleet. One for each Formic world.

And the reason they can learn from battle to battle is because they, too, have faster-than-light communication across interstellar space.

All of Bean's guesses were confirmed. He also knew the secret behind these tests. Mazer Rackham wasn't commanding a simulated Bugger fleet. It was a real battle, and Rackham's only function was to watch how it flowed and then coach Ender afterward on what the enemy strategies meant and how to counter them in future.

That was why they were giving most of their commands orally. They were being transmitted to real crews of real ships who followed their orders and fought real battles. Any ship we lose, thought Bean, means that grown men and women have died. Any carelessness on our part takes lives. Yet they don't tell us this precisely because we can't afford to be burdened with that knowledge. In wartime, commanders have always had to learn the concept of "acceptable losses." But those who keep their humanity never really accept the idea of acceptability, Bean understood that. It gnaws at them. So they protect us child-soldiers by keeping us convinced that it's only games and tests.

Therefore I can't let on to anyone that I do know. Therefore I must accept the losses without a word, without a visible qualm. I must try to block out of my mind the people who will die from our boldness, whose sacrifice is not of a mere counter in a game, but of their lives.

The "tests" came every few days, and each battle lasted longer. Alai joked that they ought to be fitted with diapers so they didn't have to be distracted when their bladder got full during a battle. Next day, they were fitted out with catheters. It was Crazy Tom who put a stop to that. "Come on, just get us a jar to pee in. We can't play this game with something hanging off our dicks." Jars it was, after that. Bean never heard of anyone using one, though. And though he wondered what they provided for Petra, no one ever had the courage to brave her wrath by asking.

Bean began to notice some of Ender's mistakes pretty early on. For one thing, Ender was relying too much on Petra. She always got command of the core force, watching a hundred different things at once, so that Ender could concentrate on the feints, the ploys, the tricks. Couldn't Ender see that Petra, a perfectionist, was getting eaten alive by guilt and shame over every mistake she made? He was so good with people, and yet he seemed to think she was really tough, instead of realizing that toughness was an act she put on to hide her intense anxiety. Every mistake weighed on her. She wasn't sleeping well, and it showed up as she got more and more fatigued during battles.

But then, maybe the reason Ender didn't realize what he was doing to her was that he, too, was tired. So were all of them. Fading a little under the pressure, and sometimes a lot. Getting more fatigued, more error-prone as the tests got harder, as the odds got longer.

Because the battles were harder with each new "test," Ender was forced to leave more and more decisions up to others. Instead of smoothly carrying out Ender's detailed commands, the squadron leaders had more and more of the battle to carry on their own shoulders. For long sequences, Ender was too busy in one part of the battle to give new orders in another. The squadron leaders who were affected began to use crosstalk to determine their tactics until Ender noticed them again. And Bean was grateful to find that, while Ender never gave him the interesting assignments, some of the others talked to him when Ender's attention was elsewhere. Crazy Tom and Hot Soup came up with their own plans, but they routinely ran them past Bean. And since, in each battle, he was spending half his attention observing and analyzing Ender's plan, Bean was able to tell them, with pretty good accuracy, what they should do to help make the overall plan work out. Now and then Ender praised Tom or Soup for decisions that came from Bean's advice. It was the closest thing to praise that Bean heard.

The other toon leaders and the older kids simply didn't turn to Bean at all. He understood why; they must have resented it greatly when the teachers placed Bean above them during the time before Ender was brought in. Now that they had their true commander, they were never again going to do anything that smacked of subservience to Bean. He understood—but that didn't keep it from stinging.

Whether or not they wanted him to oversee their work, whether or not his feelings were hurt, that was still his assignment and he was determined never to be caught unprepared. As the pressure became more and more intense, as they became wearier and wearier, more irritable with each other, less generous in their assessment of each other's work, Bean became all the more attentive because the chances of error were all the greater.

One day Petra fell asleep during battle. She had let her force drift too far into a vulnerable position, and the enemy took advantage, tearing her squadron to bits. Why didn't she give the order to fall back? Worse yet, Ender didn't notice soon enough, either. It was Bean who told him: Something's wrong with Petra.

Ender called out to her. She didn't answer. Ender flipped control of her two remaining ships to Crazy Tom and then tried to salvage the overall battle. Petra had, as usual, occupied the core position, and the loss of most of her large squadron was a devastating blow. Only because the enemy was overconfident during mop-up was Ender able to lay a couple of traps and regain the initiative. He won, but with heavy losses.

Petra apparently woke up near the end of the battle and found her controls cut off, with no voice until it was all over. Then her microphone came on again and they could hear her crying, "I'm sorry, I'm sorry. Tell Ender I'm sorry, he can't hear me, I'm so sorry . . ."

Bean got to her before she could return to her room. She was staggering along the tunnel, leaning against the wall and crying, using her hands to find her way because she couldn't see through her tears. Bean came up and touched her. She shrugged off his hand.

"Petra," said Bean. "Fatigue is fatigue. You can't stay awake when your brain shuts down."

"It was *my* brain that shut down! You don't know how that feels because you're always so smart you could do all our jobs and play chess while you're doing it!"

"Petra, he was relying on you too much, he never gave you a break—"

"He doesn't take breaks either, and I don't see him—"

"Yes you *do*. It was obvious there was something wrong with your squadron for several seconds before somebody called his attention to it. And even then, he tried to rouse you before assigning control to somebody else. If he'd acted faster you would have had six ships left, not just two."

"*You* pointed it out to him. You were watching me. Checking up on me."

"Petra, I watch everybody."

"You said you'd trust me, but you don't. And you shouldn't, nobody should trust me."

She broke into uncontrollable sobbing, leaning against the stone of the wall.

A couple of officers showed up then, led her away. Not to her room.

———

Graff called him in soon afterward. "You handled it just right," said Graff. "That's what you're there for."

"I wasn't quick either," said Bean.

"You were watching. You saw where the plan was breaking down, you called Ender's attention to it. You did your job. The other kids don't realize it and I know that has to gall you—"

"I don't care what they notice—"

"But you did the job. On that battle you get the save."

"Whatever the hell that means."

"It's baseball. Oh yeah. That wasn't big on the streets of Rotterdam."

"Can I please go sleep now?"

"In a minute. Bean, Ender's getting tired. He's making mistakes. It's all the more important that you watch everything. Be there for him. You saw how Petra was."

"We're all getting fatigued."

"Well, so is Ender. Worse than anyone. He cries in his sleep. He has strange dreams. He's talking about how Mazer seems to know what he's planning, spying on his dreams."

"You telling me he's going crazy?"

"I'm telling you that the only person he pushed harder than Petra is himself. Cover for him, Bean. Back him up."

"I already am."

"You're angry all the time, Bean."

Graff's words startled him. At first he thought, No I'm not! Then he thought, Am I?

"Ender isn't using you for anything important, and after having run the show that has to piss you off, Bean. But it's not Ender's fault. Mazer has been telling Ender that he has doubts about your ability to handle large numbers of ships. That's why you haven't been getting the complicated, interesting assignments. Not that Ender takes Mazer's word for it. But everything you do, Ender sees it through the lens of Mazer's lack of confidence."

"Mazer Rackham thinks I—"

"Mazer Rackham knows exactly what you are and what you can do. But we had to make sure Ender didn't assign you something so complicated you couldn't keep track of the overall flow of the game. And we had to do it without telling Ender you're his backup."

"So why are you telling me this?"

"When this test is over and you go on to real commands, we'll tell Ender the truth about what you were doing, and why Mazer said what he said. I know it means a lot to you to have Ender's confidence, and you don't feel like you have it, and so I wanted you to know why we did it."

"Why this sudden bout of honesty?"

"Because I think you'll do better knowing it."

"I'll do better *believing* it whether it's true or not. You could be lying. So do I really know anything at all from this conversation?"

"Believe what you want, Bean."

———

Petra didn't come to practice for a couple of days. When she came back, of course Ender didn't give her the heavy assignments anymore. She did well at the assignments she had, but her ebullience was gone. Her heart was broken.

But dammit, she had *slept* for a couple of days. They were all just the tiniest bit jealous of her for that, even though they'd never willingly trade places with her. Whether they had any particular god in mind, they all prayed: Let it not happen to me. Yet at the same time they also prayed the opposite prayer: Oh, let me sleep, let me have a day in which I don't have to think about this game.

The tests went on. How many worlds did these bastards colonize before they got to Earth? Bean wondered. And are we sure we have them all? And what good does it do to destroy their fleets when we don't have the forces there to occupy the defeated colonies? Or do we just leave our ships there, shooting down anything that tries to boost from the surface of the planet?

Petra wasn't the only one to blow out. Vlad went catatonic and couldn't be roused from his bunk. It took three days for the doctors to get him awake again, and unlike Petra, he was out for the duration. He just couldn't concentrate.

Bean kept waiting for Crazy Tom to follow suit, but despite his nickname, he actually seemed to get saner as he got wearier. Instead it was Fly Molo who started laughing when he lost control of his squadron. Ender cut him off immediately, and for once he put Bean in charge of Fly's ships. Fly was back the next day, no explanation, but everyone understood that he wouldn't be given crucial assignments now.

And Bean became more and more aware of Ender's decreasing alertness. His orders came after longer and longer pauses now, and a couple of times his orders weren't clearly stated. Bean immediately translated them into a more comprehensible form, and Ender never knew there had been confusion. But the others were finally becoming aware that Bean was following the whole battle, not just his part of it. Perhaps they even saw how Bean would ask a question during a battle, make some comment that alerted Ender to something that he needed to be aware of, but never in a way that sounded like Bean was criticizing anybody. After the battles one or two of the older kids would speak to Bean. Nothing major. Just a hand on his shoulder, on his back, and a couple of words. "Good game." "Good work." "Keep it up." "Thanks, Bean."

He hadn't realized how much he needed the honor of others until he finally got it.

———

"Bean, this next game, I think you should know something."

"What?"

Colonel Graff hesitated. "We couldn't get Ender awake this morning. He's been having nightmares. He doesn't eat unless we make him. He bites his hand in his sleep—bites it bloody. And today we couldn't get him to wake up. We were able to hold off on the . . . test . . . so he's going to be in command, as usual, but . . . not as usual."

"I'm ready. I always am."

"Yeah, but . . . look, advance word on this test is that it's . . . there's no . . ."

"It's hopeless."

"Anything you can do to help. Any suggestion."

"This Dr. Device thing, Ender hasn't let us use it in a long time."

"The enemy learned enough about how it works that they never let their ships get close enough together for a chain reaction to spread. It takes a certain amount of mass to be able to maintain the field. Basically, right now it's just ballast. Useless."

"It would have been nice if you'd told *me* how it works before now."

"There are people who don't want us to tell you anything, Bean. You have a way of using every scrap of information to guess ten times more than we want you to know. It makes them a little leery of giving you those scraps in the first place."

"Colonel Graff, you know that I know that these battles are real. Mazer Rackham isn't making them up. When we lose ships, real men die."

Graff looked away.

"And these are men that Mazer Rackham knows, neh?"

Graff nodded slightly.

"You don't think Ender can sense what Mazer is feeling? I don't know the guy, maybe he's like a rock, but *I* think that when he does his critiques with Ender, he's letting his . . . what, his anguish . . . Ender feels it. Because Ender is a lot more tired *after* a critique than before it. He may not know what's really going on, but he knows that something terrible is at stake. He knows that Mazer Rackham is really upset with every mistake Ender makes."

"Have you found some way to sneak into Ender's room?"

"I know how to listen to Ender. I'm not wrong about Mazer, am I?"

Graff shook his head.

"Colonel Graff, what you don't realize, what nobody seems to remember—that last game in Battle School, where Ender turned his army over to me. That wasn't a strategy. He was quitting. He was through. He was on strike. You didn't find that out because you graduated him. The thing with Bonzo finished him. I think Mazer Rackham's anguish is doing the same thing to him now. I think even when Ender doesn't *consciously* know that he's killed somebody, he knows it deep down, and it burns in his heart."

Graff looked at him sharply.

"I know Bonzo was dead. I saw him. I've seen death before, remember? You don't get your nose jammed into your brain and lose two gallons of blood and get up and walk away. You never told Ender that Bonzo was dead, but you're a fool if you think he doesn't know. And he knows, thanks to Mazer, that every ship we've lost means good men are dead. He can't stand it, Colonel Graff."

"You're more insightful than you get credit for, Bean," said Graff.

"I know, I'm the cold inhuman intellect, right?" Bean laughed bitterly. "Genetically altered, therefore I'm just as alien as the Buggers."

Graff blushed. "No one's ever said that."

"You mean you've never said it in front of me. Knowingly. What you don't seem to understand is, sometimes you have to just tell people the truth and ask them to do the thing you want, instead of trying to trick them into it."

"Are you saying we should tell Ender the game is real?"

"No! Are you insane? If he's this upset when the knowledge is unconscious, what do you think would happen if he *knew* that he knew? He'd freeze up."

"But you don't freeze up. Is that it? You should command this next battle?"

"You still don't get it, Colonel Graff. I don't freeze up because it isn't my battle. I'm helping. I'm watching. But I'm free. Because it's Ender's game."

Bean's simulator came to life.

"It's time," said Graff. "Good luck."

"Colonel Graff, Ender may go on strike again. He may walk out on it. He might give up. He might tell himself, It's only a game and I'm sick of it, I don't care what they do to me, I'm done. That's in him, to do that. When it seems completely unfair and utterly pointless."

"What if I promised him it was the last one?"

Bean put on his headset as he asked, "Would it be true?"

Graff nodded.

"Yeah, well, I don't think it would make much difference. Besides, he's Mazer's student now, isn't he?"

"I guess. Mazer was talking about telling him that it was the final exam."

"Mazer is Ender's teacher now," Bean mused. "And you're left with me. The kid you didn't want."

Graff blushed again. "That's right," he said. "Since you seem to know everything. I didn't want you."

Even though Bean already knew it, the words still hurt.

"But Bean," said Graff, "the thing is, I was wrong." He put a hand on Bean's shoulder and left the room.

Bean logged on. He was the last of the squadron leaders to do so.

"Are you there?" asked Ender over the headsets.

"All of us," said Bean. "Kind of late for practice this morning, aren't you?"

"Sorry," said Ender. "I overslept."

They laughed. Except Bean.

Ender took them through some maneuvers, warming up for the battle. And then it was time. The display cleared.

Bean waited, anxiety gnawing at his gut.

The enemy appeared in the display.

Their fleet was deployed around a planet that loomed in the center of the display. There had been battles near planets before, but every other time, the world was near the edge of the display—the enemy fleet always tried to lure them away from the planet.

This time there was no luring. Just the most incredible swarm of enemy ships imaginable. Always staying a certain distance away from each other, thousands and thousands of ships followed random, unpredictable, intertwining paths, together forming a cloud of death around the planet.

This is the home planet, thought Bean. He almost said it aloud, but caught himself in time. This is a *simulation* of the Bugger defense of their home planet.

They've had generations to prepare for us to come. All the previous battles were nothing. These Formics can lose any number of individual Buggers and they don't care. All that matters is the queen. Like the one Mazer Rackham killed in the Second Invasion. And they haven't put a queen at risk in any of these battles. Until now.

That's why they're swarming. There's a queen here. Where?

On the planet surface, thought Bean. The idea is to keep us from getting to the planet surface.

So that's precisely where we need to go. Dr. Device needs mass. Planets have mass. Pretty simple.

Except that there was no way to get this small force of human ships through that swarm and near enough to the planet to deploy Dr. Device. For if there was anything that history taught, it was this: Sometimes the other side is irresistibly strong, and then the only sensible course of action is to retreat in order to save your force to fight another day.

In this war, however, there would be no other day. There was no hope of retreat. The decisions that lost this battle, and therefore this war, were made two generations ago when these ships were launched, an inadequate force from the start. The commanders who set this fleet in motion may not even have known, then, that this was the Buggers' home world. It was no one's fault. They simply didn't have enough of a force even to make a dent in the enemy's defenses. It didn't matter how brilliant Ender was. When you have only one guy with a shovel, you can't build a dike to hold back the sea.

No retreat, no possibility of victory, no room for delay or maneuver, no reason for the enemy to do anything but continue to do what they were doing.

There were only twenty starships in the human fleet, each with four fighters. And they were the oldest design, sluggish compared to some of the fighters they'd had in earlier battles. It made sense—the Bugger home world was probably the farthest away, so the fleet that got there now had left before any of the other fleets. Before the better ships came on line.

Eighty fighters. Against five thousand, maybe ten thousand enemy ships. It was impossible to determine the number. Bean saw how the display kept losing track of individual enemy ships, how the total count kept fluctuating. There were so many it was overloading the system. They kept winking in and out like fireflies.

A long time passed—many seconds, perhaps a minute. By now Ender usually had them all deployed, ready to move. But still there was nothing from him but silence.

A light blinked on Bean's console. He knew what it meant. All he had to do was press a button, and control of the battle would be his. They were offering it to him, because they thought that Ender had frozen up.

He hasn't frozen up, thought Bean. He hasn't panicked.

He has simply understood the situation, exactly as I understand it. There *is* no strategy. Only he doesn't see that this is simply the fortunes of war, a disaster that can't be helped. What he sees is a test set before him by his teachers, by Mazer Rackham, a test so absurdly unfair that the only reasonable course of action is to refuse to take it.

They were so clever, keeping the truth from him all this time. But now was it going to backfire on them. If Ender understood that it was not a game, that the real war had come down to this moment, then he might make some desperate effort, or with his genius he might even come up with an answer to a problem that, as far as Bean could see, had no solution. But Ender did not understand the reality, and so to him it was like that day in the battleroom, facing two armies, when Ender turned the whole thing over to Bean and, in effect, refused to play.

For a moment Bean was tempted to scream the truth. It's not a game, it's the real thing, this is the last battle, we've lost this war after all! But what would be gained by that, except to panic everyone?

Yet it was absurd to even contemplate pressing that button to take over control himself. Ender hadn't collapsed or failed. The battle was unwinnable; it should not even be fought. The lives of the men on those ships were not to be wasted on such a hopeless Charge of the Light Brigade. I'm not General Burnside at Fredericksburg. I don't send my men off to senseless, hopeless, meaningless death.

If I had a plan, I'd take control. I have no plan. So for good or ill, it's Ender's game, not mine.

And there was another reason for not taking over.

Bean remembered standing over the supine body of a bully who was too dangerous to ever be tamed, telling Poke, Kill him now, kill him.

I was right. And now, once again, the bully must be killed. Even though I don't know how to do it, we *can't* lose this war. I don't know how to win it, but I'm not God, I don't see everything. And maybe Ender doesn't *see* a solution either, but if anyone can find one, if anyone can make it happen, it's Ender.

Maybe it isn't hopeless. Maybe there's some way to get down to the planet's surface and wipe the Buggers out of the universe. Now is the time for miracles. For Ender, the others will do their best work. If I took over, they'd be so upset, so distracted that even if I came up with a plan that had some kind of chance, it would never work because their hearts wouldn't be in it.

Ender has to try. If he doesn't, we all die. Because even if they weren't going to send another fleet against us, after this they'll *have* to send one. Because we beat all their fleets in every battle till now. If we don't win this one, with finality, destroying their capability to make war against us, then they'll be back. And this time they'll have figured out how to make Dr. Device themselves.

We have only the one world. We have only the one hope.

Do it, Ender.

There flashed into Bean's mind the words Ender said in their first day of training as Dragon Army: Remember, the enemy's gate is down. In Dragon Army's last battle, when there was no hope, that was the strategy that Ender had used, sending Bean's squad to press their helmets against the floor around the gate and win. Too bad there was no such cheat available now.

Deploying Dr. Device against the planet's surface to blow the whole thing up, that might do the trick. You just couldn't get there from here.

It was time to give up. Time to get out of the game, to tell them not to send children to do grownups' work. It's hopeless. We're done.

"Remember," Bean said ironically, "the enemy's gate is down."

Fly Molo, Hot Soup, Vlad, Dumper, Crazy Tom—they grimly laughed. They had been in Dragon Army. They remembered how those words were used before.

But Ender didn't seem to get the joke.

Ender didn't seem to understand that there was no way to get Dr. Device to the planet's surface.

Instead, his voice came into their ears, giving them orders. He pulled them into a tight formation, cylinders within cylinders.

Bean wanted to shout, Don't do it! There are real men on those ships, and if you send them in, they'll die, a sacrifice with no hope of victory.

But he held his tongue, because, in the back of his mind, in the deepest corner of his heart, he still had hope that Ender might do what could not be done. And as long as there was such a hope, the lives of those men were, by their own choice when they set out on this expedition, expendable.

Ender set them in motion, having them dodge here and there through the ever-shifting formations of the enemy swarm.

Surely the enemy sees what we're doing, thought Bean. Surely they see how every third or fourth move takes us closer and closer to the planet.

At any moment the enemy could destroy them quickly by concentrating their forces. So why weren't they doing it?

One possibility occurred to Bean. The Buggers didn't dare concentrate their forces close to Ender's tight formation, because the moment they drew their ships that close together, Ender could use Dr. Device against them.

And then he thought of another explanation. Could it be that there were simply too many Bugger ships? Could it be that the queen or queens had to spend all their concentration, all their mental strength just keeping ten thousand ships swarming through space without getting too close to each other?

Unlike Ender, the Bugger queen couldn't turn control of her ships over to subordinates. She *had* no subordinates. The individual Buggers were like her hands and her feet. Now she had hundreds of hands and feet, or perhaps thousands of them, all wiggling at once.

That's why she wasn't responding intelligently. Her forces were too numerous. That's why she wasn't making the obvious moves, setting traps, blocking Ender from taking his cylinder ever closer to the planet with every swing and dodge and shift that he made.

In fact, the maneuvers the Buggers were making were ludicrously wrong. For as Ender penetrated deeper and deeper into the planet's gravity well, the Buggers were building up a thick wall of forces *behind* Ender's formation.

They're blocking our retreat!

At once Bean understood a third and most important reason for what was happening. The Buggers had learned the wrong lessons from the previous battles. Up to now, Ender's strategy had always been to ensure the survival of as many human ships as possible. He had always left himself a line of retreat. The Buggers, with their huge numerical advantage, were finally in a position to guarantee that the human forces would not get away.

There was no way, at the beginning of this battle, to predict that the Buggers would make such a mistake. Yet throughout history, great victories had come as much because of the losing army's errors as because of the winner's brilliance in battle. The Buggers have finally, finally learned that we humans value each and every individual human life. We don't throw our forces away because every soldier is the queen of a one-member hive. But they've learned this lesson just in time for it to be hopelessly wrong—for we humans *do,* when the cause is sufficient, spend our own lives. We throw ourselves onto the grenade to save our buddies in the foxhole. We rise out of the trenches and charge the entrenched enemy and die like maggots under a blowtorch. We strap bombs on our bodies and blow ourselves up in the midst of our enemies. We are, when the cause is sufficient, insane.

They don't believe we'll use Dr. Device because the only way to use it is to destroy our own ships in the process. From the moment Ender started giving orders, it was obvious to everyone that this was a suicide run. These ships were not made to enter an atmosphere. And yet to get close enough to the planet to set off Dr. Device, they had to do exactly that.

Get down into the gravity well and launch the weapon just before the ship burns up. And if it works, if the planet is torn apart by whatever force it is in that terrible weapon, the chain reaction will reach out into space and take out any ships that might happen to survive.

Win or lose, there'd be no human survivors from this battle.

They've never seen us make a move like that. They don't understand that, yes, humans will always act to preserve their own lives—except for the times when they don't. In the Buggers' experience, autonomous beings do not sacrifice themselves. Once they understood our autonomy, the seed of their defeat was sown.

In all of Ender's study of the Buggers, in all his obsession with them over the years of his training, did he somehow come to *know* that they would make such deadly mistakes?

I did not know it. I would not have pursued this strategy. I *had* no strategy. Ender was the only commander who could have known, or guessed, or unconsciously hoped that when he flung out his forces the enemy would falter, would trip, would fall, would fail.

Or *did* he know at all? Could it be that he reached the same conclusion as I did, that this battle was unwinnable? That he decided not to play it out, that he went on strike, that he quit? And then my bitter words, "the enemy's gate is down," triggered his futile, useless gesture of despair, sending his ships to certain doom because he did not know that there were real ships out there, with real men aboard, that he was sending to their deaths? Could it be that he was as surprised as I was by the mistakes of the enemy? Could our victory be an accident?

No. For even if my words provoked Ender into action, he was still the one who chose *this* formation, *these* feints and evasions, *this* meandering route. It was Ender whose previous victories taught the enemy to think of us as one kind of creature, when we are really something quite different. He pretended all this time that humans were rational beings, when we are really the most terrible monsters these poor aliens could ever have conceived of in their nightmares. They had no way of knowing the story of blind Samson, who pulled down the temple on his own head to slay his enemies.

On those ships, thought Bean, there are individual men who gave up homes and families, the world of their birth, in order to cross a great swatch of the galaxy and make war on a terrible enemy. Somewhere along the way they're bound to understand that Ender's strategy requires them all to die. Perhaps they already have. And yet they obey and will continue to obey the orders that come to them. As in the famous Charge of the Light Brigade, these soldiers give up their lives, trusting that their commanders are using them well. While we sit safely here in these simulator rooms, playing an elaborate computer game, they are obeying, dying so that all of humankind can live.

And yet we who command them, we children in these elaborate game machines, have no idea of their courage, their sacrifice. We cannot give them the honor they deserve, because we don't even know they exist.

Except for me.

There sprang into Bean's mind a favorite scripture of Sister Carlotta's. Maybe it meant so much to her because she had no children. She told Bean the story of Absalom's rebellion against his own father, King David. In the course of a battle, Absalom was killed. When they brought the news to David, it meant victory, it meant that no more of his soldiers would die. His throne was safe. His *life* was safe. But all he could think about was his son, his beloved son, his dead boy.

Bean ducked his head, so his voice would be heard only by the men under his command. And then, for just long enough to speak, he pressed the override that put his voice into the ears of all the men of that distant fleet. Bean had no idea how his voice would sound to them; would they hear his childish voice, or were the sounds distorted, so they would hear him as an adult, or perhaps as some metallic, machinelike voice? No matter. In some form the men of that distant fleet would hear his voice, transmitted faster than light, God knows how.

"O my son Absalom," Bean said softly, knowing for the first time the kind of anguish that could tear such words from a man's mouth. "My son, my son Absalom. Would God I could die for thee, O Absalom, my son. My sons!"

He had paraphrased it a little, but God would understand. Or if he didn't, Sister Carlotta would.

Now, thought Bean. Do it now, Ender. You're as close as you can get without giving away the game. They're beginning to understand their danger. They're concentrating their forces. They'll blow us out of the sky before our weapons can be launched—

"All right, everybody except Petra's squadron," said Ender. "Straight down, as fast as you can. Launch Dr. Device against the planet. Wait till the last possible second. Petra, cover as you can."

The squadron leaders, Bean among them, echoed Ender's commands to their own fleets. And then there was nothing to do but watch. Each ship was on its own.

The enemy understood now, and rushed to destroy the plummeting humans. Fighter after fighter was picked off by the inrushing ships of the Formic fleet. Only a few human fighters survived long enough to enter the atmosphere.

Hold on, thought Bean. Hold on as long as you can.

The ships that launched too early watched their Dr. Device burn up in the atmosphere before it could go off. A few other ships burned up themselves without launching.

Two ships were left. One was in Bean's squadron.

"Don't launch it," said Bean into his microphone, head down. "Set it off inside your ship. God be with you."

Bean had no way of knowing whether it was his ship or the other that did it. He only knew that both ships disappeared from the display without launching. And then the surface of the planet started to bubble. Suddenly a vast eruption licked outward toward the last of the human fighters, Petra's ships, on which there might or might not still be men alive to see death coming at them. To see their victory approach.

The simulator put on a spectacular show as the exploding planet chewed up all the enemy ships, engulfing them in the chain reaction. But long before the last ship was swallowed up, all the maneuvering had stopped. They drifted, dead. Like the dead Bugger ships in the vids of the Second Invasion. The queens of the hive had died on the planet's surface. The destruction of the remaining ships was a mere formality. The Buggers were already dead.

———

Bean emerged into the tunnel to find that the other kids were already there, congratulating each other and commenting on how cool the explosion effect was, and wondering if something like that could really happen.

"Yes," said Bean. "It could."

"As if you know," said Fly Molo, laughing.

"Of course I know it could happen," said Bean. "It *did* happen."

They looked at him uncomprehendingly. When did it happen? I never heard of anything like that. Where could they have tested that weapon against a planet? I know, they took out Neptune!

"It happened just now," said Bean. "It happened at the home world of the Buggers. We just blew it up. They're all dead."

They finally began to realize that he was serious. They fired objections at him. He explained about the faster-than-light communications device. They didn't believe him.

Then another voice entered the conversation. "It's called the ansible."

They looked up to see Colonel Graff standing a ways off, down the tunnel.

Is Bean telling the truth? Was that a real battle?

"They were all real," said Bean. "All the so-called tests. Real battles. Real victories. Right, Colonel Graff? We were fighting the real war all along."

"It's over now," said Graff. "The human race will continue. The Buggers won't."

They finally believed it, and became giddy with the realization. It's over. We won. We weren't practicing, we were actually commanders.

And then, at last, a silence fell.

"They're *all* dead?" asked Petra.

Bean nodded.

Again they looked at Graff. "We have reports. All life activity has ceased on all the other planets. They must have gathered their queens back on their home planet. When the queens die, the Buggers die. There is no enemy now."

Petra began to cry, leaning against the wall. Bean wanted to reach out to her, but Dink was there. Dink was the friend who held her, comforted her.

Some soberly, some exultantly, they went back to their barracks. Petra wasn't the only one who cried. But whether the tears were shed in anguish or in relief, no one could say for sure.

Only Bean did not return to his room, perhaps because Bean was the only one not surprised. He stayed out in the tunnel with Graff.

"How's Ender taking it?"

"Badly," said Graff. "We should have broken it to him more carefully, but there was no holding back. In the moment of victory."

"All your gambles paid off," said Bean.

"I know what happened, Bean," said Graff. "Why did

you leave control with him? How did you know he'd come up with a plan?"

"I didn't," said Bean. "I only knew that I had no plan at all."

"But what you said—'the enemy's gate is down.' That's the plan Ender used."

"It wasn't a plan," said Bean. "Maybe it made him think of a plan. But it was him. It was Ender. You put your money on the right kid."

Graff looked at Bean in silence, then reached out and put a hand on Bean's head, tousled his hair a little. "I think perhaps you pulled each other across the finish line."

"It doesn't matter, does it?" said Bean. "It's finished, anyway. And so is the temporary unity of the human race."

"Yes," said Graff. He pulled his hand away, ran it through his own hair. "I believed in your analysis. I tried to give warning. *If* the Strategos heeded my advice, the Polemarch's men are getting arrested here on Eros and all over the fleet."

"Will they go peacefully?" asked Bean.

"We'll see," said Graff.

The sound of gunfire echoed from some distant tunnel.

"Guess not," said Bean.

They heard the sound of men running in step. And soon they saw them, a contingent of a dozen armed marines.

Bean and Graff watched them approach. "Friend or foe?"

"They all wear the same uniform," said Graff. "You're the one who called it, Bean. Inside those doors"—he gestured toward the doors to the kids' quarters—"those children are the spoils of war. In command of armies back on Earth, they're the hope of victory. *You* are the hope."

The soldiers came to a stop in front of Graff. "We're here to protect the children, sir," said their leader.

"From what?"

"The Polemarch's men seem to be resisting arrest, sir,"

said the soldier. "The Strategos has ordered that these children be kept safe at all costs."

Graff was visibly relieved to know which side these troops were on. "The girl is in that room over there. I suggest you consolidate them all into those two barrack rooms for the duration."

"Is this the kid who did it?" asked the soldier, indicating Bean.

"He's one of them."

"It was Ender Wiggin who did it," said Bean. "Ender was our commander."

"Is he in one of those rooms?" asked the soldier.

"He's with Mazer Rackham," said Graff. "And this one stays with me."

The soldier saluted. He began positioning his men in more advanced positions down the tunnel, with only a single guard outside each door to prevent the kids from going out and getting lost somewhere in the fighting.

Bean trotted along beside Graff as he headed purposefully down the tunnel, beyond the farthest of the guards.

"If the Strategos did this right, the ansibles have already been secured. I don't know about you, but I want to be where the news is coming in. And going out."

"Is Russian a hard language to learn?" asked Bean.

"Is that what passes for humor with you?" asked Graff.

"It was a simple question."

"Bean, you're a great kid, but shut up, OK?"

Bean laughed. "OK."

"You don't mind if I still call you Bean?"

"It's my name."

"Your name should have been Julian Delphiki. If you'd had a birth certificate, that's the name that would have been on it."

"You mean that was true?"

"Would I lie about something like that?"

Then, realizing the absurdity of what he had just said, they laughed. Laughed long enough to still be smiling when they passed the detachment of marines protecting the entrance to the ansible complex.

"You think anybody will ask me for military advice?" asked Bean. "Because I'm going to get into this war, even if I have to lie about my age and enlist in the marines."

24

Homecoming

"I thought you'd want to know. Some bad news."

"There's no shortage of that, even in the midst of victory."

"When it became clear that the IDL had control of Battle School and was sending the kids home under I.F. protection, the New Warsaw Pact apparently did a little research and found that there was one student from Battle School who wasn't under our control. Achilles."

"But he was only there a couple of days."

"He passed our tests. He got in. He was the only one they could get."

"Did they? Get him?"

"All the security there was designed to keep inmates inside. Three guards dead, all the inmates released into the general population. They've all been recovered, except one."

"So he's loose."

"I wouldn't call it loose, exactly. They intend to use him."

"Do they know what he is?"

"No. His records were sealed. A juvenile, you see. They weren't coming for his dossier."

"They'll find out. They don't like serial killers in Moscow, either."

"He's hard to pin down. How many died before any of us suspected him?"

"The war is over for now."

"And the jockeying for advantage in the next war has begun."

"With any luck, Colonel Graff, I'll be dead by then."

"I'm not actually a colonel anymore, Sister Carlotta."

"They're really going to go ahead with that court-martial?"

"An investigation, that's all. An inquiry."

"I just don't understand why they have to find a scapegoat for victory."

"I'll be fine. The sun still shines on planet Earth."

"But never again on *their* tragic world."

"Is your God also their God, Sister Carlotta? Did he take them into heaven?"

"He's not *my* God, Mr. Graff. But I am his child, as are you. I don't know whether he looks at the Formics and sees them, too, as his children."

"Children. Sister Carlotta, the things I did to these children."

"You gave them a world to come home to."

"All but one of them."

It took days for the Polemarch's men to be subdued, but at last Fleetcom was entirely under the Strategos's command, and not one ship had been launched under rebel command. A triumph. The Hegemon resigned as part of the truce, but that only formalized what had already been the reality.

Bean stayed with Graff throughout the fighting, as they read every dispatch and listened to every report about what was happening elsewhere in the fleet and back on Earth. They talked through the unfolding situation, tried to read between the lines, interpreted what was happening as best they could. For Bean, the war with the Buggers was already behind him. All that mattered now was how things went on Earth. When a shaky truce was signed, temporarily ending the fighting, Bean knew that it would not last. He would be needed. Once he got to Earth, he could prepare himself to play his role. Ender's war is over, he thought. This next one will be mine.

While Bean was avidly following the news, the other kids were confined to their quarters under guard, and during the power failures in their part of Eros they did their cowering in darkness. Twice there were assaults on that section of the tunnels, but whether the Russians were trying to get at the kids or merely happened to probe in that area, looking for weaknesses, no one could guess.

Ender was under much heavier guard, but didn't know it. Utterly exhausted, and perhaps unwilling or unable to bear the enormity of what he had done, he remained unconscious for days.

Not till the fighting stopped did he come back to consciousness.

They let the kids get together then, their confinement over for now. Together they made the pilgrimage to the room where Ender had been under protection and medical care. They found him apparently cheerful, able to joke. But Bean could see a deep weariness, a sadness in Ender's eyes that it was impossible to ignore. The victory had cost him deeply, more than anybody.

More than me, thought Bean, even though I knew what I was doing, and he was innocent of any bad intent. He tortures himself, and I move on. Maybe because to me the death of Poke was more important than the death of an entire species that I never saw. I knew her—she has stayed with me in my heart. The Buggers I never knew. How can I grieve for them?

Ender can.

After they filled Ender in on the news about what happened while he slept, Petra touched his hair. "You OK?"

she asked. "You scared us. They said you were crazy, and we said *they* were crazy."

"I'm crazy," said Ender. "But I think I'm OK."

There was more banter, but then Ender's emotions overflowed and for the first time any of them could remember, they saw Ender cry. Bean happened to be standing near him, and when Ender reached out, it was Bean and Petra that he embraced. The touch of his hand, the embrace of his arm, they were more than Bean could bear. He also cried.

"I missed you," said Ender. "I wanted to see you so bad."

"You saw us pretty bad," said Petra. She was not crying. She kissed his cheek.

"I saw you magnificent," said Ender. "The ones I needed most, I used up soonest. Bad planning on my part."

"Everybody's OK now," said Dink. "Nothing was wrong with any of us that five days of cowering in blacked-out rooms in the middle of a war couldn't cure."

"I don't have to be your commander anymore, do I?" asked Ender. "I don't want to command anybody again."

Bean believed him. And believed also that Ender never *would* command in battle again. He might still have the talents that brought him to this place. But the most important ones didn't have to be used for violence. If the universe had any kindness in it, or even simple justice, Ender would never have to take another life. He had surely filled his quota.

"You don't have to command anybody," said Dink, "but you're always our commander."

Bean felt the truth of that. There was not one of them who would not carry Ender with them in their hearts, wherever they went, whatever they did.

What Bean didn't have the heart to tell them was that on Earth, both sides had insisted that they be given custody of the hero of the war, young Ender Wiggin, whose great victory had captured the popular imagination. Whoever had him would not only have the use of his fine military mind—they thought—but would also have the benefit of all the publicity and public adulation that surrounded him, that filled every mention of his name.

So as the political leaders worked out the truce, they reached a simple and obvious compromise. All the children from Battle School would be repatriated. Except Ender Wiggin.

Ender Wiggin would not be coming home. Neither party on Earth would be able to use him. That was the compromise.

And it had been proposed by Locke. By Ender's own brother.

When he learned that it made Bean seethe inside, the way he had when he thought Petra had betrayed Ender. It was wrong. It couldn't be borne.

Perhaps Peter Wiggin did it to keep Ender from becoming a pawn. To keep him free. Or perhaps he did it so that Ender could not use his celebrity to make his own play for political power. Was Peter Wiggin saving his brother, or eliminating a rival for power?

Someday I'll meet him and find out, thought Bean. And if he betrayed his brother, I'll destroy him.

When Bean shed his tears there in Ender's room, he was weeping for a cause the others did not yet know about. He was weeping because, as surely as the soldiers who died in those fighting ships, Ender would not be coming home from the war.

"So," said Alai, breaking the silence. "What do we do now? The Bugger War's over, and so's the war down there on Earth, and even the war here. What do we do now?"

"We're kids," said Petra. "They'll probably make us go to school. It's a law. You have to go to school till you're seventeen."

They all laughed until they cried again.

They saw each other off and on again over the next few days. Then they boarded several different cruisers and destroyers for the voyage back to Earth. Bean knew well why they traveled in separate ships. That way no one would ask why Ender wasn't on board. If Ender knew, before they left, that he was not going back to Earth, he said nothing about it.

———

Elena could hardly contain her joy when Sister Carlotta called, asking if she and her husband would both be at home in an hour. "I'm bringing you your son," she said.

Nikolai, Nikolai, Nikolai. Elena sang the name over and over again in her mind, with her lips. Her husband Julian, too, was almost dancing as he hurried about the house, making things ready. Nikolai had been so little when he left. Now he would be so much older. They would hardly know him. They would not understand what he had been through. But it didn't matter. They loved him. They would learn who he was all over again. They would not let the lost years get in the way of the years to come.

"I see the car!" cried Julian.

Elena hurriedly pulled the covers from the dishes, so that Nikolai could come into a kitchen filled with the freshest, purest food of his childhood memories. Whatever they ate in space, it couldn't be as good as this.

Then she ran to the door and stood beside her husband as they watched Sister Carlotta get out of the front seat.

Why didn't she ride in back with Nikolai?

No matter. The back door opened, and Nikolai emerged, unfolding his lanky young body. So tall he was growing! Yet still a boy. There was a little bit of childhood left for him.

Run to me, my son!

But he didn't run to her. He turned his back on his parents.

Ah. He was reaching into the back seat. A present, perhaps?

No. Another boy.

A smaller boy, but with the same face as Nikolai. Perhaps too careworn for a child so small, but with the same open goodness that Nikolai had always had. Nikolai was smiling so broadly he could not contain it. But the small one was not smiling. He looked uncertain. Hesitant.

"Julian," said her husband.

Why would he say his own name?

"Our second son," he said. "They didn't all die, Elena. One lived."

All hope of those little ones had been buried in her heart. It almost hurt to open that hidden place. She gasped at the intensity of it.

"Nikolai met him in Battle School," he went on. "I told Sister Carlotta that if we had another son, you meant to name him Julian."

"You knew," said Elena.

"Forgive me, my love. But Sister Carlotta wasn't sure then that he was ours. Or that he would ever be able to come home. I couldn't bear it, to tell you of the hope, only to break your heart later."

"I have two sons," she said.

"If you want him," said Julian. "His life has been hard. But he's a stranger here. He doesn't speak Greek. He's been told that he's coming just for a visit. That legally he is not our child, but rather a ward of the state. We don't have to take him in, if you don't want to, Elena."

"Hush, you foolish man," she said. Then, loudly, she called out to the approaching boys. "Here are my two sons, home from the wars! Come to your mother! I have missed you both so much, and for so many years!"

They ran to her then, and she held them in her arms, and her tears fell on them both, and her husband's hands rested upon both boys' heads.

Her husband spoke. Elena recognized his words at once, from the gospel of St. Luke. But because he had only memorized the passage in Greek, the little one did not understand him. No matter. Nikolai began to translate into Common, the language of the fleet, and almost at once the little one recognized the words, and spoke them correctly, from memory, as Sister Carlotta had once read it to him years before.

"Let us eat, and be merry: for this my son was dead, and is alive again; he was lost, and is found." Then the little one burst into tears and clung to his mother, and kissed his father's hand.

"Welcome home, little brother," said Nikolai. "I told you they were nice."

Acknowledgments

One book was particularly useful in preparing this novel: Peter Paret, ed., *Makers of Modern Strategy: From Machiavelli to the Nuclear Age* (Princeton University Press, 1986). The essays are not all of identical quality, but they gave me a good idea of the writings that might be in the library in Battle School.

I have nothing but fond memories of Rotterdam, a city of kind and generous people. The callousness toward the poor shown in this novel would be impossible today, but the business of science fiction is sometimes to show impossible nightmares.

I owe individual thanks to:

Erin and Phillip Absher, for, among other things, the lack of vomiting on the shuttle, the size of the toilet tank, and the weight of the lid;

Jane Brady, Laura Morefield, Oliver Withstandley, Matt Tolton, Kathryn H. Kidd, Kristine A. Card, and others who read the advance manuscript and made suggestions and corrections. Some annoying contradictions between *Ender's Game* and this book were thereby averted; any that remain are not errors at all, but merely subtle literary effects designed to show the difference in perception and memory between the two accounts of the same event. As my programmer friends would say, there are no bugs, only features;

Tom Doherty, my publisher; Beth Meacham, my editor; and Barbara Bova, my agent, for responding so positively to the idea of this book when I proposed it as a collaborative project and then realized I wanted to write it entirely myself. And if I still think *Urchin* was the better title for this book, it doesn't mean that I don't agree that my second title, *Ender's Shadow,* is the more marketable one;

My assistants, Scott Allen and Kathleen Bellamy, who at various times defy gravity and perform other useful miracles;

My son Geoff, who, though he is no longer the five-year-old he was when I wrote the novel *Ender's Game,* is still the model for Ender Wiggin;

My wife, Kristine, and the children who were home during the writing of this book: Emily, Charlie Ben, and Zina. Their patience with me when I was struggling to figure out the right approach to this novel was surpassed only by their patience when I finally found it and became possessed by the story. When I brought Bean home to a loving family I knew what it should look like, because I see it every day.

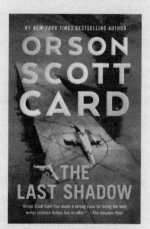